SHIRTALOON

HE WHO FIGHTS

— WITH —

MONSTERS

BOOK NINE

www.aethonbooks.com

HE WHO FIGHTS WITH MONSTERS NINE
©2023 SHIRTALOON

ALSO IN SERIES

Want to discuss our books with other readers and even the authors like Shirtaloon, Zogarth, Cale Plamann, Noret Flood (Puddles4263) and so many more?

Join our Discord server today and be a part of the Aethon community.

1

DON'T SHOW UP TO THE FANCY PARTY IN SHORTS

CONVALESCENCE WAS NOT SOMETHING THAT PEOPLE WITH THE MONEY TO AFFORD healing magic often had to deal with. Jason Asano was wealthy, even for an adventurer of his rank, yet had been experiencing a lengthy convalescence. Some wounds ran too deep, and Jason had a habit of pushing himself too hard.

Magical powers had limits, not just because they required practise to master but because the body could only endure so much. It required years to inure the body to the kinds of forces that high-ranking magic channelled through it. Jason, however, was a man for whom events would not wait for him to have the necessary strength.

On a rescue mission in a half-flooded mining complex, deep at the bottom of the sea, Jason and his team had been sent to rescue civilians. The complex had been raided by fanatical religious zealots, some of whom were exceptionally powerful. When they were trapped in a room with no escape, Jason had, characteristically, done something impossible.

There was power inside Jason that he was not ready to use. Tapping into that power, he opened a portal he should not have been able to open, rescuing his team and a large group of civilians, but the strain came exceptionally close to killing him. Only the combined efforts of his team and his familiars managed to keep him alive. The process had been so spectacular that everyone in the city of Rimaros had felt it. Jason's aura had blasted across the city and the image of his personal crest had filled the sky.

Jason's convalescence had not been uneventful either. The repercussions of what he had done to himself had precipitated a meeting with some of the most powerful entities in the cosmos. As this meeting was held in the open, the people already watching Jason became all the more interested.

Rimaros, the City of Islands, was comprised of three main islands, along with a series of artificial islands that floated in the sky atop columns of rising water. The latest addition to the city was an island that had previously been a flying fortress city, until being dropped into the ocean in a massive and costly battle.

Jason lived on one of the three main islands, Arnote. On an island of sleepy beach towns, his cloud house remained perched on a clifftop amongst more conventional homes. Looking out over a pristine lagoon, it had been a pleasant place to spend his convalescence.

The cloud house was currently in the state of a pagoda. Linked to Jason's soul, it had undergone some changes when he was close to death, including taking the form of a sinister temple-like structure. Jason's attempts to change it while in a delicate state had led to an unsettling hybrid structure, but as he recovered, he was able to restore a sensible form.

After a lengthy seclusion, Jason was finally open to meeting with some of the people clamouring for his attention. There was no shortage of them, after his series of ostentatious displays, ranging from the opportunistic to the concerned, although that concern was less *for* Jason than *about* him.

Among those seeking Jason's attention, the better-informed ones made use of people Jason was already comfortable with meeting. This started with Estella Warnock, with whom Jason was sharing lunch on a pagoda balcony that over-looked the lagoon. One of the benefits of being unable to adventure was that Jason had time to experiment with local ingredients, developing variants of dishes he knew using local ingredients. On this day, he and Estella were sharing one of his best results: a variant of shakshouka. He didn't have chicken eggs or tomatoes, which made eggs poached in a tomato sauce challenging, but the local analogues had proven successful.

Though Estella was an essence user, she was not an adventurer and had no interest in being one. When she had served as a scout to help Jason and other adventurers protect the island from monsters during the Builder's attack on Rimaros, it had not been out of any sense of civic duty. It had been at the behest of her grandfather, a former adventurer who did have the sense of duty that his granddaughter did not share.

Warwick Warnock had been one of Jason's neighbours until he died assaulting one of the Builder's fortress cities at the very same time Jason and Estella were protecting the island. Estella had inherited his home and had been at something of a loss after his death, having just given up her profession of low-stakes spy-for-hire. She had been one of Jason's few allowed visitors during his convalescence, commiserating in a shared sense of aimlessness.

"Havi Estos wants a meeting," she told him.

"Lots of people want to see me. I didn't think you were speaking to him."

Havi Estos was a major middleman for semi-legal activities to whom Jason had been introduced in his early days in Rimaros. In order to learn more about Jason, he had hired Estella to observe him, not expecting her powerful yet discreet perception abilities to be noticed. This was the very job that prompted Estella to give up the work, as it was not the first job where she got more than she bargained for. Estella had been quite nervous about encountering Jason again until her grandfather smoothed things over.

"He sought me out," Estella said. "He knows I know you and wants to make amends."

"With me or you?"

"Jason, everyone in the city is talking about you, and now he's very worried about having sent me to spy on you, and what you might do about it. No one is trying to make amends with me."

"They should. Smart, skilled, discreet people are valuable, and I'm one of those three at best."

"I'm not going back to work for Estos or anyone like him. They use people like me to catch the trouble they want to avoid."

"I wouldn't use you like that."

She gave him a long stare.

"Are you offering me a job?"

"Do you know the name Emir Bahadir?"

She thought for a moment before answering.

"Is that the guy who tried to rob the royal family a few years back?"

"He did more than try, which is why he's not allowed back in the Storm Kingdom."

"Oh, I think they'd let him come."

Jason laughed.

"Yeah, I imagine they would. Anyway, he's the one who gave me the cloud flask that produced the building we're sitting in. When he did, he told me that I should consider expanding my operation. Get some staff, the way he has for his treasure-hunting operations."

"You want to be a treasure hunter?"

"No, but have you ever heard of auxiliary adventurers? They join adventuring teams as non-combat members, providing various specialty services. My group will be doing a lot of travelling soon, and having someone outside the team proper who could get the lay of the land quickly would be valuable to us."

"You want me to traipse around the world with you and your grab-bag of lunatics who run around with diamond-rankers, gods and who knows what else?"

"Yeah, pretty much. I think things will calm down for a while, though."

"They would have to. I think you're past the point where things can escalate without the whole world getting destroyed."

"Been there, done that," Jason said. "I'm not helping my case here, am I?"

Rick Geller and his team had been in Greenstone at the same time Jason was first training as an adventurer, themselves being trained in the Geller compound. One of his team members, Jonah, had been amongst the first to be forcibly implanted with a star seed, during the same disastrous expedition where Farrah had died. The attempt to extract the star seed had been a gruesome and lethal failure. That spot on the team had subsequently been filled by Dustin Kettering.

Dustin had once been part of a three-man team with Neil and Thadwick Mercer. Thadwick's own star seed implantation had caused that group to fracture, with Neil going to Jason's team and Dustin going to Rick's. Thadwick's fate was considerably more tragic—he had become some kind of energy vampire that was still at large somewhere in the world.

Although he was now silver rank, Rick looked as uncomfortable as ever around high-rankers, being a good and obedient young man. Jason found himself grinning at Rick's uncertain expression as he watched him emerge from a flying carriage with Princess Liara, stepping onto the lawn in front of his pagoda.

Jason vaulted the balcony railing to land right in front of the pagoda's large main entrance. He conjured his cloak as he fell to slow his descent, which wasn't necessary to avoid damage to him, but to avoid dents in the lawn from a superhero landing. The new look of Jason's cloak arrested the attention of Liara and Rick, who were both familiar with its previous iteration.

"That looks creepy," Rick said. "My eyes don't want to look at it. It's wrong, somehow. Like you're wearing a hole in the world."

"It is quite unsettling to look at," Liara agreed. "I'm not entirely shocked, however, that your stealth ability is so attention-grabbing."

"Why do people keep saying that?" Jason complained as he dismissed the cloak.

"At least you're draping yourself in weird magic instead of weirdly high numbers of women," Rick observed, drawing an odd look from Liara. "When a beautiful princess attached herself to my meeting, I figured it would be the same thing all over again. What is it with you and these Rimaros princesses?"

Liara gave Jason a querying expression.

"Rick was around when I first met Zara, but I am not always surrounded by women… what's about to happen notwithstanding."

The doors behind Jason opened to reveal a group of women, including the pink-haired Estella, Farrah, Sophie, Belinda and Autumn Leal. Autumn was an adventurer whose acquaintance Jason had made, prior to his team arriving in Rimaros. She had an exotic magical frog named Neil that had perished in the defence of Rimaros from the Builder's flying fortress city. This was something Jason had discovered in the process of checking on people in the wake of the casualty-filled battle, but he had largely left her alone.

Autumn had been in mourning for her bonded companion for some time, but now, for the first time, Jason sensed at least an amount of hope from her aura, along with a solid sense of resolve. It was not the time to explore that, however, and he satisfied himself that she seemed better than she had in the past.

Rick was oblivious to this; all he saw was Jason joined by five women.

"And there it is," he said.

Jason opened a portal to Rimaros and the five women passed through. Jason didn't close it afterwards, and instead called out through the still-open doors.

"Are you coming or what?"

"On my way," a voice came from inside, shortly followed by a hustling Taika. He looked around, seeing that the five women had already departed, then his gaze settled on Liara. "Oh, hey, princess bro." He then went through the portal and Jason closed it again.

Liara shook her head.

"A bronze-ranker," she muttered. "What happened to the respect for rank?"

"It's Jason," Rick told her. "He's a bad influence."

Rick then remembered that he was speaking to a gold-rank princess and his head dipped down as if yanked by a string.

Jason chuckled. "You'd best come inside," he told them.

"Sit anywhere," Jason said as they entered a casual lounge inside the cloud structure. "I'm not really the conference table type."

The lounge, like most of the pagoda, was designed in such a way that the room had a flow leading out to an open wall balcony terrace. This particular room was made up of undisguised cloud substance rather than being masked as more ordinary material. The sprawling layout of plush couches and armchairs fell outside of the meeting etiquette that Rick and Liara were familiar with, so while they looked around for the most appropriate place to sit, Jason moved behind the bar.

After taking out a selection of fruit and two magical wands, Jason started waving the wands like a slightly confused orchestra conductor, and the fruit rose into the air. After wobbling in place for a moment, the fruit peeled, sliced, pulped and juiced itself into a pitcher. Liara and Rick gave up on finding appropriate seats for the moment to watch.

"I could be better at this, I know," he apologised. "It's something I picked up while I was recovering to practise my mana control. I know a guy who's way better at this than me, but he probably wouldn't be great at saving the world. We all have our areas."

He paused, frowning.

"Wow, that was really braggadocious. Am I a braggart? When did I start bragging about things I've actually done instead of making crazy stuff up? Oh yeah; my life caught up with the most ridiculous things I could think of. Damn, I'm great."

Jason flashed his guests a grin as he resumed moving the wands. He finished the pitcher of blended fruit drink with a bundle of ice cubes that floated in on their own, and then came out from behind the bar, looking at Rick and Liara standing around.

"Couldn't find a seat?"

With a sweep of Jason's arm, all the furniture outside of the bar area sank into the floor. Three chairs then emerged from the floor, spaced equally around a low, circular table. Jason plonked down into one of them and the others sat down after.

"I think you forgot the drinks," Rick pointed out.

"Crap, thanks."

Jason reached out with his aura, grabbing the pitcher of juice and three glasses, floating them across the room and onto the table. Liara was able to sense the aura he projected to do so and looked at him, wide-eyed.

"I wouldn't worry about it," Jason told her. "This is pretty much how it always goes. I almost die, come out of it with some weird new power, and a god or some other ridiculous thing shows up. The order changes around, but it's a pretty reliable pattern."

He filled the glasses from the pitcher.

"No exciting ingredients, just fruit. Bit early in the day, yeah?"

Jason leaned back in his seat and sipped at his drink, waiting for the others to talk. Rick was waiting for Liara to speak first, but she was looking around the room.

"Your cloud building has changed," she said. "I don't mean the shape; that's normal cloud house stuff. I mean whatever is under the surface. It feels different. Focused, somehow. Solid."

"I made some changes," Jason acknowledged.

"How bad would it be? If someone came for you here?"

"For me? Not so bad. For them? Depends on who it was."

Jason's gaze turned to Rick.

"I have to apologise," he said. "I didn't realise you were still in town. I thought you went back north after the Builder abandoned the Sea of Storms."

"I had intended to be gone," Rick told him. "You remember my sister Phoebe, yes? She's on my team but had to stay home to deal with family issues. I don't like having the team split up and wanted to head home, but we were instructed to stay. Didn't Neil tell you? He and Dustin have been spending plenty of time together since then."

"No, he didn't."

Jason looked to Liara, then back at Rick.

"Let me guess: the Adventure Society roped you in so I'd actually take a meeting, and then Princess Adventure Pants here turned up, right as you were about to set out. The royal family 'convinced' the Adventure Society to let their local representative tag along, given that I've been willing to meet with her before."

Rick gave Liara a panicked look at 'Princess Adventure Pants,' his eyes desperately trying to communicate that he wasn't responsible for Jason.

"I'm very familiar with Mr Asano's way of conducting himself," Liara assured him. "And yes, Mr Asano; that is a more or less accurate description."

She reached forward, took a glass and sipped at it, nodding appreciatively.

"Not bad. But we have to talk about this," she said, gesturing with her glass.

"We have to talk about the juice?"

"More what the juice represents," Liara said. "That is the gist of what you were sent to propose, was it not, Mr Geller?"

"Uh, yes," Rick confirmed. "Basically, Jason, everyone would be more comfortable with your level of prominence going down for the immediate future."

"Precipitously down," Liara added.

Jason looked at the juice Liara was holding, his mind ticking over what she had meant. Then a huge grin spread over his face.

"I'm in," he said.

"We haven't even told you what the Adventure Society is proposing," Rick said.

"It's a secret identity, isn't it? Jason Asano, scary god-socialiser, leaves his team for parts unknown. Then casual juice enthusiast, Bruce Wayne, joins the team as an auxiliary member in charge of cooking."

"Something like that," Liara said. "There will be a lot of details to sort out, but yes. The Adventure Society is proposing the creation of a more discreet legal identity for you to inhabit. You'll need to be more cautious when working with your team, but it should be manageable. You generally won't be observed when you're in the field, fighting monsters. It would help a great deal if your team stayed on the move, taking ordinary contracts."

"You know that won't hold up to almost any scrutiny from someone who knows enough," Jason pointed out.

"It's not intended to," Rick said. "There's no hiding you from anyone of real influence. The idea is just for you to be a lot less loud for a while. Preferably until you rank up, because the higher your rank, the more that the crazy stuff you get caught up in becomes acceptable."

"I won't be ranking up for a long time."

"The Adventure Society is very open to you spending the next decade or five being nice and quiet," Rick said.

"Fair enough," Jason said with a chuckle. "So, barbecue-Jason is roaming around with melodrama-Jason's now-former team. Where is drama-guy while this is going on?"

"He leaves with His Ancestral Majesty," Liara said. "With everything he has going on, it's time for him to go out and see some of the cosmos."

"Apprenticed to Soramir Rimaros," Jason said. "Prestigious."

"Obviously, this will work a lot better if your new identity isn't the only auxiliary joining your team," Liara said. "Before she left, your friend Dawn made some arrangements, but we can go over the specifics when we get into the details."

"The Adventure Society wants you to play up the scary adventurer before you go," Rick said. "A social event where you will need to be every bit the impressive adventurer, rather than… the other thing."

"You need to be what people imagine from a man who speaks to gods and great astral beings," Liara said. "Not the man you actually are when you speak to gods and great astral beings."

"You got a transcript from the spies floating around, then?" Jason asked. "In fairness, you have to talk to Dominion like that or he won't give you the time of day. Unless you're a king or something, I guess. Now that I think about it, maybe I should suck up to him. He might leave me alone then. I should remember to try that."

Rick was looking at Jason with the wide-eyed expression Jason was starting to think of as the 'standard Rick.'

"Anyway," Jason continued. "Don't show up to the fancy party in shorts and sandals, is what you're saying."

"That cloak of yours should do the job nicely," Liara said.

"You want me to wear the cloak to a social event?" Jason asked. "The Adventure Society is looking for me to go full chuuni, I see. I can do that."

"I don't know what chuuni means," Rick said.

"I think we can figure it out from context," Liara said. "Mr Geller, since Mr

Asano has already agreed—if your earlier acceptance wasn't merely in jest, Mr Asano?"

"I'm still in; I like this idea. And I did ask you to figure out how to reduce my profile, after all."

"Then let us take 'yes' for an answer and go, Mr Geller. Mr Asano, we'll discuss the details at a later date."

"No worries," Jason said.

"I would appreciate it if any public displays you make from here on out are more of the dramatic Jason and less of the neighbourhood barbecue Jason, if you please," Liara said.

"Oh, I wouldn't worry about that. Melodrama is kind of my thing."

"Yes, Mr Asano. We've noticed."

2

WHAT SHE WAS WILLING TO DO

"Now that Dawn has scarpered," Jason said, "I've half of a mind to do the same. Bottle up the pagoda, portal out and bunk off. No one would notice, right?"

He and his friends were sitting around a long table on a pagoda balcony, eating lunch.

"Of course someone would notice," Rufus said. "There are twelve people observing the building right now."

"Seventeen," Jason and Estella corrected simultaneously before glancing at each other briefly.

"The point is," Rufus continued, "that if you start making unexpected moves, people will get worried."

"He always makes unexpected moves," Farrah said. "And they always get worried."

"I'm not that bad."

"Bro, you went through a children's ward and made everyone think you're an angel."

"That was one time."

"You had a rolling gunfight with a motorcycle gang hopped up on vampire blood," Taika said. "On TV. And I was driving. I'm not good at dodging bullets, bro. I'm too big."

"We do have some responsibilities here before we can leave," Humphrey pointed out. "I don't feel bad about skipping this meeting with Estella's former employer, but we've agreed to help Miss Leal obtain a new familiar."

As someone with a bonded familiar of his own, Humphrey was especially sympathetic to Autumn Leal's plight. Bonded familiars were actual magical creatures that could die, compared to Jason's summoned familiars. If Shade, Colin or Gordon were destroyed, their spirits simply returned to the astral and Jason could resummon them. When Autumn lost her familiar, Humphrey could not help but think about losing Stash and how devastated he would be.

"I could go with skipping the celebration ball, though," Sophie said. "Why do the rest of us need to go?"

After months of monsters and extradimensional invasions, the dimensional membrane that normally kept such problems away had finally repaired itself, bringing the monster surge and the Builder invasion to an end. The Magic Society made public announcements and Rimaros, like the rest of the world, was in celebrations.

A lengthy festival was taking place, despite the devastation and loss the surge had brought. If only for a short time, people needed some release after monsters and death and mobile cities attacking by land, sea and air. This monster surge had been the longest and most devastating in recorded history, bringing with it not one but two interdimensional invasions, only one of which had been dealt with.

Rural populations needed to leave the cities and fortress towns, returning to what would often be monster-ravaged towns and villages around the Storm Kingdom. Infrastructure would need to be rebuilt and industries built back up. More than just the monster surge, the state of readiness the world had been in for a good five years prior to the surge had hurt economies, closed businesses and turned boom towns into ghost towns.

The repercussions would likely still be felt by the time of the next surge, but now, the repopulation, rebuilding and the messengers that had hidden themselves away could wait. The world would take a week for some much-needed celebratory catharsis.

"The festivals on the streets are the real celebration," Rufus said. "This ball for the aristocracy is just a show. The first round in the next cycle of political gamesmanship. With everything up in the air, a lot of power is up for grabs."

"So why should Jason put himself up for grabs with it?" Sophie asked. "Anyone with real power will either know Jason isn't genuinely leaving the team or be able to easily find out. So why bother with the show?"

"It's not about convincing them that I'm going off somewhere," Jason said. "It's about giving them a sense of control. These are people used to holding power, and there's been a lot going on that they don't understand and have no influence over. A lot of that is centred on this pagoda and me sitting in it. Normally, their response to something like that is to take or, failing that, kill it. By jumping through some hoops for them now, I become more of a known quantity, and demonstrate that at least someone can bring me to heel."

"Except that's total crap and you go berserk when people try to control you," Sophie said.

"Yes, but we won't be telling people that. I told you: it's a show. I don't want to spend the next few years fending off people who think that I'm some kind of rogue threat."

"You are some kind of rogue threat," Sophie said.

"Again, *please* don't tell people that at the party."

"I hope you don't think one party is going to put a stop to people thinking that they can or should come after you," Neil said.

"Of course not," Jason said. "There will always be someone with too much ambition, too much stupidity or both. But most of the people at this ball are just concerned about a loose power running around during times that are already uncertain. The Adventure Society and the royal family can parade me around, showing everyone what a good boy I am. Then I'm no longer an unknown threat to anyone's ambitions or just the general welfare of the kingdom."

"You think any nobles care about the welfare of the populace?" Belinda asked. "Good luck finding one."

"There's no shortage of selfish nobles," Jason admitted. "But some, I assume, are good people."

"Nope," Sophie said. "They all suck."

"Based on your long history of robbing them?" Rufus asked pointedly.

"Yes," Sophie said.

"You realise that Humphrey and I are both from aristocratic families, right?" Neil asked.

"Yeah, but he's pretty and you're the healer. I've seen the things they hide away. Mostly while stealing them. Your aunt Clarice has a hideous doll collection, by the way, Neil. I have no idea why she locks it up, because no one is going to steal that, trust me."

"You broke into my house?"

"There's no point breaking into poor people's houses," Belinda said. "They don't have any money. I suppose if you're crap at breaking into places."

"The point is," Sophie said, "that I've seen the things they hide. The worse they are, the harder they work to make themselves seem good. Humphrey and his mum might be nice and clean, but even Humphrey will tell you that not all of his family are like them."

"We all have secrets we hide," Humphrey said. "Things we're ashamed of."

Everyone stopped eating and turned to look at Humphrey.

"What?" he asked.

"What do you have to be ashamed of?" Neil asked.

"My entire point was that we *don't* tell people those things," Humphrey said. "That's why they're secrets."

"You keep saying 'we,' but I don't think you have anything you're ashamed of," Belinda said.

"Of course he does," Jason said. "I bet it's that one time, as a boy, he secretly pilfered some condensed milk from the pantry."

"No," Gary said. "I bet he skipped out on training once to read a book on how to maintain a humble demeanour when people won't stop looking into your sensuous eyes, like molten bowls of dark chocolate."

"Sophie," Belinda said. "What's Humphrey's deep, dark secret?"

Sophie finished chewing on a mouthful of salad as everyone looked at her.

"He accidentally killed a baby," she said casually. "This salad dressing is fantastic. Can I get some of this on a sandwich?"

As she shoved another forkful of salad into her mouth, Humphrey looked more and more like a boiling kettle until he finally boiled over.

"I DID NOT ACCIDENTALLY KILL A BABY!"

"You did say that *not* admitting it was the entire point," Jason observed.

"Yeah, he definitely killed that baby," Neil said.

"I did not kill a baby!"

"It's a helpless little baby, bro. I know it was supposedly an accident, but how could you?"

"Of course he had to say it was an accident," Gary pointed out. "Plus, it's his word against that of a dead baby, so that's probably how he got away with it."

Estella, watching the group continue roasting Humphrey, leaned towards Clive, who was also staying out of it.

"Is it always like this?"

"More or less."

"Aren't you all meant to be some group of elite adventurers?"

"I'd consider our capabilities adequate."

"I was expecting more... I don't know. Dignity, I guess."

"Admittedly, it's more like this with Jason around," Clive told her. "He has a way of setting the tone. But it's a good thing. Dignity is for outsiders; a face we put on, as needed. We let Humphrey take the lead with that. But we've seen some serious things. Lots of death, lives ruined. Adventurers often meet people on the worst days of their lives. Being able to have a little fun helps keep us sane."

"Jason knows that better than most," Farrah said from where she was sat next to Clive. "He and I were trapped in another world for a few years, and we saw some serious business. Sometimes you need people who understand and accept you, and if you don't have that, things can get extremely bleak."

"He asked me to come work for him."

"As an auxiliary, I know," Clive said. "We try to avoid letting Jason make major decisions for the team without discussing them first. Unfortunately, they keep cropping up while we're busy trying to not die. It's a good life, but even if you're not fighting for us, spying for us will be far from risk-free."

Estella looked at the boisterous people loudly devouring their lunch. Being risk-averse had always been important to her. Too much risk was the very thing that had led to her falling out with her previous employer. As she watched the group, saw their care for one another, having fun together, she witnessed something she'd never had for herself.

Estella's parents had been adventurers, dying when she was young. She had been raised by her grandfather, who never pushed her towards adventuring, not wanting to lose her the way he had his son. Estella had always been solitary by nature, but the loss of her grandfather had changed something. The absence of the one real connection she had to another person left her feeling untethered. Perhaps it was time to start re-evaluating what she wanted and what she was willing to do to get it.

"I don't like you going to him," Sophie said. "Smells like a trap."

"Everything smells like a trap to you," Neil said.

"That's because anything we run into out there is likely to be a trap."

Jason and his team, plus Rufus, Gary and Farrah, were tooling up for a fight. While they kept most of their gear in dimensional spaces, Jason had placed a ready room full of excess equipment they might need for any given mission. Their gear was stowed on the second-highest level of the pagoda, in what amounted to a locker room.

He had also installed more fireman's poles, but these were hidden behind a conspicuous bookcase that was opened by a hidden switch in an equally conspicuous bust on a small table. The poles ran from the ready room down a secret shaft to another hidden door in the atrium. Each pole was labelled with the name of a team member, except for one—Neil's pole was labelled 'Robin.'

"The possibility of a trap is why I picked the location," Jason said. "Which Estella won't be sharing with Estos until it's time for him to head there."

"You should have picked here," Sophie said.

"The only reason I agreed to this meeting is because of a name that Havi Estos dropped, and the person belonging to that name has a lot of eyes and ears. He's already in hiding, and if he hears that Estos is paying me a visit, he may disappear entirely. Again."

"And who is this mysterious person whose name you've been declining to tell us?" Sophie asked. She watched as Jason glanced at Belinda, who shrugged.

"It's Killian Laurent," he said.

"Who is Killi… wait, isn't he the guy that put a star seed in you and then vanished?"

"With a good deal of the Silva crime family's money and resources, no less," Clive said. "There was some concern you might get a little, uh, *enthused*, once you found out."

"Why would you think that?" Sophie asked.

"Because you tore half of Old City apart when Jason went missing," Belinda said.

"Well, now I can tear him apart, if we've found him."

Jason's kidnapping and star seed implantation was orchestrated by crime boss Cole Silva and local Magic Society Director Lucian Lamprey, in Greenstone. These were the enemies he had made by shielding Sophie from them, which did not sit well with her. After a lifetime of everyone trying to use her, the one person who helped change her life for no more reason than she needed it had paid the price for doing so. For all her frenzied searching, she had found nothing and failed to contribute to Jason's rescue. Silva and Lamprey had both been caught and punished, but the man who did their dirty work had escaped.

As it turned out, Silva's henchman, Killian Laurent, had been working behind the scenes on his own plan. For him, Jason had been a conveniently powerful distraction for Cole Silva, allowing Laurent to enact well-laid plans to plunder the Silva crime family and escape the city.

"Are you sure we can trust Estella?"

"She can only hide her emotions from my perception if I don't push," Jason said. "I pushed."

"That's not a guarantee," Clive pointed out. "There's a possibility that a false aura was magically overlaid on hers. Admittedly, anyone who can do that well enough to fool you, Jason, is probably more trouble than we can deal with anyway. Someone like that could probably come down on us like a hammer the moment we're away from the safety of the pagoda."

Jason moved to the bust on the table, depicting the Adam West Batman. He unhinged the head to reveal the switch that moved the bookcase, revealing the poles. Jason watched the bookcase move across with deep satisfaction.

"Jason."

"Yes, Humphrey?"

"We're portalling out of here."

"We can portal from the atrium."

"We can also portal from here."

"This room is securely shielded against portals," Jason said. "We need to leave so we can portal out. Tell him, Clive."

"He's lying," Clive said flatly. "He can portal us out of here just fine."

"Bloke, why would you do me like that?"

"How about because you have a security system that involves an illusion depicting my parents doing... things... in a giant tub of eels?"

"Hey, there was a clearly posted sign telling you to not go in there. And why. You didn't go in, did you?"

"No, I didn't go in! What kind of idiot calls *you* on a bluff?"

The rest of the group nodded their agreement.

"I can't help wondering about how active you had to be in creating that scene, Jason," Neil wondered aloud. "Did you sit down and write out how it was going to go? How detailed was it? How long did it take to craft the illusion of Clive's parents and some eels, tweaking and correcting as you went?"

"I can speak for all of us in saying that we don't want to hear the answer to that," Humphrey said. "Jason, please just portal us out."

"Actually," Belinda said, "I'd like to hear—"

"I can speak for *all of us*," Humphrey repeated, "in saying that we don't want to hear it. Portal, Jason."

Jason grinned as he went to open a portal, then stopped.

- [Astral Gate] has detected portal tracking magic. Spirit domain prevents tracking within the domain, but external destinations remain subject to tracking effects.
- Backlash from using [Astral Gate] to reconfigure portal to avoid tracking: low.

- Would you like to reconfigure portal to avoid tracking?

"Huh," he said.

"What is it?" Rufus asked.

"Someone is tracking portal use in the area. Not really a surprise."

"All portal use on Livaros is tracked," Farrah said. "The Magic Society does it, in conjunction with the Adventure Society. Part defence measure, part policing measure."

"That involves a lot of infrastructure, though," Clive pointed out. "Infrastructure that doesn't exist here on Arnote. Setting up a tracking blanket without it is fairly high-end ritual magic."

"It's not news that it's the top end of town that's paying attention to us here," Belinda said.

"We don't want to be tracked where we're going," Humphrey said. "We should call it off."

"It's fine," Jason said. "I can tweak the portal to avoid the tracking."

"How?" Clive asked. "If it was that simple, why would anyone use tracking magic?"

"Not everyone has the thing I keep behind the eel-porn doors."

Jason opened a portal, which looked normal, but his blue and orange eyes started glowing brightly and he grunted as pain racked his head. A small wall of cloud material rose from the ground and he leaned back into it heavily.

"Ow."

"Are you alright?" Farrah asked.

"Yeah. Just a minor backlash for overstepping my rank. Give me a minute."

Jason's companions looked on with worry, and while Jason had been optimistic, it was only a few minutes before the pain passed.

"Okay," he said. "Let's go."

3

MORE THAN JUST A NAME

THE STREETS OF LIVAROS WERE THRONGING WITH PEOPLE AS THE CENTRAL AREAS were overtaken by a sprawling street festival. The market district was the heart of the post-surge celebrations, but it extended into the boutique store ward and even the Adventure Society campus. Tables had been brought out and food stalls were everywhere, while the Magic Society had released thousands of colour-changing paper lanterns that drifted over the streets, illuminating everything in myriad colours.

Jason stood on a rooftop, his cloak dimmed down and blending into the shadows of the late evening. Sophie stood beside him, significantly more obvious. The rest of their companions were elsewhere, either waiting at the meeting site or in place for other tasks, all connected through voice chat.

"Ooh, the food smells wafting up here," Jason said with yearning. "I could pop down there and grab us something real quick."

"No," Humphrey scolded. He, like the rest of the team, was positioned elsewhere. "We talked about this, Jason. You agreed to play the ominous harbinger, which means no popping down to check out food stalls."

"It's not like anyone would recognise me; I'd be completely anonymous."

"That's a lie and you know it," Farrah said. "I'm betting that most of these food stalls are run by the people who run the same stalls at the market. Do not even bother trying to convince us that they won't recognise you."

"Not to mention that you have a very bad track record on staying anonymous," Clive added.

"Sophie could go down there," Jason said. "No one's looking for her."

"Thankfully," Sophie added. "I've had quite enough of that in my life, thank you."

"You want Sophie to go down there," Humphrey said. "The most beautiful woman in the city, dressed head to toe in white adventuring gear. Very subtle."

"You are such a suck-up," Jason pouted.

"I think it's sweet," Belinda said. "But yes, she does rather draw the eye."

Sophie stood out in her new armour of white with silver embellishments. Figure-hugging yet utterly flexible, like Sophie herself, it focused on mobility rather than protectiveness. She had acquired the armour while Jason was still in recovery, through Neil's looting power, from an unusual ooze-type monster. She had not enjoyed fighting the silver-star jelly, but was very satisfied with the spoils.

"There are lots of adventurers out there," Jason complained, and Sophie put a hand on his shoulder.

"I asked Belinda to go around grabbing anything that looked good," she said. "It'll come out of her storage space nice and fresh. I know it's not the same as being down there, but it's something."

Jason turned to look at Sophie, pushing the hood back off his head.

"Thank you," he said, his smile an uncharacteristic non-smirk. "That's really thoughtful of you."

After a lifetime of mistrust, Sophie was still learning about companionship, and her rare expression of bashfulness made Jason smile wider.

"Belinda was meant to be intercepting the target," Humphrey said.

"I can do both," Belinda said. "Jason's going to sense him long before I can get eyes on him anyway."

"How are we doing with that?" Humphrey asked.

"We left his warded compound in the warehouse district with a couple of bodyguards," Estella said through voice chat. "We took a carriage until we hit the festival crowds and then started moving on foot."

Estella was also included in the voice chat as she directed Havi Estos to the meeting site.

"He doesn't have a flight travel permit?" Neil asked.

"Temporarily suspended for the duration of the festival," Estella explained. "He's not happy about it either."

"Most of them have been suspended," Rufus added.

"And the guilds aren't thrilled, from what I'm overhearing," Belinda said. "You can tell a guild adventurer here more from their complaints than their gear, although anyone fully tooled up to fight monsters at a festival is probably a complete tool themselves."

"I don't like this," Havi Estos said as he made his way through the crowd. "It's the perfect chance to get in some assassinations. This week will probably see more of them than the rest of the year combined."

"You're worried about being assassinated," Estella told him. "I can't tell if you think too highly or too poorly about yourself."

"Being assassinated isn't a matter of character," Havi said. "It's a matter of being an obstacle to someone with no scruples."

"Then maybe you shouldn't surround yourself with people lacking scruples.

Look, no one is going to… oh, wow; that guy is definitely going to assassinate you."

"What? What guy?"

The two bodyguards went on alert. They had shortswords, as large weapons were generally less effective in the city, as well as being more attention-grabbing.

"That guy," Estella said, pointing. "He's hiding his aura fairly well, but I'm, you know, me."

The man in question started running.

"Don't chase," Havi ordered his bodyguards. "He might be trying to lure you away."

They carried on at a hustle, the bodyguards often rudely shouldering the way through the crowd. Only Estella noticed Belinda trailing them, occasionally changing her face.

Like the tentacles of an octopus, arms made of darkness emerged from different shadows to drag people out of sight.

"That's the fourth group that has been looking to kill this guy," Jason said as he dropped the last unconscious man onto the pile on the roof. "He's got more people after him than I do. Maybe he should be the one faking his identity and skipping town."

"The people after him are a little lower on the threat scale," Rufus pointed out.

"Still, four assassination attempts in one walk across town?"

"Not to mention the other two we stopped against unrelated people," Humphrey said. "And I know for a fact that the Adventure Society has people quietly patrolling as well, so who knows how much is going on."

"I wish you'd told me that earlier," Jason said. "I almost tried to take one of them out until I realised from his aura that he was watching for threats, not being one. That would have been embarrassing."

"Especially if you got your butt kicked," Neil added.

"Yeah," Jason agreed with a laugh.

"Estos was right about it being a prime chance for assassinations," Estella said.

"Not to mention robbery," Belinda added. "I've spotted I don't know how many pickpockets. They know their business in this city too. The deftness with which they dispel anti-theft wards is impressive. I might go find who taught them, swap some tips."

"You're not a thief anymore, Lindy," Humphrey pointed out.

"Uh, yep," Belinda agreed. "Definitely not."

"Belinda…"

"We're approaching the destination," Estella notified them.

"Site is secure," Rufus said.

"I put up some extra anti-surveillance magic," Farrah said, "but what was already in place is surprisingly thorough."

Havi Estos, Estella and the two bodyguards reached the boutique shopping district where the festival was still going on, but was a bit more subdued. This was where the festival-goers tended to be a little higher in the social hierarchy, and letting loose too much could have political repercussions. It was still a celebration, just more company barbecue than spring break in tone.

"Honestly, I didn't think we'd get this far and only see one attacker," Havi Estos said. "Perhaps I overestimated the danger."

"Exactly," agreed Estella, who had shared none of her party interface communication with him.

They arrived at a plain, cream-coloured storefront with no signage. There was only a display window with a dummy draped in a linen suit and topped with a Panama hat. The door opened at their approach, revealing a stern-faced Rufus. Havi looked at the tall, leanly muscular adventurer in front of him with midnight skin and striking good looks. The light of the colourful lanterns overhead was reflected from the man's bald head so well that Havi absently wondered if he used some kind of wax polish.

"Havi Estos?" Rufus asked in a voice that made Havi wish he could just run instead of answering. This whole night was the reason he liked conducting business from his very secure home, but he felt he had little choice. He knew enough about Asano and his associates to recognise the man standing in front of him, and who that man's grandfather was.

Havi was a very well-connected man, so he had become aware that Jason Asano was now a person of significance. Perhaps Asano didn't care that Havi once sent Estella to spy on him—he certainly seemed to have settled things with Estella Warnock. Havi didn't have a respected grandfather to mend fences, however. What he did have was information.

Like many in Rimaros, Havi had been tracking down every piece of information on Jason Asano. He had a broader base of information gathering than most, stretching from high nobility to base criminals. He was confident that no one else had yet realised the connections between Asano and local underworld figure Killian Laurent, but it was likely only a matter of time. As such, Havi needed to exploit that knowledge before it lost its value to him.

"Yes, I'm Havi Estos. Is Mr Asano inside?"

"Jason Asano has been with you for some time," Rufus said.

Havi and his bodyguard looked around and found Jason standing next to Estella. Havi tilted his head, feeling a dissonance in his mind. He suddenly realised that Asano had been walking with them for the last couple of streets, but for some reason, Havi had been ignoring his presence.

The bodyguards moved their hands toward their swords, but their silver-rank auras were suddenly annihilated and they froze, stricken with fear. Asano's presence was uncanny, almost part of the darkness as his cloak and the twilight seemed to blend together, making what was shadow and what was person unclear. How he did that while standing in the open Havi was unsure. It was like an optical illusion, his eyes sliding off as he tried to make out what was real and what wasn't. It didn't help that Asano didn't register at all to Havi's aura senses. It was as if he were looking at a picture and not the man himself.

"Jason," Havi said. "You do prefer to be called Jason, right?"

"My friends call me Jason, Mr Estos."

Asano's voice had the icy hardness of winter granite, wholly unlike their previous meeting. Havi found himself missing the man's previously friendly demeanour very much.

"Go inside, Mr Estos," Rufus ordered. "Your employees can leave."

Havi looked at the bodyguards that suddenly felt extremely inadequate to his needs.

"I need to get home safely after this meeting," he said.

"If you go home again," Jason said, "you will be delivered safely."

Havi paled at Jason's use of the word 'if' rather than 'when.' Even so, he dutifully followed Rufus inside. Waiting for them was a group of people Estos recognised from his information gathering on Asano. Just looking at the people around him was enough to know that Asano was not someone to take lightly. From prominent members of the Geller and Remore families to Clive Standish, whose relationship with the Magic Society would be a whole other investigation. If they had been in Vitesse instead of the far side of the world, no one in their right mind would dismiss the group.

The other person present was Alejandro Albericci, the proprietor of the tailor shop in which they stood. Albericci had his own formidable connections in Rimaros society and was not someone Havi would ever be interested in getting on the bad side of.

"Thank you for the use of your property, Mr Albericci," Rufus said.

"Consider it my apology for being used to political ends when you first graced my establishment. I will go now, but be assured that no sound will escape these walls. And, as Miss Hurin can attest, it would take formidable effort to observe the interior magically."

Alejandro departed through a rear door, leaving Havi surrounded. Belinda and Sophie came in to stand by Jason, with Belinda closing the door behind her. Havi steeled his nerve to speak.

"Jas— Mr Asano. I'd like to—"

"Killian Laurent," Jason said, cutting him off. "That name is the only reason any of us are here. I do hope you have more than just a name."

"He was here, in the Storm Kingdom. After he plundered the wealth of the Silva family in Greenstone, he came here and set himself up in Jaitari."

The three islands that made up the city of Rimaros were not the most populous regions of the Storm Kingdom. The largest concentrations of people were on a landmass in the centre of the Sea of Storms. Comprised of what was, in Jason's world, Cuba, Haiti and the Dominican Republic, was a single island, the largest in the Sea of Storms by far. Jaitari was the largest and most populous city on the island and the Storm Kingdom overall.

"Why here?" Jason asked. "Of all the places in the world, why the one that just happened to be where I arrived?"

"He was here long before you arrived," Havi said. "I have no idea how you arrived here, or why. I've heard rumours that Soramir Rimaros knows, but even my ability to gather information has limits. But Laurent came here because he has family. Someone in the Order of Redeeming Light. A priest. The Adventure Society has him in custody, now. Maybe he can tell you more."

"You think the priest can give us Killian Laurent?"

"I can give you Killian Laurent. When your name started spreading around, Mr Asano, Laurent heard about it and decided to get out. But that was a bad idea during a monster surge, especially this one. Too many people tracking too many things. Liquidating his assets and getting out of the region without drawing the attention of people hunting for Builder cultists or Order of Redeeming Light members meant relying on some extremely shady people. The kind of people that won't talk to the government or the Adventure Society, but will talk to me."

"You know where he is now?" Jason asked.

"No," Havi said. "By design. If I went digging, word could get to him, sooner or later. I'm not the only information broker out there, and he's an extremely cautious man. But I am certain I can find him, in fairly short order. Then it will be on you to move fast enough to get him before he moves again."

Jason didn't respond for a long time, leaving Havi to look at the alien eyes that were all that could be seen from the otherwise-impenetrable darkness of Jason's hood.

"There's something else," Havi said. He hadn't intended to share this. He had planned instead to use it to build his own influence base, but Jason's silent stare had unnerved him. "Laurent was the one who hired the adventurer that teleported the Order of Redeeming Light's people off that island. The new one that used to be the flying Builder city. He did it because his brother asked. The priest I talked about."

There was more silence. A line of dark flames moved along the ground, from which a portal arch of dark crystal noiselessly emerged. The dark flames rose to fill the arch, becoming an active portal.

"Go home, Mr Estos," Jason said.

"Do you want me to start narrowing down Laurent's location?"

"Soon. We'll be in touch."

Havi was uncertain about the wisdom of walking through a portal he didn't entirely trust, but he liked the idea a lot more than refusing to do so and staying surrounded by these people. He stepped through and emerged in his own home. The home that he had paid good money to be warded against teleportation and portals. He turned to look at the portal he had just stepped through and watched it descend back into the floor, leaving a line of dark flames that vanished in turn.

Humphrey caught Jason as he collapsed, the moment Havi had vanished.

"Yeah, that was worse," he croaked. "I have to stop using this astral gate."

"If you'd just let me study it," Clive said, "maybe we could alleviate the issues."

"If Dawn said to wait for higher rank," Farrah told him, "then it's best to wait."

"I'm going to teleport Jason back to the pagoda," Humphrey said. "Rufus, please thank Mr Albericci again and let him know that we're done."

4

THE MAKING OF THAT MAN

HAVI ESTOS WAS NOT USED TO FEELING INSIGNIFICANT. HIS CONNECTIONS SPANNED from the very top of society to the very bottom, and he was valuable enough to both that he had secured his position as the consummate middleman. He was also a successful former silver-rank adventurer. Perhaps not from a top guild, but certainly from a respectable one, and any adventurer that could hold their own in Rimaros was worthy of note.

After emerging from Asano's portal, Havi took an icy shower, then found himself staring in his bathroom mirror. He was a sizeable man, with onyx skin and gold eyes that matched his long hair. He looked at his expression and could see for himself how shaken he appeared.

He had only met Asano once, when he dropped off a package from Mordant Kerr, Havi's old adventuring friend. Kerr had been in charge of a fortress town during the surge and sent Asano with a package containing a recording of Asano wiping out a monster wave threatening that town. Havi had thought nothing of the ordinary-seeming man until he looked at the recording after he was gone.

Kerr had wanted to connect Havi and Asano, recognising that Asano could use Havi's contacts and Havi would do well to get on good terms before Asano's rise to prominence. The disparity between the amiable man he met and the slaughter machine in the recording had triggered Havi's sense of caution and he had begun investigating. Asano unexpectedly catching wind of it had cost Havi the valuable services of Estella Warnock, whose grandfather was another of Havi's adventuring contemporaries.

Asano's name came up in the course of Havi's general practice of knowing things that most people didn't, in increasingly alarming ways. Asano's connections reached the top of Rimaros society, somehow coming in a downward direction from an elusive upper echelon to which even the royal family seemed to bend.

It remained a mystery until the active presence of Soramir Rimaros, the founder of the Storm Kingdom himself, became known.

The more Asano's name came to his attention, the more Havi had grown concerned. Others were coming to him as an information broker for details on Asano, which Havi had continued to gather, albeit much more carefully than he had before. He had seen what Asano's enemies looked like, what had come of them, and worried that Asano might consider the slight of Havi sending someone to probe his aura as antagonistic.

Asano's enemies list was formidable, relative to his rank, and the mysteries surrounding him were highly suggestive. What had come of those enemies did not bode well for anyone who caught Asano's ire. What did it take to make a personal enemy of the dimensional being waging war on an entire world?

Havi was wary of approaching Asano, even though it was possible Asano hadn't given Havi a second thought. Bringing himself back to Asano's attention could have been buying real trouble to avoid imaginary danger, but it had not been something he was willing to risk. He didn't want to be on Asano's enemies list, having seen Asano's other enemies. But his enquiries into Asano's past had turned up one enemy that stood out from the others, for having gotten away.

Killian Laurent was already known to Havi, but only by reputation. Havi might work with some less-than-reputable figures, but Laurent was known for having no depth to which he would not stoop. There were no lines he would not cross, no villain he would not work with and no depravity he would not exploit.

The more he looked into it, the more that targeting Laurent seemed like the way to turn things around with Asano. He'd missed out on an opportunity to make a connection with an adventurer with mysterious influence in the corridors of power and whose rise to prominence seemed inevitable. Delivering Killian Laurent on a plate could rectify that mistake in a big way.

Havi was still making preparations when Asano's predicted leap into wider attention came both sooner and more ostentatiously than Havi's most outlandish predictions. Asano's display of his aura blanketing the sky and his transforming house was something everyone became aware of. What came next, though, didn't just grab the attention of the powerful and well informed; it scared them. Asano telling the Builder to pack up and go home was one thing. The Builder actually doing it was quite another.

It was clear to the many observers that Asano was not just dealing with gods and great astral beings but that he had been for some time. Where had he gone during the mysterious period he was believed dead? What had he done, and why was he back? Havi only had answers to some of those questions, and unreliable ones, at that.

Getting on Asano's good side had very much landed on the top of Havi's priority list, and he had accelerated his preparations to serve up Laurent. He had not pushed so hard as to spook Laurent, or so he had thought. Leaving his bathroom in a soft robe, Havi discovered that he had made two critical underestimations. One was Laurent's ability to realise he was being looked into, and the other was Laurent's ability to bypass the protection magic on his house.

"Wow, that was fast," Belinda said as she watched five men move an unconscious Havi out of his house and into a carriage. It set off down the street, in the direction of the docks. There was no shortage of drunken revellers on the streets, but the warehouse district was fairly clear and the docks weren't a festival area. The vehicle would be able to pass through without being blocked by crowds.

Jason's voice chat didn't have the range to extend from Livaros, where Belinda was, to Jason at home. He was in the pagoda that Humphrey had teleported him to, so he could recover from overstressing his portal ability again. She relayed the information through Shade, hidden in her shadow.

"Already?" Jason complained when Shade reported the information. He had barely lay down to rest. "Come on, I'm still wrecked from portalling Estos through his damn house wards. It's going to be a couple of hours before I'm combat-ready again."

"I told you it was the wrong move," Neil said. "As the team healer, I strongly advise against harming yourself just so you can show off an ability that would be better kept secret anyway."

"Agreed," Humphrey said. "Shade, is Estos still alive?"

Most of the group was in a lounge area, gathered around the reclining Jason, either portalled back by Clive or teleported in by Humphrey. Only Sophie and Belinda had stayed to watch Havi Estos' home on Belinda's hunch.

"He is alive," Shade said. "Miss Belinda would also like me to iterate that she was, indeed, correct."

As they chatted in Alejandro's store following Havi's dismissal, Belinda had voiced the opinion that Havi was underestimating his exposure to Laurent.

"We already know he's tipped off targets he's been looking into in the past," she had said. "I'm guessing that Laurent might turn the tables, maybe set a trap for Jason. I say we watch the guy and see if Laurent makes a move in the wake of Estos meeting with us."

"That would mean Laurent would have to know about Estos meeting with us," Humphrey pointed out.

"Yep," Belinda had agreed.

The result was the team's illicit activity specialists keeping a watch on Havi's place. They had barely arrived when five men moved an unconscious Havi from his home into a waiting transport.

"Tell Belinda to track the carriage," Humphrey said. "Hopefully, it will lead us to Laurent and we can jump on him before he lays a trap for us."

"Unless this *is* the trap for us," Jason pointed out. "You know, I think we might be approaching this the wrong way."

"How so?" Humphrey asked.

"I don't think Laurent is going to be a big fan of playing fair, so why should we?"

Havi was unconscious, bound to a thick metal pole by heavy chains. Even with a suppression collar, the raw strength of a silver-ranker was no small thing; both the poles and the chains had been strongly reinforced with magic. Killian Laurent took the stopper from a small alchemical vial and waved it under Havi's nose.

He awoke with a start.

"Steal some mushrooms!" he yelled deliriously.

"What?" Killian asked.

"What?" a bleary-eyed Havi asked in return, head swaying as he blinked, his senses slowly coming back. He looked around, seeing that he was in a featureless room where the walls, floor and ceiling were all metal. It had no windows but a pair of large doors, suggesting it might be some kind of warehouse.

He had a groggy recollection of being woken in similar fashion and threatened with unpleasantly specific forms of violence if he didn't go through a portal. As his senses somewhat cleared, he looked at the emaciated and sickly white man standing in front of him. He had never seen Killian Laurent, but the man perfectly fit Laurent's distinctive description.

"Oh, crap."

"Indeed," Killian agreed. "You wanted to use me as a resource? To feed me to Jason Asano? You should have stuck to information trading, Mr Estos, because information gathering is not your area."

"You won't get away with kidnapping me right out of the city."

"Oh, I know. Jason Asano has developed quite the remarkable team since I last met him. I don't know exactly how they'll track us down. Maybe the former thief secretly placed tracking magic on you during your meeting. Perhaps the astral magic specialist will trace the portal used to bring you here. My people made sure they left the city's tracking area before portalling from a boat at sea, but I don't think that will stop them. They are quite the resourceful group. Powerful as well, which is why I've taken the time to set things up quite thoroughly. The only reason I'm keeping you alive is in case there's some tracking magic I can't sense on you that will be negated on your death."

Killian moved close to Havi. He was shorter by almost a full head, but grinned malevolently as he tilted his head back to lock eyes with the former adventurer.

"Once I realised that you were looking into me, I started moving things into place. I could have run, but that was not a convenient approach, given all this monster surge unpleasantness. Instead, I made sure that it would look like I was running to anyone who bothered to investigate. I need it to look like I was being sloppy. I thought it was best to give you a little sense of urgency, so you would be the one who got sloppy. Which you did. You're a good middleman, Estos, but your expertise lies in helping upstanding citizens connect with not-so-upstanding citizens, without being seen with the riffraff. This spider-at-the-heart-of-an-information-web thing you're trying to expand into isn't going to work."

"Laurent," Havi said. "I know you're evil. You don't have to make a big speech explaining your plan to prove it."

Killian chuckled as he turned to put a little distance between Havi and himself.

"Bravado. I like it. I have a client who enjoys breaking down the tough ones, so you'll be quite lucrative for me. Once Asano and his team are dealt with, which is no small thing. You won't sense them, with that suppression collar on, but there is a coterie of gold-rank mercenaries here, waiting for the arrival of Asano and his team. I know better than to take them on directly with anything but massively overwhelming force."

Killian shook his head.

"It's unfathomably expensive to hire discreet gold-rankers who will work outside of the normal channels, you know. Fortunately, the monster surge has been very lucrative for me."

"Tragedy often is, to bastards with no scruples," Havi said, spitting out the words like a curse. "You'll work with anyone. Builder cult, Red Table, those Purity lunatics."

"Yes," Killian agreed with a laugh. "It's been working out quite nicely for me. But if I'd known he would eventually cost me this much money and attention, I'd never have left Asano alive. At the time, it seemed like a worthwhile distraction, since I didn't want his friends seeking me out in anger. I'm not sure if you know who Danielle Geller is, but she's not someone you want motivated to hunt you down, believe me."

"Neither is Asano," Havi said.

"That's certainly true now, which is why I'm going to all this effort. Who would have thought that he would fight off a star seed, even if the ritual powering it was left unattended? You know, I rather think I was the making of that man. I could never have foreseen setting in motion a chain of events that would have my dear brother helping the Builder arrange for him to arrive here from another world. Asano lives an inconveniently outrageous life, which I now need to put a stop to. Luckily, you aren't the only one with some impressive connections, and certain people are likewise eager to see Asano's demise. Otherwise, I might not have been able to arrange all these gold-rankers, no matter how much money I threw around."

"Boss," one of Killian's thuggish lackeys said. He had been monitoring a magical projection floating over a ritual on the floor behind where Havi was chained up, out of his line of sight. The projection displayed the intricate web of alarm arrays placed around their location.

"Ah," Killian said. "It seems like the guests have arrived. I assume Asano brought his full team, plus the Remore boy and his team as well."

"Boss, I'm not so sure this is Asano. The alarms are picking up a whole bunch of gold-rankers."

"What?"

5

A LESSON OF DAYS GONE

IN THE AFTERMATH OF THE FIGHTING, A SMALL ARMY OF GOLD AND SILVER-rankers swept the area for escape tunnels, traps and anyone who had managed to hide away. The adventurers were a combined force of the Sapphire Crown guild, who served the royal family, and Amouz family members. The Amouz family had volunteered in numbers that surprised even Liara, whose husband was born into it.

Killian Laurent had taken the place of Havi Estos in being chained to a thick metal pole with a suppression collar around his neck. Even more precautions had been added, in the form of a layered ritual array so sufficiently complex that Clive, Belinda and Farrah were all studying it enthusiastically. The gold-rank ritualist who had put it in place was looking harried as they peppered him with questions.

Sound could not pass through the edge of the ritual circle, which was currently empty save for Killian. Just outside it, Liara and Jason stood together, talking quietly as they watched Killian, who stared back in turn.

"I've been obsessing over finding the portal user who helped the Order of Redeeming Light for a while," Liara said. "The order members themselves still won't talk, and we've had some of them for months now. Their god wasn't even their god and they're still zealots."

"Carlos says that we need to stop thinking of them as ideologues and start thinking of them as victims," Jason said. "Just as much as people turned into vampires."

"I'm well aware of what Carlos thinks," Liara said. "The Adventure Society turned all my prisoners over to the Church of the Healer. You think this man will be more forthcoming?"

"He's practical. Self-serving. He'll be willing to make some kind of deal."

"And you're alright with that? I know what he did to you."

"Here's something that won't be in the Adventure Society's file on me," Jason told her. "While I was in the other world, one of the very few gold-rankers there killed my brother, my lover and my friend. When the time came, and I had him at my mercy, I gave him to someone else for their own revenge. I was burning so hot for vengeance at the start, but I came to realise that it's just empty."

"You had a gold-ranker at your mercy?"

"Circumstances," he said. "My whole life is exploiting circumstances to stay alive when, by every sensible metric, I should die. Or stay dead; it varies."

"You made the right choice calling us in. Not just because of what was waiting for you here, but it plays into the story we're trying to sell about your willingness to defer to the Adventure Society. Giving up personal vengeance for the communal good will sit well with people who know your going off with Soramir is just a charade. Some of them worry that you roaming around in secret is worse than letting you do so openly."

"Let," Jason repeated, dissatisfaction in his voice as he zeroed in on her word choice.

"Yes, Jason. Let. The point is to demonstrate that you're not a madman on the loose with unknown powers, answering to no one."

"Team player, that's me," he grumbled.

"If you're going to leave Killian to us, would you like to speak to him first or walk away entirely?"

"I may be willing to walk away from revenge," Jason said, "but I won't be giving up on villain banter. I don't have it in me."

She gave him a flat look.

"Yeah, I know," he complained. "No-fun, stern-adventurer Jason."

Cassin Amouz had not participated in the raid itself but had been the driving force behind the Amouz family's contribution to the operation. He arrived in the aftermath, shown into the warehouse by some of his own people. He spotted Liara speaking to a man wrapped in what looked like a portal; he had to be Jason Asano. Cassin strode over to Liara as Asano stepped inside the ritual circle and approached the prisoner.

"Princess Liara," he greeted.

"Lord Amouz. Thank you again for your support of this operation."

"Consider me motivated to root out all the people who have betrayed our kingdom and our world. This sickly thing you have chained up knows the traitor who helped take my son?"

Liara nodded as Cassin looked around.

"And the other thing?" he asked. "She's here?"

Liara nodded to where Clive, Farrah and Belinda were still badgering the ritualist with questions.

"Darker skin," she said, to differentiate the fair-skinned Farrah from the swarthy Belinda.

Cassin moved over to them. "Belinda Callahan?"

"I didn't take it," Belinda said, pointing at Clive. "I saw him doing something; I'm pretty sure it was him."

"What was him?" Cassin asked. Clive rolled his eyes and went back to examining the ritual diagram on the ground.

"Nothing," Belinda said. "I have no idea what you're talking about."

Farrah sighed, giving Belinda a look she normally reserved for Jason.

"I'm Farrah Hurin," she said. "And yes, this is Belinda Callahan. You're Lord Cassin Amouz, are you not?"

"I am. I've wanted to take the chance to thank you, Miss Callahan. The bold risk you took in infiltrating the Order of Redeeming Light's stronghold is the reason my son was brought home before they finished infecting him with their heinous magic. You have the eternal gratitude of the Amouz family, and me, his father, most of all. If you ever have need of anything at all—"

"Ooh, free stuff!"

Farrah sharply nudged Belinda with her elbow.

"I mean, you're very welcome," Belinda corrected.

"How is Young Master Gibson?" Farrah asked.

"Yeah," Belinda said, her tone suddenly less playful. "He wasn't in the best way, last time I saw him. I wasn't in time to help him."

"Yes, you were," Cassin said. "The specialist from the Church of the Healer is optimistic. *Cautiously* optimistic, as he repeatedly specifies, but it's hope."

He settled his gaze firmly on Belinda.

"Hope that you have given me," he told her. "And I meant it when I said if you ever need anything. All the free stuff you can carry."

"You may want to rethink that offer, Lord Amouz," Farrah said. "She has a storage space power and a lot of imagination."

Belinda didn't say anything glib, thrown by the sincerity of Cassin's gratitude. It was not something she was used to, and she suddenly felt awkward. He recognised that and nodded.

"I have a lot to organise here, so I shall leave you now. But the door of the Amouz family is always open to you, Miss Callahan."

When Cassin left, Farrah nudged Belinda's shoulder.

"Feels good, doesn't it? Genuinely helping someone. It's why you're better off being an adventurer than a thief."

"You're right," Belinda said, holding up a pocket watch. "You should probably have this back."

Farrah frowned as she took it from Belinda's hand.

"How did you even get this?"

Enveloped in a starry void, Jason looked more like he was floating than walking as he moved, but he dismissed the cloak as he reached Killian. He stood in front of the pale elf chained to a thick metal pole. Killian had a narrow, bony frame and pallid skin, which was unlike the normally hale appearance that even elves that weren't essence users had. Jason took a small device from his pocket and tapped it. A privacy screen manifested invisibly around them, preventing anyone else from eavesdropping on their conversation.

"You certainly look more impressive than the last time I saw you, Asano."

"You look about the same. I'm told that each time we rank up, we get closer to how we are represented in our souls. That makes your soul pretty damn ugly."

"And yours tediously vain. You're a lot prettier at silver rank, Asano."

"I look more like my brother than I used to. That used to annoy me."

Killian narrowed his eyes.

"He died, didn't he? Your fault?"

"Not my fault. It was another selfish prick like you."

"Ah," Killian said. "My mistake was that I assumed that you would seek me out in vengeance for what I've done to you. It never actually occurred to me that you would be willing to bring in outsiders and let them take that from you. But it seems you've tasted vengeance and found it not to your liking."

"You seem rather calm, given the circumstances."

"Oh, I have many secrets, many resources and contacts; knowledge and insights that are very valuable. Especially to groups that cannot do what I have done, yet desire what I have gained from doing them. Organisations tend to make deals with people as useful as me, rather than killing us for our many transgressions."

"Which is what will happen here, I'm sure. So long as they're adequately fed, I imagine you'll live long enough to finagle your freedom again, sooner or later. We live very long lives."

"And you can accept all that? I thought you were an idealist."

"I was. Still am, I hope. But I've come to realise that taking the best that things *can* be is better than lamenting the way they *should* be."

"A man of compromise now?"

"Maybe. Sometimes it feels like I'm the only one willing to do what it takes to turn what should be into what can."

"You sound tired, Asano."

"Actually, I'm better than I've been in a long time. I'm just tired of compromising with people like you. That's why the Adventure Society can have you. Make a deal, kill you, let you go; I wash my hands of it. I was done with you a long time ago."

"Yet you couldn't resist talking to me."

"It's true. I'm testing myself, I think. Can I let what you've done go and leave you to the authorities and whatever slack they may cut you?"

"And how is the test going?"

"Unremarkably. I'm a little surprised, to be honest. Until I heard your name again, I hadn't thought about you in a long time. Turns out it's because I didn't care."

"Is the same true for your pet thief with the pretty silver hair? She's been giving me a look that says she wants to kill me."

"That's because she does want to kill you. But she didn't spare you a thought either, until your name came up. You're a target of opportunity, and that's all. At the end of the day, you just don't matter. You're a lesson of days gone."

"Listen to you. You're quite the big shot now, but I've seen you naked and helpless. Not just without your clothes, but without that ridiculous mask you use to hide away the malevolence inside you."

"I don't hide it, Laurent. Not anymore. I use it, as needed, and then I put it away until the next prick like you comes along. But you know, if I asked these people to let me take you away, they would."

"I imagine so."

"But I'm not going to do that. You're responsible for enough stains on my soul already; you aren't worth another. I suppose this is the part where I tell you all the terrible things I could do to you—and they are very terrible—but I just can't be bothered."

"I believe you, Asano. I know a little about the forces with which you seem to be involved, and they're very intimidating. Why do you think I wanted to kill you? If we meet again, I'm fairly certain that goal will be out of my reach. In fact, you'll probably be able to kill me out of hand."

"You may be right. Would you be interested in garnering a little goodwill for when that day comes?"

"You want something from me."

"You secured the service of a portal user for your brother. A friend of mine would very much like to know who that was."

"And if you walk out of this ritual circle with it, it makes you look good in front of all the fancy folk who are oh-so-scared of you right now. Helps buy you the time to grow strong enough that you don't have to care what they think."

"Pretty much. But it also signals to them that you're amenable to working with them. Given the reticence of your brother and his friends, that's a valuable signal to send."

Killian and Jason looked at each other in silence for a long time.

"Despite my best efforts, I've underestimated how dangerous you are, haven't I?"

"Yes."

Killian jerked his head, indicating all the people around them in the warehouse.

"They don't know that they've done the same yet, do they?"

"No."

"And you need to become stronger before they realise. You aren't afraid I'll tell them?"

"You don't know enough to make more than baseless predictions. They know I'm dangerous enough now that they won't risk pushing. Not on your word."

"There are some who would."

"There always are."

Killian chuckled.

"Yes, there are. Esteban Galo is the name you are looking for, Mr Asano."

"Thank you, Mr Laurent. You'll forgive me if I hope we never see each other again."

"Mr Asano, you'll find my hope on that count to have significantly more fervour than yours."

6

DEAR JOHN

JASON TOSSED THE LIST OF NAMES ONTO THE TABLE IN FRONT OF HIM.

"This is what Dawn was up to," he said as he rubbed his temples. "She could have told me. It's not like I was doing much more than lounging about recovering."

He got up and moved out onto the pagoda balcony, leaning on the rail and looking out to sea. In the distance, light flared as a magical storm was absorbed by a windmill-like mana accumulator.

Farrah moved to stand next to him.

"She knew she'd have to talk you into it."

"So, she left, knowing I'd go along because she wasn't here to argue with and I'm sentimental."

"A mortal failing, she called it."

"Then I guess I'm not that mortal. We are *not* taking Zara Rimaros as an auxiliary team member. If nothing else, she's a full-blown adventurer. Auxiliaries are taken for their specialty skills, and her specialty is blowing up a bunch of monsters with typhoon powers."

Farrah took a recording crystal from her pocket and held it out for him to take. Jason groaned.

"She left a recording crystal with you and bailed again?" he asked. "These are starting to feel like Dear John letters."

"What's a Dear John letter?"

"It doesn't matter," Jason said.

"I'll give you some privacy to watch it. Just remember that we're going out to help Autumn find a familiar this afternoon."

"Yeah."

Farrah went to the elevating platform and left Jason alone in his suite. He moved inside and a crystal projector formed out of cloud stuff. It was a small plinth, capped by a pyramid, atop which was a slot for a recording crystal. Jason placed the crystal Farrah had given him and then dropped into a sprawl across a couch. A large image of Dawn's face flickered into place over the projector, making Jason feel like he was looking at a hologram of Emperor Palpatine.

"Sorry for the galactic emperor look," the projection said. "I was hoping it would make it feel less like a Dear John letter."

"We could have just had a conversation," Jason muttered.

"I know we could have just had a conversation," the recording of Dawn said, "but conversations with you always go awry from what the other person intends."

"Not always."

"Yes, always."

Jason looked at the projection, affronted. Dawn laughed.

"I wish I could see your face right now. You're not as unpredictable as you think, Jason."

Jason's mouth formed a thin line as he pressed his lips hard together in frustration.

"Yes," Dawn said, "I know you're grouchy that you can't talk back, but that's the point. This isn't a discussion. You're going to sit and listen, get crabby about it, then accept what I've done because I'm not here to argue with and it feels wrong to deny me without having me here to argue with."

"I'm starting to hate this recording."

"I've been discussing with the Adventure Society about this false identity. Since you'll be signing on with your own team as an auxiliary, it will be less obvious if your team takes on multiple auxiliaries at once."

"I know. I've seen the list."

"You're still passive-aggressively having a conversation with a recording, aren't you?"

Jason glared at the image.

"But here's the good news," Dawn said. "The list is fake."

"What?"

"I knew you'd get cranky, so I made a list of names that would annoy you, so that you'd be less angry with the real list."

"I wouldn't have to get cranky if you didn't give me a fake list full of people I'd never take. I bet you did this for laughs."

"Also, I thought it would be funny."

"I knew it! You knew you were just... and I'm still talking to a recording."

Dawn's expression softened and the image zoomed out, showing that she was sitting on the grass on a hillside somewhere, in a white summer dress. It was decorated with images of a flower known as phoenix wing.

"This is going to be a new start for you, Jason. You've told me about when you first came to this world and all the promise it held. This is your chance to have that adventuring career you were imagining back then. Maybe not exactly as you imagined it, but I suspect you won't be too unhappy with having a secret identity."

Dawn's image looked regretful, as did Jason's watching it.

"I guess I should give you the real list of names," she said. "Rufus, obviously.

He'll fight with you, but strictly speaking, he'll be listed as a trainer. You still have a lot to learn from him, and your friend Taika could benefit from his knowledge as well. Gary is another easy inclusion. Once he finds out that you can just conjure up all the rare materials he could ask for to practise his smithing, I'm certain he'll jump at the chance, even if he can't take his results out of your soul space. Just make sure he does some work where people can use the results as well. I imagine that diamond-rank mentor of his will turn up regularly to keep him on the right path."

Jason couldn't argue with those picks.

"You should consider Estella Warnock as well. I think you would be better than me making that approach, but she'll work well with Belinda and she seems a little lost. Also, I know you love her pink hair, so maybe try to hide your celestine fetish at least a little."

"I do not have a… I'm arguing with no one again. Also, I'm lying."

"Yes, you do have a fetish," Dawn said. "Stop lying to yourself."

Jason grumbled at the projection.

"Those are the easy picks," Dawn said. "Next come people you aren't so familiar with. There's a man named Amos Pensinata. He's a gold-ranker that you've probably heard of. Like you, he's had some experiences with soul trauma that left him with a more capable aura than most. I've convinced him to travel with you for a time and teach you some of the things he's learned about soul manipulation. Some of it will come from his own experiences, while others will be things you would normally learn at or just before gold rank. Fortunately, Mr Pensinata takes a more learn-as-need view."

Jason was familiar with Pensinata by reputation. He was the man who had defeated the same forces that had forced Jason to almost kill himself fleeing in the underwater complex.

"Pensinata has one condition for travelling with you, which is that he brings his nephew with him. The young man has a problem common to adventurers in high-magic zones: he was sheltered through iron and bronze rank and lacks independent experience. Pensinata wishes for his nephew to get some seasoning, away from his overprotective parents."

"He's not going to kidnap his nephew, is he?"

"Carlos Quilido can tell you more about Amos, as they have known each other for a long time."

"That wasn't a no."

"Speaking of which, Quilido is also on the list. Your soul space will be a powerful tool in researching what has been done to the Order of Redeeming Light members. Which means bringing along the captured Order of Redeeming Light members."

"How many people do you think I can fit in the cloud flask's vehicle construct?" Jason asked the projection.

"I know that means a lot of people, but you should probably keep the prisoners in your soul space anyway."

"You can sod that idea right off. I'm not turning my soul into bloody Arkham Asylum."

"I'm assuming," Dawn's recording said, "that you just went on some kind of colourful tirade because, apparently, the word 'no' is too efficient for you."

"It lacks emphasis!" Jason yelled at the projection.

"If you really can't accept the idea, I have already discussed some alternatives —less secure alternatives—with Priest Quilido."

"Damn right. Carlos can buy a prison bus or something."

"There is one more person who needs to go along, and this is the one you're not going to like. The Adventure Society wants a representative attached to your team. Something of a personal liaison to you."

"You mean a spy."

"Yes, basically a spy."

"Stop predicting what I'm going to say!"

"No."

"Arrgh!"

Jason watched Dawn's laughing figure, realising that being there, teasing his future self was possibly the last piece of unadulterated fun she had before heading off into the cosmos on Very Serious Business.

"I don't know who they're going to choose for you," she said, "but I think they know better than to make some foolish choice. They know you'll flat-out refuse if they don't find someone acceptable and that pressuring you won't work. I made sure they at least understood that much."

"Good," Jason said.

Dawn's image took on a sad smile.

"We said our goodbyes in your soul space, so I won't retread that ground," she said. "I hope that when I see you again, you don't think too poorly of me."

She made a gesture and the recording ended.

Jason still hadn't emerged from his suite since Farrah gave him the recording when Liara arrived at the cloud house. Shade led Liara to one of the mezzanine lounges, filled with leafy plants and overlooking the atrium. Although opaque from the outside, the atrium wall rising halfway up the tower was transparent from the inside and let in plenty of natural light. Farrah was waiting for her at a table, drinking a tall glass of iced tea. She poured another for Liara from a pitcher as she gestured for the princess to join her.

"What brings you here?" Farrah asked as Liara sat. "We have an activity soon and are pressed for time."

"Assisting Miss Leal with her familiar ritual, yes. Quite a small-scale activity, given surrounding events."

"We're looking for small, Princess. And we value friendship."

Liara nodded. "Mr Asano knows about the Adventure Society liaison?"

"I gave him the message Dawn left behind, but he hasn't emerged since. I don't know what his reaction will be. Dawn tried to manage him as best she could, but there's only so much managing you can do with Jason. And only so much we're willing to. He might need some rough edges shaved off from time to time, but we're on his side first. Not the Adventure Society's and certainly not your family's."

"I have no qualms with loyalty, Miss Hurin. Loyal people are reliable, and I've found over the decades of my career that consistency is more valuable than capability. If you find someone with both, you treasure them."

"Has the society come up with a liaison they think Jason will accept?"

"I have a name, but whether he'll accept it is still up in the air. But I'm here for another reason. Related to your upcoming activity, in fact."

"Oh?"

"There is a lot of talk related to Jason floating around, but the amount of accurate information varies wildly amongst different circles."

"And?"

"And when information is scarce, people have a habit of taking what they know—or what they've been told, true or not—and adding in their own assumptions to fill in the gaps."

"And then those assumptions ferment into facts in their mind."

"Just so, Miss Hurin."

"And someone has made some assumptions about Jason?"

"There are certain sectors of the adventuring community—the bottom tier guilds and other, less formalised groups—where information about Jason has taken on a certain tone. Some rather drastic assumptions have been made and are threatening to head in a less-than-ideal direction."

"How so?"

"Information on Jason's actual combat ability hasn't spread nearly as far as his name."

"I see where this is going," Farrah said. "Someone has convinced themselves that Jason is all reputation and no power, and think that taking him out is their pathway to fame and prestige."

"More or less."

"And they know what we're up to today."

"Yes."

"Did you leak it so that these idiots would be coming after us and ruining Autumn's attempt to find a new familiar?"

"Of course not."

"You know she lost her familiar defending Rimaros."

"I do."

"It's been traumatic enough for her, without some idiots coming along and ruining what's already hard enough."

"I know."

"Do you, Princess?"

"Miss Hurin, I was in the bowels of that flying city. I had friends and family convince me to let them sacrifice themselves. I would never do what you're suggesting to someone who made sacrifices for my city and my kingdom."

"But I'm not talking about you using her as bait. I'm talking about you using Jason as bait, which you've done before. Autumn would just be collateral."

"I didn't do this, Miss Hurin. It came from some Magic Society source. No conspiracy, just some administrator who saw that Miss Leal had registered she was going to go out and conduct a binding ritual, with a list of who was going to stand watch for her. An opportunist sold some information, we heard about it, and I came to warn you."

A portal opened and Jason stepped out.

"You're going to do more than warn us, Princess."

7

THIS DOESN'T FEEL GLORIOUS

THERE WAS A ROCKY OUTCROPPING ON THE SOUTHERN MAINLAND, WELL BEYOND the border of Storm Kingdom territory. Towering over the jungle, it overlooked a sweeping river and was an excellent landmark to portal to. A portal opened as someone did just that, and adventurers appeared. Emerging first were silver-rank guild adventurers, followed by Princess Liara and, finally, a visibly nervous Autumn Leal.

Autumn looked around at the guild team assigned to watch over her familiar ritual. They were from the Sapphire Crown guild, whose bronze-rankers wouldn't give her a second glance on the street, even with her silver rank. They would be polite if they ever spoke to her, sure, but why would they? And all of that was aside from the gold-rank princess.

Liara directed them to start descending the outcropping.

"Don't think about them," Liara told Autumn in a calming voice. "My understanding is that if you aren't looking to attract certain varieties of carnivore, a calm mind is best for familiar rituals."

"I don't understand what's going on," Autumn said. "I mean, I understand why I'm here, but why are you here?"

"Mr Asano was unhappy that people coming after him were going to disrupt your familiar ritual, so he told me to take you to another site while he explains things to the people in question."

"He can tell *you* to do things?"

"No, but that doesn't seem to stop him."

She didn't point out that he also told the Builder to do things, which was really how they ended up in their current circumstances.

"Mr Asano's aura is rather strong," Liara continued. "Strong enough that even I can't read his emotions. So, when enough anger slipped through that I picked up on it, it was worth paying attention to. It meant he was probably going to do something drastic, and knowing there was no stopping him, I thought it best to steer him as best I could. Fortunately, there are procedures for this."

"For what, exactly?"

"After every monster surge, there's a lot of guild recruitment as quality adventurers the guilds had previously overlooked demonstrate their ability. Many great adventurers come from outside of the guild and aristocratic families, and the surge is where a lot of them get noticed. Unfortunately, every surge also brings adventurers that failed to distinguish themselves but are unwilling to accept that. They pick someone who did and try to make an example of them. Watching out for this very thing is how we caught wind of what was happening with you and stepped in. Asano is, after all, such an obvious target."

"But even with moving my ritual, won't they still go after Jason?"

"Yes. Standard procedure is to warn whomever they've targeted, and then let them. We've found that letting people bite down on the rock is the most effective object lesson."

Autumn nodded.

"I know you're only helping me because of Jason, but I'm still not sure how I ended up here. How did I go from standing next to him in line for a scutwork delivery job to all this?"

She gestured at the other adventurers and Liara herself.

"That was Asano's choice." Liara explained. "I've studied Asano's history as extensively as anyone can, I suspect. He has a habit of going a long way for relative strangers, especially if he feels that they've been wronged on account of his actions. You have met his team members, Wexler and Callahan?"

"Sophie and Belinda? Yes."

"They were thieves when they met Asano. He and Clive Standish caught them on a contract, only to discover they were to be passed off into a fate much worse than thievery warranted. It was quite political, very corrupt and extremely unpleasant. Asano undertook actions I can only describe as characteristically drastic, and two thieves went from a disastrous fate to elite adventurers. Asano made some rather significant enemies in the process and ultimately paid a hefty price. I don't believe he regrets it, even when that price was the scouring of his soul."

"Is he going to pay a cost for helping me?"

"Not unless, as I said, he's overestimated himself. You met Asano on a fortress town delivery?"

"Yes, but it was clear things weren't normal. There was a gold-ranker on board, and not just an ordinary one. He said it was because of pirates, but you don't send the Siege Sword to guard a supply run from pirates that could be anywhere. He was there to test Jason."

"Yes, he was," Liara agreed. "I'm afraid that I am ultimately the reason for your acquaintance with Asano. I put him on that airship, although it was His Ancestral Majesty who assigned Trenchant Moore. I was using Asano as bait to catch some Builder cultists."

"His Ancestral Majesty, as in…"

"Soramir Rimaros, yes."

Liara looked at Autumn.

"I'm not helping you calm down, am I, Miss Leal?"

"Not really, no. Did you catch the Builder cultists?"

"We got Purity zealots instead. There's no shortage of people willing to go after Asano, which is what has brought us to this predicament. There are only a handful of regions ideal for seeking out familiar-appropriate magical frogs, which is why we had to portal you to a more distant one. The one you were registered to visit is currently crawling with opportunists about to find that their opportunity is eagerly awaiting them."

Eleven people were moving through the jungle on the Storm Kingdom's western mainland. They were in a region hosting a major habitat for magical frogs, around a dozen kilometres from one of the main roadways that Jason had once travelled on a delivery contract. This was where Autumn Leal had been registered as going to perform her familiar bond ritual. It was also the place where two men, Rangel and Tellez, had led their teams.

"And to think you said this helmet wasn't worth the money, Tellez."

"It wasn't worth the money, Rangel."

"We aren't the only ones out here searching for Asano. This helmet will track him down."

"Assuming he doesn't have some way to block tracking magic. There are plenty of items and abilities that can do that."

"The artificer who sold it to me said it would penetrate those kinds of protections."

"People say all kinds of things, Rangel. My wife said she'd never leave me."

"Didn't she leave that alchemy vendor for you?"

"What are you saying?"

"I'm saying there's a pattern of behaviour."

"What kind of pattern is leaving me for a guy who sells umbrellas?"

"Ella left you for an umbrella salesman?"

"During a monster surge, no less. And they aren't even magical umbrellas. They're regular umbrellas!"

Rangel and Tellez were moving through the jungle with their team members in tow. They were hunting Jason Asano, and, knowing he would have his own team with him, had grouped together. They had learned that Asano's absurdly named Team Biscuit had six, giving them almost two-to-one odds. Not everyone was on board with the plan, however, and the singular woman in the group spoke up.

"Tellez, we could still back out of this," she told her team leader.

"Escamilla, you were outvoted."

"There's a Geller on Asano's team."

"Not one of the local ones; I've never heard of him. And not every Geller is so amazing. Their reputation is overblown."

"I don't know if that's true," Escamilla said. "And Gellers don't usually let just anyone on their team."

"I haven't heard of anyone on this one's team," Rangel contributed. "Except Asano."

"Who you hadn't heard of before," Escamilla pointed out. "Just because they aren't known locally doesn't make them weak."

"You're just looking for reasons to not do this," Tellez told her.

"You're right. We're roaming through the jungle, interrupting some poor woman's familiar ritual to beat the hell out of a fellow adventurer just for the glory. This doesn't feel glorious, Tellez."

"Stop griping. We agreed to this as a team."

"I did some checking around, Tellez. This woman lost her familiar defending Rimaros from the Builder attack."

"We all defended the city from the Builder attack," Rangel said.

"Our teams were on standby on Provo," Escamilla said. "We weren't exactly beating back the cult."

"Which is why we're here," Rangel said. "To get the prestige that was denied us when we were assigned away from the battle."

"I don't think it was prestige that we were denied," Escamilla said. "I think it was casualties. A lot of people died that day. Stronger people than us."

"That's what you think, isn't it?" Tellez asked. "That Asano's team is stronger than us?"

"I don't know," she said. "That's kind of the whole point: we don't know what we're walking into. I told you I did some checking around, and I spoke to Team Work Saw."

"Team Work Saw aren't worth a damn," Rangel said.

"They're a guild team," Escamilla said.

"Yeah, the worst guild team in Rimaros," Rangel said. "We could take them easy."

"I don't think we should go underestimating any guild team," Tellez said. "What did you get from them, Milla?"

"They've worked with Asano's team. Said they're a strange group, but serious business."

"What did they say about Asano himself?"

"The usual stuff. Don't mess with an affliction specialist. They said he was kind of an odd one, though. He—"

"It doesn't matter," Rangel said. "Affliction specialists are nothing. You just punch past their protection and put them down fast."

"And exactly how many affliction specialists have you 'put down fast'?" Escamilla asked.

"First time for everything."

In a nearby shadow, Jason was starting to wonder if this entire conversation was some kind of ruse to lure him into a false sense of security.

"That's what makes this such a good plan," Tellez said, gesturing at the recording crystal floating over his head. Rangel had an identical one. "We don't have to fight Asano's team. Not really. We have the numbers to tie them up long enough to give Asano a beat down. He's silver rank, so he can take it. And then we disengage and get out. They're looking for monsters and magical beasts interrupting the ritual, not a sneak attack from two teams of elite adventurers. We blitz, beat, and bolt."

"Yes, because that's what elite adventurers do," Escamilla said. "They record themselves attacking a fellow adventurer for no better reason than to build their reputations. Do you think there won't be any repercussions from this?"

"We want the repercussions from this," Tellez said. "With footage of us kicking the goo out of the guy everyone is talking about at the top end of town, the people they'll be talking about is us. Recrimination from the Adventure Society will only help raise our profile. He has a healer, Milla. No one will be suffering anything that can't be fixed with a few minutes and a few spells. It won't be that bad. We take our lumps and come out the talk of the town."

"Even assuming that this all goes the way you think it will," Escamilla said, "I'm not so sure I want to be the subject of that kind of talk. And don't think it will go just right. When has everything gone just right on a contract, let alone this mess? If we want to end up in the upper echelons of adventurers, Tellez, we can't be stuck on basic monster hunts, which means star ratings with the Adventure Society. Every famous team is full of two-stars, and most have at least one member with three. We have one member with two stars. Me. But when what we're doing here comes out—however it goes—my second star is going away. You aren't afraid of getting demoted because you're already sitting on one star, but I'm the one with something to lose."

Tellez stopped walking and turned on Escamilla.

"And there it is," he said. "Short-term thinking is one thing, but the real problem is that it's all about you, isn't it? The unwillingness to sacrifice for the team. The selfishness."

Escamilla didn't back off, getting in the face of the man, despite being a head shorter.

"Don't talk to me about selfishness, Tellez. This whole scheme is the embodiment of selfishness. How many people are you willing to hurt to advance yourself? This woman just trying to get a familiar? The team of adventurers we're attacking? They don't know about your plan, Tellez, so they won't be playing for fun. When we hit them, they're going to hit back. Hard. And not just today either. We're making enemies here that we don't have to."

Rangel and Tellez loomed over the smaller woman.

"You don't like it, Escamilla," Rangel said, "then how about you turn around and go home? We can live without one more damage dealer. If you wanted to have people put up with your crap, you should have gone for guarding or healing powers."

Escamilla looked to Tellez, waiting, but he said nothing.

"Seriously?" she asked after a long, tense silence. "You're going to let an outsider tell a member of *your* team to go and not say a single word in their defence?"

Tellez took on an awkward expression, but then firmed it with resolve.

"You agreed to go along with the team's decision, Milla."

"I never thought the team would be this insane!"

"Then why come along at all?"

"Because you're my team! And I thought that maybe, just maybe, I could convince you to give up on this idiotic plan of yours, Tellez."

"Actually, it was my plan," Rangel said. "Well, it was Maldonado's plan, but I'm the one who stole it. And if we're going to find Asano before he does, we need to stop standing around yelling at one another and get back to the search. If Asano and his team are anywhere near here, they've heard us coming."

Escamilla glared at him but didn't respond before turning her gaze back to Tellez.

"If we want to make a name for ourselves," she asked, "how about we do it with accomplishments instead of stunts?"

"We don't have enough accomplishments, Milla! The guilds are going to be recruiting now the surge is over, but we didn't do anything that will stand out. We can't get into a top guild if no one knows who we are."

"Look at what we're doing, Tellez! You think this—*this*—is what great adventurers do?"

"Asano isn't so great, and his name is on everyone's lips right now. That's what makes him the perfect target."

"We don't know what Asano is," she told him. "But what he's not is out in the jungle, targeting other adventurers to make some kind of point."

In a nearby shadow, Jason winced, scratching his head awkwardly.

"All this has done is show us who we really are," Escamilla said. "Every other group that we're racing to find Asano is the same as us; they're either in middling guilds or none at all. Maybe the reason we didn't get the attention of a big guild, Tellez, is that we're not meant to be in one. Maybe what this whole debacle is really telling us is that this is all we amount to."

Escamilla felt the atmosphere change. She knew she'd made a mistake as the auras around her grew hostile. For the first time since being empowered by essences, she was acutely conscious of being a woman. She was the only one on either team, leaving her in the middle of the jungle, surrounded by men. She stood, tense, unease creeping into her mind when screams rang out as a member of Rangel's team was dragged into the canopy.

8

EL DEMONIO QUE HACE TROFEOS
DE LOS HOMBRES

THE ADVENTURING TEAMS LED BY RANGEL AND TELLEZ WERE IN DENSE JUNGLE. With eleven members in the combined group, it was necessary to cut a path, but magic was more than up to the task. One of Rangel's team members, Barrera, had been doing so with a conjured blade-whip that made short work of anything, from thick scrub to entire trees.

Sunlight speckled in through the canopy above, leaving the two teams in false twilight as they stopped to argue over their current endeavour. Both teams had turned on a member of Tellez's group, Escamilla, when Barrera was suddenly hauled into the canopy, screaming. He was held in place by a swarm of shadowy arms, but they were more numerous than strong. Barrera wrenched himself free, despite more arms emerging to snatch at him.

Barrera's panicked screaming turned into more of an intermittent yell until he finally yanked himself free and dropped to the ground. The others saw that he had wounds from a weapon scored into his back, sliced into the weaker fabric around the stiffer panels of his armour. The cuts were shallow, to the point that the natural recovery of a silver-ranker should have closed them, but they were freely bleeding too-dark blood.

"Poison," Rangel said bitterly. "Carilo, cleanse him."

When no answer came, he looked around.

"Carilo?"

The silence magic that had been on the throwing dart that struck Carilo was not especially sophisticated. It would not prevent spell chants from working, which were about establishing a mindset in the caster, not making sounds that triggered magic. Any properly trained adventurer could cast their spells while underwater or otherwise muffled, even if that training hadn't been with a big family or fancy guild.

Casting a spell while being dragged by the face was another matter, however. Right after the very localised silence, tough straps had wrapped around his head, wet with the coppery stench of blood. Carilo didn't panic, trying to push out with his aura senses, only to find something pushing back.

He hadn't even noticed the other aura until it started suppressing him, which was a terrifying level of control. The strength of it was no less concerning, given that he could tell it was silver rank, yet had strength more like gold. It swiftly and mercilessly crushed Carilo's aura, completely suppressing him.

Carilo felt himself being swiftly dragged into thick scrub, plants whipping at him as he was yanked across the rough jungle floor. Panic was now kicking in, but Carilo steeled his resolve and reached up to pry at the straps binding his head. He couldn't get them off his head entirely, but at least managed to peel them away from his eyes, restoring his sight. He grabbed at a tree, halting his unwilling passage across the ground. He was in the midst of heavy jungle growth, the canopy thick enough to turn daylight into near-dark.

Acting quickly, Carilo activated his shield ability. It was the common force barrier that would stop projectiles, magical or otherwise, along with powers that directly affected the target. Such direct powers were common among affliction specialists, and if it was Asano that had attacked, it should be a strong counter to his abilities.

What it didn't stop were slow-moving physical objects, along with anything already in place, such as the straps around Carilo's head. He wrapped his legs around the tree he had grabbed, bracing himself against the straps still tugging at him. He then made a concerted effort to yank off the straps. They gave way, but they didn't pull away. The force yanking at them halted and they thrashed like tentacles.

The straps looked like leather that had been saturated in blood, which started raining off the flailing tentacles in thick gobbets. The blood splashed on the rich soil, the lush jungle scrub and over Carilo himself. Each of the gobbets rapidly transformed into leeches with horrific lamprey teeth. They crawled over Carilo as he scrambled to his feet, hopping back away from the straps. It wasn't so easy, though, caught in the thick scrub, and many leeches were already burrowing into his arms, legs and torso. His healer's perception power catalogued the poisons each bite pumped into him, many of which he resisted, but fewer than he should. He suspected the aura keeping his own locked down also had some means of suppressing resistance.

Carilo was no stranger to casting spells under harsh circumstances. Though being devoured by flesh-eating leeches was harsher than most, he didn't let it distract him as he started to cast a spell that would send searing light bursting out of his body.

"Bright heart of embers, burst for—"

Because it was about the mindset, a sword passing through the back of his neck and out through his throat shouldn't, strictly speaking, disrupt the spell incantation. It was a fairly good way to distract the mind, however, and the spell failed. The magic gathered inside Carilo, ready to burst out, instead went wild in his chest. He wasn't some weak iron-ranker, however, so the damage was relatively minor.

It took more than a severed spine and a miscast spell to slow down a silver-ranker; Carilo didn't allow himself to be distracted for more than an admittedly critical moment. He ignored the sword in his neck to move forward and launch a backwards kick, just a moment after the sword slid into him. He felt the kick connect, eliciting a surprised grunt from behind him, but whirling to confront his attacker, they were already gone. Disturbingly, the kick he landed had delivered some kind of retaliatory curse that was making the leech poison worse.

He knew his attacker had hidden rather than fled as Carilo's aura was still unnervingly suppressed. Having a moment to look around, he had time to consider the aura itself. It was overwhelmingly powerful and domineering; being suppressed by it felt like being in a dark room where he could only make out ominous shapes moving in the shadows. He reached up to push the sword out of his neck, but it slid out on its own. Carilo spun to watch where it went, even as he cast a healing spell on himself. Even for a silver-ranker, powering through a severed spine on raw willpower would only work for so long.

Trying to follow the sword to its owner was revealed as a trap as once more Carilo was attacked from behind. This new attack was by two quick dagger slashes that penetrated his light armour's weaker areas. The cuts were light and in non-critical areas, but Carilo knew that poison didn't need them to be. His resistance to various afflictions was quite high, but his perception power showed him that these afflictions didn't care as a terrifying slate of them dug in with each attack.

Whirling around, all Carilo saw was a dark shape withdrawing into the shadows. He didn't try casting a cleanse, knowing that with the length of the chant, it would get it interrupted without his team to cover him. The same was meant to be true of an affliction specialist, but that didn't seem to matter to Asano. And that was who Carilo assumed he was facing, after being swiftly layered with afflictions. Until that moment, he considered it might have been some other enemy, as he had still not gotten a clear look at them.

Carilo knew there was a clock on what was happening; his team would already be looking for him and the silence effect would not last long. Instead of casting a spell, he went for a potion from his belt, the vials having endured the drag across the jungle floor just fine. Belts that magically protected potions from incidental damage were amongst the most fundamental of adventuring gear.

As Carilo moved the vial towards his mouth, a dark arm emerged from the shadows surrounding him and grabbed his arm. Many more shadow arms shot out of the dark to wrap him up like a spider web. While he was able to pull himself free, the vial was knocked from his hand.

As Carilo pulled himself free, an alien figure appeared above him, hovering under the jungle canopy. It was a blue and orange eye-shaped nebula inside an otherwise empty floating cloak. Around it floated orbs containing smaller versions of the same nebula, all of which fired blue beams that were blocked by Carilo's shield.

Six beams savaged his shield, which vacuumed Carilo's mana to maintain itself. He realised the beams were disruptive-force damage, the bane of magical barriers. Then he felt more of his mana sucked out, drained away into the shadows around him, which were indistinguishable from one another in the dark.

Carilo allowed his shield to drop, knowing that if he let his mana drain completely, he was done. To his surprise, the alien entity floating above him ceased attacking the moment the shield dropped. It turned into a cloud of blue and orange light that dashed away, vanishing into the jungle.

In the wake of its departure, Carilo finally got a good look at his enemy. Emerging from the shadows, the figure he assumed to be Asano looked only vaguely like a person. It was wrapped in a starry portal, with eyes that looked like nebulas in a distant void, identical to those of the departed entity. Asano seemed unaffected by the thick scrub, as if space itself was warping around him to permit easy passage.

Carilo suspected the figure he presumed to be Asano cast a spell, unheard in the silence, as he felt more afflictions take hold. He turned to run, knowing his team was his only chance, but again he found his enemy right in front of him. Then he felt the sword that had flown off come back, stabbing right back into the same wound it had left. The silence ended.

"Feed me your sins."

Carilo's perception power sensed all the affliction leave his body, only for others to take his place. Sensing their nature and knowing afflictions better than most, as a healer, he found these new ones terrifying. Holy afflictions were notorious for not being subject to many cleansing powers. Those powers that did work were often slower or less effective. Carilo knew this well, the healer having such an ability himself.

Carilo couldn't bring himself to call out, too shaken as the panic that had been threatening to take hold of him finally dug its claws in. He also had a sword in his throat. Then, to his staggering surprise, the holy afflictions were drained into the sword. His perception ability briefly sensed some kind of power-suppression affliction before that ability was cut off, along with all his others.

Spent, he looked at the strange man in front of him as Asano's hand grabbed him by the face.

Escamilla was forgotten for the moment as Rangel and Tellez barked orders at their teams. While the healer from Tellez's team cleansed and healed Barrera, the others shifted from alert to battle-ready, prepping items, drawing weapons and initiating various defensive powers and buffs. They didn't hare off into the jungle looking for their missing team member, knowing full well it could easily be a trap. They were cautious and methodical in their approach.

They were all Storm Kingdom adventurers and very familiar with the terrain around the Sea of Storms. That familiarity wasn't necessary to find the throwing dart that belonged to none of them, but it did help find a trail. Traces of blood and a disturbed patch of scrub showed the way, although it was a little worrying that none of them had heard Carilo get dragged away.

Unfortunately, hacking a passage through the jungle as they had before would make it harder to follow the trail. They were forced to push through the scrub at a more cautious speed instead of having Barrera carve a path. Even so, the jungle could only slow down the physical power of silver-rankers by so much, and in a short time, they found the signs of violence. It looked to have been fairly contained, but there was no shortage of blood and there were signs of physical and magical combat amidst the thick scrub.

"How did we not hear this?" Rangel asked. "Tellez, do you think it was silencing magic?"

When no answer came, he looked around.

"Tellez?"

9
OCCASIONALLY CARNIVOROUS

A SUPPRESSION-COLLARED ADVENTURER WAS TRUDGING THROUGH THE JUNGLE, BUT paused in a clearing. He looked around warily, seeing nothing but lush jungle and dark shadows. His expression was conflicted for a moment, then he turned to walk in a different direction.

"That's not the way," a cold voice said, sending a chill down his spine, despite the sweltering jungle. He looked around again, still seeing no one but himself. He turned again, resuming his original direction.

Jason opened his eyes as he stopped sharing senses with Shade, hidden in the shadow of the latest prisoner. He was deep in the jungle, but moving with caution.

"Thank you, Shade. This one took longer than the others to think about trying to go find his team."

"I believe you have them rattled, Mr Asano. That's the fourth person you've plucked from right under their nose."

"Yeah, they'll be watching for all my quiet tricks now, and they've been way too careful about shielding their other healer. Maybe we should take a run at that other pair of teams."

"You may want to leave them for now, Mr Asano. They were already at the periphery of potential sites for Miss Leal to conduct her ritual, and they're only getting further away."

"They've gone in the wrong direction?"

"It is dense jungle, Mr Asano."

"And dense adventurers, from the sounds of it."

"In which case, it may be best to let them distract themselves."

"Fair enough," Jason said. "Moving them around with portals would be so much easier, but one of the prisoners might call my bluff and refuse to go through, even if I threaten to kill them. And then there's this."

He crouched down and looked at a thread so fine it was all but invisible to even silver-rank vision. If he hadn't sensed the thrum of aura connecting it to a network of threads spread all through the jungle, he'd have never known it was there. The scope of it meant it had been put in place over the course of days, maybe a whole week, in preparation for the conflicts currently taking place in this section of jungle.

The web worked by weaving tiny threads over a vast area, imbuing them with a tiny amount of aura, to connect them to the user. Monsters, animals and essence users could walk right through a thread without ever noticing, the broken thread reconnecting itself even as the user picked up details of the oblivious wanderer.

Logistically, setting up the web net was a huge pain, but there were advantages to the laborious requirements. While wide-area tracking magic was much simpler, it was also easy to foil. The web net was triggered by contact, circumventing effects that foiled regular tracking magic. It did have tracking magic woven into it as well, but this was designed to track portals rather than people. Jason might have an ability that shielded him from tracking, but his portals did not.

"This could have tripped me up if I hadn't seen it before," Jason mused. Mr North, Jason's foe from Earth whose true form was a rune spider, had used a similar ability with significantly more finesse. Web essence abilities were also in Dawn's repertoire, which Jason had seen her silver-rank avatar use on Earth. When it came to expertise in the execution of their powers, Jason had never seen anyone come close to Dawn. Jason's sharp aura senses allowed him to navigate without tripping the thread network net unless doing so served his purposes.

"The team led by Maldonado is better than the others in preparation and ability," Shade observed. "I am being careful of the main group, so I am not always close enough to eavesdrop, but based on their activity, I suspect that they deliberately lured the other teams into this endeavour."

"They still haven't taken the bait and gone after one of my prisoners roaming around?"

"No. Perhaps if you appear on their web net in the location where you are gathering them, they will believe it to be your base of operations and strike."

"Maybe. They might think it's a trap. I'd think it was a trap. Are they still gathered at a base camp instead of moving around?"

"For the most part. The bulk of their group has vehicles ready for rapid deployment while their scouts monitor the other groups. There may be another scout moving to survey the prisoner gathering, but either they haven't gotten there yet or they are better at hiding than I am at finding."

"They're probably waiting for a confirmation of my presence. If my moves against Rangel's and Tellez's teams are going to get more overt, I'll have to take out the scout from Maldonado's team watching them first. She almost caught wind of me when I nabbed that last one."

"Mr Asano, you are kidnapping and hauling off their team members. If that does not constitute overt to you, what does?"

"Having Gordon set off an orb explosion in the middle of them and snatching someone in the chaos."

"I see. Perhaps you should move on the group going the wrong way after all," Shade suggested. "Changing up your pattern will make it harder to ambush you."

"Agreed," Jason said. "I'll have to deal with them all eventually anyway." Jason looked up at a patch of jungle canopy. "What do you think?"

The air shimmered to reveal a celestine floating in the air with a recording crystal drifting around over her head. Her hair and eyes were a pale sky blue, compared to the rich sapphire of the royal family. Her skin was also very pale, another contrast to the royal family's typical caramel.

"Oh, it's you," Jason said.

Jana Costi was a gold-rank stealth specialist from Princess Liara's team. He had not seen her in months, since before the attack by the Builder's flying city. Her brother had sacrificed himself in that battle to detonate the designed that brought the city down.

"I'm sorry about Ledev," he said. "He was a dick, but so is everyone they build a statue of, and he definitely deserves a statue."

"Thank you... I think. How did you sense me?"

"I didn't; you hid from me perfectly. You weren't quite as perfect at masking the recording crystal, though. Close, but that only counts in horseshoes and hand grenades. Neither of which you have in this world, now that I think about it. Heidel shoes and alchemy bombs? It doesn't have the same ring."

"You're still the same, then."

"Well, I am fighting people alone in the jungle while you secretly follow me around; we've been here before, haven't we? I don't suppose you want to do a little light scouting for me?"

"Your familiar seems to be doing just fine on that front."

"He is pretty great."

There was a cave in one of the tracking web's dead spots. To further shield it from prying eyes or their magical equivalent, Clive and Belinda had established several magic wards. They wouldn't last long, but they wouldn't need to. This kind of magic was a speciality of Belinda's, going back to her days of setting up operation points when she and Sophie were thieves.

Jason's team, minus Humphrey and Jason, were sitting on picnic furniture conjured up by Belinda, eating from a sandwich platter set up on a table. Along with the platter were two pitchers of iced tea and one of juice.

"Only two blends of iced tea," Neil complained. "I hate roughing it on contracts."

"After three years of spirit coins, you adapted to Jason being back on the team pretty quick," Sophie pointed out.

"You know," Neil said, "I quite like the idea of Jason being an auxiliary. More sandwiches, less trouble."

"I'll believe that when I see it," Clive said.

Humphrey wandered in with a confused-looking, suppression-collared adventurer. He was peering at the floor, surprised at the lack of a need to watch his footing. Not far into the cave, he had found where Clive and Belinda had used some simple rituals to turn rough stone into smooth floor. It made traversing the cave much less tricky, as the light stones weren't set up until far enough in that they couldn't be spotted from the outside.

"Another one?" Neil asked, then jabbed a thumb at the corner. "Over with the others."

Humphrey shoved the prisoner towards a ritual circle that had three more people sitting in it. The ritual circle caused only silence and did not restrict the occupants from leaving it. What had happened when they made a break for it did that. The others waited for him to enter the silence zone before talking again.

"Should Jason be so blatant with using suppression collars?" Clive wondered as he watched the prisoners. "I know that a lot of adventurers keep them handy, but they are, strictly speaking, restricted tools."

"It's not like that's ever enforced unless the Adventure Society is looking to harass a member in poor standing," Neil pointed out.

"The purpose is political," Humphrey said, wandering over to the table and taking a sandwich. "Showing that Jason has enough support from the Adventure Society, or just enough influence, that he can flaunt the rules. Even if everyone is flaunting that rule already, he doesn't even have to pretend to hide it."

"Hey," Neil said. "Did you just take the sandwich with willowcress and boar chunks in spicy sauce?"

Humphrey looked at the sandwich in his hand.

"Yes. You've still got half a sandwich left to eat."

"I was going to eat that one next," Neil complained.

"You realise that you're going to get fat again," Belinda told him.

"I was never fat!"

Eric Maldonado was pacing back and forth in the ready site that had been set up days earlier. It was a cleared section of jungle with a ritual-magic perimeter to stop the jungle from growing back. In high-magic zones, plant growth could be sudden, unpredictable and occasionally carnivorous.

Maldonado had sunk exorbitant amounts into this operation, from burning favours to most of the money he had earned during the surge, but he was struggling to see the value. The specialist tracker who had been so expensive to hire was completely failing to track Asano, despite her assurances that her net would work around tracking-magic countermeasures.

All she had found was the people Asano had taken from their teams and sent roaming through the jungle alone. Maldonado even had a scout to check on them as they moved through the jungle and they were, in fact, alone. As for their destination, where other prisoners had already gathered, he was yet to send a scout because it reeked of a trap. If nothing else, the tracker had detected a portal some time ago, making it Asano's likely entry point to the area.

Asano himself was a stealth user, according to Maldonado's research, but the rest of his team was not. It was Maldonado's guess that the rest of the team were in that location, guarding Asano's prisoners and preparing an ambush.

It was increasingly clear that not only was Asano aware that he was being hunted, but had cancelled the familiar ritual and was hunting them, in turn. It was only the sunk cost of the operation that had stopped Maldonado from calling an end to it.

One of the reasons Maldonado was willing to continue was that the most expensive specialist on hand was a communications specialist. This was an Adventure Society official and getting him to participate in such a shady operation had been extremely pricy. His scout being able to feed him real-time information had made Maldonado more confident in maintaining a level of control. But the longer they operated without catching Asano's tail, the more that confidence eroded.

Asano had managed to take four people from Rangel's group. Not only did he do so under the nose of the rest of the group, but also under that of Maldonado's scout, watching them. Despite his assurances that he would not let himself be distracted again, Maldonado was not confident.

"Mr Maldonado."

The communication specialist, Constantin, approached him.

"I believe that Asano has decided to change his pattern and strike the other group."

"That makes sense. His attacks on Rangel's group were becoming increasingly untenable. What do you mean by 'you believe?' What did Piera report?"

Piera was the scout observing the second group.

"Piera was removed from my communication group," Constantin said. "That she did so without reporting it suggests that the first target of the attack was her."

Maldonado ran a hand over his face.

"How long ago?"

"Moments."

"You're saying that a silver-ranker was taken out before she could even report being under attack?"

"Unlikely. It is more likely that the communication was interfered with."

"How?"

"There are spells and wards that can do so. Many dispel effects can cut an individual out of a communication link. Also, such abilities work like auras and magical senses, in that they are an expression of the soul. A sudden soul attack could account for it. You said it was an ability of Asano's."

"An unconfirmed ability. Low probability of being true, according to my source."

Maldonado shook his head angrily.

"If Havi Estos hadn't gone dark, I wouldn't have been forced to use an untested information broker."

"Perhaps that was a sign that you should not have undertaken this at all," Constantin suggested.

"You were happy enough to take the money," Maldonado said bitterly.

"It was a lot of money," Constantin replied calmly.

Maldonado sighed and ran his fingers through his hair.

"Alright," he announced loudly. "Everyone gather round."

The rest of his team moved closer and he explained the situation.

"I know this isn't what any of us wanted," he said. "But the reality is that Asano isn't the soft target we thought. We knew he wasn't going to be, whatever that idiot Rangel expected, but this is more than we thought. By a lot. He knew we were coming and the information we had about how he fights was woefully inadequate. To the point that it might have even been fed to us that way."

"You think we were set up?"

"It's clear that he knew we were coming, so it's a possibility. It may be that his connections aren't *all* at the expensive end of town."

"What about Piera?" asked Reyes, one of his team members. "We're just going to let him have her?"

"Either she's dead or she's not," Maldonado said.

"She's not," the mercenary tracking specialist said. "I've just picked her up walking in the same direction as the others Asano took out."

Maldonado nodded.

"Pull out," he instructed. "I'll stay alone and approach where the prisoners are gathering."

"The damn ambush site?" Reyes asked. "Boss, you shouldn't go up against Asano by yourself, let alone his whole team where they're set up waiting."

"It won't be to fight. If Piera and the others are alive, it's to make a point."

"I knew we should have hired a gold-ranker," said Nuñez, another team member.

"The whole point was to show that *we* could handle Asano," Maldonado said.

"Yeah, except you lured in a bunch of other teams and hired merc specialists."

"Silver-rank specialists," Maldonado said. "This whole thing is about perception, not facts, and what people care about is rank. Outside of aberrations like Asano—which is why we targeted him in the first place—people don't play outside their rank. As long as we only use silver-rank assets, we'll just be looked at as resourceful. Getting a gold-ranker would make us look inadequate."

Maldonado hung his head.

"You're all leaving," he said. "I will go to Asano and negotiate Piera's return."

"Boss," Reyes said. "That will be giving Asano all the cards."

"He already has them," Maldonado said wearily. "We bet heavy and we lost. It's time to accept that with dignity and pay up. Make no mistake: we're in the wrong. We gambled our money and our reputations, and we didn't win. I'm not sure that we ever had a chance. The stacked deck is what drove us to this in the first place, and I'm not sure we ever really did have a chance. What comes next will be bad. How bad depends on Asano."

"It won't be that bad," Jason said, stepping out of the jungle. "I respect someone who knows when to cut bait."

10

IF YOU'RE GOING TO PUNISH SOMEONE

MALDONADO'S TEAM WHIRLED AT THE UNEXPECTED VOICE. A MAN WAS WALKING out of the jungle and over the ritual line at the edge of the base camp. He wore dark red combat robes, not voluminous like a scholar's robe, but still draping loosely. He was not tall, but he had the lean athleticism of an adventurer. His features were sharp, with a pointed chin under a neatly trimmed beard. His dark hair was glossy, shining in the sunlight.

His presence was unsettling for two reasons. One was his eyes, with black sclera and irises that weren't irises. They were made up of blue and orange energy that was similar to an iris, but not quite the same. The result was an uncanny-valley alienness, something inhuman wearing human skin.

Strange eyes were far from unheard of amongst adventurers, however. What genuinely unnerved them was that they couldn't sense his aura. At all. Looking at someone and sensing nothing was something that almost all adventurers had experienced at one point or another. It was what happened when someone higher rank was about to make a point. They knew Asano wasn't higher rank than them; it just felt like it.

"He's alone," said Nuñez nervously. He was one of Maldonado's team members.

"Shut up, Nuñez," Maldonado scolded. "You don't walk out in front of this many people without knowing something they don't."

A predatory smile teased at the corners of Jason's mouth. A portal arch rose up behind him and the rest of his team emerged, forming a row behind him. Maldonado walked out from his team to meet Jason and they stopped in front of one another. Maldonado was taller by half a head, with tan skin and hawkish features. A celestine, his hair and eyes were onyx black.

"You're him," Maldonado said.

"I'm him."

"It was never going to work, was it?"

"There's always someone like you. Someone who fails to make a name for themselves during the surge, then tries to make one on the back of a more successful adventurer. They watch out for that kind of thing."

Maldonado narrowed his eyes. "But they don't stop it," he realised. "They let the successful adventurer demonstrate where their success came from."

"If it's viable. You did a lot better than most, I'm told. You did deliberately leak your plan to Rangel and the other group, right?"

"Yes. The idea was to soften you up. Draw you into the open and strike."

"You made a lot of preparations. You don't seem like someone who needs to take this approach. I'd think you would do just fine playing it straight as an adventurer. Why gamble on this?"

"Family," Maldonado said. "A nobleman married into our family and—"

"That sounds like a long story," Jason said, cutting him off. "I don't care that much. At the end of the day, what matters is what you did, what I did, and where we go from here."

"And where is that?"

Jason moved away from Maldonado, looking around their base camp as he slowly meandered. There were skimmers designed to hover over jungle canopy, crates full of resources and Maldonado's team.

"You really went all out," he observed. "There were people who suggested that the authorities deal with this, instead of leaving it between adventurers. That you'd pulled in too many people and used too many resources for me to handle. Can you guess why I insisted on doing this myself?"

"To prove that you can?"

"No," Jason said, softly enough that only the sensitive ears of silver-rankers allowed him to be heard. "That's what the Adventure Society wants. What the royal family wants. What all the people with a vested interest in me not haring off and doing something drastic want. But I'm past the point in my life where I care about proving things. It doesn't change anything and it doesn't stop people like you or the Builder or gods from interfering in my life, even though they fall short. Every damn time."

Jason paused. Despite not needing to breathe, he drew in a slow, calming breath. He turned to look at Maldonado.

"The reason I came out here myself—why I started putting people down with my own hands—is because you brought trouble to my friend to get to me. That made me angry. I wanted to punish you, no points to make or reputation to build. Just visceral self-satisfaction. My first instinct was to make sure the only part of you that left this jungle was the part I washed off my hands, after."

Jason's face took on a sincere, friendly smile as Maldonado was finally able to perceive Jason's aura. To Maldonado's senses, Jason's aura seemed as authentic and amiable as his expression. It sent chills down his back.

"I've been in this situation before," Jason said. "I spent a lot of time in an emotionally dark place because of people like you. People who thought they could get something from me and didn't care who they hurt in the process. I don't, strictly speaking, regret all the killing, but I regret that I had to do it."

Jason let out a little laugh.

"Listen to me," he said affably, as if every person in the clearing wasn't completely focused on him. "I sound like a domestic abuser. As I said: an emotionally dark place."

His smile turned sad, his aura radiating regret, but also hope.

"But I'm better now. I think. I'm trying to be, so I don't do that kind of thing anymore. It's just hard, you know? Avoiding the harmful patterns of the past. Take you, for example. You saw a pathway to something you wanted and didn't care about going through the people around me to get it. For, that is what, in my world, they call a trigger. Something that might cause me to go back to old, destructive habits. To regress."

Jason walked into Maldonado's personal space. Close enough to smell his fear, if it hadn't been plain in his aura.

"You don't want me to regress, do you, Mr Maldonado?"

Maldonado shook his head.

"Great," Jason said, beaming a bright smile as he backed away. "You saw the attention I was getting and thought it was the people watching me that made me important. That if you humiliated me, they would be watching you instead, making you important. You believed that I was vulnerable. Soft."

"And he's not soft," Belinda called out. "He's harder than a fifteen-year-old boy getting a titty massage."

Every person in the clearing turned to look at her.

"What?" she asked. "I'm helping."

"Remember the discussion we had about setting a tone?" Humphrey told her.

"Belinda," Jason called out to her, pinching the bridge of his nose. "Please refrain from using the word 'titty' while I'm attempting to monologue."

"I told you that serious Jason was never going to work," Neil muttered, earning him a glare from Humphrey.

"Well, that's ruined," Jason said. "I had this whole speech about consequences and the choice between ruthlessness and mercy. Humphrey, should I just cut my losses and kill them all? It's not exactly the point I was going to make, but it'll do."

Maldonado's team had already been on a knife's edge, and Jason's offhand comment had them reaching for weapons.

"Everyone stand down," Maldonado called out. "He's not going to kill us."

"Try and kill us, you mean," said Reyes, a member of Maldonado's team.

"You heard him talk about the authorities," Maldonado said. "They won't let him just massacre a group of adventurers. He kept the prisoners alive, remember? Whatever is going to happen, he can't kill us."

Jason stared at Maldonado for a long time as both teams looked on, ready to spring into action.

"That's sound reasoning," Jason said finally. "What do you think, Jana?"

The gold-ranker revealed herself with a shimmer.

"What I think," she said, "was that the point was to prove you could deal with them without calling on a gold-ranker. That makes this somewhat counterproductive."

"I don't need you to deal with them. I need you to tell them what happens if I kill them all."

"Well, Princess Liara is going to yell at you."

Jason gave her a flat look.

"Fine," Jana acknowledged. "She's going to yell at me. And the Adventure Society won't be happy. Or His Ancestral Majesty. Actually, I don't know about him; he lets you get away with everything. You will certainly be disinvited to the celebration ball. Well, *almost* certainly. There are things that need to be… okay, you'll probably still be invited, but you'll get some moderately disapproving looks."

"Jason," Humphrey said. "You're trying to give up killing adventurers, remember?"

"Fine," Jason unhappily conceded. "I'm not just letting this slide, though. These people have to pay."

"It was me," Maldonado said. "This was all my idea. My team, my plan. I pushed them into it. If you're going to punish someone, punish me. I'm the one behind it."

"That's noble," Jason said, looking around at Maldonado's team. "But they're all here and they knew what they were coming for. They made that choice. And you didn't come just for me, did you? Or did you forget that the only reason I was meant to be here was to help my friend?"

Maldonado grimaced, glancing at his team.

"What will you do?" he asked.

Everyone waited in silence as Jason looked at Maldonado with a contemplative expression.

"The right choice," he said, "is to wash my hands of you and leave your fate up to the Adventure Society. If it were up to me, I'd have all your society memberships revoked. It would probably happen, in different times, but while the surge is over, the need for adventurers is not. But I'm tired of people's crappy actions being overlooked because they're going to be needed."

"You're wrong," Jana told him. "The Adventure Society needs people, but they turned on their own. The society can forgive a lot of sins, but not adventurers turning on one another. How did you think you got away with killing those adventurers in Greenstone? They'd given up adventuring and went after an adventurer in good standing. If you hadn't dealt with them, the society would have."

Jason turned to her. "Really?"

"Oh, yes," she said, gesturing at Maldonado's team. "These people were gone the moment they even attempted this plan. I imagine the society will recruit the smart ones as functionaries, though. Very closely monitored, and with crap raining down on them from a very great height. If they can take that and keep their noses clean long enough, they'll get a pathway back to being adventurers. Until then, they'll be scooting around after actual adventurers, cleaning up messes like someone with a new puppy. The rest will have to find their own way in life. Where do you think the noble houses get their high-ranking house guards? Dregs that were kicked out of the Adventure Society, usually."

After Jason had ratcheted up the tension, the appearance of a gold-ranker had wound things down. Unlike Jason, the vast majority of adventurers were very respectful of rank, and the appearance of an authority figure gave them confidence that things would be settled, if not well, then at least non-violently.

Jason's team moved from where they were lined up in front of the portal to join him.

"It's time to let it go, Jason," Clive assured him, putting a hand on his shoulder. "They'll get what's coming to them, and they aren't worth our time."

"Alright," Jason said and moved towards the portal. "Jana is surprisingly good at monologuing."

"Hey!" Maldonado called out. "You have one of my team members."

Jason stopped and turned around.

"So?"

Maldonado looked to Jana.

"Don't expect me to help you," she told him. "You sent people after him. The condition you get them back in is none of my business."

Jana then vanished in a shimmer.

"I'm willing to negotiate her release with no further harm," Maldonado said to Jason, who turned and walked away.

"You don't have anything I want."

"You're not going to the party," Liara told Belinda.

"Oh, come on. You're going to make me miss the big fancy party?"

"Jason, against all odds, was actually doing what he was told for once and playing the—admittedly melodramatic—serious adventurer."

In the cloud pagoda, an angry Liara, with a nervous Rick Geller beside her, was in the middle of reaming out Team Biscuit for going off-message. Sitting with them was Jana, sharing wincing side-glances with Jason.

"Don't even get me started on you," Liara told her. "You weren't meant to be seen at all, let alone doing a double act with Asano."

"It's not like you've never been to a big fancy party before," Sophie consoled Belinda.

"Yeah, but this time, I was invited. I was hardly going to steal anything."

"What?" Liara said, wheeling on her.

"I mean, I'm not going to steal anything. Please let me go to the party."

"You should probably let her," Clive advised. "If you don't, she'll just try and sneak in."

"It's in the royal palace," Liara said. "I'm sure she's a fine thief—she's certainly an enthusiastic one—but there's no way she won't get caught."

"And would her getting caught make things better or worse?" Jason asked. "Your best bet is to let her in the door."

Liara closed her eyes and groaned.

"My preference would be that you skip this ball and leave right now," she muttered through gritted teeth.

"Done, we're bunking off," Jason said, jumping to his feet. "Everyone out of the building; I need to turn this place into a magic school bus."

"Stop!" Liara commanded. "Sit down, Mr Asano."

"Boo," he jeered as he dropped back into his seat.

"I've been telling everyone this wouldn't work," Neil said.

"Look," Liara said. "There are a lot of people doing a lot of things to make this dual-identity scenario work. I've seen plenty of follow-up plans if it doesn't, but they aren't approaches that you're going to like. They aren't approaches that *I* like, if for no other reason than you'll disagree with them and I've seen how that works out. Just stay in the pagoda, don't make trouble and we'll see to it that no one else makes trouble for you."

"Autumn got her frog familiar?"

Liara's expression turned evasive.

"What happened?" Jason asked, narrowing his eyes.

"She has her new familiar," Liara assured him. "She's still out there, in her familiar's own environment as she gets to know it. She's strengthening their bond before she brings it back to civilisation."

"Is there a problem?" Humphrey asked.

"Well, I imagine you're aware that if someone gets an essence ability for a frog familiar, such as Miss Leal with her frog essence, that ability covers a wide range of creatures. Any kind of magical frog or frog-like magical beast."

"I'm getting the impression Autumn's new familiar is more on the frog-like than the actual-frog end of the scale," Clive said.

"Her original familiar was from the region where you were all just operating," Liara said. "There were also frog-type magical beasts where we took her, but it was a different region, with different creatures. She ended up with a familiar not quite like her original one."

"How not quite like her original one?" Jason asked.

"It's a long-tongue jumping hydra," Rick said. "It's roughly the size of a two-storey house."

"Cottage," Liara corrected. "It's the size of a two-storey cottage."

11

ONE MORE LOYALTY TO BALANCE

Jason and Liara were in the pagoda, taking tea in a parlour as they discussed the Adventure Society liaison to his team.

"Vidal Ladiv," Jason said. "It's kind of an inspired choice. Someone I like and respect—when I don't, that becomes clear very quickly. But he's not someone I'm close to, who will be biased in my direction. It's a smart choice."

Vidal Ladiv was an Adventure Society official who had done very well out of the monster surge, reaching silver rank and receiving multiple promotions. Jason had only encountered Vidal a couple of times, but had been impressed with his sharp observation skills and the careful manner Jason himself could never manage to cultivate.

"He's acceptable, then?"

"I'll want to meet him again, and discuss it with the team. But provisionally, yes."

"Good," Liara said, then placed her empty teacup down and stood up. "Then I'm going to go before something ridiculous happens."

"Oh, you shouldn't have said that."

"It wasn't a challenge, Asano."

"I'm just saying that tempting fate like that is buying trouble you could have avoided for free. Use the pole if you're looking to get out faster."

"The elevating platform is fine, thank you."

She descended to the atrium and walked across it towards the open doors. She heard loud sounds of splashing from the river outside, along with laughter and yelling. Leaving the pagoda, she spotted two giant hydras splashing around in the water, to the delight of onlooking children.

One of the creatures was the long-tongue jumping hydra that Autumn Leal had bonded with, while the second was almost identical. They were enormous and they sent water everywhere, only half-submerged even in the deepest part of the river. Rather than scales like a normal hydra, they had skin like frogs, patterned in shades of green, blue, teal and yellow. Liara looked at the difference in the second hydra, slowly blinked, then looked again, confirming that she wasn't imagining it. The second hydra had what was definitely—and extremely incongruously—moustaches on each of its five heads.

Two adults stood on the riverbank, one of whom was yelling.

"No! You do not get more biscuits because you have more heads. And you don't get bigger biscuits because you're bigger. We've had this discussion before, so if you want the biscuit to seem bigger, turn into something smaller."

"It can't hurt to indulge him just this once," Autumn told Humphrey.

"Oh, it's not just this once," Humphrey said. "It's never once with him. He's a biscuit bandit."

"Well, you do what you like," Autumn said. "I'm giving Brian one biscuit per head."

"Excuse me, Princess," a voice came from behind Liara. She turned around to see Rick Geller approaching where she stood in the doorway. He was pushing a wheelbarrow full of biscuits the size of dinner plates through the atrium.

"Rick, where are the parents of these children?"

"Oh, they're used to it. Humphrey's familiar is always shape-shifting into giant monsters, apparently. Turns out kids love monsters that aren't attempting to eat them. If you don't mind, milady, can I scoot past?"

She moved out of his way, and he wheeled his burden outside.

"Rick," Humphrey scolded on seeing the wheelbarrow. "What did I say?"

"That you wanted a wheelbarrow full of giant biscuits? That's what Jason told me you…"

Rick hung his head in shame.

"I see where I went wrong now," he said.

"It's not like he's going to get fat," Autumn said.

"I'm not going to let him get greedy. It's a problem with dragons, and I promised his mum."

Liara shook her head, looking around for her flying carriage, which she had left on the lawn.

"Where's my vehicle?"

"I have no idea," the moustachioed hydra said. "It's definitely not at the bottom of the river."

As her rental carriage had become a hydra toy, Liara had to go to the compound of the royal family branch living on Arnote and borrow one. She then returned to the sky island that contained the royal palace, along with residences for the majority of the royal family and some of the most prominent diplomats.

Entry to the sky island was via the column of water that reached up from the sea like the trunk of a tree. Her flying carriage, coming from the royal family, was designed to produce a bubble shield that was carried up by the column until it passed through the bottom of the island and surfaced on a small lake. The lake was in the middle of the sky island, with the royal palace constructed around it.

Leaving the carriage where the palace stewards would deal with it, she passed through the mandatory security checks that even the Storm King had to undergo on returning to the palace. Finally, she was allowed to move through the most public and least secure section of the palace.

After leaving the sprawling palace and entering the residential outskirts, she was finally allowed to move unescorted. With the festival ongoing, security at the palace had been stepped up. The end of the surge was an unofficial end to the moratorium on political intrigue, and with so many changes, some might be tempted to do something bold and stupid. Jason Asano wasn't the only one subject to such attention, and when the noble families went at one another, the stakes were always high.

The princess moved quickly through the wide, tree-lined boulevards, not caring about decorum as she used her gold-rank speed to flicker through the streets. She could have hidden with her prodigious stealth abilities, but on the royal sky island, that would trip alarms, rather than avoid attention.

Liara slowed down on reaching a park that many townhouses backed onto, including her own. She followed a path right up to her back door, from which delicious smells wafted the moment she opened it. She went inside and tension left her shoulders as she relaxed in the way that only arriving home made possible. It was nice having a full house again, with her husband home and her daughters still staying with them. Only her son was not living back home, having his own house on the most populous of the three Rimaros islands, Provo.

Liara was royal family, as were her children, but theirs was a minor branch of the Royal House of Rimaros. Compared to Vesper or Zara, who came from the main branch, Liara was barely royalty at all. Although technically a princess, she shouldn't even be referred to as Her Royal Highness. Outside of formal events, though, she would never be dinged for failing to correct that common mistake of protocol.

Liara's closeness to the dealings of the royal family proper came from one minor factor and one major one. The minor one was that her hair and eyes were the full, vibrant sapphire that was the signature of the royal family. Many branch family members lacked it, so it made others instinctively connect her with the main family line.

The major factor contributing to Liara's importance in matters of state was her accomplishments. She had a long and successful career, both as an adventurer and an Adventure Society official. She was known as a woman who got things done, and her accomplishments and importance within the Adventure Society made her a useful asset to the royal family. Her ability to straddle the line of her various obligations without violating any lines of loyalty was also highly valued. When holding seats in multiple camps, integrity went from desirable to necessary.

Inside the back door of her townhouse was a mudroom, where Liara slipped off her shoes and placed them on a rack. There was a laundry basket where she dropped her outer garments as she stripped down to slim pants and a simple shirt before going into the house proper. It was her husband and eldest daughter cooking, rather than using the servant automaton. Baseph insisted the food was better when cooked themselves, and while Liara could never tell the difference, she didn't point that out.

Liara and Baseph had an arranged marriage in their youth, which was normal in their society, and neither resented it. They had liked each other well enough and loved their children, and their relationship had grown into a comfortable friends-with-benefits arrangement.

Then came the death of Vesper Rimaros, who was only a distant relative but a close friend, and her team member, Ledev Costi. They had died together at the heart of the Builder's floating city, their bodies never recovered before they turned to rainbow smoke and vanished. The Church of Death had been needed to confirm that neither had made a miraculous last-minute escape.

After that came Baseph's ordeal with the underwater complex he had been managing being raided by the Order of Redeeming Light. With gold-rank threats literally hammering at the door, only another of Jason Asano's impossible absurdities had seen him escape safely. Asano had paid the price of that, not just by nearly dying but in drawing attention to his many secrets, now being eyed-off by the powerful and ambitious. Liara would always be grateful for that sacrifice, though it gave her one more loyalty to balance.

The result of these trials was that, in their wake, Liara and Baseph's marriage had become much more of a loving one after decades of casual relations. The losses and dangers that they faced made them confront how much they had come to mean to one another over the years.

Liara entered the kitchen, snaked a slice of vegetable and popped it into her mouth before kissing her husband on the cheek. He held his hands, wet and sticky from mixing ingredients, away from her.

"Have those hands been washed?" he asked her. "In the blood of the wicked does not count, by the way."

"Your father thinks he's funny," Liara told Dara, her eldest.

"You think I'm joking." Baseph went back to mixing stuffing in a bowl. "Hands off my chopping board until those hands have been cleaned, wife."

"Will Joseph and Zareen be joining us for dinner?" Liara asked as she sat at the kitchen table. Baseph and Dara shared a look, and Liara narrowed her eyes at them, resisting the urge to peek at their emotions through their auras.

"Joe is on his way," Dara said as she chopped vegetables. "Zareen wasn't sure if she'd be back in time or not."

"Back from where?" Liara asked. Zareen had been close to Vesper, picking up her relative's taste for the politics that Liara disdained but could never seem to escape.

"She went to see someone," Baseph said. "I'm sure she'll be back soon."

"Someone," Liara repeated, latching onto the word. As an investigator with decades of experience, she could recognise when a word was hiding multitudes of sin. "Please tell me that this has nothing to do with Jason Asano and the kind of kingdom-sized mess that follows him around like a hydra with five moustaches."

"I wouldn't say—" Baseph said before stopping short. "Wait, what did you just say?"

"I'll tell you about it later," Liara promised. "Where is Zareen?"

"Hydra with moustaches?" Dara mused. "Maybe I should be spending more time with Asano."

"Don't even joke about that," Liara said. "I do *not* want you getting involved with Asano and his nonsense. You remember meeting Rick Geller?"

"The one from up north," Dara said. "Has those elf twins on his team that keep teasing him?"

"I don't know about that second part, but yes," Liara said. "I saw him today with a wheelbarrow full of giant biscuits."

"What do you mean?" Baseph asked.

"I mean I watched him pushing a wheelbarrow full of enormous baked goods," Liara said, holding her hands up to indicate the size.

"Why?" Dara asked. "Something to do with that hydra?"

"It wasn't actually a hydra; it was a dragon," Liara said. "But I'll tell you about that later too. Where is Zareen?"

"Just so you know, Lee," Baseph said, "you're doing a really bad job of not of making a visit to Asano's pagoda sound anything but fascinating."

"Baseph. Where. Is. Our. Daughter?"

"She went to see someone. I told you that. Just to talk."

"And we're back to this. Who is the someone?"

"Look," Baseph said. "Zareen came to me with something she wanted to talk about, and she knew you wouldn't like it."

"What did she want to talk about?"

"An idea she had."

"That I wouldn't like."

"I think that's safe to say, yes."

"Was it something political?"

"I'd say so."

"And you told her to give up on the idea, firmly and thoroughly dissuading her?"

"Of course," Baseph said unconvincingly.

Liara looked at him from under raised eyebrows.

"I may have phrased it badly," he admitted.

"How badly?"

"He told her that if she wanted to pursue it," Dara chimed in, "she should go see Trenchant Moore."

Liara gave her husband a flat glare.

"Trenchant Moore is not a political man," she said.

"See?" Baseph said. "It's not so bad."

"With the single exception," Liara continued, "of being the contact point for His Ancestral Majesty."

"Oh, is he?" Baseph asked in a voice that might have sounded innocent if not for being an octave higher than normal.

"I think you had better tell me all about this idea of our daughter's, husband," Liara said.

"Ooh, you're in trouble now," Dara said. "That's her 'I caught you selling death essences on the black market' voice."

12

THAT BOY IN THE TENT

JASON WALKED ACROSS THE ATRIUM OF THE PAGODA AND LOOKED AT THE DOORS leading outside with a frown.

"Why do these swing open?" he mused out loud.

The doors and the section of wall around them dissolved into cloud-stuff, revealing Zara Rimaros standing outside them.

"I'll be with you in a sec," Jason said. "I'm just doing some home renovation."

The cloud-stuff re-solidified into sliding doors made of dark crystal, containing swirling blue and orange light. They slid open, revealing Zara again, but this time with a wry expression and raised eyebrows.

"Can't do just one eyebrow?" Jason asked.

"You have a very political mind, don't you, Mr Asano?"

"I have no idea what you're talking about," Jason said innocently.

"Vesper used to do that too. Provoke people socially because their reactions told her something about them, regardless of what the reactions were."

"She never did that with me. I think she just kind of hated me."

"She didn't hate you, Mr Asano. She was irked by you. I think she saw more of herself in you than she would like. It didn't help that you were a lot more brazen about it. She couldn't be as brazen because she wasn't as free. The Rimaros name has a lot of weight, and while that can be useful to throw around, we still have to carry it."

"You can call me Jason. I told you that back in the tent where we met."

"We've both come a long way since that tent."

"I suppose we have."

"You aren't as... volatile as the last time we met. You felt dangerous then."

"That's because the one I was most dangerous to was myself. I'm still dangerous to everyone else. More so than ever, in fact."

"I remember your habit of enduring tribulation and coming out stronger for it.

We met when you were on the way to see the gods, remember? They pushed you, and you suffered, but they knew that once you recovered, it would make you stronger. The next time I saw you, your aura was almost that of a different person. I realise now that what I saw then was only the beginning."

"They didn't know I would recover. It was a test as much as a gift. If I'd crumbled, they'd have moved on without sparing me another thought."

"Ours is not to question the gods."

"Ours might not be, but mine is."

"You're casual with blasphemy."

"Yep. Are you going to come in, Princess, or are we going to keep talking where all the eyes and ears watching my house can eavesdrop?"

"Your home is a little intimidating."

"Only from the outside."

Zara nodded and moved through the doors that slid shut behind her. Compared to the blank space it had been to her senses from the outside, the interior was just the opposite as Jason's aura flooded the place with a strength that even Jason at full power could not project himself. Only the fact that it was not hostile to her at all stopped her from running for the door. The exterior of the building was a literal looming tower, while the inside was a metaphorical one.

Jason actively dialled back the amount the aura of the pagoda imposed on Zara. She wasn't a gold-ranker that could shrug its influence off as easily as Liara or Carlos. Zara's lack of hostility meant that the aura of the place did not attack her, but neither was she one of Jason's friends, from whom the aura always withdrew to a benevolent background presence.

"You said it was only intimidating from the outside."

"I said it was only *a little* intimidating from the outside," Jason corrected.

Zara looked around at the open atrium, from the waterfall spilling off the mezzanine to the lush plants dividing the area into sections. The exterior wall was translucent from the inside, letting light spill in. There was a reception desk by the entrance with an alien receptionist: a cloaked shadow figure with one large eye made of energy instead of a face.

"What is this place?"

"It's a cloud house. Technically, it's a cloud palace, at this size. A fairly vertical one, but a palace. I couldn't have managed a tower this big at bronze rank."

"Jason, I am a princess of one of the most prominent kingdoms in the world. I've seen cloud palaces, and that is not what this is."

"Yes, Princess, it is. It's just not all that it is."

She looked at Jason.

"Do you ever wish you could go back to being the person you were in that tent where we first met?"

The amusement dropped from Jason's expression.

"I spent a long time wishing that. Long enough that the desire to go back turned into poison, taking me even further from who I was back then. You saw the result of that."

"I remember."

The last time Zara had seen Jason, he had been a raw nerve. Angry, violent and distrustful, using his mysterious powers to lash out at the world.

"I had to learn to accept who I've become," Jason said. "And who I'm becoming. That boy in the tent died because he wasn't ready for the path ahead of him."

"And what about the path ahead of you now?"

Jason took a long, contemplative look around at the atrium before answering. "We'll see."

He set out through the atrium, along a pathway defined by plants potted directly into the floor. Jason's adjustment of the doors was only the latest of the changes he had been making as he renovated the place to his liking. The atrium was much more garden-like than it had started out, with pathways leading to what was now an array of elevating platforms, as well as the fireman's pole. One pathway led to the wall behind which the array of poles for his team was hidden.

Following Jason, Zara looked at the brassy pole with curiosity. It ran up to the ceiling, where it passed through a hole sealed by a spiral aperture.

"What's that for?"

Jason was walking in front of her and couldn't follow her gaze, but he didn't need to. He could sense where her attention was through her aura.

"Sliding down from the upper levels."

"You have a problem with elevating platforms?"

"I might not be the boy I was when we met, Princess, but I haven't entirely lost my sense of fun."

"You can call me Zara."

They moved onto an elevating platform that rose through the mezzanine level overhead. At each floor, the aperture that the platform passed through was sealed by mist that allowed passage from below while serving as a solid floor from above. This dynamically solid-gaseous cloud-stuff was something Zara had seen in other cloud constructs, not just Jason's. It was the solid spiral doors sealing the holes for the fire pole that needed to open and close that came across as strange. Jason's cloud palace possessed strange traits and seemed exceptional, so the less elegant choice for the pole had to be deliberate. Like the pole itself, it spoke to a whimsical choice that had more meaning to Jason than practicality.

Despite the oppressive aura pervading the space around her, seeing that kind of indulgence from Jason made Zara feel a lot more secure. His angry, violent intensity during their short expedition together had been disturbing. He had left the party behind, not just annihilating Builder forces but somehow making them turn on one another. He had barely been less hostile to his fellow adventurers than the enemy.

The arrival of his team had mellowed him, but Zara had not been in contact since. Vesper's plans for re-aligning her in relation to the Irios family were overtaken by the war with the Builder and Vesper's death. It had made her nervous about the choice to see him, especially as he rejected her invitation to visit Vesper's memorial.

"I apologise for not joining you in paying respects to Vesper," Jason said. "There was a little too much attention on me for that, but I would like to do so before I go. I would be happy for you to join me, if you're open to some spontaneous scheduling."

She wondered how much he was picking up from her aura. There was clearly a profound connection between Jason and the pagoda, given that it was radiating his aura as if it were a temple to him.

They arrived at the top mezzanine level, which was a lounge area that continued the pagoda's theme of abundant plant life. Washed in sunlight passing through the huge translucent walls, Jason sat on a couch and directed Zara to an armchair.

"I'm sure you didn't come here for a raincheck on a private memorial," he said. "What brings you to my door, Zara?"

Zara looked at Jason for a moment before speaking.

"The Adventure Society is assigning you a liaison," she said.

"If by assigning, you mean looking for someone we won't dump in the ocean inside of a week, then yes."

"There has been an idea floated," she said, "of another such position. Your group is growing and the royal family would like to have a representative in it. No authority, just someone who can be a genuine auxiliary, offering specific skills that could be useful to you."

Jason narrowed his eyes as he looked at Zara.

"What we—"

He held up a hand to cut her off.

"Allow me a moment to think," he told her.

"I know you can see through my emotions. This isn't a trick."

"I didn't think it was. But I'm also not reading your emotions. I could, you're right, but my aura manipulation isn't as sloppy as it used to be. I've had time to work on it while I've been convalescing."

"You can't stop yourself from reading the emotions of others when their auras overlap with yours. Not if they can't mask them properly."

A smile crept onto Jason's face.

"You're telling me what I can't do, Princess? That, historically, has not been something people have done accurately, and things don't tend to go well for them after. My aura strength means that I've been passively intruding on the privacy of the people around me for a while. That made things hard for someone close to me and made it harder to come together. It prevented us from having more time together than we ultimately did."

It wasn't hard to see there was an unhappy story there; Zara didn't enquire further.

"Removing the unmasked emotions of others goes beyond ordinary aura manipulation," she said. "You would effectively have to partition a section of your mind to assess the incoming information and decide whether to process it into your conscious mind or ignore it. That's deft mental self-manipulation and aura manipulation."

"There are aspects of our silver-rank attributes that I think go overlooked. The agility of the speed attribute is leveraged nowhere near as much as the strength of the power attribute. Even less so is what the mind can accomplish with a silver-rank spirit attribute. It's something I've been delving into as I explore combat trances, but it seemed to me that there were further applications. Every silver-ranker can multitask quite well, but how many of us work on those aspects? Fortunately, I have a friend whose family trains adventurers. He was at least able to give me some foundational training techniques."

"I'm vaguely familiar. Mind puzzles and observational tasks that require multiple threads of attention, yes?"

"Yes, but sometimes focus is important too, or we miss details. For example, I asked for a moment to think, which you appeared to completely miss as you launched into another conversation."

Zara smiled in awkward embarrassment. "Sorry."

Jason stood up, walked to the edge of the mezzanine and leaned on the railing with his hands, looking out through the clear wall. Zara stayed where she was, not wanting to interrupt his thought again.

"Why are you here?" Jason asked without turning around.

"I wanted to talk about placing someone from the royal family in—"

"I know what your purpose is. Why are *you* here? Why not Liara? Your family has been wise in letting her be their face in this. She's someone I know, and the lingering presence of Vesper engenders my sympathies. I suppose the same is true for you, but it's more complicated."

He turned around.

"Liara didn't want to do this," he realised. "She refused to be a part of it. Why?"

Zara opened her mouth, but Jason forestalled her with a gesture.

"Not actually asking," he said. "I'm just thinking at you. If Liara is against it, that means either your family is trying to do something stupid and she knows better, or she's fine with doing it but doesn't like something about the way it's being done. Soramir would stop anything too idiotic, so…"

He grinned.

"Zareen," he said. "There's no way Liara would go with us, and who else would we put up with? They wouldn't put her eldest in that position because she's pure adventurer. She doesn't have the political sensibilities for it or any interest in cultivating them. But the other daughter was more intrigued when they came to visit us. And she was close to Vesper, I recall. Playing on those sympathies again. The only other real option would be you, Zara, and that's obviously never going to happen. There's too many complica…"

He trailed off with an awkward wince.

"Oh," he said, moving back to sit opposite her, on the edge of his couch seat. He leaned forward to look her in the eye. "You did want it to be you."

"I thought you weren't reading my emotions."

"I wasn't. Now I am. I'm sorry, Princess, but you don't get a ride on this bus. Why would you even want that? Aren't you trying to be the next queen in whatever competition thing they do here?"

"That chance died the moment I tried my idiotic plan with Kasper Irios. Vesper was trying to salvage my reputation so that I might not be completely pushed aside, but now she's gone and the relationship with the Irios family she was using as a pretext means her plan will never happen. I've already withdrawn from the contest, and with it, my title as Hurricane Princess."

"Won't that contest be going on for years? There's time to make a comeback."

"There are no comebacks. The monarch is the person who went beyond expectation without making mistakes."

"Mistakes are how we grow."

"And the people who made them will be fine advisors to the monarch who didn't."

"Ah."

"In any case, that's not my path anymore."

"I'm sorry about that, Princess. But I'm not your new path. You made some choices that caused me trouble I very much did not need."

"I thought mistakes were how we grow."

Jason opened his mouth to respond, only for nothing to come out. He closed his mouth, looking confused.

"I find myself forced to acknowledge the point."

Zara stood up.

"Zareen would be a strong addition to your group," she said. "She was already planning to move from adventuring to Adventure Society service, the way her mother did years ago. It seems she wants to pivot, however. This whole thing was her idea."

"And Liara knows my background better than most. She wants her daughter nowhere near me, and I can't say I don't empathise."

"I'm not going to try and sell you more than I already have," Zara said. "Whether you choose Zareen, myself, someone else or no one at all, I'll leave it to you. Now, if you don't mind, I'd like to try that pole."

Jason blinked his surprise, then grinned.

"I don't think your father would want that."

"My father is not as protective a parent as Liara."

"You say that, but most fathers try very hard to keep their daughters off the pole."

"Why? What's wrong with it?"

13

A DIFFICULT CHILD

THE TAILOR, ALEJANDRO ALBERICCI, HAD COME TO THE PAGODA TO MAKE FINAL adjustments on the formalwear of Jason's companions in advance of the celebration ball. They were situated in a medium-sized parlour with a transparent wall that let in natural light. Alejandro was also a fully capable dressmaker and had arranged the gowns for the female members of the group—some of whom were more open to the experience than others. Sophie glowered as Alejandro checked over Belinda's gown.

"Why would anyone wear this?" Sophie asked.

"Because maybe I'd like to enjoy myself and feel pretty every once in a while?" Belinda said. "It wouldn't kill you to let yourself be a little feminine every now and again, Soph."

"It might kill me. Stuff tries to kill me a lot."

"Can't you relax for once in your damn life? Instead of complaining, how about you just tell me I look good?"

Sophie's expression was grumpy but apologetic. She looked up and down Belinda's salmon-coloured gown.

"You do look very nice, Lindy."

"Thank you. It's kind of fun preparing to attend a ball instead of preparing to rob it. Oddly enough, the time and expense is much the same either way."

This drew an odd look from Alejandro, who was crouched down, checking her hem. He stood up in front of Belinda, giving her a firm nod.

"Miss Callahan, you are perfect."

"See?" Belinda said, leaning to address Sophie around Alejandro. "People like you a lot more when you don't have to drag compliments out of them with a block and tackle."

"It was not a compliment," Alejandro said. "Just a simple statement of fact."

Belinda shoved a finger into his face.

"You can take your sexy hair and back off," she warned him. "I'm spoken for."

Alejandro held up his hands in surrender, giving her a charming smile.

"My loss," he said. "Now, for Miss Wexler."

Alejandro opened the lengthy garment bag where he had left it hanging on the rack he had brought with him. Sophie braced herself as he slid the bag off her outfit. She was surprised to see a formal pantsuit rather than a gown.

"Mr Geller made it quite clear," Alejandro said, "that anything you could not comfortably kill people in was unacceptable. As I pride myself on fulfilling the needs of my clients in style, here we are. The magical augmentations are focused on defensive properties, with a more robust self-cleaning system than normal. This means that after any excitement, you can return to the party without having to explain away any awkward viscera stains."

"See?" Belinda said. "Now, put on your damn clothes so we can go get our hair fixed."

"What's wrong with my hair?"

"Mr Williams," Alejandro said. "Just between you and me, I appreciate your custom."

"No worries, bloke," Taika said as Alejandro telekinetically adjusted a seam. "I just like finding someone that works in my size. Getting good clothes can be a struggle back home."

"That," Alejandro said, "is precisely the point I was looking to make. I've worked with a lot of leonids, but their fashion proclivities have given me pause on more than a few occasions. No offence intended, Mr Xandier."

"No, I'm right there with you," Gary said. The two largest members of Jason's group were being fitted at the same time.

"Your lot have clothing issues?" Taika asked. "Is it because of the fur?"

"Yeah," Gary said. "Most leonids wear clothes that aren't much more than a few straps, strategically placed for the bare requirements of modesty. I've even seen some isolated all-leonid communities where they don't bother with clothes at all."

"Nudist towns?" Taika asked. "Not sure I'd be up for that."

"Nor should you be," Alejandro said. "As a purveyor of fine apparel, I protest nudity in the strongest possible terms."

"I like a nice, loose coverage," Gary said. He had taken to the local fashion in Greenstone, which was free-flowing and colourful, with decorative tassels featured heavily. His current outfit was very much a loose drape, almost in the combat-robe style that Jason favoured, but the colours and cut were neat and sober. The colours were light, as was the local fashion, with Taika in white and Gary mixing cream with grey to flattering effect.

The door to the men's dressing room slid open and Jason came in.

"Hairdresser is calling for you," he said.

"Bro, Shade is the hairdresser, and he's got like thirty bodies."

"He's mostly after Gary," Jason said.

"Why me?" Gary asked.

"Bro, you're a lion man. You've got a mane."

Amongst magically propelled carriages, the class of grand carriage was more akin to a bus, ranging from smaller ones with seating for ten or twelve through to triple-decker tour bus sizes designed as mobile homes for entire groups of people. The one that arrived on the lawn in front of the pagoda was around the size of a school bus, with ornamentation that marked it as belonging to the royal family. Jason was already waiting when a gowned Liara emerged.

"Let's go inside," she told him. "Still too many ears out here."

The atrium doors slid open to grant them passage and slid shut behind them.

"Are your people ready?" Liara asked.

"Just about. I get the feeling you want to talk about Zareen first, though."

Liara glowered, but not at Jason.

"She's a grown woman and I can't make her choices for her," Liara said. "In this case, though, you can."

"Are you asking me to say no to Zareen as the royal family liaison?"

"Are you thinking about saying yes?"

"I haven't decided to accept anyone, let alone considered who it would be. The Adventure Society representative I understand. They're going out of their way with creating a fake adventurer identity for me, and want to keep an eye on how that goes. And me, of course. But what reason do I have to let the royal family insert themselves into my affairs? Again. I don't know if you recall, but my involvement with the royal family was never something I went looking for."

"I'd be perfectly happy if you didn't take anyone. The family sees the way His Ancestral Majesty treats you and thinks that a relationship now will reap benefits in the future. When you're gold, even diamond rank."

"I'm uncertain on this," Jason said. "Having Rimaros royalty could open some useful doors for us. But it could also draw unwanted attention, especially if it's someone like Zara. But this decision isn't just mine. It's the whole team's, and when I don't have a real leaning on an issue like this, I'm inclined to defer to them. Maybe you should take the chance at this party to make your case to them individually."

"I might just do that," Liara said. "There are some things you will need to know before the ball begins."

"This is the political part?"

"This is the political part," Liara confirmed. "This ball is essentially a starting flag for the resumption of political manoeuvring. The surge is over and there's plenty of power, influence and money, all on the table. No one is exactly sure when the conflict with the messengers will start and we'll be back on a war footing, so the noble houses are eager to grab what they can, while they can."

"Oh, great. You know how much I love being treated as a tool for someone else's ambitions."

"Then don't."

Jason looked at Liara with suspicion. "What are you saying?"

"Your recent endeavour with those adventurers demonstrated that quite amply. You didn't put up with their games, or ours."

"What do you mean, yours?"

"I know that roping in Jana to your little game was improvised."

"She did very well."

"But the way Miss Callahan impulsively yelled about... well, you know what about. It wasn't quite as smooth as you might have hoped, and even if it were, do you expect me to believe she did so on the spur of the moment?"

"Yes?" Jason said optimistically, earning him a wry frown from Liara.

"You wanted to show that while you might be willing to play the game," she said, "you'll always play it your way. And that's fine. Trying to stop you from being you is an exercise in futility. We would appreciate it if you brought the right version of you to the right situations, however."

"You're not just speaking generally," Jason said. "You want me to do something at this ball."

"There are factions on factions," Liara said. "We've been very carefully looking into what various groups will be trying to do tonight. We're fairly confident that someone will challenge you to a duel."

"You're kidding. Over what?"

"They'll find a pretext. It will be someone young. Silver rank, like you. From one of the lesser houses that a greater house is using as a mask."

"What does anyone involved hope to get out of that?"

"The lesser house gets the favour of the greater one, and if their scion can make even a decent showing against you in a mirage chamber, it will bring him key prominence. As for the greater house, they're likely looking to see who will step up to support you, maybe even make hay of the situation to draw them out."

"Echo-sounding the political landscape."

"Echo-sounding?"

"Something people on Earth do to map out specific environments."

"Earth. That's the name of your world?"

"Of the other world. You don't know a lot about my time there, do you?"

"Not much more than what you've told me. Any time you would like to tell me more, I would be open to that."

"Another day, maybe. Today, I need to know what you expect me to do about this duel. Since you haven't taken steps to put a stop to it, I assume you're leaving it to me."

"I've learned that expecting things from you is not a sensible approach, Asano. Just deal with it however you see fit."

"Seriously?"

"Just remember what I said about the right version of yourself in the right situation. We've discussed fun Jason and the other Jason in the past. You keep referring to this ball as a party, but it's not. We don't want to see fun Jason. We want the other Jason."

"You're giving me open slather?"

"If I'm correctly guessing the meaning of that from context, then yes. Trying to tell you what to do never works out, Asano, be it because of you or some madness you're caught up in. I've come to realise that the best approach is to accept that and work around it accordingly."

"Huh," Jason said, his expression nonplussed. "Now you say that, I feel a bit like a difficult child."

"Really?" Liara asked lightly. "That comparison never occurred to me."

Jason and his team were far from alone on their trip to the ball. The grand carriage made a number of stops to pick up people on the way to the palace. Liara's family was already inside when it arrived at the pagoda, which was clearly for the sake of appearances. It was far from practical, given their home's proximity to the palace, to fly all the way to Arnote only to fly back.

At the pagoda, it took on Jason and his team, Rufus and his, plus Taika and Travis. In Livaros, they stopped at the Temple of the Healer to pick up Arabelle and Carlos, and from the Temple of Knowledge, they picked up Gabrielle.

Jason had barely seen Gabrielle since his first arrival in Rimaros. There was contention between them, not to mention that she was Humphrey's former lover. Jason was surprised to find that Sophie had no interest in the woman, but Travis did. Jason knew that Travis had been meeting extensively with the Church of Knowledge to determine what he could and could not bring to this world from Earth's magitech, but only now discovered that Knowledge's representative had been Gabrielle.

Arabelle sat with Jason and her son, Rufus, so that they could have a quiet discussion during the trip.

"We need to have a discussion about Callum," Arabelle said. "He has become increasingly agitated about your prisoner, especially after finding out that you're leaving. To the point that I have finally managed to have him tell me the real reason he is so emphatic about getting to her."

"Oh?" Jason asked.

"Not here," Arabelle said. "I'll find you tomorrow."

Their carriage was one of many that entered the column of water rising into the royal sky island. It docked at the side of the lake and their rather large contingent was led to the ballroom by palace stewards.

There was a lengthy process of their each being announced, during which time they stood around and waited, looking over a ballroom the size of a sports oval. Over them, the roof was domed crystal, showing off the evening sky, with light coming from levitating chandeliers.

Jason, Travis and Taika stood together, looking out at a room where most of the people were high-ranking celestines. It was a sea of beautiful people with brightly coloured hair and sculpted, athletic bodies. The three of them shared a look.

"Does anyone else feel like…" Travis said.

"…we just walked into an anime," Jason finished.

"Bro, I feel like I'm going to do something not very sensible tonight."

The other two nodded their agreement.

14

ALL SINGER AND NO SONG

THE ARENA-LIKE BALLROOM WAS SET UP IN VARIOUS ZONES, EACH OFTEN REPEATED in different places around the room. Along with long buffet tables, stewards roamed with trays of food and drink. There were dining tables and small lounging areas, each with its own high-end privacy screen. The dance floor was expansive and mostly filled with young members of society in the delicate game of courtship. The privacy screens kept any sound from getting out, but did not prevent it from getting in, and there was no shortage of people using them to politic. Aura etiquette was very strict, with auras tamped down.

The Storm King and Soramir Rimaros were in one such private lounge area, but theirs was elevated, allowing everyone to see them and them to see everyone. They sat with other core members of the royal family, chatting quietly. It was clear from the body language that the presence of Soramir, the founder of the kingdom they ruled, was not helping his descendants to relax.

Liara instructed Jason's group to not roam in a giant pack like adventurers stalking a monster. She needn't have bothered, as not only did they not pay attention to her, but they immediately split up. Clive took off in the direction of a group wearing formal versions of scholarly robes. Gary, Farrah and Neil toured the food tables while Sophie and Belinda wandered off together, looking suspiciously like they were casing the joint. Gary wasn't waiting on the palace staff and their tiny trays, having liberated a large serving tray from somewhere. He was at the buffet tables, loading it up like a giant plate.

Humphrey and Rufus, the two socialites among Jason's friends, accompanied Liara's daughters to circulate. Liara's husband and son, Baseph and Joseph, moved in the direction of the Amouz family. Baseph had come from that family before marrying into the royal house, and both men were high-ranking administrators in the family's business interests.

Rufus' mother, Arabelle, was playing guide to Carlos, a priest of the Healer who was not comfortable at fancy social events, while also riding herd on Travis and Taika. As for Jason, Liara was leading him to circulate, introducing him to a chain of prestigious citizens in rapid sequence. Most were nobles, but some, like the Remore family, held prestige and influence without holding titles.

"Jason Asano," Liara said, "I present Lady Ileana Irios. Lady Ileana, Jason Asano."

The ball had, thus far, been a rather tedious sequence of Liara introducing Jason to people and Jason not saying much as he did his best to look passive and mysterious. His usual air of general amusement at the world was not in evidence in his face or voice, both of which were blank and cold as he met person after person.

"When we were having our little reputation problem with young Kasper," Ileana said, "you suggested a meeting with our family. Perhaps we could have that meeting in the near future?"

While Jason was still embroiled in the aftermath of Zara using his name when she thought he was dead, he had run into Kasper Irios. The encounter had been engineered by Vesper for political reasons and Jason had made an overture to the Irios family that they had not taken up.

"I'm afraid my near future is occupied," he apologised. "While I had the time before I became so prominent, you unfortunately never found the chance to seek me out. My window of availability has now closed, so I'll have to accept it as a missed opportunity."

Following Jason's diplomatic rebuke, Liara quickly hustled him on, moving into the privacy screen of an empty standing table.

"If you could refrain from making personal jabs at an ally the royal family only just managed to reaffirm their ties with, that would be appreciated," she told him.

"I know you've been treating me as one since I arrived in town, Princess, but I'm not an asset for the royal family to play around with as they like."

"I know that this is all a show, Asano. You only need to play stern Jason with others."

"You've been talking about 'fun Jason' and 'stern Jason' as if they were both personas and neither was actually me. What you need to understand, Princess, is that they both are very real. I don't have multiple personalities; like anyone else, I act differently in different company. I use certain parts of myself to keep a lid on other parts where maybe I shouldn't be left to my urges. You should be very careful about asking for anything but fun Jason, Princess. He's the lid."

"Jason, the royal family is your ally."

"Yes. But I don't much care for allies, if I'm being honest. I consider you a friend, Liara, so I don't count favours. But House Rimaros is an ally, and an alliance is just a measure of relative benefits. It's a cold relationship and every-thing comes at a price. Yes, I'm here because looking like I'll answer to the royal family, even if that is a lie, is of value to each party."

"You don't like being paraded around like livestock at an agricultural fair."

"It doesn't matter if I like it because I agreed to it. But if you want me to do tricks, Princess, you'll need to feed me a treat."

"What kind of treat?"

"That's on you to figure out. I'm not looking to do tricks."

The two noblewomen moved away with wary expressions on their faces.

"Bro, stop talking about sailor uniforms."

"It just came out," Travis sobbed. "I'm not good with women."

"No kidding. You're so bad with women that now I'm bad with women. This is a new experience for me; I'm a delicious chocolate drop."

At that point, Arabelle found them again.

"You're the size of a house," Arabelle told Taika. "How do you keep sneaking off?"

"I'm like a jungle cat; lithe and stealthy."

"I thought you were a delicious chocolate drop," Travis said.

"I can be both. I've got depths."

After their discussion, Liara left Jason to his own devices for the time being. He spotted Rick Geller and wandered over to speak with him. They found a couple of quiet seats with a privacy screen and sat down.

"You really are carrying yourself differently," Rick said.

"How so?" Jason asked.

"You're not surrounded by beautiful women."

"Rick, this is a party where the serving staff are cored-up silver-rankers. Everyone around us is beautiful."

"Yes, but you don't have a personal barricade of them," Rick said. "Or your sparkly cloak, for that matter. I thought you would be using it to accessorise."

"That was your idea," Jason said. "It would be a little lacking in decorum, and Alejandro would be disappointed if I covered up his excellent formalwear."

"There's no shortage of people using their more flamboyant powers to add a little flash. Something I recall you not being above."

"Back in Greenstone, maybe. Not here."

"Didn't you paint the sky with your personal crest and blast your aura across the city? As I recall, you did that here and in Greenstone."

Jason's expression took on a warning that Rick did not miss.

"In Greenstone, Richard, I was being tested to make sure I wasn't a slave of the Builder after being kidnapped and implanted with a star seed. And here, I was unconscious when that happened, and my friends were desperately trying to save my life. I hope you haven't been telling people that was some kind of display designed to grab attention."

Rick shook his head. Jason's aura remained sealed away behind a polite facade, yet Rick still felt pressured by the sudden intensity coming off Jason. Jason saw the effect he was having and relaxed his body language.

"Rick, people who have power don't need to flaunt it. Look around at the people in here showing off. They're young, trying to stand out. Back in Greenstone, I was just like that—all singer and no song. Desperate. Always making a spectacle of myself; blustering my way through like a pufferfish. That worked in Greenstone because it's a whole town full of empty bluster. But now we're on the opposite end of the world, literally and figuratively. This room contains some of the most powerful people on the planet, and they know that the more you have, the less you need to show."

"No big stunt from you tonight, then?"

"I didn't say that. We'll see where the evening takes us."

"Zareen," Jason said. He had been sitting alone with a plate of food, periodically rebuffing social overtures when Liara's daughter approached him. He waved her to a seat.

"Mr Asano, it almost feels like my mother has been shepherding me away from you since we arrived."

"Your mother has other issues on her mind, I'm sure. And call me Jason."

"No, she doesn't. Not at the top of her mind anyway. She hates this aspect of being royalty, but she inherited House Rimaros' interest in you from Vesper. There was a sense that there aren't too many people you would tolerate, and that you would be unsubtle in making that clear."

"Which neatly brings us to the topic you really want to talk about," Jason said.

"I can be an asset to your team. I'm not as prominent as Zara, but I can offer almost as many benefits. More, without the parts of her reputation that aren't the best."

"I don't doubt it," Jason said. "But I don't like how you manoeuvred me, Princess."

"I didn't manoeuvre you."

"No? You positioned me as the person who has to say no to either you or your mother. That way, the ultimate decision was mine and not a conflict between the two of you. Whichever one of you ends up disappointed, something external is the crux of it, making reconciliation between you easier."

"You can benefit from thinking like that."

"I've tried playing politics before," Jason said. "I have a good eye for spotting political issues in time to react, but every time I try to actively participate, it goes wrong."

"It doesn't have to."

"It goes wrong," Jason reiterated, "and people get hurt. People who don't deserve it. Politics has a way of doing that. For example, I'm now caught up in the family politics between you and your mother. I don't like being in that position, Zareen. You made a bold move instead of talking to your mother about it because you knew she would be against it. I would have done that too, once upon a time. I wouldn't anymore."

"You're not going to take me."

"Do what you should have done in the first place: convince your mother. Excise me from your family politics and we can have the discussion again."

"Will you take Zara instead?"

"I don't know. Right now, I'm short on compelling reasons to take her, you, or anyone else the royal family may or may not have suggested."

"The family proposed other names? Who?"

"I never said they proposed any names. Go talk to your mother, Zareen, because you and I are done discussing this."

Zareen frowned but knew when to cut bait. She rose and left the privacy screen.

"The royal family hasn't suggested any alternative names," Shade pointed out from Jason's shadow.

"I never said they did."

"But Miss Zareen is clearly convinced otherwise because of what you said."

"Is she?" Jason asked innocently.

"You can be quite mean sometimes, Mr Asano."

"You're those thief girls trailing around after Asano, aren't you?"

Sophie and Belinda turned to face the brash young nobleman, flanked by three of his fellows. Their auras were clean of cores and Sophie could tell from the way they were standing that they were trained to fight, and trained well. She looked the boy up and down before turning away again without bothering to respond.

"Hey, I was talking to you."

"Do you think someone put him up to this to provoke us?" Belinda asked Sophie. "I can't imagine them letting anyone in here dumb enough to make the kind of scene they seem to be heading for on purpose."

"Look at you, all sophisticated," the boy said. "Not bad for someone who crawled out of the gutter."

"I know," Belinda said. "We started with nothing, and here I am at the same place, at the same rank as you, without all the money, time and effort they spent on you. Does that mean that we're amazing, or that you're just kind of a waste?"

"Don't bother," Sophie told her. "Boy, if you want to make trouble, you don't need a pretence. I'll be happy to punch your teeth through the back of your head."

"Let's go, Soph. You know Jason is the one who was going to be provoked into a duel. These idiots have obviously been sent to make trouble, so don't play along."

"Why is Jason the only one who gets to beat the blood out of someone?" Sophie complained. "I have healing potions to put the blood back in, after."

"Is that a challenge?" the boy asked.

"Y—"

"No," Belinda firmly spoke over Sophie. "It's a social event and we have no interest in socialising with you. Leave us alone."

Belinda directed Sophie away and the boys followed until the women met up with Liara coming the other way and veered off.

"Thank you," Liara said after the three women moved into a privacy screen.

"It was obvious that they were the end of someone else's stick when they made that approach outside of one of the screens," Belinda said. "They wanted an audience."

"It seems that whoever is looking to provoke Asano has realised that the best way to do it is to start with his companions," Liara observed. "You aren't the only ones being approached by less-than-polite individuals, but you all seem to be handling it well. I saw some young fool looking like he was going to cry while slinking away from Arabelle Remore."

"I'm not sure that's going to hold for everyone," Belinda said. "We might want to go find—"

A gong-like sound rang out. All eyes in the room looked to Gary, holding a dented serving platter as he stood over a man on the floor.

"And I only waited that long so I could finish the food on it," Gary said loudly. "You're worth hitting over the head with a lump of metal, but you aren't worth wasting good crab puffs. Bad crab puffs, maybe, but the catering here is excellent."

"I guess it's starting, then," Liara said, and moved to join her daughter, Zareen.

15

HEFTY NUGGETS

Unsurprisingly, the commotion in the middle of the palace ballroom drew attention from across the room. After glancing at Gary standing over some nobleman he had dropped with a serving platter, Jason's attention moved to everyone else. He watched body language and looked for aura spikes, as much as he could without pushing out his senses more forcefully. Most of the obvious reads came from younger members of the nobility, as the more experienced and high-ranking ball attendees had well-trained self-control.

Seeing Rufus making a beeline for Gary, Jason instead moved to join Princess Liara and her daughter Zareen inside a privacy screen. He asked about several people he had picked out as potentially being involved from the way they watched the scene. Some they ruled out immediately, as there was no political gain for them to prompt things from behind the scenes. Others they gave him quick introductions of, no more than name, house and known political factions.

Jason noticed that Gary and the man he hit were standing back, while Rufus and another man were talking.

"Why aren't the people involved the ones talking?"

"The etiquette, in matters of personal offence, is to have others stand for you in the discussion," Liara explained. "The idea is to maintain cool heads and allow diplomacy to rule passion."

"Does that work?"

"Not really. The real reason is to use such provocation as a political tool, as is being done here. The person standing for the 'aggrieved' pushes for a duel and stands for the person in that too."

"We have something similar in my world," Jason said. "Or we used to anyway. When we still had duels. There was a second who stood in if one of the participants didn't have the bottle to front up."

"Does that mean when they got scared and didn't show for the duel?" Zareen asked.

"It does," Jason said. "So, who is that standing for the guy Gary clocked?" Jason asked.

"I'm not sure," Liara said. "He's wearing the symbol for House de Varco."

"It's Lancet de Varco," Zareen said. "He's a tournament duellist; well known if you follow the mirage arenas, but they haven't been operating for months. He's also a sometime adventurer. His guild uses him for public recognition, and in return, they help rank him up with controlled monster encounters, the way aristocratic families do with their scions. He's one of the rare arena fighters to not use cores."

"Do you know where he was when the Builder cities attacked?" Jason asked.

"Most of his guild fought the city attacking Livaros," Zareen said. "All their 'special' members were assigned to monster watch on Provo."

"That's not so bad," Jason said. "I did that too."

"Yes, but while you were taking on gold-rank monsters by yourself, he was securing the inside of a bordello."

"It was just one monster," Jason corrected. "I'm not a madman."

Zareen and her mother shared a glance.

One of the people standing by was a gold-ranker, Quint de Varco, in the same dark maroon house colours as Lancet. He was amongst the people Jason had asked Liara and Zareen about. He stood out for having the same house colours as the man talking with Rufus, along with body language that Jason read as more anticipatory eagerness than the curiosity displayed by most of the onlookers.

"I think I'd better get in there," Jason said.

He didn't use his usual trick of aura manipulation to smoothly move past people; this was not a crowd it would work on. As such, it took him time and a little rudeness to move past the gathering onlookers. He arrived to find that the situation had been escalating.

Gary was still holding a serving tray with an almost cartoonish dent. The head responsible for that dent belonged to a sullen young nobleman, now back on his feet. Separating the two as they stood off against one another were Rufus and Lancet de Varco, whose dark maroon outfit had the symbols of his house and his guild stitched in gold. It was very flattering, matching the gold of the celestine's hair and eyes.

The adventurer facing Rufus was speaking.

"From the look of your friend, Mr Remore, I would be quite confident in presuming that no apology will be forthcoming."

"Let me guess," Rufus said. "You aren't willing to let this go unresolved."

"Your friend has humiliated mine. If no restitution is offered, then I am afraid it must be taken."

"A duel," Rufus said, blank-faced. "I assume you intend to stand for your friend."

"I am. Will you be standing for yours?"

"No," Jason said, stepping out from amongst the onlookers. "He won't."

Lancet turned to Jason.

"The storied Jason Asano."

"Yep. Don't know who you are, sorry."

"Then allow me to introduce myself. I am Lancet de Va—"

"I don't care," Jason said. "Someone put you on the end of a stick and poked you in the direction of my friend. I'm going to be honest, Lancet: I know there's been a lot of talk about me, and I'm only here so the fine upper crust of Rimaros can finally get a look at me. Get a sense of who I am. Which I suspect you're about to firsthand. I don't know if someone put you here to give me that chance or because they have some agenda, but it was the right move. When you go after me through my friends, you get to see exactly who I am."

Lancet laughed.

"You barged over here because you somehow thought this was about you?"

"I did."

"You're quite arrogant, aren't you?"

"It's kind of my thing. So, as much as I would like to watch you find out what happens when you challenge Rufus Remore, you're getting me."

"So be it," Lancet said. "We can make arrangements after the ball is finished."

"No need," Jason said. "It's a nice big room."

Lancet frowned in confusion.

"Big room?"

"For the duel," Jason said. "We'll knock it out quick and let these fine people go back to their celebration."

"Are you talking about fighting right here? We'll duel in a mirage chamber, you savage."

It was Jason's turn to laugh.

"Oh, no. You asked for a duel, not a dance. I hate to break it to you, bloke, but whoever put you up to this made you the pointy end of the stick. That's the end that gets blood on it. A duel is about putting yourself on the line for your principles."

"Putting your reputation on the line."

"And you think pretending to fight is where your reputation will come from?"

"I am an experienced arena duellist, you thug. I can assure you that it is very far from pretend and there is plenty of reputation to be had."

Jason grinned as he saw the gold-ranker from House de Varco wince. While there was no doubt that many knew Lancet's background, that was very different to making a point of it himself.

"An 'experienced arena duellist' wound up here, challenging someone to a duel in a mirage arena?" Jason pointed out, voice filled with scepticism. "It's almost like someone planned it."

Lancet blanched as he realised he'd broken the cardinal rule of the political setup by making the setup transparent. Everyone would continue to play along, but it was a minor humiliation for House de Varco. Jason wasn't going to leave the knife just sitting there and gave it a twist.

"Mirage chambers are for training. Arena duelling is a sport. I'm sure it requires a great deal of skill, but this social event is celebrating the people who put themselves on the line in the jungles and fortress towns. Who went into the depths to fight underwater monsters and stood their ground against Builder cultists and Purity loyalists. Reputation comes from what you do, not what you pretend to do in a magic playhouse. How do you fight for your principles when the fight isn't real? If you want a duel, you put blood on the line. If you don't have the courage of your convictions, you're just a coward playing pretend. So, what will it be, Lancet? Courage or cowardice?"

"Your words are just sounds of a beast, howling for blood because it's all his brutish mind understands."

"Cowardice it is."

"Refusing to participate in a backwards blood ritual does not make me a coward!"

"No," Rufus said, stepping up next to Jason. "Calling for a fight and then backing out when you actually have to risk something is what makes you a coward."

"You expect me to have a real fight with an affliction specialist?"

"What does his speciality matter?" Rufus asked. "I thought this was a matter of principle. Oh, are you worried that an affliction specialist can't face you without a team to support him? That's considerate, but unnecessary. He's an affliction skirmisher, not a traditional specialist. He'll hold his own against you, don't worry."

"I apologise," Jason said. "I mistook your concern for my wellbeing for cowardice. Now that it's settled, we can commence the duel. It looks like the dance floor has been cleared. Is that space enough for you?"

Lancet's smug expression was now pure bile.

"Rimaros is the heart of civilisation, not some frontier town. We settle our affairs like gentlefolk, not drunkards brawling in an alley."

"You're the one who picked this fight," Rufus said. "You can refuse to fight it and crawl off if you like, letting all these people know exactly what you are. That's the benefit of being in the heart of civilisation. The people in that alley you talked about? They don't get that choice. They win or die; they aren't free to be cowards."

"Stop calling me a coward!" Lancet snapped.

"Or what?" Jason asked. "You'll challenge me to a duel in a nice, safe mirage chamber?"

Jason could sense Lancet's feeling of being cornered as the young nobleman channelled his fear into anger. Jason knew that if he could sense it, so could many others in the room, which itself sealed Lancet's fate. The entire encounter was about putting on a show, and they had seen what Lancet was. As the one who had lost control of his aura, letting his emotions spill out, Lancet knew it as well.

"I guess you were right," Jason told him. "You do put reputation on the line. Your mistake was pretending to be something you're not. If you aren't willing to go all the way, you'll always come up short against someone who is."

"You're just a brute," Lancet shot back. "Everyone in here knows it."

"I don't deny it," Jason said. "Which leaves you the choice between fighting the brute or running from him."

"Refusing to spill blood in the middle of a royal ball isn't running."

"Fair enough. I'm sure we can find a training hall somewhere. Probably best."

"We don't have to find a training hall, you lunatic. That's what mirage chambers are for!"

"Mirage chambers are so you can do things without facing the consequences," Rufus said. "Duels are all about consequences, which means that, by definition, you cannot hold a duel in one. All you can do is spar."

"So, what's it going to be?" Jason asked. "We have all these people watching."

"Perhaps," a new voice interjected, "everyone can take a step back."

The crowd parted like the Red Sea to permit passage of the Storm King. The tall man had broad shoulders with bright sapphire hair spilling over in waves, a match for his gemstone eyes. He moved with absolute confidence, a vision of power both political and personal. Unlike many royal families, House Rimaros forged their scions in fire and not a scrap of monster core energy was detectable in his aura. He exuded authority, even amongst the elite of society, who scrambled to move out of his way.

"Young Master de Varco," the king said, "is here representing a powerful house and a powerful guild. I wonder if, in the spirit of celebration and reconciliation, he would be willing to withdraw his duel request. And that you, Mr Asano, Mr Remore and Mr Xandier, would be willing to accept that without blame or recrimination. No victors, no cowards and *no grudges*."

"I would," Lancet said, grabbing the lifeline.

The king looked to Jason and his companions.

"Will you accept the withdrawal of the challenge without prejudice?" he asked them.

"We would be willing to do so," Jason said, giving a short bow. "As a favour to you, Your Majesty."

They all felt the wave of whispers move through the onlookers; the favour of a monarch was no small thing, and the king would not be the one in debt. That would be Lancet and the forces standing behind him—whom the king had chosen to mention specifically.

"Then I will count it as a favour, Mr Asano. And as someone who has seen recordings of what you do to people, I'd appreciate your refraining from further attempts to do it in my ballroom. We pay our stewards well, but some things I would still feel bad about making them clean up."

"I'll do my best, Your Majesty. But some days people won't let you end it with clean hands."

The king let out a chuckle, like the parent of a naughty child.

"I think it's safe to say, Mr Asano, that after this display, anyone who comes to you looking for trouble will get exactly what they asked for."

The Storm King turned to leave, but paused as his gaze fell on Travis. The lanky, nervous Earthling had come to prominence by building the magical nuclear device that had been critical in ending the Builder's attack on Rimaros.

"Travis Noble," he said. "House Rimaros would like to again extend our thanks for designing the weapon that brought down the Builder's flying city and saved Rimaros, perhaps the entire Storm Kingdom."

"Er, you're welcome," Travis said, not sure whether to nod or bow. He ended up trying both, failed and almost fell over, drawing an amused smile from the king.

"Our door will always be open to you, young man. House Rimaros remembers the debts it owes."

He panned his gaze over the room.

"As well as the debts owed to it."

Once the king returned to the royal family's seating platform, Lancet moved off in the direction of his house members.

"It just feels awkward standing here after that," Jason said.

"We could go get food," Gary suggested.

———

Jason and his team received a wide berth after the incident. While he made a very distinct impression in Rimaros society, that wasn't the same as a good one. He was sat at a table with Liara and Zareen, sharing a large plate of food that Gary had left behind while he went to get a larger plate of food.

"That could have gone worse," Jason said. "It could have gone better, but on balance, I'd say I was happy. I'll call it a solid win."

"You would?" Liara asked. "Everyone thinks you're dangerously volatile now."

"Which matches with what they've been assuming, based on all the rumours floating around about me. I was never trying to ingratiate myself with the nobility. I was trying to cement myself as an unpredictable factor with the favour of the royal house. Between the king and people seeing us here, sharing snacks, that's coming along nicely. No one wants to interfere with me until they know more, but I've also demonstrated that I can be reined in. I've established myself as a factor best avoided, but that can be managed."

"Did you plan for the king to step in?" Zareen asked.

"That wasn't part of any plan I was told about," Liara said.

"I didn't plan it," Jason said. "It was one of several scenarios I gamed out, however. Royal intervention, the people behind Lancet popping out. I was surprised they didn't send someone more capable. I saw he was an empty shirt and ran with it."

"He's far from an empty shirt," Zareen said. "Being a successful arena fighter in Rimaros means that his skills are real."

"Yeah," Jason said, "but his spine's imaginary. He never had to scramble for his life with nothing but his own skills and tenacity marking the line between life and death. He smelled so green, it's like someone just mowed the lawn."

Liara thought back to the time she watched Jason fighting against the trio of Purity loyalists. They had been sent after him with powers and items specifically to counter him. Even so, he struggled far longer than she would have expected before they finally pinned him down. Even then, he never gave up, ultimately dragging her into it. It was as desperate a fight as she'd seen, but he treated it almost like any other day.

"I don't think they anticipated you asking for a blood duel during a royal ball when they chose him. What would you have done if he'd accepted the duel on your terms?"

"Drank the life out of him until someone made me stop."

They turned to look at a man marching in their direction. He was wearing the same outfit as Lancet de Varco, but Jason could immediately spot that this was a different kind of man. He hadn't honed his abilities in the safety of a mirage chamber. He came right up to the table, planting his feet firmly as he stood in front of them. He started with a bow to Liara.

"Your Highness."

"Strictly speaking, the correct form of address is 'milady,'" Liara told him.

"Apologies, milady," he said, then turned to Jason. "My name is Hector de Varco, and I challenge you to a duel. Right here is fine."

"Huh," Jason said. "You realise the king just stopped me from doing this, right? Bloke, you might want some looser pants if you're going to haul around hefty nuggets like those."

16

FOLLOWING YOUR CONVICTIONS
TO YOUR DEATH

JASON, LIARA AND ZAREEN WERE SITTING AT A TABLE, WITH HECTOR DE VARCO standing in front of them. The confrontation was already drawing attention, even if people couldn't hear through the invisible privacy screen. Hector was a larger man than his relative, Lancet, and less polished. His hair was trimmed short instead of a sculpted coiffure, and he had broad shoulders and an outfit that, while tailored, lacked the same flatteringly painstaking fit. Hector also lacked the gold hair of Lancet, instead sporting a deep, shining copper in his eyes and hair.

Jason and the princesses shared a look.

"Young Master de Varco," Liara said. "The king personally and specifically asked Mr Asano to refrain from duelling in his ballroom."

"Then we can take it elsewhere, milady. I am happy to let Mr Asano choose the venue."

"That is only the beginning of our concerns," Liara told him.

"Indeed," Jason agreed. "I was just telling the princesses here that I was quite satisfied with how things turned out. I'm not going to accept a duel just because you aren't happy with how your family came out after they came looking for me."

"You did nothing, Mr Asano," Hector said. "Lancet is the one who hurt the reputation of our house. I wish to show you, and all the people who saw his shameful display, that the de Varco family knows how to stand, be it in victory or defeat."

Jason narrowed his eyes. "You don't expect to win."

"I am confident in my abilities," Hector said. "But I do not fear defeat. A failure you survive is but a stepping stone to the next success."

"Your motivations are irrelevant," Liara said. "There's no way—"

"I have conditions," Jason said.

"No, you do not," Liara told him.

"Princess," Jason said, "while I ever value your counsel, the challenge was made to me. The decision is mine."

There was a delicate reverb of his aura in Jason's authoritative tone, giving it a weight that even the gold-rank princess could not ignore.

"Firstly," Jason said to Hector, "it has to be tonight. I don't have time to be running around after every noble house that wants to put me in a fight. I have gods and great astral beings lining up for that already. Second, you need the king to approve. I've already caused one commotion and I have no intention of forcing him to take things in hand a second time. I'm aware that adventurers of non-elite backgrounds are given leeway in etiquette, but I'm not that bereft of courtesy. Thirdly, I'm going to need some incentive. What you're proposing is a one-sided game. So long as you take your lumps without wetting yourself, you get the good showing for your house that you're looking for, win or lose. I, on the other hand, get nothing, win or lose. I don't need to prove myself to the people here. The only reason I showed up is to demonstrate that I'm not some lunatic who's going to start an interdimensional invasion again."

"Again?" Zareen asked.

"Pretend you didn't hear that," Jason told her, then turned back to Hector.

"In short, mate, what's in it for me? And don't say pride or honour, because I have no interest in either."

Hector frowned in thought for a moment before his eyes snapped up to meet Jason's. "Mr Asano, how familiar are you with House de Varco?"

"If I was counting the minutes since I heard about you, I'd run out of fingers and toes, but not by much. Princess Liara said you were traders."

"At the risk of contradicting the princess, Mr Asano, while we do an amount of trade, it's a corollary to our primary endeavour, which is the construction of vehicles. Everything from wagons to ships to airships; even exotic flying vessels for private buyers."

"I'm already good for transport, mate."

"Yes," Hector said. "You possess a cloud flask. But as I said, my family creates all manner of transport."

"You're offering me another cloud flask?"

"No. While the creation of such a vehicle is an ambition my family is working towards, we are not there yet. We have managed some more limited cloud constructs, although a true cloud flask remains in the realm of ambition. But our progress has produced a by-product that you may find appealing."

"Oh?" Jason prompted.

"A cloud flask can take a vehicle form," Hector said. "But those forms are basic. That's fine for a static construct, like a cloud house, but vehicles are more dynamic. The inherent property of a cloud flask is to take on materials to expand its capabilities. In their studies of cloud flasks, my family had developed the means to harness that effect. With the right materials and design matrix, a cloud flask can replicate the finest vessels that my family produces. And they, Mr Asano, are some of the finest vessels in the world."

Jason looked to Liara, who gave him a confirming nod. He then turned back to Hector and leaned forward in his chair.

"I'll admit that sounds interesting."

"I know for a fact that we have several such design matrices sitting around as the results of our ongoing experiments into cloud constructs. If you agree to this duel, I will offer you the design and materials for a land vessel. If you win, I will offer you the same for an air vessel."

"How much material are we talking about here?" Jason asked.

"I'm talking about the raw materials to build an entire airship from scratch, Mr Asano. A small one. My understanding is that you won't be able to produce the kind of massive skyships cloud flasks are known for producing until gold rank."

Jason remembered his first look at Emir's cloud ship, the size of a massive ocean liner.

"That is acceptable," he said, "but I have one more condition: It can't just be you. You have to bring three companions."

"You want to fight four of us alone?"

"No, I'll be bringing companions of my own. If I take a second opportunity to kick the crap out of someone and don't invite my friend Sophie, she'll kick the crap out of me."

"Miss Hurin," Trenchant Moore said, approaching her at the buffet table.

Farrah looked at the tall, lean, pale man with dark hair, angular features and bright blue eyes. A little too blue, in fact. She guessed that, like Jason, his eyes had diverged from their original state.

"Mr Moore," Farrah said. "Is there something I can do for you?"

"I have heard that you will be staying with us in Rimaros after your friend and his team have all left."

"For a time."

"I am... that is good."

"Wow," Farrah said. "You're really smooth with the ladies. Come on, Stretch. I don't think Jason is going to kill anyone on the dance floor, so we're probably fine taking a spin."

She grabbed his hand and dragged him in that direction as he trailed behind.

"Stretch?"

Jason and Hector approached the platform atop which was a lounge area for the core members of the royal family. There wasn't a lot of lounging taking place, however; the presence of Soramir plainly reduced the family's ability to relax. Hector was even more nervous as they approached, only four people looking unperturbed. Two were diamond-rankers: Soramir and Zila Rimaros. One was Jason, who would not have looked out of place strolling a market with his easy-going stride. The Storm King was neither relaxed nor intimidated, playing up the stern-but-benevolent monarch rather than taking it easy with family.

There were no guards at the platform. Anyone who made trouble there would either be a peer of Dawn's or swiftly scraped off the polished floor by palace stewards. Even the most casual observer noticed that no one approached the platform without a very distinct purpose. Jason reflected on the contrast between that and the people approaching him earlier at the event, before he started talking about blood duels in the middle of a society ball.

Jason didn't hesitate as he entered the platform's privacy screen, which started at the short steps leading to the platform. Hector had been rather bold earlier, but the pinnacle members of the royal family intimidated him in a way that even the gold-rank Princess Liara did not.

"Come on, bloke," Jason encouraged as he made his way up the steps, turning his attention to Soramir and the Storm King, whose name he still didn't know. He just knew that he was Zara's father.

"G'day again, your kingness," Jason said, then nodded to Soramir. "G'day, Soramir; it's been a minute."

Hector, who had already dropped to one knee, had the look of a man trying to figure out how to shuffle very quickly on one knee away from the madman next to him.

"I had rather expected," the Storm King said, "that our last conversation would be the end of you making commotions at this event, Mr Asano."

"Then you might want to skip my invite next time," Jason said. "The more I try to have a nice, quiet time, the more it ends up being one thing after another. I tried to have a simple barbecue to meet the neighbours when I moved into town, and these two showed up. Uninvited, no less."

Jason gestured at Zila and Soramir with a pointed finger. Jason hadn't seen Soramir in some time, since he was hurt escaping the underwater complex. It was plain that many members of royalty looking on were not happy about Jason's insouciance, but they were not going to speak up when the king and the diamond-rankers were willing to tolerate it, even if they failed to understand why.

"Would it hurt you to show a little deference, Jason?" Soramir asked lightly.

"Would it hurt you to offer a bloke a seat?" Jason returned. "Addressing the deference issue would involve delving into my thoughts of the relative merits of different forms of governance. I don't think this is the time and place for that particular debate."

"While I genuinely would find that fascinating," the Storm King said, "you're right that this is not the place. Which begs the question of why you have approached me, along with this much more respectful young man from House de Varco. Given our last conversation, you make for an unexpected pairing."

Jason prodded the still kneeling Hector with his foot.

"This is your show, bloke. Maybe stand up and tell the nice king what you want for Christmas?"

Hector was a silver-ranker and didn't sweat, but he felt like his body might figure out how from pure nervousness. As Jason conversed with the royals, Hector realised that his assumptions about the man he had challenged were way off. Not only was he speaking with His Majesty and His Ancestral Majesty in a way that Hector would only describe as suicidal, but *he was getting away with it.*

How was Asano not wilting under the attention of all that power? Just the passive aura interactions from having two diamond-rankers pay passing attention to him were making the hair on his arms stand on end, and they were restraining themselves. Anxiously, under the now focused attention of the king and royal family, Hector got to his feet. He steeled himself, planting his feet as he raised his eyes to look at the king.

"Your Majesty, after my house failed to comport itself in a manner that reflects well on its place in your kingdom, I took it upon myself to rectify the circumstances."

"And how did you seek to go about that task?"

"I challenged Jason Asano to a duel, Your Highness. However, Mr Asano refused, citing his respect for you and your desire that this gathering remains a peaceful one. He said he would not accept unless my challenge could be made with your approval."

"And why would I give that approval? You want to have a bloody fight in the middle of my ballroom, in the middle of my ball?"

"Perhaps you could suggest an alternate venue, Your Majesty," Jason suggested. "Somewhere roomy, since it's actually going to be four duels. Should you approve."

"Four duels?" the king asked.

"I thought that if we're going to do it, why not put on a show? So, if you have a big room somewhere that maybe you don't mind us breaking some bits off of, we could just quietly bunk off and leave your guests to their lovely evening."

"And who else would be participating in this series of duels?" Soramir asked.

"The guy who's better than me with swords, the woman who's better than me with fists and the guy who's better than me at talking to people like you."

"Those first two would be Rufus Remore and Sophie Wexler," Soramir said. "Not to put too fine a point on it, Mr Asano, but that last description does little to narrow it down."

Jason let out an easy laugh and pointed. There was no shortage of people watching, despite not hearing anything, having seen Jason and Hector approach the king.

"It's the tall, broad-shouldered bloke suddenly very aghast that I'm pointing him out to you."

"Perhaps," Soramir said to the king, "we can make some entertainment of it. The old duelling arena has seating for an audience."

"Wait, you guys have a duelling arena?" Jason asked. "You should have brought that up when the other guy was crying about mirage chambers and saved us some trouble."

"It has gone unused for many years," the king said.

"It was installed only a century or so after the kingdom was founded," Soramir explained. "Back when I still ruled the Storm Kingdom, mirage chambers were yet to be invented."

"Duelling was on the decline at that time," the king continued, "but the safety they offered resulted in something of a resurgence."

"I happen to agree with Mr Asano that there are no duels in mirage chambers," Soramir said. "They're just performances for people pretending to have courage."

"Performances that let the hot-headed young members of the houses play their little games without starting blood feuds," the king countered. "Not everything has to be about following your convictions to the death."

"As Mr Asano has done exactly that several times," Soramir said, "I don't think you will have any more luck of having him agree than you would me. So you might as well reopen the arena and let the ball attendees enjoy some sport."

"Explain to me," the king said, "how failing to convince you and Mr Asano of anything means I have to allow duels to take place."

Jason opened his mouth to respond and then stopped, frowning.

"What the…"

"Is there a problem, Mr Asano?" Soramir asked.

"I figured someone would try and break into my house while everyone was off at a party, but it just had to be while I was talking to the king, didn't it? Sorry, Your Maj; I better take a look at this."

"Your Maj?" Hector failed to stop himself from dumbfoundedly asking.

Jason dug a hand into his shirt and pulled out a necklace. It had two amulets on it: his Amulet of the Dark Guardian, and his shrunken cloud flask. Cloud stuff came spilling out of the tiny flask and formed a vertical ring the size of a portal. It wasn't portal energy that shimmered into being, however, but an image of Jason's pagoda. Four people dressed in black were on one of the lower floor balconies, where they had laid down a board and were drawing a ritual on it.

"Mr Asano?" the king asked.

"Yes?" Jason absently answered as he watched the image.

"How are you maintaining any connection to your cloud building through the very significant defences around this sky island?"

Jason went still, then turned his head to look at the king with a friendly smile.

"Uh… I'm not."

"Then what exactly is this?" the king asked, gesturing at the floating ring.

"Art?"

17

THE GOD IN THIS SCENARIO

"I can't believe His Majesty went along with this," Liara muttered as she rode an elevating platform into the bowels of the sky island.

"Dinner and a show," Jason said. "What's not to like?"

A vast amount of infrastructure was in the underground portions of the flying island on which the royal palace and residential sectors for royalty and foreign diplomats were located. A large part of that was underwater docking stations where vehicles could arrive in an airlock where the water was pumped out, allowing the passengers to disembark. This was where most of the royal palace traffic arrived, comprised of supply deliveries, palace staff and government functionaries.

The lake at the heart of the royal palace was more naturalistic on the surface, but underneath, it was a perfect ring. The sections of it not occupied by docks offered magically reinforced glass walls that made for interesting office spaces and other rooms that abutted the lake below the surface.

One such room was the old duelling area, which was, like the ballroom they had just left, a stadium-scale space, both horizontally and vertically. People were swarming down from the ballroom for a chance to watch the upcoming duels, but most were heading for the audience seating. Those heading for the main area were the royal family, various key attendants, the actual duellists and a few attendants.

"The duelling arena has been used as a training hall by the Sapphire Crown guild for years," Trenchant Moore explained. He was on the elevating platform with Jason and Liara, as well as Sophie, Humphrey, Zareen, Rufus and Rufus' mum.

"You're sure Callum isn't behind the people breaking into my pagoda?" Jason asked Arabelle.

"I've been very clear with him on this," Arabelle said. "Also, he received quite the impression last time he tried."

"That doesn't mean he didn't send someone else to try," Jason told her. "People do things that are stupid and make no sense all the time. Myself very much included."

"Jason, my job is helping people with their mental issues. You think I don't know what people are like?"

"You help people because they need it and come to you," Jason said. "I get the ones who lack that much self-awareness. Instead of going to you, they try to murder me. Or kidnap. Honestly, if you discount monsters, I see more attempts to kidnap than kill me. Does that make me popular?"

"Are you sure you shouldn't be going to deal with the people breaking into your house?" Liara asked.

"I'm a silver-ranker," Jason said. "What am I going to do to a bunch of gold-rankers?"

"You're sure they're gold-rankers?" Arabelle asked.

"I am," Jason said.

"How?" Arabelle asked.

"They're still alive. Okay, that's just me being dramatic; I can sense them."

"You shouldn't be able to," Liara said. "The defences around this sky island are as powerful as any in the world. It should cut off everything."

"Does it prevent gods from speaking with their servants?" Jason asked.

"No," Liara said.

"Then it doesn't cut off everything," Jason pointed out.

"Between you and the cloud house, who is the god in this scenario?"

"I refuse to answer on the grounds that I may incriminate myself. And it's not like they're good gold-rankers. They're all core users."

"All of them?" Zareen asked. "At gold rank, core users are less common than people who trained up properly. Are they a bunch of craftspeople or something?"

"I'll ask them when I get home," Jason said. "I have something to be getting on with first... oh, it looks like they've decided to cut their losses and get out. They've started breaking through walls."

"Then you won't be talking to them when you get home," Liara said.

"Maybe, maybe not. They haven't realised yet that I keep moving the room they're in to the middle of the building."

Four men forcefully broke through a wall, arriving in another of a series of empty square rooms.

"What did I tell you?" Jedrin asked as the wall they just broke through reformed behind them. "No one pays four gold-rankers to come a quarter of the way around the planet to rob some silver-ranker's house."

"Shut up, Jedrin."

They were all uneasy. Their senses failed to extend beyond any of the walls and they had stopped finding furnished rooms. Each wall they broke through led them to one empty box after another. There was a pervasive sense that they were trespassing and there seemed to be formidable power behind it. They couldn't even be certain that power was real, however. Their senses barely brushed against it and it was not something that belonged in a silver-rank construct. It could easily have been their imaginations, except that they had each felt it.

They quickly found themselves unnerved, and it only got worse. Once they had broken into the house, they had moved through a series of ordinary rooms until they found themselves in a room that was just a plain box. There were no windows and even the door vanished, sealing them in. That was the point they decided to call it quits and started smashing through walls to escape, but each new room was a new empty box.

"Get bent, Kirk," Jedrin said. "I should have told you to shut up when you wanted to take this job. It's not like we're some infiltration experts. The only reason to go that far for us is that it's how far you have to go to find someone who doesn't know how stupid an idea it is."

"I said shut up."

"And I asked why anyone would go that far and pay that much for us? And now we know it's because the people paying attention clearly looked into this job and said no."

"How about you both shut up," William said.

"Exactly," Ray said. "Arguing won't get us out of here."

"Neither will breaking through walls," Jedrin said. "We've gone further than the width of the entire building, yet here we are. Either the rooms are moving or there's dimensional manipulation going on."

"Which we can't tell because our senses won't go through the damn walls," William said.

"If you have a better idea, let's hear it," Ray said.

"I have a better idea," Jedrin said. "Remember when I said that getting portalled in right before the job was a bad idea because it didn't give us a chance to do any research into the target?"

"That's not a better idea," Kirk said. "That's you passive-aggressively bragging—again—about how you didn't want to do the thing that you did right along with the rest of us. Again."

"Maybe let me finish?" Jedrin asked. "My point is that I did do a little research."

"We were told not to, specifically to prevent alerting the target," Kirk said. "And now we're stuck in a trap. Good job."

"Do you seriously think that me doing some research on a different continent was enough that all this was set up specifically to deal with us?" Jedrin asked.

"He's right, Kirk," William said. "I'm pretty sure that they just didn't want us finding out why no one else took the job."

"They just didn't want to use locals so it didn't come back on them," Kirk argued.

"If you'll stop interrupting," Jedrin interjected, "I can get to what my research uncovered."

"Then stop flapping your mouth and get to it," Kirk said.

"What did you find?" William asked.

"Not much," Jedrin said. "It was short notice and I wanted to be careful. What

I did find was that the guy who owns this place won a cloud flask from Emir Bahadir in some contest in the middle of nowhere. It was a big deal, with nobles sending a bunch of their young people to compete."

"Emir Bahadir the treasure hunter?" William asked.

"That's the one," Jedrin said. "The point is that I found out that the house we were hired to rob was a cloud construct."

"Oh, that's really helpful," Kirk said snidely. "I hate to break it to you, Jedrin, but we already knew that."

"Now that we're here, sure," Jedrin said. "But I knew before. Long enough before that, I knew we'd be breaking into a cloud house, and therefore had time to bring a contingency plan."

"What kind of contingency plan?" Ray asked.

Jedrin reached into the dimension bag at his hip and pulled out a box the size of a small suitcase, complete with handle. It was made of pale grey ceramic with dark metal covering the corners. A complex array of sigils was engraved into the surface of the ceramic, on each side of the box.

"What is that?" Kirk asked.

"It's a thaumic cohesion impedance device," Jedrin said.

"A what?" Ray asked while William backed away from it.

"What in the sweet gods are you doing with that thing?" William asked. "They are very, very illegal."

"We're breaking into someone's house, William," Kirk said. "We're already doing crime."

"We're doing the kind of crime that means our families have to pay a fine if we get caught," William hissed. "Jedrin just turned it into the kind of crime where the Adventure Society crawls into our backsides and builds a rustic cottage."

Ray looked at William, then the device.

"I think you need to explain what this thing is right now."

"It's—" Jedrin began, only for Ray to cut him off immediately.

"Not you," Ray said, pointing at Jedrin before moving his finger to point at William. "You."

"It's a device for breaking down things made of magic. Not things that are magical, but things actually made of manifested magic. Conjured objects, spirit coins."

"It's the perfect thing for trashing a cloud construct," Jedrin said. "Which you all know that we could very much use right now. That's my better idea; you're welcome."

"You know what else is made of magic?" William asked. "We are. We're gold-rankers, so our bodies are made of magic. It's why we don't die when we get stabbed in the head."

"If it's going to affect us," Ray said, "then I think that more specifics on exactly what you mean by 'breaking down' would be something worth hearing."

"It means," William said, "turning manifested magic—magic that's taken solid form—back into non-manifested magic. Like when a monster dies and it turns into rainbow smoke."

Ray backed off alongside William.

"I'm not interested in turning into rainbow smoke today."

"I didn't bring something that would kill us, you idiots."

"I'm sure you didn't," William said. "That's why they made them incredibly illegal. How did you even get one?"

"I know a guy," Jedrin said.

"What guy?" Kirk asked.

"Sak."

"Sak?" Ray explained. "That guy definitely sold us out."

"To who?" Jedrin asked.

"To anyone he could," William said. "It's Sak. Why would you ever consider buying something that illegal from him? And where did he even get it?"

"He knows a guy too."

"What guy?" Ray asked.

"I don't know," Jedrin said, increasingly defensive. "He had a hat."

"A hat?" Kirk asked.

"Yes, a hat. A big hat."

"Oh," William said, his tone suddenly convinced. "You should have said that he had a *big* hat. That makes it perfectly alright to buy VERY ILLEGAL MAGIC DEVICES FROM A COMPLETE STRANGER RECOMMENDED BY THE LEAST TRUSTWORTHY PERSON IN THE ENTIRE COUNTRY!"

"Just so I'm following this correctly," Ray said, "you bought a massively illegal device that will melt us, assuming that the random man with a big hat you bought it from wasn't lying about what it is. A man you went to on the advice of a person most famous for selling out the people he works with."

"It sounds bad when you say it like that," Jedrin said. "And it won't melt us. These things are optimised to break down amorphous substances replicating rigid structures. Heavy conjured armour and cloud houses. Will it sting us a bit? Yes. But right now, we're trapped on the wrong continent for a job we never should have taken in a house of infinite boxes. A house that I'm fairly certain hates us. So, we can stay here, waiting for someone to find us with this incredibly illegal device, or we can set it off to get us out of here and wipe out the evidence in the process."

The four men looked at each other and the box they were trapped in. After more back-and-forth arguing, they finally agreed to set off the device, but not in the room they were in. They would set it to activate and breach another room, putting a wall between them and the device.

Their precautions meant little as the device detonated. The room around them was disintegrated, and plenty more besides, walls dissolving into rainbow miasma. Suddenly, there was a massive sphere-shaped absence of anything in the middle of the pagoda, everything in the space having been utterly annihilated. Partly destroyed rooms were exposed, sending furniture tumbling through levels. There was a magical reverberation thrumming through the air that left them trembling and disoriented where they had landed, several floors below their initial position. There was an acrid stench that pressed on them, coming from the rainbow haze they could barely see through.

"I feel tingly," Kirk said.

All four men had closed their eyes, wincing as it felt like sandpaper had been rubbed all over their skin. They had fallen as the room they were in was destroyed and they opened their eyes to see the destruction. The hole the device had ripped in the place had dropped them into a mezzanine level with access to a large open atrium with a wall that let them see outside. The air was filled by a hazy mist that was the dissipated remains of what had previously been walls, floors and ceilings.

"Okay, we can get out," Jedrin said. "I told you that... Kirk, where are your clothes?"

"I wear conjured clothes," Kirk said. "Just from a magic item, nothing special. Easier than owning a bunch of different stuff."

"Do you have the item on you?" Jedrin asked.

"Yes."

"Then how about you put on some damn pants before we make a run for it?"

"I think it's a little late for that," William said.

The others joined him in looking around. Dark figures, each with a large alien eye instead of a face, were swarming out of the rooms that had been rent open.

"They're silver rank," Jedrin said. "We can fight our way through."

The haze suddenly coalesced in the centre of the space forming a giant blue and orange eye. Then the four men's flesh started to rot.

18

THE ONLY PERSON WHO THINKS
IT'S OBVIOUS

ON ONE SIDE OF THE DUELLING AREA, THE ENTIRE WALL WAS MADE UP OF reinforced glass, behind which was the lake at the heart of the sky island, Rimaros. Specially reared aquatic creatures, unfazed by the regular water traffic, swam around in the water. It was an impressive backdrop for anyone viewing from the seats that made up the other side of the area, also behind reinforced glass.

There were VIP viewing booths into which the palace stewards were expertly guiding the more prestigious attendees, dealing with the etiquette protocols on the fly. There were also ready areas at each end, behind massive doors. In the one set aside for Jason, Rufus, Sophie and Humphrey, they were accompanied by their friends and several others. Trenchant Moore, Zareen and Liara were all in attendance.

Jason was staring into the middle distance, his expression blank.

"Mr Moore," he said. "I'm going to go see Young Master de Varco about final details. If you would be kind enough to lead my friend to that viewing booth you mentioned."

"Of course, Mr Asano. And Princess Liara, His Majesty has asked after you."

"What about the men in your pagoda?" Zareen asked Jason.

"They're contained," he said, his tone matter-of-fact.

"What does that mean?" Liara asked. "We're going to need to talk to them. I know your pagoda is intimidating, but it's still a silver-rank construct. Four gold-rankers will be able to break out if they're determined enough."

"I've calibrated the house to keep rotting their flesh at roughly the same rate as their gold-rank recovery attributes will heal it," Jason said. "It will keep them debilitated until I attend them myself."

"Jason…" Rufus said in a worried voice.

"Rufus, you remember the joke back in Greenstone, right?" Jason asked. His voice held the whimsy of a man certain the police wouldn't find where the family was buried in time. "It turns out I *am* the man with the evil powers. I've already taught one world that."

As Jason strode out of the room, Humphrey followed to talk to him, but Arabelle gestured him to stop. She looked to Farrah, who left to trail Jason.

"Am I missing something?" Zareen asked. "Or is he remotely torturing a group of gold-rankers? From here."

"Your mother once approached me about the gap in Jason's Adventure Society records during his time away," Arabelle told her. "I refused to share what I knew, but I advocated against Jason participating in political games. I told her that he should be sent away with his team, which I believe she agreed with, to her credit. The choice was made at higher levels within the Adventure Society and royal family both, if I'm not mistaken."

"You're not," Liara confirmed.

"You may get your wish of learning about Jason's time away after all, milady," Arabelle said. "If you put Jason in a political mess, try to exploit him and then make moves on him behind his back—"

"We didn't," Liara said.

"Someone did," Arabelle said. "And that's what happened in that missing time. It happened a lot, and now you're seeing what Jason does when that happens. Put him in that mindset and his instincts are to trust no one and kill everyone. To put aside his principles whatever it costs him because that's what it takes when the world is against you and everyone coming for you has more power."

"It's not like that," Humphrey said. "This is a different world. And he has us."

"Which I strongly advise you to remind him of before his duel," Arabelle said. "Especially if you're interested in de Varco still wanting to be an adventurer after."

Farrah followed Jason into the hall, which was a plain brick tunnel. To those who didn't know how expensive the bricks were, it lacked the opulence of a royal palace. To those who did, it was practically a treasury. Entering the tunnel, Farrah was ready to rush to catch Jason, but found him leaning his forehead against the wall.

"I thought I was better," he said.

"You are."

"I've been sitting around in the tropics, thinking I wasn't the same. But when push came to shove, it took one day. One day, and I'm back to the same savage, reactionary violence I was doing on Earth."

"You are better, Jason, even if you don't see it."

"I'm torturing a bunch of strangers as we speak."

"Then stop," Farrah said lightly.

Jason pushed himself off the wall and turned to look at her, expression cold. "No."

She flashed him a smile. "You know what you remind me of right now? You, back in Greenstone. Getting some kills under your belt and wondering what was becoming of you."

"And now we know what became of me. I wouldn't have been willing to do what I'm doing back then."

"No, you wouldn't. But on Earth, you wouldn't have been beating yourself up over it either. On Earth, you killed without a moment's consideration of whether it was right because you didn't have the luxury. You didn't have time for right or wrong, only for what was necessary."

"I took it too far, Farrah. You are what you do, and what I did was put aside my principles."

"But now you're pondering them again, and that's good. Keep questioning. But that brutal part of you, that part that can do what's necessary, is just that: necessary. Some days you're going to need it. But you can also put it back in the box, and that's the difference. On Earth, you were a diamond knife, sharp but brittle. You were never soft, and every time you got a little sharper, you also came a little closer to breaking."

He bowed his head. "You kept me from breaking."

"Barely. But you have more people now, and you are different, Jason. I see it, even if you don't. You're not as soft as you started out, but also not as hard as you became. Right now, you have a balance; you can do the hard things without losing yourself in doing them. I know you're still getting the hang of maintaining it, but we're here to help you. You just have to let us."

"Crap. I'm the fragile, high-maintenance one, aren't I?"

Farrah laughed. "You're only just figuring that out? Look, if you deny what you learned about yourself on Earth, it's going to devour you from the inside out. But you can't let it dominate you either. Compartmentalise. Keep it in the box where it belongs and pull it out when you need it. I'm not telling you anything you don't know."

"You're sounding a lot like Arabelle."

"We talked about you a lot. She wanted to know about your world and our time there from someone other than you, so she could better help you. And she did, even if you maybe don't see it right now. But I see it, so you'll just have to trust me."

Jason smiled.

"I can do that. Are you sure you won't come with us when we leave Rimaros?"

"You have a portal power and I'm inventing the magic phone. It's not like you're going back to Earth and I won't see you for a decade. Which means you'll be getting plenty more advice from me, starting with this: Don't make this Hector guy quit being an adventurer due to mental trauma. He's not the one who broke into your house."

"They set off some kind of bomb in there," Jason said. "Blew a giant hole in the middle."

"They're gold-rankers. Even if they're crap gold-rankers, they could still throw a garbage truck like a basketball."

"Did you watch a lot of sports on Earth?"

"No, Jason. There was a bunch of giant, athletic men running around in tight outfits and I thought to myself, 'that's not for me.' Of course, I watched a lot of sports. Is the pagoda intact?"

"Not really. I'm going to have to return it to the flask and reproduce it."

"Don't," Farrah said. "Pack up and go tonight. Be gone by first light. It's past time you hit the road and had those adventures we promised you back in Greenstone."

"There's still stuff to do. People to collect. I haven't even decided if the royal family get to—"

"They don't. As for the people who are going with you, I'll let them know to get ready. If they don't, go without them; they'll catch up or they won't. You're the high-maintenance one, remember? Let them work around you."

———

The arena was a vast, empty room with translucent sides shielding rows of stadium seating. The private boxes were at the top, looking down on the action. Inside the arena, Sophie was undertaking the first duel. She dashed into a forest of swords that danced through the air on their own, seeking to strike her down. Some missed, others were deflected away with a push on the flat of the blades with a hand, foot, forearm, knee or shin. Space warped in subtle but important fluctuations, making strikes that should have landed slide past Sophie harmlessly.

Sophie's opponent was an elf with the sword, shield, myriad and arsenal essences. Her fighting style combined mobility with conjured swords and shields that floated around her to fight the enemy on their own. Using quick abilities to conjure the weapons bought time for her to cast more powerful spells.

The many shields, conjured over and over, moved into Sophie's path as she attempted to slip through with her speed. At the same time, Sophie was bombarded with swords that she needed to smash out of the air. They would just keep hunting her, making it harder and harder as more swords were conjured.

Fortunately for Sophie, her Radiant Fist and Immortal Fist powers gave her disruptive-force and resonating-force damage respectively, ideally suited for crushing rigid, conjured tools. Even so, they were accumulating faster than she was breaking them down.

The early advantage was with the elf. Sophie initially dodged through the conjured defenders multiple times to attack her, but Sophie's strikes simply didn't do enough damage and she was repeatedly forced to back off from counterattacks. The elf was more of a ranged than melee combatant, but no one with the sword essence was a slouch up close. With floating swords and shields harassing her, Sophie wasn't able to push the attack for long.

The count of swords and shields slowly accumulated, making it harder for Sophie to reach the elf with raw speed, but Sophie had tricks of her own as well. Her Cloud Step power allowed her to run on air as if it were solid ground and, for brief moments, take on a mist form that made her near-impervious to most forms of damage. Her Mirage Step power allowed her to make short, blinking teleports, leaving behind afterimages that sent out dimensional blade attacks to alleviate the pressure.

Sophie also used a space-distorting power. She could manipulate space to dodge seemingly unavoidable attacks, but where Jason also used his power to obscure and deceive, Sophie incorporated the distortions into her ever-flowing movement. Adding staccato shifts to her prodigious speed made it all the harder to predict and intercept her, while incongruously never seeming erratic or disjointed.

Jason had joined the Storm King, Soramir, Trenchant Moore and Liara in a viewing booth, at Soramir's request. The king had already levied some pointed questions about how Jason was communing with his cloud house through the palace's defence magic, but to Jason's surprise, Soramir had shut him down.

"That space-distortion ability she's using," Soramir said as he observed Sophie. "That's Between the Raindrops?"

"Good eye," Jason said.

"Her mastery of it is formidable. In fact, her entire power set is dangerously skill-oriented, yet she makes it look easy. You found this girl stealing in some provincial city-state?"

"There was an open contract to catch her," Jason said. "Oddly enough, we'd met before, briefly. Friend of a friend. Once it became obvious that there was some ugly politics involved, turning her into an adventurer seemed the obvious way to get it settled."

Liara let out a snorting laugh, despite the august company.

"You're the only person who thinks it's obvious to break the thief you caught yourself out of an Adventure Society holding facility, stash her with Emir Bahadir, of all people, and then turn her into an adventurer."

"Bahadir?" the king asked with a scowl.

"He's a friend," Jason said. "I know he's not super-popular around here."

"She's quite the find," Soramir said. "I'm starting to see why Roland has always been so avid about scholarships."

"You're talking about Roland Remore?" Jason asked, referring to Rufus' diamond-rank grandfather.

"Yes. His family runs a school. He won't stop talking about it."

"Try turning it into a drinking game," Jason suggested. "It won't stop him, but it makes it a lot more fun."

As they talked, the duel below was escalating. Sophie blurred as the Eternal Moment power accelerated her personal time stream. She used the brief moment of subjectively frozen time to create a storm of wind blades that erupted when time resumed. Each blade exploded on impact, smashing many of the conjured weapons apart. It brought her precious breathing room after they had threatened to overwhelm her.

"This match is shaping up to be quite interesting," Soramir said. "Miss Wexler is getting stronger as she goes, and I believe she's inflicting escalating retributive damage. Is that something from her balance essence?"

"That's right," Jason said. "She used an awakening stone of karma to pick up that particular power. Legendary stone, but it didn't disappoint. Her opponent is interesting, though. It seems like she's being increasingly pushed, but it looks like she's using all those conjured swords and shields to set up a combat ritual. Something to flip the match in a moment, I suspect."

"You noticed that?" Soramir asked, mild surprise in his voice.

"A member of his team uses combat rituals quite heavily, Ancestral Majesty," Liara explained. "It is quite likely that Miss Wexler has likewise recognised the tactic."

"Yet, she hasn't started taking greater risks to try and close the fight out early," Soramir observed. "She should be racing to finish the battle before her opponent completes the ritual, even at the risk of taking greater damage. Yet she maintains her slowly escalating tempo."

"For all her speed," Jason said, "Sophie does things at her own pace."

"Meaning she either doesn't know about the ritual, or she has something ready herself," Soramir observed.

"Sophie used a couple of awakening stones of the moment," Jason said. "One of them gave her that self-accelerating power she used to produce all those wind blades at once. The other gave her a power she hasn't shown off yet."

Soramir tapped a finger to his lips thoughtfully, considering the powers such a stone could produce from Sophie's essences. It was a long list, even off the top of his head, but the circumstances gave him clues as to what it could be. His eyes sparkled as he made a guess.

"Moment of Oneness?"

"You know your essence abilities," Jason said.

"It will take courage and timing to pull off," Soramir observed.

"I'm not worried," Jason said. "Courage and timing are kind of her things."

The combat ritual suddenly triggered and the arena was immediately filled with so many conjured swords, it was impossible to see the combatants with the naked eye.

"Fog of Swords," Soramir said. "Dedicated combat ritual essence ability spells are extremely rare."

"Levelling that thing must be a real prick," Jason said. "The effort shows, though; she timed it well. Sophie's time-acceleration power could maybe have let her dodge it all, but her enemy made sure it was on cooldown."

The swords plunged in, too thick and too numerous for any amount of spatial distortion to let Sophie avoid. Countless swords slammed into her, each one exploding as it did. They moved with blinding speed, designed specifically to catch out even someone as fast as Sophie. In the wake of the force explosions that distorted the air, Sophie was left standing unharmed, not bothering to dodge. Her opponent's eyes went wide as Sophie blinked, arriving right behind her. Sophie's fist was a blur as it arrived at the back of the elf's head, only to be stopped dead as it was caught in a hand. The impact caused their clothes and hair to whip as if caught in a gale.

Up in the booth, Jason looked down at Soramir, blocking Sophie's punch, then to the diamond-ranker's now-empty seat.

"Miss Wexler," Soramir said. "Unless Young Mistress Draglund here objects, I am going to declare you the victor."

The elf was shaken, both from the sudden arrival of Soramir Rimaros and the blast that had gone off right behind her head.

"No objection, Ancestral Majesty."

"Excellent," Soramir said. "It was a fine match indeed. I can honestly say that you are as excellent a pair of warriors as is to be found at your rank."

The elf bowed.

"Thank you for your kind words, Ancestral Majesty. This is the honour of my life."

"You are a credit to your house, Mistress Draglund. Have you ever considered switching over to the Sapphire Crown guild?"

"I am very satisfied where I am, Ancestral Majesty."

"Well, you can't blame an old man for trying," he said, then turned to Sophie.

"I won't bother trying to recruit you," he told her. "I imagine you're at least as much trouble as your friend Asano."

"I do my best."

"From what I've just seen," Soramir told her, "your best is very good indeed."

19

UNCHARACTERISTIC SINCERITY

SOPHIE'S MOTHER, MELODY JAIN, HAD BEEN SUBJECTED TO THE MIND-WARPING effects of the Order of Redemption. She had led the local faction of the order until she was captured and locked away in the cloud palace while they sought a way to undo her behaviour modification. Her months of boredom came to an explosive end when the room she was locked in violently disintegrated.

She woke up in a small pond, her head pounding. She opened her eyes and saw massive amounts of destruction above her. She was still indoors, but something had ravaged the inside of Asano's cloud building. It had destroyed the room she was being held in and dumped her all the way down into the mostly intact atrium.

She found herself in the waterfall pond that was the atrium's centrepiece, but the damage meant the water no longer fell into it from the higher level. As she got to her feet, dripping wet, she saw the water was currently spilling from a hole in the lowest mezzanine level.

Melody had only briefly been in the atrium before this, accompanying her daughter as they talked in spaces more pleasant than her cell. Her accommodations were far from uncomfortable, but there was something about open space and natural light that even the plushest of beds couldn't make up for. She looked around, her eyes lingering on the transparent wall that showed a wide expanse of sky. Her gaze then drifted down, to the doors.

"That would be a less than ideal decision, Ms Jain," a prim voice said. Asano's shadow familiar emerged from her shadow.

"Looks like your employer is having a rough day," she told Shade.

"This is hardly a rough day for Mr Asano," Shade told her. "The day you met him was a rough day. Not in his top five, but perhaps top ten."

"He almost died that day."

"Yes," Shade said. "Almost. Now, if you'll follow me, please?"

"What's going on in here?" she asked as she followed the shadow man.

"Some gold-rankers broke in and detonated some manner of device."

"Where are they now?"

She was answered by pained screams coming from above.

"Oh dear," Soramir said as Rufus' opponent entered the arena from the large doors at the end.

"What is it?" the Storm King asked.

"If I'm not mistaken, that young man is using the classic sword master combination of sword, swift, adept and master."

"Ah," the king said.

Jason noticed that Liara looked confused.

"It's the combination used by arguably the world's greatest swordsman," Jason explained.

"What's the issue with that?" Liara asked.

"This fellow is about to duel with that swordsman's grandson."

"Oh, dear."

Different magical abilities led to different physiques amongst adventurers, although they showed up in different ways. There was something of a default—the lean athleticism of a track and field champion. The variations came with the powers that gave essence users physical prowess above their baseline attributes, and they didn't always present in the same way.

Gary, Farrah and Neil all had comparable levels of strength, yet each looked different. Gary was built like a furry powerlifter, while Neil was more like a bodybuilder who didn't know how to dress himself properly. Farrah's physique was bulked out more than the average essence user while remaining lean enough that she could hide it under the right clothes. She had nowhere near the bodybuilder physique that Neil sported.

Essence users more focused on speed maintained a healthy athleticism, but trended more sleek and lithe. Sophie's lissom body was somewhere between a nymph and a knife, and the swordsman facing off against Rufus had a similar feel. His clothes and physique were both light, and while the sword at his waist was a sabre, his body felt as sharp and pointed as a rapier.

Rufus had the standard physique for an essence user, which still made him look like an Olympic decathlete. Like his opponent, he wore light armour, but with stiffer panels over areas that could afford less flexibility. The magical materials still provided the mobility to make full use of his speed and silver-rank attributes, but forewent the absolute freedom of movement that more acrobatic power sets required.

The pale grey tones of Rufus' armour contrasted with his midnight skin and the sword he conjured into his hand. It was a golden scimitar with ornate red scrollwork etched into the blade. He held it down by his side where the air around it combusted into golden flames that flared for a moment before settling to wreath the blade.

"I wonder if he's ever set his pants on fire doing that?" Jason wondered, observing the duel from the royal viewing booth. It was rather like an owner's box at a sports stadium, with a mix of standing room, seating and a loaded buffet table. "I bet he has. What's this other guy's name?"

"Glenn Twenhey," Liara said.

"Glen 20?" Jason asked. "Where I come from, that's stuff you spray after taking a poo."

The royalty surrounding him all looked in his direction.

"What?" Jason asked. "There are fewer essence users where I come from, so toilets are a much bigger deal. Unlike you lot, even rich people need to be aware of poo-related infrastructure."

"Jason," Liara hissed. "Stop saying 'poo' in front of the king."

"Why? Does he have a weird fetish or something? Your Majesty, I'm just assuming you have a good crystal wash supplier."

"Perhaps, Mr Asano," Soramir said, "you could focus on the duel before us."

"They're still just staring at each other like anime characters."

"Then how about you stop talking about poo, shut your damn mouth and show a modicum of respect while you wait quietly?" Liara said softly but through gritted teeth. This drew all the gazes to her, but Jason quietly moved to the front of the booth, standing next to Liara as he looked out. He activated a small privacy screen to incorporate just the two of them.

"Is that better?" he asked lightly.

"You are not helping my standing in the royal family, Asano. You're a bad influence."

"Yet, here you are, alongside the king and his great-great-whatever grandad."

"Stern Jason, remember?"

"Yeah, I gave up on that. Stern Jason is for murdering people, so you really shouldn't ask for him. Also, he's kind of a prick, although regular Jason is talking in third person, so there's pros and cons either way, I guess."

"Why are you always like this?"

"Why do people participating in oppressive systems of governance always act like being too casual is some grave transgression?"

"Oh, just shut up."

"Yes, Mistress."

Liara glared at him.

"You and Baseph," he asked. "Is that an open relationship thing?"

"Asano, I was an Adventure Society investigator for longer than you have been alive, so when I tell you that I will hide your corpse where magic won't find it, you would do very well to believe me."

Like Rufus, his opponent was human. Glenn was leaning forward, almost like a sprinter on a block. He and Rufus stared at one another in a silence that extended for an entire minute, then a second and a third, neither moving so much as a tremble. Then a voice resonated through the arena.

"...just touch this crystal, right?" Jason's voice boomed.

"Get away from that," Liara's voice followed.

"They're just standing there! Get on with it, Rufus, you dill pickle! I don't have all—"

Jason's voice was cut off, but the audience and Rufus' opponent were all looking in the direction of the royal viewing booth. Stewards were escorting Jason out, with an angry-looking princess trailing behind.

"That's the man everyone's been talking about?" Glenn asked Rufus.

"Yeah," Rufus said with a grin. "It's good to have him back."

"...defeated the entire point of the exercise and ruined my reputation while you were at it," Liara railed as she led Jason into the booth where his companions were.

"I said it wouldn't work," Neil said, turning at their entrance along with the rest of Jason's friends. "I kept saying it, but did anyone listen to me? No, they did not. We should have just snuck off in the night."

"He's not wrong," Farrah said.

"Not wrong?" Neil asked. "Can't you just say that I'm right?"

"It feels like that would set a bad precedent," Farrah told him.

"Did they start fighting yet?" Jason asked, looking out the glass viewing wall.

"No," Farrah said. "And what have you been doing to Liara?"

"How he treats me is secondary to how he keeps disrespecting the royal family."

"I'm not feeling like it's a positive relationship from their end either," Jason said.

"Do you have no respect for the concept of royalty at all?" Liara asked.

"Nope."

"No."

"He does not."

"Not even a little."

"I'm a republican, bro."

"You're a Republican?" Travis asked Taika incredulously.

"Australian republican," Taika explained. "It means I want to stop using someone else's queen as a loaner."

"What they said," Jason agreed. "Didn't you read my file front to back? It should have been in there."

"It mentioned problems with authority," Liara said. "Not some kind of anti-monarchical bent."

"That's about as significant an understatement as I've ever heard," Farrah said.

"Gods and great astral beings make him their personal enemy," Humphrey pointed out. "What does he have to do, hire a town crier?"

"I respect people one at a time, Liara," Jason said. "I respect you. But if your family had left me alone, I'd be in my house that hadn't been blown up right now and wouldn't give your family a second thought."

"Asano, this isn't just some game."

"Yes, Liara," he said, the amusement in his voice turning to weariness. "It is."

"We're talking about one of the most prominent kingdoms in the world," she said.

"Yes," Farrah agreed. "And while your aristocracy was fighting over scraps of influence, Jason was fighting to save his world and blunt the invader coming for this one. What is one kingdom to him?"

Liara sighed, her shoulders slumping.

"Asano, would it really hurt you to keep your mouth shut and do what you're told for one damn night?"

"Yes," Arabelle said, turning from where she had been sitting quietly, watching her son in the arena below. "Yes, it would. Tell the good princess why, Gareth."

"From the moment he was pulled into this world," Gary said, "Jason has been told to bow to power. If he ever did, he'd be dead, I'd be dead and most of the people I love would be dead. If you ever see Jason bow, Princess, you should start running because he's probably about to kill everybody. And I think we all know by now that only being silver rank won't stop him."

"I've seen him do it," Taika added. "The killing everyone part, not the bowing. He did it on TV."

"That's like a recording crystal that everyone in the world can watch," Farrah explained. "And everyone did watch."

"He's super famous in my world," Taika said. "Controversial, sure, but famous."

"You asked for a certain version of Jason," Arabelle said, "as if he were a different person. But he's not. That part of him that is holding those men in his cloud house right now is a part of him, the way that Liara Rimaros and Princess Liara are parts of you: different, yet part of a whole. Which is why Princess Liara is unhappy about how this is going, while Liara Rimaros recognises that Jason would have been a lot better off if you and your family had left him alone. Perhaps you should do that now, and let cooler heads prevail so we can talk this through later."

"That... is sound advice," Liara acknowledged. "I will find you at your pagoda after this is all done, Asano. I want to see who these people are coming after you."

Jason nodded his acknowledgement and she left.

"Thank you," Jason said, his voice breaking a little. "I'd almost forgotten what it felt like to have people stand up for you."

"Just to be clear, I didn't," Neil said from the buffet table. "I think you should have kept quiet and gone along for once."

"Weren't you the guy who's been saying this wouldn't work the whole time?" Travis asked him.

"Someone on this team has to be the sensible one. That's why I let everyone know that I was going to be right—which I was—and then accepted the reality and made the most of this buffet."

"I'm surprised they got it set up so quick," Jason said. "Those palace stewards don't muck about."

"They are very admirable," Shade agreed from Jason's shadow.

"I suppose the rush is why there isn't much food, compared to the tables in the ballroom."

"Oh, there was plenty," Farrah said, looking at Gary.

Jason let out a sigh. "If you'd all permit me a moment of uncharacteristic sincerity, I'd like to thank you. On Earth, it was me and Farrah against the world, more often than not, and I barely made it through intact. I'm still not completely sure I did. We were both on the ragged edge."

"You more than me," Farrah clarified and Jason laughed.

"Yes, me more than you. I forgot what it was like to have a whole family who would stand up for you against anyone, whatever the circumstances. I guess I'm trying to thank you all for reminding me of that tonight."

Gary moved away from the food table to embrace Jason in a bone-crushing hug.

"Oh, hey," Clive said. "Rufus finally started fighting."

"Oh, the duel," Taika said. "I totally forgot why we were here."

20

THE ONLY WOUND YOU CAN TRULY SUFFER

JASON'S COMMANDEERING OF THE ARENA'S PUBLIC ADDRESS SYSTEM HAD BROKEN the tension between Rufus and his opponent, Glenn Twenhey. After they saw Jason escorted off, however, they went right back to staring at one another. It was more than just assessing the other by physique, clothing and body language. Their auras clashed like fencers. Each sought an opening that would make for an advantage as the fight began, or even uncovered a little extra information that could be the difference between victory and defeat.

"I should have moved when your friend provided the distraction," Glenn said.

"Wouldn't have helped," Rufus said. "And I'm sorry for what's about to happen. But you knew who my grandfather was when you picked me as an opponent, did you not?"

"I did. Hector tried to talk me out of it, but I insisted."

Rufus nodded. "I know that feeling. The need to prove yourself, only to be dismantled by an opponent you underestimated."

"Who says I'm underestimating you?"

Instead of answering, Rufus used his speed-accelerating power. Everything seemed to freeze as his subjective time stream outpaced the world around him. He used that time to close the distance between them, leaving a trail of light behind him. Time unfroze and he smashed Glenn with a head butt, without even raising his golden sword. Glenn realised that Rufus had burned a long cooldown power to effectively just flex, as a head butt was nothing to a silver-ranker. The simple surprise of it had staggered him more than the damage.

Glenn activated his own time-accelerating power, but he didn't need it to close the gap, since Rufus had done it for him. Rufus seemed to freeze, standing with his silver sword at his side, and Glenn used a trick just like Sophie's. Attacks made during the accelerated time-stream would be all but harmless, so he generated a large number of blade wave projectiles which were ready to launch as soon as normal time resumed. It was only as the acceleration was about to end that he noticed a problem.

"Wait, *silver* sword?"

Rufus had the eclipse confluence essence. It informed the way he fought both with specific powers, like the gold and silver swords he could conjure, along with the general theme of his combat style. He shifted between three combat modes based on the sun, the moon and the eclipse. The sun state was built around speed and offensive ability, while the moon was about elusiveness and stealth. The eclipse state offered powerful but short-term buffs or powerful finishers.

Each state was a combination of how he fought, the way he moved and the powers he used, some of which offered different advantages, depending on which state he was in.

His *Light of the Sun, Shadow of the Moon* ability was one of several that offered different effects based on his current state. In the moon state, it could make him intangible for a brief moment. When Glenn's mass of blade waves shot into Rufus, they passed right through him. The intangibility only lasted a few seconds, but Rufus triggered it right before Glenn had slowed time, guaranteeing it would be up when Glenn's ability ended and his attack launched.

"That was nicely done," the Storm King observed. "Luck?"

"Hardly," Soramir said. "The swift essence is a favourite amongst skill-focused melee adventurers. Personal time-acceleration powers are very common, even when not hunting for them with specific awakening stones. Even magic swordsmasters who go for other essences get them. The Remore boy gets his from the sun essence."

"And I get mine from lightning," the king said. "You're saying that Remore predicted both that his enemy would have that ability, and that he would use it in that moment."

"Yes."

"Then it *was* luck. He could have easily been wrong."

"Yes, but his odds were not as bad as they seem. This is a battle for reputation. By burning one of his most powerful abilities to make an attack that was nothing more than a statement, Remore was baiting his opponent. It began when they spoke before they fought. Then Remore disregarded Twenhey with his opening move. He was essentially telling his opponent that he could throw away key abilities and still win."

"I see," the king said with a nod. "Twenhey wanted to show up Remore by using the same ability to show him—and all of us—that he deserved to be taken seriously. Especially by the grandson of the man who stands as the pinnacle of Twenhey's essence combination."

"Exactly," Soramir said. "Instead, he was outplayed again, which appears to have set a tone."

Glenn was a human and his essence abilities were reflective of that. His power set was very strong on offence, particularly special attacks. This fit very nicely into the Rimaros adventurer ethos of ultra-specialisation, as he was a pure striker. Having so many aggressive options at his disposal meant that he could tailor the approach of his offence to the enemy he was facing. If one approach didn't work, he could pivot to another. What he had never previously encountered was a situation where none of his approaches worked.

The advantage of using one of the most common and well-researched essence combinations on the planet was that it was easy to optimise. Strategies to develop more specific power sets and synergies were more readily available. Tailoring a power set was never a perfectly reliable endeavour, but with a common combination made up of common-rarity essences, it was more reliable than most.

The disadvantage of this approach was that it had the weaknesses of its strengths. An opponent who was familiar with these strategies and techniques would, sight unseen, have a solid grasp of at least the general approaches such an essence user would take.

Rufus talked a lot about how his family ran a school, but Jason had never understood the totality of what that meant, or why it was such a source of pride. The Remore Academy studied adventurer methodology from across the globe. This helped them to educate students that came from around the world, as well as prepare their students for what they would encounter in their travels.

Remore Academy students were scions of international mercantile guilds, famous adventuring families, aristocrats and even royalty. The academy prided itself on preparing those students for whatever they might face. That could be a tricky diplomatic situation in a palace, a grim assassination attempt on a remote roadway or a pitched battle against sky pirates.

Rufus was more than just the beneficiary of the teachings of his family's academy. He had seen all kinds of adventurers from when he was old enough to be carried around by his father. Most importantly for his current situation was that Rufus had been trained in swordsmanship personally by the greatest swordsman in the world.

Glenn was exceptionally skilled. His proficiency was not just with sword technique and his essence abilities, but using them in conjunction for results greater than either would achieve alone. His efficiency was tight and his tactics were built on centuries of refinement, passed down by the masters of history. It wasn't enough. Every tactic Glenn used, every ability he pulled out, was not only something that Rufus had seen, but also had practised against extensively. Rufus knew the methods of sword masters and he knew how to counter them.

Glenn was very good and deserving of his place in a prestigious guild, but the more they clashed, the less Rufus saw him as an opponent. Glenn, in Rufus' eyes, increasingly became a collection of flaws in need of correction. Since his family ran a school, Rufus did what he knew: he put on a class.

Using his sun state, Rufus applied pressure on Glenn, baiting out techniques and provoking counters that he dismantled one by one. When Glenn shot blade waves that tracked their opponent, Rufus shifted to a moon state where he couldn't be tracked. The blades shot forward blindly, hitting walls or the floor. When Glenn incorporated special attacks into his swordsmanship, Rufus spotted the indicators and dodged, blocked or countered as appropriate.

Glenn grew increasingly frustrated as his tactics were pulled apart in front of the high society of Rimaros. Guild masters and the heads of noble houses were watching as Rufus disassembled his abilities like a watchmaker taking apart a faulty timepiece. He was on the greatest stage in his life, only for every aspect of his prowess as an adventure to be pulled out and found wanting.

As a final, desperate stratagem, Glenn drew back from Rufus and paused.

"Would you be willing to try something a little different?" Glenn asked.

"I've been waiting for something a little different this entire fight," Rufus told him.

Glenn sheathed his sword, untied the dimensional pouch bound tightly to his potion belt to avoid it flapping around, and pulled out two collars. They were comfortably padded, but still plainly suppression collars.

"Pure swordsmanship," Glenn said. "No powers. How good you are against how good I am."

Rufus blinked in surprise.

"I will say this," he said. "That is the first time since we walked out here that you've done something that I truly did not anticipate."

Rufus held out his hand and Glenn tossed him a collar. Rufus opened his own dimensional pouch and took out a sword, since he would be unable to use his conjured ones. It was a scimitar, but plain compared to those he could create through magic.

"If you want something better, I can loan you one," Twenhey offered.

"This sword was crafted especially for me by my best friend in the world. You don't have anything better."

"Friendship is all well and good, Mr Remore, but you shouldn't let it blind you to the fact that your friend is a worthless smith."

Rufus smiled.

"My grandfather has given me all manner of good advice over the course of my life," he said. "For example, he once told me that if someone provokes you, then let them. But instead of getting angry and letting it cloud your judgement, let it take away your mercy as you calmly take them apart. I was only going to take this so far, Young Master Twenhey, but I suddenly find myself short on mercy."

Glenn smiled back as he clipped on his suppression collar and Rufus did the same.

"Just so you know, Mr Remore, my sword instructor studied at your academy. He was trained personally by your grandfather and spent decades developing counters to his fighting style."

"Would that be Ayer Wick you're referring to?" Rufus asked, eliciting a surprised expression from Glenn.

"You know of him?"

"It was a guess. A lot of people develop counters to my grandfather's style, and Wick is about right in terms of age and location. My grandfather rather enjoys that they do, since it's hard to refine his style as the centuries roll on. He showed me the counters your sword instructor developed. They were... well, it's best to not be rude. I noticed you trying them in our earlier clashes, which was why I was so surprised you chose this path."

"That was with powers mixed in," Glenn said. "We'll see how you do when all you have is technique."

"Yes," Rufus agreed, his eyes glancing over the audience. "I'm going to make a point of it."

He raised his scimitar.

"With this sword."

Jason had become very, very good with the sword. Rufus had helped him to take the skill books containing the Way of the Reaper and make the technique his own. After the incredible number of battles Jason had been through, wild and desperate and strange, experience had truly allowed him to become a master of the sword.

Technique to technique, Glenn would have beaten Jason. There was only so much time to practise, and martial techniques were not as central to his abilities as they were to Sophie or Rufus. Jason's combat style intricately wove his magical powers with his martial arts, along with mobility and skirmish techniques. He was a ninja warlock, not a swordsman. Glenn's strategy of removing powers from the equation would have gotten him a win against Jason without question.

Rufus was not Jason, and there was a reason that Rufus was considered the future of the Remore family. They knew talent and had nurtured his, with training and opportunities they carefully engineered so that he would see success and failure both. When he went his own way, Rufus had setbacks.

Although they didn't push their expectations on him, Rufus knew his family anticipated great things. Responsibility weighed heavily on him, and the loss of Farrah and Jason had somewhat derailed him. But the life of an adventurer was long and his family was patient. They did not intervene as he turned to teaching over adventuring. Only his mother stepped in, and even she was a light hand.

The return of Jason and Farrah brought with it a slow change in Rufus. He wasn't sure what his future held, be it teaching or adventuring, both or neither, but he knew one thing: he wasn't letting his friends down again. During his time in Rimaros, Rufus had taken the fundamentals of training he taught Jason and followed them with relentless determination. He honed his skills, pushed his body and took contract after contract, which the monster surge offered in plentiful supply.

The weight of what Rufus had been through was different to what Glenn had done. He was not dissimilar to what Rufus would have been if he had never left Vitesse, never felt true desperation and never felt the consequences of abject failure. The pride and ambition that drove him was a gentle breeze before the raging gale of Rufus' determination.

"What's he doing?" Clive asked. "Why doesn't he finish it?"

"I don't know what you call it here, if you have even have the practice in any of this world's cultures," Jason said. "Where I come from, it's usually known as counting coup. You touch the enemy without harming them, to prove that you could have beaten them. It's a way to gather prestige or humiliate an enemy into accepting defeat. Rufus was already making a show of how much better he was than this guy, but I think slagging off your sword pushed him over the line, Gary."

"Good," Gary said. "There's nothing wrong with a plain, reliable weapon. You don't have to make it all fancy."

Jason glanced down at the scabbard on his hip.

"That one is your fault," Gary said, following Jason's gaze. "Your soul bond made it go weird."

"Making things go weird is kind of my thing," Jason said, prompting agreeing nods all around.

"I yield," a crestfallen Glenn said. He was standing in front of Rufus, shoulders sagging and stance marred by exhaustion as his sword dangled from his hand. Rufus stood casually, his sword pointed at the ground.

"I haven't even touched you with the edge of my blade," Rufus said. "You're going to quit without a scratch on you?"

"You didn't have to do it this way," Glenn told him.

"You're not going to fight on? What about the pride of your guild? Of your sword instructor? Of your house? Are you going to throw it all on the ground?"

"Why are you doing this?" Glenn asked, his voice pleading.

"We didn't ask for this," Rufus shot back coldly. "I didn't bring us here. Hector de Varco's challenge turned us into a whetstone for his house and guild to hone their reputation. Defeating you wouldn't hurt you. Humiliation is the only wound you can truly suffer. Now, if you'll excuse me, I need to go have my sword repaired."

Rufus held up his blade, peering as he inspected it for nicks and dents.

"Oh. It looks like I don't have to."

Jason and his companions were waiting, sitting around calmly as Rufus returned to the viewing box.

"That was awesome," Travis said. "I know we haven't known each other very long, but you totally educated that guy. And Jason was telling me your whole family fights like that? You should open a school."

Rufus frowned in confusion.

"My family does run a school," he said. "I thought I told you tha…"

He trailed off as Travis took a shot glass from the dimensional bag at his waist.

Everyone else in the room but Rufus himself did the same and drained their glasses. Rufus took on an aggrieved expression, his eyes landing on Arabelle and the empty glass in her hand.

"Mum, you too?"

21

MOTHER'S FAVOURITE

"HUMPHREY IS THE LEAST-SUITED TO DUELLING OUT OF YOU FOUR," NEIL assessed as they watched Humphrey enter the arena.

Jason had a lot of training and experience in the five years since his first arrival on Pallimustus, allowing him to master his own power set. But when it came to group tactics, Jason could not match the lifelong education people like Neil, Humphrey and Rufus had gone through. That big-picture understanding required exhaustive instruction on essence abilities, roles, tactics and strategy that couldn't be replaced by skill books or combat experience. It took active guidance and tutelage that Jason never had neither the time nor opportunity for. His time training with Rufus, Farrah and Gary had been a desperate rush to cram him with the fundamentals of being an adventurer.

Neil, on the other hand, was one of the handful of adventurers in Greenstone that had enjoyed that kind of training. The Davone and Mercer families had colluded to team him with Thadwick Mercer at a young age, giving Neil the same opportunities afforded to Thadwick and his sister, Cassandra. Neil had made the most of those opportunities, like Cassandra, rather than squandering them, like Thadwick.

As the healer, Neil was always watching over the team in a more holistic manner than any other member. This made his understanding of the team's strategies and tactics as comprehensive as that of Humphrey, who was the driving force in developing them. He was, therefore, fully qualified to assess the chances of his team members in different circumstances.

"Humphrey has set himself up to be very team-oriented," Neil explained to the people in the viewing box that weren't on their team. "He's developed his combat style, his tactics and his equipment around working with the group. Belinda's cooldown reductions, my buffs, Clive's mana replenishment; many of our core tactics centre on supporting Humphrey, while he has increasingly focused on making the most of those advantages. Not to say he isn't strong alone, but he has given up an amount of solitary strength to be the solid anchor of our team."

"He's the black lion," Jason said.

"A black lion?" Neil asked. He and the rest of the team were confused and would have ignored Jason like usual, if not for Taika and Travis nodding in agreement.

"That makes sense, bro."

"You're saying that he's strong on his own," Travis said, "but he's no Voltron."

"That's it," Neil said. "No more people from Earth, or this will turn into a disaster."

"I think the problem," Belinda said, "is that Humphrey isn't selfish enough. He's not a glory hound, unlike some other team members participating in these duels."

"Hey," Jason complained.

"Oh, please," Farrah said. "Your first idea on how to investigate magic in your world was to pretend to be an angel and faith-heal your way through a children's hospital. Don't even try to pretend you aren't a big, prancing attention seeker."

"And I remember how you were, back in your cage-fighting days," Belinda said to Sophie.

"Theatricality is a part of arena fighting," Sophie said. "No one loves a boring gladiator. But I wouldn't go underestimating Humphrey just because he doesn't care for putting on a show."

"She's right," Rufus said. "Jason, your skills have exploded in the handful of years since we met, but you don't understand just how deep Geller family training goes. Humphrey has been training for longer than he can remember. He's an adventurer down to the bones, and the depth of that only comes out when you start pulling away at the layers. When the Geller family train their people to handle the unusual situations, they are just as diligent as with their training for everyday activities. Perhaps even more so. They know it's the edge cases that will get you killed."

"Not to mention that our entire team is built around handling those edge cases," Clive pointed out.

"That's not a coincidence," Rufus said. "Your entire team reeks of Geller family methodology, and that's far from unique. There's a reason people scramble to be on a team with a Geller who went through their Greenstone training program. If Rick Geller announced at this ball he was recruiting a new team member, he'd be mobbed with applicants from the best families in Rimaros."

"And don't forget that the Geller family is crazy rich," Gary pointed out. "He has entire gear sets to recalibrate his strategies. Not as many as Lindy, but a lot. I made some of that gear myself."

Humphrey stood in his conjured armour that looked increasingly like Stash's natural form, compared to the lower-rank version of the power. The scale armour was glorious with iridescent rainbow scales, like a quilt made of opals. Five blue crystals floated around him, lit up with internal light as they replenished his mana. He had yet to call up either of the swords he could conjure.

"Humphrey Geller," he said, introducing himself.

His opponent was dressed in strange clothes with numerous folds that looked awkward to fight in.

"They call me the Smoke Hunter."

"Okay," Humphrey said, unfazed. He was getting a vibe of early Jason from the alchemist's sense of melodrama. "You hunt smoke? I didn't realise it was that hard to find."

"That's not what it means."

"Some people use smoke as signals. Because of how easy it is to see from far away. In fact, most people avoid using smoke when they're being hunted, specifically because of how easy that would make it to track them down."

Humphrey was not big on banter. He liked fighting monsters, not people, but his mother had still drilled into him the advantages of making an opponent emotional. So, now that he found himself in a duel, he did his best Jason impression.

"Let's see what you think of my smoke when you're choking on it!"

The Smoke Hunter plucked a syringe from the air and jabbed it into his leg. His body immediately changed and Humphrey understood what he was up against. His body was growing, the purpose of his unusual clothes revealed as they expanded to accommodate his growth. Folds unfurled and straps slipped through buckles as the loose, bunched-up outfit became fitted light armour. He became twice as tall and half again as wide as he had been moments before.

Humphrey's opponent was an alchemist, although a very different one from Belinda's boyfriend, Jory. This was a full-blown combat craftsman who sought to beat Humphrey at his own game of burst-damage in the high-damage, low-endurance mould.

Combat alchemists were rare, especially non-support variants that engaged in direct combat, so it was unusual to see one in a duel. Humphrey, by contrast, was the most orthodox member on his team, with only Neil coming anywhere close. This meant that Humphrey's power set, like that of Rufus' opponent, didn't pack a lot of surprises in his toolbox. He did have a few, though, and he would need to use them well. Otherwise, predictability would be as much a defining factor in this duel as it had been in the previous.

The alchemist's proportions became less human and more hunched over. His hands grew bigger and his arms longer. His skin became leathery, taking on the lumpen green of crocodile hide. Reinforced patches on his armour looked strikingly similar to his new skin. He did not look awkward for the transformation, however. Humphrey assessed that he was still limber for his size, like an animal ready to pounce.

Alchemy-fuelled transformation was a rare speciality, but also a famous one. It stood out from all the warrior, wizard and assassin variants, and made for popular villains in stories. It was centred on powers that required alchemical catalysts to produce extreme transformations, with the nature and potency of the catalyst defining the result. Humphrey had no doubt that his opponent had gone for maximum power at the cost of maximum side-effects in the aftermath.

The alchemist had bet everything on a short-lived burst of power, which was pure Rimaros-style ultra-specialisation. It was a fantastic choice in a duel, or as a trump card for a team large enough to not miss their absence during downtime.

Contrasting the Rimaros approach was Humphrey, who was a dedicated and practical adventurer. His Vitesse-style training was focused around covering all his bases, so as not to be caught out. It worked much better in the versatile tactics his team favoured than Rimaros teams that liked to build around supporting a single specialist.

While Humphrey's team could use a similar approach, usually focused on Humphrey himself, they would never match up to the Rimaros standard in that regard. In that way, they were like Jory compared to this alchemist—it was something they could do, but not as well as those who truly focused on it. Humphrey's duel was a microcosm of the Rimaros versus Vitesse styles of adventuring, and his opponent held the advantage.

Humphrey's approach served him well in day-to-day adventuring, which was what he cared about. In the artificial circumstance of a duel, however, it placed him at a disadvantage. He didn't have to think about secondary enemies that might be lurking nearby. He didn't have to worry about watching out for his team or reserving anything for later fights. All the time and resources he had spent on training and equipping himself for those things were useless to him here.

Combat mutagens, especially the powerful ones, were known for two things: their immense potency and their immense backlash when they ran their course. The strategy to combat them was to retreat when the alchemist was at their strongest, wait out the mutagen and strike again when they were at their weakest. But in a duel, there was no retreat. There was nowhere in the arena to hide, and no extra enemies or later fights the alchemist needed to reserve himself for. He could throw everything he had into one challenge, knowing that his opponent had to take it up.

Humphrey was aware that his opponent's enhanced body would have formidable power, resilience and regenerative properties. He had not geared himself up to maximise his offensive strength and he was now grateful for it. That was more Farrah's speciality, and while she might have had the punch to beat the mutagenic monstrosity through all of those enhancements, he did not, even with his most aggressive gear. While his attacks were powerful, they weren't lava cannon powerful.

Instead, Humphrey had selected to forgo enhancing his attack. His attacks were quite strong on their own, so he focused on defence and endurance. Hidden under his conjured armour were amulets that enhanced the resilience of his conjured objects, be they his swords, armour or wings. Enchanted armbands, rings, anklets and others all offered simple and passive, but effective, boosts to his mana recovery, stamina and certain essence abilities.

Seeing his opponent hulk out in front of him, Humphrey knew that he had made the right choice. His path to victory was holding on long enough that the power of his opponent petered out. Once the mutagenic cocktail the alchemist had taken lost its effectiveness, the backlash would leave Humphrey the victor—assuming he could last that long.

Humphrey hadn't wasted time as his opponent was transforming. He could have used that moment to launch into an attack and try to end the fight before the alchemist's transition was fully complete. That was an all-or-nothing gamble, however, and one he knew he'd lose. Any adventurer who had reached the level this Smoke Hunter had would have traps prepared for anyone looking to exploit such an obvious weakness.

The moment the alchemist injected himself and Humphrey realised what he was up against, he sprang into action himself. He pulled a gourd from his storage space, spilling bone ash from it in a circle with practised speed. He then tossed a pair of twelve-sided dice into the circle, and illusions projected from their top faces as they came to a stop. Above one die was the image of a fish, while the other showed a very pale, blue swirl.

Humphrey didn't stick around to look at the results, as the alchemical bulk of his transformed opponent was already lunging at him. He dashed to the side, the dice leaping through the air to return to him. He shoved them into his storage space while on the move, skirting away from the circle and around his opponent.

Humphrey's initial assessment of the Smoke Hunter's abilities under the effect of the mutagen proved accurate. The alchemist was not slowed down by his large body, giving Humphrey no advantage in speed. All that silver-rank speed had a lot of mass behind it, however, which was great for ramming an enemy but not for quick changes of direction. This was something Humphrey understood well, having spent years swinging a giant sword where the key was balancing mass and leverage. With every rank, Humphrey had grown stronger and stronger as his sword grew heavier and heavier, so his grasp of weight and momentum was drilled into his most fundamental combat instincts.

This innate knowledge was something Humphrey called on, not to fight, this time, but to evade, as he led the alchemist on a merry chase around the arena. It didn't take long for the alchemist to realise that Humphrey was buying time, with Humphrey still yet to pull out a weapon. He stopped in the middle of the arena and Humphrey paused, carefully out of reach.

"Coward," the monster spat in a growling, inhuman voice.

"Fighting the way you want me to would make me a fool, not a coward."

If his opponent was willing to waste time, Humphrey would accept that gift with graciousness. He did not share Jason's love of combat banter, but his mother would growl at him if he didn't use every tool available. In a demonstration of Geller indoctrination that Rufus was not familiar with, it never occurred to Humphrey that his mother might not know what he was up to at any given moment.

Sadly, the alchemist gave up on talk when his provocation failed and plucked two orbs from a dimensional storage space, each large enough to fill his giant hands. One he threw in a flat trajectory, high above Humphrey's head. Humphrey didn't know what the alchemist was up to and dodged so that it didn't pass directly over him. The other orb was tossed over the alchemist's shoulder.

Each orb was a sphere swirling with mist, both of which smashed against the large doors at each end of the arena. The strength of the monstrous alchemist was enough that even a casual toss let them cross the distance. Thick smoke started filling the arena from each broken orb, slowly expanding towards the combatants in the middle.

"What will you do when you're out of room to run away?" the alchemist taunted.

"Well," Humphrey said, "the first thing I'll do is realise that your transformation has drawbacks to go with its advantages. It's heavy, and apparently, your aura senses aren't great. I'm not sure if it also affects your intelligence or if you're just naturally dim, but either way, you haven't realised that the way I was leading you around was specifically so you wouldn't look back at the circle I left behind."

The alchemist turned to see that the circle of bone powder had turned into a pale circle of light from which strange creatures were now emerging, one by one. Rising silently into the air was what looked like air elementals, made of condensed air that was hard to spot but created a visible distortion. Easier to see were the skeletons inside them, which were like that of a shark except for being somewhat draconic in shape, mostly in the skull. The wind dragon sharks were also wearing ethereal armour, easier to spot than their airy bodies but still not as obvious as their floating skeletons.

Humphrey's summoning ability, Spartoi, called up dragon bone warriors, but his summoner's dice replaced the ordinary soldiers with more exotic forms. One die changed their shape, while the other infused them with elemental or even more exotic energies. The results were rather random, but added some much-needed unpredictability to Humphrey's orthodox combat style. The summons were then further bolstered by Humphrey's power to equip them with conjured magical gear.

A dozen of the wind dragon sharks were already floating silently in the air, gathering above and behind the Smoke Hunter as he focused on chasing Humphrey. Knowing that more extreme mutagenic shifts almost always traded off various things for greater power, and aura sensitivity was a common one, Humphrey had tried to distract his opponent as his summons emerged. To his great satisfaction, it worked, clawing back at least a little of the alchemist's advantage.

With an angry growl, the alchemist resumed his chase, moving the duel into a second phase. This time, Humphrey had much less room to move as the sickly green smoke filled more and more of the arena. He had new advantages, though, as what eventually became twenty wind sharks started harassing his opponent. They weren't a danger to the Smoke Hunter, but they were a frustrating annoyance. The flying creatures clamped onto his limbs, forcing him to smash them off or ram into the walls to crush them, whittling down their number.

Unfortunately for the sharks, their ethereal armour offered little protection against brute force attacks. Unfortunately for the alchemist, destroying that armour inflicted an affliction that left chaotic winds clinging to him and buffeting his body. The affliction was too weak to impede his monstrous strength at first, but the effect grew stronger with each destroyed wind shark, disrupting his movement, coordination and balance. Even so, the alchemist continued destroying them, as it was easier for his strength to power through some wind than deal with sharks hanging off his arms and legs.

Although he was rapidly destroying the sharks, the alchemist was aware that too much time was slipping away. He chose not to completely dedicate himself to eliminating the summons. Instead, he continued to charge after Humphrey, sharks still swimming through the air to harass him.

Humphrey tried to remain evasive and stretch out the battle further, but his free space was ever-diminishing. He finally pulled out his massive dragon sword, which wreathed itself in fire, adding defensive strikes to his dodging.

Although strength was one of the defining traits of Humphrey's power set, being on the defensive against a larger, stronger opponent was not a novel circumstance. While he was usually the adventurer with the biggest stick, most silver-rank monsters towered over him. The Smoke Hunter was more monster than adventurer at that moment, and Humphrey fought accordingly.

Humphrey's strength might not equal the absurd levels that the alchemist currently possessed, but it was still well above the silver-rank baseline. Added to his array of special attacks, the Smoke Hunter was startled at the power behind them, becoming more wary. The long arms and huge hands reaching for Humphrey were blasted away by Humphrey's sword, even as Humphrey continued to dodge. One strike carved off three of the alchemist's fingers, eliciting a howl, even if they quickly grew back.

Despite the impedance of the sharks, it was increasingly difficult for Humphrey to stay out of the alchemist's grasp as the green smoke further boxed him in. That did not mean that his small box of tricks had been emptied out, however. As he was about to get pinned against the wall, he teleported behind his opponent and a mass of spider webbing slammed into the alchemist's back, pinning him against the wall instead. The massive spider that spat it then turned back into a tiny bird and flittered away, vanishing amongst the remaining sharks.

Humphrey didn't bother to attack the entangled alchemist. He was holding a massive sword, but his true weapon was time, and cutting the alchemist free himself would be counterproductive. Even so, the Smoke Hunter made relatively short work of the webs, even pinned face-first to the wall. He wrenched his limbs free and leveraged them against the wall, steel-like webbing giving way to prodigious strength. The alchemist, now draped in webbing and the few remaining sharks, turned angrily to face his opponent. Humphrey opened his mouth, but instead of words, fire spewed out.

In the viewing room, Arabelle looked at the remnant wind sharks, the shape-shifting dragon, the enemy covered in burning webs and asked a question.

"Didn't you say he was the *most* orthodox member of your team?"

The spider form Stash had taken was called a greater firelight spider. It was known for producing sticky, inflammable webs that clung to its targets, even as they burned. The remnant webs still draped over the Smoke Hunter did exactly that under Humphrey's Fire Breath power, which itself left burning residue behind. Humphrey was under no illusion that it would take out the alchemist, but being covered in what amounted to magic napalm made it rather hard to focus.

As the fight resumed, Stash started participating more following his initial ambush. None of his silver-rank monster forms were a match for the dosed-up alchemist. Instead, he used hit-and-run attacks to harass. He shifted from one form to another, too quickly to be pinned down unless the alchemist turned his attention from Humphrey. That was something the Smoke Hunter could not afford, as while even the burnt-off skin might grow back, every passing moment was a different kind of wound. Each second ticking by brought the duel closer to a victory for Humphrey, and chasing his familiar would just be another distraction.

Humphrey continued to use every trick and tactic available to avoid being pinned down. He conjured his wings to shield him from attacks, de-conjuring them to escape when the alchemist grabbed them. But in the end, he came up short. With almost no space left to avoid the green smoke, he'd already been forced to dip into the billowing wall to avoid the alchemist and felt the poison seeping through his skin. Along with eating away at his flesh, it slowed him just a little, but just a little was enough.

With a shout of triumph, the alchemist's massive hands wrapped around Humphrey, pinning his arms to his sides. He slammed Humphrey with a pair of head butts before hammering him repeatedly into the floor. This continued until the cooldown of Humphrey's teleport allowed him to vanish, but the alchemist was ready.

There was only so much space left for Humphrey to teleport into and the Smoke Hunter predicted Humphrey's destination. He leapt up, even as Humphrey was reappearing above him and conjuring his wings to stay aloft. The alchemist snatched him out of the air. Before even dropping to the floor, the Smoke Hunter threw Humphrey deep into the noxious green gas that now almost filled the arena.

The alchemist grinned at his victory. Even if Humphrey came right out, the smoke would have done enough work to make the result a foregone conclusion. If Humphrey was foolish enough to try and wait out his transformation in the cloud, the poison would finish him off. Before that happened, one of the powerful attendees, no doubt monitoring Humphrey's condition, would step in as Soramir had in Sophie's fight.

The alchemist waited, revelling in his triumph. And he waited. And waited. Why wasn't anyone stepping in? He hunted down the last of the sharks as he looked around for Humphrey's elusive familiar, but saw nothing. It had to be somewhere, and maybe it could turn into a monster with invisibility. Or, he realised as his eyes went wide, it could shapeshift into something immune to his smoke's poison.

The alchemist snarled as he pulled an orb from his storage space, immediately throwing it into the smoke. The counteragent dispersed the noxious gas almost as swiftly as a gale, revealing not Humphrey but a giant frog with bright red and green skin.

The frog opened its mouth and Humphrey staggered out, clearly having caught a sharp dose of the smoke before hiding inside the frog. He was also dripping with the frog's viscous saliva, stumbling with weakness. His skin was marked by the toxin, splotchy with green and black marks.

"Yield," the alchemist growled.

"I accept your yield," Humphrey croaked.

"What? No, you yield! You're about to drop dead!"

Humphrey grinned. "Would you like to see my mother's favourite of all my abilities?"

The alchemist had a bad feeling and charged at Humphrey, but the frog sprang into his path. Despite having more mass, the frog was sent flying while the alchemist was only brought to a stop, but that was all the time Humphrey needed. In an earlier fight on Earth, Jack Gerling had frustrated Jason with the Immortality power, which cleansed all afflictions unconditionally, ignoring any and all effects that would normally impede or prevent cleansing. It was also one of the most powerful healing abilities in existence. When he activated it, Humphrey shone with golden light. His body was restored to near-full health in an instant, with a potent ongoing recovery effect on top. The cooldown of the power was a full day, but it was Humphrey's turn to take advantage of their fight being a duel.

The alchemist looked at the restored Humphrey and all the room he now had to evade in with half of the arena cleared of smoke. He could already feel his strength fading and knew that the backlash would soon kick in. That would leave him effectively helpless against a fully recovered opponent.

"I yield."

Palace stewards came in and cleaned the walls with magic, removing the poison residue left behind by the alchemist smoke. They also used some rituals to repair the damaged portions of the brickwork floor, although it had held up remarkably to the rigours of battle. The observation glass was undamaged, although rather in need of a clean. Once the stewards cleared the area, the doors at each end opened to admit Hector from one end and Jason from the other. The massive doors closed ponderously behind them.

Hector had changed from his formalwear into a formfitting light outfit. The material was recognisable, with woven black and blue fabric. Mimicloth was noted for its ability to endure various methods of shape-shifting and matter alteration by its wearer. In the case of Hector, Jason had already been warned of his ability to transform into living stone.

Jason was already in his conjured robes, his sword at his hip. Hector was somewhat taken aback by the strange, portal-like appearance of the cloak draped over him. With his poised gait and the cloak obscuring his legs, Jason almost seemed to float as he walked towards the centre of the arena. He and Hector both stopped when they were around ten metres apart.

"I feel it's only right to warn you," Hector said, "that this arena offers a strong advantage to me. One of my evolved racial gifts allows me to modify my earth abilities with the properties of any nearby magical stone. This arena is built of core-heart lattice granite, which is resilient and easy to repair with the right rituals.

Those properties will make my stone abilities much harder to break through, and give me some abilities that will be almost like healing to me."

Jason said nothing. His aura was invisible to Hector, as was his face in the dark hood. Only his alien eyes were visible to his opponent.

"Well," Hector said, "if you have nothing to say, I'm going to begin."

Hector fell over, foaming at the mouth as his body thrashed in a seizure until Soramir's aura pushed Jason's back, cutting off the soul attack. Soramir appeared, glaring at Jason.

"That's quite enough, Mr Asano."

Jason turned and walked back to the doors, which slowly opened to accept him.

22

A GOOD FRIEND TO HAVE

ESTELLA WARNOCK STILL THOUGHT OF IT AS HER GRANDFATHER'S HOUSE, EVEN though he was now gone. After the death of her parents, Warwick Warnock had retired from adventuring to raise Estella, never pushing her to adventure the way he had her father. Warwick had learned that lesson at the price of his son's life, and had been determined to avoid the same mistake with his granddaughter.

Warwick had only ever pushed Estella to find her passion, whatever that might be. If it turned out to be adventuring, he would have supported it, but to his relief, it had not been the case. The death of her father had strangled in the crib any desire to follow that path.

Warwick hadn't loved the path that Estella did eventually choose, as a spy for hire for shady people in the city, but he never tried to dissuade her from it. What he did do, from time to time, was nudge her toward using her skills for something a little more responsible. That was how she ended up scouting for monsters that Jason Asano or other adventurers were sent after during the Builder attack.

At the same time as she was doing a rare bit of civic duty, her grandfather had gone off to fight one of the fortress cities attacking the kingdom, but never came home. They told her he had died like a hero. It was the same thing they said about her father.

All of this came at a time when she was realising that her chosen profession was not working out. She enjoyed the challenge of it, but her sketchy clients always wanted more challenge than she did. To them, she was a cheap option for spying on those that would otherwise require an expensive and troublesome high-ranker to keep tabs on.

She had left the job after several hours playing cat and mouse with Asano's damnable shadow familiar. She had been uncertain whether or not to go back to that work and what changes to make. The loss of her grandfather had left her uninspired to return at all, and she'd been languishing in aimlessness after moving back into his empty house.

Of all people, Asano had been something of a comfort. He was neighbourly and it was refreshing that he didn't want anything from her, at least until he did. His offer of employment had sounded suspiciously like adventuring by proxy. On the other hand, it would be nice to work for someone at least partially invested in her wellbeing, compared to Havi Estos and his ilk. They were all about benefits exchange, where her interactions with Asano and companions had shown that they genuinely cared for one another.

That kind of genuine companionship was something she'd never had. Her parents died before she really gained an appreciation of trust, and only her grandfather had ever earned it. There was a distinct appeal to becoming part of a group where that trust wasn't just a factor, but the norm. For all that they regularly jabbed one another, Asano and his friends breathed in camaraderie like air.

She'd been considering Asano's offer for some time, but remained undecided. It was a path forward at a time when she felt directionless, but should she jump at the first thing that came along? Her instincts told her that it was what her grandfather would want. Despite his nudges in how she should utilise her skills, his only outright complaint was how solitary her life was.

Late one evening, she was mulling the issue over, checking if anything from her grandfather's expensive liquor collection would help resolve her indecision. It hadn't any of the other times she tried it, but she prided herself on professionalism. She had to be thorough in checking.

She turned her head, looking at the wall as her magical senses moved beyond it. Something almost undetectable was approaching: one of Asano's shadowy familiars. She'd regularly felt the shadow-being's many bodies roaming around within the scope of her prodigious senses since moving close to Asano's home, and was beginning to suspect that the familiar was using her for practise.

On this occasion, Shade made his way to her front door. He knew she was aware of his presence and did not knock, and instead, waited outside her doorway. She got up, moved to the door and opened it.

"Something I can do for your boss?" she asked the shadow man in her doorway. "Isn't he at some big fancy party?"

"He is, indeed, Miss Warnock. I have come to discuss the offer of employment he made you."

"I've been deliberating."

"You have, by my estimate, one hour and forty minutes to conclude your deliberations or the offer will be revoked."

She frowned.

"Tell your boss that I don't like being pushed."

"He is not pushing, Miss Warnock; he's leaving. Our full entourage will be gone within the next two hours."

"Did something happen at the party?"

"Mr Asano was attending," Shade said. "So, yes, but my understanding is that was tangentially related at best. He informed me that the decision to leave tonight was centred on a friend helping him to remember that which mattered and that which did not."

"Sounds like a good friend to have."

"Quite so, Miss Warnock. If you are willing to tolerate a piece of unsolicited advice, I would point out that you should perhaps consider transitioning to a position where you can make friends of your own."

The arena ready-areas were essentially large locker rooms, with projectors on one wall so anyone inside could watch the duels. Liara was alone in Jason's ready room, having just watched him not so much win a duel as look at it sternly until it slunk away in shame. She knew enough about him to know he had used a soul attack, but even her gold-rank senses had failed to pick up the spike of aura he used to do so. The sheer power and precision of it, at his rank, was almost as terrifying as the attack itself.

Fully as terrifying was Asano's willingness to make soul attacks not just in public, but in front of a prestigious and attentive audience. Soul attacks were extremely rare, almost never coming from essence abilities. They were most notoriously associated with the kind of villains that Liara had spent most of her adventuring career hunting down.

She had asked Jason to be serious and demonstrate that authority could rein him in. He had told her that it was a bad idea, and now she finally believed him. She had never imagined that he would fulfil her request by attacking someone with an attack of such sudden, violating brutality that Soramir Rimaros had to step in and stop him.

The arena doors opened to admit Jason, still in his sinister blood robes and uncanny cloak. The doors closed behind him as Jason moved towards her.

"The way you move using the cloak is unusual," she observed. "Like you're gliding."

"When I was iron rank, I spent no small amount of time developing movement techniques that incorporated various minor aspects of my powers, methodologies taken from the Order of the Reaper. It helped me to travel quickly through the Greenstone delta on foot while navigating difficult terrain and maximising my endurance. Over time, it became habitual while I was wearing my cloak."

A dark mist shrouded Jason, dispersing after just a moment. When it did, his robes and cloak had been replaced by his previous formalwear. The absence of his sinister adventuring attire did not alleviate the heavy air surrounding him. He wasn't projecting the polite subdued aura that etiquette called for. His aura was barely detectable at all, and that was by a gold-ranker standing right in front of him.

"Miss Hurin told me that you are leaving tonight."

"Yes."

"You were meant to leave with His Ancestral Majesty. Make a show of you going off into the cosmos together."

"He can come to the cloud house and put on a show if he likes."

"Soramir Rimaros doesn't go to you, Jason. You go to him."

"That hasn't been my experience."

As much as she might want to, Liara couldn't argue the point. She had been raised to venerate the absentee figure of the Storm Kingdom's founder, but meeting the real thing had upended her expectations. He was a lot more casual and relaxed than the figure depicted in history books, which, she supposed, was something you could do when you didn't answer to anyone. The fact that Soramir and Jason were quite alike in this regard was not lost on her.

"I've been making arrangements as best I can to facilitate your departure," she told him. "Vidal Ladiv is bringing everything you'll need from the Adventure Society to us here. Amos Pensinata and his nephew have been notified and are en route to your building. Carlos Quilido is also making rushed preparations, with no small number of complaints over the short notice. I was not sure if you had decided to take someone from the Rimaros family with you, be it Zara or... my daughter."

"I'm taking neither; we have complications enough. From almost the first moment I arrived here, House Rimaros has been pushing itself into my affairs or pulling me into theirs. Now that I'm leaving your family's kingdom, you will find my patience for that kind of intrusion has sharply declined."

Despite the heaviness of the moment, Liara couldn't help herself. "This was you being patient?"

Jason broke into a laugh, breaking the tension. "Believe it or not, yes. You're probably better off without me."

"No," Liara said. "You're trouble in a clearly labelled box, Asano, but you may just be worth that trouble. Without you, my husband would be dead. If your friend Belinda was still in Vitesse, the Order of Redeeming Light would still be a threat. If not for your friends Travis and Dawn, the battle with the Builder's city-fortresses would have gone very differently. If you hadn't somehow made the Builder pack up and leave, the invasion would have continued for as much as five or six more weeks."

"Princess, that's just how things go for me. The reason I'm leaving is in the slim hope that maybe it won't be, if even for a little while. I do have to save my home planet again, but I'm hoping I can do that on the down-low."

The door leading into the hallways around the arena opened and Vidal Ladiv came in.

"Good evening, milady. I apologise, Mr Asano; I didn't want to interrupt your duel preparations. They told me it was about to start, so I thought it would be underway by now. I didn't want to come in until the duel had begun, and I didn't sense anyone but you in here, Princess."

Seeing someone who was visibly in front of them but absent from their magical senses was unnerving to most essence users, and a large part of the mystique high-rankers held. Vidal showed no sign of being perturbed on his face, although both Liara and Jason could feel it in his aura.

"It's fine, Mr Ladiv," Liara said. "The duel is already over."

This time, surprise did show on his face.

"I would have expected it to take longer," he said. "Hector de Varco can turn himself into stone, isolate afflictions into small parts of his body and tear them off, replacing them with stone from the environment. It's a rather unusual form of regeneration that works very well against affliction specialists. Or is supposed to."

"Mr Asano decided to forgo afflictions for another approach," Liara said. "You can ask him about it later, if you have the courage. Right now, he needs the documentation from the Adventure Society. Did you get everything in order?"

"I did, milady. Rodney was a great help."

"You know my assistant?"

"Yes, milady. Very well, in fact."

"He never mentioned," Liara said.

"You're a princess," Jason said. "He didn't think you'd care."

Liara looked at Jason, then back to Vidal, whose face gave reluctant confirmation. She frowned unhappily.

"Mr Ladiv," Jason said to the man who increasingly looked in need of rescue. "What do you have for me?"

"Give him what he needs, Mr Ladiv," Liara said. "I'm going to go help extract Mr Asano's companions, so they don't end up in any further political messes after the duels."

Vidal nodded, moving to Jason and taking a file folder from a dimensional pouch as Liara departed.

"This is the documentation relating to your Adventure Society memberships," Vidal said, and handed over the folder. "The paperwork for your real identity and your new identity, with the alias you have chosen, is all here. By the time the sun comes up, these will all have been updated in the Adventure Society central record."

Vidal then took out a small box.

"These are your new badges, with the updated rank for your real identity and the false identity."

Vidal opened the case to reveal two silver-rank Adventure Society badges, sitting on the padded lining of the box. The badge on the right had a single star while the one on the left had three. In both cases, however, they differed from the solid five-pointed stars that Jason was familiar with. The single star on the right badge had a circle around it, while the three stars on the left badge were not solid stars, but pentagrams.

"What's going on here?" Jason asked, pointing them out.

"This," Vidal said, indicating the single star, "is the standard marker for an auxiliary adventurer. It means that they can't take solo missions; they have to be attached to a team. It's for auxiliaries that can hold their own in a fight, if necessary, and means they qualify for a share of contract awards if they participate in combat or, more frequently, other dangerous activities. An intrusion expert might need to join the team if they're breaking into some fortified lair, for example. They might not fight the things in there, but they're still going into the dangerous place to open locks and bypass traps."

"So, it's for when the cook is secretly super combat guy and there's a naked lady asleep in the cake."

"I'm afraid you've lost me there, sir."

"Don't call me sir. Call me Jason, or Asano, if you're more comfortable with that. Call me H.R. Pufnstuf if you like, but not sir. I'm not in charge of you."

"No, you're definitely in charge of me, sir."

"You're an independent liaison from the Adventure Society."

"Sir, I'll be with your team and your friends in your cloud construct. While I'm confident that most, if not all, of the rumours I've heard about that building are wrong, there are people I'm very scared of who are scared of it. Add that to you being suspicious of me as an outsider and I'm not entirely certain you won't kill and dispose of me if I stumble onto the wrong secret. You're in charge of me, if only from the perspective of my not being an idiot."

"That's fair," Jason acknowledged. "Alright, tell me about the other badge."

"Well," Vidal said in the tone of someone familiar with the term 'shoot the messenger,' "you're definitely a three-star adventurer. Three stars means dealing with contracts related to high-level politics. If Soramir Rimaros is asking about your star rating, that pretty much answers the question right there. But, the Adventure Society is also aware that you sometimes feel compelled to act against your own best interests when your principles are involved. While that is certainly admirable, the society wanted to de-incentivise you flashing a three-star badge that, officially, is in another dimension."

"You were told to say that pretty much word for word, weren't you?"

"I was, sir, yes."

"So, what do these modified stars mean?"

"They don't, strictly speaking, mean anything. This star design was made for you, and you alone."

"Oh," Jason said. "That's kind of clever. If I go trying to use the authority of a three-star as a shortcut for my team, the idiosyncratic badge will mean that an Adventure Society branch will dig deeper, opening up the whole can of worms where I'm meant to be off in another dimension. Basically, they guaranteed that any time I use my badge, it will be a whole mess, reducing my temptation to use it. If it's a sufficient pain, I'll seek out more nuanced methods first."

"Very astute, sir, which I imagine to be how you got those three stars in the first place."

"Don't patronise me, Ladiv, or I'll throw you overboard while we're in the middle of the ocean."

"I have the water essence, sir, so I would be quite fine in that scenario."

"Of course you would; I'm not going to murder you for patronising me. I'll just make you run alongside the vehicle for an hour or two."

23

PUT THE EXTRAORDINARY ASIDE

A LARGE FLYING CARRIAGE LANDED ON THE LAWN IN FRONT OF JASON'S PAGODA. Jason and his companions emerged, along with Liara. Jason immediately walked up to the pagoda doors, which opened at his approach. As soon as they did, water came spilling out onto the grass. It was far from a flood, but enough to demonstrate that the massive atrium floor had been flooded to at least a couple of centimetres deep.

Like the night outside, the interior was dark. That did not obscure Jason's vision, but he still conjured his cloak, from which a swarm of tiny star lights emerged. They swept up into the building, growing brighter as they went. The massive destruction that had taken place on the building's interior became plain for all to see. It was clear that some force, not explosive but annihilating, had essentially deleted a sphere almost as wide as the building itself. Several floors were all but absent while others were damaged to various degrees, including the mezzanine levels. The waterfall was now spilling through a hole rather than over an edge into the pool, which was the source of the shallow flooding.

"Damn," Gary said. "Are you going to deal with the guys who did this?"

High above, one of the intact sections of floor opened and a small group of rot-black meat lumps dropped out, falling some seven storeys to smack wetly into the floor.

"No," Jason said. "These people were idiots being used by someone else. Liara, you're better equipped to investigate the man behind the curtain than I am, and a revenge spree is a little public for someone who's meant to be in another dimension."

"*Now* you hand over prisoners," Liara said. "I don't suppose you want to throw in Melody Jain? Assuming she didn't take the opportunity to break out."

"Definitely not," a voice came from above. Melody dropped from a high floor, forgoing slow fall abilities to make a superhero landing before standing up and gesturing at what was left of the gold-rankers on the floor. What was left did not include limbs.

"Asano did this to people while attending a party, portal distance away, behind what has to be formidable communication-restricting magic. I decided then and there that not only was I not going to make a break for it without a lot of confidence in my plan, but also that Asano probably wasn't in the best of moods, based on what he did to these poor saps anyway."

"That was a good choice," Sophie told her mother. "He soul-attacked a guy in front of the king until Soramir Rimaros stepped in to stop him."

"And what did the king do about that?" Melody asked.

"Not sure," Sophie said. "Had another drink?"

Melody looked over at Jason, still shrouded in his cloak.

"You just keep getting scarier, don't you? Is that a deliberate thing, or does it just happen?"

Jason pushed back the hood to reveal his face, which left him looking like his head was sticking out of a portal.

"That's creepy, bro. I'm into it."

"Everyone get packing," Jason said. "I'm reconfiguring the house to a vehicle, so there'll be less room to play with."

Liara directed Adventure Society personnel to put the beleaguered gold-rankers into a secure transport carriage. Once they were clear of the cloud house, its defences stopped ravaging them. The potent recuperative strength of their gold-rank recovery attributes turned them back into recognisable people by the time the magical flying paddy wagon arrived to collect them. They were all collared as they were placed inside, completely docile. None of them were acting out or speaking at all, which was remarkable for any group of gold-rankers. They just looked relieved, even eager, to be taken away from the pagoda.

Suddenly, Soramir Rimaros was standing next to her. If she'd been silver rank instead of gold, his diamond-rank speed would have been indistinguishable from teleportation. He turned on his formidable privacy screen, cutting off the various observers still watching the pagoda.

"He's still trouble," Soramir said.

"If I might ask, Ancestral Majesty, why do you let him run so rampant? I know that there's no way the king would have put up with his antics without you telling him to."

Soramir thought about it for a moment.

"The healer from Asano's team, Neil Davone," he said. "He's a capable enough mid-rank adventurer from a minor noble house in some city-state no one would ever have heard of if not for the Geller family. Under normal circumstances, would I even know the name of the person I just described?"

"Unlikely, Ancestral Majesty."

"Out in the cosmos, that's me. There is no reason I would ever come to the attention of the First Sister of the World-Phoenix. That's who Jason's friend Dawn is. Or was. She's moved on to some more nebulous rank. In the cosmic realms, I'm just a face in the crowd and she is a blazing sun. But just as I know who Young Master Davone is because of Jason, she knows who I am because of Jason as well."

"You're saying that he operates in prestigious circles. We knew that from the great astral beings and gods visiting him. Just about where we're standing, in fact."

"I'm not sure you understand how prestigious. He's already at a level where he needs to deal with me instead of the king for his actual objectives, because the king isn't enough. The only reason he's dealing with any of our family is that we dragged him into our politics. And we still failed to marry any of ours off to him; I knew we should have focused on that more heavily. Actually, now that I say it, I heard that your daughter—"

"No."

"No?"

"No, Ancestral Majesty."

"You know I meant your younger daughter, Zareen?"

"And you know I meant that while you can order my family members as part of House Rimaros, you were also acknowledging that you cannot give orders that intervene in my family dynamic. Ancestral Majesty."

Soramir chuckled.

"Asano is a good influence on you. You're an important part of the family, with your position in the Adventure Society, but you let your peripheral position in the royal family make you timid. You're going to need to hold your ground more and more, Liara. I expect to see more of that in the future."

"I'll do my best, Ancestral Majesty."

"My point," Soramir said, "is that the troubles of a royal family are significantly below the level Asano is operating at. There are things I won't tell you, secrets that belong to Asano that would cause him no small consternation should they come out. What I will say is that Asano isn't really a silver-ranker. He's a very dangerous diamond-ranker that hasn't caught up to his natural rank yet. I'm confident that he'll be younger than you are now when he reaches diamond rank, assuming he survives that long."

"I need to go, Ancestral Majesty," Liara said, indicating the security carriage about to lift off.

"Of course. Please attend to your duties."

As Liara departed, Jason emerged from the building, entering Soramir's privacy screen.

"You know you don't need this thing," Jason told him. "You could just pop inside."

"I'll decline, thank you. And you should be careful about who you let in there, given what you've become."

"I wondered if you realised, given your experiences in the wider cosmos."

"The vast majority of astral kings are messengers, Mr Asano. With a war against the messengers in the offing, that's not going to make you a popular figure if people find out."

"I imagine it won't. But laying low is the plan, so I'll do my best to avoid standing out."

"And how good is your best in that regard?"

"It's probably best you don't ask," Jason said.

"Once you send your friends on their way, Mr Asano, come to the palace. Officially, we'll be in seclusion until our departure is announced. In reality, I will have you portalled to them."

"Rather than that," Jason said, "you can take one of my familiar's bodies back with you. He can wear my conjured cloak and occasionally be spotted in the palace after I'm gone."

"That will work?"

"He can mimic my retracted aura well enough that anyone who can see through it will have to be either rudely focused with their senses or someone like you or Amos Pensinata."

"That should suffice, then."

"Which makes this the last time we'll see each other for some time. I hope our next meeting will be as equals instead of my stature being propped up by association with the people around me."

"And by the ones that aren't people."

"Gods and great astral beings are people, Soramir," Jason said firmly. "They're just weird and powerful."

Soramir laughed.

"I said something funny?" Jason asked.

"Oh, yes, Mr Asano. I think I just understood how you came to be where you are a little better. It's one thing to say that these vast entities are fundamentally the same as us when you've never felt their power pressing down on you. I know from experience that once you have, that perspective is harder to maintain."

"Almost everyone I deal with dwarfs me in power," Jason said. "Look at you and me. You get used to it."

"If I'm not mistaken, neither of us ages anymore. I'm curious about how your point of view has shifted the next time we meet."

"If I reach that point, I'll call it a win. I seem to go from one desperate attempt to cling to life to the next."

"Which is the point of our current efforts, is it not? To put the extraordinary aside for a while and live as much of an ordinary life as you can, given secret identities and secret agendas?"

"It is. But I've had hopes like that before."

Soramir nodded. "What you've faced all came around two ranks too early."

"Tell me about it," Jason said, then looked up at an approaching flying carriage, massively oversized and covered in metal plating.

"Preparation continues unabated, Ancestral Majesty; we should go, which means it's time to drop the privacy screen."

Soramir nodded. Once it was once again possible to eavesdrop, Jason started the show.

"My cloud flask isn't developed enough to be useful where we're going," he said. "I'm going to leave it here with one of my shadow familiars, because he can use it. He'll essentially be another auxiliary, in charge of transport and accommodation."

Jason plucked the cloud flask's shrunken form from his necklace and it grew to normal size. A Shade body emerged from the pagoda and Jason handed it over.

"It won't do anyone any good to steal it," Jason told Shade, "but some idiot probably will try anyway, so don't let them."

"Of course, Mr Asano."

"I left the materials to fix it up after the damage inside, so use them before you break down the pagoda."

"Yes, Mr Asano."

After a handful of other instructions, Jason wrapped himself completely in his cloak, such that no one noticed him shadow jump and leave a Shade body in his place.

"Have you said your goodbyes?" Soramir asked.

"I did that away from prying eyes," Jason's voice came from the disguised Shade.

"Then we're done here," Soramir said.

Carlos watched them leave, having disembarked from the heavily modified vehicle that landed during Jason and Soramir's conversation. It looked like a mix of double-decker, oversized tour bus and prison transport. After Jason refused to house the Order of Redeeming Light in his soul space, Carlos had been forced to make custom arrangements. The vehicle was part mobile prison, part hospital and part accommodation for Carlos and his research assistants.

The Shade that had accepted the cloud flask led Carlos into the pagoda.

"I still don't understand why Jason wouldn't just accommodate the Order of the Redeeming Light people himself," Carlos complained. "He's already holding Melody Jain."

"Ms Jain is a special case," Shade informed him as they reached the doors. "Holding hostiles in his own home can have…"

Shade paused as the doors opened and they went inside.

"…ramifications."

Carlos craned his head back to look at the destruction to the pagoda's interior. Jason's cloak lights had been replaced with an array of floating glow stones so that no one stumbled off any ledges.

"What did this?"

"Hostiles in Mr Asano's home," Shade said. "Do come along, Priest Quilido."

24

A CHANCE FOR SOME RELATIVE QUIET

IN THE ATRIUM OF HIS PAGODA, JASON HAD SET THE CLOUD FLASK ON THE FLOOR and placed a funnel into the neck. He had a large box of quintessence gems that he tipped into the funnel.

- You have added silver-rank [Air Quintessence] to the cloud flask. Remaining materials required to replenish cloud construct fundament:

- 274 silver-rank [Air Quintessence].
- 311 silver-rank [Water Quintessence].
- 2648 silver-rank [Cloud Quintessence].

After the destruction wreaked in his pagoda, Jason needed to top off the base material the cloud flask used to generate constructs. Fortunately, the quintessence types required were extremely common in the Sea of Storms. His current notoriety had uncharacteristically proven more help than hindrance as he contacted a trade hall broker and, in less than an hour, had crates of quintessence waiting when he portalled to the Adventure Society campus.

That had been one of Jason's last jobs before pretending to go off with Soramir. He was now operating under his assumed identity and would not be emerging from the cloud house again before leaving Rimaros. Amos Pensinata arrived, along with his nephew, Orin. Estella Warnock showed up, not having believed for a second that the figure departing with Soramir was actually Jason.

Jason was in his soul space while Shade returned the pagoda to the cloud flask and replaced it with a vehicle construct. Estella, on her arrival, insisted on seeing Jason and, after some deliberation, went through the white archway to Jason's soul space.

Estella was immediately wary of the strange realm. Anyone who entered could feel its uncanny nature, but her senses were much stronger and more developed than most. She looked around the beautiful but unsettling landscape, unsure of not just where she was, but what manner of reality she had found herself in.

"Strange, isn't it?" Jason asked, suddenly standing beside her.

She could sense that this was not Jason as she knew him, as he was part of this place. Or maybe it was part of him.

"Your senses will give you more insight than most into this place," he said. "I would take it as a kindness if you would keep any such insights to yourself. Maybe tell Clive. He'd like that."

"I wanted to talk to you. Before I finally accepted your offer."

"I hope coming in here hasn't put you off."

"What is this place?"

"It's a space that belongs to me. Sadly, it doesn't translate into power outside it, except in a few specific ways."

"Like making a defence specialist fall like a chopped tree in an instant?"

"You heard about that? But no, that wasn't because of this place. I suppose you could call them fruit from the same tree."

"I want some assurances before I sign on."

"No," Jason said.

"No?"

"No. All I'm offering you is friendship and trust. Where we go from there is something we have to work out together."

"Does friendship and trust come with a salary?"

Jason burst out laughing.

"Officially, we'll both be auxiliaries," he said. "Since I'm just the cook, you'll get paid more than I will."

The pagoda dissolved into cloud stuff that swept into the flask over the course of several minutes, like a genie slowly returning to its lamp. Shade then produced from the flask a new construct, this one a vehicle. It was different from what the team was already calling the Carlos Crime Wagon, which was a massive bus in plain shades of khaki and grey, dominated by heavy bolted plates.

Until it reached gold rank, the cloud flask wouldn't be able to produce the ocean-liner-sized vessel that Emir could, but it could still manage something the size of a superyacht. It had similarities to a large leisure craft in design, but instead of tapering to a sleek hull to cut through the water, it spread out like a massive hovercraft.

Being made of magic clouds, it didn't require the engineering and storage spaces of a yacht from Earth. Along with magical propulsion that did not require an engine room, Jason had fed enough low-rank dimensional quintessence into the cloud flask that it could make modest dimensional storage cupboards. This meant a lot more internal space for accommodation and leisure, and less for cargo and space-eating cabin wardrobes.

There was still a bridge, from which Shade would pilot the vehicle. It was on the top covered deck, along with the owner's cabin, with only an open roof deck above. Open areas featured at the front and rear of the two main decks as well, set up for lounging or launching smaller vehicles. Both Clive and Belinda had obtained skimmers that were parked in dimensional bays by the lower starboard deck.

Most of the cabins were below deck, while the two main decks were defined by purpose. The lower main deck was dominated by a sprawling dining bar lounge, which was the main congregating area on board. It also contained a generous galley. The upper main deck was more for the business of adventuring, mostly taken up by a spacious training room, but also with conference and briefing rooms. It was a small command centre for the two adventuring teams that would be aboard.

Arriving shortly before the cloud yacht's departure had been Arabelle and Callum Morse, whose visible agitation was a long way from his familiar stoicism. Like Carlos, they were relegated to their own transport, with a more modest vehicle. It was a skimmer designed for both land and calm waters, with seating for two and some compact bunks. Jason wasn't going to allow Callum in the cloud yacht, even if Arabelle insisted that Jason hear the man out, sooner or later. Jason had chosen later, leaving the pair to trail behind.

Arabelle was going to be part of Carlos' team anyway, but she didn't trust Callum left to his own devices. For that reason, she stayed with him in their own vehicle instead of joining Jason on the yacht or Carlos in the crime wagon. It wasn't like she and Callum hadn't shared close confines before, in their days on the same adventuring team.

The final arrivals were the remainder of Orin Pensinata's team. Jason had been reluctant to accept their presence at first, as had Orin's uncle, Amos. Orin had proven intractable on this, however, and Jason had sympathy for someone not wanting to be separated from their team. Using the Shade body he had left with Liara for communication purposes, he had her run background on the team before accepting their presence. He had worked with the team before, and knew that while their experience was limited, their training and discipline—at least while on the job—were respectable. They were guild elites, and he'd seen their power and teamwork firsthand.

Finally, not long before the sun was due to rise, the procession of vehicles set out. They left Arnote and headed south, moving over a quiet sea to the mainland. Jason's and Carlos' vehicles could both fly in the high-magic zone, but neither did. The crime wagon and Callum's skimmer van hovered a few metres over the water, which consumed the spirit coins they used as fuel at a much more economical rate.

Jason had the advantage of feeding the cloud yacht magic from his soul space, but he had no interest in rushing. He had played enough open-world games to know that once you unlocked flying movement, the wonder of exploration became greatly diminished. As such, he let the cloud yacht rest on the surface of the water like a hovercraft, only hovering up to remain level in the face of larger waves.

As the vehicles moved away from Rimaros, Jason sat on the upper rear deck, under an awning, while most of the group was on the roof deck. He sat on a couch to watch out the back window as the island shrank from view. Farrah joined him.

"Not worried about anyone seeing you?" she asked. "There are still a lot of eyes on us."

"There are invisible screens all around the yacht that only kick in as necessary. They let in a nice breeze, for example, but keep out the rain. It's also how people can have private conversations, since they act as privacy screens as well. I added that function to the cloud flask after seeing their ubiquity in Rimaros. From the outside, anyone trying to see us will only see a blur while the privacy screen is active. And because it's part of my spirit domain, even gods can't see through it, so anyone who can spot me deserves to."

"Fair enough."

Farrah would only be joining the trip to the limits of his portal range. Once they reached that distance, he and she would portal back, where he could collect the promised rewards from House de Varco for winning the duels. While Jason and his companions set off, Liara would collect the rewards to hand over to Jason.

"How are you feeling?" Farrah asked.

They watched the island shrink in their wake. They were both thinking of their arrival in Rimaros half a year ago. They were now at the start of the wet season in the tropics, and as monsoon rain started coming down, Jason's ability to see through the dark was no longer enough to keep sight of the island behind them. The rain ran off the invisible screen, but with a thought, Jason let the rain through. It pounded onto the deck and off the awning, which shifted from cloud-stuff to mimicking canvas. The canvas started thrumming as the rain hammered it.

"I always liked that sound," he said. "When I was a kid, we went on a holiday once where it rained every day. I spent the whole time living on snack food and reading as the rain fell against the tent."

"Does it help? I know that you've set off on a lot of journeys that weren't what you wanted them to be."

"It's nice, but I'm just fine," Jason said. "I've got a luxurious magic boat, good friends and maybe even a chance for some relative quiet, at least for a while. Also, if I can avoid getting killed too often, I might just live forever. That doesn't suck."

Most of the cloud yacht's occupants were on the open roof deck until the rain started. It spilled off the invisible dome over the deck that still somehow let in the wind, but most of the people took the stairs to the lower decks. Orin Pensinata and his team did not, remaining outside.

The leader of Orin and Kalif's team was Korinne Pescos. They had first encountered Jason in a mixed-force expedition. It was a strange group centred around their team of guild elites, but also included non-guild members and a pair of princesses. Kalif had been prodding the non-guild members to see if they had any spine to them. That included Jason after Kalif noticed that the princesses seemed to at least recognise him.

"What have you gotten us into, Orin?" Kalif asked. His brief history with Jason Asano was making him uncomfortable. Kalif had first caught Jason at a bad time. It had been at the height of Jason's volatility from the continued absence of his team, even as the Builder, Purity forces and local politics all sought to harass him. His response to Kalif's provocation had been to sharply demonstrate their difference in soul strength.

Kalif and his team had worked with Asano twice. There was the expedition where they met, during which time Asano went off alone and mind-controlled a bunch of Builder constructs through means still unknown. Asano had been a savage, solitary figure at that time, barely talking and rushing off alone, with no sense of teamwork.

The next time they worked together was very different. Kalif's team leader, Korinne, had been in charge of coordinating the underwater complex rescue. Asano had been critical to portalling people in and had been with his team at that stage. Although they barely interacted, Asano had been noticeably different. He was more like an ordinary adventurer once he had his team around him.

That day, in the aftermath of the underwater complex raid, was the beginning of Asano's public notoriety. Rumours abounded, ranging from the unusual to the outright insane. Finding a way to portal past magical barriers was one thing, but who would believe that a god would visit Asano for a casual chat, like an old friend?

For many, the previous evening's ball was the first time they had caught sight of Asano while Princess Liara paraded him like a prized pet. It had deflated many of the rumours about the man until people started causing trouble. The culmination of that was Asano dropping Hector de Varco, famed for his defensive prowess, like he was culling a helpless animal. Kalif couldn't help but think of the time he provoked Asano and was stopped dead with an aura technique. In that moment, he realised how lightly Asano had let him off.

At that point, Kalif wanted nothing more to do with Asano and was relieved to hear the man would be leaving Rimaros. Then he discovered that their team would be going with him. Orin just looked at Kalif, who repeated his question.

"I'm not joking, Orin. What have you caught us up in?"

"That's enough, Kalif," Korinne cut in. "You know that this isn't Orin. It's his uncle. Our choices were to abandon our team member or to come along. Are you suggesting we should have let him go alone?"

"Of course not," Kalif said. "Of course we go. That doesn't mean we go blindly, and you know that Asano and I have bad blood."

"Then why don't we cleanse it?" a new voice said.

The team turned to look at Jason climbing the stairs. He moved in front of Kalif and looked up at the taller man.

"We didn't start off on the best foot, did we?" Jason asked. "I was in a bad place and neither of us were our best selves that day."

He held out his hand as a peace offering.

"How about we start over, and put what came before behind us?"

Kalif looked at Jason's hand for a moment before shaking it.

"Alright."

Jason flashed him a grin and moved over to the railing. The rain was thick, cutting off visibility, but he looked out anyway. Kalif and his team watched him, warily.

"I enjoyed Rimaros," he said winsomely. "I'd like to come back during quieter times. I never even met all the Al brothers."

25

SURPLUS TO REQUIREMENTS

JASON AND HIS TEAM, PLUS RUFUS, WERE SITTING AROUND THE CONFERENCE TABLE on the cloud yacht, looking at a projection of a map.

"We're freer now to make our own decisions than we've been in a while," Humphrey said. "That means literally charting our own path. We have a general plan of moving south, down this continent, before crossing over to the Great Southern Continent. We'll move across there, then cross north again to reach Hornis on our way to Greenstone. From there, we'll continue up to Vitesse and then Cyrion, where the other outworlders from Earth are located."

As he talked, Humphrey pointed with his finger and a line appeared on the map. The Earth equivalent of the path he drew out would be going from the Caribbean through South America to Antarctica, then back up to Africa before reaching Europe. The Pallimustus version of Antarctica was apparently much more hospitable than the Earth version, while the local version of Australia was just the opposite. The most notorious high-magic zone in the world, it was mostly a haven to diamond-rank monsters and anyone fool enough to hunt them.

"It's not a wildly efficient route," Rufus pointed out.

"Efficiency is counter to our purpose," Humphrey said. "It's time for this team to start seeing the world."

"Even if it means wandering over most of it like a drunkard who can't walk in a straight line," Neil added, raising a fist in the air. "I'm all in. Team Drunkard!"

Humphrey's eyes went wide and he let out a loud groan. "I forgot to change the team name after the administrative restrictions came down after the surge!"

"I think that die is cast, my friend," Jason said. "I think we're all pretty happy with the team name."

"Yeah!" cheered the moustachioed mouse dragging a biscuit the size of his entire body from the plate on the table.

"I'm afraid that battle is lost," Rufus comforted Humphrey. "Perhaps we should just move on to the specifics of our journey."

Humphrey nodded resignedly before resuming the discussion.

"The first leg of our trip is to move south. There is a great road network connecting the population hubs, whichever way we go, and our general options are the east coast, the west coast or the central regions."

"What are the differences?" Jason asked.

"The east coast is what you might call the standard route. It's the most populous, the most developed and the most stable, magically speaking. Magic strength there is in the mid-range, meaning primarily silver-rank monsters, with some large packs of bronze and the occasional gold. That's a very good starting range for where we are right now, looking to rank up long-term."

"The problem with that path," Rufus said, "is that the surge just ended. There will be a lot of adventurers hitting the road, just like us, and that will be the road most of them take. That means more competition for the best contracts at every branch we run into. Also, the locals in each branch can get resentful of all the outsiders coming in to snake the most lucrative jobs."

"The next option," Humphrey said, "is the central region. This, I think we should avoid. There's more wilderness and fewer developed areas, which isn't inherently bad, but the magic levels are. The central region is notorious for inconsistent magic levels, so one day, you're fighting iron-rank monsters and the next, gold rank."

"And the west coast?" Jason asked.

"It varies between low and medium ambient magic levels. Not Greenstone low, for the most part, but sometimes it is. There are a couple of areas that, like Greenstone, are major sites for low-rank spirit coin farms. Mostly, though, the monster level is around bronze or silver."

"That's a little too low for us," Sophie said.

"I agree," Humphrey said. "On the other hand, there will be less competition for the best contracts."

"I think east," Jason said. "We don't need the most lucrative contracts. I know the only real experience I have of standard adventuring was in Greenstone, but what I saw there was that the people who needed help the most were often overlooked. They couldn't sweeten the contract rewards over Adventure Society standard rates, so their contracts tended to languish until the society assigned them as punishment contracts."

"You want to take the worst contracts?" Neil asked.

"Worst by what metric?" Jason responded. "The unpopular contracts tend to be the ones that deviate from the standard. To me, that sounds more fun."

"Of course it does," Neil said.

"We should also look at our wider objectives," Clive said. "This is an adventuring tour. If we're going to see the world, let's see it. New towns, new people. There's more to meeting other adventurers than competing for contracts. If we want to spend the whole time slogging through unpopulated areas, we might as well fly over them."

"I'm really liking the sound of this," Jason said. "Coast roads and food markets. Yeah, I'm sold."

Humphrey looked around the table.

"If there are no objections then, east we'll go."

The door to Jason's cabin opened as Korinne Pescos approached. It was the only cabin not below decks, sharing the upper deck with the bridge. The cabin was spacious and ringed with windows, aside from the wall it shared with the bridge. Jason sat on a couch that faced starboard to enjoy the panoramic view, watching the vehicle's wake cut through the waves.

"Please join me, Miss Pescos," he said, neither getting up nor turning around. She moved slowly through the spacious cabin, which was more like an open lounge. There wasn't even a bed, but she had seen him manipulate the structure of the ship by changing the cloud-substance it was made of, so knew he could make one at need.

Korinne moved around the long couch and sat, the impossible plushness of it slightly leaching the hard edge from the attitude with which she had entered. She wondered if this was incidental or something Asano did deliberately to engineer his interactions. She had been warned that his seeming frivolity would often hide deceptively deliberate manipulation.

"What can I help you with, Miss Pescos?" Jason asked. "Refreshments?"

"No, thank you. Spirit coins are food enough for me. The plainness helps keep me sharp. It fosters an efficient mind."

"I can't argue with the results," Jason said. "I've seen you in action. I'd been told about the strength of guild elites for some time, but yours was the team that truly showed me what that meant, when we went on that expedition together. It was deeply impressive. If I'm being honest, even with my full team around me, we couldn't match the overwhelmingly comprehensive speed and power with which you tore through that pack of monsters. It was a large pack too, yet you were clean and controlled the entire time. The benefits of an efficient mind, I imagine."

"You don't consider your own mind efficient?"

"Oh, I don't think anyone does, so I might as well indulge."

With a gesture, a low table of cloud stuff formed in front of him, and he pulled items from his storage space to place on it: a tray of assorted baked goods and a pitcher of iced tea. He took out two plates and two glasses, but only filled one, which he sipped from appreciatively. He then picked up a plate and served himself one of the colourful baked slices from the tray. Korinne watched in silence as he went through the slow and deliberate motions of setting out snacks. Finally, Jason bit into his slice with an appreciative moan.

"I'm so glad this world has coconuts," he said. "I do hope you won't begrudge me indulging."

"It's fine."

"So, what brings you to my cabin?"

"Do you genuinely not know?" she asked. "I was warned by your team that you know everything that happens on this ship."

"I'm not a god who can pay attention to every follower at once, Miss Pescos. I might realise that your team is discussing something, but unless I give it my direct attention, I don't know what you're discussing. Think of it like looking down from a tower. I can see what the people below are doing in general, but without paying closer attention, I can't see the details. Did my team also tell you that they've started using privacy screens in their cabins for private moments?"

"They did, but also that they couldn't be sure if the screens actually blocked your power to observe. Do they?"

"I don't have an answer that can satisfy you, Miss Pescos. Be it yes or no, I have reasons to lie either way, which means that you can't trust what I have to say."

She nodded, acknowledging the point.

"This was all very last-moment, Mr Asano. If I'm being honest, I would prefer that my team had our own, separate transport."

"That is between you and Amos Pensinata. My understanding is that you are here because his nephew is here, and Orin being here was the condition of his uncle being here."

"And why exactly is Amos Pensinata joining you?"

"A friend of mine asked him to teach me some things. He agreed, in return for help giving his nephew some seasoning as an adventurer."

"And what makes your team qualified to instruct mine?" Korinne asked. "By your own admission, we are guild elites that can outstrip your team."

Jason smiled with infuriating self-indulgence, but didn't answer immediately. He took another bite of coconut slice, then washed it down with a sip of iced tea.

"Are you sure I can't tempt you, Miss Pescos? These refreshments are quite, well, refreshing in this humidity."

"Your boat does a fine job of keeping the humidity outside, Mr Asano."

He nodded his acknowledgement of the point, which did not stop his continuing indulgence.

"Your question was what my team has to teach you," he said, finally getting back to the point. "As your tone so clearly implied, we have nothing to teach. What I would like to correct is your claim that I have admitted the inferiority of my team. What I said was that we could not equal the speed and power you demonstrated in destroying the large pack of monsters that attacked our expedition. That is not the same thing."

Korinne let out a snort. "You're going to talk about Rimaros-style adventuring versus Vitesse-style, aren't you? Specialisation versus generalisation."

"Of those two cities, I've only ever been to Rimaros. Once we reach Vitesse, it will be my first visit, so I won't go speaking to the way they do things there. For that, you should seek out Rufus Remore. He trained me, and is steeped in the Vitesse approach. You know his family runs a school there?"

"He mentioned."

He grinned, although she was unsure at what.

"What Amos Pensinata wants for you is not training, but seasoning. Be it in

Rimaros or Vitesse, the problem with training low-rank adventurers is that their experiences must be heavily curated or the local monsters will kill them. Forgive me if I'm mistaken, but my understanding is that you and your team were quite orthodox in that regard."

"We spent the majority of our iron and bronze ranks under gold-rank supervision," Korinne conceded. "But we're silver rank now. We operated alone through most of the surge."

"And that's what Lord Pensinata wants more of. Experience, away from the safety of your guild. Facing the consequences of your choices with no recourse but yourselves. He will be there if you truly are in need of rescue, but he won't be following you around and is unlikely to make it in time if you find yourselves in truly desperate straits."

"We're hardly free of gold-rank supervision, Mr Asano. There are four of them in just this tiny convoy."

"Yes, but the only one you need to concern yourself with is Lord Pensinata. Carlos was never an adventurer, and while Arabelle Remore certainly was, she'll only help my team, and even that's a maybe. I think you'll find both she and Pensinata are giving us all enough room to live with our mistakes. They have the resolve for that; ask Arabelle's son."

"Even accepting that we are on our own, or close enough to it, how exactly does being with your team benefit us? Why does Lord Pensinata see value in bringing Orin on this journey?"

"It's a matter of experience."

"And why do we need your experience? You already said you aren't going to teach us."

"And we won't. Don't look at me and my team as instructors."

"You don't have to be concerned on that front," she said, prompting a good-natured laugh from Jason.

"We are peers," Jason told her. "Avail yourself of us as such, and expect us to do the same. Advice from those who already have experience is always valuable when going out to have those experiences yourself. I met Rufus Remore because he and his friends realised that they needed experience they could not get in Vitesse. He ended up founding a satellite school in a low-magic zone based on that very principle."

Korinne didn't respond for a long time as she processed what Jason had said. For his part, Jason ate baked goods and watched the rain pouring down outside, heavy enough that he could barely see the other vehicles.

"I've heard things about you," she said finally. "The veracity of what I've heard seems spurious at best."

"Try living through them," he said, shaking his head. "I can't speak to what you've heard, and telling my own story doesn't seem helpful. Words are easy, after all. All I'll say is that my team and I have faced situations where we had no one but ourselves to fall back on, even when the stakes were high."

"That's what Orin intimated."

"Intimated?"

"He's not a big talker. But he said he saw into your aura once, unfiltered. He said it told a story that he believed."

"Right," Jason said. His first encounter with Orin was when Vesper Rimaros had arranged a 'coincidental meeting' with Kasper Irios. It was part of her political machinations that, like Vesper herself, died when the Builder conflict reached Rimaros. Orin had been a friend of the man and Jason had picked him out as the sensible one of the group, showing him a glimpse of his real aura so they would back off quietly.

"Actually," Jason said, "I didn't show him the full thing. But if you'd like to see it, I can show you."

"You're a skilled aura manipulator," she said. "That much I've heard and believe. You could put up a façade to impress me."

"I don't need to impress you, Miss Pescos. Not to put too fine a point on it, but your team's presence is a favour for a favour for a favour. Surplus to requirements. Officially, I'm going off with Soramir Rimaros, but you and yours can't be here without knowing that's a lie, so you've been brought into that circle."

He grimaced.

"I didn't want you here, Miss Pescos, but to get Amos we needed Orin, and to get Orin, we needed you. Apparently. Someone who means a lot to me left this world recently. Literally left; not a death metaphor, but I won't see her again for some time. She was the one who wanted to connect Lord Pensinata and myself. Otherwise, I'd cut my losses and take none of you. I don't need what Pensinata has to teach that much."

"Then why put up with us? Why not stash us in the bottom of the ship in our cabins instead of letting me in here to question you like this?"

"Because you're on my boat, which makes you my guests. If you're more comfortable buying a vehicle of your own as soon as we reach a place that will sell one, you are welcome to do so. I might recommend it, in fact."

He leaned back into the plush couch, laying his arms along its back and letting them sink in.

"Cloud furniture can be hard to give up," he told her with a grin. "And if your team will be eating spirit coins, watching what the rest of us enjoy will be bad for morale."

Korinne looked at him thoughtfully, then picked out a baked slice, put it on the other plate and took a bite. She contemplated the taste for a moment.

"You're right," she said. "I don't want my team getting used to this."

26

BAD AT CRIME

THE SMALL CONVOY CARRYING JASON AND HIS FRIENDS TURNED EAST AS SOON AS it hit the coast, hovering along the wide and well-maintained network of road-ways. The immediate turn east was to Belinda's disappointment; she was inter-ested in heading further south. That way led to the famously sketchy nation of Girlano and all the opportunities it offered to an enterprising and open-minded young lady.

"I officially retract my endorsement of you and Humpy," she told Sophie. "This whole 'being a better person' thing has sucked the fun right out of you."

The pair sat on the cloud yacht's open lower foredeck. There wasn't much to see, with the wall of rain still running off the invisible cloud screen.

"And by fun, you mean elaborate schemes to steal things?" Sophie asked.

"Schemes? Now you're sounding like Jason. This whole team is a bad influence."

"In that they are against robbery?"

"Exactly."

"Lindy, we're not street rats anymore. We've met the king of one of the most powerful nations in the world."

"But I never got close enough to lift his watch, though, did I?" Belinda asked, taking out a pocket watch and turning it over in her hands.

"What's that?"

"It's a watch."

"Whose watch?"

"Remember that guy who tried to provoke us at the ball, not long before Gary bent a tray over some other guy's head?"

"Kind of. He wasn't exactly memorable. Wait, that's his watch?"

"Yep."

"Well, that's fine. Screw that prick."

"Exactly. I lifted his watch while he was busy being a turd."

"You didn't touch him. You didn't even get close."

"I know, right?"

"Damn, Lindy. That's a good lift."

"Is this rain ever going to let up?" Jason asked, looking out the window of the bar lounge.

"It is," Humphrey told him.

"It doesn't look like it. How long is it going to take?"

"About four months."

"Bloody monsoon weather."

"One of the reasons Rimaros is situated on those specific islands, instead of the larger ones, is that they see the least rain in the Sea of Storms."

"I thought those windmill-looking things were meant to stop all this nonsense."

"The storm accumulators only affect storms with a heightened ambient magic level. Regular weather is unaffected. Look at it this way, Jason: we picked a great time to get out of the tropics."

"That's why I like you, Humphrey. You look for the best in everyone, even this bloody rain."

"My homeland is a bone-dry desert, remember?" Humphrey said. "If not for the magical river creating the delta, we wouldn't get rain at all, so the goddess Rain is always welcome. She's heavily worshipped in the delta."

Belinda laughed at Humphrey's words as she and Sophie came inside.

"Remember that time Sophie didn't know what rain was?" she said.

"It doesn't rain in the city!" Sophie said.

"I knew what rain was."

"You didn't tell me."

"Well, maybe if you actually talked to people instead of punching or porking them, you might have heard about things."

"I talked to you."

"Why would I tell you things? It's hilarious when you don't know about stuff that children do. Remember the whole woollen sweater debacle?"

"We grew up somewhere very hot! Why would I know about those?"

"Again, you would if you talked to people."

"I talked to you!"

"You said that."

"You're a bad friend."

Jason and Humphrey watched the pair go below decks, still bickering.

"You did well, there," Jason said.

"I was worried," Humphrey said. "When we heard you were coming back, there was all these unresolved—"

"They're resolved now," Jason cut him off. "She latched onto me because I was the first guy who wasn't a piece of crap to her."

"Except for Jory."

"Yeah, well, that guy was far gone for Lindy from the start. But Sophie didn't just need just good, mate; she needed stable. I've been called a lot of things, Humphrey. I was called 'a small tin of marrowbone jelly' once, but I don't recall ever being called stable. You're the anchor on this team. You should have gotten a healing power set."

"That's what my mother said. The power set thing, to be clear; not about the tin of whatever that is you said. But she got a good deal on those two wing essences, and the idea of Henri and me getting the phoenix and dragon confluences appealed to her."

"How is Henrietta?"

"She was fine last I saw her in Vitesse. She made silver rank, but she's never fallen into a permanent team. She ran around with Cassandra Mercer for a while."

Humphrey frowned.

"I'm not sure how that turned out, now that I think about it. Henri always had kind of a crush on Cassandra."

"I heard about her brother," Jason said. "After the Builder possessed Thadwick, he turned into some weird vampire?"

"We're fairly certain he devoured that loose soul around the sword we found. No one at the Magic Society was ever able to figure out what was going on with that whole sword and soul thing, since Thadwick made off with the sword as well. Not a lot left to study, although Clive said something about rare magic that sent them into a frenzy. Rufus' parents were chasing Thadwick for a while, but the trail went cold."

"I imagine he'll pop up somewhere. Causing trouble for us, probably. Thadwick was always fixated on me. I think he might have had a sister complex."

"I don't know what that is, and I'm confident I don't want you to tell me."

"Fair enough," Jason said with a chuckle.

"Mr Asano," Shade said from Jason's shadow. "We will be approaching Rajoras in around five minutes."

"Thank you, Shade."

Shade, along with piloting the cloud yacht, was using vehicle forms to scout the way ahead for trouble that might otherwise be hidden in the rain. Rajoras was one of the larger cities on the southern mainland coast, making it one of the southernmost centres in the Storm Kingdom's territory.

In the wake of the monster surge, Rajoras was a major hub of activity. People needed to return home after far too long boxed-up in fortress towns and often found destruction waiting for them. Every town and village needed repair, while some had to be rebuilt entirely. That was true in a normal surge, that lasted a fifth as long as this one. People and materials were already streaming through Rajoras like a river, and the road grew increasingly busy as the team drew near, despite the weather.

The massive vehicle that was the cloud yacht did not make for practical city travel, so the trio of vehicles in the convoy stopped outside of Rajoras. They needed to visit the city, as their sudden departure from Rimaros had left them somewhat undersupplied, and the guild team were hoping to find a vehicle of their own. The convoy pulled off the side of the road, with Shade floating the cloud yacht up and over the jungle so as not to obstruct the thruway with the giant vessel.

Jason's team and the Rimaros team assembled on the lower starboard deck, rain bouncing off an invisible dome overhead. That open deck was where the vessel would dock when acting as a boat, while doubling as a launch platform for the two skimmers in dimensional storage. Clive and Belinda pulled the skimmers out, each vehicle equipped for travel over land and water, with magical spray screens that would handle the rain. Each skimmer was a decent size, able to seat eight.

"I know that Belinda and I are the designated drivers," Clive said, "but we both need to go with the Rimaros team. Sorry, I didn't catch your team name."

"Team Storm Shredder," Kalif said.

"That's so much better than ours," Humphrey muttered, to the shaking heads disagreement of his teammates.

"Anyone can drive these skimmers, though, so long as we're not in a low-magic zone," Clive said. "They'll run on spirit coins, so you just need some of them. And a local driving permit, obviously."

"A what?" Belinda asked.

"The license I told you to get," Clive said, turning to frown at her. "You did get that license, right?"

"Uh, yep."

"Can I see it?"

"I don't have it on me right now."

"You don't have it on you?"

"I do not."

"You have dimensional storage space where you keep all your worldly possessions."

"Not all of them. And I have a cabin. Some things are unpacked in there."

"Then you might want to go get it," Clive said. "They may be checking them at the city gate. This soon after the surge, they'll probably be doing extra monitoring."

"Yeah?" Belinda asked, her voice only a slightly higher pitch than normal. "I'll take that into consideration. On an unrelated note, does anyone know how local low-level officials respond to bribes?"

"Why do you two need to go with Team Storm Cutter?" Jason asked.

"It's Storm *Shredder*," Korinne corrected.

"Storm Cutter was already taken?" Jason asked.

"Yep," Kalif said, earning him a sharp glance from Korinne.

"Anyway, Clive, why do you and Lindy need to go with them?"

"We'll all be heading to the same part of the city for vehicle stuff," Clive said. "They're looking to buy a proper transport, and since we'll be here a few days, Lindy and I need a dry dock to disassemble—"

Belinda slapped him on the arm.

"…we need to buy some skimmers," Clive pivoted. "And that is all."

Clive's team all stared at him.

"We already have skimmers," Sophie pointed out, gesturing at the two vehicles resting on the deck. "These skimmers."

"We need different ones," Clive said.

"You are so bad at crime," Belinda muttered.

"We're not meant to be good at crime!" Clive hissed at her.

"Speak for yourself," Belinda hissed back.

"Whatever happened with that submarine Belinda stole?" Neil asked.

Clive opened his mouth and Belinda slapped his arm again.

"What submarine?" Clive asked unconvincingly.

"The one you took when you broke out of the Order of Redeeming Light's hidden base," Neil said.

"That sank," Belinda said. "Or I lost it. Or both. I think it was both. Yeah, I told you that it sank and I don't remember where, right?"

Kalif leaned closer to Orin.

"It's your fault that we're travelling with these people?"

Orin didn't say anything.

Korinne's team was with Clive and Belinda in a skimmer, in a queue waiting to move through the city gate checkpoint. The city walls loomed ahead, still bearing the scars of monster attacks from the surge. Clive was in the driver's seat, with Belinda beside him at the front.

"Can I ask you something?" Kalif said, leaning forward to speak. "Do you find it unnerving that Asano's aura is everywhere in that vehicle? I mean, *everywhere*. It feels like he's watching your thoughts."

"Different auras feel different to different people," Clive said. "To me, it's benevolent. Overbearing, yes, but benevolent, which is very much Jason. It's reassuring, though, after having thought we'd lost him to the Reaper."

"You get used to it," Belinda said. "There's an assurance to his presence. Like a guard dog. You can feel how far he'd go if someone came for us, and we know that feeling is real. We've seen it."

"That's what it feels like to us," Kalif said. "Except that we're the ones the guard dog is watching. It's unsettling. Makes it hard to relax."

"I don't know," said Rosa Liselos, the scout from Korinne's team. "I don't think it's so bad. I can definitely live with it if it means cloud beds and giant dinner spreads. That lunch looked amazing. How often do you all eat like that?"

"That's just normal lunch when we aren't in the field," Belinda said. "Jason has always kind of been the auxiliary member in charge of food. Why didn't you all join in?"

"Korinne," Orin said, with no more explanation than that.

Korinne's five teammates all turned to look at her, to which she didn't react.

"Discipline," Korinne answered Belinda. "Indulgence dulls the wits. Sharp, efficient minds are what we need."

"Well, I need sandwiches the size of my forearm," Belinda said. "But whatever works for you, I guess."

Jason ended up staying behind when his team went into the city. Humphrey, Sophie and Neil went in search of supplies, but Jason gave them a food shopping list instead of going himself. Between the business and the weather, it wasn't an ideal time for sightseeing, and they were close enough to Rimaros that it wouldn't offer a fascinating new culture to interact with. It also meant that Jason knew enough about the local food that most, if not all, of his list should be obtainable.

Arabelle came aboard the cloud yacht, still hovering over the jungle canopy beside the road. She found him brewing tea and they sat by the window, watching the traffic below trudge along the road, through the downpour.

"It's past time we had a talk about Callum," she told him. "I wanted to do this back in Rimaros, but you decided to leave very suddenly."

"Where is Callum?"

"He took our vehicle and went into the city. It's not the smallest, but it's not that much bigger than a large skimmer. Nothing like this monstrosity."

"I'm quite happy with this monstrosity, thank you very much."

He sipped his tea, then set it down on a side table.

"You mentioned some time ago," he said, "that you had figured out the real reason that Callum was so obsessed with Sophie's mother."

"Yes."

"And?"

"He's in love with her."

"I'm sorry, what?"

27

AN EVIL GOD SITTING ON HER SHOULDER

"The full explanation is somewhat complicated," Arabelle said.

"It'd bloody well want to be," Jason told her. "If there's a simple explanation for how your team member ended up chasing around my team member's evil brainwashed mum because he's in love with her, a lot of people have been very, very oblivious."

They were sitting in the cloud yacht as it hovered over the jungle beside the road leading into the city of Rajoras. They were drinking tea and watching traffic go past in the pounding monsoon rain.

"I'll take you through what happened, as I understand it," Arabelle said. "But know that all I have to go on is Callum's account."

"And Callum isn't at his most reliable right now."

"Just so," Arabelle said. "It's disconcerting, seeing him like this. He's never been good at dealing with people, but he's always been stoic and reliable. Now he's anxious and unreliable, and chasing around after a woman. Seeing him so different to when we used to work together is downright startling."

"Have you considered letting Carlos have a look at him? Make sure there's nothing affecting Cal beyond stress?"

"That was the first thing I did once I realised how far from normal Cal had become. I had him checked for signs of the Order of Redeeming Light's 'purification' ritual, then anything else Carlos could find. This wasn't any outside influence that he could dig out, which means that it's all but certainly not outside influence. Finding and dealing with soul influences is his specialty; he's at the top of his field. From star seeds to vampirism to plain soul trauma, he's the best there is."

"Which is why he's so obsessed with helping the Order of Redeeming Light members, I assume?"

"Yes. And why the authorities are giving him leeway to handle this. Not a lot of people would be allowed to put a group of important prisoners in stasis and haul them around in a bus."

"If he doesn't fall under Carlos' specialty," Jason said, "then he falls under yours. Good old-fashioned mental health problems."

"Yes," Arabelle said. "Strictly speaking—ethically speaking—I shouldn't be treating him, because he's too close to me. The Church of the Healer gave me special dispensation because he refused to even speak to anyone else and they thought he'd open up to an old team member."

"And he did."

"Of course he did. And it took me a while, but I teased the whole story out of him. At least, the story as it happened in his mind. I'll be interested to hear Sophie's mother's version of events, but having them meet now would be a disaster, given the states they're both in."

"Melody seems fairly together," Jason said. "Her aura doesn't match her body language, though. She's masking a lot of fear and confusion."

"Exactly," Arabelle said. "Too many unknown factors to bring them together yet, even if it would answer a lot of questions. The goal is to help the both of them get better, after all, not satisfy our curiosity."

Jason nodded. "Let's start with how things went from Cal's perspective, then, shall we?"

Arabelle nodded. "We'll start with context. Callum is part of the Cult of the Reaper. It didn't impact his day-to-day life when we were a team, so it never really mattered."

"Like Clive," Jason said. "I don't think he's formally part of whatever organisation they have on this world, but he venerates the great astral being called the Celestial Book."

"Cal's membership in the Cult of the Reaper is now very much a factor. At the same time, Melody Jain was part of the Order of the Reaper. Do you understand the difference between the organisations?"

"The cult is the ones who follow the Reaper's principles. The order is an offshoot of the cult that became an order of assassins interested in cultivating backroom political power. They split off from the cult as they increasingly moved away from its core principles."

"Yes," Arabelle said. "The story begins with Melody Jain, around a quarter of a century ago, in the city of Kurdansk. This part comes from what Callum claims Melody told him herself, from before Melody and Callum knew one another. They were each members of their respective organisations, both of which operated in secret. The Order of the Reaper was in the midst of bringing centuries of planning to fruition, and they were very particular about whom they brought into the fold. Melody was highly capable and from one of the old order families, so she was completely welcome. The man she chose for herself was not, however."

"This isn't Callum we're talking about, is it?"

"No. We're talking about Sophie Wexler's father, although his name was not Wexler then. Melody kept him a secret from the order, along with the fact that they had a child. But when the child was still small, they were discovered. The Order of the Reaper specialises in infiltrating people into organisations unnoticed.

With religions, it's essentially impossible to fake, but many religions have low-level administrative staff for their endeavours that aren't required to be deeply faithful. Someone working for the Church of Fertility in their record-keeping discovered the details of how the church had helped Melody have a child without her order overseers realising."

"What were the repercussions?"

"According to Callum, Melody was certain that the order would kill her secret husband and child. This was especially true if they discovered that Melody had been teaching him the order's method of fighting for years."

"A method he eventually passed on to Sophie."

"Yes. Melody was warned that the order had discovered her family by a woman named Marta Fries, a fellow member and Melody's best friend. Melody had Marta smuggle her husband and daughter away; even Melody herself didn't know where they went. She did not want to be captured and be forced to divulge where her family was so that the order could tie up loose ends. Even Marta Fries wasn't certain, having supplied the secret husband with just enough information and resources to disappear on his own."

"Thus, Sophie and her father wound up in Greenstone. Sophie doesn't have many coherent memories before adventurers found her in that shipwreck."

"She was young. Didn't even know that her real name is not Wexler, but Jain. It's possible her father muddled her memories, somehow. Alchemy can be effective on children that young. There are potions used to help children move past traumatic events, although I try to avoid using them. When treating children, some horrors are best put aside, but the effect of the missing memories can linger, and be harder to deal with for their absence."

"I have to wonder how much of this, and what version of it, that Melody has told Sophie," Jason wondered. "They've been talking for weeks, and I imagine it must have come up."

"You didn't ask her?"

"If Sophie feels like there is something I should know," Jason said, "she'll tell me."

"It has all been happening inside your cloud house. Couldn't you listen in?"

"I could, but I don't. I know they're talking, but I put my attention elsewhere."

"I'm not sure I could resist that temptation."

"It's not hard. You just have to decide if you want to be the person that encroached on the most private moments of a close friend."

"Ah," Arabelle said. "Letting the realisation that you would be a terrible person douse the curiosity."

"Exactly. Now, you've told me about how Sophie ended up in Greenstone, but not where Callum comes in."

"After getting her family out," Arabelle explained, "Melody knew that the Order of the Reaper would not let it go. They were obsessed with not leaving threads that could cause problems for them later, especially with their plans within decades of going into motion."

"And of all the places Sophie and her father could end up, they went to Greenstone? A place where a part of the Order of the Reaper's plan was set to play out?"

"Callum didn't know why they went there. It might have been an attempt to hide where the order wouldn't look. It could have been coincidence. The order was initiating their re-emergence in locations all across the world, after all."

"So, after getting her family out, she ran?"

"Yes. And this is where Callum finally appears."

"She went to the Cult of the Reaper."

"Yes. But the cult was not going to just take her in. The order was known for its painstaking infiltration of other organisations over the last several centuries, after all. They faked the demise of their entire order as part of a plan more than half a millennium in the making."

"But that secret isn't so well hidden anymore."

"No. Their plan was always to return to their original status of being an open secret, playing tool to those in power while pulling the levers of power themselves. The first time, they were too crude and got crushed. This time, they are being more patient, and planning things out for the start. In just the few years you were absent, they've made massive strides in this regard. And the way they've been trying to establish themselves is through making themselves invaluable. They've made critical strikes against the Church of Purity, the Cult of the Builder and other imminent threats."

"Meaning that when the rest of the world was scrambling after these enemies that blindsided most of us, the Order of the Reaper had already infiltrated them and knew what they were up to. But instead of warning people, they allowed these groups to become threats, so that they would look good by striking against those threats."

"Yes."

"But surely people saw through that?"

"Of course. But the fact remains that it was an impressive display of power. Who is to say how many infiltrators the order has, in what organisations? Anyone moving against them could easily find that someone they trusted is suddenly putting a knife in their back. We also believe that they knew about the messengers and are going to make moves against them to further cement themselves."

Jason shook his head as he refilled their teacups from the pot.

"This all sounds like trouble."

"Yes. And the Cult of the Reaper was amongst the first to realise that their former offshoot order was once again on the move, although they themselves were difficult to infiltrate. Like religious orders, authentic veneration of a great astral being is a requirement in the astral cults. It's not as reliable as faith for a god, but it's impossible to get around, long-term. Too easy to get unlucky."

"But the order was trying to infiltrate the cult anyway, yes? And then comes Melody, with a seemingly convenient offer to defect. But the cult didn't trust her."

"They did not. This is the point where she met Callum. Our team had stopped actively adventuring. Emir became a treasure hunter, while Gabriel and I took on less active roles while we raised our son. I moved from a field healer to a mental health specialist, and Gabriel started teaching at the academy. Callum, we thought, was off hunting monsters in the drive to reach diamond. That isn't the usual path, but it made sense for him."

"Hunting monsters isn't the way to rank up at gold?"

"It's a part, but not everything. You will learn more as you draw closer to gold rank. For now, such questions are a distraction. The point is that while Callum was, indeed, out hunting dangerous prey, it was not occupying anywhere near as much of his time as we thought."

"He became more active in the Cult of the Reaper?"

"Yes, as it turns out, and he was made Melody's handler. They worked together for years, both investigating the order she came from and using the skills they taught her for the cult's purposes. The cult never truly accepted her, however, always wary of the patience and long-term planning of the order. They kept her at a remove, with Callum being her only real connection. She would have left, except that, by that point, she would have both the Order of the Reaper and the Cult of the Reaper coming after her."

"And that was when she and Callum got together?"

"No," Arabelle said. "According to Cal, it was one-sided. Melody herself wanted to go find her husband and daughter, but she couldn't while under the cult's thumb. So, Callum agreed to help her, despite his feelings. He made a connection between Emir and a diamond-ranker friendly to the cult. A historian who had been digging up details of the Order of the Reaper, unaware they were still active. This man's patronage is why Emir has been looking for Order of the Reaper remnants for years, around his other treasure-hunting activities. It's why he largely employs external forces, like contracting adventurers. It leaves him to use his own people for other projects."

"Adventurers like Farrah, Rufus and Gary," Jason said.

"Yes. He knew they were looking for some independence, and the low-magic of Greenstone seemed perfect."

"That's fine, but how would all that help Callum and Melody?"

"Because Emir and his patron were looking for traces of the order, including their martial techniques, the Way of the Reaper."

"Yeah, he was collecting the skill books. I thought he just wanted them for his granddaughter."

"It was more than that. The skill books are the methodology of the Order of the Reaper we know the most about. The order's members use skill books to inculcate its vast array of techniques, then training to naturalise that information."

"Exactly what I did with Rufus' help."

"Yes. It was just a part of what they were doing, but it was what Callum and Melody actually wanted. Cal knew that between the diamond-ranker and Emir, they would have people scouring the world for traces of the Way of the Reaper. Skill books were one thing, but Melody never had the opportunity to teach her husband that way. If some random guy not attached to the order was found using their techniques, that would stand out. Callum was regularly keeping in contact with his old team member, so he could learn all about what Emir was up to."

"That's a terrible search method," Jason said. "That's knowing that somewhere in the world is a haystack with a needle in it and getting someone to check haystacks for something else, in the hope they'd stumble onto a needle."

"Yes," Arabelle agreed. "It was a terrible plan, but one that they could carry out without either the cult or Emir realising what was going on."

"Cal didn't trust Emir?"

"Melody didn't. So, they did what they could, knowing full well that they might never find them, and even if it did, it would take years. Even with the formidable search resources that Emir and his diamond-rank patron were able to put into play."

"Oh," Jason said with sudden realisation. "Melody didn't have many options beyond what she could get Cal to do. And Cal was in love with her, so he wasn't wildly invested in finding her long-lost husband."

"No. Cal said that he did genuinely attempt to find the man, but had no real expectations of finding him."

"Then Sophie must have come as a shock."

"Yes, but Callum didn't realise what Emir had found until Emir started using her as bait for the order. Sophie and Emir had managed to find Marta Fries, Melody's friend, who had helped her and her family escape the order's grasp. That was when he intervened to keep Sophie and Humphrey away from her. Emir's now-wife, Constance, had been off training with Cal to reach gold rank, and her concerns over Emir using Sophie as bait made a good cover for Cal's own intentions. He tracked down Fries himself after she fled Humphrey and Sophie arriving at her door."

"But Melody was already in the Order of Redeeming Light by then, wasn't she? She's been in the Sea of Storms for years, and other places before that."

"Yes," Arabelle said. "Going back to when Callum first hatched this plan, using one of the Cult of the Reaper's diamond-rank contacts drew the attention of the cult. They decided it was time for Melody to make a sufficiently momentous gesture that the cult would be willing to accept her, and finally let her move from the Order of the Reaper to the Cult of the Reaper."

"Infiltrate the Purity church?"

"Yes. Callum was against using her to infiltrate the Order of Redeeming Light, but it was what the cult required. The cult had been looking into the Order of Redeeming Light for some time and suspected that despite serving Purity, they were using necromancy to raise undead. Part of the Order of Redeeming Light's mandate to repurpose the tools of the unclean to serve Purity."

"That sounds like a bunch of crap. The whole redeeming light thing only came along after the real Purity was given the boot, right?"

"That is our understanding, but the cult doesn't care who is behind it, only that undead are being used. The cult often works with the Church of Death in this regard, as they are closely aligned. The church does more public-facing things for the cult, while the cult can be the church's hidden dagger."

"So, the Order of Redeeming Light was known for accepting people outside the Purity faithful."

"They did so exclusively, in fact. It seemed like a rare chance to get a foot in the Purity door."

"Except that Melody was subjected to this 'cleansing fire' or whatever it was they called it. She became an artificial zealot."

"Yes. Callum lost track of her when she stopped reporting in and has been trying to find her ever since. Sophie and Emir leading him to Melody's friend Marta Fries was the first real clue he had. Fries been doing the same thing as him in seeking out Melody's trail, while trying to avoid the Order of the Reaper's suspicions about her. Ever since Melody's defection, she had been under scrutiny. Together, pooling their information and resources, they were able to trace Melody to the Sea of Storms. Then you arrived and we're all caught up."

Jason leaned back in his chair.

"Well," he said. "You did warn me it was going to be complicated."

"And that is only Callum's side. I'll be interested in hearing Melody's. I confess, however, that I am unsure how to proceed with the wellbeing of both in mind. Melody isn't truly capable of making informed choices while still under the influence of whatever was done to her. Perhaps we can't move forward until we see if Carlos can figure out how to undo this mess."

"On Earth," Jason said, "when you are unable to make your own informed decisions for whatever reason, that power generally falls to the closest family member."

"It works much the same here, although house politics often comes into play with nobility. You're saying that we bring in Sophie to see what she thinks."

"It's her mother. It seems only right that she make decisions until Melody can make her own without an evil god sitting on her shoulder."

28

A RESPONSIBILITY AS MUCH AS A PRIVILEGE

JASON AND ARABELLE CONTINUED TO CHAT AS THE MONSOON RAINS BORE DOWN outside. Jason brought out scones to go with the tea.

"There is an option," Jason said. "Something I've discussed with Carlos before. There is a place where things that aren't usually possible become possible. Somewhere I can turn off what's been done to Melody, so long as she is there. Removing it would kill her the moment she left that place, but suppressing it should be safe enough."

"You're talking about your soul space," Arabelle said.

"Yes."

"I know there have been changes. And I know that we've barely talked about them."

"Some things I'm not even sure how to talk about. I've seen glimpses of some higher society that exists in the wider cosmos. Soramir Rimaros, and presumably other diamond-rankers, have seen it. Dawn is someone important there. She's told me snippets, tales of a great city with visitors from a million universes. That wider cosmos has reached into the worlds in which I exist, changing me in different ways. Mentally, physically, magically. I've been annihilated and remade multiple times. My soul is unrecognisable from what it was."

"You're describing changes," Arabelle said, "but how changed do you feel? Do you find yourself to be a fundamentally different person from when you were human?"

"I've changed, but everyone changes. We all become different people over time."

"Then it's a question of whether it's you that has changed or if you've been changed by outside forces."

"It's not a question. The answer is both, and that's still true for everyone else. I just think that my ratio might have been tipped a little in favour of external forces.

But the closer I come to those forces, the more I realise that I've barely caught a glimpse of a realm to which I increasingly belong. There are aspects of myself that belong to that greater cosmic society. I've got one foot out into the cosmos, with no idea what I'm stepping into."

"And with the departure of Dawn, the closest thing you have to a guide is gone."

"Yes. The next closest thing is Soramir Rimaros, and I don't trust him. I don't distrust him, but he's not Dawn. Or Farrah, or you, or anyone else that I truly trust and rely on."

"How much does Soramir know?"

"I'm not sure. Enough to hurt me, although I think he seems well-meaning. It's hard keeping secrets around diamond-rankers."

"Why did you bring this up?" Arabelle asked. "Are you concerned about stumbling into something by using these cosmic aspects of yourself? By which I assume you mean the changes to your soul space."

"Yes. I don't know if my concerns are valid or if I'm jumping at shadows."

"Are you considering leaving your soul space alone until you know more?"

"No. One thing I'm very certain of is that I need to use every advantage I can, even if that sometimes comes with a cost. Right now, that means using my soul space to try and help Carlos."

"You think you can help him heal Sophie's mother and the others?"

"I hope so. If he can reach a certain point in his understanding of their condition, I might be able to help develop a treatment."

"But you think you can help Melody now, if only temporarily."

"I believe I can help the real Melody to emerge, so long as I can get her through the portal to my soul space."

"I thought the restrictions on that portal were gone?"

"Yes, the trust restrictions are gone, but it's still a portal. You can't force anyone through without consent."

"So, will Melody concede to go through some strange portal?"

"We'll see, assuming Sophie even wants that."

"I would advise you to consider this more carefully before moving forward, especially before taking this idea to Sophie. If you build her hopes up beyond what you can deliver, it could do real damage."

"I'm not rushing into anything."

"Good." Arabelle nodded her approval. "Even if this is something that you can do, it doesn't mean you should. You cannot expect to suppress the malicious magic affecting Melody and have her just be fine afterwards," she warned. "You know better than most that after the soul trauma is repaired, the mental trauma lingers. Especially since she will know that to leave your soul space is to return to her afflicted state."

Jason winced. "That's a horrible thought. Knowing that you're about to be taken over by something else."

"Thus, I counsel caution."

"I was going to discuss this idea with Sophie. Would you help me figure out how to do that? Even do it with me?"

"I will."

"We don't need to rush into it," Jason said. "We can take the time to make considered choices, even if we're left with nothing but hope that they're the right ones."

Arabelle narrowed her eyes at Jason.

"You've embraced the idea of moving forward slowly, haven't you?"

"Should I not have?"

"You absolutely should. But you've been running from one crisis to another for long enough that I thought it would take more adjustment."

Jason chuckled.

"Slowing down is what I've been dreaming of for a while. I was so ready for this."

"Alright," Arabelle said, standing up. "Try to maintain that attitude; you're not getting any older. Ever."

The giant bus Carlos was using for the trip was not as big as Jason's hover yacht, but it was still inconveniently bulky. Even so, space inside was at a premium. Despite placing most of the Order of Redeeming Light members in stasis and efficiently racking them, space was still required for Carlos and his three assistants, also from the Church of the Healer, to live and conduct their research.

A large consumer of usable area was Gibson Amouz, whose father had supplied the vehicle to facilitate his son's recovery. Gibson was inside a large, specialised containment tank, floating unconscious. Carlos had managed to prevent Gibson's degradation following the half-complete 'purification' ritual the Order of Redeeming Light had performed. He hoped that Gibson was the key to helping the others and, in a perfect world, many more besides. Gibson Amouz was potentially the key to unravelling such seemingly permanent curses as lesser vampirism, if Carlos could crack the nature of his affliction.

Carlos was sat at a desk covered in intricate notes. He ran his hands over his exhausted face, stood up and grabbed an umbrella on his way to the door. He opened it, seeing the pounding rain he'd been listening to strike the vehicle's rigid panels all day. The only windows were for the driver at the front, so this was his first time seeing the wall of falling water.

Unlike Jason's yacht, his vehicle couldn't fly using power drawn from the astral, so it was parked between the road and the jungle. Carlos chose not to walk, and instead floated out over the mud. Levitation was easy enough, so long as he wasn't disturbed, being easier for a gold-ranker than a silver. His umbrella generated a water-repelling field and floated on its own, like one Jason once owned, before he had left his with his niece on Earth.

The air outside was wet and heavy in the pounding rain, rather than fresh as Carlos wanted. He breathed it in unnecessarily anyway, trying to clear a mind caught up in his project. He needed to untangle his thoughts before proceeding, his head feeling like a clogged pipe. The importance of his current project was adding an extra layer of pressure.

Amos Pensinata floated down from the cloud yacht, apparently not caring as he was drenched in rain. He landed next to Carlos, his heavy boots settling in the mud that Carlos was avoiding. They stood side by side, watching the traffic backed up from the city gate, which had only gotten worse as the day progressed.

Carlos absently wondered what the stoic man had been like before Carlos had met him all those years ago, in a lunatic's dungeon. Probably the same, if his equally stolid nephew was anything to go by. Now that they were away from Rimaros, Amos was no longer projecting a politely restrained aura, and was instead hiding it away completely. Asano's friend Dawn had done well in recruiting Amos, as Carlos knew very few others who even could teach Jason about aura manipulation. There were people with stronger auras at the high end of gold rank and beyond. Strength was a different thing from skill, however, and like Jason, Amos was more than raw power.

"Have you started working with Asano yet?" Carlos asked.

Amos shook his head.

"You think you can show him some things?"

Amos nodded.

"You and I should sit down and discuss some things about Asano and his aura. There are some quirks that you'll need to know. His body and soul are a single entity, like a messenger's. It means he has the potential to do the same things they can."

Nod.

"You've fought messengers?"

Amos nodded, looked contemplative and then turned to look at Carlos.

"I don't have time for day-drinking," Carlos said. "I'm just clearing my head. I need to complete this first stage of my research as quickly as possible. If we can start working out how to treat the Amouz boy, that opens up a world of possibility."

Carlos looked out from under his umbrella at the rain hammering on the road, on the vehicles traversing it, and on Amos.

"This rainy season came out of nowhere," Carlos said. "It feels like it'll never let up."

Amos shrugged, prompting Carlos to lean towards the edge of his umbrella's coverage and look up.

"This afternoon? I don't see it."

Amos made an uncertain gesture with his hand.

"It'd be nice, even if it was a little break," Carlos said. "This rain feels oppressive. Makes a break like this not so refreshing."

Amos shrugged.

"Booze won't help, as you damn well know."

A smile teased at the corners of Amos' mouth.

"Fine, booze won't help me. If you want to get sauced in the middle of the day, that's your business. I suppose you're living a bit of a lazy life at the moment. Any time you aren't teaching Asano or looking out for your nephew, you've got nothing but time, in a luxurious boat made of clouds. What are you going to do with yourself?"

"There's always work to be done," Amos said in his gravel-slurry voice.

"What work will you do on a luxury yacht?"

"Read. Train. Drink."

"In that order?" Carlos asked with a grin.

Amos' friendly chuckle was the sound people heard in dark alleys in their nightmares.

"You're going to get back into a training routine? Chasing after essence revelation again?"

Amos nodded.

"I suppose you've got the time to focus on meditation. I don't think I'll ever shoot for diamond. It's too hard when you came up using cores; I'm lucky I got to gold."

Amos gave him a look.

"Don't give me that," Carlos complained. "I know that anything you don't try is impossible, but I'm trying to cure vampirism here. Maybe let me attempt one impossible thing at a time."

The city of Rajoras sprawled inland from the coast, built around the estuary of a broad river, the Rajo. It was a major manufacturing hub for water and air vehicles, and the seat of House de Varco. This made it the perfect place for Korinne and her team to find a vehicle of their own for their time on the road. They needed something that could serve as a true world-traveller, up to the rigours of intercontinental travel, along with being a robust home for adventurers.

Korinne's team was gathered in a vehicle warehouse the size of a sports stadium, filled with various bus-like vehicles. They had been looking over different vehicles that various members of the team had been excited about for one reason or another. Korinne was yet to find something she was satisfied with, matching Orin's taciturn expression.

Whether or not Orin found something exciting remained a mystery to his team. He might not have the enhanced aura strength of Jason or his uncle, but Amos had trained his aura manipulation skills personally. Unless someone of higher rank started poking his aura, it revealed no more emotions than his blank face.

The staff member guiding the team around showed no distaste at the team's lack of unity in what they wanted from a vehicle.

"When looking for a vessel that will not just be a vehicle but a home," he said, "it's important to take your time to make the right choice. Have you considered something larger, with the capacity to meet all of your needs? There are many excellent options that fall well within your stated budget."

"No," Korinne said. "A soft environment fosters a soft will. We're travelling to train as adventures, honing ourselves to a knife's edge. We need a scabbard, not a cushion. This isn't a leisure tour."

"Couldn't it be both?" asked Rosa, the team scout.

"No," Korinne said. "Orin, what do you have to say on the issue?"

"My uncle is a hard man," Orin said.

"Exactly," Korinne said before the slow-spoken Orin could continue. "Amos Pensinata is an exceptional role model. A hard adventurer needs hard surroundings. Flint and steel. Oh, what about this one?"

The vehicle she was pointing at was the size and shape of a bread truck.

"Ah," the salesman said. "The War Band model, from House de Varco. It was designed as a budget-conscious troop transport, but it does have the option of a long-term travel configuration, with accommodation features and enhanced long-distance travel features, such as more efficient flight. It's an excellent choice for one or two adventurers, but can, strictly speaking, be set up for as many as eight. This is by replacing two bed-and-cupboard configurations this one has with racks of what aren't bunks so much as shelves. It's workable if you're silver rank and can float into the higher slots. You just can't stand more than about three people plus, plus two seated in the driver station."

"What do you mean, can't stand?" Kalif asked.

"You have to remove the seating room and the storage to fit the bunk racks," the salesman explained. "We put in a rack for hanging dimensional bags. Or we will; we haven't actually sold any of that configuration, yet. But, as I said, two people can sit in the driving station at the front."

"Oh, that's fine, then," Kalif said. "There's only six of us, and two can even sit in comfort."

"I didn't say comfort," the salesman hurriedly corrected. "You can't hold me to that."

"I want to see inside," Korinne said.

"I don't," Rosa said.

"Are you kidding?" Kalif asked.

"It costs nothing to look," the salesman said. "Let me just open it up. The current configuration is for two, and it's probably best to avoid more than two or three in there at once. It's a little snug."

"I think it's perfect," Korinne said, once she was inside. "All business, no indulgence."

"I'm not above a little indulgence," Rosa said, crammed in with Korinne and the salesman. "Somewhere to sit down, for example. Somewhere to eat."

"Indulgence makes you weak," Korinne told her. "If you have time to sit down and eat, you have time to consume a spirit coin while you train."

"You do realise the monster surge ended, right?" Kalif said, poking his head in from outside. "We made a pretty good showing for ourselves."

"Pretty good," Korinne said. "You think the messengers will let you live because you put up a pretty good struggle?"

"Korinne," Kalif said, "you've been extremely militant ever since the Builder attacked Rimaros. While I agree that diligent training and discipline is good for us, so is getting to relax from time to time. If a rope is constantly pulled taut, it's going to fray."

"I agree," Rosa said. "I know you're the team leader, Korinne, and we've been following your lead, but Kalif is right. The monster surge is over, so it's time to loosen up and enjoy what we've earned. Even if it's only a little bit."

"Adventuring is a responsibility as much as a privilege," Korinne told her.

"Exactly," Rosa said. "We've had almost half a year of responsibility and it's time to enjoy a little privilege. The occasional hot meal won't turn us into lazy degenerates."

"Actual food," Kalif said longingly.

"Having a place to sit down won't turn us into failed adventurers, Korinne," Rosa continued, gesturing at the vehicle around them as much as she could in the available space. "This is a can for storing food, not adventurers."

"Orin," Kalif said. "Would your uncle stay in Korinne's tiny metal box?"

"My uncle is a hard man," Orin said again, "but he likes soft beds."

Clive and Belinda watched as a submarine was disassembled at a dry dock by a team of professional shipwrights.

"We're not going to feed the components to the cloud flask here, are we?" Clive asked.

"No," Jason's voice came from Clive's shadow, courtesy of Shade hidden inside it. It was the Shade body that had driven the stolen submarine upriver and into the dock.

"We'll need to make sure that no individual part exceeds our storage space limit, then," Clive said. "You'll need to take the bigger parts, Belinda."

Each storage space power differed in size and weight allowance for any given object. Clive's power had the lowest capacity on the team but also the strongest other functions. Its bronze-rank effect was to open portals, while at silver, it could fuel rituals in areas normally too low-magic for them. Belinda's storage was the largest, and while its other abilities were useful, they weren't portal useful.

"Shade," Clive asked. "How did a familiar sneak a submarine stolen from the Order of Redeeming Light through the river checkpoint without the Magic Society or the Adventure Society getting up in arms about it? And where did you get the paperwork for this job to be approved?"

"Miss Belinda made the arrangements."

Clive turned to Belinda.

"What?" she asked.

"How did you manage that?"

"Do you remember when I asked about how easy it was to bribe the people here?"

"Yes."

"It was an act. I already knew."

"But we hadn't even gotten here yet?"

"You're right," Belinda agreed. "*We* hadn't."

29

FIGHTING THE POWER

Korinne glowered, complaining. "This is a bunch of lizard shi—"

"We took a vote," Rosa said, cutting off her latest complaint. "You're the team leader, Korinne, not the team queen."

"I don't feel like the leader when you all mutiny like this."

"We didn't mutiny, Korinne. We just bought a vehicle that we actually want to live in."

They were riding out of the city in a House de Varco designed Outpost Rover. It was a vehicle model that the very happy salesman described as the premier choice for the adventuring team that is looking to travel in spacious luxury. What he meant was the choice for the adventuring team that could afford it.

While unquestionably comfortable for six, it was no pleasure barge, as Rosa and Kalif kept pointing out to Korinne. It had powerful defensive measures to withstand monster attacks, features designed to facilitate training and even a prison cell that could be expanded externally to the vehicle to contain a relatively large monster of up to silver rank.

Due to the impressive size of the vehicle, which would match that of the Carlos Crime Wagon, they took the salesman's advice and obtained the required temporary permits to fly it out of the city. That came at a further and considerable expense, but was worth it to avoid having to navigate the massive vehicle through the streets, let alone the gummed-up traffic around the city gates.

The entire endeavour was extremely expensive, but this was a team of silver-rank guild elites, fresh off a monster surge. They were a long way from the only adventurers making hefty investments in their future. Successful teams often took the approach of using their success during a monster surge to set up their next decade of adventuring until the next one.

The Adventure Society bonus system rewarded those who stepped up during the surge, and Korinne's team had very much done that. With the monster surge lasting five or six times longer than normal, the rewards for active adventurers had climbed to never-before-seen heights. Fortunately, the massive number of monsters meant more loot than ever before from which to distribute those awards. Adventure Society loot teams were always deployed as part of after-action teams, cleaning up after adventurers without loot powers themselves.

Jason's team had done fairly well in terms of bonuses, although Jason himself was a bit of an oddity. While he did have some outrageous contributions, he also had lengthy dead periods where he was doing nothing but recovering. In the end, he'd been given a special assessment, which he used to claim some useful quintessence to feed into the cloud flask.

The convoy remained at Rajoras for a few days as the new vehicle was customised and a certain submarine was discreetly broken down into parts and brought to Jason, who fed them into the cloud flask. Jason never went into the city himself, although he debated it during the breaks in the rain. It wasn't likely he'd be recognised, but it was still the playground of House de Varco, so he decided to remain on the yacht until they were further from Rimaros.

The three-vehicle convoy had become four as Korinne's team eschewed the yacht for their own vehicle. They left Rajoras not by road but upriver, joining the water traffic on the way to their next destination. The short-term plan was to follow the river that curved through a valley just inland of the east coast, moving out of the Storm Kingdom's territory. Eventually, they would leave the river to head for the coast proper.

Jason and his companions were gathered in a briefing room on the yacht, along with Carlos, Arabelle and most of Korrine's team. Only Kalif had been left behind, to drive their new vehicle. He was starting to get a handle on it, and had run it into very few other vehicles on the river all day.

Humphrey was going over the convoy's immediate plans, with a map behind him showing their river route and intended path east. Korinne stood beside him. Humphrey used a thin rod to indicate their disembarkation point from the river.

"We'll be landing here," he said. "Prior to the monster surge, this was the location of the river city of Cartise. Unfortunately, the Builder cult managed to claim a nearby astral space, causing widespread destruction as the astral space separated from our world. When a diamond-rank monster manifested shortly after, the city was overwhelmed."

"Most of the population was evacuated to the large towns nearby and along the river," Korinne said, picking up the narrative. "But Cartise was the major hub in this area for trade and travel. Its absence increases the logistical strain on surrounding centres as they start rebuilding after the surge."

"Especially now that they have overpopulation issues with the Cartise refugees," Humphrey added.

"In short," Korinne said, "we're saying that there is a lot of adventuring work. The surge may be over, but that doesn't mean our jobs are done. While the monster numbers won't be as high, the problems will become increasingly about logistics. Securing supply routes, escorting specialists rebuilding infrastructure. Utility powers will be increasingly at a premium, with storage and portal powers both in high demand. It may not be glamorous work, but it's essential. People need our help just as much now as they did a month ago; it's just not about constantly killing monsters anymore."

"We're from one of the best guilds in the world," complained Polix, from Korinne's team. "You want us doing delivery runs and escorting craftspeople? That's trash adventurer work."

"Trash adventurers," Korinne said, "are defined by their attitudes, not their combat ability. Our duty as adventurers is to do what people need, not what we want."

"Exactly," Rosa agreed. "Don't be a turd, Polix."

Jason felt old as he watched Korinne's team bicker briefly amongst themselves. Like Humphrey and Neil, they were roughly the same age now as he had been when he first arrived in Pallimustus, but he wondered if he'd ever been that much of a young little prick. He thought back for a moment and then shook his head. He'd been worse.

"We've moved out of the high-magic Sea of Storms, so gold-rankers will be a lot less common," Humphrey said, continuing the briefing. "As silver-rankers, it falls to us to step up and not just do our duty as adventurers, but to set an example. With our behaviour."

Korinne's team looked sheepish. They were each from major adventuring families in Rimaros, and had been lectured their whole lives about the standards they were meant to set. But most of their adventuring careers had been under strict supervision, where they were never expected to represent adventuring as a whole to the public. They were now heading into exactly the kind of experience this self-directed tour was designed to give them.

After the briefing, Humphrey found Jason and they headed in the direction of Jason's cabin as they talked.

"Thank you for expanding the cabin sizes," Humphrey said.

"Well, with team Rain Chopper—"

"Storm Shredder," Humphrey corrected.

"With team Wet Stabber moving into their new ride, there was room to expand."

"How would you like it if people were deliberately getting our team name wrong?" Humphrey asked.

"I'm fine with that. What would they go with, though? Team Scone? Ooh, that's not bad. Maybe we should formally change the name to Team Scone."

"We are not changing it to Team Scone!"

"See, I knew you'd come to love Team Biscuit."

"We should change it to something sensible."

"You mean like team Damp Jabber?"

"Storm Shredder."

"What would we go with, using that name as a model?"

"I don't mean to copy their name."

"Team Moist Crevice? Seems a bit risqué."

"I get it," Humphrey surrendered. "We're sticking with Team Biscuit."

"Hey, Shade," Jason said. "Tell the others that Humphrey is talking about changing the team name again."

"Please don't."

"Tell them he wants to go with team Moist Crevice."

"Shade," Humphrey said, "please do not do that."

"Mr Geller, I am afraid that I am but a humble familiar, bound to my summoner's commands."

"You should tell that to Stash," Humphrey grumbled.

"Hey, since I'm changing up the cabins," Jason said to Humphrey, "did you want me to merge yours and Sophie's instead of adjoined cabins with a connecting door?"

"No, Sophie values having her own space and time to be alone. Also, if she and Belinda don't get enough private time together, Lindy starts giving me looks that worry me a great deal. Farrah's started joining them as well. I'm beginning to suspect they talk about me in there."

"Beginning to suspect? Mate, they're definitely talking about you."

"You've been listening in?"

Jason put a comforting hand on Humphrey's shoulder as they arrived at Jason's cabin.

"I don't have to, mate. They just are."

The cloud door disappeared to grant them entry. Humphrey moved to sit in an armchair while Jason moved to a cooling container.

"Can I talk you into a refreshing fruit drink?" he asked.

"Please," Humphrey said. "This endless rain and heavy air is worse than back home."

"The delta is a geographical oddity, because of an astral space spewing out water," Jason said. "It's got the heat and the humidity, but it's too far south for a monsoon season."

"You know a lot about the natural world," Humphrey said as Jason started preparing fruit for juicing. "You know a lot in general."

"Those statements are both false," Jason said. "Especially here, where magic changes rules. Back on Earth as well, now it has magic too."

"I think it's a matter of perspective," Humphrey said. "I suspect your education system is much better than ours. The Church of Knowledge does what it can, but they get a lot of pushback. At the risk of supporting your thoughts on aristocracy as a system, a lot of the nobility is resistant to widespread education beyond the reading and writing programs the church managed to make standard."

"Honestly, my home culture isn't any better. My education was good because we had money."

"Wait, after all the complaining you had about nobility this and nobility that, your way isn't any better?"

"Yeah, well… you didn't come up here to discuss school funding disproportionately being funnelled into private schools."

Jason used a pair of magic wands to juice the fruit and put it in a pitcher before taking it over to Humphrey on a tray with some tall glasses containing ice cubes. They sat in armchairs facing one another, with the drinks on a table between them.

"It's about what we were talking about in the briefing," Humphrey said. "Setting an example. And also, perspective."

"Oh?" Jason prompted as he poured drinks.

"Jason, your perspective is extremely skewed. In Greenstone, you were an iron-ranker regularly dealing with silver and even gold-rankers. That isn't normal. Then you went to Earth, where things were even more disproportional, if my discussions with Farrah are anything to go by."

"You've been talking with Farrah about my time on Earth?"

"Taika and Travis, as well. We all realised that talking about it with you wasn't a good idea," Humphrey said. "We left that to Arabelle. When we first arrived in Rimaros, you were an open wound, Jason."

"You're not wrong," Jason conceded. "And yes, I wasn't exactly a face in the crowd."

"Then you arrive in the Sea of Storms, and suddenly, it's princesses everywhere, diamond-rankers and whatever Dawn is."

"She's diamond rank. Technically. I'm still not entirely clear on what half-transcendent means."

"You shouldn't have to be," Humphrey said. "My mother has indicated enough times that there are things about gold rank that I don't know, let alone diamond. Diamond-rankers are more legend than reality in low-magic zones like Greenstone."

"What's the point you're meandering around?" Jason asked.

"Jason, you've been conditioned to interact with the world in a certain way. You're used to the people around you being far more powerful, and needing to be more than a little outrageous for them to take notice. You've always had to make bold moves so you weren't dismissed out of hand."

"But?"

"But now, you'll be meeting a lot more people to whom you are the powerful one. If you run around doing outrageous things when you're the one with all the power, that's not bold; it's maniacal. These aren't people you need to go all out with. If you treat them like you did Elspeth Arella or Vesper Rimaros, you're going to turn their worlds upside down. To ordinary people, an unhinged silver-rank adventurer is far worse than a silver-rank monster."

"Unhinged?"

"Jason, most of the people in this world are just ordinary folk, going about their lives. Silver-rank adventurers coming in and acting wild have all the power and destructiveness of a hurricane. In the places we'll be going from now on, you won't be fighting the power anymore. You'll be the power."

"You know that I was always good at interacting with normal people back in Greenstone."

"And are you the same person you were back then?"

Jason grimly nodded, conceding the point. He looked thoughtful as he sipped at his drink.

"I suppose I'm not," he said. "Since then, it's been a series of increasingly powerful people trying to yank me one way or the other, and I've become more and more extreme to face that. Now that you say it, I'm not sure I know how to be anything else anymore. But now I'm the powerful one, so I've become the thing I was always struggling against. You may be right that I don't know how to handle that."

"Yes. It's hard to see what's happening to you when you're dealing with Soramir Rimaros or you're the most famous essence user in the world. But you're probably stronger than anyone who was in Greenstone back then. Except for Thalia Mercer and my mother, but they weren't really Greenstone residents. They were just back for the monster surge that kept not coming. At least now we know why."

Jason frowned and took another sip of his drink.

"I'm not sure what to do about that. How to deal with regular people. I never wanted to be that guy so removed from regular people that he becomes detached from ordinary life."

"Maybe think of this as a chance to reconnect with that. I'm just warning you to be mindful of the power you wield, and the fact that many people don't."

Jason nodded. "Thanks, Humphrey. I appreciate you looking out for me."

"Of course."

"No, I mean it. You've helped me get over a huge hump in my mindset."

"Please don't."

"It's just good to know that I can rely on the team, instead of humping this issue alone."

"Just stop."

"The same goes for you. You don't have to hump the burden of looking out for me by yourself."

"You are my least favourite team member."

30

MAKE JASON GREAT AGAIN

"THIS VALLEY WOULD BE GORGEOUS IF WE COULD ACTUALLY SEE IT THROUGH THE rain," Jason complained as he looked out the window. The convoy was floating on or just over a rather busy river, with water traffic heading in each direction. The vision-obscuring downpour slowed progress as boats, skimmers and hover vehicles cautiously navigated the waters and each other.

The banks were dangerous to any vehicle with a draft as the river was swollen with the fresh rains. It made the river's outer reaches a dangerous and murky trap for unwary boats, but freed up space for floating vehicles.

The monsoon rains had continued, with breaks in the weather lasting an hour at most. It was as if the rain, like the people it fell on, had been waiting out the monster surge that went on for far too long. By the time the river trip moved into the second day, Humphrey had pushed the team into training.

The training room did more than provide magically enhanced weights, courtesy of the various materials and quintessence Jason had fed his cloud flask. On top of the weights, the training room could have the gravity enhanced, either across the whole room or in specific sections. The team were acclimatising to this when Jason was approached by Amos Pensinata.

"Time to get started?" Jason asked.

Amos nodded, then immediately walked off.

"I guess it's aura training for me," Jason told the others.

He followed Amos out of the training room.

"What exactly did Dawn give you that you're willing to do this?" Jason asked. "If you don't mind me prying."

"Insight," Amos rumbled.

Jason waited, but no further explanation was forthcoming.

"Enlightening," he said.

"Yes," Amos agreed.

Amos led Jason to the stairs that went up to the roof deck, and stopped.

"I saw you using your aura to deflect the rain."

"It seemed like a good way to practise."

"Lazy."

"Uh, okay. What do you want me doing?"

"You know ritual magic, yes?"

"Yes."

"Use your aura to draw a ritual circle with the rain. Get it right. Precise."

"You know I won't be able to perform a ritual doing it like that, right?"

"You don't need a ritual. Just need complexity."

Jason was floating just over the roof deck in a meditative pose, completely drenched as rain pounded down on him. He was mentally exhausted after hours of painstaking concentration, which was something he hadn't experienced in a while. His silver-rank spirit attribute enhanced his mentality in various ways, including focus, concentration and multitasking. All of those had been pushed to the limit by the exercise.

Before undertaking the task from Amos, Jason had been convinced that his aura manipulation skills had been pushed to their limit. He suspected a key purpose of the exercise had been disabusing him of that notion, which it had quite thoroughly done. Using his aura to manipulate physical objects was still something he was getting used to. Shielding an area from the rain wasn't too taxing, but pulling in small amounts of water and shaping it into an array of lines and sigils very much was. Even going for the simplest ritual circle he knew was like trying to closely observe every bee in a hive simultaneously.

His early attempts had involved the simpler method of creating invisible force moulds with his aura for the water to settle in, but he had given up on that. It felt like not only was he getting more precision by manipulating the water directly, but it was better for developing control. The purpose of the exercise was training, after all. The goal was to improve his skill, not learn to cast rituals using the rain. If nothing else, water made a terrible platform for ritual magic without specialised abilities to support it.

Jason overexerted his concentration over and over again, causing even the basic rain shield to collapse, which was how he ended up soaked to the skin. But after each failure, he took a moment to recentre himself and then started over.

Amos gestured to Rufus, who was exercising with Jason's team in the large training room. Rufus was doing a flexibility exercise, which involved swinging across the room while dangling from rings, flipping through the air as he launched from one set of rings to the next. After dropping to the floor, Rufus moved over to speak with him.

"Something I can help you with, Lord Pensinata?"

"You trained Asano."

"When he first arrived in our world, yes. I gave him his start in adventurer training, primarily in combat techniques. I've also been helping him with combat trances since he came back. My companions taught him in other areas, though. If you want to discuss his early aura training, you should speak with Farrah. She took that portion of his training and is stronger in that area than me, but she'll freely admit that Jason has moved past us both in that regard."

"It's not about his previous training. How hard can I push him before he'll balk?"

"As in, how much training you can shove him into before he quits?"

Amos nodded.

"I honestly don't know," Rufus said. "It's part of what made me realise early that he was going to be great. He has a voracious appetite for training. However hard I drove him, he was always grateful. He never asked questions about why he needed to train so hard; he kept pushing to get stronger, like any weakness inside him is a poison. So long as he believes that you have a way to push him forward, he'll take all the pushing you've got."

Amos and Clive arrived on the roof deck to find Jason sitting under an orb around which the pounding rain curved. Inside it, he was sat cross-legged, hovering just off the deck. Around him was a floating ritual circle comprised entirely of water. Jason opened his eyes at the arrival of the newcomers who were standing dry under an awning.

"I have to thank you for this, Lord Pensinata. I haven't felt anything push me this hard in a while. In training anyway."

Amos looked at Clive, who peered at Jason's fake ritual circle.

"That's pretty close," Clive said.

"Show me," Amos rumbled.

Clive pointed with his finger and started drawing a ritual circle with glowing light, overlapping with Jason's own diagram made of water. As he finished, it became evident where Jason's circle had minor imperfections.

"Let me guess," Jason said. "I have to keep going until I get it right."

"No," Amos said. "When you get it right, you pick a harder ritual."

Jason grinned, and his water circle fell to the deck in a series of tiny splashes. Droplets filtered into the orb instead of around it and started forming a new ritual circle as Jason closed his eyes.

Clive yawned as he trudged out onto the roof deck. The rain finally had a proper break as they continued south and the dark sky was lit up with stars. There was still plenty of water sitting on the deck for Jason to float into complex ritual shapes. He'd moved onto a second, slightly more sophisticated ritual after mastering the first.

"Jason, it's the middle of the night."

"Check me."

Clive overlapped Jason's ritual circle in lines of glowing light, highlighting the many inconsistencies.

"Alright," Jason said, looking around and mentally noting the problem spots.

"This is the last time, Jason. I'm going to bed."

"Good night."

"You should be going to bed as well."

"We arrive at Cartise tomorrow," Jason said. "Maybe even overnight. I need to get in my training while I can."

"Jason, didn't you say you're fairly sure that you've stopped ageing? You have time?"

"So long as no one kills me, sure. And while I might have forever, I don't have Lord Pensinata forever. The great thing about a reliable instructor is that you know that so long as you put in the work, you'll get the results. No luck, no privilege. Just work for reward. There's a comfort in that reliability."

"There's also a comfort in comfort, Jason. I'm going to bed."

The dark did not obscure Jason's vision as the yacht approached the ruins that were, until recently, the city of Cartise. He looked out from the roof deck and was reminded of old pictures of London after the Blitz. Nothing was undamaged and entire blocks of buildings were reduced to chunks of rubble no bigger than a fist.

The old docks had been destroyed, and the remains had been fished out to prevent obstructions. Jason could see the detritus that hadn't been salvaged for the new docks, piled up further along the shore. The new docks served the Adventure Society camp that had been set up to handle operations in and around the fallen city.

With the rest of the group asleep, it fell to Jason to go meet the dockmaster and secure a berth. Shade appeared and pulled the team's documentation from his dimensional space, and Jason transferred it to his own. He then took a running leap off the roof deck, sailing over the docks, and landing in a crouch on the shore, next to a stone cottage. He didn't lighten his fall, as that would require calling out his distinctive cloak.

Jason's mode of arrival did not faze the grizzled man who came out of a stone cottage. He was the dockmaster for a camp that was exclusively host to adventurers and Magic Society field agents, so he found Jason's approach downright tame. His cottage was simple and square, all of a single piece. It had the plain, rough texture of a child's clay art project, the distinctive tells of a building hurriedly stone-shaped out of the earth with magic. Jason approached the man and handed over the team's documentation and the dockmaster looked it over.

"Two silver-rank teams and an assortment of gold-rankers," the dockmaster muttered. "We can certainly use that."

"I only speak for one of the teams, Team Biscuit," Jason said. "The others you'll have to arrange with separately."

"Are you saying they came here where there's nothing but work and aren't interested in working?"

"Not at all. I'm just saying that I can't speak for them," Jason said. "I'm just a team auxiliary. You won't catch me going around giving orders to gold-rankers."

In Jason's shadow, Shade was grateful for his inability to choke, as it would have revealed his presence.

"You're the auxiliary," the dockmaster said, leafing through the documents. "John Miller, that's you?"

"It is."

"Your team feels the need to take around a silver-rank cook?"

"Just between you and me, I have a few other utility tricks up my sleeve. We just keep it quiet to avoid poaching attempts."

"You're not open to someone making a better offer?"

"I trust the people I work with. Who can make a better offer than that?"

"That's a good attitude," the dockmaster said. "It's four vehicles?"

"Yeah, the dimensions are listed there."

"That's fine. Give me a moment to copy these documents and I'll find you somewhere to put them."

"John Miller," Farrah said, pausing with a forkful of pancake. Jason and his companions were sitting around the breakfast table. "We've been wondering for days what crazy name you picked for yourself, and you went with John Miller."

"The point was to not stand out," Jason said. "That's a pretty ordinary name, even in this world, right? Vidal, you said it was normal."

"I did, yes," Vidal Ladiv said. The Adventure Society liaison was still somewhat nervous around the group, rarely speaking up unless directly addressed.

"We've been bugging this guy since we set off to tell us the name," Belinda complained, "and all he'll say is that you told him not to tell us."

"I figured you'd all have some fun with it. I assume you all made guesses."

"Captain Handsome Boatman," Neil said.

"Buck Stone, Bounty Hunter," Belinda guessed.

"Action Fighter," Travis added. "Or maybe something inappropriately exotic, like Enrico de la Fuente."

"That doesn't fit at all," Sophie said. "I can see him going for that."

"What about Karl Marx?" Humphrey suggested.

"How do you know about Karl Marx?" Travis asked him.

"Jason and I used to have discussions about aristocracy a lot. This was back before we formed the team. I'm not sure who he is, but Jason seemed very enthused."

Travis turned to look at Jason. "You don't seem like much of a socialist, having a massive buffet breakfast on your magic superyacht."

"Everyone has things they're good and bad at," Jason said defensively. "I'm a socialist, I'm just... not great at it."

"Not great?" Farrah asked. "You can create infinite amounts of money."

"What?" Vidal asked.

"Don't worry about that," Farrah said. "I was guessing on some name from Earth. Bruce Banner. Bruce Wayne. Bruce McAvaney."

"You seem obsessed with the name Bruce," Jason said. "I'm actual Australian, not a Monty Python Australian. I didn't think you'd like Monty Python."

"What kind of maniac doesn't like Monty Python?" Farrah asked.

"People who were oppressed by the British," Jason said. "There's a woman I know who used to work for my dad, and her dad wouldn't let her watch any British television growing up. She missed out on Monty Python, *The Goodies*, *Fawlty Towers*."

"Even I've seen *Fawlty Towers*," Farrah said. "And I'm from another universe."

"How much Earth culture did you absorb?" Jason asked her.

"You kept going into transformation zones and leaving me twiddling my thumbs."

"I was saving the world."

"And I was watching internet videos. The name doesn't have to be Bruce; there are plenty of other choices. Clark Kent, Ahmet Zappa, Man-E-Faces, Carlos Danger, the Artist Formerly Known as Ringo Starr. Pol Pot."

"Pol Pot?" Jason exclaimed. "You seriously think I'd go with Pol Pot?"

Farrah continued reeling off guesses.

"Maximilien Robespierre, Rolf Harris, Mother Theresa, Joseph Stalin."

"Now you're just listing terrible people," Jason complained.

"Gonk," Gary said.

Everyone at the table turned to look at him.

"What?" he asked.

"Gonk?" Rufus asked.

"As a name," Gary said. "I thought Jason might go for a mononym."

"And you thought that if I went for just one name," Jason said, "that the name I'd go for is Gonk?"

"Why not?" Gary asked. "There's no telling what you're going to do."

This drew general nods of agreement around the table, which in turn led to an affronted expression from Jason.

"I was hoping for Manny McManface," Taika said, "but I thought you'd go with Michael Long."

"I thought you had it with that one, actually," Farrah told Taika. "I was sure he'd try for some obscure alias that someone on Earth used where no one would get the reference."

"Actually," Taika corrected, "Michael Knight was the alias and Michael Long was his real name."

Farrah reached out—and up—to put a hand on the shelving unit that was Taika's shoulder.

"Taika," she told him. "I'm not sure I can fully express the degree to which I do not care."

"Not all of your many terrible guesses were aliases," Jason told Farrah. "And John Miller *is* an alias, thank you very much. And none of you did get the reference."

"An alias for who?" Farrah asked.

"Oh," Travis said. "I just figured it out."

31

NEIL'S BIG MOUTH

JASON WATCHED FROM THE ROOF DECK AS RUFUS, FARRAH AND GARY HEADED upriver on the skimmers they kept stored on the yacht. With them was Estella Warnock, whom they were escorting from the Adventure Society camp to an actual population centre. Estella would be fulfilling her role of scouting out such places, for opportunities and danger. She didn't need the escort, but it was a chance for Rufus, Gary and Farrah to work together again as a team.

Letting out a sigh, Jason couldn't help but reflect that just as his team was coming together, theirs was coming apart. It was not long after Humphrey, Jason and Clive had done their first job together that Farrah had died, which had profoundly impacted Rufus and Gary. Even though Farrah was now back, none of them had a taste for full-time adventuring anymore.

Rufus was increasingly interested in training adventurers over being one, while Gary and Farrah were focusing on their very different crafts. Gary was seeking to master the old ways, chasing perfection in the smithing of weapons and armour. Farrah, by contrast, was chasing the future, pushing magic into new fields.

This trip was an opportunity to relive the old days when all they had was ambition and each other. It was also a chance to say goodbye to those days, and fully appreciate that their futures followed paths they had not anticipated. Even when they should have because they wouldn't shut up about their family running a school.

Jason chuckled at the thought and pushed himself off the railing. He had his own team and his own adventures to have, even if he was playing the role of secretly awesome cook. He wondered again if he should have named himself after a similar character from the Steven Seagal movie.

"No," he muttered to himself. "Even my rose-tinted nostalgia has limits. A man has to have standards."

"Mr Asano, are you thinking about Steven Seagal again?" Shade asked.

"No."

Jason's team was tasked with heading into Cartise to clear monsters out of the ruined city. They were one of several teams tasked with doing so, and were being guided through their assigned sweeping route by Vestine, an Adventure Society functionary. Jason himself wasn't with them, because why would you bring the cook?

"Not to be ungrateful," Neil said, "but why do we need a guide?"

"There have been some issues," Vestine told him. "Teams getting a little over-enthused, roaming into another team's territory, and suddenly, they're fighting duels instead of monsters. We don't have time for that."

"So, you're guiding teams away from making stupid choices," Belinda said.

"I hardly think that's necessary," Clive said.

"Then you should pay more attention," Neil told him.

"I completely agree," Belinda said. "That should be the policy for all teams."

"You want someone hanging around all the time, observing what you do?" Neil asked her, and Belinda's expression went stiff.

"I formally rescind my suggestion."

"We prefer to think of it as helping the teams stay focused," Vestine said.

"I bet that's because they're already trying to ditch you and cause trouble," Belinda said. "You outright tell them you're babysitters and they're going to throw a tantrum."

A smile crept onto Vestine's face, despite her best efforts, but she didn't respond.

As they moved through the ruins on foot, the team made swift progress. Having once spent months in a city not just ruined but overtaken by jungle, the terrain was no obstacle to them. They traversed the city, alert but relaxed, Sophie only occasionally visible as she scouted around them. The team took the chance to learn more about conditions in the area by questioning their guide.

"Just so I'm getting this right," Neil said, "something is attracting monsters to the city, and we're *not* meant to stop it?"

"That's right," Vestine told him. "When the diamond-rank monster died here in the city, it left behind spots of magical resonance that still linger, and will for weeks to come. Monsters normally fear their diamond-rank contemporaries, but this resonance seems to draw them in, from a hundred kilometres away or more."

"Then why not get rid of it?" Clive asked. "Eliminating magical resonance isn't that hard. Even from a diamond-rank monster, it should be easy enough. You just have to align a purgation ritual with an amplification ritual with a—"

"How many rituals would it take in total?"

"Four, maybe five," Clive said, then shrugged. "Diamond-rank, so let's call it five. Six at the absolute most."

"And these would all be in a sequence?" Vestine asked.

"They would have to be, yes," Clive said.

"You just said it would be easy."

"Yes?" Clive asked, confusion in his expression.

"I think the lady's point," Belinda told Clive, "is that not everyone thinks that running half a dozen rituals in a unified sequence is easy."

"Really?" Clive asked.

"Yes, really," Neil told him.

"Oh," Clive said, his tone suggesting he was not entirely convinced.

"I believe that Clive's original question," Humphrey said, "was why not eliminate this resonance. The difficulty or ease of doing so aside, I imagine the reason is that the Adventure Society wants the monsters here."

"Exactly," Vestine said, still giving Clive odd looks. "The surge is over, but there are still many monsters that manifested in the wilderness that weren't dealt with because they didn't pose an immediate threat. This city is an empty ruin, while the towns and villages around it are not. Better to draw the monsters here than have them attack the over-populated and under-resourced locations that are bursting with refugees."

"Rebuilding the city isn't a priority, then?" Neil asked.

"It can't be," Vestine said. "The monster surge was five years late. Five years of the economy being strained by everything being in a state of readiness for a surge that kept not arriving. Then the surge itself lasted six times longer than it should have, and that's not even accounting for the Builder invasion. Now there's a conflict with the messengers, and who knows what trouble that will bring."

"That is a lot," Neil conceded. "I suppose you have to do what you can instead of what you want to."

"I know that story," Belinda said.

The team heard the high-pitched shrieking of monsters in the distance and rushed in that direction. They sensed auras as they drew nearer, but the auras blinked out, one by one, and by the time they arrived, the monsters were gone. There were signs of combat, claw marks raking stone, but no corpses and no blood.

"Again," Vestine muttered.

"Again?" Humphrey asked.

"The Adventure Society functionaries guiding the teams are keeping contact through a communication power," Vestine explained as she crouched to examine a claw mark. "This mark is from a skittering raker, which matches the sounds we heard. They're ambush predators, a common monster in this region. This is the third instance in the last couple of hours of monster packs disappearing before adventurers could get to them."

"Almost like someone was running around, killing and looting them," Neil said innocently, earning him a slap on the arm from Belinda.

"Maybe," Vestine said. "If so, I wish they'd report to the Adventure Society camp. Someone running rogue means that we'll have to expend time and people we desperately need to use elsewhere on a false threat. But we suspect it's another monster, though."

"Oh?" Humphrey asked.

"One of the teams reported seeing some strange butterflies near where one of the monster packs vanished. The butterflies themselves fled before anyone could get a closer look, though. They were reportedly extremely fast."

Humphrey caught Clive's eye.

"Vestine, please excuse us for a moment," Humphrey said. "I need to consult with my team member."

Humphrey and Clive walked a little way from the group and Humphrey activated a privacy screen. Clive pulled out a blue marble tablet, the engravings on which started shifting as he moved his fingers across it.

"Shade," Humphrey said. "Is this Jason?"

"No, Mr Geller," Shade said from Humphrey's shadow.

"Are you sure?"

"Quite certain, Mr Geller. Mr Asano discovered just how desperate the Adventure Society efforts in this region are for resources and decided to volunteer himself as an actual auxiliary. He's been looting monster remains brought in by other teams for materials and meat, which he is cooking in ways friendly to long-term storage. He's quite busy."

"Oh," Humphrey said. "I thought he'd gone off marauding on the sly."

"Jason's butterflies aren't fast, the way our guide described," Clive said, then held up the Magic Society monster almanac in his hands. "I think I know what this monster is."

"You just looked it up? Those almanacs are a pain to sort through. My mother used to make me go through them for practise."

"I may not be part of the Magic Society anymore, but my ability to efficiently search through their record system remains intact."

"You think it's a butterfly monster, then?"

"Yes, but let's go back to the group so I'm not explaining it twice."

Humphrey nodded and disabled the privacy screen. They returned to the others and Clive explained what he suspected to be the culprit.

"There's a kind of butterfly monster called the glorious harvester," he told the group. "It's rare, and normally shows up a decent way south of here, but there are a handful of records of them showing up almost as far north as Rajoras. It's a swarm-type monster with a few distinctive traits. One is their appearance, which is green, blue and yellow, with a golden glow. Another is that they are one of the rare monsters that hunt other monsters and mostly avoids anyone else. They produce dust that triggers a rapid breakdown in monster bodies. This breakdown continues after death, dissolving them as a looting power would. The glorious harvesters then consume the magic as it returns to a raw state. I'm more or less saying that they eat rainbow smoke."

"So, it's really a monster, then?" Neil asked. "I was sure it would turn out to be —"

Belinda slapped his arm again.

"Turn out to be what?" Vestine asked.

"You are so bad at this," Belinda told Neil, shaking her head. "And I mean *Clive* bad."

"Hey!" Neil and Clive exclaimed simultaneously, then glared at each other.

"This dust that the butterfly monster produces," Belinda said, drawing attention away from Neil's big mouth. "It dissolves monster bodies, right?"

"Yes," Clive confirmed.

"High-rankers, and even well-trained mid-rankers, have bodies that are basically the same as that of monsters," Belinda said. "Wouldn't that make us vulnerable to this dust?"

"No," Clive said, shaking his head. "Well, not as much. The almanac noted that it doesn't affect essence users the same way, which is why glorious harvesters are one of the rare monsters that hunt other monsters. I'm not sure why it's less effective on essence users; the almanac didn't say."

"There's a reason we say our bodies are 'basically' the same," Neil said. As a healer, he had the best understanding in the group of how their magical bodies worked. "There are key differences between the very similar makeup of an essence user and a monster's body. The big one is that, barring essence ability intervention, monster bodies are a lot more resilient. That's because monster bodies don't have to contain an actual soul, like an essence user, or an actual spiritual entity, like a summoned familiar. Because their bodies don't need that spiritual reinforcement, they can focus on physical reinforcement."

"Then it sounds like this dust targets whatever makes monster bodies tougher than ours specifically," Clive said. "It will affect us to some degree, but not to the same degree. It won't be as severe as… someone else's afflictions."

Belinda shook her head.

"So bad at this," she muttered. "Clive, he went off into the cosmos with a diamond-ranker, not a mystic land where saying his name will levy a curse. You can say his name."

"Ah, yes, right," Clive said. "He went off with a diamond-ranker."

Belinda groaned.

"Yeah, real convincing, Clive," she complained. "I take it back. You're not allowed to talk about him."

"Who are we talking about?" Vestine asked.

"It doesn't matter," Humphrey said. "We should get moving again if we want to complete our sweep on…"

Sophie dropped to the ground next to the group.

"I found some weird butterfly monster," she said. "It was more yellow and green than Jason's."

"Who is Jason?" Vestine asked.

"Some guy we used to work with," Sophie said. "He went off with a diamond-ranker for being an extra-special boy or some nonsense."

"Callously abandoned us," Belinda confirmed.

"Did you see which way the butterflies went?" Vestine asked.

"They didn't go anywhere," Sophie said. "They weren't very fast, so I just dealt with them."

"Wait," Vestine said. "You're saying they were slow?"

"Yeah," Sophie confirmed. "Not you people slow, but slow."

"You probably shouldn't fly around," Vestine warned. "Monsters might see you and end up following you back to us."

"Exactly," Sophie said. "You people are slow, so I rounded some up. You should sense the first group any second."

"Sophie!" Humphrey scolded. "What did I tell you?"

Sophie's face took on an expression of exaggerated uncertainty.

"That you like it when I tickle your—"

"I said stop rounding up monsters because you think we're too slow!"

"Oh, that makes more sense," she acknowledged. "The other thing is kind of private."

RAGE, AUTHORITY AND
OTHERWORLDLY POWER

JASON MOVED THROUGH THE NIGHT-COVERED CITY, FLICKERING UNSEEN FROM shadow to shadow. There was no shortage of them under the light of the twin moons, allowing him to make a blistering pace. With the blanket of stars, the city was relatively bright, given the early hours, making it a shadowy realm that was perfect for Jason.

He didn't expand his senses too far, as his magical senses were an expression of his aura. Pushing them too far would broadcast his location to any aura-sensitive being in a wide area. He wasn't worried about nocturnal monsters but the adventuring teams patrolling at all hours that hunted them. He neither wanted to explain his presence nor be mistaken for one of the monsters being hunted.

Even retracted, Jason's senses were still excellent over shorter distances, allowing him to avoid any teams he encountered. Unlike him, they were blasting their senses out to detect monsters and attract the aggressive ones. That made them easy to avoid by withdrawing the moment his senses encountered theirs; their perception was weakest at the limits of their range. He was careful, nonetheless. Not only was letting himself get sloppy a bad habit, but there was every chance an elite scout would notice him, despite his caution.

Jason's goal was the inland side of the city, the opposite end from where his ship was docked. His day spent working as an auxiliary had proven fruitful in terms of information gathering for the simple reason that if you show up, get to work and don't be a tool, people will talk to you. He had spent the day surrounded by Adventure Society and Magic Society functionaries, along with a few other auxiliaries as well. This had given Jason plenty of opportunities to learn about the situation in the camp.

Estella Warnock's job was to scout out civilian locations for the team, but she was a bad fit for a work camp at a ruined city. Instead, she had gone ahead to the team's next destination. Jason himself was much better suited to the specific circumstances, having always been good at getting along with people without the power to use or oppress him.

It took Jason very little time to fit in with the primarily low-ranked workers organising resources, logistics and food. With conditions tight, essence users were mostly getting by on spirit coins. The food Jason and his new co-workers produced was being shipped off to the surrounding areas. Jason's looting ability was useful for producing fresh meat from monster carcasses, along with other materials. His cooking magic took that fresh meat and turned it into preserved meat.

There were already resources on site that allowed Jason to get a lot of work done quickly, with smokehouses and salting sheds designed for use with cooking magic that massively accelerated the process. While Jason's mastery of such magic came from skill books and was fairly basic, it was perfect for the setup in place. The learning curve was low, and by the time he was pumping out preserved meats, the people around him had gotten chatty. The bulk of what Jason learned wasn't wildly useful to the team, although it would help them. Knowing who to go to and who to avoid in camp leadership was always valuable.

The most important information was not about the base camp but the city the camp was set up to manage. One of the tribulations that had brought the city low was the wide-scale destruction following a local astral space getting torn off the side of reality. Such devastating events had been the end-goal of the Builder; when a cell of cultists managed to accomplish this task, they usually evacuated their bases in the area.

Usually, cult evacuations would be carried out quickly and quietly, as the local adventurers were generally on the warpath by that stage. As a result, there were frequently Builder cult lairs hidden in the area that contained large and dangerous construct creatures that the cult had been forced to abandon.

From what Jason picked up, there was likely an undiscovered Builder base somewhere beyond the city's inland border. Late in the night, Jason had moved to investigate in secret, to preserve his secret identity. Jason Asano was not meant to be on Pallimustus anymore, and a cook shouldn't be able to find what teams of adventurers had not.

After reaching what should be the right general area, Jason directed his senses down, careful not to let his aura spread in any other direction. Aside from his superior aura strength fuelling his senses, Jason was also sensitive to Builder-related energy. Since losing the Builder's magic door, he could no longer manipulate that energy. His ability to sense the touch of the Builder, however, predated Jason's acquisition of the door by some time. He had been sensitive to it ever since the Builder tried to steal his soul with a star seed.

Jason turned himself into a magical ground-penetrating radar as he swept the area. He moved from the outer city into what had once been farmland, but was now a mix of withered crop remnants and bare soil. The land bore the marks of the destructive shockwave that had swept over it in the wake of the astral space being removed. The force had pushed everything out and away from the epicentre in a violent blast that had thrown boulders, flattened portions of the city and uprooted trees. And this was just the shockwave area, not the blast zone.

The dimensional scar was something that Jason could sense clearly. Even more intimate than his sensitivity to the Builder was his perception of dimensional forces. The closer he drew to the former site of the astral space aperture, the more he was horrified by the gaping wound in reality left behind.

"This has left a scar on the side of reality," Jason said. "It's already starting to warp the ambient magic seeping through the dimensional membrane. I don't think this city will be liveable for a long time."

"It will have to be rebuilt from the ground up." Shade agreed. "There is almost nothing left to repair."

Magic came into the world through the dimensional membrane that separated their physical reality from the astral. A monster surge was the result of temporary damage to that membrane, but the damage always—eventually—recovered itself. That had already happened, ending the monster surge, but to Jason's perception, an ugly scar had been left behind.

"This is going to impact the magic in this area for some time," Jason judged.

"You believe the effect will linger?" Shade asked him.

"Without intervention, yes," Jason said soberly. "It's going to affect the monsters here, I suspect, and the people using magic too. It'll be slow, over time, like a taint in the groundwater that slowly accumulates toxins in the people using the land."

Jason had a unique insight into this. His connection to dimensional forces allowed him to recognise the wound in a way that others did not, and his increasing proficiency in astral magic allowed him to at least partially understand it.

"Will you warn the locals?" Shade asked. "They may not recognise the danger."

"There are Magic Society representatives here," Jason said. "They likely know what's happened and what to look for. But I'll have Clive double-check with them."

Clive was not on good terms with the Magic Society, but he was an astral magic specialist whose expertise exceeded Jason's, despite Jason's insights into dimensional forces and being tutored by Dawn herself. Jason was already sharing his unique insights with Clive and seeing Clive make leaps that Jason himself never realised. Without his advantages, Jason wouldn't be close to Clive's level in astral magic studies.

Jason pushed his senses as far as he was willing to risk, but one hour turned into two and then three without results. The sky was starting to lighten when he finally felt a twinge. There was something below him that prevented him from getting a proper sense of what it was due to some magical screening. Only the strength of his perception and sensitivity to the Builder allowed him to detect anything at all.

"Good," said Amos, whose sudden presence behind him startled Jason. Very few people could get that close to him undetected.

"What are you doing here?" Jason asked. "You liked how I managed to find the place, did you?"

"No," Amos said. "It's good that you have so thoroughly demonstrated your shortcomings. There will be new exercises, once you've rested."

With that, Amos walked away.

"You know," Jason said after watching Amos leave. "He could have at least helped us find the entrance. Shade, spread out and take a look, if you please."

Shade bodies spilled out of Jason's shadow to search the area. The fact that the lair hadn't been found yet by someone else suggested that the entrance had been permanently collapsed. Only with a narrow area to search was it worth grid searching, even with Shade's cohort of bodies. In the end, the opening was under a cluster of heavy rocks that looked like they had been piled up by the shockwave. Instead, they had been placed to obscure a shaft that had been deliberately caved in.

While he knew the right move was to bring in the team, Jason felt a temptation to act on his own. He wanted to send Shade down so he could shadow jump into the base, keeping all of the Builder constructs to himself. He could take his time, buried and hidden under the earth. Pull each construct apart with his own two hands, stripping them down to parts, one by one. Grinding every last trace of the Builder's power out of them.

"Mr Asano," Shade said. "I remind you that it is a time for discretion, not rage."

Jason hadn't noticed the aura pulsing out of him or the growing luminescence of his alien eyes as he stared at the ground, fists balled at his sides. He drew back his aura, frowning in self-admonition at the loss of control. He concentrated his senses and felt one of the patrol teams moving in his direction.

"Time to go," he said.

"Might I suggest, Mr Asano, that you seek out Mrs Remore tomorrow, in addition to Lord Pensinata?"

"Yeah," Jason said. The ferocity that clouded his mind had passed. "I'm starting to think that I might have some unresolved issues."

"I may have noticed something of the kind myself, Mr Asano."

The patrol team reached the location where they had sensed the strange aura. The archer, the swordswoman and the guardian specialist watched the darkness around them while their scout hunted for the aura. She pushed out her senses, looking for any trace. Their Adventure Society guide also kept an eye on their surroundings.

"I'm not sensing anything," the scout said. "It's like it flared up and then vanished."

"What was it?" the team ritualist asked as he examined the ground around them. "I've never felt a monster like that, but it didn't feel like a person either."

"A priest, maybe," the guardian said as he watched the moonlit terrain. The relatively bright night and flattened terrain made watching for trouble an easier task than it might have been. "They sometimes use divine power that feels strange."

"That makes sense," the guide said. "I saw a priest of Wrath in combat once, and he felt kind of like what we sensed. Rage, authority and otherworldly power."

"There's something here," the ritualist said, crouched over a patch of ground. He pointed out the rocks scattered around. "These rocks were moved, and not long ago. I think they were piled over this."

The guardian and one of the damage dealers stayed on watch while the others gathered around.

"Some kind of filled-in tunnel," the scout said. "You don't think…?"

"The Builder cult lair," the ritualist said. "I think whatever that aura belonged to was looking for this, sensed us coming and made itself scarce."

"Good," the guardian said. "I've never felt a silver-rank aura that strong."

"It's probably just some ability to scare off other monsters," the swordswoman said. "Some kind of aura flare, more performance than power."

"More scared of us than we are of it," the archer suggested.

"I'm not so sure," the scout said. "That aura didn't feel scared."

"Wouldn't that be the whole point?" the swordswoman asked. "What kind of power to scare people off would let you know it was the scared one?"

"She's got you there," the guardian said.

"I don't think assuming it's afraid is the right move," the scout said. "What if the idea is to make us think that it's gone so it can stalk and ambush us?"

"Well, isn't that a cheerful thought," the ritualist said.

"We should go," the guide said. "We'll report this in, get someone watching the site and see if it really is the cult lair once the sun comes up."

"Shouldn't we check it now?" the archer asked.

"It's been here for a good long while now," the ritualist said. "I don't think we have to worry about constructs spilling out unless we start digging down. If we hadn't come along, whatever we sensed might have and set off gods know what trouble."

"I'm worried about what that thing was," the scout said. "It's still out there somewhere."

33

ASSET

HAVING RETURNED IN THE PRE-DAWN, JASON EMERGED FROM HIS CABIN WHEN IT was almost time for lunch.

"Oh, thank the gods you've come out," Neil said, rushing up to him.

Jason narrowed his eyes, about to probe his aura to confirm his identity as Neil continued.

"Clive made… I suppose we have to call it breakfast," Neil lamented. "Taika threw him into the river."

"Taika's only bronze rank," Jason said with a laugh.

"He's strong," Neil said. "The monster surge got him pretty close to silver. He also had the element of surprise, and Clive was very surprised."

"We probably shouldn't be wasting food when people are putting in so much effort to feed people in this region."

Jason remembered the food rationing on Earth during the monster waves when refugees were crammed into the largest urban centres for safety. Food production and distribution had broken down as even the smaller cities were abandoned due to a lack of people to protect them, let alone rural areas. Jason went for almost two years without eating anything but spirit coins.

"It was fairly basic in the first place," Neil said. "Just cereal and bread."

"He messed up cereal and bread?"

"It turns out that all Clive knows how to cook is eel," Neil explained. "I can assure you that adapting those recipes to a simple breakfast does not work."

Jason winced. He could sense Taika in the yacht, his aura strong and steady. The proto-spaces and then monster waves on Earth, plus Farrah's training, had allowed him to rocket through the ranks, especially with being human as an accelerating factor. Between that and the monster surge after switching worlds, Taika had rarely seen the less hectic conditions that most adventurers faced. His progress was faster than Jason's, whose lower rank progress was met with lengthy delays.

Taika's human abilities had been replaced with outworlder ones, but Jason had never sat down and taken a good look. He'd shared his party interface and let Rufus and Farrah manage his training and advancement, as they were both better teachers than Jason. Taika's power set was very much in line with Humphrey's, from his role as a high-mobility brawler to his mix of powerful and varied attack and defence options. They even shared the might and wing essences leading to a confluence based on a mythical creature.

In Taika's case, it was garuda rather than Humphrey's dragon confluence, which made Jason wonder. Was the garuda a real creature in Pallimustus? If so, which of the various myths, legends and RPG flying monsters was it closest to?

"Neil," Jason asked. "You ever heard of a garuda?"

"Sure," Neil said. "Big flying creatures. Lots of variants, like griffins and dragons, spread across the ranks. They aren't *real* garudas, though, the way drakes aren't real dragons. The proper garudas are a big deal. Most of the lesser variants fall in the silver-gold range, I'm pretty sure, but I've never seen one. Never been to the right part of the world. I think Pranay might have them."

Pranay was a city that Jason and his team had visited after their first trip to the Order of the Reaper's astral space. They hadn't left the massive urban centre, so the only magical beasts they had seen were familiars.

"You're thinking about Taika's abilities?" Neil asked.

"Yeah. I've never really seen him in the field since he was iron rank."

"He's got some impressive powers. Similar to Humphrey, but he's a better initiator where Humphrey has the edge as a sustained attacker. You know, with another fast and tough frontliner, and if we brought in Rufus, we'd have a monster of a team, here."

"Isn't it hard to train up in a team of eight? Don't you need to take on larger-scale contracts, which means expeditions, which means other teams which means more restrictions?"

"It doesn't have to be like that. Our team is built around different synergies. Remember when Humphrey's sister was training us? We took that road contract and she kept pushing us into different small group combinations."

"It's an interesting idea," Jason mused. "Mixing things up is always good as a training exercise. You know that Rufus and Taika are only with us temporarily, though. Rufus will go off to Greenstone, eventually, and Taika might end up with the other Earth people. I'm going to need someone to wrangle the pricks."

"What makes you think they're pricks?"

"They're from Earth."

"Not a lot of love for your own world, then."

"My old world. This is my world now."

"Well, we're glad to have you," Neil said, slapping Jason on the back. "So long as you make lunch. We need to go on afternoon patrol soon, and Belinda said that Clive was eyeing off the bread again."

"Oh crap," Jason said. "I'd best get on it, then."

The base camp for Adventure Society and Magic Society activity in the area was laid out carefully into sections, somewhere between a school campus and a military base, but all the buildings were magical tents. The tents were reinforced against the weather and included drainage, plumbing and other amenities. Many were the size of full buildings, with a few even reaching as high as four storeys. For the most part, they were all square or oblong, the rigid frames visible under the drape of the fabric.

Jason's team moved across the open marshalling area, although Jason's place in the group was taken by Rufus and Farrah. Leading them was Vestine, their assigned Adventure Society functionary. They moved towards a tent the size of a small aircraft hangar. It was the main vehicle pool for the camp, managed by the Magic Society but primarily used by the Adventure Society.

The marshalling area was a mix of adventuring teams and groups from the two societies in charge of the camp. Some were coming and going on foot, while others were using skimmers, making the yard's massive size a necessity to handle all the activity.

"This afternoon, we're heading for the other side of the city," Vestine told them as they approached. "The far side of the city is the most dangerous zone in the area. It's where the diamond-rank monster fell, making it the most concentrated source of the lingering power that's drawing in the monsters. We haven't had a gold show up yet, but we've seen silvers come in very large waves, so be ready to fall back and regroup with other teams at all times."

"Yesterday, you told us we wouldn't be assigned to the far side of the city," Sophie pointed out.

"The situation changed overnight," Vestine told them. "A Builder cult lair was found and multiple teams that normally patrol the far side of the city are currently engaging in a suppression action against lingering Builder constructs. We had to dig our way down using rituals to access the lair, as the access shaft had been completely sealed. There were so many rocks in there, it wasn't worth clearing them out, and so we dug straight through the earth."

"I remember that ritual," Humphrey said. "You could have warned me it was going to spray mud everywhere, Clive."

"It was a digging ritual in a swamp," Clive said. "Do you want me to warn you that dumplings are available in a dumpling shop?"

Humphrey shook his head.

"We were aware of the cult lair," he told Vestine.

"Word gets around a camp like this very quickly," Vestine said, her tone disapproving. "On a related note, be aware that there is an unknown, potentially hostile entity in the area, but we have little information on it. We can't even be sure if it's a monster, magical beast or essence user. It's potentially a priest from one of the dark gods, so be wary. Its aura is very distinctive, being silver rank, extremely powerful and extremely sinister."

"I don't suppose this entity happened to be found where the cult lair turned out to be?" Belinda asked.

Vestine stopped walking across the marshalling yard and turned to look at Belinda.

"Do you know something you should be reporting?"

"I've never known anything I should be reporting," Belinda said. "That's how they get you."

"Your patrol sensed a particular asset to which our team has access," Humphrey said. "It reported finding a Builder lair, but it left when it sensed a patrol approaching. Since the patrol found the lair, we didn't report the discovery ourselves."

"You're claiming this asset found the lair. Are you trying to claim credit?"

"We don't care about credit," Humphrey said. "I'm only telling you this so you don't have the patrol teams jumping at shadows."

"And what is this asset of yours? Why is it a secret?"

"It's not a secret, strictly speaking," Humphrey told her. "Our team has access to a certain special asset that people often find confronting, sinister or outright evil. It's not. But this asset is known to the Adventure Society, and the branch in Rimaros decided to keep our asset mostly off the books. If anyone were to go digging, contact the Adventure Society branch and ignore their polite suggestions that you leave it alone, you'll find the answers you're looking for. You can check all this for yourself, of course. I noticed the temporary water-link chamber that's been set up for communication, although I know those devices are extremely resource-intensive. You likely only use it when strictly necessary, which means that you can either take my word for it or not."

"The water link we have is expensive to operate," Vestine acknowledged. "We only use it when truly necessary. Lacking ready access to the Adventure Society administration in Rimaros, the best solution is that you brief me and I determine how much needs to be shared with the officials here."

"No," Humphrey said.

"And if I march a few teams onto that boat of yours to find out for myself?"

"Then that would be unfortunate," Humphrey said. "It's always sad when bad things happen to good people."

"Are you threatening me, Mr Geller?"

"No, Miss Calhoun, I am not. Imagine a mysterious pit of monsters. Imagine that anyone who manages to jump in the pit and survive will be punished by the Adventure Society, in the unlikely event of their survival. It is not a threat to warn someone of the dangers of the pit, Miss Calhoun. It is well-meaning advice that, I will admit, could easily be misconstrued as an attempt to intimidate an Adventure Society official. But I will remind you, Miss Calhoun, that all the information concerning you about this situation came from a single source: me. I could have said nothing, but I did you the courtesy of warning you in the hope that you would not waste any time and resources."

Vestine looked at Humphrey for a long time.

"Wait here," she said finally. "I'm going to consult with the chief official of the camp."

The team watched her turn and march off.

"How big a problem will this be?" Neil wondered aloud.

"Not very," Rufus said. "The Adventure Society has many secrets. She's going to ask someone in camp leadership what to do, and she'll be told to be quiet and go along. If there's no imminent threat, then anyone smart enough to be left running this place with minimal oversight knows better than to buy trouble they could avoid for free."

"And if she decides to push?" Clive asked.

"Then they'll use the water-link, regardless of the cost," Farrah said. "At which point, they will be sternly instructed to abandon their line of inquiry. They'll assume Geller family interference and leave us alone."

"And you're okay letting people think your family is engaged in corruption?" Clive asked Humphrey.

"With politics," Rufus said, "you need a little corruption. Just a little, or no one else will trust you."

"Well, that's just backwards," Clive said. "I'm really starting to detest politics."

"There are upsides," Sophie said, bumping her hip against Humphrey. "I like it when you go all officious and stern." Her voice then turned to a low whisper. "You want to get out of here?"

"No!" Humphrey said, stepping away from her. "This is not the time. Or the place. Or the circumstance."

Sophie's expression turned vulnerable and hurt.

"So," she said, her voice a trembling whisper, "you don't really like me?"

"What?" Humphrey asked, taken aback. "Of course I do."

"It doesn't sound like you do."

"It's not that! I just…"

The tension in his bunched-up shoulders relaxed as he gave her a flat, admonishing look.

"…realised that you're teasing me. Do we have to have the talk about professionalism again? There is a professional space and a personal space, and you shouldn't be bringing the personal space out on the job."

"There are lots of things you shouldn't do on the job," Belinda interjected. "You shouldn't steal your Adventure Society guide's watch."

"Lindy," Humphrey asked through gritted teeth, "did you just steal her watch?"

"No," Belinda said, the picture of innocence. "I didn't *just* steal her watch."

34

THE THING YOU PRACTISE WITH
THE MOST

IT WAS RAINING AGAIN AS A LAND SKIMMER MOVED OVER THE RUBBLE THAT WAS once a city. It hovered only a metre over the ground, but that was enough to float over almost every part of the city's inland reaches. A few buildings, once magically reinforced strongholds, had left remnants in the form of a partial wall or two.

"This side of the city was where the shockwave hit after the astral space was taken," Vestine said. She was driving the skimmer but had been quiet for most of the trip from the camp. Many adventurers had secrets, but when she stumbled on them, she did not like being told to back off. That she very much had been.

"That pond seems strange," Rufus said, pointing out a large body of water. "It's an odd shape, and doesn't fit with the surroundings."

They weren't going through a park that might be expected to have such a pond. Despite the city's annihilation, the original location of roads could be determined from the relative lack of rubble, and the pond crossed multiple of them.

"It's an indent left behind by the diamond-rank monster," Vestine explained as she redirected the skimmer to run along the shore. "The monster rampaged through this part of the city, but most of the damage was covered up. The shockwave turned a damaged city into a levelled one. That indentation was one of the few signs that remained, and it was filled in by the rains."

"So, this is where the monster fell?" Neil asked. "It was big enough to leave a crater that big when it died?"

"The monster didn't die here," Vestine told him. "That's a footprint."

Amos and Jason were floating just above the deck, cross-legged in meditative poses. They were on the training deck as it was raining heavily outside.

"What I am going to show you is the method of expanding your senses without your aura alerting the senses of others," Amos said in one of the longest sentences Jason had heard him speak. Amos was taciturn by nature, but Jason was learning he didn't fetishise silence, not hesitating to speak when it was called for.

"You are already familiar with retracting your aura," Amos said, "but that retracts your senses as well. You need to learn how to mask your aura's presence without withdrawing it. You have aura stealth techniques?"

"I have one I've developed," Jason said. "Partly, it's retracting my aura, but I have more subtle methods as well. One that I'm proud of lets me blend into crowds by adapting my aura to those of the people around me, and incorporating subtle aura suppression to make the perceptions of others pass over me. Basically, I can make people ignore me if there are other people around."

Amos nodded and unfolded his legs, dropping them to the floor he had been floating over.

"We'll go to the camp," Amos said. "You can show me."

While Jason was aura training, his team moved beyond the city ruins. The wall that had once held off monsters was now just a demarcation line between city and jungle, no taller than a speed bump. The jungle itself was little better off than the city, with trees uprooted and scattered like dandelion blossoms. Despite the flattened jungle, this was not the area designated the destruction zone.

They arrived at the official destruction zone, where the astral space aperture had been, it was clear why this place had earned the name. It was a crater, but not a concave in the ground. It looked more like someone had attempted to replicate the Grand Canyon with a giant cake tin, creating a circular hole that stretched kilometres across and hundreds of metres deep.

The skimmer stopped and the team disembarked, lining up along the edge of the crater. It was a neat and round hole, with a dark green, glassy surface. The rounded wall and flat floor were polished-marble smooth, but scattered with debris. Rocks, trees and massive clumps of earth lay on the floor, along with what was left of animals and magical beasts devoured by monsters. It was large enough that, in spite of the rain, the water collected inside was not deep enough to consider it flooded, but merely wet.

"That is a big hole," Neil said. "What does it count as? A canyon? A crater?"

"To think that this is only a fraction of the size it would have been outside of a monster surge," Clive said, shaking his head in wonder. "If not for the damaged dimensional membrane, this could have covered ten times the area."

"It makes me think of the astral space you stopped the Builder from taking near Greenstone," Rufus said. "If you hadn't, I'd be dead, along with everyone else in Greenstone and every desert village and delta town around it. This place shows just how great the deed you all did that day was."

"Well, it wouldn't have affected me," Farrah said. "I was already dead."

"You were dead?" Vestine asked, turning to look at her.

"For about a year," Farrah told her.

"Then how are you alive now?"

"I know a guy."

"What does that mean?"

"We know a guy who views death as less of an end than as a hobby," Farrah told her. "We're not really meant to talk about it, though."

"Like that asset of yours."

"Exactly," Farrah said. "The asset is something he left behind."

"It's horrifying to think that this has happened all over the world," Humphrey said.

"Most of the Builder cult's attempts to steal astral spaces were stopped," Vestine said. "But most isn't all. We were lucky here, in that we managed to evacuate the bulk of the population. The explosion erased a town and flattened several villages, but their people had left for fortress towns long before, thankfully. There are places where people had it much worse." She spat aggressively over the edge. "You're all moving south from Rimaros, right?"

"That's right," Sophie said.

"Did some guy really convince the Builder to leave early?"

"That's what we heard," Belinda said.

"Well, why did he take so long?" Vestine asked angrily. "We lost everything here. Our homes. Our pride. We might have saved most of the people, but we still lost many lives."

"You lived here?" Humphrey asked Vestine, who nodded.

"I wasn't just stationed here," she said. "I grew up here. It was my city. And now they're saying that they might not even rebuild it."

"I can't even begin to imagine," Humphrey said. "I won't even try. I've never been through what you have. Lost not just a home, but the home of everyone I know. Whole communities. All I can say is that I'm sorry."

Vestine turned and marched towards the skimmer.

"You've seen it now," she said bitterly. "We need to get back on patrol."

––––––

"Are you sure about this?" Jason asked Amos as they stood on the dock at the outer edge of the busy base camp. "There are a lot of silver-rankers here, and if they notice a cook wandering around under a sophisticated stealth technique, it'll draw attention that we don't want."

"Do you lack confidence in your ability?"

"No, I'm quite proud of the ability. It's probably the most intricate in execution that I have, and it was self-developed. But it's designed to help me pass unnoticed through crowds of lower-ranked people, not to fool people of my own rank. I've got it to the point that it can, if they're not paying attention, but if they are, the technique will draw attention rather than deflect it. It's not a matter of confidence; it's about the right tool for the right job."

"Good," Amos said.

"Good?"

"Your aura manipulation skills are barely adequate, but at least you understand the value in cultivating a breadth of nuanced techniques, even if you haven't, yet."

"Barely adequate?"

"The greater the potential, the greater the expectations should be to fulfil that potential."

"I think I get it," Jason said, still frowning over 'barely adequate.' "My skills are well above the silver-rank standard, but every rank scales, not just in power but the proficiency of those considered to be the best. The ones living up to their potential. You're saying that if I want to be great instead of just good once I hit gold rank, I need to push the limits of my capabilities."

"Good, instead of adequate," Amos corrected. "Master the basics before you start claiming greatness."

"Aim low, got it," Jason said. "This is why Dawn came to you specifically, isn't it? She knew you could get me ready for the future, at least in this regard."

"Yes. Now, show me your technique."

"But what if some silver-ranker pulls me up?"

"Then use the thing you practise with the most."

"What's that?"

"Your mouth."

"I can't tell if that's an insult or a compliment. Probably a bit of both, now that I think about it. Actually, examining it further, I'm increasingly impressed at the nuance you managed to incorporate into a simple statement and the way you both layered meaning and prompted a more in-depth exploration of the ramifications of your—"

Amos flicked Jason on the forehead.

"Ow!"

"Aura technique, not mouth technique."

"You just said—"

Amos flicked him again, his gold-rank reflexes too much for Jason, even though he was watching for it.

"You're training an essence user, not a dog," Jason pointed out, rubbing his forehead.

Amos responded only with a flat look.

"Fine," Jason grumbled as he set out into the camp, initiating his aura technique. "Woof bloody woof."

———

As Vestine had promised, the inland side of the city was more active in terms of monster activity. Humphrey and the others soon found themselves working alongside Korinne and her team, as well as one more group, in wiping out a massive pack of silver-rank monsters.

Arc lizards were among the weakest of silver-rank monsters, individually. Alone, they were weaker than upper-tier bronze-rank monsters, making them a popular choice when high-rankers were curating battles for their bronze-rank trainees. As such, the local adventurers all had experience fighting them in small numbers.

An arc lizard looked like a cobalt-blue iguana, with a rough, milky white crystal emerging from its back. Their only real form of attack was an arc of lightning they could shoot from the crystal, but it wasn't dangerous to a silver-ranker. Even bronze-rankers didn't have to be too worried if they were prepared and careful or had solid defensive abilities.

The problem with dealing with arc lizards was that they never manifested alone and they became exponentially more dangerous in number. Their electrical arcs could jump from one to another, growing in strength with each link in the chain, even splitting once they grew powerful enough. Too many arc lizards gathered in one place became very dangerous indeed.

Arc lizards were monsters that commonly spawned in this part of the world, and were normally a negligible threat. During a monster surge, however, they spawned in greater numbers than normal—often much greater. This meant that arc lizards went from a minor threat into a major problem, and while the monster surge was over, some monsters had appeared in wilderness areas and were still finding their way to population centres. Unlike short-lived iron-rank monsters, those of silver rank could easily last until the next surge, if not dealt with in the interim.

With multiple packs of arc lizards congregating, they posed a major threat to the three teams sent to eliminate them. The key was to strike hard, strike fast and deliver definitive damage. The earliest parts of the battle were most dangerous, with the lizards at their strongest. The healers on each team proved their mettle in the face of the prolific and powerful attacks, although the teams had gone in prepared.

Knowing what they were going to confront, their Adventure Society guides had prepared potions to resist electricity for each of the teams. Even so, the potions only went so far in the face of multitudinous powerful attacks, which overwhelmed magical shields and burnt through armour to scorch flesh. Only as their numbers reduced did the attacks of the lizards diminish in potency, making things easier after the harrowing start to the battle.

Korinne's team was the unquestionable star of the show, clearing out enemies faster than either of the other teams. Their specialisation was built around a pair of high-damage members with the rest of the team assembled around maximising their effectiveness. This made them something of a reflection of the lizards themselves as they focused all their efforts on unleashing powerful attacks. They even used the same chain lightning, with Kalif firing electric arrows that split and split, amplifying their power with each enemy struck.

"You'd think that electric arrows would be a bad choice against electric monsters," Sophie said as the teams rested in the aftermath of the battle.

"Silver rank is where power sets start to cover their own weaknesses," Farrah explained. "Take mine, for example. I have an ability called Child of Fire that helps me penetrate resistance to heat and fire, and even affect things that are immune. I'll need to be higher rank before I start burning fire elementals to death, but I'll get there."

"The same goes for me," Humphrey said. "I don't use fire as much as Farrah, but my Dragon Might aura transforms my regular fire into dragon fire, which is much more effective."

"It's the same for anything," Farrah said. "Korinne's lightning is the same, I imagine, but look at Jason: he can make a golem bleed now."

"This is part of what makes essence users stronger than those with inherent magic," Rufus said. "With so many powers, our abilities have breadth and synergy, but they also grow to cover our weaknesses. Very few of those with inherent magic can compare to a high-rank essence user. Of those that come close, it usually requires years of training and practise."

"Like the blood magic of the intelligent troll tribes," Clive said. "Even then, they're mostly working with variant ritual magic. That's hard to use practically in combat; take it from a combat ritualist."

Korinne's team were having their own discussion of the battle's context.

"I don't see what's so special about their team that we need to follow them around and learn things," Polix said. "We showed them up today."

"This isn't the fight we need to learn from them in," Korinne said. "This battle was exactly the right kind of fight for us. A simple, if powerful, enemy in a large group setting. I hope you noticed how the other teams saw that we were the cornerstone of the group and pivoted their strategies to let us work uninterrupted. They shepherded the lizards away from us so we could maintain our offence without needing to beat back counterattacks."

"That's what I'm saying," Polix said. "They are the ones who saw that we were the stronger team."

"Polix," Korinne said, "you need to listen to everything I say, not just the parts you agree with. We were strong today because it was our kind of fight. What Geller's team has is experience with things going wrong and working just as a team, instead of as part of a group expedition."

"The difference between adventuring approaches in Rimaros and Vitesse," Rosa said.

Polix groaned. "I'm sick of hearing arguments about one being better than the other," he complained. "It's obvious."

"I thought so myself," Korinne said. "I was taught that the Rimaros way is the superior option as well, but I've been discussing this with Orin's uncle since we came along on this journey. He pushed me to look past my own biases."

"You talked with Lord Amos?" Kalif asked. "Did he use words? With his mouth?"

"He's not a mute, Kalif," Korinne said. "He just doesn't believe in talking when it isn't necessary. An all-too-rare virtue."

"What did he say about the difference between adventuring in Rimaros and Vitesse?" Rosa asked.

"He told me that it's a difference in wider doctrine," Korinne explained. "The Sea of Storms and its surrounding region has massive tracts of undeveloped jungle and deep water. Vast leviathans and whole colonies of monsters can disappear for decades, often finding one another and grouping up before they ever move on a populated area. Because of this, the threats encountered in this region are massive, like this pack of arc lizards. As such, adventuring doctrine in this part of the world accommodates the nature of those threats by putting a large emphasis on multi-team expeditions. And when people work together but in multiple teams, it makes sense that each team has a speciality."

"You're saying that it's the Vitesse approach, but scaled up?" Kalif asked. "Instead of a team where the individual members do their own thing, we have expeditions where each team does its own thing."

"Precisely," Korinne said. "Vitesse is a much more developed region, which means the monster detection coverage is more comprehensive. Threats building up in the wilderness before being detected is rare, so teams are much more likely to operate independently, and there are even people that work alone. They don't have other teams to cover them while they focus on just one thing. They have to rely on themselves, which means they need the ability to adapt. Working with another team that covers their weakness isn't an option. They have to be able to cover their own, even if that comes at the cost of focus."

"I don't see the point," Polix said. "If the threat is smaller, then our teams can just kill it before it does anything tricky with our overwhelming power. No versatility required."

"And that attitude," Korinne said, "is the exact reason we need to follow them around and learn things."

35

JUST TO PROVE YOU COULD

"Nope," Gary said as Belinda approached him in the yacht's dining and barge lounge. He was sprawled back in a chair reading a book with a mug on the table beside him, steam rising from the piping hot contents. His vantage allowed him to look out as the hover yacht proceeded down the river toward its next destination.

"You don't even know what I'm going to ask," Belinda complained.

"I'm not making you another set of lock picks."

"Alright," she conceded, "you apparently do know what I was going to ask."

"Well, don't bother," Gary said, not looking away from his book. "The answer is no."

"Why not?"

"Because I know who broke them and under what circumstances."

"I can explain that."

"You tried to steal Amos Pensinata's watch," Gary told her. "The only thing you need to explain was what was going through your head that made it seem like a good idea."

"I wanted the challenge."

"And you got the challenge," Sophie said, walking in. "Then you got the consequences."

"What's this about?" Humphrey asked, having come in with Sophie.

"Lindy tried to steal Lord Pensinata's watch," Gary said.

"It was a bit of fun," Belinda complained. "And his response was disproportional. I was going to give it back, not smash it."

"How did he even end up breaking your lock picks when you were trying to take a pocket watch?" Humphrey asked.

"Most high-end magical clothes have protections against it," Lindy said.

"They aren't hard to negate, in most cases, but some clothes makers are different and know what they're doing."

"You learn to recognise the clothes of designers who cater primarily to adventurers." Sophie said. "And aristocrats who like wearing outfits from designers that cater to adventurers."

"If your target is wearing an Alejandro Albericci suit in Rimaros, or a Gilbert Bertinelli suit in Greenstone," Belinda said, "it's time to bring the tool kit."

"Shouldn't you just go for an easier mark?" Gary asked.

"Or no mark at all?" Humphrey suggested.

"Yes," Sophie said. "Lindy, this new habit of yours is going to get you in trouble."

"It already has," Jason said as he arrived with the rest of the team, plus most of the yacht's occupants. Travis, Taika, Rufus and Farrah, plus Estella and Vidal Ladiv, were all present, although Amos was not. Korinne, Carlos and Arabelle had also joined from their respective vehicles. The dining lounge occupied most of the yacht's largest deck with space enough to accommodate them all comfortably. There were enough plush seats and couches to go around, even without Jason reconfiguring the space to remove the dining and bar areas.

"What do you mean by saying it already has me in trouble?" Belinda asked Jason warily. "I don't think you're talking about having my lock picks smashed. Which he had to search me for, by the way."

"I don't control your actions off this boat," Jason told her. "That's for the team leader to do."

"Stop stealing things," Humphrey added, no amusement in his growl.

"But while you live on this boat," Jason continued, "there are rules. I don't actively monitor you all to check if you're breaking them, but Shade does."

"No one told me about the rules," Neil said.

"That's because he's making them up as he goes," Sophie said.

"I prefer to describe it as actively learning about boundaries together," Jason said. "But yes, I'm making them up as I go. And now we have our first hard rule: no one on this boat steals from anyone else on this boat."

"It was more like a game," Belinda argued.

"I have a lot of games, Lindy," Jason said. "They were left to me by a friend of mine. None of them involve involuntary and unknowing participation. Admittedly, some have roll-and-move mechanics, which is arguably worse."

"Try and stay on topic," Farrah suggested.

"Sorry, yes," Jason said. "So, Belinda, for violating the rules of the ship—"

"That I didn't know existed," Belinda cut in.

"Lindy, don't steal is always a rule," Clive said. "You can't plead ignorance on that one."

"For violating the ship rules," Jason continued, "your cabin will be set to winter climate settings for a week."

"What are winter climate settings?" Belinda asked.

"Full insulation," Jason said. "Drawing in as much heat as it can from outside and letting none of it out."

"Are you kidding?" Belinda asked. "We're cruising down a tropical jungle river in summer."

"You're silver rank; you'll be fine," Sophie told her. "Have you already forgotten some of the places we lived? The places we hid out? Are you unwilling to put up with anything but luxury anymore?"

"Extremely unwilling!"

"Also, Belinda," Jason added, "your shower will only work for four minutes a day."

"Oh, come on."

"And you can't access the ship's crystal wash supply."

"Now you're just being vindictive."

"And the furniture will all replicate plain wood."

Belinda's section of couch turned into an unpadded, straight-backed wooden bench. Sophie next to her was still on soft cloud material.

"What next?" Belinda asked. "Are you going to cut me off from food and make me eat spirit coins for a week?"

"Not yet," Jason said. "I'm reserving certain options for repeat offenders."

"You, Jason Asano, are a tyrant," Belinda said as if she wasn't already planning to hoard food just in case.

"So Dominion keeps telling me," Jason complained, shaking his head. "I hate that guy."

Vidal, their Adventure Society liaison, narrowed his eyes and asked Jason a hesitant question. "Do you talk with him enough that it comes up a lot?"

"No, but every time I see him or one of his priests, they always smugly imply that he's happy with my progress on the path to iron-fisted autocrat."

"Because you are," Belinda said.

"How about we shift the topic to our next destination?" Humphrey said. "Miss Warnock, what did you learn in the course of investigating the town?"

"That we should probably accelerate our progress and not bother with the towns and villages in this region."

"Oh?" Humphrey said. "They don't have a lot to offer us?"

"No," Estella confirmed. "More importantly, we don't have a lot to offer them. From what I learned, they are all in more or less the same state, which is too many people and not enough resources. A lot of places that would normally see minimal damage during the monster surge were wiped out entirely. Between the length and the severity of the surge, many people returned to find entire towns that were levelled to the ground. They were forced to turn around and go back to the fortress towns they had just left, or to other towns that weren't as hard-hit. Add that to the refugees from Cartise who fled the city before its destruction and every place still standing is overflowing with people."

"They'll need protection from monsters, though, right?" Taika asked.

"One thing they aren't short of is adventurers," Rufus said. He, Gary and Farrah had accompanied Estella in her forward scouting. "Cartise had a lot of adventurers who are now protecting the fortress towns."

"I think we all saw the same was true, even at Cartise," Humphrey said. "The Adventure Society had supplied no shortage of adventurers, so while they were happy to use us, they weren't desperate for our services. I think they were more appreciative of Jason and Vidal's efforts, frankly."

While Jason was playing butcher and/or cook, Vidal had lent his administrative expertise to the logistical efforts of distributing food and resources through the region.

"Circumstances are similar throughout this region, based on everything I've heard," Estella said. "What these places need is more of what Jason and Mr Ladiv were doing; people who can help with resources and logistics, not combat specialists."

"We do have some of that, between us," Humphrey said. "Maybe not enough to be worth the trouble, though. We'd get in the way as much as help."

"Stella is right," Farrah said. "The things we can do, those people don't need. We should just hit the road and stay there until we find people who do need a boatload of adventurers."

"It would be nice to get far enough from Rimaros that I don't have to be so careful," Jason said. "Even with what little I've done here, it wouldn't take that much poking around to put the pieces together. The biggest advantage is that no one cares that much."

"The people here just want things to get sorted out with as little extra trouble as possible," Humphrey said.

"I do have one cunning plan, should I get caught out and need to convince someone I'm not me," Jason said.

"I may regret asking this," Neil said, "but—"

"Then don't ask," Humphrey told him. "Please don't ask."

"Okay, now you have to ask," Gary said.

"I hate this so much," Humphrey grumbled, leaning forward and looking at the floor as he shook his head.

"Jason," Neil said, "what exactly is this cunning plan of yours?"

"I can just tell people I'm my own evil twin."

"What?" Rufus asked, voicing a confusion that was reflected on the group's faces. Another Jason came in, this one with a moustache. He stood next to the original Jason, who took out a bushy fake moustache and affixed it to his top lip. Then both Jasons flung out their arms like they'd just finished a performance and were waiting for applause.

"I don't get it," Carlos said. "This is your shape-shifting familiar, is it not, Master Geller? Is your familiar meant to be evil?"

"He didn't mean literally an evil twin," Travis said. "It's a story trope from our world that probably should have been explained for context."

"Oh, he did a Jason," Clive said. "I'm with you now."

"What do you mean, 'a Jason?'" Jason asked.

"A Jason," Neil explained, "is where someone says some nonsense with no expectation that anyone will understand it because the people they're talking to lack the cultural context to be able to. It's oratorial masturbation."

"Masturbation is kind of my th—"

Jason put a hand over Stash's mouth to muffle it, then handed him a biscuit.

Stash turned into a moustachioed African swallow and carried it off, flying out a window that turned to mist briefly as he passed through.

"Look what you did," Jason scolded Neil. "Stash is a pure and precious boy, and you've tainted his mind with filth."

"Lady Pescos," Humphrey said quietly to Korinne, leaning closer to his fellow team leader. "Is your team, by any chance, accepting applications to join?"

"Is this how your team operates?" Korinne asked him.

"Yeah, pretty much," Neil said.

"I'd call it a standard team meeting," Clive agreed.

"How do you get anything done?" Korinne asked.

"Dashing heroics?" Jason suggested.

"How about we put aside Jason and any idea he's ever had for a moment," Humphrey said, "and return to our actual agenda of determining our next move. Miss Warnock, you've pointed out what we should avoid, but do you have any suggestion for what we should do?"

"Actually, yes," Estella said. "I talked with a few Adventure Society officials and it seems that while their resources are understandably being deployed to the regions worst affected by the monster surge, it's left a minor shortfall of adventurers in areas where the damage was less severe. These areas still need to deal with the monsters left from the surge, though, so the arrival of some temporary assistance would be very welcome."

"You're suggesting we skip over the areas in this region swiftly and head straight for lesser-affected ones?" Humphrey asked.

"It's not out of our way," Estella said. "It just means going past a few towns instead of stopping."

"They aren't great places to resupply anyway," Rufus said. "These towns won't have anything to spare unless we start bribing people, and then we're just hurting those who would have gotten what we take."

"Not only does this plan avoid the chaotic and overpopulated messes that all the local towns are reported to be," Estella said, "but we'll find locations where your team will be a welcome arrival."

"I like it," Jason said. "Let's plot out some new destinations and I'll give them to Shade."

"Jason."

"Yes, Humphrey?"

"Take off the fake moustache."

"Belinda," Humphrey said, catching her alone on the side deck outside her now-stifling cabin. He put up a privacy screen so no one would overhear. He joined her in leaning against the railing, looking out over the river. There was still plenty of other traffic, moving supplies between the hard-hit towns.

"Is this the part where you give me the serious talk about not stealing things?" Belinda asked wearily. "Instead of Jason turning it into a comedy show?"

"Yeah," Humphrey said. "This is that part. He always gets to be the fun one."

"I suppose you have a speech about how this is hurting me more than the team?"

"No, it's definitely going to hurt the team more," Humphrey said. "I get that you're revelling in a freedom that you never thought you would have before becoming an adventurer. But when you and Sophie agreed to join us, that came with a caveat. Namely, that the consequences of your actions now fall on all of us, not just yourself."

"I don't think Sophie ever really wanted to be like me," Belinda said. "She always stood out. I mean, she always looked like she does, but she was far from the only beautiful girl on those streets. It was her attitude that drove creeps like Cole Silva and Lucian Lamprey to obsess over her. She's always had this... nobility to her, even under all the crime and the violence. They wanted to tame her, like a prize animal. Crush that defiance out of her, to prove they could."

Humphrey bowed his head, saying nothing.

"I think she was always meant for someone like you," Belinda continued. "I have a hard time thinking of anyone else good enough to deserve her. Which you don't, by the way. You're just the best we could find."

Humphrey turned to look at Belinda with narrowed eyes.

"Lindy, are you—"

"It doesn't matter what I am," she said, cutting him off. "Things are the way they are."

Humphrey let out a sigh and they stood together, watching the water go by for a long time.

"You've got more speech," Belinda said finally. "I know you do."

Humphrey nodded.

"You've been stealing things, just to prove you could," he said, Belinda flinching as her own words were used against her. "If you keep doing things like this, it's going to hurt our reputations and get us all demoted. I won't let that happen. But even if I managed to remove you from the team, that would irrevocably break it. We both know that Sophie will leave with you instead of staying with me, even if she disagrees with what you've been doing."

"It's not that bad."

"Not yet," Humphrey said softly. "But if you keep putting fissures in this team, they will widen until one day it breaks. Clive would go with Jason, to whatever his next descent into dimensional absurdity is. I would too. We might be able to rope in Rufus and Farrah. We'd need to find a new healer. Neil has had his team break apart on him before, and I suspect that if it happens a second time, he'll give up on adventuring. A good silver-rank healer will have plenty of opportunities, especially with the Church of the Healer backing him."

"Damn," Belinda said. "Stop talking about the team falling apart like it's a set deal."

"I'm not worried about the team falling apart. I'm worried about it breaking apart. I'm the team leader, Lindy. That means more than just failing to keep Jason on-topic in group discussions. It means that I have to look to the future, to the dangers that we can't fight off with swords and magic. Your behaviour threatens to become the most existential danger to our team. Maybe not now, but somewhere down the line."

"You're overstating it."

"Am I? What happens when you play the wrong game at the wrong time on the wrong person? The team gets blowback at a time when we need to be discreet, or what passes for it on this team. What happens when we let what you're doing slide and the thrill isn't there anymore? Are you going to escalate? Bigger jobs, more challenging targets? You could get all our society memberships revoked."

"They are never going to pull your or Jason's memberships."

Humphrey's hand came down on the railing hard enough that it broke, turning into mist before reforming back into its original shape.

"Belinda, listen to yourself. You're talking about the Adventure Society refusing to revoke a third of the team's memberships. Is that what you want it to come to?"

"Hey, you brought all this up. And what about Jason? He's been doing insane stuff since forever."

"Jason and I had discussions like this when we first met and neither of us knew how flimsy our principles were before the winds of practical reality. But since we formed this team, Jason has always kept the team in mind. Yes, he might have some wild ideas, but he's learned to pull back when we tell him he needs to. He trusts us for that, and that's all I'm asking for here, Belinda. Trust us."

"I don't know what you expect me to say," Belinda said. "Am I meant to break down and admit my mistakes in the face of your wisdom? That's not how it works."

"I know," Humphrey said. "I just need you to think about things. About your team and what you want your place in it to be. Maybe talk to Arabelle. She knows how to listen without having any personal stake in our team."

Belinda gave Humphrey a side glance before returning her eyes to the river.

"I'll think about it," she said.

36

A MATTER OF WHAT YOU WANT

THE CONVOY LEFT THE RIVER, PASSING BY SEVERAL TOWNS ON THEIR WAY TO THE coast. From there, they followed the coast roads for the most part, but they increasingly needed to find alternatives. Compared to the excellent road network maintained by the Storm Kingdom, these were not as wide or well-maintained as those to the north. Sometimes, the hefty hover yacht needed to float over the rain-forest canopy. Other times, they would ride along the beach, skim over a bay or take to the water, running under a shoreline of cliffs.

Jason found the variety to be welcome. Their progress was not fast, but if they needed that, they could have simply flown. Jason enjoyed the days of travel as the team interspersed training with the simple joys of luxury travel. They spent large amounts of time on the roof deck for both, especially as they left the monsoon rains behind in their continuing journey south. Jungle and rainforest continued to dominate the terrain, but they escaped the worst of the oppressive humidity.

Delays were made for day trips. If they spotted an interesting mountain, they would often pause to climb it. They explored town markets and misty gorges; even the urbanite Belinda, sullen from her punishment, was unable to keep from enjoying herself. Only Korinne managed to maintain a frown on the leisurely expeditions, muttering 'traitors' and 'mutiny.' The rest of her team were utterly won over by the relaxed approach of Team Biscuit.

Towns and villages started welcoming their arrival. Less resource-starved, their main issue was keeping up with remnant surge monsters wandering out of the wilderness. The overworked local adventurers were grateful for the relief that two elite teams brought. After several welcome receptions, Jason and Humphrey were up on the roof deck, watching the latest town seem to shrink as the convoy pulled away.

"We're doing alright," Humphrey said, "but the extra monsters from the surge are starting to thin out. We're running into the reason most adventurers find their advancement slowing down after reaching silver. It's harder to find regular challenges, which makes other interests all the more enticing."

The teams led by Humphrey and Korinne were having no trouble with the monster packs they encountered, as both teams were elite. Only the most powerful of silver-rank monsters posed any real threat, so both groups had started using only parts of their rosters for individual encounters.

"You want to change things up?" Jason asked. He too felt the urge to push his abilities forward, and not just because Dawn had told him to. His advancement had been stagnant since long before his return from Earth, and the monster surge had only done so much to help. He'd spent large portions of it in recovery.

Jason was conflicted, however, as he was quite enjoying their current pace. Travelling around in luxury, helping people who very much needed it. It was the adventuring life Rufus had promised him all the way back in Greenstone, and it didn't disappoint. Humphrey was fully aware of those feelings on Jason's part, making him hesitant to suggest a change.

"I don't want to push you," Humphrey said. "But I think we both know what we need to do to find a greater challenge. I know you've been looking forward to this travelling for a long time, though, and I'm not looking to get you caught up in larger messes all over again."

"I appreciate that," Jason said, "but I'm also past ready to push my powers to new heights. These contracts for silver-rank monsters aren't enough. Only a few of them have posed any real challenge at all; not enough to go around if we want the team to grow stronger, let alone the other team. But we aren't ready to go hunting gold-rank monsters either. Not unless it's a matchup in our favour, and the Adventure Society won't let a group of silver-rankers pick and choose gold-rank contracts."

They were both aware they could likely finagle special treatment by leveraging the Geller name and Jason's unusual status with the Adventure Society, but neither man suggested it. They both wanted to move away from politics and do some good, honest adventuring work.

"You know that even if we try and act like any other adventuring team, it probably won't work out that way," Humphrey said. "It never does with you. Once we start taking contracts related to the messengers, this may well escalate."

"If it does, it does," Jason said. "We were always going to have to go after the messengers, sooner or later. Sooner, really; I need to get something from them. Now that the surge is over, I have a job to do, and it's become more complicated now that I don't have the magic tools from the Builder and the World-Phoenix. I need the advanced astral magic from the messengers to finish building the bridge between worlds."

"Clive will be happy," Humphrey said. "I'm bringing it up now because there's something in Estella's latest report. She just got back this morning."

Estella was taking her job seriously. She spent a lot of time away from the convoy, roaming ahead to investigate their upcoming destinations. She spied potential threats, scouted potential opportunities and gave an overall assessment of the value of any given stop. Estella delivered an initial report to Humphrey and Korinne before making a broader presentation to the full teams.

"Messenger activity?"

"Reports of," Humphrey said. "Maybe two days out of our way, at our current sedate pace. A little way inland, in a magic zone at the high silver level. Even discounting the messengers, we should get stronger silver-rank monsters there. The occasional gold, although I wouldn't expect us to scoop those contracts up. The locals will get priority there."

"What kinds of activity?"

"Estella didn't get much, since she was working with third-hand information. There's a small holy army in the area, though. Goddess of Knowledge."

"Worth finding out more, at the very least," Jason said. "How about I notify the teams for Estella's briefing, and we can discuss taking the detour?"

"Very well," Humphrey agreed. "Let's go hunt some messengers."

Following Estella's presentation, Korinne's team returned to their vehicle while Humphrey's went off to pursue their own activities, elsewhere in the yacht. Korinne remained behind in the briefing room to talk with Humphrey.

"Do you object to a course that brings us into conflict with the messengers?" Humphrey asked.

"No. Given the choice, I'm confident that we would make the same one you have. My only issue is that we weren't given the choice. The thing I like the least in this arrangement is that our team lacks self-determination. We are stuck following you around."

"I understand," Humphrey told her. "But while I'm willing to hear you out on any issue, I won't surrender any amount of authority to you and your team. You are, ultimately, passengers. Passengers we will accommodate as we can, but decline when we can't."

"Or won't."

"Or won't," Humphrey conceded.

Farrah found the white archway leading to Jason's soul space on the yacht's bridge, beside the door connecting the bridge to Jason's cabin. She stepped through and felt Jason's aura wash over her. It did the same on the yacht, but here, it didn't feel like an external force. It was more part of the fabric of the world around her, as inherent as the gravity holding her to the ground. The archway deposited her in an open square, amidst estate buildings centred on a towering pagoda.

"You've been spending a lot of time in here lately," she said, despite being alone.

"Just when I'm doing my meditation training," Jason said, suddenly standing next to her. "When I'm not doing specific exercises because of Amos anyway. I'm still coming to grips with this place and what I can do with it, and I'm chasing something specific, at the moment."

"Oh?"

He gestured, she nodded, and they started walking. They left the square and entered the sprawling gardens of Jason's soul space.

"I've barely touched on what the astral throne and the astral gate are capable of," he told her. "I need more power before I can truly tap into them, especially the astral gate."

"Didn't Dawn tell you to leave the astral gate alone for now?"

"And I have been. Mostly. I'm concentrating on the astral throne, for the moment. I've come to realise that I'm going to need time as much as I need power. There is so much to learn about the nature of these items and what I can do with them."

"Do they affect anything outside of this soul space?"

"Yes," Jason said. "My spirit domains—the regions on Earth and anything I make with the cloud yacht—are directly affected by not just my power here, but also my understanding. The domains on Earth I manipulated subconsciously. I was able to actively change things, but that was all surface-level alterations."

"I'm not sure what you mean."

"It means I could change a house, not the laws of thermodynamics."

"Is that an option?"

"I think so. Eventually. When I meditate here, it's like this whole place is meditating, because it is."

"Because it's you."

"Exactly. But this place is its own physical reality. Kind of. When I meditate here, my senses expand in a way that reflects that."

"Meaning?"

"That I'm starting to understand physical reality on an intrinsic level. I only recognised it because of all the time I spent in the space opened by the Builder's door. It was an introduction to how the building blocks of reality work, and I can feel that, sometimes, when I'm meditating here. I don't know if that's because I used the authority that used to be in the door, and affected this place, but the astral throne is definitely part of it. It's designed to govern physical reality, after all, compared to the astral gate, which governs dimensional forces."

"It's not a wild surprise that you can sense the space you accessed with the Builder's door, is it?" Farrah asked. "You obtained the astral throne when the door broke down, right?"

"Yeah."

"Do you think you'll be able to access that underlying physical realm again at some point?"

"Not out in the world, no. I can glimpse it, but it's not mine to change anymore. I can feel that. What I'm looking for now is a more conscious ability to change things on that level here. Right now, I have control, but lack understanding. If you think of this place like a car, I know how to drive a car. I need to learn how to build one."

"And how are the results so far?"

"Preliminary. Not enough to make me confident of successfully helping Carlos or Sophie's mother. I'd say the biggest change is in my ability to control constructs from the cloud flask. They respond to me by design, and that control has become immensely more refined. I deepened the soul bond with my cloud flask, infused it with authority and turned the material it produces into extensions of my spirit domains. The flask has undergone a fundamental change, in more ways than is readily apparent."

"Oh?"

"Let me change the subject for a moment before I come back to it," Jason said. "While I have been focusing on the astral throne, the astral gate has brought some surprises of its own."

"I thought you weren't meant to be messing with that yet. Dawn told you to leave it alone."

"Dawn's guidance is valuable, but she's not an astral king. There are some roads she can't guide me down, but it doesn't mean I shouldn't walk them. That being said, I haven't been fiddling around with the astral gate. It's just that its power has allowed me to notice something. Bonds."

"Bonds?"

"Magical bonds. I can feel the bonds between myself and my bonded items now. I feel the bonds spanning off into the astral that connect me to my spirit domains on Earth, even if I'm too weak to feel the other end. But these are deliberate bonds. They're strong, firm and don't disconnect. I've noticed other bonds as well, that I suspect have formed incidentally."

"Such as?"

"Such as between you and me. Farrah, you and I formed a special bond."

"I don't care how powerful you are here," Farrah told him. "I'm not going to sleep with you."

"What? No. I wasn't talking about that. I'd sleep with Humphrey before you."

"It did always seem like there was something there," Farrah said.

"I know, right?" Jason asked. "He's the upright, uptown boy, and I'm the sassy girl who restores classic cars. He gets talked into borrowing a car from his dad's collection without asking by one of his gadabout friends and gets in a fender-bender. I agree to fix it without his dad finding out."

"You've put a lot of thought into this."

"No."

"What's the title of this little story you've got going on?"

"It doesn't have a title. This isn't something I think about."

Farrah gave him a flat look.

"Humphrey's Big Engine," he mumbled sheepishly.

Farrah burst out laughing and Jason joined her. The path they were on led into a cave, running alongside an underground river. Their way was lit by luminescent fungus and flowers, growing out of crevices or on creeper vines.

"I think the bond between us is a remnant of when you came back to life," he explained. "The Reaper somehow bound your soul to mine, but I don't think the bond was intended to last, like string around a delivery package. When our souls entered Earth, that bond broke, by design. It's why we didn't arrive in the same place. But the remnants of that bond are there, even now, but the connection is intermittent. Now that I can sense it, I feel it link us, sometimes, and fall away at others."

"What does this bond do?"

"Not a lot, from what I can tell. I've been using the astral gate's power to examine it, but I'm even less well-versed with that than the astral throne. All I've managed to figure out thus far is that I can use the bond to treat you, in terms of my abilities, in a similar way to my familiars."

"You're saying I'm your familiar?"

"No," Jason said. "But it means I can treat you like one in certain respects, while the bond is active. Things like having you use my portals without consuming extra energy beyond what it takes for me to go through. I think it's been going on ever since Earth, but I've only just realised it was happening, and why. As for what else the bond can do, that's something we'd have to explore. I think that, potentially, we could use it for effectively infinite range with my group chat ability. The only limits would be dimensional barriers, although the results would vary by circumstance, I suspect. The same way that Shade can sometimes connect to his other bodies through an astral space boundary and sometimes not, depending on the specific nature of the astral space."

They paused in an underground grotto, sitting on a bench that overlooked an underground pond.

"You can manipulate this bond?"

"I think that I can restore the bond to full strength," Jason said. "Make it permanent. I can also eliminate it entirely. It's a matter of what you want."

Farrah nodded absently.

"You know why I'm here," she said.

"If we're going after messengers, it means that I'm getting down to business," he said. "Which means it's time for you and Travis to head back to Rimaros and get to your own business."

"I worry about you, Jason. We've been constant companions ever since you finished your walkathon on Earth."

"Walkabout."

"Whatever. Are you going to be alright without me?"

He let out a chuckle.

"I wouldn't have gotten this far without you. Not even close. It's why they sent you to me, and if nothing else, I'll always be grateful to the Reaper and the World-Phoenix for that. But I think I'll be okay. It's not just us against the world anymore, and it's past time we stopped acting like it is."

"Oh, I'm fine," she said. "You're the wobbly one. We're here in your magic god realm and you're still anxious."

"I am not anxious."

"Of course you're not."

"I'm not!"

"Uh-huh."

WHERE WE END

Farrah and Jason emerged from his soul space, through the archway located on the bridge.

"I can kind of feel the bond, if I go looking for it," Farrah said. "It's way more subtle than my power bond ability, though. To be honest, I was expecting more."

"I know that story," Travis said sadly from the doorway. "Women tell me that all the time."

"Oh, bloke…" Jason commiserated. "You need to work on that self-confidence."

"That's never worked for me," Travis said. "You may recall the pistol I was trying to use when we met was called the compensator. That's what it was compensating for: a lack of self-confidence. Not, you know… the other thing."

"You shouldn't worry about it," Farrah told him, jabbing a thumb at Jason. "Everyone has their mindset problems. My primary job of the last few years was making sure this guy didn't murder everyone—or refuse to murder anyone—because he was a sad boy."

"Hey…" Jason whined.

"I was looking for you, Jason," Travis said, giving Farrah an odd look. "Since you intend to start seriously going after messengers, I have something I've been working on to give you."

"Oh?" Jason asked. "Alright, come into my cabin."

They moved into Jason's cabin, the cloud furniture reconfiguring as they entered. The cloud material flowed and reshaped itself, eliminating the bed and pushing back the lounge area in favour of a round table and chairs.

"Iced tea?" Jason offered and the others nodded. He took out a tray and three glasses from a cabinet, then a pitcher from a refrigerator that emerged from the wall.

"What do you have?" Jason asked as he sat the tray down and waved the others to seats.

"Well," Travis began, "I know that when you portal us back to Rimaros, you'll be picking up the designs and materials from House de Varco to spice up the vehicle forms your cloud flask can produce."

"That's the idea," Jason said. "Not sure how much they'll bring to the table, but it can't hurt."

"I was thinking about supplementing those designs," Travis said. "As you know, my specialty is magitech guns. I can work with any kind of gun or large ordnance, but great big guns are my sweet spot."

"You're talking about putting some guns on my yacht?" Jason asked.

"I know your cloud house can use magic to replicate complex technology like live televisions screens," Travis said. "I also know that you have internal defence systems, but thought that you could benefit from something more externally-focused. Didn't you wonder why I was asking all those questions about how your cloud flask worked?"

"You mean the point-zero-zero-three percent of the number of questions that Clive asks? After him, a Magic Society interrogator would just seem naturally curious."

"The Magic Society has interrogators?" Travis asked.

"It's complicated," Farrah said. "The interrogators are specialists that are part of the Magic Society, but there are rules against the Magic Society using them. They work for the Adventure Society and civilian authorities, not the Magic Society itself."

"Liara was using them to try and make the Order of Redeeming Light prisoners talk," Jason said. "Having their souls coated in vampire gunk repurposed for hardcore zealotry made them tough nuts to crack, though."

"Yeah, I'm not really interested in the whole brainwashed fanatic stuff," Travis said. "I'll stick to giant guns and trying to invent the magic phone, thank you very much."

"How are you going to do that?" Jason asked. "This world already has a few different forms of distance communication, right?"

"Yeah," Farrah said. "There's the water link system, but that's complicated, expensive and requires access to a body of water connected to all the others. Inland lakes that don't feed into an ocean or river anywhere can't support a water link station, for example. Then there's the record systems that the Adventure Society and Magic Society use to keep their records updated across branches. That system is too slow for real-time communication, though."

"It also can't transmit enough information," Travis said. "I looked into it, and while it is used for communication, it's like an inefficient telegram system. It's to the point that most communication that isn't regular record updates are shared through the water link."

"Our plan," Farrah said, "is to leverage the bones of that magic and enhance it using Travis' understanding of magitech. We're taking inspiration from the Earth's magical detection grid to set up relays to extend the range."

"Magical cell towers," Travis said. "Maybe even satellites."

Travis took on an expression Jason knew and feared from interactions with Clive.

"Did you know that each of this world's moons has very different magic levels?" Travis asked enthusiastically.

"I vaguely recall," Jason said. "The magic one is called the Mystic Moon, right?"

"Yeah," Travis said. "I've been looking into it ever since I started thinking about satellites. It has a weird regulatory effect on the tides of this planet."

"You know, I keep wondering about that," Jason said.

"I know, right?" Travis said. "The tides here are a bit more complex than on Earth, but nowhere near the level they should be with two moons…"

Once Jason and Travis started enthusiastically discussing tidal forces, Farrah went to the drinks cabinet and found something to spice up her iced tea. Jason watched her topping up her glass from a liquor bottle and mixing it in with a stirring rod.

"You don't think it's a little early?" he asked.

"Hey, I'm not the one going off to fight evil," she told him, completely unrepentant. "If you don't want to see day drinking, maybe don't make your headquarters a pleasure yacht?"

"That's a fair point, I guess," Jason said as Farrah experimentally sipped at her drink and immediately poured in more booze.

Farrah and Travis made their farewells on the roof deck.

"It looks like you've found a place for yourself here, bro," Taika told Travis as he enveloped him in a huge hug.

"There's not a lot waiting for me back on Earth," Travis said. "My family were never entirely reconciled with the choices I made and what that meant for them. I think that maybe it's better for all of us if I'm just gone."

"If that's what you feel is best," Taika told him. "But Earth is still home for me."

"I hope you get back. Mate."

"Don't use New Zealand slang. It always sounds wrong in an American accent."

"Isn't that Australian slang?"

"Do you want a smack, bro?"

After the more general goodbyes, Farrah, Gary and Rufus gathered together at one end of the deck.

"So, this is where we end," Rufus said, looking and sounding uncertain. "We came together in a town overrun by zombies, fire lighting up the dark, the air filled with ash and smoke. Now we've come to the end, on a magic land-boat on a sunny day."

"Better that than steel and blood," Gary said soberly. Their minds all drifted back to Farrah's death in an astral space years earlier, Rufus and Gary helpless to stop it.

"This way," Gary continued, his voice growing more cheerful, "we can still get together and tell stories, have a few drinks. And a few more. Now I find myself wondering why I ever thought I needed adventuring to be able to do that. All it added was the need to kill things and the chance to die."

"There's the travel," Farrah said. "You can do that without adventuring, sure, but I don't think I ever would have seen another world without it. The price was high, but here we are, more-or-less intact."

"It's a long way from what we expected when Emir asked us to go to Greenstone," Rufus said. "I'm not sure any of us expected to be on the paths we're taking from here."

"I don't know," Farrah said. "Gary was always going to be a craftsman, and I've always wanted to do some real magic study in between blowing things up. The only real surprise is you, Roo."

"You know I don't like it when you call me that," Rufus said. "And what do you mean, that I'm the surprise?"

"We never imagined you running a training centre for adventurers," she said, Gary nodding in agreement.

"Why would that surprise you?" Rufus asked. "My family runs a... oh, gods dammit."

Farrah and Gary both took shot glasses from their dimensional pouches and downed the contents at a gulp.

"Are you ever going to let that go?" Rufus complained.

"I'd say not until the day I died," Farrah said, "but even that didn't stop me."

"Don't worry," Gary said. "A couple of centuries from now, when you're dead from old age and your memorial plaque reads 'his family runs a school,' we'll be there, having a drink."

"Why am I the first one to die of old age?"

"We just have healthier diets," Gary said.

"You're constantly eating your body weight in anything warm and dead," Rufus complained. "Your idea of salad dressing is anything not worse than mildly poisonous."

"Exactly," Gary said. "I'm robust."

"You can't argue that's not the case," Farrah said to Rufus, who shook his head.

Rimaros in general had excellent defences, along with tracking systems for any teleportation or similar means of travel. This was even more true on the island of Livaros, and the Adventure Society campus itself had defences second only to the royal sky island. They were not as obvious, but no less formidable.

One of the most magically sophisticated arrays in Rimaros was a room deep in the Adventure Society campus. Setting up a place where all the defences and detection of dimensional travel did not take effect was more complex than the defences themselves. The room was also one of the most secure in the Storm Kingdom, with layers of physical and magical defences. Various fail-safes could be enacted in emergencies, from collapsing the room to exposing it to all the defences and tracking it otherwise avoided.

Just portalling into the room was tricky, requiring both magical devices and specific rituals. Jason had been supplied with both, allowing his portal arch to appear in the room. The arrival room was an empty cube, with neither doors nor windows, only flat, unbroken surfaces. After stepping out of the arch, Jason recognised the dark metal the room was built from. It secured various underground portions of the Adventure Society campus against intrusion by magic perception. As with the first time he encountered the enclosed feeling, he was tempted to push out with his senses and test how strong the sense suppression was, but he suspected the consequences would not be worth sating his curiosity.

The cube room was entirely blank, without any lighting. That didn't bother Jason or Farrah, who followed him out with her eyes glowing like embers. Travis pulled out a glow stone and tossed it into the air, but instead of floating and lighting up, it fell to the floor like a normal pebble.

Curious, Jason pushed out not his aura senses but his magic senses, paying more attention to the suppressive effects permeating the room. It occurred to him that he should ask Amos about training them as well. Their strength was fine, but their active uses were far less developed than his aura senses.

Jason used his aura as a platform to reach out to the inert glow stone. He suspected that it was not a normal expression of aura projection, as it felt rather like using his aura to produce physical force. Adapting the method he used to disable suppression collars, he pushed back against the suppressive effect of the stone and it lit up, floating into the air.

The moment it did, openings appeared in the walls. Portions of the hard metal turned to liquid and flowed through the gaps left as it did. This left doorways through which a small army of silver-rankers poured through to surround the trio, led by a gold-ranker. Each was dressed in practical black, with the crossed sword and rod emblem of the Adventure Society stitched in gold.

Jason held up his hands.

"We surrender?" he said casually, just before Liara marched in.

"Please don't poke at the society's defences for fun, Mr Asano," she told him wearily.

"Hey, I was trying to fix a busted glow stone," Jason said. "If the Adventure Society is that afraid of a little light illuminating the darkness, you might want to consider what that says about it, as a metaphor."

"And I wanted to check if I missed your presence at all," Liara said. "Unsurprisingly, the answer is a resounding no."

"That's a little hurtful," Jason said.

Liara sighed, then made a sharp command gesture. The guards wordlessly started filtering out of the room.

"Come along then, Mr Asano," she said primly. "Let's get this done so you can be back on your way."

"How's the family?" Jason asked.

"Fine," Liara said curtly.

"So stern," Jason said. "Trying to keep things professional in front of your work friends?"

Liara looked around as the guards finished filtering out and all the doors but one were resealed. Her mouth crinkled unhappily.

"Baseph and the children asked me to say hello," she said, like a prisoner in a hostage video.

Jason let out a laugh.

38

PEOPLE THAT YOU DIDN'T AGGRAVATE

A SPRAWLING, MULTI-LEVEL, SUBTERRANEAN COMPLEX EXTENDED BENEATH THE entirety of the Adventure Society campus. Large portions of it were restricted, with potent protections, including the ones through which Liara led Jason, Farrah and Travis.

"There are two things on your agenda before you go," Liara told Jason. "One is collecting your winnings from the duels, along with the additional materials from Mr Noble's list."

While Jason had been gone, Liara continued to keep one of Shade's bodies hidden within her shadow, which allowed her to communicate with Jason. He had used this link to send her a list of materials he wanted procured, mostly related to Travis' weapon designs for the cloud flask.

"I appreciate you putting in the effort to collect these things since I can't go out on a shopping trip," Jason told her.

"What makes you think I did this personally?" she asked, then looked suspiciously at her shadow.

"Shade doesn't tell me what my allies are up to while he's in their shadows," Jason told her. "Not on my boat, not in my house and not out and about."

"It was one of the earliest rules Mr Asano established," Shade said. "He said he wanted to be more ethical."

"I'm pretty sure I said more than that," Jason told him.

"That was the part I felt worthy of admiration," Shade clarified.

"What was the rest of it?" Jason wondered aloud. "Shade, do you remember?"

"My memory is sometimes disadvantageously thorough in cataloguing my experiences."

"What was the rest of what I said?"

"I believe that the selectiveness with what I chose to include and omit will present you in a better light than the unabridged version, Mr Asano."

"Not being in the best light is kind of my thing," Jason told him.

"It involved the Goddess of Knowledge, a respect for privacy, a tub of Togetherness Jelly and a sack of raisins," Shade said. "On a personal level, I would prefer not to expound on the details."

"Fine," Jason acceded. "But you know that excessive and outlandish descriptions of things is part of my charm."

"You have charm?" Farrah asked.

"Are you kidding?" Travis asked. "Back on Earth, he's a sex symbol."

Jason and Farrah both stopped dead. They turned to look at Travis, brought up short by their stopping.

"What?" Travis asked.

"A sex symbol?" Jason asked sceptically.

"Yes."

"Me?"

"Him?" Farrah asked, prompting Jason to turn to her.

"You know, I've got the incredulity covered," he told her.

"No, this much incredulity is a two-person job."

"That's a little hurtful. People are attracted to power."

"I shoot lava!"

"You're a sex symbol too," Travis assured her. "Not as big as Jason, but that's just an exposure thing. You're frequently paired together, especially if you do an image search with the safe search off—"

"NOPE," Jason boomed, cutting him off.

"Are you sure it's him more than me?" Farrah asked.

"It depends on the specifics," Travis said. "I know his body pillows sell a *lot* more."

"Body pillows?" Jason asked. "You seem suspiciously well-informed on this topic."

"If you don't mind," Liara cut in, "we're on a schedule."

"We are?" Jason asked.

"I told you that there were two things on the agenda," Liara told him. "One is the materials provided by us and House de Varco. The other is a scheduled water-link call."

"With whom?" Jason asked.

Despite her exhortations for the group to keep moving, Liara led them to collect materials before the scheduled remote meeting. She guided them to a secure storage centre on the first basement level, just underground. They saw no one along the way, which was not strange in the lower levels, based on Jason's previous visits. Once they reached the first basement level, the absence of people was more notable, and the lack of sense suppression allowed Jason to detect others in a wide area. Based on the pattern of people, he was certain that Liara had their path cleared for them.

Liara, walking beside Jason, gave him an assessing look.

"What?" he asked.

"Your senses. You're projecting them very cleanly."

"I've been working on it, but it's still early days. It'll be years before I'm even approaching a silver-rank version of Lord Pensinata."

"You realise that most people would find the idea of anyone comparing themselves to Amos Pensinata's aura abilities quite laughable."

"If I worried about what people thought was and wasn't possible, my world would have been annihilated. Next to that, what is some aura training?"

Liara's thoughts drifted to her husband being trapped in an underwater complex with gold-rank enemies pounding on the door. If Jason hadn't found a way to portal from a place where portalling was impossible, she would be a widow.

"Thank you, Jason," she said quietly.

"No worries," he said with a smile. He didn't need to ask what her thanks were for.

As they approached their destination, Jason sensed a presence he recognised and stopped.

"Hector de Varco?" he asked Liara.

"You were warned that any family with enough power and influence would find out what you were really doing if they looked hard enough. Did you think the de Varco family wouldn't be looking at you hard after what happened?"

"I suppose not," Jason said.

They entered the basement warehouse where crates, sacks and barrels were piled up. There were two people present: Hector de Varco and a gold-rank woman. She had the look shared by many gold-rankers; she appeared around thirty years old at a glance, but with an uncanny agelessness, especially in the eyes. She wore practical adventuring leathers, with a sword on her hip. She reminded Jason of Sophie with her tied-back hair and sense of readiness to spring into lethal action.

The woman moved to meet the group while Hector remained where he was, looking slightly cowed. Jason could sense Hector's wariness of him and the woman.

"So, this is Jason Asano," the woman said.

"And this is some random lady," Jason shot back. "We meet at last."

"Do you think that your childish antics impress anyone?" she asked him.

"No, they're just for fun," Jason said. "I don't much care what random people think about me."

"You are not here to vent your frustration, Lady Astasia," Liara said. "You are here to fulfil a wager."

"There is something that needs to be settled first," Astasia said. "This boy may have won his duel, but by the means of necromancers and soul-warpers. Who knows what foul tricks he knows and where he learned them?"

"I know," Liara said. "That should be sufficient to lay any concerns you have, if not to rest, then at least into a discreet silence."

"We never saw what he can do outside of his illicit powers," Astasia said. "What assurance do I have of his true strength? If he gets bested by some worthless fool, what does that say of my son, who lost to him? That is the perception, even if the duel was hardly legitimate."

"I didn't seek out you or your family," Jason said. "Your son came looking for trouble, so you have no grounds to blame me for his ability to find it."

"You didn't have to handle the fight the way you did," Astasia said.

"No," Jason agreed. "But your son came to me because he had a point to make. It turns out that I had a point to make as well. I made mine better."

Jason's and Astasia's auras clashed as they stared at one another.

"I will test you," Astasia said, her hand drifting to the sword at her hip. "We shall see if you should be left free to roam about with the potential to harm my son's reputation."

Jason knew, that for all his aura strength, he was only equal to the trashiest of gold-rankers. He still fell short of true elites, which he immediately understood as he felt Liara's aura unleashed in full force for the first time. Cold and sharp, it made the conflict between his and Astasia's auras look like the squabbling of children.

"Lady Astasia," Liara said, her voice carrying the same knife-edge warning as her aura. "This is not your house. This is the Storm Kingdom and this is the Adventure Society, which means that it is *my* house. You were allowed to come here as a courtesy, and my courtesy is now exhausted. You will give Mr Asano what you owe him and Mr Asano will keep his mouth shut and not provoke you or your family any further. Isn't that right, Mr Asano?"

"Yes, ma'am."

Astasia looked at Liara for a long time before finally speaking.

"People were starting to talk about you going soft, Liara."

Liara walked up to Astasia until they were face to face, almost touching.

"Do you think I'm soft, Asta?" Liara said, her voice barely a whisper.

"No."

"Then leave what you brought and leave this room. And say hello to Gregor for me."

Astasia snorted a surprised laugh.

"We should have dinner sometime, Liara. It's been too long."

"Call my assistant, Rodney. He'll set something up."

Astasia stepped back, turned and nodded at Hector. He moved forward and handed Jason a dimension bag. Jason held out his hand for the other man to take. Hector looked at Jason's hand for a long moment before hesitantly shaking it.

"You didn't lose," Jason told him. "You were caught up in something bigger than yourself and got hammered. It happens to us all."

Hector gave Jason a little nod before backing off without saying anything and he followed his mother out.

"Well, that was fun," Jason said when they were gone. "I assume you knew that she would react like that."

"Astasia was the driving force behind House de Varco's contributions to resource distribution during the monster surge, which were not small. She's a good person who genuinely did her part during the surge, and pushed her house into doing so as well. But she's very protective of her children, and you spiked one of them in the soul."

"So, you let her in here to vent?" Jason asked, then shook his head. "No, maybe a little, but that's not enough. You let her in here so that you could stop her when she did vent on me."

"My reputation needs some rehabilitation," Liara said. "The family wants me taking on some of Vesper's old responsibilities, which means more of a public face."

"And people think you've gone soft since your necromancer hunting days. You do seem to have changed a mind, there. She's looking to get on your good side before everyone else realises that it's a good place to be."

"People think that some silver-ranker that I was meant to be in charge of made me look like a buffoon in front of the king and His Ancestral Majesty. Your behaviour in the royal viewing box reflected very poorly on me."

"Yeah, I blew it there," Jason said morosely. "Getting involved in Rimaros politics meant so much to me as well. The effort I put in to insert myself into the affairs of the royal family, all wasted. What was I thinking? It was me who wanted to get involved in—"

"Fine," Liara said. "Your point is taken. You should collect all this before your scheduled call."

"This is all for me?" Jason said, looking around at the crates and sacks and barrels. "Then what's in this dimensional bag?"

He rummaged through and pulled out some orbs, handing one each to Farrah and Travis.

"This is interesting," Travis said, pulling out a device to examine the orb with.

"Is that a tricorder?" Jason asked him.

"No," Travis said unconvincingly, before changing the subject. "This orb is some kind of design matrix. The biggest challenge when I designed the guns for your cloud flask was making sure that it would be able to infer the designs from the materials fed into it. These things allow for significantly more sophisticated outcomes, which I guess you need. Reworking the whole boat is more complex than running out the cannons."

"You should talk to House de Varco if you're interested," Farrah said. "Maybe they'll be willing to trade some secrets. I'll bet you they'll climb over themselves to learn some magitech tricks."

"Sounds like you two will be having fun here in Rimaros," Jason said.

"I think the biggest challenge," Farrah told him, "will be getting anyone to work with us. We need to find some people that you didn't aggravate."

"What are you talking about?" Jason asked. "People love me."

"Can we please just go?" Liara asked.

"Liara," Jason said. "People love me, right?"

"Well," Liara said, "I've comprehensively studied your activities and you've done a lot of impressive things for many, many people. Yet, all the evidence points to everyone wanting to kill you, have you killed, kidnap you, ostracise you, hand you over to the Builder to get your soul taken over…"

"You could have just said no," Jason said sullenly, then raised his hand, palm up. Blood seeped out of his skin, coagulating into the form of a leech with terrifying rings of lamprey teeth.

"You love me, don't you, Colin?"

The leech unleashed a hideous screech that sounded like a clothes hanger shoved into an overcharged garbage disposal.

"That means yes," Jason said.

While the Magic Society operated the water-link infrastructure and the majority of the water-link chambers, major families all had chambers of their own. The Adventure Society likewise maintained several chambers with additional security measures to prevent eavesdropping. The Magic Society regularly assured the Adventure Society that they had no way to tap into those calls.

Jason entered one of the Adventure Society's chambers, which was a large, tiled booth. The floor was divided in half, with one side a dry floor and the other a pool of water. The dry side had a low, round platform onto which Jason stepped. He waited for around a minute until the water in the pool floated up, taking on a human shape. Once it had, the water started filling with colour, like ink had been spilled into it. The colours swirled and became more complex until Jason was standing in front of a water clone of Emir Bahadir.

"Jason," the clone said with a grin. "I hear you've been renovating that cloud flask I gave you."

39

NOT YOU

"That's the first thing you ask about?" Jason said. "My cloud flask? After I go off into your astral space and die?"

"You're going to talk to me about causing trouble?" Emir asked. "There are about a hundred outworlders who arrived in the wake of you coming back, and you've just left them on the other side of the world while you're playing with your great astral being friends. Since you keep not showing up, who do you think people bother about it? Anyone in the area who knows you, that's who. Vitesse isn't even that close."

"The great astral beings are not my friends. They're... business acquaintances."

"I've been hearing something about a diamond-ranker you've been running around with. Doesn't she work for one of them?"

"You mean Soramir? No, he doesn't work for them."

"You know full well I do not mean Soramir. You remember that Arabelle is one of my closest friends in the world, right?"

"I also know that Callum is one of your closest friends, and that guy has been all sorts of trouble. And Arabelle has strict rules about confidentiality, so don't try to goad me into spilling the beans that way."

"There are beans to spill, then?"

Jason laughed. "What are you reaching out for?"

"Something that is better discussed in person," Emir said. "There's a few too many ears on these water-link chambers, whatever they tell you. There's a city called Isart that you should arrive at on your procession south."

"Yes, although we're about to detour, so we won't be racing down there."

"Detour?"

"Messenger activity," Jason said. "We're going to take a look at what we're up against."

"Just be careful. I'll meet you in Isart when you're done and we can talk about a job."

"I don't have a job for you," Jason told Emir. "Still, I'll keep your application on file, and if anything comes up…"

"I see that going up a couple of ranks hasn't managed to instil a reverence for higher-rankers. I imagine that was inevitable, given the stories floating around about you."

Emir smiled, but there was a grimness to his eyes.

"Do me a favour and don't take too long to get to Isart," he told Jason.

"Oh, bloody hell," Jason complained. "I'm getting that fate-of-the-world feeling again. Does it really have to be me?"

"Nothing that drastic," Emir said. "But there's something out there that will cause a major shift in some of the foundational elements of society. We need to find it before someone who shouldn't does, and they're already ahead of us in the search."

"Emir, that sounds exactly like what I'm trying to avoid. I just want some good, honest adventuring."

"That's exactly what this is. It's not about you, Jason. It's a good old-fashioned race to the magical treasure. You and your team just happen to be the best people for the job."

Jason perked up. "Okay, now I'm more interested."

"Then meet me in Isart. I'll be arriving there in about two weeks. Also, I'll have the person who made our cloud flasks with me. She's very interested in what we've been hearing about what you did to yours. I think."

"You think she's very interested?"

"No, I'm certain about the interest; I'm just not certain she's a she. She keeps changing it up on me."

"Gender fluid diamond-ranker? That is interesting. Having some trouble with your pronouns, Emir?"

Emir's water clone looked surprised.

"I thought I was going to throw you off with that."

Jason laughed.

"You have no idea how many people back where I come from would appreciate having magic to help them transition," he said, then frowned. "Actually, that's probably becoming more of an option now, which will be a giant political garbage fire. I bet they find some way to blame me."

Liara returned Jason to the room in the Adventure Society campus from which he could portal out.

"Any word on those idiots that broke into my cloud house?" Jason asked Liara.

"Yes," she said with a nod. "As far as we can tell, they're a bunch of idle rich kids from extremely wealthy families. Too important to not foster, thus getting them to gold rank on cores, but too incompetent to give any actual responsibility.

It seems that they got it into their heads to prove themselves and started taking work for hire, as a group."

"And, despite their idiocy, they're gold rank," Jason mused. "People will overlook a lot if it lets them hire a gold rank team on the cheap."

"Yes, but we don't think the person that sent them after you was concerned with their ability. We haven't determined who it was yet, but the motivation seems related to their local politics, not you. You were chosen because you were far enough away that the fools wouldn't know they were jumping into the shark's mouth while being important enough that it would be an embarrassment to their families."

Jason groaned as he ran his hands over his face.

"Is this going to be yet another thing I'm caught up in?"

"Actually," Liara said, "if you're willing to let this go, you'll find some powerful families owe you a favour if you ever find yourself in that part of the world."

"Let this go, meaning walk away and not have anything more to do with it?"

"If you're willing to give up revenge, yes."

"Yeah, let's do that," Jason said hurriedly. "Just warn me before any blowback from this hits me, yeah?"

"As best as I am able," Liara said. "I handed it off to the royal family's political specialists once we knew that your involvement was peripheral. They will keep looking into the situation."

"You talk about the royal family a lot, as if you weren't a part of it."

"A peripheral branch. And I need to keep my perspectives separate, given that I do a lot more in my role as an Adventure Society executive than as a royal."

Jason drew out the ritual circle required to circumvent the protections and open his portal arch. He didn't go through immediately, and instead turned to face Travis and Farrah. He shook Travis by the hand and shared a hug with Farrah.

"Just don't go off and die the second I'm not watching over you," she said. "You have the life expectancy of a friend of Jessica Fletcher's who is visiting from out of town."

Jason chuckled as he went through the arch, which then vanished into the ground.

"Who's Jessica Fletcher?" Travis asked.

"From *Murder She Wrote*," Farrah said. "How can you not know that show?"

"When was it on?"

"1984 through 1996. They made twelve seasons. It's a cultural touchstone."

"Before I was alive, maybe. That bond ability of yours that lets you take information out of people's heads; I'm not sure you should have ever used it on Jason."

Jason stepped out of the portal arch in his cabin on the cloud yacht and it closed behind him. He could have spoken to Farrah, their new bond allowing him to open up a voice chat over large distances, but he resisted the urge. The bond was there if he went looking for it, but was otherwise unnoticeable. He let out a sigh.

"Are you alright, Mr Asano?" Shade asked, emerging from Jason's shadow.

"Yeah. It just feels like... I don't know. Like a clean cut has been made. Farrah and I have been running around together for a long time now. I guess the ground just doesn't feel as stable without her here. Even with the bond, her absence seems palpable. I know I've always got you, but, no offence, you're a spirit of darkness and death older than the human race. On Earth, at least. Your perspective isn't something a flickering candle like me can always relate to. Even if I end up living for millennia, right now, I'm not even thirty."

"I understand, Mr Asano. I have found that there is a strange dichotomy between existing for epochs, yet living moment to moment, like everyone else. My perspective, as an ancient entity, puts me at a separation from most beings. I suspect it is what has driven me to become a familiar. To insert myself into the lives of the short-lived and immerse myself in their cultures and interests. You will find, Mr Asano, that even when you can survive for millennia, you have to live day by day, just like everyone else."

"You know what, Shade? I take it back. You are relatable. Thanks for sticking with me through so much nonsense."

"Immortality can be hard sometimes, Mr Asano. I hope that you will live long enough so that I can help guide you through it. It becomes isolating as you find yourself slipping further and further from the concerns of mortality. Miss Dawn understood this. You have put her on the start of a journey I began a long time ago."

"Shade, have I ever told you that you are amazing?"

"Many times, Mr Asano."

"Good. Because you are."

One of the reasons that the Storm Kingdom stood out on the global stage was that there were very few regions with a celestine majority, and it was the largest of them by far. Having moved south of there, the convoy found itself increasingly in elf-held territories. This excited Jason less because of the elves themselves, of whom he had known many, and because of the differences in culture that came with encountering them on home turf. Instead of having their own enclaves in places where they were a minority, this was the elves in their element, and Jason was not disappointed.

The smaller towns and villages hadn't been a lot different to what he had seen elsewhere, but as the convoy approached a small city, Jason watched from the roof deck in wonder. To Jason's eyes, the architecture poking up out of the rainforest was a mix of ancient civilisation and absolute modernity, with ziggurats built from the shining glass of skyscrapers and gothic towers of gleaming metal.

The city materials seemed dominated by metal and glass from a distance, although only the uppermost building areas could be seen above the rainforest. Much of it had a green tint, reminding Jason of Greenstone. Here the shades were much darker than that city's signature stone, but the bright sunlight drew out gorgeous colours.

From what Jason could see, the city was not exclusionary of the rainforest, which was let into the city and incorporated into the city planning. He presumed it was in a carefully controlled fashion and he looked forward to going in and looking around for himself. Before that, however, he had a task ahead of him.

The convoy split up at the city outskirts. Arabelle continued forward with her relatively modest vehicle, while Carlos and Korinne left their vehicles behind. Carlos cadged a ride with Korinne's team on the more manageable skimmer docked on the roof of their new vehicle.

The passengers of Jason's hover yacht all exited, including Melody under Sophie's watchful eye.

Jason plucked the tiny cloud flask from his necklace and sat it on the ground as it grew to its regular size of a large chemistry flask. The hover yacht dissolved into a wispy cloud that flowed into the flask. Everyone stood around watching the process, which would take around ten minutes. In that waiting time, Jason started pulling out the crates, sacks and barrels he acquired in Rimaros from his inventory. Melody approached him while he did so.

"My daughter tells me that it was your idea to add windows to my cabin," she said.

"Your daughter said you were getting a little antsy."

"Do you expect me to be grateful? That amenities and little luxuries you've provided will win me over? Do you think I don't see that it's an easy way to build up a sense of thankfulness that makes up one of many steps to you having me open up and give you what you want?"

"I don't want anything from you, Mrs Jain. What I want is relaxing days spent visiting interesting places, with no hassles. You are a hassle. I'd be happy to throw you in a box and forget about you, or hand you over to any of the many people that want to get their hands on you. As we speak, my familiar is scouting the area in case someone is following us, waiting for the chance to pounce and take you away. You got those windows because it makes your daughter happy. I couldn't care less about you. I checked."

"Do you practise these little speeches in case the right situation comes up, or is it all off the top of your head?" Melody asked. "I'm not sure which one is worse. They both require a profoundly pompous mindset."

Jason laughed. "I won't argue with that, Mrs Jain. Now, if you'll excuse me, I have to put a very large number of things into a very small bottle."

Once the flask had been refilled, Jason started opening containers full of materials. Sheets of metal, bags of powder, magically crafted crystals and barrels of alchemical liquids were tipped into the flask. Some went in via a funnel, like powder and water. For solid objects, Jason poked them at the flask and they slowly dissolved into a mist that the flask then sucked into itself.

This went on for several hours as Jason pulled the many containers Liara had prepared from his inventory. Belinda and Clive took out all the disassembled submarine parts they had as well. Once all the materials were finally consumed, Jason was about ready to test out the new potential of his cloud constructs. Before he began, he turned as he sensed Korinne's team returning from the city.

On their arrival, Korinne's team found Jason waiting with a scowl. They disembarked from the skimmer, which had all eight seats filled. There were the six members of Korinne's team, plus Carlos and one more person.

"Care to explain yourself?" Jason demanded of Korinne, not looking at the newcomer.

"We found a new team member," Korinne said.

"I'll remind you, Lady Pescos, that while you are operating as a part of this convoy, you are under certain restrictions that you would otherwise not be, should you be operating alone."

"I'm well aware of the need for secrecy," Korinne said. "But she already knows your secrets, so there isn't a problem."

"Explaining the full inaccuracy of what you just said will take no small amount of time," Jason said. "For now, go back to your vehicle and we'll discuss this later."

"This convoy might be built around you, Mr Asano, but you don't tell my team what to—"

Korinne stopped talking as she felt the pressure of an aura she had thought Jason could only produce with the aid of his massive cloud construct. It carried the cold anger of an icy hell and had Korinne's team reaching for weapons until it receded after a short moment.

"Go back to your vehicle, Lady Pescos," Jason repeated softly.

Korinne and her team looked to Amos Pensinata for support but saw nothing beyond his usual stoicism. Orin was the first to follow Jason's directive, but the others soon followed. Korinne was the last to move, none of the fear in her aura showing in her expression or body language. The newcomer moved to follow.

"Not you," Jason said, turning his gaze on her.

He looked her up and down, his expression fierce. Her adventuring gear was plain and practical, mostly covering her smooth, caramel skin. Her milky-teal hair spilled down past her shoulders and her matching eyes stared back at Jason. Despite himself, Jason couldn't help but reflect that the young woman in front of him was more beautiful than the nineteen-year-old girl she had been when they met in a tent five years earlier. She might have changed her distinctive sapphire hair and eyes, but there was no hiding the exquisite beauty of Zara Rimaros.

40

INVENTING A MAN IN YOUR HEAD

RAINFOREST ENCROACHED ON BOTH SIDES OF THE WIDE ROAD LEADING OFF towards the elf city in the distance. Glass ziggurats and polished towers of dark metal poked up over the canopy; Jason had been looking forward to exploring such a large city built into, rather than over, the environment.

He had stopped outside the city first, after finding a rare clearing by the side of the road. While other members of the convoy moved forward, he had loaded up his cloud flask with materials brought back from Rimaros. He was about to check the results when some members of the convoy came back from the city early, having acquired a new member.

Zara Rimaros was someone with whom Jason had a complicated history. They had met early in their adventuring careers, before the traumas that had come to define Jason. She had used his name, thinking him dead, for political purposes that complicated things for them both when he turned up alive. It embroiled him in machinations he had no interest in, at a time when he desperately needed to be left alone, eventually bringing him to the edge of breakdown.

For her, Jason's resurrection finalised a fall from grace that began when she used Jason's name in an ill-conceived attempt to help a friend. As the king's daughter, she had been in a prime position to vie for the crown of the Storm Kingdom, one of the most powerful nations in the world. That was never going to happen now. Instead of staying in Rimaros, she had gone south alone. Now, she found herself standing in front of Jason Asano once again, against his express desire to be done with the royal family.

Jason looked Zara up and down, his gaze lingering on her hair and eyes. As a celestine, hers matched, but the royal family's signature sapphire she once sported had become a milky teal. As Jason looked over her new look, the people around them watched as they stared at each other. The princess' return had come as most of the convoy was waiting on Jason to remake their mobile accommodations using the cloud flask. It was no secret that Zara had requested a place amongst them, or that Jason had refused, leaving her behind in Rimaros.

The people watching knew that Jason was still volatile, despite his ongoing mental recovery, and the tension was thick as both they and Zara waited for his reaction. They had felt the power and fury in the aura spike Jason had used to dismiss the team to which she had attached herself as a pretence. As the moment dragged on in an increasingly weighty silence, Zara finally spoke up herself, launching into an explanation.

"You need to know that—"

"Copper," he said, cutting her off.

"Copper?"

"Your hair and eyes. It will stand out less than the teal."

"I've adopted into my mother's family. This is their colouration."

"I don't care. Change it."

A portal arch of white stone rose from the ground, filling with rainbow light.

"Jason, I—"

"My friends call me Jason, Princess."

"I'm not a princess anymore. I'm Zara Nareen now."

"Then call me Mr Asano, Miss Nareen. Even better, don't call me anything at all."

Jason stepped through the portal to his soul space and the rainbow light flickered out, leaving the arch standing empty. The nearby cloud flask started spewing out cloud stuff as it began the process of forming a new vehicle.

There was an awkward atmosphere in the wake of Jason's departure. Zara felt isolated and scrutinised as the assembled people split their attention between her and the cloud vessel taking shape nearby. Scrutiny was something she was used to as a former princess of the Storm Kingdom, but she felt the absence of the usual support that role offered. She moved towards Jason's team, who were not looking on her with kindly expressions.

"Keep walking, lady," one of them said.

Zara knew from her investigations into Asano's team that the speaker was Belinda Callahan, a thief turned adventurer. Zara turned her gaze to Humphrey Geller, the team leader. She had met him back in Greenstone and knew he had the trained manners of high society.

"You heard her," Humphrey said coldly. "You'd best join your new team, Miss Nareen."

Zara moved to the vehicle into which her new team had gone. It was a large vehicle designed for overland travel as well as flight, with room enough for privacy. She was admitted by Korinne Pescos, who took her into a kitchenette with a dining booth. Zara sat down at an inviting gesture from Korinne, who started brewing tea.

"I think we need to have that longer talk now, Your Highness."

"It's not 'Your Highness' anymore, Lady Pescos. It's Lady Nareen or, preferably, Zara."

"I think you may have understated what Asano's reaction would be, Zara. I always knew that there was history between you and him, but I never put much stock in rumours. I saw the two of you interact when we were all on that expedition together. It had the feel of a show to me, a political game your aunt concocted."

"It was."

"Then it's time you told me the truth, if you genuinely want to be a part of this team. I welcome your presence, as do the others. Your wide-area damage specialisation is a good fit for our team and, princess or not, having you on the roster will open a lot of doors when we go back to Rimaros. Assuming you want to stay with us at that stage."

Zara thought back to Asano's team outside. The unified front they put on, defensive of their friend and teammate, resonated with her. Her political upbringing always upheld the idea of compromise with both allies and enemies, who could easily switch from one day to the next. The idea of genuine commitment felt forbidden and enticing.

"I'm looking for a place to belong," she told Korinne, after thinking about it long enough that Korinne brought the tea and sat it on the table before sitting opposite Zara in the booth.

"Are you sure we're not a way station until you can talk Asano around?" Korinne asked as she poured the tea. "I'm not saying that's unacceptable, but I need to know where you stand in relation to my team."

Zara nodded as she held her cup, waiting for it to cool. While it was hot outside, the temperature and humidity inside the vehicle had both been set low.

"Honestly," she admitted, "I don't know. Unless my rushed approach and less-than-terrific reception here didn't make it clear, I'm somewhat floundering. I have to find something new. A new way to live my life."

"And you think Asano is the answer? Are you in love with him?"

"No," Zara said, shaking her head. "I've only ever met him a handful of times, which may be part of the problem. I'll confess to a certain fascination, and the mysteries surrounding him is a big part of that. Perhaps if I knew him better, I wouldn't be so compelled."

"You're drawn to trouble."

"No. Yes. I don't know, probably. Have you ever felt completely lost, Lady Pescos?"

"Korinne. If you're going to be in our team, you should call me Korinne. But no, sorry. I don't think I can empathise. I've always known my direction, ever since I was a girl. Even through detours like this, it doesn't derail me."

"I remember that feeling," Zara said with an envious smile. "That comforting certainty of where every foot forward was going to fall. I've been wondering a lot where I lost that, even though I knew the answer the whole time."

"Oh?" Korinne prompted.

"It was my first time far from the Storm Kingdom. The other side of the world. My aunt Vesper was the chaperone, but it was really me and some other iron-rankers from the Sapphire Crown guild. Royal guards my father assigned as a team, but not like yours. There was no camaraderie there. They were servants, but also minders. They weren't even companions, let alone friends. I've never actually had a team."

"So, it's true? You met Asano on the other side of the world and—"

"No," Zara said. "I met him, yes, but only a couple of times. We certainly never…"

Zara smiled.

"I was a girl. I don't think I'd ever felt like one before. I was always a princess. And an adventurer. A future leader. Then this man came bursting into my tent, all swagger and rakish charm. Exactly the kind of man my father would never let get anywhere near his precious daughters."

"Your guards wouldn't stand for that, surely?"

"They didn't, but he was unfazed and I told them to stop. He had no idea who I was. It was the first time I'd ever been treated as anything but a princess. He was this wild, crazy man, a few years older. He gave me a plate of baked slices. My guards destroyed half of them testing for toxins. I'll confess that my head was turned. Then I heard that he ran into me on his way to meet a whole group of gods, who had asked for him specifically."

"Why?"

"It doesn't matter. That just seems to be the circles he moves in."

"That is an absurd thing to say."

"He's an absurd man. I saw him again, at a party, but nothing came of it. I've been trained my whole life to handle politics and relationships, so I was aware of what was driving my feelings. I kept my distance and returned to Rimaros. Then I heard that he died. After that, he occupied this strange place in my mind. Or a version of him did anyway; one who was at least as much my own invention as true to the man."

"It's easy to idealise the dead. The living can never compete with a story in your head."

"No, they can't. When I came up with my terrible plan to get Kasper Irios out of our arranged marriage, I invoked Asano's name, which was an idiotic thing. He just fit so well. There was so little information about him and he had died on the far side of the world, in a sufficiently heroic fashion to impress. He also had impressive connections, but no family. He was exactly what I needed in a dead fiancé."

"And did you come up with this plan and he happened to fit, or did you come up with the plan because he fit? And which Asano was it? The real one or the one in your head?"

Zara let out a self-mocking chuckle.

"I think you know the answers, although I'd have denied it flatly at the time. Even to myself. Of course, it was a massive mess."

"I remember. Royal scandals get around, although how much of it is true is a very different question."

"It had all just about died down and my fake period of mourning was about to end," Zara said. "That's when he came back, but he came back different. Not like the way he was in my head, of course, but also not the way I knew him. The first time I saw him again was the day you first saw him as well."

"The expedition."

"When I met him, he was playful. Roguish. He was also ordinary in his power. But you saw what he was like that day. Angry, powerful."

"He wasn't powerful when you knew him?"

"No more than any capable adventurer. But you've felt what he's like now. What he can do with his aura. And I've heard other things. Things I can't talk about. And he certainly wasn't playful. His anger at me was genuine, whatever political show we put on."

"Why would he even agree to that?"

"Because of the damage my mistake would cause if he didn't. Whatever his flaws, he's a good man."

"So you say."

"Yes, I do say. I've looked into everything I can find about him, since he came back. And I could find more than most, as you'd imagine. There are sharp edges to him, but he's a good man. Willing to sacrifice."

"Are you sure you're not inventing a man in your head again?"

"No," Zara admitted. "I know that coming here was foolish. The attempts to rehabilitate my reputation were overtaken by events. The last hope I had was joining Asano as a royal liaison. He's always in the middle of something, and if I could be a part of that…"

She shook her head.

"When I was rejected, I knew it was time to move on. I was the last person to accept that I was long out of contention to be the next queen, but once I did, it was oddly freeing. Putting down a kingdom's worth of responsibility opened a world of possibility. I adopted into my mother's house to signal my withdrawal from the contest for the crown."

"If you have a whole world of opportunity, what are you doing here?"

"You're completely right," Zara said, nodding. "This was a terrible choice. I should have run far from Rimaros and far from Asano to find… whatever it is I'm looking for. A new way to live, I guess. I have this idea in my head that Asano is at the centre of things in a way that might let me find it."

Korinne shook her head. "I do not see the appeal of that man."

"That's not what this is."

Korinne drew a long breath and let it out slowly, then stood up.

"Temporary member or not, Princess, you'll be valuable to our team. But you are in desperate need of getting your head straight, and that's dangerous. There's a healer in this convoy who specialises in the mind. Seek her out. Until she tells me you're up for it, you can travel with our team, but I won't let you fight with it."

41

DOING THINGS THAT YOU SHOULDN'T

THE ASTRAL REALM THAT JASON'S SOUL SPACE HAD BECOME WAS AN ESTATE OF cloud buildings that sprawled through strange and varied gardens. It all centred on a dark crystal tower in a pagoda style that loomed over everything. Completing the dark lord motif was the giant blue and orange eye floating over the tower that regularly prompted unwelcome Sauron comparisons.

In a garden that looked something like an English country pond, Jason had created an avatar of himself. The avatar was floating cross-legged over the pond while Jason sat on a wooden bench on the shore. He alternately probed and bombarded the avatar with aura attacks and aura probes. The exercise itself had been devised by Amos as part of his training, serving several purposes. It helped him develop his aura defences and aura masking techniques, but these were areas where Jason was already strong.

The training method Amos had shown him was also designed to teach him how to do radically different things with his aura in rapid succession or even simultaneously. Jason had thought himself quite adept at manipulating his aura, which Amos quickly remedied by showing him how much he had left to learn. Rather than be disheartened, Jason had been excited at all the new possibilities laid out before him.

For the training method to be effective, Jason had initially required the more powerful Amos to switch between probes and bombardment to apply sufficient pressure. But inside his soul space, Jason had far more power than he did outside it. Once he figured out how to accurately replicate his outside power levels with an avatar, he was able to use the method through self-study, attacking his own avatar. As the avatar was still a part of himself, everything it learned, he did as well.

The training Amos was giving him, this method included, was comprehensively advancing Jason's aura manipulation skills, and the results were already showing. When Jason had first arrived in Rimaros, he'd attempted to create an identity mask by manipulating his aura. He was only now realising the many reasons his sloppy attempt had aroused the suspicion of even someone of lower rank than himself, cringing at his crude, earlier attempt.

Jason sensed the presence of Arabelle standing in front of his portal and he opened it to let her inside. He opened an arch next to himself so she would arrive next to him. She looked around before sitting down beside him on the wooden bench, joining him in observing the avatar.

"It unsettles me, coming here," she told him. "The Healer is one of the more hands-off gods, but I'm still used to his presence in the back of my mind."

"And here I was thinking that having someone taking up residence inside your mind would be the unsettling part."

"There's a comfort in faith, Jason. For some. Not those favoured by Dominion, of course. He likes the ones who refuse to kneel."

"Ugh, don't talk about that guy. And who said I won't kneel? I'll take scuffed knees over a severed neck."

"Is that a lie or selective memory?"

"I was younger then."

"How long ago did Shako kill you for your insolence?"

"About a year. And I wouldn't describe it as insolence. If some prick is telling you what to do for no better reason than they have the power to do so, they need mouthing off to."

Arabelle turned to look at him from under raised eyebrows.

"I'm aware of the irony," he said, not turning to meet her eyes.

"You told her to change her hair and eyes? You shouldn't be trying to take away people's body autonomy, Jason. Especially as a punitive measure."

"I know. I was angry. It's why I walked away."

She nodded.

"Your friends are concerned that you're moping in here. You shut them out, literally and figuratively. I was a little surprised you let me in, but it's a good sign that you did."

Jason let out a sigh.

"I know. Back in Greenstone, this was the part where I'd go off and clear adventure board notices until I'd worked through my problems. Keep busy doing something worthwhile as I was getting my head straight. I can't just leave everyone now, though. So, I'm just taking some time while I do some training."

Arabelle turned her gaze back to the avatar.

"One of Lord Pensinata's training exercises?" she asked.

"Yes."

She nodded her approval. "Separating yourself as you process emotions in your own time has always been one of your healthier defence mechanisms. Just make sure not to cut yourself off from your support structure. Too much separation has turned poisonous on you before, as you well know. Don't recreate your conditions on Earth for yourself."

"I know."

"Knowing something and using that knowledge for self-improvement are very different things, Jason."

"I know that too."

"I'm not sure that girl does. She clearly has some kind of fixation on you."

"Are you telling me that I should be happy I have a pretty stalker?"

"You know that I'm not. I find it interesting that you chose to point out that she was pretty."

"Anyone with eyes can see that."

"You're avoiding a response to my observation. We've talked about that."

Jason grumbled.

"Are you interested in this woman?"

"I don't know her."

"That isn't what I asked. It's plain that there is some manner of compulsion there. She's no prettier than Miss Wexler, yet Zara Rimaros gets under your skin in a way that Sophie never has."

"It's not Rimaros anymore. It's Nareen."

Arabelle turned to look at Jason again, this time her eyes narrowing in suspicion.

"Jason."

"Yes?"

"Are you spying on the other team?"

"What do you mean?"

"Have you been observing the goings-on inside their new vehicle?"

"I'm claiming this conversation under the confidentiality of a healer consultation. You can't tell anyone about the things I tell you."

"It's between you, me and my god."

"They don't count, the privacy ignoring... that doesn't matter. I just want to know you won't tell people what I tell you."

"I won't. Even if I think that you're keeping secrets and doing things that you shouldn't."

"I had Farrah and Belinda take a look at the defences of the other team's vehicle when it first joined the convoy. I had the girls put a hole in the protections so Shade could slip in and out to observe them."

"You've been spying on them."

"Shade operates under certain strictures, you know that. He won't tell me anything unless there is a security threat or something else I need to know."

"Or unless you ask him."

"Yes."

"And have you?"

Jason didn't answer for a long time. Arabelle waited him out.

"I listened in on a conversation between Zara and Korinne."

"That's a wildly inappropriate use of the power you have over the people in this convoy. It's a violation."

"I know," he said softly. "I have a bad habit of becoming the thing I hate, the moment I get the chance."

"Your actions towards this woman are setting up a power imbalance, Jason. The kind of imbalance that you described between yourself and Asya."

The avatar over the pond dissolved into nothing.

"I'm not in a relationship with Zara Rimaros."

"You weren't with Asya for a long time, from what you've told me. She was a young woman chasing you around in a position where you held all the power. Does that sound familiar?"

"She wasn't chasing me around. I never said anything like that."

"Farrah did. I learned more about your time on Earth from her than I did you, Jason. Even after all this time, you are more withholding than you should be."

"You shouldn't be talking to other people about me."

"I wasn't. I was listening."

"What's going on here is nothing like what happened with Asya."

"Not yet."

Jason stood up, storming back and forth. He didn't seem to notice when his sharp pacing took him onto the surface of the water, which held him like solid ground. Suddenly, he stopped, his back to Arabelle.

"My fears have always been narcissistic," he said, not turning around. "I've been confronted with them magically, more than once, and they're always about myself. Fear of what I'll become. Fear of how I'll fail, and what my actions will cost. Frankly, they've all been very well-founded. And now I have a new fear."

"And that is?"

Jason turned, holding out his arms to indicate the space around them. "Do you understand what this place is?"

"Not really. Some kind of astral space created by your soul."

"This isn't a place I created. This place *is* me. I'm as much geography as I am a person."

"Ah."

Arabelle nodded, having realised Jason's issue.

"You've finally returned to your friends, but you're afraid that your path will take you away from them again."

"They're essence users. It defines their power and their path forward. Even if they manage to follow that path to the end, it makes them like Soramir. That's not where my path leads. Many of the gold- and diamond-rank secrets are still hidden from me, but I'm an astral king. I'm still not sure exactly what that means, but I do know it puts me on a different path from anyone I care about. Even Dawn."

Arabelle nodded again.

"Sit down, Jason."

He did as instructed.

"Your fears aren't as self-involved as you seem to think."

"The nightmare hags I've met say differently."

"And you think some monster you met understands you better than I do? Such creatures latch onto the fears closest to your sense of self-identity. Of course, what they dig up is about you."

"That's not what I was told."

"And when did you, of all people, start believing whatever you were told? How many times have we discussed what happened to your brother, your friend and your lover over the last few months? About your fear of losing other people close to you?"

"A lot of times," he begrudgingly acknowledged.

"You seem to have gotten it into your head that losing them is inevitable, and you're mentally preparing for that severance by distancing yourself from them emotionally."

"That's not what I'm—"

"Yes, it is. You're convinced that you'll become so alien that you won't care about them anymore."

"What if that is what's going to happen? What if it's inevitable?"

"What you do is obvious: you choose for it not to happen."

"I just choose?"

"Since when has impossible or inevitable stopped you from doing anything? Are you, of all people, going to tell me that powers on the level of a great astral being are too much to fight against?"

Jason blinked.

"Huh."

"Yes."

They sat side by side for a long time as Jason realigned his thoughts. Arabelle felt his body language shift as he nodded to himself.

"What are you going to do about your pretty young stalker?" she asked. "It's clear that she's in a very uncertain place with her own self-identity. You could potentially do some real damage there."

Jason nodded his agreement. "She seems to have latched onto the idea that I can somehow show her what's next for her."

"And what will you do about that?"

"I'm not ready to be anyone's purpose, or even to show them theirs. I think only Shade has a better understanding than you of what a mess I am right now."

"That doesn't change the question. What will you do about her?"

"She's gotten it in her head that I can do something for her, but the person she needs is you. Do I send her away to take myself out of the equation? Point her at one of your colleagues? Or do I let her stay and confront whatever has gotten her fixated on me? This is not rhetorical, by the way. I'm genuinely asking you as a mental health professional."

"You should not be the one to handle her situation if she stays."

"Oh, I completely agree. I think regular sessions with you should be the condition of letting her join the convoy. I'll stay well out of it."

"I'm surprised you're willing to tolerate her presence at all."

"I'm sympathetic to her personal brand of damage, even if we came to it from opposite directions. I understand doing reckless things because it seems like the only path forward, but I let her stay for Korinne's team. They got kind of a rough deal in terms of determining their own fate. They didn't ask to be stuck dealing with me lording over them."

"Then perhaps you should give them some more autonomy."

"No. But having Zara on their team will be a boon for them when this is done with and we part ways. I can give them that much."

When Jason and Arabelle emerged from his soul space, no one else was around, barring the traffic moving down the road they were parked next to. Jason found his new cloud vessel had completed its formation and his companions had already boarded to explore their new home.

The result of the House de Varco's purpose-built design looked more akin to Earth design than it had before, being something like a sleek white pleasure yacht sitting on top of a giant hovercraft. Jason could feel the changes through his connection to it having been produced by the soul-linked cloud flask.

In terms of speed and manoeuvrability, there were only minor enhancements. The larger differences came from the protective properties of the exterior and the integrity of the structure. The materials that had been added to the cloud flask had been selected to enable the vessel to produce specialised defences that optimised both the protective properties of those materials and the cloud vehicle's ability to dissolve and reconstitute its structure. The result was both resilient to attack and able to repair itself in real-time during an attack.

The other new feature, also oriented towards combat, was the speciality weapons designed by Travis. Large ordnance was his speciality and he had developed an array of weapons that would enhance Jason's cloud vessel should they find themselves in combat. As they were heading in the direction of a potentially large conflict with the messengers, Jason was happy to have potent new weapons in his arsenal.

Certain design elements in the reformed vessel were similar to those in the vehicle recently purchased by Korinne and her team. Like the modifications to the cloud vessel, its design came from House de Varco, although the end results were very different. The cloud vessel was larger and a visibly hybridised vehicle. The other was made entirely from conventional materials and was only as big a vehicle as Korinne's team could convince her to buy. Even then, she had only capitulated since the team had all supplied funds in equal measure.

The door to the vehicle Korinne's team now called home opened. The top of the door came out and down, extending to form a ramp. Zara emerged, her hair and eyes now looking like polished copper. Her hair was loose, parted in the middle as it fell to her shoulders, framing the caramel skin of her face. Jason clamped down his aura, but he gave Arabelle a side glance, knowing she'd caught his reaction to Zara's dark beauty.

"This is Arabelle Remore," Jason introduced coldly. "She will ask you some questions and decide if you can remain as a part of this convoy. If you lie to her, you're out. If you evade or refuse to answer her questions, you're out."

Jason turned and marched up the ramp leading into his own vehicle.

"Mr Asano," Shade said once they were inside the vessel. Another innovation from the de Varco designs was an automated privacy screen in corridors and cabins for soundproofing. That made the entry foyer they were in secure against prying ears.

"Yes, Shade?"

"You seem to be having an outsized reaction to Lady Nareen."

"I noticed that myself."

"Perhaps you should have yourself tested for external influences."

"If something was affecting me, I'd know."

"Perhaps. On the other hand, you and your abilities are well known enough that an enemy could have designed a subtle attack with properties to avoid detection, allowing it to bypass your system notification ability."

Jason frowned, considering the idea.

"I think if there was anything, I would have realised it in my soul space."

"Perhaps it is related to your soul space, and not necessarily malign. The lingering effects of such a different state of being could still be affecting you. Or the link with the avatar you created could potentially have left you more open to altered emotional states."

Jason frowned.

"That sounds dishearteningly plausible."

"Perhaps you should seek out Mr Standish and Mr Davone, to see if they can find anything."

"I don't like that idea."

"An astral magic specialist and a healer would be the appropriate people to consult, Mr Asano."

"Yeah, but I don't want to go to Clive and Neil to ask if my private god realm is making me horny."

42

QUIET PROFESSIONALISM

THE ORIGINAL DESIGN OF JASON'S CLOUD CONSTRUCTS ALLOWED TWO MODES. ONE was overtly made of cloud substance, while the other looked traditionally constructed by the vessel replicating ordinary materials. This could be a false façade or truly mimic the properties, so long as the materials had been fed into the flask.

Over time, the binary nature of the constructs had become more fluid as Jason made many alterations to the cloud flask that produced them. Between deepening his bond to it, filling it with myriad new materials and altering it using authority stolen from the Builder, the cloud flask had undergone extreme changes.

The culmination of this was a third form of cloud construct that used a hybrid of replicated materials and cloud substance in equal measure. The inclusion of House de Varco's modification designs had made it possible, allowing the vessels to use the best of both worlds. Not only could it enjoy the exceptional properties of any materials it reproduced, but also the mutable and self-repairing properties of cloud substance.

Belinda ascended stairs that were rigid platforms that seemed like white marble, both to the eye and to the touch. They floated on cloud-stuff that offered just a tiny bit of give, balancing comfort and support. That support modulated itself automatically, whether the person walking it was as heavy as Gary or as light as Belinda. Light was a relative term, however, as high-rankers weighed more than normal people of identical builds. Belinda's small frame looked very light, while her actual weight was more than Taika's had been, pre-essence.

Belinda made her way up the stairs to the top deck, where a cabin door opened at her approach. Jason's master cabin looked different every time she went inside as he frequently shifted it around, and this time, it was empty save for Jason himself. He was standing in front of the window, back to the cabin as he looked out at the city in the distance. Dark structures of glass and metal poked through the rainforest canopy in the distance to gleam in the harsh summer sun.

"I have them," Belinda said, stepping into the cabin. "They'll stop working if you use your more overt magical abilities, but that shouldn't be an issue for you. Humphrey would have more to worry about in that regard."

"What about using my aura?" Jason asked without turning around. "It's a little more forceful than the norm."

"I've never tested this kind of device with an aura like yours. I'd keep it tamped down, just to be safe. That shouldn't be a problem if you're laying low, right?"

Jason turned around, flashing her a smile.

"Exactly right," he agreed as she handed him a pair of blue coins. "I just put them in place?"

"I like to keep devices like this one simple. It's important to be able to change appearances quickly and easily when you're avoiding pursuit."

"I'm not looking to steal anything," Jason told her, a hint of good-natured scolding in his voice.

"I'm just saying that you should keep your options open."

"Is this what the princess uses to change her appearance?"

"I'm fairly certain she uses some ritual magic designed especially for celestines. Not quite as convenient, and needs regular reapplication, but it will hold up under stress in a way that these won't. But as long as you avoid your big finisher spells or any of your wide-area powers, these should be fine."

"I'm not looking to get in any fights," Jason said.

"You never are," Belinda said.

"You didn't see me back on Earth," he said, then placed the blue coins over his eyes. The coins immediately vanished, revealing not Jason's alien eyes but ordinary dark brown ones, much as they'd been when he was human. "I wasn't mellow the way I am here."

"Are you sure you don't want your eyes to be a piercing, icy blue or something?" Belinda offered. "I can tweak them very easily."

"No, thank you," Jason said, prodding around his eyes. The coins had truly disappeared, not just turned invisible.

"They'll reappear if you use too much magic," Belinda said. "Just channel mana into your eyes if you want to take them off."

Using most magic items was a fairly instinctual process of feeding them with mana to form a magical link. Jason did just that with his eyes and they went back to normal as the coins reappeared.

"That will do nicely," he said. "Thank you, Belinda."

The city of Yaresh was relatively small in terms of population, having only a few tens of thousands. The design, deeply accommodating the natural environment, led to a small population density, however. Geographically, Yaresh had the footprint of a much larger centre.

Humphrey, Clive and Neil had gone ahead to the Yaresh Adventure Society branch to gather information. The information they brought back spoke to a situation more complex than originally anticipated, which they gathered everyone together to explain.

Almost every member of the convoy was present in the cloud vessel's briefing room, even the gold-rankers, including the less-than-stable Callum Morse. Absent were the Order of Redeeming Light prisoners, all in magical stasis save for Melody, locked in her cabin in the cloud house. Carlos was present, but his assistants were not, leaving only two last absentees.

Humphrey, Clive and Neil stood at the front of the briefing room, the others sitting in rows watching them.

"Where's Asano?" Korinne asked from the first row, the team leader sitting alongside the gold-rankers.

"Jason and Estella Warnock," Humphrey told her, "have headed for the city, where they will remain for what we estimate to be two weeks. For the duration of that time, our teams will be working in close cooperation with other teams in the area. That means avoiding questions about why the cook is killing so many monsters, or why a mysterious figure keeps slaughtering monster packs before we arrive. Until we can operate more independently, Jason will be working in the city."

"Warnock I understand," Korinne said. "Scouting out urban areas is her job. Asano doesn't strike me as much of a spy."

"Jason will surprise you when it comes to blending in with regular folk," Gary said. "When he doesn't have to get involved with kings and gods and high-rank adventurers, he can blend in just fine. Especially for someone from another world. He doesn't run around doing outlandish things around normal people because he doesn't have to."

"Mostly doesn't," Rufus qualified. "Depending on your definition of outlandish."

"He's far more normal around regular people," Gary said. "Remember that village, right after we met him. He was just meeting people and being social. While gathering information, I'll remind you. Completely sensible."

"Are you talking about the village where he was blasted off the side of a mountain by a malfunctioning waterfall before saving the village from a bunch of shabs?" Rufus asked him.

"It's not his fault the waterfall wasn't working properly."

"Standing in front of it when it wasn't working was."

"Jason isn't going into the city to spy," Arabelle spoke up, cutting them short. "He presented a new idea for refining his aura control to Lord Pensinata, who approved of his exploration of the concept."

"What concept?" Korinne asked.

"Integrating aura-echo interrelation with interpersonal magic," Clive explained.

"What does that mean?" asked Kalif, a member of Korinne's team. "Interpersonal magic?"

Clive took on an uncomfortable expression.

"Interpersonal magic is known by a wide variety of colloquial terms," he said. "One of which is carnal magic."

"Wait," Kalif said. "We're going to be working for the next two weeks while Asano is off knocking boots with the cute pink-haired woman?"

"Miss Warnock and Jason will be operating separately," Humphrey said. "Miss Warnock will fulfil her role as a spy while Jason undertakes his own endeavour."

"Plus, Stella likes girls," Sophie added.

"So much for that, then, Polix," Kalif said to another member of his team who had a disappointed expression. "Hold on, if Asano isn't taking someone with him, how is he going to use rumpy-pumpy magic?"

"Firstly," Clive said, "please don't call it that. And secondly, I imagine he'll seek out volunteers."

"Meaning he'll have to pick up women himself?" Kalif asked. "Who's going to go for that guy? If he had his Rimaros reputation to play off, he might get a pity rub, but he's playing a cook now, right? He's going to spend the next two weeks going home alone."

"I completely agree," Belinda said. "What woman will go for a guy with laid-back charm, absolute confidence, a mysterious dark side and hidden secrets? Plus, he can cook and dance, which are traits that famously repel women."

"I bet he doesn't go for those stuffy society dances," commented Rosa, the scout from Kalif's team.

That earned her a glare from Kalif.

"I mean, who cares?" Rosa covered lamely.

"I think that's quite enough about Jason," Humphrey said. "We need to focus on our own activities in the coming weeks and potentially months. The conflict with the messengers in this region has proven significantly more complex than anticipated."

"The Adventure Society more or less told us to shut up and do the contracts we're told," Neil said. "They're on a war footing and are looking for soldiers who will obey, not adventurers causing trouble."

"Fortunately," Humphrey said, "we were contacted by a priest of the Church of Knowledge. He gave us a much more thorough appraisal of the situation and background to how it reached this point. He also told us that if we can, not to make a fuss and follow the Adventure Society's orders for a couple of weeks, at which point the Church of Knowledge will requisition us for the main conflict. They already know about Jason, so they'll set us up on missions where he can work with us almost openly. They regularly requisition teams, so it won't look too out of place if we've proven ourselves reliable."

"Why would it look outlandish if they just call us up now?"

"Because there are plenty of teams that have already proven themselves and want a place in the big fight," Neil said. "If we come in out of nowhere and take a slot, people will start looking at us closer than we want to be looked at."

"The Church of Knowledge reached out because of Jason's relationship with the goddess," Clive said. "But Jason is also the reason we don't want too many eyes on us."

"Relationship with the goddess," Belinda repeated. "And this guy thinks he'll have trouble picking up women."

"It's not that kind of relationship, Belinda," Clive said. "Also, I'm fairly certain that implying it is counts as blasphemy."

"So?" she shot back. "Gods and their churches never did a damn thing for me."

"You do know that I'm a priest of the Healer, don't you?" Neil asked.

"You've got an imaginary friend; we're all very proud," Belinda told him. "Get on with it."

"The Healer is not imaginary! And you're the one who interrupted in the first place."

"Belinda," Humphrey admonished, his tone making it plain that he was not willing to brook further nonsense. "If silence is as much professionalism as you can muster, then do so. Clive, please explain what is going on."

Clive nodded as Belinda gave Neil a smirk but held her tongue.

"Some of what we're about to tell you is information we had already gathered from various sources," Clive said. "Some of it comes from the priest of Knowledge we just met. As you should all be aware, the Church of Knowledge has been mustering forces in certain areas around the world."

"What most of you won't know," Humphrey followed on, "is the scale and scope of the church's activities, and how long they've been going on."

"The groundwork for the church's activities," Clive picked up, "turns out to have been going on for decades. Large troupes are being established piecemeal, so as not to attract attention. Monster cores have been used to create expansive forces of essence users, under the command of more conventionally trained adventurers. Each and every one, faithful to the Church of Knowledge. Only the god War was aware of the magnitude of Knowledge's plans, and remained silent for reasons unknown, at least to us."

"A number of years ago," Humphrey said, "they started to mobilise and gather at locations around the world, chosen by no means anyone could determine. It took a while to realise what was happening and on what scale, but if you track the activity back to when the forces that Knowledge had built up started moving, it was all on a single day. A day after which the Church of Knowledge apparently no longer cared about being noticed."

"Given that you've made such a point of it," Korinne said, "I assume there is something significant about that day."

"It was the same day Jason Asano first arrived in this world," Clive said. "Knowledge knows more than even the other gods. She knew the messengers were coming, and she knew that Jason would be the one that opened the window through which they would come."

"Are you saying that Asano is responsible for the messenger invasion?"

"No," Humphrey said. "Jason and Farrah were the ones who triggered the monster surge."

"The monster surge that had been artificially delayed for years," Clive added. "The longer it was stalled, the worse the surge that came with it would be when finally unleashed. And the longer the Builder would have to plunder our world. Jason and Farrah put an end to that delay and prevented it from getting worse, but some amount of damage was inevitable. It was a plan that came into effect years before Jason ever encountered magic."

"And the same window used by the Builder," Humphrey said, "allowed what we thought was the Church of Purity to help the messengers in coming to our world. And that is where everyone learned what Knowledge had been preparing for."

"Where Knowledge had gathered, other forces gathered in reaction," Neil explained. "And in every region where that happened, messengers were summoned. Knowledge has been preparing to defend this world for decades, building the force we would need but have no time to establish once the threat was revealed."

"This brings us to what the priest in Yaresh told us," Humphrey said. "A few hours from the city, Knowledge's military force set up a camp. The God of War did the same, and then the messengers came. The government in Yaresh as well as the Adventure Society were both concerned about each of these developments, and then things got worse."

"There is an extremely rare natural magic event that can happen," Clive said. "It's called a natural array. To excessively simplify, it means that, over time, essences, awakening stones and quintessence manifested, undisturbed, in a very specific pattern. The convergent magical energies within that pattern combine to create unconventional effects. The nature of those effects is defined by the size and nature of the pattern, as well as the elements that make it up."

"Can someone simplify that some more?" Kalif asked.

"It means that sometimes magic stuff happens," Clive said, exasperated. "If you can't follow more than that, then I recommend staying quiet and asking your team leader after the briefing."

"I'm not an idiot," Kalif said sullenly.

"Then do the smart thing and be quiet," Clive said, "or we'll be here all day."

"I don't like how you're speaking to my team member," Korinne said warningly.

"And I stopped caring what you liked the moment your new team member arrived," Clive shot back. "Shut up and listen or get out."

Humphrey put a hand on Clive's shoulder.

"Clive—"

"No," Clive said, shrugging off his hand, and turned on Amos Pensinata. "You were brought on to help Jason, not make things worse. But your baggage..."

He waved a hand at Korinne's team.

"...has only made things worse. So, fix it or get off this boat and take them with you."

With that, Clive stormed out, Humphrey wincing as he watched him go.

"What about the briefing?" Neil asked. "Clive was meant to cover the magic stuff."

"We'll postpone," Humphrey said. "We've covered what we need for the next couple of weeks, which is that we'll be given contracts that we should carry out with the kind of quiet professionalism that we have failed to demonstrate today. We can reconvene the briefing once we're in the city and everyone has cooled down."

At the back of the briefing room, Zara shrank into her chair, trying to make herself as small as she felt.

43

A MAN OF MANY TALENTS

AFTER INCREASING DELAYS, THE CONVOY WAS FINALLY PREPARING TO HEAD DOWN the last stretch of road leading into the city of Yaresh. Part of the delay was making sure they had a place waiting to stow their large vehicles for the duration of their visit. They had settled on a fairly low-end camping ground as space was currently at a premium. Many travelling adventurers had already arrived in Yaresh, looking to join the conflict with the messengers. Humphrey's and Korinne's teams were far from the only ones to travel in what amounted to ambulatory houses.

Before they left, Humphrey approached the vehicle used by the other team, stopping at the bottom of the ramp that led inside. He waited, knowing that the magic defences would have already alerted the occupants to his presence. He was left standing for several minutes before Korinne appeared at the top of the ramp.

"What can I do for you, Master Geller?"

"After the failed briefing, I thought it would be a good idea for us to discuss the friction between our teams. May I come in?"

Shortly thereafter, Korinne was sitting across from Humphrey in a booth. Unlike when she had been there with Zara, she did not make tea.

"I think it's clear that our teams are having some issues operating together," Humphrey said. "As the leaders, I thought you and I should figure out together if this is something we can remedy, or at least ameliorate, or if the differences are irreconcilable."

"Your team members seem to be blaming us for Asano running off to get his dongle wet instead of working with his team."

"That is not your fault and they know it. But your decision to take on Zara Rimaros has got them riled."

"Are you telling me to kick her out?"

"No. Jason decided that she stays. He's aware that you and your team are not in ideal circumstances and that your involvement with the princess will serve as some manner of compensation."

"He said that, did he?"

"Yes. I'm not putting words in his mouth to try and make you think he's less difficult than he actually is."

"Why is it his decision to make in the first place? Which one of you is the team leader?"

"On our team—our team, not my team—we each take the roles we need to take."

"That's a good way to get yourselves killed, dithering when everyone tries to take control in the heat of battle. Command structures agree for a reason."

"And we've found what works for us. I won't claim it will work for your team any more than yours will work for mine."

"Why are we even talking about this anyway? Didn't Asano leave the decision about the princess to Lady Remore?"

"It's Mrs Remore," Humphrey corrected. "And you'll find that Jason does things to achieve the outcome he wants, not to say what he means or speak the truth."

"You're saying he's duplicitous."

"We each have our roles. I already told you that."

"Fine. But how are we supposed to trust someone who lies to us?"

"We don't want your trust, Lady Pescos. We want your cooperation or, failing that, for you to stay out of our way. Zara Rimaros used Jason's name dishonourably, and it dragged him into the exact trouble he wanted to avoid, at the time he most needed to avoid it. That is why having her on your team has put my team at odds with you. We are sensitive about losing Jason because we've done it before. He can be fragile in certain regards, and if something happens because of your princess, you'll find that we are bad enemies to have."

"Then why let her stay in the convoy at all?"

"Because Jason told us to, and he's the one she makes trouble for. You wanted to know why Jason gets to choose? That's why."

Korinne sighed. "My team is resentful of yours. It feels like we're secondary. Tacked on."

"You are," Humphrey said. "Do with that what you will."

Korinne started pacing in thought, a scowl plastered on her face.

"Genuine contention will only drag us both down," Korinne said. "But a rivalry could be a push that moves us all forward."

The smile that spread across Humphrey's face made Korinne suspect he'd been waiting for the suggestion all along.

"I couldn't agree more," he said. "And Jason's absence might just give us the breathing room to find a balance that is beneficial to us all."

The city walls of Yaresh were a line of massive trees with walls of glossy black stone filling the gaps between them. Tunnels passed right through the trunks, allowing passage from one section of wall-top to the next. A black land skimmer arrived at the wall where vehicles were queued up at the gate, awaiting inspection. In the driver's seat was Jason, with Estella Warnock beside him.

Most of the vehicles were hauling cargo on magically powered wagons, some of which were almost the size of a semi-trailer truck. Bulk land freight was inefficient compared to the alternatives magic offered, but was cheap and seemed common locally, based on the vehicles lined up at the gates.

"That's a lot of land transport," Jason pointed out.

"I was thinking the same thing," Estella agreed. "Could be something about local magic conditions that makes other methods less viable. The magic is more than high enough to support airships, though, so I don't know. I'll look into it and see if there's anything going on we need to concern ourselves with."

"I have to say, Miss Warnock, I am increasingly satisfied with the choice to bring you aboard."

"Don't be too happy," Estella said. "I'm calling dibs on your princess."

"What?"

"You heard me."

"You're talking about Zara?"

"Yep. Come down in the world, low self-esteem. That's my zone."

"That's pretty despicable."

"You had your chances."

"I don't mean calling dibs. I mean preying on someone at their lowest."

"Oh, yeah, she's really hurting, with all her money and connections. Not all of us can just adopt ourselves into one of the most prestigious families in the kingdom because being a princess was harshing us out."

"It doesn't sound like you want to chase after her."

"I'll admit I'm not great at pursuing relationships."

"Have you considered maybe trying charm? Getting to know them honestly? Basic decency?"

"None of those are my strong areas."

"Then maybe figure out what your strong areas are and find someone who finds those appealing."

"As it turns out, I'm not really into the people who are into my strengths. My standards are too high to include anyone who'd settle for me."

"You weren't kidding about low self-esteem being your zone, were you? Watch out for the landing."

The skimmer turned into a cloud of swirling darkness that was drawn into Jason's shadow. Jason moved from sitting to standing with practised ease while Estella fell on her rear before getting up and brushing road dirt off her pants.

"I did say watch out for the landing," he told her.

"I didn't know that meant the vehicle would disappear out from under me."

There were two queues for people wanting to enter the city. Rather than joining the vehicle queue, they moved to the shorter queue for those with other means of transport, usually mid-to-high-rank adventurers. These were people that flew under their own power, rode familiars like Jason did or portalled into a nearby open area designated for that purpose.

Jason and Estella produced their Adventure Society badges and identity papers. Like Jason's current identity, Estella was registered as an auxiliary that was not required to mobilise, despite the city's adventurers being on a war footing. They were told that the team they were attached to would need to report to the Adventure Society by the end of the day after their arrival. After that notification, the pair were allowed through a tunnel that brought him into the city proper.

"Oh, yeah," Jason said as he emerged from the tunnel and looked around. "Travis won't be happy about missing a proper elf city."

They were in a warehouse district centred around the city gate. A four-lane boulevard ran from the gate into the city, but didn't follow the plumb-straight line typical of urban areas. It was instead split into a pair of double-lane streets, each following one side of a mostly straight creek. The sides of the street were lined with trees and the space around the buildings was filled with grass.

The buildings were all made from brick in various shades of black, yellow, grey, red and brown, suggesting a wide variety of local stone. Vines crawled up the walls of every building and the roofs were gently sloped and covered in live grass, bushes and other small-to-medium plants. The air was thick with rainforest smells, damp and earthy. Looking down the boulevard and further into the city, they saw much taller buildings in the distance where stone gave way to glass and metal.

Panning his gaze around, Jason saw very little lumbered wood. What wood he did see looked either natural, with the city accommodating its growth, or having been shaped into highly specific forms as it grew. The buildings were spaced out, with rainforest growth burgeoning up in between them.

The street was busy with vehicles entering through the city gate next to the tunnel from which they had just emerged. Taking more of a look, Jason noticed that many of the vehicles were made from more of the specifically grown wood. Metal-wheeled carriages had wooden frames that not only looked to have been grown that way but also had the faint aura of living plants. The frames were filled out with metal and draped cloth. Other vehicles had similar designs, from three-wheeled single-seaters to bus-like contraptions that had a dozen massive wooden legs instead of wheels.

Other vehicles that Jason was more familiar with were also in evidence. Land skimmers, more conventional carriages and personal floatation discs were all on display. They were minimally present, however, and never driven by the elves that made up the bulk of the population. The local elven ethnicity had skin tones ranging from almond to milk chocolate, while their hair ranged from honey to rich brown. Straight hair was either out of fashion or not natural, with styles ranging from cascading waves to ringlets to explosions of frizzy waves.

Jason and Estella moved out of the way of others emerging from the tunnel and Jason closed his eyes. He took a deep breath, letting it out slowly with a huge grin.

"Do you still have lungs?" Estella asked him.

"No."

"Then how are you breathing like that?"

"I just do. Doesn't your body just do the things you want it to?"

"No. My grandfather showed me some techniques for body manipulation, but if I wanted to breathe, I'd have to concentrate to make it work."

"You should practise those techniques some more. It's nice to be able to sigh sometimes. Studies have shown that sighing is an important component of personal well-being, helping to alleviate stress and recalibrate your mood."

"I'm going to go now. See you in two weeks."

"Don't forget that Shade is there if you need to signal for help."

"You thought I'd forget the person you left hiding in my shadow?"

"You might have."

"He watches me sleep."

"Yeah, he mentioned that you snore."

"What?"

"Mr Asano," Shade said from Jason's shadow. "I will thank you for not impugning my character. Miss Warnock, I can assure you that I told Mr Asano nothing about your snoring."

"I don't snore."

"I acknowledge that you assert that, Miss Warnock."

"You two are as bad as each other," Estella said. She stormed off, leaving Jason standing at the side of the street.

"Does she really snore?" Jason asked.

"Mr Asano, you were the one who told me not to divulge personal details unless relevant to security. Even if those details sound like someone sawing lumber in a tunnel."

Jason spent the day walking through the city, taking things in. Beyond the unconventional architecture, the warehouse district had little to offer and he didn't tarry. The neighbouring entertainment district proved much more interesting, even early in the day, with bars, cafes and places offering delights ranging from the chaste to the downright saucy. Jason was looking for the place he could sample the local cuisine when he spotted an elf rubbing out the menu board from the outside wall of a small pub.

"Food's off?" he asked.

"Most of the kitchen crew got in a brawl playing tri-ball," she said without turning around. "The city militia threw both teams in the cells until tomorrow. Chef's still in, but unless you know of four at least halfway-decent cooks who'll work for cheap on short notice, there won't be enough hands to do food service."

Still with her back to him, she didn't see the huge grin overtake Jason's face.

Bellory had been sceptical of the strange human, but she stood transfixed as she watched the bustle of activity in the kitchen. As the chef issued directions, a forest of shadow arms poked out from under shelves, out of cupboards or anywhere else a shadow could be found. They also reached out from her new temporary employee, chopping up ingredients, working the grill and frying with pans or plating meals.

"Are you sure it's okay for those things to touch the food?" she asked the chef, Kellance. He was her cousin.

"The conjured arms are very sanitary," Jason said.

"Also, I have an active sanitation ritual," Kellance said. "More sariantes, please, Mr Miller."

"Call me John," Jason told him. "Which ones are the sariantes? Oh, the shallot-looking things, no worries. They taste good."

"Have you been sampling ingredients, Mr Miller?"

"Er... no."

The rainforest-riddled city offered little in the way of light pollution, making it easy to see the stars shine once the sky grew dark. After the evening rush died down, Jason and Kellance retired to the roof of the pub, in lounge chairs with naturally grown frames slung with light, comfortable fabric. Between them was a side table with a bottle and two glasses. Once the pub closed for the night, Kellance went home and his spot on the roof was taken by Bellory. The bottle was emptied, followed by two more.

"I didn't realise that elves could put away so much liquor," Jason said. "I've got poison resistance and this stuff still has a kick."

"Do you know a lot of elves?"

"I haven't done a lot of drinking with them, it's true," Jason said. "Although I'm just realising that I might have and don't remember it because they drank me under the table. I did make some elven friends, though, when I was living in a port city a few years back."

"And now you're following adventurers around?"

"Strictly speaking, they're following me. They haven't even arrived yet. Or maybe they have; I've been here all day. And I think I just drank all my wages."

Bellory laughed, a tinkling water sound.

"You don't mind just being an auxiliary?" she asked. "Waiting back at camp while the others go off and do the fighting?"

"Well, for one," Jason slurred, holding up a slightly wobbly finger, "have you ever seen adventurers fight monsters? You're best off staying away from that, believe me. And for a third thing, I serve an important function."

"You do seem like an important man," Bellory said unconvincingly.

"Do you know what a bulvrath is?"

"I don't."

"It's a bog monster. Likes to ambush travellers on roads that go through swamps and mangroves. Very good at hiding, very cautious. Good at telling the difference between a wagon full of juicy victims and a wagon full of adventurers coming to kill it. Takes days to pin them down, and that's when you know what you're doing."

"And what's that got to do with cooking? Are they delicious?"

"I haven't checked. They make nests out of their own poo."

"I don't think I'd check either."

"The point I'm making is that after hunting down a bulvrath, an adventuring team has spent days roaming around a filthy bog, living on spirit coins, for the chance to kill a monster while wading through waist-deep filth. When they come back from that, do you think they'd rather wash themselves off with soap potion, eat a spirit coin and go to bed, or have a nice, crystal-wash-infused shower followed by a delicious hot meal?"

"You provide showers as well as cook?"

"I'm a man of many talents. I cook, I dance, I provide amenities and I…"

He frowned.

"…I'm a man of three talents."

Bellory laughed again as she emptied the last bottle, splitting the dregs between their glasses.

"So, will you be going back to your amenities?"

"I don't, strictly speaking, know where they are right now," he said, not exactly lying. Knowing the precise direction and distance wasn't the same as knowing what the location in question was. "I'm sure they've arrived somewhere. My friend Hump said something about a camping ground."

"You have a friend named Hump?"

"You wouldn't like him. He's definitely not super-handsome. I'm sure I can find my way back to them."

"You know," she said, her voice growing husky. "It's awfully late to go looking for your friends, especially in your condition."

"I'm fine," Jason said, his sing-song voice not assisting his plausibility. "I'm fine to go roaming the streets at night, as surely as I'm standing here."

"You're sitting."

"You might have a point, then. Are you inviting me to stay?"

"Maybe."

"I'd best take this off, then," he said, reaching under his shirt collar to unclip a small suppression collar.

- Multiple resistances have increased. All relevant afflictions will have their duration reduced according to new resistance levels.

- Poison [alcohol (silver rank)] has ended.
- Poison [alcohol (silver rank)] has ended.
- Poison [alcohol (silver rank)] has ended.
- Poison [alcohol (silver rank)] has ended.

Jason shook his head to clear it, then turned to Bellory, who was giving the suppression collar a flat look.

"I told you I had poison resistance," he said. "Does this mean I'm uninvited?"

"No," she said, climbing out of her chair and on top of him in his, making the frame squeak. "It means you better remember what that fourth talent is."

THE SAME THING AS TELLING THE TRUTH

JASON WAS COOKING BREAKFAST IN THE PUB'S KITCHEN WHEN THE CHEF, Kellance, arrived through the door leading directly into the kitchen from the alley. In Yaresh, alleys were much nicer than the norm, usually having more in common with a garden. In this case, a gravel path meandered through long grass and around a couple of trees with long leaves of lush green.

Jason had learned the day before that the elven chef was the cousin of Bellory, the pub's owner.

"Morning, bloke," Jason said as he entered, only briefly glancing from the frypan in front of him.

"John, you're still here," Kellance said. "I had a feeling you might be."

"Oh?"

"Bell likes men she knows for sure won't stick around longer than it takes fruit to go bad. Her husband running off, leaving her with this place and a pile of debt did some damage. She's scared of opening up again, you know?"

"I can imagine. She glossed over it last night, but I got the impression that there was a wound there. I hope you don't mind me plundering the kitchen to make breakfast."

"That depends. Did you make enough for three?"

"As a matter of fact, I did. If you want to grab some…"

Jason trailed off, frowning as he looked at the wall.

"What is it?" Kellance asked.

"Three men are coming this way, and I don't think it's for a breakfast fry-up."

The pub, like most buildings in the area, was made of dark grey stone. The door to the alley was a rectangle of wood that looked to have grown into that shape, with some kind of light ceramic used to fill it in. There was a window in the top half that Kellance looked out through, swearing under his breath.

Almost immediately after, a trio of elves moved in front of the door. They had looks typical for the locals and wore neat casual suits that Jason recognised as fitting the local fashion. They looked something akin to business suits but worn loose, with long, tapered sleeves and coattails. He had seen the pub's more upscale clientele wearing similar outfits the night before, although most of what he'd seen had been in light colours. These three wore significantly darker shades. The one in front was clearly the leader, flanked by the others. He grinned at Kellance through the window before pushing the door open.

"Hello, Kell," he said, his voice snide. "Something smells good."

It was clear to Jason that the newly arrived elves were local thugs that delighted in the petty power they held. If their body language wasn't enough, their auras reeked of insecurity and glee at holding power over anyone. Jason tapped the crystal that turned off the stove's heat stone and moved the frypan onto a wooden board.

"And who do we have here?" the lead elf said, looking over at Jason.

"A temporary cook," Bellory said as she came down the stairs. Jason noticed that the pub owner had quickly tossed on the same clothes she'd been wearing the night before.

"And here we have it," the lead thug said. "Bell and Kell. Why would you need new kitchen staff, Bell?"

"The rest got caught up in that tri-ball brawl yesterday."

"Oh, I heard about that. It's the very reason my father sent me along. Wanted to collect early, make sure that you didn't come up short after having to cancel food service."

Jason had been wondering how a sports punch-up had led to arrests when Pallimustus was usually so open to violence. He had put it down to local laws or culture, but now he realised that there had been outside intervention. He guessed the thug's father was some local boss, shaking down Bellory's pub and other local businesses. For whatever reason, he wanted extra pressure put on Bellory.

"I've got your loan repayment, Emresh," Bellory told the thug. "Just give me a minute to get it together."

"Take your time, Bell," Emresh said as he sauntered up to Jason. "Gives me a chance to get to know your new employee."

"He's just a drifter passing through, Emresh," Kellance said as Bellory left for another part of the pub.

Emresh got right up in Jason's face, sniffing him like an animal. Like the thug and his offsiders, Jason's aura was silver rank with a heavy mark of monster core use. He'd been practising his aura masking a lot, and Amos Pensinata had especially helped him refine it.

"Silver rank, not bad," Emresh said. "Is that right, kitchen boy? You just passing through?"

"I'm an adventuring auxiliary," Jason told him. "I'll only be around as long as my team."

"Well, look here, boys. We've got ourselves a big-time adventurer. You fight any monsters, adventurer?"

"I'm a cook."

"And how's your cooking?" Emresh asked. "Good enough that your team will come looking for revenge when we make an example of you?"

"If you want to try my cooking, it's right there," Jason said, nodding at the frypan on the bench.

Emresh laughed.

"I like this one."

He plucked a piece of fried vegetable from the pan with his fingers and popped it into his mouth. His eyebrows went up and he laughed, turning around to look at his flunkeys.

"You know what? He's pretty good. Shame, really."

Emresh turned back to Jason, the insincere friendliness dropping from his face.

"You think my father is afraid of some wandering adventurers?"

"I don't know," Jason said. "I haven't met him."

"Oh, you're funny," Emresh said.

"I have my moments."

Emresh drove a fist into Jason's gut and he doubled over. He leaned down to speak into Jason's ear.

"Is this one of your moments, adventurer?"

"Sorry, what was that?" Jason croaked. "I couldn't hear over the sound of how small your dick is."

One of the lackeys snorted a laugh, earning a glare from Emresh.

"You should not have done that," the other flunkey said.

Emresh stamped his fist down on the back of Jason's head, dropping him to the floor. He then followed up with a savage boot to the gut. Jason let out a retching sound, but pushed himself and got to his feet.

"You should have stayed down," Emresh said.

"You were going to kick the crap out of me either way," Jason said.

"Most people would have run if they figured that out."

"You'd only beat me harder if you had to chase me down first."

Emresh let out his snide laugh once more.

"That's true," he said. "But do you know what I hate more than someone that makes me chase them before a beating?"

Jason theatrically sniffed the air. "I'm going to say soap."

Emresh gave him a malevolent smile.

"Someone too smart for their own good."

"I can see how you'd resent smart people."

When Bellory returned with a bag of spirit coins, Emresh and his lackeys were repeatedly kicking Jason who was curled up on the floor.

"I've got the money," she yelled. "What are you doing?"

"Call it an object lesson," Emresh said, not pausing from the assault. "If my father decides your kitchen is closed, then your kitchen is closed."

Bellory bit back her retort. There was no point asking how she was meant to meet her loan payments—the answer was that she wasn't. She wanted to intervene, but the attempt would be as pointless as the repercussions would be severe. Finally tiring of their game, the thugs admired their handiwork as Jason was left moaning softly on the ground. His face was red from the pummelling and his skin abraded from their boots; the damage to the covered parts of his body was likely far worse.

"Silver-rankers," Emresh said. "They can take much more of a beating, so you have to put more effort in. Still, they don't accidentally die on you, so there's that."

He pointed a finger in Bellory's face, snatched the bag of money from her hands and roughly opened the door before swaggering out. Bellory looked to the still-moaning Jason but was surprised to see him looking up at her, waggling his eyebrows. He tapped a finger to his lips so she'd stay silent even as he continued letting out light moans.

Bellory and Kellance watched him, seeing the injuries on his face swiftly healing. He stopped moaning and sprang to his feet.

"Bloody silver-rank hearing," he said cheerfully. "Had to make sure they were out of earshot."

"John, are you alright?" Kellance asked.

"I've had worse than that, believe me," Jason assured him. "That was practically a massage."

Bellory cupped a hand to his face where the most visible damage had been, now completely unblemished.

"Why would you provoke him like that?"

"He was here to make a point, one way or another. Best if it's on someone who can take his lumps."

Jason turned his gaze to the door.

"I gather that he's the son of whoever holds your loan? Someone not above interfering so he can use that loan to snake this whole place out from under you?"

Bellory nodded, bowing her head in shame, resting a gentle hand on Jason's arm.

"I pulled you into my troubles," she said, her voice filled with self-recrimination.

"I've pulled myself into worse, believe me. It's kind of my thing. But you should tell me who that bloke's father is."

She looked up sharply. "Don't get your adventurer friends to go after him."

"I'm not looking for revenge. I know that will just bring trouble down on you."

"You could have taken those guys apart, couldn't you?" Kellance asked as he gave Jason an assessing up-and-down look.

"It doesn't matter," Jason said. "I'm only passing through. Anything I did today, you'd pay for tomorrow. But I need to know who I'm dealing with, so I can at least stay out of their way until I'm gone."

"Thank you," Kellance said. "That was Emresh Vohl. His father, Urman Vohl, is a major figure in the entertainment district."

"Crime lord?"

"Not exactly," Kellance said. "The city administration doesn't let crime bosses grow too strong without slapping them down. Vohl is legitimate in his actual business interests, even if the way he conducts them is criminal. So long as he doesn't trample on the interests of anyone who can match or exceed his influence, he can run his legitimate interests in a less-than-legitimate way."

"That's pretty much what I guessed," Jason said, then sighed as he looked at the cooling food in the pan. "So much for breakfast. I should go."

"I feel bad just letting you leave after that," Bellory said. "But you're probably right."

"Are you sure you're alright after all that damage?" Kellance asked.

Bellory reached out to Jason's face again, running a delicate thumb over the scar on his chin. Her thoughts went to his other scars, revealed to her the night before.

"He is," she said. "He's not just a cook."

"Yeah," Kellance said. "I'm getting that impression."

He looked at Jason's blood on the floor.

"I'll go get a mop."

Jason smiled after Kellance left.

"Tell him to keep the mop outside for an hour or so," Jason said. "My blood will dissolve and leave the worst stench you've ever smelled behind."

"We get a lot of scarlet-comb beetles here."

"Beetles?"

"I kill lesser monsters with my broom a couple of times a month. I know to air it until the rainbow smoke clears. Your body is that magical?"

"You tell me," he said with a sly grin. "You checked pretty thoroughly."

She failed to stop her snort of derision from becoming a laugh as she withdrew her hand from his face.

"John," she said, "if I went looking into that tattoo on your back, would I learn who you are?"

"Yeah," he said softly. "I'm not hiding anything you can't figure out if you try. I'm hoping you won't, though. I like the idea of living in your memory as a mysterious stranger who passed through one day."

"Oh, you think you're worth remembering?" she teased.

"I don't imagine you forgetting someone who can conjure that many magic hands."

She gave him a beaming smile, but with a hint of sadness in her eyes.

"How many lies did you tell me?" she asked.

"Two. But not telling lies isn't the same thing as telling the truth. The things I didn't say have hidden a lot."

"I don't need your life's story. Your name was one of the two lies, wasn't it?"

He nodded.

"And the other one was about only having four talents."

"I only have four that I like."

He leaned in for a lingering kiss that tasted like goodbye.

Jason wandered down the street, letting his feet guide him as he explored the city.

"Shade," he said. "Estella will be looking into local power brokers as part of her work, right?"

"She already is, Mr Asano."

"Do me a favour and have her take a closer look at Urman Vohl, will you? As much detail as she can get without alerting them to her interest."

"I shall let her know, Mr Asano."

"How do you think she snores if she doesn't have her body control techniques completely down? Something to do with half-learned methodology?"

"I never told you that she snored, Mr Asano. That would be an invasion of privacy."

"Maybe she has a secret familiar and that snores."

"I do not think she has a secret familiar."

"Like a gerbil. A gerbil that snores like a lumberjack choking on a peach pit."

"What relevance would a person's profession have on the sound they make while choking?"

"I don't know," Jason said, rubbing his chin thoughtfully. "It feels like a lumberjack would snore worse than a ballet dancer, though. Am I subconsciously conforming to gender norms or am I just thinking about the difference in diet? Diet's a factor in snoring, right?"

"I don't know, Mr Asano."

"Could you find out?"

"Yes, Mr Asano."

Jason stopped and stared accusingly at his shadow.

"*Will* you find out?"

"No, Mr Asano."

45

THE POINT OF SACRIFICE

On Earth, the Asano clan had a deficit of silver-rankers. Taika had been amongst the first trained in Farrah's methods that did not use monster cores, placing him in the first wave of non-core essence users. The monster waves and proto-spaces were both outstanding places to grind out experience, working alongside the Network, before the factions fragmented and his association with Jason became a problem.

Once magic came out into the open, Taika had moved his family, first to Asano Village, and then to Jason's spirit realm in France. He had already blazed into bronze rank by that time and continued pushing towards silver. The revelation that the US and Chinese had cracked non-core training long ago and had hidden their elites from the rest of the world only pushed him harder, especially with Jason's departure.

Advancement slowed down once Jason stabilised the Earth's dimensional barrier and left. This brought an end to both proto-spaces and monster waves, and instead caused ordinary magical manifestations. Monsters could randomly appear anywhere, along with essences, awakening stones and quintessence. They had none of the concentrated numbers of a monster wave or proto-space, however, and were considerably weaker in most zones. Only a handful of places had sufficiently high magic to produce genuine threats.

Opportunities to use combat for advancement became more scarce. That changed when Taika was drawn through the anomaly into Pallimustus, but not in an entirely welcome manner. Suddenly, the level of everyone around him, bar his fellow Earth refugees, was higher than ever before. After reuniting with Jason, his training stepped up, guided once more by Farrah, as well as Rufus. Humphrey also made a helpful guide.

Taika's power set fell under the same broad category as Humphrey's. They were both high-mobility brawlers, even sharing similar essence combinations. Not only did they both have the might and wing essences, but also confluence essences of magical flying creatures. For Taika, it was garuda, with dragon for Humphrey. They even had abilities that were alike, such as conjuring wings, and both possessed the potent survival power called Immortality.

Taika's biggest issue was finding appropriate challenges. With all his friends and allies at silver rank, he'd been stuck in Rimaros taking what bronze-rank contracts he could. Given the team and multi-team approach favoured in the Storm Kingdom, as a teamless bronze-ranker, Taika regularly found himself sidelined and stuck as a guard or a lookout.

It was only late in the monster surge that it started to change. As Jason rose to prominence, suddenly, Taika found himself getting contract after contract that seemed custom-made to give his advancement the push it needed. Combined with the training from Rufus and Farrah, Taika pushed himself achingly close to silver while Jason was variously unconscious or healing after his latest insane feat.

By the time the monster surge ended, Taika was on the very cusp of silver, but had not quite made it. As the convoy made its way south, Taika was on the lookout for opportunities to get over that line, finally becoming an asset that Jason's team could make use of.

During the convoy's first night in the city of Yaresh, Taika found himself alone on the roof deck, lying back in a lounge chair. In the cheap camping grounds on the city outskirts, there was little to look at, aside from the enclosing rainforest and other large vehicles, no few of which belonged to other adventuring teams. That left the stars above as the only appreciable vista.

Rufus made his way up the stairs, taking a lounge chair next to Taika, but not lying back. Instead, he sat on the edge, looking at Taika.

"Humphrey's a pretty good adventurer," Rufus mused, as if the thought had just struck him. "He's dedicated. Like me, he has that human advantage of his essence abilities advancing a little faster than most. Not much good at low ranks, but it really starts to shine at silver. But he made silver rank in good time."

"Okay," Taika said, unsure of what Rufus was leading up to but knew it was something.

"Jason and Humphrey reached bronze rank close enough to simultaneously as to not matter," Rufus continued. "And as I said, Humphrey made silver in good time. Jason beat him by about a year and hit the wall fast. He's been sitting there ever since, waiting for the rest of us to catch up, which most of us have, more or less. The ridiculous duration of the monster surge helped, especially given how much of it Jason spent lying around healing up."

"Jason did a lot of fighting back on Earth," Taika said. "A proto-space or a monster wave is like monster surge concentrate. That's even without a ghoul army, hundreds of thousands of zombies or whatever weird stuff he went through in those transformation zones."

"So Farrah has told me. At length. Adventurers manage their risk, but that wasn't an option for him, from what I can tell."

Taika sat up, turning so that he was also sitting sideways to his lounger, now face to face with Rufus.

"I know all this, bro. What's your point?"

"At this point, Jason has probably faced more exotic and deadly combat situations than anyone of his rank that I've ever heard of. I don't think anyone with less than a half-dozen years of experience has come that close to death so many times without falling off. Not even Jason himself."

"I'm still waiting on that point."

"We're all chasing him now, and it's not just about rank. He's run a gauntlet and come through it hurt. He's with us now, but not completely, because we haven't seen what he has. None of us but Farrah."

"She seems pretty strong."

"She seems that way, yes. But she's not here, is she? Jason is dramatic, and the way he handles damage is too. Farrah's quiet about her wounds, but they run deep and are hidden well. She needs time, but only limited guidance, at least according to my mother. As you said, she's strong. But Jason needs coddling, or he might break. Have you noticed how he's withdrawn? How he spends more and more time with the higher-rankers?"

"The ones who've been around enough to see the kind extreme situations that he has," Taika realised.

"Exactly. So we're all chasing Jason, not just in powers, but in experience. I know it's been rough, being bronze when everyone around you is silver. That feeling is the reason that Farrah, Gary and I left Vitesse. But you're just about ready to cross that threshold into silver now, and I want you to be ready for the change."

"The change?"

"You'll be able to fight with us, but that feeling of trying to catch up won't go away. The power difference won't be so great, and you'll reach the advancement wall before any of us have put much of a dent in it. Instead, you'll be chasing something more ephemeral: a sense that you're just as ready to face what's out there as the people around you."

Rufus smiled, but his eyes were staring at the floor without really seeing anything.

"The pursuit never ends," he continued, "even when the thing we're chasing is imaginary. You chase us, and we chase Jason. I can't even imagine what Jason is chasing. But we never feel ready, not really. Not unless we're willing to stop moving forward."

"What if I do want to stop?" Taika asked. "I never wanted to come here, and I want to get back to my family."

Rufus nodded.

"Perhaps you're closer to catching Jason than the rest of us," he said. "He never asked to come here either, and found himself scrambling for power to survive. He has talent, and so do you, but it was desperation and challenge that let him grow so strong so fast."

"I don't think I can come back from the dead, bro."

"You're an outworlder," Rufus said. "You've done it once. But don't worry about that. Keep putting one foot in front of the other and you'll get where you're going eventually. The next step is silver rank, which is why I wanted to have this talk."

"You think I'll cross over here in Yaresh?"

"I do. The magic here is lower, and the Storm Kingdom's ways aren't as prevalent here. High-end bronze and low-end silver monsters are the bread-and-butter contracts here. It's perfect for someone looking to cross the line. Go hard while we're here. We want you standing beside us when we wind up fighting the messengers."

"I don't... you said I might be closer to Jason than the rest of you, but I don't want to be the next Jason. I like him, bro, I really do, but he's damaged. Even when I first met him, there was something about him. I saw him let it out once, not long after we met. I saw him cow a room full of the hardest, cruellest people I've ever met, just by not hiding what he was underneath. He didn't show me, though, and I sometimes wonder if I wish he had."

Taika shook his head.

"I've seen his family look at him and be afraid," he continued, "and I'm not sure they were wrong. I don't want power or to be important. Not if it leads to my family looking at me like that. Yes, they were sorry when he was gone, but he was gone. It's easier to be sorry when they aren't right in front of you."

Taika let out a sigh.

"I'll stand by Jason to the end," he said. "He's more than earned it. But I don't want to make the sacrifices he made."

Rufus grinned.

"That's good," he said. "The point of sacrifice is that others don't have to make it. You seem to have figured out that you don't have to walk the path life puts you on. It took me a lot of failure and loss to realise that. I guess you're wiser than I am."

"So, what now?" Taika asked.

"Well, you can step off the path, but you have to find the right spot. Otherwise, you'll end up in the weeds, and some of those weeds are prickly."

"Bro, if I hear one more metaphor, I'm going to stab you in the eye."

Rufus chuckled.

"I'm saying get to silver. We'll find your way home, but you have to live long enough to see it."

The revelation of a sprawling underground beneath the city was an enticing lure for Jason. He was shoulder to shoulder with young elves dressed in garish colours, some kind of punk trend, as they shuffled through tunnels where cheap plaster sealed the walls and ceiling between the roots of the trees above. The floor was hard-packed dirt, pressed almost to a stony firmness by countless feet. Cheap glow stones were embedded in the walls, some flickering, others fading and some missing altogether, pry marks around the indentations left behind.

The tunnel sloped down sharply and drunken young people slipped regularly, stirring confrontation as they tumbled into the people ahead of them. Eventually, the tunnel led out into a large subterranean chamber that looked to be one of several connected together. The walls and roof were made from sturdier brickwork, although patches of plaster with root systems poking through were still present. Brickwork columns supported the ceiling, placed regularly through the chamber.

Four of the columns marked out a square in the middle of the chamber, the sides of the square being metal cage walls. People crowded around the walls, cheering and jeering at people fighting inside. Amongst the crowd, it was easier for Jason to watch the fight with his magical senses than with his eyes, and he quickly took stock. The combatants were bronze rank but wearing suppression collars, fighting it out with only their enhanced attributes.

Jason was using the crowd to practise extending his senses without a commensurate extension of his aura, which he was still only beginning to learn. As such, he could only just sense similar spectacles in other chambers, all of which seemed to have bronze- or silver-rank combatants.

There seemed to be some order to the proceedings that the locals knew, while the non-elves like himself seemed lost and confused. Jason didn't rush; he used his aura senses, along with his ears to make sense of the madness. The first thing he found was a bar, where he discovered that cheap elven hooch had a sickly sweet nature that he was completely on board with.

From there, he got a sense of the fights, how they were bet on and how they were organised. Eventually, he realised that hapless outsiders were regularly recruited into fights, relying on bravado and drunkenness to lure in the punters. The fighters were amateurs, for the most part, judging by their skill and the auras he sensed once the fights were over and the collars came off. It was in the deeper chambers where he found the real fighters.

The deeper chambers were less crowded, courtesy of the need to pay for entry. They were also better organised, with an audience that was both older and more conservatively dressed. The security staff could have passed for fighters themselves in the other chambers, where the standards were lower, but not here. Jason could tell that the people in these cages were trained, experienced or both, and he guessed many of them were adventurers. There was even assigned seating, where the other areas had been standing room only. Jason discovered that most of the audience here did not come in with the rabble as Jason had, and had some manner of exclusive entry.

Jason froze, startled as he sensed something extremely unusual: an aura belonging to a species called the valash, who were not native to Pallimustus. Jason had only seen them when humans had been turned into them by transformation zones on Earth. He had needed Shade to give name to them.

They were a comical-looking species to human sensibilities, with skinny bodies and Chihuahua-like heads. Jason sensed the valash navigating the crowd in his direction, wondering if he had somehow seen through Jason's aura mask. What truly startled Jason about the valash wasn't his species, but something that made sense, given he should not have been present in this world. The valash was an outworlder.

46

WHAT YOU WANT INSTEAD OF
WHAT YOU NEED

JASON HAD ACCESSED THE RESTRICTED SECTION OF THE FIGHTING DENS WITH A payment that was outlandish to the rebellious youths packed shoulder to shoulder in the main area, but negligible to any mildly successful adventurer. The restricted area was the largest of the subterranean chambers, with four cages surrounded by chairs. It was less crowded than the open areas, due to the exclusivity, while still being relatively packed.

The clientele wasn't any kind of city elite, based on what Jason could tell from their clothes, auras and the general presence of thugs. He suspected this was where the mid-to-high-level members of the local underworld congregated. Jason made his way slowly and carefully, even using some of his aura tricks for moving through a crowd, although he was careful about that as well. He didn't notice anyone that would be able to sense his manipulations, but that didn't mean they weren't present. They could be better at hiding themselves than he was.

Jason's attention was drawn to a valash, a skinny sapient species not native to Pallimustus. The male was not just lean but downright skinny, even shorter than Jason and with a chihuahua-like head. He wore a pristine white suit, not in the local style but more fitted. Compared to the flowing, tapered lines of local elf fashion, this outfit would have been more at home in a Miami nightclub in the eighties.

The valash slipped through the crowd with practised ease. He was obviously familiar with the environment and making the most of his small stature. Despite being diminutive, he was not pushed, shoved, or disrespected by the people around him. His silver-rank aura meant more than shoulders the size of a park bench, especially as it had no signs of core use. Arriving in front of Jason, he looked him up and down.

"How do, new meat? Did the burly fellows at the entrance tell you the rules, or just take your money and usher you through?"

Jason was surprised on hearing the smooth, deep voice that came from the tiny man, suddenly imagining him and Taika in a body swap movie.

"They didn't tell me anything but the price of entry," Jason said. "Which makes me wonder if they were negligent or if you're trying to lure me into a game that isn't real."

"Disappointed as I am that you're not the ever-pleasant conglomeration of money and stupidity, I'm afraid you really do have some issues you'll need to work through."

"I already have a mental health professional for that."

"Not those kind of issues." The valash held out a hand for Jason to shake. "I'm Zolit. Zolit Kreen."

"John Miller," Jason said, shaking the man's hand. "How did you pick me out as a first-timer?"

"There's only so many silver-rank auras floating around in here," Zolit explained, "and I know all the others. Plus, they don't come in through the public entrance, especially without an entourage."

"I should have people with me?"

"I told you about those rules, right? Rule one is that if you're new, you either put up a fighter or you fight yourself."

Zolit looked him up and down.

"Human, core user, but your body language tells me that you aren't some wilting leaf. You know where the boot goes if it comes to it. Adventurer auxiliary?"

Jason nodded.

"Sharp eye. I'm the cook for a team passing through the city. They want in on the messenger fight."

"Them and every other team in this town. You know where glory leads? A glorious death."

"I know that better than most," Jason told him with complete sincerity.

"So, a cook, huh?" Zolit asked.

"Yep," Jason said. "Cooking, grocery shopping. Knife skills."

Zolit grinned; Jason was surprised at how easy it was to read expressions on the small man, despite his unusual appearance. He suspected that Zolit was very good at showing exactly what he intended, especially given the tight rein he had on his aura. Jason wouldn't be able to read the man's emotions without pushing hard enough that someone would notice.

"You don't have anyone with you, do you, Cook? That means you either need to get out fast or get in a cage. You'll need a fight organiser for that."

"Which you just happen to be?"

"One of life's funny little coincidences," Zolit said with another grin.

"And what if I say no?"

"One way or another, you fight. Do you think you can carve your way out past everyone here, with those knife skills you mentioned?"

"No," Jason lied.

"Then you need to secure a slot in the fight slate. Single-round elimination, matched by rank and collared so no one gets killed."

"Do I get paid if I win?"

"You get a slice of the betting take, so you want to put on a good show. Silvers can take a lot of punishment and no one wants to watch two of them slapping each other pointlessly for an hour. But something tells me you've got something ferocious inside, even without your knives. To be clear, you can't take your knives, and don't worry so much about winning. Some proper adventurers fight here; mostly locals, but some outsiders come too, looking to make extra cash. You manage to make a decent showing against one of them and you can make some good money, even on the losing end."

"So, how does it work?"

"Sixteen fighters, four rounds, single-round elimination. You fight until you lose. Come with me and I'll get you set up."

Jason was in a chamber underneath the cages. It was a changing room with a shower made of partly tiled-over brick. It also served as a waiting room for the fights above, with stairs leading up to a sliding panel that went directly into a cage. The only other exit was a heavy sliding door, also made of brick, opened and closed by a touch crystal on the wall.

With Jason and Zolit was an elf that worked for him. She was a silver-rank core user with plain, dark brown clothes and a big duffel bag.

"This is Bennie," Zolit introduced.

"Benella," she corrected with an annoyed shake of her head.

"Bennie will help you find your look since you don't want to fight in your regular clothes," Zolit said. "Unless you want to end the night dressed in bloody rags, although maybe that's a look you want to go for. The savage brute who lives only to fight can be a good angle, especially for a walk-in like you. I'm not sure you have the size to sell it, though."

"Let's try something else," Jason said.

"Alright, then," Zolit said. "Bennie?"

Jason was given a variety of options, pulled from Benella's duffel. Her offering ranged from gi-style outfits to things closer to regular athletic wear, as well as combat robes and flashy lucha-libre style costumes, complete with masks. There were far more clothes than would fit in a non-dimensional bag, which made Jason wonder why it was so big. He guessed that making it that large was less expensive, as opposed to the extravagant dimensional coat that Emir possessed.

Jason went for shorts and a top made from clingy, slick fabric that would resist being grabbed. The result made him look like a professional bicyclist. As he was changing, he did not miss the looks shared by Benella and Zolit when they saw his scars, but he kept the soul crest on his back out of their sightline.

"Okay," Zolit said after he changed. "We're going to head back upstairs and watch how you do. Just wait until that panel opens and go on through. You can figure out what to do from there."

"What are the rules of the fight?" Jason asked.

"You'll get stopped before anyone dies," Zolit told him.

"The crowd usually doesn't like eye-gougers unless things get desperate," Benella added. "They have no problem with a little brutality, though. They want to see a fight."

"Or a lot of brutality," Zolit said. "Once the fight is done, the panel will open back up so you can come back down. Or get carried down, depending on how it goes. You can't have familiars up there, by the way; the magic in the cage will sense them. If you have any, leave them behind in here until you come back."

Zolit and Benella made their way to the large stone door that slid open or closed with a touch crystal set into the wall.

"Zolit," Jason called out.

"Yeah?"

"I don't like it when people run around asking questions they shouldn't."

"Is that so?" Zolit asked lightly.

"It inclines a man to start asking questions of his own."

Zolit laughed, touching his face.

"You wouldn't be the first to wonder what I am, Cook."

"I know what a valash is, Zolit. My questions would be significantly more pointed."

Zolit's face went blank as Benella looked between the two men with curiosity. Zolit left, Benella in tow, the door closing behind him.

"A cook, my narrow ass," he muttered.

For Jason, it was refreshing to practise his unarmed techniques against someone other than Sophie, who regularly disassembled him without hesitation or mercy. His first opponent was clearly a cage fight veteran, given his theatrically aggressive tactics and use of the space. The cage walls, as it turned out, were barbed chain links. As the other fighter slammed Jason into it, his flesh was gouged when the opponent pushed him along it.

Jason's slick, flexible clothes didn't rip, their frictionless surface helping him as it slid across the razors. Only his exposed arms and legs were slashed. For Jason's part, he played possum at the start, feeling out his enemy. He made the most of his silver-rank resilience to tease out his opponent's weaknesses, which quickly became evident.

From the way the man fought, Jason guessed he was more cage experience than trained technique. Of the two, the experience was the better to have, but he also had weaknesses that Jason was able to exploit. After taking the time to feel out his opponent and let the bets stack up against him, Jason began his counterattack.

The critical strength of Jason's fighting style, the Way of the Reaper, was the versatility that allowed it to be adapted to different circumstances and different approaches. Sophie used it in a domineering fashion, relentless hammering on an enemy's weak point. Jason took a very different approach, employing deception and baiting his opponents into exposing themselves to counterattack.

Soaking damage, Jason set up rope-a-dope counterattacks that inflicted injuries that would have crippled an iron-ranker and debilitated a bronze. Baiting his enemy into an overreaching lunge, Jason stomped hard on the side of his knee. If he was going to take down a silver-ranker, it would take that level of attack over and over, which he proceeded to do.

It slowly dawned on Jason's opponent that his hits were landing less and less often, and not hitting as hard when they did. Jason was no longer letting himself get rammed into the cage, and the aggressive assaults exposed opportunities for Jason to counter with brutal hits to knees, elbows or bell-ringing head strikes.

The audience watched as the initially aggressive cage fighter became more and more cautious, as if he were fighting a trap golem instead of a man. He didn't realise that he was instinctively backing off as Jason walked slowly across the cage until he heard the jeers of the crowd.

Knowing he needed to turn the momentum back in his favour, the fighter resumed his aggressive attacks, but, by this point, Jason had his measure. Experience had taken the man a long way, but his range of attacks was limited and Jason had read them all. That was not to say that it was completely one-sided; the man certainly landed hits, but they weren't hard or repeated enough to take down a silver-ranker. Jason's counters, by contrast, involved bending wrists, knees and elbows in directions they weren't meant to, and hammering other joints to slow down the opponent.

Jason had to admire the man's tenacity to keep attacking, but by the culmination of the fight, it was like watching someone charge into an industrial wheat thresher over and over, coming out more broken and bloody each time. Finally, it became a one-sided beatdown of a man broken in body but not in spirit, refusing to surrender. As he demolished the man, blood painting his forearms, Jason absently thought back to a time his actions would have filled him with horror.

"Yield," Jason said coldly, getting only a snarl in return.

He repeated the offer before he broke each limb, at which point the fight was called in Jason's favour. The floor panel opened and he glanced at the other three cages before descending. He had been ignoring the familiar presence in one of them, even though it meant he had no chance of winning overall. The Nightingale's grace, speed, beauty and expertise put every fighter to shame.

Jason shook his head and descended to where his familiars were waiting for him. He stopped in front of Shade, blood dripping from his hands.

"Am I broken?" he asked, more curious than fearful.

"Everyone is broken, Mr Asano, and anyone in that cage has chosen to be there. Life is about working around the damage. You don't have the luxury of showing mercy to those who choose pride over wellbeing."

"But I want to be the guy that does. I like mercy."

"There is a reason I called it a luxury, Mr Asano. If you do what you want instead of what you need to, it all goes wrong."

SETTLING DIFFERENCES WITH A NICE CHAT

THE BRICK LOCKER ROOM UNDER THE FIGHTING CAGES WAS SMALL, AS THERE WERE two for each of the four cages. They weren't much different from domestic bathrooms in size and layout. Jason emerged from the shower having washed off the blood, of both himself and his opponent. His regenerative abilities had already healed his injuries, the biggest factor being Colin.

Jason's clingy cyclist-style outfit was surprisingly resilient and hadn't ripped, so after washing it off in the shower as well, he yanked it back on, ignoring the wetness of it. He didn't bother with crystal wash for himself or his clothes as they would soon be bloodied again. Just as he was awkwardly yanking the wet top into place with sharp tugs, the door opened to admit the chihuahua-headed outworlder Zolit.

"Not bad, Cook," Zolit told him as he strode inside. "The bookmakers let people keep betting into the start of the fight because there are always those chumps who think they can read how it goes from the opening moves."

"Does that mean I get a bigger slice?" Jason asked, not bothering to look at the skinny man in the white suit.

"Sure does. Of course, being your first fight, there's only so much going around."

Jason turned to stare at the little man.

"Hey, I'm not responsible for the betting, and the later rounds are where the real money is. Everyone is paying attention to this Nightingale girl, and that's where all the money is going. Even putting aside what she looks like, which is just... wow, she's really good. I mean, no offence to your respectable skills, but she is just plain better than you. You get a lot of travelling adventurers trying their hand in the cages, and most don't do that great. In a box, with no powers, it's a different fight. But this girl knows her way around a cage."

"I'm well aware of her competencies."

"You know her?"

"I'm a cook for an adventuring team. She's on that team."

"No kidding. Think she'll go easy on you if you get matched up?"

"I do not."

"Good thing you weren't matched up until the final round, then. You're up against some adventurer next, but people saw you both fight and the odds are pretty even. Maybe take a few hits early so the bookies can roll up some chumps? Keep up the turnaround fights if you want to fatten up your piece of the pudding. I know that means taking an extra beating and I was even bringing you a potion to kick that healing into action. You don't appear to be having any problems in that regard, though."

"Isn't it about time you left so I can get in the right headspace?"

"Okay, I'll go. I think you've got this next fight, but try and make it look like a struggle. It'll help shift the betting odds for the fight after, and that's where you'll make your money."

Jason didn't respond and Zolit left. The small man concerned Jason in that his aura showed nothing but what Jason would expect from a mid-tier underworld fight promoter. Since he was an outworlder like Jason, it was more strange for him to be ordinary than not, especially given his unusual appearance. Jason's Eurasian features didn't match any of the human ethnic groups he'd encountered on Pallimustus, but there were enough variations that he didn't especially stand out. The little chihuahua-faced man would have had much more trouble blending in.

The upcoming fight was not preying on Jason's mind. Win or lose, it was just an experience for him. More pressing was the question of what to do about Zolit. While it wasn't a rule that outworlders had to get involved in exceptional events, it was his understanding that it was almost always the case.

There had been another outworlder in Rimaros when Jason arrived, but they had never gotten to meet. From what he discovered, she had become embroiled in a conflict between some lesser elemental gods and had left the city early in the monster surge in an attempt to broker peace. The monster surge was bad enough without a holy war involving powerful elemental forces.

She had apparently achieved results, as some of the priests in question had been on hand to help shield coastal communities from the backlash of the Builder's flying city crashing into the sea and causing a tsunami. The outworlder herself had not returned and Jason hoped to meet her in the future.

Compared to that, Zolit was a more curious proposition. On one hand, Jason wanted to reveal his full identity and learn all about the man's experiences. On the other, he seemed a relatively ordinary and not wildly trustworthy person. His instincts told him not to break cover, as flimsy as his false identity was. There was a big difference between a mysterious stranger who quickly moved on and hanging out his secrets for the world to see.

Jason pushed the small man out of his mind, shifting his concentration to the fight ahead. Zolit could wait, although Jason wondered if he was letting the other man make the choice for him. The emotions he read in the man's aura held disproportionately more curiosity than caution.

Zolit returned to his reserved seating, mildly annoyed at its location. The four cages were placed in a square, with seating around and in between them. He was on the opposite side from the fight everyone wanted to watch, anticipating the Nightingale again making absolute brutality seem graceful. Instead, he was stuck watching the cook with his strange scars and air of mystery.

Plonking down next to Benella, Zolit sat with a sullen expression as the panels in the cage floor opened to admit the fighters. It went about as Zolit had predicted, with the adventurer's inexperience operating without his powers showing in his messed-up rhythm.

The cook fought a little differently, to Zolit's mild surprise, although the start was quite similar. The opponent was aggressive but lacked the same mastery of the cage that the cook's previous opponent had. This new one had more skill, but failed to make use of the confined space and sharp boundaries of the cage.

Rather than unveil a countering strategy that slowly increased the wariness of his opponent, the turn in the fight came suddenly. After feeling out his opponent for a while, the cook aggressively leapt on every mistake his opponent made. Those pacing issues became glaring weaknesses as the cook used each one to launch not just attacks but entire attack sequences. Caught on the back foot, the opponent was pounded repeatedly; it was the kind of hammering it took to deal with a silver-ranker.

Zolit observed as the cook's style went through subtle changes throughout the fight, shifting his approach to keep his opponent off-balance, every time the adventurer started adapting to the cook. He wondered if the cook had been playing possum long before Zolit suggested it.

As the fight continued, Zolit was joined by an unexpected guest. Claiming the seat next to his was a prestigious figure of the underground fight scene, a priest of the Warrior called Kraysch. The priest was an elf, who were naturally slender as a people. Like Neil and Lucian Lamprey, however, Kraysch was unusually bulky for his kind. He was tall but not towering, broad-shouldered but not hulking. His loose clothes, the standard informal outfit of his church, looked similar to martial arts training gear.

"What brings you by, honoured priest?" Zolit asked, straightening his posture.

"My god is very happy with this place, Mr Kreen. Battle is rarely fair, so places like this, which are as close to fair as you are likely to find, fall under his favour."

"We are blessed," Zolit said, his tone almost a question as he tried to figure out what the priest wanted.

"Being under my god's favour means that he doesn't like things disrupting it."

"Apologies, honoured priest, but I am not a man of political mindset. I'm not sure what you're getting at."

Kraysch sighed.

"There is a certain kind of story," he said. "I'm sure you've heard some variation. It's about a man whose true skill in life is killing, so he kills and he kills and he kills until all that he is is a killer. Until all that he has is killing. So, he gives it up, in search of something else. Anything else. He becomes an unremarkable man doing an unremarkable job."

The priest gave Zolit a smile that didn't reach his eyes.

"Of course," Kraysch, "he's not really an unremarkable man, and he gets remarked upon. Someone notices something and starts digging deeper. And stories being stories, the man gets dragged into something he shouldn't, and is forced to resume all the killing he tried to leave behind. Are you familiar with this kind of story?"

"I am, Priest Kraysch."

"And are you a smart man or a wise man, Mr Kreen?"

"I aspire to each of them, honoured priest, but fear I fall short of both."

"Then perhaps you would be open to some spiritual guidance."

"Of course."

"When an ostensibly unremarkable man, with an unremarkable job—say, a cook for instance—tells you that he doesn't like questions, you have a smart path and a wise path. The smart path is to ignore him and learn all you can, as there are dangerous secrets lurking about. The wise path is to let go of your curiosity and leave it be."

"The Church of the Warrior is interested in the cook?"

Kraysch bowed his head, saddened. "Curiosity it is, then." He stood just as the cook's opponent fell, too beaten and exhausted to continue.

Zolit stood as well. "Priest Kraysch, I wouldn't want to do anything that would frustrate your deity."

"I have already told you of my god's feelings. But since you have already asked the question, then no. The only interest the Church of the Warrior has in your fighter is not getting involved with him. Faith does not always need to be smart, Mr Kreen, but it should be wise whenever possible."

The priest walked away leaving a confused Zolit behind. The hitherto silent Benella, Zolit's aide, only spoke once he was gone.

"Do you believe him? That the church isn't involved with your cage-fighting cook?"

"I think it's likely he's telling the truth, if only because I'm not important enough to lie to. But it's not just that. I think he came to me like this because the church isn't involved and doesn't want to be."

"You think the cook is some secret super-warrior? That he's hiding his real skills?"

"No. I think the danger is if he starts using his powers."

"You think he would start using his powers and go on a rampage here?"

"How would I know? I met the guy, what? An hour ago? And I'm already starting to hate this guy. If you want people to think you're a cook, maybe don't join a fighting tournament and flash your scars, you stupid…"

Zolit let out a little growl, and Benella successfully hid her reaction to the tiny-dog adorableness of it.

"What are you going to do?" she asked. "This fighter is starting to sound like trouble."

"Starting? A church full of combat fanatics doesn't want him making a mess at an underground fighting area. That isn't the way trouble starts, Bennie. That's how trouble ends."

"Then I'll ask again: what will you do?"

"Did you notice what Kraysch said about the cook not liking questions? That was something he said in the prep room, which has a privacy screen. A good one."

"Meaning?"

"His god has blessed this whole place. Warrior probably directed his priest to come over here and talk to me. I do not want gods paying attention to me, for a variety of reasons. I've already got a bad feeling that the cook is better at reading me than he should be. And if this guy is a big enough deal that gods are moving, I'm moving out of the way. I'm going to take the advice of my fine local clergyman and not ask any questions. I'm going to pay the cook what he earns and send him on his way, in the hope that he takes the money and leaves. If someone else wants to make trouble, that's their problem; I just want to avoid anyone blaming me for it, be it the top fight organisers or Warrior, the god of not settling differences with a nice chat."

48

THE SEX MAGIC THING

JASON'S SECOND OPPONENT IN THE UNDERGROUND CAGE FIGHTS HAD BEEN CAPABLE enough, but suffered from a critical flaw in his fighting techniques. This was due to an absence of the essence abilities he normally had access to, and Jason completely sympathised. Combat styles interacted with essence powers on a spectrum, with one end having the fighting style as the skeleton, with the essence powers building off of it. This was Sophie's end of the scale, and when deprived of their powers, such adventurers fared the best.

At the other end of the scale was Jason, whose essence abilities were the fulcrum of his combat style. He had developed his martial arts specifically to work around his powers, rather than his powers working around them. When deprived of his essence abilities, such as in the cage fights he was undertaking, he was forced to heavily adapt his normal style.

Jason had the good fortune to have enjoyed Rufus as a teacher and Sophie as a sparring partner, which meant he had the practise adapting his style. Rufus, as a magic swordsman, fell in the middle of the spectrum, where skill and powers both needed to be mastered in order to thrive.

Rufus had been adamant about preparing for the worst-case scenarios, such as being forced to fight while power-suppressed. Given that Jason had met Rufus in that exact situation, he understood why Rufus had been so emphatic about it.

His second opponent clearly fell on Jason's end of the spectrum, but without the benefit of having his training under Rufus Remore. He also lacked the time sparring with Sophie, who relished hammering every gap in Jason's techniques caused by the absence of his powers. After feeling out his opponent, Jason dished out the same treatment. When he was done, he looked over at where Sophie had already finished her opponent and was watching him from her own cage.

"Took you long enough," she called out to him.

"I'm a lover, not a fighter," he called back.

"And how's that working out?"

"Well, I'm fighting, so… not great."

Sophie let out a laugh that startled Jason by how free she seemed. Although she was using the Nightingale name again, as she had in the fighting pits of Greenstone, she was a world away from the prickly creature he remembered. He flashed her a grin and then walked down the stairs revealed by the opening floor panel, into the changing room below.

"You really do know the Nightingale, don't you?" Zolit asked.

"I already told you that," Jason said as he emerged from the shower with a towel around his waist, using a second towel to dry his hair. Zolit ignored his nakedness, but his aide did not, her eyes wandering over Jason's scarred torso. The lean, sculpted muscle was unremarkable for a silver-ranker, but the permanent marring of his flesh was not.

"My eyes are up here, lady," Jason told her.

"I'm not looking at your eyes."

"*Bennie*," Zolit hissed sharply, and she sullenly stalked off.

"You seem worried, Zolit," Jason said. More than his body language, there was a change in Zolit's aura since their last encounter. Someone or something had put a proper scare in the little man.

"I'm just nervous about your next match," Zolit lied. "Two rounds are enough to make sure no one is left standing through luck."

Jason's ability to read the complex emotions of people through their auras had rapidly grown over the years. On Earth especially, where most people had little to no power to shield it, he had learned to dig through the nuances of what their auras revealed. Jason had a feeling that Zolit had some inkling of either Jason's real identity or had become aware of how dangerous learning it could be.

Underneath that surface concern, though, was a deeper worry. He was repressing it well, leaving Jason with no sense of what it was, but there was a fear that any trouble coming from Jason would bring it to light. Odds were that it was just some criminal activity making Zolit nervous; the cage fights were literally underground, but not against the law. If there was something shadier going on as a side business, that would explain the small man's wariness.

Zolit left and Jason's familiars re-emerged. His gaze lingered on the door that had closed behind the fight promoter.

"Do you think Mr Kreen is related to our real purpose here?" Shade asked.

"It's worth checking, but probably not."

"An outworlder might be more aware of how dangerous the messengers could be than the people native to this world," Shade suggested. "Such knowledge could make them more amenable to being an agent for the messengers, should they come calling."

"That's good enough for me. Have Stella look into him, but have her focus on the aide more than him. What did you make of her aura?"

"It seemed easy enough to read," Shade said. "You noticed something suspicious?"

"The thirsty vibes she was giving me seemed a little performative. I haven't been paying that much attention, focused as I've been on Zolit, but that may be the point."

"You think she is masking her aura and using Zolit as a distraction, so no one looks too closely at the ordinary elf standing behind him?"

"Anyone with halfway decent aura senses will mark him as an outworlder, and that draws attention. It certainly drew mine. But I think whatever spooked Zolit may have worried her a little and she overcompensated. I'm not saying that means she's what we're looking for, but she seems a better candidate than Zolit. I think that guy really is just an outworlder who found his calling as a small-time crook."

"Do you want me to surveil her?"

"Let's hold off on that for now. If she is masking her aura, then she's very good at it. And if she's that good with her aura, she might spot you. Let's give Estella time to do some professional spying before we make any more moves."

"Are you implying that I'm an amateur, Mr Asano?"

"I'm saying that I'm an amateur and you're stuck with me."

"Very astute, Mr Asano. Self-awareness is the path to enlightenment."

"You are terrible at giving compliments, you know that?"

"I work with what I have."

Above them, the panel at the top of the stairs slid open.

"Alright," Jason said, looking up. "Time to go beat up a girl."

Jason groaned as he tried to get up, only to have a foot on his torso shove him back to the floor.

"You know," he croaked, "I could probably keep this up for a while. I'm in a lot of pain, it's true, but being in pain is kind of my thing."

"You're a masochist, are you?" the woman looming over him asked. She was an unusually tall elf, muscular, like Neil, but she wore it a lot better, at least in Jason's opinion. Proportionally, she was similar to other elves he'd seen but fifteen percent larger, like looking at her through a zoom lens.

"I prefer to think of myself as open to new experiences, but looking back, I can see how—"

Jason yanked on the leg pressing into him as his hand pushed the back of her knee. His body spun like a top and flipped away from her in a display of acrobatics only available to silver-rankers or people bitten by radioactive spiders. His opponent was already moving, a foot catching him in the gut as he landed on his feet.

Jason let the momentum carry him, softening the blow as he started a one-handed backflip but then shoved himself into the air. She had predicted the backflip with her follow-up lunging kick that hit nothing but air. She threw out a punch as Jason pivoted in the air, twisting to catch her in the chest with a kick. It did no damage, having been launched from the air with no leverage, but it shoved her away long enough for him to land.

Jason held up his hands.

"Can we just pause for a moment to appreciate how awesome this fight is?"

He failed to block her straight punch to the face and he reeled back.

"No," she said and kept coming.

The level of the training and experience his opponent possessed was thoroughly imprinted on Jason as the fight continued, lasting well past Sophie's match. In most cases, a drawn-out match was not enjoyed by the crowds, but this fight had the audience fully engaged. The elf's relentless, efficient attacks clashed with Jason's shifting styles and tricky counterattacks. There were wild acrobatics and frenetic exchanges of strikes, punctuated by lulls as they felt each other out. Jason attempted distracting banter in such moments, usually followed by his receiving a sharp blow to the head.

Jason had trained to adapt his skills for when he didn't have his powers, but the results were not flawless. Slowly but surely, the elf picked him apart, the way Jason had done with his previous opponent. It was just a much longer and more even affair, where Jason landed more than a few brutal attacks of his own.

Both combatants were heavily pummelled, but Jason's stamina was the first to give out. Even so, he desperately clung on, used to fighting on the ragged edge. He even managed to surprise his opponent, who had previously broken apart every trick and tactic Jason had thrown out and baited her into.

Back to the wall and giddy from a merciless pounding, Jason's not entirely lucid mind put him into fight or flight, and he drew on old experiences. The cage fight didn't have much in the way of rules, but he had still been treating it as a sport, albeit a brutal one. The savagery that came from Jason entering survival mode startled the elf.

Taken aback, a fist to her face included a knuckle to the eye. Jason yanked her arm straight and twisted it before bringing his elbow down on hers, bending it the wrong way. Jason almost turned the fight around through raw aggression before she countered. His onslaught was vicious but also sloppy, both from the mindless approach and his still-exhausted body. Even so, he didn't stop until she hammered his body so badly it would no longer move. She stood over him, staggering, blood dripping from her mouth and fists.

The door to the changing room opened, admitting not Zolit but Sophie. Jason was already healed, largely due to the recuperative powers provided by Colin. He was still painted red, however, as he had not yet taken to the shower.

"I can't believe you cheered for the other person," he groaned.

"I have no idea what you're talking about," she said innocently.

"I heard you yelling 'kick him in the bits, random lady!'"

"That could have been anyone."

"Uh-huh."

"She was pretty okay, I'll admit. It took me a lot less time to handle her than for her to handle you, but still, not bad."

"Oh, that's how it is?"

"You couldn't even make it to the final round."

"Oh, you want to go find a mirage chamber and see how that goes?"

"Absolutely."

"Ugh, I forgot I was talking to someone who kicked me in the face the moment we met."

"I could have kicked you in the face again today if you hadn't lost to a girl."

"You're a girl."

"I'm a woman."

"So was she, believe me."

Sophie narrowed her eyes.

"How is the sex magic thing going?"

"It's mostly been me getting the crap kicked out of me."

"That wasn't the first time?"

"It was not."

"How about the other thing? Stumbled across anything yet?"

"I might have something. My promoter's aide tweaked my spider-sense."

"Your what?"

"Never mind. Estella will look into it."

"Then you're free to come drown your sorrows. All the arena big nobs are throwing a party for the fighters who managed to avoid embarrassing themselves."

"And that includes me?"

"No. You kept getting punched in the face midway through a pathetic banter attempt. But I can get you into the party."

"What do you mean by pathetic?"

49

THE POWER AND THE CONTROL

JASON HAD YET TO ENTER ANY OF THE TOWERING GLASS AND METAL STRUCTURES he had seen from a distance while approaching the city. This would soon change as the clientele of the underground arena departed, Jason amongst them. As he had speculated on finding the VIP area, there was a private entrance aside from the tunnels he had shuffled in through himself, shoulder to shoulder with the crowd. Rather than just a less crowded set of stairs, the private exit was an underground tram station.

Two lines connected the arena chambers to the city's underground tram network. As Jason let Zolit guide him, the fight promoter answered Jason's questions about the tramway. Jason listened closely, careful not to give his aide, Benella, any undue attention. The entertainment district was the most outlying section of the tram network, which mostly serviced the affluent inner districts. The lines out to the entertainment district were restricted to at least the semi-elite, so they didn't have to mix with the rabble. Jason's silver-rank adventurer badge, even being an auxiliary one, was enough to get him aboard.

The ride had Jason reminiscing about the submerged subway in Greenstone, which was more impressive than the dark tunnels of the tramway. By leveraging the property of the region's unique magic stone, Greenstone's city founders had created a fascinating train made up of submarines. Absently, he wondered how long it would be until he saw it again.

Jason missed those early days of admittedly repressed fear and panic, but also wonder at a world full of magic and possibility. He carried so many responsibilities now, but he also longed to travel the world and find all the things his imagination had conjured. He hoped that this was just one of many experiences to come.

The station they eventually arrived at was disappointingly similar to a subway station on Earth, even to sporting plain white tiles covering the walls. The main difference was that this station was cleaner than what he would have expected on Earth.

"Private station, for the building above us," Zolit explained to Jason. "It's the biggest hotel in the region; lots of mercantile river barons."

They stepped onto an elevating platform, crammed in with other lesser lights of the underground fighting scene. Sophie was nowhere to be seen; she had been taken on one of the earlier tram rides that were less crowded. Zolit's aide begged off for the night, leaving him and Jason to ride the platform together. It moved swiftly up through the building until it arrived at a floor that appeared to be a private club.

It was not as raucous as a nightclub but was more vibrant than a country club. There was a small section where a slew of attractive young people danced. They were generally low rank and in clothes that were fashionable but not expensive, akin to what he had seen in the entertainment district. The people watching from the mezzanine floor above were dressed in more expensive and conservative attire, and the way they looked at the dancers reminded Jason of people eyeing a buffet.

Masking the distaste in his aura, Jason panned his gaze slowly around the room, taking it all in. There was a double-wide spiral staircase leading up, next to the elevating platforms at the centre of the room. Music that was an odd mix of classical and old-school electronica to Jason's ears came from oversized recording crystals floating in the air. They served double-duty, also shedding the light that illuminated the room. The light was bright over the bar, dim over the sitting areas, with shifting colours over the dance floor.

Columns, booths and tables made the room an obstacle course, which patrons traversed to reach the four bars, each placed against one of the four walls. The room was a perfect square, with walls made entirely of glass. The dance floor was likewise square, in the centre of the room. The four bars were situated such that the walls behind the bartender offered panoramic views from the tall building, obscured by various colourful bottles. Jason intended to investigate them shortly.

Before that, he made his way to the south wall to take in the view, Zolit trailing behind. It was Jason's first real look at the heart of the city, having only seen the dark metal towers and glass ziggurats from afar. It turned out the club was in one of the ziggurats, with Jason's floor being the lowest level of the cube sitting atop the building.

Just to the south of the building, a wide river flowed toward the west. The river docks were lit up, operating through the night, but the river also had more decorative stretches. Many sections had trees lining the banks, with multicoloured lights painting them with rainbows. Jason couldn't help but wonder about the value of riverfront property left undeveloped for the sake of aesthetics, but could not deny his appreciation of it. The outer reaches of the city, visible from the height of the building he was in, only showed sporadic lighting. The inner districts, however, were lit up like an Earth metropolis.

"I have to say, Zolit, you've found a pretty nice place to call home."

"Yeah." Zolit moved to stand next to Jason as they both looked out over the city. "We endured the monster surge better than most, but this mess upriver..."

"The messengers," Jason said.

"Right now, it's only the adventurers getting worked up," Zolit said. "The Adventure Society is talking about war, but it hasn't affected the rest of the city quite yet. If anything, people are scrambling for lucrative contracts to supply the conflict."

"People ignore disaster in the face of profit," Jason said. "I've seen it in my homeland."

Zolit opened his mouth to ask where that was, then restrained himself.

"I think the government and the Adventure Society are trying to shield the populace," he said instead. "People aren't ready for another conflict when they aren't done recovering from the last."

"That's what the Adventure Society is for, right?" Jason asked. "Protecting people?"

"That's what they say," Zolit scoffed. "You know the society controls all the suppression collars we use in the arena?"

"They are regulated magic," Jason pointed out.

"Regulated my bony rump," Zolit said. "I could find someone to sell you an unregistered suppression collar without leaving this room."

Jason didn't argue. The person Zolit found could even have been Jason himself, having accumulated his own notable collection of suppression collars over the years.

"The Adventure Society makes a big show of bringing in auditors to make sure none of the collars have gone missing, as if the arena was where they all leak from. What they really want is to remind everyone who has the power and the control."

"I thought power and control were the Church of Dominion's, er... dominion."

"I don't see them speaking up. The Adventure Society has been telling everyone what to do for years now. Surge readiness, then the surge, then the Builder and now these guys with wings? There's always a new reason they get to tell everyone what to do. The society has been encroaching more and more, and I've never even met a priest of Dominion."

"You're better off," Jason said. "Their boss is annoying."

"Boss?" Zolit asked before stopping himself.

Jason could feel in the small man's aura him forcibly staunch his curiosity. Zolit couldn't entirely help himself, though, for all the good it did him. The penetrating look he gave Jason was spoiled by his big chihuahua eyes.

"If a man was looking to stay out of trouble, he'd move along nice and quick," Zolit said. "If he stays in a place like this, it could be the man is just telling himself he wants to stay out of trouble when what he really wants is to find it. However much damage it does."

Jason glanced at Zolit and chuckled.

"Someone put the wind right up you, didn't they, mate? I've got no problems with you, Zolit. But I'm not the danger you should be watching out for."

"And what should I be watching out for?"

"Best you don't watch out at all, lest you draw its attention. If you are what you seem, then the safest move for you is to stick to your normal routine. Just avoid any uncertainty as much as you can."

"Avoiding uncertainty is my normal routine. But normal is in short supply these days."

"Isn't it just?" Jason agreed with a chuckle. He then turned his gaze from the window to the bar. "I think I might get myself a drink."

"Stick to the bar down here or one floor up," Zolit said. "Higher than that is for the big-timers, not the likes of us. Maybe your Nightingale friend can get you up there. They like winners, and they love big-time adventurers, and she's both. She'll be enjoying a sickening amount of adoration right now. The top end of this club is still the bottom end of high society, and important adventurers are famous for opening doors."

Jason could feel Zolit's frustration, which was causing him to prod at Jason, even knowing that anything he learned was trouble. Jason mercifully left the man behind and made his way to the bar, flashing the elven bartender a smile.

"What'll it be?" she asked.

"I don't know the local beverages very well. Something colourful and sweet?"

"What rank, and how fancy do you want to go?"

"Silver," he said, "and as fancy as it'll go."

"You should go one floor up," she said. "That's where they keep the stuff the people down here can't afford."

"Good to know, thank you." He climbed off his stool as he flashed another smile. "Shame, though. What I've seen down here seems quite enticing."

Jason made his way to the stairs, following them up to another level. The only overt difference from the floor below was the additional bouncers in front of the stairs leading further up, as well as at the elevating platforms. None of the bouncers were elves, and instead were mostly imposing leonids, plus one of the rarely seen draconians.

Jason headed for one of the bars and his eyes landed on the bartender, who looked identical to the one below. Peeking closer with his aura, he sensed they were definitely different people, but with a subtle bond between them.

"Oh no," he muttered as he wandered over.

The bartender came to serve him.

"You have a familiar face," he told her.

"You met my sister downstairs? She's Isabelle, and I'm Mirelle. But everyone calls me Elle."

"There aren't eight of you, are there?"

"Just twins, sorry. You're an ambitious one."

Jason laughed.

"On the contrary; I've been having trouble keeping up."

"I'm not quite sure what that means," she said, narrowing her eyes as she looked him up and down. He noticed her gaze paused on the scars on his face, as well as the larger one at the base of his throat.

"Adventurer?"

"Sort of."

"Sort of?"

"I cook for adventurers. There's still stabbing, but it's safer."

"You don't look like someone who avoids danger. You came in with the cage arena crowd?"

"I did."

"You're a fighter?"

"No one told me the rule about needing a flunkey to fight for you. I fought, but I'm not sure that makes me a fighter. A fighter would end up with sore fists instead of a sore head."

"Get dropped in the first round?"

"Third."

"At silver rank? That's suspiciously good for someone who got pushed into a cage for not knowing the first rule."

"I had it on good authority that the first rule was to not talk about fight club. I don't suppose you have something for a sore head?"

"Not a problem," she said. "Everything I've got back here will give you a sore head if you drink enough of it."

He snorted a laugh. "I'm going to have a rough morning. Alright, set me up with something colourful, sweet and expensive."

"It's not that kind of establishment, fighter boy," she said with a cheeky smile.

He flashed her a grin. "I'm just looking for drinks; I'll make my own arrangements for the other thing."

"Good to know," said a handsome man with midnight black skin and colourful beads woven through his hair. He slid onto the stool next to Jason. "Are you going to be monopolising this lovely young woman all night?"

"That's up to her," Jason said, holding his hand out for the other man to shake. "John Miller, nice to meet you."

"Emir Bahadir."

"I think someone like you belongs on the higher floors, Mr Bahadir."

"I was looking for my friend Jason. We were meant to meet in a couple of weeks, but then I heard he was running off to hunt a species of dangerous and aggressive birds."

"I have it on good authority that he won't be available until the end of next week. Maybe you should take that time to visit other old friends."

Emir stood up, sliding a gold spirit coin onto the bar that only lasted a moment before vanishing into the barkeeper's hands.

"I'm confident that John here can more than cover his own drinks," Emir told her, "but it's always nice to give a gift when making new friends. I'll see you again, John."

Jason shook his head.

"You know who that was, right?" Mirabelle asked once Emir was gone.

"He did just tell me his name. Emil something?"

"That's Emir Bahadir. The treasure hunter. You know him, don't you? Don't play dumb."

"Oh, I'm not playing. We may have crossed paths in another life. Since he already paid you, let's go ahead and rack up some drinks."

Mirelle gave him another assessing look.

"Colourful, sweet and expensive, was it?" she asked.

"It was indeed. I'll trust your judgement."

"Oh, you probably shouldn't do that," she said with a sly grin. She turned around to pull one colourful bottle after another from the shelves behind her.

"You know, a lot of the out-of-towners like that awful, throat-burning stuff," she said. "I like amber as much as the next girl, but who needs a hundred varieties of throat fire?"

"I have always enjoyed elven liquor, ever since I first discovered it," Jason told her. "A sweet rainbow of drunkenness for me, thank you."

"I can arrange that. A lot of the fighters like to one-up each other with the nastiest drinks anyone will sell them."

"I've had to drink quite enough bitterness in my time."

Jason watched as she poured out a row of expensive drinks. The kind of specialised ingredients that went into high-rank liquor, at least anything that was more drink than boat polish, cost the kind of money that regular people used to renovate their homes. High-end spirit coins were not used for ordinary transactions. They were used to buy things like buildings and skyships, or the kind of indulgences that powerful adventurers enjoyed.

"I'm making what we call a rainbow wave," Mirelle told him. "There are countless variations, based on price and availability, but the idea is for each drink to be enhanced by the one that came before it. A good rainbow wave is how you tell the difference between a real bartender and someone just handing you drinks for money."

"Well, you certainly ain't that," a voice slurred from a few seats along the bar and Jason glanced over at the drunken leonid. "I've been waiting for you to serve me, but you just keep talking to rich pricks."

"I'm not the only bartender," Mirelle said, gesturing at the other staff. "In fact, I watched you wave one of them off. Also, you seem to have had quite enough."

"I want to be served by you. I like pretty elf girls."

"Well, if you want them to like you back," she told him, "I suggest spending less on drinks and more on soap."

The man bared his teeth with a snarl until a massive hand covered in dark green scales arrived on his shoulder. It belonged to a bouncer who was all the more intimidating for being a draconian. Jason had only seen a few of them before, but they were as big as leonids, if not bigger, with swept-back faces and tiny scales instead of skin.

"There are three kinds of people in this club," the draconian said with a deep hissing voice. "Those important enough that they can be obnoxious and those that aren't. You're coming with me."

"Is the third kind the ones who aren't obnoxious at all?" Jason asked.

"It is," Mirelle said.

"Well, that's not me. I think I'll have these drinks and then get thrown out. Will you put in a good word for me?"

"Drink up and we'll see," she said as she went to serve another patron.

As Mirelle moved away, a tall elf claimed the barstool to Jason's left. Jason looked over and then up at the woman who had beaten him in the third round.

Unlike Neil, whose bulk shifted his proportions from the elven norm, this woman looked like a normal elf but scaled up.

"This yours?" she asked, nodding at the yet-untouched row of drinks.

"It is," Jason said. "You like a rainbow wave?"

"Gods, no," she said, then nodded at Mirelle, who was coming back. "Give me a hursketh claw."

Jason watched as Mirelle mixed a drink that smelled like aviation fuel.

"I'm Avale," the large elf said.

"John Miller."

"You fight well, John Miller."

"You fight better."

"That's why I came and found you," she said. "I like drinking with good fighters, but I also like being the best."

"Then this might not be your night," Jason said, leaning forward to look past her. "Hello, Sophie."

Avale turned to watch Sophie slide onto the barstool on her left.

"Damn it."

50
DISTANT POWER

WITHIN THE RELATIVELY CONFINED AREA OF A CITY, SWIFT TRAVEL WAS A SIMPLE matter for Jason. Being able to shadow jump respectable distances through Shade's bodies meant that Jason could deploy his familiar around the city and jump to those locations, sight unseen. Because of this ability, Jason had never gone the long way to the camping grounds just inside the city wall where merchants, adventuring teams and other travellers left their sizeable vehicles. In his brief visits to his team, he would slip in and out using a Shade body.

In the kitchen of Jason's hover yacht, he emerged from a Shade body to find Taika and Gary assembling a hillock of slices and pastries.

"That is not the basis for a healthy breakfast," he scolded.

"Bro, it has to be this way. Rufus threatened to cook again, and you were off making whoopee with twins. Congratulations on that, by the way."

Jason scowled and flung out his arm in an angry gesture. The floor opened up and Sophie passed up through it on a moving section of floor. She had a confused expression and a magically enhanced dumbbell in one hand.

"Firstly," Jason said, "it wasn't twins. It was one woman who happens to have a twin. Her twin was not involved."

"I'm sorry, bro. You must be disappointed."

"That I didn't lure sisters into sharing a sexual encounter with one another?" Jason asked. "That's not okay."

"Oh," Taika said, his brow creasing in thought. "It's kind of creepy when you think about it like that."

"It's extremely creepy when you think about it like that," Jason said before wheeling on Sophie. "What are you telling people?"

"What makes you think it was me?"

"Because you were there."

"So was Emir."

"We all have our flaws," Jason said. "I imagine that Emir's makes for a fascinating list that does not include a lack of gentlemanly decorum."

"What's he even doing in Yaresh?" Neil asked, walking in with a dumbbell in his hand. "And why did Sophie just pass through my cabin?"

"Why weren't you wearing a shirt?" Sophie asked him.

"Because I was in my cabin. You dropped this, by the way."

He tossed the dumbbell lightly through the air and Sophie staggered as she caught it. Unusually for a healer, one of Neil's elf abilities had evolved to give him strength akin to Gary's.

"I think if we're going to discuss Emir's presence, we should include him in the conversation," Humphrey suggested as he also entered the kitchen. Being Jason's kitchen, it had plenty of room to accommodate the increasing population. "Also, Jason, what's this I hear about you making sisters do inappropriate things to one another?"

Jason turned a flat glare on Sophie.

The camping grounds where Jason's cloud vessel was parked had a panoply of other vehicles occupying space. The magical vehicles varied widely in size, design and colour, with the result looking like a wizard shantytown.

Jason hadn't reconfigured the cloud vessel to a cloud palace form, despite the stationary nature of the team's current activities. It had a much larger footprint in that form, and he felt it would be obnoxious to take up even more of a space already crowded with vehicles. They already stood out enough with the hybrid cloud vehicle, although it was far from the only exotic means of transport on display. Jason especially admired an artificial beetle even larger than his own vehicle.

Emir did not share Jason's compunction about overt ostentation. His massive cloud palace required a large enough space that it had to go hard up against the city wall, some way from Jason's vehicle.

While Jason's cloud vessel had gone through extreme changes since Greenstone, Emir's was almost exactly as Jason remembered it. The only differences were minor ones, mostly around the base where it rested on land instead of sea. Emir's palace was larger than Jason's, even when it was on full display.

Emir's preferred design was a castle with five grandiose towers, topped by shimmering domes and connected by bridges. It made no attempt to hide its nature, and the cloud material it was made from flaunted brilliant sunset colours.

"I guess I don't need to ask where he parked," Jason said as he and Humphrey walked down a ramp from Jason's vessel. Emir's palace loomed over everything else in the grounds, even obscuring the wall behind it. They looked at the maze of vehicles between them and Emir's palace, then up.

"Fly?" Humphrey suggested.

"Fly," Jason agreed.

Humphrey conjured his dragon wings, air surging as they launched him into the air.

"I shouldn't pull out the cloak," Jason said. "Let's just do a flight suit."

"Are you certain, Mr Asano?" Shade asked from Jason's shadow, his voice tinged with concern. Since leaving Earth behind, Shade had not taken a single form based on the vehicles there, even when it was more convenient. Jason had never asked him to either.

"It's fine," Jason said, not entirely convincingly, but darkness swirled from his shadow to surround him in a hover suit. Jason immediately thought back to his niece flying around over the water, giggling like a fool.

"Mr Asano?"

"It's fine," Jason repeated and took to the air, quickly catching Humphrey's slow progress. They weren't the only ones eschewing ground travel through the grounds, and everyone moved at respectful speeds.

"What is that thing?" Humphrey asked.

"It's something they make on Earth to let people fly without magic."

"That works without magic?"

"Shade does the magic version," Jason said. "It's a lot more convenient and a lot less loud."

They passed over the grounds before arriving at the massive double doors to Emir's front tower, their flight aids disappearing as they landed. The doors opened to reveal Emir standing behind them in a cavernous atrium.

"Hello, boys," he said with a grin. "Come on in."

"Has Arabelle spoken to you about Callum?" Jason asked Emir as they rode up an elevating platform.

"She's kept me apprised," Emir said. "I never realised he was already deeply involved when I invited him to join me in Greenstone. He's always kept so much hidden, even when we were at our closest. You're still deciding whether to give him access to Miss Wexler's mother?"

"Yes, although that comes down to what Sophie wants and Arabelle thinks is best. It's for them to decide, not me."

Emir nodded.

"I know that story. You get a cloud flask and start accumulating people, but you have to realise that your roof doesn't always mean your rules."

"He needed help to finally figure that out," a melodious voice said as the platform arrived at the top of the tower. Under the translucent dome was Emir's sprawling office of mutable cloud furniture, subtly shaped to draw the eye to a massive desk at the back. Sitting behind it was Emir's chief of staff and now wife, Constance.

Emir and Constance had been moving around each other for years, but the power imbalance had sat between them like a wall. Not only was Emir her employer, but also gold rank to her silver. Over the years, she had become more and more indispensable to Emir's operations, more partner than employee. Her ascension to gold rank had signalled the final boundary between them falling away, and they married during Jason's time on Earth. She rose and crossed to meet them, looking contrite in front of Humphrey.

"I owe you and Sophie an apology, Master Geller. I genuinely believed that Callum was trying to protect you, not act on an agenda of his own."

Constance had been training with Callum to finally reach gold rank, returning just as Sophie and Humphrey discovered that Sophie's mother was still alive. Callum had let their best lead get away, ostensibly to shield them from dangers they were too low-rank to confront.

"Yes," Jason told her solemnly. "I hope you learned your lesson that teenagers are always right and you should let them do whatever they want."

Emir snorted a laugh as Constance shook her head. Humphrey gave Jason a flat look.

"Sophie is your age," he pointed out.

Jason frowned, looking Humphrey up and down.

"That's a good point," Jason said. "She's bit of a cradle-snatcher, isn't she?"

Constance gave Humphrey an amused smile.

"If it makes you feel any better," she said, "the difference between Emir and myself is more than the full age of either of you."

Jason and Humphrey both turned to give Emir disapproving looks.

"Oh, come on," he said. "I knew her for twelve years before anything happened."

"Humphrey," Jason said.

"Yes, Jason?"

"Does your world recognise and condemn the concept of grooming?"

"Yes, it does," Humphrey said.

"Now, that's not fair," Emir said jabbing a finger at them. "She was an adult when we met."

"Uh-huh," Jason said.

"I'm sure everything was fully completely legitimate," Humphrey unconvincingly added.

Constance chuckled at Emir's scowl. He threw out an angry gesture and all the office's cloud furniture dissolved. It reconstituted around them as a series of comfortable chairs with a table in the middle. A hole opened up in the table and a drinks tray rose through it, much as Sophie had done earlier in Jason's cloud vessel. They sat down around the table and Emir poured himself a glass of amber liquid as the others looked at him.

"I'm not sure that's what I'd go for this early in the morning," Jason said.

"The greatest joy of power," Emir told him, "is not having to conform to what anyone else wants from you."

"Put it away," Constance told him.

"Yes, dear," Emir said without missing a beat.

The drinks tray, complete with Emir's poured drink, descended back into the cloud table that reformed over it.

"I think we should put aside the issue of Callum for the moment," Jason said. "As I said earlier, that is the decision of people not currently with us."

"Which leaves the question of what brought you here," Humphrey said. "I didn't think you'd be in the region for another week and a half."

"Once we heard that you were going after messengers," Emir said, "we felt that it was best to see you immediately."

"This is about the mysterious job you have for us?" Jason asked. "Is it related to the Order of the Reaper?"

"No," Emir said. "That has taken on some complex and political elements that I am very wary of wading into. Especially until I figure out just how much trouble Callum's meddling has caused. For which reason, I would like access to both him and your prisoner, Melody Jain."

"Again, that's up to Sophie and Arabelle," Jason said. "I won't help or hinder you in that regard. But Sophie remembers that you gave her shelter when she needed it most. At the very least, she'll be willing to hear you out."

"I can't ask for more than that," Emir said, which prompted a cough from Constance.

"Well, I *won't* ask for more than that," he corrected. "What I will ask you for is help with something new. You may recall that the scythe that you, Jason, ultimately brought to me, was the culmination of a years-long search that involved dozens of teams contracted to search remote reaches and fallen ruins the world over."

"I do."

"I have something similar in the works. A treasure hunt for something even more elusive and valuable, with no idea where in the world it is."

"Or if it even exists," Constance added.

"It doesn't matter whether it exists or not," Emir said. "It matters if we get paid to look for it."

"That sounds ethical," Jason said.

"Being serious," Constance said, "if this thing is real, then it could change the course of history."

Jason went very still.

"No," he said, his voice icy.

"Jason," Emir said. "You don't even—"

"I said no."

Jason leaned forward in his chair, rubbing his face in his hands and then staring at his feet. His aura retracted until even Emir could barely sense it. Constance, who had only been gold rank for a couple of years, couldn't detect his aura at all.

"Jason," Emir said again. His voice reflected that he realised he'd stepped on a landmine. "Arabelle gave me some indication of what you've been through. She didn't give me specifics, but instructed that I was, under no circumstances, to put you in the middle of important events. And I'm not. This is important, yes, but I only intend to put you at the periphery. You and your team will just be one set of adventurers amongst many. It's how I operate. I hire teams of adventurers and send them out. It's an ordinary job."

Jason looked up at Emir, his eyes no longer masked by the magic coins Belinda gave him. It was the first time Emir had seen their true state, and though his senses didn't pick up anything strange about them beyond their appearance, his instincts made him flinch. Jason's expression was cold, and his nebula-like eyes with their black sclera felt like a mercifully distant power in an unfathomable abyss. When he spoke, his voice was gravel being poured over a winter grave.

"An ordinary job?"

"Yes," Emir said.

"Tell me."

51

WHO YOU TRULY ARE

EMIR HAD KNOWN JASON BEFORE MANY OF THE TRIBULATIONS THAT RESHAPED HIM from the soul out. Gods marking his soul, in the way overbearing deities would see as a reward. The Builder, using a star seed to try and force Jason into accepting slavery. The long, slow recovery from that, and his struggles against powerful political forces.

Emir himself was responsible for placing Jason into situations he should not have been. It was Emir's search for the Order of the Reaper that ultimately sent Jason into the astral space where he died. Now Jason was back, not just from another world but from death itself. Despite having seen Jason's formative experiences, Emir had been startled by how different Jason was.

At a glance, Jason was much the same; when they spoke over a water link connection, it was little different to the past. But water links did not transmit auras, and a brief conversation did not reveal that damage, waiting just a scratch beneath the surface. It was their short encounter in the club that had changed Emir's perspective.

Emir's intention had been to have a little fun with Jason, who was clearly terrible at maintaining a cover identity. Flashing his scars and proving his skills in a cage fight was the opposite of how to sell himself as an unassuming cook. When he met Jason, however, he had been startled. The strength and clamp-tight control of Jason's aura had meant that even Emir, a veteran gold-ranker, could not see through him at all.

Even so, Emir had not realised the degree to which he no longer understood the manic, plucky outworlder he had once known. Jason had always put on a good front of being unconcerned about the powerful people around him. The gold-rank Emir had always known, though, that Jason's feelings were consumed with worry over that power imbalance. Jason was always in a manic scramble to somehow level the odds, be it through nonsensical behaviour or bold, unexpected moves.

From the way he strode through Emir's imposing cloud palace to his utter disregard for gold-rankers, Emir could tell there was no façade at play anymore; Jason was genuinely unintimidated. It was sitting across from Jason, looking into eyes that spoke of power waiting in the void, when Emir truly realised he no longer knew the man in front of him. Jason's aura was politely restrained, yet an ominous feeling teased at Emir's senses. It was like knowing there was a predator hidden somewhere in the bushes, waiting for a moment of vulnerability in which to strike.

"Tell me," Jason said in a voice of stone closing over a tomb. "Tell me about the messengers, Emir. Tell me what you want."

Emir suddenly felt that telling Jason anything was a terrible idea. Arabelle had warned him, but Jason's reaction was much worse than he imagined. He glanced at Humphrey, whose face revealed nothing. He reached out with his senses to explore Humphrey's emotions, only for a hard wall to spring up in his way.

Jason's face showed no change for having blocked Emir, who suspected that Humphrey hadn't even noticed the high-level aura clash. Emir was startled that Jason was even capable of the feat. Blocking the senses of others in such a way was normally only taught to gold-rankers. It wasn't an especially difficult technique for someone of that rank, if they had the right skill foundations, but the power, confidence and precision with which Jason executed it was intimidating.

"I've clearly approached this very wrong," Emir said. "We can do this another —"

"I said tell me," Jason commanded. His voice was soft but with an inexorable force at its core.

Emir pushed down his anger at being told what to do in his own house, knowing that it wouldn't be productive. He was not used to being the responsible one, which was Constance's job, but he was the older man and the higher-ranked one. He glanced at his wife, who nodded her approval. Emir then turned back to Jason, who was watching him with those unsettling eyes.

"You're aware of the problems surrounding the Church of Purity," Emir told him. "People all over the world are trying to figure out exactly when and why the original Purity was sanctioned by the other gods. The churches either haven't been told by their gods or are telling us they haven't. I do know the diamond-rank community has been looking into it."

"There's a diamond-rank community?" Humphrey asked.

"Diamond-rankers are powerful," Emir said. "Their numbers are limited, and things like distance and money are almost irrelevant as problems. They keep in contact with one another, most of them, and they barter in favours and rarities rather than money. I have more contact with them than most, but I've only seen glimpses and don't know exactly how they operate. What I do know is that they've been digging into what happened with Purity, and I know what they've found."

Jason didn't react, still watching Emir with a silent, unblinking stare. Emir waited only a brief moment for a reaction before giving up and continuing.

"They've asked me to leverage the networks that I use for treasure hunting to seek something out. I'm not the only person they deployed, not by any measure, but they want to cast as wide a net as they can without causing a commotion. For that reason, people like me aren't telling the adventurers we hire what they're looking for. When we get a lead, we give them the details we have and send them out without knowing what they're truly looking for, or why."

"That seems dishonest," Humphrey said. "Not to mention, inefficient. Adventurers deserve to go into any contract knowing everything they can."

"That's true when hunting monsters," Emir said. "Hunting treasure is a different game, and what I've just described is standard. Ask any teams that specialise in treasure hunting, and they'll tell you the same."

"How do they know what to look for?" Humphrey asked.

"They don't," Emir told him. "Even *I* don't know what to look for. I'm just a middleman, passing on what clues I've been given."

"That doesn't sound reliable," Humphrey said.

"I'm not oblivious to that fact," Emir said with a chuckle. "All we can do is throw as many trustworthy adventurers at this as we can. I'm just asking for your team to be amongst them, and knowing more than the rest, at that. We're not even talking about sending you somewhere. It's just that if you happen to converge on a point of interest, I may ask you to make a slight detour to check something out. From time to time."

"And now is one of those times," Jason said, finally speaking. "Because it involves the messengers, doesn't it?"

"Yes," Emir admitted. "As I said, I'm not telling anyone what we're after. But I've received permission to tell you."

"From whom?" Humphrey asked.

"Diamond-rankers," Jason answered, pre-empting Emir. "Someone told Emir, here, that I have some business with the messengers. He wants me to see what I can find about his mysterious goal while I'm at it."

"Yes," Emir said.

Jason continued to look at him, blank-faced, but at least with Humphrey, Emir could see his words having an impact. Jason felt more like another gold-ranker, and a hostile one at that.

"Even the diamond-rank community doesn't have an answer for exactly what happened to the God of Purity," Emir said. "Not one they're telling me anyway. But there is a belief that it was related to something. A device, a substance, a process; we don't know its nature. But whatever it is, it can achieve a goal as old as essence magic: cleansing the effect of monster cores."

Humphrey rocked back in his chair, eyes wide. Jason didn't move.

"You think this is what the messengers are here for," Jason said, less question than statement.

"Yes," Emir said.

"Why?" Humphrey asked. "Don't messengers look down on essence users as belonging to inferior species?"

"Power," Jason said. "Power and control. If you have a monopoly on turning core users into regular essence users, you're holding a hand down over the entire essence-using world."

"You could have all the people who regret using cores become able to train like adventurers again," Humphrey said in hushed tones.

"That's only the beginning," Emir said. "From an objective perspective, the difference between core and non-core users is negligible. But the idea of that difference being real is a cornerstone of society's upper reaches. Something like that could throw the levers of power into disarray, and that's assuming whoever controls this cleansing power is benign. If this power is real, the world will change, one way or another. The nature of that change will depend on where this power comes from, what is it and how it works. And, most importantly—"

"Who controls it," Jason finished.

"Exactly," Emir said.

"Jason," Constance said, speaking up for the first time since the discussion began. "We're just looking for adventurers. Lots of adventurers, of which your team would be one of many. That is what Emir meant when he said you would be on the periphery. Resolving this is not your responsibility. We're just looking for people we can trust."

"That might not be me," Jason said. "My judgement can be compromised when it comes to the dissemination of power. If I find something like that, I won't just obediently hand it over to whoever hired me. I'll do with it what I decide is best, and I haven't always been right about that."

"That's why it won't be you making that choice," Humphrey told him. "It will be us."

Jason turned to Humphrey, his expression finally softening.

"Are you making the call, team leader?"

"I am."

Jason nodded.

"Alright then."

Jason got to his feet, Humphrey following suit.

"Always a pleasure," Jason told Constance and Emir, but it was unconvincing since his tone still sounded like a threat. "I'll see you again at the end of next week."

"I'll show you out," Constance said.

"It's fine," Jason said. "I'll portal directly."

"You won't be able to portal out of the palace," Emir said.

Jason pulled the necklace holding his two amulets from under his shirt. One was his Amulet of the Dark Guardian, while the other was his shrunken cloud flask. Cloud stuff spilled out and formed a portal that filled with darkness that Jason stepped through. Emir watched the darkness vanish and the cloud stuff disperse, his eyebrows attempting to climb off the top of his head.

"How the fu—"

———

Unsurprisingly, the city of Yaresh had no shortage of parks. They featured expanses of thick, soft grass, dotted with lush plants, and vibrant flowers. After getting riled up by Emir, and then angry at himself for getting riled up and treating his friend like crap, Jason found a park and started meditating to resettle himself. It also gave him a chance to rest after he tapped into his astral gate to punch a portal through Emir's cloud house defences. While his cloud flask absorbed most of the impact from tapping into that energy, even the little left over had shaken him.

Jason lost track of time as he allowed his mind to quiet into an empty peace. He had learned many meditation techniques, but he ignored them for the moment, seeking only pure calm. When he opened his eyes, the sky was a gorgeous sunset orange. In equatorial Rimaros, the sunset had been like flipping a switch off. They were now far enough south that it was still quick, but offered fleeting moments of glory at the end of the day.

Rather than leave in search of accommodation as the city passed into night, Jason closed his eyes again, returning to meditation. This time, he practised a technique Amos had taught him, expanding his senses such that it didn't project his aura in an easily detectable way. It was the most difficult form of aura manipulation he had learned, representing a more advanced technique than anything else he knew.

Learning the technique involved simultaneously concentrating his focus and a meditative relaxation of the mind, which left him feeling like he needed two heads. The spirit attribute enhanced the mind in certain ways, including improved multitasking, but this was pushing his silver-rank abilities to the limit.

Much of the aura manipulation Amos was teaching Jason was normally reserved for gold rank. When those techniques relied heavily on raw power, Jason picked them up easily. When it was more about skill and he couldn't lean on his strength, it was much more of a struggle. Even if he couldn't master the techniques through a limitation in his rank or just his aptitude, grasping just the fundamentals would be a massive boon once he ranked up.

Jason slowly and carefully expanded his senses, making sure that his aura was undetectable to all but the most sensitive. In almost every adventuring scenario, moving so slowly would be fairly useless, but Jason continued to act with patience. Even if he didn't use what he was practising in the field for a decade, after he'd ranked up, he knew he was building the foundations of something amazing.

One of the things Amos had taught him was to pay more attention to the differentiation of his various senses. Most adventurers, Jason included, lumped their senses into two boxes: natural and magical. Neither of these was strictly correct, as even the 'natural' senses of sight, hearing, taste and touch were powerfully enhanced by magic.

The physical senses were also increasingly refined with each rank, as Jason could expand them into spectrums unavailable to normal humans. Mostly, though, he used that refinement to filter input. His mind didn't actively perceive things on the limits of the visual and audible spectrums unless they stood out for some reason, and he didn't process the bulk of the tastes and aromas wafting on the air. That saved him from nauseating experiences that normal people were mercifully spared from.

Magical perception was made up of two senses: the ability to sense magic and the ability to sense auras. All essence users understood there was a difference between them from an absolute perspective, but treated them as one from a practical perspective. This was as true for Jason as it was for most, although he did have an advantage in differentiating them, as his aura sense was much stronger than his magic sense.

Even so, Jason had rarely utilised them separately until Amos pushed him to do so. It was the first step in increasing what Jason thought were already highly refined senses. As he became increasingly proficient at using them separately, he discovered that doing so made them much more sensitive. This was the key to expanding his senses without what he now thought of as crudely shoving them with his aura. There was a lot of practise ahead of him, but even his early results had him excited.

Once again, Jason lost track of time. He fell into a meditative cycle as his senses expanded at a crawl, moving out centimetre by centimetre. His perception glacially expanded to encompass the park and he could sense the few people in it, late into the night.

This was the point where he realised it was the early hours of the morning, as everyone left in the park was engaged in behaviour he would rather not pry into, be it sketchy or amorous in nature. He sensed a familiar aura, though, and that had his eyes snap open.

"Mr Asano?" Shade asked.

"It's the outworlder's aide, Benella. She has some other silver-rankers with her."

"You think she is here for you?"

"Yep."

"I am somewhat concerned that she was able to find you."

"I may be practising at hiding my aura as my senses expand, but my efforts are still sloppy and crude. To someone with sufficiently sensitive perception, I was closer to being a beacon than being hidden."

"How are you going to react?"

"Well," Jason said, "I see us as having three options. One, scarper before they get closer. Two, try to turn it around and sneakily follow them. Three, fight."

"The second option offers the greatest benefits," Shade pointed out. "We could learn who this woman truly is. But the sufficiently sensitive perception you just mentioned would be a threat."

"Agreed."

"Of the remaining options, Mr Asano, escape is the more sensible approach. Fighting gets you nothing except showing this woman who *you* truly are."

"I'm not going to lie," Jason said. "That holds a certain appeal."

"But it only holds consequences with no upsides, Mr Asano."

Jason grumbled, but nodded. "Alright, but we are officially hunting this woman back."

Shade emerged from Jason's shadow and Jason stepped into him, vanishing.

52

THE GENUINE ARTICLE

BENELLA WAS ANXIOUS AS SHE RODE A SKIMMER BIKE CAREFULLY THROUGH THE rainforest. There were no roads to her destination and she wouldn't risk being observed flying out over the canopy, so she took a small bike and made her cautious way along the animal trails. Fortunately, there were enough large magical beasts amongst the local fauna that the trails were generously wide, if quite meandering. Early morning light only partially broke through the canopy, drenching everything in a beautiful twilight she was unable to appreciate, with her mind occupied by what was coming next.

She reached her destination, a small clearing with a creek babbling past a rocky outcropping. She parked the bike in the shadow of the rock and leaned up against it herself. As she waited, she nervously checked her watch over and over, wondering how time seemed to tick over so slowly.

Finally, there was a shimmer in the air and a glorious being became visible. Descending slowly, he looked like a celestine with alabaster skin and long hair of spun gold. It spilled down the back of his shirtless, hairless torso and gleamed under the sun. His eyes were solid gold orbs. He was too tall to be a celestine, however, standing some eight feet high, as well as having a pair of wings spread out behind him. His legs were covered in loose teal pants with gold trim.

He descended, stopping to float in place just before his bare feet reached the ground.

His wings were pristine white, aside from yellow and orange feathers along the bottom.

They were clearly not responsible for his flight, at least not by physically holding him aloft. As he floated magically in the air, the wings were open behind him, gently undulating.

When he spoke, his voice was deep and resonant, to the point of having an almost unnatural reverberation to it.

"I sense your fear, elf. Why are you here alone?"

"Haresh refused to come."

"What failure makes him unwilling to face me?"

"There is a man in the city. I suspect that he noticed the mask placed over my aura."

"A gold-ranker?"

"Only silver."

"That should not be possible."

"I was uncertain. But there are other indicators that the man is unusual. Certainly more than what he claims. He is attached to a group of adventurers, and not inconsequential ones, I discovered by making some discreet inquiries. But Haresh insisted on eliminating the threat, and he is the one you gave final authority."

"ARE YOU QUESTIONING MY JUDGEMENT?"

The messenger's voice went off like a bomb, shaking the trees and plants around the clearing and causing loose stones to tumble down the outcropping. Benella stumbled back, putting a foot into the creek and tripping, landing on her back. She was disoriented for a moment, and when she looked up, the messenger was floating over like the blade of a guillotine.

"I would never, Lord Fal. I only sought to clarify, believing that my explanation was flawed. I acknowledge my failing."

Fal scowled, floating back.

"Tell me of what happened."

"Haresh insisted that we eliminate the threat, but this man proved hard to find. He is resistant to tracking magic and seems to have some means of teleportation. We only got lucky and found him at all because he was practising an aura technique of some kind in a public park at night. His aura was almost completely different from the mask I had seen when I first encountered him."

"Then how did you know it was him?"

"The aura mask you gave me. It reacted to his aura the same way both times."

"Reacted how?"

Still sprawled, half in the creek and too scared to move, Benella winced, looking away.

"Tell me!" Fal demanded, his voice reverberating like a command from the heavens, projected into the clearing through some magical channel.

"A different way to the other servant races," she said, dragging the words out of herself. Her head was still turned from Fal, her eyes clenched shut like a child anticipating a beating.

"I did not ask what it was *not* like, servant. I asked what..."

He paused, his eyes narrowing as they focused not on Benella but her shadow. He moved in a flash, reaching into her shadow and pulling something out.

"Reaper spawn," he said as Shade dangled from a massive fist. Benella scrambled out of the way. "Who do you serve, familiar?"

"You will learn soon enough," Shade said calmly. "He has business with your kind."

"He's watching, isn't he?"

"Yes."

Fal then did something that neither Shade nor Jason realised was possible, launching a soul attack on Jason through his connection to Shade. Then it was Fal's turn to be surprised as Jason not just easily fended it off but retaliated, pushing the messenger's aura away from Shade.

The messenger tossed Shade aside.

"You should stay out of our affairs, shadow. The Reaper does not govern my kind; we do not grow old and die like the lesser races."

"You may not age, but you do die," Shade told him. "You claim to be the superior beings, yet you all seem to meet someone stronger eventually, and find your way to my progenitor."

"The Builder was of my kind, shadow. You think he will die too?"

"Have you ever wondered why he has been so obsessed with building his own world? What has been done once can be done again, or undone entirely, and he is not the only one creating a universe. The Builder has enemies, and one of them is right here. Do you believe that the likes of you can face someone that the Builder acknowledges as a personal foe? I suggest you run from this place, lest your time to meet my progenitor comes soon."

Fal moved in a blur and was once again clutching Shade, this time squeezing hard. Shade retaliated by draining mana; the alabaster skin of the highly magical messenger grew dull, starting with the hand and slowly crawling over the wrist and up the forearm.

"I am of the greatest people in the cosmos," Fal snarled. "We are without equal, let alone superiors. Your words are simply the bluster of the helpless."

Power surged down Fal's arm, and while the blackening from the mana drain accelerated, it did not stop Shade's body from being destroyed.

Jason was sitting in an office in the Yaresh Adventure Society branch, high in a tower of dark, glossy metal. Most of the Adventure Society campus in Yaresh was actually buried underground, with one tower for public-facing operations. With Jason was Humphrey, Estella and a high-level Adventure Society official named Fiora Luth. Like Jason and Humphrey, she was silver rank, although she had gotten there entirely through cores.

Fiora was a lifelong administrator, rarely seeing combat outside of a monster surge, and even then, it was usually indirect. She had been a logistics officer during the latest surge, whose risks weren't confronting monsters but getting supplies through monster-infested areas. While waiting for Benella to arrive at her destination, she and Jason had shared their experiences of supply-running during the surge.

Once Jason saw the interaction through Shade's perception, he confirmed that a messenger was present and the room fell silent. He had seen false messengers before, created by a transformation zone or summoning ability. He had to admit that they paled in comparison to the genuine article, even just a silver-rank one.

Although it was the lowest rank at which adult messengers were to be found, it still made quite the impression.

As soon as Jason confirmed there was a messenger, Fiora sent a signal. Adventurer teams moved on the network of associates Estella had managed to dig out since first investigating Benella at Jason's instigation. It had barely been a day and a half since then, but Estella had been quick to map out her key associates. The fact that Benella had called them together right after she parted from Jason and Zolit had been a help.

Jason opened his eyes after his link to Shade's body was cut off by its self-destruction.

"It's over?" Humphrey asked.

"He found Shade," Jason said. "We expected as much. It was a gamble sending him in Benella's shadow."

"It was the right move," Fiora said. "The messengers now know that we know they have agents in the city, but they'll have to be more circumspect. Hopefully, we can root them out while they're laying low by following the trail from this Benella woman."

"It was quick thinking to have the Shade body in your shadow jump to Benella when you saw she was leaving the city," Humphrey told Estella.

"I wasn't sure if it was the right move," she said.

"I agreed with it," Jason said.

"As did I," Shade agreed from Jason's shadow. "Consulting Mr Miller was the correct instinct."

"And in the days you've spent in large social gatherings," Fiora said to Jason, "you haven't seen anyone else that you suspect?"

"No," Jason said, "but I could easily have missed someone. The aura mask she was wearing was incredibly good. It took multiple direct interactions before I even noticed it, and even then I wasn't certain. The most worrying part, though, is that it wasn't even her aura mask. I always suspected that the messengers would outclass us when it came to auras, but not to this degree. Whether it's an item or a technique, their aura-related magic beats us out handily."

"Why would you suspect that they had superior auras?" Fiora asked.

"Because of their nature," Jason said. "Most entities are living beings with souls inside. For messengers, their bodies and souls are one thing, not two. Since auras are projections of the soul, their gestalt nature gives them access to abilities those with body-soul duality do not have."

"Are there any vulnerabilities to this nature?" Fiora asked.

"Only if you can convince them to be self-destructive," Jason said.

"Surely we should explore this more," she said.

"My understanding is that the topic is already being studied," Jason said. "There is a gold-rank healer in our convoy, Carlos Quilido. He knows more on that topic than I."

Humphrey was watching Jason warily. Jason's reaction to Carlos asking Jason to be a test subject for how to harm body-soul gestalts had ended violently. No sign of disturbance appeared in Jason's expression, body language or aura, but Humphrey kept a close eye on him.

Jason not only noticed Humphrey doing so, but also saw Fiora notice the dynamic. She didn't ask, despite the curiosity Jason felt from her. Jason sensed Fiora's self-control as she pushed her curiosity aside to refocus her attention.

"I'll admit I was sceptical when the director suggested you might be able to dig out some of the agents working for the messengers in the city," she said.

"I was lucky," Jason said. "She made a mistake and drew my attention. The odds of finding another by just randomly going to places with lots of people are slim at best. Chasing down the people associating with Benella will result in much better leads."

"What was her objective?" Humphrey wondered. "Working as assistant to some mid-tier fight promoter doesn't seem to have much in the way of benefits for the messengers."

"I imagine that many of their agents are low-level people placed in roles where more powerful people are around them," Fiora said. "Assistants, housekeepers, low-level bureaucrats. The ones that powerful people pay no more attention to than a lamp or a chair."

"It could be the person she's an aide to," Jason said. "He seems innocuous, but he's an outworlder. That's not something to ignore when dealing with a big dimensional mess. A bunch of messengers turning up, for example."

"I did know there was an outworlder in the city," Fiora said. "The society keeps track of people like that. I've glanced through the report logs on him, but the only thing that stuck out was that, for an outworlder, he's been unusually sedate. Some minor criminal activity that we let go. We'd rather he stick to that than look for something more exciting. My investigators are looking closer now, of course, and I have analysts combing these reports for any less-obvious indicators that he's been up to something."

Fiora leaned back in her chair.

"We've been lucky that the messengers are fighting on multiple fronts," she said. "You're aware of the natural array?"

"We are," Humphrey said. "Our magical researcher is downright eager to see it. He's been a little cranky since his intended lecture about it to my team and the other group with us was derailed."

"We're currently invested in keeping the fighting centred on the messenger strongholds and away from the city. They're keeping us from the only access to the array, deep underground. The people here, behind the walls, don't understand how bad the fighting is. If the messengers can cut off the supply lines coming out of the city, though, our forces will have to pull back. Then the fighting will be at our walls instead of theirs."

Jason felt her lock down her emotions, and she stood up. Humphrey and Jason did the same, and she shook both of their hands.

"I will confess that you have left me quite curious, Mr Miller. The director said that if I looked deeper into your identity, I would find it, so he asked me not to. I wouldn't ordinarily let that stop me, but you've done us a service, so I'll respect that."

"I appreciate it," Jason said. "But it's the Adventure Society, Mrs Luth. Service is the point."

53

STORIES ABOUT FUNGUS

URMAN VOHL HAD PULLED BACK TO THROW THE FOLDER FULL OF PAPERS ACROSS the room when he stopped himself, closed his eyes and put the folder back down on his desk. His sons, Valk and Emresh, stood anxiously in the middle of the office.

"Another one," Urman snarled. "That's two in the time it's taking the broker to get here. You are certain he's coming, aren't you, Valk?"

"Yes, Father," the older brother said.

Urman's office was midway up one of the inner-city towers, prestigious but not overreaching. Understanding where to headquarter oneself was an important part of maintaining a reputation in Yaresh. It demonstrated a self-valuation that could hurt one's interests if they were to over- or under-evaluate their position in society.

A knock at the door was followed by some of Urman's less thuggish men escorting a small elf in a well-made but not ostentatious suit. Like Urman's office, his clothes were carefully aligned with his societal position. Despite being in Urman's office and surrounded by his people, the elf looked unperturbed. He was a silver-rank core user, but his aura was sharply controlled, giving away none of his emotions.

"Mr Vohl," the small elf said. "Your people bringing me here is pushing quite firmly against the boundaries of propriety."

"Jasich Tovill," Urman said with a glower. "You're going to stand there and talk about pushing boundaries when you have been interfering with my business?"

"I have nothing to do with your business, Mr Vohl."

"In the last three days, no fewer than nineteen of my debtors have paid their loans in full, immediately after getting loans from you."

"You are incorrect in two regards, Mr Vohl. Firstly, the loans facilitated by myself have nothing to do with your loans, simply because they went to the same people in several instances. If you disagree, you will find my legal advocates downright eager to explain the difference before a civil magistrate. Secondly, they are not my loans. Loans have been executed through me, but it is my client from whom the loans are issued, not me."

"And who is your client?"

"None of your business, Mr Vohl."

"Father," Emresh said angrily. "Let me—"

"Quiet," Urman commanded dismissively.

"Yes," Jasich agreed. "You've done your father quite enough damage."

"What does that mean?" Urman asked.

"I apologise," Jasich said. "I spoke out of turn."

"My father asked you a—"

"Shut your mouth!" Urman snapped at Emresh, then turned his gaze on Jasich.

"I have no patience for your games, broker. Tell me who your client is or you'll find unfortunate coincidences befalling your interests."

Jasich sighed.

"As it happens," he said, "my client anticipated a scenario quite like this and issued directions accordingly. I have been given, should I be put under duress, permission to reveal that my client is a member of the Nareen family, out of Rimaros."

"The Storm Kingdom?" Urman asked. "What do they want with a handful of businesses in the Yaresh entertainment district?"

"My client, as it happens, is also a go-between. She has no interest in the entertainment district or the business involved."

"She's doing this for someone else?"

"Yes."

"Why?"

"She has only involved herself to protect someone."

"Protect who?" Urman asked. "My debtors? This mysterious person behind her?"

"No, Mr Vohl. She's doing this to protect you."

"Me? Who and what do you think I need protection from?"

"Someone within your organisation has offended a person they very much should not have."

Remembering the broker's earlier statement, seemingly made offhand, Urman looked to his younger son before turning back to Jasich as he continued his explanation.

"Mr Vohl, the offended party knows that if they retaliate against this member of your organisation, events would escalate to the point where they would be required to kill you and everyone around you before there were no more people to come seeking revenge."

"Even if this person could do that," Urman said, "the city authorities wouldn't just sit back in the face of that much killing."

"I don't know the identity of the person in question," Jasich said, "but I am assured that he is unconcerned about any authorities. It seems an outlandish claim, but given the identity of my client, not one I can entirely dismiss. However, doing all of that would go against the person's current desire for anonymity. He, therefore, decided that he shall satisfy his need for revenge by interfering with your interests rather than melting down your flesh and carrying you around in a bucket. That is a direct quote, by the way, and one I am assured can be taken quite literally, other than potentially requiring multiple buckets or perhaps a barrel. My client is attempting to prevent that person from deciding you are worth casting aside their anonymity over. She knows that going through me is something you would be willing to do, but going through her is not."

Urman leaned back in his chair, considering the broker's words. Jasich stood in place, patient and unconcerned, while Emresh was agitated, unable to keep his hands and feet still without fidgeting. His older brother, Valk, was more composed, but still showed signs of uncertainty in his expression. During the long silence, Emresh looked like he was about to speak several times before either stopping himself or being stopped by a harsh glare from his brother. Finally, Urman spoke.

"Broker. Sell me the loans you have issued."

"As I have already explained, Mr Vohl, they are not my loans. I merely administered them."

"You're a smart man, Mr Tovill. I'm sure you can figure something out."

"What I have figured out, Mr Vohl, is that if you keep pushing, your best result would be humiliating failure."

"You think failure is the best I can do?"

"If you do anything, Mr Vohl, I am the only person in this room who will still be alive at week's end."

Urman grimaced but refrained from another outburst.

"Take Mr Tovill home," he told his minions. They took Jasich out, leaving Urman and his sons. "Emresh, what did you do?"

"Nothing."

"Don't lie to me, boy."

"Really, nothing. It was a normal week."

"You didn't hurt anyone?" Valk asked. "Make anyone angry?"

"Of course I hurt people," Emresh said. "I just said it was a normal week."

"Who were these people you hurt?" Urman asked.

"I didn't make a list."

"Emresh," Valk said. "You are the only one of us that spends time in the entertainment district. You know the people there, yes?"

"Of course I do."

"Out of the people you hurt, which ones were strangers?" Valk asked.

"What makes you think it was someone I hurt?" Emresh asked. "The broker said offended, and how would I hurt some death-dealing savage who could take us all out?"

"It was probably some kid from a powerful family out for fun," Urman mused. "Too prideful to drop their name, perhaps, or not wanting to drag that name into a petty mess."

He looked at Emresh.

"Some people know better than lay their mistakes at the doorsteps of their families."

"It could have been anyone he encountered," Valk said. "The best move, for now, is to find out more about the broker's client."

Urman nodded.

"Valk, look into any members of House Nareen in the city."

"What do I do?" Emresh asked.

"Go home," Urman said. "My townhouse, not your place in the entertainment district. Stay there until I tell you otherwise. I'll have my men make sure you go, and tell your mother you aren't to leave."

"You're telling Mum on me?"

Jason's team was in Clive's skimmer, moving south over the forest canopy. For once, Jason himself had joined them.

"While it's good that we're operating alone so you can come with us," Humphrey told him, "this isn't a low-stakes contract to slowly get used to working together with. We're one of seven teams, four of which have gold-rankers attached. We're all scouting out the region south of the city. No one has heard anything from anyone in that direction for days, including from the first two teams sent to look into it."

"Why split up all the teams?" Belinda asked. "Isn't that asking to be picked off in isolation?"

"Because the area we're covering is so large," Humphrey told her. "As far as anyone can determine, the entire southern approach is cut off. The Adventure Society wants this dealt with before a panic starts."

"*Should* a panic be starting?" Neil asked.

"That's what we're trying to find out," Humphrey said. "The local teams are checking the main thoroughfares south. We've been assigned to hop between smaller and more isolated communities, along with Korinne's team and another group of out-of-towners."

"So, we get the low priority tasks," Neil griped.

"Be grateful," Humphrey said. "The teams with gold-rankers are going after the main routes, which is where the most dangerous threats are likely to be. Otherwise, the larger towns would have gotten the word out before going silent."

"We can handle dangerous," Sophie said. "Unless it's something gold rank."

"Rank isn't the only source of danger," Clive warned. "Yes, we could handle most silver-rank monsters, but the Magic Society's monster almanac is filled with exotic threats. Not everything can be solved by punching."

"That depends on how good you are at punching," Sophie told him.

In their own skimmer, Korinne's team was also moving over the rainforest, trees just below them.

"Why couldn't we just take the roads?" Polix wondered aloud. "It would take longer, yes, but we could have just left earlier."

"The Adventure Society wanted us to avoid trouble on the way to the population centres," Korinne said. "The comprehensiveness with which the southern region has gone silent suggests that the roads are compromised."

"But running these skimmers in flight mode consumes a lot of spirit coins," Polix said. "The Adventure Society is reimbursing us, right?"

"Of course they are," Rosa said. "Isn't that right, Korinne?"

"It is," Korinne said. "They will fully reimburse us."

"Why do you not sound convincing?" Polix asked.

"They will reimburse us," Korinne said. "More or less."

"More or less?" Kalif asked. "We're fuelling this thing out of party funds. What does more or less mean?"

"It means that the society is currently funnelling supplies to the conflict with the messengers," Korinne said. "They're still paying out contracts, but non-urgent reimbursements are being paid out in credit bonds."

"What are credit bonds?" Kalif asked.

"It's a token that you can use to reclaim an owed amount at a later date."

"How much later?" Polix asked.

"A year."

"A year? We won't be around in a year!"

"You can claim them at other branches," Korinne said.

"Do we still have to wait the year if we do that?" Polix asked.

"Only if you want the full eighty-five percent," Korinne said.

"What do you mean, eighty-five percent?" Polix asked.

"There's a slight fee for claiming the token at a branch other than the non-issuing one," Korinne said.

"We should never have taken this contract," Polix complained. "Self-funding a trip into some vaguely defined area where people keep vanishing? Including adventurers?"

"Maybe the whole region is overrun with something," Rosa suggested. "I've heard stories about fungus that can overtake whole towns in one night."

"I once saw a carnivorous vine the size of a large town," Zara said. "It was in an astral space, part of the mass expedition that Emir Bahadir arranged five years ago. Iron-rankers only, with promising young teams from across the world. It was a good chance to meet with other royalty."

"Did you kill the vine monster?" Kalif asked.

"It wasn't a monster," Zara explained. "It was some kind of alchemically modified plant creature that had been left to grow wild for centuries. It had buried itself underground, but had vines on the surface, amongst the regular overgrowth. It would attack anyone that entered its territory. Dozens of adventurers teamed up to deal with it."

"A single giant organism?" Polix asked.

"Yes," Zara confirmed.

"Affliction specialist," Polix said. "Even a whole bunch of adventurers won't get it done. You need someone that can keep scaling damage endlessly to handle something that big."

"Except that it wasn't that easy," Zara said. "We were iron-rank, and you know what affliction specialists are like at that rank."

"Crap area specialists," Kalif said. "No iron-rank monster is tough enough to make afflictions worthwhile and no bronze-rank affliction special survives a bronze-rank monster. Not without a lot of backup. Faster and easier to just run around killing stuff the regular way."

"Yes," Zara said. "It's why only a few teams brought them. And they were all specialised in area afflictions, which don't have escalating effects until higher rank. Fortunately, there was one focused affliction specialist, part of a local team."

"A focused affliction specialist?" Korinne asked. "They're even weaker than area affliction specialists at low rank. And as for high ranks, they're just worthless against anything but one giant creature."

"If they really are affliction specialists, yes," Zara agreed. "The person in question became an affliction skirmisher."

Everyone except Polix, who was driving, turned to look at Zara.

"Yes," she said with a small, weary sigh. "I was talking about him. It was the first time I saw him, although we never actually met until later."

"You need to get over that guy," Rosa said. "I don't think he's especially keen on you, Princess."

"It's not princess anymore," Zara said.

"Which I believe about as much as you not being obsessed with the guy you joined our team over," Rosa told her. "Maybe try to avoid letting out a little sigh when you talk about him and it might come across as more believable."

"You realise he's probably listening to all of this," Kalif said. "That shadow familiar of his is sneaky."

"I keep sensing him skulking around," Rosa said. As the team scout, she had the best perception amongst them. "I'm sure he's getting harder to spot, though."

"I appreciate you saying so, Miss Liselos," Shade said from her shadow. "I need to refine my skills again with each summoner I am familiar to, and you have been very good practise."

54

VAMPIRE MONSTER SLAVES

Korinne's team paused their progress over the rainforest to fend off a large group of spider monkeys. These were not like the spider monkeys of Earth, as they had four extra arms, shot webbing from their hands and poison barbs from the tips of their tails. They also were more aggressively omnivorous, still enthusiastic about fruit while also mixing anyone they could catch into their diet.

The rainforest canopy was an environment that was a mixed bag for the team. They could all get by on silver-rank agility, but some fared better than others in the trees.

Rather than slaughter all the monkeys, the team drove them off with a show of force, with only a few of the creatures dying. They were not monsters but native magical beasts, and the rainforest canopy was their natural habitat; they were only a threat to anyone roaming the treetops, who would generally be able to handle themselves.

The team was returning to the skimmer hovering over the canopy, making their way up through the shadowy canopy, when Rosa, the scout, froze. She turned to peer into the shadows as the rest of the team readied themselves. They took tactical positions, floating in the air or perched on branches. Only Zara was out of step, not having the years of training and working together that kept the others in perfect sync.

Two blue and orange eye-shaped nebulas appeared in the dark. Realising it was Jason didn't do much to relax the team, and they remained on alert.

"How did you get so close?" Rosa asked. "You didn't use to be this good."

"The entire reason we're all together like this is so that Lord Pensinata can train my aura use," Jason told her. "It would be a little strange if I wasn't improving."

"But this fast?"

"Wait until you see a messenger," Jason said. "You'll realise that this isn't fast enough."

"What are you doing here, Asano?" Korinne asked. "You should be with your own team."

"I just wanted a word with your newest team member."

"Last I heard, you wanted nothing to do with her."

"Yes, well," Jason said, his voice embarrassed. "I kind of have this thing where I make grandiose statements of principle and intent, only to immediately realise I have to go back on them for practical reasons. Lady Nareen has undertaken a task at my behest and I wanted to discuss it."

"I don't think now is the best time," Korinne said.

"Yeah," Jason acknowledged, "but we're off to fight evil and I've learned it's best to seize the moment. I die kind of a lot."

"It's fine," Zara said. "I'll catch up."

The team shared unhappy glances but made their way up to the skimmer while Zara activated a privacy screen. She stood on a small floating cloud that roiled like a storm. Jason emerged from the shadows, sitting casually on a branch as he pushed the hood back off his head.

"There are a lot of conveniently strong and horizontal branches up here," he observed. "Is that normal? I don't know a lot about trees outside of their use in landscape architecture, and I mostly forgot all of that stuff. It's what my dad did for a living."

"Did, past-tense? Your father died?" Zara asked.

"What? No, there was a monster apocalypse and he's fixing one of my places. A bunch of gold-rankers dug it up looking for treasure, the pricks. I'm not sure I was paying him, now that I think about it. I probably should be. He's going to have some wages racked up by the time I get back."

"Did you just come here to talk nonsense?" Zara asked.

"It's generally a safe bet," Jason said with a disarmingly vulnerable smile. "But this time, I came to thank you for helping me with that property developer thug."

"You supplied the money," Zara said. "All it took me was a couple of hours and my name."

Jason nodded. "And you got to see what a hypocrite I am. I was against you joining the convoy because your background would bring trouble. And then I asked you to flaunt your name the first chance I got."

"That's not why you didn't want me to join," Zara said softly. "You weren't thinking of the trouble I'd bring, but the trouble I already had. That my whole family brought you, but you never would have been involved with us, if not for me."

Jason knew that was wrong, as Soramir had been watching him from the moment he and Farrah returned to Pallimustus. He doubted Zara was faking ignorance, which meant that Soramir had not told her, leading to more self-recrimination than was entirely warranted. He knew himself well enough to realise that not telling her that was petty, but he could live with being a little petty.

"Probably," Jason agreed.

Zara sat down in her floating cloud, Jason laughing as her legs dangled out of the bottom.

"You know that I can do things for you without drawing too much attention," she said. "For example, I didn't need to throw my identity around. The name of House Nareen was plenty to settle the issue."

"It's not settled," Jason told her. "Vohl is looking into you."

"People, especially ambitious ones, don't eat a loss quite so willingly," Zara said dismissively. "It's in hand. I'm not done with Mr Vohl."

"Are you sure?"

"Yes."

"Your plan doesn't involve marrying any dead people, does it?"

"I learned that lesson," she said, shooting him a flat look. "I think it's time we both got back to our teams. I don't know about yours, but mine is waiting."

"Oh, mine doesn't even know I'm gone," Jason said. "But genuinely, thank you for handling the business with Vohl."

"It's not that big a concern," she said. "It's not like if I didn't then you would *really* go ahead and kill them all."

"No," Jason said, his aura showing nothing but sincerity. "Of course I wouldn't."

Jason emerged from one of Shade's bodies, arriving back on his team's still-moving skimmer.

"Where did you go?" Humphrey asked in his best disappointed-mother voice.

"I didn't go anywhere," Jason said. "I've been here the whole time."

Humphrey turned his gaze to Jason's seat. Sitting in it was what looked like a mummy from an old movie, made up of bandages bound tightly around a roughly human-shaped cluster of leeches. Pinned to its forehead was a note with the word JASON written on it.

"In my defence," Jason said, "I thought he'd take the blood clone form."

"You thought that you, but red and mute, would be convincing?" Humphrey asked.

"Red, I might believe," Sophie said. "Mute? No."

"Come on, Colin," Jason said, gesturing at his familiar. "The cat's out of the bag."

Colin suddenly lurched to his feet with a burst of enthusiasm.

"No," Jason said. "I don't have an actual cat in a bag for you to eat."

The mummy's shoulders slumped, prompting Jason to wonder why a bound-up swarm of leeches had collective body language.

"I may have a fresh spider monkey," Jason told him.

"He is not eating that in the skimmer," Clive called out from the driver's seat. "Not unless you're supplying the crystal wash to clean it."

When Jason and his team drew closer to their destination, they slowed to a stop. Clive carefully descended the skimmer below the canopy but paused high above the forest floor, out of the sun to hide amongst the trees. Jason went over the side, vanishing into the shadows as Shade's bodies poured from his cloak to do the same.

The rainforest floor was a metropolis of shadows and obstacles; precisely the kind of place it would be foolish to fight someone like Jason. His team waited for Jason and Shade to scout the way forward, flickering from shadow to shadow in the gloom. Their destination was a small town, a dozen kilometres ahead, that had not been heard from in days. That was not unusual, as it was a small and relatively isolated place, but with the region increasingly going dark, Jason's team had been sent to check. Every location they were scheduled to check was the same.

Jason didn't go the entire way shadow jumping, as even his mana would suffer without a source of replenishment. He drew on his old techniques for navigating the Greenstone delta on foot, adapted as he ranked up, but never as practised as in his early days as an adventurer. With the hot, humid air, it almost felt like he was back there.

One of Shade's tertiary powers was the ability to be the locus of Jason's non-combat abilities. Because that included his map ability, sending out Shade bodies was an excellent way to map out an area. It was Shade who first encountered the town, after which his other bodies swept around it.

The town was surrounded by crop fields, divided by lines of trees rather than fences. Rice paddies featured heavily, with many shade houses lined up in rows for crops that weren't as fond of the blazing sun. There were people working the fields, although most of the labour was being performed by construct creatures, built for this purpose and directed by elf supervisors.

It looked normal at a glance, but something was tweaking Jason's instincts. He kept himself hidden and his magical senses restrained. He made his way forward using the lines of trees that divided the fields, as well as the shade houses. He found a spot close to the town, inside a cluster of shrubbery at the end of one of the tree lines.

The town was unremarkable, with simple wooden buildings, often open-sided. Airflow and minimal obstruction seemed to be key to the design principles, and all of the buildings were painted the same dark green. It looked like the whole town had been repainted recently as well. Jason could see right through many of the buildings, especially the houses. They were furnished in the same minimalist principles in which they were constructed. The internal spaces were open, with racks instead of cupboards, hammocks instead of beds, and open sides instead of walls.

Once again, the town populace seemed normal, but Jason's instinct that something was off was growing, even if he couldn't figure out what was tripping alarms for him. Before taking the risk of expanding his supernatural senses, Jason enhanced his physical ones. He started by pushing his vision into the thermal range. The immediate detail that stood out was the fact that every building had a heat bloom radiating from the new paintwork. It was counteracting the design of the buildings, making it harder for the airflow to cool them down.

Jason next turned his enhanced vision on the people. Elves were very much like humans under thermal vision, barring essence-related exceptions. The towns-folk all had unstable temperatures, with points all over their bodies soaking heat as if they were feeding on it.

As he focused on the people, it finally clicked for Jason what his instincts were picking out as wrong. Every person moved in the exact same way, from body language to simple gestures to stride. They greeted one another the same way, walked down the street the same way and picked out items at the small market the same way. It was as if the whole town was the same person with many different bodies.

"Bloody Stepford elves," he muttered.

"Mr Asano?" Shade asked.

"I think we've got a pod people situation," Jason said.

"Will you use the technique Lord Pensinata taught you to expand your senses without alerting people to your presence?"

"No," Jason said. "I'm still too inconsistent with it. I'll discuss it with the team before making any moves that could potentially set them off."

"We definitely need a closer look," Jason said after explaining what he saw to the team back at the skimmer. "I have an idea in my head, though, and if I'm right, these people might be able to sense me. The outworlder's aide, Benella, was almost certainly wearing some kind of aura mask that was applied from the outside, instead of being created by her."

"Is that even possible?" Belinda asked.

"Not using the magic we know," Clive said. "But the last few years have seen our world flooded with outside magic. It only makes sense that the messengers have some as well."

"These elves may be using aura masks as well," Jason said. "They wouldn't even have to be as good as the one Benella has. They would only need to hold up long enough to lure unsuspecting people into an ambush. For victims to wander into town and get taken out or taken over by whatever has a hold of those elves."

"Why would the messengers want a town that occasionally kidnaps people passing through?" Sophie asked.

"To keep everything quiet while they build up a secret army. It prevents anyone from going home with stories about some weird stuff they saw in the town, plus the populace itself is the goal, so a few extra recruits would be welcome."

"If they're doing this all over the southern region," Humphrey said, "then a massive army has formed on the borders of Yaresh without the city noticing. And if enough of the southern region was affected that the city did finally notice, then that army is basically in place. If someone sets them off, they may turn overt and move on the city."

"Someone like any of seven teams roaming around right now, looking for bears to poke," Jason said. "Now that the city has noticed something is going on, we have to assume these hidden enemies will move sooner rather than later."

"Which leaves the question of what we do now," Humphrey said. "Looking closer may trigger them, but we need to know what we're dealing with."

"From what Jason described," Clive said, "I would assume some manner of body control."

"Like that spider in the Order of the Reaper's astral space?" Sophie asked. "The one that turned all those monsters into an army of vampire monster slaves."

"Oh, great," Neil said. "I can't wait to relive the horrifying pitched battle where we almost died after fighting for hours against a relentless horde."

"It might be worth enquiring with Carlos," Clive suggested. "Jason's observations suggest a heat-consuming parasite that takes over the body. As Carlos specialises in things that take over the body, he might have some insight into what we're dealing with."

55

THE FACE OF INSURMOUNTABLE POWER

MESSENGER ARCHITECTURE WAS OBSESSED WITH CIRCLES. THEIR BUILDINGS WERE circular, as was the pattern in which they were laid out. The wall around each of their strongholds was also a circle. The wall was only ten feet tall, which would hardly even slow down a silver-rank adventurer, but the wall itself was not the obstacle. It was a platform for the powerful defensive screen that tapped into the combination of aura projection and ritual magic used by the messengers.

Benella was unnerved by the ritual magic used by the messengers. Pallimustus had rituals and magical devices that created artificial auras, like aura beacons used for signalling. Compared to what the messengers could do, however, the Magic Society were children playing in the mud. Their ritual magic was able to not just produce artificial auras, but even take on and reproduce actual auras, as well as use them in more sophisticated ways.

The messengers could actively enhance protection arrays with their auras. This improved both offensive and defensive capabilities, and was the key to their success in fending off regular Adventure Society assaults. In addition to the walls around the stronghold, the circular buildings could each serve as a sturdy fort or bunker, depending on their size.

The buildings constructed by the messengers trended large, with a lot of open space. Columns rose from the top of the circular walls, creating a gap between the wall-tops and the conical roofs. The flying creatures often used this gap for entry and exit, although there were also arched double doors. Aside from that, smaller doors were used by servants of what the messengers called the 'lesser races.'

The messengers had five strongholds scattered to the west and south of Yaresh, all of which had come under attack multiple times. Each stronghold was made up of round buildings, surrounded by a neatly circular wall. In one such stronghold, Benella was waiting in a large, round and almost empty building.

Inside the building were three chairs that would best be described as thrones, which were favoured by the messengers. The backs of the thrones curved in an hourglass shape to accommodate their wings. Benella knew that messengers could absorb their wings into their bodies, having seen them do it herself. They almost always did not, however, although she was unsure why.

Amongst the non-messengers like Benella, who had chosen to serve them, the best guess was that the messengers did not want to resemble celestines so closely. There was little chance of that, even discounting the wings, as the messengers were around half again as tall as a celestine. Even so, the servants were careful to avoid even the implication. If a messenger thought they were being compared to their 'lessers,' any servant that did so would be annihilated, irrespective of their value.

In the community of servants, rumour and speculation would rapidly spread. This was because the messengers felt no need to explain themselves to those they considered lesser, which was everybody. Their inherent superiority was a key part of their quasi-religious philosophy. Benella and the other servants tried their best to learn such philosophy, despite the messengers having no interest in teaching it.

Benella had found that the messengers' refusal to explain themselves in any instance and on any topic extended to the point of impracticality. All the servants had made mistakes due to a lack of information a messenger could easily have provided. The punishment for these failures was always violent, often lethally so, despite the lack of fairness.

Benella had seen that the danger level differed from messenger to messenger. Since joining the stronghold full time, she had realised that the messenger she primarily served, Fal Vin Garath, was one of the more erratic. He was more prone to violence, and what exactly would set him off was less predictable—most servants took 'everything' as the default assumption.

The need to find a new place for herself was why she was waiting in the large building with the three thrones, which looked tiny in the high, open space. The only other thing in the building, other than Benella herself, was a crystal recording projector on a small plinth.

She could no longer go back to Yaresh, having been exposed by John Miller or, as she now realised, Jason Asano. She still maintained contact with certain people in the city, and while they were now laying low, she had managed to get the results of enquiries she had already made into John Miller. It took very little effort to discover Miller's true identity; he was almost flaunting it. Between the scars, the skills and the team he was attached to, almost any investigation would quickly reveal the truth. Whether he realised it himself or not, Benella knew that Asano was aching to cut loose.

Benella's utility to the messengers as one of their agents inside the city was gone. Gathering information from overheard conversations in the cage-fighting arena had only gotten her so far anyway. She had managed to dig out a few useful titbits from attendees networking and making deals at the fights, but nothing wildly important or revelatory.

Her main value had been in managing Zolit. He would become increasingly unstable without her there to reinforce the right behaviour and administer doses, now that she could no longer return to the city. That problem was no longer hers, however, and the messengers would solve it as they saw fit. They certainly wouldn't bother telling her what was happening.

The presentation Benella was waiting to give was her chance to maintain relevancy to her winged masters. They had no sense of loyalty to those they considered lesser, so any accomplishments in the past had earned her almost nothing. At most, it demonstrated that she was still potentially useful moving forward. If she could show the messengers her value, she would be assigned to a new role. If she could not, her best case was being an ordinary stronghold servant. They could easily decide she knew too much and eliminate her as a potential liability.

Benella's most recent results had been extremely patchy. Things had gone wrong from the moment she met Asano, and the key to her future was demonstrating that he was a significant threat. If she could convince the messengers that Asano was a threat they needed to deal with themselves, she would be absolved of blame. The advantage to the superiority with which the messengers viewed themselves was that their expectations of others were low. If they were required to handle an issue, then it logically followed that a servant was insufficient to the task. One thing the messengers never blamed their servants for was not being their equals.

The key person Benella needed to impress was a messenger ritualist who was relatively new to the stronghold, Jes Fin Kaal. She had been dispatched by messenger leadership and was referred to by the other messengers as Voice Kaal. From what Benella could tell, she was something between a general and a priest. How that worked with the messengers' religious philosophy she was unsure, as the only thing the messengers seemed to worship was themselves. What Benella did know was that if she could get the favour of Kaal, she might escape the capricious attentions of her current master, Fal.

In the face of insurmountable power, the only choice was to surrender to it or be crushed by it. Watching her adventuring team get annihilated one by one had engraved this onto Benella's soul. In the wake of that, she had betrayed her own kind and her own world to enter the dangerous servitude offered by the messengers.

Benella was utterly convinced that the conquest of her world was inevitable. If she wanted any place in it, then service to the new rulers was the key, and the earlier the better. Only one thing had ever given her any uneasiness in this conviction, and he was what had led her to her current position. She had come to believe that the messengers were right about their superiority, but Jason Asano gave her much the same feeling they did. It left her uncertain about her choice, wondering if she had betrayed everything and everyone, only to be wrong.

Like Benella, the messengers were also seeing a shift in their circumstances. The arrival of Voice Kaal had led to speculation amongst the servants that the messengers were primed to escalate the conflicts they were involved in. Benella didn't know much, but was aware that at least some of the strongholds were fighting enemies that went beyond the adventurers of the city.

Three messengers flew into the building through the roof gap: two male messengers of silver rank, flanking a third who was shorter and had no aura that Benella could detect. The messenger on the left was Lord Fal, while the one on the right she had seen in the stronghold, but didn't know the name of. Messengers rarely deigned to introduce themselves to the servant races.

Compared to the fair-skinned, golden-haired Fal, the messenger on the right was dark-skinned, with silver hair and solid silver orbs for eyes. His wings were black, with white feathers along the bottom edge. His hair draped down his back in strings of tight braids.

Both men were shirtless, showing off lean muscle but an odd absence of nipples. Their lower bodies were covered by loose, flowing pants of dark teal with gold trim. Their feet were bare but didn't touch the ground, which was typical. The messengers frequently floated in the air rather than set foot on the ground. Their wings did not work like a bird's, and they levitated around using their auras.

Silver-rank essence users could levitate using their auras, and golds could float around in slow flight. Compared to what the messengers could manage, however, it was a pale imitation. Not only could messengers move faster and with more control, but they were not easily disrupted by almost any intervention.

Benella presumed the messenger in the middle was Jes Fin Kaal. She was smaller than the others, barely taller than seven feet, and she lacked the domineering presence of the other two. Benella couldn't magically detect her presence at all, despite Kaal being gold rank. All she sensed were the silver-rankers beside her.

Kaal's clothing was also different, being a loose robe of deep red, with white trim that matched her pristine white wings. Only a few wisps of black hair escaped the hood, which shadowed her pale, delicate features. Compared to the solid gold and silver orbs that the other messengers had for eyes, Kaal had more human eyes, albeit supernaturally blue. They stood out in the shadowy hood even more than her bright red lips.

Despite the auras radiating from the two messengers beside her, Benella could not take her eyes from the woman in the middle. Her compelling presence did not seem aura-related, although perhaps it was some subtle effect, beyond Benella's ability to recognise. Her thoughts drifted back to Asano, whose presence had been similarly mysterious.

The three thrones rose into the air for the messengers to sit on. After being seated, Fal looked down on Benella imperiously, which was almost comfortingly normal.

"You have asked to present to us information of a particular threat," Fal told her. "You speak of the man whose familiar followed you to our meeting."

"Yes," Benella said, steeling her nerve. "I had already determined this man was suspicious, and suggested investigation. The decision was made to move directly to elimination, but he detected our approach and fled. I had already initiated an investigation of him on my own initiative at that point, so I was able to gather a good amount of information. Then I contacted Lord Fal, and made the grave error of allowing the man to follow me using a shadow familiar."

"We expect our servants to serve to the best of their ability, no more and no less," the dark-skinned messenger said. "There is no admonition required in a failure to notice a child of the Reaper."

Relief flooded Benella, but she was not fool enough to thank the messenger.

The implication that her consideration would matter to him would get her punished and possibly killed outright.

"After collating the information on this man from my various sources," she continued, "it became evident that he poses a potential threat. I believe that further investigation is warranted, but in the wake of my failure, I am unable to do so. Due to the Adventure Society learning that I serve you, I cannot return to the city and my associates are either going into hiding, fleeing the city or have already been snatched up."

"And what of these contacts?" the dark-skinned messenger asked. "What would be your recommendation?"

"Leave them be," Benella said. "If I were an Adventure Society officer looking into this, I would be laying traps for when agents come to tie off loose ends, compromising us further. There is a reason that agents in the city are not given critical information."

Benella was under no impression that they were looking for actual advice. The question had been a test, which was good. It meant that they were genuinely considering Benella for a position of actual relevancy. She still had a chance to get out of the building alive, if she could convince them that Jason Asano was a genuine threat.

56

EVEN THOUGH YOU FEAR

THE ROUND BUILDING WAS LIKE A SILO: WIDE, HIGH AND ROUND, WITHOUT ANY internal structures. Standing in the middle of it, next to a small crystal recording projector, Benella felt tiny. The three powerful beings looming over her, floating in the air on thrones, did not help.

Benella had one chance to prove herself still valuable to the messengers. What she had gone with was presenting Jason Asano as a potential threat to the agenda of the messengers, which was a risky play. Her initial investigation into him had all stemmed from a chance encounter with him in an obviously fake guise, and an instinctive sense that he was dangerous. The more she dug up, however, the more her sense that he was a large problem grew. The messengers, as far as she knew, remained unaware of him. She managed to hold her nerve as she explained everything she had found, advocating for further investigation into the man. Once she was done, she could only wait like a prisoner about to be sentenced.

Thus far, only the two silver-rank messengers had spoken. Fal Vin Garath was Benella's master, who was abusive but not outside the bounds of acceptability to his fellow messengers. He was free to treat the servant races however he pleased, so long as it did not impinge upon the interests of other messengers.

The other messenger she did not know, although she had seen him moving around the stronghold. He seemed to be of equal status to Fal, while being his physical and temperamental counterpart. Dark-skinned and silver-haired, compared to Fal's fair complexion and golden hair, he was composed and civil in his conduct. This was true even to servants, although there was no question that he demanded nothing less than total obedience. But while his tone always carried an implicit warning when speaking to servants, Benella much preferred it to Fal's open threat.

The third messenger, dominant amongst the three, had yet to speak. Jes Fin

Kaal had, thus far, allowed the others to ask the questions, although Fal had said little of use. It was the other messenger who seemed to be her primary representative. Fal was about to speak when Kaal made a silencing gesture. Then, for the first time since her arrival, she spoke.

"I am aware that your primary purpose in bringing this information to us is to prove your worth for self-serving reasons," she said, her voice an ominous melody. "This is acceptable, as your goal is to prove yourself a worthy servant. But of all the ways you could have chosen to approach us, why did you choose this one? You could have brought any number of issues to us. Why is this the one that will show you are an asset to be valued, and not a liability to be excised?"

Benella didn't even consider denying her motivations.

"I…"

She frowned, hesitant. She knew that her next words would be life or death.

"In my ignorance," she said, "I do not know how to address you."

The standard mode of address for messengers was lord, be they men, women or androgynous. Benella was aware that Kaal was part of a select group within the messengers, and feared offending her.

"I am Voice Kaal, and you may address me as such."

Benella neither apologised nor thanked her, being worthy of neither. Fearing that she was subconsciously stalling for time, which Kaal would notice, she steeled her nerves again.

"This is the thing that matters," Benella said, her voice firming. "Yes, there were many ways to show my value. Many issues I could bring to your attention, but they did not warrant such an approach as this. The leadership amongst the servant races would have been sufficient to address them, and bringing them to you would have been a waste of your time. But this man is someone I suspect will be beyond the ability of the servant races to handle."

"Did you bring it to the servant leadership?"

"I did."

"They agreed with your assessment?"

"They agreed that I should present this issue to you personally, Voice Kaal."

It had taken significant insistence on Benella's part to address the potential threat of Asano. The leadership had many calls on their time as events were escalating in the stronghold. They had not only refused to look into one silver-rank auxiliary adventurer, but would not even listen long enough to discover why. Benella understood; she was far from the only servant looking to advance themselves with 'important issues for the messengers.' She finally managed to convince someone to allow her to present her case. That way, she would be the one killed for wasting the messengers' time, being neither the first nor the last to meet their end that way.

Benella was unsure why Kaal was so interested in her thought process in reaching that decision. Kaal's seat descended partway to the floor and she leaned forward, examining Benella. She could feel the messenger forcefully probing her emotions with her aura. Could the voice even read her thoughts? She had heard rumours from other servants, although nothing reliable.

"Why?" Kaal asked again. "Something very specific convinced you that this man should be brought to our attention. I can feel it digging at your insides like a burr. What is it? Why are you afraid of it? It's not what you found when you looked into him, is it? It's the thing that made you dig deeper in the first place. For all that you found to support your instinct, it was something at the beginning that convinced you. It drove you to bring it to us, even though you fear what doing so will mean for you."

Chills ran through Benella's body as the messenger rendered her transparent, seeing through her thoughts and motivations. She bowed her head, knowing she had to answer the question she had fervently hoped would not be asked. It made sense that someone who could see through her like a window would dig it out. Squaring her shoulders, she continued.

"I told Lord Fal that I first gained this man's attention when I noticed something about him. That the aura mask he gave me reacted unusually."

"But there is more to it than that," Kaal deduced, her voice certain.

Benella nodded, still not meeting her eyes.

"I felt something from this man. Something like I have never felt from any of the servant races. I have only ever felt it from…"

Benella braced herself, squeezing her eyes closed.

"…from your kind. From messengers."

Benella felt air wash over her, but nothing else. She opened her eyes to see the dark-skinned messenger's back in front of her, his wings spread out to shield her. Past him, she saw Lord Fal, arrested mid-lunge by a restraining hand on his chest. Fal still had a fist raised, ready to crash down on Benella.

"Return to your seat."

"This creature just compared one of the lesser races to us," Fal snarled.

"She was asked a question and answered it honestly," Kaal said. "If she lied, would you have struck her down for that?"

"Of course."

"And I am certain this woman knew you would. That she came here, knowing she would likely be asked that question, where both answers carried a death sentence. Yet she came. I will not allow you to kill what may be a surpassing servant. Not yet."

"How can you tolerate her insolence?" Fal asked in a shout.

"However I see fit. Return to your seat, Fal Vin Garath. I will not tell you a third time."

Fal openly glared at Kaal but obeyed as he did so, returning to his seat. The other messenger did as well.

"Thank you, Hess Jor Nasala," Kaal said to him.

Benella was frozen as the two messengers floated back to their chairs. She was at least glad that she had found a name for the third messenger, although she still offered no thanks. He may have saved her life, but all he was safeguarding was her potential value. Her gratitude meant nothing to him.

Kaal rose from her seat, floating past the other as they returned to theirs. She stopped when she reached Benella, looming over her. Benella did not look up to meet her eyes.

"You are a gambler, elf. You have bet your life on the suspicion that this man you have told us of is of sufficient value that we need to investigate, if not intervene ourselves. That you did not take a safer approach to secure a place in our service interests me. What about this man has so shaken you?"

"I know my power to assess is lacking," Benella said. "I know he is not the match of the gold-rankers arrayed against you. But of all the adventurers I've ever encountered, this man is the only one my instincts told me was like you. The messengers."

"Like us?" Fal roared standing up in his seat. "You would compare—"

"Quiet," Kaal said, her voice soft but with an almost physical power behind it.

Fal complied in an instant, sitting back down, although he continued to glower.

"Explain," Kaal commanded Benella. "How is he like us?"

"I'm not sure exactly how to explain it," she said. "There is an otherworldliness to him. Beyond anything I've felt even from Zolit. Oh, Zolit is—"

"I am familiar with the Zolit project," Kaal cut her off. "Continue."

"I'm not sure quite how to say it."

"Yes, you are," Kaal told her. "You simply fear what will happen when you do."

Benella nodded her admission.

"This man feels on a level with your kind that goes beyond rank," she said. "I spoke of otherworldliness, but it was not like what I had felt from other messengers. It's like he has the same thing that makes you special but…"

Her voice broke, knowing she could well be about to die.

"…even more so."

"She thinks some lesser being is—"

He was cut off as Kaal turned to look at him and his mouth sealed up, like a wound healing over.

"I have taken your power to speak," Voice Kaal told him. "What I have left you with is the power to think and the power to act. In the future, use them in that order. If I become convinced that your mouth can produce anything worthwhile, I shall return it to you. Until then, I suggest you study the value of silence."

That her abusive master had been admonished and punished did not make Benella feel better. Fal no longer had a mouth, but the glare in his eyes spoke loudly. He was not happy about being chastised over one of the lesser races, and in front of her, no less. The idea of being shamed in the face of an inferior poured through his eyes as rage, although he was not fool enough to suppress her with his aura. For the moment, the presence of Kaal was keeping Benella safe, but she knew that should she ever be in his power again, she would die. He wouldn't even need an excuse, given her status. If a messenger wanted her dead, it was his right to kill her.

That put all of Benella's hopes on Kaal. She was not only of higher rank than the other messengers in the room but was able to control the very nature of their bodies. She had been the one to erase the mouth from Fal's face. If Benella could become the property of Kaal, Fal could not touch her without cause.

Done with Fal, Kaal turned to the terrified Benella and crouched down, as if approaching a skittish animal. Even so, the robe that was low enough to hide her feet never quite reached low enough to brush the floor.

"You said this man is like us, but more?" Kaal asked softly.

Benella nodded.

"You believe this man is a threat to us."

"Potentially. I would not presume to equal your judgement, and merely wish to point out that he is out there."

"And you have seen in him the same thing you see in us?"

"Not exactly," Benella said. "But there is something there. My instincts screamed at me that he…"

Benella trailed off, having realised what she was about to say before she stopped herself.

"That he what?" Kaal demanded.

"…that he was on the same level as you. Your people, I mean, not you, specifically."

Benella waited for the death blow, but it never came. Then she felt Kaal's presence with her magical senses for the first time. They had been extended gently and she realised it was for her benefit. Despite that gentleness, however, there was an unflinching imperiousness to it. It was also something different in her aura, compared to the other messengers: a thread of power whose source seemed distant and endless.

"What do you feel?" Kaal asked.

"It's closer to what I felt from Asano," Benella said. "Not the same, though. It feels like the power inside you is anchored somewhere else, while his... It's as if you possess power, but he *is* power."

Kaal's eyes widened for just a fleeting moment. Benella would have missed it if Kaal had not been crouched down in front of her. The messenger floated back to her throne and sat down between Fal and Hess.

"You brought this man to our attention, seeking to rise within our servant hierarchy."

"Yes, Voice Kaal," she said.

"You had best tend your garden with caution, child. A misstep could see everything you have grown pulled up by the roots and burned to ash."

Benella wordlessly acknowledged Kaal's guiding words with a nod. She tried to avoid getting excited, realising that she had accomplished her goal. She knew the messengers would sense her relief and joy, and thought for a moment that she saw the tiniest smile tease the corners of Kaal's lips, then told herself she was imagining it.

"Tell us about this man," she instructed Benella.

Benella gave a jerky nod, her whole body trembling.

"He is travelling under the identity of John Miller," she said. "He is ostensibly the cook of a team of travelling adventurers. This is an obvious falsehood, as even the short time I had to investigate was sufficient to reveal his true identity. His real name is Jason Asano, an adventurer belonging to that same team to which he is ostensibly an auxiliary. The purpose of the false identity, given its transparency, seems to be to garner less attention after the events in Rimaros surrounding him. It is not a complex identity designed for infiltration."

She tried to calm herself by keeping her hands busy, giving her attention to the crystal recording projector.

"It was difficult to obtain imagery of Asano, especially on short notice. I did manage to obtain one recording with his appearance, which matches the man I encountered. This is all I could get, as he has an item or ability that interferes with recordings unless he allows them."

She finished calibrating the projector and pulled out a crystal.

"What I have here is something he did allow, from a meeting that is believed to have been held out in the open for the very purpose of being observed. He is meeting with two people, both believed to be diamond-rankers from outside of this world. One arrived and was taken away later by a third entity. The other spent some time in Rimaros and is believed to be close to Asano. I do not know her identity, but I heard reports that Soramir Rimaros was deferent towards her. Soramir Rimaros is a diamond-ranker, and officially, has taken Asano out into the cosmos. This was when I became certain it was right to bring Asano to your attention."

"When I asked you why you brought this to me," Kaal said, "surely this would have been reason enough to offer me, rather than risk angering us."

Benella clenched her hand in a determined fist before turning from the projector she was setting up to look at Kaal.

"You did not ask for *a* reason I decided to bring this to you, Voice Kaal. You asked for *the* reason. If I had told you this was it, it would have been a lie."

Kaal gave a slight nod that Benella would have interpreted as approval if she hadn't known better. Benella slotted the crystal into the projector and an image came up.

"Stop!" Kaal commanded immediately.

A startled Benella was only frozen for a moment before she paused the recording. Kaal floated out of her chair to peer closely at the now-still projection.

"You were quite right that this warrants further examination," Kaal said. "You have done well."

"What is it?" Hess asked.

He also left his throne, and moved closer to examine the paused projection. It showed Jason, Dawn and Shako sitting in chairs on the lawn in front of Jason's cloud house in Rimaros.

"Who are those people?" he asked.

"This will be Asano," Kaal said, pointing to Jason. "The others are the now-former prime vessels for the World-Phoenix and Zithis Carrow Vayel."

The other two messengers stirred.

"Why would they be on this world?" Hess asked. "Are they interfering in our affairs?"

"I doubt they would do so directly," Kaal said. "The great astral beings are more concerned with one another than us, although we cannot be certain when Vayel is involved."

"We cannot base our activities on doubts and assumptions," Hess said. "We should investigate this matter further."

"Agreed," Kaal said, "but the timing is poor. We are too close to the next stage. Once the assault of Yaresh begins, we can seek this man Asano out more actively."

5 7

MOCKERY

THE STASIS CABIN OF THE CARLOS CRIME WAGON WAS AN ADAPTED BUNK ROOM filled with stasis pods. Each pod contained a member of the Order of Redeeming Light, and Carlos regularly serviced the pods to make sure they were operating properly. Space being at a premium, it was a narrow cabin, making the maintenance work rather awkward.

Carlos grumbled under his breath as he worked. He'd been preparing for the next major step in his research, to which Jason was critical. That was the exact moment that Jason had chosen to ramble away and test his aura techniques on any woman that wandered into view. Now he'd gone off with his team on some ill-defined contract to find possibly nothing.

After finishing, Carlos left the cabin for the small washroom and was wiping pod gel off his hands when one of his assistants appeared at the door.

"Boss, that weird shadow guy is at the door."

"Show him in," Carlos told his assistant.

"He said you should come out."

Carlos grumbled as he made his way to the exit of the vehicle, through the hatch and down the metal stairs.

"What is it, Shade?" Carlos asked irritably.

"Mr Asano and his team have a question for you, Priest Quilido."

"Is it 'why did we go off on some pointless mission when we could be participating in world-changing research?'"

"No," Shade said. "It is not."

"Carlos," Jason said, projecting his voice through Shade's body. "Let me tell you about something I saw."

Jason explained what he'd seen in the town he scouted, from the heat-producing paint to the uniform mannerisms and strange heat signatures of the residents.

"What you're describing sounds like a heat-consuming parasite with a swarm hive mind," Carlos said. "I have a lot of research on creatures and objects that take people over in various ways, so I might be able to find something more specific."

"How long would that take?"

"A few hours. In the meantime, any information you could get from the auras of the people would help."

"Alright, I'll discuss it with the team."

With the skimmer floating in the rainforest canopy, Jason and his team sat and discussed their next move. As they went through various approaches, Jason pushed back against going in and scouting with his aura.

"You seem uncharacteristically nervous about using your aura," Clive told him.

"Yeah," Jason said as he absently nodded. "I've grown accustomed to my aura being an absolute advantage. Something I can always rely on being the best at. Now I'm starkly aware that isn't true and it makes me feel uneasy. I only caught a glimpse of the messenger, through Shade, and it still shook me. Even passively sensing the refinement of his aura through Shade's senses spooked me."

"You can't let anxiety over someone being better at one thing stop you," Humphrey told him.

"I know," Jason said. "But I've also realised how much my aura powers have been a crutch. I need to prove that there's more to me than that. To use every tool in the toolbox before I forget how."

"Good," Rufus said. "That's exactly what I taught you."

"There's another thing, though," Jason continued. "It's been a while and we've barely worked together out in the field."

Like Zara in Korinne's team, Rufus was a late and temporary addition to Team Biscuit. He lacked experience working with the team and would eventually go back to his training centre in Greenstone.

Jason had a similar problem around teamwork, having been away for so long. Compared to Rufus, though, he still had the months in the Reaper's astral space with the others. That time had welded the team into a cohesive unit. They still needed to kick off the rust and learn all the changes to each other's powers, but those ingrained patterns were still there.

The team had spent good chunks of Jason's convalescence going over their powers and formulating new strategies and tactics around them. Now they needed to get out in the field and use them.

"Someone got stomped and had to sit out most of the contracts," Neil pointed out.

"I know," Jason said. "I'm nervous about messing up. Making everything go wrong. And what if it isn't like before? What if—"

"I'm not a big worshipper of the gods," Sophie cut in. "But for the love of the gods, please shut up."

"What?" Jason asked.

"We get it," she said. "You're in touch with your feelings, and that's great, but you are spending too much time with Rufus' mother."

"That's what I've been saying," Rufus said.

"For different reasons," Belinda told him. "Quiet, you."

"Jason, there's been too much talking and too much thinking. That's always been an issue for you, but now it's reaching the point where you're getting in your own way. So, here's what's going to happen. We're going to go to that town and you're going to look at the auras of all the creepy people. Then something is going to go wrong, they're all going to attack us and we're going to kick everyone's insides out. Everyone agrees with this plan."

"We do?" Neil asked, earning him a gentle elbow jab from Belinda.

"I'm not sure that's—" Clive began.

"*I said*," Sophie cut him off, "everyone agrees with this plan."

The group all turned to Humphrey, who was both team leader and Sophie's lover. He looked between Sophie and the rest of the team.

"Don't look at me," he said. "I heard everyone agrees with the plan."

"You know," Neil said, "Humphrey's mother is almost always right."

"What's she got to do with anything?" Humphrey asked.

"I was just thinking," Neil said. "Sophie may not always be right, but she'll punch people until they admit she is. She's kind of like a violent version of Humphrey's mother."

Humphrey's face was stricken with wide-eyed horror.

Jason was the only one to draw close to the town, again making use of the shade houses and tree lines in the agricultural flatlands around it. The others waited in the edge of the rainforest for Jason to examine the town with his aura senses.

"I'm a little worried about Jason," Clive said. "It's not like him to be so hesitant."

"He's been anxious and fearful from the start," Rufus said. "Gary and I didn't see it at first, but Farrah saw through him. He's always had a knack for using aura masks, even before he knew what they were. It's like he tricks himself into becoming this outlandish person. Someone who can survive in the madness he always seems to find himself in."

"That persona is how he gets there in the first place," Neil said.

"Yes," Rufus said. "But I'm thankful for it. Jason's willingness to insert himself into a situation he could walk away from saved my life."

"It saved me from worse," Sophie added.

"We were low rank," Rufus said. "Our aura senses weren't as sharp as they are now and we didn't see through him. But Farrah trained his aura, and she saw how scared he really was. How fragile. But after he came back from Earth, it's different. He can't—or maybe won't—hide his feelings. He lashes out like a cornered animal."

"He's getting better," Humphrey said. "But that wound is still there. I think he scared Emir."

"My mother likes to say that we can never go back to what we were," Rufus said. "The best we can do is decide who we'll be next."

"Talking to your mum is why everything takes so damn long," Sophie said. "How long does it take to aura scout one small town? It's barely more than a village. I think Jason may have missed the key element of the plan."

"Which is you running in and punching people?" Neil asked.

"Exactly," she said. "Simple is best when it comes to plans. I learned that from Humphrey. His mum made him read lots of books about strategy written by people who went on to die in battle. It doesn't say a lot about the value of their books if you ask me."

"They didn't *all* die in battle."

"Actually, the women writers mostly seemed to live," Sophie mused.

"I bet it's a pride thing," Belinda said.

"It's not a pride thing," Humphrey asserted. "They were warriors. It makes sense that they died in battle."

"I'm with Lindy," Clive said. "I never understood the whole male pride thing. Seems like a good way to get yourself killed for stupid reasons."

"Yep," Belinda agreed as she and Sophie nodded.

"Speaking of the plan," Rufus said, "I think we should make some clarifications. Specifically, regarding the kicking-out of people's insides. The people in this town are more likely victims than perpetrators."

"If they're full of heat-sucking parasites," Belinda said, "they're probably past saving."

"That's most likely the case," Clive sadly agreed.

"We'll know more once Jason is done," Humphrey said.

"If he ever is," Sophie complained.

"Give him time," Humphrey said. "He said that technique takes a long time to use properly. I know Jason can be a bit frivolous, but you heard him earlier. I'm sure he's completely focused on the task at hand."

"That was a good sandwich," Jason mumbled as he sucked sauce off his fingers. "I need to find out what was in that sauce."

"Mr Asano," Shade said.

"I have to say, I'm loving how the elves around here do food. Sweet drinks and spicy tucker."

"Mr Asano."

"I wonder what they use to make bread. It's not wheat, and it's not what they used in Rimaros either."

"Mr Asano, Miss Wexler is rapidly shifting from impatient to violently impatient."

"This technique takes time," he said. "I have to slowly and carefully expand my senses, unless I want people to notice my aura immediately. Even then, I'm still learning. I'm certain that's how Benella and her rental henchmen found me at the park."

"Rental henchmen?"

"I can only assume that's what they were."

"Why would that be the only possible assumption?"

"There's no other reasonable explanation for how she ended up with flunkies."

"We spied on people who confirmed they were working together."

"That kind of thing is easily misinterpreted."

"I cannot imagine why your team would worry that you aren't giving this task your focus."

"Because I ate one sandwich? I don't need my hands or my mouth to expand my aura."

"But you do need concentration, Mr Asano."

"And a sandwich helps me get into a balanced state of mind. Nagging does not, by the way."

Despite his teasing of Shade, Jason had, indeed, been slowly and carefully expanding his senses into the town from his hiding place in a shrubbery on the outskirts. He was taking it even slower than he had while practising, in the hope of going undetected. This approach bore fruit as Jason extended his aura senses over the closest of the townsfolk as they walked by. They showed no reaction to his aura but, despite going unnoticed, Jason's expression filled with sadness and rage.

"I got a closer look at one of the elves," Jason told the team through voice chat. "I don't think there's any rescuing them. They have a death aura with some kind of swarm aura inside them. I'm fairly certain they're walking corpses filled with parasites."

"Can you get any more details?" Clive asked. "Anything you can pick up will help Carlos identify what we're dealing with. Maybe even find a weakness we can exploit, or at least get a sense if whatever this is could be widespread enough to cover the southern region."

"I'm looking," Jason said. "Slow and careful, though, so give me some more time."

Even Sophie didn't complain at that, after the revelation that everyone in the town was dead.

Jason continued expanding his senses, examining the auras of other parasitised residents. Comparing them, he felt a familiar sensation from them, but only passingly so. It teased at his mind until he finally realised what it was: all of these people had creatures living inside them.

Unlike Jason's symbiotic relationship with Colin, these were parasites. They took and gave nothing back. In Jason's mind, Colin had given him far more than Jason had ever returned. Colin had kept him alive time and time again, not just staving off death but healing him up enough to keep fighting when he would have fallen.

When the Builder's star seed tried to take over Jason's body, Shade and Gordon had been banished back to the astral, their vessels destroyed. It was Colin who slowed the star seed as it claimed Jason's body, helping him to hold on. It was Colin, nestled inside Jason's soul, who offered support in his darkest moments. Without Colin, Jason would be dead or a slave, not unlike the residents of this village.

The creatures that had taken the people of the town, both killing and enslaving them, were a mockery of what Colin and Jason shared. It filled him with a burning desire to go on a rampage, digging the parasites out of the townsfolk and annihilating every last one. He didn't, but his fury flowed out through his aura.

His partially mastered aura-hiding technique was disrupted and the town was alerted. As one, every elf in it threw back their heads and let out an inhuman screech.

58

DIE IMMEDIATELY WITHOUT PROMPTING

JASON'S TEAM EXPLODED OUT OF THE RAINFOREST AS INHUMAN SCREECHING came from the town ahead. Sophie was nothing more than a flickering blur while the others thundered over rice paddies, the terrain barely hindering the superhuman pace of silver-rankers. Following them out of the rainforest were the twenty draconic bone spiders in magic armour that Humphrey had summoned while they waited. Behind them was Neil's lumbering chrysalis golem, a monolith of crystal that sank heavily into the mud, quickly getting left behind.

They felt Jason's aura flood out, infused with blind rage.

"That's not good," Neil said as they dashed.

Then they felt the rage vanish.

"Okay, that's *really* not good," Neil said.

Jason had carefully hidden his aura as he extended his senses over the town. It was the revelations of what had happened to the people in it that made him lose control. He could mask even strong emotions from showing in his aura under normal circumstances, but his new sensory technique was a work in progress. When using it to expand his senses stealthily, he lacked the same rigid control.

When his senses revealed that the townsfolk were actually dead people being puppeteered by some kind of parasite, that control slipped. His hidden aura was revealed as it flooded with rage, revealing his presence.

The townsfolk tossed aside their too-perfect normalcy on sensing Jason's rage, letting out a chorus of alien shrieks. They started rushing to Jason's location, faster than their ranks should have allowed. In doing so, their bodies moved in an awkward and off-putting manner, as if filmed in crude stop-motion. It was damaging their bodies, some even breaking bones and falling over as they over-taxed themselves.

They had completely transformed from the pleasant façades they had been displaying to wild and twisted berserkers. Their uncanny-valley appearance made plain that the elves were no longer people. Something stranger and more insidious was inside them, wearing them as suits.

Although this infuriated Jason, he managed to rein in his anger, rather than let it drive him. Oddly, his earlier explosion at Emir helped him regain control instead of letting his rage run rampant. Following that encounter, he had been dwelling on the anger waiting just below the skin, ready to erupt at any provocation. It wasn't a revelation, but it was a wake-up call that he was not as mentally recovered as he'd previously believed.

Jason had been letting his anger control him for too long, and it was past time to get it in order. For all that fury felt strong, he knew that was a trap. It narrowed his vision, blinded his judgement and led him to choices he would come to regret. It also blocked him out of the powerful combat trance technique, which he could only achieve with a calm and balanced mind.

Now there was an enemy more than deserving of his anger, but he refused to let himself indulge in the emotion. He concentrated on all the training he had gotten from Rufus and Farrah about fighting with a cool head. Even with the enemy rushing at him, he closed his eyes and took a long, slow breath. Breathing was unnecessary, but made for a good meditative tool, helping him achieve a flow of calm. He let the breath out and his anger with it, allowing it to drift away.

Sophie arrived at his side, having moved across the entirety of the fields surrounding the town faster than the parasitised elves could reach Jason. She peered into his hood when she couldn't see his glowing eyes.

"What are you doing?" she asked.

In response, he drew his sword.

"These people are dead," he told her. "I'm preparing to free them."

The oncoming enemy didn't give him any more time for explanation than that as they charged in on Jason and Sophie. There was no pattern to the attacks, just dozens of parasitised elves. They launched themselves through the air the moment they were close enough, literally jumping at them in wild, artless attacks. The elves dashed through the streets and out of buildings, quickly forming a mob.

Whatever intelligence had been guiding them to fake the role of a pleasant populace had turned to mindless frenzy like someone had flipped a switch. Their only tactic was to assault Jason and Sophie with a wall of bodies.

Before the mob could form too tight a pack, Jason and Sophie moved from the tree line and into the town, kicking off a melee in the middle of a street.

Aware that something had taken over the townsfolk, the entire team knew to be careful. The unknown parasite could potentially infect them, so until they were certain of what it was, caution was the first priority. Humphrey hadn't allowed the rest of the team to charge blindly in after Sophie. The fields they were crossing had elves that moved towards them in a frenzy. While Sophie was past them before they had even really started to stir, the rest of the team was not.

Humphrey led the team forward more cautiously, trusting Jason and Sophie to hold their own. Their ability sets were both well-suited to this early stage of the conflict, before too many elves gathered.

Sophie was always elusive in the face of the enemy, with abilities that would shield her from retaliatory effects. So as long as she was the one hitting and not being hit, she knew that she should be fine. She did not take the risk, however, regardless of how minor it was. Instead of landing hits, she chose to miss each target by a close margin.

Wind Blade was one of only two special attacks Sophie possessed, and the only one whose use was unconditional. It allowed her to make slashing gestures with any part of her body that launched blades of razor-sharp wind. Large gestures created long, slow-moving blades, while short, sharp gestures fired off small-but-swift projectiles.

Sophie making her attacks miss every enemy meant that she could instead use the motions to fire off wind blades at point-blank range, meaning that even the slow blades hit home. She soon started increasing her range when possible, given the unskilled mass of bodies being thrown at them.

The wind blades did not end their effectiveness by cutting into enemies. The silver-rank effect of the ability triggered a ring of cutting force from each target struck. Sophie had practised long and hard to master the nuances of this ability, actively negating the blades and rings before they struck herself or any friendlies. She could even eliminate just a part of a blade or ring, allowing two sides of a blade to pass around an ally.

Jason knew this, but was still rigorous about checking for friendly fire. Humphrey and Clive had been fighting alongside Sophie for the past few years, but Jason was still fitting back into the team's rhythms. He didn't trust himself for pinpoint coordination just yet.

Like Sophie, Jason's style was inherently evasive, but in a different manner. There were similarities, such as a reliance on skill and uncanny dodging through space displacement powers. But Sophie's approach was a domineering mix of raw speed and unmatched skill, challenging any foe to strike her down. Jason was very different, relying on obfuscation, disruption and erratic unpredictability unnerving his opponents over the course of the battle.

Jason's tactics began by sending a herd of Shade bodies to mix into the elves. With the sun high in the sky and the battleground a wide street of dry dirt, there was little in the way of natural shadows, so Shade would serve instead.

Shade and Jason had worked on tactics to make Shade less vulnerable when the familiar was serving as a shadow-jump platform. The more Jason ranked up, the more enemies were able to affect Shade's incorporeal form, making it a less reliable defence than it had been in the past.

One of the ways that Shade did this was by moving his bodies in and out of shadows. While a shadow might be too small for Jason to jump through, Shade had no such restrictions. For the elves, though, it quickly became evident that they had no way of harming the familiar, which gave Jason the chance to use another tactic.

Jason conjured copies of his cloak on a multitude of Shade bodies, which danced through and around the elves. Even the wild, seemingly mindless enemy was thrown off as Shade variously ballooned out the cloak to block their view, sent blinding star motes flashing into their eyes and displaced space itself.

The space displacement had minimal effect, just enough to turn an attack on Jason from a near-miss into a full-miss. When two dozen cloaks were using it at once, however, it left the crowd of elves stumbling into one another, as what should have been sound hits missed entirely, sending them off balance. This had no effect on the incorporeal Shade and his intangible cloaks, leaving elves scattered about on the ground. This offered critical breathing room for the high mobility approaches of Jason and Sophie, who fared much worse against a shoulder-to-shoulder mob.

As for Jason himself, his cloak danced around him like a hazy cloud of darkness and stars. Along with hiding Jason's movements, it shifted between tangible and intangible. In one moment, it was grabbing or blocking enemies, and in the next, letting go, causing them to lose balance as they tried to pull free or yank at the cloak, only to find the resistance gone. That was the instant Jason would strike, his sword unseen until it passed through the cloak.

When Shade's antics weren't enough to stop the constantly growing mob from clustering up, Jason and Sophie would both escape, buying time and space to make a fresh approach. Jason used Shade bodies to shadow jump, while Sophie employed her Mirage Step ability.

Mirage Step was not a true teleport ability, but a time-manipulation power involving near-instantaneous movement. Like Eternal Moment, Sophie's main power for accelerating her personal time stream, the effect of Mirage Step seemed like stopped time. She was progressing through time so much faster than the world around her that everything else seemed frozen.

Mirage Step was even more limited than Eternal Moment, in that the time displacement between herself and the world around her made it hard to interact with. All Sophie could do while Mirage Step was active was move, but it had other advantages, especially after ranking the power up. These advantages were centred on the after-image left behind when she used the power, and for which the ability was named. The after-image would send out blades of dimensional force, similar to Sophie's wind blades. It also disoriented anyone who attacked the image, through short-lived mental illusions.

The elves that attacked the after-image triggered an unusual reaction. Normally, there would be visible coloured light around the head of an enemy, indicating that they were caught up in illusions. For the elves, however, lights appeared all over their bodies. The disorienting effect was also unusually potent, causing the elves to collapse into thrashing heaps. Sophie took immediate advantage and used her Wind Wave power to gather them all up in a pile.

Wind Wave was a versatile ability that she could use for personal mobility, to deflect magical projectiles, or herd enemies, as she was currently doing. With the elves piled up, she used her personal time acceleration, Eternal Moment, to produce a storm of wind blades and launch them all at once. The blades slammed into the pile like an angry swarm of buzz saws, cutting first with the blades, then the secondary cutting rings. The result was an ugly meat grinder, the foul stench of death carried on the gusty air that came in the wake of the exploding wind blades.

Sophie was no offensive specialist, and her perfectly executed synergy of attacks were not enough to destroy most of the parasite-infested elf bodies. What she did gain by piling them up and slaughtering at least an appreciable number was one of the most valuable resources in any battle: time. Jason had deployed his affliction-spreading butterflies that were multiplying on the beleaguered elves.

Another benefit from all the slicing that Sophie did was that she and Jason got a look at the parasites that crawled out of the chopped-up bodies. Many had been immediately cut into pieces as well, but there were more than enough to get a look, with dozens of worms pouring out of every dismembered elf.

The parasites were brown worms, looking much like garden worms but around the length of a forearm. Their most notable feature was at the tip of each worm: a triangular chitin cap, almost like a drill bit. As the worms became afflicted by butterflies, Jason learned the ominous name of the creatures.

- You have inflicted [Blood From a Stone] on [Parasitised Elf (host)].
- You have inflicted [Inexorable Doom] on [World-Taker Worm].

The initial cluster of elves had been handled by Jason and Sophie, but it was only a fraction of what Jason sensed coming their way. With his senses now openly spread over the town, he sensed a larger population than the town should have. This confirmed that one of the reasons the town had gone silent was that the world-taker worms were claiming anyone that passed through.

Jason backed off as his team arrived, led by Humphrey and followed by Humphrey's summons. Sophie's efforts to gather and slice up the elves had brought them a brief moment to regroup.

"I sensed something in the town," Jason told Humphrey. "I'm not sure what; it seems shielded against magical perception and I barely noticed it at all. Now you're here, I'd like to take Clive and check it out."

"It could be important to handling these things," Humphrey agreed. "If not to this fight, then to the larger one, if there are more towns like this. Any clues on what these things are?"

"Something called a world-taker worm," Jason told him.

"That's not the kind of name I wanted to hear," Neil said. "I guess a 'die immediately without prompting worm' was too much to hope for."

"Clive can fight with us while you investigate," Humphrey told Jason. "You move better alone. Just open a portal when you find something for him to look at."

"Will you be alright without me?" Jason asked.

Humphrey looked at the magical butterflies already moving to intercept the approaching elves.

"Your presence will be felt."

59

THE OLD GROOVE

THE TEAM ONLY HAD A BRIEF RESPITE FROM THE WORM-HOST ELVES THAT WERE inundating them, rushing from every street and building in the town to hunt them down. While Humphrey and Jason quickly discussed Jason's departure, Clive drew out a ritual circle. Golden lines were left behind by the edge of his staff as he used it to draw, like scratching in the sand with a driftwood stick. The ritual, like the golden light itself, was an aspect of Clive's most fundamental ability.

Ability: [Enact Ritual] (Rune)

- Special ability.
- Cost: varies.
- Cooldown: None.

- Current rank: Silver 4 (12%).

- Effect (iron): Manifest lines of magic to draw out ritual diagrams. Materials required for a ritual may be used directly from a dimensional storage space instead of being placed within the diagram.

- Effect (bronze): Create simple ritual diagrams to alter the parameters of magical items.

- Effect (silver): Conjure mana lamps with enhanced efficiency and accumulation rate. Refined mana from the lamp can be used to enhance ritual magic.

The ritual was designed for Clive and Belinda to stand on, altering the parameters of their magical weapons. Belinda was using her Specious Sorcerer ability to take on a spellcaster role, avoiding getting too close to their enemies.

Ability: [Specious Sorcerer] (Charlatan)

- Special ability.
- Cost: Very high mana.
- Cooldown: 6 hours.

- Current rank: Silver 4 (09%).

- Effect (iron): Gain a significant increase to the [Spirit] attribute and the ability to use magical tools. Your maximum mana increases and you gain an ongoing mana recovery effect.

- Effect (bronze): Gain the ability to cast a number of basic spells.

- Effect (silver): Gain the ability to cast additional spells, based on the gear you have equipped.

With a robe, plus a wand in one hand and a staff in the other, she was equipped much like Clive. She had supplied herself with decent-quality items, albeit not the equal of the weapons and armour Gary had crafted to use with her Counterfeit Combatant power. They certainly weren't a match for Clive's staff and wand, which were a legendary growth item set he had picked up at iron rank, before Belinda had even joined the team.

Both Belinda and Clive's weapons would be affected by Clive's ritual. Instead of the normal bolts and beams of force for Clive, and fire for Belinda, their staves and wands would produce cold attacks. They didn't know much about the parasites infesting the townsfolk, but they seemed to feed on heat. That made cold Clive's best guess as to what would be the most harmful to them.

Clive finished his preparations by using another ability to attach ritual circles to their weapons directly, the floating magic diagrams, somewhat akin to Jason's system windows. Not wasting time, Clive and Belinda were already on the attack by the time Jason vanished into the shadows, blasting the onrushing elves with bolts and beams of magic.

The team set up so that Sophie, Rufus and Humphrey moved in a circle to shield Neil, Clive and Belinda from attacks on each side. Stash and Belinda's familiars were inside the circle as well, while Humphrey's dragon-bone spiders roamed out to run interference.

With the numbers they were facing, efficiency in both time and mana was important. In extended fights, especially against so many opponents, they needed to make the most of their big-ticket abilities, and even their mid-range heavy hitters. The right abilities needed to be ready, with enough mana to use them, when the optimal moments arose.

Managing this for the team had become Belinda's job. Their time apart meant that the team had to learn all new ways to work together. Not only was their teamwork out of practise, but their old bronze-rank strategies were no longer sufficient. They and their power sets had gone through massive changes, and it was taking time to find the old groove.

One of the more defining changes to how they worked together was that Belinda had taken on a tactical director role. While Humphrey generally called the play, it was Belinda who helped the team execute the details. She was always tracking who could do what and when, courtesy of Jason's interface, and the team's efficiency was spiking as a result.

Belinda had fallen into this role for several reasons, starting with her power set. Her powers placed her in a position to facilitate the rest of the team in various ways, and ranking up had only amplified that factor. She could reduce or entirely reset cooldowns, as well as duplicate key abilities.

Even Belinda's magic tattoo could reset some of her cooldowns, being the silver-rank version of the one she had at iron rank. She had been careful to get it after what happened at bronze. After a night drinking with Sophie, she woke up with a magic tattoo that produced hot sauce.

Judgement was key to Belinda's power set, as almost every power she used to assist the team would live or die on the timing. The only exception was her aura.

Ability: [Masterful] (Adept)

- Aura (recovery).
- Base cost: None.
- Cooldown: None.

- Current rank: Silver 4 (11%).

- Effect (iron): Abilities of allies within the aura come off cooldown more quickly.

- Effect (bronze): Mana and stamina costs for the essence abilities of allies are slightly reduced. Has greater effect on abilities with ongoing costs than instantaneous costs.

- Effect (silver): Boons affecting allies have slightly increased effect.

The reliable but generalised bonuses were nice, but weren't anything that would turn a battle on its head. It was Belinda's active powers that could make for clutch plays, where the trump card of an ally became a handful of trump cards and clinched a win.

Belinda's ability to manage not just her own abilities but those of the team was key, but only the start of why she was now the tactical centre. Every essence user had their mind enhanced by their spirit attribute, but there were differences in how that applied specifically. Clive had always been the smartest guy in the room when it came to deciphering the complexities of sophisticated and exotic magic. Ranking up had only enhanced his ability to comprehend the most sophisticated nuances of magic. Jason's mental advancements were perceptual, allowing him to better process sensory input greater than others of his rank. In Belinda's case, it was a peerless ability to multitask. The return of Jason and his party interface made that trait not just valuable but the centrepiece for her new role on the team.

Jason's party interface was one of the most impactful contributions he brought to the team, now that they were silver rank. It provided so much information that when the whole team was in a party, there was too much visual clutter to even see.

From health condition body indicators to mana and stamina bars to cooldowns for every active ability, each team member had to customise the interface to their own needs.

Humphrey, Sophie and Jason himself had the most pared-down interfaces. They all had to move fast and get deep in the action, so minimum obstruction was the goal. Being the healer, Neil maintained a more robust interface so he could monitor the team, but that did not compare to Belinda. She tracked every active cooldown of every team member in real-time, along with the mana they had to use their powers.

It was a mess, but one that gave Belinda an unrivalled tool for enhancing her effectiveness. Only she was able to parse all that data, let alone do so while actively participating in combat. She was the one who saw the gaps and plugged them, either by directing a teammate or by employing her own versatile power set.

Belinda's new authority in the team came with growing pains. Jason's interface gave Belinda the metrics to dig out the team's inefficiencies and zero in on their inefficient habits. It was good in the long run, but no one enjoyed having their shortcomings pointed out.

"Neil, throw out some more spells," she instructed. "Your mana is too close to full. Use Verdant Cage on cooldown to slow down the incoming elves as much as you can. Focus on the fields, where the existing plants will strengthen the power. Then use Reels of Fortune to dump mana; my power is ready to help you with the cooldown so you can triple-cast it."

Ability: [Blessing of Readiness] (Adept)

- Special ability (recovery).
- Base cost: Moderate mana.
- Cooldown: Varies.

- Current rank: Silver 4 (10%).

- Effect (iron): This spell can only affect an ally and not yourself. The cooldown of the next ability used by the target is reduced by up to one minute. The cooldown of this ability is equal to the time taken from the cooldown of the target ability.

- Effect (bronze): The affected ability can have the cooldown reduced by up to ten minutes.

- Effect (silver): This spell can be used one additional time while on cooldown. The cooldown incurred by the second use is added to the original, and the spell cannot be used again until the full cooldown is complete.

Rough edges were no surprise after the team had spent years apart. It was more than Jason's absence; the rest of the team had drifted apart in the wake of his loss. Neil and Belinda had worked together, protecting Jory as he roamed the world in dangerous times. As for Sophie, Humphrey and Clive, they had pursued their vendetta against the followers of Purity and the Builder. Clive had played third wheel for almost two years as he watched the other two awkwardly circle one another, the ghost of Jason between them. Even worse were the regular debriefs on their relationship progress, demanded of Clive by Belinda every time they all met up.

"I thought your job was to make us efficient," Neil complained to Belinda. "Explain to me how having almost full mana is an efficiency problem and not just efficiency."

"Your aura is feeding us way more mana than normal from all these worms dying," she said. "You're letting mana go to waste because you can't hold any more."

Ability: [Spoils of Victory] (Prosperity)

- Aura (recovery, conjuration, boon, drain).
- Base cost: None.
- Cooldown: None.

- Current rank: Silver 4 (02%).

- Effect (iron): Allies within your aura recover mana and stamina for each enemy that dies within your aura, also receiving a minor healing effect. You can loot enemies that die within your aura.

. . .

- Effect (bronze): Your [Spirit] attribute is temporarily increased each time an enemy dies within your aura.

- Effect (silver): Enemies that die within your aura leave behind orbs of health and mana that can be collected by allies to gain healing and recovery effects.

"Thank you for the orbs, by the way," Humphrey chimed in. As the most mana-hungry member of the team, as well as being highly mobile, finding mana boosts scattered around the battlefield was a massive boost. Neither the healing nor the mana gains were exceptional, but especially against a swarm monster, like the worms, they added up.

"Your aura should have maxed out your spirit buff as well," Belinda told Neil. "Only using that power on shields and healing is a waste."

The rest of the team was also giving their all, adventurers and familiars alike. Belinda's astral lantern familiar fired off its own force bolts, focusing on any worms attempting to sneak up on the team while they were distracted. Worms that had escaped both Sophie's wind blades and Jason's afflictions were already crawling along the ground, seeking out the team in moments of inattention.

Humphrey was the most vulnerable to the swarm, as he was a melee fighter. Sophie and Rufus were as well, but her grace and speed, plus his elegant elusiveness, made them untouchable. They moved like dancers on fast-forward, reminding everyone that no one else on the team could touch them for pure skill.

Humphrey was also highly skilled, but so much of how he fought was about the application of power, which was not useful against enemies that were weak and numerous. It also didn't help that his powerful attacks sent worms spraying out of the elves he cut apart. Without the evasiveness of Sophie and Rufus, he found the worms splashing over him.

To minimise his exposure, Humphrey was modifying his usual combat style. His usual fast-paced aggression was not ideal for defending, and his heavy attacks were overkill against the worm-laden elves. He focused more on lateral movement than charge-forward aggression, and on skill rather than overwhelming power. It's not that Humphrey didn't have the skill—his mother would never have stood for it —but it wasn't his strongest area. Key to making his adapted style work was his sword. Of his two conjured weapons, he usually favoured the largest. For his current situation, however, the smaller sword was the right choice.

Ability: [Razor-Wing Sword] (Wing)

. . .

- Special ability (conjuration).
- Cost: High mana.
- Cooldown: None.

- Current rank: Silver 4 (11%).

- Effect (iron): Conjures a sword in the shape of a wing. Movement powers are enhanced while wielding it. Ineffective when used with special attacks best suited for large or heavy weapons.

- Effect: (bronze): Feathers from the wing sword can be used as projectiles.

- Effect: (silver): Feathers from the wing sword can be animated to intercept physical projectiles.

The Razor-Wing Sword was stylised as an angel wing of white and gold, with glossy metal feathers. It could fire razor feathers from the blade, which Humphrey was making the most of to pick off loose worms. As of silver rank, it also produced feathers that floated around him to intercept projectiles. As this included worms flinging themselves at him, Humphrey was able to fight in relative safety.

Humphrey was still effective, despite changing up his style, but he was not fighting at full effectiveness. He was forced to be careful instead of bold, passive instead of taking the fight to the enemy. He had to be constantly vigilant, even with his defensive measures. This was especially true when he had to stand his ground between parasitised elves and his team members.

Neil took some of the load in those moments, dropping a characteristically well-timed shield over Humphrey. That was when Humphrey deployed what was his most useful power, given the circumstances. His Fire Breath power sprayed out like a flamethrower, burning up waves of elves and eliciting shrieks like those Jason's aura had drawn out. It was extremely effective, despite the worms feeding on heat, because it was not ordinary fire.

Ability: [Dragon Might] (Dragon)

- Aura (recovery).
- Base cost: None.
- Cooldown: None.

- Current rank: Silver 4 (13%).

- Effect (iron): Allies have increased [Power] and [Spirit].

- Effect (bronze): Fire created by your essence abilities becomes dragon fire.

- Effect (silver): Allies have increased resistance to effects that reduce the [Power] and [Spirit] attributes.

Humphrey's aura turned any fire produced by his abilities into dragon fire, which was significantly more troubling to deal with. It was certainly beyond the power of the parasite worms to feed on.

The biggest problem with Fire Breath, and the reason Humphrey didn't usually rely on it as a mainstay, was that it was extremely mana-hungry. Fortunately, the team had many methods of replenishing mana. Clive's aura and Belinda's astral lantern familiar both did so, as did the crystals floating around Humphrey from his own Crystallise Mana ability. Neil's orbs were a boost, and Humphrey's equipment also leaned heavily into retaining or replenishing mana. The net result was Humphrey possessed an extraordinary amount of sustain for someone with his power set.

Humphrey's greatest advantage, however, was not his powers, his training or his gear; it was the humility to recognise that he was not the critical figure in this combat. He didn't make any bold rushes or seize any perceived opportunities. He did the work, stayed the course and trusted in his team.

60

GRISLY CHORE

Wʜɪʟᴇ Hᴜᴍᴘʜʀᴇʏ ᴡᴀs ᴏɴʟʏ ᴀᴅᴇǫᴜᴀᴛᴇ ᴀs ᴀ ᴘᴇʀsᴏɴᴀʟ ᴘᴀʀᴛɪᴄɪᴘᴀɴᴛ ɪɴ ᴛʜᴇ battle against the parasitised elves, his contribution was still large. This came through the other assets he brought to the combat, starting with his cohort of summons.

Humphrey's dragon-bone soldiers, the spartoi, had been modified by his powerful, if unpredictable, summoner's dice. In this case, the soldiers had been called up in the form of spiders with fire powers. It wasn't ideal for fighting their current enemy, but randomness was the price of such a potent item. At least they had managed to slog through the fields, unlike Neil's golem. That had been left behind after it half sank into a rice paddy.

Humphrey directed the soldiers to form a cordon, intercepting the elves approaching from all sides. Only twenty summons was not enough to block them all, but they at least helped prevent the team from being overrun. Unfortunately, Humphrey had to command them to stop spitting burning webs over the elves.

The flames his summons could create were too removed to count as Humphrey's own fire. As such, Humphrey's aura did not transmute it into dragon fire, and the heat-hungry worms absorbed it. The affected elves had their flesh burned, but, being dead, were unaffected unless they were low rank enough that it burned them away entirely.

Like other forms of conversion they had seen, becoming a corpse-host for worms seemed to rank up the body. Most of the elves being slaughtered were ordinary people ranked up to iron. Their main threat came from the worms that shot out when the bodies were cut apart. While the higher-ranked ones were burned by the flames of Humphrey's summons, though, the worms inside didn't care. They devoured the heat, which gave their scorched hosts a burst of strength and speed. After witnessing that only a couple of times, Humphrey ordered his spartoi to stop using fire.

Although the summons had the numbers, the most powerful member of Humphrey's cohort was naturally Stash. The mirage dragon had taken on the form of a monster called a spriklish, which was essentially a massive sea urchin atop three giraffe legs. Its main body was the size of an economy hatchback, and it attacked by shooting spines that weren't especially dangerous, at least to an appropriate-rank adventurer. It also had many weaknesses. The long legs were slow and thin, making it easy to topple the creature. Even better, leaving the body up on its high legs made it easy pickings for ranged powers. It had the ability to rapidly heal, but not fast enough to overcome the attacks of a ranged adventurer.

What made the spriklish a valuable form was that it could shoot spines very rapidly and with pinpoint accuracy. Against the multitudinous-but-frail worms, it left them pinned to the dirt road by spines. Rapid spine regrowth meant that endurance wasn't a problem either.

Stash proved so effective at eliminating the growing sea of loose worms that Belinda sent her echo spirit familiar to mimic him. A second spriklish appeared, looking like a cheap hologram replica. The spines it fired were magical force rather than physical spines, but they worked just as well.

Clive also had his familiar, Onslow, but was holding him in reserve. He wanted the tortoise fully charged up so that he could cover for Clive once he joined Jason. There was one more support, though, who arrived late to the combat.

Neil's chrysalis golem was slow and lumbering. Too slow to keep up with the team as they crossed the rice fields, it had last been seen sinking into a paddy, abandoned to the tender mercies of the parasitised elves. It at least had distracted some of the elves who had gone from farming to frenzy, chasing after the team as they made their way to the town.

The golem's singular power was to shroud itself inside a chrysalis that was near-indestructible, at least to attackers of its own rank. It underwent a transfiguration inside before emerging in a new form, adapted to the battle at hand. Going through the process was not swift, and the golem was ill-suited for short battles. More often than not, they would be over before the summon had undergone its transformation.

As was normal for a power with so many disadvantages, it was formidable should the right circumstances appear. At silver rank, the golem was far better at adapting to enemies and environments, compared to the crude attack reactions that had shaped its lower-rank transformations. When the transformed golem finally appeared over the battlefield, its crystal body glimmered brightly in the sun.

The golem's new form was a giant, crystalline wasp, the size of a bread van. It had sixteen long, multi-jointed arms, each ending in a hand of narrow, barbed fingers. The wasp came buzzing over the trees and hovered over the battle briefly before descending into the fray.

Wholly unlike its ungainly initial form, the giant insect darted around like a dragonfly, wings buzzing as they flapped in a rapid blur. Its hands reached out and plunged into one elf after another, jabbing in and out. Each time a hand emerged, dead worms dangled from the barbs on its fingers.

Neil's transfigured golem marked a turning point in the fight. Having configured itself to annihilate hosts and pluck out the parasites within, it alleviated the pressure on the team. They still had to fight and be careful about it, but they were less worried about running into desperate moments.

There were still more and more elves emerging from across the town, however. With a population of several thousand, there was no shortage of bodies. The team even had to move, having no interest in using the piled-up dead as a bulwark. They crossed a field of corpses to an empty stretch of wide road and then proceeded to create a fresh charnel house of elven bodies.

The team were all aware that the elven corpses they were laying out were not monsters but victims. They were adventurers, used to laughing in the face of death, but only Rufus had witnessed such a scene before. Years earlier, he had met Gary and Farrah in a town of around the same size, where the population had also been turned into walking corpses.

With the push of the enemy lessened by the arrival of Neil's devastating golem, the fight had lulls that were not entirely welcome. The team bantered as if they were not surrounded by death, trying to keep their mind off the horror they were participating in. The townsfolk had been dead before the team arrived, but they were still aware that they were cutting down mothers and brothers. They all turned their eyes from the reality of how many of the bodies belonged to children.

"Whoever did this is going to burn," Sophie growled.

Not even Humphrey disagreed with Sophie's sentiment of revenge, but the moment was soon over as more elves ran to the slaughter.

"It feels like they'll never stop coming," Neil grimly opined.

"They will," Humphrey said, but he was unable to muster anything but weariness to his tone.

The fight turned from a dangerous battle to a grisly chore as the team eliminated one parasite host after another. Jason's butterflies still flew around, but many worms managed to crawl away. If they ended up needing to hunt them all, it would be a tedious task.

The worm parasites had apparently turned mindless when triggered, despite having been able to mimic the townsfolk at least enough to lure visitors to their doom. It led the team into a false sense of security, and the most dangerous moment of the battle came as they thought it was reaching a clean-up stage. Whatever intelligence drove the worms held back a large number of hosts, sending out just enough to keep the team active. Then they rushed in to swamp the team with pure numerical advantage.

Despite being surprised, the team reacted with professionalism, their readiness never having truly slacked off. Rather than push back hard, Humphrey instructed the team and his bone spiders to stop warding off elves and let them cluster up. Sophie even helped, rounding them up with her Wind Wave power. Once they were nice and collected, it was Neil's turn to step in.

Of everyone on the team, it was Neil who had the hardest time ranking up. More than any other member, his power set had abilities that were high-cooldown, circumstantial or both, making them difficult to use on a regular basis. Even his summon was hard to raise up, with battles often ending before the summon could enter its chrysalis, let alone exit. As for his healing and support powers, the excellence of his team actually hurt him. In more fights than not, there was little call for Neil's abilities.

Neil was best served in critical fights, but constantly chasing the edge would get the team killed, sooner or later. The rest of the team had a variety of attack powers they could use. The biggest problems were Humphrey, Belinda, Clive and Rufus, all of whom advanced an extra step faster because they were human.

At low ranks, the human advantage in ability growth speed mattered little, but now they were at the wall. When ranking up abilities took exponentially longer, even a minor advantage would add up over time.

Like many healers, Neil used a lot of his downtime to raise his healing powers slowly but reliably on civilians. It was also fulfilling to help people in need, reminding Neil why he'd joined the Church of the Healer in the first place.

Even so, many of Neil's powers could only be deployed in action. Without the team falling into dire straits, many of Neil's powers went unused. From his overwhelming single-target buff to wide-area heals and cleanses, all of Neil's big spells had an impact, but only when the circumstances were right. Even though such abilities inherently rose more quickly than others, it still made them awkward to use.

Ability: [Reaper's Redoubt] (Shield)

- Special ability (dimension, disease, unholy).
- Cost: Extreme mana.
- Cooldown: 6 hours.

- Current rank: Silver 3 (98%).

- Effect (iron): Take allies into a dimensional space briefly while flooding the area with death energy, dealing disruptive-force damage, necrotic damage and inflicting [Creeping Death] on everything in the area.

- Effect: (bronze): Allies undergo extreme mana replenishment while in the dimensional space.

- Effect: (silver): Enemies are afflicted with [Death's Grip]

- [Creeping Death] (damage-over-time, disease, stacking): Inflicts ongoing necrotic damage until the disease is cleansed. Additional instances have a cumulative effect.

- [Death's Grip] (unholy): The effects of healing are reduced. This effect is initially weak but is enhanced by any necrotic damage suffered by the victim.

As a healer, Neil had little in the way of destructive power, but the one ability he did have was devastating. Although more and more elves continued to rush at them, his power provided the team with a reset. When they emerged from the dimensional space Neil created, the worms and their elven hosts in a wide area were rotted and dead. The same was true of plants, trees and even the wooden buildings, the closest ones having collapsed.

"Did I just sense our healer blanketing the area in death and murdering everyone and everything?" Jason asked through voice chat.

It was light and jovial, as if they weren't surrounded by death, even though he mentioned it specifically. They each knew from Farrah that Jason had once encountered what they'd all gone through on a much wider scale. They realised he wasn't being flippant about death, but telling them to do what they could to put it out of their minds until the job was done.

"I had to do it," Neil said. "Someone ran off by himself and left us to do all the fighting."

"Hey, I have an important role," Jason said defensively. "On an unrelated note, chewing sounds don't come through my voice chat, right?"

"Not the time," Humphrey scolded.

Unable to put all the deaths aside, even for the moment, his face was filled with rage with nowhere to put it. He could kill townsfolk victims and massacre worms all day, but it wouldn't give him the person behind it all. The hope was that Jason found them, although that wasn't why he reached out.

"I just talked with Carlos," Jason reported. "I updated him on what we've seen."

"And?" Humphrey asked.

"He said that world-taker worms are bad."

"Oh, they're bad," Neil said. "I'm glad we figured that out. Extremely helpful."

"More helpful than sarcasm," Belinda muttered.

61

INFERIOR

Nervousness was not a normal sensation for a messenger. When the adventurers arrived, Pei Vas Kartha had been in her hidden underground lair, as usual, managing the worm implantations. She was confident that they would not sense her presence, as any non-messenger perception would be firmly but subtly blocked. The sophisticated aura magic rituals had been inscribed into the facility by someone far stronger than Pei herself.

It was not the first group of adventurers to arrive. Pei remained until she sensed an absurd aura flood the town. It was angry and startlingly powerful, but that was not what disturbed her. The aura was not that of a messenger, yet it undeniably carried properties that belonged to messengers.

There were several elements of that aura that Pei found unnerving. One was that she was not used to anyone of her rank having a stronger aura than her. She knew it was possible for non-messengers to have stronger auras than normal, but seeing it for herself was unsettling. Then there was the nature of the aura. Not only did it carry something akin to that of a messenger, but it was so oppressive that it cast a looming shadow over her soul.

She caught herself shrinking her shoulders and then pushed them back up, angrily reasserting her posture. She was not going to bow down to some random aura. It wanted her to feel small and unworthy, as if she had been judged and found wanting. As if she had sinned. That the person it belonged to would not even be able to sense her made it even more galling.

Then she remembered that odd strain in the aura of messenger-like power. She wondered how well-hidden she truly was and, in a moment of crippling shame, found herself thankful to be shielded from even such powerful senses.

The word 'inferior' slithered into her mind, like one of the worms she'd been implanting into the elves. She snarled, feeding her weak emotions into the flames of rage. Even so, she did not lose control and lash out. She extended her senses past the protection of her lair, careful not to expose her aura. She needed a better sense of what was happening above.

She sensed the adventurers fighting the worm-host, realising they were stronger than the last ones. They were violently undoing so much of Pei's work by slaughtering the hosts, but she did not rush out to intervene. While she had the pride of messenger superiority, she was not fool enough to confront such a powerful team, at least while they were fresh. She would wait until the battle had exhausted them before looking for opportunities to pick them off.

The town's elven population had been overtaken by parasitic worms that were using the townsfolk as host bodies, pretending everything was still normal. The arrival of Jason's team had changed that. The townsfolk became frenzied berserkers, throwing themselves at the team from every direction.

Jason and Sophie fended off the first wave until the rest of the team turned up. Once they did, Jason went off in search of something that had tweaked his senses. It was faint enough that he wasn't entirely certain that he wasn't imagining it at first. He methodically searched, using his stealth abilities to avoid the enemies charging his team.

While he moved, Jason relayed what the team had learned about the worms through Shade to Carlos, still in the city of Yaresh. Carlos had a decent amount of notes about world-taker worms, and once he had a name, he was able to dig out some research records. This was specifically because of his research into various means of taking over the bodies of innocent people; world-taker worms were one example. He had collected notes from other researchers as part of his own endeavours.

"I knew I had these," Carlos relayed back through to Jason. "Interestingly, this particular breed of worms has colour gradations that indicate—"

"I'm more in the market for practical facts that will help me right this second," Jason interrupted him. "Basically, how are they going to try to kill us? Also—and this is the big one—how do we make them not do that?"

While Carlos took him through the salient points, Jason continued his search. Around the time he found what he suspected he was looking for, Carlos had moved from more practical details and on to 'interesting points of note.' Jason contacted the team to share what he knew, while Carlos headed for the Adventure Society. With seven teams all searching the same region, it was critical to disseminate the information.

"The worms maintain the host body's functions," Jason explained to the team through voice chat. "Enough to make a passable facsimile of being alive anyway. That's why they don't have the zombie look, even though they're dead."

"And how they pass themselves off as people," Rufus said. "At least long enough to get people close enough to infest them as well."

"I'd assume so," Jason agreed. "You want to avoid the worms digging into you. You can't heal them out because they'll just absorb the life magic and multiply. You need to physically gouge them out of the body and then heal the wound after doing so, once you've extracted all the worms."

"Charming," Belinda said. "Any good news?"

"Actually, yes," Jason said. "They like to go after critical organs, like the brain and the heart."

"How is that good news?" Sophie asked.

"We have neither," Neil said. "We're all basically sacks of magic, blood and meat. No critical organs they can devour to kill us instantaneously."

"It's a problem if too many of them get inside you, though," Jason said. "It's harder to take over essence users of our rank, but not impossible. If enough of them get inside you, they can hijack the magical matrix that makes your sack of blood and meat work. That means taking control of you."

"You know, my mum wanted me to be a merchant," Neil said bitterly. "Travel, money. Not being eaten from the inside out by worms."

"I did say they were bad," Jason said. "Carlos said that they're classified as an apocalypse beast."

"That would suggest these worms are what's responsible for the whole region going silent," Clive said. "Which leads to the question of whether this is just the next disaster in the queue, or if the messengers brought them here."

"I'm hoping you can help me figure that out," Jason said. "I'm going to open up a portal, so come on through."

A dark portal opened up next to Clive, but he didn't step through immediately. Magic light seeped through the front of his robe and quickly coalesced into a tortoise shape. Clive's familiar, Onslow, was a tattoo on Clive's torso when not manifested. When he appeared, he was a flying tortoise that could change his size and wield potent attack magic. Each segment on his shell bore a glowing rune, representing one elemental power he could use. Clive patted Onslow affectionately on the neck.

"I'll need you to cover for me, buddy."

One of the runes on Onslow's back stopped glowing as a lightning bolt shot out, chaining between enemies.

"That's the way," Clive said and went through the portal. He emerged from the other end of the portal in some kind of underground space. Light filtered down through cracks between a wooden floor above, dust dancing in the beams. The floor and three of the walls were hard-packed dirt, and an old ladder led up to an open trapdoor.

The last wall in the room was very different, being made of polished slate bricks. Set into it was a pair of double doors made of carved wood.

Unlike the boards above, the wood of the door was extremely well made and fitted, with no cracks to peer through. It also wasn't painted in the same heat-radiating green paint as the town buildings, and was instead covered in elaborate magic sigils. They glowed very faintly and shifted under his gaze, the lines slithering like serpents. He glanced at Jason, who was standing in front of the doors.

"What do you think?" Jason asked as Clive moved to examine the doors, fascination lighting up his expression.

"I have no idea," Clive said excitedly as he opened his storage space.

Clive's storage power, Rune Gate, was a little less convenient than Jason's, Belinda's and Humphrey's. Where they could all just pluck items out of the air, Clive needed to open a miniature portal, ringed by floating runes, that he could reach into and take things out of. Even so, Clive had arguably the most useful storage ability, as it could also be used as a regular portal power or to enhance the strength of his ritual magic.

Plucking out strange devices one by one, Clive used them to examine the door before shoving them back into storage. One looked like an hourglass and another like a magnifying glass. There was an opaque orb that flashed various colours and a set of large crystals, strung together on a line. Clive threw various powders at the door from bags, from ground-up lesser monster cores to chalk powder mixed with salt and infused with magic. All the while, Clive jotted notes into a book he left on a small levitating table.

"You know this isn't an academic exercise, right?" Jason asked him. "Our friends are fighting up there."

"It's fine," Clive said absently, not looking away from his work. "Most of those elves were normal people. The worms might be silver and bronze rank, but artificially ranked-up bodies are much weaker than the genuine article. You've fought enough of the converted to know that."

"Yeah," Jason said. "You know that I fought a new kind of converted on Earth, right? Not based around the Builder's clockwork cores, although the higher-ranked ones used modified cores to stabilise their own conversion process."

"You've mentioned," Clive said.

"I'm not sure that I mentioned that the guy who ran the organisation they came from left me a vault full of secrets. Including all the research on their conversion project."

"Are you saying you can make converted?"

"No. Well, maybe. But I think he was hoping that I could refine the process."

"Why you? That's not your area of expertise."

"I think his choice was more to do with trusting me to use it properly. I'm pretty sure he wanted me to find a way to give regular people powers, without needing a truckload of essences. They wouldn't match an essence user, sure, but sometimes quantity over quality is the way to go."

"Why would he want that?"

"I'm not sure. Both he and Dawn have made it clear that somewhere down the line, I have another fight coming. What that is, I don't know, but everything this psycho did was in preparation for it. He wanted me to take over for him after he was dead."

"You killed him?"

"He killed himself because he knew that I wouldn't let him live."

That finally caused Clive to pause and he turned to look at Jason.

"Farrah never told us that."

"Farrah wasn't there for everything. How is that door going?"

Clive turned his attention back to the door.

"This is a ritual magic paradigm, unlike anything I've ever seen. This is otherworldly ritual magic, like the astral magic the Builder cult was using."

"Not like the local stuff, then."

"Even more so than what the cult was using. We have magic that interacts with auras, but it's simple and crude."

"Like the aura beacons used for signalling over long distances."

"Exactly. The water link system is as elaborate as it gets, and there's a reason Farrah and Travis are looking to replace it. The efficiency and practicality leave a lot to be desired."

"And this magic does it better?" Jason asked.

"It makes sense that messenger ritual magic interacts with auras in far more sophisticated ways than any of ours, given what we know about them. This is beyond my expectations, though."

"Do you even know what this magic is doing?"

"Oh, that's simple enough. The door just has some simple locking magic. The fancy part is the anti-detection magic that is shrouding whatever is behind it. Frankly, I'm amazed you noticed this was here."

"Can you open it?"

"Oh, that's not a problem," Clive said. "It's essentially the same magic we use in this world. The problem is that the alarm is part of the anti-detection magic. I don't understand enough about how it works to stop the alarm from going off. It incorporates the intrinsic properties of messenger auras, which I can't replicate. At least this seems to confirm that whatever's going on here, the messengers are behind it."

"Would I be able to replicate the messenger aura?"

"I was wondering the same thing," Clive said. "It'll take time and study, though. It's not something we can quickly knock out in a dirty basement. I don't see any way of opening this door without triggering the alarm."

"Okay," Jason said.

"Then how do we open the door?" Clive wondered.

"Kicking?"

"You want to kick it open?"

"If there's anyone in there, I'm pretty sure they know we're here."

"Shouldn't we wait for the team?"

"What if someone's fleeing down an escape tunnel, or preparing something that will let the worms overrun the team?"

"What if it's twenty people waiting for the door to open so they can kick the snot out of you?"

"Then I'll run away."

"You're a lot better than me at running away."

"There's a portal right there. Actually, hold on a tick."

Jason went through the portal to where his team was still fighting the worm-host elves, but the enemy numbers were diminished as the town's population was finally nearing depletion. Standing near Neil and Belinda, Jason held his hands up over his head and chanted a spell.

"*As your lives were mine to reap, so your deaths are mine to harvest.*"

Red lights, the remnant life force of countless dead worms, shone across the charnel house of a battlefield. They then started streaming into the air, all converging on Jason, who absorbed it all.

- You have used [Blood Harvest] on multiple [World-Taker Worms].
- Your health, mana and stamina have been replenished.
- You have gained multiple instances of [Blood Frenzy] from [Blood Harvest].
- Maximum instances of [Blood Frenzy] have been reached. Additional instances will be converted into [Blood of the Immortal].
- You have gained multiple instances of [Blood of the Immortal] from [Blood Harvest].

- Maximum health, mana and stamina have been exceeded. Ability [Sin Eater] has temporarily raised your maximum, health, mana and stamina to accommodate. These maximums will diminish over time.

"Jason?" Humphrey asked. "What are you doing that you felt the need to come back and gain a massive amount of temporary life force?"

"Clive is making me kick open a magic door."

"I am doing no such thing," Clive denied through voice chat.

"He also said he was going to run away if something scary is in there," Jason added.

"Can we please save the pithy banter for when we're not fighting evil?" Rufus asked.

"Have you never seen an action movie," Jason said.

"No!" Rufus yelled. "No, I have not!"

"For a guy ostensibly against it," Jason told Rufus, "your pithy banter is on point."

"Jason…" Humphrey growled.

"Fine," Jason said, returning through the portal. "Clive, unlock this door so I can kick it."

Clive grumbled but put away the instruments he used to examine the door. He then took out a clear crystal rod and pointed at the door. The rod started glowing in a mix of swirling, strobing colours that slowed down their strobing over time. The colours dropped out one by one until the rod was glowing solid blue. Then the light stopped shining altogether, leaving clear crystal once again.

"I didn't think you approved of shortcuts like unlocking rods," Jason said.

"Taking the easy path is the wrong move when the hard one has something to teach you," Clive said as he stepped well back, ready to jump through the portal. "I don't have anything to learn from simple lock magic, so why waste the time?

You remember that the rest of the team is still fighting, right? Now, if you insist on kicking the door open, kick away."

"Now that I think about it," Jason mused, "what is that alarm magic going to do? Will it be attached to a trap?"

"Probably," Clive said. "Also, we've been out here talking for a while. If anyone inside didn't know we were out here, they do now."

"Good point. Any suggestions on how we should approach it?"

"Yes," Clive said, eyeing the open trapdoor above them as he pulled out his wand. "You go first."

Jason chuckled as he strode over to the double doorway. He lifted a leg, about to kick it open when the doors were flung wide on their own. A wall of worms poured out, like water through the sluice gate of an overflowing dam. It was swift enough that Jason was inundated, toppled over and completely buried. Clive was saved by silver-rank reflexes and agility, as well as his extra distance from the door. He had a scant moment to react and he used it, leaping up through the trapdoor in the ceiling.

In the building above, Clive immediately crouched to look down through the trap door. The wave of worms was flattening out, but Jason was still unseen, buried beneath them.

"I think we might have a problem," Clive said through voice chat. "Jason, are you there?"

"What's the situation?" Humphrey asked.

"Jason just got buried in worms."

"How buried?" Belinda asked. "Are we talking just a lot of worms, or full bathtub?"

"More like swimming pool," Clive said. "Jason?"

There was still no response.

"We can't come down," Humphrey said. "If any more of us break off, we'll get overrun."

"I'll take a closer look and see what I can figure out," Clive said, leaning in to get a better viewing angle through the doorway below. From what he could see, it was a tunnel made of the same slate bricks as the wall into which the door was set.

A figure stepped up to the now-open door, the worms parting before it like the Red Sea. The creatures maintained a circle of clear space, not around the person but an orb she held out in front of her.

As the figure came fully into view, Clive spotted the wings folded on her back. It was a messenger with nut-brown skin and dark hair. Her wings were also brown, with tan speckling. Her clothes consisted of a short, loosely draped top and loose, flowing pants, both fawn-coloured. Her bare feet floated just off the floor.

The object she was holding looked like a ball of overlapping leather straps, around twice the size of a fist. The worms would not go near it and Clive got to see an unmoving Jason as the messenger drew close. The worms slithered off of his body and outside of the circle around the orb.

Jason's conjured cloak had vanished, but his conjured robes had not. Despite what was going on, Clive's analytical mind couldn't help but absently posit that while Jason himself conjured the cloak, the robes were conjured by one of his familiars. While the robes remained in place, however, it was covered in holes. The skin visible beneath each hole had a small wound mark.

Still holding the orb in one hand, the messenger conjured a spear in the other. Clive raised his wand and fired, but a wing moved out to block the beam. She brought the spear down. She was not the only one with protection, however. A nebulous eye manifested in front of Jason, then expanded into a shield that blocked the attack. Gordon manifested behind the shield with five more eyes, all of which shot beams at Jason's attacker. She blocked by wrapping her wings around in front of her, which she could barely manage in the enclosed space of the doorway. She then floated backwards, out of Clive's sight.

Clive saw that the worms flowed back from the edges of the room where they had been driven, but they now avoided Jason, just as they had done the orb. Then worms started crawling out of Jason's body, tunnelling free of his flesh. Many dug their way out through the wounds they had presumably entered by, while others poked new holes in his skin and robes with their drill-bit heads. Dozens of them emerged from all over Jason, and Clive flinched as one pushed its way out from his eye socket, squeezing around the eyeball, like a horrifying, fleshy tear.

Then the worms that had refused to move closer to Jason started twitching and thrashing, like a rat pit after a snake was dropped in. They pushed against the walls as if trying to climb up them, or started digging into the dirt. The worms crawling out of Jason, half-emerged, flailed as they were pulled back into his body, as if plucked by the tail.

Clive spotted one worm that managed to escape and start crawling away, only for a strip of red leather to extend from Jason's robe, wrap around the worm and pull it back. A leech with rings of savage lamprey teeth emerged from the same wound the worm had escaped from, and when the worm was dragged back, the leech brutally devoured it.

62

APOCALYPSE

BURIED BENEATH A TOWN WHERE THE POPULACE HAD BEEN BODY-SNATCHED BY parasitic worms was a hidden chamber. The messenger, Pei Vas Kartha, had been operating there for months, luring the town elders into what they had believed to be lucrative-but-ordinary treason. They had helped her to magically excavate under a building, in the dead of night, installing the facility.

The hidden chambers were topped by an ordinary building, with the unordinary doors set into the brick wall of a basement otherwise made of hard-packed dirt. The doors led to a tunnel and then stairs going down to the main facility. There, Pei had bred more worms from the initial stock she was given, preparing to take over the town. She started with one breeding vat in a hidden room, so as not to spook her accomplices, but when the elders grew wary, they became the first worm-hosts.

After that, the vat came out into the main chamber and Pei's operations expanded. More vats were added, along with implantation chambers to infest the local elves in batches. The actual implantation of the town was accomplished in only a few days, the time spent breeding a worm supply paying off handsomely. Once enough of the town had become hosts, they were able to monitor the others and lure in any visitors.

Pei herself was not immune to the worms, but the vats, chambers and tubes allowed them to be moved around without setting them loose. As a failsafe, she had the orb created by the messenger who had given her the initial batch of worms. A similar device was in the possession of every messenger infiltrating the towns and villages along the southern reaches of Yaresh.

After months of everything going exactly to plan, genuine trouble was overdue. Even the adventurers that arrived had been successfully swept up. The real threat began with a dangerous aura that washed over the town above, now fully converted to worm-hosts.

The man to whom that aura belonged had somehow found her hidden facility and had been about to kick the doors open. By that time, however, Pei had long-ago installed worms in vats by the door, rigged to the magical alarm. The man had been buried in worms, but she decided to finish him off anyway. His aura had been like nothing she'd ever experienced and she needed him dead if only to quash the insidious doubts it had infested her with.

Although the man was unconscious, worms digging through his body, even his passive aura was incredibly hard to read. What she could glean from it only unnerved her more. She moved to strike, conjuring her spear. She could sense the other adventurer in the building above, but dismissed him. His aura marked him as a capable but ordinary adventurer. It was the anomaly on the ground in front of her that needed to be eradicated.

What came next only solidified her certainty that the man needed to die. She casually deflected a wand beam from above and brought her spear down, only to have it blocked. The unconscious man had an avatar of doom as a familiar, which was shocking enough on its own to warrant reporting this man to the messenger leadership.

There were very few forces that the messengers actively avoided. Even the agents of most great astral beings were opponents to be wary of, but not to back away from. Amongst the very few forces that the messengers were careful to avoid belonged to the Eye of Annihilation and the Sundered Throne. These were the only two forces known to regularly employ the reality assassins, the avatars of doom. While it wasn't unheard of to see them elsewhere, it was rare enough to warrant very close attention. And now one of them was floating in front of her, protecting a man that worms would soon take over.

The avatar was only a familiar, restricted to Pei's own silver rank. Otherwise, she would have been annihilated in an instant. The beams it shot at her were resonating force, unpleasantly penetrative but not the transcendent damage the avatars possessed at diamond rank. They burrowed into the magical metal she transformed her wings into as shields, but did not punch through them immediately.

The messenger withdrew into the tunnel, not wanting to face the avatar and the other adventurer, who was shooting beams through the trapdoor. She retaliated by firing a swarm of feathers from her wings that danced around, attacking from every angle. This forced the avatar to switch its orbs from beams to barriers, and it seemed satisfied to remain on the defensive, shielding its summoner. She knew this was a mistake on its part, as the worms inside the man would soon take him over.

Even knowing this, the man on the ground had Pei shaken, despite what had to be his inevitable demise. Did the avatar know something that she didn't? This rank-diminished avatar was not her match and she kept her senses trained on the man it was protecting. The other adventurer was staying above, likely wary of the worms, but the worms were not behaving as they should.

Her withdrawal should have had the worms swarming back over the man, who was no longer warded by the orb she carried. But, if anything, they had started avoiding him more than the orb. The individual worms were mindless creatures, directed by the intelligent brood mother in the chambers below. Yet she sensed that they were scared of him when fear should not have been possible at all.

That was when things got worse. Not just the worms around the man, but the worms inside him radiated fear, and she sensed them struggling to escape. They started digging out of his body, dozens of them, but they were yanked back as if something inside was devouring them. Then one managed to escape and something came out through the wound to get it. When she saw the large leech with the ringed rows of lamprey teeth, a chill ran through her body.

Messengers were the pinnacle beings of the cosmos, dominating the sky of countless worlds. Now the messenger Pei Vas Kartha found herself in a hole in the ground, stricken with... fear? Though she had sensed fear in others, she had never felt it herself, so she could not be sure.

She was surrounded by dangerous creatures. One was an apocalypse beast swarm that conquered worlds from the inside of their populations, and would hollow her out like any lesser being if they got the chance. The creatures were piled up around the walls, held off only by the magical orb in her hand. But for all that such creatures had conquered worlds, they alone weren't close to enough that she would fear them. They might be the nightmare of entire civilisations, but to the messengers, they were just another weapon.

It was the being in front of her that made her scared for the first time even though he lay unconscious on the ground. He had been drowned in the apocalypse worms and should be quite thoroughly dead. Yet the creatures were even more fearful of him than of the orb she held, climbing the walls and digging into the dirt to escape him.

The worms had burrowed into the man, as was their nature, but they had found something inside him even more terrifying than themselves. Pei Vas Kartha had understood immediately when she saw it. It was not the first time she had seen a sanguine horror.

Even though she was the lowest caste of messengers, never surpassing silver rank, Pei had seen many worlds. She had joined numerous conquests, serving minor but valuable roles, such as worm breeder. In her experience, she had encountered worlds ravaged by apocalypse beasts of different types. Fungal vultures that devoured the atmosphere, choking out the inhabitants. Primeval serpents that burrowed into the core of planets, triggering a volcanic apocalypse that choked with ash, cutting off the sun.

The messengers knew these apocalypse beasts. Many, they even used themselves, deploying them as weapons of mass destruction. This was the case with the world-taker worms as well. But some apocalypse beasts were never used. Too uncontrollable and too hard to stop if they got loose, the danger was not worth the reward. When Pei saw the sanguine horror crawl out of the man in front of her and devour the world-taker worm, she was shaken. First an avatar of doom, and now this?

Only once had Pei seen a world where a sanguine horror had been loosed. Conquered by the messengers, the native population had summoned a sanguine horror from whatever nightmare realm where the Limitless Legion met the Final Domain. The natives had believed they could control the swarm monster and use it to drive the messengers off their planet. They had been half right. A sanguine horror was hunger incarnate, and once it reached its full strength, the only way to stop it was to starve it out. It multiplied too fast, devouring life to fully replenish itself from even a single leech.

The surviving messengers, including Pei, had abandoned the planet. They hadn't taken any of the natives as slaves because there weren't any left. She had been shaken to her core by the experience, and not just from the horrors she had witnessed. It was the first time she had seen the messengers run.

It was not that they could not fight the sanguine horror. Pei had slaughtered countless of the leech-lampreys herself, let alone what the higher-caste messengers of gold and diamond rank had slain. But no matter how many they killed, the apocalypse beast didn't stop. They would sweep through a town, devouring every living thing. The people, the animals, the plants. They dug up the roots in the ground and consumed the algae growing in the wells. Everything they consumed was fuel to increase the leech mass.

The messengers had started burning whole cities in the path of the swarm, like a fire break before an inferno. They tried to isolate the swarm from its food supply so they could cut off its ability to reproduce. They were partially effective, reducing the swarm's size, but had been unable to quash it entirely. While the messengers had been struggling to contain and eradicate the remnants, they were unaware that their efforts were futile. Too late, they realised that the sanguine horror swarm covering the land was only a fragment of what occupied the planet. In the lowest fathoms of the oceans, the swarm devoured every living thing, from fish to coral to leviathans of the deep.

Only as the swarm cleared out the furthest depths and moved closer to the surface did the messengers sense its presence. With the ubiquity of the swarm, the leeches under the oceans had been hard to sense until they moved closer. Even the diamond-ranked messengers had failed to recognise the true threat until it was too late. Once the swarm grew and reached the shallower portions of the ocean, they finally realised that attempting to stop it was futile.

It might have been possible to stop the swarm before it turned the planet into a lifeless husk, but what remained in the aftermath would not be worth keeping. Pride in their superiority over every other living thing in the cosmos had cost the messengers lives, but they were not so blinded by it that they would fight to the death over a worthless rock. They gave up and left what remained of the planet to the horror.

Sanguine horrors did not take hosts the way world-taker worms did. Somehow, this man had claimed, as a familiar, the only thing Pei had seen the messengers surrender to. That was not the only reason that she was discovering fear for the first time. Once she started exploring the unconscious man with her magical senses, she realised the sanguine horror was only one of several bizarre things about him.

Firstly, his aura. Even dormant, while the man was unconscious, it was incredibly hard to read. The more she gleaned from it, the more she was startled. For one, he was not a dual-entity comprised of body and soul, but a gestalt physical and spiritual being. He was no messenger, but he shared that trait with them.

As their special nature was one of the cornerstones of their superiority, the fact that this unconscious adventurer shared that nature rocked not just Pei's mind but her faith. Once again, she found a blasphemous idea creeping into her mind, despite trying desperately to shut it out. The idea that perhaps she, as a messenger, was inferior to someone that wasn't.

The other things she sensed in his aura only made it worse. Scars from battles he had no business surviving. The touch of transcendent beings. Power that even she didn't recognise. More than anything else, however, what scared her was a power that she did recognise. Something no silver-ranker should be able to possess. It was a power granted to the Voices of the Will, except that it was not the remote, bestowed power granted to the voices she had met. This was the other end of that power, not the recipient but the source. The power she sensed in him belonged not to the servants of the astral kings, but to the astral kings themselves.

It shouldn't have been possible. For all that this man's aura reflected a toweringly powerful soul, he was definitely only silver rank. How could there be a silver-rank astral king? But as her senses probed his astounding familiars, she grew all the more certain. The bestowed power that should belong only to the voices resided within them.

The astral kings of the messengers exclusively took other messengers as their voices. Not only had this man become an astral king at least as early as silver rank, but had claimed an apocalypse beast and a reality assassin as his voices. That was more than a little disturbing, as a voice was the mouth of an astral king to the world. What kind of astral king had, as his voices, beings who variously devoured all life and annihilated that which should have been immortal? Looking at the avatar of doom still shielding the man from her storm of feathers, she was disinclined to ask.

Pei was still contemplating these questions when the man's eyes shot open.

63

SUPERIOR

As she pelted his familiar with metal feathers, Pei Vas Kartha watched when the unnerving man opened his eyes. He rose to his feet, not by pushing himself up but tilted as though on an invisible slab. She could sense the way he moved with his aura, and it was not the crude inefficiency of an essence user. He used it in the clean, smooth manner of a messenger. His gaze moved up and down her body, his eyes like nebulas in a void. It did not escape her attention that they were mirrors of the nebula eye floating in the avatar of doom's body, as well as each of its orbs.

Pei withdrew her feather storm for the moment and the avatar vanished. She felt the man's aura absorb it and grow even stronger in the process. Two of the orbs were left behind, orbiting the man as they had the avatar. As the man made no move to attack yet, she allowed her wings to recover from the avatar's attacks.

He looked past her at the tunnel descending to the main workrooms, and then at the alcoves to either side of the doorway he was standing in. The vats that had once held worms in those alcoves were smashed, the worms having spilled over the floor like a carpet. Only two circles of the floor were empty of worms, where Pei stood with her orb and the man with his hungry familiar.

Seeing Pei floating just off the floor using her aura, the man did the same. In the back of her mind, she had been clinging to some hope that her senses were being deceived. Seeing him move like a messenger and watch her with cosmic eyes, that hope died. She knew then that she would soon die with it, in a hole in the ground. At the hands of a superior being.

Pei was not going to give up without a fight, however. Once more, she blasted out her metal wing feathers, but this time, they did not dance around, looking for an opening. They shot straight and fast, her wings glimmering with the speed at which her feathers had to regrow to keep it up.

What looked like a void portal manifested into being around the man, shrouding him like a cloak. Her feather storm fell into it as harmlessly as rain falling into a pond. He did not retaliate, but continued to float in place. The only difference was the cloak was wrapped around him, hiding his body aside from the eyes that stayed locked on her. The cloak flapped in some non-existent breeze as if touched by astral rather than mortal winds.

She gave up on the attack and instead spoke to him, the rage in her voice mostly covering the tremulations.

"What are you?" she asked, despite knowing the answer. She was unable to make her conscious mind believe it, even with her gut screaming that it was true.

Instead of an answer, the man asked his own question in a stony voice. His tone held no fear, no malice and no anger. It was hard, immutable and uncaring as a mountain.

"Are there more like you?" he asked. "More towns, more world-taker worms?"

"Why should I tell you anything?"

"Because you're a messenger. Your entire philosophy is that the inferior being serves, is it not?"

She threw her spear down the tunnel and it multiplied into nine, and the nine into eighty-one, filling the space. She bolstered each one with physical force by sheathing them with her aura. She felt his aura move out like the tide, stripping hers away. The spears slowed under the physical force produced by his aura but did not stop. The two orbs floating around him became shields to intercept them.

The spears hammered down on the shields and, even without her aura infusion, there were too many for the shields to take. It was the ability she had intended to eliminate the avatar with, but doing so to its summoner was even better. Without the aura enhancement, the shields did not break until most of the spears had shattered against them, but around a quarter turned the man into a pincushion.

He was impaled many times over, even through the head, right below his left eye. Even so, his gaze never left hers. He didn't even move as the spears exploded, shredding his robes and his flesh. His cloak could absorb fragmentation attacks, but not when they came from inside his body.

Even so, his eyes stayed on hers as she conjured a fresh spear and the ones she had already thrown disappeared. She dashed forward, plunging her spear through his face, yet somehow, she missed.

She kept her range, launching spear jabs. He was using space displacement to defend, but every technique had weaknesses. Enough attacks, and some would land. She expected him to draw the sword at his side but instead stopped her spear by the simple method of letting it hit him. He grabbed it, not letting her pull it away.

They stayed locked in front of one another for a moment. She could already see his wounds closing and his robes mending. She remembered the power of an astral king and had a terrifying thought. Was he immortal? Was this some kind of incarnation? It would explain the silver rank.

She yanked her spear free and floated back. Beyond putting up shields and grabbing her spear, he hadn't even fought, as if combat with her was below him.

"You are not superior to the messengers!" she said, spitting the words defiantly.

"Your mouth speaks, but it's your aura that tells the truth. I can feel your faith shaking like a naked child in a storm. By my reckoning, you are right; I'm not superior to the messengers. But in your philosophy, I am. Good for us both that I don't share it. If I did, I would have to acknowledge vampires as superior to the people they feed on."

"What are you talking about?" Pei asked, even as she dreaded the answer.

"You are the first of your kind that I've met in person," he said. "I've seen familiars, replicas and encountered one through a remote-viewing medium, but you are the first messenger I've ever had placed in front of me like a dinner."

"I am not your food."

"No?" he asked, pushing his hood back to reveal a predatory grin. The hole in his face from her spear had already closed and the red mark it left behind was fading. "Now that I've seen you with my own eyes, and tasted you with my own senses, I've come to realise something. I was told that the messengers believed themselves the foundational species of the cosmos. I always assumed they were deluding themselves, but to my great surprise, it may well be true. I, at least, now believe it to be possible."

"Why?"

"Do you know what a reality core is?"

"No."

"It's one of the fundamental elements of every physical universe. The power source of reality. You feel very much like one of these reality cores. Not quite the same, but close. And the thing is, it turns out that I can devour life-force that has been infused with reality core energy. I found that out after some vampires got a hold of these cores I'm talking about. They started infusing the power of them into the blood they were consuming. And when I consumed the vampires, that power became mine."

"You ate vampires?"

"The meat held no appeal. The essence of a vampire is the life force, so that is what I devoured. Now I find myself wondering what will happen when I do the same to yours. You won't know, as you'll be dead by then. The very fact that I can is why the messenger claims of superiority don't hold up, according to your own standards. I don't hold with that master race nonsense, be it from your kind or any other. But how can you be the master race if you aren't at the top of the food chain?"

"You are strange," she responded. "Your nature, however you have come to be that way, is powerful. But I suspect it is also unique and I am but the lowest caste of messenger. You are an anomaly, and even then, your power is far below others of my kind."

The man let out an executioner's laugh.

"You're whistling as you pass a graveyard, messenger. I can feel your fear. I can feel you trying to burn it as fuel for your hatred, and the despair that won't let you. True superiority has no qualifiers and you know it. You're reeling inside, knowing that everything you believed—the very foundations of your identity—is wrong. A lie. If you were still the proud messenger, dealing with a lesser, would you have stopped at such a token resistance? Where's the fight in you? It's nowhere, because you know it would be futile. An ageless life of superiority has engraved what being the lesser means into your soul. Now that it's you, you can't even bring yourself to fight."

He floated towards her at a crawl, barely moving in his ominous approach.

"If you still have faith that you are superior," he challenged, "then show me."

He glanced at the conjured spear in her hand.

"Take your weapon and strike me down with all your hatred."

When Pei had tried to execute the man using the spear, the avatar blocked it. She had various ways of empowering the spear, as well as other supplemental powers, but the man was right; inside, she had already acknowledged her defeat. The conjured weapon clattered briefly on the slate brick floor, then dissolved into nothing.

"Why are you doing this?" she asked, almost begging.

"Because this is not the first time I've seen whole populations wiped out by those who cared nothing for the lives they were taking. So, I'm going to kill you, eat you, and send what's left to the Reaper. And before I do, I'm going to make sure that you understand that your entire life leading up to this moment was a pointless lie. That every life you took, every time you stood over someone and proclaimed them to be below you, it meant nothing. Your life was a waste, your existence means nothing, and now it will end. You will be the equal of all those you killed. I don't know what the Reaper has in store for you, but I'm going to hand you over rough."

Pei steeled her aura, launching it at the man in a last-ditch effort to fight not just for her life, but for her faith and for her soul. It slammed into an iron wall and the man laughed cruelly. She felt his aura wrap around hers like a hand and slowly start to squeeze.

"The messenger aura," he mocked. "So special. So unique. So powerful. I'd ask how it feels to have the embodiment of what makes you superior broken down to nothing, but I can feel it. I can feel your faith dying, and you'll follow it soon. In not much better condition either."

Pei rallied her strength, pushing everything she had into her aura, but the man was right. He couldn't injure her soul directly, but her faith was shattered, which cut deeper than any wound. As the source of her aura, she could no longer muster the strength she once had. Even so, her aura didn't collapse completely. Then, in a final moment of crushing despair, she realised she was not holding him off at all. He was finishing her slowly, just because he could.

The final straw came when another outrageous familiar, a shadow of the Reaper, emerged from the darkness. Her defences collapsed and she fell to the floor, dropping not just to her feet but to her knees.

"You may be getting carried away, Mr Asano," the shadow warned, finally letting her know the name of her murderer.

"Your father will get his due, Shade."

Pei realised that it wasn't just any shadow of the Reaper, but the astral being's famous wandering child. Who was this Asano, to have such a retinue?

"I am not concerned about my progenitor, Mr Asano. I am concerned about how far you are going."

"So am I," another voice came from behind Asano. It was the other adventurer, still looking in from the trapdoor. "Jason, you remember that the whole 'guy with evil powers' thing was a joke, right?"

The man named Asano turned away from her to look at the newcomer.

"Put her down, Jason," the adventurer said. "Quick and clean. You don't have to rip her soul out while you're at it."

"She is her soul, and I can't destroy it," Asano said. "All I can do is consume her residual life force as she transitions from a physical and spiritual gestalt to a purely spiritual entity. It won't be pleasant, but I'm not sucking anyone's soul out."

"Jason, what you were talking about sounds a lot like an energy vampire. Like whatever Thadwick turned into. Do you want that?"

Asano didn't respond, but his cloak vanished, revealing the back of his blood-red robes to her. The robes grew slick and wet as a thick coating of blood seeped from them.

"Feed," Asano commanded. "The woman and the worms."

On the planet that the messengers had abandoned to the sanguine horror, she had never been in real danger. She'd always been protected because she wasn't powerful enough for the heavy fighting. For that reason, she had never feared, even as she had watched millions of natives be devoured, and even some of her own kind that were caught out. She had watched them scream as they were devoured, musing over their lack of equanimity as they suffered the price of their failure. The same failure that was now hers.

As leeches poured out of the slick red robes, Pei Vas Kartha screamed for the first and last time.

64

SIGNIFICANTLY MORE POWERFUL

CLIVE WINCED AT THE GRISLY SOUND OF CHEWING THAT FILLED THE TUNNEL. THE worms were being merrily devoured by toothy leeches that grew in number as they ate. The sound of fleshy consumption was accompanied by a muffled screaming that came from the largest pile of leeches, under which the messenger was buried. The pile undulated with the messenger's helpless thrashing.

The auras mixed up in the tunnel were unsettling. The strongest was Jason's, which loomed like a prison tower. Although it was not directed at Clive, it filled him with unease, like an authoritarian monument. Next was the aura of the sanguine horror.

Clive knew that the familiar was an apocalypse beast. He remembered hearing about it in the beginning and being disturbed, but somehow it had become normal to him. Jason had a way of hiding the disturbing things, such as giving the creature an innocuous name. But as Clive felt the fully unleashed hunger of it, the need to consume without end, he recalled the dread that had struck him on first learning about Colin.

In that way, summoner and familiar were alike: easy to forget what lay underneath the smiles and the jokes. Jason watched his familiar feed, the hood of his cloak pushed back to reveal his stony expression. The impassive manner in which he watched the heaping mounds of bloody monsters chew up flesh was almost as confronting to Clive as the scene itself. He searched in Jason's expression for the laughing man he had met back in Greenstone, but he had trouble finding it.

Clive thought of the mirage chamber recording from Greenstone where Jason fought Rick Geller's team. Jason was embarrassed by it and the way he played up his monstrous behaviour. The act had been enough to intimidate inexperienced teenagers, at least for a little while. But what Clive had just seen in the tunnel wasn't an act. There was something in Jason now that he'd had to fake back then.

Something all too easy to take out. Clive hoped that it would be as simple to put away again.

"I'm fine, Clive," Jason assured him, although his granite-hard voice was unconvincing. It wasn't the cold malevolence with which he had broken down the will of the messenger, but echoes of that cruelty remained. Jason's gaze did not flinch from the bloody pile of creatures beneath which the messenger was dying.

"It's rude to read my emotions, Jason."

"How could I not when your aura is all but shouting them? It's time for more team exercises in aura control, I think."

The other auras in the tunnel, aside from Clive's own, were of the worms and the messenger. The worms were also an apocalypse beast swarm, yet it seemed like little more than feed before the sanguine horror. The worms exuded animalistic terror as they attempted in vain to escape the all-devouring familiar.

As for the messenger, Clive tried to shut out her aura from his senses. He had seen a lot of combat and death, even for a silver-ranker, but he had never felt a death. Her aura felt broken, shattered by helplessness and despair that dwarfed even the pain of being consumed alive.

"Jason, please just end this."

"They're connected," Jason said in reply.

"What?"

"The messengers. I don't know how it works exactly, but it's to do with an astral king."

"Like you."

"Significantly more powerful than me."

"You think one of them is here? In this world?"

"No. It's a servant of some kind. It's connected to the astral king, the way Colin and Gordon are connected to me, but deeper than that. Because their king is stronger, so is the power it can give its servants. And one of those powers is influence over those who subject themselves to that astral king. Including this messenger."

"So, this servant knows what's happening here?"

"I don't think so, not entirely. Just what's happening to this one. It can feel her pain, her despair."

"So, that's what you're doing? Sending a message to the messengers?"

"Yes."

"I think they've probably gotten it, Jason. So put an end to this."

"Clive, they've killed who knows how many people, turning them into nothing but places to stash these worms."

"Yes, Jason. They're callous and evil. Are you fighting them because we're better than they are, or to prove that you can be worse?"

Jason finally turned from the leech mound the messenger was buried under to look at Clive.

"I don't know," he said in little more than a whisper.

He turned back to the pile.

"*Mine is the judgement, and the judgement is death.*"

Blue, silver and gold light came beaming down from the ceiling and into the leech mound. The leeches were unaffected aside from the mound deflating as the transcendent damage eradicated the messenger.

Ability: [Verdict] (Doom)

- Spell (execute).
- Cost: Moderate mana.
- Cooldown: 30 seconds.

- Current rank: Silver 4 (87%).

- Effect (iron): Deals a small amount of transcendent damage. As an execute effect, damage scales exponentially with the enemy's level of injury.

- Effect (bronze): Damage scaling is increased by instances of [Penance] on the target.

- Effect (silver): Inflicts or refreshes [Sanction] on the target.

- [Sanction] (affliction, holy): Healing, recovery and regeneration effects have diminished potency. Base strength of this effect is very minor but scales exponentially with the enemy's level of injury. Scaling is affected by [Legacy of Sin] in the same way execute damage is. Cannot be cleansed while any instances of [Penance] are present.

After the light of the spell ended, smoke seeped out of the leeches. This was not the rainbow smoke of a monster, however, but akin to the transcendent light of Jason's spell. The smoke itself was blue, with gold and silver light sparkling inside it. Clive postulated that the magic from which a messenger's body was made was more refined than that of a monster. He had heard of similar phenomena around the deaths of very high-rank essence users.

There was also a red haze mixed into the smoke, wet and heavy like the air before a storm. The haze was slowly fading, turning into more sparkling light. Clive could sense the remnant aura of the messenger within it. Jason held out his hand and chanted another spell.

"*As your life was mine to reap, so your death is mine to harvest.*"

The red haze moved towards Jason's hand but struggled like a dog pulling against its leash. Clive felt Jason's aura push out, unleashing a soul attack against the aura. The leash was cut and the life force was dragged out of the aura and into Jason. Clive watched as Jason's nebula eyes glowed bright and his starlight cloak flared out, becoming a shadowy cloud. It took on a shape like a bird silhouette, the stars inside it glowing brightly before the bird shrank down to a cloak once more.

- You have drained life force using [Blood Harvest].
- Health, mana and stamina have been replenished.
- You have gained multiple instances of [Blood Frenzy].

- You have absorbed physical matter with inherent spiritual properties.
- Your readiness to enter a star phoenix state has increased.

- Current star phoenix state readiness: 0.3%

Jason looked down at his glowing hands, his body electrified as if he'd mainlined a bolt of lightning. Clive looked on in concern as a predatory grin crossed Jason's face. The star phoenix state was what Jason turned into rather than dying when his body was killed. It should have been unavailable to him again until he reached gold rank, but now he had a new path forward. That it went through the middle of the messengers did not bother him in the least. If they were going to run around wiping out whole towns to use the people as weapons, he had no qualms about devouring them.

Shade, who had been watching silently, finally spoke up.

"Mr Asano, while I recognise that you are simply accelerating her transition from a physical-spiritual gestalt to a purely spiritual state, the process is extremely traumatic to the soul."

"I know," Jason said softly. "I can feel it."

"Mr Asano, I've warned you in the past about there being some things you don't come all the way back from."

"I'm not coming back. On Earth, people came after me time and time again because they didn't respect me as a threat. You think Jack Gerling would have been so cavalier about killing Kaito, Greg and Asya if he thought I'd peel his soul like a grape in return?"

"Escalation is not a good way to handle a situation, Mr Asano."

"I know. I'm going to need you to stop me from going too far, like when you stopped me from ripping that guy's soul out."

"What?" Clive asked, but Jason ignored the question.

"But I have to be willing to go far enough," Jason continued.

"Is that the person you want to be?" Shade asked.

Jason gave Shade a sad smile.

"You know how much time I've spent brooding about what I was going to turn into," he said. "That time is over. Now the question is about living with what I've become."

This time, the smile he gave Clive and Shade was genuine.

"Sometimes I'm going to have to do things that aren't very nice, and I'm done struggling against the parts of myself that let me do them. I've always been afraid of how easy is to take those parts out when I need them. But accepting them is the only way I'll be able put them away again when I'm done."

Jason looked around at the leeches that grew in number as the number of worms lessened. Some of the worms had fled further into the tunnel and down the stairs leading deeper. A pile of Colin glooped after it, also spilling down the stairs into the areas neither Jason nor Clive had yet seen. Other worms had dug into the hard-packed dirt, digging neat, thin holes. The leeches had followed by digging rough, ugly burrows. Even with many of the leeches departing, there was no shortage left.

- Familiar [Colin] has reached maximum potential biomass for its current rank.

Unlike the world-consuming terror that a sanguine horror could become, Colin was limited by the power of the vessel Jason created for him. He was also infused with Jason's power as an astral king, however, and Jason decided to test what he could accomplish with that. He opened the gate to his soul space and had the excess Colin crawl inside.

Jason followed, arriving in the extradimensional realm within his soul, where he possessed god-like power. They were in one of the many cloud buildings, this one round and empty, with a transparent roof. Colin conglomerated from a leech pile into a blood clone of Jason, looking at his summoner.

"You trust me to try something?" Jason asked.

Colin nodded immediately.

"Just to be clear, I don't know exactly what I'm doing," Jason warned him. "I may be winging it a bit."

Colin opened his mouth to emit a nails-on-chalkboard shriek.

"Hey," Jason complained. "I do so know what I'm doing most of the time. Some of the time, definitely. I make plans."

Another screech.

"My plans are just fine, thank you."

Shriek.

"I'll have you know that I haven't died in more than a year."

Snarling screech.

"Okay, yes, that one was quite close. But I lived. I will admit that the recovery time was longer than I would have liked."

Jason frowned at the blood clone.

"Don't give me that look. I'm just going to start, alright?"

Jason didn't reach out with his senses as, in his soul realm, his senses were already everywhere. Instead, he concentrated on the portion of Colin that was in the realm with him. He explored the nature of the familiar, from the core astral entity to the vessel containing it to the two links that bound it to Jason.

One was the familiar link, which was strong but contractual and impermanent. The other was more tenuous and crudely forged, but permanent. Jason explored that link further as he tapped into the astral throne and astral gate. These two elements of his soul were the core of what had turned his soul into a physical domain.

The crude link was something that Colin had initiated himself while Jason was unconscious, struggling to survive after pushing his limits. What Jason had done to put himself in that position had broken down two extremely powerful items inside his soul. One of these items had been given by a great astral being and the other taken from one by Jason. Each item was intended to be used in specific ways, with specific limitations, but when Jason managed to damage his very soul, the items were damaged with it.

This resulted in the power driving the items being loosed as the items themselves broke down. Jason's soul absorbed large amounts from both, with the rest triggering Jason's loot power, which saved the leftover power from killing him. Jason traded that leftover power away, but what he absorbed had changed him on a fundamental level. It was responsible for the astral throne and astral gate that now resided in his soul, reforging it into a physical realm. And he was the astral king of that realm.

Jason was still in the earliest stage of learning what that meant. Before he had even awoken, however, two of his familiars had made use of it. As Jason was just learning, astral kings could bestow powers through a bond. His existing familiar bonds served as an invitation, allowing Colin and Gordon to accept that bond while Jason remained unconscious.

Jason had never actively attempted to manipulate that bond, but now did so for the first time. Working by instinct and moving with caution, Jason tapped into the astral throne and astral gate. He was still inexpert in wielding their power, which Dawn had cautioned him to leave alone, especially the astral gate. Naturally, that was what Jason had used the most.

The astral throne governed matter and physical forces, and Jason used it to refine Colin's physical vessel. The astral gate affected the spiritual, and dimensional forces, which he used to modify the nature of the connections between Colin, Jason and the physical vessel Colin inhabited.

- You have attempted to disconnect the portion of familiar vessel [Colin] in your astral kingdom from the main host.
- If disconnected, the portion of the vessel can be claimed by the main host by entering the astral kingdom, up to the biomass limit for its rank.
- Disconnected vessel portions will not count against the biomass limit of the main host.
- Destruction of the main host vessel will result in the main host returning to the astral kingdom and claiming the disconnected vessel portion, up to the biomass limit for its rank.

The blood clone splashed down as it turned into blood, Colin's consciousness no longer contained in that portion of it. Jason used his ability to control physics to avoid any landing on him. He then manipulated the large, round building around him. The walls turned from cloud stuff to black brick with a dark red sheen. The translucent ceiling turned into dark greenhouse glass and the floor into thick, rich soil. A pit formed in the middle of the room and the blood immediately flowed into it, barely covering the floor at the bottom. The air grew hazy and humid as plants grew from the soil, dark green, lush and leafy.

The end result was like a dark jungle greenhouse, built around an almost empty pit of blood. Jason was confident that Colin would like it. Jason's experiment worked out quite well, as his intention was to create a storehouse of biomass for Colin. The leech familiar frequently had much of it destroyed in combat, and replenishing it took time.

Having a storehouse of it meant that Colin could be ready to return to the fight much faster. That was predicated on taking the time to fill the pit, however. Colin would be working on that right now, feeding on the worms outside of Jason's soul realm.

Or was it astral kingdom? Jason had changed what he called the dimensional space inside himself several times. This was partly as it developed and changed, and partly as the names for all Jason's interdimensional assets blurred into a confusing mess. Was 'astral kingdom' what the realms of astral kings were properly known as? Was it what the messengers called it? Jason's interface had shown the ability many times to properly label things when even Jason didn't know the name.

Gordon manifested, floating over the blood pool. The eye-orbs around him rapidly flickered in complex patterns.

"Yes, I'll see what I can do for you too," Jason told him. "Not right now, though. We have to go fight more evil."

More flickering.

"Yes, I know I took the time with Colin, but he has all these worms to eat and he'd already gained his maximal biomass. It was the perfect time to try."

Flickering, with long, bright pauses.

"No, I'm not going to do Shade first. For one, he isn't linked to me the way you are. And I can promise you, he does not want the ability to turn into Herbie the Love Bug. He even threatened to do that once."

Flickering.

"Yes, it would probably be in shades of black and dark grey."

65

EVIL LAIR

JASON EMERGED FROM HIS SOUL SPACE, CLOAK AND HOOD BACK IN PLACE. IN THE tunnel beneath the town, Clive was looking at the empty space where the messenger had died. There was no visible trace after Jason's execute spell left not so much as a single drop of blood. Instead, there was a pile of dirty clothes and the orb she had used to avoid the worms. Clive was searching her clothes for anything else left behind, but stood up on Jason's return.

"You handled that with unexpected ease," Clive said. "I expected more from the messengers."

"It didn't feel so easy. I was impaled a lot of times. There was a spear inside my head and it exploded."

"Now that our bodies are generalised magical flesh, your ability to infuse yours with additional life force is more useful. You can shrug off formidable injury."

"Exactly. That would have been rough if I hadn't topped up before coming down here. Also, I think she was as weak a messenger as we can expect to face," Jason said. "The one Shade and I spied on was stronger, even within the same rank. And she didn't lose because of a lack in power. She lost because of a weak mentality."

"You played on the messenger superiority fixation," Clive said. "Used the various quirks you possess to shake her."

"That will only work on the weak-minded ones," Jason said. "I sensed a vulnerability in her emotions and exploited it. She was lesser amongst her kind, so she already had a subconscious inferiority complex. Most won't break as easily, and I won't often get the chance to try."

"So, you saw a weakness and preyed on it," Clive said. "How much of what you said to her did you mean?"

"I played up the melodrama, but it all came from somewhere. I may have embellished, but I didn't lie."

"Jason, are you alright?"

"I'm fine."

"You didn't sound fine. You sounded ready to twist the heads off puppies and drink their insides."

"I just told you about the melodrama. I'm okay, Clive, really. I've put the evil hat away for now, and my familiars helped me stay balanced. I'm about as good as you could ask for, given the horrors that have taken place in this town. I'm more worried about you."

"Me?"

"Clive, the entire population of this town were killed and turned into meat puppets for alien worms. It won't be the only town like this either. I don't know how much you've sensed about what was happening up there while we were down here, but the team cleared out all the hosts. I imagine that with everything going on down here, you subconsciously suppressed your sense of smell."

Clive concentrated on his olfactory senses, realising that Jason was right. His nose was immediately choked with the cloying stench of death, drifting down from above. His tongue was coated in the coppery taste of blood and he almost gagged. It was not a physiological reaction but a mental one, driven by disgust. His supernatural senses expanded, filling him in on the killing field that had once been a town.

As shaken as Clive was, he had only seen the early stages of the fight. He could feel the team's unstable emotions, ranging from numb horror through grim determination to burning rage. Suddenly, Jason breaking the will of the messenger responsible before killing her did not seem like such an overreaction.

"The messenger didn't go up in rainbow smoke," Jason said.

Clive knew his friend was only trying to distract him, but welcomed it.

"Refined magic in their bodies," Clive explained. "I'm more interested in the red haze that was in their death smoke."

"Remnant life force," Jason said. "Normally, transcendent damage would wipe that out when the body is completely eradicated, but the life of messengers is not just physical. It's tenacious, which is why I had to fight her soul down to take it. Resurrection magic doesn't work on messengers. Or anyone like them."

"Like you?"

"Yeah. But I have my own thing going on."

"Is that what that bird form your cloak took on was? That looked like a star phoenix."

"You know star phoenixes?"

"They're a symbol commonly associated with the Celestial Book."

"I forgot you were in the bag for a great astral being. Didn't really know what that meant when you told me. You're not in a cult or an order or something, are you?"

"No. Those of us that venerate the Celestial Book maintain a loose network, with ties to the Magic Society and the Church of Knowledge. I haven't been keeping in touch very often since the Magic Society and I parted ways. They'd be very interested in you."

"There's a little too much of that going around," Jason said. "Thus, the false identity."

"You aren't hiding your real one very well."

"If the fake story falls apart, then fine," Jason said. "These may be the only real adventuring years I have. I'm not going to waste them pretending."

"What do you mean, the only real adventuring years?"

"I don't know what Dawn told you about what's coming," Jason said. "She didn't want me to ask, so I didn't. But something's waiting for me down the road, Clive, and it's not good."

"I'm not meant to talk about it," Clive said. "But Dawn excluded me when she talked to the others. I don't know why."

"Because she knew that you'd figure out something you shouldn't. Shouldn't yet, at least."

"It's not like you to accept secrets being held over your fate, Jason."

"I trust Dawn. Not her boss, but her."

Jason turned to look down the tunnel, but instead of heading in, reached out to Humphrey through voice chat.

"You need us to come up?"

"You're alive, then," Rufus said. "We were sensing the fight down there."

"I told you he'd be fine," Neil said. "Probably got another stupid power out of it."

"More like a new way to use an old one," Jason said.

"Wait, you actually did?" Neil exclaimed. "That is a pile of heidel sh—"

"What about the messenger?" Humphrey asked, cutting Neil off. "Was that her dying we sensed?"

"Yeah," Jason said.

"Felt like she went out rough," Sophie said. "Good."

"We're mopping up out here," Rufus said. "We're definitely not done, but it's finally looking like the town is running out of hosts. I don't think we need the help."

"We can't spare anyone, but I don't think we need the help," Humphrey said. "Explore the hidden area and see if there's anything else we need to deal with."

Jason and Clive shared a grim look. While they both hoped to find little downstairs, they feared encountering fresh horrors.

"Let's go," Jason said. "I have a bad feeling that the other adventuring teams are finding much the same right now, all across the region."

"Will that be alright with just the two of us? At the very least, a lot of worms escaped down there."

"Any that haven't been eaten yet will be too scared of Colin to come for me," Jason assured him. "And as for you..."

Jason looked at the messenger's clothes, piled at Clive's feet with the orb on top of them. Using his aura, Jason floated it up in front of Clive.

"...that should keep you safe."

Clive reached out and took the ball.

"Are you worried about how much you're like them?" he asked.

"I can't change it, so there's no point worrying about it," Jason said. "I'm trying to make that my new personal philosophy. See if I can't cut back on the brooding."

Jason flashed Clive a smile, but it wasn't quite right. They could both still smell the blood and death in the air. Clive nodded at him and they set off down the brick tunnel.

"If being like the messengers gives me something I can use," Jason said, "I'm going to use it. So long as I don't end up hurting people the way they do."

"I don't think it's their powers," Clive said as they reached the top of the stairs and peered down. "I think they just have a culture of being detestable scum."

The large slate bricks from which the hidden basement was built continued down the stairs and into a wide chamber lit by glow stones in a ceiling that stood two storeys high, with catwalks roaming around the upper level. Arched doorways led into side chambers, but the main chamber itself had plenty to look at. Clive knew a magical workshop when he saw one, with workbenches, freestanding magical tools and magically driven vents in the ceiling and walls. Most prominent were massive vats, some empty and some teeming with worms swimming in sickly yellow fluid.

Even at a glance, it was clear that this was the centre in which the worms had been bred, and not just because of the worms crawling around, being hunted and devoured by Colin. The stairs were slick with ichor from where worms had already met their end.

As they descended, they spotted four glass cylinders that had been obscured by the vats from their initial vantage. These were just the right size to hold people, and three of the vats had elves inside. Jason and Clive extended their senses, quickly realising that the occupants were dead.

They moved towards the centre of the chamber, which had an open workspace with long, clean tables. Worms writhed around the room with leeches in pursuit, but they avoided Jason and the orb in Clive's hand.

"What do you think?" Jason asked, standing in the middle of the chamber. "My magical studies were all astral magic, not whatever passes for biological sciences. I know an evil lair when I see one, though. Catwalks over monster breeding vats are bit of a giveaway."

Clive looked at the catwalks, which had no ladders or stairs to reach them. He guessed that the messenger, who could float around everywhere, had only used them to rest objects on while working. This was reinforced by the crates on them that he guessed were filled with whatever served as nutrient supply for the vats. He desperately hoped it wasn't chunks of people.

"Am I imagining it," Jason asked, "or do the messengers have much better aura shielding magic than us? My senses can't get out of here any more than they could get in."

"The party interface is still active," Clive observed. "It can't be a complete seal. But if you can't extend your senses past these walls, that's probably the case. Securing an area against perception requires a lot of infrastructure and special materials, at least by any magic we know. I'm guessing this place just has ritual circles in place behind these slate tile walls."

Clive's senses weren't as strong as Jason's, but his perception power excelled at recognising and analysing in-place magical effects, like rituals. That allowed him to notice things that even Jason's perception missed.

"There's something going on with that section of wall," he said, pointing. "Also, in the floor, in the middle of the room. You want to take the floor while I look at the wall?"

"Belinda will be of more use to you than me," Jason said. "I'll swap out with her."

He opened the voice chat to the rest of the team again. "How is it going up there?"

"We think we've just about run out of townsfolk," Humphrey said in a haunted voice. "It's... it's bad up here."

"I know," Jason said softly. "I'm sorry you had to go through that."

His own voice was haunted by the thousands of dead he'd been unable to save in Broken Hill and Makassar on Earth. Just as he'd had to fight the victims after they were brought back to life, Humphrey and the team had cut down all the townsfolk already reduced to hosts for the worms.

"We're going to get the messengers back for this," Sophie snarled. "They think they can just use people however they want."

"Getting the messengers back doesn't matter," Humphrey said. "What's important is stopping them from doing this again. But if that means killing them all, then that can't be helped."

Jason couldn't think of anything that marked the severity of what the team had been through more than a bloodthirsty Humphrey. Even under the current circumstances, it came as a shock.

"I'll come up, and swap out with Lindy," Jason said. "We've found some kind of magic workshop, so she'll be more use than I am down here."

He extended his senses through the room, determining that few of the worms remained. Colin, on the other hand, was growing close to his maximum potential biomass again.

"Colin, leave enough to clean up the last worms and have the rest follow me. Gather yourself together so we can go outside."

All around the room, leeches melted into pools of blood. Wet strips of ragged bandage shot out of them, tangling together at the bottom of the stairs. The blood pools flowed quickly along the bandages, swiftly coagulating into Colin's blood clone form. It followed Jason up the stairs.

66

IMPERFECT RESPONSES

THE MESSENGER JES FIN KAAL HOVERED JUST OVER THE FLAT ROOF OF A circular tower in a messenger stronghold. She was looking out over the rainforest contemplatively when another messenger floated up through the round hole in the middle of the roof. It was the dark-skinned and silver-haired Hess Jor Nasala, who was subordinate to Kaal. Not only was Kaal gold rank to his silver, but she was also a Voice of the Will.

"Our agents in the city have reached out," he reported. "The investigation into them has been suspended for the moment as the Adventure Society moves to respond to the world-taker worms. As you predicted, they are committing significant forces to the eradication, now they have discovered the threat. They are moving even more quickly than anticipated."

"Will that affect the readiness of our forces?" Kaal asked, not turning her eyes from the vista.

"It will not, Voice. The wing leaders are prepared to move on the city at your command."

Kaal nodded. "Inform the wing commander that he may move at his discretion," Kaal ordered. "But first, I would like to hear you out on something."

"It would be my honour, Voice Kaal."

"Since my arrival here, I have found your counsel to be sound, Hess Jor Nasala. I am grappling with an issue and would value your perspective."

"Of course."

"Pei Vas Kartha is dead."

Hess frowned in thought until he recalled the name.

"One of the worm breeders? My understanding is that we assigned the least of us to those positions exactly because of the risk."

"Indeed, we did," Kaal said. "That choice, however, has now presented us with an unanticipated problem."

"There was an issue with Pei Vas Kartha's death?"

"Yes. We have an enemy who, through intention or happenstance, has found a way to bring us trouble."

"How so?"

"I felt Pei Vas Kartha's death. It was ugly, but that, in and of itself, is not the concern. The problem is that before she died, her will was broken. She came to accept that something stood above the messengers in superiority."

"Then she was deserving of death. I see now why sending the least of us was a problem. What of the others?"

"Most escaped. Several died, but none in shame, like Pei Vas Kartha. I believe what happened to her does not reflect a new approach by the enemy forces, but an individual within them."

"You believe it is this man Asano?"

"I consider it likely. I have dangerous suspicions about him."

"Dangerous?"

"Do you think it is possible for there to be a silver-rank astral king? One that does not come from within our own kind, no less?"

"In my experience, Voice, it is best not to count anything as wholly impossible."

"Wise," she said with a nod. "What do you see as the central problem in finding an approach to deal with Asano?"

Hess did not respond immediately and gave the question consideration.

"Ambiguity," he said after thinking it over. "Any action we take has the potential to ripple negatively through our people. If he truly is an astral king, do we venerate him or strike him down? If we venerate someone not a messenger, it undermines the core tenets of our people's pride and self-image. If we eliminate him, it undermines the absolute authority of the astral kings."

"Yes," Kaal agreed. "But there is an aspect that makes that question of whether to kill him not a question at all."

"That if he truly is an astral king, he deserves veneration."

"Exactly. If he is not, that simplifies things. If he is, he is more complicated to respond to as a threat."

"Do we need to respond at all?" Hess asked.

"Yes," Kaal said. "The death of Pei Vas Kartha is the beginning, not the end. If we leave him free to wreak havoc, he will."

Hess frowned.

"If we are going to target him, the knowledge of what he did to Pei Vas Kartha may give our less strong-willed people reason to hesitate. If one of us is willing to acknowledge this man as superior, what if he is? Allowing seeds of doubt to be planted into the soil of our faith is dangerous."

"But if we keep what he did a secret, it will be fine so long as it remains a secret. If not, we'll be seen as tacitly acknowledging his superiority, seeking to crush him before the truth spreads."

"Are our people so weak-willed that they would be swayed so easily?"

"We are a people built on a faith that everyone we oppress seeks to challenge. Doubt is no more than a pinprick to the faithful, but a pinprick that carries poison.

Enough poison will bring down even the mightiest beast. And even in our own ranks, there are those who would question our values."

"The unorthodoxy," Hess said, his expression troubled.

"This man who killed Pei Vas Kartha, be it Asano or someone else, offers us only imperfect responses to his deed. Whatever we do, including nothing at all, will bring complications. My greatest concern is if this was their intention. That suggests an enemy not to be taken lightly."

Hess did not respond, knowing better than to talk for the sake of it. Instead, he considered the problem at hand while gazing out from atop the tower. After musing on it for some time, he spoke up.

"Perhaps we need to recontextualise how we see him," he suggested. "While the forces of the astral kings may come into conflict, we are unused to viewing an astral king as an external enemy. If we can resolve his identity as an enemy with his identity as an astral king, it may be possible to turn him from a problem into a solution."

"Go on," Kaal told him.

"The Adventure Society and the rulers of the elven city know about the natural array and the threat it poses, not just to us but to them. They have even sent diplomatic envoys more than once. The wing commander executed them, of course. While assistance would be useful, we cannot be seen working with the servant races. But we need essence users to deal with the array, which is why we have been enslaving them."

"I have seen these servants," Kaal said. "Those who will kneel before us are too weak-willed to resist the array's effects."

"But if an astral king were to be the representative of the local denizens, that would be an acceptable alliance. We can have them send those with the required strength of will."

Kaal finally turned to look at Hess.

"An interesting idea. An astral king is an acceptable ally, but we must be sure that it is an astral king we are dealing with. He needs to be tested."

"Use Fal Vin Garath. He lacks leadership and strategic abilities, but every messenger is superior in their own way. Even if he dies to Asano, he will die fighting, not kneeling."

Kaal nodded. "Have the wing commander detach a group in the city attack to target Asano specifically. If he is hard to track as our agents have suggested, target his team."

"And if Asano hides during the attack?"

"Then that itself is an answer."

The town was a killing field, blanketed in dead. The elves had been enemies, but really, they were victims. The worms had not just killed them but had driven their bodies to attack the team. As a result, the people Jason and his companions had been there to save were stacked in corpse piles across the town.

The powers of essence users were unkind in their violence. Bodies were piled up in mounds, men, women and children left in states that were chilling to look at. Flesh scorched or rotted black. Severed limbs, hewn torsos and heads cleft apart.

Now that the fighting was mostly over, the team had time to see what they had made of what had looked like an ordinary happy town on their arrival. Knowing that the parasitic worms had sealed the fate of the town long before their arrival was cold comfort as they made their way through the thousands of dead that carpeted the streets.

At some stage, whatever mind that controlled them decided to take what hosts remained and fled. This left the team to the grim task of hunting them down, which felt uncomfortably like following up a massacre of civilians by eliminating the fleeing witnesses. Jason returned to the team, who were moving as a loose group through the town.

"We're not having trouble catching the elves serving as worm-hosts," Humphrey told Jason. "The elves can't outrun me, let alone Sophie. The problem is the worms that have been crawling off on their own. They've gone into the trees, the houses, the rice fields; we're pretty sure some of them just started digging down. With your senses and Shade's bodies for mobility, you can find and deal with them quicker than the rest of us combined."

Sophie returned in a blur, stopping in front of Jason. She peered into his dark hood.

"What are you doing?" he asked.

"I noticed this earlier," she said, "but I can see your head."

"I can see your head too," he told her.

"You can see his head?" Humphrey asked as the others crammed themselves next to Sophie to look into Jason's hood.

"What exactly is going on?" Jason asked, acting disgruntled. He knew the team was trying to distract themselves from the horrors around them and the part they played in it. If ignoring it with a little forced humour helped them cope even a little better, he was happy to play along. He remembered his own similar experience on Earth and wanted the team to deal with it better than he had under similar circumstances.

"Your hood used to completely hide your head," Humphrey said. "It was just darkness in there. Then you came back and we could see your eyes, but nothing else. Now we can see your head. Kind of. The silhouette of your head."

"Especially your chin," Sophie said. "With your rank-ups and your beard, it seemed a lot less pointy than before. Seeing it stick out of the dark like that, though, you're really reminded that you could put someone's eye out with that thing."

"It does not stick out," Jason insisted. "If it did, you'd have noticed it long ago. My cloak's appearance changed back in Rimaros, and you're only spotting the difference now?"

"In fairness," Rufus said, arriving to join the group, "your cloak also looks like you're wearing a portal now. You can't blame us for missing a relatively minor detail."

"I don't know that 'minor' is the word," Belinda said.

"Lindy, go help Clive," Jason told her. "He found some magic doors."

"I'll head off, then," she said agreeably. "If I need to pick a lock, I'll call and you can bring your chin."

While most of the team continued to round up elves, Jason went hunting worms that had left their hosts. He swept his senses over the town to find them and deployed Shade's bodies as shadow-jumping targets. As for dealing with the worms, that was Colin's area, with occasional help from Gordon. Most of the worms were making their way through the rice paddies, where Jason would sprinkle a few leeches and move on. Whether hidden in the water or buried in the mud, Colin would find and devour the lesser apocalypse beast.

Some of the worms had climbed into trees, hiding in the upper reaches. Gordon used his beam to cut off branches or even topple the entire tree, giving Colin easy access to them. It was a similar case in buildings where worms had hidden under floorboards or between wall panels. Gordon opened them up and Colin happily undertook his grisly work.

They wanted to be thorough in eradicating the worms, as there were uncertainties about how they reproduced. They did not match Colin, who could eat to multiply, but they had at least some means of self-replication. The worms could soak up the life energy in healing magic used on their hosts to reproduce, although there were possibly limits to that. Otherwise, what was the point of the underground breeding centre?

Carlos had given them some information about the creatures, but his knowledge was far from comprehensive. The worms were not a native species to Pallimustus, which was fortunate but made information hard to come by. Hunting down the errant worms might have been critical or futile; they just didn't know. It was more likely than not that there were many towns in similar situations.

Jason made several wide-ranging passes over and around the town to be sure as he could that he'd gotten them all. He then reconvened with the team back in the underground worm-breeding facility. Colin had finished the last of the worms there, the leeches Jason left behind clearing out the last ones that had escaped down the stairs. Colin had then moved onto the ones floating in vats, swimming through the unappealing yellow liquid.

Clive and Belinda spent that time assessing the place. The two anomalies that Clive had spotted were places where hidden doors would open by shifting sections of wall or floor. Belinda had traced out the doors and the opening mechanisms, but hadn't triggered them yet. She wanted to carefully assess them for traps and other fail-safes before taking any action.

"Why secret doors?" Neil wondered. "This place is secret already, right?"

"Maybe it was from when they were first setting up," Clive postulated. "There's no way all this was put in place without people noticing things, even using magic. They would need collaborators with authority, like the mayor or some influential local elders. Whatever is behind these doors might have been the things the messengers were worried would give the collaborators second thoughts."

"Once you're helping someone turn everyone in your town into a worm-incubating corpse," Neil said, "I think you're past the point of second thoughts."

"Perhaps that was the point," Belinda suggested. "These vats are all in the open now, but there are signs of them having been moved. The messengers might have convinced the collaborators that it was a more conventional attack. Stockpiling weapons or something, good old-fashioned treason. In the meantime, the first batch of worms was being cultivated in the hidden rooms. Once the collaborators don't matter, are in too deep or have just been infested themselves, the operation expands and the vats come out."

"Would they actually work with elves, though? Aren't all we non-messenger races too unworthy to work alongside?"

"Given that any collaborators are doubtless worm-filled corpses right now, I doubt the messengers thought of it like that. They wanted it to be secret, so they used the people of this town as necessary. I doubt they even thought of turning on them as a betrayal."

"It doesn't matter what happened or why," Sophie said. "The Adventure Society will be crawling over this place soon enough. Let them figure it out. I just want to find the ones who think they can do this to people and bury my fist in their heads."

"We'll have some answers once we open these doors," Belinda said. "Maybe that will help us find a head for you to put a fist inside of."

She was crouched down in front of the secret door set into one of the walls. She had drawn a variety of sigils around it and left strange-looking magical tools lying around.

"I don't know enough about their aura magic to stop the trap on this door from being triggered when we open it," Belinda explained. "I'm disconnecting the trap altogether, so we should be able to trigger it and have nothing happen."

"*Should* be able to?" Neil asked.

"If you don't think I'll get it right," Belinda told him, "you can disconnect the trap yourself. You want to take over?"

He held up his hands in surrender.

"That's what I thought," she said, turning back to her work. "This trap is a bit funny, though."

"Funny how?" Humphrey asked.

"The trap isn't pointing out."

"Not pointing out?" Humphrey asked. "What do you mean?"

"I mean that this door was rigged so that if you open it, you kill whoever is inside, not whoever is out here."

"That implies prisoners," Rufus said. "I think we'd best get that door open as quickly as it can be done safely."

"And here was me about to take a sandwich break," Belinda said.

"It's not necessarily prisoners," Humphrey said. "The messengers are happy to use an apocalypse beast as a weapon. It could be some other dangerous creature."

"Using an apocalypse beast," Jason muttered reproachfully, shaking his head. "The maniacs."

The team all turned to give him a flat look.

"What?" he asked innocently.

67

TRIAGE

In the worm-breeding facility hidden under the town, Jason and his team gathered around as Belinda prepared to open the hidden door. Inside could be anything from an empty room to a wildly dangerous entity, so they were prepared to spring into action. When she finally triggered the door, a whole section of the slate brick wall shifted backwards and to the side, revealing a large opening.

The room inside was dark, with only the floating lights from the main chamber outside the door providing any illumination. That didn't stop Jason as he took stock of the room, his Midnight Eyes power easily piercing the dark. The chamber was large, at least half the size of the facility's central space. Cages were set out in rows, overstuffed with squalid, miserable elves.

Motes of starlight lifted off from Jason's cloak and floated into the room, filling it with a soft, silvery light. Not only did this allow the rest of the team to see, but caused a stir amongst the prisoners. Few of their auras flickered with hope, however, and the sounds were mostly fearful whimpers.

The elves were dirty from living in their own filth; men, women and children were all crowded with barely room to sit, their knees pulled up against their chests. Their auras shouted out their misery and suffering, but also that they were alive and not worm-hosts. There were dozens of survivors, all crammed into cages.

Jason noted that if the cages were absent, they would have been no less trapped, but conditions would have been far more humane. They would have had room to lie down for what sleep they could manage on the cold slate floor. They could have relieved themselves on one side of the room and stayed on the other, instead of being forced to go where they sat.

Jason felt his rage echo through the auras of his companions, but none of them let it leak out. They were not going to spook the prisoners that had been through more than enough already. Instead, they took joy in the fact that anyone survived, even if it was just a fragment of the town's population.

The team immediately went to work, Neil taking charge as the team healer. Humphrey and Neil used their superior strength to pull open cages. Sophie heavily pushed out her aura while the others withdrew theirs. Out of everyone in the team, Sophie's was the most reassuring and calming of the group.

Ability: [Cleansing Breeze] (Wind)

- Aura (recovery).
- Base cost: None.
- Cooldown: None.

- Current rank: Silver 4 (12%).

- Effect (iron): Allies within the aura have increased resistance to curses, diseases, magic afflictions, poisons and unholy afflictions. Cleansing abilities used on allies within the aura have increased effect. Toxins are purged from the air within the aura.

- Effect (bronze): Allies within the aura are continually cleansed of curses, diseases, magic afflictions, poisons and unholy afflictions. Mana and stamina recovery effects on allies have greater effect.

- Effect (silver): When this ability cleanses an affliction from an ally, they gain an instance of [Integrity].

- [Integrity] (heal-over-time, mana-over-time, stamina-over-time, holy): Periodically recover a small amount of health, stamina and mana. Additional instances have a cumulative effect.

Despite the name, Sophie's aura didn't create a literal breeze. Instead, a refreshing spiritual wave passed over the caged prisoners, purging the toxins and diseases that had accumulated while they were all crammed in together. It was an incongruous power within Sophie's set, which primarily focused on speed and violence.

The aura was the most direct expression of her soul, but was also shaped by the tools used to unlock her aura power. The essence and awakening stone involved were large factors, but even so, aura powers were considered to be the ones most impacted by the nature of the person awakening the power. For Sophie, most of her power set reflected the face she showed the world: swift and untouchable. Yet the power that should represent her the most was nurturing and protective.

An awkward expression crossed Sophie's face as she pushed her aura out, as if exposing a vulnerability. Belinda gave her a quick, reassuring hug from behind and Humphrey flashed her a beaming smile.

The others also employed the power of their auras, careful to avoid being imposing. Sophie's aura turned the diseases and toxins the elves suffered in their squalor into healing boons, and Belinda's aura enhanced those boons. Humphrey's aura gave them a much-needed boost in strength and stamina. It seemed they had been fed and watered, but just enough to keep most of them alive. The team found dead amongst their number as well, two elderly people and a young child.

The team's auras were far from enough to settle the prisoners after all they had been through. Even though the team was clearly not the messengers, the prisoners became agitated at the new intruders into their hell. Sophie's aura at least managed to prevent things from escalating; a panicked stampede could easily have led to deaths. Most of the people in the cages were normal townsfolk, without the constitution to endure such conditions for long.

The way the team had been built from the outset, back in Greenstone, meant that leadership did not always fall to Humphrey. The team took Neil's directions as he started the process of triage. His abilities, along with Sophie's aura, would help the initial management of the prisoners as they extracted them from the tight cages.

Neil specifically had Jason not help, despite the usefulness of his cleansing power. The nature of Jason's powers would do more harm than good when dealing with these people, already teetering on a ragged edge. The last thing they needed was an ominous man feeding on their sins.

Jason joined the others, helping to clear space in the main room. Jason, Rufus and Humphrey shifted tables and equipment under Clive's direction, as only he and Belinda could point out which things were dangerous to move. Belinda started by conjuring tarps that she tossed over the worm vats, now empty courtesy of Colin. They still contained sickly yellow fluid, streaked with red.

They made a space at the side of the room near the stairs, where Belinda conjured bunks and a treatment table for Neil to use. The team was not ready to lead the people up those stairs, for two main reasons. One was that many or most of the prisoners weren't in a state to climb them. The other was that the space upstairs was filled with dead, which was bad for both mentality and hygiene.

Despite the horrifying conditions, and the doubtless horrifying circumstances that brought them about, the prisoners were the lucky ones. The people above, who had already been implanted with worms, would never get any chance to recover.

Most of the people the prisoners knew were scattered around the town above, not just dead but violently torn apart while fighting the team. Jason and the others were not going to let them see that, and a gruesome stew of pity, anger and shame sat heavy in their bellies.

Aside from one special group that Neil had quickly assessed as being in no danger, they started moving patients to the treatment and recovery area the team had set up. Neil went to work in earnest as he directed the rest of the team to manage patients. First step was a cursory assessment by Neil, followed by a quick shower. A simple cistern shower was about as much complexity as Belinda could conjure, but it was enough. Jason pulled out a barrel of crystal wash to fill it, making the shower cool but effective. Priority went to the next person on Neil's triage list for focused treatment, followed by anyone else who had been through his initial assessment. A few he determined too weak for the shower, so Belinda conjured a bath. While she managed the shower, Jason washed the more delicate people, his telekinetic aura gentler. It didn't disturb those being washed, because they were the ones too far gone to notice what was happening to them. It was hidden from onlookers by the deep bath.

The recovery beds were bunked by necessity of space. Bottom bunks went to the most delicate patients, usually after Neil was done with them. Others had been deemed by Neil to not require treatment. A few were able to climb the bunk ladders, but most were carefully assisted onto the higher bunks by Humphrey and Rufus.

Clive had been directed by Neil to warm up the cold room with ritual magic. The adventurers were unconcerned by the cold chamber, but the prisoners were mostly normal people covered in filthy rags. Clive drew out a ritual in the air over the treatment area. The golden light of the ritual drawing turned to a warm glow as Clive chanted out the final element of the ritual.

"Is that the Healer's Hearth ritual?" Neil asked him, neither his hands nor eyes leaving the patient on his table.

"Yes," Clive confirmed. "Rather than radiate warmth, it will gently impart it directly into their bodies."

"Good job."

Once they had processed the bulk of the prisoners, Humphrey pulled Rufus and Jason aside to discuss their next move. Humphrey activated a privacy screen so the prisoners wouldn't overhear them.

"What are we going to do with these people?" Humphrey asked. "Those beds will do for now, but we can't leave them there. We can't take them upstairs, though. Should we leave them here until support arrives from the city?"

"I agree we can't take them up into the town," Rufus said. "If they see what's happened to their town, their friends and their families, they'll suffer all the more."

"Their reaction to that would be unpredictable," Jason concurred. "We need to keep them as calm as we can manage, under the circumstances. We got lucky with Sophie's aura power being so out of character for her."

"It's not out of character," Humphrey said. "It's who she is behind all the spikes and walls. She's always wanted to be good, but the world never gave her that chance."

He looked at Jason.

"You gave her that. I wish it had been me."

"You shouldn't," Jason told him. "It sets up an uneven power dynamic. If you'd been the one to get her out of her old life, that would hang over you your whole lives."

"He's right," Rufus said. "It creates an imbalance that I've seen poison relationships, but this isn't the time for that conversation; stay on task."

Humphrey nodded.

"We need to open the floor in case there are more prisoners," he said. "But we can't do that while the prisoners we've already released are still here. It could be anything down there, and if something comes out, looking for a fight, we can't guarantee their safety. We also have to deal with any complications from the prisoners we left in the other room."

"Sending them to Yaresh with your team's ridiculous number of portals and teleport powers has to be the way to go," Rufus said.

"Portalling them is the obvious solution," Jason agreed. "Assuming they can handle the trip."

Humphrey queried Neil through voice chat after glancing to make sure the distraction wouldn't be harmful.

"They should be able to endure it, once I'm done," Neil said. "We can space out the most delicate ones and make sure I'm waiting on the other side."

They left Neil to his work, resuming their private conversation.

"We need somewhere to portal them to," Humphrey said. "Somewhere that we all know well enough to set as a destination."

"That pretty much means the camping ground where the vehicles are parked," Jason said.

"It's not a bad choice," Rufus said. "Open space, away from the heart of the city. We just need to have them make some room and set up a camp. The Church of the Healer are the people to approach for that."

"That'll work," Jason said. "I've had to portal survivors out of a wiped-out town before, and that's how we did it. Shade, you know what we need. Can you get Rufus' mum to light a fire under the Church of the Healer?"

"I already have, Mr Asano."

"Good man."

UNQUESTIONABLY AUTHORITARIAN

Neil was checking the low-priority patients at his triage station. The more critical cases were already stashed on bunked recovery beds, with the remainder those who were comfortably self-mobile. These were the people that had endured the best and gotten the most from what Sophie and Humphrey's aura powers offered. In most cases, this was the handful of iron-rankers who had lived in the town. Not adventurers, but agriculture specialists with essences like earth and plant.

Sophie continued to assist Neil while the rest of the team returned to the cage room and the last of the prisoners there, where one cage still contained people. Unlike the townsfolk, who were all elves, this group of five had only two elves, plus a human, a celestine and a smoulder. They weren't just caged but unconscious and chained up, with magical seals on the shackles around their wrists, ankles and necks, chaining them to the cage. The cage itself was also the most heavy-duty one in the room.

The shackles suppressed their auras, which had allowed them to go unnoticed until the team found them while shuffling out prisoners. They were stripped naked and filthy, but the athletic physique and attractive features of essence users shone through. They reminded Jason of when he had first met the infuriatingly handsome Rufus, who had looked good even after climbing out of a cannibal's cage.

"An adventuring team?" Humphrey posited.

"We need to get those shackles off to check their rank," Clive said. "Lindy, think you can pop them?"

"Hold on," Jason said and pushed his senses out.

He forced his aura through the suppressive effects of the shackles to touch their souls directly.

"Bronze rank," he said.

The others turned to look at him.

"What?" he asked.

"I might have to ask Lord Pensinata if I can join in that aura training," Rufus said.

Belinda entered the cage; the door had already been yanked off by Humphrey. She examined not the shackles first, but the people.

"Drugged, I think," she said. "These shackles seem to be preventing Sophie's aura from purging whatever they've been dosed with."

She then moved on to the bindings themselves.

"Usual suppression shackle situation," she said. "Forcibly remove them and it'll kill the wearer. Straightforward locks, though. Generic keys should handle it."

Belinda took out a set of magic keys, similar to ones Jason had occasionally crafted in the past. In addition to Belinda's being higher rank, the craftsmanship was far superior to Jason's crude efforts. She used the keys on the shackles, setting loose the probable adventurers. Humphrey took blankets from his inventory to cover their nakedness as they started to stir. Sophie's aura was now affecting them, eliminating the toxins keeping them knocked out.

"Let's leave them to the friendly guy," Rufus said. "Waking up to a bunch of silver-rankers looming over them probably won't be helpful."

"Who's the friendly guy?" Humphrey asked, prompting the others to all turn and look at him. "It's me?"

"Yes, Humphrey, it's you," Jason said. "You're nice and handsome in a way that makes others feel comforted. Which is way better than someone so handsome you just look at them and feel bad about yourself as a person."

"That is the single worst compliment I have ever gotten," Rufus said.

"And what makes you think I was talking about you, Mr Vain?"

Rufus raised an eyebrow at Jason.

"Fine, I was talking about you."

"They're waking up," Humphrey said. "Go away."

Jason gave a derisive snort as he turned to leave.

"Rude. So much for being the nice one."

The team had little more to do than wait, trying not to let their minds dwell on the dead, scattered in piles throughout the town. Humphrey got the story from the adventurers, whose tale was as expected. The group had arrived at the town and quickly sensed something off about the residents. Investigating, they were ambushed by the silver-rank messenger and subdued to await implantation.

The one piece of new information was that they were being prepared to host worms that were not the same as the others. As the team had yet to come across any worms outside the norm, they suspected them to be in a lower level of the basement workshop, through the hidden door in the floor.

Humphrey guided the adventurers to Neil to receive a thorough examination. By the time he was done, Shade had notified Jason that the Church of the Healer had arrived at the Yaresh campgrounds and started clearing space for a refugee camp. It was intended to accommodate not just the people rescued by the team but by all the scout teams sent to investigate the towns and villages of the southern region. Reports were already coming in to confirm that worm infestation was not an isolated incident.

Jason portalled through to assist with the setup. The camping grounds where foreign adventurers left their magical mobile homes had ample open space for a camp once the vehicles were cleared out. The church started kicking people out to commandeer ground and Jason returned the land yacht to the cloud flask.

The church officials were initially not interested in using Jason's cloud palace, as Jason himself was an unknown quantity. Things changed when gold-rank members of the church, Arabelle and Carlos, both stepped up, vouching for him. Jason then produced a cloud palace specifically designed for the intake of people into the camp being organised.

The church officials weren't ecstatic about the cloud palace after sensing Jason's aura permeating it. They were quickly forced to acknowledge, however, that the amenities of the palace were exceedingly useful. Also, while Jason's aura was unquestionably authoritarian, the benevolent protectiveness of it proved comforting to people in desperate need of feeling safe.

Jason and Clive started portalling people in, though Humphrey did not use his teleport. Mass teleportation was less convenient than portals, being better suited to strategic than utility purposes. As most of the people were normals, the two portals were more than sufficient.

Once the former prisoners were all transferred, the team returned to the workshop and the hidden floor opening. The exception was Neil, who stayed with his fellow Healer church members. Not only had he started building a rapport with the prisoners, but he understood the amenities the cloud palace offered. Even so, a portal was left open so he could rejoin the team at need. The team expected more vats with some speciality worms, but if something nasty leapt out instead, they wanted their healer able to swiftly come to their aid.

In the workshop, the rest of the team stood around as Belinda went to work on safely opening the hidden floor panel.

"I'm curious about these special worms that those adventurers mentioned," Clive said.

"I'm just looking to crush them underfoot," Sophie said.

"Assuming they fit under your feet," Jason said. "For all you know, we've got a 'worms of Arrakis' situation going on down there."

"Is that a monster from your world?" Humphrey asked.

"Not my world. It's one you want to stay away from. The worms are bad enough, but what you really have to watch out for is an oily Sting."

"You mean a monster with an oily stinger?" Humphrey asked.

"No," Jason told him. "No, I do not."

The opening in the floor of the worm-breeding workshop was an elevating platform that descended a long shaft. It came to an end in an alcove set into the wall of another chamber, another plain room with the same slate brick. Glow stones were set into the ceiling, revealing the worm vats they had been expecting. The central vat was too large to fit on the elevating platform, and the glass sides filled with murky yellow fluid. This made it hard to see what was inside. The other five vats were smaller, each into its own alcove around the walls.

The team quickly took stock of the chamber, spotting no immediate threats as they swept the area. They then turned their attention to the vats, starting with the large one in the middle.

"This vat is way too big for the platform," Clive observed. "My guess would be that this large worm is some kind of brood queen, brought down here when it was smaller. The vat would have either been built here or carried in dimensional storage."

They spotted something shifting inside the liquid; it wasn't long before they saw what they were dealing with. It was a massive worm, forced by its size to coil up, even in a vat several metres across. The lack of room often left it pushing against the glass, which is how the team could see it through the ghastly yellow fluid.

This worm was quite unlike the ones they had dealt with so far, but size was far from the only difference. Where the others had been thin, this one was bloated into obesity, with corpse-pale skin. It also lacked the drill-bit head of its smaller brethren. Instead, it had a flat, fleshy head with a puckered sphincter. The team also spotted a few normal worms swimming in the goo, and they watched as one crawled out of the big worm's sphincter.

"Is that its face or its... other end?" Belinda asked.

"It seems to be some kind of brood queen," Clive assessed. "Not to mention the ugliest worm we've run into, although that fluid it's in doesn't help. It seems to be a more concentrated version of what we saw in the vats above."

He then turned to the other vats, which were smaller cylinders, also with glass sides. Jason found himself ominously thinking they were the perfect size to hold children, but did not voice the macabre thought. Inside each vat was a single worm, much closer to the normal worms than the bulbous queen. Only slightly larger than normal, they retained the drill-bit heads. The most notable difference was that each one was a bright colour: blue, green, red, and yellow.

"I'm more concerned about these colourful worms than with the chunker in the middle," Jason said.

"Why?" Clive asked.

"My first concern was getting caught up in a gritty *Power Rangers* reboot, but then I remembered something far more terrible. One of the most famous and deadly monsters in my world is called a Dalek. A while back, a bunch of Dalek variants in bright colours like this turned up, and it was... not good. Like these worms, they were created by those caught up in hubris, willing to inflict terrible damage in the pursuit of their own mad ideas. Just one look at those things, and you immediately knew someone had undertaken a truly horrifying act of creation."

"What happened?" Humphrey asked.

"We managed to go on, and eventually, the people behind it were removed from power. But as these things so often go, someone else took their place. Someone who would go on to do worse things than we imagined possible."

Jason turned away, looking off at nothing with a haunted expression.

"Jason?"

"Yes, Clive?"

"Are you talking a bunch of crap again?"

"Yes, Clive," Jason said gravely. "Yes, I am."

Clive shook his head and turned his attention back to the vats.

"These are obviously the specialty worms that the messenger was breeding for the adventurers," he said. "It seems that the messengers cultivate different worms for different purposes, and I wonder how expansive that program is. Do they just have these for implantation into higher-rank hosts, or is it more? Are there speciality infiltration worms that can do a better job of pretending to be people? Is Yaresh already facing an infestation?"

"A grim thought, but one for the Adventure Society to explore," Humphrey said. "I'm just glad we didn't face adventurers with enhanced worms inside them while we were cleaning out this place."

"How powerful do you think they would be?" Jason wondered. "According to Carlos, most conversion processes rank-up whatever they convert, but they're relatively weak for their rank. At least compared to essence users."

"Well-trained essence users," Rufus corrected. "These world-taker worms would tear through Greenstone like a sickle through grass."

"I have to imagine these specialty worms are stronger than the ones we encountered thus far," Humphrey said. "They were little more than corpses being thrown at us. Most likely, these would be closer to vampires, or the Builder's clockwork converted."

"Which would have made fighting through the worm-hosts an uglier affair," Rufus said. "If we had to deal with anything that posed an individual threat, we could have been easily overrun."

"It would have been uglier for the adventurers in question," Belinda pointed out. "They aren't in great shape, but these worms look fully grown, or close to it. It might not have been long before implantation."

"Maybe," Clive said. "We can't be sure how large they are fully grown."

"Carlos said that the hosts they occupy are for a secondary incubation cycle," Jason said. "It wasn't relevant to the fight, so I didn't bring it up, but they are inside people trying to turn into something else. He didn't know what, though. Anywhere that finds out tends to be eradicated."

"Perhaps something to do with how the worms self-propagate," Clive guessed. "Something that will allow them to spread without needing breeding centres like this one."

"Or maybe they just turn into fatties, like this one," Belinda said, tapping on the glass of the tank. She placed her palm against the glass. "It's warm. Feels gross."

"We know that the worms can consume heat," Clive said, also shifting his gaze to the central vat. "It might be part of the reproductive cycle."

"That would make sense," Jason said. "Did you notice how all the buildings had been magicked-up to radiate heat? I bet that's part of the incubation cycle."

"I wonder if the aspects of intelligence we saw all came from the larger worm," Clive said. "Colin has a decentralised hive mind, but I suspect the world-taker worms operate differently. My guess would be that any higher-order mental capacity comes from this queen worm, and she directs the worms like a general."

"But we didn't see a lot of intelligence from the worms," Belinda pointed out. "They made one strategic move the whole time, and it was a very simple one."

"Maybe it needs these," Rufus suggested, tapping one of the smaller vats. "Maybe they serve as officers under the general."

"Relay nodes, able to mediate between mindless worms and the higher mind of the queen," Clive said. "That would make sense. But this is all speculation. Whether the queen is truly sapient or just possesses some level of animal cunning I can only guess. With study—"

"No study," Sophie said. "We kill every one of these things we can find."

69

VOICE OF THE WILL

S<small>OPHIE WAS TAKING A FIRM STANCE AGAINST STUDYING THE WORMS RATHER THAN</small> eradicating them on sight.

"Do you want some lunatic researcher trying to do what the messengers did and use them as a weapon?"

"It's a good point," Belinda agreed. "Imagine what Evil Clive could do if he got his hands on these things."

"Evil Clive?" Clive asked.

"Lindy, I thought you *were* Evil Clive," Jason said.

"Oh, that's sweet of you," Belinda happily replied, touching his shoulder briefly.

"Sophie's right," Humphrey said. "All it takes is some duke who wants to turn his city-state into a kingdom and has more ambition than morals or good sense. They set up their own breeding program, somewhere no one finds it. It gets out of control, the worms get loose and by the time anyone realises, it's too late. The world-taker worms have too much momentum and live up to their name. Even if they can be stopped, the price in lives is high. I'm not saying that our actions alone will be enough to avoid that outcome, but I'm not willing to do anything to make it any more likely."

"Do you practise portentous monologues in the mirror for when these situations come up?" Jason asked. "Because seriously, that was on point. I've tried practising sinister lines that I can use later, but I had to knock it off because I'm waaay too melodramatic. It should be simple and concise, like 'I'm Batman,' but I always end up veering into 'I am the terror that flaps in the night' territory. So now I just wing it so I don't get carried away."

"You still get carried away," Belinda said.

"I do?"

"A bit."

"A bit nothing," Clive said. "Do you want me to play the speech you gave that messenger?"

"Play it?"

Clive pointed to the mana crystals floating over his head from his Crystallise Mana ability.

Ability: [Crystallise Mana] (Magic)

- Conjuration (restoration).
- Base cost: Low.
- Cooldown: None.

- Current rank: Silver 4 (04%).

- Effect (iron): Create a crystal that floats around you, accelerating mana recovery. Crystal is impervious to damage, but vulnerable to dispel effects. If dispelled, crystals grant an immediate burst of mana. You can have a single mana crystal at a time.

- Effect (bronze): Crystals can intercept magical projectiles, negating their effect. For a period after negating a projectile, a crystal becomes inactive, unable to produce mana or intercept further projectiles. Maximum crystal count is increased to three, with each active crystal cumulatively increasing mana recovery.

- Effect (silver): Each crystal can absorb one projectile while negating its effect. Crystal with an absorbed projectile will consume the projectile's energy to increase mana production. Absorbed projectiles can be redirected at enemies, with the effects diminished based on the amount of projectile energy converted into mana. Maximum crystal count is increased to five.

Humphrey had the same; he and Neil both shared the very common ability with Clive. But where five crystals were floating over Humphrey's head, Clive had a sixth. When he pointed this out, they all recognised it as a recording crystal.

"Do you want me to show the others?" Clive asked.

"It wasn't that bad," Jason insisted.

"Why don't we let the others see it, then?"

"Because it's embarrassing, and they know how dramatic I can get. And we need to deal with these worms, which leads to an important question: Do I feed Colin the colourful ones first or the big one?"

"There's a lot of Colin to go around," Belinda said. "Why not both?"

Jason shrugged and started moving from vat to vat. They each had a sealed opening on the metal top that Jason presumed was for extracting worms and feeding nutrients. He used it for dumping in leeches, most of which went into the central vat. The smells that came out from the vats as he opened the seals were rancid.

"Ooh, that's rough," Jason said. Then he took a step back as the obese worm in the central vat banged against the inside of the glass.

"Are we okay with it doing that?" Clive asked. "Things breaking containment in magical laboratories have historically had less-than-ideal results."

"I'm open to suggestions," Humphrey said.

"Is running away on the table?" Belinda asked. "I did not like the smell coming out of those tanks. Couldn't we just go back up the entry shaft and drop stuff down to kill the worms?"

"I'm not running away from what amounts to a giant sausage," Sophie said. "A sausage that is being enthusiastically devoured, no less."

As Sophie said, the leeches in the vat were aggressively chewing into the worm. Red blood stained the sickly yellow fluid, making the contents of the vat murkier with each passing moment. Gaping wounds were easy to spot as the worm slammed itself against the glass of the vat, sometimes squashing leeches in the process. The amount of life force Colin was consuming allowed him to reproduce faster than he lost leeches.

"There's a lot of life force in that worm," Jason observed. "I don't think I've ever felt Colin quite so enthused. You show them who's the best apocalypse beast, Colin! Also, please don't eat any planets."

The others all turned to look at him.

"What?" Jason asked. "I said *don't* eat any planets."

"Are we all sure we aren't the villains here?" Belinda asked. "Am I Evil Clive?"

The worm slammed its torn and bleeding body against the vat again, causing spiderweb cracks to appear.

"That's not good," Jason said as the cracks rapidly spread.

The team all floated off the floor and away from the cracking portion of the vat.

Any well-trained silver-ranker could slowly move themselves around, just without the speed, power and control of Jason or a messenger. They also had to maintain careful concentration or they would drop.

As the worm banged against the side again, the vat broke, spilling yellow liquid onto the floor. It was thick, almost slime, and heavily streaked with red. The worm only half emerged, getting caught on the broken glass and cutting itself open. A foul smell emerged the moment the vat broke, but when the worm suffered deep lacerations, it became excruciatingly pungent. It was the only stench any of them had encountered that was worse than rainbow smoke. They all shut off their sense of smell as soon as the wall of stench struck them.

"Okay, Lindy," Sophie choked out. "I was wrong. We should have run away."

"I have no expertise in magical research, or in eating worms," Rufus said. "I'll leave this to Jason and Clive."

With that, he floated himself up through the elevating platform shaft in the ceiling, Sophie, Belinda and Humphrey following close behind. Jason looked at Clive, whose expression was torn. There might be something to learn if he stayed, or it might just be some leeches eating some worms, which he could happily imagine in the fresh air.

"I think whatever's in those vats is making my eyes sting," Clive said, making his decision. "Tell me if anything interesting happens."

Jason shook his head with a chuckle as Clive made good his escape. The leeches in the side vats had finished their meals and he let them out, but didn't absorb them immediately.

"If you think I'm letting you inside me while you're covered in gunk," he said, holding up a leech with his thumb and forefinger, "you've got another think coming."

With the elevating platform still downstairs, the shaft was open and Jason was able to extend his aura through it. He used it to grab the barrel of crystal wash, left over from cleaning off the prisoners, and float it down the shaft. A little of the wash went a long way, so it was still mostly full. While Jason was moving the barrel, Colin finished off the large worm.

- Familiar [Colin] has consumed [World-Taker Worm Matriarch].
- [Colin] can use the devoured power of the [World-Taker Worm Matriarch] to awaken as a Voice of the Will. This will require extended hibernation in the astral kingdom to which it is connected. Only passive, unmanifested abilities will be available during this time, and manifestation will be impossible.

- Familiar [Colin] must fully return to the Astral Kingdom to initiate awakening.

"Voice of the Will? I keep adding to the list of things I need to ask the messengers. I'll have to leave one alive. Eventually. If I can find one that isn't in the middle of committing war crimes. Still, far be it from me to look a power upgrade in the mouth. Come and get cleaned up, buddy."

Jason floated individual leeches into the air with his aura until they surrounded him like a swarm of bees.

"Hey, I think we might have just found a great new tactic, Colin. This is going to scare the crap out of people."

While holding the leeches in the air, Jason used his aura to lift droplets of crystal wash from the barrel to clean them.

"You know what? This is pretty good aura manipulation practise. You're so useful, Colin. Good boy."

Jason emerged from the shaft into the workshop. Belinda and Clive were exploring the messenger's work while Sophie, Humphrey and Rufus stood around. The underground workshop was hardly pleasant, but it was a better place to wait for the Adventure Society than the town full of corpses. Just as Jason reached the top of the shaft, Neil appeared through the portal Jason had left open.

"Lindy," he said. "We could use some logistical aid. The Adventure Society has been expanding the refugee camp in the camping grounds with people evacuated from other towns and villages. The cloud palace is being used for assessment and treatment, but we could use some housing."

Belinda nodded and followed Neil back through the portal. Neil had grabbed Belinda for her ability to conjure simple items. That ranged from tools like a sword, a pickaxe or a wall to soft items like curtains or bedding. With Belinda at silver rank, she could conjure a vast number of simple objects that would last for a considerable time. Knocking out what amounted to a series of pre-fab dormitories would be well within her abilities, freeing up time and resources that local authorities could expend on longer-term solutions.

At the same time, more adventuring teams were heading for towns like the one Jason's team had purged. Following close behind were support teams from the Adventure Society, Magic Society, various churches and the Yaresh civic authorities. Reports had come in quickly, from Carlos and others connected to alternate scout teams. Once the magnitude of what was going on had been revealed, resources and personnel were deployed in far greater numbers than the original scout teams. More towns needed to be checked, some teams required backup and everywhere would require management in the aftermath.

"What will the messengers do, now that their plans have been revealed?" Humphrey mused.

"I don't know," Rufus said. "Given the scale of this operation, though, they had to have known that exposure was inevitable. The question is what they planned to do when that happened. This isn't anything the Adventure Society won't have considered, though. They'll be reinforcing the operation sites for the clean-up in case the whole idea was to bait out teams that could be taken down in isolation by messenger strike groups."

"But doesn't that draw a lot of forces out of the city?" Jason asked. "What if that's the whole point of all this?"

"It's not like the city will be emptied out," Rufus said. "I guarantee you that forces in less critical operations are being recalled as we speak. Plus, the city's defensive infrastructure is a massive impediment to even a concentrated messenger assault."

"Does that make anyone else feel like messenger saboteurs are bringing down that infrastructure as we speak?" Jason asked.

"Now that you say it, yeah," Sophie said. "Good job, Rufus."

Rufus gave Jason a flat look.

"Where did you even learn all this about city infrastructure and defence protocols and the like?" Jason asked.

"My family runs a... get bent, Jason."

The others all laughed as Jason headed for the stairs. As the one with the strongest senses, he would be the one to first notice the reinforcements. The workshop was impeding his perception, so he needed to go outside.

"I could have used a drink too," he muttered.

70

HE HIMSELF DOES NOT BECOME
A MONSTER

JASON DIDN'T LINGER DOWNSTAIRS WITH THE OTHERS FOR LONG. HE HAD NO interest in facing the town filled with dead, but didn't want his aura restricted by the underground facility. His aura could somewhat escape the workshop's inhibition magic with the doors open, but it still greatly impeded his senses. He went up the stairs, through the tunnel into the dirt basement, and then up the ladder to the trapdoor.

This returned him to the building that served as the secret entrance to the underground facility. It was one of the few buildings in the town that did not have open-sided walls, and was used as a storage shed. Judging from the layer of grime coating empty barrels and broken farming tools, it was one that saw little use.

Jason went outside, once more taking in the stomach-churning scene of bodies littered around the town. Although he knew they had been worm-hosts, dead before the team even arrived, it still rattled Jason to look at. It was not the first time he had seen the dead piled high—tragically, far from it. He desperately hoped he would never become accustomed to the sight.

He would rather have stayed downstairs. He could join the others in distracting themselves from the dark reality with light banter, pushing the dark thoughts away until the job was done. There would be ample time to sit with the horror in the sleepless nights Rufus had warned Jason about. That had been Jason's very first night in his new world, and felt like a million years ago.

Jason thought back to that night and didn't recognise that person he had been anymore. Idly wondering about the choices he made, he wondered how things could have been different. He'd made a lot of mistakes and seen a lot of death, some of which was on his head.

But the big things had gone well enough. Better than could be expected in most cases. Earth wasn't in precipitous danger. The days of proto-spaces threatening to spew forth dangerous monster waves were over. The monsters would manifest directly now, and mostly far weaker. They would not be contained in the proto-spaces, but it was good enough.

Pallimustus had weathered the monster surge and the Builder invasion. Jason had even managed to push the Builder into leaving a little early. He would never know how many lives even a few weeks without fighting had saved, and while that did not make up for the dead scattered before him now, it was at least some consolation to his soul.

Jason and his friends had to live with cutting down the people of the town, and while they were already corpses, that wasn't how it felt. Even accepting that, they were desecrating the remains of innocent strangers, people they had not been able to protect. This was sadly not new for Jason and Rufus, but the others would need to come to terms with that.

Jason knew that his team would endure, however. He'd done it. Not well, but he'd done it. He hoped he could help them do it a little better. It was the people of the town he felt bad for. The few dozen that had survived were not going to feel like they had. Their world had just been destroyed. Almost everyone that each of them knew was lying in front of Jason, hacked to pieces, burned to ashes or torn apart.

These were small-town people and their town was over. How could they ever come back to this nightmare place after what happened? Even if they did, there were not enough of them left to revive it. It was a ghost town now, and the memories would haunt them. The blood and the bodies could be cleared away, but their presence would linger. The town was done.

A grim future awaited the survivors. Many of them may never have even left the town before, and now their lives would change forever. Compared to them, Jason and his team had places to go and homes to return to. Even when they suffered losses, they had the power to minimise them and seize a path forward. The surviving townsfolk were the pawns of fate, stuck in a world of magic they didn't have and monsters they couldn't fight. Whatever their future would be, it was not theirs to choose.

For all that Jason had faced hard times since arriving in this world, he at least had made his own choices along the way. He had the agency to seize his own destiny, even with forces beyond comprehension arrayed against him. Determination and far more luck than he had any right to expect had carried him along. The survivors of the town had no such agency. Their lives were not theirs to choose and would never be the same.

This was the distillation of something Rufus warned Jason of, on that first night, and why Jason dwelled on it now. That grim days were ahead, but if he ceded control to others, he wouldn't have any choices at all. He would be left only able to wait and see what happened to him, with no power to change it. That was how Rufus convinced Jason to be an adventurer.

Standing, looking out at the dead, Jason thought about how many lives and deaths had passed through his hands. He remembered the waterfall village where, for the very first time, he had made the choice to stand between innocent people and the violence that was coming for them. Doing it again in the very same village, he had earned his first and largest scar.

As his powers grew, so did the challenges. Protecting Greenstone from the Builder. Broken Hill, Makassar. The entire Earth threatening to tear apart from dimensional forces. The dangers escalated more quickly than his powers did, and he'd had to become something further and further from human to meet them. More than once, it had cost him his life. But at least he came back, when so many others did not. This town that he didn't even know the name of was just the latest to host the mounds of dead that he had failed to save.

There was nothing Jason could have done for the people in front of him, but what about the dead that lay behind him? The people who died at Broken Hill? Makassar? His brother, his lover and his friend? How did the ones he saved balance against the ones he failed to? The loss of each had galvanised Jason, prompting spikes in his strength that he used down the line. Were those losses worth the things Jason had accomplished? Were all those people sacrifices or just helpless victims?

"It's a bleak equation," he pondered.

Shade emerged from Jason's shadow to stand beside him.

"You can count the dead, Mr Asano," Shade said, knowing Jason's mind, "but it accomplishes nothing. All you can do is move forward, doing the best you can with what you have. I've heard you say that many times, and of all your..."

Shade's pause was rich with disapproval.

"...*catchphrases*, it is the one I prefer. The one that has wisdom."

"You think I'm wise?"

"No, Mr Asano. No. Dear goodness, no. Which is why you should always remember those sparkling moments when you manage to achieve them."

Jason let out a soft chuckle, not enough to wipe the sadness from his expression.

"Are you alright, Mr Asano?"

"You know what, Shade?" Jason asked, looking out over the dead. "To my own surprise, I actually might be. I don't ever want to get used to scenes like this, but I'm not going to let them break me either; I'm going to use them. Let them remind me of why I have to keep pushing, of why I have to get stronger. Of who and what I'm going to face, and the lengths they are willing to go."

He bowed his head.

"I've got this voice inside me, telling me that if I become worse than the things I fight, they'll be too scared to do what happened in this town. I've been so angry for so long now that I don't even remember when I started listening to that voice. But it's wrong. It never works like that, does it?"

"No, Mr Asano. It does not."

"I've been heading down a certain road for a while now, but it doesn't lead anywhere I want to go. It's time to take a different direction. Maybe find some of that naïveté that I discarded along the way."

"Your treatment of that messenger—"

"That was the line. That's how far I can go without losing myself. I let myself go right up against it with her. But I think that's okay. I've been telling myself that's not where the line is for a long time. That I'm a good person who is only doing these things because I have to, and when the world stops dumping on me, I'll stop. But the world never stops dumping, does it?"

"No, Mr Asano. It does not."

"It's time to accept that my line is where it is. To stop deluding myself over who I am and moping over how bad things are. The people of this town, living and dead, have gotten it far worse than me, and I owe it to them to stop this from happening somewhere else. I have so much power. So many good people around me. So many things to be thankful for. So much I can do."

"If what you did to the messenger was the line, Mr Asano, does that mean you'll be stepping back from it?"

Jason nodded. "Once I accept where my line genuinely is, instead of telling myself where it should be, I feel like it will be easier to avoid pushing up against it. Not unless I need to."

"Do you regret breaking her will before you killed her?"

"I don't know. No, I think. I probably should. It was anger that drove me, and anger is always hungry for more. But I'm willing to go that far, after what she did. She had a rough time, but I was just talking up my power. A bit. The essence ability I used on her is a vulture, picking the bones clean; it can't damage the soul. It might be a little rough-and-tumble on a gestalt entity like a messenger, but she'll find her way to your dad fully intact. It's not like when you stopped me from using that guy's star seed to peel the body off his soul. That would have been over the line."

"Yes, Mr Asano. That would be more than I was willing to tolerate."

"I'm not done giving the messengers a hard time, though. They have a lot of things that I need. Advanced astral magic. Understanding of what an astral king is. Knowledge of whatever Emir is looking for."

"You may need to leave some of them alive for that."

"True. But they also have a power inside them that I can use. If I have to crack them open like eggs to get it, then so be it. They came to this world, looking for trouble. After seeing how far they'll go to find it, I'll happily oblige them."

"Will you dedicate yourself to pursuing them, then?"

"I don't need to. They came here in numbers, and they came to stay. The conditions they used to get here ended with the monster surge, so while I'm sure they have the means to leave, I doubt they can do so easily or en masse. Even just living the adventurer life, I'm going to be hunting them for a good, long time."

"And if they hunt you back?"

Jason's grin belonged on a comic book cover, and not on the face of the hero.

71

AN EGG STARTING TO HATCH

Standing in the town filled with fallen elves and annihilated parasite worms, Jason looked off to the distance. Something had pinged his aura senses, somewhere out in the rainforest, and he withdrew his magical perception. It was a gold-rank adventurer, and Jason wasn't sure if he had been noticed in turn, but the person was making a beeline for the town.

"Time to make myself scarce," he said.

In the workshop under a nearby building, meanwhile, Jason's team were having a discussion.

"Is he even going to keep up the hidden identity?" Clive asked. "They don't care here about what happened in Rimaros."

"He kicked the Builder off the planet," Sophie said. "I think they might care that the guy who did that is running around."

"Even so," Clive said, "the locals have much more immediate concerns. The messengers and these worms are problems now, while the Builder invasion is history."

"Extremely recent history," Rufus said. "There are still pockets of Builder cultists scattered around the world. Even here, you know that."

"We need to finish briefing Korinne's team," Humphrey said. "They need to know the complexity of the situation when we go after the messengers."

"We don't even know if we'll still be sent after them," Clive pointed out. "These worms are going to shake up whatever plans the Adventure Society had. I don't think Jason will have the luxury of hugging the shadows for much longer. And it's not like he's doing a great job at playing nondescript cook. He's terrible at playing any roles other than lunatic or monster."

The others nodded their agreement.

"Lindy always complained about me when I was on the job," Sophie said. "I used to play socialite a lot when we were preparing to rob a place, and she always said I wasn't embodying the role enough. But at least I wasn't joining cage fight tournaments."

"You weren't?" Humphrey asked.

"Well, once, and she didn't let me hear the end of it. The job did not go well."

"Jason isn't on some infiltration mission," Rufus said. "It's not about him maintaining some rigid identity. Most adventurers have secrets; Jason himself is ours. When people see a cook who is obviously more than he appears, it's not anything to worry about. They'll assume he's someone like the princess hiding out in Korinne's team, some spoiled aristocrat looking to avoid the trouble that comes with their name. Jason just needs to avoid inspiring too many powerful people into looking closer. If adventurers went looking into every person with obvious secrets, they'd never have time to do any actual adventuring."

"Exactly," Jason said, coming down the stairs. "It's okay to be shady, so long as we don't step on the toes of anyone who can make trouble for us. Where I come from, we call it plausible deniability."

"And when the people we rescued are debriefed?" Clive asked. "What happens when they mention the guy with the starlight cloak that doesn't match any member of our team? It's not a huge leap to someone looking up our team members, present and former."

"Clive," Rufus said. "You were the one who pointed out how busy things will be for the locals. I doubt they will have the time to go looking into Jason with everything going on. Even if they do, Jason's record has been sealed. The whole thing now, not just sections, the way it was in the past. And the classification of those restrictions is high enough that someone important has to really want it before the Adventure Society will give them anything."

"Plus, the locals don't know us," Humphrey said. "Any power the prisoners describe will be passed off as belonging to any one of us."

"Why are you so keen on me giving up the identity anyway?" Jason asked Clive.

"I just think it would be better if you were back with the team properly."

"I can't argue with that," Jason agreed.

"Also," Clive said, "Colin might be useful to clean up worms in other places. I'm guessing that worm eradication will be a big priority. If you weren't hiding, you could use him more."

"Colin can't replicate enough to be effective on that scale," Jason said. "At best, he can double his standard mass, which he can only maintain while actively feeding anyway. Besides, he's sleeping off Christmas dinner."

"What does that mean?" Sophie asked.

"You never been in a turkey coma?" Jason asked.

"What's turkey?" Clive asked.

Jason looked back up the stairs. "We can talk about this later," he said. "You're about to get visitors, so it's time for my portal and me to scarper."

Jason and Clive still had active portals that they had funnelled the prisoners through, along with Belinda and Neil. Jason went through his portal and it vanished behind him.

Jason had returned to Yaresh previously, just long enough to reconfigure his cloud construct from land-yacht to palace. He had greater control over the specifics of the design than when he first obtained the cloud flask, and was able to lay it out like a hospital. The palace took the appearance of a hospital as well, with a white, square exterior arranged into three connected wings. The interiors were likewise white, with square tile patterns.

The design was to best facilitate the needs of the camp, being set up to screen, treat and manage the evacuees from worm-infested towns and villages. The ability of the cloud palace to utilise different amenities, as well as clean anything inside it, would be a boon for medical work.

The palace was situated at one end of the space being cleared for the camp, with the other end near Emir's cloud palace by the wall. Two front-facing wings marked the border of what would become the camp, with one rear wing away from the camp. The rear and one of the front wings each had three storeys; the remaining front wing had a fourth.

The rear wing contained living space for Jason and his companions. This included Melody, who had remained under Jason's watchful eye while her new secure room was formed. The private wing for Jason and his friends was the only part of the palace that continued to serve as Jason's spirit domain, where his influence was sufficient to impinge upon the natural laws within it.

Jason withdrew his full influence from the front wings, having it operate more like a normal cloud construct. This was critical for allowing in the priests from the Church of the Healer, as they would be cut off from their god's influence in the spirit domain.

This was something that Arabelle and Neil had gotten used to, but they did not have powers directly bestowed through divine essences or awakening stones. They also knew Jason. Explaining why their god was not welcome to a group of clergy while they were busy setting up an evacuee camp was not an efficient use of time. And if they had divinely granted powers on top, it would be even worse.

Jason knew that leaving the area of a god's influence did not prevent essence abilities with divine origins from working. He had seen that in astral spaces where the influence of gods did not reach. If anything, it might mean that it was harder for the gods to revoke those powers, although Jason couldn't be sure. Another thing he was uncertain about was the degree to which he could interfere with those powers should they be used in an area over which he had dominion. He suspected he could have an influence, but he also suspected that running tests was a bad idea.

The front wings still retained Jason's aura, but he tamped it down to the minimum. Carlos, Arabelle and Neil, all members of the Church of the Healer, were already at work and gave him suggestions for facilities he should include. One wing was designed for intake, with treatment rooms and spaces to organise people that were divided by what looked suspiciously like cattle-yard railings. There were also secure screening rooms for checking people for worms, and cells to hold any that did.

The other front wing was designed around secondary services, such as cafeterias and shower rooms that people in the camp would need to visit once or more per day, for as long as the camp was set up. This was the wing with the extra storey, which contained administrative spaces. The people running the camp had needed a place to retreat to and organise things out from the chaos the camp could be in.

The palace had only so much space within, however, especially as Jason's palace was smaller than Emir's. Part of that was the rank difference, with his palace being silver rank currently, compared to Emir's gold. He suspected that the unique nature of his palace had an effect as well. Given the additional energies being fed into the cloud flask from Jason's soul realm, he guessed that more of the flask's resources were required to contain it.

Because of the size limitation, Jason had abandoned dormitory space entirely to focus on facilities that would benefit from the amenities his cloud palace could offer. Places for the evacuees to live and sleep were being arranged by the churches, civic authorities and the Adventure Society, all of whom had become involved in organising the camp. The Magic Society was also present, but they were in no danger of being put in charge. No one believed that they were interested in the welfare of the evacuees over studying any worms they brought with them.

Jason had no interest in their jostling over influence and had left them to it, returning to his team. Now that he was back at the camp, he went to check the results. He had to admit that whoever was in charge worked fast, as the camp had sprawled out in the short time he was away. The area around the palace had been cleared of other vehicles to make room to set up the expansive evacuee camp. That space was already filled with a mix of tents and prefabricated buildings, conjured by Belinda and others with similar powers. The conjured items mostly had a matte plastic look to them, in various colours, and Jason recognised the dark green that belonged to Belinda.

Activity was hectic both inside the palace and out in the camp. People rushed around, Jason picking up auras that ranged from normal through to gold. He identified the familiar ones, including Amos Pensinata, and Taika, who was meditating in the private section of the palace. Jason was startled to realise that Taika's aura was so close to breaking through to silver that it was like an egg starting to hatch. Jason quietly withdrew his aura and left him to it.

With so many people hurrying everywhere, it was easy for Jason to tweak his aura such that others overlooked him as he roamed around. This was especially true within the cloud palace, where he could blend into the surrounding aura. He sent Shade's bodies out as well, taking stock of the camp. If anyone was trying to exploit the chaos to work against the camp, the city or Jason, he wanted as much warning as he could get.

After roaming the camp, Jason made his way up to the administrative area on the fourth storey, to a private office he had set aside for his own use. The room was empty and he moved to the front wall, a single giant window overlooking the camp. Shade emerged and floated next to him.

"How are the organisers making use of the palace amenities?" Jason asked.

"Mrs Remore has been appointed facility liaison, to help make the most of the resources at hand. I have been assisting her, naturally, and she has been making sure the palace is being used efficiently. Some assets are unavailable outside of the spirit domain, of course, such as your avatars."

"I don't think a bunch of cycloptic shadow monsters would help the situation, even if they are practical. I'm pretty sure they would just start a panic."

"I concur, Mr Asano."

"Is there anything that would benefit from my personal intervention? In the kitchens, maybe?"

"The procurement, preparation and distribution of food is being handled by the city authorities. They have the cafeterias well in hand and their own personnel in charge. Attempting to take over management would disrupt more than help."

"I don't have to manage things; I could be an extra pair of hands."

"That would require taking orders, Mr Asano."

"I can take orders."

Instead of responding, Shade turned his head toward Jason.

"Yeah, alright," Jason grudgingly conceded. "Just keep scouting the camp outside the palace and let me know if anything crops up. Actually, position some bodies around the city as well, and maybe a few to patrol outside the city walls."

"You are concerned that the messengers will attack?"

"Rufus doesn't think so, but I can't shake the idea."

"Why not?"

"Because that's what I'd do."

"What would you do about the city defence infrastructure?"

"Not sure. I'm guessing readiness levels would make sabotage unreliable. Maybe set up something inside the city to draw defenders from the walls, then hammer one point hard. I'm no strategic genius, so maybe I'm all wrong. It's not like my suspicions are specific enough that I can check them out."

"Mrs Remore is working with the camp leader to help make the most of the palace's facilities," Shade said. "Shall I mention to her that if something does happen, she should be ready to evacuate the palace so it can be reconfigured?"

"That's a good idea, Shade. It's probably nothing. I hope it's nothing, and not just because I don't want to see the city attacked. I don't want to find out that I think like a messenger."

"I suspect, Mr Asano, that they would be more alarmed to discover they think like you."

"Was that a compliment or an insult?"

"Yes, Mr Asano. It was."

72

WHAT THE SWARM CAME TO CURE

JASON STOOD IN AN EMPTY ROOM, LOOKING THROUGH A WINDOW WALL DOWN AT the evacuee camp. It was far more than just the few dozen people from the town Jason and his team had gone to, as towns across the southern region likewise had adventurers investigating. The expedition had started with seven teams and expanded once the truth was discovered.

Through Shade's eavesdropping, Jason was keeping an ear out for how things were going. Jason and his team had encountered one of the worst-gone towns, almost entirely taken over. Other towns were thankfully only in the early stages and had been saved by adventurers who drove off or killed the messengers in them. Unfortunately, it was not all good news.

"Of the seven teams initially deployed, two of them lost members in the process of killing or driving off the messengers they found," Shade reported. "In both cases, it was in larger towns than we were sent to, where multiple messengers were present and the teams did not have a gold-ranker with them. Also, one team was lost entirely. Their deaths have been confirmed using their tracking stones."

Each Adventure Society branch maintained tracking stones connected to the adventurers operating in that area. One of the first things Humphrey had done on the team's arrival at Yaresh had been to visit the Adventure Society and notify them that the team would be operating in the area so that local tracking stones could be produced. This was based on soul imprints taken by the Magic Society.

As souls shifted over time, the imprints required refreshing, especially after rank-ups. This was why Farrah had extra problems when identifying herself on her return from death. Also, other changes in the soul could invalidate an imprint, which was very much the case for Jason. The solution was to obtain a personal crest, which was only possible while at iron rank. It was common amongst nobility and provided a fixed marker for soul imprinting. The Adventure Society had simply copied Jason's imprint when creating one for his John Miller alias.

"If someone was able to take out an entire adventuring team," Jason said, "are they thinking that location is the central hub for worm production?"

"There has been speculation, but I don't have access to the full information," Shade said. "I am only going by what the Adventure Society officials here in the camp have been discussing. I do know that the location in question was one of the larger towns."

"So, there might have been a whole messenger contingent there. There certainly had to be a gold-rank messenger."

"From early reports, Mr Asano, there is a particular messenger tactic that the team will need to be wary of."

"Oh?"

"Messenger abilities vary quite a lot, but many seem to be able to isolate themselves and an enemy such that neither can leave until the other is dead."

"Allowing them to take out critical enemies," Jason said. "Healers, glass cannons and the like. Any restrictions, or can they just go in and pluck people out of our formation?"

"It seems to require a certain level of physical isolation. So long as you keep the core members together, it is likely that they will be stuck targeting your more mobile members."

"That's acceptable," Jason said. "Rufus, Humphrey, Sophie and I can all handle a one-on-one. Lindy, in a pinch, although best if we can avoid it. If we keep her, Clive and Neil together, we should be alright."

"From what I can tell, it is a category of ability the messengers possess, not a specific power. Each messenger who possesses such a power will have their own variant, so there is no predicting exactly how that power will work. I think it is inevitable that you will encounter such a power, Mr Asano, but there is no telling what the exact effects will be."

"You picked up all this from hearing about just a few encounters?"

"These powers are responsible for the two deaths in the teams that lost members but weren't wiped out," Shade explained. "It has been a topic of some discussion, and this is far from the first time that the locals have clashed with the messengers."

"I see."

Jason continued to watch the camp's activity. There was an arrival area where portals or flying vehicles brought in survivors from the towns and villages. They were brought into the cloud palace where Jason had set up screening and treatment rooms. Jason couldn't see this process through the window, but could observe anything happening in cloud palace, should he desire.

The screening rooms were a redundancy measure, as sufficiently close observation should allow worm-hosts to be picked out from their auras. Jason fully agreed with the measure anyway, because of the specialty worms. They had yet to be implanted in the adventurer prisoners Jason's team had found, but there was no telling what the results would have been. The disappearance of several adventuring teams had been the original prompt for the sweeping investigation into the towns, which left others potentially infested with the special worms.

The precaution proved valuable when a group of liberated adventurers was brought into the cloud palace. Jason detected an aura mask placed over them, subtle enough that he might not have even noticed in person. In his cloud palace, however, very little escaped his perception. As they entered, Jason sensed an aura mask similar to the one used by Benella, the elf who had been a spy for the messengers.

At a mental command from Jason, an image of a hallway appeared on the window in front of Jason. It was the group of liberated adventurers being escorted down a hall by a woman in Church of the Healer robes and a man wearing an Adventure Society emblem. They were all bronze rank, according to their auras, and were on their way to the screening rooms.

A second mental command brought up a second live image from within the palace. This one showed Arabelle Remore, in one of the palace's administrative offices. She was standing over a desk with a scowl on her face as she organised procurement lists.

"Arabelle," he said.

She looked up, glancing around. "Jason?"

"You're working with the person running the evacuee operation, right?"

"Yeah," she confirmed, half-groaning. "I'm in charge of making the most of your magic cloud hospital. Right now, supplies are being brought in as quick as people can get their hands on them, which is not the basis for an efficient system. I'm trying to make sure things go where they're needed without too much getting lost in the shuffle."

"Unfortunately, I need to add to your load. I'm sorry."

"Can it wait?"

"I think there is a group of worm-infested adventurers in the building."

"So, 'no' is what you're saying."

"Pretty much. A group of rescued adventurers just came in, but they're all wearing aura masks. The sophisticated kind I've seen the messengers use."

"And you think they've been infected."

"It could be something else. They could be magically disguised messengers for all I know. Unless I poke them hard enough that they notice, I can't tell what they're hiding."

Arabelle left the room, the image on the window moving to track her quick stride.

"We have a team of Adventure Society enforcers on standby for this reason," she said. "They're stationed by the screening rooms."

"I know, but they won't act on my say so."

"I'll get them moving; if something is going to happen, it will be in the screening rooms or on the way. Whoever or whatever we're dealing with, they'll get violent once they realise their disguises won't hold up. Can you use the building to assist?"

"Of course. I just didn't want to contain them out of nowhere and alarm the people working here."

"I'm pretty sure they'll be alarmed anyway."

"But at least about the right thing. I want people worried about intruders, not the building randomly eating rescued adventurers."

"That's not my responsibility. Once we've contained these adventurers, I want you to meet Hana Shavar, the woman in charge. I don't have time to be your mouthpiece all day."

"Yes, ma'am."

Five elite worm-hosts were moving down a hall, in a building with white walls that looked like smooth tiles but were actually absorbent cloud-substance. The hosts communicated silently, much like Jason's voice chat, wary of their situation. The facility all the rescuees were being taken into was beyond expectations, preventing their magical senses from moving beyond what they could see.

Unlike slave worms, the elite worms only needed one worm to the host, and each had an independent mind. While they were capable of commanding slave worms and communicating with the matriarch, they could operate independently, without control. They were independent minds within the swarm.

They had realised that the messengers had never intended to leave this world to the worms once attackers started descending on the initial breeding sites. As the matriarchs started dying, with minimal reaction from the messengers, the worms realised that their agenda no longer aligned with that of their winged allies.

The elite worms had no recourse but to go along, looking for an opportunity. They at least still possessed the aura masks left on the host bodies by the messengers; they could look for the chance to slip away. If they could rejoin the other elite worms in the city, they could begin to work on redeeming a situation that had turned dire. They had not yet had a chance to quietly escape, with so many eyes on them.

Now they were in this strange building, with walls that could block their senses and soft floors that muffled sound—any corner could have people just around it. At least there were only the two people moving with them, now. Even better, they were the same bronze rank as the aura masks inscribed into the host bodies. With the host bodies enhanced to silver, they could put their escorts down quickly and move on.

From what the worms gathered, one of their escorts was a kind of healer, Gloria. The other, Lomius, had a role that was alien to the worms. He seemed to have been given the task of helping others of his kind organise one another, which was the kind of inefficiency that only came from creatures with isolated minds. Without the swarm to guide them as a colony, their fractious psyches would quickly fall to confusion and disarray. They even had to designate one another with names, just so they could effectively interrelate. The swarm memory had seen this over and over, with countless worlds and countless species. This was what the swarm came to cure.

If the worms were going to move before they reached their destination, the timing was as good as it was likely to get. The two weaklings with them would offer minimal impediment.

"Where are you taking us?" one of the elite worms asked.

"Just a screening to double-check you don't have any of those foul worms in you," Lomius said. "Frankly, I think it's a redundant time-waster, but does anyone listen to me? No, and now you poor sods are stuck jumping through rings instead of getting cleaned up and fed. You've been through enough already, without any extra poking and prodding."

The elite worm made the host give a friendly smile. "I don't suppose you could skip it, then? We've already been through so much."

Lomius looked to the healer. "What do you say, Gloria?"

"No."

"Come on."

"No."

"You know they don't really expect to find anything. Otherwise, they'd have more than just us escorting them."

"Lomius, if we had the people, we would have."

Gloria shook her head firmly.

"My Adventure Society colleague may think that this step is unnecessary," she told the worm-hosts, and then her expression softened. "I truly am sorry to stretch things out for you, but when the cost of a mistake is so high, redundancy in safety measures is exactly what you want."

"Oh, come on, Gloria," Lomius said. "Do they look like dead bodies being puppeteered by worms to you?"

"No, Lomius, they don't. Which is why we have a screening process instead of having you and me eyeball it."

Lomius shrugged at the worms. "Sorry, but you heard the lady. Rules are rules."

Without warning, the smiling worm shot into motion. A hand was flung at Lomius, drill-bit-like spikes emerging from its fingers like claws. A wall of cloud stuff coalesced between the host and the elf, but was not enough to stop the attack. It did slow it down, at least; only the finger spikes were buried in Lomius' head. The silver-rank strength of the host would have otherwise buried its entire hand into the bronze-ranker's head, leaving him very dead instead of just injured.

Another worm-host went for Gloria, but another cloudy barrier gave her time to toss up a magical shield. The single strike was enough to break it, but there was no follow-up. The air around the worm-hosts had rapidly grown opaque, condensing into thick cloud-substance. Like a mix of marshmallow and concrete, it left the worm-hosts stuck, with only the two arms that had made attacks visible. They jutted comically from the cloud-stuff, thrashing impotently.

Gloria only stared for a moment before turning to Lomius on the ground. She threw out a fast healing spell and assessed his injuries. He was conscious but incoherent, having had several three-inch spikes puncture his head. Bronze-rankers usually still had brains as a massive physical vulnerability, especially non-adventurers.

Another glance at the now-blocked hallway told Gloria that the adventurers were not likely to get free. She examined Lomius and realised he had dangerous puncture wounds to the brain that her quick heal hadn't come close to fixing. She assessed that immediate treatment was more important than evacuating him from danger and potentially exacerbating the wounds, so she went to work on a more powerful, ritual-assisted healing ability.

Gloria was still working on the ritual when the Adventure Society enforcers arrived, only moments after the attack. The team leader directed her people to protect Gloria, but wasn't sure what to make of the white wall with two arms sticking out. They had spike-claws jutting from the fingertip and were jerking helplessly.

"What do we do with this?"

73

A MORTAL PERSPECTIVE

From his room overlooking the camp, Jason watched a combination of Adventure Society enforcers and Magic Society functionaries take away five cylinders on a floating platform. Each cylinder was a stasis pod, containing a worm-host that could be vaguely made out through the blue liquid in the pod.

Someone appeared in the room and joined Jason in staring out the window. It wore brown robes and sported a neat grey beard, appearing as a handsomely middle-aged man. Jason knew that it was neither middle-aged nor a man, and didn't react to its arrival. It was only able to appear there because Jason had withdrawn his spirit domain from the bulk of his cloud construct.

"Just because I happen to have left the door open," Jason said, "that doesn't mean I want just anyone wandering in."

"Thank you for giving my people access to these facilities. It has given us the most precious resource when it comes to healing: time."

"You don't need to thank me for basic decency. If you can help, you help. That's obvious. Besides, I'd rather knock up a quickie hospital and help people than carve up people I was too late to save."

"You've had a grim day."

"Lots of people have, but that's adventuring. We meet a lot of people on the worst days of their lives and hope to make them a little less awful. Didn't do so well today."

"Not every adventurer sees their role in that light."

"Enough do. I know a lot of us get changed by the money, the power, the influence. I certainly was; just ask your boy Dominion. But when the time to step up comes, most adventurers put all that aside. Is there a lot of ambition wrapped up in that? Sure. But they answer the call; the monster surge proved that. There's a lot of hope to be found there."

Healer smiled. "I am glad that you can find optimism on such days as these. I wondered if there was any left in you when you first came back to this world."

"Is that what you're here for? To cheer me up? I don't think providing a few amenities for the camp here warrants the personal thank you."

"You are in a strange position, Jason. May I call you Jason?"

"Since when does your lot ask permission for anything?"

His laughter was warm and comforting, like a roaring fire in a snow chalet.

"I suppose we don't. Not with mortals, but you don't fall neatly into that box. You are certainly and most enthusiastically mortal, yet you have a foot firmly planted in our realm."

He glanced sideways at Jason.

"Thank you for opening your space to my people. Domains are tricky things, and I can easily see how you might be reluctant to withdraw it."

"Making your people come in and deal with the presence of a spirit domain would only cause problems. It would promote distrust and soak up valuable time while I convince your people to use the building. Seems obvious to take a step back."

"Even so, it is not easy to forsake control, even for a short while. *My boy Dominion* does not approve."

"I don't approve of him either, so fair enough. If you really are grateful, though, I don't suppose you'd be open to a few questions?"

"I can give you *some* answers, but the areas I can speak on are limited by my role. I am not Knowledge. Also, will you trust anything a god has to say?"

"You may not be a bloke, and you may not have a heart, but you seem like a bloke with his heart in the right place. And as for a topic, surely a god can talk about god stuff."

"Yes, but my advice is to concentrate on mortal affairs. The rest will come to you naturally as the incongruity in power between your aspects of self grow smaller."

"Oh, I'd be more than happy to wait until I naturally get to cosmic affairs, but you may have noticed that they're not waiting for me. I've got a great astral being with a personal grudge. I've got gods paying way too close attention—no offence —and I had to start re-writing reality to save the world. Twice. And I cannot understate the degree to which I do not know what I'm doing with that, and I've still got a dimensional bridge to finish. For which I need to go poking around a messenger invasion, which is pretty tame by comparison. And yeah, the messengers aren't mine to deal with, but then there's the whole bit about me being an astral king. Even if I'm willing to put that aside, I don't think they will."

"Then use it; they will respect that status. It won't stop them from trying to kill you, but there can be advantages to being a respected enemy."

"What happened to focusing on mortal affairs?"

"The messengers are mortal. More or less. But I cannot give you more advice on that than I have. I don't want War complaining to me about encroachment."

"How does that work, exactly? What happened with Purity? Why didn't your lot tell anyone?"

"It is not for the rest of us to reveal the deceptions of the god Deception, or unveil the disguises of the god Disguise."

"Tell that to generations of people who were worshipping the wrong god."

"We did. To gods, the limitations of mortals seem strange. They seem like nothing to us, often meaningless or even contradictory. We, in turn, have limitations that make no sense to mortals, yet to us are as binding as the inevitability of death is to them."

"You might be talking to the wrong guy about the inevitability of death."

"As I said, Jason, you are in a strange position. Your nature is liminal, which makes it hard to know how to deal with you."

"Isn't there a God of Truth who could have told everyone about Purity?"

"It is far from that simple. Fire and water may seem like oppositional forces at a glance, but in reality, their interactions are complex and not always obvious. In the same way, Truth and Deception are not simple antagonists. And even if they were, would you, of all people, want them playing out their conflict in the mortal realm?"

"Isn't that exactly what Disguise did by taking over the Purity church? That's a lot of mortals being played with like pieces in a game."

"And if gods were constantly making proxy war of the physical realm, then all mortals would be but pawns, moving back and forth. We gods choose our moments and take our turns, by our own measure."

"And Truth didn't get a go in however long since the rest of you ganked Purity?"

"We did nothing to Purity. Most mortals believe that we did, but no. He sanctioned himself."

"And what is sanctioning, exactly? I've been wondering about this for a while."

"Sanctioning is an extreme change in the nature of a transcendent being, through a comprehensive shift in their authority."

"Just to be clear, when you say 'authority,' you're talking about the power to fundamentally reconfigure reality and unreality both, creating or recreating elements of cosmos, be it part of a physical universe or the deep astral, right? Or is it more of a 'permit to host a charity sausage sizzle' kind of authority?"

"The first one."

"I figured, but thought it was worth making sure. I'd feel like an idiot if I got it in my head that the old Builder was banished to the depths of the astral when he was outside a hardware store, fundraising for the local girl's cricket team."

Healer turned to look at Jason, who looked back.

"What?" Jason asked.

"You are an odd person."

"I'm not that odd. You just need to talk to more mortals."

"That is not so easy. The direct attention of a deity can be hard to withstand. We once gave you that attention, to harden your soul for the challenges to come. There is a reason our appearances in the worship squares are brief and focused on crowds. Unless a mortal is within my spirit domain, or part of my clergy and inured to my attention, even speaking to a projection like this for too long is harmful."

"Should I be worried? We've been here for a while. I feel fine, but are you pulling a spiritual silent-but-deadly on me?"

"As I have said before, you are unusual. Not many mortals have a nascent universe inside them."

"Mum always told me I was special. That's not true. She said my brother was special. Hey, did you change the subject? We were talking about sanctioning, and suddenly you're bringing up my mum."

Healer raised an eyebrow, but Jason shamelessly ignored him.

"You were saying something about sanctioning being a shift in authority."

"Yes. A transcendent entity is, by nature, either largely or entirely comprised of authority. Very little of that authority is boundless, however, and most of it has specific affinities. This is how gods come to have areas of influence."

"So, you're pretty much a sentient bundle of authority with a healing affinity?"

"Putting it that way is rather rude, but yes. To the degree that a mortal mind can comprehend the nuances, that is somewhat accurate."

"And sanctioning is changing the affinity of someone's authority?"

"Yes. As the name 'sanctioning' implies, this is normally a punitive act, imposed by other transcendent entities. You know of the new Builder. The previous Builder had its authority forcibly transmuted until it could no longer serve as the Builder."

"So, the old Builder is out there somewhere."

"Yes, although I shall speak no further on that. It is not for me to tell or for you to hear. Yet. The higher-order secrets will come to you as you progress as an astral king."

"And you said that you and the other gods *didn't* do that to Purity?"

"No. Gods can alter their own nature, but it is hard to do so without encroaching on other gods. Purity did it not by changing the affinity of his authority but by expending it."

"He used up all his power?"

"Yes."

"Why?"

"I do not know his reasons. As a god, I am content, but I know that others are unsatisfied with their lot. Purity took all his power, transmuted all that he was, and channelled it into an act of creation."

"Creation? You're saying that the God of Purity made something so hardcore, he had to top himself to get it done?"

"Yes."

"What could possibly require a god killing themselves to make?"

"Something that would inspire the messengers to invade a world."

Jason's eyes went wide.

"Someone told me that the messengers were here looking for something. Something that can purge the monster core effects out of someone's soul. You're telling me that it's some kind of artefact that a god killed himself to make?"

"That's not strictly accurate, but is broadly correct, yes."

"So, to sum up, the God of Purity got ennui and committed suicide by MacGuffin."

"That is not how I would describe it, but I can see how that could be seen as the case. From a very specific perspective."

"You know, I was wondering if my friend was overstating what a big deal this monster core purification thing is."

"He was not."

"Yeah, I'm getting that."

"Into whose hands this object falls is important, yes."

"Are you asking me to go look for the thing? Is that why you're here?"

"No. You have no place amongst the forces that will clash over this."

"Diamond-rankers."

"Yes. You can participate in the search, should you desire, but once it is found, run far and fast. I would advise staying out of the chase altogether."

"Do you know where this divine relic is?"

"Yes."

"Are you going to tell anyone?"

"No. After reluctantly going along with Deception and Disguise, the gods have unilaterally decreed that none of us shall interfere with the search for the artefact Purity left behind, or the fight that takes place over it. We shall leave its fate to mortals to determine for themselves."

"Even though it's some kind of divine relic?"

"If a new Purity rises, they may intervene. It is unlikely one will before the issue is settled, however."

"If you're not here to get me to involve myself, why are you here?"

"To express my gratitude, as I said. I also have something for you. Consider it both a thank you for your accommodations to my people today, as well as a welcoming gift for your first step into the immortal realm, as tentative as that step is."

He held out a fist-sized orb, clear but filled with sparks of blue, silver and gold. The moment Jason took it, the god was gone.

Item: [Genesis Command: Life] (transcendent rank, legendary)

The authority to create a life. (consumable, magic core).

- Effect: Give true life to an astral construct created from a dimensional space. The construct becomes a true astral entity, bound to the dimensional space.

- Uses remaining: 1/1

"Holy crap, guy," Jason muttered. "I think you're overpaying just to rent out some space."

74

MR ASANO WILL SEE YOU NOW

Jason looked at the orb in his hand, given to him by the Healer. He wasn't certain exactly what it would do, but with the power of his soul space, he was certain he could figure it out. He was tempted to do so immediately, but instead, put it into his inventory. There would be time later, and he couldn't help but feel there was another shoe left to drop with the messengers.

Rufus had posited that the messengers might strike the teams investigating the worm-infested towns. Jason wanted to be able to portal in and rejoin the team in an instant if that happened, but his instincts told him it wouldn't. It could just be his imagination, but he felt an uncomfortable affinity with the messengers, and he couldn't shake the idea that they would come for the city.

If and when the messengers made a move on the city, there was only so much Jason could do. Compared to the city's defence infrastructure, one cloud palace would not make a big impact. He certainly couldn't compare to the high-ranking defenders, but he was prepared to make the most of what he could offer. Shade bodies were already placed throughout and around the city.

For the moment, he stayed where he was, looking out over the evacuee camp. He could sense Arabelle moving through the administrative area of the cloud hospital, alongside another gold-ranker. It wasn't someone Jason knew, but had sensed roaming around the hospital. They were heading for Jason's location and would shortly arrive. Jason weighed his options for a moment between politeness and being needlessly dramatic before deciding to be true to himself.

"Shade?"

"Yes, Mr Asano?" Shade asked, emerging from Jason's shadow.

"Please show the ladies in when they arrive."

Shade's silhouette form did not have a face with which to give Jason a flat look, yet somehow his pause managed to convey the feeling of one.

"Must we, Mr Asano?"

"What?" Jason asked innocently.

"I know that tone, Mr Asano, and I know what you want."

"That saves time, then."

"I'd rather not."

"It's kind of your job."

"Mr Asano, it's a terrible movie."

"I know it's a terrible movie."

"And a worse book."

"It's a much worse book, yes."

"I'm not doing it. If you wanted to do this, you should have chosen Christian Grey as your alias."

"Shade, you understood the job when you became my familiar."

"Mr Asano, I don't understand the job *now*."

"Just get out there; they're about to arrive."

Shade did not grumble and Shade did not sigh. Even so, and looking in the other direction, Jason felt their heavy implication.

"Will the high priestess be meeting Mr Asano or Mr Miller? And what will he be wearing?"

"Good question," Jason said, and removed the coins that disguised his eyes. "Asano, I think. I don't think lies will help smooth out my relations with the lady."

Jason was shrouded in dark mist for a moment, and when it faded, his clothes had been replaced with a sharp grey suit from his Alejandro Albericci collection. He then turned back to the window and looked out into the middle distance.

"Better?"

"Much. You realise that this world has barely started recording theatrical productions for public viewing. They won't understand the reference to a movie poster from another universe."

"They never do, Shade."

"Then why do you insist on doing this?"

"Because it's fun."

"Is that entirely appropriate today, Mr Asano? Not long ago, we were standing in a town filled with the dead."

"It's not appropriate, but I'm going to do it anyway. You know I've tried brooding on the dark days, and you know how that worked out."

"I do."

"It didn't make me feel better; I just spiralled. You know that better than anyone. So, I'm going to remind myself that while life can be a crap sack of death and misery sometimes, I don't have to let those times define my life. I tried that and it sucked."

"Very well," Shade acceded. "I approve of your attitude, Mr Asano, although I must stress the opposite about the means by which you have chosen to express it."

His voice dripped so heavily with disapproval, despite its formality, that Jason was inclined to ban Shade from watching British television.

"When we go back to Earth, I hope your niece is in need of a familiar," Shade muttered as he disappeared into Jason's shadow.

"What was that?" Jason asked.

"I have no idea what you are talking about, Mr Asano."

Hana Shavar was the High Priestess of the Church of the Healer for the city of Yaresh. When people had started arriving, after being rescued from towns and villages across the southern region, she personally took charge. Scrambling for resources was difficult as they were already being sent off as fast as they could be, to supply the fight with the messengers.

Tapping into the local adventurer resources was a typical approach in such circumstances, although the building from which the evacuee camp was run left her uneasy. On the surface, it was perfect, with a slew of amenities that were a boon to her work, but she could not shake a nebulous suspicion about it.

Something about the building tickled Hana's senses. That there was an aura, heavily tamped-down, was normal for a soul-bound item like a cloud flask. The aura itself even felt protective and benevolent, but something told her that something else lay dormant, like a sleeping dragon.

Arabelle Remore had been a useful asset, both in making the most of the building and assuaging Hana's unease. As a follower of the Healer, Remore's mental health specialty was not as immediately useful as others might have been, but would be critical in the days to come.

Healing magic would swiftly bring the survivors of the towns and villages to full physical health, but what they had been through would take a much longer recovery. There was no healing spell for the memory of everyone you know being killed and their bodies paraded around in a mockery of life.

Even so, Remore did not entirely settle Hana's concerns. While she had never been outright evasive with Hana's questions about the building and its owner, Hana got a definite sense that important things were going unsaid. For this reason, Hana wanted to meet the owner of the building, so when Remore asked if she would, she immediately agreed. Although she was busy, the chance to alleviate her concerns was worth a little time.

Hana was dealing with a few last issues around the infested adventurers that had been caught when she sensed the presence of her god. Where she couldn't be certain, but he was definitely projecting himself somewhere in the building. With all the work they had to do, it was welcome, although she could not help but feel disappointed that he hadn't appeared before her.

One of the building's amenities was a communication system that allowed Hana to see and speak with her key subordinates in the building, but checking around, she could not find where the god had shown himself. That was when she discovered that the others hadn't felt his presence, only Hana herself.

Remore took Hana to the top floor of the building, which had the most space currently unused. It was tagged for the kind of long-term treatment that Remore and others like her would need to conduct once things slowed down enough to make that possible. They arrived at a door with a shadow creature standing outside it. Most shadow entities blurred into the gloom around them, but this one was neat and clearly defined, looking almost officious despite being little more than a silhouette.

"High Priestess Shavar, Mrs Remore," it greeted them in a male voice with formal intonation. "Welcome. I am Shade."

"Shade," Remore said. "Why are you playing doorman? Is something the matter?"

"Yes, Mrs Remore," the shadow said, paradoxically sounding both extremely polite and extremely disgruntled at the same time.

"What happened?" Remore asked.

"The usual," the shadow said.

"Ah. Would I even understand if I asked?"

"No, Mrs Remore. I would apologise for Mr Asano, but I do not wish the responsibility and he has no intent to contrition."

Hana had seen nothing but professionalism from Arabelle Remore, so was surprised to see her let out a long-suffering sigh.

"Alright," Arabelle said. "Let's get it over with."

"Very well," Shade said.

The shadow creature was not easy to read, yet Hana had the sense he was steeling himself with a rigid pause. There was a shared camaraderie between Remore and the shadow that Hana recognised from warriors facing grave odds together, which was more than unusual for what should be a mundane meeting.

"Is something the matter?" she asked.

"I do so hope not, Priestess Shavar. Mr Asano will see you now."

Hana couldn't be certain that she didn't imagine the very slight shudder that seemed to pass over the shadow creature as he spoke and the door opened. The first thing she noticed was the lingering presence of her god; this was the room in which he had appeared.

Inside, the room was empty save for a man standing with his back to the door, hands in pockets as he stared out the window wall. The window itself was tinted, leaving the camp outside and the sky beyond it pale and washed of colour. After a moment, the man turned, giving her the same assessing look she gave him.

Startlingly, his aura was a closed book, despite being only silver rank. Hana's senses were sharp, even for a gold-ranker, but all she got from him was the same muted aura she sensed from the building itself. If there was any difference, it was that her sense of something dormant and dangerous lying within that aura only grew stronger. If she wanted any more than that, she would have to force her senses onto him, crashing through the boundaries of politeness.

That left his appearance by which to judge him. Asano's expression was that of faint amusement, as if thinking of a joke only he understood. From the exchange with the shadow creature, she imagined that was the case, although whether the joke was at her expense she could not tell. From Arabelle's reaction, she guessed it was a self-indulgence of the man himself.

Sharp features were softened by a neatly trimmed beard, with glossy black hair the standout feature. He had the usual polished symmetry of silver rank but was not stand-out handsome. She guessed that his face had been a little too angular before the polishing effects of ranking up. His suit was neat-casual in the Rimaros-style, expensive without the need to flaunt it, which meant *really* expensive. He wore it well enough, but it had the feeling of a costume. Something in his expression told her that he liked costumes, the more flamboyant the better.

Asano's eyes were flagrantly magical, but what drew her attention were his scars. Small marks stood out, bisecting one eyebrow and gouging a thin, hairless mark in his beard. A more substantial mark was on his throat, plainly visible with the open collar of his shirt.

Finally, she turned to the eyes, blue and orange with dark sclera. They gave the sense of distant power, off in a void, and Hana immediately concluded that this was the most honest thing in his appearance.

Looking into his eyes, something finally clicked about the building. It was hard to notice, barely registering on her magical senses, but something was feeding power to the building from somewhere. If she hadn't been intimately familiar with the process, as a channel for divine power, she wouldn't have recognised it at all.

This time, she did push her senses beyond the limits of propriety, exploring the link between the man and the building. She traced the link back to some kind of power inside him that she didn't recognise, her aura recoiling at the touch of it. He showed amusement rather than offence.

"Rude," he said, the edges of his mouth curling up in a slight smile. "Your aura is strong for your rank."

Despite outranking him, his words felt patronising after what she'd just sensed. Even without the power that tossed her perception back, the aura she had dug through to find it had been impossibly potent for a silver-ranker.

"Who are you?" she asked bluntly. After what she'd just done with her aura, there was little point in the pretence of manners.

"Jason Asano."

She frowned.

"*What* are you?"

"Team chef."

"Liar."

"Frequently. Drink?"

A drinks cabinet made of clouds rose from the floor. A bench slid out of it with three glasses and Asano started mixing drinks, not waiting for a response.

"I have concerns about this building," Hana said. "And about you."

"And I have concerns about you," he said, not looking up from his task. "Arabelle, your friend's manners leave something to be desired."

"You're right," Hana acknowledged. "But while you're standing there, playing games, people with intense trauma are being brought in here. I need to know that you are genuinely trying to help and not setting us up for something that will only make things worse."

"I've seen what's inside them, Priestess," Jason said. "I'm not sure it can get much worse for these people. If I have some political agenda, what do they care? And if I was in league with the messengers, enacting some wildly convoluted scheme, do you think some lady interrogating me in my own house will bring it all down?"

There was flinty rebuke in his final words, but when he looked up from the drinks, there was still nothing but faint amusement on his face while his aura was as unreadable as ever. The beverages in front of him were in wide, short glasses, clear to show off colourful layers of liquor. He took one of the glasses from the bench and the other two floated off as the cabinet descended into the floor. Hana realised that he was levitating the glasses with his aura. Like a messenger.

"I have too many questions to be able to trust you," she said, leaving the glass floating in front of her.

"Oh, you have no idea how many reasons there are not to trust me, Priestess."

Arabelle grabbed her drink and took a heavy gulp, shaking her head at the both of them.

"Mr Asano, you should be taking things seriously on a day like today."

"I disagree," Jason said. "I've seen many days like today, and I've taken them very seriously. I'm not going to go roaming past the survivors, whistling a jaunty tune, but I won't wear a dark cloud over my head like that will somehow make things better either. As for trust, that's up to you."

"You just told me not to trust you."

"No, I said there are many reasons not to trust me, not that you shouldn't."

Hana narrowed her eyes as she ran another assessing look over the infuriating man.

"I understand that you have seen a lot of death today, Mr Asano."

"That's right."

"You seem very frivolous for someone encountering such a thing."

"I do, don't I?"

"Do you think that those deaths mean nothing?"

"That would make me a monster."

"Which is exactly why I asked."

"The deaths matter. They all matter."

"Then how is it that you seem so unaffected?"

"Practise."

"How can you use your aura like a messenger?"

"Also practise."

"Why was my god here?" Hana asked, which drew a raised-eyebrows expression from Arabelle. "I sense his lingering presence in this room."

"Fashion advice," Asano said. "He's looking to switch the church robes from brown to a pale blue. I'm trying to talk him into a floral print, but he's proving reluctant."

"You're veering in the direction of blasphemy."

"I'm Jason Asano, pleased to meet you. That's twice I've introduced myself, by the way, which you have yet to do. If your god left anything here that you can sense, I can't imagine he did so by accident. You might want to spend some time contemplating why."

Hana frowned.

"I am Hana Shavar. High Priestess of the Church of the Healer, Yaresh."

Instead of the slight, rather smug smiles he had shown thus far, his sudden and genuine-seeming smile lit up his face.

"Have a drink, Priestess. This might be your camp, but this is my house and you're a guest. A rude one, as we've already established."

Cloud furniture rose from the floor, a seat behind Jason and a couch behind Hana and Arabelle. Jason and Arabelle sat, then Hana took the still-floating glass and sat as well, glowering at Jason.

She looked at the glass in her hand. Did it have some undetectable poison whose fumes were affecting her? She barely recognised her own behaviour, realising that this man and his strange building unsettled her much more than she had originally realised. Was it the strange power inside him, or some childish jealousy over her god appearing in front of him without letting her know why? Was it as simple as a personality clash? There was just something about the man that made her want to punch him in his smug face, but she was far better than that. Scolding herself, she schooled her emotions.

"I apologise, Mr Asano. You have been generous, and I have been discourteous."

"It's a rough day, Priestess; I won't begrudge you a little stress. And call me Jason."

"My behaviour notwithstanding, I have a responsibility to this city and the people we are attempting to help here. I cannot allow any potential dangers, and this building troubles me. Its owner troubles me more. I've seen cloud palaces before—there is one nearby for direct comparison—but this one is different. I don't know what power you are using to feed it, or how, but it's close enough to a divine connection that I keep coming back to my original questions: who and what are you?"

Asano crossed his legs and leaned back in his chair, relaxed. He took a sip of his drink.

"To sum up, Priestess, you want me to tell you all my secrets before I'm qualified for the privilege of lending you what I'm confident you've already found to be an exceptionally useful building."

"Yes. Mr Asano, what are your thoughts on mysterious powers that you don't understand, with motives you don't know?"

"I'm against them, as a rule, but as they try to kill me on a regular basis, I'm somewhat biased. As someone who encounters them on a regular basis, though I've learned that sometimes you have to suck it up and do the job in front of you."

"And how has that worked out for you?"

"Very mixed," he said, frustration poking through his façade as he turned to Arabelle. "Is this what I'm like? Marching into places to make rude and outrageous demands?"

"Yes," Arabelle said absently, peering into her glass with a sceptical expression. "How is this so sweet? It's like syrup."

"I think I'm starting to see why people don't like me," Jason said, then turned his attention back to Hana.

"If you don't trust this building," he told her, "don't use it."

"That would make the camp activities far less efficient," she said. "Especially given that we are already using it quite heavily."

"Then you have a choice. Give it up and make things worse, or keep using it and live with the mystery. I'll leave the decision up to you."

Jason and his chair both descended into the floor, vanishing. Arabelle immediately turned to Hana.

"If I might ask, High Priestess, are you alright? I've been watching you act with decorum all day, in the most hectic of circumstances. Jason was as I expected, and I know he can be hard to deal with, but if you'll allow some blunt honesty, it was your behaviour that surprised me."

Hana looked into the glass in her hands, still untouched. Her expression reflected her thoughts, uncertain and troubled.

"I'm sorry, Priestess Remore. I'm not sure exactly what has gotten into me. I think it is an accumulation of things. Also, I don't think I've ever had someone infuriate me so quickly. The arrogance and the smugness of him. What we're doing here is important and he treats it like a joke. That is not an excuse for my behaviour, I know. Do you think he will withdraw his use of this cloud building?"

"Oh, don't worry about annoying Jason. Being rude will get you on his good side faster than being polite, if anything. I'm more worried about what's going on with you. When was the last time you slept?"

"I don't know. Three, four days? We assaulted the messenger strongholds in sequence. Wanted them on the back foot in case the problems to the south were part of some plan of theirs. I was barely back in the city when the call for the camp came in. But again, that's a reason, not an excuse."

"You need to rest."

"There's too much work."

"And there are people to do it, at least long enough for you to sleep. I'm not asking, High Priestess. This is an order from your mental care specialist."

Hana nodded, still staring into the colourful liquid in her glass. She closed her eyes as she lifted it to her lips to take a sip. As the thick sweetness of the liquor spread over her tongue, her eyes shot open.

"This is amazing!"

75

HOT CHOCOLATE

J ES F IN K AAL WAS NOT PRONE TO NERVOUSNESS. A S A MESSENGER, CONFIDENCE was ingrained. More than that, she was a Voice of the Will, a representative of her people's most powerful beings. But as much as she might have tried to bury the memory, she remembered the sense of inferiority that had defined the final moments of Pei Vas Kartha as she died at Jason Asano's hands.

While being a Voice of the Will was an unquestionably powerful position, there was no escaping the fact that it was a state of permanent subordination. Even if that was to an astral king, serving anyone did not come naturally to messengers. While ordinary messengers might obey her now, each one of them was looking towards the day when they surpassed her, reaching the pinnacle of their kind. That only a minuscule few would ever reach those heights meant little, so long as the potential was still there. For all the power that a voice commanded, they did not have that potential. Their power ultimately came from another.

The messengers had never been able to determine what set the limits to their individual power. They did not even learn those limits until they hit them. For those who discovered themselves unable to surpass silver rank, there were only two options. One was to accept their status as the least of their kind, and live with being superior to everything that wasn't a messenger. The other was to seek out an astral king that would have them, allowing them to artificially surpass their limits.

While other messengers might serve an astral king, and be subject to their power, they could always escape it if they themselves grew powerful enough. For a Voice of the Will, there was no going back. Silver and even gold-ranked messengers might show deference to a Voice of the Will; those who reached diamond looked at them with disdain. Diamond was the hard limit for voices, while messengers who reached that point on their own had the potential to become astral kings, however unlikely that was. For that reason, diamond-rank messengers looked down even on voices that had reached the same rank.

Jes Fin Kaal was a gold-rank voice, and while she had claimed command of the messenger forces in the region, there was a diamond-ranker amongst them who could take that right from her whenever he liked. That he had chosen not to was typical of diamond-rank messengers. While they might be forced to capitulate to the agendas of astral kings, their obsession was transcending mortality to become one themselves.

Unsurprisingly, the diamond-ranker, Mah Go Schaat, had claimed the largest and tallest building in the stronghold as his own. Jes flew up and hovered around the domed pinnacle. She waited to be acknowledged, one minute turning into ten and minutes becoming an hour. Everyone in the stronghold could look up and see her being left outside, waiting on an audience.

Jes did not mind; it was both a childish power play and a chance to rest her mind in meditation. Between the attacks on the messenger strongholds, organising the upcoming attack and reacting to the adventurers hitting the worm nests, she could use the rest. As for the idea of being shamed in front of the entire stronghold, she did not care what the people below or the one she was waiting on thought of her. She neither needed their praise nor feared their scorn.

Finally, a panel in the dome slid open to allow her entry. Inside was a library with bookshelves and tables covered in tomes. Freestanding magical writing boards were scrawled with notes and had papers pinned to them, showing scraps of map or magical diagrams.

There was only one chair. It was a massive throne of dark leather in the messenger style, with an hourglass back to allow for wings. Mah Go Schaat sat in it, his brown wings with dark yellow speckling spread out behind it. He was a massive figure, even for a messenger, being almost as tall sitting as Jes was when floating upright, just over the floor.

The chair faced the door, but he did not look up as Jes entered. His gaze was locked onto a many-faceted crystal he was holding in one hand. She waited patiently, just as she had outside. Finally, Mah's eyes shifted from the crystal to her.

"Why do you interrupt my contemplation, Voice?"

"The time approaches to attack the city. We launch our attack in the hours before dawn."

"You would presume to have me move at your word?"

"I am only the voice. The word is that of the astral king."

"Is it? This is your plan, Jes Fin Kaal."

"If you wish to claim my position, you have the power. I can let the astral king know that you will be enacting her agenda in my place."

Mah glowered and Jes did not let her disdain reach her face. Mah was a typical, unthinking thug who believed that being a messenger and being powerful was all he needed to embody their superior ideals. Jes knew that superiority was not just a birthright, and that their actions were needed to maintain it.

Jes knew that it was foolish to prod Mah, yet she could not resist the urge. The more powerful a messenger became, especially one like him, the more they chafed any time they were forced to acknowledge any will but their own. Being a voice, and no longer the instrument of her own will, had given Jes what she believed was a more objective perspective. The myopic power obsession of too many messengers left them with no sense of what truly made their kind great. They had faith just as blind as the fools who worshipped gods.

Mah not only lacked the inclination to administer the messenger strongholds but also the ability, and he knew it. Like Fal Vin Garath, whom Jes would be sending to test Asano, Mah was a brute who saw value in nothing but power. It was only on realising that martial power alone would not allow them to transcend immortality that they started looking further afield. Jes had seen more than one diamond-ranker suddenly immerse themselves in study after hitting the barrier that lay between diamond rank and transcendence.

"Very well," Mah finally said through gritted teeth.

"If I may," Jes said with deference, knowing when to step back, "I would like to submit a role in the attack for your approval."

"Speak on it," Mah ordered.

"The weapon we placed in the city years ago is no longer under containment," Jes said. "I was going to place someone new to contain the change, but as the timing was right, I decided to exacerbate it instead. Once the weapon awakens, the city will deploy their forces against it, as it is already inside the defences. That is when we will attack weak points in the city infrastructure that we have identified. My hope is that you, as the supreme power in this conflict, will occupy the city's diamond-rank defenders. If you can kill them, all the better, but containing them is enough to let our forces rampage."

"It will be two against one, in their territory. I am stronger than either, but not both together."

"That is why we let them tire themselves fighting the weapon. You come in and clean them up."

"What is your goal?"

"The city has been the feeding point for the forces that have been harassing us. We seek to ruin and sow chaos, to bring the war they have pressed on us to their doorstep. They coddle their weak masses, who will demand their power be used as a shield they can huddle behind, no longer sent to the attack. We can then turn our attention to the Builder's remnant forces, the Ashen and the tainted."

"Then what solution have you found to the natural array? Have you finally accepted it for the crucible it is?"

"I still oppose a mass attack. There is no telling how many more of our people will suffer the taint."

"Which is how we cull the weak and inferior. The ones who fall to the taint— as you doubtless would, without the astral king's power—are not worthy to be counted as messengers."

"We will let the essence users deal with the array."

"You would let them destroy it? What of your astral king's plans?"

"The enemy will carry them out for us."

"Having your foe act when you lack the strength. Pathetic."

"There are many kinds of strength."

Mah snorted derision.

"How will you even manage that?"

"What does it matter, so long as it works?"

Mah's lip curled in a sneer, but he didn't push.

"Go, then. Send word when the time comes, and I may deign to join your attack."

Jes gave him a short bow. "My gratitude for your benevolence, Mah Go Schaat."

The rear wing of the cloud hospital Jason created was the private residence and provided facilities for Jason and his team, still fully within his spirit domain. Jason waited, leaning against a wall with two fruit drinks in large steins, one of which he was sipping from through a metal straw. On the opposite wall, a doorway opened as the cloud door dissolved into nothing, revealing an exhausted-looking Taika.

The big man was stripped down to the waist, his dark, tattooed torso almost large enough to seal the doorway again. Gone was the roundness that he had when they first met, his body instead sporting the sculpted muscle of a professional wrestler.

Jason held out the spare drink, Taika taking it eagerly.

"Thanks, bro," Taika said as he plucked the straw from his stein, then heavily gulped down half of the drink at a go, juice running down his chin. He let out a breath as he grinned and wiped his chin with the back of his arm. "That's the stuff."

"For a guy who's been meditating," Jason said, "you look a lot like someone who just finished a session at the gym."

"Meditation isn't exactly the same for an essence user as for a lady who buys a lot of crystals at a new age store," Taika said. "You know that. I've seen you doing that Dance of the Sword Fairy technique that Rufus taught you."

"Yeah," Jason agreed.

The availability of more effective meditation techniques for adventurers was one of the fundamental differences between the essence users of Earth and Pallimustus. As one of the pillars of non-core advancement, such techniques were also the least intuitive to develop. Pallimustus had been refining them for millennia, whereas Earth had almost nothing.

Even the US Network only had a few basic techniques, but that had still put them in a globe-dominating position amongst the magical factions. Those techniques had come from the Network founder when his familiar—who would go on to become Mr North—betrayed him.

As essence users ranked up, their minds changed, becoming capable of more. Meditation techniques needed to change accordingly, taking in elements of internal mana manipulation, martial arts katas and plain physical exertion, depending on the nature and purpose of the exercise. Jason relied heavily on different versions of the sword dance meditation Taika mentioned.

"Did Humphrey show you something new?" Jason asked.

As Humphrey and Taika had similar roles, Humphrey had supplied Taika with more appropriate techniques than Jason or Farrah had to offer him back on Earth.

Without anything specialised for him, he had been using the same general techniques Farrah taught all her Network trainees.

"Actually," Taika said, "I met this bloke when I was coming back into the city from a solo job."

While Jason had been doing sexy aura training over the past week, Taika had been taking solo contracts, pushing himself to finally cross the line into silver. As a result, his aura was almost trembling with how ready he was to take the final step.

"We got to talking," Taika continued, "and he ended up showing me this meditation technique that meshes perfectly with my garuda essence. It's called Golden Wings Transcending the Heavens. Sounds pretty sweet, right?"

"It does. And it looks like it works pretty sweet too, if your aura is anything to go by."

"Hell yeah, bro. You ready to have me on the team?"

"That, I'm not so sure about," Jason said.

Taika frowned. "Are you saying I'm not good enough?"

"No, I'm saying that between you and Rufus joining, there's too many sexy brown people. I'm worried Belinda will have the team name changed to Hot Chocolate."

The messenger forces were preparing to leave their strongholds. The attacks from the city had been an impediment, but not a critical one, and the messengers were aching to pay what they thought of as the servant races back in kind.

Not far from one of the marshalling yards, Jes looked at Fal Vin Garath, who still didn't have a mouth after she had taken it from him. She was somewhat surprised that he had managed to endure, not thinking the brute would tolerate what she had done to him for long. Her ability to affect him in such a way was tied directly to Fal's acceptance of the authority of the astral king she served. The moment he rejected that authority, his mouth would have returned. She would have subsequently killed him, but he'd have died with his mouth back.

It was a test in and of itself, as even a moment's disloyalty would have been enough. Yet he stayed true, despite the inherent ambition and demonstrated arrogance of the man. Although Fal was her least favourite kind of person, Jes was forced to acknowledge at least a modicum of grudging respect.

"We are going to attack the city," she told him. "You've already been given your task. Hunt down Asano and kill him. If you can, all well and good. If not, do your best to withdraw and regroup with our regular forces. Do you understand?"

Fal's blank lower face morphed back into a mouth, yet he silently nodded.

"Good," she told him. "Now that you have a mouth again, do you have any questions?"

"If this man truly is somehow a silver-rank astral king, are you certain you want me to kill him?"

"If he is someone that you can kill, Fal Vin Garath, he isn't worth using."

She felt the anger suffuse his aura.

"You don't like it," she said. "You don't like that this man is already on the path that is the goal of every messenger. You don't like that I'm using you as a tool, as if he is more important than you. I am curious if you will let that anger rule you. If you do, you will die. It might be because you fight Asano to the death, or perhaps you will lash out at me and be struck down."

She grinned.

"Prove me wrong," she told him. "Show me that you're more than a mindless thug, and you will find that I can be a valuable ally in your quest for advancement. We did not start off on the best foot, Fal Vin Garath, but do well here and this could go very well for you."

SADNESS PORRIDGE

Hana Shavar let out a happy moan as she stirred in half-slumber before her head cleared as she came fully awake. Despite herself, she couldn't help but stretch out, luxuriating in the cloud bed that felt far too light to support her weight, while doing so perfectly, moulding to her body.

Propping herself up on her elbows, she looked around. The room was small, one of several on the hospital's top floor set aside for the people running the camp to get some rest. Arabelle Remore had sent her stumbling in, following Hana's afternoon meeting with Asano. She barely managed to yank off her clothes before collapsing into the cloud bed, hardly registering the enveloping softness before sleep took her. Taking her first proper look around, she noticed that although the room was small and almost featureless, it was cosy, with a soft light that slowly grew brighter, allowing her sleepy eyes to adjust.

The room was quite different from the clean and clinical décor that comprised the rest of the hospital. While this room contained only a bed and a bedside table, the cloud-construct nature of the building was on full display. While white was the predominant colour, soft hues of blue and orange gradated softly to break up the monochrome.

She looked to the bedside table where the clothes she had roughly pulled off before falling into slumber had been cleaned and neatly folded. She grabbed her pocket watch, sitting atop the clothes, and frowned as she checked the time. After meeting Asano in the afternoon, she'd spoken with Arabelle, issued some directives for while she was resting, and been asleep within half an hour. One of those directives had been to wake her in the evening, but she had been left to rest for hours past the turn of midnight.

Navigating her way out of the cloud bed was a little odd, like escaping the fluffiest of marshmallows. Her feet sank ankle-deep into the lush, airy softness of a floor that was almost as luxurious as the bed. The pull to let herself fall back and return to slumber was so strong that she examined her aura for undue external influence, before scolding herself for laziness.

She glared at her clothes on the bedside table. She had been half-dead on her feet, but she clearly remembered leaving them crumpled on the floor. Even in the depths of exhausted sopor, anyone approaching her should have stirred her to wakefulness. Who had managed to come in, take her clothes, wash, and then return them, all without tweaking her aura senses? The obvious candidate was Asano, despite his silver rank. The combination of his remarkable aura and dominion over the cloud house might have made it possible. After all, the one aspect of the room she was in was that her senses could not penetrate the walls.

She swept her magic and aura senses over the clothes, looking for any trace of tampering. After finding nothing, she pulled them on, ignoring the pang of regret as her shoes went on, separating her feet from a floor she would have happily slept on every night for the rest of her life.

She needed to get out of the room and clear her head before she took her clothes back off and crawled back into bed. She looked to the door, delineated in the blue and orange of a winter sunset. The door didn't have a handle but a patch on the wall next to it that emitted a gentle glow. She pressed her hand against it and the doorway dissolved into mist, revealing Jason Asano leaning against the opposite wall. He held out a plate with a gently steaming fried sandwich on it.

"Morning, sunshine."

Jason watched as the door dissolved to reveal the high priestess. Her clothes were neat and clean, but she herself looked drowsy, eyelids drooping heavily over vibrant green eyes. Her light brown hair was only slightly mussed, despite falling well below her shoulders, somehow looking more sensual than dishevelled. He wondered absently if that was a gold-rank thing or if she was just one of those people, like Rufus, who looked great under any circumstances.

If Jason looked even close to that astounding, first thing after waking up, he wouldn't have needed to get so good at cooking breakfast food. But he did, which inspired his confidence in the fried vegetable and egg sandwich with spicy relish he held out for her.

"Morning, sunshine."

"Did you take my clothes?" she demanded.

He looked her up and down.

"You're wearing your clothes."

"My clean, pressed clothes. Someone came into my room and did that."

"That would be Shade, my shadow familiar. I have no interest in the goings-on inside your room."

"Then how did you know I was waking up, to be here with a hot sandwich?"

"This is my house, Priestess. I see everything."

"I just woke up in my underwear," she pointed out.

"Uh... well, when I say 'see,' that's more of a metaphor. I *knew* that you were awake and getting dressed, but I wasn't actually watching."

"But you could look if you wanted to? Without me knowing?"

"I could."

"Then I just have to trust that you didn't?"

"You do. But don't flatter yourself, Priestess."

Her eyebrows shot up and he flashed her a grin.

"Are you the one who stopped me from being woken up, Mr Asa... Mr Miller?"

"That was your designated mental health professional," Jason told her. "Who I see explained my identity situation."

"Why did you even tell me your real name?"

"I like to put an honest foot forward," he said. "What you see is what you get with me."

"I have no idea what I'm seeing when I look at you."

"Which is exactly what to expect going forward, from what I'm told. Are you going to take this sandwich, or should I eat it myself?"

"I'm fine eating spirit coins."

"Not in this house."

Jason didn't have the time he would like to focus on magical cooking. Experts could produce moderate but long-lasting boons with their food, but Jason focused elsewhere. By giving up on the trickiest part of cooking magic, he was able to use high-rank ingredients for the most fundamental aspects of cooking: taste and nutrition. As such, the sandwich on the plate he held could be swapped out for the gold coin or ten silver coins a gold-ranker needed.

Such food also cost noticeably less than the coins it replaced, with the added benefit of tasting like food and not like a car battery. This was one of the key reasons that gold-rankers favoured high-magic zones, even if they weren't actively adventuring. Where the production of high-ranking food ingredients was viable, the cost of gold-rank living went down while quality of life went up.

Jason contemplated this as he watched her peer at the sandwich with suspicion, even as her nostrils flared at the delectable smell of it. She took the plate from his hands.

"Thank you, I'm going to eat it walking," she said and immediately set off down the hall.

"Uh, Priestess?"

She stopped and looked back.

"Yes?"

"Elevating platform is in the other direction."

"I'm certain it was in this direction."

"It was, yes. When you went to sleep."

"It moved?"

"Yes. As did the room you were sleeping in. Cloud-stuff makes renovations fairly easy."

"I didn't think you could make major structural changes to a cloud construct on this scale without breaking it down first."

"Mine is a little more flexible than most, although there are still some hard limits."

"Why would you change things around?"

"Some of the teams found towns where people were in the process of having worms implanted. My friend Carlos figured out how to extract the worms without killing the host if they catch the process early enough, if you have the right facility, so I had to make room. The administration area's a bit crowded now, the shower queues are a little longer and there's not quite as much space for frozen food. Also, I had to give up my big empty office for watching the camp from."

"Your friend Carlos? Do you mean Priest Quilido?"

"That's the bloke."

"You are friends with a lot of powerful and prestigious healers."

"I've taken a few hits in my time."

He felt her gaze rest on his scars.

"Why did my god visit you?" she asked softly.

He almost gave a flippant answer but stopped himself.

"I'm not going to tell you that," he said gently. "You have to get to know me better before I'll talk about something like that, and you won't even eat my sandwich."

"Why are you so concerned with this sandwich?"

"Because you're wasting the sandwich. The plate is enchanted to keep it warm, but it's fried food. It's pretty light, but you'll still see some congealing if you just let it sit there."

"Why are you always trying to make me eat and drink?"

"Feeding people is kind of my thing. I made that myself, just so you know. The sandwich, not the plate. It's a lot better than the food they're getting down in the cafeteria."

"What they're getting in the cafeteria has nutrition, energy and even mild healing properties. It was designed specifically for normal-rank people that have experienced trauma and is what their bodies need."

"Their bodies, sure, but gruel is not what their souls need."

"It doesn't matter how it looks or tastes."

"That came through very clearly when I tried some. While you've been asleep, I've been working with your head of food distribution to fix the recipe."

"This may be your house, Asano, but this is my camp. Who gave you permission to do that?"

"Arabelle. She shares my opinion that people will recover faster if their food doesn't taste like it was made in a gulag."

"What's a gulag?"

"A forced labour camp. These people have been through enough without feeding them sadness porridge."

"Just direct me to wherever the administration area is."

"We have to talk first."

"About what?"

"Arabelle tells me that you've been in the fight against the messengers?"

"Yes."

"The messengers haven't attacked the teams handling the towns in the south where worm-breeding sites have been found. What does that tell you?"

"The attacks on their strongholds may have put them on the defensive. They may not have been ready for us to hit the towns where they were infesting the people with world-taker worms. Or, potentially, this all fell within their plans and they are looking to strike at the city while so many adventurers are clearing out those towns."

"And if they intend to attack the city?"

"Then the best time will be leading up to dawn."

She checked her watch again.

"Most likely within the next few hours," she added.

"City administration has put the city on a heightened alert level, just in case. Preparations to get the population into the monster attack bunkers as soon as an attack begins were started yesterday. The Adventure Society is organising combat response teams and the Magic Society is keeping a close eye on the defence infrastructure."

"I need to organise the evacuee camp response."

"Already being done. You have effective subordinates, which is the mark of a good leader."

"Why are you the one telling me all this, instead of one of those subordinates?"

"Because the plan, if there is an attack, is to reconfigure the two cloud palaces into defence bunkers for the people in the camp. And there are things you will need to know about that before it happens."

"Such as?"

"If I turn this place into a bunker, your god won't be able to reach you inside. That goes for every priest and every god, but yours is the one with the most people in camp."

Jason could see the walls go up in her body language.

"What are you talking about?" she asked.

"Just what I said. Your powers should still work fine, but you won't be able to hear the voice of your god."

"I've experienced that before when I went into astral spaces to confront the Builder cult. Does your cloud house have the power to create a dimensional space outside the world?"

"No. It's more like... have you ever entered the core areas of another god's temple?"

She narrowed her eyes at him. "That isn't a dimensional effect. That is a god being shut out because they don't have permission to operate in a space dedicated entirely to another deity."

"You'll be dealing with much the same thing. I'm just letting you know so your people don't freak out at a more inopportune moment. I'm not waiting until the middle of a messenger attack for you to declare me an abomination unto Nuggan. You can take your people into Emir Bahadir's cloud building if you like. He'll be making a bunker as well, and it will be gold rank. Mine is only silver."

"I strongly suspect there is not 'only' when it comes to this building, Mr Miller. What you have just told me raises many questions."

"Sure does," Jason laughingly agreed. "And you're probably going to get annoyed that I'm not going to answer any of them."

"Why not?"

"Because I don't have to. I don't have to do any of this. I could have kept to myself and not gotten involved. But I didn't. I stepped up because people needed help, even when it meant my secrets poking out of the shadows. You'll have to forgive me if getting suspicion instead of gratitude for my trouble is starting to make me cranky."

He walked over to her and reached for the plate, but she moved it out of his reach.

"I'll eat it," she said. Good to her word, she picked up one of the triangular cut halves and bit off a corner, her eyes lighting up. "This is good!"

"You don't have to sound *that* surprised," he grumbled.

77

THE BETTER ADVENTURER

ONE BUILDING ON THE ADVENTURE SOCIETY CAMPUS OF YARESH WAS OLDER THAN all of the others. It had been the entire headquarters for the Adventure Society in the early days of the city, and the defensive measures built into it were formidable. As Yaresh grew, and its branch expanded from a building to a full campus, the building and its defences had been repurposed. It now served as a set of secure residences, for those who needed to be kept safe, along with those who needed to be kept secure, but the campus prison tower was not appropriate. This was the case for Zolit Kreen.

Zolit was not just an outworlder but one that had originally been a valash: a species that did not natively appear on Pallimustus and looked like a humanoid chihuahua. Both of these things made him attention-grabbing, and he had spent years working very hard to undo that damage. Zolit had been a run-of-the-mill adventurer by intention, slowly but surely ranking up to silver while remaining as unremarkable as he could. He did his part during the monster surges while doing his best not to stand out.

After attaining the wealth and extended lifespan that came with being silver rank, he'd retired and found a comfortable niche as a fight promoter. It was an environment where everyone was a little bit strange, looking for a gimmick so his idiosyncrasies didn't stand out as much. Everyone had their thing, and being a valash outworlder was his.

It had all gone wrong the moment he set eyes on the other outworlder. He'd become complacent, forgetting the importance of being ordinary. The next thing he knew, Adventure Society enforcers were dragging him out of bed in the middle of the night and locking him up in an admittedly lavish suite that was, nonetheless, a prison. They were asking him about the outworlder and, for some reason, his assistant, Benella. They were talking nonsense about messengers and Zolit had no answers to give.

What was worse was that he was starting to feel ill and he didn't have any more of his medicine. One of the problems with not being native to this world was that there was an incompatibility between himself and the magic of Pallimustus. It was something he was sensitive about, as he was always wary of the Adventure Society grabbing him and handing him over to the Magic Society for experimentation. He'd decided to reach out to the other outworlder about it, but he didn't get the chance. Benella disappeared and he'd been snatched up by the Adventure Society.

Benella's disappearance had been the biggest problem as she had been the one procuring his medicine for years. He didn't know which alchemist she used or what exactly was in the medicine; it was one of countless things he'd relied on her for in the early days. His memories of that time were hazy at best, and the ones from his old world were gone entirely. This was another side effect of the magic incompatibility for outworlders, according to the expert Benella had found.

Zolit groaned, pacing around in the secure but opulent suite, barely dressed. For as long as he could remember, Benella had been managing his life. Without her help in the beginning, when his magic incompatibility kept leading to blackouts, he never would have managed at all.

Now she was gone, and some kind of traitor? She was the main thing that the Adventure Society interrogators asked about. They didn't call themselves interrogators, but that's what they were. And Zolit was terrified to talk about his medicine lest they turn their attentions on him rather than her. Or worse, hand him over to the Magic Society. They might claim that they didn't do unethical research on innocent people, but he knew what obsessed researchers did behind closed doors. It was one of the main things Benella had warned him about in the early days.

He needed them to let him go so that he could track down the medicine for himself. He was feeling worse and worse by the hour, his thoughts increasingly scattered. He couldn't sit still and his body was releasing sticky sweat. He shouldn't sweat at all, as a silver-ranker, let alone this strange, tacky substance. Three showers with little more than an hour between, scrubbing the residue from his body. He should ask for some crystal wash, but he didn't want to draw attention to his condition.

Sleep wouldn't come, his mind racing and scattered. He was hungry too, more and more as the night moved into the early hours of morning. At least they were feeding him properly, and he'd just asked for another meal.

An Adventure Society functionary, Argrave Mericulato, pushed a trolley of food down a hall of the secure residence building. His aura mask hid the seething anger that was always inside of him at being reduced to such menial tasks, while he kept his expression easy and friendly. He never used to suppress his emotions, but it was something he had to learn. Fortunately, no one paid that much attention to servants, which was what he amounted to, in spite of his silver rank.

He wasn't a traitor. Any reasonable person would see that the Adventure Society were the traitors, having been the ones to turn on him. They didn't care that he had been a celebrated adventurer in his own right; the moment his father had died in the One Day War, everyone had turned on him. They treated him as if only his father had any value, ignoring his own accomplishments.

His team had just up and left. It wasn't his fault that the right tactical decision in the moment was to make a strategic withdrawal without them. He was the most important team member, so obviously, they should be the distraction that let him go to safety. There was a flying attack fortress, gold- and diamond-rankers battling about, and the dimensional pocket device his father had given him only had room for one. His father had died in that battle, so waiting it out in safety was the responsible move, for the family. Not that his sister saw it that way.

The team hadn't even come looking for him in the aftermath. They left Rimaros almost immediately, pausing only long enough to have him listed as missing, presumed dead. The pocket dimension device had messed up his tracking stone and they didn't even come looking to confirm. Instead, they had him formally struck off their team list. By the time he went through the massive amount of paperwork to get himself re-listed as alive, they had a new team member. They had refused every water link request and sent him a letter that read 'Sorry: team full.'

Four years together and they ended it with three words. Years of treating him like a prince, only to reveal their true faces the moment they heard about his father. Finding another team should have been easy, and it had been the first time. Once they heard his now-dead father's name. How was Argrave to know that the incompetents would demand too much, and then blame their failures on him?

After that, teams had been harder to come by, even with so many looking to fill slots in the wake of the monster surge. It was not Argrave's fault that these pathetic adventurers didn't understand how to properly support what should obviously be the new core of their team. Four teams, none of them worth a single damn.

The Adventure Society was worse than no help. Time and again, Argrave went to them with the perfectly reasonable demand of being placed on a team that was worthy of him. And each time, the society was duped, bamboozled by the lying teams that sought only to cover their own incompetence. With each new team that scapegoated him, Argrave's eloquent arguments fell on increasingly deaf ears until he was forced to move on, looking for an Adventure Society branch that wasn't full of idiots.

Unfortunately, idiots flocked together. He moved south, from one branch to another, encountering nothing but fools, incompetents and those who undermined him out of jealousy. They went so far as to poison his name so that each branch already knew of the teams he'd been in, along with the lies they'd told. But did they listen to what really happened? Of course not. The simple-minded fools believed the first thing they heard and were too stupid to recognise the truth when they heard it.

It was in Yaresh that Argrave realised that he was the one who had been the fool. He should have realised from the start that it wasn't a few bad apples. The entire Adventure Society was made up of petty idiots, saddling him with one pathetic team after another because they were jealous of his talent. They knew they would never reach his potential, leaving him no choice but to roam from one branch to the next, looking for honest people.

Finally, he was forced to admit that there were no good people in the Adventure Society. If they had even a scrap of Argrave's potential, they would be adventurers themselves, not bureaucrats using their petty power to bring down their betters. But even in bad teams, Argrave's light was too bright to hide. In the end, they had to strip him of his status as an adventurer, denying him the chance to shine.

Adding insult to injury, they had the temerity to offer him the role of a menial functionary that he only took due to his financial needs. It was not cheap to travel in the manner he deserved, and his pathetic sister had cut him off before their father's body had turned to rainbow smoke. It wouldn't surprise him if the bureaucrats knew this and took shameless advantage.

Argrave did not betray the Adventure Society because that wasn't possible. The Adventure Society betrayed him first. Every snub, every team member who didn't understand how to properly support the hero their team had been graced with. He came into these groups who had lost a member in the surge, and it was little surprise they had. And when he told them as much, they had the gall to get angry at *him*.

The messengers understood his value. He'd only met one briefly, when his aura mask had been applied, and the intimidating being had been brusque, it was true. But they were from beyond the borders of the world and radiated glory; they would learn that Argrave was glorious too. It was only a matter of time until they realised and Argrave stood among them. Their philosophy of superiority resonated with him, and finally, there would be someone to recognise that some people were just better than others.

Of course, being from another world, they would need to see his superiority in action. He had leapt at the chance to use the menial task the Adventure Society had given him, as what had meant to be a humiliation would be the instrument through which he would prove his greatness. They had tried to make him a servant, but the cream would always rise to the top, and there was nothing they could do to stop it.

The fool guard was one of the Adventure Society enforcers who clearly couldn't hack it as a real adventurer. His senses swept rudely over Argrave but didn't penetrate the aura mask. It was more proof which of them was the better adventurer, not that any more was needed. The guard looked Argrave over and gestured at him to stop the cart and checked each of the covered trays.

"He's agitated again," the guard said. "He hasn't slept at all, and I think he might be sick. We're waiting on a healer, but the priority is some kind of evacuee camp. The messengers did something to the towns south of the city. I'd advise leaving the cart and getting out quick."

Argrave swallowed a retort about the guard looking after himself and instead gave him a smile.

"Thanks for the warning," he replied.

The guard opened the door to let him wheel the trolley in, then closed it behind him.

Through the door was a well-appointed room containing a creature that Argrave found disgusting, but he plastered on a smile. The tiny man with the emaciated dog head was unpleasant to look at, but Argrave didn't let his revulsion show. Fortunately, the aura mask meant he only needed to school his expression.

"Hello again, Zolit," he greeted.

The agitated little man was visibly unhealthy. He had been pacing around the room wearing shorts and a robe left hanging open. His skin glistened and he looked sticky, although whether that was natural for whatever he was or some odd condition, Argrave didn't know. He didn't particularly care either.

Zolit ignored him, moving to the cart and lifting lids from trays that he awkwardly picked up all together before moving them to a table, spilling bits of food as he went. Argrave shook his head as he watched Zolit sit down, facing the other direction. The idiot could have had him move the trolley to the table and transfer the trays across neatly, but it worked out well for Argrave's own plans. He opened the narrow panel hidden on one of the trolley legs and withdrew a long needle.

Zolit didn't turn as Argrave approached. The little man was shoving food into his mouth in an agitated frenzy, only letting out a muffled yell as Argrave's hand slipped over his mouth. Argrave jammed the needle into Zolit's spine, through the slats in the back of the dining chair.

To Argrave's complete startlement, Zolit shrank to the size of a marble in the time it would have taken to snap his fingers, with a wet sucking-slapping sound. The marble fell to the chair and rolled onto the floor.

Argrave turned to look at the door, but the guard outside did not make an appearance. The thick walls and heavy doors of the building had long-standing enchantments to prevent eavesdropping. After waiting an extra moment, just in case, he moved to where the tiny sphere had settled in the carpet and leaned over to peer at it.

He'd been told that the device he was given would make it possible to take Zolit away, sneaking him out of his prison. He had been expecting it to knock the little man out and turn him invisible, allowing Argrave to wheel him out on the cart. Having the man turn into a tiny brown ball was certainly more convenient, although he would have appreciated a warning.

He reached down to pick the ball up and discovered it was astoundingly heavy. Not too much for his silver-rank strength to lift, but the marble-sized object weighed as much as a heavy person. He'd have to keep it in his hand, as it would weigh down any pocket enough to be glaringly obvious and he hadn't been allowed to bring a dimensional bag.

Argrave held the orb up in front of his face, peering closely. It was warm and leathery to the touch, looking like it was made of tiny leather strips wrapped around one another. Jason would have recognised it as a tiny version of the orb the messenger had used to ward off the world-taker worms.

The door opened and the guard stepped inside.

"You really shouldn't linger... where's Kreen?"

"Uh, shower. He was all sticky with something and wanted to wash it off."

"Yeah, I told you he was sick. He's been showering every few hours. What's that thing you're holding?"

Argrave had done his best to casually move the hand holding the tiny sphere casually to his side, but he'd been peering closely at it when the door was opened, so the guard saw it plainly.

"Just a personal keepsake," Argrave told him, but saw that there was an unfortunate limit to the guard's credulity. The guard placed a hand on his sword hilt and took a wary stance.

"Step back into the middle of the room, Mericulato."

"I don't think—"

The guard drew his sword.

"Step back into the middle of the room. I won't ask again."

Argrave did as instructed, moving into the lounge area as his mind scrambled for an appropriate response. He would need to take out the guard quietly and get off-campus before anyone realised. As he was thinking, the guard moved into the room and checked the only other door, which led into the bathroom. He saw that it was empty and levelled his sword at Argrave, touching his other hand to a brooch on his chest at the same time.

"Where is Kreen?" the guard demanded. "And what was that thing you were looking at?"

"Oh, this?" Argrave asked.

He held up the sphere between his thumb and forefinger. He was careful not to let the guard see how heavy it was, then tossed it at him. The guard moved to intercept it with his sword but the sphere stopped dead, floating in the air between them.

"What is…"

"What the…"

The orb started to grow and pulsate. It looked as if a tiny creature was rapidly growing inside a leathery egg, trying to claw its way out. For all either man knew, that was exactly what was happening. The guard brought his sword down on the sphere and it slid off, not so much as budging it from where it hung in the air. The growing orb started emitting an aura, silver and weak but rapidly growing stronger.

"I think we might need to get out of here," Argrave said.

"What is it?"

"I don't know, but I don't want to stay and find out."

"You're not going anywhere."

The sphere had grown to the size of a basketball and glowed faintly with golden light as the aura transitioned from silver to gold. The surface of it, still covered in leathery strands, was writhing and undulating.

"I really think we need to…"

Argrave trailed off as something started pushing its way out of the orb. On opposite sides, each facing one of the two men in the room, something scaly was shoving through the leathery strands. Argrave chanted a quick spell as the guard swung his sword again. From either side of the orb, snakes shot out. The sword blow and Argrave's firebolt glanced off harmlessly. The snakes latched their fangs into the two men.

78

BRAVE BECAUSE IT CAN WIN

As the night moved closer to dawn, the most likely time for a messenger attack grew imminent. Jason floated, cross-legged and eyes closed, over the roof of the cloud hospital as he projected his senses through the Shade bodies scattered around the city. His eyes shot open when he noticed something approaching the cloud house. He was alarmed because all he sensed was a small dead spot within his perception, subtle enough that he'd almost missed it entirely.

Jason unfolded his legs, dropped his feet to the roof from where he was floating above it and dashed to the edge. What he spotted below was Taika standing with another man at the edge of the camp, both looking up at him. Jason focused his senses, hearing the other man laugh.

"You're right," the man told Taika. "He does have sharp senses."

Astoundingly, the man was a head taller than even the mountainous Taika. His hair was a golden mane with long sideburns, while his eyes were green and sharp. He had craggy features and a hawk nose, with none of the polished perfection typical of high-rankers. None of his massive physique was fat, but he was a slab of a man, more powerlifter than bodybuilder.

The man was bare-chested and bare-footed, with loose, rough pants held in place by a piece of rope used as a belt. Hanging from the belt was a gourd and he held a closed umbrella, slung over one shoulder.

Jason leapt off the roof, using his aura to slow himself as he approached the ground and lightly land in front of the two men. Jason had picked up a few extra centimetres from ranking up, but in front of Taika and the stranger, he looked like a 50% scale model.

"G'day, I'm Jason."

No one around them cared about Jason, even after he'd leapt from the roof. The camp workers were busy and the evacuees had more on their minds than some adventurer. As for his lack of subtlety in front of Taika's companion, Jason was entirely confident that lying was pointless. There was little point trying to be less prominent when Jason's instincts screamed that this man was an absolute powerhouse.

"Haliastur," the man introduced himself in a rumbling voice. "You've got quite the odd friend here, Taika."

"And here was me about to say the same thing," Jason said.

The man in front of him did not register on Jason's magical senses at all, to the point that he suspected the man only revealed himself at all as a test. Even so, there was a presence to him that transcended auras and magic. For most, that would be something that didn't consciously register, but Jason recognised the sensation.

Jason had encountered diamond-rankers, gods and great astral beings often enough that he had a decent sense of what he was dealing with when encountering entities vastly above his own power level. This was true even when their auras were far beyond his ability to read; there was something about their presence they couldn't entirely hide. Consciously recognising it was there required the kind of regular exposure that very few people below diamond rank had. Most would pass it off as inherent charisma, or some kind of subtle aura manipulation, if they noticed it at all.

Jason had come to think of it as a transcendent presence, but that didn't mean it only belonged to transcendent beings like gods and great astral beings. Both Shako and Dawn displayed it, and Jason suspected that he himself had the barest skerrick from his nature as an astral king. But neither Zila nor Soramir Rimaros had it, suggesting that the key was to touch the transcendent. That was something most essence users would only do at the peak of diamond.

This man had it as well, and Jason gauged him to be roughly on Dawn's power level, although that was admittedly a guess. His measure of transcendent presence was still crude and operating from an extremely low vantage point. Another guess Jason had about the man was that he was not an essence user.

Jason was certain that Haliastur saw through him completely while he saw very little. The man confirmed as much immediately.

"Blessing of the Reaper. Blessing of the World-Phoenix. Astral king, that's an odd one. You're the one building that half-assembled dimensional bridge between this world and some other one. Jumping on the back of the link that idiot Builder got himself sanctioned over. And you're the one Shade is attached to right now."

Shade emerged from Jason's shadow.

"Good day, Haliastur."

"Shade. I thought you might be embarrassed to show yourself after getting bound to some astral space for a few centuries."

"You've been talking to Umber. Shame is something you have for your choices, where I have no embarrassment over mine, even when the outcomes were not what I had hoped for."

"A healthy attitude."

"You two have met, then," Jason said.

"We have," Haliastur said. "It's a big cosmos, but the most powerful in any given region are relatively few in number and immortal, so we all meet eventually.

Once you get to diamond rank, Shade can guide you to Interstice. I'll introduce you around."

"Interstice. That's the cosmic city-universe, right?"

"Yes."

"And what brings you to this world?" Jason asked. "Is this something to do with the former First Sister of the World-Phoenix? She already left."

Haliastur raised his eyebrows.

"Little Dawnie was here? What for?"

"Him," Taika said, nodding at Jason.

"I'm just another pawn the World-Phoenix pushed into place," Jason said.

"I imagine you're not used to people seeing through your lies," Haliastur said, his voice showing no signs of taking offence. "How does a silver-ranker know Dawn?"

"He more than knows her," Taika interjected. "He…"

Taika's chocolate skin turned milk chocolate as he paled under Jason's glare.

"…knows her quite well," he finished lamely.

Haliastur glanced at Taika with another chuckle.

"How did you and Taika meet?" Jason asked.

"How did you and Dawn meet?" Haliastur countered.

"The World-Phoenix sent her to make me save the world. Not this one. The one at the other end of that link."

"And did you?"

"Twice. Working on a third time, which should be the end of it."

"The bridge."

"Yep."

"It's an incomplete mess."

"Tell me about it. I don't suppose you know how to finish it?"

"Sorry, I'm less a dimension engineer than an invincible paragon of speed and power."

"And modesty," Jason added. "I guess it's back to the plan of beating astral magic out of the messengers."

Haliastur threw back his head and let out a laugh that felt like an earthquake.

"I like you, Jason Asano. You have a fun friend here, Taika."

"And how did you meet?"

"I've been looking for something for a couple of decades and received word that it is in this city. Someone has lured me here as part of some game, but that matters not so long as my objective is met. I came across Taika and saw him using his powers, and as I happened to have some insights, I introduced myself. It turns out that we get along quite well."

"This thing you're looking for," Jason said. "Is it a threat?"

"Oh, yes," Haliastur said, then gestured at the camp. "You've seen that the messengers like to use apocalypse beasts as indiscriminate weapons."

"Unfortunately," Jason said.

"You will find that what they have done here is not unique. Such disasters are being launched all over this world. They aren't likely to actually cause an apocalypse, as the messengers know better than to use something that they can't control."

"I get the impression that they dislike an absence of control."

"Very true. But they will cause considerable damage and the messengers don't always get it right. I recall a sanguine horror getting out of hand and scouring a planet only a few decades ago. But you wouldn't know anything about that, would you?"

"I wasn't alive a few decades ago."

Haliastur snorted but didn't push.

"I have been pursuing one of these apocalypse beasts for a little time now," he said. "Have you ever heard of a naga genesis egg?"

"No," Jason said. "Shade?"

"I know of it by reputation," Shade said. "My understanding is that it consumes flesh and converts it into a serpent race called the naga. It can wipe out an entire world, replacing it with the serpent people."

"We have myths about them in my world," Jason said. "Not the egg bit, that I know of, but the serpent people. If we're about to have an army of naga to deal with, what we really need is…"

Jason looked to Taika, thinking about his confluence essence. How would Haliastur, who Jason was convinced was not an essence user, be able to help Taika, who was? He looked at Haliastur, the gourd at his belt and the umbrella slung over his shoulder. Haliastur, who had been chasing a naga egg for decades.

"I don't suppose that there's amrita in that gourd?" Jason asked.

Haliastur let out another laugh.

"Amrita?" Taika asked. "I have an essence ability called that."

"Your friend here has figured me out," Haliastur told him.

"Are you going to help us?" Jason asked.

"I am here for the naga egg, which is not so slight a thing as world-taker worms. I do not know how they've been keeping it dormant or hidden from my senses, but if it becomes active, removing it will be help enough, believe me."

"I do," Jason said. "If it comes to—"

Jason and Haliastur both turned towards the centre of the city with stern expressions.

"What is it?" Taika asked. He wasn't quite silver yet, and even if he had been, he would not match the aura senses of either of the others.

"Some manner of aura burst," Haliastur said. "It started at silver rank and grew to gold very quickly. I believe it is the egg."

"I know that aura," Jason said. "Or I did before it became warped and turned gold. It belonged to another outworlder. He used to be a valash."

Haliastur's eyes went wide.

"So that's how they did it."

"Meaning?" Jason asked.

"I think that the messengers took a soul, modified it, wrapped it around the egg and shoved the egg into this world. Artificially creating an outworlder whose soul served as a barrier to contain the egg."

"Can they do that to a soul?"

"Difficult. But possible, if you're willing to perform soul engineering. The astral king who rules the local messenger forces, Vesta Carmis Zell, is a known practitioner, so I believe we have our answer. She's a proper astral king, not a baby one like you, Jason Asano."

"Where do they get the soul? It would have to be a volunteer or they couldn't touch it, right?"

"Yes, but you can torture someone's soul until they become a volunteer."

"I'm familiar with the process," Jason said with a glower.

Haliastur looked Jason up and down again.

"So I see."

"I once saw a disembodied soul used as a magical barrier," Jason told him.

Haliastur nodded. "Soul engineering. It can be used for various purposes. Where did you come across something like that?"

"An astral space that used to be an astral vessel of the Builder, until the Reaper's people stole it."

"What happened to it?"

"The Builder was trying to take it back and fire up some of those world engineer golems he uses, so my friends and I broke the place and shut it down. He didn't take it well."

Haliastur laughed.

"You live an interesting life, Jason Asano."

"Something tells me that tedium isn't a problem for you either. Why aren't you rushing over to where that aura surge was?"

"The egg is awakening. If it senses my presence while it is still taking its initial form it will panic and expend all of its gathered power immediately. That will cut off its potential for overrunning this world, but flood the city with serpents. The people of this city will die before I can stop them all."

"So, you let it grow up into a monster brave enough to take you on and then kill it?"

"That is the idea."

"Uh, what if it's brave because it can win?" Taika asked.

"It can't," Jason and Haliastur said simultaneously.

Haliastur grinned.

"That should be long enough," he said. "Genesis eggs experience explosive growth. I will try to minimise the damage to the city, but you should stay clear."

"Oh, that's all you, bloke. If that thing is kicking off, the messenger attack probably isn't far behind."

Haliastur launched into the air, transforming into a golden bird.

"What the hell is that bloke?" Taika asked. "And why were you so sure he can win?"

"He's a garuda. Or *the* garuda; I don't know how the real thing differs from the myths. But garuda is the devourer of serpents. Naga in particular, which is how I figured out what he is."

"Garuda is my confluence essence."

"Yep. That's why your new meditation technique works so well."

"That's pretty sweet, bro. I do have one question, though."

"What's that?" Jason asked.

"What's a garuda?"

Jason turned to look at him.

"Seriously? You have the garuda confluence and you don't know what a garuda is?"

"I got an ability from it called Feaster of Serpents, so I thought it was a specialty chef thing."

"A chef thing? Why would you think that?"

"Your sister has chef powers."

"My sister's a chef. What other powers did you get from that confluence?"

"Amrita. It summons a jar of stuff to drink."

"Okay, that's fair. What else?"

"One is called Brother of the Dawn. Unbowed is the one I got when I first absorbed the essence."

"They don't sound very culinary. What about the last one?"

"It's called God-Striking Fist."

"God-Striking Fist?"

"Yep."

"And you thought it was some kind of cooking confluence?"

"You never know with awakening stones. I thought it might be an *Iron Chef* thing."

"What awakening stone did you use to get that?"

"Defiance."

"You thought an awakening stone of defiance gave you an ability from a chef-type essence called God-Striking Fist?"

"Some of those chefs are pretty rough. What about that bloke who swears all the time?"

"Taika?"

"Yeah, bro?"

"By any chance, did it just reach the point where it's been long enough since you got your essences that you were too embarrassed to ask what your confluence was about?"

Taika bowed his head. "Yeah, bro."

Jason gave a good-natured chuckle, reached up to pat his shoulder, gave up and patted him on the bicep.

"That's nothing to be ashamed of, mate. You have no idea how many times I've ended up looking like an idiot."

"Sure I do. I know your sister pretty well."

Jason groaned.

"Mr Asano," Shade said.

"Yeah, what's up, Shade?"

"Messengers have just been spotted by the city scout patrols. The city alarms will be activated very soon, so it is time to take down the cloud hospital and establish a bunker."

"Right," Jason said. "Let the high priestess know it's time to evacuate the hospital so I can take it down. I just hope that—"

An explosion sounded in the distance and all heads turned to look towards the centre of the city. Dozens of giant snakes had risen over the city like the heads of a hydra, looming as tall as the city's towers. Light from the towers lit the snakes in ominous silhouette, making their visage all the more menacing.

"…something like that doesn't happen."

As they watched, another monstrous form grew to the size of a building. It was roughly humanoid but with an eagle's head, four arms and golden wings spread out from its back. It was draped in golden robes and its skin was emerald-green. One hand held an umbrella and the other held a gourd.

"Bro, I can turn into something like that. I can't get big like that, though. Do you think I will after I rank up?"

Despite the spectacle in the distance, Jason turned to look at Taika.

"You thought it was a chef essence?"

"That power is from the wing essence, bro. Calm down."

"Taika?"

"Yeah, bro?"

"Have you been messing with me this whole time?"

"Yep."

"Seriously?"

"Did you really think I believed that garuda was a Gordon Ramsey essence? How dumb do you think I am? It's a little hurtful, bro."

79

A MAN THAT WILL INSPIRE COURAGE

THE CRASH OF WOOD SMASHING APART AND STONE BEING PULVERISED FILLED THE air with noise, dust and splinters as Jason dashed through it. He dodged falling sections of ceiling and leapt through holes in once-intact walls, his cloak deflecting much of the debris filling the air.

"You'll try to avoid damaging the city my arse," he grumbled, his voice lost in the noise.

Outside of the central city area, most of the architecture in Yaresh was built with living trees as a core, moulded into elaborate shapes and supplemented with brickwork. The trees were usually of the magic variety, outside of the poorer districts, and held up to impacts very well. This was important when some of them were being ripped out of the ground, used as crude clubs and tossed around.

The building-sized garuda, Haliastur, was savaging what looked like an even larger hydra whose main body was an arena-sized orb and whose heads counted in the dozens. Prehensile necks were grabbing whole tree buildings and launching them at the garuda, who deflected them away. They crashed into other buildings, chunks bouncing off to inflict more damage as they broke apart.

The results were that the evacuation of people in the area was not going well; the casualties were mounting. Adventurers rushed in to get people out alive, but the adventurers themselves were facing casualties. The closer anyone came to a fight between diamond-rankers, the more the difference between life and death became luck. The spreading disaster zone at the heart of the city was an ample demonstration of that.

The unconventional structure of the tree buildings held up better than traditional designs, at least at first. Once their integrity was finally compromised, however, they collapsed much faster. Jason rushed through a building that was crumbling under the weight of most of another building, tracking civilians with his aura senses. He found them huddling under a table as he dashed into the room, watching the ceiling collapse.

Pushing his silver-rank speed to the limit, he launched himself across the room. He kicked away the table that would not shelter the woman and two boys from tons of stone and wood. Standing over them and spreading his cloak wide, he pushed against the falling ceiling with his aura, which wasn't close to strong enough.

His aura slowed the fall only a little, but it was just enough for Jason to interpose himself between the ceiling and the people as it slammed into his back. His legs almost buckled but managed to barely hold, trembling at the weight. He formed a shelter for the people he was leaning over, his cloak draped around him. Cloud stuff emerged from the bottle hanging around his neck, plugging the gaps between his cloak and the floor, filtering out stone dust and splinters.

"HUMP!" Jason bellowed, his voice carried on his aura to boom through the building, overwhelming even the sounds of destruction. Moments later, the weight threatening to push Jason down grew lighter as huge chunks of brickwork and broken tree trunk were tossed away.

Humphrey raced against time as the floor under Jason and the civilians threatened to give way, just as the ceiling above had. As he had to be careful not to bring even more of the ceiling down, it was a race that Humphrey lost. The children let out startled screams as the floor fell out of under them and they were grabbed in a net of shadow arms, dangling over the hole now below them. Finally, Humphrey cleared out enough space that Jason could hand the children up to him.

Humphrey took the kids and Jason the mother as they leapt from the building that continued to crumble like a biscuit behind them. It was a tall residential treehouse, which was how it had caught debris from the diamond rank battle taking place in the distance. Humphrey had a kid slung under each arm, flying clear with his conjured dragon wings. Jason held the mother using shadow arms while his cloak spread out into wings of darkness, speckled with stars.

They flew into an area where the adventurers had set up a staging point in an open market. It left them somewhat exposed to debris thrown off by the diamond-rank battle in the distance, but there were no buildings tall enough to tumble onto it.

The staging area was covered by a dome of shimmering pale blue energy set up by Clive. Inside was Clive's portal, through which civilians were being sent to the nearest monster attack bunker. The dome had no chance of stopping the larger chunks of rubble and collapsing building, but could keep out choking dust and at least some of the smaller debris.

"If I had a portal instead of a teleport, I could do more," Humphrey complained.

"Say that when a building is about to fall on a bunch of people and you teleport them all out. Portals aren't fast enough to do that."

They didn't have time to stop for banter and both left after that quick exchange. Jason shadow-jumped through a Shade body and Humphrey leapt away as if shot from a cannon.

There was another portal site shielded by Clive's rituals, this one with Jason's portal. This allowed the team to spread out, giving them two options for where to take the people they found or rescued. Until messengers attacked and made it into the city, the team was spreading out, operating alone but with others close enough to offer backup at need.

Each team member had their own specialties, and they used voice chat to call in the right person for any job. Humphrey's strength and ability to fly were obviously useful, and he was able to dig out trapped people the easiest. The ability to teleport into spaces that he could see but not access was also a boon. Neil had the strength but not the flight, but his ability to shield and heal made him arguably the team's most critical member.

Sophie, Rufus and Jason all used their excellent mobility for rapid response. Sophie's speed meant that she could get to the people most in need while Rufus could use his two short-range teleports, Moonlit Step and Flash Step, to navigate buildings in the process of collapsing. Jason's biggest advantage was that his aura senses could pick people out that the others might have missed. In all the chaos, it was easy to overlook normal-rank people whose weak auras were on the verge of winking out. But Jason was able to track them down and feed them a potion, get them to Neil or both.

Clive was in charge of watching the bigger picture and focused on maintaining the extraction areas around his and Jason's portals. He had set up as many rituals as he could cram into the area without them interfering with one another. Mostly, they were designed to shield the people from the smaller things that were harmless to a silver-ranker but could still hurt normal people.

Belinda's role was to assess and extract people from the trickiest situations. Her versatile skill set and power selection meant that she had the best toolkit for the trickiest work. Many civilians were trapped under rubble that was difficult to extract them from. Some were in danger of it collapsing on them while others were injured and almost any shift could kill them. Belinda assessed their needs and either extracted them herself or called in the right team member to help.

The one Belinda called on the most was Gordon, whose pinpoint beams were ideal for cutting through debris. All of the familiars were proving their worth, either subsumed into their summoner or actively taking part. Belinda's astral lantern familiar was inside her, allowing her to use eye beams similar to Gordon's. They couldn't cut away debris as fast as Gordon's half dozen powerful beams, but for delicate work, they were ideal.

Stash, like Belinda, was incredibly versatile. For clearing heavy rubble he used the form of a fifteen-foot gorilla with a face on its chest and a third arm where its head should have been. For snaking through tight spaces to reach people, he could take the form of a mouse or, indeed, a snake. From there, he could take a form like a dungeon beetle to extract them.

Dungeon beetles were predatory creatures with a very hard and mostly hollow carapace. They were known for taking their prey, entrapping them in their carapace and then burrowing deep underground, letting their prisoners slowly die of thirst before consuming them. As grim as this was, the hollow but very strong body and the burrowing power were ideal for digging people out.

Onslow, Clive's flying tortoise, was flying around the areas furthest from the extraction points. This was where Rufus, Jason and especially Sophie were to be found, and they could hand over civilians to Onslow to be carried to safety. Onslow was able to shuck off his shell which became a large and sturdy flying transport. Without his shell, the rest of him became a tiny and adorable green tortoise-man, which was perfect for calming down scared children.

With large chunks of falling debris bouncing heavily off his shell, keeping people calm was important. Onslow used his elemental powers as best he could, throwing out water barriers and exploding chunks of stone with lightning bolts, but his indiscriminate powers weren't the best for the situation. It was getting people to safety that was his most valuable role.

Colin was still hibernating in Jason's astral realm, with no indication of rousing. Shade, on the other hand, was characteristically valuable. He could scout spaces that even Stash couldn't squeeze into and allowed Jason easy mobility around the zone.

Jason found another group of civilians, trapped at the bottom of a hole. It was just wide enough to pull people out from, but too narrow to go down and get them. This was a problem that simply lowering a rope couldn't solve because the sides of the hole were sharp and jagged. Anyone coming out would require delicate extraction to avoid being lacerated to death on the way.

Jason called on Belinda's echo spirit familiar, Gemini, who could mimic the team's abilities. They both used Jason's ability to call up shadow hands, essentially creating a tunnel of dark hands that could lift the people out while shielding them from the sides of the hole.

"Mr Asano," Shade said.

"What do you need?"

"Both cloud palaces have completed the conversion to bunkers and High Priestess Shavar is ready to start moving evacuees into them."

"Alright. I'll be along as soon as we get these people out."

Once again, Taika felt the frustration of still being bronze rank. He was so close, and if he'd managed to cross that line, then he'd be out in the city instead of playing usher to evacuees, leading people into the two cloud buildings as the camp was organised. Lines of people clustered together, snaking through the camp and leading up to the bunkers.

Emir Bahadir's cloud bunker was the larger of the two by a solid margin. The five-tower configuration of the palace was still echoed in the bunker, which was a smooth dome with five spires jutting up and out at angles, like leaning towers. Spaced evenly around the dome, the spires had a massive ritual diagram floating between them: an elaborate pentagram using the spires as anchor points. Glowing with shifting colours, the brightness of it painted the area in rainbow hues.

Jason's bunker was a pyramid covered in interlocking hexes of matte black, with blue and orange light glimmering in lines between the hex panels. The top of the pyramid did not reach a point and instead formed a cup over which a giant version of one of Jason's eyes floated ominously. Notably, the rainbow light from

Emir's palace stopped dead as it approached Jason's, stopping as it hit an invisible wall that shimmered faintly when the rainbow light struck it.

Taika let out a sigh as he looked at the power the two buildings displayed. He was not a man with a hunger for power, but when people needed help, he couldn't help but feel inadequate when confronted with such displays.

"Your frustration is understandable," Hana told him.

He had felt her approach as, like him, she was actively using her aura to calm the crowd. These people were only hours from having their towns wiped out by alien horrors and their nerves were raw.

"While this task is not as exciting or dangerous as running through the periphery of a diamond-rank battle," Hana said, "that does not make it unimportant. Panic could easily set in, and that will be a disaster. For all the power I possess, people would get trampled and die before I can restore order. I am grateful for your reliable presence, not just for your aura, but for you."

Ability: [Unbowed] (Garuda)

- Aura (Boon).
- Base cost: None.
- Cooldown: None.

- Current rank: Silver 0 (0%).

- Effect (iron): You and allies within your aura have enhanced [Power] attribute and resistances.

- Effect (bronze): You and allies within your aura gain one or more instances of [Courage] when performing acts of courage within your aura.

- Effect (silver): Negate the effects of afflictions that penalise attributes or reduce damage inflicted. The afflictions remain in place but do not take effect on you or any ally within the aura.

- [Courage] (boon, holy, stacking): Negate the next instance of significant damage you would suffer or the next affliction that would be applied to you. If a single attack or effect causes both and/or multiple afflictions at once, the entire effect is negated. Minor instances of damage and less impactful afflictions will not trigger this unless sufficient instances of those afflictions are applied at once to have a cumulatively significant impact. Additional instances of this boon can be accumulated.

The high priestess was a tall woman, although Taika still towered over her. She placed a comforting hand on his forearm.

"Remember that the powers we gain are not just about essences and awakening stones, but about who we are. This is true for our aura powers most of all. Your aura is inspiring, and that isn't just a power that you have. It's a reflection of something inside you. I've always held that as we gain power, it doesn't change us, but concentrates us. It takes who we are, shaves away the fluff at the edges and leaves behind the distillation of our core natures. You are a man that will inspire courage. Lift people up. That is a very fine thing. Not everyone's reflection is so uplifting."

She turned her gaze to the ominous eye looming over the camp. Jason's aura did not push out beyond the boundaries of the pyramid to impose on the camp, but essence users with aura senses could easily detect it. Even more than Jason's aura in person, the building was portentous, benevolent but also judgemental. It radiated a sense that to enter it was to abide by its rules, that transgressors would pay the price of their sins.

"I can see why Asano warned me," Hana said. "I'm not sure I want to send anyone in there after all."

"I'm not sure you want to go in there yourself," Taika said. "Jason has… views about gods."

"My god seems to like him. Which is strange, given what I know of Asano. Certainly given that aura."

"How much do you know about Jason's background?"

"Not much. I can tell he's an outworlder. Like you."

"We come from the same world. Jason had responsibilities there, ones that shouldn't have been his to bear. What our world taught him was that he couldn't allow anyone to stand in his way when things absolutely needed doing, even if that meant becoming a tyrant. Jason is always the first one to stand between people and the bad things coming after them, which I think that's why your god likes him. But he got used to people standing in his way, even when he was killing himself to save them."

"And who keeps him in check if he won't listen to anyone?"

"No one," Arabelle told her as she approached the pair. "And that's the problem. He never trusted authority in the first place. The other world taught him, when the stakes were at their highest, that he had to become the authority. One that no one can command. So now, he defies everyone. Kings, diamond-rankers. Gods, great astral beings."

"That sounds like a path to a quick death."

"It is," Taika said. "He doesn't let death command him either."

"Everything's ready with Emir's bunker," Arabelle said. "We should start moving people into the bunkers."

"We're waiting on Asano to open his building back up," Hana said. "He wanted to show me in himself. He thought that there would be an issue with our priests."

"He's right," Arabelle said. "You'll see for yourself what it means to defy even gods in there. It's unsettling, being cut off from the comforting presence of your god when you've gotten so used to it. You might want to put the priests in the other bunker."

"We need people in both, so I'll lead the ones in Asano's bunker myself. Once he opens it up."

Shade emerged from Arabelle's shadow and Jason stepped out of the familiar's shadowy form.

"Sorry I'm late. Dashing heroics; you know how it is. Anyway, shall we?"

80

LUCK THAT GOOD

THE SKY RANG WITH NOISE DESPITE THE BATTLE AT THE CENTRE OF YARESH BEING a dozen kilometres away. Even from the outskirts, barely within the outer walls, the titanic figures could be seen looming over the towers at the heart of the city. The eagle-headed garuda was entangled with snakes wrapping around his body, as if a basket of them had been tipped over him. There was also a cluster of serpents of almost unbelievable enormity, as if sea monsters had risen from the deep and merged into a leviathan hydra.

The air thundered as the colossal adversaries destroyed buildings of metal and stone as if they were cardboard. Debris flew out over the city, chunks of masonry whistling like bombs as they fell from the sky. The garuda was diamond rank and its opponent was the same, having rapidly passed through silver and gold rank as it grew.

At the outskirts of the city, just inside the outer walls, was the refugee camp for people who had been displaced from towns to the south. The camp was a flurry of activity as the people shuffled into the two cloud palaces that had been converted into bunkers. The larger bunker, belonging to Emir Bahadir, was a dome from which five leaning towers extended up and out. The other was a pyramid made up of matte-black hexes with blue and orange light glowing between the panels. The pyramid did not rise to a point, instead having a cupped top. Floating over it was a giant eye made up of nebulous blue and orange light.

Hana Shavar looked up at the ominous eye as her people led civilians into the wide doors at the base of the pyramid. She was the High Priestess of the Healer for the city-state of Yaresh, but she had sent most of her own people into the gold-rank bunker belonging to Bahadir.

There was a reason she directed all the clergy, both from her church and others, away from the bunker belonging to Jason Asano. When it had taken the form of a hospital, she had found the building to have an unnerving quality she couldn't quite place. Now it was in full defensive mode, the power lurking within no longer hidden. Somehow, Asano's building could place a barrier between priests and their gods, cutting off the voices of the deities.

The constant presence of her god's power had always been a comfort to Hana, watching over her in her greatest moments and darkest hours alike. Only in a few rare moments had she been cut off from him, in an otherworldly realm or the heart of another god's sacred ground. Those times were the worst for any priest.

For those who had felt the direct touch of their deity, every feeling and instinct told them it was a power without limit. An all-seeing, all-powerful force, beyond the petty concerns of the mortals that served them. When that presence was cut off, the fact that even the gods had limits was a harsh reality to face. Ground that should have been solid underfoot suddenly lurched, unstable.

Hana had experienced it enough times that, while uncomfortable, she had grown used to it. Grappling with the knowledge that her instincts and reality conflicted had challenged her faith, but ultimately came to reinforce it. She realised that her god not being all-powerful meant that he was not simply an omnipotent, benevolent force, bestowing grace on small mortals. He had limits, albeit extreme ones.

The revelation that strengthened her faith was that her god had limits, her faith was not just some game he was playing; her position as a priestess was not pointless in the face of ultimate power. He might not need her as much as she needed him, but he did need her. She wasn't just taking from this great being, but also had something to give. Her purpose, her life's work, was true and good.

This was what gave her comfort in those moments when she was somewhere beyond her god's power. She could be his hands when he could not reach, his eyes when he could not see and his voice when he could not speak. She was a priestess. The representative of her god, and that was never more important than when she was cut off from him.

Not every priest had come to this conclusion, however, with the revelation having taken Hana years to not just reach but truly internalise. It was not something she could offer her fellow priests in the middle of a refugee evacuation, so she pushed all the priests into Bahadir's bunker, where just walking inside would not threaten a crisis of faith.

There was no shortage of secular staff to guide people into Asano's sinister lair, although Asano himself was no longer present. He had shown up long enough to reconfigure the building from a hospital into the menacing pyramid bunker it was now, but he had immediately returned to rescuing people caught up in the battle of colossi.

In his place was Jason's familiar, Shade, although most of the shadow-creature's multiple bodies were apparently busy. Shade directed a larger group of shadow entities, whose presence neither Shade nor Asano had explained beyond referring to them as avatars. They were dark silhouettes that looked like people in hooded cloaks, with a large single eye instead of a face. It was hard to miss that those eyes were reflections of both the giant orb floating over the bunker, and with Asano's own eyes.

Hana had checked the bunker before allowing anyone inside and now Shade led her back into the building. They moved past the lines of people heading in through the large doorway, directed by Asano's dark avatars.

The walls, floors and ceilings were cold, hard and empty. They were made from dark crystal flecked with blue, silver and gold. There was no decoration and none of the leafy green plants that had been found all throughout the hospital variant of the building. Having seen inside the dormitory sections, she knew that they were at least furnished with plush cloud furniture.

"The dormitory spaces set aside for the refugees may not offer a lot of room," Shade assured her, "but they are more comfortable than the hallways suggest."

Hana glanced at the shadow familiar, not for the first time wondering if he could read minds.

"I appreciate that," she told him, "but safety is the priority, not comfort."

"Do not worry on that front, Priestess Shavar. I would say gods help those who come here looking for trouble, but they will need more than gods in Mr Asano's domain."

There was an undercurrent of ominous glee to the familiar's polite tone that was sufficiently subtle that she may well have been imagining it. She could believe his words to be false bravado if not for the gaping hole in her mind where the presence of her god was normally settled.

Various passages and rooms had a wall of mist blocking them off. These walls were as impermeable to Hana's senses as the rest of the pyramid, which was another reason it unnerved her. Magical senses that could take in the city at a glance were stopped by the walls as surely as her vision. It left her feeling as isolated from the world as she was from her god.

"The walls serve to secure the civilians in the dormitories," Shade explained, once more anticipating her concerns. "While the outer walls are strong, a sufficiently dedicated attack will penetrate them, especially if gold-rankers are involved. The dormitories are the most reinforced internal spaces, making the empty corridors a more appealing path for enemies traversing the inside. It will give the defences time to deal with them."

"Can the defences deal with gold-rankers that can punch their way in?"

"I am quietly confident, Priestess Shavar."

"I suspect, Shade, that you are quietly everything."

"That is very kind of you to say, Priestess."

They arrived at an elevating platform at the centre of the pyramid that was also shrouded in mist. They stepped through the mist and the elevator ascended higher into the building.

"Beyond myself and the avatars, only you have access to this central shaft," Shade explained as the platform passed through more mist barriers in each floor. There were only four, with the platform stopping in a room with no ceiling. Above their heads was the open cup with the nebulous eye floating over it, and high above that, the city's barrier dome. From the open ceiling, the walls of the room sloped down, being the outer walls of the pyramid.

"This room seems like an invitation to break in," Hana said, looking up at the ominous floating eye.

"It does, doesn't it?" Shade said. "Let us hope the messengers are polite enough to accept."

Images appeared in the air around them. Most showed scenes from inside or around the buildings, mostly people shuffling into the bunkers in queues or settling into the dormitories. One showed a man arguing with one of the camp staff, and as soon as she focused on it, sound started playing. The man was complaining about the constricted space, apparently convinced that some people were being given private rooms.

"There's always a few," Hana muttered, the sound dimming as her attention moved on.

Her gaze fell on a zoomed in perspective of the distant battle. The eagle-headed giant was ravaging the hydra heads and the serpents crawling over it, often devouring them outright. Even so, they seemed to replenish themselves endlessly, more snakes appearing as the hydra heads rapidly healed or grew back entirely. She again glanced up.

"Is that vision coming from the large eye?"

"It is. This room can show anything from inside the building or that the eye can see. You can monitor the bunkers and the surrounding conditions from here. If you fight in here, you will have an environmental advantage, although I advise you to withdraw if and when attackers break in. The elevating platform will safely extract you."

"Assuming that the messengers really do attack the city."

"They are already assembling. Mr Asano has arranged for you to extend your senses beyond this room if you filter them through the eye."

It took Hana a moment to figure out how, but passing her aura and magic senses through the eye before extending them over the city was fairly intuitive. She quickly sensed the battle of diamond-rank titans, overshadowing everything else. She sensed adventurers around the city, scrambling to rescue citizens or prepare for attack. Her senses passed through the city's active barrier magic far easier than they should have and she sensed the messengers gathering around the city on every side.

Having taken part in attacks on the messenger strongholds, Hana understood their strategies. Each messenger was at least a little different from the others, but they fell into several broad roles. One of the most important, at least for large scale operations, were the summoners.

Summoners amongst the messengers had many advantages over their essence-user counterparts. Not only were their powers more convenient to activate, requiring no summoning circles, but they also summoned creatures in greater number. Their creatures might be less individually powerful, but that was an acceptable trade-off when it allowed them to balloon the relatively small number of messengers.

Hana could sense them building up their forces, not far from the city walls. It was close enough to be a real threat, but not so close as to be attacked without people leaving the protection of the city. Only a few skirmish specialists were out making trouble amongst the enemy, while the rest waited for the attack. The number of defenders was unfortunately low, with many adventurers still in the towns to the south.

"That's not good," Hana said as she used the giant eye to pan her senses over the messenger forces. "It doesn't look like they've managed to infiltrate the shield infrastructure nodes to sabotage them, but they clearly understand how the city barrier works."

"There is a flaw in the city defences?" Shade asked.

"Not a flaw, but there are only so many ways to shield an entire city, and no solution is perfect. Every system has weaknesses, and knowing how they work means those weaknesses can be exploited. In this city, the defensive screen is adaptive, meaning that it focuses the shield energy to any areas under attack in any given moment. It excels against monster attacks, which are sporadic by nature. It's why this type of barrier is so common in cities and fortress towns. But if you have the numbers to assault the entire shield all at once, instead of staging sporadic attacks like monsters do, you reveal the weakness."

"I believe I see," Shade said. "If you take a shield designed to focus its power on places it is attacked, and then attack everywhere, the shield becomes thin all over. It then becomes vulnerable to big, instantaneous attacks."

"Exactly. The shield won't collapse if you punch a hole in it, but it will take time to self-repair the breach. Long enough that you can get a good number of people through all at once. And we know for a fact that the messengers have at least one diamond-ranker. I'm guessing they're going to spread the attacks of all their summoned creatures to thin out the shield. Then they'll punch through various spots with simultaneous attacks from their diamond-ranker and stronger gold-rankers. The openings will only be temporary, but enough for their strongest forces to come through, along with enough summons to serve as fodder."

"I assume the people commanding the city defences are well aware of this," Shade said.

"Of course; they'll be watching this far closer than us. They would have already sent people out to disrupt the enemy, if we had the people to send. It's looking more and more like the worm-infested towns to the south were never meant to be the real invasion force."

"Or they were and this attack is a contingency for if they were discovered prior to being ready."

Hana shook her head. "Multiple-stage plans with integrated contingencies. I do not like smart enemies."

"For a smart enemy, the strategy you have posited seems like an all or nothing proposition. If the strike forces who breach the city fail to conquer it, they will be cut off once the barrier repairs the holes."

"They're not here to conquer," Jason said as he stepped out of Shade's body like the shadow creature was a doorway. "They're here to sow terror. We may not have the people to take the fight to them, but we can at least see where they are setting up their strongest attackers."

Jason casually gestured with his arm as he tugged the hood back from his head to reveal his face. The images floating around the room all shifted, their original depictions getting replaced. The new ones showed various locations outside the city, as seen through the slight shimmer of the defensive barrier. It was a dome that rose up from the city wall, and now it was surrounded by enemies.

Messengers only made up a minority of the forces, and usually hovered somewhere near the top of the city wall. Their summons, all of which could fly, surrounded the domed barrier from all angles, including directly above. The summoned monsters were strange to Jason's eye, divergent from the normal pattern. Most monsters looked like they could appear in the environment in which they spawned, so long as there was enough magic. Aquatic shark-crab hybrids on the coast. Swamp monsters with sodden bark-like skin. Even the more bizarre ones that were mostly mouths and tentacles appeared in magically corrupted lands, dark caves or the depths of the ocean, where such entities were unwelcome, but not unexpected.

The messenger summons were different. They didn't look like anything that would be naturally produced in any environment not created by MC Escher. One was a set of concentric metal bands, floating in the air. They spun around one another, their edges covered in eyes that flicked gazes all around. Another looked like a single closed eyelid with wings sticking out either side, but when the lid opened, it revealed not an eye but a mouth with rows of dagger teeth. They were all similarly alien, although eyes and wings featured heavily. Some were geometric, looking like floating sigils. Jason spotted a giant disembodied hand with a mouth on the palm and eyes on the fingertips.

Hana realised that the images in the pyramid's viewing room were not picking out random strange monsters, but instead what was most likely the strike teams. She could sense their strength, with gold-ranked messengers gathered into clusters around the city.

"See where they're positioned?" Jason asked Hana. "Do you see what those locations have in common?"

Hana extended her senses again, focusing on those areas. In each one, she sensed lines of civilians streaming in those directions, along with the powerful magic of the permanent bunkers designed for monster incursions on the city.

"They're going after the bunkers," she said in a horrified whisper.

"Yep," Jason said. "I think they want to break through the defence barrier, inflict as many civilian casualties as possible and get out before the barrier stabilises. I don't know if this was always the plan or if it's a backup once they saw our new bird man friend fighting their snake monster. Either way, I think it's what they're up to now."

"Do you know where the city's diamond-rankers are?" Hana asked.

"Helping out the garuda, last I saw," Jason said. "Fortunately, the garuda is doing the heavy lifting. If our diamond-rankers had to deal with that *and* the messengers, this city would be done."

"Then we are extremely lucky he is here," Hana said.

Jason frowned.

"Yeah," he said unhappily. "We'd have been completely buggered if he wasn't here. I don't trust luck that good."

NICE AND GRUNTY

THE CITY OF YARESH WAS UNDER SIEGE BY MESSENGERS AND THEIR SUMMONED monsters. It was Jason's first time participating in the full-blown defence of a city, and a high-magic one at that. During the defence of Rimaros, he had been working monster clean-up on another island.

If not for the danger to the people of the Yaresh, he would have enjoyed being an unremarkable cog in the big machine, one of many silver-rankers recruited to the task. As the messengers and their summons were silver rank at a minimum, bronze-rank adventurers would only be a liability in battle, despite their numbers. They were relegated to support roles, which worked well for healers but reduced combat adventurers to glorified ushers, leading civilians into bunkers.

Silver rank was considered the threshold for becoming a real adventurer in high-magic zones. The leap in power from bronze to silver was far greater than anything that came before, as bronze-rankers were just too easy to kill. Silver rank represented the stage at which a well-trained essence user took their first major step away from frail mortality, their bodies transforming from a sack full of weak points into a sack full of hit points.

Silver was also a stage that any adventurer could reach if sufficiently resourced. Outside of magically desolate zones like Greenstone, an active adventurer could go from bronze to silver in five to ten years. For guild elites, three years was the norm, and many went faster. There were always circumstances that provided opportunities for the bold, with the extended monster surge Pallimustus had been through an extreme example. There were now more newly minted silver-rankers than any other period on record.

Even the gold-rankers had seen their numbers grow, although to a far lesser degree. The gold-rankers of Yaresh were the true power in the city's defence, with Jason's gold-rank companions already having joined them. Emir, Arabelle and Callum Morse were three-quarters of their old adventuring team, with the slot of

Arabelle's absent husband filled by Emir's wife, Constance. They had moved out with Amos Pensinata, who was famously powerful even by gold-rank standards.

Carlos Quilido was a healer, and not a combat one like Arabelle. He had been deployed to assist dealing with the many injured by the battle taking place at the centre of the city. The building-sized garuda still fought the serpent apocalypse beast, even as the messengers gathered outside the city.

The native gold-rankers of Yaresh were in charge of the city's defence. The Deputy Director of the Adventure Society had a communication power not unlike Jason's, but more powerful by virtue of rank. He had used it to connect every team leader in the city of silver rank and above, coordinating the city's defenders.

Jason had taken a brief pause from rescue efforts to check that his cloud palace had formed a defensive bunker properly, having never properly tested the defences. He was in the observation room at the peak of the pyramid-shaped building with Hana Shavar and Shade, eyes closed as he explored the building with his magical senses. The structures all looked good, the weapon systems ready and waiting. They were the contribution of Travis Noble, the magical ordnance specialist from Earth. Jason had thought the results would be more gun-like, but instead were clearly shaped by Jason's own proclivities.

He could also sense the people in the bunkers. The civilians were filling up the dormitories, and he could sense Estella Warnock and Taika in the small quarters he had set aside for them. Estella paced nervously while Taika was meditating. Jason guessed that Taika was hoping to break through to silver in time to join the fight, and as close as he was, he might even do it. Jason didn't think leaping straight into a fight from a rank-up was a good idea, but he was in no position to criticise reckless leaps into combat.

Humphrey reached out through Jason's party chat ability. As team leader, he was the one taking directives from city defence command and relaying them to the group.

"Jason, the evacuation of the civilians into the city defence bunkers is in full swing. They're directing everyone to prep for incursion, assigning teams to the bunkers they expect to be attacked."

"Have we been assigned to the refugee camp?" Jason asked.

"No, the refugee camp is surrounded by adventurer vehicles, plus the two cloud palaces. The entertainment district has bunkers that are some of the largest but weakest in the city, so we're being sent there along with many other teams. We're already headed there, so can you meet us on the way?"

"No worries, mate."

Jason stepped out from one of the bodies Shade had stationed on a rooftop. Most of Shade's bodies remained with Jason for combat purposes, but a handful were stationed in the cloud palace or in strategic locations around the city. This allowed Jason to quickly shadow jump to any of them, navigating around the city without putting his portal on cooldown.

It was not hard to orient himself after appearing on the rooftop; the diamond-rank battle between the garuda and the endlessly spawning serpent creature was impossible to miss. The eagle-headed humanoid was taller than the towering buildings of the city centre, and every time it struck at the hydra-like serpent heads it fought, thunder rumbled across the city. Even some ten kilometres away, air that should have been still under the city's barrier dome was stirred by the shockwaves of the fight.

After sparing the battle a quick glance, Jason ran to the edge of the building and leapt off. His cloak of darkness and stars took the form of sweeping wings, undulating as they pushed him through the air.

He looked over the city from his high vantage. Much of Yaresh was built around living trees, magically shaped and then filled out with stone. The heart of the city contrasted this as living buildings gave way to polished metal and shining glass towers. Many of these had been damaged or toppled entirely by the garuda and its serpentine foe fighting amongst them.

The city was washed in a blue tint as sunlight passed through the dome of the city's defence barrier. Normally visible as little more than a heat-haze shimmer, it now glowed blue as it fended off attacks all across its surface. The messengers had begun their assault and their summons were gathered around it like a swarm of angry bees.

Jason was far from the only airborne traveller as the sky was filled with adventurers alone or in teams. Most rode personal vehicles of various types, from flying skimmer cars like a *Star Wars* character to floating clouds like Sun Wukong. Others rode on familiars, had magical wings like Jason, or simply flew around like superheroes. Sophie was one of those, catching up to Jason as she easily outpaced him in the air. The rest of the team trailed behind in Onslow's expanded shell.

Clive's familiar, Onslow, could expand his shell into an open-sided flying craft, the unshelled tortoise taking the form of a small green humanoid. Wearing child's clothes provided by Clive, he looked like an adorable team mascot. He was still more than capable of directing deadly elemental attacks from the glowing runes atop his shell, however.

Jason and Sophie slowed to join the others in the shell. Clive had purchased some furniture for travelling inside Onslow's shell, but as they were headed for combat, he had left most of it in his storage space. He had only put out a plush rug that the team sat on as Humphrey briefed them. Sophie and Jason flew in and sat with the others and Stash, in the form of a puppy, crawled into Sophie's lap for head scratches.

"The messengers have several aspects broadly in common with essence users," Humphrey explained.

He wouldn't be introducing anything too revelatory, but was a big believer in reiterating information until it stuck. As the team's primary strategist, he had studied their future enemies more than anyone else on the team.

"The messengers all have unique power sets," he continued. "Not as many or as varied as essence users, but don't underestimate their versatility. Also like us, their power sets tend to fall into roles, so look out for what they're doing and react accordingly. Strikers are high damage but not as resilient, so prioritise them."

He nodded at Sophie.

"Defenders are a lesser danger, but hard to kill. They're also good at occupying multiple attackers, so they won't go after the others. Sophie and I will be largely responsible for occupying them so the rest of you can go for softer targets, but be ready to focus defenders down if that's the right play. Belinda will take on the field tactician role as normal, so she'll be looking for opportunities we can jump on."

"Healers are the top priority, right?" Rufus asked.

"As always," Humphrey said with a nod. "Healers are rare amongst the messengers, but if we spot one, it goes to the top of the list. Be aware that they will be the most heavily defended, so we only go after healers as a team, and with a plan. Or we send Jason by himself."

"You're just going to throw me in there?"

"Yes," Humphrey said. "And you're not a pinpoint assassin, so I expect you to kill more than just the healers while you're at it. Next up, we have summoners, who are the weakest of the messenger archetypes individually, but critical to their forces. Killing them won't get rid of the summons, but it will reduce the cohesiveness of their summoned monsters. Low priority, but take the chance if it's there."

He looked at Neil and Clive.

"The key thing to watch out for is that many messengers have the power to isolate individuals, forcing a one-on-one confrontation. Neil and Clive, you're our weakest solo fighters, so stick together with Belinda in Onslow's shell. Clive, I want you focused on setting up big hits against any messengers you can get a line on through the wall of summoned monsters. Lindy and Neil, boost him when you aren't focused on healing or protecting the group. Lindy, I want you to hold your tricks for when we can make the most of throwing the messengers a surprise or two. Stash, I want you to stick to them and keep them safe."

Stash let out an affirmative yip.

"If they can't get you alone," Humphrey continued, "they can't use those isolating powers on you. Just watch out for area attacks, since you'll be clustered up. You know what to do, Neil."

Neil nodded.

"I can't afford to just stand still," Sophie said. "I'm useless that way and might as well have stayed back at the cloud house."

"You're right," Humphrey agreed. "Everyone not sticking to Onslow will be on the move, operating with some degree of independence. You and I will be staying relatively close, running escort for the others. I'll be sweeping summons that get near Onslow, and I want you getting in the face of any messengers, Soph."

"I take the big ones and you take the little ones," Sophie told him.

"Essentially, yes," he confirmed. "The messengers have the intelligence to make strategic and tactics choices their summons won't. I want you getting in their faces, disrupting whatever they're trying to do and setting them up for big hits from Clive."

"You don't want me to kill them?"

"Focus on disruption, at least at the start. You'll have plenty of fight to power up and you'll be nice and grunty in the late stages."

"Oh, I'll be the grunty one, will I?" she asked, and Humphrey's face reddened.

"Time and place," he told her through gritted teeth.

"What about the one-to-one powers the messengers have to isolate?" Rufus asked.

"As long as the group stays together, all the information we have says they'll be fine. For those of us moving alone, we have to assume that some or all of us will be hit by them eventually. Most likely after the messengers realise they can't break off Neil or Clive to target."

"Will they even go for us?" Sophie asked. "They have to assume that we know about their powers, so anyone going it alone can handle themselves in a duel."

"Don't underestimate messenger arrogance," Jason said. "Our side might rate the messengers as slightly below a combat-focused adventurer in a one-to-one comparison, but I'll bet you they do the opposite. And I honestly don't know which side is right. I promise you that their auras will be a critical factor."

"We can't just hunker up in fear of solo fights," Humphrey said. "As Sophie said, if we don't fight our way, we might as well not have come. These enemies are too strong to bring anything but our best. We just have to trust that we can take them alone and get back to the fight."

"Which means some of us will be relatively alone," Rufus said.

"Yes," Humphrey agreed. "Especially you and Jason, Rufus. You don't have your own flight power, so I want you on the ground. Messenger summons are all flyers, but they'll be trying to break into the underground bunkers."

"I can clear out summons while simultaneously setting up my powerful attacks for the messengers," Rufus said. "Maybe catch some of those defenders by surprise with big hits."

"Jason," Humphrey said. "I know you don't like talking about Earth, but from what Farrah has told me, you should be just fine in the middle of the enemy. Is that something you can handle?"

"No worries. Being alone in the middle of thousands of monsters is kind of my thing."

"Just don't die again," Neil told him.

"No promises."

"Jason, you're out of resurrections," Humphrey pointed out.

"I hate to break to you, cobber, but so is everyone else. Even your Immortality power won't get you back up until gold rank."

"He's not wrong," Neil said. "Resurrection magic has been harder for a few years now. Even at gold rank, you have minutes at best, and only the most complex and difficult healing magic can do it."

"Sorry about that," Jason told him.

"It was something that the gods of healing and death did to how magic works," Neil said. "It wasn't your fault."

Jason's expression became an apologetic wince.

"It wasn't *not* my fault. I thought I told you this. The whole bit with the Reaper making a deal so the World-Phoenix wouldn't keep bringing me back from the dead."

"I thought that was a joke."

"Why would that be a joke?"

"Because it's insane."

Neil let out a sigh.

"Look at who I'm talking to. Shade, please tell me the Reaper didn't have the gods change how magic works because of Jason."

"The Reaper did not have the gods change how magic works because of Mr Asano."

"Thank you," Neil said, his voice relieved.

"Mr Asano was more of an inciting incident that pushed the Reaper to act on something he has been concerned about for quite some time."

Neil gave Shade a flat look.

"Is it too late for me to go find energy vampire Thadwick and join his team again?"

82

BREACH

Jason and his team were riding inside Onslow's expanded shell towards the entertainment district. Buried under the taverns, clubs, theatres and nightclubs was a massive subterranean bunker, one of the least secure in the city. It was large and magically reinforced, but mostly relied on a sturdy roof, with no active defences that could deter attackers from digging in eventually.

That was usually fine if a monster spawned in the city or some managed to break in during a monster surge, but messengers were more intelligent foes. Not only would they bother to go after the people in the bunker but would also realise its relative vulnerability. Jason's team and others like it were tasked with holding off the messengers once they made it into the city. Eventually, they would be forced to either retreat through the breaches they created in the barrier dome or be trapped inside when they closed.

Jason stood at the edge of Onslow's shell looking out at the dome that spanned over the city. The barrier had already turned from clear to blue as summoned monsters attacked the entire surface of the dome. As it became increasingly stressed, it started buzzing like wet power lines, even giving off a similar ozone smell. Most people wouldn't detect it, but Jason's silver-rank olfactory senses could smell the tang of it, even from far below.

Humphrey tilted his head, listening to a voice in his head. He was currently under two communication powers: Jason's linking him to the team, and a gold-ranker coordinating the city defences.

"They're expecting breaches at any moment," he warned. "We'll be on site in only a minute or two, but we may be arriving at a fight already in progress."

Gary picked his way along a street far closer to the centre of the city than Jason and his team. This was a part of Yaresh where buildings were made of polished metal and stone rather than living wood. The buildings were also taller, at least the ones that had more than a shattered base pointing jaggedly upward like the hilt of a broken sword.

The street was in ruins, entire sections of building having fallen to the street. Navigating them alternately meant clambering over, skirting around or even going through them, entering through a shattered section of wall and exiting through a door or window that somehow remained intact.

Gary was travelling with other essence users specialised in various crafts, moving closer to the great battle at the centre of the city than most adventurers. The craftspeople had little to no combat experience other than Gary, but that barely mattered. Anyone short of diamond rank who got involved in the fight between the garuda and the serpent monster would die helplessly, combat veteran or not.

Cresting a toppled tower, Gary paused to look up. Debris was raining from the sky as titanic beings smashed apart buildings. Some of the debris *was* the buildings, landing on other buildings or the wide boulevards like bombs. Dust choked the air, acrid in the lungs of any low-rankers caught in it.

The air was filled with shrill cries from the serpents and the thunderous crashes as the fight destroyed yet more of the city. Behind those irregular sounds was a sonorous hum, growing louder as the barrier endured attacks from the outside. The light filtering through the dome had become a deeper blue, lending the city around Gary the feel of an underwater ruin. He briefly thought back to the village under the lake he, Farrah and Rufus had discovered near Greenstone, shortly before they met Jason for the first time.

He shook his head, his mane dancing around his head. He looked down at where the others were making their way over the obstruction. They may not have been fighters, but they still had silver-rank strength, endurance and agility, so they needed no help. The support team of bronze-rankers with them were actual adventurers and were likewise capable.

The only member of the group that had any trouble negotiating the terrain was Gary's summon. A ten-foot-tall forge golem, it was a humanoid construct of grime-black industrial metal. The glow of molten metal radiated from the joints, between the metal panels and in the eye holes that were the only features on an otherwise blank face. It was not a great climber, but Gary's almost gold-rank strength was able to haul the six-ton golem with no concern. In many cases, the golem went through, rather than over obstacles.

Gary and the other craftspeople were all volunteers looking to help with the evacuation. Their powers were more effective than the average adventurer's for dealing with widespread destruction. They could meld stone, reinforce buildings in danger of collapsing and use other techniques to extract any survivors who had become trapped. The support team of bronze-rank adventurers with them were assigned by the Adventure Society, as they had powers well-suited to getting the rescued civilians to safety once free from whatever had them trapped. Most had vehicle or speed powers, but the Adventure Society had even managed to spare a portal user and a healer.

The healer was especially useful with the thick dust that tightened the lungs of the normal-rankers they found. Children were especially vulnerable, often unconscious until subjected to a healing or cleanse ability. Luckily, low-rankers were not taxing on a bronze-rank healer's mana reserves.

The group had little time to spare. Once the messengers and their summoned monster army broke through, there would be no safe evacuation of civilians through the streets. Waiting out the rest of the attack buried where they were was not a great option, especially for those with injuries, but travelling through the open streets would not be safe.

It was already proving dangerous even before the dome was broken through. Twice Gary's group had encountered naga—people with the upper body of an elf and the lower body of a serpent. These were lesser beings created by the serpent-spawning apocalypse beast the eagle-headed garuda was fighting. Fortunately, the freshly created beings had been disoriented by their coming into being. He guessed that was why they'd wandered off. One had been bronze and another silver, which Gary had easily dispatched, but he dreaded meeting a gold.

At this point, the streets were mostly clear of civilians not in need of rescue, as they had already evacuated to the bunkers. The bunkers were designed to withstand monster attacks and the civilians had been drilled in swiftly heading to them when anything threatened to get past the walls. This usually meant monsters manifesting inside the city, but soon after the monster surge, those drills were fresh in everyone's mind. With magical assistance to organise everything, evacuating the populace into the bunkers had gone smoothly in most of the city.

The place this wasn't true was the centre of the city. Groups like Gary's were risking extreme danger to rescue people trapped in fallen buildings or cut off on blocked streets. What should have been easy terrain had turned harsh and was getting worse by the moment as debris rained from the sky. Anything from loose rubble to the better part of entire buildings were leaving massive craters or obstructing entire streets.

More than once, Gary had to interpose himself to shield another craftsperson, getting hammered into the ground for his trouble. After each instance, he had needed a healing potion and to conjure a fresh shield. As they moved, they saw many people who had been struck down while attempting to escape.

Gary and his group reached the next building where they sensed the auras of trapped survivors and went to work. Gary had the hammer, iron, fire and forge essences. His powers were better suited to smithing weapons than reinforcing buildings, but fortunately, he had experience to draw on. In the years leading up to the monster surge, Gary had spent time moving between isolated towns, helping them prepare. Not only had he supplied them with weapons but he had also worked on reinforcing walls and other defensive infrastructure.

The craftspeople shaped stone, reinforced structures and opened up pathways to dig out trapped people. These were people either too low-rank to escape themselves or people trapped with low-rankers. A silver-ranker pushing their own way out could easily cause a shift in debris that killed the people with them. Sadly, Gary had already encountered some who had made that mistake.

Each situation required its own adaptation to the specific conditions, testing the creativity of the craftspeople. As they went from rescue to rescue, they discovered which approaches worked best in most circumstances, refining their use each time. A common tactic was for a tunnel into a fallen building to be stone-shaped into place. The two-piece chest plate of Gary's forge golem then opened to spray a layer of molten metal across the surface in a surprisingly well-controlled stream. A water user then cooled the molten metal to reinforce the tunnel.

The silver-rank conjured metal was thin but strong, and while it would vanish along with the golem in time, it was more than enough to evacuate whoever was at the end of the new tunnel. Rough and ready construction was the order of the day at every site as jury-rigged girders and iron walls only had to hold long enough to get trapped civilians out.

The group realised their time was up from the hum of the barrier dome. A constant drone behind the crashes of debris and thunderous sounds of diamond-rank combatants, it had been consistently rising in pitch. Once the hum started to pulse, they knew the breach was about to happen. Gary looked up but couldn't see more than a hazy blue through the dust.

"Time to get to the bunkers ourselves," he declared, his tone brooking no dissention.

As a group, they headed for the nearest bunker. It wasn't too far, as the city centre had a number of them. In normal conditions, a silver-ranker on foot could reach one in minutes, if not seconds, but conditions were far from normal. The terrain was one thing, but in short order, they heard sounds in the air that were something between electrical discharges and breaking glass. They couldn't see it, but they knew the barrier protecting the city had been breached.

<hr>

Jason and his team had managed to reach the sky over the entertainment district just in time to see the breach occur. The breaches were centred over the bunkers, so the team had a clear view as the barrier dome rippled like water. The rippling magic energy shifted from blue to clear as monsters pushed against it, but then suddenly pulled back.

The summoned creatures moved from the other side of the dome and a messenger gathered energy over his head, arms raised. It formed an orange, red and yellow ball, glowing like a sun, the colours plain through the now-clear section of barrier. Other messengers fed streams of power into it and it slowly grew larger.

Jason and his team watched and waited; they were far from alone in doing so. The air was not as thick with adventurers as the other side of the barrier was with monsters, but it was far from empty. Many teams hovered in the air, in vehicles and on personal flight devices. More adventurers were on the rooftops far below, waiting to protect the bunker beneath the ground.

There was a moment of stillness on both sides of the barrier dome. It was not quiet, with the distant thunder of diamond-rank battle, but the air was thick with tension. The fireball grew larger than the messenger creating it, until it was finally unleashed.

The flaming sphere did not rush forward, moving slowly towards the barrier dome. It struck the clear, rippling section of the barrier, which went hard like glass. It then shattered, though it did not sound quite like glass with a sharp electric crash. A jagged hole appeared in the barrier, but it did absorb all the power from the fireball before breaking. Fragments of brittle magic, temporarily made solid, fell a short distance before dissolving into nothing.

Monsters poured through the breach like pressurised water through a sudden leak. The summoned creatures were all bizarre flying entities, moving through the air and firing projectiles or swooping to the attack. A one-eyed griffin with four wings that looked freakishly like human arms dove into the attack with lion-like forelimbs and eagle talon hind legs. A large uncut crystal, purple and floating in the air, was orbited by magic sigils carved from what looked like rubies and sapphires. The sigils conjured rings of flame and razor-sharp circles of ice that were shot at the adventurers.

Like all the others, Jason's team moved forward to meet them. Humphrey and Sophie launched out of Onslow's shell, while Rufus stepped off and dropped down. Jason stepped into Shade and vanished. As soon as they were gone, a shimmering wall of air swirled around the shell. Onslow could use various elemental powers by activating the glowing runes on the segments of his shell, and as a silver rank, Clive could enhance them. He was using ritual magic to enhance the wind shield as Belinda, dressed in a robe and pointy hat, was shooting blasts of magic from her staff and wand. Neil was taking stock of the battleground forming in the sky, saving his mana for when his team needed it.

Along with Onslow, Belinda and Humphrey's familiars were at the ready. Stash was currently retaining his puppy form as it allowed him to stay out of the way. His task was to guard the shell and its occupants, and he would shapeshift as and when needed. Belinda's astral lantern, Shimmer, was pumping out mana to the team. Given that the battle would be a long one, that would pay off more and more the longer the conflict continued. Her other familiar, Gemini, was a blurry replica of Clive. It was better at replicating abilities than before, now that it was silver rank, and shared Belinda's knack for doing more of the best thing anyone else was up to.

The team was variously ready and waiting, or already on the move. The Battle of Yaresh had begun.

83

GARY GOES TO WORK

B<small>REACHES TO THE BARRIER WERE HAPPENING ALL ACROSS THE CITY, BUT ONE WAS</small> unlike any of the others. Seen and heard from across the city, the messenger's only diamond-ranker came down through the peak of the dome like an anvil through glass. The dome being penetrated released sound that reached the outer walls and force that shattered windows for kilometres. Adventurers were avoiding the central part of the city because of the ongoing garuda battle, but even at a distance, many flyers were knocked out of the sky.

For most of the city's adventurers, the highest-level conflicts were more like a fireworks show than a battle they were participating in. Distant explosions made for a spectacular view, but getting too close held nothing but danger. Jason and his team paid minimal attention, trusting the city's own diamond-rank defenders to intercept. All they could do was hope that the city wasn't levelled in the process.

The high-level fights were mercifully out of reach of Jason's team in the entertainment district, and they had more than enough to be going on with. Enemies gushed through the local breach like water through cracks in a dam, mostly monsters but with a solid contingent of messengers. The adventurers outnumbered the messengers, but the monsters were a countless swarm.

No one on the field was lower than silver rank. While both sides had gold-rankers, Jason was relieved to see that the adventurers had a slim advantage in that regard. None of the monsters were gold rank, only messengers. His aura senses told him that the most powerful combatant was on the other side, however. Auras were far from a perfect measure of power, but Jason's instincts warned him about one of the messengers.

It was the man who had conjured the fireball that breached the barrier. His skin was light brown and his hair dark. He wore light leather armour, but any protection at all was rare amongst the messengers, as if to admit the need was to show weakness. The man's wings were shades of brown and grey, more like a bird than an angel.

Both sides were led by their gold-rankers, although very little in the way of orders were going out. Summoned monsters swarmed down towards the adventurers defending on the ground, while the ones in the air thinned them out as best they could. The messengers sought to impede the adventurers as much as they could, with the gold-rank battles especially settling into a détente.

The gold-rankers of one side could swiftly decimate the other if they weren't forced to negate one another. It was a tense conflict that no smart silver-rank went anywhere near, largely taking place in the higher reaches of the battle. At the low end, the advantage of flight the summons had against many ground defenders was ameliorated by their goal. If the monsters couldn't dig down to the bunker they had failed, so they were forced to come to the defenders. The result was a massacre, although not without adventurer casualties. No matter how many monsters fell, however, there were always more pouring down.

Jason's team went to work, sticking to Humphrey's outlined strategy. Belinda and Clive made use of the rituals Clive had set up inside Onslow's shell that enhanced the beams and blasts coming from their magical staves and wands. Arrays of nested ritual diagrams were difficult to integrate without them interfering with one another, but Clive had spent much of the past few years perfecting the unusual practice of combat rituals.

Clive had been well aware that while he was a utility asset to the team, he was the least useful member when it came to combat. He had a few support abilities and one very powerful attack spell, but he often found himself feeling more like an auxiliary member than a full one. As such, he had spent much of the time Jason was absent working to improve his combat effectiveness.

He was never going to match Humphrey, Sophie and Jason, who were the combat mainstays. Belinda's versatility meant that she was always filling a gap, disabling enemies or making a team member even better than they already were. As for Neil, his value as healer was obvious. Clive couldn't change his powers and he was never going to be a solo combat star, so instead of trying to expend his abilities, he narrowed them.

Clive had long used combat rituals to enhance his effectiveness, largely inspired by his acquisition of very powerful staff and wand weapons. Combat rituals were largely looked down on by adventurers and magical researchers alike, but Clive was determined to take them as far as they could be taken. The result was a collection of rituals that could be nested in tight arrays, turning a largely ignorable beam attack from his staff into an attack that rivalled an essence ability.

The result of Clive's efforts was that he and his familiar had become a turret bunker, pouring out attacks that ravaged the summoned monsters. At the same time, it was efficient enough that the barrage could be maintained for hours. Clive had mana enough to spare that he could feed extra to Onslow, resetting and enhancing the familiar's magic powers. As for any monsters that tried to assault them, Onslow's elemental powers could fend off any but the most concentrated assaults. While it took some preparation time, Clive finally felt that he could contribute to battle without absolutely needing the support of the team.

Gary's group of craftspeople and low-rank adventurers were navigating a city that looked like it was going through the apocalypse. Thunder pealed, not from storms but from the battle of behemoths only vaguely visible through the choking dust. Stones that ranged in proportion from the size of a fist to the size of a house fell from the sky at random; the sky had to be watched at all times.

The biggest problem facing the group was that their destination, a bunker, was the same place the messengers were targeting. The craftspeople and their adventurer support team hurried through the city, picking up straggling civilians as they went. Fortunately, this didn't slow them too much as the adventurers had all been chosen for their ability to hasten others. One had an aura that enhanced movement speed while another had a pack of rideable lizard familiars. One adventurer picked up civilians and carried them telekinetically.

It did not take long after hearing the barrier broken open before the monsters found them. Gary knew that he would not be able to shield the civilians and bronze-rankers against the summoned creatures. They were all silver rank and he was the only real combatant, so he would need to take the fight to the monsters. The other craftspeople were of at least some help, conjuring ice barriers and water shields or raising up walls of earth. They even managed to fight back—shooting obsidian spears and other projectiles— but they were not fighters.

Under Gary's direction, they strove to keep moving rather than secure kills. Any monster that wanted to slink back into the sky, Gary was happy to let go. The group sustained injuries and lost a couple of civilians to a monster that fired sonic blasts. That one was left struggling to fly back into the sky, after being weighed down with a coating of molten metal.

Gary's senses told him that the whole city had become a war zone as adventurers, messengers and monsters clashed. Hard-hit streets became even worse as powers flew off in every direction, tearing up pavement and hammering buildings. Scattered civilians too slow or stubborn to reach a shelter were pummelled by stray magic or collapsing buildings.

Despite losing a couple of civilians, the group was largely optimistic as they drew close to the bunker. The craftspeople had done a surprisingly good job of deterring the monsters, even if they mostly escaped alive. Gary was about to warn the group to be wary as they rounded the next corner when an aura emerged from the throng of monsters that stood out from the others.

A messenger flew around a building and descended to float just above the ground in front of them. Gary could sense he was of the summoner type from the way his aura interacted with the monsters in the area. He was slightly taller than even Gary's height. Beautiful, with golden hair and pale skin, his sculpted body delicately draped in loose clothes of white and gold. His bare feet floated just over the flagstone street, the pristine white wings spread out behind him undulating softly. The dust that clung in Gary's fur and on his armour did not touch the messenger, as if afraid to soil it.

Gary knew that the messenger being only a silver-ranker did not mean the adventurers' numbers were an advantage. He was certain the summoner could call on the monsters with swiftness, and probably even boost their power. Even if he could seize the momentum before the summons were brought into play, messengers were no joke to fight alone.

"I have sensed you driving off my creatures," the messenger told them, his voice a melody of the heavens. "That will end here."

There was almost pity in the messenger's voice; Gary's hackles rose as the beautiful man looked down on them. The messenger looked at him and smiled, then pushed out with his aura. Despite being one man, he suppressed the silver-rank craftspeople who had never trained their auras for combat. The messenger's aura was unlike anything they had encountered, a brutal and almost physical force. Compared to delicate appearance of the messenger, his aura was that of a savage thug.

Only Gary's aura held strong, the benefits of training with Jason. Jason's aura was even more brutal than this man's, with many of the same traits yet even more oppressive. Jason had been ruthless in training his companions to resist aura suppression, and none of them shirked. They all knew how dangerous auras could be.

The others in Gary's group did not fare as well. The civilians collapsed outright, one of them going into a seizure, but Gary had neither the time nor the power to help them. The bronze-rankers and the craftspeople fared about the same, the adventurers better trained while the craftspeople were stronger. They all turned pale as their auras shrank like mice under the gaze of a hawk.

Gary's aura wasn't suppressed, but he was definitely outmatched, even when the messenger was simultaneously suppressing the others. His aura wavered but held, trembling under the strain. Many of the others had dropped to one or both knees under pressure that was spiritual rather than physical. Gary squared himself, planting his feet. His right hand held his hammer, the head glowing red-yellow with heat. His armour and shield did the same, glowing between plates of dark metal. His head was bare; he had not conjured his helmet so as to not restrict his line of sight on the sky.

The messenger looked at Gary with surprise, as if at a pet that had demonstrated an unexpected trick. He floated forward, stopping directly in front of Gary.

"Kneel, savage, and you shall live. Serve me, and I shall even spare these... people... out of respect for your value as a slave."

Gary grinned defiance through lion's teeth. What he'd heard about the arrogance of messengers had proven true, as had the fact that it could lead them to make tactically unsound choices.

"You want savage?" he growled.

Gary's roar hit the messenger like a cannon, the pure sonic force of it shooting the messenger back faster than the bronze-rankers could even track. The messenger smashed through the wall of the building it had just come around, while the building itself was covered in spiderweb cracks.

"Pull it out," Gary snarled.

The foundry golem at the rear of the group opened its chest cavity. Glowing hot chains shot out of the golem and into the hole made by the messenger entering the building. They stopped for a moment and then started pulling back rapidly.

The only light they could see through the hole was the glow of the chains, wrapped around something in the dark. They hauled it out with industrial inevitability as the chains went back into the chest cavity of the golem. The messenger became visible as he reached the hole, looking far less untouchable. He was caked with dust and grime now, sear marks burnt black into white wings where the chains were binding them.

The messenger did not allow itself to just be dragged along, ignoring the sizzle from his hands as he gripped the chains. He twisted himself as he was dragged, planting his feet at the edge of the hole and hauling back against the golem. For a moment, his movement was arrested as he struggled for control.

Gary stood next to the chains that extended from the golem behind him. He tossed his hammer casually in the air, grabbed one of the chains and yanked, sending the messenger hurtling in his direction. Even bound, the messenger's wings managed to turn his tumble in the air into a glide, but it came to an unceremonious end before he could arrest his momentum. Gary snatched his hammer out of the air and brought it down, smashing the messenger into the ground.

The winged man's face had hit hard enough to crack a flagstone, but Gary was far from done. He grabbed a wing and flipped the messenger like a steak. He felt the beleaguered man's aura reaching for the monsters nearby and distracted him with a hammer to the face. The shield dropped from Gary's arm, pinning the messenger's chest and arms when Gary planted a foot on it. His head visible, the messenger glared up at Gary as he tried to push him off, but the leonid was intractable as a mountain.

Gary looked back at the people behind him, under his protection. His mind flashed to Farrah's death, when he could do nothing but watch helplessly as dimensional invaders killed her in front of him. He looked down at the messenger, gripped his hammer in both hands and went to work.

84

THE LADY SHOOTING
HURRICANES AT PEOPLE

BELINDA WAS MIMICKING CLIVE, BLASTING AT SUMMONED MONSTERS WITH HER own staff and wand, but she was a pale imitation of the real thing. She could also make use of Clive's rituals, boosting her weapons to deal more damage and chain their attacks from enemy to enemy. The problem was that her weapons were not able to make as much use of the rituals as Clive's were. Her staff and wand were both quality items, but if she let the rituals overcharge them as much as Clive did his, they would swiftly break down.

Clive had discovered his legendary-quality growth items in an astral space and nothing available on the market could match them. They could take more punishment than ordinary weapons and were the crux of his combat effectiveness. Belinda didn't begrudge him such a key tool, but was feeling a little wasted as a second-rate imitation.

Watching how the monsters moved, she looked for fresh options. Her power set was versatile, but didn't do well when coming into direct combat without time to prepare. If she had time to study the area, rig the terrain or at least lure enemies into a favourable environment, her charlatan and trap essences were incredible assets. When the fight was open and sudden, however, her effectiveness dropped. To have a real impact, she had to get opportunistic, finding the right moments to make an unexpected move.

The monsters poured through the breach in the barrier dome, hundreds of metres above. They immediately dropped towards their target, the bunker buried beneath the ground. Adventurers in the sky did their best to thin them out for the other adventurers at ground level, while the messengers sought to distract them, letting the monsters go through unimpeded.

Area attacks were the most valuable asset to the adventurers, given the circumstances. This was not her team's strong point, but they did have a few powers that had taken on area effects as they ranked up. The most spectacular was Sophie's wind blades, which were usually too slow for area attacks. She tended to use them at point-blank range, being a melee fighter, but she did get the occasional chance to truly unleash. With the monsters clustered so thickly together, it was shooting fish in a barrel.

Belinda watched as Sophie periodically shot her wind blades at the torrent of creatures descending through the sky. Her blades grew wider as they travelled, and for each enemy they hit, they triggered a secondary ring of cutting force. In normal circumstances, most silver-rank monsters had the reflexes to dodge, but with a curtain of monsters falling from the sky, it was harder to miss them than to hit.

The results were incredibly destructive, but using any individual power was like trying to divert a river with a bucket. Only a lot more people with a lot more buckets would get the job done, and other adventuring teams were doing better jobs of widespread devastation. Team Storm Shredder fought nearby, demonstrating this as they made good on their name. Their core strategy was built around stacking buffs on powerful attacks; in this case, electric arrows chaining from monster to monster. The result did look like a thunderstorm shredding monsters.

Their already impressive area attack powers were given a powerful and thematic boost by the inclusion of Zara Rimaros. She might have been adopted into another family with another name, but she lived up to her former title of Hurricane Princess as she unleashed localised storms of hurricane-force wind and water. Monsters were left battered, disoriented and soaking wet, set up for an electrical blast.

Even so, the monsters did not stop pouring in through the breach like beer from a keg. Truly clearing out the monsters would require the slow-but-extreme area attacks of affliction specialists. These were people with entire teams built around keeping them safe as their afflictions escalated in reach and power.

Jason and Rufus both had slow-burn affliction powers, but Rufus used them more as a platform to set up finishing moves on individual targets. His afflictions were used to charge up powerful attacks that could take down even silver-rank enemies, if there were enough weaker enemies to load up with afflictions. One-shotting a silver-ranker was something few could manage, even assassination specialists and gold-rankers. As Rufus was no assassination specialist, the setup required was slow and required a small army of enemies to afflict so he could build power up from them. Even if he met these requirements, he had to roam amongst those enemies, which was always a dangerous proposition.

Belinda knew that Rufus was far below them, working on that at that very moment. Jason was somewhere in the middle of the enemy, starting the destructive butterfly chain that could, if it got up and running, rival some of the full-blown affliction specialists. If the butterflies weren't stopped from spreading early, they would eventually get way beyond anyone's ability to suppress.

That would take time, though, and time was in short supply as the monsters descended to the ground and the bunker beneath it. Immediate area attacks were what would buy the affliction specialists time. Belinda's powers were all about using them in the right context; as she looked again at the descending monsters, that might be exactly what she needed. All she had to do was convince someone to do something very stupid.

"Hump," she reached out through party chat. "I'm seeing a very solid opportunity to do some damage."

"I take it that there's a complication." Humphrey said. He sounded perfectly calm, even though Belinda saw him carve a monster in half as he spoke. "I'm guessing you want me to do something very stupid. Also, don't call me Hump."

"You still have those floating discs I gave you, right?" she asked him.

"I do," Humphrey said, his voice wary. "I don't see how they would do you much good without them being right in amongst the monsters."

"Very astute," Belinda praised.

"Jason is better suited to diving in amongst the monsters," Humphrey pointed out.

"Little busy," Jason said, sounding strained even through voice chat.

"I could do it," Sophie said as she kicked off a messenger's back to go sailing through the air. The messenger turned and fired a thick beam of energy from its hands, striking Sophie square on. He had struck an after-image, the beam passing through and punching a hole through a summoned monster as Sophie appeared behind the messenger again, kicking him in the head.

"You need to keep anyone from focusing on Onslow," Humphrey told her. "I'll do Belinda's madness run, but I'll need some extra attention, Neil."

"Don't worry," Neil assured him. "I'll keep you alive."

"I'd have preferred if you said you'd keep me safe," Humphrey told him.

"I didn't say safe," Neil told him. "You can't hold me to that."

"See?" Belinda said. "You'll be fine, probably."

There was no response for a moment.

"Did you just make a grumbling sound and then realise you couldn't figure out how to send it through voice chat?" Sophie asked.

"No," Humphrey said unconvincingly.

"Oh, look out," Sophie said. "Messengers high and right."

The group's attention turned to a trio of messengers that had taken notice of the flying shell from which adventurers were safely spitting out attacks.

"How is that fair?" Clive complained. "Why aren't they going after the lady shooting hurricanes at people?"

"I think you'll find that some of them jumped her a while back," Belinda said, pointing.

Clive looked to where Zara's team was fending off a half-dozen messengers. "Oh. I guess that is fair."

Humphrey rocketed through the air to engage the three messengers moving in on Onslow's shell. Even propelled by a special attack designed for rapid air strikes, however, he still arrived after Sophie. Her first two kicks landed on their heads before they even registered her presence, a perfectly timed distraction for Humphrey's arrival. His Dive Bomb attack was a combination power, allowing him to link it with his Unstoppable Force ability and land a devastating hit. Combined with his ability to sacrifice life force to enhance his power, his massive sword blasted into all three like an explosion, sending them flying.

Despite being robbed of the initiative, the messengers were undaunted. One of them conjured scale armour stylised like feathers that covered him head to toe. Only magic giving the rigid armour flexibility made movement possible, as ordinary armour with the same design would have left the wearer unable to move.

The other messengers fell back behind their armoured companion, one conjuring a bow stylised like a wing. The other had feathers fly from her actual wings, turn to metal and combine to form a sword. Humphrey and Sophie ignored the defender, both teleporting behind the trio to engage the strikers. Humphrey dropped his heavy sword and conjured his lighter one, the messenger swordswoman in front of him frowning at it. Humphrey's Razor Wing Sword power created a sword that looked a lot like a messenger's wing, rendered in metal.

Sophie and Humphrey played out a dance in the air with the messengers as they manoeuvred for position, the defender trying to reposition himself to protect the others. Humphrey, with his conjured dragon wings, was the most awkward of the group. He swiftly found the armoured messenger interposed between himself and the others. Sophie was the opposite, a leaf on the wind with her flight power, Leaf on the Wind. She harried the two strikers simultaneously, especially the archer.

"You have strength and skill," the armoured messenger told Humphrey, "but it will not be enough this day. Withdraw, wait out the battle, and you will live to see tomorrow."

They hovered in the air facing one another. They both had wings out, but it was magic holding them aloft, not aerodynamics.

"But if I do that," Humphrey told him. "Who will distract you three?"

"What?"

Sophie and Humphrey teleported away, just as a prismatic beam washed over the messengers.

Clive stopped firing off his weapons and started gathering mana the moment Sophie warned them about the messengers.

"Set them up for a big hit, if you please."

"Let us know when to get out of the way," Sophie said through voice chat, already landing kicks on their heads.

Jason's party chat was useful for keeping contact through loud battles and across large distances, but it was also a powerful tool for silently communicating tactics. Humphrey and Sophie held the messenger's attention while Clive charged up his strongest offensive ability.

- You are preparing to cast [Wrath of the Magister]. Select the variant you wish to cast.
- Variant one: [Prismatic Affliction].
- Variant two: [Prismatic Void].

- Variant three: [Spell & Weapon Enhancement Ritual]. This variant is already in place. Multiple effects do not stack but additional casts may be used to cover additional areas.

"Jason," Clive said into party chat as he looked at the system box, "I am so glad to have you back."

"Still busy," Jason said. "I hope these guys have seen my powers before, because otherwise, they researched me personally."

"Are you alright?" Clive asked him.

"Yeah, no worries. I just need to—"

"Jason?"

"Can't really talk. Stitch this, you birdman-rally-looking mother fu—"

Jason cut off his chat channel mid-sentence.

Clive turned his attention back to the spell he was gathering mana for. It was the slowest ability in his arsenal by far, but the payoff was commensurately impressive. It was one of the unconventional powers, usually belonging to spellcasters, that offered variations of the ability to choose from with each use. At lower ranks, the void variant had been a mana-intense trump card that could kill anything at bronze-rank that would stand still long enough to charge up the spell. Now that the enemies were silver, Clive found more value in the debilitating effects of the affliction's variant.

- You have selected the [Prismatic Affliction] variant of [Wrath of the Magister]. Select any or all of the following colour effects, with each colour additional mana costs:

- [Red] (high mana): Target's temperature is significantly increased (high-damage frost burn if combined with blue).
- [Yellow] (high mana): Target's abilities have increased mana cost.
- [Pink] (moderate mana): Target's resistances are reduced.
- [Green] (moderate mana): Target's blood is poisonous to itself.
- [Purple] (very high mana): Expending mana harms the target.
- [Orange] (very high mana): Target suffers increased damage from all sources.
- [Blue] (high mana): Target's temperature is significantly decreased (high-damage frost burn if combined with red).

Although it was the early stage of the battle, Clive didn't hold back.

- You have selected all colours. Total mana cost has increased to beyond extreme.

Clive had a larger mana pool than normal, courtesy of a blessing from a great astral being. It had triggered a human gift evolution, turning the normal human affinity for special attacks into one for spells. Combined with his ability to accelerate mana recovery and burn health for mana, Clive was built for big, expensive spells.

Clive warned Sophie and Humphrey at the last moment and did not wait for them before unleashing the spell. Silver-rankers had lightning reflexes and he didn't want to miss, trusting his teammates to get out of the way.

From where he stood at the edge of Onslow's shell shelter, a prismatic beam as wide as the shell itself blasted from Clive's outstretched hands, blasting over and past the messengers. Clive had deliberately aimed to avoid any adventurers, but the beam washed through the throng of summoned monsters behind them.

Humphrey and Sophie dove back in, pouncing on the now severely debilitated messengers, Belinda and Clive backing them up with ranged attacks.

The two strikers fell, mostly from Humphrey's attacks. He burned life force to inflict massive spikes of damage, Neil restoring it with healing magic. It was too early in the battle for Sophie to kill quickly, not having built up her magical buffs, so she focused on preventing the withdrawal the savaged messengers were attempting to make. Even so, the defender managed to escape into the summoned monsters. Sophie started to chase them, but Humphrey called her back.

"We dropped two of them," he told her. "Keep the victory rather than chasing defeat. No good will come of diving into all those summoned monsters."

"Speaking of which," Belinda told him, "can we get back to our conversation about you diving into all those summoned monsters?"

85

HUMPHREY'S NEW NORMAL

CLIVE LOOKED AT THE BREACH IN BETWEEN BLASTING AT MONSTERS WITH HIS staff and wand.

"They must have summoners stationed outside, sending more in as we kill these ones."

"I'd say a lot of summoners," Belinda agreed. "I know their summoners can call up more than even Humphrey, but these numbers are beyond anything they told us to expect. Which means we could really use *someone* diving in there to help me use my power effectively."

"Yes, I'm going," Humphrey grumbled through voice chat.

"Have you got the discs?" she asked him.

"Yes, I still have the discs."

"Did you pack a lunch?"

Humphrey's sword claimed the last head of a monster that looked like conjoined triplets carved out of marble, with three wings at equidistant points around its body. It didn't look like it could function, let alone fight, but it was more intelligent than most monsters and even could cast a handful of spells. Humphrey had charged at it through a rain of projectiles, his mana crystals absorbing some and the others blasting his armour with elemental attacks of fire, ice and lightning. Once he got within arm's reach, it was a short fight.

"If you're ready, I'm just going to go," Humphrey told Belinda. "You alright with that, Neil?"

"I'm ready," Neil confirmed.

Humphrey plunged into the torrent of monsters spilling in through the breach and dropping like a waterfall towards the ground. He cleared a path as best he could with his fire breath and swept enemies away with his massive dragon-wing sword. Neil's shields snapped into place every time they came off cooldown, but attacks still rained down on Humphrey's dragon armour.

Neil was a skilled adventurer, but in a very different way to Sophie. He had two quick-use shields that were his most commonly deployed abilities. They were short-lived but exceptionally effective when timed correctly. Neil's skill was not demonstrated in martial or acrobatic prowess but in situational awareness, judgement and timing. Knowing when to use an ability and when to hold it for a few seconds later. Reading the fight to predict what his teammates would face. Understanding exactly what his companions could and could not endure.

Neil's quick-shield abilities both had cooldowns of twenty seconds, with one being more tactical and the other focused entirely on protection. The tactical power, Burst Shield, blasted away enemies that attacked the barrier. It could be used to give the recipient respite from attack, room to manoeuvre or the opportunity to make a counterstrike. This shield was useful as Humphrey was swarmed with enemies, but the protective shield was more critical.

Ability: [Absorbing Shield] (Shield)

- Special ability (recovery, retribution, drain).
- Cost: High mana.
- Cooldown: 20 seconds.

- Current rank: Silver 4 (07%).

- Effect (iron): Create a short-lived shield that negates an incoming attack and generates mana-over-time with a strength that scales with the amount of damage negated. High-damage attacks of gold-rank or higher may not be entirely negated.

- Effect (bronze): Attacks made against the shield drain health and mana from the attacker and bestow it upon the recipient of the shield.

- Effect (silver): The recipient gains [Priority Ward].

- [Priority Ward] (boon, magic, stacking): When [Absorbing Shield] is used on a target with this boon, the cooldown is reduced by one second for each instance of [Priority Ward]. Additional instances of this boon may be accumulated.

Absorbing Shield not only protected but even had some healing and recovery effects. Most importantly, repeated uses meant the short-lived shield could be used on closer and closer intervals. The counterbalance to this was the high mana cost, which could rapidly stack up with sequential uses.

Belinda and Clive's auras both reduced the mana cost of the team's abilities, and Clive's replenished mana at the same time. Even so, Neil was swiftly burning through mana as he cast Absorbing Shield over and over.

"Clive," Neil said as he threw the absorbing shield on Humphrey again. He could barely see Humphrey through the throng of monsters to put the shield up. "Humphrey is taking a pounding out there and I'm going through a lot of mana to keep him up. I'm going to need a tide."

"If I use Mana Tide now, that's it for the fight unless Belinda uses her reset on it."

"If I don't get some more mana," Neil told him, "that's it for Humphrey."

"Alright," Clive agreed, pausing from his attacks to cast a spell.

"*Let the astral tides bestow their bounty on the chosen.*"

Ability: [Mana Tide] (Balance)

- Special ability (recovery).
- Cost: low mana.
- Cooldown: 4 hours.

- Current rank: Silver 4 (02%).

- Effect (iron): Draw mana from the astral to replenish allies. Mana recovery begins slowly and escalates over time. Local dimensional conditions may impact the rate of recovery.

- Effect (bronze): Allies affected by this ability increase their mana recovery by spending mana. The more mana spent, the greater the recovery increase. Abnormal local dimensional conditions may produce positive or negative side effects.

- Effect (silver): When allies affected by this ability use powers that cost mana, the effect of those abilities is enhanced. Enhanced abilities will be affected by environmental factors.

Mana started trickling into the team, over a widespread enough area that even Jason and Rufus were affected. The trickle grew swiftly as the dimensional membrane between the universe and the astral was still thin and patchy following the monster surge.

Neil continued tossing Absorbing Shields on Humphrey, finding that they were lasting longer than they should. Mana Tide caused abilities to be impacted by the environment, such as ice spells being stronger in the cold or fire spells stronger in the desert. To Neil's delight, the city barrier, throwing off loose energy from where it had been breached, seemed to be boosting his shields.

The rest of the teams opened up with their strongest abilities, so as not to waste the extra mana. Belinda was waiting for her opportunity, which came as Humphrey emerged from amongst the monsters, job done. He crash-landed inside the shell, bloody and bedraggled despite Neil's best efforts. His rigid dragon-scale armour was shredded, draping off him like rags. It was clear that he had been chum in the water to that many monsters without the elusiveness of Sophie, Rufus or Jason.

What Humphrey had been doing amongst the monsters was deploying small discs, looping through the horde and leaving them behind like breadcrumbs. The palm-sized objects were unremarkable, with barely enough magic to float in place. Humphrey had left a trail of them behind, and while a handful were destroyed by the monsters, most were ignored. The orders of their summoners to reach the ground and dig through to the bunker were more important than a few small, unthreatening devices.

As Neil healed Humphrey, who was conjuring a fresh set of armour, Belinda's attention was on the discs. She had crafted them personally with cheap and easy magic, looking for something unremarkable and inexpensive as she wouldn't be getting them back.

Far more expensive was the looking glass that allowed her to spy on her discs from a moderate distance and, more importantly, allowed her to use her abilities on them. It was a simple device, the range was fairly short and only worked on two of her abilities. Even so, the price for devices that would break the line-of-sight limit that most abilities had was always a costly proposition, and in more ways than one. Such items required an intrinsic link to the user, meaning that if someone hostile got a hold of them, they had grasped a dangerous vulnerability.

The looking glass wasn't actually glass but a hoop of moon silver, threaded with sun gold. The image that appeared as she activated it was an illusion it produced of the closest disc. Extending her power through the hoop, Belinda used her Lightning Tether power. A rod rose from the disc and an arc of electricity jumped to the nearest monster. The arc stayed in place as another arc jumped from that monster to another, repeating in a chain until seven monsters were linked.

The nature of the power was to inflict very little damage close to the rod, little more than a static shock. The further the targets moved from the rod, however, the larger the damage from the lightning arcs linking them together. Further, the arcs would fire off electricity at other nearby enemies. Given that the monsters were hurtling towards the ground at breakneck speed, the damage swiftly became immense. As myriad arcs of electricity crackled and seared through the monsters, from the outside, it looked like a waterfall of lightning.

Such a spectacular display quickly drew attention. The monsters avoided the lightning and the rod to which it was tethered, although they were so tightly packed, there was only so far they could go. The messengers did not avoid it, recognising it as a threat. One of them acted to stop it, shooting a razor-sharp feather from a safe distance. Weaving through the monsters, the feather struck the lightning rod, which immediately detonated in an explosion of electricity and force. Even having given the rod distance, the radius was large enough that many monsters were severely burned. There were no immediate fatalities, but some lost the ability to fly, be it through scorched wings or electrical paralysis.

Belinda shifted her looking glass to another disc and called up another rod.

***

Belinda activated all the discs left by Humphrey that hadn't been taken out by monsters before she got to them. By the time she was done, the team had once again drawn the attention of the messengers. They had been left alone for a time after killing two and driving off a third, but after Belinda's lightning waterfalls, their interest was renewed. Fortunately, they were mostly still focused on the big area attackers like Zara and some of the local guild teams. The most they did, for the moment, was redirect more of the monsters to attack the team. It was only a tiny fragment of the numbers continuing down from the cracked dome above, but it was enough to put the team under real pressure.

Humphrey had fully recovered, while Belinda worked her magic. With a few healing spells, freshly conjured armour and a quick splash of crystal wash, he was once again looking like the imposing team leader. After getting tossed around by the monsters when he went to them, he was looking to even the score now that they were coming to him. He was going to show them what he could really do, force more messengers to show up themselves and then kill them too.

Humphrey flew around on his conjured wings, the mana drain of doing so reduced by one of the many expensive items he possessed. One of the benefits of coming from a wealthy and connected adventuring family was the ability to source the perfect items, making him the best-geared member of the team. He used his connections to help the others, but nothing could match the efforts Danielle Geller spent on equipping her children.

Humphrey had struggled on first reaching silver rank. At iron and bronze, the power of his attacks was overwhelming, butchering all but the sturdiest of monsters in a few blows. His strongest attacks could wipe out multiple targets at once. Silver rank was the threshold at which the resilience of bodies, especially those of monsters, outstripped even the strongest of attacks. One-hit kills became a thing of the past and Humphrey had needed to correct some bad habits.

It was a lifetime of training, plus his dedication and experience that helped him push past his initial problems and find his new normal at silver rank. He did so by taking the opposite approach to the rest of his team, which, as a whole, specialised in fighting the least common and most exotic enemies. Humphrey doubled down on his role as the team's anchor, bringing a conventional speed and power approach that was a foundation for many of the team's strategies.

Adventuring at silver rank was a different proposition than what came before. Many adventurers in high-magic zones never saw an unsupervised contract before silver-rank. Most monster encounters fell into three categories: swarms of weaker monsters, packs of balanced monsters, and the most powerful monsters, spawning alone or in pairs.

At lower ranks, the powerful monsters were the most dangerous, with the strongest bronze-rank monsters outstripping many of the weaker silvers. The difference only really mattered to bronze-rank adventurers who had to be wary of the damage reduction and resistance bonuses that came with rank disparity.

At silver rank, the solitary monsters were no longer the key threat. With even weak monsters being startlingly resilient, the standard shifted away from the once invincible attacks that had cleared out monsters like sweeping a dirty floor. A good team could leverage their numbers to gang up on one or two targets effectively, or use superior strength to clear out weaker monsters, even if they were tougher than before. Although their team makeup was rather unusual, Humphrey and his team were not so bizarre as to escape that dynamic.

The most dangerous monsters, then, were those too numerous to gang up on, yet too tough to be handled quickly. This was the dynamic that Humphrey had prepared himself for. He might not slay every monster with a single sweep of his sword anymore, but he still hit harder than most adventurers, and could move around quickly while doing it. With potent, unrelenting attacks, supplemented by a moderate amount of area damage, he was a square peg in a square hole when it came to the most common and dangerous of monsters.

Humphrey was perfectly suited to the level of power displayed by the monsters summoned by the messengers. The messengers used middle-ground monsters exclusively, but had somehow managed them in massive numbers, making it the worst of all worlds. With extra monsters now focused on Onslow's shell as the team's primary platform, Humphrey got busy.

NOT ENOUGH MONSTERS TO FIGHT

For Humphrey and his team, the fight had reached a new peak of intensity. After Belinda's wide-scale destruction using her lightning tether, the messengers had sent a storm of summoned monsters to assault Onslow's tortoise-shell mini-fortress. Rather than being placed on the defensive, however, they were taking the fight to the enemy. Clive's Mana Tide spell had the team operating above and beyond their normal levels, giving them the mana to throw everything they had at the enemy.

Humphrey cut a spectacular figure, hurling himself at the monsters while spraying out dragon breath. He dashed through the air, unloading blow after blow from his humungous dragon wing sword, spinning like a top as his Unstoppable Force attack carved troughs through the bodies of the monsters that dove in to surround him.

Once his mainstay attack, Unstoppable Force could no longer one-shot monsters the way it did at low ranks, but it still excelled when many monsters fell within reach. Not only did it blast concussive force out with every hit, extending the reach of the attack, but the cooldown was reduced for every enemy struck. With monsters all around, he was able to burn through mana and stamina firing it off again and again.

The monsters quickly learned that being too close to Humphrey was a good way to get their faces carved off, or whatever the bizarre creatures had instead of a face. Their over-eagerness to box him in waned and they dropped back to make ranged attacks, forcing him to engage only a couple of them at a time.

Humphrey was unperturbed. Humans were masters of special attacks and Humphrey had a variety of them for every situation. Rising to the fore in his reper-toire was an attack that had gone largely overlooked when his rank was lower and the monsters weaker. Relentless Assault had no cooldown and increased in damage every time it was used in quick succession. This let Humphrey chop his way through monsters like a lumberjack felling a tree before using a dash attack or teleport to keep his sequence going with the next monster.

There were so many monsters in the air that Humphrey had no trouble maintaining his attack sequence. As the special attack reached certain thresholds, it added resonating and disruptive force to his blows, smashing apart armour and magical shields respectively. As the messengers' strange summons often had one or both, it made Humphrey all the more effective.

His Relentless Assault escalated in power beyond anything he had seen before as he went through monster after monster. It landed with explosive force, eliminating summons in just a handful of hits. There was a commensurate cost, however, as the ability came with a stamina cost, rather than mana. The more he used it, the faster Humphrey exhausted himself. This was where one of Humphrey's human gifts came into play.

Ability: [Magic Warrior]

- Transfigured from [Human] ability [Essence Gift].

- You may expend stamina in place of mana and mana in place of stamina.

Humans were unique amongst essence-using species in that none of their inherent abilities did anything without essences. Where every leonid was strong and every elf graceful, humans got nothing until they absorbed an essence. The most representative powers humans had were four blank powers, called essence gifts, that would evolve automatically, one-by-one as essences were claimed.

That Humphrey, on absorbing the magic essence, gained a power that would let him throw everything he had into his endeavours before he dropped surprised absolutely no one. The ability to use mana and stamina interchangeably meant that he could keep throwing out powers when the mana or stamina to fuel them was depleted, until he had absolutely nothing left.

Relentless Assault was growing more expensive with every strike, the stamina cost growing and growing. But so long as Clive's Mana Tide lasted, so would Humphrey.

Marek Nior Vargas was the messenger leading the breach force over what the people of Yaresh called the entertainment district. It was no surprise that the inferior species would dedicate so much time and resources to pointless frivolity. He was happy enough to be the one to make an example of the base creatures, quivering underground like rodents, even if he did not care for the operation as a whole.

There was little to be gained in making the attack on the city, whatever the Voice of the Will, Jes Fin Kaal, might say about morale. He had seen over and again that, when pushed, even the least of sapient species would push back. Only a prolonged, inter-generational oppression could truly break a people, which Marek had seen for himself over and again. So had Kaal, so he knew that her assertions were a lie.

Marek was not above participating in politics, if only to protect himself. He detested the ambitions that led to political games. They, in turn, led to internecine sniping that only served to weaken the messengers as a whole. As a realist, Marek recognised that most messengers gave little more than lip service to serving their kind as a whole. They were obsessed with standing at the top as individuals, rather than standing together as a people. This was as true of the least silver-ranker all the way up to astral kings.

It was hard to blame them. Every doctrine the messengers held told them that they were superior simply by existing, so what did they have left to overcome but one another? Marek was not so foolish as to accept the indoctrination, however. He had seen much, from messengers stricken with fear to members of the servant races as powerful as any messenger. This man Asano was just another example, wherever he was.

Marek was high above the city, just below the barrier dome. He and his fellow gold-rankers clashed with their adventurer counterparts, reaching a stalemate for the moment. Marek was fine with this state of affairs, as his priority was not the success of their objective. He was not going to sabotage the directives he was given, but neither would he take any undue risk to see it done. Ending the raid with minimal messenger casualties took precedence over killing a few livestock in a hole.

His fellow gold-rankers were smart enough to know the city was not worth their lives and acted with appropriate caution. The silver-rankers, on the other hand, needed to be reined in. Seeking glory and caught up in ideas of their own invincibility, some of them had already fallen. Despite his directives that they take no risks, many had overreached when sent to impede any adventurers too effective at thinning out the monsters.

Marek's attention was drawn to one particular group. They were far from the most effective at slaying monsters, although that trick with the lightning tethers had earned Marek's approval. He appreciated a power used well over one that was mindlessly strong, and, unlike many messengers, could respect a capable enemy. They had already killed a couple of messengers that had gone after them, gaining Marek's attention. The survivor of that sortie had raved when forbidden from gathering more messengers and attacking again.

Marek judged that the group was more of a threat to individual messengers than the monster horde. Even after the trick with the lightning, he did no more than send additional monsters to harass them. Clearly they had skill, but without the ability to produce regular attacks on the scale of the lightning, their threat to the operation was limited. The girl throwing around miniature hurricanes was much more of a problem, which was why he had sent one of his more reliable teams to harass her. It didn't matter if they failed to secure the kill, so long as she wasn't rampantly tearing apart their summoned forces.

Another concern was someone even Marek had a hard time pinning down. Operating amongst the monsters, what he presumed to be an adventurer was moving through their forces with seeming impunity. The adventurer's aura was difficult for even Marek to sense, but the glimpses he caught confirmed it was silver-rank, and highly unusual for an essence user. He suspected this was the man Asano that Jes Fin Kaal was interested in, but Marek did not care. Until it was confirmed and he was forced to act by order, he would not take action personally.

Instead, he sent some messengers to contain the man. He had somehow gained the disturbing ability to produce Harbingers of Doom, the cataclysmic butterflies that should not be found on a world like this. The fact that a cosmic weapon was not only being used in an isolated universe but at such a low rank was further evidence that the man was Asano.

Marek was not going to check unless he absolutely had to. He deployed a few messengers to keep things under control, as the butterflies were not dangerous if caught early. He again sent some of his more reliable people, however; if the butterflies were allowed to propagate, it would spell doom for the operation. He knew from experience that if not stopped quickly and thoroughly, they would eventually spread faster than the summoners could reproduce the monsters the butterflies destroyed.

He passed his attention over the area, seeing a dangerous spread of afflictions, but nothing that couldn't be absorbed. So long as the butterflies were contained, he need pay it no more mind for the moment. He returned his attention to the group centred on a flying tortoise shell, considering if they were worth more attention after all. He could sense some manner of ability drawing magic through the dimensional membrane, fuelling an escalation in their battle that was overwhelming the additional monsters he had sent. Out of curiosity, he directed even more monsters their way to see how they performed.

As the most straightforward team member, Humphrey was easy to overlook. Jason, Clive, Belinda and Sophie were all various levels of unconventional, while Humphrey was a textbook brawler. But as a fresh wave of monsters broke off from the main force to assault Onslow's shell, he took centre stage. The monsters were numerous, but he was no longer alone amongst the horde. He was also no longer relying on his own power alone.

With the support of the team, Humphrey became an engine of monster annihilation. Buffs turned his special attacks from weapons into ordnance. Neil's shields, themselves boosted by Clive's Mana Tide spell, meant Humphrey's armour was not under constant barrage. He also had a mantle of glowing runes, courtesy of Clive, but the most important boosts came from the stacked aura powers.

Humphrey's own aura boosted his power and spirit attributes. Belinda and Clive boosted mana recovery, reduced ability costs and reduced cooldowns. Neil's caused enemies to drop floating spheres of life force and mana that anyone in the team could absorb, while Sophie's power enhanced other forms of mana and stamina recovery, boosting what the others offered. On top of all this was Clive's Mana Tide, increasing mana recovery with each passing minute.

Humphrey's items further reduced the cost of his powers; his powers cost far less than the baseline while his resources to spend on them were overflowing. Humphrey had the chance to do something he had never been able to do before: go completely wild. No cooldown management, no mana management; he was throwing out special attacks as fast as he could swing his sword.

The Relentless Assault ability proved more and more aptly named. He blasted his Fire Breath power without pausing, his sword still swinging as flames poured from his mouth. He used other special attacks like Flying Leap and Dive Bomb to move between monsters, but these were combination attacks. He was able to link them to his Relentless Assault, the sequence never stopping.

The rest of the team also opened the taps to full, making the most of the deluge of mana. Sophie had the least advantage—she already had enough mana efficiency that she couldn't empty her mana pool if she tried. Try she did, however, and was almost impossible to see as she flickered through the sky like a wind spirit. She grew stronger as the fight wore on but, for the moment, was focused on preventing monsters from overrunning Humphrey or Onslow's shell. Clive and Belinda focused on finishing off monsters left in Humphrey's wake, so as to save Humphrey from needing to slow down for clean-up.

Clive overcharged his combat rituals, pushing the limits of what even his exceptional weapons could handle. He shot down stragglers while Belinda cleared any that reached Onslow's shell in fighting shape. She made excellent use of her Force Tether and Lightning Tether powers, while also shooting off her staff and wand, interspersing those attacks with attacks she stole from the summons using her Power Thief ability.

Clive fired off his prismatic Wrath of the Magister spell, which Belinda copied with her Mirror Magic ability. At silver rank, she could even use the copied spell twice, then reset Clive's cooldown with Blessing of Readiness. He cast it again as she used her magic tattoo to reset Mirror Magic. They cast their spells again, turning what should have been a single spell with extreme power but a long cooldown into six geysers of rainbow annihilation. With so many monsters, it once again demonstrated that the team could output periodic area damage, and at far greater power levels than normal widespread attacks.

The final piece of their combat puzzle was one of Neil's powers. The unflashy healer had one very flashy ability called Reels of Fortune. Intensely mana hungry, it conjured a set of intangible slot reels that rolled every time he fed it enough mana, the results random. At silver rank, there was a second set of reels and the results could potentially be much stronger, although the chance for dud rolls remained.

With more mana than he could ordinarily spend, Neil dumped it into the reels over and over. Some rolls were just wasted mana for no effect, while others ranged from moderate team buffs to chain lightning that dashed through the monsters, striking them dead with every stroke. Then Neil finally rolled a jackpot.

Reel of Fortune: Jackpot

- Select a single target ability to affect all enemies and/or allies in the area as appropriate to the chosen ability.

- Duration will be extended or the effect of instantaneous powers will be increased. This will not cost mana or trigger cooldowns.

- Any negative aspects for allies normally produced by the ability will not take effect.

Neil goggled at the system window for a moment, even as his instinctual understanding of the spell confirmed what was written. This was a result he had yet to see from the reels, one of the new results possible at silver rank. As for the spell to choose, he didn't consider anything but one. He made his choice, not even needing to cast the spell. The entire team then had system windows pop up.

- You have been affected by [Hero's Moment]. All benefits of this ability operate multiplicatively with existing bonus.

- All attributes are increased.
- All resistances are increased.
- Damage reduction is increased.
- Maximum mana is increased.
- Maximum stamina is increased.
- Mana and stamina recovery are increased.
- All essence ability cooldowns are reduced.
- All essence ability effects are enhanced.

- The normal duration of this ability is extended.
- The debilitation suffered after this ability ends will not occur.

There were not enough monsters to fight to take advantage of this turn of events. The waves sent their way had been thoroughly disposed of, many of the team's attacks taking out parts of the main horde as collateral. Humphrey didn't wait for more to arrive, plunging into the torrent of monsters still streaming through the breach. The rest of the team, centred on or inside Onslow's shell, followed.

87

THE DIFFERENCE IN
CONVICTION

HUMPHREY'S SECOND FORAY INTO THE MAIN FORCE OF THE SUMMONS WAS markedly different from the first. His Relentless Assault attack had reached such levels of power that his silver-rank sword broke apart every dozen or so strikes, the forces passing through it too much for it to endure. It didn't stop Humphrey; he didn't miss a beat, conjuring the sword anew each time and continuing his assault. Every swing of his blade left a monster debilitated or dead, the toughest finding half their body turned into scattered chunks. The weaker ones were reduced to a fine mist, drifting on the air.

While Humphrey was revelling in a level of power he had never imagined, he was fully cognizant that it was a fleeting moment, one that would pass sooner rather than later. Clive's Mana Tide had reached peak output as the spell's duration drew close to the end, while Neil's buff was not a long-term one, even with the duration extended. Most of all, Humphrey had maintained his Relentless Assault to the point that even with multiple significant mana sources and an expanded mana pool, it was becoming too expensive to sustain.

With each swing, a noticeable chunk of his mana pool was emptied. It was like nothing Humphrey had even experienced, and he was feeling the strain. Something deeper than exhaustion of his stamina and mana, the meridians that were the pathways of magic in his body were becoming strained. Jason had an affliction that replicated this, making abilities more costly to use, but this was no attack. Humphrey had just overextended the magical matrix, the underlying framework that was the core of his body. All he needed was a good rest, but he wasn't ready to rest yet.

There was also something else, another effect that Humphrey had heard of but never seen. There was so much power piled up on him, from potent boons to a constant influx of shields and healing. Most of all, it was Humphrey's attack. The build-up power was thankfully centred on the sword Humphrey kept swapping out because, like his swords, Humphrey was silver rank. Even his tenuous connection to the magic of the attack, just enough to guide it, was leaving him shaky. If he, instead of the weapon, was the main conduit, that much power would break him down. And unlike his sword, his body couldn't just be conjured fresh. That was more Jason's area.

The accumulated power of Humphrey's special attack had started to feel unstable to the point that others were noticing more effects than just how much power it had built up.

"Humphrey," Clive warned through voice chat, although the signal was patchy with so much magic around them. "If the magic comes close to triggering a backlash, just let it go. Silver-rank magic becomes extremely volatile if it reaches gold rank and might do something."

"Something?" Sophie asked.

"It's magic," Clive told her. "It's inherently unpredictable. People like me work very hard to take small parts of it and make them predictable."

"Tell that to Jason's aura," Neil said. "Humphrey's like the Jason's aura of hitting people right now."

"You're making my point," Clive said. "Look at how wrecked Jason always ends up after one of his stunts. Do you want to be lying around for three months? Do you want to die? Because that's kind of his thing, and not all of us come back from the dead recreationally."

"It's not a hobby," Jason complained through voice chat. "That's just something I tell people."

"I thought you were busy," Belinda said to him.

"I am, but I still have time to defend my...crap; no, I don't."

He started yelling through voice chat.

"Stop eye-beaming my butterflies, you messenger prick! I'm going tear your head off, shove it up the other end and watch you eyebeam your own insides! Then I'm going to drag you over to that monster with the one antler sticking out of its forehead and... wait, *is* that an antler? That can't be a... oh, that isn't right. That is not right. Who summoned that? There might be kids watching this battle, you depraved pricks! Humphrey, this monster has a big, multi-pronged—"

Humphrey muted the chat channel with a thought as he kept fighting.

Sophie, like Humphrey, was deep inside the monster torrent. After the lengthy fighting they'd done, she had finally built up enough power to be a genuine threat, while being even more elusive and harder to kill than ever. She was no match for Humphrey's power, but at that stage, there *was* no match for Humphrey's power at silver rank.

She was pinballing between messengers, trying to disrupt them from controlling the summons. If she could break their concentration enough, it would buy the defenders much-needed time to thin the monsters out.

Neil, Belinda and Clive were still in Onslow's shell, floating around the outer edge of the horde. Belinda had conjured a massive, flat metal plate, hooked onto the underside of Onslow's shell. She had then cast her Pit of the Reaper ability on it, facing down. The ability created a pit that was not a hole but a dimensional space, which could be placed on anything roughly level, even the surface of still water. Belinda's custom-conjured plate was a purpose-built surface, sized just right. Shadowy tentacles reached from the pit like a nightmare kraken, snatching anyone or anything that got too close to Onslow's shell and wasn't part of the team. The monsters quickly realised that too close was a significant radius, as many of them were dragged into the darkness of the pit. Despite it being upside down, nothing dragged in fell back out, only tentacles re-emerging in search of fresh meat.

The rest of the team were far from idle. Neil concentrated on Humphrey, who Clive was worried would explode despite the fact that he was so powerful; he was still being hammered by monsters. He threw out shields and healing as fast as he could while dumping mana into his Reels of Fortune as fast as they would take it, trying not to waste the mana coming in from Clive's spell. He knew that once the Mana Tide was over, he would miss the near-infinite stream it had become.

Belinda's tentacle pit snatched monsters out of the sky and dragged them into the void where they suffered massive necrotic damage. Each time the duration ended, the pit spat out whatever was left of the monsters that had been dragged in. Some two thirds survived, at least until she cast the spell again and they were drawn back inside.

Even with the fake death kraken plucking monsters out of the sky, the sheer density of monsters meant that Onslow's shell came under constant barrage. Clive had used ritual magic to enhance the wind barrier surrounding the shell and powers launched from the glowing runes marked on it. Each one launched fire, lightning, a hailstorm or some other elemental power, the runes fading as each was expended to produce an attack. Clive constantly restored them with his own over-flowing mana, allowing Onslow to keep up the barrage.

Belinda didn't just use her Pit of the Reaper spell, which she had no need to supervise. She also used her two tether powers on the top of Onslow's shell, leaving the enemy with an unpleasant situation. Force Tether dragged enemies towards it, dealing damage to any that resisted. Those that managed to overcome its strength suffered the damage of that, along with an unhealthy dose of electricity from the Lightning Tether. Anyone who did escape took increasingly more severe electrical burns the further they got from the tether rods planted on the shell.

Staying on the shell was not a valid option either, as that left them as sitting ducks for the dark tentacles looking to drag them into the pit. The monsters tried destroying the rods anchoring the tethers, which then exploded with startling force. That was enough to inflict massive harm, and Belinda immediately created fresh tethers.

As for Belinda's familiars, her lantern had returned to her eyes, allowing Belinda to fire eyebeams at stray monsters between copying Clive's Wrath of the Magister spell, restoring her detonated tether rods or refreshing the Pit of the Reaper. Any gap periods she filled by simultaneously blasting bolts of force from her wand and beams from her staff and eyes.

Her echo spirit was also mimicking Clive's Wrath of the Magister. Unlike Belinda's copy, however, the familiar's version was more illusion than reality. It did inflict a respectable amount of force damage, but nothing compared to the real thing with its massive damage and debilitating effects. It looked real enough, though, even to magical senses. That forced monsters and messengers alike to scatter out of its way.

Stash also moved into action, doing his best impression of Sophie. This meant imitating her speed by turning into a flitter drake, which looked like something between a lizard and a hummingbird. It somehow took the worst aesthetic elements of each, turning into a grotesquery that looked both too small and too large at the same time. It had not endeared Stash to Sophie when he first used the form, explaining that it was the way he could be most like her.

The ugly form was hard to make out, however, as Stash did indeed move through the battlefield in a blur. He specifically went after the monsters that managed to avoid Belinda's defensive measures as they continued to harass Onslow's shell with attacks.

The messenger, Marek Nior Vargas, absently blocked a projectile fired by a gold-rank adventurer with his wing, his attention on the adventurer that had dived deep into the monster horde for the second time. He had grabbed Marek's interest the first time because the move had made no apparent sense. The man had escaped, a worthy enough feat, although the attempt had unsurprisingly left him beaten and bloodied, for what seemed like no result. Marek's confusion had lasted until the lines of lightning had started raining down into the horde, originating from points along the path the man had taken.

Marek did not fear a fool who overestimated himself and learned a brutal lesson. But a man with the conviction to take that kind of beating because he knew it was worth the risk was another prospect entirely. The conviction to get things done, and the wisdom to make sure the things getting done were right, *was* something that Marek feared.

He had no interest in the attack on the city and whatever schemes the Voice of the Will was using it to enact. The people defending the city, by contrast, could not have cared more; to retreat was to abandon their homes and their families. Marek had seen time and again the flame that lit inside people, and how that flame became a forge producing heroes and martyrs. The difference in conviction could easily be the deciding factor in the battle.

Marek was confident in his superiority over the servant races here, but he knew that passion and commitment could close that gap in the face of Marek's disinterest. If the defenders of Yaresh started throwing themselves at the enemy with truly reckless abandon, the tenor of the battle would change. Those willing to accept casualties for victory had a grim but powerful advantage, even if any victory they earned became a pyrrhic one.

Seeing the man plunge back into the descending torrent of monsters once again had Marek concerned. Strategic decisions were all well and good, but if the enemy was willing to go to lengths that he was not, then his part of the raid could be brought undone. Marek might not care about the success of his part in the mission, but neither would he ignore a threat. Marek focused his attention more directly onto the man and immediately realised that a threat was exactly who and what he was.

The sheer number and power of magical effects on the man had surpassed silver-rank power levels, to the point of bordering on outright volatile. It was rare for that kind of power escalation, but Marek had seen it a number of times. The result would go one of two ways.

If the magic got out of control, the results would annihilate a goodly part of the horde of summons, given the man's location within it. Of course, the man himself would die with them, but that might even be his purpose. But if he held on, any silver-ranker wielding that kind of power would be something to behold.

Marek watched in wonder as he tore through the summons like a wildfire through dry grass. That his fellow messengers could see that display and remain convinced of their inherent superiority amazed him. Standing above all others took work. No one just stumbled arse-backward into the kind of power that let them stand at the peak of the cosmos.

Elsewhere in the battlefield, Jason sneezed.

88

SOMETHING TO TURN THE TIDE

JASON SNEEZED.

He was standing on the corpse of a monster as it fell through the sky, using shadow arms to hold himself in place. Shade and Gordon flew next to him as he rode the monster downward, away from a spear-wielding messenger flying above.

"Mr Asano, did you just sneeze?" Shade asked.

"I did. That's weird, right?"

"Given that you do not have sinuses, I would say yes."

"Maybe someone is talking about me."

"I don't see the relevance."

"Sometimes you sneeze when someone is talking about you."

"That does not sound likely."

"It's a thing."

"I do not believe that it is a thing."

"It's totally a thi—"

Jason shadow-jumped using his cloak, leaving it behind as a spear made of fused-together teeth passed through it, thrown by the messenger. She was rocketing down headfirst, wings back and tight to avoid drag, another spear appearing in her hand as she conjured a fresh one.

A Shade body emerged from a small shadow cast on her body by her arm. Jason jumped out of Shade's body, conjuring a new cloak around him. Shadow arms shot out of it to grab the messenger and drag Jason down to slam his feet into her back. He pushed his feet in hard as he grabbed her wings and hauled back on them, yanking her body into an arch.

The messenger went from a controlled dive to an uncontrolled plunge. It was a peculiarity of messengers, Jason had discovered, that damaging or constricting a messenger's wings impeded their ability to fly. This had surprised him, as he had always assumed that their wings were unrelated to actual flight. He didn't know much about aerodynamics, but he knew an eight-foot-tall woman with bird wings was not going to fly around without a good lot of magic. Their flight magic was apparently seated in their wings, however, and he was appreciative of the weakness.

With the messenger's ability to fly curtailed, they were heading for the ground at a rapid pace. Jason continued to pull on her wings while pushing his feet into her back, holding her in place. She reached back and grabbed his ankles, but lacked the leverage to dislodge him. Bone spikes shot out of her fingertips and dug into his legs, but he ignored them.

Numerous shadow arms coming from Jason help him maintain his position, mounted on her back like a sky surfer. One arm held his conjured dagger, making rapid, shallow stabs like a sewing machine. As the dagger loaded her up with special attacks, Jason chanted a spell.

"Bear the mark of your transgressions."

A small amount of transcendent damage seared a brand onto her face, making her yell all the louder. Jason cast another spell.

"Your fate is to suffer."

"GET OFF ME, YOU FILTH!"

"If you'd warned me you were attacking the city," Jason shouted over the rush of air as they fell, "I would have had time for a bath. That's on you."

She had dropped the conjured tooth spear to grab at his legs, the lengthy weapon having no good angle. When stabbing his legs accomplished nothing, she let them go and conjured a new weapon. This one was a giant blade made from jagged, yellowing bone. It was a vastly oversized sickle with a deeply curved hook; the tip was covered in sharp, irregular barbs. The messenger was holding it so the point was aiming back at herself. It was sized just right to swing at her back and the man perched upon it.

"Lady, has anyone ever told you that your powers seem kind of evil?"

"DIE!"

She swung the sickle back over her head to stab at Jason with pinpoint accuracy. The viciously barbed tip looked like it passed through Jason, as if he were a ghost. In reality, a combination of a subtle back-sway and his cloak bending space meant it passed through the air in front of him, jabbing into the messenger's own back. She screamed, more in rage than pain, and the weapon vanished.

"You realise that was a terrible plan, right?"

Jason felt a mass of power building inside the messenger, but he wasn't quick enough to escape before bone spikes erupted from every part of her body. They tore through her flesh and thin, practical clothing to jab in every direction. Jason was impaled dozens of times by thin bone spikes that broke off inside him as he moved, the fragments crawling through his body like worms.

"I already have worms for that, you hag," Jason said through gritted teeth.

The messenger didn't respond, having gone limp. Her aura had also greatly diminished and Jason realised that the attack had taken large amounts of her reserves. After madly chasing Jason around the entire battle, her body wasn't up to the expenditure when it was being ravaged by Jason's afflictions already. He suspected the main culprit was his Tainted Meridians affliction, which forcibly raised mana costs. It made the massive attack consume even more mana than the messenger had realised and she passed out from mana exhaustion.

Jason forcibly pushed himself off the spikes, more of them breaking off in the process. He used his cloak to float, letting the unconscious messenger drop. He knew she would likely wake before hitting the ground, even if there was only a short drop left. Messengers recovered even faster than adventurers, so she would

—

Jason watched her crash into the ground, limbs in that awkward sprawl of a thing that wasn't alive anymore.

"Huh."

Valk Vohl was far from a stand-up citizen of Yaresh, but there was a difference between being a criminal and not standing up when angels and their strange pet monsters invaded. Not when he could fight. He was no adventurer, but he'd done his part during the monster surge and he was doing it again now. He was back to back with some adventurer whose name he'd forgotten, controlling what looked like a giant stick figure made of swords as it swung its arms at the monsters.

It wasn't enough. The monsters kept pouring out of the sky, no matter how many the people of Yaresh killed, and they were close to the point of being over-whelmed. He and the adventurer were both low on mana, their armour rent and skin wet with blood.

When one of the messengers splattered onto the broken flagstones of the road, bone spikes sticking out and limbs awkwardly splayed, he was only startled for a moment. It, possibly she, wasn't getting up to kill him, so he turned his attention back to the things that were. Then he saw a figure emerge from the shadow of a half-collapsed bordello.

There was something about the man that unnerved him, and he realised that he couldn't sense the man's presence, even looking right at him.

"Gold-ranker," he said, the words arresting the attention of the other adventurer.

"Where?" he asked, looking around.

Valk watched the man who had come from the shadows walking over to the dead messenger. He was calm in the chaos, wearing a robe the colour of dried blood. His eyes were inhuman, glowing blue and orange. His features were just a little too sharp for a truly classic high-rank handsomeness, the neat beard failing to entirely hide the lengthy chin.

"We could use a little help here!" the adventurer with Valk called out and the man turned his gaze to them. Then his gaze moved upward, to the monsters above. That was when Valk and his companion felt the man's aura. It rolled out like a physical thing, making the air around them seem heavy. They realised he was no gold-ranker, but he didn't feel like an essence user either. His aura was tyrannical, as if everything belonged to him by virtue of his existence. Valk feared for a moment that he was some kind of wingless messenger, until he saw how the monsters reacted.

They fled.

The creatures flew off, crashing into their fellows still coming down in a mad panic to run from whatever the man standing over the dead messenger was. Valk watched them go, then felt his gaze drawn to the man as if by a magnet. He watched as the man held a hand over the messenger and chanted a spell, his voice winter cold.

"*As your life was mine to reap, so your death is mine to harvest.*"

Transcendent light of blue, silver and gold was drained from the corpse, into the man's hand as the body dissolved into rainbow smoke. As the man drained the messenger's energy, Valk thought he heard a scream, but it was somehow picked up with his aura senses, not his ears. An image formed over the man, that of a shadowy bird speckled with silver stars. The man finished claiming the messenger's energy and the image vanished.

"Who are you?" Valk asked him.

"I only drove the monsters off for a moment," the man said, his voice hard but lacking the malevolence with which he had chanted the spell. "Get what rest you can and be ready for their return."

"Will you stay and help?"

"More messengers are coming for me. I won't bring them down on you."

Shadows rose up to wreath his body, becoming a shadowy mantle. A dark figure rose from Valk's own shadow and the man stepped into it, vanishing. The shadow figure then retreated into Valk's shadow, also disappearing. He stared at his shadow warily, wondering what else was in there.

Jason emerged from Shade's body on a rooftop, looking up. He could sense Rufus not far off, and an army of monsters glowing with Rufus' silver and gold flames. Soon enough, Rufus would use his zone power, Eclipse, and consume those afflictions, hopefully shooting a few messengers out of the sky.

Jason wished that he had been as effective. He had taken out one of the messengers harassing him, but they had won and he had lost. It was almost certainly too late for his butterflies to spread properly, even if he managed to get them going now. The messengers had shut down every attempt to get them going, killing the butterflies and even slaughtering their own monsters that Jason afflicted to produce them. He'd been pointlessly running around the whole battle, accomplishing nothing.

Jason had not felt inadequate in his power set in years, since he had been a green iron-ranker with half his power set yet to awaken. But he could sense the places around the city, and even this battle over the entertainment district, where affliction specialists were succeeding where he had failed. It was the first time that he felt lesser for being an affliction skirmisher.

For all that they were forced to build whole teams to hide behind, it was here, in open war, that such adventurers showed their true worth. Left alone they would die quickly, where Jason would thrive. But where he had stealth powers, they had afflictions. Where he had utility powers, they had afflictions. And where he had affliction, they had afflictions.

Jason had to find ways to make his powers work in any situation, where they simply picked the appropriate ones from their selection. They weren't restricted to complicated butterfly-based delivery systems that could be shut down by an enemy that knew what they were doing. If an enemy stopped one approach, they could simply use another.

Jason had already given up on wiping out huge waves of monsters with his butterflies some time ago. It wasn't going to work and there were other afflictions for that. Instead, he decided to focus on wiping out the messenger team that had been sent after him. The monsters were ultimately a disposable force, but if enough messengers went down, the enemy would pull out.

His efforts to put a stop to the messenger team had not gone as well as he had hoped at first. They were quite capable, working together well and harassing him without any exploitable overextensions. They even had one of the messengers' rare healers, meaning that chipping away at them was pointless.

The group of messengers were a team and their practised cooperation showed as they swiftly eliminated any butterflies, along with any monsters that were spawning them. In response, Jason had spread out his attempts to trigger a butterfly chain.

The biggest advantage Jason had over them was that they absolutely had to shut down the butterflies and anything producing more of them—ideally including Jason. This meant that he could leverage his mobility to force them to split up.

Eventually, he had allowed their most aggressive member to get what seemed like a clear shot at Jason's back. She overextended, a little too far from where the others were quashing butterflies, allowing Jason to counterattack. Now she was dead and devoured, her remnant life force getting him a little closer to another chance to resurrect.

He looked up at the teeming monsters, sensing the messengers amongst them. They would stick together now that he'd taken one of them out; they had to know as well as he did that it was too late for the butterflies to have a massive impact. They would most likely stay as a group, eliminating butterflies as best they could, but letting some of them go rather than compromise their safety again.

Shade stood next to Jason as he watched the sky.

"Thinking on it, Mr Asano, I may have been wrong."

"About what?"

"The sneeze. We know that your powers often interpret themselves in a way that has meaning to you, and we know that you have some powerful sensory ability that you are unable to consciously use. Perhaps your sneeze is a manifestation of that mysterious sensory power, revealing that someone actually was talking about you."

"I have an extra sense I don't know about?"

"The capabilities demonstrated by your original power called the Quest System prove that. It was your ability, yet it knew things that your conscious mind did not."

"You're right," Jason mused. "Do you think I'll be able to use the sense that made that power work once I'm higher rank?"

"Perhaps. Or perhaps that sensory power is long gone and it really was just a sneeze. That power may have been fuelled by lingering astral energy from when you first became an outworlder. The ability may have evolved for the simple reason that the fuel ran out and you couldn't use it anymore."

"You'd barely signed on as my familiar when I lost that ability, right?"

"That is correct, Mr Asano."

"How did you even think of that ability, to draw that conclusion? You barely saw it in action."

"It is not a conclusion, Mr Asano, but a postulation. As to why I thought of the ability, it is arguably the most startling one in your repertoire. A sensory ability that powerful, even when you were normal rank? Clearly, it was not tied to your aura or magical senses as you had neither. I am very old, Mr Asano, and there is very little that I am unable to at least postulate on. Whatever sense fuelled your Quest System ability is outside even my experience."

"So, you have no idea?"

"At best, I could guess at something that I cannot be certain is even real. If anyone, it would pertain to you, but I hesitate to speak on it. It is more myth than anything, and less the 'heroes and gods' kind of myth than the 'man in a trailer with a foil hat' kind of myth. Although it usually does involve heroes and gods."

"You'll have to tell me about it some time we aren't in the middle of a city invasion."

"I had been wondering why you were just standing here. Are you attempting to confront the remainder of the messenger team?"

"No, they'd kill me. But I want them close enough to really see what they've chosen to pit themselves against."

"I thought you were saving that for when they—"

"They will. Soon. I might have been shut down, but plenty of others weren't. My biggest contribution was tying up a bunch of messengers so they couldn't harass other adventurers. The adventurers here on the ground are feeling overwhelmed, but they're holding on. People like Zara and the affliction specialists are doing work, and the messengers' commander will need something to turn the tide."

89

THE STRONGEST ARROW IN HIS QUIVER

MAREK OFFERED A MENTAL SALUTE TO THE MAN RAMPAGING THROUGH THE monster horde. He had managed to overhear one of the man's companions call him Humphrey, and Marek hoped he would survive to eventually reach gold rank. He would like to face him in battle, perhaps finding a clue in that confrontation to push his own advancement forward. He lamented that while this battlefield had many exceptional silver-ranked enemies, the golds were only passable. It seemed that the defenders of the city had limited care for the civilians of the entertainment district.

With the gold-rankers being adequate but unexceptional, Marek wished he'd been chosen for other battlefields. He could sense more impressive essence users in other parts of the city, including one whose aura was a match for most messengers.

He turned his attention to the silver-ranker he suspected of being Asano. Two people with such unusual auras implied they were connected, perhaps with the gold-ranker instructing the silver. If he personally intervened, would the gold-ranker move to assist, giving him the chance for a more exciting battle?

Marek shook his head, scolding himself. Compromising the strategic situation for personal ends was the kind of behaviour he despised in a certain breed of messenger that he looked down on. That most of his fellow messengers fell into that group was a misfortune he lamented regularly.

Marek frowned as he sensed the team he sent to harass Asano lose one of their number. He was impressed; he had sent neither rash nor weak people to contain the man. Even so, the harbinger butterflies were still not establishing themselves, so the situation required no further intervention. Marek did not want to lose people, but some casualties were inevitable.

The man Humphrey also did not require Marek's intervention. For all he was impressively carving a path through the monster horde, time would put an end to the rampage more effectively than a costly confrontation. The unstable power driving him would soon come to an end, one way or another. Humphrey was certainly destructive, yet still failed to impact the battle as much as the wide area attack specialists amongst the adventurers. Marek's messengers were of more use containing them than going after Humphrey. He could easily kill messengers in his current state, but Marek could afford to lose however many summoned monsters he took down.

The monsters were not infinite, however, for all the expense they had employed to make it seem so to the defenders. The Voice of the Will, Jes Fin Kaal, had brought in the artefacts that were enhancing the number of monsters the summoners could call up at once. The acquisition was made against the advice of Marek and other gold-rankers, but she had overruled them. Even so, she never explained what made them worth the resources and favours expended to obtain them, significant even to the messengers.

At least the expensive artefacts were located outside the barrier. If the adventurers were able to reach them and shut off the monster spigot, the raid would come to a swift end, the costs coming to nothing. He wondered if Jes Fin Kaal would see it that way, since the success of the city raid was clearly not her true objective. Whatever political game she was playing, it unfortunately had the approval of the astral king, or his disinterest at the very least. Otherwise, he would have stopped her already.

Again, Marek told himself not to dwell on it. All he had to do was an adequate job and get as many of their people out alive as was viable. If he started digging into whatever plots the voice was carrying out through the city invasion, it would only cost him, and get him nothing. He was sure that she was scheming against someone amongst the messengers, but equally confident it was not him. He was carefully apolitical as a defence mechanism.

This was part of why he had been so reserved in directing his portion of the raid, even as those under his command chafed at his conservative strategy. The gold-rankers were alright, being seasoned warriors, but Marek could feel the hunger in the silver-rankers under his command. They were straining like an untrained beast on a leash, eager to cover themselves in glory and adventurer blood.

They were going to be disappointed. Marek was never going to let the most reckless element of his forces do as they wished and, if the adventurers managed to force a direct conflict with the messengers, he would signal the withdrawal. He wasn't sacrificing anyone he didn't have to on the altar of Jes Fin Kaal's schemes, even if she was voice of the astral king's will.

He could sense that in other battlefields, some commanders had made different decisions, chasing the same glory as their silver-rank subordinates. That was far from enough to convince him to let his messengers loose. It accomplished just the opposite; the casualties he sensed under more proactive commanders were exactly what he wanted to avoid.

It was, however, time to make a change. The adventurers were starting to press in, their affliction specialists taking hold in spite of the messengers working to suppress them. Unlike the man working alone behind enemy lines, these were people with a frustrating variety of afflictions and delivery systems, as well as entire teams dedicated to making sure they were used.

It was time to draw the strongest arrow in his quiver. This was one that most other commanders had already fired, to what Marek considered insufficient effect. While Marek was forced to concede that aura superiority had its advantages in the establishing moments of a conflict, he saw using it immediately as a waste. Essence users had demonstrated time and again that when given time to adjust, they could fight at near-full capability under aura suppression.

Compared to that, a sudden and well-timed aura wave could finish an enemy already under pressure, or reverse a disadvantageous trend. That was what Marek faced in his own battlefield, so it was time to turn the tide.

A large wave of destructive magic headed for Marek, his gold-rank opponent having cast a large spell while Marek had been contemplating his options. He glanced up at a house-sized sphere of blue-gold flames barrelling down on him, burning through monsters as it went. Marek fed mana into his wings and flapped them a single time in the direction of the fireball. It was blasted back the way it had come, causing the gold-rank adventurers to scramble out of the way.

Marek sighed with boredom, wishing that the only capable adventurers in his battle hadn't been silver rank. He took out his communication stone and issued a directive to every messenger under his command.

"Unleash your auras."

In the early stages of the battle over the entertainment district, the area-specialist teams had started off strong. They had been carving large chunks out of the monsters, which earned them the focused attention of messengers, suppressing their effectiveness. Then, slowly but surely, they started pushing back the messengers, once again thinning out the monsters seeking to descend and dig through to the civilian bunker.

The adventurers were becoming so effective that more monsters arrived at the ground dead than alive. As one of the adventurers working at ground level, Rufus had to watch out for monsters falling like rain. Despite operating at ground level, though, Rufus was spending little time on the ground. He moved through the air with a combination of silver-rank acrobatics and short-range teleport powers. Many adventurers failed to fully leverage their new physical limits after ranking up, but Rufus was too well-trained for that. He used the monsters themselves as platforms, hopping between them like a frog moving between lily pads.

Rufus didn't use the buildings often despite the frequent convenience of a rooftop. The entertainment district looked like a bombing site, with no building escaping damage. He didn't trust any of them to not collapse under him.

The monsters often didn't react when Rufus landed on them, lacerated them with his gold and silver swords before moving on, and left gold and silver flames in his wake. The summoned creatures were under a compulsion to dig down to the bunker, mostly hovering in the air and firing ranged attacks at the ground. Many didn't even fight back against the adventurers, simply drilling down as far as they could before being taken out.

Rufus' afflictions were useful for setting up the big attacks that would hopefully shoot down messengers, but ineffective at clearing out monsters. The disadvantage of Rufus' eclectic power set was that any individual element was somewhat weak, requiring skill to draw out the potent synergies.

The main work of handling the monsters was being done by an affliction specialist. Rufus didn't know the woman, but she was clearly effective, which both sides had come to recognise. A full dozen messengers had been deployed to suppress her, but three full adventuring teams had moved to counter.

The messengers had been well-chosen, all being protective types that appeared to have healthy amounts of defence, affliction resistance and even self-healing and cleansing. That was something an affliction specialist could overcome, given time and protection, but the more focus she had on the messengers, the less time she spent clearing out monsters.

As a result, the adventurers on the ground were increasingly feeling the pressure. Monsters dug down, through layers of street, rock and buried magical protections, slowly uncovered and broken. Rufus picked a building that looked reasonably intact to land on and paused long enough to look over the situation. He opened a voice channel.

"Jason, are you busy?"

"No, actually. Things are swinging our way, so you can expect the messengers to drop the aura hammer soon. I'm getting ready for when that happens."

"Ready how?"

"The usual."

"Something stupid, self-destructive and absurdly attention-grabbing?"

"Pretty much."

"Do you have a few moments before that happens?"

"I can spare a little time. I should probably scoot off before the messengers hunting me get here anyway. What do you need?"

"I've got an affliction specialist dealing with her own set of messengers. She'll get through them, but they're pretty shielded up, so it's taking longer than we need it to. Any chance you could come in and brighten the messengers' day?"

Jason stepped from the shadow of a broken section of wall.

"I can do that," he said.

"It's over—"

"I can sense it," Jason said before Rufus had a chance to point.

Rufus could barely sense anything amongst the mess of auras that was a magical battlefield, but Jason turned his gaze the right way immediately. He moved back to the shadow he had appeared from and vanished into it.

Elseth Culie was frustrated. The teams defending her were doing an excellent job, but she wasn't doing her part as fast as she needed to. Some of the messengers had flexible but comprehensive full body armour that had to be dug through before she could afflict them directly. Others had classic bubble shields, while the more annoying ones had both. Some pushed off the afflictions on to proxies, such as the one who created clones of herself and the one who collected afflictions into her feathers, shooting them back at Elseth's defenders.

She had answers to all of these, from resonating or disruptive force afflictions to spells that replaced afflictions on a target the moment they were disposed of. But with the messengers also purging, dispelling and cleansing, as well as replacing dissolved shields and disintegrated armour, it was taking too long. With each passing moment, she more desperately needed to refocus on monster slaying.

Suddenly, someone was next to her, startling her with its lack of aura. At first, she thought it was a monster, draped in what were clearly magic shadows. It glanced at her with alien eyes from within a dark hood.

"I'm going to eat your afflictions," the man said. His tone was cold with a hint of apology, but the clear intention was to do as he said, whatever she might have wanted. His shadow rose up like a living thing and he stepped into it, disappearing. Then he was amongst the messengers, loudly chanting a spell.

"Feed me your sins."

The transcendent light of messenger life force shone from within the messengers, tainted by Elseth's afflictions. She was familiar with the spell he was using. It was a rare spell that was usually awakened by those with bright intentions but dark powers. She was unsurprised, then, as her afflictions were devoured and transcendent damage was left in their place.

Transcendent damage ignored any protections and dug right into the messengers, who immediately retreated. Elseth was certain they were going in search of the healing and cleansing they would need to survive. With all the afflictions she had dumped on them turned transcendent, it would take a lot.

As the messengers fled upwards, the shadowy man floated down. Her defenders let him through as they looked to her for new direction.

"We need to get back to clearing monsters," she declared. It was an obvious statement, but the first part of command was being certain and confident. Knowing what she was doing was also useful, but lower priority.

The man landed gently next to her and pushed the hood from his head. He had sharper features than humans preferred, but his human face had an exotic appeal to elven sensibilities.

"Prepare your people for an aura assault," the man warned her. "You reclaiming control over the ground level will probably be the final straw that provokes…"

He trailed off as an aura dropped down like a hammer. The messengers in the battlefield had all unleashed their auras at once, silver- and gold-rankers harmonised in a symphony of power. The auras of the messengers were fundamentally different to those of essence users, as if they were not just spiritual but physical. There was a weight to their suppressive force, and Elseth felt her aura suppressed as if the titanic hand of a god was reaching down to cover her.

That was when she finally sensed the aura of the man in front of her. It swept out like a colonial power, claiming territory as it pushed out what was there before. He created a bubble that felt more like the messengers than his fellow essence users, and while Elseth's aura was freed up, she still did not feel comfortable. There was an overwhelming sense of domination, her spiritual senses telling her that she was safe only by the benevolence of the power controlling the area around her. A power that demanded obedience.

Elspeth and the other adventurers looked at the man with unease as he tilted his head to look up. A strange monster that looked like an empty cloak surrounded by floating orbs appeared. She felt some of the others tense, but they quickly felt the link between the man and his familiar.

"Gordon," the man said. "Let's get to work."

90

WIN A FIGHT

Fal Vin Garath was not having a good day. He detested being forced to act at the behest of the Voice of the Will, Jes Fin Kaal, and this mission was exactly why. She had sent him to kill Jason Asano, but she clearly expected him to not come back. He would relish the look on her face when he dropped Asano's head at her feet.

Fal could not openly defy the voice. Like all messengers, he needed to be sworn to an astral king, lest he wither and die. It was one of the strongest drives to become an astral king, as only then could they truly stand with no one and nothing above them. Until then, the astral king had influence not just over his actions but his very being. And as a voice of the astral king's will, Jes Fin Kaal shared that influence.

Having his mouth sealed closed was a humiliation, especially when it did not even come from the king herself but one of her voices. Fal was at the start of his journey, still silver rank, but he already had a long list. When he stood at the peak, everyone on that list would pay.

For now, however, Fal was stuck obeying the voice of the astral king to whom he was sworn. He was unable to defy her voice, but that did not mean he could not undermine Jes Fin Kaal. She had plans for the outworlder and saw Fal as meat she could feed to him. But Fal would be the one to feed, and Kaal's intentions for Asano would die with him.

The first step was finding the man inside the city. He was quite elusive and the city was in chaos, making an individual aura almost impossible to pick out. Unless he forcibly manifested his aura on a large scale, which would be insane in this circumstance, Fal would have to hunt him down.

That meant starting with the most likely place to find him and then torturing answers out of the people there. Either Asano would be drawn in or he would get information that drew him closer. The best information the messengers had was that Asano and his team were based out of a large adventuring vehicle, located alongside those of the other foreign adventurers.

Fal went through the breach closest to the area. There was a large zone of eclectic vehicles, many of which were the size of buildings. It amounted to a city district comprised of mobile forts, centred around a sprawling refugee camp. The camp had been emptied, leaving no one behind and there were no defenders out in the open. He could sense adventurers inside the vehicles, most of which were unable to block his aura senses. Either the district had minimal defenders or they were gathered in the vehicles that could block his perception.

The leader of the contingent to which Fal had been attached issued orders as soon as they were through the barrier.

"Watch out for countermeasures from the adventurer vehicles. Eliminate any that are impacting the monsters, but watch out for ambushes. They may have greater numbers than we can sense."

Monsters had poured through the breach before any of the messengers, to absorb any ambushes and reveal emplaced defences. This proved wise as the defenders remained in their mobile forts, letting the vehicle weapons do the work. With the larger vehicles especially, they boasted heavy-duty weapons that could eliminate a silver-rank monster with a well-placed shot, and make a gold-ranker take notice.

Vehicle weapons were not designed to take out people or smaller monsters, however, which was why adventurers only used vehicles when hunting large monsters. Only the fact that the monsters were an unmissable curtain made hunkering down in the vehicles a viable strategy. The messengers, once they made their appearance, had little trouble avoiding the vehicles' weapons, at least for the most part. Several vehicles had more pinpoint weaponry, especially the two that were not, currently, vehicles.

Although they both completely blocked magical perception, the two buildings were plainly cloud constructs currently configured as buildings. And those buildings were configured for war. The messengers were appropriately wary of the two buildings, as cloud flasks were the tools of the most well-resourced adventurers. There was no telling what manner of weapons and defences they had been equipped with.

One of the buildings was gold rank and the other silver. The gold-rank one was a dome with five heavily leaning towers jutting out. The towers themselves were capped with domes that blasted out various attacks. There were explosive fireballs and armour-piercing ballista bolts that were conjured already in flight. The most common attack was a chain lightning that hopped between monsters, eradicating one with each jump. The gold-rank attacks of a giant magical fortress were too much for silver-rank monsters.

The various attacks also had the accuracy to strike out at messengers, especially the lightning blasts. Unlike the summoned monsters, however, the messengers had exotic powers and intelligence. They used magical barriers, conjured armour and used the summons as living shields, meaning that while messengers certainly took hits, they weren't slaughtered like their summons.

The other building was a pyramid with a cup instead of a peak. Over the cup floated a massive, ominous eye. The sides of the pyramid were covered in matte-black hexagonal panels set into cloud-substance underneath. The cloud-stuff shone blue and orange in the seams between the dark hex panels.

Like the gold-rank cloud building, the pyramid had not just attacks but ones that could effectively target messengers. Some of the hexes withdrew, sinking into the cloud-stuff behind them. Rising in their place were complex arrangements of metal set into the surface of the cloud-material like eye-shaped mosaics. The eyes contained components of blue, orange and black metal, but each was dominated by a single colour. There was one eye of each colour set into each side of the pyramid, firing beams of different coloured energy.

Fal recognised that the design of the eye weapons was not native to this world, but used elements of techno-magic it had yet to develop. The beam fired by each eye-weapon corresponded to the main colour of that eye. They fired in quick succession, the efficient downtime a result of combining magic and technology to create something better than either could do alone.

This alone made it plain that the pyramid belonged to the outworlder, Asano, although that was hardly necessary. While the other cloud construct had a detectable aura from being soul-bound to an essence user, the pyramid used its aura as a weapon. It blanketed the entire city district, amplified strongly enough that the gold-rankers' attempts to suppress it fell short. They perhaps could have managed it if that was all they did, but they needed to fight.

What the aura did was make any monster or messenger that attacked suffer a retaliatory affliction. That affliction didn't do anything by itself, but despite its rarity, Fal knew of it and the danger it presented. The affliction was called Sin, and it escalated any necrotic damage suffered. It was a rare affliction known to be employed heavily by Jason Asano.

One of the three beam colours, black, directly delivered necrotic damage to take advantage of the affliction. This was less effective against those with potent armour or magical barriers, but that was where the other beams came in. The orange ones were resonating force, rapidly breaking down physical armour, while the blue disruptive-force beams had a similar effect against magical barriers.

The beams all ignored the monsters to target the messengers, although they mostly struck monsters anyway. There were just too many of them, and the messengers quickly learned to interpose a solid wall of monsters between themselves and the pyramid. For this reason, the extra power and unpredictable lightning arcs made the gold-rank building the greater threat.

While the beams attacked the messengers, the giant eye above the pyramid was the most effective weapon for eliminating monsters in the district. Its gaze took the form of a massive beam that grew wider the further it projected. The beam itself was barely visible, a heat-haze shimmer tinted faintly blue. The results were likewise subtle, with no immediate impact. It bestowed afflictions, what Fal suspected to be the ones in Asano's own repertoire.

The messengers were able to easily avoid the eye's gaze, but it affected the monsters in droves. After the eye's gaze had moved on, the monsters left behind were soon melting in the sky, gobbets of wet flesh rotting away to fall like raindrops. Even with the lack of empathy quintessential to messengers, it was a horrifying sight. The information they had on Asano suggested a foolish hero complex, but this was not the power of a hero. It wasn't even the power of a villain. As dead flesh rained across the entire city district, it felt like the punishment of a vengeful god.

Fal scoffed at his own thought. Messengers were not afraid of gods and Asano was not one in any case, even if his pyramid felt like a temple. Despite its bizarre power, he knew the building could not project Asano's aura without Asano being present, meaning he had found his target. A soul-bound item lacked a strong enough connection to the soul to be a source of the true aura being projected by the building. Asano had to be inside, using the building to amplify his power.

The messengers continued to throw their summons at the vehicles below, cannon fodder they were happy to let die. While the defenders had not yet been forced to emerge, their weapons proving so successful, the situation could only be sustained for so long. Most weapons on adventurer vehicles were designed to fend off the odd monster attack and make the occasional hunt. They were not built for war or the sustained fire they were currently pumping out. Whether their power supplies ran low or the weapons were overtaxed and shut down, they would only last so long.

Fal guessed there would be a few exceptions, almost certainly including the two cloud buildings, but, inevitably, most of the vehicles would stop firing before the summoned monsters stopped coming. Then the defenders would show themselves, and things would go badly for them. This particular attack force included a higher proportion of gold-rankers than normal, so they could reliably break into the vehicles once they were exposed.

Fal had his own mission that only required cracking open one of the vehicles. He sought out the gold-rank commander of the messenger forces.

"We need to invade the pyramid," Fal told him. "The outworlder, Jason Asano, is in there. The Voice of the Will wants—"

"I agree," the commander said, cutting him off.

Fal had been expecting more of an argument.

"The voice made it clear that Asano is the priority in this zone," the commander continued. "My orders are to facilitate a confrontation between you and Asano where you can use your isolation power to duel him. Even if that was not the command, that pyramid is a problem. It isn't as much of a threat to us as the gold-rank cloud building, but it's killing the summons far too quickly. I want it dealt with before the adventurers are forced to come out and face us, so we have as much fodder as possible."

"You'll gather the gold-rankers for an attack, then?" Fal asked. The higher percentage of gold-rankers reflected Jes Fin Kaal's priorities.

"My information is that Asano is arrogant and likes to make public demonstrations. You may be able to lure him from the building for a duel. If you kill him, his building will be greatly diminished, perhaps even going dormant entirely. If he kills you, we will catch him outside the building if we can and chase him into it if we can't."

The commander was testing his nerve. It was clear enough that the man was one of the voice's lackeys, which was shameful for a gold-ranker. His job involved making sure that Fal did as instructed. Fal didn't care, as he only had to do one thing to spite the commander and the foul woman he served: win a fight.

91

KING OF THE SKY

FAL VIN GARATH SNEERED AND HEADED IN THE DIRECTION OF THE PYRAMID. Although no one saw it, the sneer was for his commander, for his astral king's Voice of the Will and for Asano, who would soon be dead. Fal's wings spread out as he wove his way through the battlefield, the image of grace and elegance as he glided through the chaos. He seemed untouchable, yet there was no frenetic dodging as he moved through the monsters; attacks from the vehicles below passed him by. He danced through the sky. One moment, he was swooping down or shifting his angle as he descended in a graceful curve. At other times, he tucked in his wings and plunged downwards, spinning in an inverted pirouette as energy beams and explosions went off around him as if avoiding his path.

Fal was big, even for a messenger, but he was no thug; his large size belied his swift and graceful powers. Any fool could blind-fire a storm of razor-sharp feathers and be effective. It required true superiority, even amongst messengers, to take simple enhancements to agility and spatial awareness and become an effective force on the battlefield.

Fal's fighting style was a reflection of his flight: open, graceful and mobile. If he was forced to fight Asano inside a building sized for humans, his own body would be an enemy as he was boxed into small rooms and tight hallways. While there was glory to be found in fighting on the enemy's terms and winning anyway, Fal knew that Asano was not a foe on which to build extra accolades. Jes Fin Kaal knew what Fal could do, and at least some of what Asano could do. Even if she was underestimating Fal, her confidence that Asano would beat him meant that the outworlder was not to be taken lightly.

As he drew closer to the pyramid, the beams from Asano's building increasingly focused on him. They prioritised messenger targets, so most of the others were giving it a wide berth, letting the monsters take the hits. Despite the increased attention from the beams, Fal eluded them easily.

He did not yell out his challenge to Asano. Any animal could bellow. Fal had a point to make: messengers were different. Not just stronger but inherently better. When Fal called out to Asano, he did so in a way that the servant races could not replicate. Projecting his aura, he laced it with physical force, the signature trait of messenger auras. He created vibrations in the air that manifested as words, rumbling loudly across the battlefield. The result was Fal forging words as thunder, crashing down imposingly on the defenders hidden in their fortresses.

"JASON ASANO. COME OUT AND FACE ME!"

The beams stopped targeting Fal, instead going for other messengers that were more distant. This allowed Fal to hover in place, his eyes glaring challenge.

In the entertainment district, Jason was chatting with Rufus as they watched Gordon draw out a massive magical orrery.

"Placed in an extreme circumstance, with power levels far above your own," Rufus told him, "you do something spectacularly outlandish that you probably shouldn't."

"There you go, then," Jason said. "You just said I shouldn't do it."

"Are you going to do it?"

"Of course I'm going to... sorry, give me a sec. I've got a thing."

Jason looked off into the middle distance.

On each side of the pyramid, a hex panel opened and a metal object slid out. They were simple metal arms with a small pyramid made of clear crystal seated on the end. The four pyramids glowed with soft light and a massive image appeared in the sky, over the giant eye. It was a cloaked figure that looked to be standing on the eye, although its translucency demonstrated that it was only a projection. The cloak's hood was pushed back from the figure's head, revealing Asano's face. His eyes, reflections of the image orb his image was standing atop, glared up at Fal Vin Garath, who was floating some distance from the pyramid.

A voice spoke, but it did not come from the image of Jason. The same technique that Fal had used was replicated, but on a much larger scale. The aura coming from the pyramid covered the entire city district, strong enough that the gold-rankers had not managed to suppress it.

The entire battlefield shuddered with physical force as Jason crafted his words, the walls of the sturdy fortress vehicles shaking. The air itself trembled, the summoned monsters panicking as messengers halted in the air, unnerved. They could feel something in the aura, something that resonated inside them and told them to obey. They shook it off immediately, but it left them unsettled.

When the words came, they did not come from any one place. They were not spoken at all. They just came into being, like an act of creation.

IF YOU WANT TO FIGHT ME, THEN COME IN HERE AND GET ME.

The words were inescapable, yet they went precisely as far as the aura and no further. They covered the battlefield, yet instead of thundering across the city, the sound stopped dead beyond the area Jason chose.

Fal felt hesitation for the first time. He knew that it was an intimidation tactic, having just used it himself, but the comparison was humbling. Messengers did not handle being humbled very well. Fal knew that he had accomplished the display only by using the pyramid to somehow amplify his aura, but it didn't matter. Once enough people were involved, image became truth, which was why Fal had made such a public challenge in the first place.

To the defenders, Asano's words had been a rallying cry. To the summoned monsters, it was confusion, the voice of a master scolding them in anger. The summoners quickly reasserted control, but there was no denying the influence Asano had. This was even true of the messengers. The entire reason Fal had been sent after him was because he was somehow an astral king.

Fal realised that, on some level, he had been denying what Asano was. Though he'd been told, the very idea was absurd. But now he had felt the truth shuddering through his body, and there was no part of him that could deny it anymore. And he knew that every messenger on the battlefield was experiencing the same thing.

As the giant projection of Asano vanished, Fal considered ways to undercut him. He was tempted to mock him, to try and lure him out where they could fight on Fal's terms, but he knew that it wouldn't work. After Asano's display, shouting mockery at the pyramid would be like a drunkard shouting at a temple, a worthless buffoon.

Even the slender chance of it working was gone once a contingent of gold-rankers moved to join Fal. There was no way he would come out to face that. Fal had no doubt that the sudden show of support was designed exactly to make sure that Asano did not emerge. The Voice of the Will had plans for Asano, and Fal was the sacrificial lamb that would prove his worth to the other messengers.

Asano proving himself against a messenger was a pointless exercise in show-manship. Many messengers had died to adventurers; it was happening at that very moment, all around the city. Any fool would see through it, but that was politics. So long as she could sell the pretence, Jes Fin Kaal got what she wanted. Which now meant Fal had to enter the pyramid and fight Asano under the worst possible conditions.

"Well?" the commander asked. "Aren't you going in? We all heard that impressive invitation."

The commander's voice was steady, but Fal knew he would be roiling inside. Fal knew how galling it was that an astral king at his own rank existed. Astral kings were the peak that every messenger strove to ascend, yet here was someone who had reached it, without being a messenger, and at *lower rank.*

Fal turned to speak to face the commander, unable to resist delivering a jab.

"I didn't hear my name," he said. "He didn't sound like he was any more worried about you than me. Or did Asano's display leave the mighty commander of all these gold-rankers scared?"

"You would be wise to watch your words, Fal Vin Garath."

"Or what? You'll have the Voice of the Will send me on a suicide mission? You're just a servant. You might as well be one of the lesser races, huddling in their vehicles."

The commander smiled instead of retorting, which unnerved Fal in the fleeting instant before he realised why. The reflexes of a gold-ranker could have deflected the harpoon shot from the pyramid before it impaled Fal, but he hadn't even warned him, let alone moved.

The harpoon yanked back with blinding speed, dragging Fal with it. The chain to which it was attached led into the cloud stuff of the pyramid where a hex panel was absent. In the moment it took for the harpoon to pull back inside, Fal struggled pointlessly against the huge barbs holding the harpoon in place. He could have gotten free with a few extra moments, but he didn't have them. He disappeared, dragged into the pyramid and the hex panel slid back out to cover the place he had entered.

Fal fell through a misty wall that immediately turned solid behind him. The harpoon had vanished somewhere during his passage through cloud-substance that made up the building, itself turning ephemeral.

Impaling was a negligible wound to a messenger, the damage already healing by the time Fal floated off the floor and into a more dignified position. The floor was already slick with his silver-gold blood, shining like metal with a faint blue sheen. It stained his clothes, loose and white with gold embellishments that set off his gold hair.

Fal pressed his hand onto the wall he had just passed through, finding it now cool and solid to the touch. It was some manner of smooth-cut stone or crystal, or perhaps some substance in between. He took in his surroundings, a hallway that would have been generously sized for humans. To Fal, it was cramped, his impressive height almost brushing the ceiling and his wings unable to unfurl at all.

He looked each way down the corridor; one way led to a turn and another to a dead end. He wondered at the odd design choice, thinking about how it would be the worst place for him to fight. That immediately triggered a realisation that came too late as something struck him from behind like a meteor. He was smashed into the wall at the dead end of the hallway, spiderweb cracks appearing in the stone from the impact. That was a hard hit, even for a silver-ranker, and Fal slumped to the ground again. He rallied instantly, looking up to see what had hit him.

It looked like a human, only bigger. The dark-skinned man was not as tall as Fal himself, but Fal was towering even by the standards of his own kind. This man may have been a full foot shorter, but with his sculpted muscle and majestic size, a pair of wings would have let him pass for a messenger himself.

Fal again rose up, not pushing himself to his feet like an animal but floating with his aura. It was hard, as the aura permeating the building was hostile and oppressive. It wasn't enough to entirely suppress him, but it made using his aura a struggle. Even so, he used it to stand to his full height, feet floating just off the floor. He looked down at the man who was in no apparent rush to continue his attack.

The man's body might not have matched Fal for height, but he was just as wide, if not wider, with shoulders that were geographical in magnitude. He wore loose pants but neither shirt nor shoes, although he did have a towel draped over his shoulders. Intricate tattoos marked his chocolate skin; while Fal didn't recognise the Māori designs, he correctly guessed that they were tribal in origin. The man's short-cropped hair was wet. He had the blank scent of someone who had just used crystal wash, although his natural scent was beginning to assert itself. It was the springtime freshness that marked an outworlder, and a glance at the man's aura confirmed it.

As Fal examined him, he examined Fal in turn. Although Fal doubted that the huge man had to look up at people very often, he showed no concern in doing so with Fal. His expression said that he didn't see anything interesting and his gaze turned to his own body. He frowned with displeasure at Fal's blood from the impaling wound, which had gotten onto his arm and chest during their impact.

"Bro, I just showered," the man complained.

Fal knew that if the man was willing to converse, he might well lead him to Asano.

"You took a shower in the middle of a battle?" Fal asked.

"I was covered in rank-up goo. Have you smelled that stuff? It's chemical warfare, bro."

"You just ranked up to silver?"

Fal's aura senses were massively suppressed in this building, barely able to glean the most basic information about the man. He pushed a little harder and saw the tell-tale signs of a very recent rank gain. For all the man looked unperturbed, his body must have been aching for rest.

"Who are you? Where is Jason Asano?"

"I'm Taika Williams, and Jason's not in. That giant battle you just mentioned, remember? If you're looking for him, just wait. He'll do something pretty attention-grabbing sooner or later. It's kind of his thing."

"You're lying."

"No, it really is his thing. And I'm not even counting that big projection he just did. How he managed that from across the city, I have no idea."

"I mean that you're lying about him not being here. There's no way he can project his aura at a remove. Not unless this pyramid is a lot more than a cloud building."

Even as he said it, Fal realised that it almost certainly was. There was an oppressive power, a sense of dominion that he normally associated with ground sanctified to a deity.

"I'm telling you the truth," Taika said. "You're pretty rude, bird man."

"I am not a bird man," Fal said, forcefully enunciating each word. For all his conflict with his own kind, Fal was still a messenger, with a messenger's pride.

"I am one of the supreme beings of every reality blessed enough to be graced with our presence."

"You've got giant bird wings, bro. Not a criticism; I'm just saying that you need to accept yourself in order to love yourself."

"These wings are the symbol of my glory as a messenger."

"They're bird wings, bro. Just big and on a man, so... bird man."

Fal conjured a curved sword and swung it at Taika's neck. Taika held up an arm to block it and the sword bounced off. The skin was unblemished, although the area around the strike point had turned jade-green. It swiftly faded back to Taika's normal chocolate colour. Taika didn't retaliate.

Fal frowned.

"Is that the Emerald Skin power?" he asked.

"You know your essence abilities, bro. Not your weapons, though. That curved blade is for slicing, but you went for the chop. Can you conjure a machete? It might work better for you; I'll wait."

Fal ignored Taika's words, instead focusing on his own aura. He pushed it out to wash over the other man, through the interference of the building around them. His aura flinched back as soon as he tried to suppress Taika at all, his instincts screaming at him to kneel before the king of the sky.

As he had feared, this man had the powers of a garuda.

92

A PRETTY CREEPY DUDE

Taika had both hands against the shower wall as the water sluiced the ichor from his trembling body. Nothing short of crystal wash would get the foul, clinging gunk the body produced during a rank-up off, but that was fine. The cloud palace showers had the water infused with crystal wash. Jason was surprisingly free with the stuff, given how there had been a shortage in Rimaros.

"Oh," Taika said to himself, suddenly realising why.

He scrubbed away the foul black-green residue with a cloth that he was going to dispose of, crystal wash or no. He knew he shouldn't go straight out and fight, but he was going to anyway, the moment he stopped looking like a swamp monster. His body was still strained from the rank-up and what he needed was sleep. But that was not going to happen with a war raging outside.

Jason also knew that Taika shouldn't fight. He had told him as much, but also knew that his friend would not be deterred. Or so he thought. His body had mostly stopped shaking by the time he emerged from the shower to find, instead of his fresh clothes, Shade.

"You forgot a change of clothes, Mr Williams."

"I did not forget a change of clothes."

"I suspect that Mr Asano forgot for you," Shade said, his tone soaked in disapproval. "This building tends to eat things he wants to disappear. He has, however, provided you with what he declared to be an appropriate outfit."

Taika looked at the purple stretch pants that Shade held out for him.

"Seriously?"

"I can assure you of my firm protestation, Mr Williams. But you know how he gets."

Taika chuckled, took the pants, slid them on and tied off the waist cord.

"Yeah, I know. Good looking out, bro."

"Now that you are fully attired," Shade said inaccurately, "Mr Asano has something he would like you to handle, Mr Williams."

"He doesn't want me to fight."

"He does not."

"I managed to rank up in time, and I won't be fobbed off. Unless what he has for me is a fight, I'm not interested."

"Which he anticipated. This task is, indeed, a fight."

"What kind of fight?"

"I mentioned that this building tends to eat things that Mr Asano does not like. There is a messenger floating around who fits that description."

"He wants my first fight after ranking-up to be a messenger?"

"Yes. I would add that I do not care for this particular messenger either."

Fal Vin Garath's day was only getting worse. He was trapped inside Jason Asano's pyramid, boxed into a dead-end corner by a man with garuda powers. If it came to a fight, Fal's quick and mobile style would be all but useless. His only advantage was that the man in front of him had only just ranked up. Even so, fighting would be a bad choice until he could find a better battlefield.

Garuda powers were a problem. The garuda were natural-born kings of the sky, and whether it was a garuda in person or an adventurer tapping into their power, they were some of the worst enemies that messengers could face.

Fighting an adventurer with garuda abilities would bring Fal prestige. He could add it to the list of reasons that winning fights in his current circumstances would bring him glory. That was also the list of things he desperately needed to avoid today, but he didn't seem to have much choice.

With the worst possible opponent in the worst possible place, talking was the better strategy. This was not a strong area for Fal, and for most other messengers as well. Messengers didn't negotiate with the servant races. That was beneath them. Should the servant races be graced with the presence of a messenger, all they required was the honour of obeying whatever directive they were issued. Reality, however, was not always kind. Fal, given his current circumstances, would need to talk this man, Taika, around. He did his best to not show his annoyance at needing to learn the man's name.

"Your aura power comes from the garuda essence," Fal said.

"Yep," Taika confirmed.

"And you're an outworlder. Did the garuda bring you here? Or did it come here looking for you in the first place and only stumble upon the egg?"

"I barely know that bloke. He came here for the evil egg you lot had hidden away. I have met him, though. He saw me doing the garuda thing and gave me some tips."

Fal didn't let a grimace cross his face. Not only did this man have garuda powers, but guidance, however brief, from an actual garuda. That was even assuming the man was telling the truth. Fal had not developed the gift of reading people from their body language, as very few could hide their emotions from his senses. In this place, though, his magical senses were impeded, along with his aura.

"We don't have to fight," Fal said. "I'm here for Asano, and not even to assassinate him. I've been instructed to test him. With a duel. No tricks, just honest combat. Honourable combat. I'm led to believe he'll go for that."

"I wouldn't go trying to predict Jason unless you predict he'll do something insane and then make a sandwich. I don't think he'll go for your honourable duel, bro; he doesn't much like honest combat. He's more into shameless cheating. Back stabbing. Poison. Luring people into his evil magic pyramid."

"Harpooning someone through the chest is a rather unsubtle lure."

"You think that's bad? Get a look at his floral shirts, then you'll know what unsubtle is."

"We don't have to fight. What would you get out of it?"

"Cardio? But you're right, we don't have to go at it. You could surrender. Jason wants us to take any messengers we fight alive if we can. That being said, you might want to fight to the death instead."

"Why? What does he want us for?"

"I'm not going to lie. I stopped paying attention pretty early when he explained it to us. It's always 'astral this' and 'spirit that' with him. I think you messengers have some kind of energy he can... well, he didn't use the word *eat*, but it sure felt like he was talking around it."

"Eat?"

"I know, right? Jason can be a pretty creepy dude. I mean, he's probably not going to *eat you* eat you, but he is big on sucking the life force out of people. Which he insists is not the same as drinking blood or eating people, but I dunno, bro. There are only so many times a bloke can tell you he's not eating people before you start to think he's definitely eating people."

"Eating is a disgusting practice, whatever you eat. We messengers sustain ourselves on the power of the cosmos."

"Jason too. It's a little weird how much you guys are like a copy of him."

"We are a copy of no one. My people are ancient, while he is less than three decades old. He is a copy of us."

"If you say so, bro," Taika said sceptically.

"Why don't you take me to Asano? He and I can settle things between us."

"I told you he's not here."

"But he is somewhere."

"Sure, but he doesn't want you there. He wants you here. You think he can't kill you with this building? The only reason you aren't a puddle of gooey flesh soup right now is that he doesn't want you to be. He's waiting for your gold-rank friends to come in here too. As for you, he fed you to me."

"Are you saying you eat people as well?"

"What? No, gross. It's an intimidating metaphor, bro. Was it scary? This is my first time bantering with a supervillain. It kind of sucks that you're basically evil Angel, though. He's the worst X-Man. People might tell you it's the guy whose only power is to blow himself up the one time, but at least that's interesting.

Angel's just got wings. He should start a courier service or something, not fight evil. Why are you looking at me like you have no idea what I'm talking about?"

"Because I have no idea what you're talking about. You and I may well fight to the death and you're babbling nonsense."

"Can't take yourself too seriously, bro. I watched Jason do that and it kind of messed him up. So, yeah, it's a little bit gallows humour, but I'll get by. So long as you're the one swinging on the gallows."

"Again, we don't need to fight."

"Bro, you and yours just smashed your way into this city. As we speak, you pricks are trying to break into the places the innocent people are hiding so you can kill them just to make a point."

Fal saw a potential way forward in Taika's words. It could be considered traitorous, but he'd never been ordered not to voice conclusions he came to on his own. And since the Voice of the Will had thrown him to the wolves, he had no loyalty to her.

"That's not really what's happening," he told Taika. "The woman who masterminded this attack doesn't even care about what happens. She's just using me, like she is you. She doesn't tell me anything, but her plans go beyond this attack, and I know what she really wants. It's all internal messenger politics and her own ambition."

For the first time in their encounter, Taika looked hesitant.

"Then what's it really about?" he asked.

"I know why she wants Asano. Take me to him and we can talk about it. Work out something that forwards all our agendas, rather than those of the people that sent me here."

"The best I can do is lock you up until he comes to you. I mean, you're locked up already, if I'm being honest. Jason could just seal off the hallway and leave you in there. Or make your body rot away, although I hope he doesn't. Not for your sake, but I just had a shower. Washing off this blood will be bad enough, but I don't want melty messenger on me. It should be fine, though. He decided to let me test out my new power level on you, where he can keep me safe. It's a little condescending, but he means well. Unlike you."

"We may be on different sides, but we at least have some common interests."

"Mate, I'm hearing words, but it's not your mouth you're speaking out from. You're talking about some kind of what? An alliance against your bosses? You think I'm that easy to manipulate? That you can lure me into that kind of trust? You didn't even tell me your name. It didn't even occur to you that it might be a good idea, when you're trying to suborn some bloke, to give him the basic courtesy of an introduction."

"I am Fal Vin Garath."

"I don't care what your name is. You missed your window to paint yourself as anything other than a piece of crap that knows how long his odds are. Jason put me here to kick the crap out of you, and that's what I'm going to do. You're training wheels, bloke."

"I can be far more valuable to you than that. I have to serve the messengers above me, but they've sent me here to die. We can work something out. You, me and Asano. The attack on the city doesn't matter."

Fal immediately saw that he'd made a mistake as Taika's expression went from amiable to stormy.

"Doesn't matter?" he growled, his normally high-pitched voice taking on the deeper timbre of rage. "People are dying. Innocent people. There was never a single second where you thought of their deaths as a bad thing, was there? You don't think their lives matter any more than I matter enough to give me your name."

"Yes, we come at this from very different perspectives. But perhaps we can find a way to an ending we both want. If you take me to Asano—"

"You don't get Jason," Taika said, his voice ominously soft.

Even Fal, oblivious to social cues, could sense the lurking violence. He didn't wait, making the first attack himself.

He conjured a second sword into his other hand and swept both at Taika's neck. Each was blocked by a huge forearm but, this time, Fal did not stop at a single strike, launching into a combination of flashing moves, up and down Taika's body.

To Fal's surprise, Taika didn't keep blocking. Where a blade struck without active blocking, his flesh still turned emerald green and resisted the damage, but wasn't as resilient. Fal's blades managed only shallow cuts, but they successfully scored Taika's flesh.

It only took a moment for Fal to realise what Taika was doing as the already big man grew to match Fal's height. His head became that of an eagle, red and gold feathers running down to his shoulders like a mane. His body retained its chocolate colouring and tattoos but became leaner, sleek yet powerful. Taika went from bodybuilder to boxer, his physique optimised for quick, explosive power. His fingers and his feet became more talon-like, and wings appeared on his back. They were feathered in red and gold, but, like Fal, he had to keep them tucked away.

The change took less than a second, but Fal's reflexes were fast even for a silver-ranker. He tried to use the moment to slip past Taika and escape the dead end, but it was a hard task. Taika, as it turned out, also had superior reflexes, and superior strength to go with it. He grabbed Fal by the face and slammed him back into the wall, his feet no longer floating but dangling from where Taika held him in place.

Fal dropped his swords, grabbed Taika's arm and used one of his powers. A spiral blade of force shot its way up Taika's arm, which immediately turned green and hard. Even so, the corkscrew of energy wound its way up his arms, spraying blood as it gouged a deep, razor-thin wound in stony green flesh.

Taika's grip loosened as his arm flinched. Fal slipped out and again made to escape past Taika. Taika grabbed at a wing, but another of Fal's powers rendered it almost frictionless, as if greased. It slid through Taika's fingers and Fal managed to slide around him, his wings brushing against the wall. The open corridor was still restrictive, but at least he wasn't boxed into a dead end. He conjured fresh swords as Taika turned on him, glaring with eagle eyes.

Garuda were paragons of speed, power and fortitude. Fal considered himself their match in pace and mobility, but he and Taika both had their speed constrained by the environment. That left Taika with strength and resilience, and Fal with a massive disadvantage. His best bet was to hope that Taika felt pressured by the restrictiveness of the space.

"I will face you in honourable combat," Fal declared. "But this tunnel is unworthy of our duel. Surely this place has at least one room large enough for us to fight in."

Taika didn't sneer, refuse or mock. He didn't say anything. His fist broke the speed of sound, the pressure wave hitting Fal like a compressed hurricane.

Ability: [God-Striking Fist] (Garuda)

- Special attack (dimension, holy).
- Cost: Extreme stamina, extreme mana.
- Cooldown: Six hundred and sixty-six minutes.

- Current rank: Silver 0 (00%).

- Effect (iron): Make a hard, fast punch. Time and space manipulation will not function in the vicinity while the punch is being swung.

- Effect (bronze): Cooldown is reduced based on the condition of the enemy after the attack. More resilient enemies results in a shorter cooldown time. An amount of stamina and mana is refunded based on the condition of the enemy. A sufficiently resilient enemy may trigger a refund of stamina and mana greater than the initial cost.

- Effect (silver): Damage inflicted is transcendent.

The very air thundered at the passage of Taika's fist as it broke the sound barrier. Fal, astoundingly, was fast enough to start dodging, but not enough to completely avoid it. He bounced off the wall and the ceiling before hitting the other end of the hallway like a bomb.

Taika whispered urgently under his breath. "Please don't get up, please don't get up."

For all the power of Taika's hit, the messenger floated up from the floor for a third time since being dragged into Jason's pyramid.

"That sucks, bro," Taika told him. "If you'd stayed down, I could have totally been One-Punch Man."

93

SECURITY OVERSIGHT

TAIKA LOOKED DOWN THE HALLWAY AT THE MESSENGER FLOATING AT THE END OF it. After being impaled and smashed into walls multiple times, the once glorious being now looked like a bird that couldn't stop flying into windows. As for Taika himself, he was in a strange state where he was both exhausted from his recent rank-up and simultaneously tingling with energy from his shape-change ability.

Ability: [King of the Sky] (Wing)

- Special ability (shape-change).
- Cost: High mana.
- Cooldown: None.

- Current rank: Silver 0 (00%).

- Effect (iron): Take the form of a garuda. [Power] and [Speed] attributes are increased. Wings allow for gliding but not flight without an additional power. Powers that conjure wings instead use the wings of this form and have significantly enhanced flight speed and manoeuvrability.

. . .

- Effect (bronze): Aura suppression and suppression resistance against any creature with wings or that is currently flying is significantly increased.

- Effect (silver): Certain other abilities have enhanced effects. Affected abilities: Emerald Flesh, Grace of Garuda, Golden Wings, Block Out the Sun, Feaster of Serpents, Amrita, Brother of the Dawn.

Taika was reminded of a time before he knew magic was real, fending off sleep deprivation with enough coffee to animate the dead. His poison resistance would now put paid to any effect caffeine once had on him, yet he found himself with that same odd sensation. His body was heavy, yet an electric charge ran through it.

He was starting to think that Jason may have been right to warn him against going outside in his current state. Even so, he still had a ragged bird man to deal with before he sought out precious slumber.

Fal glared back at Taika, conjuring fresh swords yet again. Then he glanced down the passage where the hallway turned, leading elsewhere in the building. Taika saw him looking and burst out laughing.

"Are you gonna leg it? If I were you, I'd definitely scarper, but I'm not a messenger. Where's the pride, bro? If you run, that kind of makes me look superior, and I once squashed my plums trying to sit on a chair like a guy from *Star Trek*. You wouldn't know him."

Fal faced Taika, his conciliatory façade completely gone. Although bloodied and beaten, his eyes stared imperiously, his pride and disdain no longer hidden away. His arms became a blur, firing off blades of wind that rushed unavoidably down the corridor at Taika.

Taika didn't try to dodge or even stand his ground and endure. He launched himself down the hallway, not running, not even really flying. He shot like a bullet.

Ability: [Momentous Charge] (Swift)

- Special attack (movement, combination).
- Cost: High mana and stamina.
- Cooldown: Four minutes.

- Current rank: Silver 0 (00%).

- Effect (iron): Charge attack. Rapidly gain [Momentum] during the charge. Can culminate in a non-combination special attack.

- Effect (bronze): Can cover extreme distances and move through the air. The speed of the charge escalates over the duration of the charge.

- Effect (silver): The damage from [Momentum] is enhanced by your speed at the moment the attack lands.

- [Momentum] (boon, magic, stacking): When making an attack, all instances are consumed to inflict resonating-force damage. Multiple instances can be accumulated and instances are lost quickly while not moving.

Fal's wind blades exploded onto Taika in rapid succession but failed to penetrate his skin as it again turned green to resist the damage. With hits landing all over his body, Taika had turned almost entirely emerald, his tattoos standing out in stark contrast. Damage was not the primary purpose of the wind blades, however, which exploded with force that pushed back against Taika's forward motion. Taika saw the surprise on Fal's face when he didn't slow down at all.

Ability: [Unstoppable Strike] (Swift)

- Special attack (movement).
- Cost: Moderate mana and stamina.
- Cooldown: One minute.

- Current rank: Silver 0 (00%).

. . .

- Effect (iron): Melee attack. If any instances of [Momentum] are triggered by the attack, they deal an amount of disruptive force equal to the resonating-force damage.

- Effect (bronze): When combined with a movement-combination special attack, the physical momentum of that attack is extremely hard to impede. Physical barriers and constraints are struck with resonating-force damage. Magical barriers and constraints are struck with disruptive-force damage. Resistances to any effect that impedes motion are significantly increased for the duration of the combination attack.

- Effect (silver): The cooldown of this ability is reset when using a movement-combination special attack, allowing this ability to be combined with that attack.

Fal managed to interpose his wings between himself and Taika, snaking them around his body from where they were tucked behind him. They absorbed the damage, but the damage was still enough for blood to stain where the blunt attack crashed into them. Fal bounced off the wall behind him like a ball as Taika threw aside the protective wings. The beak of his eagle-headed face came down like a pickaxe digging for ore.

Fal's skull was hard and the beak slid across it and down the messenger's face. The result was a massive gouge that took one of his eyes with it. Taika didn't waste time, immediately following up with rapid punches. Despite his wound, Fal was just as fast, his short swords clashing with Taika's fists. Even boxed into a hallway, both men showed off blinding speed, their movements a blur as they clashed.

Ability: [Grace of Garuda] (Wing)

- Special ability (movement).
- Cost: None.
- Cooldown: None.

- Current rank: Silver 0 (00%).

- Effect (iron): [Speed] attribute, reflexes, movement speed and perceptual speed are increased.

- Effect (bronze): Mana and stamina costs of movement abilities are reduced. Gain instances of [Momentum] while moving at high speed.

- Effect (silver): Instances of [Momentum] gained from other abilities take longer to drop off when not moving. When [Momentum] is triggered, instead of all instances being immediately consumed, they begin rapidly dropping off one at a time. This continues until all instances are gone or additional instances are gained.

The difference between the combatants swiftly became apparent. While Fal did have a slight edge in speed, he didn't have the room to dodge that was a hallmark of his elusive fighting style. They traded blows at staggering speed, with Fal coming out the worst. Forced to block a much stronger opponent, he was constantly being hammered with fists that landed like wrecking balls. When he got a blade past Taika's blocking arms, by contrast, they managed little more than shallow cuts in jade flesh. If Taika got an arm in the way, they did nothing at all. The only real damage Fal managed to inflict came from magical attacks, his spiral cutting magic proving the most effective.

Bleeding from spiral cuts, Taika managed to body-press Fal into the wall. He then conjured an amphora to drink from while keeping the messenger pinned. As soon as he drank, his wounds healed faster.

Ability: [Amrita] (Garuda)

- Special ability (conjuration, restoration).
- Cost: Varies.
- Cooldown: Varies.

- Current rank: Silver 0 (00%).

- Effect (iron): Conjure a jar containing one to five doses of restorative elixir that bestows an ongoing health and mana recovery effect. The elixir may be shared and does not interact toxically with other potions. Cooldown is predicated on how many doses are conjured, from one minute for one dose to fifteen minutes for five doses. Mana cost is low, moderate, high, very high or extreme, depending on the number of doses conjured.

- Effect (bronze): For the duration of the elixir's recovery effect, abilities that provide damage reduction are enhanced.

- Effect (silver): Duration of the elixir's ongoing recovery effect is increased. The elixir can be converted to a life elixir at an extreme mana cost per dose. Life elixir has no effect when consumed but does not disappear after being removed from the amphora and may be used as a material in rituals and crafting.

Fal's body turned slick while Taika was drinking from the amphora. He slid from between Taika and the wall, dashing down the hallway Taika had goaded him into not using earlier. Taika dropped the amphora, which vanished before it hit the ground, but he didn't rush after Fal.

"Drinking with a beak is tough," he observed to himself, then looked down the hall.

Fal was swift; he had already vanished around a corner. Taika glanced at the trail of blood left behind.

"I don't know where you think you're going, bro. There's no way out and you're Hansel & Gretelling pretty hard."

"I feel obligated to point out, Mr Williams," Shade's voice came from Taika's shadow, "that 'Gretelling' is not a verb. Or a word."

"Bro, have you been in there the whole time?"

"Mr Asano has given me strict instructions not to explain when or where I may be at any given point. He likes people to realise I could always be watching."

"The panopticon effect, I get it. That's a rude thing to do to your friends, bro."

"Indeed," Shade concurred. "Mr Asano has some rather authoritarian tendencies. But your attention should be on the blood trail, Mr Williams."

Taika looked at the blood trail and saw the floor turn from hard stone to soft cloud material and siphon the blood away. A glance at the wall he had smashed Fal into showed that it was likewise being automatically cleaned and repaired.

"Oh, bloody oath," Taika muttered and then rushed off, following the rapidly disappearing trail of blood.

Fal realised in short order that not only was the pyramid all hallways and no doors, but it was also changing as he moved through it. Dead ends forced him to backtrack into places that were not the same as when he had passed through moments earlier. He recalled what Taika had said about Asano waiting for the gold-rankers to invade. He didn't know if the pyramid was powerful enough to contain them, but knew that they would test it sooner or later. He would not be getting out. They would assume he died and come after, to eliminate the pyramid as a threat.

Fal was recovering swiftly. His burst eye had grown back, but its vision was still blurry. Even if he was fully restored, however, it didn't matter. There was no door he could break through in search of hostages or a better place to fight. His most powerful attacks had bounced off the walls in his attempts to breach them. Taika had made some serious dents, mostly with Fal's head, but Fal himself lacked the strength. Powerful attacks were not his strong point. There was no escaping Taika in these halls, and Fal had accepted that, in these halls, he couldn't win. All that remained was choosing the most dignified manner in which to lose.

Taika followed the blood trail being rapidly devoured by the cloud palace's passive cleaning functions.

"I suggest you hasten, Mr Williams. The gold-rankers have decided to invade the building. The gap at the top was apparently too tempting to resist."

"How's it going?"

"They rushed in deep before they realised that walls were closing behind them. The afflictions are just starting to break past their resistances and they are debating whether to smash walls to go deeper or smash walls to get out."

"Which one do you want them to do?"

"It doesn't matter. They don't realise that Mr Asano can reorient the chamber they are in, gravity included. Whatever wall they break through, he will choose where it leads. They will need to rapidly break through walls in a straight line if they want to get out. Mr Asano will allow that, so long as they don't head in the direction of one of the dormitories where people are secured."

"How is he doing all this? Doesn't he have his own thing going on elsewhere?"

"Mr Asano's unusual nature includes a certain level of multitasking. It's similar to how gods watch all of their followers and sacred grounds. On a much more limited scale, obviously."

Taika rounded a corner and found Fal waiting for him. The messenger was looking much restored, but his former glory remained buried under a coating of blood, pounded out of him by Taika's fists. His swords were in his hands, which dangled loosely at his sides.

"I won't surrender," he said, resignation in his voice. "There is no shame in failing an impossible task, only in giving it up."

"Cool story, bro."

Taika was leaving a fresh trail of silver-gold blood as he dragged Fal through the hallways by his hair. Along with the thick line on the floor, marks punctuated the walls where Taika occasionally slammed the messenger's head. The fast-healing messenger kept blearily rousing. Shade had emerged from Taika's shadow to move alongside him.

"You did very well, Mr Williams."

"These are pretty controlled conditions," Taika said. "I don't think anyone needed me to deal with this guy."

"Will you go out to join the fight, then?"

"Nah, bro. I got that out of my system. I'm barely staying on my feet here. I'm glad you kept me from going out, so thanks. It would have been pretty rough."

Fal moaned insensibly as he threatened to rouse again. Taika was about to slam the messenger's head into the wall again when Jason's aura surged. This wasn't the background aura that always suffused the cloud palace but something coming from further away. It was a deeper, richer aura projection than anything Taika had experienced.

"Is that Jason himself?" Taika asked.

"Boosted, but yes," Shade said. "I believe his pursuers will be able to find him now."

The messenger thrashed like a fish on a hook, his hair still gripped in Taika's hand. Taika wasn't sure if it was some kind of frenzy or if Fal was having a seizure, but it stopped when the messenger's head hit the wall hard enough to crack the dark stone. The stone turned into mist briefly, drawing away the blood and restoring the wall to a clean, undamaged condition.

"Do you think I could get that installed at my mum's house?"

"Perhaps not that exact thing, Mr Williams, but I imagine something similar. You should talk to Miss Farrah or Mr Standish once we make our way back to Earth."

"Bro, why do you only ever use women's first names? I've heard you call Emi and Erika and Farrah by their first names, but you even use Jason's surname, and you're his familiar."

"I don't use all women's first names," Shade pointed out. "Only the ones I like the most. Also, it made things easier when everyone was named Asano."

Taika gave Shade a side glance.

"Jason still doesn't let you spy on people in bathrooms, right?"

"It's observing, Mr Williams, not spying. But, no; that security oversight remains."

94

I HAVE TO GO FIGHT EVIL

THE COMMANDER OF THE ADVENTURER FORCES DEFENDING THE ENTERTAINMENT district was Eilaf Hayel, a gold-rank elven adventurer and Yaresh native. He was a veteran of fighting the messengers, having assaulted their strongholds more than a dozen times. He was extremely familiar with the aura suppression tactic they employed and how it impacted the morale of adventurers. The fact that they hadn't used it from the opening moments of the battle was not a relief but a concern.

Eilaf's gold-rank senses allowed him to monitor the auras around the city. In most of the battlegrounds, the messengers had deployed their auras immediately. This had helped them gain a foothold as they came through the breach, but Eilaf had seen in his own battlefield that the ceaseless torrent of monsters didn't need the help.

That the commander he was up against held their auras in reserve suggested that he was not underestimating the adventurers, which was unfortunate. One of the weaknesses common to messengers in Eilaf's encounters with them was an overwhelming arrogance that led them to underestimate opponents. He had hoped a messenger that didn't undervalue their opposition was weak enough that they had to act with caution.

That hope was forlorn. The messenger commander was not just powerful, but the single strongest messenger Eilaf had ever seen. Most messengers were marginally weaker than a well-trained adventurer, and while there were certainly exceptions, he had never seen anything like this.

The commander was shrugging off the most powerful attacks that Eilaf and his fellow gold-rankers could throw at him, and sometimes throwing them right back. Fortunately, the messenger was more interested in commanding his forces than pressing the adventurers by attacking in person. He was likewise directing his forces conservatively, a situation Eilaf wanted to continue for as long as possible.

The Battle of Yaresh, not just in the entertainment district but across the city, was essentially a race. The messengers were trying to dig out and slaughter as many civilians as they could before the city barrier restored itself, trapping them inside. Eilaf didn't know why his counterpart did not push for speed, but as it was the only mistake the man seemed to be making, Eilaf wanted to capitalise on it.

Eilaf had his own gold-rankers pressure the other gold-rank messengers, prioritising them over the commander. Aware that the conservative strategy could be a trap to lure them in, Eilaf didn't let his people push too hard and overextend themselves. Both sides being conservative was to the adventurers' advantage, so he would let that play out as long as he could.

The move proved a sound one. Eilaf came to suspect that the enemy commander was less than enthralled with his assignment and was more interested in running out the clock than pushing for success. If the man would rather keep his people alive and leave unsuccessful than sacrifice them for victory, Eilaf was the last person who would get in his way. He just made sure that the commander was occupied keeping his gold-rankers alive rather than interfering with the silver-rankers.

Things continued to go well for Yaresh, as there were some real gems amongst the silver-rank adventurers. The more the battle turned in favour of the adventurers, however, the more Eilaf anticipated the aura drop. The adventurers had all been warned about messenger auras and many were veterans who had experienced them already. Even so, Eilaf wished he could warn them all again. That was not practical in a battle, but he could at least prepare his gold-rankers.

Eilaf was unsurprised when their foes finally unleashed auras that hit the adventurers. It was like a physical force, to a small degree, albeit not enough to cause any harm. The real impact was spiritual, with just enough kinetic force to show the essence users that messenger auras were fundamentally different.

It was a subtle but effective intimidation tactic, which was ultimately the purpose of the aura wave. Suppressing the auras of adventurers did have a tactical impact as aura essence abilities were shut off, but it wasn't the main goal. Having their auras pushed down left the adventurers feeling weak and helpless, like bullied children.

That reaction wasn't universal amongst adventurers, with many fighting on, unconcerned. Those were mostly veterans who had besieged messenger strongholds and tasted their auras in the past. For most, however, a suppressed aura left them feeling vulnerable and exposed. Such tactics were key means by which the messengers propagated their sense of superiority.

The adventurers didn't collapse under the assault, but it certainly arrested their forward momentum. Eilaf and his gold-rankers had the edge in both numbers and —discounting the enemy commander—individual strength. The combat power became less relevant as the gold-rankers on both sides moved to pure spiritual conflict, floating in place as it looked like they were trying to stare each other down. If not for the advantage in numbers, the adventurers would have been overwhelmed by the messengers' advantage in spiritual strength.

The silver-rankers were likewise clashing aura-to-aura, and the adventurers were struggling. They did not give up the physical conflict the way the gold-rankers had, but their spiritual battle was reflected in physical combat. The previous advance of the adventurers had come to a halt, while the messengers went from holding back to pushing forward, taking the fight to their enemy.

Elite adventurers were well-trained in aura use, but the messengers simply had a higher baseline. Not only were their auras stronger, but even the least messenger had a refined grasp of how to use it that few could match. Adventurers were used to heavily outclassing any individual foe, and often found themselves taken aback at how close messengers came to matching them. As a result, first encounters with messengers were the ones most likely to go poorly.

Eilaf had seen green adventurers struggle against messengers time and again. He felt unease in the auras of adventurers, and doubt could be a plague in a fighting force, and panic was a wildfire. Morale was the key to any battle, and the side that lost it was the side that broke, regardless of relative strength. The monster torrent was gaining ground against adventurers suddenly struck with hesitation. Unfortunately, all Eilaf could do was hope that his adventurers had the steel to hold on.

Elseth Culie was finally getting back to clearing out monsters after the messengers fled to seek healing. Her task became more urgent as the adventurers on the ground became less effective under the aura suppression blanketing the battlefield. Elseth and the teams protecting her were in a bubble that held the suppression off, centred on a man currently looking up.

Asano's aura was not unlike that of the messengers, if not even more domineering, but she quickly stopped worrying about that and focused on killing more monsters. Asano himself was not moving, watching as his alien familiar drew lines and symbols in the sky that glowed in blue and yellow. The creature Asano called Gordon was orbited by six blue and orange nebula orbs in the pattern of eyes. Each orb fired beams of blue or orange energy, leaving glowing shapes in the sky like fireworks that didn't stop lingering.

All six eyes drew intricately intersecting lines, the beams implausibly managing to never cross one another. The familiar was drawing a massive ritual circle, not just on a flat plane but in a sphere. Lines, runes and sigils were woven together in a floating sculpture of light.

The summoned monsters did not interfere with it or anyone inside Asano's aura, visibly fleeing from it. This left the other adventurers protected by the aura free to pour out attacks. Elseth made up for lost time as best she could, giving no thought to her dwindling mana reserves as her spells pumped out mass afflictions that were already spreading through the monsters.

She only paused to pull out her most expensive mana potion and chug it down, taking the chance to look over what Gordon was doing. It had completed its sphere and started crafting smaller ones around it, connected by lines. The smaller spheres drifted around the central sphere on their own.

"An orrery?" she said, not realising it was out loud.

The finished magical sculpture had formed an intricate and startlingly beautiful orrery, the smaller spheres moving around the larger central one. It was a massive creation, the size of a wealthy townhouse, and as she looked at it, she realised that the sculpture was a ritual magic diagram, but unlike any she had seen before.

Like many adventurers, Elseth had a decent grounding in ritual magic. Even so, she failed to grasp even the most basic principles of what the familiar had crafted. She suspected that it operated on some magical paradigm completely outside of her experience.

"Gordon turned out to be something of a magic artist," someone said.

She looked over, not recognising the voice. It was Asano, proudly watching his familiar. She hadn't realised it was him because his icy voice had thawed, speaking warmly of Gordon. He turned to look at her.

"You should probably get back to the afflictions," he suggested, his voice still soft. The friendly smile was completely undercut by the aura pouring out of him, oppressive and territorial. She was equally parts glad and astounded that it was holding off the messengers' collective aura, but she also wanted to leave it as soon as possible.

***

While Gordon continued to draw the most outrageous and elaborate ritual Jason had ever seen, he concentrated on maintaining his aura against the messengers. They had somehow managed to blend their auras together into a singular force, a technique Jason would ask Amos Pensinata about later. The messenger aura was spread not just across the entire entertainment district but also the battlefield filling the sky above it. This dilution of power meant that Jason was able to push it back over a moderate area, only possible because the gold-rankers from each side were negating each other. He managed a sufficient range to shield the affliction specialist and the adventurers supporting her, with space for more adventurers who found them to take shelter. She went back to dosing monsters while the rest lashed out with ranged attacks or left to guide other adventurers to the safety of Jason's aura.

There had been very few occasions in which Jason had truly opened up his aura, projecting it with as much strength as he could muster. It had reached the point of being too powerful, a danger Farrah had warned him of on the day she introduced him to auras. His aura also covered too much ground, pushing through all but the most extreme measures to constrain it. If not for the suppressive force of a full contingent of messengers, it would have spread out across the city, likely harming any normal-rankers that had not yet reached a bunker.

While he regretted that there would be collateral damage once Gordon was done, Jason's resolve did not falter. He could sense the messengers pushing back against the adventurers, allowing more and more monsters to safely descend. They had already started digging through the ground at an accelerated rate, growing closer to a breach of the bunker's defences. If he had even a chance to arrest the aura advantage of the messengers, he would take the chance.

Rufus arrived next to him in a flash of light, startling the adventurers whose defensive perimeter he had circumvented.

"You're doing something about this, right?"

"You expect me to stop the collective aura of who knows how many messengers, all by myself?"

"Yes."

"You have some pretty outlandish expectations there, mate."

"Yes. I hate to break it to you, John," Rufus said, using Jason's fake name due to the nearby adventurers. "But you're the one who set up those expectations. Placed in an extreme circumstance, with power levels far above your own..."

He threw his arms out, indicating the wider battle.

"...you do something spectacularly outlandish..."

He pointed to the giant glowing orrery over their heads, then looked flatly at Jason.

"...that you probably shouldn't."

"There you go, then," Jason told him. "You just said I shouldn't do it."

"Are you going to do it?"

"Of course I'm going to... sorry, give me a sec. I've got a thing."

Jason looked off into the middle distance, glaring at nothing.

"If you want to fight me, then come in here and get me," he declared to no one, then turned back to Rufus.

"Sorry about that. Anyway, shouldn't you be taking out some messengers about now?"

"That's why I'm here," Rufus told him. "I want to time it for right after you do whatever you're going to do. I'm hoping to take out a few in single shots."

"How many afflictions have you left out there to absorb?" Jason asked.

"A lot," Rufus told him. "So, get to it."

"I'm waiting on Gordon to finish. He's doing an amazing job, right?"

"It's amazing to look at," Rufus agreed. "What kind of magic is that?"

"I have my suspicions. I'm pretty sure Shade knows and isn't telling me."

"That is for the best, Mr Miller," Shade asserted as he emerged from Jason's shadow.

"So you say."

"Since we're waiting," Rufus said, "do you have any sandwiches?"

"Who are you talking to?" Jason asked, pulling out a sandwich wrapped in paper and handing the slightly larger half to Rufus. They both looked up at the monster-filled sky.

"Have you ever seen this many monsters at once?" Rufus asked, then bit into his sandwich.

"Yep," Jason said. "Not all flyers, like this, though. There was a vorger swarm that came pretty close."

"In that astral space?"

"The one the Builder tried to take back? No, this was a transformation zone. I told you about those, right?"

"When you explained them, they just sounded like astral spaces."

"Bloke," Jason scolded. "I'm starting to see why Clive gets cranky when people don't understand astral magic. A transformation zone is a defence mechanism of reality, when the dimensional membrane has a localised catastrophic failure."

"But they're still a dimensional space you can go into, right? Does that just make it a kind of astral space?"

"You can go into a bath and you can go into the ocean, Rufus. Yes, you can slowly soap up your taut, black body and bald head with a sponge in both, but that doesn't make your bathtub an ocean."

"I'm not entirely comfortable with that analogy."

"The point is, they're different. But if you get both in the same space, you've got maybe a month before it blows a hole in the side of reality large enough to suck a planet into the astral. Where it stops existing, because there is no physical reality in the astral."

"Yes, Jason, I know you saved the world. You mention it quite a lot."

"You're damn right I do. Do know how awesome that is? I do wish I could stop saving it from this dimensional nonsense all the time. I want to fight a guy with a weather machine."

"Are you in any danger of getting to a point?" Rufus asked.

"About what?"

"You were telling me about when you saw a massive vorger swarm."

"Oh, right. So, I was in a transformation zone, patching a hole in the side of the universe. I was just about done when a bunch of vorger came through. There was a nightmare hag too."

"Another one? What did it show you that time?"

"It was kind of embarrassing, so I don't want to say."

"It's fine. I'll ask Farrah."

"I didn't tell Farrah."

Rufus gave him a flat look.

"Please don't ask Farrah."

They realised that someone was staring at them and turned to look at the affliction specialist.

"What?" they asked simultaneously.

"Who are you people?"

"This is Rufus and I'm Ja... John. It's not a fake name."

Rufus shook his head. "May I ask your name?"

"Elseth Culie."

"It's lovely to meet you," Rufus told her. "I've noticed you're the main reason the monsters haven't cracked the bunker yet, so thank you."

"Who are you?" she asked him.

"He's a teacher and I'm a cook," Jason told her.

"You were just talking about saving the world," she said.

"I'm a very well-paid cook. Also, it wasn't this world, so you don't have to worry. Probably."

Jason looked to his right as Gordon floated down next to him, his work completed. They looked up at the final result, a glowing orrery like a solar system make of fireworks that refused to fade. Each sphere was comprised of a complex, nested array of lines, runes and sigils.

"Clive is going to be sorry he missed this," Jason said as his cloak billowed around him and he rose up into the air.

"You could use a recording crystal," Rufus suggested, calling up after him.

"No time," Jason yelled back. "I have to go fight evil."

"Some of my people have recording crystals," Elseth offered. "A lot of teams are recording the battle for analysis and posterity."

"I might take you up on that," Rufus said. "Thank you."

"Is your friend going to be able to make sense of that thing? It's a ritual diagram, right?"

"It is," Rufus said. "And no, he won't know how it works. He'll love it."

9 5

STRAY THOUGHT

JASON FLOATED UP, HIS CLOAK SHAPED INTO GENTLY BEATING WINGS AS THEY carried him into Gordon's ritual diagram. His eyes swept over the sophisticated magical orrery, his body tingling as he passed through the glowing lines. He moved to the centre of the large, central sphere. He had the unnerving impression of being inside a complex machine, the operation of which he didn't completely understand. But he did have a basic grasp of how it worked, enough that he could take his place as the final component of the ritual.

Gordon's ritual magic was foundationally different to what Jason had been taught. The same was true of every ritualist on Pallimustus and Earth. Neither Dawn nor Shade had been willing to explain it to him, both transparently feigning ignorance. He, in turn, declined to tell them something that neither seemed to have realised: Gordon's ability to use that ritual magic was somehow bound to Jason.

Gordon had become even more linked to Jason than an ordinary familiar. It was when he had done so that Gordon unsealed the ability to use the strange ritual magic. Their link gave Jason some instinctive insight into how it worked, but nowhere near enough to attempt using it himself. It wasn't knowledge but an instinctive feel, similar to what he had for astral forces.

Jason was not entirely without knowledge, however. He had spent a year roaming around Earth, using the Builder's magic door to access the fundamental underpinnings of reality. He had been crudely repairing the link between worlds, working with trial and error, without any theoretical framework. In that time, he had slowly and fumblingly obtained some understanding of the fundamental mechanisms of reality. In Gordon's magic, he recognised the framework that he had lacked. By his own admission, his comprehension was that of a monkey attempting to do maths, but at least he could make the attempt. Also, he loved bananas.

It would take years of study that Jason wasn't even sure how to do before he would gain any real comprehension of the alien ritual magic. But all he needed today was the means to trigger Gordon's ritual, and for that, he knew enough. Just. He was pretty sure. Worst came to worst, he could ask Gordon for a hint.

This was only the second time that Gordon had used this kind of ritual magic. The first had been when Jason had flooded himself with reality core energy that needed to be bled off. Gordon had used an aura projection ritual that drained the power out of the very unconscious Jason to fuel itself, blasting his aura across Rimaros. That ritual had been inefficient by design, so as to drain the excess power killing Jason.

This new ritual was the same basic concept, a significantly more sophisticated refinement of the original. Along with being orders of magnitude more efficient, it did not replicate the same aura projection that ordinary ritual magic could accomplish. It was designed to draw out and project Jason's aura far more comprehensively. More than simple aura amplification, it would dig out every element of Jason's soul and put it on display, impressing exactly who and what he was on everyone within range. And that range would be enormous.

This time, Jason was an active participant. Floating in the air, he nervously opened and closed his fists. He thought back to his early days on Pallimustus, desperately trying to hide the vulnerability he felt. Confidence was something with which he had taken a hard 'fake it until you make it' approach. He had hidden his fear and confusion by making everyone else fearful and confused, veering manically between movie monster impressions and babbling nonsense.

Somewhere along the way, the version of himself that was cranked up to eleven had stopped being a mask. As he prepared to become more vulnerable than he ever had, it was time to find out if he had the resolve; if he'd finally made it or, deep down, he was still just faking it. This would, quite literally, announce himself to the world. No hiding behind bad manners, manic behaviour or thirty-year-old television references. His soul would be on display for all to see, allies and enemies alike.

When Gordon had suggested this, Jason had recognised the value. Especially after his abject failure to get Gordon's butterflies up and running, this was the only way for Jason to make a substantive impact on the wider battle. Despite his self-assurances that he was happy just being one more adventurer, it never occurred to him *not* to do something outrageous and stupid to help sway the battle on a wider scale.

While Gordon's new ritual magic was unquestionably powerful, Jason could already see reasons it would never replace the ritual magic he already knew. Firstly, the complexity was absurd. Instead of relatively simple diagrams that could be drawn on a flat surface, these rituals were three-dimensional structures. Without a power like Clive's to draw them in the air, anyone using them would need to assemble actual sculptures.

The real killer, though, was in how the rituals were powered. Ordinary rituals drew on ambient magic, meaning that all most rituals needed was to not be in a magical dead zone. Gordon's rituals required a different source. That had been the reality core energy inside Jason for Gordon's first ritual, but he was definitely not trying that again. He didn't need that level of power anyway, as this new ritual was far more efficient. This time, he was going to do something that Dawn had explicitly told him not to: tap into his astral gate.

The astral gate inside his soul was, along with the astral throne, one of the things that fundamentally changed Jason's nature. They were the tools of astral kings, who forged their very souls into physical universes, creating domains where their power was unassailable and all-but-unlimited.

Dawn had told him that he should experiment with the astral throne, which governed physical aspects, while leaving the astral gate alone. It tapped into the deep astral, the infinite plane of raw magic and dimensional forces that Jason was far from ready to handle. After his first time tapping into it had left him convalescing for months, she had advised him to leave it be until he had ranked up. Preferably, all the way to diamond. That it had taken him months after she left before he completely ignored her warning was something of a personal triumph.

She hadn't been wrong, and he knew it. The astral space was the sea on which every universe in the cosmos sailed. What would opening the gate to that infinite power do?

"Explode me like an overfilled water balloon, probably."

"Mr Asano, you're talking to yourself again," Shade said as he emerged from Jason's cloak to float next to him.

"I know," Jason said. "I'm a little distracted trying to use a giant alien magic ritual. Which looks awesome, thank you, Gordon."

"The looks are not the point, Mr Asano," Shade said.

Jason turned his gaze from the glowing ritual sphere to look at Shade from under raised eyebrows. Despite being a blank-faced shadow with just enough softly glowing white to imply a butler's tuxedo, Shade managed to look embarrassed.

"Apologies, Mr Asano; I'm not quite sure what came over me."

"It's a big day," Jason told him. "Just don't let it happen again."

Jason relaxed some of his built-up tension at the banter with Shade, but strain and worry still marked his expression. Around them, the orrery clamoured for power like an insistent pet at mealtime. This was his last chance to back out.

"What do you think, Shade? Do I tap into the astral gate and risk getting completely wrecked?"

"You know the price for what you are about to do, Mr Asano. You've paid it before. Channelling more power than you can handle has hurt you in the past, but I'm not telling you anything you don't know. It isn't the first time you've made this choice. You're just wasting time now when we both know that this isn't really a choice for you."

"It kind of is."

"We don't have the time for you to lie to me, Mr Asano, let alone yourself. I've seen you choose between the safety of others and the safety of yourself time and time again. Stop dithering and get to work."

"Strict nanny," Jason said with a chuckle.

He sighed, nodded and closed his eyes as he pushed his senses into the orrery. This was not a simple amplification ritual that would passively affect his aura, and he had to feed his aura into it, like loading a cannon. It was a simple enough process, using the same fundamental aura control techniques that Farrah had taught him years earlier.

Jason was connecting with the ritual, which was far more reactive than an ordinary one. He was loading it with his aura, but that was the cannonball and it needed the gunpowder. The orrery was *hungry* and ambient mana was not what it needed. Jason reached into his soul, sending his will through his spiritual realm to where his astral gate rested. He understood its functions only a little more than he did Gordon's ritual magic, but he didn't need to. Today, all he had to do was open it.

Jason's spirit realm had been tapping into the infinite power of the deep astral since before it became a place that others could enter. It started as a trickle of power, replacing his need to feed himself spirit coins or magically rich food. Beyond that gentle, passive stream, drawing on the astral for any more power than that had not been an option. Then came the astral gate. The hole in the wall through which power trickled had now become a tap. And a tap could be opened.

He reached out with his will to open the astral gate the barest sliver. It was the tiniest gap he could manage, and yet a torrent of raw magic geysered into his soul. Like drinking from a fire hose, his senses were overwhelmed, as all he could sense was the spray of it striking him like a weapon. Although the impact was spiritual, he almost fell from the sky in his disorientation. That would drop him out of the orrery and collapse the ritual.

He steeled his resolve, concentrating on shaping himself into a conduit, feeding power into Gordon's ravenous orrery. He immediately understood that if he didn't have that outlet, the magic would have ravaged him. Attempting to use the same method to fuel his essence abilities or ordinary rituals would probably kill him, with neither being designed for that kind of power.

Even with the outlet of the orrery, Jason struggled to remain conscious. The power pounded its way through his soul, and as his soul was also his body, he felt it as a physical impact. He shook like an old pipe with too much water pressure, his eyes glowing bright like beacons.

The orrery also shone brighter and brighter. The sigils and lines of the central sphere blurred, melding together and hiding Jason's presence, transmuting into a heatless orange sun, stained with ominous swirls of dark blue. The spheres orbiting it also turned solid and took on the familiar nebulous eye shape of Gordon's orbs.

Jason's aura didn't blast out immediately, the orrery building up power like a charging battery. As the source of that charge, Jason floated within the sun, now inundated in blue and orange light. He clenched his fists, holding on as magic continued to explode through him. He maintained a tenuous grasp on lucidity, tapping into meditation techniques to maintain a grip on reality. Even so, his mind was scattered, odd thoughts popping in and out. He absently compared the sensations he was feeling to getting a colonic irrigation from a hurricane and started brainstorming business names for the service.

Jason was barely clinging to sanity by the time the orrery was fully powered. He closed the astral gate more from instinct than conscious command, drooping in the air as he felt like a cored apple. Then the orrery flared to life and Jason snapped back to alertness. He felt his soul pulse like a heartbeat, swelling with each thump.

The aura projection rituals Jason had experienced before were just that: projections. They cast an image, compared to now where Jason felt like he was genuinely expanding, spreading out over the city. It reminded him of when he had formed his spiritual domains, taking over the transformation zones and remaking them in his image.

This was a declaration. Jason's soul was showing everyone exactly who and what it was. His aura flooded the city, even the areas where gold- and diamond-rankers held sway. He was not taking over the territory, but simply announcing himself. It was not the formation of a new spirit domain—yet, his mind added, and he scolded himself for the thought. He hoped Knowledge wouldn't tell Dominion about the stray thought.

There was a moment of stillness across the city as the fighting stopped. It was a fleeting instant, less than a second, and then the adventurers, messengers and monsters went back to thrashing one another. But in that instant, something had changed. The summoned monsters became erratic, their summoners struggling to keep them under control. As for the messengers, some became hesitant, but many more became enraged, thrown into a berserker frenzy by what they had just sensed. Some attacked their opponents with renewed vigour, while others left their own battles to hunt down the source of the aura.

In any case, Jason had succeeded in his goal. Whether cowed or inflamed, the harmonic interlinking of messenger auras had been disrupted, not just in the entertainment district but across the city. The adventurer commanders didn't waste the opportunity, pushing themselves onto the front foot. The messenger auras weren't gone, but they were no longer a unified front. As for the messengers themselves, they were not thinking tactically, which the better adventurers made the most of.

Unfortunately for the adventurers, their leaders had held their nerve. The gold-rankers were simply too strong to fall under Jason's influence and were screaming orders and dominating their silver-rank kin, pulling them into line before they gave away too much of an advantage.

In the entertainment district, the orrery faded away, dissolving into the air as Jason floated back to the ground. Jason landed, disoriented, as he looked at his hands held out in front of him, the fingers flexing open and closed.

"How are you holding up?" Shade asked him.

Jason turned with a confused expression before his eyes focused. He looked back at his hands.

"I'm fine," he said. "I mean, barely standing up, but I'm pretty sure that all I need is a good rest. I think I've finally hammered my own soul so much that it's gotten used to the abuse."

His expression creased into a scowl.

"That doesn't make me sound good."

96

HERETIC

THERE WAS A SINGLE DIAMOND-RANKER AMONGST THE MESSENGER FORCES, MAH Go Schaat. He had no interest in the astral king's goals, and longed for the day he would no longer have to take the woman's directives. He was already powerful enough that she could only ask so much of him, and he gave no more than was strictly required. He was still bound to her service, however, until he finally found the path to astral king for himself. In the meantime, he was stuck servicing her agenda, as delivered through her Voice of the Will, Jes Fin Kaal.

He was under no requirement to handle any issues below diamond-rank. In his current deployment, this meant countering the native diamond-rankers when they participated in raids on the messenger strongholds. Now that the messengers were the ones on the attack, he would be part of it. The diamond-rank adventurers would doubtlessly participate in the defence of their city, meaning that Schaat was obligated to join the attack.

The natives had two diamond-rankers. They were weak for the rank, but Schaat was not a fool. He knew that even the weakest diamond-ranker was one of the deadliest entities in any world, even if they weren't a messenger. He had no intention of taking them lightly, and if the attack plan had not involved softening them up with an apocalypse beast, he would not have participated at all. His obligations to the astral king did not include suicide missions, which meant that Jes Fin Kaal had been careful to hide that this mission was exactly that.

Schaat did not realise the duplicity of the voice until he had breached the barrier from above and his senses spread across the city. He didn't care about the operation, or how it served the astral king's goals. Beyond what the astral king demanded of him, Schaat didn't care at all. Even so, using four life-forge gates to attack this unimportant city struck him as wasteful. He had wondered what the voice saw in the place that was worth the expenditure, but not enough to interact with his lesser and ask. It was only after he breached the barrier from above that he realised he should have.

With the barrier stained blue and covered in monsters like bees on honeycomb, he could not see inside. Neither did his formidable magical senses reach through the barrier, such was the strength of such a formidable emplacement. The presence of the garuda had been hidden from him.

That the garuda was here now, right as the genesis egg was activated, was too staggering a coincidence. Someone who knew about the egg must have leaked that information at just the right time to coincide with the attack. As a result, the diamond-rankers had been spared from pushing into that chaotic clash.

That left the question of what anyone got from leaking that information. The answer, to Schaat's mind, was obvious: it got him. He was inside the barrier, now, with two diamond-rankers to deal with. As for who had set it up, that was equally obvious.

While the management of the astral king's local operations fell to Jes Fin Kaal, she was ultimately a gold-ranker, Voice of the Will or not. She had neither the power nor the right to overrule Schaat on almost any matter, should he take an interest. Nor could she make major decisions without passing them by him. He had been willing to overlook the costly life-forge gates because he liked that she didn't bother him with every little thing. But he now understood that he should have paid more attention.

Schaat had been expecting the native diamond-rankers to have expended significant resources fighting the naga genesis egg, making them easy pickings for Schaat to deal with. Instead, he found a gods-bedamned garuda eating the egg like it was breakfast, the remains of countless serpents demonstrating the epic battle it had waged on the egg's spawn to reach that point. Even now, giant serpents attacked the garuda while smaller ones rushed off into the city. The garuda allowed it for the moment as it finished off the egg, tearing chunks off with its beak, which would cut off the serpents at the source.

The entire raid was a trap. It was an assassination attempt disguised as a city invasion, so that Schaat would die and Jes Fin Kaal would no longer be under his thumb.

It grated, but did not surprise, that the astral king permitted this. The Voice of the Will would never go after a diamond-ranker without her approval, however deniable the plan might be. Schaat avoided politics entirely, so he had no idea what schemes Kaal and the astral king were working on. He was focused on becoming an astral king himself, but clearly, he had been remiss in his narrow focus. While he had been in study, she had obviously been making back-handed deals that would forestall any backlash from the upper-tier messengers at the attempt to kill him off. Arranging the death of a diamond-ranker was no small thing, even if it was unlikely to stick.

Schaat's first thought had been to abandon the raid. The barrier breach was right there, as he had just made it. But that, in itself, was a trap. He was obligated to participate in the attack because of the diamond-rank adventurers and the garuda's presence didn't change that. Kaal would deny arranging events, and now that Schaat had joined the fray, flight would be seen as cowardice. Kaal could claim he fled in fear and have him neatly removed from authority, which equally got her what she wanted. If anything, that was an ideal outcome for her, as it avoided any chance of backlash from getting him killed.

Only if Schaat could prove she arranged everything would he have a case to defend his reputation, and it would not entirely erase the sting of having fled. Kaal was also not sloppy enough to leave threads for him to pull on after the fact. If things had reached this stage, he was certain she had already cleaned up after herself.

That left Schaat with an unenviable choice. If he left, he would be safe but disgraced. While he did not enjoy his responsibilities, the authority that came with them was essential to his efforts in becoming an astral king. If he was branded a coward, his status as a diamond-ranker would hold less weight, leaving him even more subject to the astral king's control.

The only option that remained was to fight. Fortunately, the garuda would not participate. He was here for the serpents and no garuda would fight on Kaal's behalf. Schaat imagined the garuda had seen through Kaal's manipulations and only gone along with them enough to get what he wanted. Kaal would get no more out of him, of that Schaat was certain.

That still left two diamond-rank adventurers. Schaat had clashed with both in the past and was confident that he could deal with either one alone, but not both together. They knew his strength as well, and working as a pair in their own territory, they would be able to fight him to a stalemate. For them, keeping him from rampaging through their gold-rankers was enough.

This was not a situation where Schaat could kill one quickly and move on to the other before the first revived. Even if the one he killed lacked a power to accelerate his resurrection, there was no way to kill a diamond-ranker quickly. It was why the high-rank effects of assassination powers moved away from damage and into escape prevention and revival negation.

Killing diamond-rankers took planning. Getting them to stay dead was often the result of decades, if not centuries, of elaborate plotting. Schaat was confident that even if he died here, the most Kaal could have arranged was for his resurrection to be delayed, not shut down entirely. That would have been too traceable, and all she needed was him gone long enough to carry out her plans, whatever they were. Whether he was trapped in death for a while or disgraced into irrelevance, she got what she wanted.

He wasn't going to let that happen.

Schaat still had certain advantages. Even if he was just stumbling onto Kaal's schemes, by analysing them he would be able to discern her strengths and weaknesses. Some were easy enough to infer already. She wouldn't be able to get the garuda or the diamond-rank adventurers to actively participate in her plans as that would be too easy to trace back to her. Instead, she would have had to align their agendas with hers, which could only go so far.

Schaat considered the people in play. The garuda knew better than to interfere too heavily in a universe the World-Phoenix had isolated from the wider cosmic community. Although they were famously individualistic, they would not fly in the face of a great astral being's agenda the way the messengers would.

The World-Phoenix would not object to it hunting down the naga genesis egg, as that was their purview. It would even allow some nudging of locals in one direction or another, in moderation, but starting a war with the messengers was too far. The messengers had paid a price for defying the World-Phoenix and invading this world that the garuda would not. As for the diamond-rank adventurers, they would be satisfied if Schaat left their city, having no need to see him dead.

The path to frustrating Jes Fin Kaal's plans, then, was to stall. He couldn't ignore the diamond-rank adventurers or the voice would rightly claim dereliction of responsibility. But he didn't have to kill them, or even really hurt them. All he had to do was occupy them, keeping them off the gold-rank messengers. So long as he did that, he could ignore everything else and then withdraw with the rest of the messenger forces at the end of the raid.

He would accomplish no more than the bare minimum in assisting the raid, making sure the diamond-rankers were occupied and no more. He had no investment in the operation even before it turned out to be a pretence to kill him. If he came out unscathed, and the voice claimed he hadn't done enough, he could simply state that the adventurers were too challenging. No, why sacrifice his pride over it? He would claim that the voice's plan was flawed. If anything, the more messengers that died, the worse Jes Fin Kaal looked. So long as those deaths weren't laid at his door, it was the first step in turning the tables on Kaal and having her removed.

He wouldn't be allowed to kill her outright, as she belonged to an astral king. But this was the start of a path by which he could reveal her machinations and duplicities, forcing the astral king to revoke her protection. It meant dirtying his hands in politics, but after this, he would do just that. He could wash them clean in her blood when she was the one disgraced and he was finally free to kill her.

Schaat engaged the diamond-rank adventurers, as was required. He was overtly cautious, his opponents quickly realising that he was stalling for time. They were suspicious of diamond-rank reinforcements, at first, but eventually realised the truth: that he wanted to leave the city as much as they wanted him to go.

Both sides still clashed. Schaat had to keep up appearances and the adventurers would not leave him be in case his disinterest was a ploy. They took no incautious chances, fully expecting a no-score draw once the raid was done. If they could avoid a diamond-ranker rampaging through the city, they would. The garuda was closer to fighting for them than not, and yet had done more damage than all the messengers and their summoned monsters combined.

The intermittent combat, with neither side overcommitting, left Schaat with the spare attention to watch the city with his magical senses. Some of the more powerful gold-rankers—from either side—might have been tempted by the voice to intervene, despite the danger. Reaching diamond rank was not as hard as transcending it, but it was still a threshold that most failed to cross. The insight an astral king's servant could offer, garnered from her mistress, would sway the hearts of many.

There was no sign of further duplicity, however, and Schaat did not expect it to appear. The temptation to keep adding more complexity to a plan was how it unravelled, and Schaat acknowledged that Kaal was not so foolish. But the gold-rank adventurers seemed to be paying their diamond-ranked compatriots very little attention, concentrating on the defence of their city. As for the messengers, they were revelling in getting back at the servant races. Schaat could only agree that the servant races needed to be shown their places after having the temerity to attack messenger strongholds.

Marek Nior Vargas caught his eye, the gold-rank commander seeming to have as little interest in the attack's success as Schaat himself. Schaat saw the man as a potential rival, should he ever reach diamond. He was smart, straightforward and mostly avoided politics. He also hated Jes Fin Kaal, meaning that of all the commanders, he was the least likely to be part of her plot. Schaat didn't entirely dismiss the possibility, though, as strange things were happening in the commander's battlefield.

Although remaining slightly wary of Marek, Schaat dismissed the strange activity, as it was only occurring amongst the silver-rankers. While some gold-ranker could potentially pose a threat, however negligible, nothing from two ranks below could be a danger. Nothing from two ranks down could even surprise him, or so he thought until he sensed something in Marek's zone. It was close to the ground, some manner of ritual magic, but not of a kind that should exist in this world.

It was a kind of magic he had only encountered in his studies of transcendent power, in his pursuit of astral king status. More astoundingly—he would say impossibly, if not sensing it at that very moment—it was silver rank. How was anyone in this world, even the diamond-rankers, using intrinsic-mandate magic?

"Kaal, what did you do?" he muttered with a grin. It didn't matter what she was scheming now, because this was a step too far.

"No," he corrected himself, realising that Kaal was not behind it. There was no way she would risk getting caught dabbling with intrinsic-mandate magic as a Voice of the Will. Even if she was careful and used foes of the messengers as proxies, it was too dangerous. If the astral king she served found her meddling with a different higher-order power, her privileged position and everything that came with it would be instantly revoked.

This made whoever or whatever was using that magic a curiosity. Not a threat, as it was still silver ranked, but perhaps a warning of greater threats to come. He wondered if the garuda was behind it. It wouldn't make a lot of sense, but the messengers, the garuda and the naga genesis egg were the only cosmic-level forces in play. If it was actually coming from some local silver-ranker, that represented something outside of Schaat's knowledge, experience or studies.

Schaat waited for the magic to trigger, hoping the result would give him more clues. If he was smart about it, he could potentially leverage this to get his revenge on Jes Fin Kaal. He absently wondered how they were even feeding it the required power. Examining it with his senses, he discovered it was some manner of aura projection ritual, and immediately wondered why. It would only be able to affect a silver-rank aura, and what silver-rank aura was worth that kind of magic?

The answer exploded across the city, blanketing every battlefield inside the barrier. It was the most comprehensive aura projection Schaat had ever encountered, fully revealing every nuance of the projected aura. And the aura itself was startling, from the strength relative to its rank to the scars that marked it. They spoke of spiritual battles no silver-ranker should have encountered, let alone endured. Each one told a story of tribulations faced and overcome. Gods and great astral beings; unwinnable fights and world-shaking resolve.

There was more to it as well. The base nature of the aura was a grab-bag of cosmic forces. The gestalt nature of the messengers and the nascent realm of an astral king. The spiritual domains of divine territory and the intrinsic mandate of the great astral beings.

Schaat was staggered at what he sensed. This was the embryo of something beyond monstrous. It was a power that crossed cosmic lines, a myth from before the sundering. He doubted that anyone else on the battlefield even realised what they were sensing.

There were five diamond-rank beings in the city, counting the garuda and the remnants of the egg. Normally, any aura ranked below theirs would shrivel back like a withering plant. A silver-rank aura should be washed away like words in the sand as the tide rolled in, yet it did not. It could certainly not push back such auras, but it shared the space they occupied, utterly unyielding.

Schaat knew that the messengers throughout the city would be rattled. They wouldn't understand all of what the aura contained, but what they could was enough. That it possessed their gestalt physical-spiritual nature meant that it shared their inherent superiority. Some might even think it *was* one of them.

That realisation was nothing, however, next to the unmistakable nature of an astral king. Mortals might not recognise it, but no messenger could miss it, even if the astral realm behind it was incomplete. It was an astral king, at silver rank, flying in the face of everything the messengers knew. It mocked their ambitions, everything they strove for. Only those who knew the origin of their kind would realise what the owner of that aura was. But as Schaat himself had only uncovered that secret in his studies of transcendent power, he was likely the only messenger on the field that did.

Across the city, messengers froze in place. Even some of the gold-rankers were affected. It wasn't any kind of magical compulsion, and it certainly couldn't suppress their interlinked auras. It was simple shock. The very existence of whatever was behind that aura was a challenge to everything the messengers believed about themselves, their ambitions and the superiority that defined them.

Schaat was past the blind indoctrination of his youth. He knew the origins of his kind and the lies that governed their society. He knew that the messengers, as a whole, were not inherently superior. Superiority was for individuals, like him. But for those blinded by self-aggrandisement, being confronted by someone that seemed to share their nature, yet was an astral king at silver rank, in defiance of it? He knew that for those without the will to adapt, it would be an almost religious experience, and not a positive one.

Messengers neither worshipped gods nor venerated great astral beings. They obeyed the astral kings, but did not pray to them. Messengers worshipped themselves and their faith was towering. But for messengers all across the city, that tower had just shifted at the foundations.

Although it felt like an eternity, the strange stillness that spread over the city lasted only a fleeting moment. Barely a second went by before the messengers were moving again, most now overtaken with rage. The gold-rankers held themselves together, but many of the silver-rankers were behaving strangely.

A few scattered handfuls were listless, not resuming the fight. Around half of the silver-rankers were doing the opposite and going berserk. Some left their battlefields to seek out the source of the aura. Others were too caught up in fights and launched themselves at their enemies in frothing zeal.

The messengers, who had no religion, had found their first heretic.

AN EXTREMELY ANNOYING
CATALYST

SOPHIE AND HUMPHREY RETURNED TO THE RELATIVE SAFETY OF ONSLOW'S hollow flying shell. Jason performing some insane act was an inevitability, and once he had, the monsters went mad. Some continued towards the ground, the control of the summoners managing to hold. Others snapped the leash and fled back up the way they had come, or flew about randomly in a confused frenzy.

"I have a feeling we should get to Jason," Humphrey announced. "I suspect that he'll soon be the centre of some extremely unpleasant attention."

"We can barely tell which way is up," Clive said, right as the shell was rocked by an impact.

"I'm confident we'll find which way is down if we don't do something," Belinda said as she looked out the side.

"Did a monster just ram us?" Sophie asked.

"Yes," Neil said, also leaning to peer out and up. "A particularly large summoned monster has rammed the wind barrier protecting the shell and had its face shredded for the effort."

"At least it had a face," Belinda said. "How is the barrier holding up?"

"Onslow can maintain it so long as I keep feeding him mana," Clive said. "The ritual enhancing his ability is inside the shell, so we don't have to worry about that unless the monsters use some extremely powerful dispel magic. I have no idea if the messenger summons can do that."

"These messenger summons are weird," Belinda said. "Have you seen the ones that are just a bunch of metal rings spinning around each other? How do they even fight?"

"They slowly charge up infrequent but extremely powerful force beam attacks," Humphrey said. "I was prioritising any that targeted Onslow, and I saw Sophie deflecting the others that I didn't get to."

Another heavy impact rocked the shell.

"Onslow isn't indestructible," Sophie pointed out. "We need to move."

Clive gave Onslow's shoulder a reassuring squeeze. His familiar, when separated from his shell, was a child-sized humanoid tortoise. In that form, Onslow supplemented his usual elemental attacks with weaponised adorableness. Stash, who currently looked identical except for a bushy moustache, handed Onslow half of a salad sandwich.

"Where did you get that?" Neil asked Stash.

"Uncle Jason."

"Did you just call him *Uncle* Jason?" Neil asked.

"No," Stash said with the complete yet casually dismissive conviction of an inveterate liar.

"Not exactly the most time-critical conversation," Humphrey told Neil.

"I know. But where was he keeping the sandwich, though?"

"Onslow," Humphrey said, "please take us down, towards Jason and Rufus on the ground."

"Stash doesn't have a dimensional space," Neil said.

"We've been headed down for a while," Clive told Humphrey. "It's just hard to tell amongst all these summons."

"Or a dimensional bag," Neil continued.

"Is anyone else sensing those messenger auras in amongst the monsters?" Sophie asked.

"Not even a regular bag."

"We can all sense the messenger auras," Belinda said. "We've been able to since they started suppressing all the adventurers, and it's even worse now half of them have gone berserk."

"Maybe a discreet satchel? Stash, do you have a satchel?"

"Neil, could you maybe let it go, just for now?" Humphrey asked.

"You know, don't you?" Neil accused Humphrey. "Does he keep his sandwiches somewhere disgusting?"

"It could be a shape-shifter thing," Belinda suggested. "Maybe he shape-shifts a hidden orifice every time he changes form. A secret flesh crevice."

"Ew," Sophie said. "Please never say 'flesh crevice' again. That's gross."

Belinda gave Sophie a disbelieving look.

"What?" Sophie asked her.

"I once saw you beat a man's head to pulp using a different man's head," Belinda said.

"So?"

"So, being disgusted by the term flesh crevice seems a little odd after some of the stuff you've done."

"I just asked you not to say that again."

"HEY!" Humphrey bellowed. "Can I remind you that there's still a battle going on?"

"Oh, yeah," Belinda said. "Sophie, you said something about the messengers... Neil, what are you doing?"

Neil and his moustachioed twin looked up guiltily from where they were peering suspiciously at each other's bodies.

"What?" they asked simultaneously.

"The messengers," Sophie said. "They were holding back before Jason's little display. Now there are a bunch of them dropping like stones right towards him. It's easy to spot them because their auras are spiked with rage."

They all turned their attention to the auras of the messengers, glowing like embers amongst the summoned monsters. As Sophie had pointed out, a good number of them had lit up their auras and started plunging towards the ground.

"We should move faster," Humphrey said. "Onslow, can you speed up?"

"He's a tortoise," Clive said. "Slow is, dare I say it, kind of his thing."

"He also flies and shoots lightning bolts, Clive," Humphrey pointed out. "I can confidently state that Onslow is superior to the ordinary tortoise."

"I'll ask," Clive said sceptically and turned to Onslow. "What do you say, little buddy? Can you get us down any faster?"

The diminutive familiar threw his arms up and let out a sound that was something between a chirp and a cheer. Then the team hit the ceiling in undignified fashion as the shell dropped like a missile. Only Onslow and Sophie were the exceptions, with Onslow remaining adhered to the floor as if glued. As for Sophie, in the instant of acceleration, her reflexes and agility allowed her to flip and land on the ceiling in a crouch.

Marek Nior Vargas wasn't happy. There was no longer any denying that the man he suspected to be Jason Asano actually was. He was also, like an extremely annoying catalyst, the cause of Marek's other problems. Asano's spectacular reveal meant that the Voice of the Will would have some uncomfortable questions as to how Marek had failed to notice Asano before he had blasted his presence across the city.

Marek lamented that he wasn't a diamond-ranker that could put in the absolute minimum effort, the way he sensed Mah Go Schaat doing. He would need to go investigate Asano, as instructed, despite not caring at all about the man or Jes Fin Kaal's plans for him. If he was lucky, the voice would deploy someone herself before he had the chance.

As commander of a portion of the messenger forces, Marek was going to get his silver-rankers in order. Strictly speaking, Asano was the priority, but Marek had the discretion to reorder priorities in the field should events grow sufficiently extreme. With a full third of his messenger subordinates gone berserk or near-catatonic, he counted that as meeting the sufficiency threshold.

He proudly noted that none of his personally trained troops had lost their minds except for Mari Gah Rahnd, and she was always somewhat unique. He strongly suspected that she was fine, faking a berserk rage so she could rush down at Asano because it seemed interesting. If she wasn't the best fighter he had by far, Marek would have kicked her from his personal cadre long ago.

Marek ordered the messengers that had retained their equanimity into action, sending them to round up the others. He did not begrudge the frenzied messengers their rage as he fully understood it. Those who broke, either driven to fury or left reeling and immobile, were the ones whose worlds had just been shaken to the core. Astral kings were very big on indoctrinating fresh messengers, keeping them compliant with promise and purpose.

Once they left the shelter of the astral kingdoms, the sense of superiority now instilled in the messengers kept them dismissing anything that contradicted what they had been taught. Marek knew from experience that without a good leader to help break those dangerous ideas, a messenger was left with the exact mental fragility that Asano had just exploited.

Despite himself, Marek found him respecting the tactic. Asano had demonstrated an understanding of both the nature of the messengers and the exploitable nature of blind faith that was surprising, allowing him to turn that insight into a weapon. Marek was no uncritical believer in standard messenger doctrine, but even he was shaken by what the man had shown off.

What Asano demonstrated flew wildly in the face of what freshly created messengers were taught. Marek had been lucky enough to find himself under a leader who showed him that the indoctrination was judicious with the truth, but he never imagined the reality he saw now. While he accepted that the truth had been bent, he at least believed in the path of power laid out before them. Asano was a living impossibility, showing what may well be an alternate pathway not just for himself, but for any messenger that could snare those secrets.

Marek felt the temptation to go after Asano himself and quickly realised that he was not the only one to have that thought. All around the city, he sensed gold-ranked messengers abandoning their stations and heading in Asano's direction, their adventurer counterparts either charging after them or exploiting their absence. None of that compared to Mah Go Schaat, however, the diamond-ranker moving so fast, he almost vanished from Marek's senses. It was a speed that, for most practical purposes, was the next best thing to teleportation.

Mah Go Schaat was certain that the thoughts going through his mind were replicated in most, if not all of the gold-rank messengers in the city. They all knew that the Voice of the Will had placed the utmost priority on Asano, and it was becoming evident why. Even if they didn't understand what he was, the way Schaat did, they saw that he represented: a path to power that was alike, yet also different from that known to the messengers. In difference, there was knowledge, and that knowledge might help them unlock the secrets that would lead them to become astral kings.

Jes Fin Kaal had not told Schaat about Asano, but little escaped the attention of his diamond-rank senses. As soon as the aura projection happened, he heard the name on the lips of the gold-rankers under instruction to capture the man. Many of the gold-rankers were already moving, but he suspected they might not be so eager to share Asano with Kaal, now that his potential had been revealed.

That the gold-rankers had the jump on him mattered nothing to Schaat. The busy city would obstruct them, however little that might be, but it was a problem he did not share. No gold-ranker was a match for his speed and he could barrel through any obstacle like it was vapour.

Schaat started to move and the world slowed down around him. The effect wasn't a power but a passive effect of his diamond-rank speed. His perception accelerated to match his pace so he didn't just crater into the ground. He flew through the forest of monsters, messengers and adventurers, the two diamond-rank adventurers moving in pursuit. He stopped for no obstacle; any monsters, messengers or adventurers he struck turned into blood mist without so much as bumping him slightly off angle. He passed through a building, leaving only a dust-filled tunnel in his wake.

He found Asano standing on the ground, the remnant energy of his intrinsic-mandate ritual hanging in the air above him. When he stopped, the world should have returned to a normal pace as his perception normalised to a practical speed. Instead, everything that was moving slowed even more, the world around him coming to a halt.

"Mah Go Schaat," a voice said from behind him.

He didn't sense anything, which was terrifying for a diamond-ranker. He turned, focusing his attention on the woman standing there. With something to focus on, his magical senses managed to pick her up, albeit barely. As best he could tell, she was a half-transcendent, having reached the maximal stage of diamond rank. That left Schaat in the extremely unusual position of coming second in power.

He looked around at a world that had completely frozen, at least to his subjective senses. This woman had accelerated both of their time streams enough that they were operating outside of normal time. His gaze ran up and down her body, which was that of an elf in simple tan pants and a pale green blouse. Her hair was a lighter brown than her skin, and flecked with green. Her eyes were amber, bright to the point that they almost seemed to be glowing.

He frowned as his slow examination ended without his time-stream returning to normal. She seemed satisfied to wait.

"Your ability to manipulate time is good," he said. "Too good. You serve the Sand."

"I do," she said. Her voice was soft and melodious. Schaat could not help but feel that she was tamping down a natural playfulness to her tone.

"What do you want?" he asked.

"A favour."

"What favour do you want from me?"

"The favour isn't from you, Mah Go Schaat, nor is this the time to request it. Leave Asano be. Turn around and leave this city."

"There is more than I coming for him."

"The rest he can handle."

"Are you sure? It's a lot of people who are a lot more powerful than he is."

"It always is, and he always manages."

"Who are you, and what do you want with him?"

"I am Raythe, and I have told you as much of my intentions as you need to know. Leave or die."

"I'm not so easy to kill, even for someone like you."

"That's alright," she told him. "I have time."

Jason and Rufus were looking up at the sky along with the elven affliction specialist, Elseth Culie. There were other adventurers scattered around them, having taken shelter from the messenger auras in the protective bubble of Jason's spiritual aegis. Monsters were still coming down, although in far lesser amounts, and seemed to be focusing on any area except where Jason was.

Elseth quickly directed the adventurers to spread out and fight. Those who had not been shielded by Jason were still woozy from the messenger auras, and it impeded their combat effectiveness. Elseth herself was already sending out affliction-laden spells.

"The messengers will get them back under control sooner rather than later," Rufus said. "We need to be ready for a fresh surge."

"I still don't understand what just happened," Elseth said between incantations.

"You remember how I said I was a cook?" Jason asked her. "This was basically a Friday night fry-up, except it was war. I grabbed what I had, chucked it together and did my best."

"That was terrible," Rufus told him. "That analogy doesn't land at all."

"I know," Jason said with a grimace. "I could tell while I was saying it, but I thought I could turn it around. Be cool with understated mysteriousness, you know?"

"They can't all be winners," Rufus said. "I think the monster attacks will be more intense than ever, once the summons are back under messenger control. And if I can sense the messengers that are coming, I know you can."

"I don't know if I can handle them," Jason admitted. "I never did get the butterfly thing working."

"There is one thing you could try," Rufus said.

"What's that?"

"Stop spending the whole battle trying to get one power from one of your familiars to do all the work for you and do it yourself."

"You make me sound like a slacker."

"Fighting smarter rather than harder is a good thing, Jason, but don't let yourself become obsessed with any specific tactic. You lose the big picture and start overlooking good opportunities. Stop messing about with something that doesn't work and remember how you used to do things before your extradimensional friend started shooting butterflies at people."

"You two are extremely strange," Elseth told them.

"No, I'm normal," Rufus said.

"If you were normal, Rufus, you would have pants that tight enchanted so they're flexible in a fight. Which you're about to have, by the way. There's a lot of stuff coming, and not just from our battlefield. Gold-rank messengers and adventurers are bearing down on us, and the diamond-rank messenger just vanished."

Just as he said it, a messenger corpse appeared at their feet, still radiating diamond-rank power. Rufus and Elseth immediately staggered back, the aura forceful even in death. Jason raised his eyebrows, then grinned.

"Well, that's the biggest freebie I've gotten since the World-Phoenix token."

"What do you think happened?" Rufus asked.

"I think we just got deus-ex-machinised, but I'm going to take the win and leave the how and why to later."

He held a hand out over the corpse and chanted a spell.

"As your life was mine to reap, so your death is mine to harvest."

Rufus watched transcendent energy flow out of the body and into Jason as the corpse dissolved into rainbow smoke. The dark image of a bird, speckled with starlight, appeared above Jason, growing stronger as he drained more of the corpse's astounding remnant life force.

"I don't think his life was actually yours to reap, Jason."

"It's a spell, Rufus. I just have to say it; it doesn't have to be true."

"That's an attitude you've thoroughly taken to heart, haven't you?"

98

TEACHING MOMENT

MESSENGERS AND ADVENTURERS ALIKE RUSHED TOWARDS JASON. FOR THE highest-ranked people, traversing the city was not a lengthy exercise, and the diamond-ranker adventurers pursuing Mah Go Schaat arrived first.

The diamond-rankers were both elves, a man and a woman. Her name was Allayeth and his was Charist. They found Schaat's corpse, dissolving into rainbow smoke. A sharp-featured silver-ranker was extracting and devouring the remnant life-force. As he drained the diamond-ranker's power, a dark shape looming over him grew more and more distinct. It was quickly becoming void black, speckled with stars.

"Star phoenix," Allayeth whispered. She had heard of them but not seen one; they were creatures of the wider cosmos, not native to Pallimustus.

"What's going on here?" Charist demanded.

"I just got food delivery," the silver-ranker said. "You know how it is. You're fighting a battle, you get peckish, but you don't have time to cook."

He gestured at the monster-filled sky above them.

"Because of the battle, obviously," he continued. "I have to say, I was hesitant about raw messenger, but it was totally worth going diamond rank. There really is satisfaction to be found in top-quality ingredients."

"You're making jokes?" Charist asked incredulously.

"You get used to it," another silver-ranker called out. "Sorry about him."

The second speaker was a dark-skinned and extremely handsome human. He and a third silver-ranker had backed off from the intensity of the dead diamond-ranker's aura. The man devouring the life energy from the corpse seemed unaffected. A glimpse at his aura revealed that it was the same one that had been projected over the city, sending the messengers and their summoned monsters into a frenzy.

The first man turned around to shout back at him while still draining the immense life force of the messenger.

"Don't apologise for me!"

"Then don't be rude," the handsome man called back. "These are busy people with a lot going on right now. They were probably chasing whoever that messenger you're eating was."

"I'm not eating him! Look, the life force is going in through my hand."

"If you want to avoid having to explain so often that you don't eat people, maybe don't make food delivery jokes."

"Okay, that is fair," the first man acknowledged.

The two diamond-rankers shared a confused look. They were used to the silent adoration of silver-rankers, who were honoured simply to be in their presence. That was the reaction they were getting from the third silver-ranker, an elf. She looked equal parts in awe of them and horrified at the other two. The diamond-rankers turned to her.

"What is your name, adventurer?" Allayeth asked her.

"Elseth Culie, Lady Allayeth."

"A local girl," Charist said. "Your father is known to me. Convey my regards."

"It will be his honour and mine, Lord Charist," Elseth said, bobbing her head nervously.

"What is happening here?" Allayeth asked.

"This man is called Miller, although I don't think that is his true name. He and his familiar worked a ritual using some manner of magic I have never seen before. Then the messenger arrived, dead, moments before you. Miller proceeded to drain its life force."

"I do appreciate you turning up," Miller said cheerfully. He was still draining silver-gold life force, the messenger's reserves seeming limitless, even in death.

"Should we stop him?" Charist asked his companion.

"No," Allayeth responded.

"It is unlikely that a silver-ranker can keep the messenger dead," Charist said, "but it will likely be some time before the messenger reconstitutes if his life force is drained entirely."

"Will the silver-ranker be able to hold all of that power?"

"He shouldn't be able to contain what he's taken already, yet he seems unperturbed. I imagine one of his essence abilities allows his life force reserves to expand when he drains excess."

"Yep," the man going by Miller announced. "I guess I'm no mystery at all to you lot."

They looked at him draining the power of a diamond-ranker whose seemingly instantaneous death at his feet remained wholly unexplained. The man wore a cloak that matched the starry void of the star phoenix image forming above his head.

"If the messenger is dead," Charist said, "then we are free to go after their gold-rankers."

"A lot of their gold-rankers are coming here," Allayeth pointed out. "Our presence is the only reason they haven't arrived already."

"So, what's it going to be?" Miller asked them. "Are you going to use me as bait and clean up the gold-rankers that come after me? I've been bait before, it's cool. You should probably run around, intervening where the fight's not going so well for our side, though. If you do, I'd appreciate you leaving us some gold-rankers to fend off theirs."

Allayeth looked thoughtfully at Miller but spoke to Charist.

"He's got a point. I was inclined to, as he said, use him as bait, but killing gold-rankers isn't why we're here. The priority is defending the city. Even with their diamond-ranker dead, they could still break into the bunkers."

"Very well. Miller, or whatever your name is, you'll have some questions to answer when this is done. I will redirect enough gold-rankers here to achieve parity with the incoming messenger forces, but no more than that. It is a large city and this is far from the only battleground."

"Tell me about it. I've got a pyramid with a bunch of gold-rank messengers in one room and a bunch of civilians in another. I'm one quirky neighbour and twenty-three minutes plus ads short of a hit family sitcom. Oh, I think this bloke is finally running low."

The diamond-rankers watched as the last of Mah Go Schaat's corpse dissolved into rainbow smoke. Miller finished draining the energy, the image above him now seeming completely solid. It shrank down, sinking into Miller's body.

Jason had drained a lot of life force over the last few years, including from messengers. None of it prepared him for what came out of the diamond-ranker.

"Are you alright?" Rufus asked. He was able to move closer now that the remnants of the messenger and the two diamond-rank adventurers were gone. Some of the messenger's aura remained, an echo of his formidable power, but it was fading fast.

"I'm good," Jason said, his expression wide-eyed manic.

"It's just that you look a little intense. Like you're on something that maybe you shouldn't be."

"Yeah, that checks out," Jason told him. "That guy's life force was like main-lining distilled lightning. In a good way."

- You have drained life force using [Blood Harvest].
- Health, mana and stamina have been replenished.

- You have exceeded maximum levels of life force, stamina and mana.
- Ability [Sin Eater] has temporarily increased your maximum levels for life force, stamina and mana. These maximums will decline over time.

- You have gained multiple instances of [Blood Frenzy].
- Maximum instances of [Blood Frenzy] have been reached. Additional instances will be converted into [Blood of the Immortal].
- You have gained multiple instances of [Blood of the Immortal] from [Blood Harvest].

- You have absorbed physical matter with inherent spiritual properties.
- You have accumulated sufficient spiritually active matter to enter a star phoenix state.

- Current star phoenix state availability: 1.
- Next star phoenix state readiness: 14.8%

"What was that bird thing?" Rufus asked.

"A visual representation of my ability to self-revive," Jason said. "I've got another resurrection in the chamber now. I'm just hoping I don't get crushed to death by a chunk of falling building and have to use it right away."

Jason and Rufus looked at each other, then both turned their gazes slowly upwards.

"It's fine," Rufus said with relief. "Still just a bunch of monsters. But there's something going on up there. It's hard to tell through all the monster auras."

"It's gold-rankers," Jason said. "They're all clashing in the sky already. The team is dropping down through that, so I hope they're okay."

"It's getting rough out there," Humphrey said. "Lindy, time to pull out one of your tricks."

"I'll try and clear up a path, sure," Belinda said. "Get over to the edge."

Humphrey moved to the open side of Onslow's shell and Belinda conjured a massive, heavy plate into his hands. It was as large as Onslow's shell itself and Humphrey had to brace his feet so the weight didn't tip him out. Belinda used her Pit of the Reaper ability on it and Humphrey tossed it down with all his considerable strength. If he hadn't, it wouldn't have been able to outpace the plunging shell.

The plate dropped vertically, its surface containing an aperture to a dark dimensional pit. Tentacles darted in and out, snatching anything they could reach and yanking it into the void. Monsters, messengers and adventurers alike sensed it coming and moved out of the way, clearing Onslow's shell for an unmolested descent.

This tactic worked well until they were closing in on the ground and a messenger directed monsters to swarm the shell, clamping onto it. They ignored the wind barrier that scraped at them as if they were pushing themselves into a wheat thresher. Onslow was forced to a halt and even more monsters piled on. That was when Neil used his Reaper's Redoubt power. The team were all drawn into a safe dimensional space as death energy flooded a massive area centred on their original position.

Onslow's shell and its occupants reappeared in a cleared airspace, the survivors of Neil's ability having fled. Many didn't make it, having already been afflicted with Sin from Jason's aura, making them vulnerable to necrotic damage. The shell descended once more, finding the battle on the ground as frenetic as the one in the air, if not more so.

The monsters that were still on task continued to dig into the earth of an entertainment district that had become unrecognisable. It was now little more than rubble and excavated pits, monsters digging as adventurers fought not just them but also the messengers.

Most of the silver-rank messengers that had arrived were operating at or near ground level, fighting with savage abandon. After spending much of the battle holding back, they were mad with zeal as they sought out Jason and fought anyone who impeded their search.

Jason was teleporting across the battlefield so as to spread out the messengers pursuing him. He led them around the ruins of the entertainment district and into the path of scattered adventurers. The gold-rankers of both sides remained in the air, countering each other as they had for much of the battle. This left the main battle to the silver-rankers, but the golds could not be ignored. Every so often, a gold from one side or another would fire off a powerful attack or even break loose, attacking some silvers before returning to the fight above.

Jason wasn't just fleeing as he shadow-jumped back and forth. He frequently doubled back on messengers that he'd already led into adventurers. Between their distraction and his surprise attacks, he was able to swiftly leave a slate of afflictions before most had time to react. Enhanced by Blood Frenzy, Jason's speed outstripped most silver-rankers.

- [Blood Frenzy] (boon, unholy, stacking): Bonus to [Speed] and [Recovery]. Additional instances have a cumulative effect, up to a maximum threshold.

Even with his enhanced speed, Jason was still taking hits. This was partly because he went rampant, ignoring wounds and incoming attacks in pursuit of getting as many afflictions laid on as possible. The gold-rankers were not entirely out of the fight either, with one firing a long-range assassination power that caused Jason's head to explode. He was staggered but didn't stop, still swinging his sword through the brief moment it took his head to grow back. The life force flooding his body made him, for the immediacy, all but unkillable. Not only was he flush with life force from draining Mah Go Schaat, but he also gained more as he went.

- [Blood of the Immortal] (boon, healing, unholy, stacking): On suffering damage, an instance is consumed to grant a powerful but short-lived heal-over-time effect. Additional instances can be accumulated but do not have a cumulative effect.

While he did manage to swing his sword without his head, the precision was significantly lacking. More frustrating for Jason was waiting for his mouth to grow back. He yelled out a battle cry the moment it was restored.

"'Tis but a scratch!"

"Maybe draw less attention to yourself," Rufus suggested through voice chat.

"No idea what you're talking about," Jason responded innocently.

"Someone just blew up your head!"

"No, they didn't."

"I just watched it happen."

"It was just a flesh wound."

"Yes. The flesh of your entire head."

"I've had worse."

The messengers pursued Jason around the battlefield as monsters continued their directive to dig their way down. Adventurers like Elseth Culie were working to stop them, but the messenger presence made crucial demands on their time. More often than they would like, they were forced to face messengers instead of clearing the monsters from their assault on the underground bunker.

Slowly but surely, the messengers were boxing Jason in. Had their minds not been clouded with zeal, they might have wondered how they were managing to herd someone who could teleport that freely. When Jason decided enough of them were in range, he used his Feast of Absolution power.

From across the battlefield, the life force of the messengers lit up, as Jason revoked all the afflictions that had built up on them. Even the ones he never faced had gained afflictions for each attack they made against an adventurer. Poison, disease and unholy power were drained from all of them, bruise-coloured lights of sickly green, bruise purple and ugly yellow. The afflictions flowed through the air on streams of silver-gold, matching the life force of the messengers. From above, Jason looked like an eldritch spider, draining his victims through his arcane webs.

In the place of the removed afflictions, inside Jason's enemies, he left the blue, silver and gold glow of transcendent power. It ate them from the inside, irresistible and all but unstoppable.

Jason was not the only adventurer making a good showing for himself. Rufus was on a rampage, finally triggering his zone magic that turned the sky over the battlefield dark, lighting it up with a false moon. Containing all the power Rufus had been building up since the start of the battle, it fired beams of immense power, crippling or outright killing messengers. He only managed a few shots before the power was gone, but his display roused the adventurer morale. Seeing a solid win heartened the adventurers to push back against the zealot messengers.

Seeing their forces being overpowered, the gold-rank messengers issued a directive. The raging zealots weren't doing a lot of listening, but this was an order that suited their current state just fine. From the start of the battle, the adventurers had been wary of the isolating duel powers the messengers possessed. Suddenly, each of the messengers that had them, which was most, used them all at once.

Just before they did, a gold-rank messenger had taken note of Onslow's shell. Half of Jason's team was using it as a bunker, even inviting a few glass-cannon adventurers to join them. The messenger broke free of his opponent and dropped on the shell like a hammer. It broke apart, sending adventurers scattering just as the silver-rank messengers were launching their duel powers.

Only those standing alone could be targeted, or the isolation powers failed. Humphrey and Jason were both hit, while Sophie dodged and found Belinda, causing the messenger targeting her to waste his power. Neil was grabbed by Stash, in the form of a hopping insect that pulled him out of a messenger's path.

Clive landed hard after Onslow's shell shattered. His arms wrapped around Onslow's humanoid form, whimpering from having his shell smashed apart. A silver-rank messenger found him like that and activated his challenge power, drawing them into a dimensional space. It was clearly an artificial area, consisting of a flat white circle, floating in a void.

Clive looked up, dazed, just a spear came down and skewered Onslow through the head.

"Face me, human."

Clive pushed himself to his feet with his staff, his wand having been lost somewhere in the breaking of Onslow's shell. He looked down at his dead familiar; the vulnerable humanoid form could not resist the messenger's spear.

"No familiar," the messenger sneered. "One look and I can see that you are a weak spell caster. You will never leave this place."

Clive looked up at the messenger, blank-faced, then again down at Onslow.

"Sentimental," the messenger mocked, then lunged with his spear.

Clive's staff shifted, and the spear slid along it, making the messenger slightly off-balance. The end of the staff slipped between the messenger's legs and Clive gave it a little leverage that turned the hovering charge into an ugly tumble.

Clive didn't follow up as the messenger floated to his feet, more hurt by the indignity than landing on the ground. Clive looked at him, blank-faced, took out a recording crystal and tossed it into the air.

"I need to record this," he told the messenger, his voice flat and emotionless. "It's going to be a teaching moment."

99
RIGID FLAWS

CLIVE WAS TRAPPED IN A DIMENSIONAL SPACE BY THE DUELLING POWER OF A messenger. Until one of them was dead, neither was able to leave. The space was an empty void, the only object being a massive flat disc on which Clive stood. The remains of his precious familiar, Onslow, lay at his feet.

Facing off against Clive was a spear-wielding messenger whose sneer had turned into a glare. He had lunged at Clive, only to discover the adventurer could use his staff for more than blasting force bolts.

Item: [Spell Lance of the Magister] (silver rank [growth], legendary)

The staff of an ancient sorcerer, this weapon is focused on priming enemies for a potent magical assault (weapon, staff).

- Requirements: The power to wield magical tools.
- Basic attack: Explosive disruptive-force bolt. Inflicts [Spell Impetus].
- Basic attack: Disruptive-force beam. Consumes mana. Sustaining the beam on a target periodically inflicts [Spell Impetus].
- Effect: Increase the mana consumption when casting a spell to increase the effect. Effect is further enhanced if wielding both [Spell Lance of the Magister] and [Magister's Tithe].
- Effect: Can be used as a focus for the unique ritual [Magister's Ballista]. This ritual is not possible without the staff.
- Effect: When used to strike an enemy in melee gain an instance of [Power of the War Magus].
- [Spell Impetus] (affliction, magic, stacking): All resistances are reduced. When the recipient suffers an offensive spell from someone

wielding [Spell Lance of the Magister], all instances of [Spell impetus] are consumed to increase the effect of the spell.

- [Power of the War Magus] (magic, stacking): Gain a body-hugging barrier that resists damage. When a force bolt is fired from the staff, all instances are consumed to increase damage.

Clive didn't have the matching wand, Magister's Tithe, which had fallen from his grip when the gold-rank messenger smashed apart Onslow's shell. The silver-rank messenger he now faced had trapped Clive before he could retrieve it. The messenger continued to glare at him, hefting his spear. A system window appeared, flickering on the verge of collapse.

- Party leader [Jason Asano] has had all abilities negated.
- Party has been disbanded.
- Ability [Party Interface] has ended.

The window blinked out of existence.

Humphrey stood with each foot pinning a wing as he drove the point of his sword down on the messenger's throat. The point of his stylised dragon wing sword was essentially blunt, so he had to ram it down over and over, committing decapitation by blunt object.

For most of the time Jason spent on Earth, Clive had adventured as a trio with Sophie and Humphrey. His powers were not suited to frontline combat, but without a full team to shield him, coming face-to-face with danger was inevitable. Clive's preferred solution was to pre-empt such situations with comprehensive planning, but even he acknowledged that it was impossible to be ready for everything.

Even if he had been willing to ignore this truth, Sophie and Humphrey were not. They drilled him on fighting up close and personal, where he was least comfortable. He would never choose to take the fight into melee, but he could hold his own far better than the messenger he faced had expected.

They moved around each other in a dance, the messenger's spear alternately jabbing, lunging and spinning. Clive moved through the patterns Sophie and Humphrey had drilled into him, the tips of his staff leaving trails of gold light behind them. They lingered in the air as the pair clashed, and soon the air was littered with golden streaks.

Clive's powers were far from ideal for this kind of fight, but he had a number that were strikingly effective. His Mana Shield power allowed him, as the name implied, to soak damage by draining mana from his fortunately enormous pool. It was a costly draw when under repeated attack, but the silver-rank effect at least included a mana drain field that leached it from his enemies. With only one foe on hand, however, its efficiency was not the best in a duel.

His main source of replenishment was the silver-rank effect of the Blood Magic ability. The base effect was to trade health for mana, which was the opposite of his current requirements. As of his last rank-up, though, he could turn other people's health into mana with a ranged drain attack. Every time his opponent was fool enough to give him some distance, Clive drained his mana in a bright blue stream.

The messenger quickly learned not to let Clive have any distance. Along with mana drains, Clive used each reprieve from melee to bolster himself with more spells. A few abilities from the balance and karma essences left Clive almost more trouble than he was worth to attack.

Rune Mantle inflicted random retaliatory effects, from explosive knock-back damage to strength-enervating afflictions. Mantle of Retribution was more simple and direct, applying retribution damage in response to every attack. It wasn't only defensive powers either, as any chance to cast was an opportunity for the Instant Karma spell. This was an attack spell that dealt damage to the target based on how much damage they recently inflicted themselves.

In the early stages of the fight, attacking Clive seemed pointless as he soaked all the damage and dealt more back. Even the special attacks that punched through Clive's Mana Shield were returned twice over, each one more powerfully than the original.

Ability: [Vengeance Mirror] (Karma)

- Special attack.
- Cost: Varies.
- Cooldown: Varies.
- Current rank: Silver 4 (01%).
- Effect (iron): Replicate the last spell or special attack used on you or an ally by an enemy within the last few moments. Cost and cooldown are the same as the replicated attack. You may still use this ability if the triggering effect was negated. The replicated ability functions at your rank, not the rank of the enemy that originally used it.
- Effect (bronze): You may use the replicated ability a second time.
- Effect (silver): The ability replicated has enhanced effects if used against the individual it was copied from.

Clive's close-quarters techniques were not built for extended use, however. They were designed to get him out of danger or to hold on until help arrived, neither of which was going to happen here. The messenger simply took Clive's hits and bulled through the retaliatory effects.

The messenger's powers leaned towards decent resilience and rapid healing, allowing him to eat the punishment and keep going. Clive, on the other hand, was heavily reliant on his mana pool. While it was far larger than a normal adventurer, it could hold up only so long when his Mana Shield was under constant barrage.

The main factor swinging the fight away from Clive's favour, however, was that the messenger was starting to read Clive's patterns. Clive may have been heavily drilled by Sophie and Humphrey, but even highly effective patterns were no match for experience, and many of Clive's patterns were ineffective, inefficient and seemed to make little sense.

The messenger was battered but healing fast, while Clive was increasingly just battered. More and more attacks were punching through his barrier as his mana ebbed, making his shield weaker. The messenger recognized that his enemy could no longer afford to copy his attacks and returned to throwing out powerful special attacks, his spear glowing and vibrating with power. Sensing his impending victory, the messenger started to gloat.

"You fight well for a spellcaster, human, but your skills are shallow. You cannot hide behind your magic shell forever."

Clive remained silent, just as he had since tossing out the recording crystal. If the messenger wanted to gloat, that was fine. All the more pride to strip away, and better that than wonder why Clive's fighting technique had so many fixed patterns and rigid flaws. The two continued to dance through air now thick with the golden lines still being left behind by Clive's staff.

The messenger had realised the floating, glowing lines were harmless and that Clive was trying to use them to bait him onto Rune Traps. The messenger was too attentive, however, and ignored the golden lights as he watched carefully for the traps. He even remembered where the traps were after they vanished, not triggering any of them.

Sensing that the spellcaster's exhaustion was bringing the battle to its climax, the messenger moved to finish it in one glorious strike. A powerful beat of his wings threw him high into the air. The spellcaster took the chance to shoot a force blast from his impressive staff, boosted by consuming the charges it had built up from every melee strike landed throughout the duel. The messenger quickly folded his wings in front of him, absorbing much of the damage, but the heavy impact still sent him tumbling back, feathers scattering from pummelled wings.

It was not enough. All it accomplished was making the messenger even more determined to finish the spellcaster with his ultimate attack. He glared down at the man, who had moved into the centre of the glowing lines that marked the progress of the battle. Glowing lines, the messenger realised, that looked very different when viewed from above.

At ground level, the lines were nothing but random shapes, left behind by Clive's staff as it moved. From above, viewed as a flat plane instead of in three dimensions, it looked suspiciously like a ritual circle. Suddenly, he remembered all the moments of strange, impractical movement the spellcaster had gone through in the battle. He had put it down to inexperience and adhering too closely to fixed forms, and he suspected that truly was the case.

Somehow, the spellcaster had managed to do something else as well.

He would have needed to remember every required nuance, adding to the ritual diagram opportunistically as the fight allowed. The kind of mind that could keep all that together was staggering, and the messenger hoped that the spellcaster had made a mistake in the process. He almost certainly had. Getting it perfect should be near impossible, yet the messenger was certain, deep in his gut, that there weren't any mistakes.

The messenger met the man's eyes. The spellcaster's expression had been blank throughout the battle, but now it was not. The messenger's blood turned cold on seeing the gleeful malevolence on the spellcaster's face as he held up his staff and chanted a ritual trigger.

"Let loose wrath's ascension: Magister's Ballista."

The messenger initiated his ultimate attack power. It didn't, strictly speaking, have a name, but he thought of it as Descent of the King. He did not tell anyone about the name. The power launched him towards the ground, but surprise had cost him. The spellcaster began his short chant as the messenger was startled by the revelation of the ritual, hesitation costing him in the critical moment. His plunging attack was gathering what he thought of as unstoppable momentum when a force spear shot up and stopped it.

The spear had shot from the end of the spellcaster's staff, and it did not just stop the messenger but sent him tumbling up in the other direction. The momentum of his attack was easily overwhelmed, and the spear was far from done. It turned around and then shot into the messenger again. Over and over it landed, never giving the messenger a chance to recover as it grew weaker and weaker. He was bloodied and beaten by attack after attack, juggled helplessly in the air. The spear impaled a wing on one pass and half-blinded him on another. He was too disoriented to see the man on the ground directing the spear, waving his arm like a conductor.

Clive didn't stop the spear from juggling the messenger until the magic of the ritual was expended, even though he was sure the messenger was long dead. What he did do was have the recording crystal zoom in as the messenger went from glorious warrior to avian roadkill. Clive felt the dimensional space dissolving around him and he released the magic of Onslow's vessel. Normally, that would return the familiar to a tattoo state on Clive's chest, but the dead vessel was empty now. Onslow's spirit would not return until Clive summoned a fresh vessel, the old one dissolving into rainbow smoke. Clive didn't even remove himself from the stench of it.

"I'll bring you back to me, little buddy," he whispered.

Many other adventurers had been caught up in the wave of messenger isolation attacks, some coming out on top and some coming out dead. Humphrey had escaped fairly quickly, having taken his messenger apart. He and the rest of the team continued to fight messengers and monsters as they waited for Jason and Clive to escape.

Jason's isolation was a type that others could see but not interfere with, those making the attempt finding themselves damaged and tossed away by a barrier surrounding each combatant. They could see Jason and his opponent, however, and were not especially worried. The mix of indignation and frustration on his opponent's face told them that Jason was doing what Jason did.

The one they worried about was Clive. Not only was he one of their weaker individual combatants, but they couldn't see what was happening. He had vanished into a dimensional space and they dreaded seeing a messenger reappear with his corpse. Instead, Belinda was startled as Clive reappeared right in front of her, battered but alive. Also, alone.

"Nice one," she said nodding. "What happened to the messenger? You don't have a looting power; shouldn't there be a corpse?"

Clive shoved her backwards and a wet mass of flesh and feathers fell from above, spraying silver-gold blood when it crashed between them with a juicy splat.

100

DOUBT, FEAR AND HESITATION

A MESSENGER SLAMMED INTO JASON AND THEY BOTH WENT TUMBLING TO THE ground. Similar attacks had struck Humphrey, Clive and other adventurers around the battlefield. Jason and the messenger rolled away from one another and he felt some manner of power settle over him. His magical buffs vanished. His conjured items, cloak and robe, crumbled into dust. His aura was fully restricted, but not exactly suppressed. It felt more like there was an invisible cloud surrounding his entire body, preventing him from projecting any aura through it. That cloud felt familiar, like the boundary of a soul, meaning it was most likely impregnable.

A system window appeared, flickering like a TV with a bad signal.

- All magical effects have been negated. This does not trigger any secondary effects.
- All conjured items have been eliminated. This does not trigger any secondary effects.
- All magical items have had their abilities suppressed. This does not trigger any secondary effects.
- None of your familiars can manifest. All existing familiars have been unmanifested and passive familiar abilities have been disabled.
- All magical abilities have been suppressed. This does not trigger any secondary effects.

Jason barely had time to read it before the window sputtered and blinked out entirely. He pushed himself to his feet, watching the messenger do the same. That was something he'd never seen before, as messengers always floated to their feet using their auras. Yet, here was one who pushed herself up with her hands and stood with her feet on the ground instead of floating over it.

Jason noted that her appearance also diverged from the standard for many messengers. They frequently favoured diaphanous materials with little practical or protective value, more concerned with their image as beings of power and glory. This messenger looked more like an adventurer, with practical leather armour and a pair of long-handled axes. Her elbow-length leather gauntlets had reinforced knuckles and serrated blades running up the outside of her forearms. This matched the blades of her axes, the edges also serrated. They very much looked like the intention was to maximise not damage, but fear and pain, making shallow tears in flesh rather than deep cuts.

Her gear was incongruous with her facial features. She was beautiful, as all messengers were, but it was not the sharp beauty of a sword. Her face was cute, sweet and soft, her dark hair cropped into a short and practical pixie cut. Standing at more than seven feet tall did oddly little to change the impression. She looked, to Jason's eyes, maybe sixteen or seventeen, although he knew she was likely much older.

"How old are you?" he asked.

"By the reckoning of this world, it is my eighteenth year. I will be young to have such glory as will come to me today."

Jason sighed.

"This one's going to feel bad," he muttered to himself.

At that moment, Sophie and Rufus attacked her from each side in a pincer strike. Both were blocked by an energy barrier that froze them in place for a moment before hurling them both away.

The messenger looked at them with a scoffing laugh before turning back to Jason.

"I am Tera Jun Casta," she announced proudly, "and it is your ill fortune to meet me. I was not the one chosen to test you, Jason Asano, but I will be the one to kill you. It is I that will wipe clean the stain of your heresy and reap the glory that comes of claiming your head."

"Okay," Jason said with the resignation of an office worker being handed a fresh stack of paperwork. "Good luck with that."

He was now garbed in boxer shorts, boots and a potion belt with his scabbard hanging from it. His sword dangled loosely in his hand and the necklace with his magical amulet and shrunken cloud flask hung from his neck.

"You may be arrogant now, Asano, but—"

"If I'm being entirely honest," he interrupted her, "I was pretty arrogant before now as well. My surname is Asano and my personal name is Jason, and I have a slight flaw in my character."

"You will not be so glib once you realise the situation you are in!" she declared in a hurried half-yell, as if to preclude his butting-in again.

"You clearly don't realise who you're dealing with," he told her. "Glib is kind of my thing. And I understand the situation perfectly well."

"Is that so? You are in for a rude surprise, Asano."

"I love surprises. And rudeness, for that matter. What have you got for me?"

She scowled. "You are no doubt confused as to what has happened to your powers."

"Nope. You used an ability that encapsulated us each in some kind of barrier that seems to hug our bodies. My guess is that the barrier is made from your soul, meaning that nothing can affect us except each other. We'd probably make good battering rams, if what happened to my friends is anything to go by. We're impervious to outside harm unless they bury us alive or something. I imagine that both our power sets are fully suppressed and that we'll stay sealed away until one of us is dead. Maybe there's a secondary release mechanism where, after a certain time, either we both get released or both get killed."

The messenger's eyes went wide.

"How can you possibly know that?"

"It's called context clues. I think you need to get out and see the cosmos a bit. Does inter-dimensional conquest have a gap-year program? Have you ever heard of Rumspringa?"

"I don't understand your foolish prattle. Speak plainly."

"You messengers travel between universes, right?"

"That is within our power."

"You should find a quiet one and try a little self-discovery. Have you read *Eat, Pray, Love*? You could do a liberal arts degree. You need to expand your horizons is what I'm saying."

"I see what you are doing. Babbling to mask your fear."

"Actually, I'm stalling while I check if I can do anything about this barrier with my aura. No luck, sadly; your soul has us locked down tight."

"You will be free when I wrench your head from your body."

"Try and get the spine to come with it if you can. Hold it up and let it dangle for a moment. If I've got to go, there are worse ways than a classic fatality. I don't suppose you have ice powers by any chance?"

Elseth Culie, the elven affliction specialist, was doing her best to slow down the fresh wave of monsters digging at the bunker underneath the ruined entertainment district. With the messengers having given up their safe but conservative strategy, they were suffering more losses, but their summoned minions were freer to complete their task.

Rufus and Sophie had taken on the role of shielding Elseth as she worked, her previous guardians scattered or occupied fighting messengers. In between spells, Elseth looked over at where John Miller and a messenger were shrouded in a power that had deflected both Sophie's and Rufus' attempts to intervene.

"Most of the messengers and adventurers started fighting right away," Elseth pointed out. "What do you think they're talking about? And why is he in his underpants?"

"The answer to almost any question you have about Jason," Rufus told her, "is that it's better if you don't know."

"He's probably telling her that something is kind of his thing," Sophie added, eyes scanning the sky above them for threats.

"What is his thing?" Elseth asked.

"Melodrama," Rufus said. "And I hear the messengers are just as bad. Their fight may come down to who can best capture a sense of mournful longing as they stare off into the middle distance."

"Yeah, like you've never done any brooding," Sophie told him.

Tera Jun Casta tired of Jason's words and lunged to the attack. He immediately recognised that she seemed comfortable fighting with her abilities suppressed, which was hardly a surprise given the nature of her duelling power. Her style was practised but orthodox, for the most part. She didn't try anything elaborate, simply trying to make her serrated axes meet flesh as efficiently as possible.

The wild card was her wings, which she used to supplement her clean, efficient axe work. Her feathers were a dark red-brown, like her hair, with a tough, leathery texture. The wings held up well to slashes from Jason's sword as she made liberal use of them. Whether as a weapon to batter him, an obstacle to lead him or a shield to block him, she made the most of the advantages they offered.

While she used the wings effectively, it was not a tactic that Jason found overwhelming. He had fought bizarre creatures by the thousands in six years of adventuring, and it had been a long time since he considered a humanoid, even a tall one with wings, as exotic.

Without his powers, Jason was forced to become more aggressive. This was where sparring with Sophie, Rufus and Humphrey paid off, as they were all aggressive in different ways. His model for this was Sophie, as while their styles had diverged over time, they retained the same root in the Way of the Reaper.

Rufus had always been ruthless about Jason training for the worst-case scenarios, but he had trouble getting him to be more straightforward. Jason always got caught up in tricky strategies and roundabout tactics, which he infused into every combat scenario.

Jason had full access to the Way of the Reaper's techniques, courtesy of the largest skill books he had ever seen. The reality was, however, that there were only so many that Jason had mastered. While he had made the techniques he used the most his own, the majority he could use, but with a rote-learning comprehension that anyone truly skilled would look down on.

Jason switched up his style frequently to keep the messenger on edge, not knowing how he would face her next. One moment, he was fighting at the limits of her reach, and the next, dashing in past the long hafts of her axes. A backflip kick to the chin led into a more acrobatic style, leading her on a merry dance through the levelled buildings of the entertainment district.

At first, it worked. The impetuousness of youth quickly had her frustrated and making mistakes, although Jason failed to capitalise. The weakness of his overelaborate approach meant that he wasn't landing the kind of heavy, repeated hits required to take down a silver-ranker. They were extremely tough and healed fast, making a victory without powers to amplify damage hard to achieve.

Jason's failure to do significant damage turned the balance of the fight against him. While Tera was young, she had been fighting her entire life, giving her triple Jason's combat experience, at least in years. Once her mind settled, she realised his flaws and that she did not share them. Her vicious weapons and straightforward style were built around winning this kind of fight.

Jason realised that he needed to stop getting caught up in flights of fancy about how to fight. Time and again, Rufus had told him that there were times when all the tricks in the world didn't matter. Sometimes it was about the willingness to be brutal and the resolve to endure brutality. Some fights couldn't be danced around or subverted. Sometimes you had to stand up, take the hits and hit back harder.

When he finally accepted this, the tenor of the fight changed. Jason faced off against Tera inside what he guessed had once been a tavern. It seemed like it had been an open space, but too little remained to tell. What was left of the walls wasn't even as tall as he was, barring a chimney that threatened to crumble at any moment. Outside, what had once been a street was now a pit dug by monsters trying to drill into the bunker below.

Jason and Tera started wailing on each other with their weapons. Tera's serrated axes and gauntlet blades were brutal and flesh-tearing, while Jason's was refined and elegant. The sword had its powers suppressed, leaving the runes running down the black blade in their basic white. Even so, it remained a masterful weapon of near-limitless potential, forged by Gary with the assistance of his diamond-rank mentor. It was a sword whose construction was guided by the power of Jason's soul flowing through it, making for the ideal melding of wielder and weapon.

The duel had become simple and savage, painting both combatants in their own and each other's blood. Tera's twin axes were suited to this kind of fight and had torn ragged gashes in Jason's flesh. In their brutal stand-up fight, she had taken the early advantage because of her weapons, but she felt that start to shift. Her axes had taken a beating from Jason's sword, with heavy nicks and even losing some of the edge serrations.

As the fight was a marathon, rather than a sprint, she was forced to be less aggressive with her weapons. Jason's sword, on the other hand, was marred only by blood. Whether clashing blade to blade, slicing through her tough armour or missing and striking a wall, nothing left so much as a scratch on the blade. This allowed Jason to continue being as aggressive as he liked.

Even though she had to be mindful of her weapons, Tera continued the exchange of relentless attacks. She and Jason both grew more savage, striving to inflict damage faster than natural silver-rank healing could undo it. Like lumberjacks hand-sawing a tree, they fell into a rhythm of attack and counter-attack until they were both torn and ragged.

Tera's armour was all but ribbons, the skin beneath it not much better. Jason was, if anything, worse for not having armour in the first place. The love hearts on his boxer shorts were now invisible, the white cloth soaked entirely red.

An unspoken agreement formed between the pair: the one with the will to keep

standing and take it the longest would be the one to survive. This was only a realisation for Jason, as Tera had always known things would come to this. Jason could
see the manic glee in his opponent's expression as the duel reached this stage. It
was her power that had put them here, after all, and this was the kind of fighting
she knew.

For her part, Tera was surprised that Jason had lasted this long. His foolish
early strategy was something she had seen before, and each time her enemy had
crumbled on realising it would utterly fail. Every trickster she had fought lacked
the resolve for this kind of fight. But not only did this adventurer engage fully in
the ugly slugfest, but he was grinning like a snake after an egg rolled into its lair.

Tera was starting to feel an uncharacteristic sensation she realised, after a
moment, was worry. It was only a tiny amount; this was her kind of fight and it
was playing out just the way it should. Asano's tricky fighting had been annoying,
but he finally realised that without a way to finish the job, all his fancy dancing
meant nothing. The only way to win was to stand there and take more punishment
than the enemy.

Tera loved her isolation power. It stripped away all the tricks and all the magic,
leaving combat in its purest form. Victory wasn't about weapons or skill unless
one person massively outclassed the other. It was about resolve. The ability to take
the hits unflinchingly, not letting it affect hitting the enemy back.

This was why Tera chose not the weapons that inflicted the most harm, but
those that instilled the most fear. In every duel Tera had initiated with her power,
the fight had come down to crudely hammering each other until her enemy lost
their nerve. As the damage built up, they realised that to keep fighting it would
only get worse and worse. That was when the fear crept in. Then there was the
pain. The mind could block out pain, she had learned, but the ragged wounds left
by her serrated axes were ugly. They *looked* painful, which helped force the idea
of pain into the mind.

Once fear and pain crept in, the fight was all but over. They would hesitate,
just a little, not even realising they were doing it at first. But it was enough to sap
their strength and make them shrink back, just enough to make a difference. That
was when she dominated. Every moment made it worse until they finally
collapsed, often literally. More than a few opponents had knelt and waited as she
took their heads, spirits broken.

But it had been too long. None of the signs were there. Asano was looking
more like a market-stall meat skewer now, but he kept coming at her harder than
ever. His eyes sparkled with inhuman light from a face caked in blood. There was
no fear of death, no grimacing through the pain.

Tera had fought fear, pain and death for her entire life, but now she faced a
man who had walked beside them until they were boon companions. Looking into
his eyes, Tera realised that the summoned creatures her kind had brought with
them were not monsters. *This* was a monster.

With that revelation, the doubt, fear and hesitation finally arrived. But to her
horror, they came from within her, not him, her mind and body betraying her.
They saw what she had brought out in this man and knew that he would never
stop. She was somehow certain, against all sense and reason, that even killing him

wouldn't do it. She might as well have duelled the sky, for all her axes could cut it down.

Tera refused to let fear rule her. After using her power so many times, she had now found an opponent that would not fall in the kind of fight she had engineered. Instead, she had to change it. She had to gamble on a decisive move before her growing fear left her paralysed.

Behind her opponent, a deep pit lay where there had once been a road. Monsters had dug it as they strove to breach the underground bunker, and were probably down there, digging still. It would be a tight space where long weapons would be useless and her gauntlet spikes would be the weapon of choice. Dropping her axes, she launched herself into a crash tackle.

Her wings lacked the magic to fly, but one heavy beat from them was enough to throw her forward like a battering ram. Jason's sword went tumbling from his hand as they barrelled over the edge of the pit to plummet down. When they reached the bottom, they crashed hard into a summoned monster.

The monster was a cube with an arm emerging from each side and an eye in the palm of each hand. Beams from those eyes had been drilling through a metal plate it had dug up when Tera and Asano landed on it hard. To Tera's surprise, the impact and their combined weight finished the job, breaching the bunker and dropping them all inside.

101

NO

THE BUNKER BENEATH THE ENTERTAINMENT DISTRICT WAS SET UP AS A SERIES OF dormitories, punctuated by various service rooms. As the occupants were primarily not essence users, there was a need for food preparation and toilet facilities for thousands. Those facilities, in turn, required logistics and utility infrastructure to service them.

Jason, Tera Jun Casta and a confused summoned monster crashed through the ceiling and into a warehouse filled with massive crates and barrels. They hit a rack hard on their way down, sending several crates tumbling to the floor. The crates broke open and spewed out compressed rations, more than the crates should have been able to hold. Cheap but mediocre dimensional magic had been used to increase storage space, but that magic broke along with the crates, depositing the contents onto the floor.

Jason and Tera were both bloodied, having finally fought hard enough to overcome each other's inherent toughness and rapid healing. Jason's sword was back outside; it had been dropped when Tera rammed them both into the pit. She had already dropped her axes and lost one of her gauntlets during their descent. The other had lost one of its serrated arm blades, but it was now the only weapon that either of them had.

Alarms blared at their intrusion and, as they got to their feet, a pair of silver-rank adventurers burst through the warehouse doors, a squad of bronze-rankers behind them. One of the silver-rankers dove at Tera and was hurled into the wall hard enough to leave cracks for his trouble. The other fired a stream of frigid wind, laden with icicles at Jason. Jason turned to look at the man as the beam stopped dead around arm's length away.

"I know I'm in rough condition," Jason understated, "but of the three intruders, one has wings and another is a monster. You can't figure out which one is the adventurer?"

Tera looked at Jason and then at the door, making her choice and bolting for it, past the adventurer picking himself up off the floor. The bronze-rankers split like bowling pins as she barrelled through, bouncing off the barrier that shielded her from everything but Jason.

"Deal with the monster, then seal and barricade the room," Jason commanded the silver-ranker. "I'll handle her."

Jason had no aura to back up his words, yet the man who had just attacked him found himself moving to obey. There was something in Jason's voice that dared him to disobey, and he was not taking that dare. He was not an expert fighter, which was why he'd been assigned to the bunker. He wouldn't be missed in the battle above, and if the bunker was breached, it was unlikely to matter how strong the on-station defenders were.

Jason swiftly pursued Tera, following a trail of silver-gold blood. He moved through a short series of utility corridors until he found her shoving open a pair of double doors. They looked heavy and were doubtless magically reinforced, but the people behind them had failed to close them in time. She shoved the unlatched doors wide, scattering the people on the other side before dashing inside.

Jason pursued her into a massive dormitory that held hundreds of people. Rows of bunks filled the far end while closer to the door, cafeteria-style tables were lined with people. Tera glanced back at Jason and he saw the fire in her eyes had dimmed. She was no longer willing to face him, even if she did have the only weapon.

He would have let her live if he could, but she had taken that option from him. He didn't know whether her power would release or slay them if it expired before one of them killed the other. He wouldn't trust her word on it, and he wasn't willing to wait when monsters would soon be pouring into the shelter through the hole.

He watched Tera look from him to the people who were scrambling to move away from them, climbing over tables and each other to head for the bunk end of the massive room. He realised that she wasn't seeing people fleeing for their lives; she was seeing hostages. They were her path to evening the odds, making up for her lost confidence.

She would be able to get to the closest people before he could get to her, and they both knew it. Even if he did reach her first, the fight would come with collateral damage, and quite likely a lot of it. The normal-rank civilians would most likely be killed just from impacting the barriers around her and Jason. If she forced the fight amongst them, they would both be slaughtering the people he was there to protect. The room was full of hostages.

When she moved in their direction, Jason knew that there was little point in chasing. All he could do was try and talk her down, but the idea of civilian casualties he was helpless to stop clouded his mind. Memories of people dying in Broken Hill and Makassar because he wasn't strong enough flashed through his mind.

"Don't. You." **DARE.**

He didn't even speak the last word. It vibrated through the air on a wave of aura and Tera stopped dead, jolted in shock. She stared at Jason, who was equally surprised. What he just did shouldn't have been possible with his power sealed by the soul barrier still around him.

They stared at each other as Jason's mind raced through the possible explanations, rejecting all but one. His astral realm wasn't just a place he could go, a place that belonged to him. It *was* him; it was his soul. And just like a messenger, his soul was his body. Her challenge power might suppress his essence abilities and even his aura, but it could not suppress his entire astral realm. That power was far too great, and in his fury, he had tapped into it, shucking off the suppression on his aura for a brief moment. Now he knew that was possible, the situation had reversed. He just had to figure out what he'd done and how to do it again.

Jason examined the sensations shooting through him, but it was hard to pick out any unusual sensations through all the damage. He managed to pick out an odd tremulation, his body quivering ever so slightly in reaction to the power that had just surged through it. It was a similar sensation to overcharging his portal ability with energy from his astral gate.

"How?" Tera asked in breathless disbelief, still shaken by Jason's use of his aura.

For once, Jason did not respond with a pithy line. He was concentrating on how he could actively tap into that power, replicating what his rage had done unconsciously. He knew he couldn't call up a portal to his astral realm to draw power through. He had tried that while stalling for time with banter at the beginning of the fight. But he was his astral realm. Did he even need a conduit? Could he *be* the portal? Not to travel through, but to tap into his full reserve of power.

He saw the shock fading from Tera's face and she was eyeing the civilians again. They had managed to flee further down the room while Jason and Tera stared at each other, but it wouldn't stop them from getting caught up in it if the fight continued. He didn't have time for careful experimentation, to see if he could do the thing that popped into his mind without harming himself. That was nothing new. Concentrating on the feeling he had when he'd spoken out in anger, he reached inside to draw out power in a way unlike any he had attempted before.

Tera's attention was arrested again as she felt Jason's aura brush against her, faint but unmistakable. She told herself it wasn't possible, despite it being unmistakable. She felt his aura surge again, just like when it had flooded the city. His power and his rage towered over her, diminishing everything she was and belittling her ambitions. Just as it had the first time she felt his aura, fury rose within her to fight back.

From the day she was brought into being and her training began, Tera had been told that she was the pinnacle of creation: a living embodiment of the will of the cosmos. That nothing, save for her own kind, was her equal. She was power and glory manifest, at the beginning of a path that would lead her to stand at the top, even amongst the messengers. To become an astral king. The path was known, but it was rigid and hard. Only a messenger could walk it.

In eighteen years, not a single day went by where she doubted her path for a moment. She met every challenge and accomplished every feat presented to her. She would reach gold and then diamond, and then become the pinnacle of her kind that, in turn, was the pinnacle of all kinds.

Then came Asano. He was no messenger, yet everything that made her special, she could feel within him. The body-spirit gestalt. The aura that could grasp physical reality, even stronger than her own. Most of all, he wasn't struggling to climb the tower to astral monarchy; he was inside it, walking up easy stairs at his leisure. He was incomplete, but unmistakably an astral king.

It was perversion. Heresy. The only path to astral king should be a messenger transcending diamond rank. This man made a lie of everything she knew. Everything she had been told, every single day of her life. Most of all, it made her feel small. Lesser. How could she be the pinnacle of creation with this abomination roaming the cosmos, making a mockery of who and what she was? And it wasn't just an astral king either. She didn't recognise exactly the other elements of his aura, but at the very least, she felt the echo of divinity. Was he on a path that went beyond even astral king? If such a person could exist, a supremacy that she could never reach, then not only was she not superior, but she never could be. If so, then what meaning was there in her own experience?

The fear and doubt that had plagued her were gone. She did not need hostages or weapons. All she needed was Asano's ruined corpse beneath her feet, dissolving into rainbow smoke. His existence must come to an end. She was poised to launch herself at him when her entire universe became pain.

Jason had known from the start that this fight would be bad. He had, for all intents, been pushed into a death match with a teenager, born and raised in a cult. Like any cult, the doctrine seemed transparently foolish from the outside, the ideology crumbling at the first sign of critical thought. Their superiority obsession was clearly nonsensical, falling apart when contrasted with almost any information not sourced from their own insular community.

But to those born and raised in a cult, or who had found something in it that filled a deep need, the incongruities didn't matter. They had been primed from the beginning to ignore the lies of outsiders, however compelling they might seem. But when they were forced to confront those problems, they did not rationally accept what the outsiders saw as logical, self-evident conclusions. They got angry and they got violent.

Tera's power made the fight kill or be killed. One of them would die; there was no room for mercy. But, like anyone, Jason did not like being forced into corners where every choice was bad. He had become so tired as he kept falling short on Earth, stuck between bad and worse decisions. He had been faced with one hard choice after another as the people that should have been helping stood in his way.

The Network betrayed him over and again, but he kept working with them because that was what it took. He failed the living as the victims piled high in Makassar, then had to destroy what was left when the bodies were turned into unliving monstrosities. He had to make deals with the very enemies behind those previous events, all the while planning to turn on them. In doing so, he became that which he hated most: a betrayer of trust.

He was improved from what he had become at that time. Not recovered, not entirely; there was no going back to what he was before, but he was able to live with himself again. Mended enough that he could put the hard choices of the past behind him, even if they would always be there. But now, once again, he was faced with a bleak proposition: kill a woman—a girl—that he saw as a victim. It wasn't even really an option, as the alternative was to die.

No.

The refusal was a declaration, not just to himself but to the universe. He wasn't going to let it happen. Yes, this girl was an enemy. Yes, she had probably killed countless innocent people. Yes, many were more worthy of being saved than she was. But here and now, he was done. The world had bent him to the point of breaking and it was trying to bend him some more. It wanted him to kill this girl, but he was going to give her mercy.

This time, the world was going to bend.

Jason's spiritual battle against the Builder he remembered not with his mind, but with his soul. His body had not been his own and it had been a spiritual war, in any case. One that a mind seated in the physical matter of a brain was inherently incapable of comprehending. But Jason was not the same man that warred with the Builder over his soul at iron rank. He didn't even have a brain anymore, and his soul was not just a spiritual entity lurking behind his body. His soul and his body were one.

Jason still didn't remember much of what happened, like hearing echoes from the other end of a long tunnel. The memories were emotion more than anything; fear, resolve. A seemingly limitless will that screamed for him to capitulate with the force of a typhoon. Colin, joining him in the last stand for his soul. Defiance.

The one thing he had come to fully remember was a sensation. The Builder had not been able to harm his soul, but he could inflict a pain that transcended anything a physical body could experience. Jason's own spiritual attack was a paltry echo of that, something he had learned from that scathing sensation, barely remembered as it was.

The Builder had scoured Jason's soul, trying to force him to open it up and accept his oppressor. Jason had not. And now he fully remembered that pain, exactly what the Builder had done to him, and how. He had resolved to never use it. It was not something to inflict even on an enemy. He had thus far drawn the line at far less savage soul attacks, even if sometimes he had needed a friend to help him not cross the line.

But that was not enough for what he needed to do now. He had to become like the Builder and inflict a suffering he had promised himself he never would. He wondered what Shade would say, but he only had himself in that moment. His own judgement that had failed him in the past. Jason could feel his familiars inside, locked away and unable to advise him as he crossed a line he had resolved not to.

He could only tell himself that while he was replicating the Builder's actions, it was not with the Builder's intentions. That this was the only path to mercy. Was it a justification? He knew that, whatever he told himself, he had a hunger for power and control. The god Dominion had seen it from the beginning.

In the end, all he could do was the best he could with what he had. And what he had was a girl whose soul had trapped them both and would not let go until one of them was dead. He was certain that if she had the power to end it, she would have. So he had to reach inside her soul and end it for her. But first, she had to let him in.

The only way he could shut off her power was to force his way into her soul and do it himself. He couldn't break in, any more than the Builder could with him. She had to let him, and there was no way she trusted him enough to allow that, whatever the circumstances. Sometimes, even when the mind said yes, the soul said no.

He would have to do what the Builder did to him. Make her suffer, as he had, until she capitulated. *If* she capitulated. And even then, he couldn't be sure it would work. He had never rummaged around someone else's soul.

He could just kill her. He knew what he was about to do and that, in the face of such miserable suffering, killing could be seen as a mercy in itself. But Jason wouldn't allow it. Fate had put this girl in his path and decreed that one of them would die. Fate could go fuck itself.

Transcendent light of blue, silver and gold shone through Jason's skin as he lit up like a beacon. He drew on the power of his astral realm, his body shaking as he turned himself into something like a portal that only his power could pass through. It clashed with Tera's soul, the very thing that bound him. This meant he didn't need to push through the suppression to attack it; it was right there waiting for him.

Tera fell but didn't hit the ground, instead floating up. Her spine arched and her wings, head and limbs were all yanked in the direction of the ground as if something was holding them while brutally pushing into her back. Her mouth opened in the image of a scream, but at first, none came. Then there was a sonorous hum, building with every passing second, slowly rising in pitch as it grew louder.

Emresh Vohl was huddled with the civilians, despite his silver rank. The adventurers had tried to recruit him in case of something breaking into the bunker, but he had refused them to their derision. But he was no adventurer, having ranked up on cores. He'd never fought anything more dangerous than a stable hand a rank lower than he was.

His choice had been validated when the ragged angel had barged into the room, battered and bleeding. The bronze-rankers trying to close the door on her had been thrown back as she shoved it open and stormed in, dripping silver-gold blood.

He knew that she was one of the messengers that people had been talking about, not an angel from the old elvish stories his mother told him as a child. But even as injured as she was, she still looked like one. There was something glorious about her, even under the blood, the wounds and the tattered armour.

The man that followed her was no such thing. He was all but naked, the blood painting his body covering him more than his red-stained under shorts. He was in even worse condition, his body covered in savage lacerations.

Emresh had not wasted time using his silver-rank physicality to rush past others, not caring if a few children or old people were knocked aside. But he kept his gaze on the two figures, and he did not like the way the messenger looked at them. He'd seen that look on his father many times; it was the look of a man who saw assets and not people. It was not an outlook he'd ever had a problem with until he was the asset.

The two intruders had a short exchange, him warning her in a voice that rang like a gong. She looked at him in shock and he seemed equally surprised. For a long moment, they just stared at one another. Then he started to glow and she was dragged into the air by an unseen force, her arms, legs and wings pulled downwards as if trying to drag her back.

The room was eerily quiet, civilians and bronze-rank adventurers equally huddled in silence as they looked on. Then came a base hum, slowly growing louder and higher until people started to moan and Emresh felt a pricking in his ears and eyes. A child cried as the rising pitch of the hum left blood trickling from her ear, more joining her as blood started seeping from the eyes, noses and ears of the young and the elderly. Then an aura washed over them, domineering yet protective, the authority of a benevolent dictator.

The sound stopped affecting the civilians, who looked on at the suffering angel and glowing man who was also floating into the air. Dark red leather appeared on his body, draping him in a robe. It soaked away the blood left on his exposed hands and face. When his face cleared, Emresh's blood ran cold.

Silver-rankers had excellent memories. Emresh knew that face, even if the dark brown eyes were now an alien blue-orange. He had last seen it on the floor of a tavern, shielded by the man's arms as Emresh and his boys kicked the man over and over.

Things started clicking into place. The mysterious person who had severely damaged his father's business interests, for some unknown slight. The way the man had taunted Emresh, all but asking for a beating. Emresh had gone to the tavern looking to beat someone and he now realised the man had offered himself up because he could take it.

He watched as the man's face vanished into a dark hood as a cloak that was not fabric but a living void manifested around him. He could just make out the silhouette of the man's sharp chin, beneath the glowing eyes.

Essence users rarely exhibited the base physiological functions of a normal body. They hardly ever blushed, hardly ever cried and never went to the toilet. Especially by silver rank, only extremes of emotion could make their magical bodies replicate the base nature they had left behind. This left Emresh confused at the warm trickle he felt in his pants.

The most infinitesimal portion of power the Builder could exert would still be enough to annihilate a universe. Jason couldn't comprehend power on that scale, let alone match it. Yet, even at his power level, his facsimile of the Builder's assault on his soul was a horrifying thing to do to a person. Jason himself knew this better than anyone, and as he flayed Tera's soul, he felt an intense revulsion he had to push through to keep going.

It was the only potential path out that he saw leading anywhere but to her death, but he wondered again if death was not the greater mercy. He knew what the treatment he was giving her would do. It had taken him months and some of the best experts in the world to recover. He doubted the messengers would give her the same care that he had received.

He kept pouring on the pain, willing her to surrender. The faster she let him in, the quicker the pain would end, and if she didn't surrender at all, he would have to kill her anyway. Then, instead of mercy, he had taken her from death to excruciatingly miserable death. He had to steel his resolve over and over to continue, redoubling his efforts as his will squeezed her soul like a ball in his fist.

Jason didn't have a star seed, but he wasn't looking to take her over once he was allowed into her soul. All he needed was a connection, and in the course of his torturing her, he realised that it was already there. He could feel a link, not between Jason Asano and Tera Jun Casta but between astral king and messenger. He could tell immediately that it had always been there, waiting. It was strange and made him feel uncomfortable. It was almost like messengers were built to be controlled.

Jason poured his will into that connection, every ounce of soul strength he could muster assaulting her anew. Finally, he felt the first, tiny tremble in her will to resist. Whatever that connection was, it left her hard-wired to obey, so long as he could activate it. That she was able to resist the inherent urge to surrender that came through it deeply impressed Jason, even if he wished she didn't. He desperately wanted to stop, although not near as much as she did, he knew.

He had to finish it. He had to push through, and make her give up. He floated over to her, his cloak drifting loosely around him. He had pushed away the power of her soul enough that he could use at least some of his powers. He reached out a hand, palm down in the space where her torso was arched up.

Yield. Your. Soul.

Her body trembled, then shook. Then she fell to the ground.

102

A FIGHT TO THE PAIN

OUTSIDE OF THE BARRIER DOME SURROUNDING YARESH, THE COMMAND COUNCIL, the strategic command for the messenger raiding force, floated in the air. Information from the field commanders within the city was relayed to them through speaking stones, a magical device this world did not possess. Communication was one of several odd points of ignorance in this otherwise magically developed world, alongside their dearth of dimensional magic.

One of the commanders left the group to move in the direction of the Voice of the Will, Jes Fin Kaal. Although in charge of all the messenger forces in the region —undisputedly, with the death of Mah Go Schaat—she had been leaving the direction of the raid to the gold-rankers that made up the strategic command. They were both surprised and grateful, as they knew their people and how to lead them far better than an outsider, even one sent by the astral king.

The voice had been satisfied setting objectives and then leaving the commanders to determine how best to carry them out. She only made a few stipulations, although they ranged from small to fundamental in their impact on the strategic approach to the raid. Attaching one messenger to the troop most likely to encounter one specific adventurer was a confusing but easy-to-accommodate directive. Employing the great summoning gates, on the other hand, defined the manner in which the attack was conducted.

The commander approached Jes Fin Kaal and made a status report. Kaal listened without looking at the man, her eyes locked on the city barrier, despite seeing little more than a blue blur through its surface.

"...being pushed back across the city," the commander reported. "We had believed that the gods would largely remain out of the conflict, but not only have the churches mobilised extensive forces, but those forces have proven suspiciously strong and well-informed."

"The goddess Knowledge," Kaal said, her voice unconcerned. "We have long known that she was preparing for our arrival in this world. She pushed the boundaries of what information she was able to spread, but our collaboration with the Church of Purity has given her leeway."

"The command council is advising withdrawal, Voice," the commander said. "The barrier breaches are repairing themselves quickly and the defenders are taking the upper hand as the summoning gates reach their limits. They are close to breaking down and we cannot replace the summons being destroyed as quickly as before. The fall of Mah Go Schaat has also freed up the local diamond-rank adventurers, and we've started losing gold-rankers. Casualties are already shifting away from the summoned fodder and onto our actual forces."

"You have confirmed the aura event was Jason Asano?"

"Yes, Voice. Also…"

Kaal finally turned to look at the commander.

"What?" she demanded.

"We have been unable to determine how Mah Go Schaat died. As best we can tell, he was rushing towards Asano in the wake of the aura events. The next moment, he was dead. At Asano's feet."

The voice blinked in confusion.

"Just like that?"

"Yes, Voice. And then… Asano devoured the life force left in his corpse."

Kaal's eyebrows shot up and then, to the commander's surprise and mild terror, she burst out laughing.

"Voice, we lost the diamond-ranker."

Kaal gave him a friendly pat on the shoulder.

"And we likely won't be seeing him again for some time. Such a shame. What is Asano's current disposition?"

"One of our silver-rankers caught him in a duelling power. We have been unable to ascertain his status from that point."

"He was drawn into a dimensional space?"

"No, Voice. It was the power type that wraps each duellist in a soul shell, allowing them to fight each other, but anyone else coming into contact is forcibly thrown away."

"Then why do we not know his status?"

"Their duel moved into a breached bunker. It is likely their fight created massive casualties amongst those sheltering inside. These soul shells can hurt a silver-ranker; they'll kill the frail servant race civilians."

"The bunkers don't matter. What about Asano?"

"Forgive me, Voice, but were the bunkers not the entire objective in attacking the city? To sow terror?"

"What? Oh, yes, of course they were. What are you doing to get eyes in that bunker?"

"The commander for that district is Marek Nior Vargas. He has secured the entrance with his personal forces only, not the ones that were assigned to him. But he is denying entrance to our forces, along with the city defenders."

Kaal's face took on a contemplative expression.

"Interesting," she mused. "I knew many of our gold-rankers would fight over

Asano once they realised what he was, but Marek Nior Vargas being one of them is a surprise."

"His actions could be seen as traitorous."

"They could. But, equally, he may simply be taking care in securing Asano. He's always been a careful one, and I suspect not all of our people are acting with duty utmost in their minds. He does not act without due consideration, and he knows I will allow only silver-rankers the chance to kill Asano."

"From our ongoing assessment of him, I'm not sure any of our silver-rankers *can* kill Asano."

"Precisely."

"Then why did you specifically direct them to try?"

"Because our people are slow to learn when it comes to respecting those who come from outside of our ranks. An unfortunate side effect of the learning programs. But now, they will respect the threat he poses and, more importantly, his potential when directed to our ends."

"You have your own intentions for him, then?"

"I have all manner of intentions, Commander, as those who whisper behind my back are all too ready to point out. Remember that we are not in this region to wipe out a servant-race city. That is why we are raiding it instead of razing it to the ground. Our objectives are greater, which is why the gold-rankers were instructed that Asano be either captured or left alive, and Marek Nior Vargas knows this."

"But if he *is* a traitor, he might try to kill Asano, or seize him for his own ends."

"He is a cautious man, and is unlikely to make a sudden, bold move now."

"But if he does?"

"Then it will be an unexpected but not unacceptable outcome. Marek Nior Vargas won't kill Asano, because that gets him nothing. And he has no information he can share with Asano that will interfere with the astral king's agenda. He may even streamline the transition to the next phase."

"The next phase, Voice?"

She focused on the commander again.

"The Command Council will be informed as necessary. For now, the council recommendation has my approval. Signal the full withdrawal."

"Thank you, Voice."

Jason projected his will into the soul of the messenger, and the result was disorienting. His magical and aura senses showed the inside of Tera Jun Casta's soul, while his ordinary senses still showed the inside of the bunker. He could barely comprehend what his spiritual senses perceived. It was more vast and complex than his mind could parse, with only glimpses of partial understanding.

Being inside her soul did show him enough to disprove a hypothesis he had formed while he was attacking it from the outside. He had started to suspect that the messengers were some kind of artificial race, created by the astral kings or some other beings, behind the scenes. What he discovered inside her soul disabused him of that notion. It felt messy and organic; everything was in a constant state of flux, yet it all worked in harmony. It was like hearing a hundred songs that seemed discordant, yet when played over one another, produced a heavenly chorus.

The elements of her soul ranged from completely incomprehensible to *almost* completely incomprehensible. The exceptions were three things that stood in stark contrast for the simple reason that Jason had a solid and immediate understanding of them. In all three cases, it was a connection to things outside of her soul that helped Jason both to find and to understand them.

The first element appeared to be the very core of the messenger's existence: a nexus hub for the body-soul gestalt that comprised her very being. Onto that central nexus, someone had placed a mark. From what he was seeing, Jason guessed that the mark was placed while the soul was still forming, like branding a newborn calf. It was placed before the soul became an impregnable whole, granting whoever placed the mark continued access.

Looking at the mark and how it was impacting the soul, it clearly did more than grant access. It had become an intrinsic part of the soul by the time it finished forming, like an internal organ. Now, if the mark was removed, the result would be a spiritual wound that would eventually be fatal.

The next aspect that stood out was what he identified as her potential. This was where her power slowly accumulated, not unlike where Jason's essence powers grew. She was not an astral king, however, so instead of the garden inside Jason's soul, she had a kaleidoscopic churn. That churn, however, was not growing. There was a seal placed on it, leaching power out of her soul entirely. Once again, Jason recognised the power of an astral king at play; just glancing at it showed him how he could use the same thing.

The seal drawing out power meant that Tera was eternally trapped at silver-rank, the power that would accumulate and trigger her advancement siphoned off. The astral king was taking the power that should have slowly let her grow to gold rank and beyond, claiming for himself. Jason realised that this must be a standard practice; every messenger unable to move beyond a certain rank was not held back by some inherent limitation. They were unwitting power batteries for the astral kings they served.

Jason's mind went through what he knew about the messengers. The Voices of the Will had chosen to serve the astral kings in return for the chance to advance further than their natural limits. But now Jason realised that those limits weren't natural at all. The great gift of raising a messenger's potential was nothing more than adjusting the seal to let more power accumulate before siphoning it off.

Although startled, Jason moved his attention to the third aspect of her soul he recognised. This was easy enough because it was the mechanism that drove Tera's duelling power. As Jason was currently fending that power off with power-boosted suppression resistance, he was able to trace the power right back to the source and immediately reached out with his will to turn it off. It didn't budge, leaving him no more able to disable it than the messenger herself.

Jason turned back to the first element he'd recognised, the marked core of her being. He could feel the control that brand had over her, and realised that if he had that control, it should let him end the duelling power. It was a move that filled him with revulsion, but it was necessary. Now that he had seen the underlying mechanism of the power, he could tell that if neither of them died first, it would kill them both within minutes.

He examined the mark, seeing that it was similar to writing he had seen before. There was an ancient and mysterious ideographic language that Jason had seen other examples of. His sword had the name written on the blade in those ideographs, and when he branded enemies with his Mark of Sin power, that brand also used the same language. The exact meaning of the symbol was multi-layered, but it roughly translated as 'soul-shaper.'

Hoping his own would sound at least a little less villainous, he searched his own soul for a similar mark and found it immediately, appearing the moment he willed it. He let out a sigh in his mind when he saw that it translated to 'hegemon.' Because of course it did.

Replacing the other astral king's brand with his own proved startlingly easy, the original shifting into the new shape with the barest expression of his will. When he did so, her entire soul shook like a shanty in a hurricane, but he ignored it and immediately turned off the now-compliant duelling power.

He was about to withdraw from her soul, then stopped himself. He looked again at the brand, now his own, on the core of her being. He knew he couldn't remove it; there had to be a brand now or it would destroy her slowly, like a spiritual gut wound that was unable to heal.

He cast his senses out, looking to see if he could find her own mark, somewhere in her soul. It was far harder than finding his own, and not only was it not his soul, but she wasn't an astral king. She didn't even have the potential to become one, with that seal in place, capping her potential.

The most he could find were dregs of what had once been the start of a mark, but both the brand—now his—and the seal were suppressing it. Jason willed his brand to stop doing so, and it did. Then he turned his attention to the seal and found that, unlike the brand, it was a simple matter to remove. He could sense her soul already trying to throw it off, and all he needed to do was give it a little help. He channelled some of his own strength into Tera and the seal pulsed like a heart before bursting.

Vesta Carmis Zell was an astral king, comfortably residing in her astral kingdom. She was watching servant race armies battle to the death, resurrecting them and bestowing on them different abilities to keep things interesting.

When she felt one of her seals disappear, she went deathly still.

It was a silver-rank seal, one of countless, but there was only one way for it to be removed: for an astral king to be allowed into a soul to remove it.

"HALLAS!" she bellowed, shaking her entire realm with such power that the servant races all died. She revived them again as her servant, Hallas, arrived. Hallas was one of her more satisfactory experiments in soul engineering: a living soul bound into a golem. The golem was seven feet tall and humanoid, wrought from white and gold materials that would be coveted even in the cosmic city of Interstice.

"Hallas," she commanded. "Reach out to the others. I am calling the Council of Kings."

With the seal gone, Jason cast his senses through Tera Jun Casta's soul once again, looking for the mark that represented Tera herself. The nascent aspects he had sensed were already moving, coming together and refining themselves. He waited, but while the mark quickly took an initial form, it was far from complete. It did not develop to the degree Jason's or the other astral king's had because Tera was no astral king.

It wasn't enough for Jason to use. Tapping to his own power, he took some of his own presence and radiated it through her soul, doing his best to give her an understanding of an astral king's nature. He focused it on her nascent mark and she responded, her soul instinctively using him as a blueprint to further develop it. The moment he sensed her not just reference him but copy him outright, he cut off the power and retracted his presence. He was trying to help her, not remould her in his own image.

Her mark remained incomplete, but he was sure it was enough to work, given it was her own soul. He reached out to her brand, his will again guiding her unconscious instincts to replace his mark with hers.

Once again, her entire soul shook. Jason felt an immediate sense of rejection from her soul and he withdrew his presence from her soul entirely.

Near-silence reigned in the dormitory bunker. The sound of a few wailing children was the only noise, and they sounded small in the vast chamber. The sound of the messenger falling to the floor was a punctuation mark to her conflict with Jason, and in its wake, everything went still.

The people there hadn't seen the bulk of the conflict between Jason and Tera, and while they had seen the end, they did not know what to make of it. From the perspective of those huddled in the bunker, Tera had burst in, followed by Jason. He'd scolded her in a voice that rang out in their souls like the command of a god, started glowing, and then, so far as anyone could tell, broke her with his mind.

Jason slowly descended from the air as the light shining from within his body dimmed. It was gone completely by the time he stopped, hovering with his feet just above the floor. He floated over to the unconscious messenger and lowered himself onto the floor in a kneel. This was partly to examine her and partly because he wasn't certain he could stand on his own two feet. The power he had just finished channelling hadn't crippled him, but it left him exhausted and hollow, like a pitted olive.

Shade manifested from Jason's shadow.

"G'day, bloke," Jason said, his voice straining to maintain its trademark casual relaxation.

"How are you, Mr Asano?"

"Between you, me and the huddled masses wondering if I'm going to kill them next? Pretty knackered."

"Events have progressed in your absence. I recommend you take stock, Mr Asano."

Jason fully expanded his senses for the first time since he had been caught up in her duelling power. He grunted, what was normally effortless giving him an immediate headache. His senses did not extend beyond the bunker's protective magic, even though it had been breached at the point where he and Tera had entered. But what he sensed inside the bunker was alarming enough.

Jason pushed himself unsteadily to his feet.

"Shade, did you happen to retrieve my sword with one of your bodies?"

"Of course, Mr Asano." Shade produced Jason's sword from his dimensional space and Jason took it. Immediately, his arm dropped, the sword tip scraping the hard tile floor as his arm dangled.

Jason and Shade both turned to the still-open doors. Moments later, a gold-rank messenger floated through, a silver-rank adventurer dangling from each hand. They were the pair Jason had encountered on entering the bunker. His senses told him that they were unconscious, not dead.

Jason recognised the commander of the messenger forces in the entertainment district. Like Tera, this man dressed more like an adventurer than a typical messenger, eschewing the impractical drapery for plain, practical armour. He was very brown, from his light skin to his dark hair, to the grey-tipped brown feathers of his wings.

His aura was intimidating. Like his appearance, it was imposing but not flashy. Jason didn't try to move as the messenger floated over to him at a walking pace, more messengers filing through the doors behind him. He was flanked by two more gold-rankers, with silvers forming up in a tactical wedge. All that power was directed at one very tired Jason and his shadow familiar.

"My name is Marek Nior Vargas," the commander told him. "Put your sword away, Jason Asano; you barely have the strength to stay on your feet, let alone lift it. You couldn't fight one of my silvers, let alone all of us."

Jason slowly lifted a hand to push the hood of his cloak back, revealing his face.

"Then again," Jason told the commander, "perhaps I have the strength after all."

He floated into the air to match Marek and lifted his sword, holding it level and steady, pointing at the messenger as he made a steely-voiced demand.

"Drop. Your. Sword."

"I... don't have a sword," the unarmed Marek told him.

103

ONE LUDICROUS ENCOUNTER TO THE NEXT

JASON DROPPED BACK TO THE FLOOR, LANDING IN A SUPERHERO CROUCH, THEN toppling over.

"Yep," he grunted, lying sprawled on the ground. "I'm pretty much spent. Hey, commander angel pants, what are you doing here? You know the diamond-rankers won't let you roam free in a bunker for long, right? You've kind of boxed yourself in."

One of the other gold-rank messengers moved closer to Marek and whispered, although silver-rank hearing meant that Jason heard it perfectly.

"Are you certain we should risk everything by betting on this… person?"

"We need something different, Payan," Marek told him. "He is different."

"I'm not sure that is the kind of different we want."

"It's the kind of different we have."

Marek floated over to Jason, looking down at him. "We are wagering heavily on someone protecting us from them."

"Please tell me that someone isn't me."

"It is you."

"Then you may be out of luck unless both those diamond-rankers have a deathly vulnerability to snoring. It's really starting to feel like nap time."

Marek floated down until his feet touched the ground, then reached down to offer Jason his hand. Jason groaned, accepted it, and allowed the messenger to pull him to his feet. The messenger was a good two feet taller, forcing Jason to crane his head back to look at him.

"I pretty much get it," Jason said. "You're unhappy with your current astral king service and are looking to switch to a new provider."

"Your phrasing is unusual, but you have deduced the situation with accuracy."

"Then you're going to need quite the sales pitch, bloke. I'm not a fan of the Nazi-scientist deal."

"I would like nothing more than to sit down and discuss many things with you at length. Unfortunately, time is against us. This was not a move I anticipated making, and it is only a matter of time before my fellow messengers realise what we are doing."

Jason stood upright, his tired slouch vanishing and the expression on his face turning hard. He slid his sword into its scabbard before responding to the messenger.

"You being in a hurry doesn't change the fact that you came here to kill the people huddled at end of this room. It doesn't change the fact that good people died stopping you. You saw what was left of this district after the monsters you sent were done with it. Even the ones that got out with their lives have had their homes and livelihoods destroyed. You came here for no other reason than to destroy. To sow fear and leave scars across the city that would remind the people here what it means to fight the messengers."

"I was reserved in my actions. I think you know this."

"Not out of any consideration for the people you were attacking. You think slaughter and destruction carried out with diffidence instead of enthusiasm means you aren't responsible for the lives you've taken?"

"How many lives have you taken?"

"Plenty, and it's messed me up pretty bad. I don't imagine you lose a lot of sleep over it, though."

"No," Marek conceded. "I won't pretend that I am something I'm not, but—"

Marek stopped as a chime sounded from each of the messengers present, including the unconscious Tera. Marek took a stone from a small pouch on his belt. It was strobing red.

"And our time is almost done," Marek told Jason. "That is the signal for a general withdrawal. The attack on your city is over."

"You think the defenders of this city will let you just waltz out? You can't come and go as you please, killing whoever catches your eye. You think I'll let you go?"

Marek's gold-rank offsider, Payan, floated up to them.

"You can barely stand and you think you can do anything to us? Any of us could kill you in an instant."

"Go for it; I've been killed plenty. The Builder killed me. His prime vessel killed me. I imagine you've heard of Shako. Every time the Builder wants one thing and I want another, I get hurt or I get killed. But I get what I want, and he doesn't. You think I'm scared of a few messengers? Why? Because you're all standing in a triangle?"

The messengers floating in a wedge formation bristled but went still when Marek held up a hand.

"We have no time, Jason Asano," Marek said. "I do not like to do it this way, but I will give you a simple choice. Your world has the concept of political asylum. I wish to claim it. I want to defect."

"Leaving aside how much you know of my world," Jason said, "you're not talking about asking the city for asylum, are you? You're asking me."

"Only another astral king can harbour us."

"Yeah. As it happens, I just found out why."

Jason turned to glance at Tera Jun Casta, still sprawled unconscious on the ground. Marek followed his gaze and then narrowed his eyes as he peered at her.

"What did you do to her?"

Marek moved to her side in a blur of motion, kneeling to place a hand on her forehead.

"You know her?" Jason asked him.

"She was under my command, but no. You changed the astral king she belongs to."

Marek stood, turned and looked over Jason with a freshly assessing gaze.

"What astral king does she belong to? It's not you; I could tell with both of you in front of me. But she does not belong to Vesta Carmis Zell anymore either. I would feel it, the same connection I have. And how are you even both alive? She used a duelling power."

"I thought you didn't have time for questions."

Marek stood up, frowned, and then nodded.

"You are right; I do not. I need asylum, for myself and my people. I can promise you that there are benefits to be had for doing so."

"I'm not looking for a bribe."

"And I do not offer one. These are benefits you will want not for you, but for all the forces arrayed against my kind."

"So, your pitch is that you'll do something super impressive if I take you in, but you don't have time to explain it right now."

"The withdrawal has been called. If you will not accept us, we will have to leave before the city barrier closes. That will be bad for both of us."

Jason sighed.

"Shade, thoughts?"

"He claims to need time, Mr Asano. You could offer him that, if you are willing to stand up to the diamond-rankers who will demand you hand them over. I think we both know that will not be a problem for you."

Jason sighed again, then turned back to Marek.

"Give me one reason," he said. "Not vague promises. Give me one good, solid reason that I should even entertain the idea of helping you."

Marek paused for a long time, his expression thoughtful. Finally, his gaze came to rest on Tera Jun Casta, lying on the floor. He closed his eyes for a moment, opened them and then turned to Jason.

"Because you have chosen mercy," he said.

Jason locked eyes with Marek for a long time, needing to crane his head back to do so. Then he turned, just as Marek had earlier, to contemplate Tera's prone form.

"Bloody hell," he muttered unhappily.

A portal arch rose from the floor, filled with gold, silver and blue light. It started off human-sized, but grew to accommodate messengers at a gesture from Jason.

"You know where that goes, right?" Jason asked.

"Your astral kingdom."

"Get your people inside. It will keep everyone off you until we can have that long talk you mentioned."

Marek ordered his people in, the messengers looking decidedly uncertain but doing as they were told. More messengers came through the doors when Marek called them with his communication stone. They had been the ones blocking the hole in the bunker's ceiling against other intruders, and Jason's team was hot on their heels. They found Jason standing with Marek as the messengers filed through what the team recognised as a portal to Jason's astral realm. The team knew Jason in the middle of his latest insanity when they saw it, and since the messengers weren't attacking the civilians or Jason, they looked on warily from the door.

When Marek was the only one remaining, he turned to Jason.

"Do not leave us for long. Our current astral king will likely revoke our patronage, and that will kill us."

"I'm aware," Jason told him, then gestured at Tera. "Take her with you."

"She's knocked out. If she does not subconsciously consent to move through the portal, I can't."

"Then try. Or would you rather leave her to the mercies of my side, after what your side just did?"

Marek floated over to Tera, gently knelt down and picked her up. He moved back to the portal and they both disappeared into it.

"You could have at least let me fight," Melody said to Sophie as she and Emir led her from Emir's cloud palace to Jason's. "I could have fought messengers."

"I wouldn't trust you to use your mouth when eating a sandwich," Sophie told her. "There's no way we would let you loose in a city-wide battle. How many times have I explained this in the last few weeks?"

"So why did it take so long to put me back in Asano's cloud palace? This man's is tedious."

"I have an extensive library."

"Asano has television. I've been learning the language of his world by watching stories about a man with a moustache and a sleek red carriage. The gold-ranker's palace lacks innovative amenities."

"That he lets you see," Emir said. "And the gold-ranker has a name."

"And if he also had a personality instead of colourful hair beads, someone might care," Melody told him.

Emir raised his hands to his bead-laced hair with a hurt expression.

"I like my hair beads."

"Be nice," Sophie admonished Melody.

"Of course, you like the boring guy," Melody said with a groan. "Are you still seeing that Lump guy?"

"It's Hump... it's Humphrey," Sophie said.

"I am not boring," Emir insisted. "In fact, you'll find that a great many people's most fervent wish is that I was more boring."

They approached Jason's cloud palace, which was once again set up to serve refugees. Instead of just the towns to the south, much of Yaresh's population was now homeless, making them refugees in their own city.

In the weeks following the battle of Yaresh, countless tons of rubble and ash had been collected and repurposed in construction projects that were rebuilding the city at a startling pace. Even so, tent cities still dominated, both inside and outside the city walls. Sophie, Emir and Melody had been walking through what amounted to a tent district that had grown up around all the parked adventurer vehicles, including Emir's and Jason's.

"You're going to see Jason?" Sophie asked Emir as they neared the entrance. They didn't pause in the doorway itself, as there was a stream of people coming in and out.

"If he refuses to leave his soul space, or whatever he's calling it now, then I'll have to go see him."

"You're not going to try and get him to see the diamond-rankers, are you?" Sophie asked. "They're the reason he's not coming out."

"Not the Yaresh diamond-rankers, no," Emir said. "There's another one that has come here to see him."

"Just don't cause him any trouble," Sophie warned. "Your wife still feels guilty about going along with…"

She glanced at her mother.

"…your old teammate. She'd be more than happy to do me a favour."

Emir held his hand up in surrender.

"No trouble for Jason," he promised.

Sophie took her mother inside as Emir wandered over to a nondescript woman who was splitting her attention between the cloud palace and a cube-shaped device in her hands. She looked to be a well-preserved forty, although Emir knew she was many times older than that. He grinned as he saw the frustrated expression on her face.

"I see you're still a woman," he said by way of greeting.

"What? Oh, yes," she said distractedly. "A couple of years, now. I've been thinking it's time for a switch again. Not a man, though. Somewhere in the middle, I think. Young."

Emir looked down at the device. "No luck?"

"It works on yours."

"Oh, I'm aware," he said. "I was in the bath when you decided to return my palace to the cloud flask to make sure your override still worked."

"I made the damn thing; of course I should be able to control it. What has this boy of yours done to his? I know I designed them to be adaptive, but this is outside all of the parameters I set."

"I was about to go in and ask if he'd speak to you. He's been dodging the local diamond-rankers, so he's been reluctant to come out."

"They're diamond-rankers. Why don't they just break in, if they're that determined?"

"They did, after the first week. He's retreated into a dimensional space."

"You can force open dimensional spaces."

"Not this one. The Builder tried, once, and even he couldn't manage it."

"Who is this boy?"

"Someone who has a habit of being the right person in the very wrong place."

"Really? Did he start off ordinary and get caught up with something powerful? Properly powerful, I mean, not just some diamond-ranker?"

"Actually, yes."

She made a sound of mild surprise.

"Fate senses, probably. That would explain the strange, disparate powers I'm reading from this cloud construct. You would have to go from one ludicrous encounter to the next."

"That certainly describes Jason," Emir said. "What are fate senses?"

"Just the knowledge that it's possible to survive without astral king patronage will be a revelation," Marek said. "It is the fact that the kings are artificially limiting our advancement that will be the match that turns the Unorthodoxy from dead wood to raging inferno."

"The Unorthodoxy," Jason said. "That's the messenger rebellion against astral kings you were talking about?"

He and the messenger sat on a long park bench in a wild garden of plants flowering vibrant red.

"It is far from a rebellion," Marek said. "You cannot rebel against those without whom you will die. But what you've done for us shows that we can live without astral kings."

"So long as you have an astral king to put your own brand in place," Jason pointed out. "I'm not going to be your one-stop-shop for messenger refurbishment, if that is what you're thinking. We both know that wouldn't work."

When Jason changed the brands on the souls of Marek and his people, it was not a smooth process. Opening up their souls to Jason was difficult for them, their unconscious reluctance overriding their conscious minds. In the end, only one had been unable to will themselves into opening their souls to Jason, and he had died several days after the astral king he previously served removed his own mark.

Even at the end, in the face of death, the messenger had not opened his soul. Marek had asked Jason how he did it with Tera and suggested he do the same, but Jason flatly refused. With Tera, he needed to save them both, and even then he still felt revulsion at the act. More than once in the subsequent weeks, he'd jerked awake from a flashback nightmare. As she was still to wake, there was no telling what trauma she had survived.

"I am not asking you to free more souls," Marek said. "The first step must be showing my kind that it is possible. Then we can work at suborning astral kings. Those not on the Council of Kings won't challenge the council under current conditions. If the messengers as a whole discover what the kings have been doing, that will change. I am certain that some will be willing to go along, if only to use the rebellion to build a power base the council cannot undermine."

"That is your affair; I want no part of it."

"I am surprised that you placed our own marks to free us, when you could have branded us with yours. We were in no position to argue. It was let you into our souls or die."

"I'm not taking anyone as a slave, no matter what they've done. I'll kill them if the consequences of leaving them alive are worse, but I won't enslave anyone. Again. It was strictly a one-time thing."

"Then you will let us leave?"

"Slavery is not an option. Imprisoning, I'm more open to. Being secret rebels or whatever doesn't absolve you of the things you've done. You may not care, but I do."

"Then what will it take for you to release us?"

"I don't know," Jason admitted. "I'm not big on incarceration either, if I'm being honest."

"Letting us go is only good for your side. We will be undermining messenger power structures."

"So you've told me. Repeatedly, and at length. I'll continue to consider your arguments."

Before Marek could answer, Jason was gone.

104

THE FOOLISH CHOICE

INSIDE JASON'S ASTRAL REALM, MAREK NIOR VARGAS WAS WALKING WITH HIS friend and companion, Payan Nior Roel. Having bloomed in the same district of the same garden world, they had known each other for all but the first few days of their lives. They had served under the same commander, who had helped break their indoctrination. They had confided their doubts in one another and secretly sought out the Unorthodoxy together.

"We need to leave this place," Payan said, far from the first time.

"And I am asking you to wait," Marek said patiently. "Again. And I have been asking him to release us, but really I am laying a foundation for the relationship. It's going to take time for him to see us as anything other than superiority-obsessed zealots."

"We're free of the astral kings, except we're trapped in the astral kingdom of this one. Do you not realise what the revelation of not needing astral kings to survive will mean? Let alone that the astral kings have been imposing the limits on us while claiming they were natural."

"I do realise what it means," Marek said. "It means that our deaths will come extremely fast if we are not extremely careful. And while we can demonstrate our freedom simply by existing, we have no proof that the kings are limiting us. The astral kings will call us liars and aberrations."

"But that isn't true. Our people will see that."

"People will choose what they want to be true over what is, given even the flimsiest excuse."

"The servant races, yes, but we are talking about messengers."

"You shouldn't call them servant races, Payan. Not only will our host not like it—and there is no place we can hide from him here—but think about the revelations we have just learned. The reality is, Payan, that *we* are the true servant race."

"Which is why we need to get out there and start changing things."

"Which we will, but I think you've failed to realise that the most important gift that our freedom gives us is time. Time to hide. Time to plan, prepare and gather resources. No Voice of the Will to answer to. No astral king spying on our souls. That means we can finally hide. We've never had that before."

"And you would hide in a prison?"

"Yes, I would. Don't squander this chance, Payan. This astral kingdom is tiny and incomplete; it's more of an astral estate. When will you ever get another chance to see an astral kingdom as a work in progress? You should take it all in, learn as much as you can and be grateful for the time you get to spend here. This time will pay itself back a thousandfold when we are seeking to construct our own astral kingdoms. Think of Mah Go Schaat, cloistered away in his study. How many centuries had he spent chasing rumours that would give him a fragment of what is all around us?"

"But what does Asano want of us while we are here? What is his agenda?"

"You have already given Asano your trust, Payan. You let him into your soul."

"Against every instinct screaming at me not to. If the alternative was anything but death, I don't know that I could have. Pios Val Haat couldn't, even then, and it killed her."

"Yet, all he did was free us, when he could have made us slaves. He did not even leave himself a way back into our souls, which he equally could have. He had no need for schemes because we were perfectly vulnerable and he had all the power. What could he have done that showed his lack of ill-intent more clearly than that? I'm actually asking because I cannot think of anything."

"But that's the issue, isn't it? He's made it clear that he sees us as enemies. You think he wants to play us against the astral kings?"

"I think he does now, after I've put the idea in his head."

"Then why did he help us?"

"I don't know. When I was trying to convince him, asking for mercy felt... wrong. I haven't thrown off the superiority doctrine as thoroughly as I like to tell myself. But I saw Tera Jun Casta who, by all rights, should have been dead. And I saw Asano, exhausted from the effort of circumventing a duel power, which shouldn't be possible. He should have killed her. Could have killed her. He had the power and she was an enemy. Why he made that choice, I don't know. But it feels important that I find out."

"Then perhaps," Payan said, "you should ask him."

"I hate that shadow," Charist said.

He and his fellow diamond-rank adventurer, Allayeth, had just come from Asano's cloud palace. Again. Asano's familiar had politely told them that he would inform Asano of their 'request' as soon as he was able. They had returned to the Adventure Society's main building, one of the few that was essentially intact in the wake of the raid, taking tea in a private parlour.

"I told you that we shouldn't have broken into the cloud palace," Allayeth said. "He wasn't in there and it only made things worse. The High Priestess of the Healer has filed multiple formal complaints to the Adventure Society."

"We're diamond-rankers; what do we care?"

"We decided to stay here for some time, Charist. The people of this city love Hana Shavar, as does the Healer. Causing her trouble is trouble for us. Unless you're looking to rule with an iron fist, we can't just squash the city authorities."

Charist's face took on a contemplative expression. Allayeth saw it and groaned.

"No," she told him. "We are not going to rule with an iron fist."

"You're the one who brought it up."

She gave him a flat look.

"Fine," he reluctantly acceded. "But I won't have this Asano running over us the way I'm apparently not allowed to with the city's precious authority figures."

"He is a concern. Have you read the testimonies from the people in that bunker?"

"You mean where he tells the messenger to give up her soul and it looks like she does? Clearly, Asano is someone who needs to be brought to heel."

"No," Allayeth said. "I spoke to Soramir Rimaros again this morning. He said that force is a very bad idea."

"Well, we're not in the Storm Kingdom. We don't have any places named after Soramir Rimaros down here."

"Actually, there's a trade town just upriver called Rimarino that—"

"Are you kidding me?"

There was an aura pulse from behind the door and Allayeth responded in kind. An Adventure Society functionary came in.

"It's time?" Allayeth asked.

"They should be portalling in six minutes from now," the functionary said.

"I can't believe it's come to this," Charist muttered as he rose from his chair.

"If it worked in Rimaros, it should work here," Allayeth told him.

In a city far to the north of the Storm Kingdom, Rick Geller was dressing up.

"They're treating me like a translator that speaks Asano," he complained. "This is a steaming pile of heidel shi—"

"Diplomacy, Rickard," his teammate and girlfriend Hannah told him as she adjusted his collar. "We're about to meet with diamond-rankers."

"Oh, so now it's Rickard. I know you were the one who told the protocol officer at the royal palace in Rimaros that my name was Richard."

"And I know that you won't stop talking about how Asano is always surrounded by beautiful women whenever you get near him."

"Said like someone who didn't have her own little crush on him."

"I have no idea what you're talking about," she said airily.

They walked out of their bedroom in the Geller family compound and made for the teleport zone where the compound's defences wouldn't interfere with a portal. With a sizeable messenger stronghold not too far away, the compound was always on low-level alert. Dimensional interference was normally too expensive to leave running, but the compound leveraged peculiarities of the local magic to make it work.

The rest of Rick's team joined him and Hannah on the way. Phoebe Geller was Rick's sister, now back on his team, and Claire was Hannah's twin. The last member of the team was Dustin Kettering, the only non-local. They had picked him up in Greenstone after their original fifth, Jonah Geller was killed during a failed star seed extraction. Dustin had been on a team with Neil Davone and Thadwick Mercer, who had disbanded the team while also under star seed influence.

"We're barely back from Rimaros and now we're going south again," Claire complained.

"I didn't get to go last time," Phoebe said, "so I'm looking forward to it. It will be nice to see how Sophie is coming along."

"I'm looking forward to seeing Neil again," Dustin said. "Also, being somewhere less dusty. None of you warned me that they call this region the dust basin. It's easy to get magic that shrugs off humidity, but for dust, you have that annoying air magic blowing over you the whole time."

"That's why I told you not to buy the cheap anti-dust bracelet," Claire told him.

"I'm not going to pay that much money for a dust bracelet. It's like those humidity bracelets back in Greenstone all over again. At least there my name wasn't Dustin in a place full of dust. People keep trying to give me terrible nicknames."

"Work faces on," Rick interrupted as he led them through the door and into the courtyard they would be portalling from. The gold-ranker, his aunt, gave him a wink as she opened the portal. This involved a gelatinous blob appearing that swiftly expanded into a ring shape, floating in the air. The space in the middle of the ring filled with green glowing energy.

Inside Jason's astral realm, Marek was explaining what he knew of Jes Fin Kaal's intentions to Jason and his team. They were in a grassy area, splayed out in lounge chairs. The two exceptions were Marek, floating just off the ground at the front, and Gary, cooking at the back. The smell of grilling meat wafted over the team.

"The astral king is after something buried deep underground," Marek explained. "She has known about it for decades, which is why she had the naga genesis egg placed here. I suspect the astral king will not be happy about the voice expending so many resources on the Yaresh raid, but I could just as easily be wrong. Astral kings are known for massive expenditures when they want something."

"And what is it that they want, exactly?" Humphrey asked.

"I don't know," Marek said. "But I think your Goddess of Knowledge does. She's been building forces up here for years, which is the only reason we didn't wipe out Yaresh on our arrival."

"It's something to do with the natural array, isn't it?" Clive asked.

"I believe so," Marek said.

"Can somebody explain what that is again?" Sophie asked. "The last time we were meant to be briefed, Clive threw a tantrum and stormed off."

"It was not a tantrum," Clive said. "But ignoring that, a natural array is a magical array —a permanently emplaced ritual—except it occurs naturally instead of being crafted through ritual magic. The elements that make it up are essences, awakening stones and quintessence that have manifested normally over decades or even centuries. They just happen to have manifested in exactly the right proximity and arrangement that their magical energy interacts to produce a ritual-like effect."

"That can't be common," Sophie said.

"It's breathtakingly rare," Clive agreed. "Magic Society researchers have murdered one another over the chance to study one. Not only does every element need to be positioned with excruciating precision, but it must do so without being interfered with in the many years it takes the natural array to form."

"And being made up of valuable materials," Belinda said, "anyone that finds it will plunder it."

"It got away with it here by all the bits appearing deep underground?" Neil asked.

"Exactly," Clive said. "The essences, stones and quintessence that make up the array will be what you'd expect from manifestations that far underground. Earth, fire and iron will make up the vast majority, I imagine."

"The astral king knew of its existence," Marek said. "I do not know how, when even the elf city almost on top of it was oblivious. The original intention had been to conduct a mining operation and excavate down, setting off the naga genesis egg in the city if they discovered the operation. But obstacles arose and things became significantly more complicated."

"Complicated how?" Humphrey asked.

"We were expecting an array buried in solid earth, doing whatever it was doing. What we found instead was a subterranean city centred around it, with a population that had been there for centuries. What's more, there is an astral space down there that the Builder cult somehow managed to find and occupy. They've been fighting the locals ever since. When our forces arrived, not only did we find ourselves stumbling into what was now a three-way war, but Knowledge's army was waiting to strike from behind. Even worse, the effects of the array were impacting our forces. We were forced to withdraw with considerable losses."

"I have heard the early stages of the conflict went poorly for the messengers," Humphrey said.

"Yes. Significant reinforcements were sent by the astral king. That was when I arrived with my people. We set up the strongholds, but aside from the various factions in the conflict, there was another major impediment. The nature of the array seems to imbue individuals with elemental magic."

"And what does imbuing people with magic do?" Belinda asked.

"Those living down there were smoulder," Marek said. "That makes sense as they have strong earth and fire affinities. They are an essence-using people, but those who live there now are not. Centuries of exposure have turned them into a more magical sub-species. They can no longer use essences, but their inherent powers have grown considerably."

"There are other cases like that," Clive said. "Moonstalker Elves. Thunder King Leonids."

"The subterranean residents have adapted well," Marek continued. "Those who already have high levels of inherent magic are less positively affected. The messengers sent down swiftly started mutating into elemental variants."

"I bet that went down great with team 'we are the superior race,'" Neil said.

"It did not," Marek agreed. "Especially as the changes cause intelligence to rapidly and precipitously devolve. Most of the initial force of silver-rankers were lost and even some of the golds failed to escape before being affected."

"And that's when you started suborning essence users," Jason said.

"Yes," Marek confirmed. "We discovered that essences users and the Builder's converted are both resistant to the effects. Not immune, but there was no concern on our part for casualties amongst the…"

"Say it," Jason told him.

"…servant races," Marek continued. "There were a number of problems, however. One was that our efforts to recruit and suborn essence users were not resulting in the numbers we required. The other was that the main component of successfully resisting the array's effects, at least amongst essence users, was willpower. That, as it turns out, is something that those willing to serve us tend to lack."

"No surprise there," Taika said. "That bloke you all sent after Jason tried to get me onside. His arguments sucked, bro."

"That was when the stalemate with the local forces settled in. We had our fortresses, with the Knowledge army and Adventure Society war camps pressuring them. We also had to periodically deal with incursions from below, through the very access shafts we had dug."

"You had dug?" Jason asked pointedly.

"That our slaves had dug," Marek corrected. "To end the stalemate, the astral king sent Jes Fin Kaal. She is a Voice of the Will, one of the astral king's personal servants, imbued with a portion of her power. She did not come to fight, however, but to plan. She brought the world-taker worms and the infested proved resistant to the array's effects."

"They weren't meant to be an invasion force?" Rufus asked.

"Something important to understand about Jes Fin Kaal is that she never does anything for just one reason. Every resource has an alternative use. Every plan has contingencies and synergies; every objective has alternatives. When something goes wrong, she adapts, turning adversity into opportunity. You, Asano, are the perfect example. She wants to use you, and she is keeping her options open as to how."

"She must have gotten a surprise when you sold out instead of capturing him, then," Neil said.

"No," Marek said. "Her orders to the silver-rankers were to kill him, so as to prove his worth to the rank-and-file messengers. His actions during the raid more than accomplished this. The gold-rankers were under orders to capture Asano if possible, and leave him alive and free if not. She does not need you captured, Asano. She believes she can get what she wants from you without forcing you into it."

"How?" Jason asked. "And what does she want from me?"

"She will attempt to use you to retrieve whatever it is she wants from the subterranean city. I suspect she will make an enticing offer to secure your participation. With you ostensibly in command of an essence user force, she can make it work. She will, of course, have plans contingent upon your refusal as well as your acceptance."

"Why me? The astral king thing?"

"Yes. The indoctrination of my kind excels at instilling obedience, but it does have its drawbacks from a control perspective. My kind are unwilling to work with what they see as their lesser. Any attempt at collaboration inevitably descends into abuse for the sake of amusement. If they are going to work with essence users, there needs to be an essence user they acknowledge. She was going to have you prove yourself in a duel, which would hopefully demonstrate your astral king nature. Your aura displays during the raid served her purpose far better than she could have hoped."

"She's going to send someone to make an offer," Jason said.

"Yes. Most likely, she will approach the city itself, rather than you directly. Leverage their influence to pressure you into action."

"That's idiotic," Sophie said. "The city is already pressuring him, and it's getting them nowhere."

"That's because what they want right now is control," Jason said. "They want the messengers I have and to know whatever they think I know that they don't. That's easy to refuse. But what if they want something that will help the city? The people? Civic authority holds minimal leverage over me. Moral authority is harder to resist."

"Jes Fin Kaal must meet the needs of the astral king," Marek said. "It is the only time you can find her acting on a single objective because she has no choice. It's the only condition under which she becomes predictable. I promise you that whatever she offers the city, it will be hard for you to refuse."

"And the astral king wants the natural array?" Clive asked.

"There is something else down there she wants," Marek said. "I know that it is not the array, nor the elements that make it up. Whatever it is, the astral king wants it very badly."

"The messengers are here for Purity's legacy," Jason said. "Is that down there? It would be quite the hiding spot."

"No," Marek said. "This is something the astral king wants for herself, to the point of letting the other kings vie over the Purity relic. I don't know what, but everything else is secondary to her."

"Then all Jason has to do is say no," Sophie said. "Plan stopped."

"Plan altered," Jason corrected. "I don't think this Jes Fin Kaal will move forward with an absolute failure point in her plan, especially such a predictable one."

"Then we go along with her?" Humphrey asked. "It seems that if we want to have the ability to influence events, we need to be part of them."

"To put out an idea that no one seems to have considered," Rufus said, "what if we actually go along with the diamond-rankers? Telling them what we know and giving them what we have? They are on our side."

Dark clouds gathered in the sky above them.

"I've tried working with the organisations on my side before," Jason said, his voice rumbling with the echo of thunder.

"That is a no, then," Rufus said. "I just thought I'd ask."

Marek and Jason were on a balcony on the pagoda tower at the heart of Jason's astral realm, looking out over the gardens and buildings. Jason was leaning casually against the rail while Marek was upright, floating just off the floor. The grounds in front of them shifted and changed in a constant state of flux. Buildings grew larger or smaller, disappearing or new ones suddenly being there. The flowers in the gardens changed colours and the pathways and streams shifted location.

Marek never noticed any of it happening. He would simply realise the difference without having seen it change. He was looking right at it and yet failed to perceive it, his senses lying to him that it had always been that way.

"Why are you helping us?" Marek asked. "Why was asking for mercy what convinced you, when the sensible choice was to use us? To hand us over to the rulers of Yaresh?"

"I might still do that."

"I don't think you will, but I don't understand why not. And I feel like it is somehow important that I should."

Jason turned to look at Marek. He didn't speak for a long time as he stared at the messenger. Finally, he turned his gaze back out towards the grounds.

"When I first started to realise that I was more powerful than I was moral," Jason said, "I asked my father for advice."

"Is your father a powerful man?"

"No. What he told me was that when I have someone at my mercy, and I'm faced with the choice between ending them or not, that is a chance to decide who I am."

"The wise decision is to kill your enemies unless you need them for something. Kill the root and the plant will not grow again."

"The wise decision, you say. I think that depends on the kind of wisdom you're talking about. But I did make your wise choice. Or rather, I just killed and didn't even think of it as a choice. I don't know why it was different with that messenger girl. She wasn't different, not really. A little young, but definitely not innocent. But for some reason, that was the moment. I've been thinking about what my dad told me lately, and that was the moment I decided to listen."

Jason ran a hand over his face, took a deep breath and let it out in a slow sigh.

"Maybe it was just because I'm contrary by nature," he continued. "Mercy was the hard path and I don't know how to take the easy one anymore. Everything pointed to killing her, and for whatever reason, I decided I wouldn't. It's not like I'm a good man; that ship sailed far too many corpses ago."

"We each have our values," Marek said. "Yours and mine are quite different, but we both, I think, lament our failures to live up to them."

Jason nodded.

"I don't even know if what I did to her was mercy. I might not know even after she wakes up. I may have destroyed her more horribly than death could have, but that might not show itself for months or even years. There's no fully predicting damage of the mind. But I hope I did right. I can't tell anymore, and I'm not sure I was right when I thought I could."

"Then why try?" Marek asked. "Why make a fool's choice you can't be certain of instead of the smart choice you can confirm?"

"Because I've been down what you call the smart choice, and I do mean down. It only gets darker the longer you walk it. Making things worse and getting what you want out of that is easy. Making things better is hard and often uncertain. And yes, it means making the fool's choice. It's harder and you might get it wrong. But if no one dares to be a fool, then all there will end up being is darkness. I'm sick of darkness, and I like being a fool, so that's what I'm going to be."

"You do not think anything like my people."

"Your people could stand to think more like me, from time to time."

"I think you are right. I see now, I think. It is aspirational, yes? You want to make the foolish choice the right one, even if that always means taking the harder path. I too have a hard path if I want to save my people. To redeem them."

"Then I wish you success. But you should know that it will be even worse than you think. Sometimes, the world will try to break you. Either you have to bend, or you make the world bend."

"Bend the world? If that is your goal, you will need almost inconceivable power."

Jason smiled and Marek's gaze moved from the silver-ranker to his astral kingdom laid out before them.

"I may have just started to understand you, Jason Asano."

———

Jason Asano will return in He Who Fights With Monsters 10!

THANK YOU FOR READING HE WHO FIGHTS WITH MONSTERS, BOOK NINE.

WE HOPE YOU ENJOYED IT AS MUCH AS WE ENJOYED BRINGING IT TO YOU. WE JUST wanted to take a moment to encourage you to review the book. Follow this link: He Who Fights With Monsters 9 to be directed to the book's Amazon product page to leave your review.

Every review helps further the author's reach and, ultimately, helps them continue writing fantastic books for us all to enjoy.

Want to connect with Shirtaloon?

Discuss He Who Fights With Monsters and more, join Shirtaloon's Discord!

Follow him on www.HeWhoFightsWithMonsters.com where you can find great HWFWM merch and other great content.

HE WHO FIGHTS WITH MONSTERS
BOOK ONE
BOOK TWO
BOOK THREE
BOOK FOUR
BOOK FIVE
BOOK SIX
BOOK SEVEN
BOOK EIGHT

BOOK NINE
BOOK TEN

Looking for more great books?

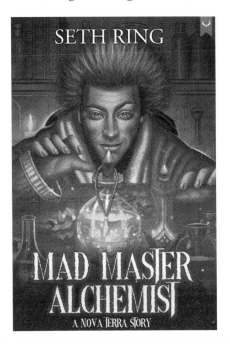

Alphonso Richt— **Expert botanist. Genius chemist.**
Recently unemployed. Burning down the lab will do that.
But every cloud has a silver lining, and after being let go from
his most recent job for unsanctioned experiments, Alph is
given the chance to blow off a little steam with a cutting edge
new game that isn't even out of beta. It's called Nova Terra.
Logging into a fully developed fantasy world, Alph discovers
a new field of study called Alchemy that instantly captivates
him, allowing him to bring his unique insights and scientific
knowledge to bear as he explores the wonders of magic.
Plus, no one really cares if his potions explode in the game.
Mad Master Alchemist is a new LitRPG story from Seth
Ring, bestselling author of *Battle Mage Farmer* and *The*
Titan Series. Set in the world of Nova Terra and starring
the unforgettable Alph, if you like immersive storytelling,
rich fantasy, and epic adventures with a slice of
friendship thrown in, you'll love this novel. Pick up Mad
Master Alchemist today and uncover the mystery of Nova
Terra!

Get Mad Master Alchemist Now!

He *WILL* protect this town. Glenn Redwood has longed to become an Adventurer since he was a young boy, and has focused every waking moment since he turned 14 on leveling and growing stronger. Answering the challenge of the Gods of Luxtera, he has fought Monsters to prove himself again and again. He has earned the right to travel the world and protect its people... but the Gods have other plans. After they choose Glenn to become a Town Guard, he is charged with protecting his small town and everyone within. His dreams of traveling the world seem all but impossible. Even so, as he upgrades his new Town Guard Class, Glenn learns that one doesn't need to travel abroad to find challenge, adventure, friendship, and even love. And the people he wants most strongly to protect may have been in his small village all along. *Don't miss the start of a new action-packed LitRPG Adventure with strong-to-stronger progression, strategic battles, endearing characters, and slice-of-life elements.*

Get Town Guard Now!

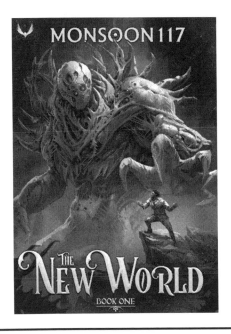

For all our LitRPG books, visit our website.

ABOUT THE AUTHOR

Shirtaloon was working on a very boring academic paper when he realised that writing about an inter-dimensional kung fu wizard would be way more fun.

To discuss He Who Fights With Monsters and more, join Shirtaloon's Discord!

Made in the USA
Middletown, DE
02 November 2024

PAROCHIAL LIBRARIES

Vid. Sᵗⁱ Aug. Confess. Lib. 8. Cap. 12.

This Book belongs to
the Parochial Library
of Irthlingborough in the
County of Northampton.

A DIRECTORY OF THE

PAROCHIAL LIBRARIES

OF THE CHURCH OF ENGLAND AND

THE CHURCH IN WALES

FIRST EDITED BY NEIL KER

revised edition edited by

MICHAEL PERKIN

LONDON
BIBLIOGRAPHICAL SOCIETY
2004

© The Bibliographical Society 2004

Published by the Bibliographical Society

ISBN 0 948170 13 1
A CIP Catalogue record for this book is
available from the British Library

Designed by David Chambers
Printed and bound in Great Britain at the
University Press, Cambridge

Half-title: the smaller Bray bookplate, 1709
(see pp. 14, 47-8)
Frontispiece: general view of part of
the chained library at Wimborne Minster

To *Margaret*,
field-trip companion, and patient
observer of 'breeding' files,
with love

CONTENTS

ILLUSTRATIONS

FOREWORD

The impetus for the original publication in 1959 of *The Parochial Libraries of the Church of England* was concern at the neglected state of so many of these libraries. The stress and strain of modern life to which Archbishop Fisher drew attention at that time in his foreword have in no sense diminished. Our national heritage of church furnishings and fittings, monuments and stained glass continues to be vulnerable, and to this list we must now add collections of, often, valuable books.

Care of these collections of books has, however, improved since 1959, and it is clear from the significant number of additions to this new edition of the directory that our knowledge of the content of these collections, and their whereabouts, continues to grow.

The motives of those who established parochial libraries, both large and small, are sometimes tantalizingly obscure. The continuing education and improvement of the clergy is a recurring theme where information does exist, but it is also clear that, where conditions for lending survive, these collections were intended for a wider readership.

Many of the books, as one would expect, are theological, but other subjects can be found. At Hatfield Broad Oak, for example, there are books on history, biography, medicine, philosophy and travel, and multilingual dictionaries. At Heathfield the collection includes books on classical scholarship, and works on agriculture, household management, carriers' timetables, heraldry and English literature. These were – and are – 'accessible' collections and we can only speculate today on their original use and influence.

The Council for the Care of Churches is particularly grateful to Michael Perkin for all that he has done to produce this new edition of *Parochial Libraries*. He has enlarged the scope of the original work significantly, and brought to fruition a study which will be the standard reference point on parochial libraries for many years to come. The work involved many years of painstaking research and scholarship, much letter writing and visits to many of the libraries recorded, and we are grateful to those charities that gave money to cover the expenses of this study.

Raymond Furnell
Dean of York
Chairman, Council for the Care of Churches

ACKNOWLEDGEMENTS

I am greatly indebted to the Bibliographical Society, and to the Idlewild Trust, the Pilgrim Trust, the Radcliffe Trust, the SPCK, and the Yapp Education and Research Trust, for generous grants to cover the cost of travel and other expenses incurred during the compilation of this Directory.

In a survey carried out to a considerable extent by correspondence it will readily be apparent that I owe a great debt of gratitude also to the many librarians and archivists who have responded so patiently to my requests for information and photocopies: my sincere thanks to all. Similarly I express my warmest thanks to all incumbents, churchwardens, and other curators of collections, who have replied to a questionnaire or request for information, sometimes at length.

Over six plus years I have received help from many people: some are acknowledged under entries in the Directory, others I fear I may have missed from the following list (and I hope they will accept my apologies and general thanks at this point). I would like to thank, especially, the following:

Bernard Barr and Deirdre Mortimer, for information on parochial collections deposited in York Minster Library; Barry Bloomfield, for sending me disks of the 2nd ed. of the Directory of Rare Book and Special Collections before publication; Dr Ian Doyle, for information on Durham and other NE libraries; Phyllis DuBois, Secretary, for sending me detailed lists of pre-1700 books now in the care of the Bishop of Norwich's Committee for Books and Documents; Jane Francis, for much information on Bucks. parochial collections; Jonathan Goodchild (Deputy Secretary) and Janet Seeley (Librarian) of the CCC, for information, advice and encouragement when flagging; Sheila Hingley (Librarian) and Dr Michael Stansfield (Archivist), Canterbury Cathedral, for information on Kent collections; Peter Hoare, for information on Tenison's library and E. Midlands collections in general; Brian North Lee, for sharing lists with me, for information from his forthcoming book on parochial library bookplates, and for loaning those from the Bray library for reproduction; Paul Morgan, for sending me his personal CCC Committee files, information and encouragement; Dr Richard Palmer, librarian, and the staff of Lambeth Palace Library; Charles Parry, of the NLW, for much information on Welsh libraries, and for reading through the Welsh section; Dr Nigel Ramsay, for numerous references to libraries and books; Wendy Thirkettle and Alan Franklin, of Manx National Heritage, for information on Isle of Man library survivals; Michael Tupling, for much information on Suffolk parochial collections; Canon David Weston, Carlisle Cathedral, for information on parochial libraries in Carlisle and in the NW generally; David Williams, former Deputy Secretary, CCC, for starting me off on a long trail (see Postscript, pp. 56-8).

I am especially grateful to Peter Hoare for reading the whole text and making useful suggestions for its improvement, and for numerous corrections; and to Michael Twyman for taking on the onerous task of reading proofs.

Finally, I owe a great debt of gratitude to David Chambers, not only as designer, for the elegant appearance of the book, but for his many practical suggestions for correcting, arranging and improving the original, undoubtedly 'raw' text.

March 2003   Michael Perkin

The larger Bray bookplate, 1709
(see pp. 1, 47-8)

REFERENCES
& THEIR ABBREVIATIONS

This list is of books, articles, etc., cited more than once in the Directory entries, with their abbreviations, and other works (not abbreviated) referred to in the Editorial and Historical introductions (except those expanded in the footnotes) and Postscript. Other books and articles on, or relating to, specific libraries are listed under place-names in the Directory.

Allison & Rogers   A. F. Allison and D. M. Rogers, *A Catalogue of Catholic Books printed Abroad or Secretly in England, 1558–1640*, 1964.

Barr   C. B. L. Barr, 'Parish libraries in a region: the case of Yorkshire', *Proc. of the Library Association Study School and National Conference*, Nottingham, 1979, pp.32–41.

Barr, York Minster   C. B. L. Barr. The Minster Library. In: *A History of York Minster*, ed. G. E. Aylmer and Reginald Cant, Oxford, 1977, ch. XI, pp.487–538.

Best   Graham Best, 'Books and readers in certain eighteenth-century parish libraries' (PhD. Loughborough U. of Technology, Dept. of Library and Information Studies, 1985).

Bill Report, 1970   E. G. W. Bill, Report on Parochial Libraries, 1959–69. TS. CCC, 1970.

Blades, BIC   William Blades, *Books in Chains* (Bibliographical Miscellanies, 2–5), 1890; and as: *Books in Chains and other Bibliographical Papers*, 1892.

Blades, *Book-Worm*   William Blades, 'A list of minor libraries in England and Wales, ecclesiastical, parochial or scholastic', *The Book-Worm* (1866), Sept.–Nov., pp.134–5, 157–8, 172–3.

Boase   F. S. Boase, *Modern English Biography . . . since 1850*. 6v. Truro, 1892–1921.

Bodl. MS.Eng. Misc.c.360   Catalogues of parochial libraries deposited with the Bodleian Library by Dr Neil R. Ker.

Bodleian Library   *Fine Bindings 1500–1700 from Oxford Libraries: catalogue of an exhibition*. Oxford, 1968.

Bray Associates Records   USPG Archive, Bray Associates Records, 1729–1940. Rhodes House Library, Oxford.

Cameron   Andrea T. Cameron, 'Some parochial libraries of south-west Middlesex', *Ealing Occasional Papers in the History of Libraries*, no.1 (1972), pp.5–8.

CCC Questionnaire   Replies to a questionnaire on books in churches circulated by the Council for the Care of Churches in 1950 and listed in Lambeth Palace MS.3224, ff.124–.

Christie   R. C. Christie, 'The old church and school libraries of Lancashire', *Chetham Soc. N.S.* 7 (1885).

Clark, John Willis, *The Care of Books*, 2nd ed. Cambridge, 1902.

CLC   *The Cathedral Libraries Catalogue: books printed before 1701.* 2v. in 3. Ed.-in-Chief, David J. Shaw, 1984–98.

Cox, J. Charles, *Churchwardens' Accounts*, 1913 (ch.8 includes lists of books chained in churches).

Cox, J. Charles, *English Church Fittings, Furniture and Accessories*, 1923 (ch.xi. Chained books and church libraries).

Cox, Notes   J. Charles Cox, *Notes on the Churches of Derbyshire.* 4v. Chesterfield, 1875–9.

Cox & Harvey   J. Charles Cox and A Harvey, *English Church Furniture*, 1907. (ch.xi. Church libraries and chained books). Supplementary lists in: *The Library*, v.3 (1891), pp.179, 270–3, 441–5; *N & Q*, 12 ser. v.12 (1923), pp.493–6.

Crockford   *Crockford's Clerical Directory*, current edition.

Day   John C. Day, 'Parochial libraries in Northumberland before 1830', *Library History*, v.8:4 (1989), pp.93–103.

DNB   *Dictionary of National Biography.*

DRB   *A Directory of Rare Book and Special Collections*, ed. M. I. Williams, 1985.

DRB2   *A Directory of Rare Book and Special Collections*, 2nd ed., ed. B. C. Bloomfield, 1997.

DWB   *The Dictionary of Welsh Biography down to 1940*, ed. J. E. Lloyd and R. J. Jenkins, 1959.

Evans   David Roderick Evans, 'The five parochial libraries founded by Humphrey Chetham in 1653' (Dissertation, M.A. in Information and Library Studies, Manchester Metropolitan University, 1993).

Ferguson   James P. Ferguson, *The Parochial Libraries of Bishop Wilson.* Douglas, Isle of Man, 1975.

Fitch, 1965   J. A Fitch, 'Some ancient Suffolk parochial libraries', *Proc. of the Suffolk Inst. of Arch.*, v.30, pt.1 (1965), pp.44–87.

Fitch, 1977   *Suffolk Parochial Libraries: a Catalogue*, ed. A. Elisabeth Birkby, 1977. (Introd. by John Fitch).

Fletcher, Canon J. M. J., 'Chained books in Dorset and elsewhere', *Proc. of the Dorset Nat. Hist. Soc. and Antiq. Field Club*, v.35 (1914), pp.21–6.

Foster   J. Foster, *Alumni Oxonienses . . . 1500–1886.* 8v. Oxford, 1891.

Franks Collection   E. R. J. Gambier Howe, *Franks Bequest. Catalogue of British and American Book Plates bequeathed to the Trustees of the British Museum by Sir Augustus Wollaston Franks.* 3v. 1903–4.

Gibson   Strickland Gibson, *Early Oxford Bindings*, 1903.

Hastings, Paul, 'Parochial libraries in the nineteenth century', *Local Historian*, v.15 (1983), no.7, pp.406–13.

Hobson   G. D. Hobson, *Blind-Stamped Panels in the English Book-Trade c. 1485–1555*, 1944.

Howells   William Henry Howells, 'Anglican libraries in the diocese of St. David's in the eighteenth and nineteenth centuries'. 2v. (M.A. College of Librarianship Wales, University of Wales, 1982).

Kelly   Thomas Kelly, *Early Public Libraries: a History of Public Libraries in Great Britain before 1850*, 1966.

Kelly, Shrops.   *Catalogue of Books from Parochial Libraries in Shropshire*, ed. Miss O. S. Newman, 1971. (Introd. by Thomas Kelly).

Ker, MLGB2   *Medieval Libraries of Great Britain: a list of surviving books*, ed. N. R. Ker. 2nd ed. 1964. (Suppl. to the 2nd ed. by Andrew Watson, 1987).

Ker, MMBL   *Medieval Manuscripts in British Libraries*, by N. R. Ker and others. v.1–4, Oxford, 1969–72.

Ker, Pastedowns   N. R. Ker, *Fragments of Medieval Manuscripts used as Pastedowns in Oxford Bindings with a Survey of Oxford Binding c. 1515–1620* (Oxford Bib. Soc. Publications, N.S.5, 1951–2).

Lambeth Palace MSS   MS.3094: a collection of library catalogues and lists mainly collected by Dr E. G. W. Bill for the survey of parochial libraries reported on in 1970 (see: Bill Report); MSS 3221–4: notes and lists of the contents of parish libraries in England and Wales made by N. R. Ker (1908–82) both before and after the publication of PLCE1 in 1959.

Lee, British   Brian North Lee, *British Bookplates: a Pictorial History*, 1979.

Lee, Church   Brian North Lee, *Some Church of England Parochial Library and Cathedral Ex-Libris* [forthcoming].

Lee, Early   Brian North Lee, *Early Printed Book Labels*, 1976.

McKerrow, Dict.   R. B. McKerrow, ed. *A Dictionary of Printers and Book-sellers . . . 1557–1640*, 1910.

Manley   K. A. Manley, 'The SPCK and English book clubs before 1720', *Bodl. Lib. Record*, v.13 (1989), pp.231–43.

Martin   Christopher Martin, 'The care of parochial libraries'. [Unpublished TS, 1979. Copy in King's Lynn PL].

Morgan   Paul Morgan, 'Nineteenth-century church lending libraries', *Proc. of the Library Association Study School and National Conference*, Nottingham, 1979, pp.29–31.

Nicolson   William Nicolson, Bishop of Carlisle. Miscellany Accounts of the Diocese of Carlisle, [1703], ed. R. S. Ferguson. *Cumb. and Westm. Antiq. and Arch. Soc.* Extra Ser. v.1, 1877.

Nicolson & Burn   Joseph Nicolson and Richard Burn, *The History and Antiquities of the Counties of Westmorland and Cumberland*. 2v. 1777.

Notitia Parochialis, 1705   A collection of 1579 replies to the queries of an unknown 'Divine of the Church of England'. Bound up in 6v. by A. C. Ducarel. Lambeth Palace MSS. 960–5.

Oldham, Blind-Stamped   J. B. Oldham, *English Blind-Stamped Bindings*. Cambridge, 1952.

Oldham, Panels   J. B. Oldham, *Blind Panels of English Binders*. Cambridge, 1958.

Palmer, PLCE1   Annotations made by John Palmer in a copy of PLCE1 (BL Staff copy).

Pearce Survey, 1949–50   John Pearce, 'A survey of parochial libraries in the diocese of Truro compiled on behalf of the Archdeacons of Cornwall and Bodmin'. TS, Lambeth Palace MS.3224, ff.85–.

Pearson   David Pearson, *Oxford Bookbinding 1500–1640, including a Supplement to Neil Ker's Fragments of Medieval Manuscripts used in Pastedowns in Oxford Bindings*. (Oxford Bib. Soc. Pubns. 3 ser. v.3, Oxford, 2000).

Pevsner   Nikolaus Pevsner, and others, *The Buildings of England*.

PLCE1   *The Parochial Libraries of the Church of England*, 1959.

Plomer, Dict.   Henry R. Plomer, *A Dictionary of the Booksellers and Printers . . . 1641–1667*, 1907.

Read   E. Anne Read, *A Checklist of Catalogues and Periodical Articles relating to the Cathedral Libraries of England*. (Oxford Bib. Soc. Occasional Pubns. no.6, 1970).

Read   E. Anne Read, 'Cathedral libraries: a supplementary checklist', *Library History*, v.4:5 (1978), pp.141–63.

Richards   Raymond Richards, *Old Cheshire Churches*, rev. and enlarged ed., Didsbury, 1973.

Savage   E. A. Savage, *Old English Libraries*, 1911.

Scott   Graham K. Scott, 'English public and semi-public libraries in the provinces, 1750–1850'. (Library Association Final Examination, pt.6, 1951.) Unpbd TS.

Select Committee Report, 1849   *Report from the Select Committee on Public Libraries, together with the Proceedings of the Committee, Minutes of Evidence, and Appendix*. Printed 23 July 1849.

Shore   T. W. Shore, 'Tabular list of old parochial libraries in England and Wales; notices of other old church libraries; Bray libraries in Great Britain'. *Trans. and Proc. of the Library Assoc. United Kingdom Conference*, 1878–9, pp.145–53.

Shrops. PLC   *Catalogue of Books from Parochial Libraries in Shropshire*, prepared by the Shropshire County Library, 1971.

Smith   [Samuel Smith], *Publick Spirit illustrated in the Life and Designs of the Reverend Thomas Bray*. 2nd ed. 1808.

Southam, B. C., 'Chained libraries', *N & Q*, 12 ser. v.12, 23 June 1923, pp.493–6: 'A list of some churches possessing books in chains which are not in Blades' list'.

STC2   *A Short-Title Catalogue of Books printed in England . . . 1475–1640*. 2nd ed, ed. Katharine F. Pantzer. 3v. 1976–91.

Streeter   B. H Streeter, *The Chained Library: a survey of Four Centuries in the Evolution of the English Library*, 1931.

Suffolk PLC   *Suffolk Parochial Libraries: a Catalogue*, ed. A. Elisabeth Birkby, 1977.

Tallon   Maura Tallon, *Church in Wales Diocesan Libraries*, Athlone, 1962.

Venn   J. A. Venn, *Alumni Cantabrigienses* [to 1900]. 10v. Cambridge, 1922–54.

Weinreb & Hibbert   Ben Weinreb and Christopher Hibbert, *The London Encyclopaedia*, 1983.

Whitaker   *Whitaker's Almanack*. Current edition.

Williams, David M., 'The establishment and maintenance of the English parochial library: a survey'. (M.A. thesis, University College, London, 1977.)

Williams, David M., 'English parochial libraries: a history of changing attitudes', *ABMR*, v.5, no.4 (1978), pp.138–47.

Williams, David M., 'The use and abuse of a pious intention: changing attitudes to parochial libraries', *Proc. of the Library Association Study School and National Conference, Nottingham*, 1979, pp.21–8.

Wing   *Short-Title Catalogue of books printed in England . . . 1641–1700*, compiled by Donald Wing, 2nd ed. 3v. New York, 1972–88.

Woolf   D. R. Woolf, *Reading History in Early Modern England*, Cambridge, 2000.

Yates   Nigel Yates, 'The parochial library of All Saints, Maidstone, and other Kentish parochial libraries'. *Archaeologia Cantiana*, v.99 (1983), pp.159–74.

ABBREVIATIONS
& ACRONYMS

ABMR	Antiquarian Book Monthly Review
Arch.	Archaeological
Archit.	Architectural
Ass.	Association
augm.	augmented
AV	Authorized Version
b.	born
B & W	Diocese of Bath and Wells
Ban.	Diocese of Bangor
BCP	Book of Common Prayer
Bib.	Bibliographical
Birm.	Diocese of Birmingham
BL	British Library
Blackb.	Diocese of Blackburn
BLR	Bodleian Library Record
BM	British Museum
Bodl.	Bodleian Library
Bradf.	Diocese of Bradford
Bris.	Diocese of Bristol
Cant.	Diocese of Canterbury
Carl.	Diocese of Carlisle
Cat.(s)	Catalogue(s)
CCC	Council for the Care of Churches
CCT	Churches Conservation Trust
Chelmsf.	Diocese of Chelmsford
Ches.	Diocese of Chester
Chich.	Diocese of Chichester
CL	Cathedral Library
Co.L	County Library
Cov.	Diocese of Coventry
CRO	County Record Office
d.	died
ded.	dedicated / dedication
DeskL	Desk Library (see pp. 23–4)
Dur.	Diocese of Durham
ed.(s)	edited / edition / editor(s)
est.	established
ESTC	English Short-Title Catalogue
Ex.	Diocese of Exeter
FFC	Friends of Friendless Churches

fl.	flourished
Glouc.	Diocese of Gloucester
Guildf.	Diocese of Guildford
Heref.	Diocese of Hereford
HMC	Historical Manuscripts Commission
Hist.	Historical
imp.	imperfect
Jnl	Journal
LAR	Library Association Record (now CILIP *Update*)
Leic.	Diocese of Leicester
Lib.	Library
Lich.	Diocese of Lichfield
Linc.	Diocese of Lincoln
Liv.	Diocese of Liverpool
LL	Lending Library
Llan.	Diocese of Llandaff
Lon.	Diocese of London
Mag.	Magazine
Man.	Diocese of Manchester
Mon.	Diocese of Monmouth
M.P.	Michael Perkin
MS(S)	manuscript(s)
NADFAS	National Association of Decorative & Fine Arts Societies
N & Q	Notes & Queries
Nat.	Natural
n.d.	no date
Newc.	Diocese of Newcastle
NLW	National Library of Wales
Nor.	Diocese of Norwich
NRC	No reply to correspondence
N.S.	New series
NT	New Testament
OPAC	On-line Public Access Catalogue
OT	Old Testament
par.	parish
ParL	Parochial Library
ParLL	Parochial Lending Library
PCC	Parochial Church Council
Pet.	Diocese of Peterborough
pl.(s)	plate(s)
PL	Public Library
PLCE1	Parochial Libraries of the Church of England, 1959
Portsm.	Diocese of Portsmouth
Rec.	Record
red.	redundant

Ripon	Diocese of Ripon and Leeds
RO	Record Office
Roch.	Diocese of Rochester
RTS	Religious Tract Society
S & B	Diocese of Swansea and Brecon
S & M	Diocese of Sodor and Man
Sarum	Diocese of Salisbury
ser.	series
Sheff.	Diocese of Sheffield
Shrops. RRC	Shropshire Records and Research Centre, Shrewsbury
Soc.	Society
SPCK	Society for Promoting Christian Knowledge
St.Alb.	Diocese of St. Albans
St.As.	Diocese of St. Asaph
STC	Short Title Catalogue
St.D.	Diocese of St. Davids
St.E.	Diocese of St. Edmundsbury and Ipswich
S'wark	Diocese of Southwark
S'well	Diocese of Southwell
tp.	title-page
Trans.	Transactions
TS	typescript
U	University
UL	University Library
unpbd	unpublished
USPG	United Society for the Propagation of the Gospel
V & A	Victoria & Albert Museum, National Art Library
VCH	Victoria County History
Wakef.	Diocese of Wakefield
Win.	Diocese of Winchester
Worc.	Diocese of Worcester

EDITORIAL
INTRODUCTION

This book is a revised edition of *The Parochial Libraries of the Church of England: Report of a Committee appointed by the Central Council for the Care of Churches to investigate the Number and Condition of Parochial Libraries belonging to the the Church of England, with an Historical Introduction, Notes on Early Printed Books and their Care and an Alphabetical List of Parochial Libraries Past and Present*, published in 1959 by the Faith Press in conjunction with the College of Faith. Most of the work of compiling and editing the entries for the List was completed by F. C. Morgan (d.1978); Notes on Early Printed Books and their Care and the Index were drawn up by Joan M. Peterson; the Historical Introduction was drafted by Sir Frank Francis (d.1988) and Neil Ker (d.1982); and Neil Ker edited and prepared the book for publication. Information for this new edition has been obtained by personal visits, replies to a questionnaire and correspondence, and from printed and manuscript sources.[1]

Scope. In this edition the Directory has been revised and expanded to include the following additional categories:

1) libraries established up to *c.* 1900 (with a few after that date);
2) all libraries recorded as established by the Trustees for Erecting Parochial Libraries, and later by the Associates of Dr Bray, up to *c.* 1900;
3) the Trustees, Bray and SPCK libraries established in Wales (9 only were included in PLCE1, recorded from the replies to a questionnaire sent out to the Archdeacons of the Church in Wales in 1950);
4) some libraries with less than 'a dozen books printed before 1800' (excluded from PLCE1);
5) a broad sample of desk-libraries (see p.31), with one or more pre-1700 prescribed books. Only a few examples were included in PLCE1 (e.g. Ecclesfield, Sleaford, Sutton Courtenay, Wootton Wawen), because of their size, or because they were the beginnings of a larger library formed at a later date (e.g. Cartmel, Bridlington). Those newly recorded in this edition must of necessity be only a small sample of libraries with surviving books, since, as has been noted, most parish churches from the mid-16th to the end of the 17th century would have had one or more books, in many cases chained. While a great many have been reduced to fragments, lost, or destroyed, many do still survive, often in poor condition, some in churches, perhaps as many deposited with parish records in Diocesan Record Offices. It is not my contention that

---

1. Details of publications referred to in brief in this Editorial Introduction will be found under References and their Abbreviations.

these books can be said to form 'parochial libraries' of the kind established by Humphrey Chetham in the 1650s and later: the question of when any collection of books can be said to form a library is not one that can be easily resolved. The broad sample is included for the same, mainly historical, reasons as books in later collections (see p.29, & n.1). How such small collections of prescribed liturgical and other books, and indeed the private collections of the clergy from the same period, affected the general pattern of book provision, and the growth of libraries, is a question which can only be resolved by a much broader study of such holdings still in churches, and in record offices and other repositories throughout the country, which was not possible in the course of this revision. The information on those listed in the Directory is derived from a wide variety of sources. It is clear that some of the surviving books, perhaps many, must be later replacements or modern donations (the sources are rarely specific on this point). How the books were acquired is described on pp.30–1 and by Kelly (pp.48–50), and there is a useful account in Best, pp.4–10. The books prescribed from *c.* 1536 to 1586 by Royal Injunctions and Proclamations, by Canons, and by the edicts of successive archbishops, included the Bible, 'both in Latin and also in English', and 'of the largest volume in English', Erasmus' *Paraphrases* in English (1548–); Bishop John Jewel's *An Apologie . . . in Defence of the Church of England* (1562–), and his *A Defence of the Apologie* (1567–), and *Works* (1609–); John Foxe's *The Actes and Monuments . . . (Book of Martyrs*, 1563–);[2] and Henry Bullinger's *Fiftie Godlie and Learned Sermons* (1577–), and other works, added well into the 17th century. (Some popular, not always helpful, names given in sources for Bibles in these collections include: Bishops' Bible, 'Breeches' Bible, Cranmer's Bible, Geneva Bible, Great Bible, 'Treacle' Bible, 'Vinegar' Bible, etc.)

An analysis of some 132 inventories of parish churches in Bucks. in the 1780s listing books reveals that 127 held copies of Bibles (11 parishes with 2), and the same number held copies of the BCP (many with 2 to 4 copies, Amersham had 7). There were 18 parishes listing other service books; 39 had copies of the Book of Homilies; 7 had copies of Bishop Jewel's *A Defence of the Apologie*, or *Works*; 4 had copies of Foxe's *Book of Martyrs*; 2 had copies of Erasmus' *Paraphrases*; 1 had a copy of Bullinger's *Sermons*; and 1 a copy of Aquinas. Currently, 16 parishes in Bucks., included in this Directory, have one or more pre-1700 survivals from such desk-libraries, 7 with books on deposit with their records in the Bucks. RO, and a further 9 have books still in situ or on deposit elsewhere. This pattern of books[3] in Bucks. parishes once extant,

2. The canon of 1571 with respect to Foxe's work applied only to cathedral churches but, notwithstanding, the *Book of Martyrs* is by far the most commonly found historical item in parochial and desk-libraries up to the late 17th century. (Woolf, p.190)

3. I am greatly indebted to Jane Francis for passing on to me the tabulation of her research on these inventories in Bucks. RO (D/A/GT)

and surviving now, can perhaps be regarded as typical of the survival rate for other counties in England and Wales.

Desk libraries with surviving books were listed in *N & Q* from the 1850s onwards, and by William Blades in 1890; Cox & Harvey produced lists in 1907 (which were supplemented in *The Library* and *N & Q*, particularly by B. C. Southam), Cox again in 1913 and 1923, and Canon J. M. M. Fletcher in 1914. The furniture and fittings of chained libraries in parish churches were discussed in J. W Clark in 1909, and in detail by B. H. Streeter in 1931.

Additional locations for surviving books have been drawn from lists of books noted in replies to the Pearce survey of the diocese of Truro (1949–50), and, country-wide, in replies to a CCC Questionnaire of 1950 (the results recorded in Lambeth Palace MS.3224, ff.85–96 and 127–36, respectively); from lists of books now in the care of the Bishop of Norwich's Committee for Books and Documents; from the Records of Parish Churches provided by voluntary recorders for NADFAS (using the set of reports in CCC for Berks., Bucks., Hants., Oxon., and Warwicks.), and from the lists of parish deposits in Record Offices for these counties; and from other sources noted under individual entries.

6) One library included in PLCE1, King's Cliffe, has been omitted from this edition as having no parochial links.

Revised and new matter. Sections I and II of the Historical Introduction have been lightly revised to reflect changes of location and new information, but are substantially unchanged from PLCE1 (the footnotes are re-numbered, and changes and additions are signalled in new footnotes enclosed in square brackets and signed: M.P.). A new Postscript and Chronological Table are provided as sections III and IV, followed by a new Table of Libraries by Counties. Information on medieval and later MSS is included in entries in the Directory, with references to fuller descriptions elsewhere, and the list on pp.108–11 of PLCE1 is omitted. Some MSS in parish churches, or once in parish churches, in that list, and later listings, are recorded under place-names in the Directory, even though they did not form part of a library in the church then or subsequently (e.g. Appleby Magna, Wollaton). The Appendices which follow the Directory contain: A, the Act of 1709 (reproduced as in PLCE1); B and C, the Bishop Wilson List, and the Oley, Bray and Wilson table, both new in this edition; D, Notes on Parochial Collections and their Care, a new version of this section in PLCE1; and E, Reports and recommendations, a summary of the 1959 Report, with later Reports and legislation.

Order of information in each Directory entry. The **Place-name** is given as in Crockford (with some variation in Welsh place-names), but the qualifying element is not placed after the main element, e.g. East Bedfont, not Bedfont, East. Some places in Wales in English dioceses are listed under England, e.g. Church Stoke, Mont. and Trelystan, Mont. (both in Heref. diocese). Churches in London filed in Crockford under areas of London, e.g. Bloomsbury, are listed here alphabetically by dedication. The **County Name** is that before the 1974 boundary changes (with the present-day names of counties and shires in brackets).⁴ The **Dedication** is as given in Crockford (unless an earlier or pre-amalgamation of livings name is recorded). Redundant churches are noted here, e.g. CCT, Churches Conservation Trust, etc., and the present **Diocese** in abbreviated form as in Crockford (see Abbreviations, pp.20–2). In the next line the **Number of Surviving Volumes** is given in brackets. As far as possible a distinction is made between the number of titles and the number of volumes; where this distinction is not made the total could be either. Information supplied in response to a postal enquiry to the incumbent, or other person looking after the library, for this edition (or in some cases PLCE1) is indicated by an **Asterisk**. NRC = no reply to correspondence. The **Present Location** of surviving books from the library is in the same line. In the **Body of the Entry** an attempt is made to provide a concise chronological history of the collection, with special attention to origins, founders and donors (with their dates where they can be provided from standard sources, e.g. DNB and the Oxford and Cambridge University lists), buildings, furniture and fittings, followed by notes on contents, the number of books from different periods, individual books, subjects, bindings, manuscripts, etc. Cross-references to other place-names in the Directory are printed in bold. Then follows a listing of known **Catalogues** of the collection and their location (with shelf-marks if known), and lastly, the **References** used to create the entry, either in full or abbreviated form, in the approximate order of their use in the entry.

After working on this revision for over six years I have come to realize the impossibility of 'completeness' in a compilation of this nature: the picture is constantly changing. Similarly, with information from such a wide variety of sources, achieving complete accuracy and consistency is unlikely. I have made endeavours towards both, and errors and inconsistencies that remain are entirely my responsibility.

4. As listed in Whitaker, 2001, p.552.

STATISTICS
PAROCHIAL LIBRARIES, *c.*1800–2000[1]

Parochial Libraries Report, 1959 (PLCE1)

Total no. of libraries listed:	253
Total no. of libraries with books:	146

	PLCE1 *c.* 1800–1959	Bill Report 1959–70	Directory[2] 1970–2000
Libraries deposited in:			
Cathedral libraries	5	6	35
(desk-libraries)			84
College libraries	2		12
County Hall			1
County libraries	2	8	
Chapter libraries			1
Diocesan House	1		1
Heritage Centre			1
Institutes (desk-libraries)			2
Lambeth Palace Lib.			4
Museums	2		3
(desk libraries)			2
National libraries : England			4
(desk-libraries)			1
: Wales			11
: Ireland			1
: France			1
Private houses			5
(desk-libraries)			1
Private libraries			3
Public libraries	13	9	5
(desk-libraries)			1
Record Offices	2		38
(desk-libraries)			60
Rectories (not of parent church)			2
Religious communities	1		
Representative Body of the Church in Wales			1

1. The figures in this table represent any holdings from a single volume to a whole library.
2. The present location only is recorded for libraries with several institutional moves since 1959. Totals in this column include some deposits not singled out in earlier reports.

	PLCE1 *c.* 1800–1959	Bill Report 1959–70	Directory 1970–2000
Schools	3		
Subscription libraries	1		
Theological Colleges			1
University Libraries: England	5	14	46
(desk-libraries)			3
: Scotland			1
: Belgium			1
: U.S.A.			13
(desk-libraries)			1

Subsequent fate of other libraries:

sold (part-sold)	14	5	6
sold (part-sold) at auction			9
destroyed (part-destroyed) by fire or in WW2	14	3	11
dispersed /disposed of			4
stolen (part-stolen)	1		2
lost (part-lost)	2	5	3
lost but now found			6

Additions to the Directory, 2000:

Bray Trustees' and Associates' Libraries, *c.* 1720–1900:	
England (including 3 SPCK libraries)	185
Wales (including 4 SPCK libraries)	97
Bishop Wilson libraries, Isle of Man	19
Other libraries to *c.* 1900	143
A sample of desk-libraries	354

Directory, 2000:

Total no. of libraries listed:	1061
with books	558
in England:	920
with books	538
still in situ	67
in the Isle of Man:	19
with books	8
still in situ	3
in Wales:	122
with books	12
still in situ	3

HISTORICAL INTRODUCTION
I. LIBRARIES IN CHURCHES & PARSONAGES
FIFTEENTH TO TWENTIETH CENTURIES

I

Many parish churches contain a number of books which varies in different places from two or three volumes to several hundreds. It is often asked how they came to be there, and why dusty, shabby, and apparently out-of-date books should be preserved. It is the purpose of this publication to show that these books are important possessions, handed down from the past, to be valued in the same way as other treasures. They are part of the cultural heritage of which we are now the trustees. Their interest is great, for they are evidence of historical events, and give us glimpses of the way our forebears dealt with the problems of their time, as well as material for the study of social and political life.[1]

As we would expect, these libraries were mainly theological.[2] We find Bibles in English, Hebrew, Latin, Greek, or in two or more languages arranged in parallel columns; also commentaries on the Bible. The Fathers of the Church, such as Augustine, Chrysostom and Ambrose, are represented, and from the 16th century onwards, there was a continuous stream of theology including doctrine, exposition and controversy. The Roman claims naturally demanded attention, and works on both sides survive. There are collections of sermons, many of which show an unexpected wealth of imagery and force of expression. It has been said of 17th century sermons that 'they are grave, dry, abstruse, dreadful; to our debilitated attentions they are hard to follow . . . they are devoted to a theology that yet lingers in the memory of mankind only through certain shells of words long since emptied of their original meaning. Nevertheless, these writings are monuments of vast learning, and of a stupendous intellectual energy both in the men who produced them and in the men who listened to them. . . They were conceived by noble minds; they are themselves noble. They are superior to our jests. We may deride them if we will; but they are not derided'.[3]

1. [Other reasons can be given, e.g. i) the inscriptions and notes in individual books can provide important historical evidence for provenance research, especially at the local level, but also sometimes on the national level; ii) a knowledge of the holdings of mss, and perhaps unique or rare early printed books, will promote research, especially when recorded in catalogues, union catalogues and computer databases; iii) they contribute to the history of the book and the history of libraries at all periods; iv) they contribute to the continuing study of the book as a physical object, particularly in the areas of descriptive bibliography and bookbinding research. M.P.]
2. [But, in the later collections, especially, there are surprising 'pockets' of books on a wide range of non-theological subjects: see the Index under subject headings. M.P.]
3. M. C. Tyler, *A History of American Literature*, v.1, 1607–76, 1879, pp.192–3.

2

The keeping of books in parish churches was a common practice in the Middle Ages, as appears from wills and inventories. Probably most churches possessed some books other than service-books in the 15th century. There were, for example, a dozen such at St. Margaret's, New Fish Street, London, in 1476. They are listed, together with 47 service-books, in the churchwardens' records, and, as commonly, were chained.[4] Probably most churches had fewer books than this, but the principal churches are likely to have had more. Thus Boston church had a 'libraria' in the second half of the 15th century. Copies of the Polychronicon and Dieta Salutis and other books were bequeathed to it in 1457.[5] A common-law book was bequeathed to it in 1469.[6] These books were, no doubt, part of a larger collection.

Medieval manuscripts like those at Boston were already old-fashioned by the time of the Reformation. The invention of printing, not the change of religion, was primarily responsible for their disuse. But it is likely that in most places such books as there were, whether printed or manuscript, were thrown out, along with the old service-books, at or soon after the Reformation. Incumbents had no longer any use for a popular priest's guide like Pupilla Oculi, whether in print or in manuscript. A few medieval service-books and Bibles belong now to the churches to which they belonged before the Reformation, but the churches have not owned them continuously since the Reformation. No church possesses any of its pre-Reformation library books, except possibly All Saints, Bristol.

3

During the half century after the Reformation, the only institutional libraries in England were those which had survived from the Middle Ages, often in a rather struggling fashion, in the two universities and attached to the ancient cathedrals and to the colleges of Eton and Winchester, and those established in a few of the colleges and schools founded in the middle and second half of the century. Nothing that we should call a library is known to have existed in a parish church in this period. Reading matter for the clergy was provided, however, to some extent in the old way, by bequest, and reading matter for the laity was provided by authority. An order of 1538 required the placing of English Bibles in churches.[7] In 1547 King Edward's injunctions required incumbents to provide the Bible 'of ye largest volume in English' and 'the

4. C.Wordsworth and H. Littlehales, *The Old Service-Books of the English Church*, 1904, pl. II.
5. *Richmondshire Wills*, Surtees Soc., v.26 (1853), p.2.
6. *Registrum Cancellarii Oxoniensis 1434–1469*, v. II, Oxford Historical Soc., vol.94, 1932, p.307.
7. Second Royal Injunctions of Henry VIII, 1538. 'Item, that ye shall provide on this

Paraphrasis of Erasmus also in Englishe vpon the Gospelles, and the same sette up in some conuenient place, with in the sayed Churche, that they haue cure of, whereas their Parishioners maye moste commodiously resorte vnto the same, and reade the same'.[8] These injunctions were repeated by Queen Elizabeth in 1559.[9] The repetition was necessary because what had been 'sette up' by King Edward had been taken down again by Queen Mary. The following note may not refer to books in a church, but it probably shows what happened to books in many churches between 1553 and 1558: 'Memorandum that i burnyd all the boockes. In primys a bybyll of rogers translatyon the paraphrases yn Englysche A communyon boocke Halles cronekylles the byshop of canterberyes booke Latimers sermonttes Hopers sermontes A psalter'.[10]

In Elizabeth's reign and James's and later, the Bible, the Homilies of the Church, the *Paraphrases* and some other books, notably Foxe's *Book of Martyrs,*[11] and Jewel's *Works,*[12] were so widely distributed by injunction and otherwise, that an appreciable number have survived the wear and tear of three or four hundred years. They were, and in a few cases still are, chained to reading desks. Lists of these 'desk-libraries' have been compiled, but these are necessarily far from complete, since no reliable list can be made except after a detailed survey, county by county. Very few of these 'desk libraries' have as many as a dozen books.[13]

side the feast of Easter next coming, one book of the whole Bible of the largest volume in English'. See *Visitation Articles and Injunctions of the Period of the Reformation,* ed. W. H. Frere, v.2 (Alcuin Club Collections, v.15, 1910), p.35.

8. *Iniunccions geuen by Edward the sixte,* 1547, sig. a.iiii verso. These are also given by Frere, *Visitation Articles,* p.117.

9. *Iniunccions geuen by the Queenes Maiestie,* 1559, sig. A.iii.

10. A note at the end of *Autores Historiae Ecclesiasticae,* Basel, 1557, in a contemporary London binding, no.211 of the books in the parochial library at Cartmel, Lancs.

11. The Canons of 1571 required that the Archbishops and Bishops, Deans, Canons, and Archdeacons should possess at home, in the hall or dining room, where they could be perused by visitors, 'the Bible of the largest volume', (i.e. the Bishops' Bible of 1568), Foxe's *Book of Martyrs* and 'alios quosdam similes libros ad religionem appositos'. Deans were required to provide the same books in the cathedrals, but the churchwardens of parish churches were only required to provide, in addition to the Prayerbook and Book of Homilies, the 'Bible of the largest volume'. Some, no doubt, thought it wise to place a more liberal interpretation on the Canon. Thus, according to the vestry minutes of St. Michael, Cornhill, in the city of London, it was agreed on January 11, 1571–2, 'That the Book of Martyrs of Mr Foxe and the paraphrases of Erasmus shal be bought for the church and tyed with a chayne to the Egle bras'. See *Accounts of the Churchwardens of St. Michael, Cornhill, 1456–1608,* ed. W. H. Overall, 1871, p.167.

12. Archbishop Bancroft wished that 'every parish in England' should have a copy of Jewel's *Works* (letter of 27 July 1610 printed by E. Cardwell, *Documentary Annals,* 2nd ed. 1844, II, 160.

13. [For the scope of the sample in this Directory see the Editorial Introduction, pp.23–5, and the references given there. See also plate, p.157. M.P.]

4

Early libraries end 916[c]

The first establishment of libraries of some size independent of universities, cathedrals, colleges and schools, comes not surprisingly in the great period at the end of the 16th century, which is in Oxford especially notable for the foundation of the Bodleian Library, and the thorough reformation of the libraries at Merton College, All Souls College and St. John's College. We read of a room called the library in the church at Leicester in 1586–7 and in the church at Newcastle in 1597. At Bury St. Edmunds various donors combined to form a church library in 1595: contemporary records of the foundation are lacking, but the facts can be ascertained from inscriptions in the books themselves. At Grantham Francis Trigge founded a library in the church by will dated 20 October 1598. At Ipswich William Smarte bequeathed books to the church by will dated 8 January 1598–9.

The common goal – a library for the clergy

The wording of wills and other records of the use and ownership of these libraries and other libraries founded in the next century in towns suggest that town libraries and church libraries are not easily distinguishable.[14] It is no coincidence that, except at Norwich, town libraries were not set up in towns where there were already cathedral libraries. There is no distinction, except in the placing, between Trigge's gift of a library to the Alderman and Burgesses of Grantham for the use of the clergy and others in the town and soke of Grantham and in the County of Lincoln, and Archbishop Harsnett's gift of a library in 1631 to the Bailiffs and Corporation of Colchester for the use of the clergy of the town and other divines. Trigge's was put in the church, and is usually thought of as a church library, Harsnett's was not. A convenient place for a library was all important. Henry Bury's bequest of money to buy books for the common use of the parish of Manchester in 1634 was conditional on their having 'a convenient place of their owne'. The libraries kept in buildings apart from the church, Norwich, Ipswich (after 1612), Bristol, Colchester, and Leicester (after 1632);[15] the libraries kept in parish churches but under lay control, having been formed by the citizens or entrusted by their donors to the town governors, Barnstaple, Grantham, King's Lynn, Manchester, Marlborough, Newark, Newcastle, Totnes, Wisbech; the libraries which seem to have been in the control of the church, Bury, Oakham, Stamford, all contained the same sort of

14. School libraries and town libraries may also be difficult to distinguish. The library founded by Bishop Parkhurst at Guildford Grammar School in 1573 is, and was already at the end of the 16th century, considered to be a school library, but according to the terms of Parkhurst's will, his gift was 'to the Lybrarie of the same Town ioyning to the schole' (G. C.Williamson, *Guildford in the Olden Time*, 1904, p.105).

15. For the history of the Norwich, Bristol, and Colchester libraries, see G. A. Stephen, *Three Centuries of a City Library*, 1917; N. Mathews, *Early Printed Books and Manuscripts in the City Reference Library, Bristol*, 1899; G. Goodwin, *Catalogue of the Harsnett Library at Colchester*, 1888.

books and were formed with the same object, the advancement of learning. The books are for students, and, to a large extent, in Latin. They are, in fact, a selection of the books which would have been found at this time in a college library at Oxford or Cambridge, and may be thought of as college libraries in miniature transported to the provinces for the use mainly of the local clergy.

At the end of the 17th century libraries were to be found in the parish churches of a score of towns. A dozen more came into existence at the turn of the century. Of these Reigate, founded in 1701 for the use of the 'freeholders, vicar and inhabitants', is the best documented and perhaps the most interesting.

5

Outside the towns only a very small number of libraries were founded, so far as we know, before the last two decades of the 17th century. The founder of one of them, Tankersley (1615), used a phrase which was much used later: the books were given to the incumbent 'and his successors for ever'. At Langley Marish (1631) the library was for the 'perpetual benefit' of the incumbent and other clergy. At King's Norton (1662?) the library was given to the parish and kept in the Grammar School in the churchyard. At Chirbury (1677) the library was 'for the Use of the Schoolmaster or any other of the Parishioners': it, too, was to be placed in the schoolhouse in the churchyard. These are all libraries in which books in Latin were numerous. In contrast to them, the libraries founded by Humphrey Chetham, d.1653, in the churches of Bolton, Gorton, Turton, Manchester and Walmesley contained only books in English and were 'for the edification of the common people' – in the words of Chetham's will.

Chetham's foundations are parochial libraries in the sense which seems now the obvious sense. The term was not, however, used at this time, nor at all, as far as can be discovered, until the last years of the 17th century, when it was applied to the type of library then in favour, that reserved for the exclusive use of the incumbent and his successors.

6

A crisis in the history of libraries in churches occurred about 1680. Before this time only a few libraries had been founded and most of these were in towns. During the next half-century, however, many libraries were founded and mainly in those churches where the incumbents were least likely to have books of their own. The idea of placing libraries deliberately in the poorer livings throughout the country occurred, it seems, to Sir Roger Twysden (d.1672).[16] It was put into practice in a small way by Barnabas Oley in 1685 and later by

16. T. Bray, *Bibliotheca Parochialis*, 1697, sig.a.3 verso.

the Trustees for Erecting Parochial Libraries.[17] Its best known and most enthusiastic advocate was Thomas Bray (1656–1730), whose writings encouraged many people to found libraries. The provision of a parochial library became a proper object of charity. 'Have you a Parochial Library?' was a question asked at episcopal and archidiaconal visitations.[18] Some of the country clergy left books to their successors for ever, and some of the nobility and gentry founded libraries in their local churches, for example at Astley, Bassingbourn, Bromham, and More. The number of libraries thus founded in country churches and parsonages 'to be an agreable Companion to a Man of Letters destitute of Books in a solitary Country'[19] was no doubt much larger than would appear from the Directory in this book. Many unrecorded 'standing' libraries are likely to exist in parsonages and many, once there, are likely to have perished from the ordinary causes or because they were dispersed with the goods of deceased incumbents (cf. Flaxley, Sible Hedingham, Tideford). Many of the existing libraries are of particular interest, because they introduce us to the books of the individual donors, usually a mixture of Latin and English, including pamphlets and schoolbooks. Inscriptions often show that books were bought during their owner's tenure of a college fellowship at Oxford or Cambridge. Thus we have the books of John Okes of St. Edmund Hall in the Wotton-under-Edge collection, the books of Cavendish Nevile of University College in the Norton collection, and the books of William Beasley of King's College, in the Mentmore collection.

7

In 1685 Barnabas Oley, fellow of Clare College, Cambridge, prebendary of Worcester and vicar of Great Gransden, required his executor to give 16 vols. to each of ten poor vicarages in the diocese of Carlisle, 'the several books . . . to be kept within the church . . . for the use of the vicars there for the time being and their successors for ever'. The books thus given were (1–4) either Hammond's *Works* in four vols., or four vols. to an equivalent value, Jackson's *Works* (three vols.) and Towerson's *Works*; also (5) Andrewe's *Sermons*, (6) Mede's *Works*, (7) Sanderson's *Sermons* and (8) his *Nine Cases of Conscience*, (9) Pearson *On the Creed*, (10) Usher's *Body of Divinity*, (11)

17. [PLCE1 has 'a committee of the Society for Promoting Christian Knowledge', but, as Thomas Kelly pointed out in a letter to N. R. Ker, 14 April 1965, 'the libraries you describe as SPCK libraries were not in fact promoted by the SPCK but by a special body (consisting, it is true, substantially of the same people) known as the Trustees for Erecting Parochial Libraries and Promoting other Charitable Designs. Newman himself in his correspondence insists that the SPCK had no responsibility for these libraries: the libraries it promoted were the lending libraries in each of the four Welsh dioceses between 1708–11'. (Letter in Lambeth Palace MS.3224, and see Kelly, pp.107–9. This correction has been made throughout this edition.) M.P.]
18. For example in 1716 (Canterbury, Norwich), 1722 (Oxford), 1735 (Bristol), 1759 (Oxford).
19. See p.46.

The Works of the Author of the Whole Duty of Man, (12) Sparrow's *Rationale* and (13) his *Collection of Canons*, (14) Cave's *Primitive Christianity*, (15) Herbert's *Country Parson* and (16) Walton's *Lives*. These books cost £10. 10s. 8d. per set of 16. They were duly distributed in 1687 to the churches at Ainstable, Askham, Burgh-by-Sands, Crosby-on-Eden, Crosby Ravensworth, Dalston, Dearham, Isel, Thursby and Wigton. In 1703 when Bishop Nicolson made a primary visitation of his diocese the Bishop caused the titles of the books and the articles of agreement drawn up at the time of their distribution to be entered in his journal, so that he could make careful enquiry concerning them in each of the ten parishes.[20] What he found was not very satisfactory.[21] In 1959 eight vols. survived at Dalton and four at Ainstable: these have now disappeared, but 11 vols. have been found from Crosby Ravensworth, now on deposit in Carlisle Cathedral library. It is not surprising that most of them have now vanished, since no provision for the housing of the books had been made by Oley's executor. The appearance of the books at Isel in the 18th century is recorded in a draft letter from one of the rectors: 'These Books are kept in a little study along with my own; and are sufficiently distinguished from them by the manner of their Binding. For they are all bound after an uniform manner which I take to be calf dressed in imitation of Buff. They have all been letter'd on the Back with these letters B:Oley, but the lettering is so tarnished by the length of time that (it) is now scarce legible'.[22] Evidently the books were then in the rectory.

8

Bray's enthusiasm for libraries is well known.[23] He was appointed rector of Sheldon, near Birmingham, in 1690, at the age of 34. He took an active interest in social affairs and as a result of this, he was picked out by Henry Compton, Bishop of London, 'to model the infant church of England in the province of Maryland', and was offered the position of bishop's commissary there in 1696. Before accepting, however, he seems to have investigated whether he could get sufficient clergymen to go to the colonies, and to have formed the opinion that the only volunteers were poor men, not in the position to buy the books necessary to keep up their education. This state of affairs Bray reported to the Bishop, and recommended that libraries were both necessary for the well-being of the clergy going to America, and an encouragement to them. His recommendations were accepted, and he proceeded to

20. *Miscellany Accounts of the Diocese of Carlisle*, ed. R. S. Ferguson for the Cumberland and Westmorland Antiquarian and Archaeological Society, 1877, pp.7–8.
21. *ibid*, pp.7, 14, 20, 22, 74, 77, 80, 110.
22. The letter is kept in the church safe.
23. For Bray see the DNB (J. H. Overton); E. L. Pennington, *The Reverend Thomas Bray* (Church Historical Society [U.S.A.] Publication, no.7), 1934; G. Smith, 'Dr. Thomas Bray', *LAR*, v.12 (1910), pp.242–60; H. P. Thompson, *Thomas Bray*, 1954.

Bray's
plans
for
libraries
in England
+ America

Maryland, where he set up a library, named the Annapolitan Library after Princess Anne of Denmark, at Annapolis. In furtherance of his plans he published *Proposals for the Encouragement and Promoting of Religion and Learning in the Foreign Plantations,* 1696?, setting out a scheme for a parochial library in every parish in America. Another book, *An Essay towards promoting all Necessary and Useful Knowledge, both Divine and Human In all parts of His Majesty's Dominions, both at home and abroad,* 1697, contained proposals to the gentry and clergy for purchasing lending libraries for all the deaneries of England where the author had also found many clergymen too poor to own books. Bray went into details of administration, suggesting titles of books recommended, a preliminary classification scheme, the marking and care of books. It was his suggestion that five parishes should be grouped together as a deanery with a decanal library to serve as a lending library 'to allow (both clergy and gentry) to carry the books to their homes', while the parochial libraries would form 'standing' libraries. His *Bibliotheca Parochialis,* published in 1697, and his *Apostolick Charity,* published in 1699, were both intended to promote his library projects. In furtherance of the same ends and owing to the growth of his schemes, he prepared the first sketch of the Society for Promoting Christian Knowledge, a society with the objects of setting up libraries at home and abroad, charity schools, missions, etc., which held its first meeting in 1699, and two years later he obtained the charter for the Society for the Propagation of the Gospel throughout the British Plantations. His advocacy of parochial libraries continued throughout his life. In 1704, in *An Introductory Discourse to Catechetical Instruction . . . in a letter to the clergy of Maryland . . . with a preface to . . . the parochial clergy and school masters in this Kingdom,* he wrote, 'I would recommend the having a book press with a lock and key, fixt in the vestry, or chancel of every Church'. In 1709 Bray put out a broadsheet, *Proposal for erecting Parochial Libraries in the Meanly endow'd Cures throughout England,* the contents of which were summarized by William Blades in the following words:

'Many will be surprised to hear, that in England and Wales there are above 2,000 parishes where the income is under £30, of which 1,200 are under £20, and 500 under £10. Of necessity these are without books, a deficiency which good men have often tried to supply. A committee of clergy and laity have met to promote the good work, and so far prospered that they have got together over 3,000 folios, 4,000 4tos. and 8vos., besides having put to press many books now out of print. Fifty-two libraries are now nearly complete and 500 more proposed. An Act of Parliament has been passed for the better preservation of Parochial Libraries, and those who are willing to be benefactors to this charity, are desired to pay the sum they shall contribute to Mr. Henry Hoare, in Fleet Street, London'.[24]

The Act of Parliament mentioned in this *Proposal* was passed on 4 March

24. Quoted from Blades's preface to the reprint (1889) of *An Overture for Found-*

1708–9.[25] The preamble includes the following passage: 'Whereas in many Places . . . the Provision for the Clergy is so mean, that the necessary Expence of Books for the better Prosecution of their Studies cannot be defrayed by them; and whereas of late Years, several charitable and well-disposed Persons have by charitable Contributions erected Libraries within several Parishes and Districts in *England,* and *Wales*; but some Provision is wanting to preserve the same . . . from Embezilment; Be it therefore enacted . . . That in every Parish or Place where such a Library is or shall be erected, the same shall be preserved for such Use and Uses, as the same is and shall be given, and the Orders and Rules of the Founder and Founders of such Libraries shall be observed and kept'. The following are its main provisions:

(2) Every incumbent, rector, minister, or curate of a parish, before he shall be permitted to use and enjoy such library, shall give security for the preservation of the library and due observation of the rules and orders belonging to it.

(4) The incumbent shall make a catalogue of the library to be delivered to the ordinary.

(5) Where a library is already erected, the catalogue shall be ready before 29 September 1709, or in the case of a new library, within six months of its foundation.

(6) Upon the death of an incumbent, the library shall be locked up by the churchwardens.

(8) The incumbent shall enter the names of benefactors in a book.

(10) Books shall not be alienated without the consent of the ordinary, and then only if they are duplicates.

9

Some of the information given in Bray's *Proposal* and in the Act may have been based on the replies to a printed Advertisement by 'a Divine of the Church of England' inserted at the foot of a broadsheet royal Brief. The Brief, dated 28 February 1704–5, was issued to raise money, 'upwards of £4,800', for the rebuilding of All Saints' Church, Oxford.[26] The Advertisement is addressed, 'To the Reverend the Minister of every Parochial Church and Chapel in England'. Bray himself replied to it as minister of Sheldon. It asks ten questions. Ministers were requested to answer them on the back or at the foot of the Advertisement. Question 6 is, 'What library is settled or settling in

ing and Maintaining of Bibliothecks in every Paroch throughout this Kingdom (i.e. Scotland), a pamphlet printed in 1699 and attributed to James Kirkwood, minister of Minto.

25. For the full text of the Act see Appendix A (pp.439-42).

26. A copy of the Brief and Advertisement returned from Gotham, Nottingham-shire, without contribution to the fund or a reply to the Advertisement, is now Bodl. MS.Rawlinson B.407a f.144.

your Parish, and by whom?' Question 7 is, 'If the yearly Value of your
Rectory, Vicarage, or Chapelry be under £30, how much?' On the return of
the Briefs 1579 replies to the Advertisement were detached. They now form
the document known as 'Notitia Parochialis'.[27]

Nearly all the incumbents who replied to the Advertisement either did not
answer question 6 or said that there was no library settled or settling in their
parish. 31 of them gave positive answers, saying that they had or were getting
a library (23), or that there was a school library (2) or a town library (1), or
some other sort of library (2) in the parish, or referring to individual books in
possession of the incumbents for ever (3).[28] What they have to say is often of
interest to us. It was, no doubt, of interest to Bray and his friends.

10

The Committee of laity and clergy to which Bray referred in his *Proposal* and
of which he was a member functioned from 1705 until 1729. Henry Newman,
the able Secretary of SPCK, was also Secretary of the Committee, and its
activities are set out in his admirable minutes and in the full record of
correspondence which he kept. The Minute Book, called 'The Proceedings of
the Trustees for Erecting Parochial Librarys; and Promoting other Charitable
Designs', the correspondence, and the accounts reveal the care with which the
Committee furthered its scheme.[29] They reveal also that important as Bray
was as a promoter of parochial libraries, it is wrong to say, as has commonly
been said, that he himself founded them. The 64 or more libraries established

27. Lambeth Palace MSS. 960–5. The replies were bound up in these six volumes by
A. C. Ducarel, Lambeth Librarian. He had bought them in 1760 from the Revd. Mr
Entick of Stepney, who had bought them in the Harleian sale.
28. The 'Notitia Parochialis' contains information about the following libraries
included in the Directory: Beccles, Bicester, Bilston, Bury (Lancs.), Chirbury, Costock,
Denchworth, Frisby-on-the-Wreak, Hull (St. Mary Lowgate), Hurley, Leicester,
Nantwich, Newcastle upon Tyne, North Grimston, Reigate, Sheffield, Sheldon,
Skipton, Sleaford, Stainton, Warwick, Womersley, York (St. Mary Castlegate); and
also about school libraries at Cheltenham and at Newport, Shrops. (nos. 1485,
1311); about a library in the town at Gainsborough 'settled by the voluntary
Subscriptions of several persons which was begun A.D.1696' (no.879); about a
library at Bishops Castle, Shrops.: 'We have no public library, only a private one for
the use of neighbors given by Charles Mason Esq. one of or Representatives in
Parliament' (no.358); about the library in the collegiate (and parochial) church of
Southwell 'settling by ye Prebendaries and Neighbouring Gentlemen, but it advances
slowly' (no.1252); and about individual books at Myndtown, Shrops. – 'but one
book of Dr Braye's gift'– (no.418); at Crosthwaite, Cumberland, a Josephus in Greek
and Latin by Mr Appleford of St. John's College, Cambridge (no.1182); and at
Greenford, Middlesex, Walton's Polyglot and Castell's Lexicon, donor unknown
(no.546). The other libraries founded before 1705 (see pp.59–64) were in parishes
from which no reply to the advertisement was made, except Halifax (no.397), whose
incumbent did not answer the question about the library.
29. [Now deposited in Cambridge UL. M.P.]

between 1710 and 1729 were the Trustees' libraries. Two of the Trustees were men of substance, Henry Hoare, and Robert Nelson, and they were in their way no less vital than Bray to its success.[30] Contributions received on 50 occasions in the years 1706 to 1710 amounted to £1,738. 8s.[31]

The first meeting of the Trustees was on 30 July 1705. The minutes of this meeting begin with the words 'Whereas the Reverend Dr Bray has communicated to Sr Humphrey Mackworth, Mr Nelson, Mr Hoar, and Mr Brewster a Proposal for encouraging and erecting Parochial and Lending Libraries'.[32] The Trustees soon decided that parochial libraries, permanent and inalienable, were to be preferred to lending libraries.[33] 'A Catalogue of Books suitable for a Parochial Catachetick Librarie' was produced at the meeting on 8 March 1705–6. Thereafter four years were spent in preparing libraries for despatch. At first the foundation of not less than 500 libraries was thought of, but the number was soon reduced to 52, approximately two to each diocese. The first two libraries were sent to Evesham and Henley-in-Arden in March 1710. In all 22 were sent out in 1710, 15 in 1711, and 14 in 1712.[34] The 52nd library was sent to Oldbury in August 1713. With one exception,[35] each of these 52 libraries consisted of either 72 or 67 volumes[36] and cost with binding, travelling cupboard, and carriage, between £21. 10s. and £22. 11s. Of this sum, £5 was required from the incumbent of each parish to which a library was sent.[37] The rest was defrayed by the Trustees.

After the completion of its immediate task the Trustees continued to function, but with less vigour. Enough books were collected and bound to allow the despatch of eight libraries, numbering 55–62,[38] in 1720 and 1721. No.63 went to Fluckburgh in 1725 and no.64 to Shustoke in 1727. In 1729 preparations for ten more libraries were made and two libraries seem to have been sent to St. Mary's in the Scilly Isles and to Burwell in Cambridgeshire.[39] The 110th and last meeting of the Trustees was on 3 March 1730, a fortnight after Bray's death. Subsequently a new body was formed, The Associates of the late Reverend Dr Bray. The Associates founded 73 small parochial

30. See p.44.
31. Minutes of Library Committee 1705-1729/30, to the end.
32. Minutes, p.1.
33. Cf. p.36.
34. See pp.64–5.
35. See pp.116–7 (Alcester).
36. See p.48.
37. The £5 was sometimes paid by a benefactor. Thus Sir Thomas Lowther appears to have paid for Flookburgh (see p.212) and Mr Wentworth of Wentworth Woodhouse for Bolsterstone, Harrowden Parva, Irthling-borough, Tinsley, Wentworth, and Wollaston (Bodl. MS. Rawlinson D.834, f.6).
38. The libraries sent to Virginia and Montserrat were numbered 53 and 54.
39. Minutes, pp.167–70. The libraries sent (about this time?) to How in Norfolk 'at the request of Lady Betty Hastings' and to Streatley in Bedfordshire are known only from catalogues found recently by the Revd. H. P. Thompson among loose papers belonging to the Associates of Dr Bray.

libraries between 1757 and 1768, mainly in North Lancashire and Wales. Later their foundations were, as they still are, lending libraries.

The Associates stopped founding parochial libraries at about the time when there is a marked falling off in the number of parochial libraries founded by individuals, and the question about parochial libraries ceased to be put to the clergy at visitations. The library at Finedon founded in 1788 was 'for the sole use of the Ministers of Finedon for ever, the Foundation Book being Dr Thomas Bray's *Bibliotheca Parochialis*'. A century later the gifts to Prees (1883) and Eastbourne (1890) have the same restricted use. On the other hand, the libraries at Elham (1809) and Castleton (1819) were for the use of the parish, and the library at Bewdley (1819) was for the clergy and 'respectable inhabitants' of the town and neighbourhood. The library at St. Peter's-in-the-East, Oxford (1841) is of special interest as an 'Oxford Movement' library. On the whole the learned character of the libraries was maintained in these 19th century foundations, and in the additions made at this time to the few older libraries which had funds at their disposal, for example, Holy Trinity, Hull.

By 1849 when the Select Committee on Public Libraries was taking evidence and preparing its Report, [40] many of the old libraries were suffering from neglect and had fallen into disuse. The Select Committee in its Report depended largely on the evidence of Edward Edwards and the Revd J. J. Smith. It noted that 'Parochial Libraries once prevailed to a considerable extent throughout England, Wales and Scotland . . . Their foundation was, in the first instance, due to individual benevolence; but subsequently and principally, to the efforts of Dr Bray and his "Associates," at the beginning, and in the middle, of the last century. They were generally intended for the use of the clergy . . . Of many of these Libraries, it is stated that "the books lie exposed to chance, and liable to be torn by the children of the village." In one, however, that of Beccles, in Suffolk, the books have been rescued from danger. They have been deposited in a room in the town, and "made the commencement of a Town Library." Your Committee cannot but recommend that the example of the people of Beccles should be imitated whenever there is an existing parish library'.[41]

Possibly arising out of this Report there was a considerable correspondence about parochial libraries in the pages of *Notes and Queries* in the years 1852–9. William Blades listed many of them under the heading 'Minor Libraries' in *The Book-Worm* for 1866, and in 1879 another list was prepared by T. W. Shore at a conference of the newly formed Library Association.

The renewed interest in the fabric of churches extended sometimes to their

40. [Details of publications referred to in brief in this Historical Introduction and not listed in full in the footnotes will be found under References and their Abbreviations, or under individual Directory entries. M.P.]
41. Reports from Committees, 1849, pp.vi,vii.

libraries. From time to time during the last century and a quarter individuals have described them, catalogued them, and cared for them. There are particularly good descriptions in print of Denchworth (1875), Doncaster (1882), King's Lynn (1904), Tiverton (1905), Marlborough (1947) and of the libraries in Lancashire.[42] At least 44 church libraries have been catalogued in print since 1820, if sometimes very badly catalogued. Jacob Ley had the books at Wendlebury rebound at his own expense in 1840. G. J. French restored the chained library at Turton in the fifties, and the library at Henley-on-Thames was put in order and labelled at about the same time. Canon Fletcher made Wimborne the model library it now is during the time he was vicar there. We owe the continued existence of the interesting library at Marlborough largely to Mr E. G. H. Kempston. In recent years the libraries at Langley Marish, Maldon, and Reigate have been assisted by the Pilgrim Trust. Maldon and Reigate are receiving annual County Council grants.

Neglect, not care, is, however, the usual story. Many libraries have vanished mysteriously, some of them, like Brent Eleigh and Northampton, in the not very distant past. In many, the books have become gradually less in number. Libraries at Broughton, Durham, Effingham, Flaxley, London (St. George the Martyr, Queen Square, and St. Martin-in-the-Fields), Manchester, Milden, Norton and Lenchwick, Reepham, Royston, Shipdham, Stanground, and Whitchurch (Hampshire) have been sold: of these the St. Martin's, Shipdham, and Whitchurch collections were important. Libraries at Coniston, Hillingdon, Llanrhos, Milton Abbas, North Walsham, and Wendlebury, and parts of libraries at Bushey, Lanteglos-by-Camelford, Mentmore, and Steeple Ashton, have been destroyed deliberately. Libraries at Doncaster, Liverpool, and Willen, and part of the library at Great Yarmouth, have been destroyed by the accidents of war and fire. Probably the neglect of books kept in dry conditions has been harmless, but damp has caused damage at, for example, Bury St. Edmunds and Norton (Derbyshire).

II

The neglect is understandable. By the second half of the 18th century the permanent parochial library founded by an individual with his own books was beginning to be out of fashion. People who wished to read beyond their own shelves and could afford the money were able in many places to subscribe to a lending-library of modern books. Libraries of this sort were formed under various auspices, often not ecclesiastical, in at least most towns, and in many villages. At Witham and perhaps at Caerleon and Llanbadarn Fawr a church lending-library was founded before 1800.[43] At Bridgnorth and at Stockton-on-

42. R. C. Christie, The old Church and School Libraries of Lancashire, *Chetham Society*, N.S., vol.7, (1885).
43. The books in the parochial and lending libraries founded by the Associates of

Tees, the old parochial library was turned into a subscription library in the 19th century, increased in size, and for a time flourished. The parochial library founded at Bromfield in Cumberland in the middle of the 19th century may be taken as an example of a subscription library under church patronage. The Bishop of Carlisle was patron and all parishioners subscribing one shilling annually were members. There were about 1,000 volumes and 192 subscribing parishioners in 1853, when a catalogue was printed.[44] The intention was – in the words of the Address prefixed to the catalogue – not only 'to open to the Parishioners at large the sources of innocent gratification which properly directed Reading is capable of affording, but also to offer the means of self-instruction to those, who might have but few other opportunities for the improvement of the mind'. No doubt many other libraries with these aims were founded at this time. In 1873, at a visitation of the diocese of Canterbury more than half the incumbents answered the question 'Have you a library in your parish?' in the affirmative.[45] These libraries were useful, especially in country districts, in the days before County Library services existed, but most of them have disappeared without leaving any trace of their existence. They do not concern us here.[46]

I 2

Book-rooms, furniture, and chains. Research on parochial libraries suggests that nothing has been so important to them as a good home. Their founders were often aware of this and prepared special rooms for the safe keeping of the books. Some of these rooms still exist, as at Hatfield Broad Oak and Langley Marish. Others, as at Denchworth, Henley-on-Thames, and Rougham were destroyed during alterations to the church, leaving the library homeless. In many churches the room over the south porch was a ready-made library room; in some there was a room over the vestry fit for the purpose. These upper-storey libraries are often charming. They are attractive even when neglected. They are as a rule dry and the books in them, on shelving against the walls, have often kept well, with no greater enemy than dust. It is easy to think of them as happy summer refuges for the married clergy.

The best known libraries now are the chained libraries. People with no

Dr Bray from 1753 onwards (see pp.68–82 and Samuel Smith, *Publick Spirit*, 1808, pp.81–3) did not belong to the parish to which they were sent, but remained the property of the Associates, returnable if no longer required.

44. *A Catalogue of the Bromfield Parochial Library*, Wigton, 1853. A copy to which Mr G. K. Scott drew attention is in the Public Library, Carlisle.

45. The Returns are in the library of Lambeth Palace.

46. Incumbents replying to a questionnaire sent out by the Central Council for the Care of Churches in 1950 referred to modern libraries in active use at St. Olave's, York, St. Martin's, Hull, and Westcliff-on-Sea (Essex), to the specialist collection of liturgical books at Wellingborough, and to the local collection housed in the 'scriptorium' at Selby Abbey.

interest in old books are prepared to be interested in chains. Wimborne, Grantham, and Hereford (All Saints) have many visitors. The two first are doubly attractive, being chained in an upper room.

In parsonages, 'standing' libraries have not been happy as a rule. To Heathfield in Sussex a wise founder left not only the books in 'my press', but also the press itself 'for ever to be kept in a dry convenient place in the Vicarage House'. In most other parsonages the books have been probably eyed with disfavour by one or more in the long series of incumbents. They have tended to find their way to an attic, if not to an outhouse or a sale room. The sale or sub-division of over-large parsonages has not made them more secure in recent times.

Most of the libraries included in the Directory, and still *in situ*, fall, as to their placing, into one of four divisions. They are in an upper room, or the vestry, or the body of a church, or in the parsonage.[47]

(i) **In the upper room of a church.** Ashby-de-la-Zouch, Astley, Bloxham, Boston, Bromham, Broughton, Chelmsford, Finedon, Grantham, Loughborough, More, Nantwich, Newark, Newport (Essex), Ottery St. Mary, Oxford, Reigate, St. Neots, Stoke-by-Nayland, Swaffham, Wimborne, Wotton-under-Edge.

(ii) **In the vestry.** Amberley, Bassingbourne, Beccles, Bradfield, Bury St Edmunds, Cartmel, Hackness, Hatfield Broad Oak, Hull (St. Mary Lowgate), Kildwick, Stamford, Tiverton, Tong, Woodbridge.

(iii) **In the body of a church.** Denchworth, Feckenham, Hereford (All Saints: in the Lady chapel, which was formerly a vestry), Oakham.

(iv) **In the parsonage.** Ainstable, Bampton, Chirbury, Coddenham, Coleorton, Crundale, Dalston, Darowen, Doddington, Donington, East Harlsey, Heathfield, Lanteglos-by-Camelford, Lawshall, Plymtree, Steeple Ashton, Tortworth, Whitchurch (Shrops.), Woodchurch, Worsbrough, Yelden.

At Halton and Maldon, the library is in a special building apart from church and parsonage. At Leicester in 1632 and at Brent Eleigh in 1859 the library was moved from the church to a building specially constructed for it in the churchyard. At Bicester, Chirbury, and King's Norton, the library was attached to a grammar school in close proximity to the church.

Since 1800 many libraries have been moved from their original homes in churches, rectories or vicarages. For details see the Directory and Index under their names, and for general statistics see the Table on pp.27–8.

---

47. [The following lists do not aim at completeness. For the more recent history and locations of libraries in this list see the Directory. They are reproduced here as in 1959 as part of the historical record. However it must be emphasized that some libraries are no longer in the locations given, e.g. Ashby, Hereford, Loughborough and Oakham. M.P.]

II. THE TRUSTEES' LIBRARIES
1705–1729[48]

1. LETTERS FROM HENRY NEWMAN, SECRETARY OF THE SPCK

Four letters written by Henry Newman in the summer of 1725 are of particular interest. In two of them Newman informed his correspondent, Thomas Sharp, Rector of Rothbury and Archdeacon of Northumberland, about the Trustees and their aims. The other two illustrate the whole business of sending out a library, that sent to Flookburgh in North Lancashire which still remains in the church there. Extracts from the two letters to Sharp will suffice:

Letter I (extract). Newman to Sharp, Middle Temple, 27 May 1725[49]

In answer to yours of the 21st Currt the design of Parochial Libraries is still carry'd on, but with less Vigour than it us'd to be when Mr Nelson, and Mr Henry Hoare were living, who were great Benefactors to it out of their own Pockets.[50]

I have Part of the Material for 20 Libraries by me, upon the same Model as those already sent out, 10 of which are far advanced; and, if Mr Hoare had liv'd, I believe, would have been compleated this Summer, but now I don't know when they may be compleated, unless kind Providence should raise up some Friend to the Undertaking like those I have mentioned.

If You please to signify the Name of the Place you would recommend for a Library, and who will engage for the Payment of the Five Pound Praemium, when a Library can be had, I will take Care to recommend it to the Gentlemen concern'd in Promoting this Charity at their next Meeting.

I must acquaint You with the Qualifications expected in ye Livings where these Libraries are bestow'd. Viz^t

That they do not exceed £30 per Annum, certain Value to the Incumbent; And that the Incumbent be resident, and give Bond, with the Penalty of £30. to the Bishop of the Diocese for observing the Rules prescrib'd by Act of Parliament and the Founders.

---

48. See pp.38–9.
49. Archives of the SPCK, EL.1 CS/1, p.201. This and the other letters are in the hand of Newman's clerk.
50. For Robert Nelson, 1665–1715, see DNB; Henry Hoare, died in March 1725, aged 48, and bequeathed large sums to various charities: see J.Wilford, *Memorials and Characters*, 1741, p.778. He suggested the inclusion of Bishop Beveridge's *Private Thoughts* in the libraries and paid for the 52 copies bought by the Committee (Minutes, 1705–30, p.58).

Letter 2 (extract). Newman to Sharp, Middle Temple, 17 July 1725 [51]

At first the Gentlemen concerned did indeed propose the placing of 2. Libraries in each Diocese, as a Specimen of the Charity they intended, but they soon found themselves oblig'd to break thrô that Design; some Bishops entertaining the Proposal very coldly, while others were very eager in Promoting it, among the last of which was the late excellent Arch-Bishop Sharp, and his Successor, and therefore there are as many Libraries of this kind in your Diocese as in any two Dioceses in the Kingdom, except Worcester, the late Bishop of which was a zealous Promoter of them. [52]

Letter 3. Newman to Richard Hudson, curate of Flookburgh, 'in Cartmell, near Lancaster', Middle Temple, 12 June 1725 [53]

Revd Sir,
    Yesterday there was deliver'd to Mr Knowles Junr, the Lancaster Carrier, a Parochial Library for yor Chappel at Flookborough, in 2 Cases, cover'd with Matts, and directed to You.
    They are a present to yor Chappel from some Gentlemen who are Founders of several Parochial Libraries, and, at the desire of Sir Thomas Lowther, who has been a Benefactor to the Undertaking, this Library is sent to You, in Hopes You will take due Care of it, as the Rules direct, so that the Books may be all safely transmitted to yor Successor. I have sent, in the least Case, 2. Catologues, with a Receipt endors'd, which you are to desir'd to sign in the Presence of your Church-Wardens, or other noted Inhabitants in your Parish or Neighbourhood, and to send one them (*sic*) to your Diocesan, and the other when sign'd to me, under Cover to Sir Thomas Lowther in Red Lion Street.
    The Key of both Cases is fasten'd to the under Part of the Least Case under the Matt.
    Sir Thomas Lowther desires You would give Directions for conveying ye Cases from Lancaster to Flookborough, at the first of which Places Mr Knowles has promis'd to deliver it next Monday Sennight, to which Place also, i.e. Lancaster, the Carriage is paid here.
    Pray let me here from You as soon as You receive the Library if not before, because I am to fill up a Bond, in the Bishop's Name, in the Penalty of £30. only, which You are to execute, as all the Security the Founders require of You, that You will not embezzle or destroy the Books, but preserve them as the

51. EL. 1 CS/1, p.205.
52. Bishop Lloyd of Worcester contributed books to the value of £30 in 1706 (Minutes, 1705–30, p.5).
53. EL. 1 CS/1, p.203.

Act of Parliament, and the Rules of the Founders prescribe for your own Use, and the Use of your Successor.

I wish them safe to You, and am,
Revd Sir,
Your most humble Servant
Henry Newman.

You will see the Form of the Bond which You are to execute in the Register which accompanies the Library.

Letter 4. Newman to Hudson, Middle Temple, 13 July 1725 [54]

Reverend Sir,

I have Yours of the 24th past under Cover to Sir Thomas Lowther, with the Catalogue of the Library sign'd; and as You make no Complaint of the Books not being in good Order, I hope they were carefully deliver'd.

I herewith send the Bond, which you are to sign and execute in presence of Your Church-Warden and principal Parishioners, which, when done, I must desire You to send under Sir Thomas Lowther's Cover to me: for thô it be taken in the Bishop's Name, I am to lay it before the Founders of the Library for their Directions to transmit it to the Bishop of the Diocese, but the other Catalogue, which I sent to You, You are desir'd to send to his Lordship, as mention'd in my Letter of the 12th of last Month.

I wish you may long enjoy the Effect of Sir Thomas's Kindness to You, which must be an agreable Companion to a Man of Letters destitute of Books in a Solitary Country, and, if rightly used, must enable You to do more good, as a Minister of the Gospel, to feed with Heavenly Truths the Flock committed to your Care.

Please to let me know where they are plac'd, whether in the Vestry or your dwelling House, that I may be able to inform the Founders thereof being,
Revd Sir,
Your most humble Servant
Henry Newman

54. EL. 1 CS/1, p.204.

2. BOOKS, BOOKPLATES, CATALOGUES, CUPBOARDS, & BONDS

The surviving books, bookplates, catalogues, book-cupboards, and bonds illustrate the matters referred to in the Minutes and Accounts and in Newman's letters.

A. **The books and their bindings.** Substantial remains of ten of the 62 libraries founded between 1705 and 1727 still exist. They are at Bridlington, Darlington, Darowen, Dudleston, Feckenham (nearly complete), Flookburgh, Poulton, Preston-by-Wingham, and St. Neots, and, transferred from Newport (Mons.), at Llandaff Cathedral.[55] Other libraries existed into the 19th century, but from 1868 onwards the secretary of the Associates of Dr Bray made strenuous and on the whole successful efforts to secure the return of old books: 'Our great object is to get rid of the libraries which are useless and at least of all the useless books out of the libraries which the Clergy value'.[56] Many of the clergy objected to this policy,[57] which should have been applied, if at all, only to libraries founded by the Associates themselves and not to the older and inalienable parochial libraries founded by the Trustees. The North Walsham library was dispersed as recently as 1938.

The books still surviving *in situ* are mostly in good condition and are almost without exception in their original calf bindings, plain except for small corner-ornaments.[58] The accounts show that the Committee first employed John Worall as their binder, then F. Fox, and finally and chiefly Philip Cholmondeley. The books they bound are named individually. Thus Worall was paid £8. 5s. for binding 52 copies of Eusebius in 1709 and Cholmondeley was paid £2. 7s. 8d. for binding 52 copies of Placette and Godeau in 1710.[59]

B. **Bookplates.** A bookplate was placed in each volume sent out and is still to be found in most of the books in existing libraries. The plate in the larger books shows St. John on Patmos and an angel giving him a book with the words 'Accipe Librum et devora illum' (Revelation 10:9): the book-cupboard shown in this design is an accurate reproduction of the cupboard in which the books actually travelled from London. The plate in the smaller books shows a kneeling figure and is inscribed 'Tolle Lege' and 'Vid.S^{ti} Aug. Confess. Lib. 8 Cap.12'.[60] Both plates were printed in 1709 from copper-plates designed by

55. For details see the Directory under these places, and also for a few surviving books, Alnwick, Newport (Essex) and Lostwithiel.
56. The quotation is from a letter lying loose at p.134 of a manuscript volume of 'Review Papers' belonging to the Associates, dated 1868–75.
57. See Directory: Corston.
58. On 44 books at Bridlington there seem to be 15 different corner-ornaments and on 40 books at Darlington 11 different corner-ornaments, three of which are different from any of those at Bridlington.
59. Accounts, 1706–11.
60. Reproduced in the Annual Report of the Associates for 1944 and some other years after 1944.

Simon Gribelin. The 'Accounts, 1706–11', ff.6v, 8v, and the Minutes, pp.52–3, where specimens of the bookplates are inserted, record that 8,000 copies were printed. The Franks Collection of Bookplates in the British Museum contains examples of the plates from books formerly in Trustees' libraries at Evesham, Henley-in-Arden, and Tinsley (nos. 33850, 33854, 33865).

Variants of these, and a number of typographic labels, were subsequently produced, details of which will be found in Brian North Lee's forthcoming *Some Church of England Parochial Library and Cathedral Ex-Libris*.

C. **Catalogues.** (i) Shelf-catalogues of each of the 52 libraries sent out in the years 1710 to 1713 are to be found in a single volume now belonging to the Associates, who received it as a gift from the SPCK. The catalogues show that the stocks of books assembled by the Committee were made up into 32 identical libraries, each of 72 vols, and into 20 substantially identical libraries, each normally of 67 vols.[61] Each library was given a reference number from 1 to 52 and this number was written at the head of the catalogue. The numbers bear no relation to the order in which the libraries were sent out. (ii) One vol. in each library was called 'The Register'. The surviving 'Registers' of Alnwick (now at Newcastle), Corston, Preston-by-Wingham, Darlington, Trevethin, North Walsham, and Wollaston (now in the Bodleian) are vellum-covered blank-books of about 85 leaves, containing a catalogue of the books, and in front of the catalogue printed copies of the *Proposal for erecting Parochial Libraries in the Meanly endow'd Cures throughout England*,[62] of the Act of 7 Anne 'for the better Preservation of Parochial Libraries', and of 'Rules for the better Preservation of Parochial Libraries',[63] Most of the leaves remain blank. (iii) Besides the 'Register' two catalogues were sent with each library. They were to be signed by the incumbent in the presence of witnesses and returned by him, one to his bishop and the other to the secretary of the SPCK. The catalogues returned to Newman from Over Whitacre, Chepstow, Oldbury, Whitchurch, and Malton are now in the Bodleian, MS.Rawlinson D.834 ff. 13–14, 20–21, 24–5, 31, 34.

The catalogue of the library sent to Oldbury is here printed from the Bodleian manuscript, ff.24–5, as a specimen of the 72 vol. library sent to the incumbents of 32 churches: Brewood, Bridlington, Bolsterstone, Brookthorpe, Chepstow, Darlington, Detling, Dudleston, Dullingham, Elmley, Feckenham, Flaxley, Irthlingborough, Kilmersdon, Kingsbridge, Llanbadarn Fawr, Llanrhos (Eglwys Rhos), Lostwithiel, Marske, Monmouth, Newport (Essex), Newport (Mon.), Oldbury, Oundle, Over Whitacre, Oxenhall, Prendergast, St. Neots, Slapton, Tinsley, Trevethin, and Wollaston.

61. 66 volumes at Kirkoswald and St. Bees; 74 volumes at Alcester.
62. See p.36.
63. The Act (see pp.439–42) and the Rules are printed in Samuel Smith, *Publick Spirit*, 1808, pp.69–7.

A CATALOGUE of the Parochial Library at OLDBURY
in Shropshire No. 38

Diocese of Worcester	I. SHELF	£	s	d
1	The Ecclesiastical History of Eusebius &c	1		
2	A:Bp. Tillotson's Works in folio 7. Edit		18	
3, 4	Dr. Whitby's Commentary on the New Testament 2. Vol.	1	15	
5	Chillingworth's Works		12	
6 Bound {	Dr Bray's Catechetical Lectures		8	
	Allen's Discourse on the two Covenants		2	
7 Bound {	Allen's Discourse on Faith		8	
	Kettlewell's Practical Believer			
8	Bp. Pearson's Exposition of the Creed		10	
9	The Register		4	
10	Dr. More's Theological Works	1	1	6
		6	18	6

II. SHELF

		£	s	d
11	A.Bp. Leighton's Comment. on part of the 1st Epistle of S. Peter		5	
12, 13	Reeve's Translation of the Apol. of Iustin Martyr; Tertullian and Minutius Fælix &c. with the Commonit. of Vinc. Lirin. 2.Vol.		9	
14	Dr Bray's Bibliotheca Parochialis		4	
15 Bound {	Placette's Christian Casuist		5	
	Godeau's Pastoral Instructions			
16–20	Dr. Scott's Christian Life in 5.Vol.	1	1	
21	Ostervald's Causes of Corruption among christians		5	
22	—— of Uncleaness		3	6
23–4	Bp. Beveridge's Sermons the two first Vol.		8	
25	Howell's Discourse on the Lord's Day		4	
26	Bp. Stillingfleet's Vindication of the Doctrine of the Trinity		3	6
27	Dr. Goodman's Penitent Pardon'd		4	
28	—— Winter Evening Conferences		3	6
29	Reform'd Devotions published by Dr. Hickes		3	
30	Grotius de Veritate Religionis Christianæ		2	6
31	Dr. Lucas's Practical Christianity		3	
32	Bp. King's Inventions of Men in the Worship of God		1	
		4	5	

	IIId SHELF		£	s	d
33	A:Bp. Tillotson of Sincerity in Religion	15. Sermons		4	
34	Ditto's Posthum. Sermons on several Subjects	16. Serm. 2. Vol.		4	
35	Ditto	16. Serm. 3. Vol.		4	
36	Ditto	15. Serm. 4. Vol.		4	
37	Ditto	13. Serm. 5. Vol.		4	
38	Ditto on the Attributes of God	14. Serm. 6. Vol.		4	
39	Ditto on Ditto	15. Serm. 7. Vol.		4	
40	Ditto on Repentance	15. Serm. 8. Vol.		4	
41	Ditto on Death, Iudgem^t. & future State	15. Serm. 9. Vol.		4	
42	Ditto on the Life, Sufferings &c of Christ and the coming of the Holy Ghost	15. Serm. 10.Vol.		4	
43	Ditto on several Subjects	15. Serm. 11. Vol.		4	
44	Ditto	15. Serm 12. Vol.		4	
45	Ditto on the Truth of the Christian Religion	15. Serm. 13. Vol.		4	
46	Ditto on several Subjects	6. Serm. 14. Vol.		4	
47	Kettlewell on the Sacrament			3	6
48	Ditto's Measures of Christian Obedience			5	
49	Bishop Burnett's Abridgement of the History of the Reformation			5	
50	Dr. Gastrell's Christian Institutes			3	6
51 Bound	Bp. Beveridge's private Thoughts Publick Prayer frequent Communion			5	

		3	18	

	IVth. SHELF	£	s	d
52, 53	Jenkins's Certainty of the christian Religion in 2.Vols.		9	
54	Nelson's Feasts and Fasts of the Church of England		5	
55	Bp. Stillingfleet concerning Christ's Satisfaction		5	
56	Dr. Comber of Ordination		5	
57	Wheatly's Harmony and Excellency of the Common Prayer		3	
58	Bennett's Abridgement of the London Cases		3	6
59	Confutation of Popery		3	6
60	Confutation of Quakerism		3	6

61	Bp. Wilkin's Natural Religion	4	6
62	Dr. Cave's Primitive Christianity	5	
63 Bound	{ Dr. Hickes's Apolog. Vindic. of the Church of England	2	
	Bp. Ken's Exposition on the Church Catechism	1	
64 Bound	{ Dr. Worthington on self Resignation	2	6
	Spinckes of Trust in God	3	
65	Bonnel's Life	2	6
66 Bound	{ Dr Bray's Catechetical Institution / Baptismal Covenant / Pastoral Discourse to Young Persons }	5	
67 Bound	{ Short Method with the Deists and Iews	2	6
	Stearne de Visitatione Infirmorum	1	
68 Bound	{ Dr. Clark's three practical essays	1	
	Wall's Conference about Infant Baptism	1	
69 Bound	{ Herbert's Country Parson	1	6
	The Country Parson's Advice to his Parishioners	1	6
70 Bound	{ Allen's Discourse on Divine Assistance	1	6
	Harrison's Exposition of the church Catechism	1	6
71	Kettlewell on Death	2	
72 Bound	{ Io. Elis Articulor. 39 Eccl. Angl. Defensio	1	6
	Thomæ a Kempis de Imitatione Christi	1	6
		3 19	6

		£.	s	d
Brought from Shelf 1st.		6	18	6
Ditto	2	4	5	
Ditto	3	3	18	
Ditto	4	3	19	6
The Case		1	5	
Packing, Carryage &c of Incidental Charges		1	5	
		21	11	—

Received the withinmention'd Parochial Library into my Custody, which I promise to keep safe for the Benefit of myself and my Successors pursuant to the Rules prescrib'd by the Act of Parliament and the Founders. I say receiv'd this Third day of September: 1714

In presence of   per Me Edward Hale Curate

Tho: Pearsall junr. } of the parish of Halesowen [64]
Jonathan Carpenter }

64. The receipt is written on the otherwise blank fourth page (f.25v).

19 of the remaining 20 libraries sent out in these four years differed from the Oldbury library only in the contents of the second shelf, which held 16 instead of 21 vols. Instead of nos. 16–32 on this shelf (from Scott's *Christian Life* to King's *Inventions of Men*), costing £3. 2s., these libraries had the following 12 vols, costing £4. 2s. 6d.

		£	s	d
16	Bp. Patrick's Commentary upon Genesis		8	
17	Exodus		8	
18	Leviticus		8	
19	Numbers		8	
20	Deuteronomy		8	
21	Ditto on Joshua, Judges and Ruth		8	
22	Ditto on the 2 Books of Samuel		8	
23	Ditto on the 2 Books of Kings		8	
24	Ditto on the Books of Chron: Ezra, Nehem' and Esther		8	
25	Bellarmine's Notes of the Church Examined etc.		7	
26	Camfield of Angels and Their Ministries		2	
27	Bp. Beveridge's Explanation of the Church Catechism	1		6

This selection of books was sent to the incumbents at Alnwick, Bampton, Burgh-by-Sands, Corston, Darowen, Dorchester, Evesham, Henley-in-Arden, Harrowden Parva, Kirkoswald, North Walsham, Preston-by-Wingham, Pwllheli, St. Bees, Sudbury, Tadcaster, Wentworth, Weobley, and Wigton. Basically the same selection went to Alcester but with additions which raised the total number of volumes to 74 and the price to £29. 16s. 6d.

Ten libraries were founded in the years 1720–7, at Llantysilio, Poulton-le-Fylde, Shepshed, Skelton (near Guisborough), Stowey, and Whitchurch (Hants) in 1720; at Malton and St. Martin's in 1721; at Flookburgh in 1725; at Shustoke in 1727. The contents of only two of them are known from catalogues. The catalogue of the 81 vols. sent to Whitchurch is here printed in an abbreviated form from the printed sheet in Bodleian MS.Rawlinson D.834, f.31. The Malton catalogue, also on a printed sheet, is identical with it.[65] To judge from the extant books, the collection at Poulton-le-Fylde was the same and the collection at Flookburgh nearly the same as that at Whitchurch.[66] Titles which do not occur in the Oldbury catalogue are printed in full. For other titles the reader is referred to the Oldbury catalogue (above pp.49–51).

65. MS. Rawlinson D.834, f.34.
66. See pp.212 and 388–9.

A CATALOGUE of the Parochial Library
at WHITCHURCH in Hampshire

SHELF I.	1	Eusebius, *Oldbury*, no.1	1	1	6d
	2–4	Archbp. Tillotson's Works, 3 Vol. in Folio	2	8	
	5,6	Whitby, *Oldbury*, nos. 3,4	2	2	
	7	Pearson, *Oldbury*, no.8		10	6
	8	Bray and Allen. *Oldbury*, no.6		10	0
	9	Allen and Kettlewell. *Oldbury*, no.7		8	
	10	Dr. More's Collection of Philosophical Writings		9	
	11	More. *Oldbury*, no.10		16	
	12	The Register. *Oldbury*, no.9		4	
			8	9	

SHELF II.	13	Bp. Bradford's Sermons at Mr. Boyle's Lectures		5	
	14	Mason's Sermon concerning the Authority of the Church in making Canons, etc.			8
	15–22	Bp. Blackall's Practical Discourses upon our Saviour's Sermon on the Mount. 8 Vol.	1	14	
	23	Comber. *Oldbury*, no.56		5	
	24–5	Jenkins. *Oldbury*, nos. 52–3		9	
	26	Nelson's Address to Persons of Quality		3	6
	27	Nelson. *Oldbury*, no.54		5	
	28–31	Lucas's Sermons, 4 Vol.		17	
	32	Kettlewell. *Oldbury*, no.48		5	
	33	Kettlewell. *Oldbury*, no.47		3	6
	34	Placette and Godeau. *Oldbury*, no.15		5	
			4	12	8

SHELF III.	35–8	Abp. Sharp's Sermons, 4 Vols.	1		
	39–40	Arndtius de Vero Christianismo, 2 Vol.		11	
	41–42	Reeve. *Oldbury*, nos.12, 13		9	
	43	Bennet. *Oldbury*, no.60		3	6
	44	Bennet. *Oldbury*, no.59		3	6
	45	Bennet. *Oldbury*, no.58		3	6
	46	Ostervald. *Oldbury*, no.21		4	
	47	Ostervald. *Oldbury*, no.22		3	6
	48	Dunster's Drexelius on Eternity		3	6
	49	Howell. *Oldbury*, no.25		3	6
	50	Bp. Smalridge's Sermons		5	
	51	Dr. Isham's Divine Philosophy		3	

	52	Goodman. *Oldbury*, no.27	4	
	53	Wilkins. *Oldbury*, no.61	4	
	54	Cave. *Oldbury*, no.62	5	
	55	Spinckes. *Oldbury*, no.64 (ii)	1	6
	56	Worthington. *Oldbury*, no.64 (i)	3	
			4 10	6
SHELF IV.	57	Abp. Wakes's Sermons	4	6
	58	Dr. More's Divine Dialogues	4	
	59	—— Life	3	6
	60	—— Enchiridion Ethicum	2	6
	61	{ Mr. Le Fevre's Sufferings on Board the Galleys in France, and his Death in a Dungeon	1	6
		An Apologetical Vindication of the Church of England. *Oldbury*, no.63(i)	1	6
	62	Bonnell. *Oldbury*, no.65	3	
	63	Bp. Burnett's Pastoral Care	2	6
		Goodman. *Oldbury*, no.28	3	
	64	Mocket's Politia Ecclesiae Anglicanae	1	
		{ Zouch's Descriptio Juris et Judicii Ecclesiast. secund. Can. Anglic.		9
		—— Decriptio Juris et Judicii Temporalis secundum Consuetudines Feudales et Normanicas		9
	65	March's Sermons	3	
	66	Nelson's Practice of True Devotion	2	6
	67–70	Dupin's Church History abridg'd, 4 Vol.	10	
	71	Allen. *Oldbury*, no.70(i)	1	6
	72	Lucas. *Oldbury*, no.31	2	6
	73	Clarke. *Oldbury*, no.68(i)	1	6
	74	Wall. *Oldbury*, no.68(ii)		4
	75	King. *Oldbury*, no.32	1	6
	76	Kettlewell. *Oldbury*, no.71	1	6
	77	Addison's Christian Daily Sacrifice	1	0
	78	Gastrell. *Oldbury*, no.50	2	6
	79	Bray. *Oldbury*, no.66	4	
	80	{ Bp. Beveridge's Church Catechism explain'd		9
		Ostervald's Grounds and Principles of the Christian Religion explain'd	2	
	81	Beveridge. *Oldbury*, no.51	3	
			3 6	1

Brought from the	I. Shelf	8	9	
	II. Shelf	4	12	8
	III. Shelf	4	10	6
	IV. Shelf	3	6	1
The Case		1	6	
Packing, Carriage, etc. of incidental Charges		1	5	
		23	9	3

D. **Book-cupboards.** Each library sent out in 1710–13 was packed in a wainscot cupboard of 'best Season'd Oak' (Minutes, 1708, p.37) costing 25s. The cupboards had handles for easy transport and contained four shelves. The bottom shelf was made tall enough to take Henry More's *Works*, a fairly large folio. The other shelves were for small books. The cupboard for the church at Preston-by-Wingham still contains its books. At Bridlington books and cupboard were kept separately. Cupboards without books are at Llanrhos in the church and at Flaxley in the rectory. The upper half of the cupboard remains in All Saints' Church, Evesham. A catalogue of the books and a copy of the Act of 7 Anne were pasted inside the door of each cupboard. The number 32 painted on the outside of the door of the cupboard at Evesham is the number assigned to the library sent to Evesham. The library sent to Flookburgh in 1725 was in '2 cases cover'd with Matts'.

E. **Bonds.** The Rules of Parochial Libraries and the form of words whereby the recipients of a library promised to observe the Rules under pain of a penalty of £30[67] were printed on a pair of leaves and sent to incumbents, who signed them in the presence of witnesses and returned them to Newman. Copies of these bonds signed by the incumbents of Alcester, Llanrhos, Malton, Poulton, Shepshed, and Whitchurch are in the Bodleian Library, MS. Rawlinson D.834, ff.18, 23, 34, 28, 26, 32.

67. See p.45.

III. POSTSCRIPT
2000

General Studies and Sources. Since 1959 a considerable amount has been published on the history, description and cataloguing of parochial libraries. There was no general survey of English library history available when the Historical Introduction in PLCE1 was prepared, and the only regional survey completed was that by R. C. Christie, on 'The old church and school libraries of Lancashire', published by the Chetham Society in 1885.[1] In 1966 Thomas Kelly published his *Early Public Libraries*, in which the growth of parochial collections from the medieval period onwards is described in the cultural and historical context of libraries in general. The appendices in this book, containing various checklists of endowed and Bray libraries, underpin the entire revision of this Directory. The notes and lists of contents of libraries, made by Neil Ker both before and after the publication of PLCE1, subsequently mounted in 3 vols. and placed in Lambeth Palace Library (MS.3221–4), have been an invaluable source of information in the preparation of this revision, as has the collection of library catalogues and lists made by Dr E. G. W. Bill (Lambeth Palace MS.3094, and see Bill Report). David Williams, until 1986 Deputy Secretary at the Council for the Care of Churches, in his M.A. thesis of 1977, and in two articles of 1978–9, broadly surveyed the establishment, use and maintenance of parochial libraries. He also started the collation and filing of new information in preparation for this revision, a task which I took over from him in 1994.

Union Catalogues and Regional Studies. The Committee's wish in 1959 for 'a more detailed combined descriptive catalogue of the libraries and of the books which they contain' has been met, in part at least, by the publication of two union catalogues published by Mansell, that for Shropshire (11 libraries) in 1971, with an introduction by Thomas Kelly, and that for Suffolk (8 libraries) in 1977, with an introduction by Canon John Fitch. Other studies of parochial libraries on a regional basis include Canon Fitch's detailed article on 'Some ancient Suffolk parochial libraries' in 1965, Andrea T. Cameron's account of 'Some parochial libraries of South-West Middlesex' in 1972, Bernard Barr's fully referenced paper on 'Parish libraries in a region: the case of Yorkshire' in 1979, and John C. Day's article on 'Parochial libraries in Northumberland before 1830' in 1989.

---

1. Full details of publications cited in brief in this Postscript will be found under References and their Abbreviations, and under place-names in the Directory.

17th and 18th Century Studies. Parochial libraries on the Isle of Man were not included in PLCE1. Thomas Wilson (1663–1755), Bishop of Sodor and Man 1698–1755, took up Thomas Bray's scheme for establishing parochial libraries and, beginning in 1699, founded 16 libraries on the island, which were aided with grants from Bray ranging from 15s. to £6 (Kelly, p.107 & n.3). The full story of these libraries, included in the Directory, is given in James P. Ferguson's *The Parochial Libraries of Bishop Wilson*, 1975. Some 44 libraries founded by the Trustees, 1710–21, and 70 by the Associates of Dr Bray, 1757–68, were noted in the Chronological Table but not in the Alphabetical Table in PLCE1. They are included in this edition, as are later Bray Associates' foundations, as listed in Samuel Smith's *Publick Spirit*, 1808, the Select Committee Report of 1849, Shore's list of 1879, and the Bray Associates Annual Reports, 1850–1905.

19th Century Studies. The Associates of Dr Bray continued to establish parochial lending libraries in the 19th century: 102 in England (especially in the 1840s) and 36 in Wales (especially in the 1890s). Very few of these libraries still survive: they were the property of the Associates and certainly from 1868 onwards (see p.47) they were often reclaimed when no longer of use; some were merged with other collections, others were lost or destroyed. The remnants of others may perhaps be discovered by a systematic inspection of all deposits of parish records in Diocesan Record Offices, a task attempted for only a few counties in this revision. There were a number of other schemes to provide parochial libraries for poorer parishes and clergy in the first quarter of the 19th century at the diocesan and archdeaconry level, notably in Wales and Northumberland. Bishop Shute Barrington (1734–1826) devised the scheme for Northumberland, entrusting the work to Archdeacon R. G. Bouyer (*c.* 1742–1826), who, in conjunction with the SPCK, by 1823 had personally bought 150 lending libraries to distribute to the 92 parishes in his archdeaconry (see Day, p.100). However, the foundation of other parochial collections steadily dwindled, mainly because of the availablity of reading matter from other sources. Even earlier in the 18th century, because of the growth of subscription libraries and book clubs, some parochial libraries had been taken over or converted to a subscription basis. But there were many informal collections of books kept in church or parish rooms for lending to parishioners, village lending libraries (which might also be parish lending libraries), and Sunday School libraries. The Select Committee Report lists *c.* 5410 by 1849, but they have now largely disappeared. Paul Morgan in his paper on 'Nineteenth century church libraries in England', 1979, describes surviving references to three, at Bristol, St. Mary Redcliffe, Dursley, and Stratford-upon-Avon. All these libraries owed much to the work and publications of the RTS, which distributed *c.* 4,000 libraries in England, Scotland and Wales, 1832–49, and the SPCK, with distribution on a similar scale (Kelly, pp.202–3). Further survivals are described in Paul Hastings' article on 'Parish libraries in the nineteenth century', 1983.

Individual Libraries. Since 1959 there have also been a number of studies and catalogues of individual libraries, or groups of libraries, sometimes in the form of essays towards library science degrees (e.g. Best, 1985; Evans, Chetham libraries, 1993); and sometimes in articles in journals, especially *Library History* (e.g. More, by Conal Condren; Oakham, by Anne L. Herbert; Grantham, by Angela Roberts; and Steeple Ashton, by William Smith.)

IV. DATES OF FOUNDATION
OF LIBRARIES

(Excluding desk libraries, and other collections for which no date of foundation can be given: these are included in the Table of Libraries by Counties, which follows). The dates of foundation for some libraries referred to in the Historical Introduction but not included in the Directory have been included (in italic), with page references to the Introduction. The county name is that in use before the 1974 boundary changes. Abbreviations used:

Bray A	Founded by the Bray Associates after 1730
Bray F	Assisted by Bray funds, 1695–9
Bray P	Founded or assisted by Bray personally, by gift or bequest
Bray T	Founded by the Trustees, 1705–30
Chetham	Founded by Humphrey Chetham
Oley	Founded under the will of Barnabas Oley
r.	Recorded by this date
Wilson	Founded by Bishop Wilson

Date	Place	County	Type
1300, r.	Oxford. St. Mary	Oxon.	
1369	Crediton	Devon	
1369	Ottery St. Mary	Devon	
1378	Newcastle upon Tyne	Northumb.	
1394	York. St. Mary Castlegate	Yorks.	
1416	Bristol. St. Mary	Glos.	
144-	London. St. Peter's Cornhill	London	
1455	Ottery St. Mary, augm.	Devon	
1464	Bristol. All Saints	Glos.	
1464, r.	Warwick	Warwicks.	
1481	Buckingham	Bucks.	
1496, r.	Bristol. St. Mary	Glos.	
15--	Addington	Bucks.	
15--	London. St. Saviour	Lon.	
1527, r.	Derby. All Saints	Derbys.	
1549, r	Ecclesfield	Yorks.	
1557, r.	Ludlow	Shrops.	
1567, r.	Bristol. St. Thomas	Glos.	
1568, r.	Steeple Ashton	Wilts.	
1570	Toddington	Beds.	
1573 (see p.32, n.14)	*Guildford*	Surrey	
1586, r.	Leicester	Leics.	
1586, r.	Norwich. St. Andrew	Norf.	

59

1593, r.	Brockenhurst	Hants.	
1595	Bury St. Edmunds	Suffolk	
1598	Grantham	Lincs.	
1599	Ipswich	Suffolk	
16- -	Greystoke	Cumb.	
16- -	Hadleigh	Suffolk	
16- -	Maidstone	Kent	
16- -	Marske	Yorks.	
16- -	Painswick	Glos.	
16- -	St. Saviour's, Guernsey	Channel I.	
160-	Kirkham	Lancs.	
16- -	Stamford	Lincs.	
1608 (see p.32)	*Norwich*	Norf.	
1613 (see p.32)	*Bristol*	Glos.	
1615	Tankersley	Yorks.	
1616	Oakham	Rut.	
1617	King's Lynn. St. Nicholas	Norf.	
1618, r.	Abingdon	Berks.	
1619, r.	Bath	Somerset	
1619	Totnes	Devon	
1622, r.	Repton	Derbys.	
1624	Ripon	Yorks.	
1628	Halifax	Yorks.	
1628, r.	Norwich. St. Andrews	Norf.	
1631	King's Lynn. St. Margaret	Norf.	
1631	Langley Marish	Bucks.	
1632 (see p.32)	*Colchester*	Essex	
1633, r.	Newton Kyme	Yorks.	
1634, r.	Boston	Lincs.	
1634, r.	Bury. St. Mary	Lancs.	
1634, r.	Hurley	Berks.	
1636	Ottery St. Mary, augm.	Devon	
1637	Spalding	Lincs.	
1640	Manchester	Lancs.	
1645, r.	Great Torrington	Devon	
1646	Southampton	Hants.	
165-, r.	St. Saviour's, Guernsey	Channel I.	
1651, r.	Wisbech	Cambs.	
1652	Wooton Wawen	Warwicks.	
1655, r.	Frisby-on-the-Wreake	Leics.	
1658	Gorton	Lancs.	Chetham
1659	Marske	Yorks.	
1659	Turton	Lancs.	Chetham
1659	Walmsley	Lancs.	Chetham
1659, r.	Wrington	Somerset.	

1661	Birmingham. St. Martin	Warwicks.	
1661	Newcastle upon Tyne, augm.	Northumb.	
1664	Barnstaple	Devon	
1664	Bishop's Stortford	Herts.	
1665	Hull. Holy Trinity	Yorks.	
1665	King's Norton	Warwicks.	
1665	Manchester	Lancs.	Chetham
1668	Bolton-le-Moors	Lancs.	Chetham
1670, r.	Sherborne	Dorset	Bray F
1670, r.	Southwell	Notts.	
1671	North Grimston	Yorks.	
1673	Worsbrough	Yorks.	
1675	Wrington	Somerset	
1676, r.	Lund	Yorks.	
1677	Chirbury	Shrops.	
1678	Marlborough	Wilts.	
1679	Chelmsford	Essex	
1679	Swaffham	Norf.	
1680	Milton Abbas	Dorset	
1680	More	Shrops.	
1682, r.	Hull. St. Mary Lowgate	Yorks.	
1684	Horsted Keynes	Sussex	
1684	London. St. Martin-in-the-Fields	London	
1684, r.	Wethersfield	Essex	
1685	Ribchester	Lancs.	
1686	North Grimston	Yorks.	
1686, r.	Sutton Courtenay	Berks.	
1686	Tamworth	Staffs.	
1686	Wimborne	Dorset	
1686, r.	Sutton Courtenay	Berks.	
1687	Ainstable	Cumb.	Oley
1687	Askham	Cumb.	Oley
1687	Burgh-by-Sands	Cumb.	Oley
1687	Crosby Ravensworth	Cumb.	Oley
1687	Crosby-on-Eden	Cumb.	Oley
1687	Dalston	Cumb.	Oley
1687	Dearham	Cumb.	Oley
1687	Isel	Cumb.	Oley
1687	Thursby	Cumb.	Oley
1687	Wigton	Cumb.	Oley
1688, r.	Newbury	Berks.	
1689	Stainton	Yorks.	
169-	Stansted Mountfichet	Essex	
1690	Assington	Suffolk	
1690	Salford	Lancs.	

1691	Bicester	Oxon.	
1693	Denchworth	Berks.	
1694	Stainton	Yorks.	
1695	Cudworth	Somerset	
1695	Martock	Somerset	
1695	Willen	Bucks.	
1695	Wimborne, augm.	Dorset	
1695–9	Andover	Hants.	Bray F
1695–9	Bamburgh Deanery	Northumb.	Bray F
1695–9	Bishop's Castle	Shrops.	Bray F
1695–9	Bromsgrove	Worcs.	Bray F
1695–9	Buckden	Hunts.	Bray F
1695–9	Buttington	Wales. Mont.	Bray F
1695–9	Carlisle	Cumb.	Bray F
1695–9	Chester	Ches.	Bray F
1695–9	Chirbury (?)	Shrops.	Bray F
1695–9	Church Pulverbatch	Shrops.	Bray F
1695–9	Churchstoke	Wales. Mont.	Bray F
1695–9	Coleshill	Warwicks.	Bray F
1695–9	Corbridge Deanery	Northumb.	Bray F
1695–9	Coventry	Warwicks.	Bray F
1695–9	Deal	Kent	Bray F
1695–9	Forden	Wales. Mont.	Bray F
1695–9	Huntingdon	Hunts.	Bray F
1695–9	Kimbolton	Hunts.	Bray F
1695–9	Kirkoswald	Cumb.	Bray F
1695–9	Llanfyllin	Wales. Mont.	Bray F
1695–9	Llanidloes	Wales. Mont.	Bray F
1695–9	London. St. Botolph	Lon.	Bray F
1695–9	Ludlow	Shrops.	Bray F
1695–9	Mancetter	Warwicks.	Bray F
1695–9	Montgomery	Wales. Mont.	Bray F
1695–9	Morpeth	Northumb.	Bray F
1695–9	Myndtown	Shrops.	Bray F
1695–9	Nantwich	Ches.	Bray F
1695–9	Newbury	Berks.	Bray F
1695–9	Newtown	Wales. Mont.	Bray F
1695–9	Norbury	Shrops.	Bray F
1695–9	Northampton	Northants.	Bray F
1695–9	Ratlinghope	Shrops.	Bray F
1695–9	Shap	Westm.	Bray F
1695–9	Shelve	Shrops.	Bray F
1695–9	Sheldon	Warwicks.	Bray F
1695–9	Sherborne	Dorset	Bray F
1695–9	St. Ives	Hunts.	Bray F

1695–9	St. Neot's	Hunts.	Bray F
1695–9	Stoke-by-Nayland	Suffolk	Bray F
1695–9	Tamworth	Staffs.	Bray F
1695–9	Trelystan	Wales. Mont.	Bray F
1695–9	Warwick	Warwicks.	Bray F
1695–9	Wigton	Cumb.	Bray F
1696	Gainsborough	Lincs.	Bray F
1696	Goosnargh	Lancs.	
1697	Cartmel	Lancs.	
1697	Tong	Shrops.	
1698	Coleshill, augm.	Warwicks.	
1698	Garsdale	Yorks.	
1698	Newark-upon-Trent	Notts.	
1698	Womersley	Yorks.	
1699	Beverley	Yorks.	
1699, r.	Coniston	Lancs.	
1699	Gravesend	Kent	Bray F
1699	Nantwich, augm.	Ches.	
17--	Broughton in Furness	Lancs.	
17--	Bushey	Herts.	
17--	Gorton	Lancs.	Chetham
17--	Kildwick	Yorks.	
17--	Nayland	Suffolk	
17--	Rivington	Lancs.	
170-	Caddington	Beds.	
1700	Bedford	Beds.	
1700	Hackness	Suffolk	
1700	Nantwich	Ches.	
1700, r.	Plymouth	Devon	Bray F
1701	Durham	Durham	
1701	Kendal	Westm.	SPCK
1701	Reigate	Surrey	
1701	Warwick	Warwicks.	
1702, r.	Costock	Notts.	
1703, r.	Basingstoke	Hants.	
1703	Bilston	Staffs.	
1703, r.	Crosby Garret	Westm.	
1703	Milden	Suffolk	
1703, r.	Orton	Northumb.	
1703	Sleaford	Lincs.	
1703, r.	Welford	Northants.	
1704	Lawshall	Suffolk	
1704	Maldon	Essex	
1705, r.	Beccles	Suffolk	
1705	Bilston	Staffs.	

1705, r.	Bishop's Castle	Shrops.	
1705, r.	Crosthwaite	Cumb.	
1705, r.	'Elm Green'	Worcs.	Bray P
1705, r.	Frisby-on-the-Wreake	Leics.	
1705, r.	Greenford	Middx.	
1705, r.	Sheffield	Yorks.	
1705, r.	Skipton	Yorks.	
1705	Southwell	Notts.	
1705, r.	York. St. Mary Castlegate	Yorks.	
1706, r.	London. St. George	London	
1707, r.	Barton-upon-Humber	Lincs.	
1707, r.	Presteigne	Wales. Radnor.	
1708	Carmarthen Diocesan Library	Wales. Carm.	SPCK
1708	Hatfield Broad Oak	Essex	
1708	Lewes (projected)	Sussex	Bray T
1709	Bangor Diocesan Library	Wales. Caer.	SPCK
1709, r.	Rougham	Norf.	
1709, r.	Wrexham	Wales. Denbigh	SPCK?
171-	London. All Saints	London	
1710	Beetham	Westm.	
1710	Brewood	Staffs.	Bray T
1710	Bridlington	Yorks.	Bray T
1710	Corston	Somerset	Bray T
1710	Darowen	Wales. Mont.	Bray T
1710	Detling	Kent	Bray T
1710	Dorchester	Dorset	Bray T
1710	Evesham	Worcs.	Bray T
1710	Flaxley	Glos.	Bray T
1710	Halifax, augm.	Yorks.	
1710	Henley-in-Arden	Warwicks.	Bray T
1710	Irthlingborough	Northants.	Bray T
1710	Kirkoswald	Cumb.	Bray T
1710	Llanbadarn Fawr	Wales. Card.	Bray T
1710	Lostwithiel	Corn.	Bray T
1710	Monmouth	Wales. Mon.	Bray T
1710	Newport	Essex	Bray T
1710	North Walsham	Norf.	Bray T
1710	Oxenhall	Glos.	Bray T
1710	Prendergast	Wales. Pembs.	Bray T
1710	Preston [near Wingham]	Kent	Bray T
1710	Slapton	Devon	Bray T
1710	Tadcaster	Yorks.	Bray T
1710	Weobley	Heref.	Bray T
1710	Wigton	Cumb.	Bray T
1710	Wotton-under-Edge	Glos.	

1711	Alnwick	Northumb.	Bray T
1711	Bolsterstone	Yorks.	Bray T
1711	Cowbridge Diocesan Library	Wales. Glam.	SPCK
1711	Darlington	Durham	Bray T
1711	Ely	Cambs.	
1711	Harwich	Essex	
1711	Kilmersdon	Somerset	Bray T
1711	Kingsbridge	Devon	Bray T
1711	Leek, r.	Staffs.	
1711	Little Harrowden	Northants.	Bray A
1711	Llandaff Diocesan Library	Wales. Glam.	SPCK
1711	Newport	Wales. Glam.	Bray T
1711	Over Whitacre	Warwicks.	Bray T
1711	St. Asaph Diocesan Library	Wales. Flint.	SPCK
1711	St. Neots	Hunts.	Bray T
1711	Tinsley	Yorks.	Bray T
1711	Trevethin	Wales. Mon.	Bray T
1711	Wentworth	Yorks.	Bray T
1711	Wollaston	Northants.	Bray T
1712	Alcester	Warwicks.	Bray T
1712	Bampton	Westm.	Bray T
1712	Brookthorpe	Glos.	Bray T
1712	Burgh-by-Sands	Cumb.	Bray T
1712	Chepstow	Wales. Mon.	Bray T
1712	Dudleston	Shrops.	Bray T
1712	Dullingham	Cambs.	Bray T
1712, r.	Earl Sterndale	Derbys.	
1712	Elmley Castle	Worcs.	Bray T
1712	Feckenham	Worcs.	Bray T
1712	Llanrhos (Eglws Rhos)	Wales. Caer.	Bray T
1712	Marske-by-the-Sea	Yorks.	Bray T
1712	New Malton	Yorks.	Bray T
1712	Pwllheli	Wales. Caer.	Bray T
1712	St. Bees	Cumb.	Bray T
1712, r.	Stockton-on-Tees	Durham	
1712	Sudbury	Suffolk	Bray T
1713	Oldbury	Shrops.	Bray T
1713	Timsbury	Hants.	
1714	Ashby-de-la-Zouch	Leics.	
1714	Doncaster	Yorks.	
1715	Brent Eleigh	Suffolk	
1715, r.	Cranfield	Beds.	
1715	Hereford	Heref.	
1715	Liverpool	Lancs.	
1715, r.	Llandrillo-yn-Rhos	Wales. Denb.	

1716, r.	Huntingdon	Hunts.	
1716, r.	Poslingford	Suffolk	
1716	Tiverton	Devon	
1716	Winslow	Bucks.	
1717	Bassingbourn	Cambs.	
1717	Lewes	Sussex	
1717	Whitchurch	Shrops.	
1717, r.	Withington	Heref.	
1718, r.	Ashton	Northants.	
1718	Gillingham	Dorset	
1718, r.	Newcastle Emlyn	Wales. Carm.	Bray T.
1719	Boston, augm.	Lincs.	
1719, r.	Faversham	Kent	
1719	Heanton	Devon	Bray (projected)
1720	Bradfield	Yorks	
1720	Llandysilio	Wales. Denb.	Bray T
1720	Ormesby	Norf.	
1720	Poulton-le-Fylde	Lancs.	Bray T
1720	Shepshed	Leics.	Bray T
1720	Skelton	Yorks.	Bray T
1720	Stamford, augm.	Lincs.	
1720	Stowey	Somerset	Bray T
1720	Whitchurch	Hants.	Bray T
1721	Crediton	Devon	
1721	Hillingdon	Middx.	
1721	Oundle	Northants.	Bray T
1721	Oxford. St. Peter-le-Bailey	Oxon	Bray T
1721	St. Martin's	Shrops.	Bray T
1721, r.	Swinderby	Lincs.	
1723, r.	Bamburgh	Northumb.	
1723, r.	Bothal	Northumb.	
1723, r.	Gosforth	Northumb.	
1723, r.	Llysfaen	Wales. Denbigh	
1724	Basingstoke	Hants.	
1724	Effingham	Surrey	
1724	Slaithwaite	Yorks.	
1725	Aylesbury	Bucks.	
1725, r.	Douglas	I of M	Bray P
1725	Flookburgh	Lancs.	Bray T
1726	East Harlsey	Yorks.	
1727	Ashby-de-la-Zouch	Leics.	
1727, r.	Box	Wilts.	Bray T
1727	Coleorton	Leics.	
1727	Great Yarmouth	Norf.	
1727, r.	Hounslow	Middx.	

1727, r.	Reading. St. Giles	Berks.	Bray T
1727	Shustoke	Warwicks.	Bray T
1727	Woodchurch	Ches.	
1728	Rotherham	Yorks.	
1728–9	Crundale	Kent	
1729	Burwell	Cambs.	Bray T
1729	Corbridge	Northumb.	
1729	Howe	Norf.	Bray T
1729, r.	Lezayre	I of M	Wilson
1729	St. Mary's	Scilly I	Bray T
1729, r.	Streatley	Beds.	Bray T
173-	Royston	Herts.	
1730, r.	Amberley	Sussex	Bray P
1730	Bilston, augm.	Staffs.	
1730	Ledsham	Yorks.	Bray P
1730	London. St. Botolph, augm.	Lon.	Bray P
1731, r.	Chertsey	Surrey	
1731, r.	East Bedfont	Middx.	
1731, r.	Feltham	Middx.	
1731	Newport Pagnell	Bucks.	
1731	Whitchurch	Hants.	
1732	Elston	Notts.	
1733	Birmingham. St. Philip	Warwicks.	
1733	Bishops Lydeard	Somerset	
1733	Halton	Ches.	
1733	Sible Hedingham	Essex	
1734, r.	Astley	Lancs	
1734	Willen, augm.	Bucks.	
1735, r.	Kirkbride	I of M	Wilson
1735	Maidstone, augm.	Kent	Bray P
1735	Newcastle upon Tyne, augm.	Northumb.	
1736	Fersfield	Norf.	
1737	Broughton	Hunts.	
1737	Henley-on-Thames	Oxon.	
1737	Newent	Glos.	
1737	Skipwith	Yorks.	
1738, r.	Arbory	I of M	Wilson
1738, r.	Ballaugh	I of M	Wilson
1738, r.	Braddon	I of M	Wilson
1738, r.	Douglas	I of M	Wilson
1738, r.	German	I of M	Wilson
1738, r.	Jurby	I of M	Wilson
1738, r.	Lonan	I of M	Wilson
1738, r.	Malew	I of M	Wilson
1738, r.	Marown	I of M	Wilson

1738, r.	Maughold	I of M	Wilson
1738, r.	Michael	I of M	Wilson
1738, r.	Onchan	I of M	Wilson
1738, r.	Patrick	I of M	Wilson
1738, r.	Rushen	I of M	Wilson
1738, r.	Santan	I of M	Wilson
1739	Bromham	Beds.	
1740	Daventry	Northants.	
1740	Douglas, augm.	I of M	Wilson
1740	Heathfield	Sussex	
1740, r.	Horwich	Lancs.	
1742	Newark-upon-Trent, augm.	Notts.	
1743, r.	Amersham	Bucks.	
1743	Bridgnorth	Shrops.	
1743	Doddington	Kent	
1743	Mentmore	Bucks.	
1745	Droxford	Hants.	
1745	Tong, augm.	Shrops.	
1746, r.	Andreas	I of M	Wilson
1746, r.	Riccall	Yorks.	
1747, r.	Bubwith	Yorks.	
1747	Llanteglos-by-Camelford	Corn.	
1749	Bratton Fleming	Devon	
1749	Norton	Derbys.	
1750, r.	Chippenham	Cambs.	
1751	Bampton	Westm.	
1751, r.	Thurnham	Kent	
1751, r.	Witham	Essex	
1752, r.	Ecton	Northants.	
1752, r.	Great Ayton	Yorks.	
1754	Campsall	Yorks.	
1754, r.	Dent	Yorks.	
1754, r.	Ramsey	I of M	Wilson
1754	Stanground	Hunts.	
1754, r.	Tunstall	Lancs.	
1756, r.	Alston	Northumb.	
1756, r.	Enstone	Oxon.	
1756	Ulverston	Lancs.	Bray A
1756	Westerham	Kent	
1757	Admarsh-in-Bleasdale	Lancs.	Bray A
1757	Askrigg	Yorks.	Bray A
1757	Caerleon	Wales. Mon.	Bray A
1757	Crook	Westm.	Bray A
1757	Dalton	Lancs.	Bray A
1757	Ellel	Lancs.	Bray A

1757	Ingleton	Yorks.	Bray A
1757	Lowick	Lancs.	Bray A
1757	Old Hutton	Westm.	Bray A
1757, r.	Patrixbourne	Kent	
1757	Poulton-le-Fylde, augm.	Lancs.	Bray A
1757	Selside	Westm.	Bray A
1757	Setmurthy	Cumb.	Bray A
1757	Silverdale	Lancs.	Bray A
1757	Staveley in Cartmel	Lancs.	Bray A
1757	Thwaites	Cumb.	Bray A
1757	Tortworth	Glos.	
1757	Waberthwaite	Cumb.	Bray A
1757	Witherslack	Westm.	Bray A
1757	Woodplumpton	Lancs.	Bray A
1757	Wythop	Cumb.	Bray A
1758	Bampton, augm.	Westm.	Bray A
1759, r.	Mugginton	Derbys.	
1759, r.	Penshurst	Kent	
176-	Norwich. St. Martin-at-Oak	Norf.	
1760	Ford	Shrops.	Bray A
1760	Llandaff	Wales. Glam.	Bray A
1761	Arkengarthdale	Yorks.	Bray A
1761	Bolton-le-Sands	Lancs.	Bray A
1761	Cockerham	Lancs.	Bray A
1761	Crosscrake	Westm.	Bray A
1761	Leck	Lancs.	Bray A
1761	Lindale	Lancs.	Bray A
1761	Littledale	Lancs.	Bray A
1761	Mallerstang	Westm.	Bray A
1761	Pilling	Lancs.	Bray A
1761	Richmond. Holy Trinity	Yorks.	Bray A
1761	South Cowton	Yorks.	Bray A
1761	Ulpha	Cumb.	Bray A
1762	Allendale	Northumb.	
1762	Cockermouth	Cumb.	Bray A
1762	Gressingham	Lancs.	Bray A
1762	Hoole	Lancs.	Bray A
1762	Ravenstonedale	Westm.	Bray A
1763	Bala	Wales. Mer.	Bray A
1763	London. St. Leonard	London	
1763	Stonehouse	Glos.	
1764	Cilmaenllwyd	Wales. Carm.	Bray A
1764	Lancaster	Lancs.	Bray A
1764	Llanwnog	Wales. Mont.	Bray A
1764	Shipdham	Norf.	

1764, r.	Wendlebury	Oxon.	
1765	Abernant	Wales. Carm.	Bray A
1765	Cardigan	Wales. Card.	Bray A
1765	Cellan	Wales. Card.	Bray A
1765	Ciliau Aeron	Wales. Card.	Bray A
1765	Eastwick	Herts.	
1765	Grantham	Lincs.	
1765	Lampeter	Wales. Card.	Bray A
1765	Llanbadarn Trefglwys	Wales. Card.	Bray A
1765	Llanddewi Aberarth	Wales. Card.	Bray A
1765	Llandyfaelog	Wales. Carm.	Bray A
1765	Llandysul	Wales. Card.	Bray A
1765	Llanfihangel-ar-arth	Wales. Carm.	Bray A
1765	Llanwinio	Wales. Carm.	Bray A
1765	Llanwnnen	Wales. Card.	Bray A
1765	Offord Cluny	Hunts.	
1765	Penboyr	Wales. Carm.	Bray A
1765	Stone	Staffs.	
1765	Tre-lech a'r Betws	Wales. Carm.	Bray A
1765	Trefilan	Wales. Card.	Bray A
1765	Westerham	Kent	
1766	Clydau	Wales. Pembs.	Bray T
1766	Cyffig	Wales. Carm.	Bray A
1766	Dalton, augm.	Lancs.	
1766	Eglwys Gymyn	Wales. Carm.	Bray A
1766	Field Broughton	Lancs.	Bray A
1766	Graveley	Cambs.	
1766	Grayrigg	Westm.	Bray A
1766	Hardraw	Yorks.	Bray A
1766	Heversham	Westm.	Bray A
1766	Laugharne	Wales. Carm.	Bray A
1766	Little Newcastle	Wales. Pembs.	Bray A
1766	Llanarth	Wales. Card.	Bray A
1766	Llandawke	Wales. Carm.	Bray A
1766	Llanddowror	Wales. Carm.	Bray A
1766	Llandeilo Fawr	Wales. Carm.	Bray A
1766	Llandysilio	Wales. Pembs.	Bray A
1766	Llandysiliogogo	Wales. Card.	Bray A
1766	Llanegwad	Wales. Carm.	Bray A
1766	Llanllwchaearn	Wales. Card.	Bray A
1766	Wasdale Head	Cumb.	Bray A
1767	Coddenham	Suffolk	
1767	Deuddwr	Wales. Mont.	Bray A
1768	Bangor Teifi	Wales. Card.	Bray A
1768	Egremont	Wales. Pembs.	Bray A

1768	Llandyfriog	Wales. Card.	Bray A
1768	Llandygwydd	Wales. Carm.	Bray A
1768	Llanfair Caereinion	Wales. Mont.	Bray A
1768	Llangathen	Wales. Carm.	Bray A
1768	Llanwnda	Wales. Pembs.	Bray A
1768	Narberth	Wales. Pembs.	Bray A
1768	Royston	Herts.	
1768	St. Clears	Wales. Carm.	Bray A
1769	Caernarfon	Wales. Caer.	Bray A
1769	Llanbadarn Fawr, augm.	Wales. Card.	Bray A
177-, r.	Bloxham	Oxon.	
1770, r.	Caddington	Beds.	
1770	Llandysilio, augm.	Wales. Pembs.	Bray A
1770	Pwllheli, augm.	Wales. Caer.	Bray A
1772	Broughton, augm.	Hunts.	
1773	Woodbridge	Suffolk	
1777, r.	Kirby Lonsdale	Westm.	
1777	Northampton.	Northants.	
1778, r.	Garsdale	Yorks.	
1778, r.	Tatham Fells	Lancs.	Bray (?)
1780	Knutsford	Ches.	Bray A
1780, r.	Norwich. St. Martin	Norf.	
1781	Bewdley	Worcs.	Bray A
1782	Ross-on-Wye	Heref.	Bray A
1783	Smarden	Kent	
1783	Wigton	Cumb.	Bray A
1784	Abergavenney	Wales. Mon.	Bray A
1784	Norton and Lenchwick	Worcs.	
1785	Loughborough	Leics.	
1785	Redmire	Yorks.	Bray A
1785	St. Neots, augm.	Hunts.	
1786, r.	Buckland	Berks.	
1786	Crosthwaite	Cumb.	Bray A
1786	Keswick	Cumb.	Bray A
1786, r.	Newbury	Berks.	Bray F
1786	Tortworth, augm.	Glos.	
1787	Cardington	Beds.	
1788	Finedon	Northants.	
1788	Heversham	Westm.	Bray A
1788	North Walsham, augm.	Norf.	Bray A
1788	Wentnor	Shrops.	
1792	Brampton	Westm.	Bray A
1792	Bridgnorth, augm.	Shrops.	
1792	Wedmore	Somerset	
1793	Swansea	Wales. Glam.	Bray A

1793	Woodchurch	Ches.	Bray A
1794	Llanrwst	Wales. Denb.	Bray A
1794	Swansea, augm.	Wales. Glam.	Bray A
1795	Beetham	Westm.	
1795, r.	Flamborough	Yorks.	
1795	Oswestry	Shrops.	Bray A
1796	Beaumaris	Wales. Ang.	Bray A
1796	Dolgellau	Wales. Mer.	Bray A
1796, r.	Plymtree	Devon	
1797, r.	Banbury	Oxon	
1797	Mold	Wales. Flint.	Bray A
1798	Stowey, augm.	Somerset	Bray A
1799	Much Wenlock	Shrops.	Bray A
18--	Alwinton	Northumb.	SPCK
18--	Appleton le-Street	Yorks.	
18--	Aymestrey	Heref.	
18--	Carleton Rode	Norf.	
18--	Clifton	Westm.	
18--	Dufton	Westm.	
18--	Evington	Leics.	
18--	Hughenden	Bucks.	
18--	Newquay	Corn.	
18--	North Piddle	Worcs.	
180-	Rhos	Wales. Pembs.	Bray A
1800	Stockton-on-Tees	Durham	
1801	Llandeilo Fawr, augm.	Wales. Carm.	Bray A
1801, r.	Steeple Morden	Cambs.	
1802	Llandeilo Tal-y-bont	Wales. Glam.	Bray A
1804	Heversham, augm.	Westm.	Bray A
1804	Ingleton, augm.	Yorks.	Bray A
1806, r.	Thornham	Norf.	
1807	Bacup	Lancs.	Bray A
1807	Elham	Kent	
1807	Hunmanby	Yorks.	
1807, r.	Pen-bre	Wales. Carm.	Bray A
1807	St. David's	Wales. Pembs.	Bray A
1808	Haverfordwest	Wales. Pembs.	Bray A
1808, r.	Henbury	Glos.	
1808	Ystrad Meurig	Wales. Card.	Bray A
1809, r.	Lutterworth	Lancs.	
1809	Ystrad Meurig, augm.	Wales. Card.	Bray A
1810	Rhayader	Wales. Radnor.	Bray A
1810	Sandbach	Ches.	Bray A
1811	Llangynllo	Wales. Radnor.	Bray A
1811	Temple Sowerby	Westm.	Bray A

1812	Cannock	Staffs.	Bray A
1812	Hunmanby	Yorks.	Bray A
1812	Leominster	Heref.	Bray A
1812	Newchurch	Staffs.	Bray A
1813	Tilshead	Wilts.	Bray A
1814	Denbigh	Wales. Denbigh.	Bray A
1814	Lampeter, augm.	Wales. Card.	Bray A
1814	'Lane End'	Staffs.	Bray A
1815	Cockermouth, augm.	Cumb.	
1815	Penistone	Yorks.	Bray A
1815	Wasdale Head, augm.	Cumb.	Bray A
1816	Princes Risborough	Bucks.	Bray A
1817	Castleton	Derbys.	
1817	East Haddon	Northants.	Bray A
1817	Ewell	Surrey	Bray A
1817	Guilden Morden	Herts.	Bray A
1817	Prees	Shrops.	
1818	Accrington	Lancs.	Bray A
1818	Burton-on-Trent	Staffs.	Bray A
1818	Pudsey	Yorks.	Bray A
1818	Rampisham	Dorset	Bray A
1818	St. Bees, augm.	Cumb.	Bray A
1818	Stokesley	Yorks.	SPCK (?)
1819	Bewdley	Worcs.	
1819	Eastwood	Notts.	Bray A
1819	Haslingden	Lancs.	Bray A
182-	Allesley	Warwicks	
1820, r.	Clapton in Gordano	Somerset	
1820	Marsden	Lancs.	Bray A
1821	Aldbury	Herts.	Bray A
1821	Muker	Yorks.	Bray A
1821	Norton St. Philip	Somerset	Bray A
1821	St. Mary's	Scilly I	Bray A
1822	Alnwick, augm.	Northumb.	Bray A
1822	Lillington	Warwicks.	
1822	Spondon	Derbys.	Bray A
1823	Ashurst	Kent	Bray A
1823, r.	Bolam	Northumb.	
1823	Bury. St. John	Lancs.	Bray A
1823	Cardigan, augm.	Wales. Card.	Bray A
1823, r.	Corbridge Deanery	Northumb.	
1823, r.	Cornhill	Northumb.	
1823	Cradley	Worcs.	Bray A
1823, r.	Exeter	Devon	
1823, r.	Ford	Northumb.	

1823, r.	Gosforth	Northumb.	
1823, r.	Haltwhistle	Northumb.	
1823	Kings Bromley	Staffs.	Bray A
1823, r.	Kirkby-in-Cleveland	Yorks.	SPCK
1823	Llangefni	Wales. Ang.	Bray A
1823, r.	Long Benton	Northumb.	
1823, r.	Long Horsley	Northumb.	
1823, r.	Mitford	Northumb.	
1823, r.	Morpeth	Northumb.	
1823, r.	Netherwitton	Northumb.	
1823, r.	Newbiggin-by-the Sea	Northumb.	
1823, r.	Norham	Northumb.	
1823	Old Malton	Yorks.	Bray A
1823, r.	Shilbottle	Northumb.	
1823, r.	Staunton	Glos.	
1823, r.	Tynemouth	Northumb.	
1823, r.	Whalton	Northumb.	
1823, r.	Whittingham	Northumb.	
1823, r.	Wooler	Northumb.	
1824	Alconbury	Hunts.	Bray A
1824	London. St. Mary Aldermary (?)	London	
1824	Ulverston, augm.	Lancs.	Bray A
1825	Great Driffield	Yorks.	Bray A
1825, r.	Hooton Roberts	Yorks.	
1825, r.	Iron Acton	Glos.	
1825	Myddle	Shrops.	
1826	Barnstaple	Devon	
1826	Newchurch- in- Pendle	Lancs.	Bray A
1826	Stokesley	Yorks.	Bray A
1827	Cowbridge	Wales. Glam.	Bray A
1828	Haltwhistle, augm.	Northumb.	
1828, r.	Misson	Notts.	
1828, r.	Much Marcle	Heref.	
1828	Steeple Ashton	Wilts.	
1828	Usk	Wales. Mon.	Bray A
1829	Llanover	Wales. Mon.	Bray A
183-	Wirksworth	Derbys.	
1830	Bradford	Yorks.	Bray A
1830	Hadleigh	Suffolk	
1830, r.	West Wickham	Cambs.	
1831, r.	Bradfield	Berks.	
1831	Dewsbury	Yorks.	Bray A
1832, r.	Bassingham	Lincs.	
1832	Deptford	Kent	Bray A
1833, r.	Bangor Monachorum	Wales. Denbigh.	

1833	Llanboidy	Wales. Carm.	Bray A
1833	Milnrow	Lancs.	Bray A
1833	Roos	Yorks.	
1834	Brecon. St. Mary	Wales. Brecon	
1834	Newport, augm.	Essex	Bray A
1834	Newport	I of W	Bray A
1835	Great Driffield	Yorks.	Bray A
1836	Admarsh-in-Bleasdale, augm.	Lancs.	Bray A
1836	East Retford	Notts.	Bray A
1837	Birch	Lancs.	Bray A
1837	Dursley	Glos.	
1838	Ainsworth	Lancs.	Bray A
1839	Melton Mowbray	Leics.	
184-	Llanfyllin	Wales. Mont.	SPCK
184-	Warwick	Warwicks.	
1840	Ashworth	Lancs.	Bray A
1840	Beaumaris, augm.	Wales. Ang.	Bray A
1840	Bradford, augm.	Yorks.	Bray A
1840	Caernarfon, augm.	Wales. Caer.	Bray A
1840	Denbigh, augm.	Wales. Denb.	Bray A
1840	Dolgellau, augm.	Wales. Mer.	Bray A
1840	Frome	Somerset	Bray A
1840	Goodshaw	Lancs.	Bray A
1840	Illingworth	Yorks.	Bray A
1840	Llanrwst, augm.	Wales. Denb.	Bray A
1840	Newcastle upon Tyne	Northumb.	Bray A
1840	Plymouth	Devon	Bray A
1840	Preston	Lancs.	Bray A
1840	Rochford	Essex	Bray A
1840	Southampton	Hants.	Bray A
1840	Warminster	Wilts.	Bray A
1840, r.	Whitford	Wales. Flint.	
1841	Devizes	Wilts.	Bray A
1841, r.	Fishguard	Wales. Pembs.	Bray A
1841	Huddersfield	Yorks.	Bray A
1841	Hungerford	Berks.	Bray A
1841	Oxford. St. Peter-in-the-East	Oxon.	
1842	St. Bees, augm.	Cumb.	Bray A
1842	Truro	Corn.	Bray A
1843	Bakewell	Derbys.	Bray A
1843	Bradford-on-Avon	Wilts.	Bray A
1843	Macclesfield	Ches.	Bray A
1843	Portsmouth	Hants.	Bray A
1843, r.	Reepham	Norf.	
1843	Stockport	Ches.	Bray A

1844	Cockermouth, augm.	Cumb.	Bray A
1844	London. St. Matthew	London	Bray A
1844	Warrington	Lancs.	Bray A
1845	Leeds	Yorks.	Bray A
1845	St. Columb Major	Corn.	Bray A
1845, r.	Stetchworth	Suffolk	
1846, r.	Kerry	Wales. Mont.	
1846	Oldham	Lancs.	Bray A
1846	Shaftesbury	Dorset	Bray A
1846	Warton	Lancs.	Bray A
1847	Ashton-under-Lyne	Lancs.	Bray A
1847	Bury. St. John, augm.	Lancs.	Bray A
1847	Lancaster, augm.	Lancs.	Bray A
1847	Leigh	Lancs.	Bray A
1848	Cheadle	Staffs.	Bray A
1848	Ilminster	Somerset	Bray A
1848	St. Albans	Herts.	Bray A
1848	Stoke Damerel	Devon	
1849, r.	Derby. Holy Trinity	Derbys.	
1849	High Wycombe	Bucks.	Bray A
1849	Holyhead	Wales. Ang.	
1849	Keswick	Cumb.	
1849	Llanfaelog	Wales. Ang.	Bray A
1849	Torquay	Devon	· Bray A
1849	Yelden	Beds.	
1850, r.	Derby. St. Peter	Derbys.	
1850	'North Craven'	Yorks.	Bray A
1851	Ludlow	Shrops.	
1851, r.	Llansantffraid Glyndyfrdwy	Wales. Mer.	Bray A
1852	Chipping Sodbury	Glos.	Bray A
1852	Halstead	Essex	Bray A
1852, r.	Odiham	Hants.	
1853, r.	Bromfield	Cumb.	
1853, r.	Chirk	Wales. Denbigh.	
1853	Embsay	Yorks.	Bray A
1853	Leamington Priors	Warwicks.	Bray A
1853	Otley	Yorks.	Bray A
1853	Tiverton	Devon	Bray A
1854	Bengeworth	Worcs.	
1854	Cuddesdon	Oxon.	Bray A
1856, r.	Halifax	Yorks.	
1856	Llanelli	Wales. Carm.	Bray A
1856	Warminster, augm.	Wilts.	Bray A
1857	Ampthill	Beds.	Bray A
1857, r.	Derby. St. John	Derbys.	

1857, r.	Staunton	Glos.	
1857, r.	Westwood	Warwicks.	SPCK
1858, r.	Addington	Bucks	
1858	Bolton [-le-Moors]	Lancs.	Bray A
1858, r.	Cornhill	Northumb.	
1858	Gressingham	Lancs.	Bray A
1858, r.	Huggate	Yorks.	
1858	Norham, augm.	Northumb.	Bray A
1858	Yarnton	Oxon	
1859	Douglas	I of M	Bray A
1859	Norwich. St. Stephen	Norf.	
186-	Eardisley	Heref.	
186-	Llanfyllin	Wales. Mont.	SPCK
1860, r.	Ash	Kent	
1860	Friezland	Yorks.	Bray A
1861	Bristol. St. Mary, augm.	Glos.	
1861	Newport, augm.	I of W	Bray A
1861	Pwllheli, augm.	Wales. Caer.	Bray A
1862	Halifax	Yorks.	
1862	Brompton	Yorks.	Bray A
1862	Kirkby Fleetham	Yorks.	
1862	Olney	Bucks.	Bray A
1864	Blandford Forum	Dorset	Bray A
1864	Monmouth, augm.	Wales. Mon.	Bray A
1865	Blandford Forum, augm.	Dorset	Bray A
1865	Devizes, augm.	Wilts.	Bray A
1865	Llanelli	Wales. Carm.	Bray A
1865	Middlesborough	Yorks.	Bray A
1866	Hull. St. Mary, Lowgate	Yorks.	SPCK
1866, r.	Pilton	Somerset	
1866, r.	St. Peter Port, Guernsey	Channel I	
1868	Docking	Norf.	Bray A
1869	Ampthill, augm.	Beds.	Bray A
1869	Brompton, augm.	Yorks.	Bray A
1869	Canterbury. St. Augustine's Coll.	Kent	Bray A
1869	Donington	Lincs.	
1869	Macclesfield, augm.	Ches.	Bray A
1869	Newport, augm.	I of W	Bray A
1869	St. Bees, augm.	Cumb.	Bray A
1869	St. Neots, augm.	Hunts	Bray A
1869	Ulverston, augm.	Lancs.	Bray A
1869	Warton, augm.	Lancs.	Bray A
187-	Stratford-upon-Avon	Warwicks.	
1870	Accrington, augm.	Lancs.	Bray A
1870	Alnwick, augm.	Northumb.	Bray A

1870	Ashurst, augm.	Kent	Bray A
1870	Bewdley, augm.	Worcs.	Bray A
1870	Bury. St. John, augm.	Lancs.	Bray A
1870	Cannock, augm.	Staffs.	Bray A
1870	Cockermouth, augm.	Cumb.	Bray A
1870, r.	Compton	Surrey	
1870	Deuddwr, augm.	Wales. Mont.	Bray A
1870	Devizes, augm.	Wilts.	Bray A
1870	Dewsbury, augm.	Yorks.	Bray A
1870	Dolgellau, augm.	Wales. Mer.	Bray A
1870	Evesham, augm.	Worcs.	Bray A
1870	Gressingham, augm.	Lancs.	Bray A
1870	Haslingden, augm.	Lancs.	Bray A
1870	Hungerford, augm.	Berks.	Bray A
1870	Kirkoswald, augm.	Cumb.	Bray A
1870	Leicester, augm.	Leics.	Bray A
1870	Llanarth, augm.	Wales. Card.	Bray A
1870	Llandysilio, augm.	Wales. Denb.	Bray A
1870	Llanfair Caereinion, augm.	Wales. Mont.	Bray A
1870	Llanfihangel-ar-arth, augm.	Wales. Carm.	Bray A
1870	London. St. Matthew, augm.	London	Bray A
1870	Newcastle upon Tyne, augm.	Northumb.	Bray A
1870	Newchurch-in-Pendle, augm.	Lancs.	Bray A
1870	North Walsham, augm.	Norf.	Bray A
1870	Oldham, augm.	Lancs.	Bray A
1870	Oswestry, augm.	Shrops.	Bray A
1870	Otley, augm.	Yorks.	Bray A
1870	Over Whitacre, augm.	Warwicks.	Bray A
1870	St. Albans, augm.	Herts.	Bray A
1870	Spondon, augm.	Derbys.	Bray A
1870, r.	Stratford-upon-Avon, augm.	Warwicks.	
1870	Tinsley, augm.	Yorks.	Bray A
1870	Torquay, augm.	Devon	Bray A
1870	Usk, augm.	Wales. Mon.	Bray A
1870	Wall	Staffs.	Bray A
1870	Warminster, augm.	Wilts.	Bray A
1871, r.	Brattleby	Lincs.	
1871	Bridlington, augm.	Yorks.	Bray A
1871	Cardigan, augm.	Wales. Card.	Bray A
1871	Dolgellau, augm.	Wales. Mer.	Bray A
1871	Ellesmore	Shrops.	Bray A
1871	Norton St. Philip, augm.	Somerset	Bray A
1871	Raughton Head	Cumb.	Bray A
1871	St. Columb Major, augm.	Corn.	Bray A
1871	Shepshed, augm.	Leics.	Bray A

1871	West Alvington	Devon	Bray A
1871	Westwood	Warwicks.	
1872	Birkenhead	Ches.	Bray A
1872	Cheadle, augm.	Staffs.	Bray A
1872	Cuddesdon, augm.	Oxon.	Bray A
1872	Darowen, augm.	Wales. Mont.	Bray A
1872	Docking, augm.	Norf.	Bray A
1872, r.	Draycott-le-Moors	Staffs.	Bray A
1872	High Wycombe, augm.	Bucks.	Bray A
1872	Huddersfield, augm.	Yorks.	Bray A
1872	Laugharne, augm.	Wales. Carm.	Bray A
1872	Llandaff, augm.	Wales. Glam.	Bray A
1872	Llanwnog, augm.	Wales. Mont.	Bray A
1872, r.	Painswick	Glos.	
1872	Penistone, augm.	Yorks.	Bray A
1872	St. Martins, augm.	Shrops.	Bray A
1872	Stockport, augm.	Ches.	Bray A
1872	Stratford	Essex	Bray A
1872	Tiverton, augm.	Devon	Bray A
1872	Ystrad Meurig, augm.	Wales. Card.	Bray A
1873	Beverley	Yorks.	Bray A
1873	Haverfordwest, augm.	Wales. Pembs.	Bray A
1873	Ross-on-Wye, augm.	Herefords.	Bray A
1874	Coventry	Warwicks.	Bray A
1874	Docking, augm.	Norf.	Bray A
1874	Lancaster, augm.	Lancs.	Bray A
1874	Middlesbrough, augm.	Yorks.	Bray A
1875	Bradford, augm.	Yorks.	Bray A
1875	Llanfihangel-ar-arth, augm.	Wales. Carm.	Bray A
1876	Leeds, augm.	Yorks.	Bray A
1876	Sutton St. Mary	Lincs.	Bray A
1877	Aylesbury, augm.	Bucks.	Bray A
1877	Great Yarmouth	Norf.	Bray A
1877	Otley, augm.	Yorks.	Bray A
1877	Pershore	Worcs.	Bray A
1878	Bakewell, augm.	Derbys.	Bray A
1878	Beverley, augm.	Yorks.	Bray A
1878	Bolton [-le-Moors], augm.	Lancs.	Bray A
1878	Burgh	Lincs.	Bray A
1878	Cuddesdon, augm.	Oxon.	Bray A
1878	Dewsbury, augm.	Yorks.	Bray A
1878	Newchurch, augm.	Staffs.	Bray A
1878	Newport, augm.	I of W	Bray A
1878	Olney, augm.	Bucks.	Bray a
1878	Oswestry, augm.	Shrops.	Bray A

1878	St. Albans, augm.	Herts.	Bray A
1878	St. Bees, augm.	Cumb.	Bray A
1879	Frodsham	Ches.	
1879	Llanfaelog, augm.	Wales. Ang.	Bray A
1879	Newport	Essex	Bray A
1879	Penrhyndewdraeth	Wales. Mer.	Bray A
1880	Conwy	Wales. Caer.	
1880	Criccieth	Wales. Caer.	Bray A
1880	Llandudno	Wales. Caer.	Bray A
1880	Monmouth, augm.	Wales. Mon.	Bray A
1881	High Wycombe, augm.	Bucks.	Bray A
1881	Pershore, augm.	Worcs.	Bray A
1883	Cardigan, augm.	Wales. Card.	Bray A
1883	Dowlais	Wales. Glam.	Bray A
1883	Monmouth, augm.	Wales. Mon.	Bray A
1883	Newport, augm.	Wales. Mon.	Bray A
1884	St. Asaph	Wales. Flint.	Bray A
1884	High Wycombe, augm.	Bucks.	Bray A
1885	London. All Hallows	London	Bray
1885	Reading. St. Giles	Berks.	Bray A
1886	Huntingdon, augm.	Hunts.	
1886	Llanfihangel Genau'r-Glyn	Wales. Card.	Bray A
1886	Prees, augm.	Shrops.	
1886	Riccall	Yorks.	
1887, r.	Carbrook	Norf.	
1887	High Wycombe, augm.	Bucks.	Bray A
1888	Bolton [-le-Moors], augm.	Lancs.	Bray A
1888	Dewsbury, augm.	Yorks.	Bray A
1888	St. Clears Deanery	Wales. Carm.	Bray A
1888	Slaithwaite, augm.	Yorks.	
1889	Birkenhead, augm.	Ches.	Bray A
1889	Cardigan, augm.	Wales. Card.	Bray A
1889	Carlisle	Cumb.	Bray A
1889	Darowen, augm.	Wales. Mont.	Bray A
1889	Dolgellau, augm.	Wales. Mer.	Bray A
1889	Dudleston, augm.	Shrops.	Bray A
1889	Kirkoswald, augm.	Cumb.	Bray A
1889	Llandudno, augm.	Wales. Caer.	Bray A
1889	Llanfihangel-ar-arth, augm.	Wales. Carm.	Bray A
1889	Newport, augm.	Essex	Bray A
1889	Newport, augm.	Wales. Mon.	Bray A
1889	Penrhyndeudraeth, augm.	Wales. Mer.	Bray A
1889	Pwllheli, augm.	Wales. Caer.	Bray A
1889	St. Asaph, augm.	Wales. Flint.	Bray A
1890	Crewkerne	Somerset	Bray A

1890	Denbigh, augm.	Wales. Denbigh.	Bray A
1890	Eastbourne (see p.40)	Sussex	
1890	Fenton	Staffs.	Bray A
1890	Liverpool	Lancs.	Bray A
1890	Llanddeusant	Wales. Carm.	Bray A
1890	Newcastle upon Tyne, augm.	Northumb.	Bray A
1890	Pentre	Wales. Glam.	Bray A
1890	Trowbridge	Wilts.	Bray A
1890	Warrington, augm.	Lancs.	Bray A
1891	Lincoln	Lincs.	Bray A
1891	West Mersea	Essex	Bray A
1892	Ampthill, augm.	Beds.	Bray A
1892	Birkenhead, augm.	Ches.	Bray A
1892	Bishopthorpe	Yorks.	Bray A
1892	Liverpool, augm.	Lancs.	Bray A
1892	Porthmadog	Wales. Caer.	Bray A
1892	Truro, augm.	Corn.	Bray A
1893	Guildford (see p.32, n.14)	Surrey	Bray A
1893	Wrexham	Wales. Denbigh	Bray A
1894	Pontlottyn	Wales. Glam.	Bray A
1895	Carmarthen	Wales. Carm.	Bray A
1895, r.	Cawthorne	Yorks.	
1895, r.	Islip	Northants.	
1896	Alltwen	Wales. Glam.	Bray A
1896	Carlisle, augm.	Cumb.	Bray A
1896	Dolgellau, augm.	Wales. Mer.	Bray A
1896	Ebbw Vale	Wales. Mon.	Bray A
1896	High Wycombe, augm.	Bucks.	Bray A
1896	Lancaster, augm.	Lancs.	Bray A
1896	Liverpool, augm.	Lancs.	Bray A
1896	Llanelli, augm.	Wales. Carm.	Bray A
1896	Llanfihangel-ar-arth, augm.	Wales. Carm.	Bray A
1896	Llantrisant	Wales. Glam.	Bray A
1896	Llanwnog, augm.	Wales. Mont.	Bray A
1896	Newport, augm.	Essex	Bray A
1896	Otley, augm.	Yorks.	Bray A
1896	Penrhyndeudraeth, augm.	Wales. Mer.	Bray A
1896, r.	Preston Gubbals	Shrops.	
1896	Pwllheli, augm.	Wales. Caer.	Bray A
1896	Stratford, augm.	Essex	Bray A
1896	Usk, augm.	Wales. Mon.	Bray A
1896	Warminster, augm.	Wilts.	Bray A
1896	Warrington, augm.	Lancs.	Bray A
1896	Warton, augm.	Lancs.	Bray A
1896	Welshpool	Wales. Mont.	Bray A

1896	Yaxley	Suffolk	
1897	Ellesmere, augm.	Shrops.	Bray A
1897	Tredegar	Wales. Mon.	Bray A
1898	Kendal	Westm.	Bray A
1898	London. All Hallows, augm.	London	Bray A
1898	St. Clear's Deanery, augm.	Wales. Carm.	
1899	Liverpool, augm.	Lancs.	Bray A
1899	Llangattock	Wales. Brecon.	Bray A
1899	Manchester	Lancs.	Bray A
1899	Pontlottyn, augm.	Wales. Glam.	Bray A
1899	Sedburgh	Yorks.	Bray A
19--	Mere	Wilts.	
1900	Menai Bridge	Wales. Ang.	Bray A
1900	Pontardawe	Wales. Glam.	Bray A
1900	Swansea, augm.	Wales. Glam.	Bray A
1902	Kingsbridge, augm.	Devon	Bray A
1938, r.	Dedham	Essex	
1970, r.	Seathwaite	Lancs.	

TABLE OF
LIBRARIES BY COUNTIES

This table includes desk-libraries and other libraries for which no date of foundation can be given, omitted from the preceding chronological table. The county name is that in use before the 1974 boundary changes.

Symbols employed:
B   Libraries with surviving books
D   Desk-libraries (solely, or as part of a later collection)
§   Libraries recorded as possessing, or once possessing, chained books
I   Libraries recorded as holding incunables
S   Libraries recorded as holding STC books
W   Libraries recorded as holding Wing books
C   Libraries recorded as holding 16th – 17th cent. continental books
Information on holdings is derived mainly from the Directory entries and, espccially under columns I, S, W, C, is certainly incomplete. (See also Table of Oley, Bray and Wilson libraries, pp.444–52)

	B	D	§	I	S	W	C
ENGLAND							
Bedfordshire							
Ampthill							
Bedford	B			I			
Bromham	B				S		
Caddington							
Cardington	B						
Cranfield							
Streatley							
Toddington							
Yelden	B						C
Berkshire							
Abingdon	B	D	§		S	W	
Aldermaston	B	D				W	
Binfield		D					
Blewbury	B	D			S		
Bradfield							
Buckland	B				S	W	C
Caversham	B	D				W	

Berkshire, *continued*

	B	D	§	I	S	W	C
Denchworth	B		§	I	S		
Didcot	B	D					
East Challow	B	D			S	W	
Hungerford	B	D					
Hurley							
Longworth	B	D				W	
Newbury	B		§			W	
Reading. St. Giles	B				S		
Reading. St. Lawrence	B	D			S		
Shellingford	B	D			S		
Sparsholt	B	D			S		
Sutton Courtney	B		§		S	W	
Wantage		D					

Buckinghamshire

	B	D	§	I	S	W	C
Addington	B						C
Amersham					S	W	C
Aston Abbots	B	D					
Astwood	B	D			S		
Aylesbury							
Bledlow	B	D				W	
Bletchley	B	D			S	W	
Broughton	B	D			S		
Buckingham	B						
Cheddington	B	D			S		
Crowmarsh Gifford	B	D			S	W	
Cublington	B	D	§		S	W	
Great Brickhill	B	D				W	
Hedgerley	B	D				W	
HighWycombe	B						
Hughenden							
Langley Marish	B				S	W	C
Lathbury	B	D			S	W	
Mentmore							
Milton Keynes	B	D	§				
Newport Pagnell			§				
Olney							
Oving	B	D				W	
Princes Risborough							
Quainton	B	D				W	
Willen							
Winslow	B				S	W	C

Cambridgeshire

Bassingbourn	B				S		C
Burwell							
Cambridge. St. Benet	B	D			S		
Chippenham							
Dullingham							
Ely							
Graveley	B				S	W	
Impington	B						
Steeple Morden							
West Wickham							
Wisbech	B			I	S	W	C

Channel Islands

St. Peter Port, Guernsey
St. Saviour's, Guernsey

Cheshire

Alderley	B	D			S		
Astbury	B	D					
Backford	B	D	§		S		
Barthomley	B	D					
Birkenhead							
Bunbury	B	D			S		
Burton	B	D	§		S		
Chester							
Frodsham	B			I	S	W	
Halton	B				S	W	C
Knutsford	B	D				W	
Lower Peover	B	D	§		S		
Macclesfield		D	§				
Nantwich	B			I	S	W	
Nether Tabley	B	D			S		
Plemstall	B	D	§		S		
Sandbach							
Stalybridge	B	D			S		
Stockport							
Tarvin	B	D			S		
Warmingham	B	D			S		
Weaverham	B	D					
Whitegate	B	D					
Woodchurch	B					W	C

Cornwall

Landewednack		D		
Lanteglos by Camelford	B		S	W
Lostwithiel				
Newquay	B		S	W
St. Columb Major				
St. Dominic		D		
Tideford				
Truro	B			

Cumberland

Ainstable				
Askham				
Bowness		D	§	
Bromfield				
Burgh-by-Sands	B			
Carlisle	B			
Cockermouth				
Crosby-on-Eden				
Crosthwaite				
Dacre	B	D		S
Dalston				
Dearham				
Greystoke				
Isel				
Keswick				
Kirkoswald	B			
Mungrisdale	B	D		S
Raughton Head	B			
St. Bees				
Setmurthy				
Thursby				
Thwaites				
Ulpha				
Waberthwaite				
Wasdale Head				
Wigton				
Wythop				

Derbyshire

	B	D	§	I	S	W	C
Bakewell	B						
Breadsall		D					
Castleton	B				S	W	
Derby. All Saints							
Derby. Holy Trinity							
Derby. St. John the Evangelist							
Derby. St. Peter							
Dronfield	B	D	§				
Earl Sterndale							
Egginton	B	D	§				C
Mugginton							
Norton	B			I	S	W	
Repton							
Shirland	B	D	§		S		
Spondon							
Wirksworth							

Devon

	B	D	§	I	S	W	C
Barnstaple	B			I	S	W	
Bratton Fleming	B						
Crediton	B			I	S	W	
East Budleigh	B	D	§				
Exeter							
Great Torrington							
Hartland							
Heanton							
Kingsbridge	B						
Kingsteignton	B	D	§			W	
Ottery St. Mary	B		§	I			
Plymouth							
Plymtree							
Slapton							
Stoke Damerel							
Tavistock	B	D	§		S		
Tawstock	B	D					
Tiverton	B				S	W	
Torquay							
Totnes	B				S	W	
West Alvington							

Dorset

Blandford Forum							
Dorchester		D					
Gillingham	B				S	W	
Ibberton	B	D	§			W	
Lyme Regis	B	D	§		S	W	
Milton Abbas			§				
Purse Caundle	B	D	§			W	
Rampisham							
Shaftesbury							
Sherborne	B				S		
Spetisbury	B	D	§		S		
Wimborne Minster	B	D	§	I	S	W	C

Durham

Darlington	B				W
Durham	B		I	S	
Egglescliffe	B	D			W
Stockton-on-Tees					

Essex

Chelmsford	B				
Colchester	B				
Dedham	B			S	W
Halstead					
Harwich					
Hatfield Broad Oak	B		I	S	W
Hornchurch		D			
Maldon	B				
Newport	B		§		
Rochford					
Sible Hedingham					
Stansted Mountfichet	B			S	W
Stratford					
West Mersea					
Wethersfield	B				
Witham					

Gloucestershire

Ashchurch	B	D			S	W	
Bledington	B	D			S		
Blockley	B	D	§		S		
Bristol. All Saints	B			I	S	W	
Bristol. St. Mary							
Bristol. St. Thomas	B						
Brookthorpe							
Bushley	B	D			S		
Cam	B	D			S	W	
Chalford	B	D			S		
Chedworth	B	D			S		
Chipping Sodbury							
Cirencester		D					
Coates	B	D			S		
Cromhall	B	D			S		
Dursley	B	D					
Fairford		D	§				
Flaxley							
Frampton Cotterel	B	D			S		
Henbury							
Iron Acton							
Mickleton	B	D	§				
Newent							
Newnham	B	D			S		
Oxenhall							
Painswick	B	D			S	W	
Prestbury	B	D			S	W	
Ripple	B	D	§				
Staunton	B						
Stonehouse					S	W	
Tortworth	B				S	W	C
Upleadon	B	D			S		
Westbury-on-Severn	B	D					
Wotton-under-Edge	B				S	W	

Hampshire

Andover					
Avington	B	D			
Basingstoke	B			W	
Bentley	B	D		S	
Boldre	B	D		S	
Bournemouth	B	D(?)		S	

Hampshire, *continued*

Brockenhurst	B						
Christchurch			§				
Crofton	B	D					
Droxford	B				S	W	
Hordle	B	D				W	
Lasham	B	D				W	
Lymington	B	D			S	W	
Milford-on-Sea	B	D			S		
Odiham							
Porchester	B	D			S		
Portsea	B	D			S		
Portsmouth	B	D			S	W	
Sherborne St. John	B	D	§			W	
Southampton	B		§		S	W	
Stratfield Saye	B	D			S		
Timsbury	B	D			S	W	
Whitchurch	B				S		
Wootton St. Lawrence	B	D					C

Herefordshire

Abbeydore	B	D				W
Aylton	B	D			S	
Aymestrey						
Canon Frome		D	§			
Eardisley						
Hereford	B		§	I	S	W
Kinnersley	B					W
Ledbury	B	D			S	W
Leominster						
Much Marcle						
Ross-on-Wye						
Weobley						
Weston Beggard						
Withington						

Hertfordshire

Aldbury					
Barley	B	D		S	W
Bishop's Stortford					
Bovingdon	B	D		S	
Bushey		D			

Hertfordshire, *continued*

Eastwick	B				
Guilden Morden					
Hemel Hempstead	B	D			
Royston	B			W	C
Sacombe	B	D		W	
St. Albans					
Stevenage					

Huntingdonshire

Alconbury					
Broughton	B				
Buckden					
Great Gransden	B	D		W	
Holywell	B	D	S	W	
Huntingdon	B				
Kimbolton					
Offord Cluny	B			W	
Ramsey		D	§		
St. Ives					
St. Neots	B				C
Stanground					

Isle of Wight

Arreton	B	D		W	
Newport					
Shorwell	B	D	S		

Kent

Ash [-by-Wrotham]			S		C
Ashford	B	D	S	W	
Ashurst					
Bekesbourne	B	D			
Borden		D			
Canterbury. St. Andrew	B	D	S		
Canterbury. St. Augustine's Coll.					
Canterbury. St. Margaret	B	D	S		
Canterbury. St. Mary Breadman		D			
Chislet	B	D		W	
Crundale	B		S	W	C
Deal					

Kent, *continued*

Deptford						
Detling						
Doddington	B			S	W	C
Dover	B	D				
Elham	B			S	W	
Faversham						
Graveney	B			S		
Gravesend						
Maidstone	B		§	S	W	C
Margate	B	D		S		
Patrixbourne						
Penshurst	B				W	C
Preston [near Wingham]	B				W	
River	B	D		S		
Smarden	B					C
Sturry	B	D			W	
Thurnham						
Westerham						

Lancashire

Accrington						
Admarsh-in-Bleasdale						
Ainsworth						
Ashton-under-Lyne	B	D		S		
Ashworth						
Astley						
Bacup						
Birch						
Birch-in-Rusholme		D				
Bolton [-le-Moors]	B		§	S		
Bolton-le-Sands						
Broughton in Furness	B					
Bury. St. Mary	B					
Bury. St. John						
Cartmel	B		§	I	S	W
Cockerham						
Coniston	B					
Dalton						
Didsbury		D	§			
Ellel						
Field Broughton						
Flookburgh	B					

Lancashire, *continued*

Goodshaw						
Goosnargh						
Gorton	B		§		S	W
Gressingham						
Haslingden						
Hoole						
Horwich						
Kirkham						
Lancaster						
Leck						
Leigh	B	D	§			W
Leyland	B	D	§			
Lindale						
Littledale						
Liverpool			§			
Lowick						
Manchester			§			
Marsden						
Milnrow						
Mitton	B	D	§			
Newchurch-in-Pendle						
Oldham						
Pilling	B	D	§		S	
Poulton-le-Fylde	B					W
Preston						
Ribchester	B					W	C
Rivington						
Salford	B		§		S	W
Seathwaite	B					
Sefton						
Silverdale						
Staveley in Cartmel						
Tatham Fells						
Tunstall						
Turton	B		§			
Ulverston						
Walmsley	B					
Warrington	B					W
Warton	B					
Woodplumpton						

Leicestershire

Appleby Magna	B						
Ashby-de-la-Zouch	B				S	W	
Coleorton	B						
East Leake		D	§				
Evington							
Frisby-on-the-Wreake							
Leicester	B		§	I	S	W	
Loughborough	B				S		C
Lutterworth	B						
Melton Mowbray	B		§				
Shepshed	B				S	W	

Lincolnshire

Barton-upon-Humber							
Bassingham							
Boston	B				S	W	
Brattleby							
Burgh	(?)						
Donington	B					W	
Gainsborough							
Grantham	B		§	I	S	W	
Horncastle	B	D	§			W	
Lincoln							
Sleaford	B	D				W	
Spalding	B			I	S	W	
Stamford	B				S	W	C
Sutton St. Mary	B						
Swinderby							
Uffington							

London

All Hallows by the Tower	B	D			S	W
All Saints (Chelsea Old Church)	B	D				W
St. Andrew Undershaft	B	D	§		S	W
St. Bartholomew the Great	B	D				W
St. Botolph without Aldersgate						
St. Edmund the King	B	D			S	W
St. George the Martyr						
St. Helen, Bishopsgate	B	D				W
St. Leonard, Shoreditch	B				S	W
St. Martin-in-the-Fields	B	D				W

London, *continued*

St. Mary Abchurch	B	D		S	
St. Mary Aldermary					
St. Mary Woolnoth	B	D			W
St. Matthew, Bethnal Green					
St. Michael Cornhill	B	D	§	S(?)	
St. Peter's Cornhill	B				
St. Saviour	B				
St. Saviour, Pimlico					

Middlesex

East Bedfont	B				
Feltham	B				
Greenford					
Hillingdon	B	D			
Hounslow					

Norfolk

Aldborough	B	D			
Ashby St. Mary	B	D		S	
Baconsthorpe	B	D		S	
Bacton	B	D		S	
Barnham Broom	B	D		S	
Barningham Winter	B	D		S	W
Beeston next Mileham	B	D			W
Blakeney	B	D			
Brunstead	B	D		S	
Burnham Deepdale	B	D			W
Burnham Overy	B	D		S	
Burnham Sutton	B	D		S	
Carbrooke	B	D		S	
Carleton Rode	B	D		S	
Claxton	B	D			W
Cranwich	B	D			
Diss		D			
Docking					
East Carleton	B	D			W
East Dereham					
East Winch		D	§		
Fakenham		D			
Fersfield	B	D			W
Field Dalling	B	D			W

Norfolk, *continued*

	B	D	§	I	S	W	C
Filby	B	D				W	
Florden	B	D				W	
Fransham	B	D				W	
Gissing	B	D			S	W	
Great Melton	B	D			S		
Great Snoring	B	D			S		
Great Yarmouth	B				S	W	C
Guist	B	D			S	W	
Halvergate	B	D				W	
Hapton	B	D			S	W	
Hassingham	B	D				W	
Hethersett	B	D			S		
Hindringham	B	D			S		
Hockering	B	D				W	
Howe	B						
King's Lynn	B			I		W	C
Lakenham	B	D			S		
Lessingham	B	D	§		S		
Loddon	B	D			S		
Marlingford	B	D			S	W	
Mautby	B	D				W	
Merton	B	D			S		
Necton	B	D			S		
North Walsham	B	D			S		
Norwich. St. Andrew	B						
Norwich. St. Augustine	B	D			S		
Norwich. St. Clement	B	D				W	
Norwich. St. George, Colegate	B	D			S		
Norwich. St. Giles	B	D			S	W	
Norwich. St. Gregory	B	D			S	W	
Norwich. St. John de Sepulchre	B	D			S	W	
Norwich. St. John Maddermarket	B	D			S		
Norwich. St. Martin-at-Oak							
Norwich. St. Michael-at-Plea	B	D			S		
Norwich. St. Peter Mancroft	B	D			S	W	
Norwich. St. Stephen	B			I	S	W	
Ormesby							
Paston	B	D			S		
Ranworth	B	D					
Reepham							
Reeps with Bastwick	B	D			S		
Rougham							
Salthouse	B	D			S		

Norfolk, *continued*

	B	D	§	I	S	W	C
Sculthorpe	B				S		
Sedgford							
Shelfanger	B	D			S		
Shelton	B	D			S		
Shimpling	B	D				W	
Shipdham	B	D			S	W	C
Smallburgh	B	D			S		
South Burlingham	B	D			S		
South Walsham	B	D			S	W	
Spixworth	B	D			S	W	
Stanfield	B	D			S	W	
Starston	B	D			S		
Stoke Holy Cross	B	D			S		
Stokesby	B	D			S		
Strumpshaw	B	D			S		
Swaffham	B			I	S		C
Thornham	B	D			S		
Thorpe-next-Haddiscoe	B	D			S		
Thurgarton	B	D			S		
Thurlton	B	D			S	W	
Thuxton	B	D				W	
Tibenham	B	D			S		
Upwell		D					
Whinburgh	B	D			S		
Wiggenhall		D	§				
Winfarthing	B	D			S	W	
Worstead	B	D			S	W	

Northamptonshire

	B	D	§	I	S	W	C
Ashton							
Burton Latimer		D					
Collingtree	B	D			S		
Daventry	B				S	W	
East Haddon							
Ecton							
Finedon	B			I	S		
Geddington	B	D	§		S		
Great Doddington	B	D	§		S		
Irthlingborough							
Islip							
Kingsthorpe		D	§				
Little Harrowden							

Northamptonshire, *continued*

Northampton			§			
Oundle						
Overstone	B	D				W
Peakirk	B	D			S	
Steane	B					W
Towcester	B	D	§		S	W
Walgrave	B	D	§		S	W
Welford						
Wollaston						

Northumberland

Allendale			
Alnwick	B		
Alston			
Alwinton			
Bamburgh Deanery			
Bolam			
Bothal			
Corbridge			
Corbridge Deanery			
Cornhill			
Ford			
Gosforth			
Haltwhistle			
Ingram		D	
Long Benton			
Long Horsley			
Mitford			
Morpeth			
Netherwitton			
Newbiggin-by-the-Sea			
Newcastle upon Tyne	B	D	§
Norham			
Shilbottle			
Tynemouth			
Whalton			
Whittingham			
Wooler			

Nottinghamshire

Costock						
East Leake		D	§			
East Retford						
Eastwood						
Elston						
Misson	B				W	C
Newark-upon-Trent	B			S	W	C
Southwell	B			S	W	C
Wollaton	B	D			W	

Oxfordshire

Banbury	B	D	§	S	W	
Bicester		D	§			
Bloxham	B		§	S		
Cuddesdon						
Cumnor	B	D		S		
Ducklington	B	D				
Enstone	B	D	§	S	W	
Ewelme	B	D				C
Hardwick						
Henley-on-Thames	B			S	W	
North Marston	B	D		S		
Oxford. St. Mary the Virgin						
Oxford. St. Peter-in-the-East	B	D		S	W	
Oxford. St. Peter-le-Bailey						
Shiplake						
Shipton-under-Wychwood	B	D				
Souldern	B	D			W	
Standlake	B	D		S		
Stanton Harcourt	B	D		S	W	C
Steeple Aston	B	D			W	
Swinbrook	B	D			W	
Upper Heyford	B	D				C
Wendlebury				S		
Witney	B	D			W	
Yarnton	B					

Rutland

Barrowden		D	§			
Hambleton	B	D		S		
Oakham	B		I			C

Scilly Isles

St. Mary's

Shropshire

Atcham	B		§		S	W	
Baschurch	B	D	§				
Bicton	B	D(?)					
Billingsley	B						
Bishop's Castle	B						
Bridgnorth	B				S	W	
Chirbury	B		§		S	W	
Church Pulverbatch							
Dudleston	B						
Ellesmere	B	D					
Ford							
Hodnet	B	D	§	I	S	W	
Holdgate	B	D				W	
Ludlow	B			I			C
More	B	D		I			C
Much Wenlock							
Munslow	B	D			S		
Myddle	B	D					
Myndtown							
Norbury	B					W	
Oldbury	B				S		
Oswestry							
Prees	B					W	
Preston Gubbals	B						
Quatford	B	D			S		
Quatt	B	D					
Ratlinghope							
St. Martins							
Shelve							
Tilstock	B	D	§			W	
Tong	B				S	W	
Wem	B	D					
Wentnor	B					W	
Whitchurch	B				S	W	C

Somerset

Bath	B			I	S	W	
Bishops Lydeard							

Somerset, *continued*

Cannington	B	D			S	
Chew Magna	B	D			S	
Chew Stoke	B	D			S	W
Chewton Mendip	B	D			S	
Clapton in Gordano						
Corston						
Crewkerne						
Cudworth						
Frome	B					
Huntspill	B	D			S	
Ilminster						
Kilmersdon						
Martock	B				S	W
Minehead	B	D	§		S	W
Norton St. Philip						
Pilton				I		C
Selworthy	B	D				
Stowey						
Ubley	B	D	§		S	
Wedmore	B					C
Wells	B	D			S	
Winsham	B	D			S	
Wrington	B	D			S	W

Staffordshire

Bilston	B		
Brewood			
Burton-on-Trent			§
Cannock			
Cheadle			
Darfield	B	D	§
Draycott-le-Moors			
Fenton			
King's Bromley			
Kinver		D	§
'Lane End'			
Leek			
Newchurch			
Stone			
Tamworth			
Wall			
Wolverhampton	B	D			S

Suffolk

	B	D	§	I	S	W	C
Ampton		D					
Assington	B			I	S	W	C
Beccles	B			I	S	W	C
Bramfield	B	D			S		
Brent Eleigh	B						
Bury St. Edmunds	B			I	S	W	
Cavendish	B	D	§				
Chediston	B	D			S		
Coddenham	B				S	W	
Hadleigh							
Ipswich	B			I	S	W	
Ixworth	B	D				W	
Lawshall	B				S	W	
Milden	B				S	W	
Nayland	B		§		S	W	
Pakefield	B				S		
Poslingford							
Sotherton							
Sotterley	B				S		
South Elmham	B	D			S		
Stetchworth							
Stoke-by-Nayland	B				S	W	C
Sudbury							
Walton	B	D					
Weston	B	D				W	
Woodbridge	B				S	W	
Yaxley							

Surrey

	B	D	§	I	S	W	
Chertsey							
Compton							
Crondall	B	D			S		
Effingham	B					W	
Epsom	B	D					
Ewell							
Guildford							
Lingfield	B	D	§		S	W	
Little Bookham	B	D					
Reigate	B			I	S	W	

Sussex

Amberley						
Brede	B	D				W
Eastbourne	B					
Heathfield	B					W
Horsted Keynes	B					W
Lewes						
Rye	B	D			S	

Warwickshire

Alcester	B	D			S	W
Allesley						
Astley	B	D			S	
Austrey	B	D			S	W
Baginton	B	D			S	
Barcheston	B	D			S	
Berkswell	B	D				W
Birmingham. St. Martin	B					
Birmingham. St. Philip	B					
Coleshill	B	D				W
Coventry	B	D			S	
Halford	B	D				W
Hampton in Arden	B	D				W
Henley-in-Arden						
King's Norton	B			I	S	W
Leamington Priors						
Lillington	B					
Mancetter	B	D			S	
Meriden	B	D			S	
Monks Kirby	B	D			S	
Nuneaton	B	D				W
Over Whitacre						
Sheldon	B			I		W
Shipston-on-Stour	B	D			S	W
Shustoke						
Smethwick	B	D				W
Solihull	B	D				W	C
Stratford-upon-Avon	B	D	§		S	
Tredington	B				S	
Warwick	B		§	I	S	W
Wasperton	B	D				W
Westwood						
Whichford	B	D				W

Warwickshire, *continued*

	B	D	§	S	W
Whitchurch	B	D			W
Wootton Wawen	B		§		

Westmorland

Ambleside	B	D		S	
Appleby	B	D		S	
Bampton	B				
Beetham	B			S	W
Brampton					
Brough	B	D			
Brougham	B	D			
Clifton	B				
Colton	B	D		S	
Crook					
Crosby Garrett					
Crosby Ravensworth	B				W
Crosscrake					
Dufton	B				
Grayrigg					
Heversham	B				
Kendal					
Killington	B				W
Kirkby Lonsdale					
Mallerstang					
Old Hutton					
Orton					
Ravenstonedale					
Selside					
Shap					
Temple Sowerby					
Windermere	B	D	§	S	
Witherslack	B				W

Wiltshire

Box					
Bradford-on-Avon					
Chippenham					
Devizes			§		
Durnford		D	§		
Hilmarton		D	§		
Malmesbury	B	D		S	

Wiltshire, *continued*

Marlborough	B				S		
Mere	B						
Steeple Ashton	B				S	W	C
Tilshead							
Trowbridge							
Warminster							

Worcestershire

Bengeworth	B				S	W	
Bewdley	B			I	S	W	C
Bransford	B	D					
Bromsgrove	B		§		S	W	
Cofton Hackett	B	D			S		
Cradley							
'Elm Green'							
Elmley Castle							
Evesham							
Feckenham	B						
Fladbury	B	D			S		
Great Malvern	B	D	§				
North Piddle							
Norton and Lenchwick	B					W	
Pershore							
West Malvern							
Wolverley	B	D			S		
Worcester	B	D	§		S		

Yorkshire

Acaster Malbus	B	D				W	
Appleton-le-Street							
Arkengarthdale							
Askrigg					S		
Bagby	B	D					
Beverley	B				S	W	C
Bishopthorpe							
Bolsterstone							
Bolton Percy	B	D	§		S		
Bradfield	B				S	W	
Bradford							
Bridlington	B	D	§		S	W	
Brompton							

Yorkshire, *continued*

Bubwith	B					
Campsall	B					
Cawthorne						
Coxwold	B	D			S	
Darton	B	D	§			
Dent	B					
Dewsbury						
Doncaster						
Easington	B	D				W
East Harlsey	B				S	W
Ecclesfield	B		§			C
Embsay						
Emley	B	D				
Flamborough						
Friezland						
Garsdale	B					W
Great Ayton	B					
Great Driffield						
Grinton	B	D	§			
Hackness	B					
Halifax	B		§	I		
Hardraw						
Hatfield						
Hooton Roberts	B					
Huddersfield						
Huggate						
Hull. Holy Trinity	B				S	W
Hull. St. Mary Lowgate	B				S	W
Hunmanby	B	D	§		S	
Illingworth						
Ingleton						
Kildwick	B				S	W
Kirkburton	B	D			S	W
Kirkby Fleetham	B				S	
Kirkby-in-Cleveland						
Kirklington	B	D				W
Ledsham						
Leeds						
Linton in Craven	B	D			S	
Lund						
Marske						
Marske-by-the-Sea	B					
Middlesbrough						

Yorkshire, *continued*

Muker						
New Malton						
Newton Kyme	B					C
North Craven						
North Grimston						
Old Malton						
Otley	B					
Penistone						
Pudsey	B					
Redmire						
Riccall	B					
Richmond. Holy Trinity						
Richmond. St. Mary	B	D			W	
Ripon	B					
Roos						
Rotherham	B				W	
Sedbergh						
Selby	B					
Sheffield	B					
Sheriff Hutton	B			S		
Skelton	B					
Skipton	B					
Skipwith	B					
Slaithwaite	B			S	W	
South Cowton						
Stainton	B		I	S		C
Stokesley						
Tadcaster						
Tankersley	B				W	C
Tinsley	B				W	
Wakefield	B	D		S	W	
Wentworth						
Womersley	B					C
Worsbrough	B			S	W	C
York. All Saints' Pavement	B	D	§	S	W	
York. St. Mary Castlegate	B			S		

ISLE OF MAN

Andreas	B
Arbory	
Ballaugh	B
Braddan	
Douglas	B
German	
Jurby	B
Kirkbride	B
Lezayre	B
Lonan	
Malew	B
Marown	
Maughold	B
Michael	
Onchan	
Patrick	
Ramsay	
Rushen	
Santan	

WALES

Anglesey, Isle of

Beaumaris
Holyhead
Llanfaelog
Llangefni
Menai Bridge

Breconshire

Brecon. St. John
Brecon. St. Mary
Llangattock

Caernarvonshire

Bangor
Caernarfon
Conwy
Criccieth
Llandudno
Llanrhos
Llanystumdwy
Pothmadog
Pwllheli   B

Cardiganshire

Bangor Teifi
Cardigan
Cellan   B   W
Ciliau Aeron
Lampeter
Llanarth
Llanbadarn Fawr
Llanbadarn Trefeglwys
Llanddewi Aberarth
Llandyfriog
Llandysiliogogo
Llandyssil
Llanfihangel Genau'r-Glyn
Llanllwchaearn
Llanwnnen
Trefilan
Ystrad Meurig

Carmarthenshire

Abernant				
Carmarthen	B		S	W
Cilmaenllwyd				
Cyffig				
Eglwys Gymyn				
Laugharne				
Llanboidy	B			
Llandawke				
Llanddeusant				
Llanddowror	B			
Llandeilo Fawr				
Llandyfaelog				
Llandygwydd				
Llanegwad				
Llanelli				
Llanfihangel-ar-arth				
Llangathen				
Llanwinio				
Newcastle Emlyn				
Pen-bre				
Penboyr				
St. Clears				
Tr-lech a'r Betws				

Denbighshire

Bangor Monachorum		
Chirk		
Denbigh		
Llandrillo-yn-Rhos		
Llandysilio		
Llanfwrog	D	
Llanrwst		
Llysfaen		
Wrexham		

Flintshire

Hanmer	D	§
Mold		
St. Asaph	B	
Whitford		

Glamorganshire

Alltwen					
Cowbridge	B				
Dowlais					
Llandaff	B		S	W	C
Llandeilo Tal-y-Bont					
Llantrisant					
Pentre					
Pontardawe					
Pontlottyn					
Swansea	B	D			

Merionethshire

Bala			
Dolgellau	B		W
Llansantffraid Glwyndyfrdwy			
Penrhyndeudraeth			

Monmouthshire

Abergavenny			
Caerleon	B		W
Chepstow			
Darowen	B		
Ebbw Vale			
Llanover			
Monmouth			
Newport			
Tredegar			
Trevethin			
Usk			

Montgomeryshire

Buttington			
Churchstoke			
Darowen	B		W
Deuddwr			
Forden			
Kerry			
Llandysul			
Llanfair Caereinion			
Llanfyllin	B		

Montgomeryshire, *contued*

Llanidloes
Llanwnog
Montgomery
Newtown
Trelystan
Welshpool

Pembrokeshire

Clydau
Egremont
Fishguard
Haverfordwest
Little Newcastle
Llandysilio
Llanwnda
Narberth
Prendergast
Rhos
St. Davids

Radnorshire

Llangynllo   B   D
Presteigne
Rhayader

DIRECTORY OF
PAROCHIAL LIBRARIES
PAST AND PRESENT

ENGLAND

ABBEYDORE, Heref.
St. Mary. Heref.
[8v.] Heref. & Worcs. RO
DeskL: containing books dated 1657–1788, including a vol. of the *Works* of Bishop Jewel (AG18/8), a BCP, 1707, given by the Duke of Norfolk on the request of the rector, John Duncomb, 1810 (AG18/2), and a book with the inscription of 'Robt Mallory Jn, 1672' (AG18/4).
Catalogues: Heref. & Worcs. RO list, Abbeydore, AG18/1–8 (copy in CCC).

ABINGDON, Berks. (Oxon.)
St. Helen. Ox. *
[35 items in 12v., but see below] Reading UL; and in situ
A ParL, chained, founded c. 1618, possibly by the gift of Laurence Stevenson (d.1623). Blades listed 11 items and noted their bad condition: they had been placed in an aisle under a defective roof; Streeter recorded 11 items in glass cases in poor condition. The books were transferred to Reading UL, via the Bodleian, on permanent deposit in June 1962. They have been cleaned, treated and boxed but not restored; some chains, hooks and rings remain. All the books are 17th century English, theological and ecclesiastical. There are 7 STC and 28 Wing items. Abingdon 6 and 7, two vols. containing 25 quarto pamphlets, are almost certainly an edition of *A Collection of Cases and other Discourses* lacking the general title-pages.
St. Helen's Church contains: Bible. A. V. London, R. Barker, 1611 (chained); Bible, ed. Beza. 1611.
Catalogues: Blades lists 11 titles; The Bodleian's original TS list is in Reading UL (copies in Lambeth Palace Lib. and CCC); Lambeth also has a MS list of 12 items (MS.3221). A revised handlist is in progress.
References: Blades, *BIC*, p.13; Streeter, p.290; Cox & Harvey, p.338; Cox, p.195; D. H. Knott, *Rare Book Collections*, Reading UL, 1980 (& revisions).

ACASTER MALBIS, Yorks.
Holy Trinity. York
[2v.] York Minster Lib.
DeskL: Mark Frank, *LI Sermons*, 1672; Edward Stillingfleet, *Fifty Sermons*, 1707. In poor condition.

ACCRINGTON, Lancs.
St. James. Blackb.
[nil] *
A ParL of 76 vols. was est. in 1818 by the Associates of Dr Bray, and augm. in 1870.
Catalogues: Bray Associates Records, f.40, pp.17–19.
References: Shore, p.152; Kelly, p.262.

ADDINGTON, Bucks
St. Mary. Ox.
[7 titles in 6v.] Lambeth Palace Lib.
The books were found in the chancel wall during restoration work, deposited with the Bucks. Archit. and Arch. Soc. in 1858, and then in Lambeth Palace Lib. in 1989. They are all 16th cent. continental imprints and include a rare Sarum Primer, 1541, and contemporary bindings.
Catalogues: list in Lambeth Palace Lib. (copy in CCC).
References: Bill Report, 1970.

ADMARSH-IN-BLEASDALE, Lancs.
St. Eadmor. Blackb.
[nil] *
A ParL of 29 vols. was est. in 1757 by the Associates of Dr Bray, and augm. in 1836 (107 additional vols.) It is not recorded after 1880.
Catalogues: Bray Associates Records, f.38, p.48; and f.40, pp.269–72.
References: Bray Associates Annual Reports, 1880.

AINSTABLE, Cumb. (Cumbria)
St. Michael and All Angels. Carl.
[nil]
One of the 10 parishes in the diocese of Carlisle given 16 books in 1687 under the will of Barnabas Oley (see pp.34–5, and table on pp.444–52). At Bishop Nicolson's visitation in 1703 13 vols. were present 'all in the same abused condition' and the other 3 vols. were lent out. In 1959 4 vols. remained in the vicarage (nos 1–3 and 5). The Wigton parish records show that a bequest of books was also received in 1687 from another source. All books were reported missing in 1970.
Catalogues: MS list in Bodl.MS.Eng.Misc.c.360 (copy in CCC).
References: Nicolson, p.74; Kelly, p.246 & n.1; Bill Report, 1970.

AINSWORTH, Lancs.
Christ Church. Man.
[nil]
A ParL was est. in 1838 by the Associates of Dr Bray. It is not recorded after 1900.
References: Bray Associates Annual Reports, 1900; Kelly, p.262.

ALCESTER, Warwicks.
St. Nicholas. Cov.
[3v.]
DeskL: Bible, BCP, *c.* 1610; 2 other books: Samuel Clarke, *The Saints Nosegay*, 1641; Thomas Brooks, *An Arke for all Gods Noahs*, 1662, were 20th cent. gifts.
A ParL was est. by the Trustees for Erecting Parochial Libraries in 1712 with

74 vols. (not quite the usual selection since it included the 5 vols. of Pole's *Synopsis*, and cost £29.16.6). The books were reported in 1872 as having been returned to the Associates when about 70 vols. of the Library of Anglo-Catholic Theology were substituted for them. No vols. seem to have survived from the library noted by Richard Hurd, Bishop of Worcester (1720–1808) during his visitations: 'Lord Brooke gave 10s. yearly and a small library, common to Alcester, Exhall and Wixford'.

Catalogues: Bray Associates Records, no.34, f.39, pp.205–8.
References: Report, 1849 (states that the library was founded *c*. 1705); Kelly, p.263; Mary Ransome, ed., 'The State of the Bishopric of Worcester, 1782–1808', *Worcs. Hist. Soc.*, N.S. v.6 (1968), p.188.

ALCONBURY, Hunts. (Cambs.)
St. Peter and St. Paul. Ely
[nil] *
A ParL of 134 vols. was est. in 1824 by the Associates of Dr Bray.
Catalogues: dated 1825, Bray Associates Records f.40, pp.113–6.
References: Kelly, p.262; an oval Bray Associates bookplate completed in ms. '1825' is reproduced in *Ex Libris Jnl*, v.12 (1902), p.81.

ALDBOROUGH, Norf.
St. Mary. Nor.
[1v.] Norwich CL
DeskL: BCP, 1683.

ALDBURY, Herts.
St. John the Baptist. St.Alb.
[nil]
A ParLL of 83 vols. was est. in 1821 by the Associates of Dr Bray. There were no books by 1950.
Catalogues: 'for clergy of parishes within deaneries of [ ], Berkhamsted & Dunstable', Bray Associates Records f.40, pp.49–52.
References: Blades, *Book-Worm*, p.135; CCC Questionnaire, 1950; Kelly, p.262.

ALDERLEY, Ches.
St. Mary. Ches.
[2v.] *
DeskL: Geneva Bible, 1560; 'Vinegar' Bible, A.V.1717, in two display cases.

ALDERMASTON, Berks.
St. Mary the Virgin. Ox.
[1v.] Berks. RO
DeskL: Homilies, 1683, and 18th and 19th cent. forms of service.

ALLENDALE, Northumb.
St. Cuthbert. Newc.
[?] NRC
By his will proved York, 18 Aug. 1756, the Revd John Toppin, minister of Allendale, left 'to the ministers of Allendale and Alston, each £20, to buy books of practicall and usefull divinity for the use and instruction of the people of each parish, in their Christian duties . . . hoping that each parish will provide a vestry, proper chest of convenience for the preservation of the said books, to be lent out and taken in again by the ministers, among such of the people of each parish as are poor . . .' An agreement for setting up a ParL was drafted in 1762. Some books were still present in 1903.
References: *History of Northumberland*, v.4 (1897), p.84; agreement: Northumb. RO: EPi/44 (copy in CCC); G. Dickinson, *Allendale and Whitfield*, Newcastle, 1903, p.77; Day, pp.96–7.

ALLESLEY, Warwicks.
All Saints. Cov.
[nil] *
A bookplate of the 'Rev. W. T. Bree, M.A. Allesley' is illustrated in Lee, below. William Thomas Bree (*c.* 1785–1863) was rector of Allesley from his father's death in 1826. There is another state of the plate reading 'Allesley Rectory'.
References: Lee, British, no.95.

ALNWICK, Northumb.
St. Michael and St. Paul. Newc.
[iv.] Newcastle UL
A ParL of 68 vols. was est. in 1711 by the Bray Trustees for Erecting Parochial Libraries, augm. in 1822 and again in 1870. The books were transferred to Newcastle Cathedral Chapter Library in or shortly before 1889, and that library was placed on permanent loan in Newcastle UL in 1965. Of the original Bray Trustees Library nos.1, 3–8, 10–25, 27, 42–45, 47, 53, 56, 57, 60, 62, 64, 67 are recognizable in the Hicks and Richmond Catalogue, 1890. A copy of Hicke's *Vindication*, 1706, bound with Ken's *Exposition on the Church Catechism*, 1703, with the Bray bookplate, is still in this collection but until it is fully catalogued other vols. cannot be identified.
Catalogues: No.13. Bray Associates Records f.39, pp.157–60 (copies in Northumb. RO and CCC); Alnwick Deanery LL (assisted by Bray from funds at his disposal, 1695–9): catalogue 1822 (134 vols). Bray Associates Records, f.40, pp.57–63; E. B. Hicks and G. E. Richmond, *A Catalogue of the Newcastle Chapter Library and of the Churchwardens' or Old Parish Library*, 1890.
References: George Tate, *The History of . . . Alnwick*, 1868–9, v.2, pp.149–50; Kelly, pp.259, 263; E.L. M. Selfe, '19th century libraries in Morpeth, and Alnwick, Northumberland', *Ealing Occasional Papers in the History of Libraries*, v.1 (1972), pp.23–4.

ALSTON, Northumb.
St. Augustine. Newc.
[?] NRC
John Toppin, minister of Allendale, by his will proved at York, 18 Aug. 1756, left £20 for each of the incumbents of **Allendale** and Alston to purchase books.
References: *Northumberland County History*, v.4,1897, p.84; Northumb. RO: Allendale parish EPi /44; Day, pp.96–7.

ALWINTON, Northumb.
St. Michael and All Angels. Newc.
[?] NRC
In the Northumb. RO is a copy of 'Rules of Alwinton Parochial lending library', n.d. [19th cent., SPCK].
References: Northumb RO, EP 99/3. (copy in CCC).

AMBERLEY, Sussex (W.Suss.)
St. Michael. Chich.
[nil]
Perhaps est. *c.* 1730 as a result of a clause in Bray's will bequeathing a box of books 'towards a library of Lady Blount's or Mr. Stephen Hale's nomination to a parish near Arundel in Sussex'. ' Stephen Hale' is perhaps Stephen Hales (1677–1761). In 1865 the collection numbered 31 vols, dating between 1691 and 1728. In 1959 one vol. was noted in the vestry, a copy of *Apparatus Biblicus*, vol.2, 1728; in 1970 this was reported as missing.
Catalogues: in Notes on Amberley, 1865, reference is made to a catalogue listing 38 vols. 'for the use of the Incumbent for the time being and his successors for ever' and to Bray bookplates in some of the books. An example of the Bray bookplate, for Amberley & Houghton, is in the Franks Collection, no.33846.
References: DNB: Hales; Smith, p.58; *Sussex Archaeological Collections*, v.17 (1865), p.236, Notes on Amberley; Bill Report, 1970.

AMBLESIDE, Westm. (Cumbria)
St. Mary. Carl.
[2v.] *
DeskL: Bible. A.V. 1611; and an 18th cent. Bible. [Selections].

AMERSHAM, Bucks.
St. Mary the Virgin. Ox.
[nil]
Benjamin Robertshaw (1679–1744), rector of Amersham, 1728–43, in his will dated 20 July 1743 bequeathed 'all my books, book cases, shelves and bureaus . . . to my successor and successors the Rectors of [Amersham] . . . And my meaning is, that the said books may be a foundation or beginning of a Parochial Library . . . to be managed as near as may be, to the Stat.7 Anne

c.14 concerning Parochial Libraries'. There is no evidence that it was ever est.
Catalogues: A catalogue of books in Robertshaw's library, in an 18th cent.
hand, is in Bucks. RO (PR4/28/4; copy in CCC): this lists a substantial library
of *c.* 448 pre-1800 books, including 3 English and 29 continental 16th cent.
items; 145 English and 104 continental 17th cent. items; and 89 English and
26 continental 18th cent. items.
References: Will: PRO: PROB 732 (I am indebted to Jane Francis for this
reference).

AMPTHILL, Beds.
St. Andrew. St.Alb.
[nil] *
A ParL was est. in 1857 by the Associates of Dr Bray, and augm. in 1869 and
1892. Registers of books for the period 1858–92 survive in Beds. CRO. Those
with the Bray bookplate were returned to the Associates in *c.* 1956; the rest
were sold.
Catalogues: Registers, Beds. CRO, P30/28/2–3.
References: Shore, p.151; Bray Associates Annual Reports, 1895.

AMPTON, Suffolk
St. Peter. St.E.
[?] NRC
DeskL: in 1950 two books were noted: 1. BCP, 1662, known as Ampton
'Sealed Book' (bearing signed and sealed Certificate of Royal Commission of
1662 (Wing 2nd ed. B3622–3625?, now in Lambeth Palace Lib.); 2. *The Great
Historical, Geographical and Poetical Dictionary.* 2nd ed. . . . enlarg'd to the
year 1688, by Jer. Collier. 2v. 1701.
References: CCC Questionnaire, 1950; H. M. Cautley, *Suffolk Churches and
their Treasures*, 3rd ed. 1954, p.219; *Book Collector*, v.50, no.3, Autumn
(2001), p.408.

ANDOVER, Hants.
Church not identified. Win.
[nil?] NRC
A grant of £2. 10s. towards the cost of a ParLL was awarded by Bray from
funds at his disposal, 1695–9.
References: Kelly, pp.106 n.3, 258.

APPLEBY, Westm. (Cumbria)
St. Lawrence. Carl.
[6v.]
DeskL: (incorporating books from St. Michael's, now closed): Foxe's *Book of
Martyrs*, 3v. 1631 (given by Richard Mores, 'citizen and stacioner' of London
in 1632); Bible, 1617; BCP, 1783; BCP (Queen Anne).
References: Blades, BIC, p.13.

APPLETON-LE-STREET, Yorks.
All Saints. York
[nil?]
A list of books from a 19th cent. parish lib. is in the Borthwick Institute.
References: C. C. Webb, *A Guide to Parish Records in The Borthwick Institute of Historical Research*, 1987, p.5.

APPLEBY MAGNA, Leics.
St. Michael and All Angels. Leic.
[1v.] Leics. RO
A 13th cent. ms. Bible was given by John Mould 'in usum Ecclesie de Appleby', 8 Feb. 1701/2.
References: John Nichols, *History of Leicestershire*, v.4, pt.2, 1811, p.434; Ker, MMBL, II, 1977, pp.45–6.

ARKENGARTHDALE, Yorks. (N.Yorks.)
St. Mary. Ripon
[nil
A ParL of 13 vols. was est. in 1761 by the Associates of Dr Bray. In 1849 this library was reported as being one of those 'either wholly lost or reduced to a few tattered volumes'.
Catalogues: sent in 1762, Bray Associates Records f.38, p.82 (an identical library was sent to Trinity Chapel, **Richmond**, Yorks.)

ARRETON, IOW
St. George. Portsm.
[3v.] *
DeskL: Foxe, *Book of Martyrs*. 9th ed. 3v. 1684.

ASH [-BY-WROTHAM], Kent
St. Peter and St. Paul. Roch.
[nil] *
Books 'attached to the rectory' were kept there until 1942 when the old rectory was sold. They were then stored until 1947 when they were deposited in Maidstone Co.L. as 'belonging to the Rector and Patron of Ash-by-Wrotham for the time being'. By tradition they were thought to be part of a larger library belonging to the family of Fowler of Ash, and came to the Ash Rectory in the 1860s, though for what purpose is not known. During a vacancy in the benefice in 1970 the books were withdrawn by the churchwardens and put up for sale without a faculty. The collection was sold by Phillips, Son & Neale in conjunction with Puttick & Simpson, 30 June 1970, lot nos. 173–233 (*c.* 367v.). A sum of £1280.10s was raised and used to augment the benefice endowment. The collection was strong in classics (15 16th cent. continental editions, 1 STC), English literature, history and travel.
Catalogues: a file relating to the sale and a marked-up copy of the sale

catalogue is in the Kent Archives Office: P8/5/4 (copy of the catalogue in CCC).
References: Yates, pp.165–6; Martin, pp.69–70.

ASHBY-DE-LA-ZOUCH, Leic.

Transferred

St. Helen. Leics.
[c. 1250 works in c. 800v.] Loughborough UL
Some books were given in 1714 and later years but the library was largely formed by Thomas Bate (1675–1727), Rector of Swarkestone, and bequeathed by him 'for the use of the parishioners and others'. There was a building erected near to the vicarage with a Latin inscription over the door to house the 'Bate Library'. Some further books were added in the 18th cent. by the Revd Peter Cowper (c. 1706–82) and others, but it was then badly neglected. It was deposited in Loughborough Technical College in 1970 and moved to Loughborough UL in 1987.
There are 66 STC items in the collection (including a fragment of St Albans printing), and 700 Wing items; apart from theology, there are 18th cent. locally printed sermons and other local books; most of the books bear the name 'Tho. Bate' on the title-page (some he notes belonged to his father), and a few have his bookplate.
Catalogues: a TS catalogue by L. J. Mitchell, c. 1959, is in Leicester Museum.
References: N & Q, 6 ser. 6 (1882), pp.11, 52; J. P. Rylands, 'An eighteenth-century Leicestershire church library', *Jnl of the Ex Libris Society*, v.15 (1906), p.23; W. Scott, *The Story of Ashby de la Zouch*, 1907, pp.337–8; Kelly, pp.94, 249; Venn: Cowper; Graham Best, 'An eighteenth-century Leicestershire parish library: St. Helen's, Ashby-de-la-Zouch', Loughborough U Dept. of Library & Information Science, 1980; Geoffrey Wakeman, 'Bookbinding styles in the Loughborough and Ashby-de-la-Zouch parish libraries' in: G. Wakeman and G. Pollard, *Functional Developments in Bookbinding*, New Castle and Kidlington, 1993; Pearson A235.1.

ASHBY ST. MARY, Norf.

St. Mary. Nor.
[3v.] Norwich CL
DeskL: Erasmus, *Paraphrases*, 1548; Bible, 1617; Jewel, *Works*, 1617.

ASHCHURCH, Glos.

St. Nicholas. Glouc.
[3v.] Glos. RO
DeskL: Foxe, *Book of Martyrs*, c. 1610; Geneva Bible, 1608; Richard Hooker, *Ecclesiastical Polity*, 1682.
Catalogues: list in Glos. RO, P19 MI, 2–4 (copy in CCC).

ASHFORD, Kent
St. Mary the Virgin.
[2v.] *
DeskL: Foxe, *Book of Martyrs*, 1568 (very imp.); Book of sermons and homilies, 1640; and copies of BCP, 1708, 1718.

ASHTON, Northants.
Ashton Chapel, near Oundle. Pet.
[nil]
Probably the Ashton referred to in SPCK MSS, Abstracts of correspondence, v.8, no.5646, 21 July 1718, as having 'a sort of lending library established by the pious gentlewoman who built the chapel'.
References: Kelly, p.251 & n.1.

ASHTON-UNDER-LYNE, Lancs.
St. Michael and All Angels. Man.
[2v.] *
DeskL: Geneva Bible, 1576; Bishops' Bible, 1603.
No books survive from the ParL est. in 1847 by the Associates of Dr Bray.
References: Kelly, p.262.

ASHURST, Kent
St. Martin of Tours. Roch.
[nil] *
A ParL of 68 vols. was est in 1823 by the Associates of Dr Bray, and augm. in 1870. It is not recorded after 1890.
Catalogues: Bray Associates Records, f.40, pp.65–8.
References: Kelly, p.262; Shore, p.150; Bray Associates Annual Reports, 1890.

ASHWORTH, Lancs.
St. James. Man.
[nil] *
A ParL was est. in 1840 by the Associates of Dr Bray.
Catalogues: 1840 for 'Ashworth Chapelry, par. of Middleton, Lancs'. (116v.) Bray Associates Records, f.41, p.4–5.

ASKHAM, Cumb. (Cumbria)
St. Peter. Carl.
[nil] *
One of the 10 parishes in the diocese of Carlisle given 16 books in 1687 under the will of Barnabas Oley (see pp.34–5 and table on pp.444–52). Bishop Nicolson reported the books safe in the vicar's care 'having never had a repository in ye church'.
References: Nicolson, p.74.

ASKRIGG, Yorks. (N.Yorks.)
St. Oswald. Ripon
[nil] *
A ParL of 40 vols. was est. by the Associates of Dr Bray in 1757. In 1849 this library was reported as one of those 'either wholly lost or reduced to a few tattered volumes'.
Catalogues: 'Ashrigg' [sic] York (40v.) Bray Associates Records, f.38, p.41; W.Yorks. Leeds District Archives glebe terriers: CD/RG3 1778, 1789 have lists of the books with brief author / title entries.
References: Select Committee Report, 1849; Kelly, p.264.

Transferred

ASSINGTON, Suffolk
St. Edmund. St.E.
[369 works in 362v.] Suffolk RO, Ipswich
The library was founded in 1690 under the terms of the will of the Revd Thomas Alston (*c.* 1609–90?), incumbent: 'I . . . do give & bequeath . . . unto ye vicar incumbent of Assington . . . & to his successors in ye said Vicaridge for ever for & towards a standing library for their use'. The books were housed in the rectory until it was sold in *c.* 1945. They were then transferred to the church and in 1959, after being discovered in a deplorable condition, suffering from damp and worm, they were transferred to the Bodl. for safe keeping. From 1959 to 1964 many books were cleaned, refurbished and repaired (7 non-Alston books were destroyed as being beyond repair). They were deposited in Bury St Edmund's CL in 1964, transferred to the Central Library, Ipswich in April 1983 and finally deposited in the Suffolk RO, Ipswich.
The collection contains one incunable, Lyndwood's *Provinciale,* Oxford [1483?], 220 STC and 130 Wing items; and 20 17th cent. foreign imprints. About 190 books are identifiable as being Thomas Alston's; nearly all are theological (a few political) and contain his scholarly marginalia; many are stamped 'T.A.' on both covers. Other former owners include members of the Gurdon family (Philip Gurdon owned the Assington estate from 1679 to 1690), Sir Thomas Abdy (1685); Anthony Sparrow (1612–85), Bishop (ex dono authoris, 1657). There are two early 16th century bindings with panel stamps, and some gold-tooled bindings, e.g. that on a copy of Eikon Basilike, 1649.
Catalogues: Thomas Alston's own 12p. catalogue ('Register book') listing 280 vols. (191 of which still survive) is Suffolk RO, Bury (FL/521/11/2, formerly EL/5/12/1; copy in Lambeth Palace MS.3221, ff.13–); Suffolk PLC, 1977; a MS catalogue made by Canon J. A. Fitch in Oct. 1986 (copy in CCC).
References: Foster: Alston; DNB: Sparrow; Lambeth Palace MS.3221, ff.13–45: notes and rubbings of bindings by N. R. Ker; Fitch, 1965, pp.55–6; Pearson 122.1, 586.1, A207.1.

ASTBURY, Ches.
St. Mary. Ches.
[?] NRC
DeskL: John Jewel, *Apologia*; Foxe, *Book of Martyrs* in a contemporary (?)

binding, one cover only, with a label under horn, 'This is the gift of Humphrey Lowndes citizen and stationer of London, the son of Hugh Lowndes, Esq. while he lived in this parish'. Humphrey Lowndes was active in London, 1587–1629.
References: CCC Questionnaire, 1950; Richards, p.26: McKerrow, Dictionary, p.178.

ASTLEY, Lancs. (G.Man.)
St. Stephen. Man.
[nil]
In the 1880s a collection of 16th and 17th cent. books was kept in the vicarage; by 1959 they were kept in the church and remained there until the entire collection was destroyed by a fire in June 1961. In Christie's time there were 27 titles in 64 vols; in 1959 there were *c.* 200 vols. The name 'Thomas Mort', presumably Thomas Mort, Lord of the Manor of Astley, d.1734, was in nearly every vol. and 1734 is perhaps the date when the library was est.
References: Christie, pp.69–75; Bill Report, 1970.

ASTLEY, Warwicks.
St. Mary the Virgin. Cov.
[1v.] Warwicks. CRO
DeskL: John Jewel, *Defense*, [1567]: a few leaves only.

ASTON ABBOTS, Bucks.
St. James the Great. Ox.
[1v.]
DeskL: BCP, 1776 (?), in an elaborately gold-tooled red leather binding.

ASTWOOD, Bucks.
St. Peter. Ox.
[2v.] Bucks. RO, Aylesbury
DeskL: Erasmus, *Paraphrases*, 1548; Jewel, *Works*, 1609: both with MS bookplate of Charles Ware, vicar, and some notes of Roger Baker, vicar, 1616–41.

ATCHAM, Shrops.
St. Eata. Lich.
[78v.] Shrops. RRC

In situ

A collection of mainly 16th and 17th cent. books which were found among the effects of the late vicar in *c.* 1970. Shelved with them are a few examples of books from a DeskL, e.g a chained copy of Jewel's *Works*, 1609; other vols. show no evidence of chaining but many are lettered on the fore-edge as well as being neatly labelled on the spine. The previous history of the library is not known.
Catalogue: Shrops. PLC
References: Kelly, Shrops., p.x.

ATHERSTONE, Warwicks.
ParLL: see under **Mancetter**.

AUSTREY, Warwicks.
St. Nicholas. Birm.
[2v.] Warwicks. CRO
DeskL: Jewel, *Works*, 1609; John Pearson, *An Exposition of the Creed*, 5th ed, 1683.

AVINGTON, Hants.
St. Mary. Win.
[?] NRC
DeskL: 'Vinegar' Bible, Oxford 1716–17; two 'beautifully bound' BCP: both given in 1770 by the Marchioness of Caernarvon.
References: CCC Questionnaire, 1950.

AYLESBURY, Bucks.
St. Mary the Virgin. Ox.
[nil?] NRC
In 1725 Ralph Gladman (*c.* 1658–1725), last schoolmaster of Aylesbury Old School, by his will bequeathed his books to the library of the free grammar school, both those relating to grammar and school learning and books on divinity 'for the use of such poor clergy whose livings will not allow them to buy such books'. It appears that the library was located in the church, since a faculty dated 1727 mentions the 'newly erected' library at the N. end, and there is a similar reference in 1743. A ParL of 146 vols. was est. in 1816 by the Associates of Dr Bray at **Princes Risborough**, and augm. in 1870: in the Bray Associates Report of 1877 it was noted that this library had been amalgamated with that at Aylesbury. The Bray library is not recorded after 1900 but in 1907 there was still 'in a wainscote press in the north transept . . . a small collection of theological books'.
Catalogues: 1816 Princes Risborough: Bray Associates Records, f.38, pp.262–6.
References: Bucks. RO MS Wills Peculiar 25/5/30; Faculties 1727 (D/A/X/9/35) & 1743 (D/A/X/(/130); Cox & Harvey, p.332; Shore, p.152; Bray Associates Annual Reports, 1900; Kelly, p.261; unpublished notes on Aylesbury by H. A. Hanley drawn from minutes of the Trustees of the School (copy in CCC).

AYLTON, Heref.
'A chapelry of Ledbury'. Heref.
[1v.] *
DeskL: Book of Homilies, 1623.

AYMESTREY, Heref.
St. John the Baptist and St. Alkmund. Heref.
[?] NRC
A list of 78 undated titles for an early 19th cent. lending library, mainly pastoral and evangelical survives in the Heref. RO: mainly books from the 1820s and 1830s with some earlier.
References: list, Heref. RO, F/71/151.

BACKFORD, Ches.
St. Oswald. Ches.
[4v.] *
DeskL: Bible, 1617 (chained and in the church from the 17th cent.), and 4 18th cent. Bibles, liturgical works.
References: Cox & Harvey, p.338; Cox, pp.193–8; Richards, p.34.n.

BACONSTHORPE, Norfolk
St. Mary. Nor.
[1v.] Norwich CL
DeskL: Bible, 1617.

BACTON, Norfolk
St. Andrew. Nor.
[4v.] Norwich CL
DeskL: *Articles agreed . . . in 1562, 1630;* BCP, 1662; *Certain Sermons or Homilies,* 1623; Erasmus, *Paraphrases,* 1548.

BACUP, Lancs.
Bacup Chapel. Blackb. (now Man.)
[nil] *
A ParL of 87 vols. was est. in 1807 by the Associates of Dr Bray; it is not recorded after 1880.
Catalogue: of books sent to Bacup Chapel in chapelry of New Church, parish of Whalley, Lancs., Feb. 1807, Bray Associates Records, f.38, pp.214–5.
References: Bray Associates Annual Reports, 1880.

BAGBY, Yorks. (N.Yorks.)
St. Mary. York
[4v.] York Minster Lib.
DeskL: Bible, 1613/11; BCP and Psalms, Cambridge, 1622–3 (2 copies); BCP, n.d., and Psalms, Cambridge, 1767 (deposited 1988).

BAGINTON, Warwicks.
St. John the Baptist. Cov.
[1v.] Warwicks. CRO
DeskL: Bible, BCP, *c.* 1633.

BAKEWELL, Derbys.
All Saints. Derby
[2v.] *
A ParLL of 167 vols. was est. in 1843 by the Associates of Dr Bray, and augm.
in 1878; it is not recorded after 1890, but 2 vols. still survive in situ.
Catalogue: Bray Associates Records, f.41, pp.98–101.
References: Bray Associates Annual Reports, 1890.

BAMBURGH, Northumb.
St. Aidan. Newc.
[?] NRC
A ParLL for the Deanery of Bamburgh was assisted by a grant of £1. 10s. from
Bray from funds at Bray's disposal 1695–9.
Archdeacon Thomas Sharp noted in his visitation return of 1723 'a parochial
library of about 60 volumes lately beginning and now increasing by ye
voluntary contributions'. It was housed in a press in the vestry.
A MS transcript of rules, subscribers and books, undated, but in a blank
baptism register with the date 1758 on the front cover, is headed 'Copy of a
paper affixed to the door of the press belonging to the parish library, wch
stands in the vestry of Bambrough church' and is signed at the end ' Thos.
Sharp, curate of Bambrough'.
There were 24 original subscribers, each contributing £1, which would suggest
that this was also a subscription library from the beginning. The books were
almost entirely theological; a MS catalogue of 1723 lists fewer than 40 vols.,
a 2nd MS catalogue of 1792 reveals no losses but no additions. Archdeacon
Thomas Singleton at his visitation in 1828 noted 'about 60 volumes in the old
parochial library – but they are not in a creditable condition'.
Catalogues: 1758 list: Northumb. RO, Corbridge parish: EP59/82 (copy in
CCC).
References: Sharp visitation records; Newcastle Diocesan Records: terriers,
ser.1, no.7 (1792); Kelly, p.259; Day, pp.97–9.

BAMPTON, Westm. (Cumbria)
St. Patrick. Carl.
[c. 1200v.]
A ParL of 67 vols. was est. in 1712 by the Bray Trustees for Erecting Parochial
Libraries, and a ParLL of c. 302 vols. by the Associates of Dr Bray in 1758. In
1751 Jonathan Tinclar, rector of Addlethorpe, Lincs., gave to three yeomen of
Bampton £50 in trust to purchase estate and to apply profits to the purchase of
a library for the benefit of the vicar of Bampton. The library was housed in
Bampton vicarage until c. 1992 when the vicarage was sold and the books
were transferred to custom-built oak cupboards in the parish room next to the
church.
Nos. 12, 13, 58, 59, and 65 from the Bray Trustees library were present in
1965 (with Bray bookplates) and possibly the Bray copies of nos.2, 15 and 52.

About 100 books have an 18th cent. label 'Tinclars Library / Bampton Vicarage. / Westmoreland'; later 19th cent. books have the label 'Tinclar's Library, Bampton Vicarage, Westmorland'. About 125 vols. are pre-1800. There is now a support group co-ordinated through the Trustees of the Tinclar Library.

Catalogues: 1712: ms. cat. no.51. Bray Associates Records f.39, pp.189–92; 1758: 'with the remainder of Dr. Evan's library, with the books sent by Mr Lee of Kingston, Mr. Barnard, Mr Cross . . . to which the Associates . . . [made] a considerable addition from their own subscriptions & store'. Bray Associates Records, f.38, pp.51–58; complete TS cat. by G. E. Marrison, *c.* 1992, with the collection (copy in Cumbria RO, Kendal).

References: Tinclar Library: trust deed, rules, accounts, etc. Cumbria RO WPR/15; Kelly, pp.255, 261; M. E. Noble, *History of Bampton*, 1901, pp.139–44; Charity Commissioners, 7th Report (1822), pp.567–8 (the Tinclar library then held 337 vols).

BANBURY, Oxon
St. Mary. Oxf.
[13v.]
Probably in origin a DeskL. St. Mary's church was rebuilt after a fire in 1797 and at that time the residue of the library was donated to Banbury PL. At the time of county amalgamation it was proposed to dispose of the collection but the vicar intervened and asked for its return to the church where it is now housed in the 'Caxton Room' over the vestry, together with some 18th cent. books and several shelves of 19th cent. theology and lectern Bibles. There are 5 STC and 3 Wing items, including: a Bishops' Bible, 1586; Jewel's *Apology*, 1685, and *Reply to Mr Harding's Answer*, 1565, and 2 works by William Whateley, a former vicar of Banbury; 5 items have chains, or traces of chains and hasps.

References: accounts and lists of books purchased, 1850–1902: Oxfordshire Archives, MSS.D.D. Banbury.d.16; DRB2, p.488.

BARCHESTON, Warwicks.
St. Martin. Cov.
[3v.] Warwicks. CRO
DeskL: Erasmus; Musculus, etc., 1578; Jewel, Sermon, 1611; all chained.
References: Blades, BIC, 1890, p.16.

BARLEY, Herts.
St. Margaret of Antioch. St.Alb.
[7v.] Herts. RO
DeskL: of works dating 1608 to 1702 written by three former rectors, Andrew Willet (d.1621), rector 1599–1621, Mark Franck (*c.* 1612–64), rector 1662–64, and Joseph Beaumont (1615–99), rector 1664–99, and probably donated by them.
References: Foster: Willet; Venn: Franck, Beaumont.

BARNHAM BROOM, Norf.
St. Peter and St. Paul. Nor.
[1v.] Norwich CL
DeskL: *Constitutions and Canons Ecclesiastical*, 1633.

BARNINGHAM WINTER, Norf.
St. Mary the Virgin. Nor.
[2v.] Norwich CL
DeskL: *Certain Sermons or Homilies*, 1673; Bible, 1617.

BARNSTAPLE, Devon
St. Peter. Ex.
[*c.* 250 works in 350v.] Exeter UL, and in situ.
Judge John Dodderidge (1555–1628) gave 112 vols. to the town in 1664, and
the Corporation in 1665–7 built a room to house them adjoining the church,
which later became the vestry room, described in the Wase MSS (below):
'Bibliotheca Doddrigiana . . . engraved on high over the Library-Dore in great
Romane Letters in gold'. The collection was transferred to the North Devon
Athenaeum, Barnstaple in 1888, and then in 1957 to Exeter UL on permanent
loan. The Dodderidge collection includes 2 incunables, *c.* 50 16th cent. and
c. 200 17th cent. books on mainly religion and philosophy, but also classics,
geography, history and science. There are many late 16th and early 17th cent.
Oxford bindings and a Hereford binding; there are various donors and many
inscriptions from the 2nd quarter of the 17th cent.
A Barnstaple Clerical Library was founded in 1826 from a dated armorial
bookplate (copy in the Franks Collection, no. 33769) and *c.* 120v. are still
retained in St. Peter's Church.
Catalogues: 1739 catalogue (328v.) under the names of the donors; this
catalogue was revised by H. Luxmoore, vicar in 1824 (271v.), see Chanter,
Memorials, below; and a 1909 catalogue (see Dodderidge, below).
References: Bodl.Wase MSS CCC390, v., p.39; Lambeth Palace MS 3221:
notes and rubbings of bindings by N. R. Ker; Minute book of Barnstaple
Archdeaconry Clerical Library, 1840–1947 (Devon RO 3061E/1–); J. R.
Chanter, *Literary History of Barnstaple*, 1866, pp.73–5, and his *Memorials of
St. Peter's Church, Barnstaple*, 1881 (1824 catalogue, pp.166–72); S. E.
Dodderidge and H. G. H. Shaddick, *The Dodderidges of Devon*, 1909
(catalogue, pp.42–51); Kelly, pp.80, 246; Exeter University Library, *Special
Collections and Manuscripts in the University Library*, 1991; Pearson A129.2.

BARROWDEN, Rut.
St. Peter. Pet.
[nil]
In 1907 there were old chained books in a bookcase made out of a Jacobean
pulpit; they were no longer present in 1950.
References: Cox & Harvey, p.338; CCC Questionnaire, 1950.

BARTHOMLEY, Ches.
St. Bertoline. Ches.
[4v.] *
DeskL: Foxe, *Book of Martyrs*, 2v. 1632; 'Commentary upon the Holy Bible called Assemblyes notes', 2v. 17th cent. Very imp.

BARTON UPON HUMBER, Lincs. (E.Riding of Yorks.)
St. Mary. Linc.
[nil]
A terrier of 1707 at the Lincoln Diocesan RO lists probably 45 books: none remain.
Catalogues: TS copy of the list in CCC.

BASCHURCH, Shrops.
All Saints. Lich.
[3v.] *
DeskL: Bible (chained); BCP, Articles of Religion, Bible, 1770 (chained); BCP, 1799.

BASINGSTOKE, Hants.
St. Michael. Win.
[*c.* 110v.] Southampton UL (but not kept as a collection).
A library is mentioned in the church accounts, 1703–5, and in 1707, when a catalogue was made. In 1724 Sir George Wheler (1650–1723), vicar 1685–94, bequeathed his divinity books for the use of the vicar and clergy of the diocese. They were housed in the rectory until it fell into disuse in 1968 when the books were moved to Church Cottage adjoining the church, and finally deposited in Southampton UL in *c.* 1983. More than half were in poor condition. The books are mainly puritan theology and classical texts, especially in Dutch editions; there is a copy of Walton's Polyglot Bible. Wheler's bookplate is in the Franks Collection: no. 33770. One book was given by James Rolstone, citizen of London.
Catalogues: Glebe terrier listing the books in the Basingstoke Parochial Library May 1721. Hants. RO 35SPM48/17–20; TS shelf-list of the books in the church, *c.* 1969 (copy in CCC); TS handlist of the books as deposited in Southampton UL, 1975 (copies in CCC and Winchester CL). Since 1981 items have been recatalogued on Southampton UL OPAC.
References: DNB: Wheler; Kelly, p.247; Bill Report, 1970; Woolf, p.184, n.63.

BASSINGBOURN, Cambs. (Herts.)
St. Peter and St. Paul. Ely
[786v.] Cambridge UL: 412v.; Essex UL: 374 titles.
A tablet in the vestry records that Edward Nightingale of Kneesworth Hall founded the library in 1717; additions to the collection were made by two 18th

century vicars, Gilbert Negus (d.1763) and John Williams. The collection was first housed in four cupboards in the tower vestry. In 1969 the surviving vols. were purchased jointly by Cambridge UL and Essex UL, with assistance from the Pilgrim Trust. The collection contains: STC: 94 vols.; 16th cent. foreign: 34; English and foreign, 1601–1700: c. 590; 18th cent.: 200; mainly theology, but some history and classical literature. A stray vol. from the collection was recorded at a sale before 1853. There are some roll-tooled bindings, and an oval stamp of J. Lindsay on a book of 1575.

Catalogues: MS 'Library of printed books in Bassingbourn Church. Catalogue compiled in 1959', by H. M. Adams, as 'arranged in cupboards under the tower' (copies in Cambs. CRO: P11/[R93/39], and CCC; copy of 'select list of 21 items' in CCC); handlists of their respective portions of the collection at Cambridge UL and Essex UL.

References: *N & Q*, 203, 17.9.1853; Lambeth Palace MS.3221: rubbings of bindings and notes on provenances by N. R. Ker; Kelly, p.245; Venn: Negus.

BASSINGHAM, Lincs.
St. Michael and All Angels. Linc.
[nil] *
References: 'Parochial Library rules and catalogue of a lending library, 1832'. Central Reference Lib., Lincoln, UP/1420.

BATH, Somerset
Bath Abbey of St. Peter and St. Paul. B & W
[281 titles in 349v.] Wells CL
A library was begun in the church in c. 1619 by Arthur Lake (1569–1626), Bishop of Bath and Wells, who gave the works of James I. It was deposited at Bath PL in 1895, where it was housed in two Chippendale cases in the vestibule, and, minus the cases, deposited on long-term loan in Wells CL in October 1982. Three vols. were returned to Bath Abbey in 1994, including Voragine's *Golden Legend*, Wynkyn de Worde, 1493, and are now on permanent exhibition there. With a few exceptions all the books were printed before 1750: STC, 78 vols.; Wing, 85; 1701–1800 English, 21; pre-1800 continental, 93. There are many early medical and scientific books. Some pamphlets were given by William Prynne (1600–90), M.P. for Bath in 1660, and by his associate, the publisher Michael Sparkes (d.1653). Bookplate: Bath Abbey Collection at Wells Cathedral.

Catalogues: MS 'Catalogue of the benefactors towards the librarie in the church of saint Peter and Paule in the cittie of Bath', c. 1620–1715; a MS catalogue of 1657 (or earlier); a photocopy of an 1879 handlist; and a full MS author catalogue compiled by W. M. Wright, the librarian, 1953, are kept with the collection (the latter included names of donors and dates of presentation when known, and a list of 78 books included in the Benefactors' Book, but is now missing). The 17th cent. catalogue lists 2 or 3 medieval MSS, including a Polychronicon, now missing.

References: DNB: Lake, Prynne; *Proceeedings of the LA*, 1878, p.128; R. E. M. Peach, *The Bath Abbey Library, with notes thereon; reprinted from the Bath Chronicle*, Bath, 1709; V. J. Kite, 'Libraries in Bath, 1618–1964', LA Fellowship thesis, 1965, pp.4–11; Plomer, Dictionary: Sparkes.

BECCLES, Suffolk
St. Michael the Archangel. St.E.
[100 titles in 139v.] 2v. in situ; Suffolk RO, Lowestoft, the remainder.
The library was begun by the Revd Thomas Armstrong, rector 1671–1715, who replied in Notitia Parochialis, 1705 (no.962), 'there is a library setling by the Minister there'. In a MS memorandum of *c.* 1717 headed 'A representation of the state of Beccles library' (possibly by Thomas Payne, 2nd rector, 1715–64) it states that 'he did about the year 1707 at great charge and trouble collect books for a parochial library and having obtained many benefactors in books and money to buy books, the same was laid out accordingly, and the parishioners at their own cost and charge fitted up a room over the south porch of Beccles church for the same designation'. In 1840 the library (then 148 vols.) was deposited in the recently opened Beccles PL, the rector and church-wardens stipulating that 'the books be open to all the inhabitants of Beccles for inspection and perusal'. After the closure of Beccles PL the books were returned to the church and housed mainly in cupboards in the vestry against a damp north wall, where they deteriorated rapidly. In 1962 the books were again transferred to a shelter in Ipswich to prevent further damage: 8 vols. had to be destroyed (but 5 title-pages were later salvaged and bound together); the remaining 137 vols. were restored and repaired by East Suffolk RO and rehoused in Bury St. Edmunds CL. From April 1985 they were deposited in the Strong Room of Ipswich PL, and they are now, finally, deposited in the Suffolk RO at Lowestoft.
The contents include 1 incunable (Nicholas de Lyra, *Postilla on the Old Testament*, 4 vols., Nuremberg, 1497), 8 STC books, 30 Wing, 12 16th cent. (some rare early 16th cent.) and 33 17th cent. continental works. The Fathers are well represented, as are continental and English theology and philosophy of both the Reformation and Counter Reformation, and classics. The outstanding book is probably the copy of one of the 1549 first editions of the BCP, London, Edward Whitchurch (retained at St. Michael's Beccles); 9 leaves from a 14th cent. Digest were paste-downs in St. Jerome, *Works,* 5v. Basel, Froben, 1525–6. Marks of ownership are plentiful: all the dated gifts are between 1706 and 1712 (see Fitch, below). A number of vols. are stamped in gold on black on the covers 'E Bibliotheca Becclesiana' and on some smaller books 'E B B'. There is a contemporary Cambridge stamped binding with the devices of Henry VIII and Katherine of Aragon (on the St. Jerome, see above); a 1571 roll-stamped binding; and a handsome Oxford binding on Cicero, *Opera*, Lugdunum, 1578.
Catalogues: a catalogue printed in 1816 (and its MS version): Beccles Town Hall, Rix Collection (quoted in Ellwood, below); *A Catalogue of the Beccles*

Church Library, 1840, lists 148v., mostly in Latin and all, except 5, earlier than 1700 (TS copy in CCC); *Catalogue and Laws of the Beccles Public Library*, 3rd ed., Beccles, 1877 (pp.65–70, Catalogue of the Beccles church library); Suffolk PLC, 1977; MS list made by Canon J. A. Fitch, 1986 (lists 139 vols. with cross-references to the nos. on slips in the books: copy in CCC).
References: Venn: Armstrong; Notitia Parochialis, 1705: no. 962; Norwich Diocesan Registry, Norfolk & Norwich RO, DN/MSC 239; *N & Q*, 8, 1853, p.62; Lambeth Palace MS.3221: rubbings of bindings and provenance notes by N. R. Ker; Fitch, 1965 (especially for details of provenance); Kelly, pp.195 & n.6, 253; Michael Ellwood, 'Library provision in a small market town, 1700–1929', *Library History*, 5.2 (1979), pp.48–54.

BEDFORD, Beds.
St. John the Baptist. St.Alb.
[*c.* 825v.] Bedford Central Lib.
A library was founded in 1700 'by the contributions of the gentry and clergy' and was settled by deed, dated 20 October 1704, 'for the use of the rector of St. John's and his successors and also of the present and all future contributors and benefactors to the value of 10s'. There were more than 130 trustees and the books could be borrowed. (One of the trustees was Archdeacon Thomas Frank (d.1730) who reported on a Clerical Book Club in Bedford in 1709 to the SPCK, which was probably not continued because of the existence of the parochial library.) The books were kept firstly at St. John's Church, then, from 1713 to 1748, in a specially erected Library and Register Office to the south of St. Paul's churchyard, from 1748 to 1831 in St. Paul's Church itself, and in 1830 in the newly-founded Bedford Literary and Scientific Institute and General Library, later Bedford Public Library. The present collection was transferred to the new Central Library in 1973.
The Council of the Institute sent up the library's copy of Caxton's Royal Book for sale at Sotheby's, 17 March 1902, lot 897, and it is now in the Pierpont Morgan Library: its binding leaves, taken from two copies of an Indulgence printed by Caxton in 1481, were lots 985–6 in the same sale, and are now in the Pierpont Morgan and British Library; 7 other printed books and 4 medieval MSS were sold at Sotheby's, 15 June 1904, lots 447–57; 3 of the MSS, lots 445–7, are now respectively BL Add.36984, 36983, and Manchester, John Rylands lat.176. Bunyan's copy of Foxe's *Book of Martyrs* was sold in 1910. There was a further sale at Sotheby's, 1 Aug. 1935, lots 465–75. The books that remained in 1946, *c.* 550 vols., some in bad condition, were handed over to Bedford Corporation as a public trust and are housed in the John Bunyan room. The subject content is mainly theology, including *c.* 100 Bedfordshire sermons and charges, and 53 bound vols. of tracts and sermons.
Catalogues: *A Catalogue of Books in the Library at Bedford*, 1706 (shelf order, no index; publicized by the SPCK along with the rules of the book society); MS catalogues of the early 18th cent. (822v.) and of 1807 (703v.); *Catalogue of the Circulating and Reference Libraries of the Old Library*

founded in 1707, 1892 (pp.235–72); duplicated list in the Central Library.
References: Beds. CRO: foundation deed of St. John's church library (1703): PI/28/3; Bedford Library foundation deed (1834): X825/4; Foster: Frank; Seymour de Ricci, *Census of Caxtons*, 1909, pp.69, 89; T. A. Blyth, *History of Bedford*, 1873, pp.166–7; *Gentleman's Mag.* (1817), pt.2, pp.135–6, 578; *Bedfordshire N & Q*, v.3 (1891), p.29; H. M. Walton, 'The Old Bedford library', *LAR*, 4 ser., 2, 1935; A. Baker, *The Library Story: a History of the Library Movement in Bedford, c.* 1958; W. J. H. Watson, 'The community libraries of Bedfordshire, from 1830 to 1965', FLA thesis, 1972; Kelly, pp.91, 96–7,135–6, 244; Manley, pp.234–5.

BEESTON NEXT MILEHAM, Norf.
St. Mary the Virgin. Nor.
[1v.] Norwich CL
DeskL: *Certain Sermons or Homilies*, 1683.

BEETHAM, Westm. (Cumbria)
St. Michael and All Angels. Carl.
[*c.* 295 titles in *c.* 408v.]. Lancaster UL
The earliest gift towards a library at Beetham was made by James French from 1710–14, consisting of 18 vols. of the works of William Beveridge (of which 14 are left, all lettered with the donor's name). William Hutton (1735?–1811), antiquary, vicar of Beetham 1762–1811, gave over 130 vols. from his personal library to Heversham Grammar School, Westmorland, in 1768; in 1795 he deposited the remaining 260 vols. in the vestry of Beetham Church 'for the use of the schoolmaster and vicar in being', specifying that the books should also be for the use of the schoolmaster of Heversham. They were kept on shelves with mesh doors some 7 feet from the ground. (The Heversham Grammar School books were later acquired by Newcastle UL.) Some books were added in the 19th and 20th cents. The Beetham library was deposited with faculty in Lancaster UL in 1987. The collection contains 23 STC books, 41 Wing books and 75 sermons or tracts, 1710–1803, mostly bound-up in sets. Hutton was a scholar and author and his books include not only theology but history, antiquities and science, especially geology and entomology. A copy of *Certain Sermons or Homilies*, 2v, 1633, contains the bookplate of George Hutton, citizen and stationer of London (fl.1636–41), William's father, given in 1634. Later donations to the library were made by Alfred Balleine, vicar 1907–29 (65 vols. mostly of the 19th cent., 49 still present) and Philip Kirkham, vicar 1930–46 (10 books).
Catalogues: listed from Hutton's notebook, The Beetham Repository, *Cumb. and Westm. Antiq. and Archaeol. Soc.*, Tract ser. no.7 (1906), pp.157–9; TS shelf-list, no index, 1959 (copy in CCC); TS report and full catalogue by G. E. Marrison, April 1987 (copies with the collection and in Cumbria RO: WPR/43).
References: R. D. Humber, *Heversham: the Story of a Westmorland School*

and Village, Kendal, 1968; Edgar Hinchcliffe, 'The Bainbrigg Library of Appleby Grammar School' (*History of the Book Trade in the North*, PH73, 1996, p.6); Kelly, p.255; Lee, Early, no.100 (not illustrated); DRB2, p.54; Plomer, Dictionary, p.105: George Hutton; DNB: William Hutton.

BEKESBOURNE, Kent
St. Peter. Cant.
[1v.] Canterbury CL & Archives
DeskL: 'Psalmody', n.d. The Psalter of Tattershall, dated 1794 in St. Peter's parish records, printed by subscription as a gift to the parish, probably from the vicar of the time, Robert Phillips.

BENGEWORTH, Worcs.
St. Peter. Worc.
[1,000v.] Birmingham UL

The bookplate describes the collection as 'the library left by the late Rev. John Shaw [*c.* 1793–1854] for the sole use of the incumbents of the parish of Bengeworth for ever. 1854'. The books were housed in Bengeworth rectory until 1962 when they were deposited in Birmingham UL. There are a few 16th and 17th cent. books but the majority are 18th and early 19th cent. Each vol. has a bookplate, a stamp on the title-page: 'Shaw's Vicarage Library', and, as in the catalogue, a number on the spine. One book is inscribed ' Sam: Bernard Magd.', a 16th cent. schoolmaster.
Catalogues: *Catalogue of the Library of the late Rev John Shaw left for the Use of the Incumbents of Bengeworth for ever.* Evesham printed, 1859.
References: Foster: Shaw; Lambeth Palace MS.3221: provenance notes and rubbings of bindings by N. R. Ker; J. P. Shawcross, *Bengeworth*, Evesham, 1927.

BENTLEY, Hants.
St. Mary. Win.
[2v.]
DeskL: Bible, 1560; BCP, 'including Apocrypha and NT', 1636.
References: NADFAS Report.

BERKSWELL, Warwicks.
St. John the Baptist. Cov.
[3v.] *
DeskL. Foxe, *Book of Martyrs*, 9th ed. 3v. 1684 (lacking title-pages).
References: *N & Q*, 9 Nov.1912.

BEVERLEY, Yorks. (E.Riding of Yorks.)
St. Mary. York
[16 titles in 22v.] York Minster Lib.
The library was est. in 1699 with the gift of Walton's Polyglot. Some 446 vols. given over the next 10 years, mainly by Thomas Alured, recorder of Beverley 1688–1700, in 1701 and 1708, and by Charles Warton (c. 1657–1708) of Beverley, are recorded in an early catalogue. The books were increasingly neglected over the years; in 1856 they were used to light the church fires. In 1959 32 vols. remained, in bad condition; by 1970 some were inappropriately or incorrectly rebound or rebacked and displayed in a specially built showcase in the south transept; 5 vols. were stolen from the church in 1977 but subsequently recovered. In 1983 17 vols. were deposited in York Minster Lib., and a further 5 vols. in 1986 (the 5 books stolen from the church).
A ParL was est. in 1873 by the Associates of Dr Bray, and augm. in 1878, of which nothing remains.
Catalogues: MS Donors' book, 'May 25th. 1699. Henry Jefferson, Rectr of St. Nicolas, and Vicar of St Maries', united churches in Beverley, gave this paper book for the use of the library in St Marie's aforesaid; viz, for recording the names of benefactors, and their several & respective gifts to the said library'; also used from the other end as 'A copy of the catalogue of the books in the library of St Maries' church in Beverley, as the same was taken Septembr 20, 1709, and given to the Registry of the ArchBp's Court at York'; TS catalogue of the remaining books, Nov. 1956 (32v.), with notes on 6 bindings (including a Cambridge binder of the 1620s; Ker, Pastedowns, pl. IX, no.XXV; and a London binder 'R.B.' Oldham HM.h.10), and a list of 19 donors, 1699–1727, according to the MS catalogue; copy in CCC); slip catalogue with the collection (photocopy in CCC).
References: Venn: Alured, Warton; *N & Q*, 3 ser., 5 (1864), p.51; 6 ser., 6 (1882), p.294; Shore, p.150; Bray Associates Annual Reports, 1880; Kelly, pp.91 n.4, 255; Bill Report, 1970; Barr, pp.34–5.

BEWDLEY, Worcs.
St. Anne. Worc.
[c. 3,000v.] Birmingham UL
Thomas Wigan of Bewdley (d.1819) bequeathed 'to the rector of Ribbesford and to the master of the Free Grammar School at Bewdley for the time being and their successors for ever, all my books which at the time of my death I may be possessed of at Bewdley aforesaid, in trust for the use of the clergy and other respectable inhabitants of that town and neighbourhood as a public library'. The books were available for loan; many had belonged to Wigan's uncles and grandfather. They were kept in the Grammar school and elsewhere in Bewdley until 1950 when they were transferred on loan to Birmingham UL.
A ParLL was est. by the Associates of Dr Bray at Bewdley in 1781 (augm. in 1870); it is not recorded after 1900 and no books have survived.
Catalogues: Catalogue printed by Sir Thomas Phillipps at Middle Hill in

1859; a full TS catalogue was compiled by Paul Morgan at Birmingham UL in 1955; Catalogue of books belonging to the lending library, 1801 (*c.* 151 titles). Bray Associates Records, f.38, pp.172–5.

References: Charity Commissioners, 26th Report, 1833, p.562; Bray Associates Annual Report, 1900; Paul Morgan, 'Wigan's Library, Bewdley'. *Trans. of the Worcs. Arch. Soc.* N.S. 35 (1958), pp.61–66.

BICESTER, Oxon.
St. Edburg. Ox.
[nil]
This library was est., apparently, by 1691 (see below: Blomfield). 'A catalogue of the parochial library of Burcester, 5 Octr 1757' in the Bodl. (MS. Oxf. Archd. Papers, Oxon. b.22, ff.249–52) lists 128 titles. This collection probably belonged to the Grammar School, and was housed in a room adjoining the church which was taken down when the church was restored in 1862. The surviving books were then placed in the care of one of the churchwardens. In 1705 there was no library 'worth notice' according to the incumbent.

Catalogues: Blomfield, below, refers to a catalogue of 1691, listing 150 books and 71 benefactors; catalogue of 1757 (above).

References: Notitia Parochialis, no.237; J. C. Blomfield, *History of Bicester*, 1884, p.34; Lambeth Palace MS. 3224 notes that A. N. L. Munby once owned a chained copy of Burton's *Anatomy*, 2nd ed., 1624, from Bicester library, which was sold *c.* 1950.

BICTON, Shrops.
Holy Trinity. Lich.
[6v.] Shrops. RRC
Part of a DeskL.? With notes on 7 items.

BILLINGSLEY, Shrops.
St. Mary. Heref.
[1v.] Shrops RRC
Part of a Desk.L.?

BILSTON, Staffs.(W.Mids.)
St. Leonard. Lich.
[nil]
John Tomkys (d.1703), vicar of Snitterfield, Warwicks., 1682–1703, by his will dated 14 June 1703, left his books to the minister of Bilston and desired that a catalogue of them should be 'Registered in parchment . . . that a view may be made upon the removeall of every Minister that they may not be alienated from the uses intended'. A copy of the will was entered by Richard Ames, curate of Bilston, in the parish register; in the Notitia Parochialis of 1705, Ames notes that the library 'is now in my possession'. A table formerly

in the church states that Ames (d.1730) 'by his last will, left his lib. of bks., for the use of the curts of B. for ever'.

References: Venn: Tomkys; Notitia Parochialis, no.1133; Bilston Parish Register, Staffs Parish Registers Soc., 1938, pp. 220–1; G. T. Lawley, *History of Bilston*, 1893, p.238; Kelly, p.253.

BINFIELD, Berks.
All Saints. Ox.
[nil] *
DeskL. 'Breeches' Bible, 1560; Erasmus: both present in 1950, stolen in 1984.
References: CCC Questionnaire, 1950.

BIRCH, Lancs. (G.Man.)
St. Mary (ded. uncertain). Man.
[nil]
A ParLL of 141 vols. was est. in 1837 by the Associates of Dr Bray; it is not recorded after 1880.
Catalogues: Catalogue of Birch 'in par. of Middleton, Lancs', Bray Associates Records, f.40, pp.295–7.
References: Bray Associates Annual Reports, 1880.

BIRCH-IN-RUSHOLME, Lancs. (G.Man.)
St. James. Man.
[nil ?] NRC
DeskL: copies of a Bible, 1611; a Beza version of Bible; and Homilies were recorded in 1950.
References: CCC Questionnaire, 1950.

BIRKENHEAD (Claughton), Ches.
St. Aidans's College.
[?]
A ParLL was est. in 1872 by the Associates of Dr Bray, after removal from **Woodchurch**, and augm. in 1889 and 1892. The Library was deposited firstly at Church House, Liverpool, then at Liverpool CL.
References: Bray Associates Annual Reports, 1895; Shore, p.151.

BIRMINGHAM, Warwicks. (W.Mids.)
St. Martin. Birm.
[12+v.] Birmingham PL
Thomas Hall (1610–55), appointed curate at St. Nicholas church from 1640 until he was ejected in 1662, bequeathed books to form a library for the use of the ministers of Birmingham. The will, dated 1664, and 'A catalogue of those books wch are given to the library at Birmingham 1661' are in Dr. Williams's Library, London (MS.61.1:Baxter MSS). This collection of books became part of the Governors' Library at King Edward's School, Birmingham, and the

remains of it are now housed with that library in Birmingham PL. The main part of Hall's bequest was deposited at **King's Norton.**

Catalogues: the 1661 catalogue above was printed by F. J. Powicke in *Bull. of the John Rylands Lib*, v.8 (1924), pp.186–90 (299 entries).

References: J. E. Vaughan, 'The Hall manuscript, containing the life, will and catalogues of the library of the Rev. Thomas Hall, B.D. (1610–1665) transcribed with introduction and notes' (M.A. Univ. of Bristol, 1960); Kelly, pp.80, 254; Audrey H. Higgs, 'Two parish libraries and their founders', *Open Access*, N.S.16, no.3(1968), pp.2–7.

BIRMINGHAM, Warwicks. (W.Mids.)
St. Philip (from 1904 the Cathedral). Birm.
[*c.* 300v.] Birmingham PL; [*c.* 150v.] Queen's College, Birmingham
A library 'free to all clergymen in the Church of England in the town and neighbourhood' was est. by the first rector, William Higgs (*c.* 1678–1737), in 1733, and was housed after 1792 in a special room adjoining the parsonage house in St. Philip's churchyard. This library was closed in *c.* 1927 and some 300 vols. were presented to Birmingham PL (and recorded in the official Donation Book); the remaining 150 vols. or so were deposited in Queen's College, Birmingham (where a Bray Associates LL had been est. in 1866). The books in Birmingham PL are not kept as a collection but dispersed throughout the reference collections.

Catalogues: A Catalogue [and Rules] of the Parochial Library, in St. Philip's Church Yard, Birmingham, 1795 (lists 550v; the copy in Birmingham PL has MS addns to *c.* 1810); catalogue, *c.* 1795–1810. Birmingham City Archives, 339921 22 32; catalogue, including rules. Lichfield RO B/A/22/1; Books presented by the Trustees of the Higgs Library, 1927 (TS inserted in Birmingham PL Donations Book). A copy of the pictorial bookplate is in the Franks Collection, no. 33847, and it is reproduced in *Ex Libris Jnl*, v.12 (1902), p.79.

References: Foster: Higgs; W. Hutton, *History of Birmingham*, 1795, p.357; Shore, p.153; R. K. Dent, 'Birmingham: its libraries and its booksellers', *Book Auction Records*, 4 (1906–7); Kelly, p.254; Audrey H. Higgs, 'Two parish libraries and their founders', *Open Access*, N.S.16, no.3 (1968), pp.2–7; Read, Supplement, p.158.

BISHOP'S CASTLE, Shrops.
St. John the Baptist. Heref.
[6v.] Shrops. RRC
A private, non-parochial lib. was est. by Charles Mason. M.P. 'for the use of neighbours' before 1705 (see p.38, n.28). Mason became M.P. for Bishop's Castle in 1695, so this may be identical with the lending library aided by a grant of £1 by Thomas Bray from funds at his disposal, 1695–9. Nothing further is know about Mason's library; the surviving vols. are probably from the Bray library. In 1950 a copy of Wollaston, *The Religion of Nature Delineated*, 1759 was reported at Bishop's Castle, but is no longer present.

References: Notitia Parochialis, no.358; CCC Questionnaire, 1950; Kelly, pp.252 & n.3, 259.

BISHOPS LYDEARD, Somerset
Blessed Virgin Mary. B & W
[nil]
John Geale (b. c. 1685), vicar from 1714, bequeathed by will proved 22 Dec. 1733 'my books to remain in the library that I have erected in the parish church of Bishops Liddeard'.
References: *N & Q*, v.154 (1928), p.123; Foster: Geale.

BISHOP'S STORTFORD, Herts.
St. Michael. St. Alb.
[nil] *
A library was est. apparently in 1664, 'formerly in the tower of the parish church, also in the endowed Grammar School'. Books from the library were sold at Sotheby's, 27 July 1893. There were no books reported at the church in 1950.
Catalogues: Catalogue & bibliography of books at Bishops Stortford. n.d. Herts. R.O. D/P21/29/44. In two hands, the last dated book is 1907; c. 235 books and a list of prints, engravings and tracts; there are few dated items, but c. 4 17th cent. and 27 18th cent., mainly local sermons (copy in CCC).
References: *Gentleman's Mag*, (1795), v.ii, p.892; Blades, *Book-Worm*, p.135; CCC Questionnaire, 1950; Lambeth Palace MS.3224: extracts from the Wace MSS. I am indebted to Dr D. J. McKitterick for information in this entry.

BISHOPTHORPE, Yorks. (N.Yorks.)
St. Andrew. York
[nil] *
A ParLL was est. in 1892 by the Associates of Dr Bray.
References: Bray Associates Annual Report, 1895.

BLAKENEY, Norfolk
St. Nicholas. Nor.
[5v.] Norwich CL
DeskL: Bibles, 1569, 1578; 1606; Jewel, *Works*, 1611; *A Replie unto Mr. Hardinge's Answeare*, 1565.

BLANDFORD FORUM, Dorset
St. Peter and St. Paul. Sarum
[nil]
A ParL was est. in 1864 by the Associates of Dr Bray, and augm. in 1865; it is not recorded after 1900.
References: Shore, p.152; Bray Associates Annual Reports, 1900.

BLEDINGTON, Glos. (Oxon.)
St. Leonard. Glouc.
[2v.] in situ; [4v.] Glos. RO
DeskL: Foxe, *Book of Martyrs*, 1631–2; Bible & BCP, 1712; Bible. 2v. 1763–7.

BLEDLOW, Bucks.
Holy Trinity. Ox.
[2v.] *
DeskL: Foxe, *Book of Martyrs*, 2v. 1641; the 18th cent. Book of Homilies reported in 1950 is now missing.
References: CCC Questionnaire, 1950.

BLETCHLEY, Bucks.
St. Mary. Ox.
[3v.] [1] in situ *; [2] in Bucks. RO
DeskL: BCP, Bible, Psalter, Cambridge, Buck and Daniel, 1638, in a red velvet binding with silver clasps and engraved silver plates on both covers, 'alleged to have belonged to Charles I' (probably a volume from one of the Chapels Royal); BCP, Psalms, London, 1687, in a black leather binding with gold-tooled covers and lettered 'Liber Parochialis Ecclesiae B. V. M. de Blecheley in Comitatu Buckingham': the tools are also found on books bound by an unidentified Oxford shop in the 1670s and 1680s. Both vols. were given by Browne Willis (1682–1760), in 1709–10, who paid £6.5.0 for the binding. An 'oaken case made skilfully to fit it' was lost by 1828. Two other vols. listed in a Visitation inventory of the 1780s in the Bucks RO have not survived; still in St. Mary's Church is: Samuel Hieron, *Works*, 1619.
References: William Bradbrooke, 'The reparation of Bletchley church in 1710', *Records of Bucks*, v.12 (1927–33), pp.239–60; DNB: Browne Willis; Paul Morgan: notes on bindings, etc., in CCC file (citing H. M. Nixon, *English Restoration Bookbindings*, 1974, pp.14–19).

BLEWBURY, Berks. (Oxon.)
St. Michael and All Angels. Ox.
[7+v.] *
DeskL: Bible, 1613 (in a converted 17th cent. sloping desk); Jewel's *Defence*, 1567, and *Reply to Harding*, 1565; Erasmus, *Paraphrases*, v.1, 1548 (in a late Victorian display cabinet); Bible, Oxford, 1739; BCP, 1709, and Psalms, 1706; BCP, 1752; BCP, Oxford, 1788, and Psalms, Oxford, 1787, together with other 19th and 20th cent. prayer books, in a 14th cent. chest.

BLOCKLEY, Glos.
St. Peter and St. Paul. Glouc.
(1v.) *
DeskL: Bible, 1617, in a contemporary binding, chained and in a display case.

BLOXHAM, Oxon.
Our Lady of Bloxham. Ox.
[*c.* 40v.] *
A small miscellaneous collection, the earliest bequest dating from the 1770s, kept in a room over the south porch, in a display case and in the clergy vestry. Includes Johan Piscator, *Commentaries*, 3v., 1638–58 (2 sets); a 10v. set of Cornelius à Lapide, *Commentary on the Pentateuch*, Venice, 1740, and a very imp. Foxe, *Book of Martyrs*, 6th ed., 1610.
Catalogues: TS list (copy in CCC).

BOLAM, Northumb.
St. Andrew. Newc.
[nil] *
One of 92 parishes in the Northumberland Archdeaconry granted a ParLL under a scheme devised by Bishop Shute Barrington, carried out by Archdeacon R. G. Bouyer by 1823 (see p.57), and recorded as still possessing books in visitation returns, 1826–8.
References: Day, pp.99–103.

BOLDRE, Hants.
St. John the Baptist. Win.
[2v.]
DeskL: Bibles, 1579, 1613 (the gift of Lt. Cmdr. A. B. Wood).
References: NADFAS Report.

BOLSTERSTONE, Yorks. (S.Yorks.)
St. Mary. Sheff.
[nil]
A ParL of 72 vols. was est. by the Bray Trustees for Erecting Parochial Libraries in 1711. The library was given up as 'lost' in 1895, and any remaining obsolete books were to be returned to the Associates.
Catalogues: MS. catalogue no.8. Bray Associates Records, f.39, pp.133–6.
References: Bray Associates Annual Reports, 1895.

BOLTON [-LE-MOORS], Lancs. (G.Man.)
St. Peter. Man.
[56v.] Bolton School.
One of the 5 parochial libraries provided for under the will of Humphrey Chetham in 1651 (see under **Manchester**; the others were at **Gorton**, **Turton**, and **Walmsley**). It was not until 1668 that 117v. (93 titles) were chosen for St. Peter's Church, listed, and chained 'in Mr Cheethams chappell in the deske there pr'pared for them'. The library was augm. by some gifts over the years, including 3 vols. presented early in the 18th cent. by Thomas Bray. A ParLL was est. in 1858 by the Associates of Dr Bray, and augm. in 1878 and 1888. The surviving books (in poor repair) were removed from the church for safe-

keeping and it was not until 1885 when Christie's work (below) was being prepared for publication that 56 vols. of the church library were discovered in the school's chained library (which had been presented, with a chest, by James Leaver in 1694).

Catalogues: the 1668 list is printed in Christie, pp.51–5, and Evans, Appendix 2, pp.39–40, below; a ms. shelf-list of 1702 (copy in CCC); Lambeth Palace MS.3094, ff.22–9: TS list of 6 chained books [dated 1624–53]; TS: A catalogue of books belonging to Bolton School, 1727; TS: H. W. D. Sculthorpe, The chained library of Bolton School, Lancs., 1969 (copies of last two in CCC); Wendy J. Sherrington, 'A catalogue of the chained library at Bolton School' (U. of Sheffield, M.A. in Librarianship, 1979); included in Evans, below, in a union cat. of extant books in the 5 Chetham libraries, pp.45–53.

References: Christie, pp.51–5, 119 (and frontispiece photograph of bookcase); Blades, BIC, pp.16–17, and pl. IV, a photograph of the bookcase; Streeter, pp.300–1; Evans, pp.16–17, 39–40; G. W. Daniels, 'The chained library', St. Peter with Holy Trinity Bolton Parish Magazine, Jan.1981, pp.12–15.

BOLTON-LE-SANDS, Lancs.
Holy Trinity. Blackb.
[nil]
A ParL of c. 15 vols.was est. by the Associates of Dr Bray in 1761; in 1849 this library was reported as being one of those 'either wholly lost or reduced to a few tattered volumes'.
Catalogues: sent in 1762 to 'Bolton by the Sands'. Bray Associates Records, f.38, p.90.
References: Report, 1849; Kelly, p.262.

BOLTON PERCY, Yorks.
All Saints. York
[iv.] York Minster Lib.
DeskL: Jewel, Works, 1611 (rebound in 1728 locally in a reversed calf panel binding, metal corner mounts and iron cleat from original chained binding transferred); 4 early 19th cent. Bibles and copies of the BCP also in deposit.

BORDEN, Kent
St. Peter and St. Paul. Cant.
[nil]
A BCP and a copy of Comber were chained to a stand in the chancel in 1853; and a chained Foxe, Book of Martyrs was recorded in 1923.
References: N & Q, no.210, 5.11.1853; Blades, BIC, p.17; Cox, p.196.

BOSTON, Lincs.
SS. Botolph. Linc.
[c. 1500v.]
The Boston Assembly Book for 12 Dec. 1610 states: 'item at this assembly it is

Boston: a bookcase, perhaps one of the original cases built to house the books of Edward Kelsall, vicar 1702–19

agreed that the room over the south porch of the church of this Borough shall be prepared and made ready at the charge of this Borough ffitt and meet to make a library in'. One of the orders made by Sir Nathaniel Brent as commissary of Archbishop Laud in his visitation, 20 Aug. 1634, required that 'the room over the porch . . . shall be repaired and decently fitted to make a library in which to keep books given to the use of the parish'. This was carried out at the request of Anthony Tuckney (1599–1670), vicar 1633–70, who gave many books; others were bought with money subscribed. In 1719 the Corporation paid £50 for the books of Edward Kelsall (d.1719), vicar 1702–19, and added them to the library, and in the following year the churchwardens paid for 'classis' to be made to house them, presumably book cases or pressses. In 1819 over 150v. were sold; a report in 1853 has a detailed account: 'two or more cart loads of books from this library . . . sold by the churchwardens, and, as he believes, by the then archdeacon's order, at waste paper price; that the bulk of them was purchased by a bookseller then resident in Boston, and re-sold by him to a clergyman in the neighbourhood of Spilsby'. The library was restored c. 1950. The collection contains one medieval MS, a 13th cent. works of Augustine from the Cluniac priory of Pontefract, the gift of William Skelton, rector of Consby (persons of this name rectors of Coningsby, Lincs. d.1610, 1660, 1679). Most of the books were printed before 1700 and consist mainly of patristic, scholastic and pre-Reformation theology, including a BCP, 1549, and a first edition of Foxe's *Book of Martyrs* (Foxe was born in Boston). Other books include Camden's *Britannia*, Heylyn's *Cosmography,* and 2 rare 16th cent. editions of Chaucer. Most of the books bear evidence of having belonged to Edward Kelsall ('F. Kelsall, St. John's College Cambs.'). There are 4 identified Oxford bindings of the period c. 1515–1620. The library received grant aid from the CCC for repair work to the books in 1996; in 1997 the Boston Parish Library Project Group was formed for the care, cataloguing and maintenance of the books and the library room.

Catalogues: a 1702 terrier containing a list of books 'belonging to ye parish church of Boston', arranged by size and language (Lincs. RO: TER 10/121, copy in CCC); catalogues made in 1724 and 1819; a catalogue of c. 1893 by A. E. Bernays (Cambridge UL: Add.MS.2716(2): c. 330 vols.); TS catalogue of 1948–50; card catalogue with the collection.

References: William Laud, *Works*, 1847–60, v.5, p.499; Vestry Minute Book, 1705–76; Venn: Tuckney, Kelsall; Pishey Thompson, *History of Boston*, 1856, p.187; *TLS*, v.49 (1950), p.192 (recent restoration); Kelly, pp.75, 195, 249; Ker, MMBL, II, 1977, pp.150–1; Ker, *Pastedowns*, 274a–b, 1587a, 1902a; Pearson 830.5; Lambeth Palace MS.3221, ff.83–9: rubbings of bindings and notes on provenance by N. R. Ker; M., T. N. *A Concise Sketch of the History of St. Botolph's Church*, Boston, 1895; *Lincoln Diocesan Mag.,* v.66 (1950), pp.21–3; Pilgrim Trust 38th Report, 1968, pp.28–9; Mark Spurrell, *Boston Parish Church*, 3rd ed., 1987, p.19. *Boston Parish Church Library in St. Botolph's Church* (leaflet, n.d. 2001?).

BOTHAL, Northumb.
St. Andrew Newc.
[nil ?] NRC
After his visitation in 1723 Archdeacon Thomas Sharp noted 16 vols. of the Fathers, in continental editions, 1571–1603; in 1826 Archdeacon Thomas Singleton noted only 6 vols. remaining. In 1830 3 curators were appointed for the parish library but there was no mention of titles.
References: Northumb. RO: M91, Sharp visitation returns; ZAN M16 B31, Singleton visitation returns; Bothal parish records: EP 164/43, 1830; Day, p.94.

BOURNEMOUTH, Hants. (Dorset)
~~Holy Trinity~~ (closed 1973) Win.
[33v.+] Winchester CL
DeskL: in origin (?): Bible, 1613, and 19th cent. books on theology deposited in Winchester CL in 1973 (not kept as a collection).

BOVINGDON, Herts.
St. Lawrence. St.Alb.
[2v.] St Albans Abbey Lib.
DeskL: Erasmus, *Paraphrases*, v.1, 1551 (rebound 1946), and a copy of Foxe, *Book of Martyrs*.

BOWNESS, Cumb. (Cumbria)
St. Michael. Carl.
[nil]
DeskL: in 1923 there were chained copies of Erasmus, 1516–20, Jewel, *Works*, 1609, and a *Book of Homilies*, 1543, but no longer.
References: Blades, BIC, pp.17–18; Cox & Harvey, p.338.

BOX, Wilts.
St. Thomas à Becket. Bris.
[nil]
In the Minutes of the Bray Trustees, 23 Aug. 1727, a gift of surplus books to Box is recorded.
References: Kelly, pp.255 & n.5, 264 n.1.

BRADFIELD, Berks.
St. Andrew. Ox.
[nil ?] NRC
'A catalogue of books in the Parish Library, Bradfield, 1831', listing c. 150 titles, and rules for the use of the library, is held in the Berks. RO. A copy of the pictorial bookplate is in the Franks Collection: no. 33772.
References: catalogue: Berks. RO, D/ESv(B) Q3.

BRADFIELD, Yorks. (S.Yorks.)
St. Nicholas. Sheff.
[91 titles in 39v.] Sheffield UL
The Revd Robert Turie, one of the chaplains at the parish church of Sheffield, and incumbent curate of Ecclesall from 1695 to 1720, by his will in 1720 gave 'all my books, and the press wherein they are (excepting six octavo English books to be chose thereout by Mr Steer of Ecclesfield, for the use of my wife, and excepting the Bibles and Common Prayer Books, and such little pamphlets as my wife shall desire for herself), unto the Minister of Bradfield Chapel, in the county of York, and to his successors there; and I direct and appoint that a catalogue shall be taken of the said books, and that a true copy thereof shall be entered in the Archbishop's Register at York, to prevent their being embezzled'. In the catalogue of 1720 some 117 titles (137v.) are listed; some books were evidently added to the collection since in 1859 there were 149 titles (see Eastwood, below). By 1959 there were only 49 surviving vols. They were deposited firstly in Sheffield PL, and then in 1993 in Sheffield UL, when there were only 39 vols. The collection, which is mainly theology and the classics, contains books dated from 1600 to 1764, including 5 STC and 22 Wing items.
Catalogues: Catalogue of 1720, copy in the Archbishop's Register (i.e. Registry) is in the Borthwick Institute, Bp.C and PII/18; 1859 catalogue (see below); checklist compiled by Richard Turner, 1977; MS catalogue by C. J. Ewbank and S. E. Boorman, 1980 (copy in CCC).
References: J. Eastwood, *N & Q*, 2nd ser. 7 (1859), p.473, and *History of the Parish of Ecclesfield*, 1862 (including a catalogue of the books 'as they existed May 23 1859', pp.541–5); John C. Wilson, *The Parish Church of St. Nicholas, Bradfield*, Sheffield, *c.* 1970; Barr, p.37; the 1720 cat. is analysed in Woolf, p.192–3.

BRADFORD, Yorks. (W.Yorks.)
St. Peter (from 1919 the Cathedral). Bradf.
[nil] *
A ParLL was est. in 1830 by the Associates of Dr Bray, augm. in 1840, and again in 1875.
Catalogues: 1830 (190v.) Bray Associates Records, f.40, pp.187–92; 1840 (132 vols.), Bray Associates Records, f.41, pp.12–15.
References: Shore, p.152; Kelly, p.264.

BRADFORD-ON-AVON, Wilts.
Holy Trinity. Sarum
[nil]
A ParLL of 169 vols. was est. in 1843 by the Associates of Dr Bray; it is not recorded after 1890.
Catalogues: 1843: Bray Associates Records, f.41, pp.102–5.
References: Bray Associates Annual Reports, 1890; Kelly, p.264.

BRAMFIELD, Suffolk
St. Andrew. St.E.
[1v.]
DeskL: Erasmus' *Paraphrases*, 1551, in original binding of leather and wood.

BRAMPTON, Westm. (Cumbria)
St. Martin. Carl.
[nil]
A ParLL was est. in 1792 by the Associates of Dr Bray; it was still recorded in 1849, but not after 1880. It was probably one of those libraries intended for the joint use of the school and the parish (**Beetham** was another).
References: Bray Associates Annual Reports, 1880; Kelly, p.261; Select Committee Report, 1849; letter from Edgar Hinchcliffe, 2 Jan. 1970 (CCC file: Beetham).

BRANSFORD, Worcs.
St. John the Baptist (chapel). Worc.
[1v.] Heref. & Worcs. RO
DeskL: Bible, Cambridge, Baskerville, 1763.

BRATTLEBY, Lincs.
St. Cuthbert. Linc.
[nil?] NRC
The Lincs. RO holds a list of rules, lists of books, and lists of borrowers and subscribers, 1871–3, for a parish library.
References: Lincs. RO: Brattleby 23.4.

BRATTON FLEMING, Devon
St. Peter. Ex.
[*c*. 190v.?] NRC Gonville and Caius College, Cambridge
A monument in the chancel records that Bartholomew Wortley (*c*. 1655–1749), rector 1705–49, bequeathed 'Bibliothecam et supellectilem omnem futuris huius ecclesiae rectoribus in perpetuum'. The parish records for 1910, p.33, state that Wortley 'left a library containing 214 vols'. Wortley's will indicates that he had been for several years Senior Fellow in Gonville and Caius College and had bequeathed money to found 2 fellowships there. The college has been patron of the living since 1706. A visit by Dr Margaret Lattimore in 1984 disclosed the residue of this library in an attic room at the rectory in a purpose-built mid-19th cent. bookcase. She reported that about 190 vols. of those found were uniformly bound in dark calf (the large folios in parchment with paper-covered boards), with gilt spine-lettering and the Gonville and Caius College coat of arms on the front board, together with a label reading: 'Cai. Coll. Cant.'. On the lower board was Wortley's coat of arms and 'Barthol. Wortley' in gilt. On the back of most title leaves was a

Bratton Fleming: a monumental inscription relating to the founder,
Bartholomew Wortley, rector 1705–19

label: 'This book is to be preserved at Bratton Fleming Parsonage, for the use of the incumbent for the time being'. From the date range it is clear that not all the books can have been in the original 1749 bequest, and only *c.* 28 vols. in the collection, mainly theology and sermons, were published before his death. The remainder, mainly theological works, *c.* 1800–40, were probably purchased and not donated. There were also post-1850 Bibles and service books. The surviving vols. were transferred to Gonville and Caius College, Cambridge, in 1997.

References: Bodl. MS. Top. Devon, c.8, f.94; Shore, p.145; Kelly, p.246; Lattimore TS report 1984 (copy in CCC).

BREADSALL, Derbys.
All Saints. Derby
[nil?] NRC
DeskL: of 8v. dated 1609–1702, 'chained to a unique double reading-desk, on the two folding lids fastened at the top by a padlock, but this was wickedly and wantonly destroyed by the militant suffragists when they set fire to the church in July 1914'. Drawings of the desk were reproduced in the 1856 vol. of the Anastatic Drawing Society, and the 1866 vol. of the Fac-simile Society.
References: Cox, Notes, v.3, p.61; Cox & Harvey, p.338 (where the vols. are listed).

BREDE, Sussex (E.Sussex)
St. George. Chich.
[3v.]
DeskL: George Petter (rector 1610–54), *Commentary on St. Mark's Gospel*, 1661, 2v.; 'Vinegar' Bible, 1717.
References: Venn: Petter.

BRENT ELEIGH, Suffolk
St. Mary. St.E.
[*c.* 17v.] Suffolk RO, Bury St. Edmunds (and see below)
The library was est. by Henry Colman (*c.* 1670–1715), a fellow of Trinity College, Cambridge from 1694, rector of Harpley, Norfolk from 1706, and of Foulsham from 1713 until his death. In a codicil to his will proved 9 Nov. 1715 he states: 'as to my library of books I leave then altogether and dedicate and consecrate them to the use of the Church of Brentily that is the incumbent minister there for ever'. A bond of 1720 tells us that his widow-executrix has delivered her husband's library to Thurloe [Nicholas Thurloe, vicar] for safe keeping, and a parchment catalogue of 1719 lists *c.* 1500 titles in a little over 1700 vols. This catalogue shows that the library was strongest in divinity, classics, and English and European history, the earliest printed book being a Latin Bible of 1524. An 1801 Brent Eleigh parish terrier describes the brick library built by Mrs Colman onto the east end of the chancel, demolished in 1859. The books were then transferred to another building near the church-

yard gate, itself taken down before 1926. The sale of the MSS, through the agency of M. R. James, began in 1887. The entire library of printed books disappeared without trace some time after 1891, perhaps as late as 1900. There is no record of any faculty having been granted. Largely through the efforts of Canon John Fitch some 17 books have so far been traced from the library (see Lewis below).

8 vols. are deposited in Suffolk RO, Bury St. Edmunds; there are 8 medieval and 2 later MSS, most of which belonged to Fane Edge (d. at Lavenham in 1727), and a vol. of collections by Nicholas Roscarrock (d.1634?). 2 of the MSS were in Sotheby's sale of 26 July 1887, lots 104 (now Bodl. Lat. liturg.f.5, Queen Margaret's Gospels) and 268 (now Cambridge UL, Add.3327); 6 were acquired by Cambridge UL in 1891 (Add.MSS.3037–42); 1 was acquired by the Fitzwilliam Museum in 1891 (MS.17).

Catalogues: parchment catalogue, 1719 (Norfolk & Norwich RO, Diocesan Registry Box, Misc. 1705–30; copy in Suffolk RO, Bury: HD915/1); an 18th cent. catalogue, Sotheby's, 26 July 1887, lot 304, is now Bib. Nationale, MS.angl.221.

References: W. A. Copinger, *The Manors of Suffolk*, v.1, 1905, p.43; H. R. Barker, *West Suffolk Illustrated*, Bury St. Edmunds, 1907; H. W. Tompkins, *In Constable's Country*, 1906, pp.177–8; Thomas of Monmouth, *The Life and Miracles of St. William of Norwich*, ed. A. Jessop and M. R. James, Cambridge, 1896, p.1; M. R. James, *Eton and King's*, 1926, pp.205–6; Fitch, 1965, pp.69–74; Fitch, 1977, p.xv; Fitch, *N & Q*, 120 March 1979 (2 books traced, one in Urbana UL and one in Glasgow UL); Roy Harley Lewis, *Book Collecting: a New Look*, Newton Abbot, 1988, pp.81–5 (an account of the 17 vols. so far traced in private and institutional hands). Another vol. has recently been identified in the Wellcome Library (information from H. J. M. Symons, Curator).

BREWOOD, Staffs.
St. Mary and St. Chad. Lich.
[nil]
A ParL of 72 vols. was est. in 1710 by the Trustees for Erecting Parochial Libraries, and reported as 'lost' in 1878.
Catalogues: no.41. Bray Associates Records, f.39, pp.41–44.
References: Bray Associates Annual Reports, 1878.

†ransf

BRIDGNORTH, Shrops.
St. Leonard. Heref.
[2,310v.] Shrops. RRC
The library was est. by Hugh Stackhouse (*c.* 1684–1743), master of the Free Grammar School and rector of Oldbury, d.1743, who bequeathed his 'Study of books and pamphletts' to the Society of Clergymen in and about Bridgnorth. The foundation deed of 1 July 1743 includes a list of *c.* 1,500 books and some pamphlets, and its wording suggests that the Society may already have

possessed a library, perhaps a subscription library on the lines of that formed in 1714 by the Society of the Clergy of Doncaster which established a library in the parish church there with the vicar as librarian. Thomas Lyttleton, rector of Oldbury 1743–93, bequeathed £30 in 1792, the interest on which was to provide for the upkeep of the books and of the library-room attached to St. Leonard's Church. In the 19th cent. the Bridgnorth library was run on a subscription basis, and many books were added to it (e.g. runs of Record Commission publications, and periodicals), and by 1971 contained *c.* 5,000 vols. It was deposited firstly in Shrops. Co.L and then in the Shrops. Records & Research Centre. After Whitchurch this is the largest surviving ParL in Shrops. There are many fragments of medieval MSS bound up with Hebrew and Latin eds. of the Bible; part of a fine missal forms a cover for Laertius, *De Vita Philosophica*, 1524. The 2 surviving MSS are 1. De Speculum Moralium. s.xiii, and, 2. Statuta Angliæ, etc. s.xiv.in. There are two identified Oxford bindings of the period *c.* 1515–1620.

Catalogues: in Foundation Deed (see below); *Catalogue of books belonging to the library previous to the year 1796*, printed, with MS notes and additions (copy in: Lambeth Palace MS.3221, ff.91–); *Rules and Catalogue of the Stackhouse Library, Bridgnorth*, Wolverhampton, 1838 (The Bodl. copy contains printed additions to 1846, pp.32–44, and corrections and additions in manuscript); The Stackhouse Library Bridgnorth, Shropshire County Library, 1964 (TS, copy in Lambeth Palace MS.3221); Shrops. PLC, 1971.

References: Foster: Stackhouse; Venn: Lyttleton; Foundation Deed (19th cent. copy): BL MS.Add.28732, ff.13–21; Lyttleton bequest: *ibid.*, f.24; Ker, MMBL, II, 1977, pp.164–9; Ker, Pastedowns, 181–2; Kelly, pp.91 n.4, 252 & n.4; Lambeth Palace MS.3221, ff.91–150): rubbings of bindings and notes on provenance by N. R. Ker.

BRIDLINGTON, Yorks. (E.Riding of Yorks)
St. Mary's Priory Church. York
[*c.* 60v.] York Minster Lib.
A ParL of 72v. was est. by the Bray Trustees for Erecting Parochial Libraries in 1710. (Listed in some early sources, e.g. Report, 1849, as 'Burlington'.) In 1959 46 vols. remained in the church: nos. 1, 3–8, 10–13, 15–21, 26–9, 31, 35–44, 47, 50, 52, 55, 58, 61, 63–5, 67, 69 and 70, together with 8 vols. of *Critici Sacri*, Amsterdam, 1698, given by the Associates in 1871, the cupboard in which the books were sent to Bridlington, and 5 17th cent. vols., chained, probably part of a DeskL (including Jewel's *Works*; Hooker's *Ecclesiastical Polity*; Heylin's *Works*; Comber's *Companion*). The surviving books were deposited in York Minster Lib. in *c.* 1992. The cupboard (illustrated in PLCE1) was removed from the church in 1989 or earlier and its present whereabouts are not known. A copy of the bookplate is in the Franks Collection: no. 33858, and in the John Johnson Collection.

Catalogues: catalogue no.25: Bray Associates Records, f.39, pp.57–60; a ms. catalogue of 1719–20 listing *c.* 60 books is in the Borthwick Institute, York:

R.VI.D.13, f.48; list of DeskL books (copy in CCC).
References: Blades, BIC, p.18; Cox & Harvey, p.338; Kelly, p.264 & n.3; Lambeth Palace MS.3224, ff.153–5: notes and rubbings of bindings by N. R. Ker.

BRISTOL, Glos. (Bristol)

tranf

All Saints. Bris.
[48v.] Bristol RO
Five early printed books (dating from 1481 to 1503) and 3 medieval MSS (14th and 15th cents.) are traditionally regarded as survivors of the Guild of Kalendars' Library, est. by John Carpenter (d.1476), Bishop of Worcester, in 1464. The remaining part of the collection consists of Bibles from 1537 to the 20th cent. (including Tyndale's trans. 1537, and the 1602 ed. with preface by Cranmer); copies of the BCP from 1677 to the 20th cent.; and other theological works, including prescribed works, e.g. Erasmus, *Paraphrases*, 1548, and *Certain Sermons or Homilies*, 1562, reprinted 1683, and 19th cent. pamphlets. Deposited in Bristol RO some time after 1969.
The medieval MSS are: 1. W. Peraldus, Sermones, etc. s.xv; 2. G. Zerbolt, De spiritualibus ascensionibus, etc. s.xv; 3. Augustinus, De Trinitate, etc. 1465. There is one identified Oxford binding of the period c. 1515–1620.
A printed catalogue of 1861 is evidence that there was a lending library of c. 300 vols. est. by that date, on a subscription basis, open only for a short time once a week. The contents included a large no. of RTS and SPCK publications.
Catalogues: MSS described briefly in Williams, below; handlist of all items in Bristol RO (copy in CCC); printed cat., 1861.
References: DNB: Carpenter; T. W. Williams, 'Gloucestershire medieval libraries', *Trans. of the Bristol and Glouc. Arch. Soc.*, v.31 (1908), pp.87–90; Kelly, pp.32–4 & n.2; Ker, MMBL, II, 1977, pp.183–6; Ker, MLGB, 1964, p.13; Ker, Pastedowns, 26; N. Orme, 'The Guild of Kalendars, Bristol', *Trans. of the Bristol and Glouc. Arch. Soc.*, v.96 (1978), pp.42–3; *The Church of All Saints, Bristol* [guidebook], [1973–]; Lambeth Palace MS.3221, ff.151–3: rubbings of bindings by N. R. Ker; Morgan, p.30.

BRISTOL, Glos. (Bristol)
St. Mary the Virgin (Redcliffe). Bris.
[nil?]
Cox & Harvey record that: 'Belinus Nansmoen, a British merchant, left by his will of 1416 to the church of St. Mary, Redcliffe, the Sixth book of the Decretals & the Constitutions of Pope Clement V, to be shut up in that church so that the vicar & chaplains might study them when they pleased'. Jo. Mede, a merchant of Bristol in his will proved 2 May 1496 requested burial in St. Stephen's aisle next to the 'library' there [in St. Mary Redcliffe]. A printed cat. of 1861 is evidence that there was a ParLL of c. 300 vols. est. by this date, on a subscription basis, open only for a short time once a week. The contents included a large no. of RTS and SPCK publications.

Catalogues: printed, 1861.
References: Cox & Harvey, p.331; Morgan, p.30; I am indebted to Dr Nigel Ramsay for the reference to Mede.

BRISTOL, Glos. (Bristol)
St. Thomas the Martyr. Bris.
[iv.] Bristol RO
A medieval MS: Biblia, s.xiv/xv, 'restored to St. Thomas's in 1567 and rebound in that year according to inscriptions' is deposited in Bristol RO: P/St.T/PM/1, accompanied by a detailed analysis (copy in CCC).
References: Ker, MMBL,II,1977, pp.212–3; T. W. Williams, 'Gloucestershire medieval libraries', *Trans. of the Bristol and Glouc. Arch. Soc.*, v.31 (1908), p.90.

BROCKENHURST, Hants.
St. Nicholas. Win.
[iv.] Winchester CL
A Cassiodorus fragment found in a parish register of 1593 is now Winchester CL MS.XXV, Cassiodorus, S.IX.

BROMFIELD, Cumb. (Cumbria)
St. Mungo. Carl.
[nil] *
A printed *Catalogue of the Bromfield Parochial Library*, published at Wigton in 1853, includes lists of donations and subscriptions.
References: Lambeth Palace MS.3221.

BROMHAM, Beds.
St. Owen. St.Alb.
[*c.* 860v.] Bedford Central Lib.
The library was est. in 1739 (from the date in two catalogues) or 1740 (from the inscription on the wall outside) by Thomas, Baron Trevor (1658–1730) 'for the use of the parish and ministers of Bromham', and was added to later by members of the Trevor family and others up to the mid 19th cent. In 1959 it consisted of *c.* 800v. kept in a small room over the south porch accessible only by outside steps. It was deposited in Bedford Central Lib. in 1984. There are a few late 16th cent. books, but they are mainly late 17th and 18th cent., with an emphasis on theological, literary and historical subjects; classics and travel are also represented. The charms of the library are celebrated by Robert Hampden-Trevor in his Latin poem, *Villa Bromhamensis*; a copy of his *Poetical Works*, printed at the Bodoni Press at Parma, is also in the library. The bookplates of Thomas Trevor and John Trevor often occur; there are no early bindings, save a few in vellum, but there are many handsome 18th cent. bindings with gold-tooled spines.
Catalogues: three 18th cent. lists were kept with the collection; a TS catalogue compiled by E. C. Cooper in 1959 listing *c.* 860 vols. was privately published

as *Catalogue of the Books in the Library of the Parish Church of St. Owen, Bromham, Bedfordshire*, Bromham, 1959 (in shelf-list form: copy in CCC). This catalogue refers to the sale in 1809 of Walton's Polyglot Bible and Castell's *Lexicon* from the proceeds of which a further 53 vols. were purchased.

References: DNB: Trevor; Foster: Hampden-Trevor; *N & Q*, 6 ser. v.6 (1882), p.258; H. C. Brooks, *Compendiosa Biblografia di Edizione Bodoniane*, Florence, 1927, no.470; *Beds. N & Q*, v.2 (1889), pp.18–20; Lambeth Palace MS.3221, ff.154–5: notes on content and provenance by N. R. Ker.

BROMPTON, Yorks. (N.Yorks.)
St. Thomas. York
[nil] *
A ParL was est. in 1862 by the Associates of Dr Bray, and augm. in 1869. It is not recorded after 1880.
References: Shore, p.150; Bray Associates Annual Reports, 1880.

BROMSGROVE, Worcs.

St. John the Baptist. Worc.
[114v.] Worcester CL
The early history of the library is unknown, but provenance information about many of the books is given in the catalogues listed below. It may be the library granted £2 by Bray from funds at his disposal, 1695–9. The books are mainly 17th cent. Blades reported in 1890 that there was a copy of Jewel, 1609, chained to a desk in the church. Deposited in Worcester CL in *c.* 1997.
Catalogues: listed (partially) by W. A. Cotton, *Bromsgrove Church*, 1881, pp.39–41 (91 vols.) and subsequently in *The Bibliographer*, v.1 (1881), p.134, with some provenance notes (copy in CCC); full TS catalogue by B. S. Benedikz, 1993 (114 vols.) gives provenances for each book. Many books belonged to Thomas Tullie and John Waugh I (*c.* 1703–65) and II, vicar 1754–77.
References: Foster: John Waugh I (?); Venn: John Waugh II; Blades, BIC, p.18; Kelly, pp.106 n.3, 255 & n.6, 259; Cox & Harvey, p.338; Lambeth Palace MS.3221, f.56: rubbings of bindings by N. R. Ker; Pearson 1772.1.

BROOKTHORPE, Glos.
St. Swithun. Glouc.
[nil]
A ParL of 72 vols. was est. by the Bray Trustees for Erecting Parochial Libraries in 1712; in 1849 it was one of those reported as 'either wholly lost or reduced to a few tattered volumes'.
Catalogues: MS cat no. 17 'Brockthorp'. Bray Associates Records, f.39, pp.177–80.
References: Report, 1849; Kelly, p.362.

BROUGH, Westm. (Cumbria)
St. Michael. Carl.
[5v.] Cumbria RO (Kendal)
The Report of 1849 states that a clerical library was est. *c.* 1705 by Dr Bray, but there is no evidence for this.
DeskL: BCP, 1683; Foxe, *Book of Martyrs*, 3v., 1610; Jewel, *Works*, 1681.
References: Select Committee Report, 1849.

BROUGHAM, Westm. (Cumbria)
St. Wilfrid Chapel. Carl.
[2v.] Cumbria RO (Kendal)
DeskL: BCP, Cambridge, 1754; Bible, 18th cent.

Broughton (Bucks.): a copy of Erasmus, *Paraphrases*, 1551, chained to a wooden desk near the chancel arch (photo: copyright Paul Morgan)

BROUGHTON, Bucks.
St. Lawrence (CCT) Ox.
[2v.]
DeskL: John Jewel, *A Defence of the Apologie . . . and Answeare to . . . M. Hardinge*, London, Henry Wykes, 1567; bound with his *A Replie unto Mr Hardings Answeare*, London, Henry Wykes, 1565; and, Erasmus, *Paraphrases upon the Newe Testament*, London, Edward Whitchurch, 8th ed., 1551 (imp.), chained to wooden desks on the north and south sides of the chancel arch. The desks and chains are possibly 19th cent. local work, but the Erasmus has the inscription 'This booke belongs to the parish churche of Broughton, bought in the year of our Lord 1632. Richard Radborne Rector'. Radborne was curate of Broughton, 1606–18, and Rector, 1619–32, and the book was evidently a replacement for an earlier copy.
References: notes by Paul Morgan after a visit in 1995 (CCC file).

BROUGHTON, Hunts. (Cambs.)
All Saints. Ely
[c. 582v. + pamphlets] Cambridge UL; 18v. and 12 pamphlets in situ.
William Torkington (d.1737), rector of Wistow, Hunts., 1705–37, left his books to Robert Hodson (d.1774), rector of Broughton 1713–74, 'towards the setting up of a public library'. In Hodson's will, dated 8 Jan. 1772, he left his books to Philippe Holmes 'to be by her plac'd in my library in the chancel of the parish church of Broughton' and £40 for the provision of bookcases, but a codicil of 19 Nov. 1773 revoked this last bequest 'I having in my lifetime been at the expense of procuring proper cases for their reception'. The sequestrator informed the Central Council in 1950 that the books had been sorted by Dr R. H. Murray, rector 1922–8, and that 'those of no consequence were disposed of'. Except for 18 books and 12 pamphlets retained at the church, the whole collection was sold with faculty to Cambridge UL in 1958. (The books at Broughton are now in a display case given by Cambridge UL, and the original bookcases are stored in the tower.) About half the collection, duplicates of books in the University Library, was then resold to a bookseller, H. W. Edwards, Ashmore Green, Newbury (catalogues 84–90, 1958). Most of the books bear either the name or bookplate of Torkington, or the name of Hodson.158
Catalogues: TS catalogue of those books and pamphlets sold by Cambridge 5UL, and those put aside for return to Broughton, by N. R. Ker, together with rubbings of bindings (copy in CCC).
References: Venn: Torkington, Hodson; copies of wills: Hunts CRO, TORK 15/45; Lambeth Palace MS.3224: notes by A. N. Munby.

BROUGHTON IN FURNESS, Lancs. (Cumbria)
St. Mary Magdalene. Carl.
[5v.]
In 1950 it was reported that 13 books were given in the 18th cent. by Dr Stratford, and Dr Bray's Associates, for the setting up of parochial libraries; and a 'Breeches' Bible was presented 'recently' by Sir Robert Rankin. The 'Breeches' Bible was stolen in 1994, and 2 other vols. are lost; 5 vols. dating from 1749 to 1784 are retained in the church.
References: CCC Questionnaire, 1950.

BRUNSTEAD, Norf.
St. Peter. Nor.
[1v.] Norwich CL
DeskL: Bible, 1617.

BUBWITH, Yorks. (E.Riding of Yorks.)
All Saints. York
[6v.] York Minster Lib.

a catalogue 'properly engrossed on parchment' of a large collection of books formerly at Bubwith. This catalogue 'of the books in Bubwith Library taken the sixteenth of April 1747' lists some 689 titles with dates between 1512 and 1706, but there is very little later than 1680. Raine saw some of these books 'some thirty years ago . . . in a tattered and neglected condition'. They were used to light the vestry fires, until 'the sole remnant of some six or seven hundred volumes were some six or eight', which the incumbent 'picked up in the village and wisely offered to the Dean and Chapter of York for preservation in their library'. Four have been identified in Raine's catalogue: copies of Alstedius, Chemnitius, Douza and Malcolm, and there are two other very imperfect vols. They were deposited by 13 Dec. 1892 according to 'Liber Donorum', f.96–7, by the Revd W. F. H. Campbell, vicar of Bubwith.

Catalogues: 1774 catalogue: York Minster Lib. BB.10.1; James Raine, *Catalogue of the Printed Books in the Library of the Dean and Chapter of York*, 1896, introduction, p.xvii, catalogue, pp.8, 99, 142, 284.
References: Barr, p.35; Kelly, p.247.

BUCKDEN, Hunts. (Cambs.)
St. Mary. Ely
[?]
A ParLL was granted £1 by Bray from funds at his disposal, 1695–9. The bishops of Lincoln (who kept a palace in Buckden) donated books to St. Mary's church for the use of the congregation, especially John Kaye (1783–1853), bishop, 1827–1853, and the library was administered by the vicar from 1837. The complete library was transferred in 1874 to the **Huntingdon** Archdeaconry Library. In the mid 1960s the bishops' papers at Huntingdon were transferred to the Cambs. RO, and the residue of books to Cambridge UL, where they are stored as 'Huntingdon Rare Books' in the Bible Society Library. Books from the Bray library can no longer be identified.
References: Shore, p.151; Kelly, pp.248, 258; letter from Barry Jobling, St. Mary's historian (CCC file).

BUCKINGHAM, Bucks.
St. Peter and St. Paul. Ox.
[iv.]
A 14th cent. Latin Bible, given probably in 1481 by John Rudyng (d.1481), but later alienated, was restored by gift in 1883.
References: Ker, MMBL, II, 1977, pp.215–16.

BUCKLAND, Berks. (Oxon.)
All Saints. Ox.
[70 titles in 58v.] Reading UL
Archdeacon Onslow's visitation book, 1786, records under Buckland: 'A parochial library . . . founded by Dr John Burton of Eton consisting of near a hundred volumes but the books are all lost, except a Greek testament or two

and an old volume of the Fathers'. None of the surviving books bear any evidence of ownership by Burton, presumably John Burton (1696–1771), Fellow of Eton in 1733, and vicar of Mapledurham, 1734–6. There is no record of the founding of a Bray library at Buckland but 3 vols. have Bray Trustees bookplates and two other vols. are uniformly bound after the pattern of Bray Trustees' libraries. There are a number of books and pamphlets by Bray in the collection. John Burton was interested in Bray's schemes and published *An Account of the Designs of the late Dr Bray* in 1764 (often reprinted). The books were transferred in 1951 to the Old Manor House, Buckland, for safe-keeping, and in 1969–70 to Reading UL on permanent deposit. The books are mainly theological, ecclesiastical, 18th cent. and in English. There are 2 STC, 10+ Wing, 35+ ESTC, 5 16th cent., and 9 17th cent. continental books in the collection. The library includes a copy of the 'Breeches' Bible, Geneva, 1560. Some 4 vols. have the armorial bookplate of the book collector, Robert Hoblyn (1710–56), and a number of other vols. have the signatures of John Rogers, 1669, vicar of Eynsham, and John Rogers, 1708, his son, Fellow of Corpus Christi College, Oxford, 1706, and shortly afterwards curate of Buckland 'between five and six years'. There are 11 vols. of sermons by John Rogers, the son, in the collection (published between 1728 and 1784). Many of the books are inscribed 'Belonging to the the Lib: of Buckland'. There is an Oxford binding, probably by John Westall, on Casaubon, *De Rebus Sacris*, 1614 (Gibson: roll 25).

Catalogues: TS list by N. R. Ker of 19 items (Bodl.MS.Eng.Misc.c.360, copies in Lambeth Palace MS.3221 and in CCC); complete TS list with the collection (including provenances); not yet re-catalogued.

References: Visitation book, 1786 (Berks. RO: D/EX1324/1, f.58v.); DNB: John Burton, Robert Hoblyn; D. H. Knott, *Rare Book Collections*, Reading UL, 1980 (and revisions).

BUNBURY, Ches.
St. Boniface. Ches.
[6v.] 4v. in the church; 2v. in Cheshire RO
DeskL: 'Breeches' Bible, chained; Bible, n.d.; Birkett's *Commentary on the New Testament*, 18th cent.; copies of BCP, 1752, 18th cent., and 1801.
References: Cox & Harvey, p.338.

BURGH, Lincs.
(Ded. unknown). Linc.
[?]
A ParL was est. at the 'Mission House' in 1878 by the Associates of Dr Bray. An uncertain place-name: possibly Burgh le Marsh (St. Peter and St. Paul) or Burgh-on-Bain (St. Helen).
References: Bray Associates Annual Report, 1880.

Burgh-by-Sands (in Carlisle Cathedral Library): a book-cupboard (not the traditional pattern) designed for the Bray Trustees library established in 1712, with 39 of the original volumes, and later volumes, a list of the books on the inside of the upper door, and evidence of where the Queen Anne Act of 1709 was pasted on the inside of the lower door

BURGH-BY-SANDS, Cumb. (Cumbria)
St. Michael. Carl.
[42v.] Carlisle CL
One of the 10 parishes in the diocese of Carlisle given 16 books in 1687 under the will of Barnabas Oley (see pp.34–5 and table on pp.444–52). A ParL of 72v. was est. by the Bray Trustees for Erecting Parochial Libraries in 1712. In 1703 William Nicolson, Bishop of Carlisle, enquired after the Barnabas Oley books with disquieting results: at Burgh-by-Sands he retrieved 5 vols. from the house of widow Matthews, another had been lent to a neighbouring rector, etc. By 1959 all books from both deposits were reported as missing, but in 1968 some 39 vols. of the Trustees library were located and deposited in Carlisle CL: nos. 1, 2, 4, 5, 6/1, 7/1, 8, 11 (vol.2), 12–14, 15/1, 16, 18–20, 22, 27–8, 30, 48–53, 56–62, 63/1, 65, 66/1, 67/1–2, 69/1, 70/1, 71, 72/1 (see p.52), together with 3 other 18th cent. theological works. The books are housed in 2 book-cupboards, each of 2 shelves, one above the other. The upper cupboard has the no. 52 stamped on it and a copy of the ms. cat. pasted inside the door. They are probably original but are not of the same pattern as other surviving Bray book-cupboards.
Catalogues: Catalogue no.52 for 'Brough by the Sands, Cumb.', Bray Associates Records, f.39, pp.193–6; Handlist of 'Burgh by Sands in the vestry' (Bodl.MS.Eng.Misc.c.360, copy in CCC): this would appear to be a mid-19th cent. general library (24v. + 58 RTS tracts, 1820s to 1850s).
References: Nicolson, 1703, pp.15, 20; Kelly, pp.105, 246 & n.1, 261; Barr, p.35; *Library History*, v.1, no.55 (1969), p.170.

BURNHAM DEEPDALE, Norf.
St. Mary. Nor.
[1v.] Norwich CL
DeskL: *Certain Sermons or Homilies*, 1676.

BURNHAM OVERY, Norf.
St. Clement. Nor.
[2v.] Norwich CL
DeskL: Antonius Corvinus, *A Postill or Collection*, 1550; Jewel, *Works*, 1611.

BURNHAM SUTTON, Norf.
St. Ethelbert. Nor.
[1v.] Norwich CL
DeskL: Bible, 1634.

BURTON, Ches.
St. Nicholas. Ches.
[1v.] *
DeskL: Foxe, *Book of Martyrs*, London, Daye, 1562–3, formerly chained to a
Bible desk.
References: Richards, p.84.

BURTON LATIMER, Northants.
St. Mary the Virgin. Pet.
[2v.] 1v. in situ; 1v. in Northants RO. *
DeskL: in 1950 a leather-bound box dated 1615 in the parish chest contained a
copy of a Book of Homilies: the box is retained but not the book; leaves from
an illuminated 14th cent. service book found in the binding of the churchwardens' account book for 1559 are now in the Northampton RO.
References: CCC Questionnaire, 1950.

BURTON-ON-TRENT, Staffs.
St. Modwen. Lich.
[nil]
A ParL of 74v. was est. by the Associates of Dr Bray in 1818; it is not recorded
after 1880.
Catalogues: Bray Associates Records, f.40, pp.21–3.
References: Bray Associates Annual Reports, 1880; Kelly, p.263.

BURWELL, Cambs.
St. Andrew. Ely
[nil] *
A ParL was est. in 1729 by the Bray Trustees for Erecting Parochial Libraries;
it is not recorded after 1880.
References: Bray Associates Annual Reports, 1880; Kelly, p.261 & n.3.

BURY, Lancs. (G.Man.)
St. Mary the Virgin. Man.
[3v.] Bury Grammar School
Henry Bury (d.1638), clerk, at some time before 1634 gave more than 600
vols. 'to certain ffeoffees in trust for the use of Bury parish and the cuntrie
therabouts of ministers also at ther metinge and of schole maisters and others
that seek for learninge and knowledge'. The tradition at Bury in 1705 as
recorded in Notitia Parochialis was that Bury's library passed to, or was
actually intended for, the grammar school which he had founded in 1625 (two
books with Bury's name and one with his initials survive at the school) and
that the best of the books had been stolen in the Civil War. Bury also
bequeathed money to buy books for a library at **Manchester**.
References: Christie, p.139; Notitia Parochialis, 1705: no.219; Kelly, p.76;
Alan Hitch, 'Books in Bury: a history of libraries in Bury, Lancashire, to 1900'
(Library Association, FLA thesis, 1973).

BURY, Lancs. [G.Man.]
St. John. Man.
[nil] *
A ParL of 92 vols. was est. in 1823, and a ParLL of 83 vols. in 1847, augm. in 1870, by the Associates of Dr Bray.
Catalogues: sent in 1824: Bray Associates Records, f.40, pp.107–9; 1847: 'opened for use of clergy of town & neighbourhood, originally a parochial library for use of incumbents of St. John's', Bray Associates Records, f.41, pp.182–5.
References: Kelly, 1966; Shore, p.152; Kelly, p.262.

BURY ST. EDMUNDS, Suffolk
St. James (the Cathedral from 1914) St.E.
[365 titles in 502v.] Suffolk RO, Bury St. Edmunds
The library was est. in 1595 with the gifts of books by Samuel Aylmer (of Mowden Hall, Essex), and by other local laymen and clergy. In a catalogue of 1599 some 133 titles in c. 200 vols. are recorded, and further items were added by gift up to 1764. Most of the titles and 41 donors in this cat. have been identified by J. S. Craig in his 1992 thesis, below. From 1846 to 1865 the library was removed to the Guildhall to form part of the Bury and Suffolk Lib. Sometime after 1865 the books were returned to the church and housed on the north wall of the vestry where they suffered badly from damp. St. James's Church became the Cathedral Church for the newly-formed diocese of St. Edmundsbury and Ipswich in 1914, and the books were first rescued from the damp vestry in 1960, and finally, in 1963, transferred to a library room specially built over the north west porch. Later the collection was deposited in Bury St. Edmund's RO.
This is the largest, earliest, and most valuable of the surviving Suffolk parochial collections. It consists mainly of divinity and Church history, with Greek and Latin strongly represented, and with a good range of miscellanea, e.g. Moses Pitt's *Atlas*, 1680–3, Dodoen's *Herball*, 1578, and Bacon's *Novum Organum*, 1620. There is an impressive range of Fathers, Eastern and Western, and, for a post-Reformation library, surprisingly strong holdings of medieval doctors of the Church, Reformation and Counter Reformation theology. A wide range of European printing presses is represented. There are 5 incunables, 45 STC and 53 Wing books; 7 music MSS; and 2 identified Oxford bindings of the period c. 1515–1620. The four medieval MSS and their provenances have been fully recorded: 1. (a) Bede, Historia Ecclesiastica, etc. c. 1400; (b) Bede, Commentaries on Acts and Catholic Epistles, 13th cent. 2. Cassian, Collationes, 15th cent. 3. Pauline Epistles, glossed, late 12th cent., given in 1639. 4. Medical texts, etc. 12th and 13th cents., partly in Beneventan script, from the Abbey of Bury. Nos. 1–3 were sold at Sotheby's, 12 July 1971 (1. to the Huntington Library, California; 2. to Leyden UL, and 3. to Bibliothèque Royale Albert Ier, Brussels); no.4 was bought by private treaty by the Wellcome Foundation, London.

Catalogues: parchment shelf-list (138 books) of 1599 (Bury RO: FL541/13/1); MS list of 18 books given by Samuel Aylmer, 1599; a parchment catalogue of 1716 (Norfolk RO: DN/MSC/2/38); shelf-list in a paper book of the late 18th cent. (Bury RO: B.87.2, and on microfilm: J528); MS catalogue by C. M. Neale, 1911 (Bury RO: FL541/13/3); F. K. Eagle, *Catalogue of the Library of St. James Church, Bury St Edmunds, now deposited in the Guildhall. Bury St Edmunds*, 1847; Suffolk PLC, 1977 (includes 30v. added in recent years); STC and Wing items are included in CLC, v.1, 1984; and pre-1701 continental items in CLC, v.2–3, 1998.

References: Manuscripts: nos. 3 and 4 are noted briefly in M. R. James, 'On the Abbey of St. Edmund at Bury', *Camb. Antiq. Soc.* Octavo ser. v. 28 (1895), pp.50, 53, 67; and all 4 in Historical Manuscripts Commission, 14th Report, App. pt.8, pp.121–2, pl. I(b); Ker, MMBL, II, 1977, pp.216–17. **General**: Fitch, 1965, pp.44–87 (especially for a detailed account of donors and content); Sears Jayne, *Library Catalogues of the English Renaissance*, 1956, rev. ed. 1963, p.87; *N & Q*, 6 ser. v.2 (1883), p.117; C. M. Neale, in *St. James's Parish Mag.* for 1911, nos. 344–6; Lambeth Palace MS.3221, ff.164–79: rubbings of bindings, photostats of MSS, and provenance notes by N. R. Ker; Ker, Pastedowns, 275, 469; J. S. Craig, 'Reformation politics and polemics in sixteenth century East Anglian market towns', (PhD, Cambridge University, 1992), pp.105–8 and Appendices IV, V and VII; J. S. Craig, 'The Bury Stirs revisited: an analysis of the townsmen', *Proc. of the Suffolk Inst. of Arch and History*, v. 27 (1992), pp.215–16; Read, Supplement, p.159 (for references to the pre-Reformation library); Woolf, pp.192–4.

BUSHEY, Herts.
All Saints. St.Alb.
[?] York UL
A library of 18th cent. (?) books was an heirloom in the rectory until soon after 1943. About half the books, mostly sermons, and many 'damp and dilapidated', were then destroyed, and the rest, largely canon law, were given to the Community of the Resurrection at Mirfield, Yorks., sometime between 1943 and 1950. The Mirfield collection, all pre-1800 books with some later sets of historical Record Society publications, was deposited in York UL on permanent loan in 1973. The Bushey books were not identified at Mirfield and cannot be identified at York. A stray vol. in the Bodl., *Clergyman's Vade-Mecum*, 1723, has inside the cover 'The Rector of Bushey, County of Herts', (Bodl.Vet.A.4.f.453).
References: Lambeth Palace MS.3224: notes by N. R. Ker.

BUSHLEY, Glos.
St. Peter. Worc.
[1v.] *
DeskL: Erasmus, *Paraphrases*, Basel, 16th cent. (? imp.)

CADDINGTON, Beds.
All Saints. St.Alb.
[nil]
In Beds. CRO there is a document with information concerning the removal of a parish library from the church in 1770; the library possibly dated from the time of Mr Bibby, 1702–9, and was probably transferred to London.
References: Beds. CRO: ABC 323–5; H. M. Prescott, *Notes on Caddington Church*, Luton, 1937, p.49.

transf.

CAM, Glos.
St. George. Glouc.
[11v.] Glos. RO
DeskL: 11 vols. including 4 STC items, and 1 Wing item, on temporary deposit in Glos. RO from Aug. 1997.

CAMBRIDGE, Cambs.
St. Benet. Ely
[5v.] *
DeskL: 4 STC items including Jewel's *Apologie*, 1571, and Bibles of 1611 and 1635.

In situ

CAMPSALL, Yorks. (S.Yorks.)
St. Mary Magdalene. Sheff.
[154 items in 121v.]
Founded by the Revd Thomas Cleworth (*c.* 1698–1754), vicar 1702–54, who by a clause in his will of 1749 gave 84 books 'for the use of the minister of the said parish and his successors, and do vest them in Thomas Yarborough of Campsal Esq. & Richard Frank of Campsal and their successors in trust . . . with power to them to agree upon and settle such rules and orders for the purpose afore said as to them shall seem meet'. Cleworth's own catalogue is now lost but some of his books are presumably those referred to in later terriers of the land and property of the church, e.g. those of 1770, 1777, 1786 and 1825. There is no evidence of any additions after 1770 and the library seems to have fallen into disuse until the 1970s. The spines are numbered and the original collection has lost at least 18 vols. and probably numbered *c.* 150 vols. at its largest. The greater part of the library consists of orthodox Anglican theology, Bibles, prayer books and service books, with some works on ecclesiastical history, philosophy, science and literature. Other owners include Thomas Yarborough (d.1772) and Henry Yarborough (d.1774), and members of the Ramsden family.

Catalogues: a 'Catalogue of books in the vestry' is in the terrier of 29 June 1770 (83 titles); a TS list was made in 1959 (copies in Sheffield PL and CCC); Michael Gallico, 'A catalogue of the library of Campsall church' (M.A. Librarianship, U. of Sheffield, 1980): TS (copy in CCC).
References: Venn: Cleworth, Yarborough, Thomas; Foster: Yarborough, Henry; terriers deposited in Doncaster Archives Department; Kelly, p.256; Barr, p.37.

CANNINGTON, Somerset
Blessed Virgin Mary. B & W
[1v.] *
DeskL: Bible, London, Robert Barker, 1617.

CANNOCK, Staffs.
St. Luke. Lich.
[nil] *
A ParLL of 100 vols. was est. in 1812 by the Associates of Dr Bray, and augm. in 1870.
Catalogues: sent in Nov.1812. Bray Associates Records, f.38, pp.248–9.
References: Shore, p.151; Kelly, p.263.

CANON FROME, Heref.
St. James. Heref.
[?] NRC
DeskL: *An Account of the Societies for Reformation in England and Wales*, 5th ed. 1701, with chain, was seen by F. C. Morgan in 1951.
References: CCC Questionnaire, 1950.

CANTERBURY, Kent
St. Andrew (red.?) Cant.
[1v.] Canterbury CL & Archives
DeskL: Erasmus, *Paraphrases*, Edward Whitchurche, 1548.

CANTERBURY, Kent
St. Augustine's College. Cant.
A lending lib. was est. in 1869 by the Associates of Dr Bray. The College library, which also included books from **Smarden**, was closed in 1993. The books were dispersed: some went to Canterbury CL, and to Pusey House, Oxford; others were sold.
References: Shore, p.150.

CANTERBURY, Kent
St. Margaret. Cant.
[2v.] Canterbury CL & Archives
DeskL: Erasmus, *Paraphrases*, 1548; Foxe's *Book of Martyrs*, 1570

CANTERBURY, Kent
St. Mary Breadman. Cant.
[nil]
DeskL: an extensive library is recorded in the Churchwardens' accounts, 4
April 1629, including Foxe's *Book of Martyrs*, Erasmus, *Paraphrases*, 'the
newe booke of Bysshop Jewels', statutes, articles, books of canons, homilies
and prayer books. The church was pulled down just before 1900.
References: accounts, Canterbury Cathedral, CCA U3/2/4/1.

CARBROOKE, Norf.
St. Peter and St. Paul. Nor.
[14v.] Norfolk RO and Norwich CL
DeskL: 7 printed books, including 4 STC items; 4 vellum leaves from a 13th
cent. MS Antiphoner, framed (Norfolk RO); Erasmus, *Paraphrases*, 1548;
Bible, 1541; 1574; 1585; 1611 (Norwich CL).
Miscellaneous documents dating from 1887 to 1912 relating to a parochial
library are also housed in the Norfolk RO.

CARDINGTON, Beds.
St. Mary. St.Alb.
[*c.* 157v.]
The books are housed in a glazed mahogany bookcase in Trinity House (the
old vicarage) bearing the inscription: 'This bookcase with books for parochial
use the gift of Samuel Whitbread [1758–1815] and John Howard [1726?–90],
the philanthropist, stood from 1788 in the vestry of Cardington church . . .'
The books are mainly 18th and 19th cent. theology. Each book in the original
collection has a printed bookplate 'Cardington Library MDCCLXXXVII
The gift of' with the name of the donor added in manuscript. The library is
now administered by Beds. Co.L.
Catalogues: Notes on the library and list of books, etc. Beds. CRO (CRT 130
CAR 28); a list of books in an 1822 terrier was published in *Beds. Hist. Rec.
Soc.*, v. 73 (1986?), pp.163–4; a TS list of 22 titles [pre-1800], 1978 (copy in
CCC).
References: DNB: Howard, Whitbread; DRB2, p.12.

CARLETON RODE, Norf.
All Saints. Nor.
[3v.] Norwich CL *
DeskL: *Certain Sermons or Homilies*, 1635 [1633]; Wolfgang Musculus,
Commonplaces, 1578; John Whitgift, *Defense of the Answere*, 1574. A printed
label exists, reading 'The Lending Library Carleton Rode Rectory', probably
early 19th cent. from the ornaments used. No books survive at the rectory.
References: I am indebted to Brian North Lee for the reference to this label.

CARLISLE, Cumb. (Cumbria)
Dedication not known. Carl.
[36v.] Carlisle CL
A grant of £1 towards the est of a ParLL was awarded by Bray from funds at his disposal, 1695–9. No books from this period survive but 36 vols. from a Clerical LL est. by the Associates of Dr Bray in 1889 (augm. in 1896) have been discovered in the Prescott Library in the Carlisle Diocesan Resources Centre, and are now deposited in Carlisle CL on permanent loan. The Carlisle Bray library incorporated that of **Raughton Head** by 1890 and **Kirkoswald** and **Temple Sowerby** by 1900. Some vols. also have the bookplate of 'The Free Library for the Clergy of the Archdeaconry of Carlisle'.
References: Bray Associates Annual Reports, 1890, 1900; Kelly, pp.106 n.3, 258.

CARTMEL, Lancs. (Cumbria)
St. Mary and St. Michael. Carl.
[334 titles in 335v.] Lancaster UL
The books were mainly bequeathed by Thomas Preston of Holker (*c.* 1648–97) and were to be 'to be placed in the new vestry', built in 1677 in place of the old sacristy. Some 10 vols. of a DeskL, a few with chains, are recorded in an inventory of 8 July 1642 and are still present. Blades reported that there were 294 vols. in his survey of 1890. The collection (apart from some MS and archival material retained at Lancs. RO) was deposited in 1974 in Lancaster UL. There are two incunables, 123 STC, and 58 Wing items in the collection. The books are mainly theological, but there are few puritan writers. Most of the Fathers and great 16th cent. theologians are present, with some books in German, unusual in an English 17th cent. library. The earliest book is Niccolo Falucci, *Sermones*, Venice, 1491. There are 3 identified Oxford bindings, *c.* 1515–1620; a comprehensive provenance index is included in the Taylor / Ramage catalogue, below.
Catalogues: 'A catalogue of books in ye vestry of Cartmel-church given by Tho: Preston of Holkham Esqr.', 1698, was drawn up by John Armstrong (d.1698), vicar of Cartmel, 1665–1698, and transcribed by William Field, 1854 (TS copies in Lambeth Palace MS.3221, ff.180–, and CCC); Sam. Taylor and David Ramage, *The Ancient Library in Cartmel Priory Church*, 2nd ed. enlarged and corrected, Durham, 1959.
References: Venn: Preston; Blades, BIC, p.19; Christie, pp.82–93; Kelly, p.249; Woolf, p.195 & n.86; Ker, Pastedowns, 485, 1589–90; Lambeth Palace MS.3221, ff.180–203: notes and extensive rubbings of bindings by N. R. Ker; some fragments of medieval MSS, notebooks and lists are held in Cumbria RO (Kendal) WPR/89 I67–72.

Castleton: open bookcases

CASTLETON, Derbys.
St. Edmund. Derby
[881 items in 700v.]
A collection made and bequeathed to the church by the Revd Frederick Farran,
vicar 1780–1817, and augm. later by his brother-in-law G. J. Hamilton, the
books being distinguished by their respective engraved bookplates. A brass
plaque in the chancel is inscribed '1819. The books deposited here are a gift to
the parish from the late vicar the Revd F. Farran. They are to be lent at the
discretion of the vicar'. They are housed in a specially built room next to the
vestry, paid for by Farran's sister, Frances Mary, containing glazed cases and

Castleton: a folding eighteenth-century library chair-cum-steps,
as chair; as steps

a handsome folding library chair-cum-steps. There are 100+ STC and Wing
items.   The main part of the collection consists of 18th cent. theology,
doctrinal and controversial books, and pamphlets (there are 30 vols. of bound
pamphlets and sermons). There are also a good number of books on philosophy, history, travel, essays, and biography, and more than 70 vols. of
non-religious works from the first two decades of the 19th century, including
works of general interest, often finely illustrated. There is a borrowers' register
with entries from 1852–87, and a 'Graph to show the number of books
borrowed from Castleton Parish Library for the period 1854–1886'.
Catalogues: 'Farran Collection', a MS catalogue in at least 3 different hands,
n.d. (copies in Lambeth Palace MS.3094, ff.43–85 and CCC); a 'Vestry
catalogue', 1832 (incomplete); Joan E. Friedman, 'Castleton parish library:

the Farran collection' (Catalogue). Sheffield U Postgraduate School of Library & Information Science thesis, 1977.

References: Kelly, p.197; E. D. Mackerness, 'The Castleton parish library', *Jnl of the Derbyshire Arch. and Nat. Hist. Soc.*, v.77 (1957), pp.38–48.

CAVENDISH, Suffolk
St. Mary. St.E.
[2v.] *
DeskL: two-sided wooden lectern on display which formerly held chained copies of Jewel's *Apology*, 16-- on one side, and a Book of Homilies on the other (the books are now kept elsewhere in the church).

CAVERSHAM, Berks.
St. Peter. Ox.
[1v.] Berks. RO
DeskL?: A Protestation Roll, 1641.

CAWTHORNE, Yorks. (S.Yorks.)
All Saints. Wakef.
[nil]
An intact ParL. in 1895 was converted by W. S. Stanhope into a village library, which has now vanished without trace.
References: note by N. R. Ker in Lambeth Palace MS.3221.

CHALFORD, Glos.
Christ Church. Glouc.
[3v.] Glos. RO (transfer to Gloucester CL agreed)
DeskL: 'Brccches' Bible, 1614, and 2 other works on temporary deposit from Aug. 1997.

CHEADLE, Staffs.
St. Giles. Lich.
[nil] *
A ParLL of 111 vols. was est. in 1848 by the Associates of Dr Bray, augm. in 1872 by a library removed from **Draycott-le-Moors** and improved. By 1890 it had been incorporated into **Fenton**.
Catalogues: 'Cheadle, & its vicinity', Bray Associates Records, f.41, pp.206–7.
References: Bray Associates Annual Reports, 1890; Shore, p.151; Kelly, p.263.

CHEDDINGTON, Bucks.
St. Giles. Ox.
[1v.] Bucks. RO, Aylesbury
DeskL: *Certain Sermons or Homilies*, 1623.

CHEDISTON, Suffolk
St. Mary. St.E.
[IV.?] NRC
DeskL: a copy of Erasmus, *Paraphrases*, 1548, is inscribed 'Hic liber appertat ad ecclesiam Chestoni', with the autograph of Thomas Claxton (churchwarden?), and with original brass and leather clasps, and a Tudor rose design on the cover (repaired in 1864; further repairs under consideration).
References: Fitch, 1965, p.47.

CHEDWORTH, Glos.
St. Andrew. Glouc.
[IV.]
DeskL: Geneva Bible, 1583 (and 3 1800–50 service books), reported as in situ in 1997 by Glos. RO.

CHELMSFORD, Essex
St. Mary (from 1913 the Cathedral). Chelmsf.
[581 items in 405v.]

There are now 405 vols. surviving from the library of the Revd John Knightbridge (d.1677), given by his older brother Anthony to St. Mary's Church in 1679 'in usum vicinorum theologorum'. The original press-marks indicate that there are now considerable gaps in the holdings and that there were probably *c.* 600 vols. in the foundation collection. They were housed firstly in a small building on the north side of the church then, after the rebuilding of 1801–3, in a room over the vestry, and finally, by 1882, in a room over the south porch. There have been many later additions to the collection (and from 1901 a separate collection of books from the Associates of Dr Bray and the SPCK). The books are mainly 16th and 17th century theology, with some Patristics and other early books. There is a good collection of bound pamphlets dealing with the revision of the BCP printed in 1661. One Oxford binding of *c.* 1515–1620 has been identified.
Catalogues: MS Index to the library at Chelmsford Church, Essex, 1815; Andrew Clark, 'Knightbridge Library, Chelmsford: catalogue, 1903' (Bodl. MS.Eng.Misc,*c.* 42–3); an author card catalogue; pre-1701 books are included in the CLC, 1984–98.
References: Philip Morant, *The History and Antiquities of the County of Essex*, 1768, p.8; *N & Q*, 6 ser. v. 6 (1882), p.15; Read, Supplement, pp.159–60; Andrew Clark, 'Notes on the Knightbridge pamphlets', *Essex Rev.* v.12 (1903), pp.238–42; A. J. Morley, 'Our cathedral library re-opens', *Essex Churchman*, no.80, Feb.1959, p.[2]; Ker, Pastedowns, 1681a; Martin, pp.28–37; Pilgrim Trust 51st Report, 1981, p.37; DRB2, p.78 (for details of individual books); Notes on Knightbridge Library, including accessions 1901–1934: Essex CRO, Chelmsford, T/P 157/9; DNB: Knightbridge.

CHERTSEY, Surrey
St. Peter with All Saints. Guildf.
[nil]
A catalogue of the library provided *c.* 1731 by Lady Anne Hollis and Lady Blount is in Phillipps MS.31985, which later belonged to Wilfred Merton (unlocated).
References: Lambeth Palace MS.3224 (a letter from A. N. L. Munby to N. R. Ker, 16.9.1959, describing the MS above).

CHESTER, Ches.
St. Mary on the Hill (ded. uncertain). Ches.
[nil]
A ParLL for the Bishop and Archdeacon of Chester was awarded a grant of £10 by Thomas Bray from funds at his disposal, 1695–9. Books from an unrecorded later foundation were returned to the Associates in 1872.
References: Bray Associates Annual Reports, 1872; Kelly, p.258.

CHEW MAGNA, Somerset
St. Andrew. B & W
[2v.] *
DeskL: Jewel, *Defence,* 1560; Bible and Metrical Psalms, 1591.
References: Blades, BIC, p.20; Cox & Harvey, 1907.

CHEW STOKE, Somerset
St. Andrew. B & W
[3v.] *
DeskL: *Annotations upon all the Books of the Old and New Testaments,* 1651 (2 copies); Bible, black letter, James I.

CHEWTON MENDIP, Somerset
St. Mary Magdalene. B & W
[1v.] *
DeskL: Bible, 1611.

CHIPPENHAM, Cambs.
St. Margaret. Ely
[nil]
'A good collection of books in the chapel, at the east end of the south isle' was reported in *c.* 1750.
References: Francis Blomefield, *Collectanea Cantabrigiensia,* 1750, p.194.

CHIPPENHAM, Wilts.
St. Andrew (ded. uncertain). Bris.
[?]
Known only from the Bray Library bookplate in the Franks Collection: no.33848.

CHIPPING SODBURY, Glos.
St. John the Baptist. Glouc.
[nil] *
A ParL was est. in 1852 by the Associates of Dr Bray; it is not recorded after 1900.
References: Bray Associates Annual Reports, 1900; Shore, p.151.

CHIRBURY, Shrops.
St. Michael. Heref.
[194v.] Shrops. RRC
This is probably the oldest Shropshire parochial library, but its origins are obscure. It consists mainly of books bequeathed by Edward Lewis, vicar (d.1677) who asked that they should be placed in the schoolhouse built by him in the churchyard, 'for the use of the schoolmaster or any other of the parishioners who shall desire to read them'. The library was noted in the Notitia Parochialis of 1705. Marton, a hamlet near Chirbury, was the probable birthplace of Thomas Bray and it is perhaps this collection which was granted £1 from funds at his disposal, 1695–9. Shortly before his death in 1730 a proposal was provisionally approved to supplement its resources by the allocation of a Bray parochial library, but there is no evidence that this ever happened. In 1890 207 vols. were recorded by Blades, originally all chained, but by then only 110 vols. retained them, with signs of chaining on the others. They were later kept in the vicarage and subsequently deposited in the Shropshire Records Centre. The books have been described (in a note by N. R. Ker) as 'an intensely protestant collection', and are dated from c. 1530 to c. 1684. Some of the books bear signatures of members of the Herbert family. Three Oxford bindings of the period c. 1515–1620 have been identified.
Catalogues: a list of the books taken 10 Feb.1859 is printed in Wilding, below; a list of the books was printed in a Charity Commissioners Report of 1914; Shrops. PLC, 1971.
References: Foster: Lewis; William Wilding, 'On a library of chained books at Chirbury', *Jnl of the Brit. Arch. Ass.*, v.39 (1883), pp.394–401; Blades, BIC, p.20; Flora Macleod, ' The history of Chirbury', *Trans. of the Shrops. Arch. and Nat. Hist. Soc.*, 3 ser. v.6 (1906), pp.227–376; Notitia Parochialis: no.357; Kelly, pp.80, 82, 252, 259, 260; Streeter, pp.293–4; *N & Q*, 12 ser. v.12 (1923), p.495; Ker, Pastedowns, 814, 1682, 1834; Lambeth Palace MS.3221, ff.209–13: notes and rubbings of bindings by N. R. Ker.

CHISLET, Kent
St. Mary the Virgin. Cant.
[7v.] Canterbury CL & Archives
DeskL: Homilies, 1673, 1726 and 1833 (and 4 books 1800–1850).

CHRISTCHURCH, Hants. (Dorset)
Holy Trinity. Win.
[nil] *
DeskL: in 1907 it was reported that there was 'a library of about 100 chained volumes'.
References: Cox & Harvey, p.334.

CHURCH PULVERBATCH, Shrops.
St. Edith. Heref.
[nil]
A grant of 15s. towards the costs of a ParLL was awarded by Bray from funds at his disposal, 1695–9: (the name in the MS is 'Poulderbatch'). The library founded by Edward Rogers at **Wentnor,** because of the amalgamation of livings, was also lodged here and at **Myndtown** and **Norbury** before return to Wentnor.
References: Kelly, pp.252, 253 n.3, 259; Crockford: now 'Pulverbatch' alone.

CHURCHSTOKE, Mont. (Powys)
St. Nicholas. Heref.
[iv.] *
A grant of £6 towards the cost of a ParL was awarded by Bray from funds at his disposal, 1695–9. Bray's *A Course of Lectures upon the Church Catechism,* vol.1, 1696, still survives.
References: Kelly, p.259.

CIRENCESTER, Glos.
St. John the Baptist. Glouc.
[?] NRC
DeskL: a copy Foxe, *Book of Martyrs,* given by John Chandler in 1632, was noted by Blades as having disappeared at the restoration of the church in 1867; BCP, 1731.
References: Blades, p.20; CCC Questionnaire, 1950.

CLAPTON IN GORDANO, Somerset
St. Michael. B & W
[nil] *
The Clapton in Gordano parish register book includes a notice relating to the founding of a parochial library from the estate of the late Mrs Susanna Colston, 1820, confirming that the books had arrived and had been circulated among the inhabitants of the parish in accordance with the rules.
References: parish register: Somerset RO, D/P/c in g2/1/4.

CLAXTON, Norf.
St. Andrew. Nor.
[1v.] Norwich CL
DeskL: Bible, 1617.

CLIFTON, Westm. (Cumbria)
St. Cuthbert. Carl.
[2v.] Cumbria RO, Kendal
A book label reading, 'Clifton Parish church. Lending Library', probably 19th cent., still survives; there are two copies of the BCP, dated 1770 and 1846, deposited in the Cumbria RO.
References: I am indebted to Brian North Lee for the reference to this book label.

COATES, Glos.
St. Matthew. Glouc.
[3v.] Glos. RO
DeskL: Erasmus, *Paraphrases*, 1551; Jewel, *Works*, 1609; BCP, 1811.

COCKERHAM, Lancs.
St. Michael. Blackb.
[nil]
A ParL of *c.* 9 vols. was est. in 1761 by the Associates of Dr Bray; in 1849 this library was reported as being one of those 'either wholly lost or reduced to a few tattered volumes'.
Catalogues: sent 1762. Bray Associates Records, f.38, p.94.
References: Select Committee Report, 1849.

COCKERMOUTH, Cumb. (Cumbria)
All Saints. Carl.
[nil] *
A ParLL of *c.* 159 vols. was est. by the Associates of Dr Bray in 1762, augm. in 1844 (by 97 vols.), and again in 1870. In 1815 under the management of trustees originally appointed by Edmund Keene (1714–81), Bishop of Chester, the library was enlarged, and by 1849 contained *c.* 500 vols. It is not recorded after 1880.
Catalogues: Bray Associates Records: 1762, f.38, pp.73–8; 1844, f.41, pp.118–20; *c.* 1815: Bodl. Lib. John Johnson Collection.
References: Bray Associates Annual Reports, 1880; Kelly, p.261; Shore, p.151; Charity Commissioners 5th Report, 1857–8, p.52; letter from Paul Kaufman to N. R. Ker, 15 Aug. 1962 (CCC file).

Trans

CODDENHAM, Suffolk
St. Mary St.E.

[325 titles in 365v.] Suffolk RO, Ipswich

The collection was formed by Balthazar Gardemau (c. 1656–1739), born in Poitiers, vicar at Coddenham, 1689–1739, and was given by his successor John Bacon (who added 12 vols.) to Basil Bacon of the Inner Temple, his executors and administrators in trust. The trust deed dated 30 Dec. 1767 endorsed 'The Revd Mr Bacon's gift of the books in Coddenham vicarage house in trust for the use of the vicar'. The books were kept in the vicarage until it was sold in 1964 when they were transferred on permanent loan to Bury St Edmund's Cathedral Library, and finally to Suffolk RO, Ipswich. The portrait of Gardemau, formerly in the vicarage, was removed to the church vestry. The collection reflects Gardemau's Huguenot origin, and includes c. 50 vols. of French protestant and Catholic theology. There are 3 STC and 175 Wing items, and c. 100 'controversial tracts', c. 1685–7, but most books are dated c. 1670 to 1800. The contents, and provenances, are described in detail in Canon Fitch's article, below.

Catalogues: an imperfect MS catalogue was made by Nicholas Bacon in 1780 (Suffolk RO, Ipswich: 50/19/4.7(10)); a list was made by the Revd Walter Wyles (rector, 1890–1930) in c. 1902; MS catalogues were made by Canon J. A. Fitch in 1962 and 1986 (copies in Lambeth Palace MS.3221, ff.215–, and CCC); Suffolk PLC, 1977.

References: the trust deed, and a letter on the books in the library, 1744, are in the Suffolk RO, Ipswich (HA 24 50/19/23, and HA 24 50/19/4.7); Fitch, 1965, pp.77–83; Kelly, p.253; Canon J. A. Fitch, 'Balhasar Gardemau: a Huguenot squarson and his library', _Proc. Huguenot Soc. of London_, v. 20 (1968), pp.241–72; DRB2, p.549.

COFTON HACKETT, Worcs.
St. Michael. Birm.

[2v.] *

DeskL: Great Bible, 1539; BCP, 1752 (with Companion to the altar, 1782, and Metrical Psalms, 1783).

COLCHESTER, Essex
St. Mary. Chelmsf.

[1v.]

A 13th cent. Bible belonged to a 15th cent. rector, William Kettell. It was bought for the church at Sotheby's 29 Nov. 1949, lot.1. The personal library of Samuel Harsnett (1561–1631), Archbishop of York, while for the use of 'the clergie of the towne . . . and other divines', was in fact bequeathed to 'the bayliffes and incorporacn of the towne' and was never a parochial library.

References: Ker. MMBL, II, 1977, pp.409–10; in Gordon Goodwin, _A Catalogue of the Harsnett Library at Colchester_, 1888; DRB2, p.79; DNB: Harsnett.

COLEORTON, Leics.
St. Mary the Virgin. Leic.
[*c.* 500v.] Coalville PL; Southfield PL
A collection of *c.* 500 vols. was given by William Hunt (b. *c.* 1677), rector
1700–1727. In *c.* 1957 it was transferred from the rectory to Church House,
Leicester; at a later date it was deposited on permanent loan in Leics. Co.L.,
and finally transferred to Coalville PL; *c.* 20–30 vols. in poor condition were
removed to Southfield PL.
Catalogues: a loose leaf catalogue was compiled by Loughborough College
Library students in the 1960s (copy with the collection).
References: Venn: Hunt; Lambeth Palace MS.3221, ff.242–3: notes on provenance and rubbings of bindings by N. R. Ker.

COLESHILL, Warwicks.
St. Peter and St. Paul. Birm.
[2v.] Warwicks. CRO
DeskL: 2 works by John Kettlewell (1653–95), vicar 1682–90: *A Funeral
Sermon for . . . Lady Frances Digby*, 1684, and *A Sermon . . . Death of Simon
Lord Digby*, 1686. A grant of £5 towards the cost of a ParLL was made by
Bray from funds at his disposal, 1695–9. However, 'the lending or publick
library of Coleshill', to which Bray bequeathed 31 vols. of Aquinas and
Lorinus in 1730, was that founded by William, 5th Lord Digby (1661–1752) in
1698. Digby initially gave 'twenty pounds to buy books; besides all materials
& workmanship of a large frame wth. shelves on wch. the said books might be
conveniently plac'd'. The catalogue of 1698 (see below) includes 9 'Rules for
the lending library in the town of Coleshill founded by the Right Honble. Wm.
Ld. Digby Ano. Dni. 1698 & enlarged by severall benefactions from the
gentry & clergy'. Rule 2 states that all clergymen in the Hundred of
Hemingford could borrow, but laymen only if they had subscribed in some
way. Several undated and incomplete 18th cent. catalogues are included in the
document: the first lists 171 vols., those which are dated are mainly 17th cent.
There is no evidence as to where the library was originally housed. Certainly
by the 1830s it was in Coleshill Grammar School where a ms. catalogue
(undated) was produced listing 441 titles. A letter in the Coleshill Grammar
School Records of 21 Oct. 1833 on behalf of the Charity Commissioners draws
attention to the 'many valuable books' in the library with recommendations
that they be 'placed in cases at one end of the Upper School room where they
would be accessible at convenient times to such gentlemen of the town &
neighbourhood as the Trustees might allow to have access to them', strongly
implying that they were in a neglected state. The books were eventually
relegated to a cellar, and finally, on the authority of the Trustees, sold at
auction in *c.* 1909. The 1698 catalogue lists the early subscribers or donors of
books to the library including Thomas Bray, Sir William Dugdale (1605–86),
and, notably, Edward Maynard (1654–1740), 'a worthy friend to the library,
for he not only took extraordinary pains to lay out ye much greater part of

such moneys as were given by the several benefactors upon very choice books which he procured at very cheap rates, but he also gave . . . these following books . . .'.

Catalogues: 1698 cat. Warwicks. CRO, CR 1740; 'A catalogue of books in the library of Coleshill, Warwickshire', n.d. Warwicks. CRO, Coleshill Grammar School records, H2/220.

References: Smith, p.58; Kelly, pp.254 & n.4, 259; letter, 1833: Warwicks. CRO, Coleshill Grammar School records, H2/212/1; *Birmingham Daily Mail*, 8 Sept. 1909, 'Romance of an old library' (also in *The Coleshill Chronicle and Nuneaton Standard*, 11 Sept. 1909); DNB: Digby, Kettlewell, Dugdale, Maynard.

COLLINGTREE, Northants.
St. Columba. Pet.
[4v.] *
DeskL: Erasmus, *Paraphrases*: autograph of William Smyth, rector, 1578; Jewel, *Defence*, 1567; *Homilies*, 1623; BCP, 1700.

COLTON, Westm. (Cumbria)
Holy Trinity. Car.
[1v.] Cumbria RO, Barrow
DeskL: Bishops' Bible, 1577.

COMPTON, Surrey
St. Nicholas. Guildf.
[nil]
Charles Kerry recorded in *c.* 1870 that 'the remains of an old library were preserved in the upper story of the church', before its restoration; at that time the larger books had been lost but *c.* 30 smaller books in very poor condition were kept at the rectory, including J. Mollerus, *Fasciculus Remediorum*, Basel, 1579; *Dormi Secure*, and a book which had belonged to Edward Fulham (*c.* 1608–94), of Eastbury Manor, in the 17th cent.
References: Derby PL, Kerry MSS, v.2, p.136 (reference supplied by T. E. C. Walker in 1950); Foster: Fulham.

CONISTON, Lancs. (Cumbria)
St. Andrew. Carl.
[1v.] *
DeskL: BCP, 17th cent. Roger Fleming of Coniston Hall gave money in 1699 and bequeathed money in 1703, out of which 8s. 4d. was set aside annually for buying books. In 1885 there were *c.* 100 books which 'are, or were formerly, lent out at Easter to any of the inhabitants who wished to read them'. Some 133 vols. were listed in a terrier of 1778. The books were destroyed, probably in 1957, as being dirty and unread.
References: Christie, pp.95–6; Charity Commissioners, 3rd Report (1820), p.224; Lancs. RO, Preston: Ulverston terrier, 1778 (DRC/3).

CORBRIDGE, Northumb.
St. Andrew. New.
[nil] *
12 books of divinity and 7 prayer books were sent by Mrs Alice Colpitts of Newcastle in 1729 'to be put in the church for the use of the parishioners in common for every person'. The books were listed in the parish register. Corbridge was one of 92 parishes in the Northumberland Archdeaconry granted a ParLL under a scheme devised by Bishop Shute Barrington, carried out by Archdeacon R. G. Bouyer by 1823 (see p.57), and recorded as still possessing books in visitation returns, 1826–8.
Catalogues: list of books donated to Corbridge parish, 1729 (Northumb. RO: EP57/2).
References: *N & Q*, v.10 (1854), p.213; *History of Northumberland*, v.10, The parish of Corbridge, by H. H. E. Craster, 1914, p.217; Day, pp.95–6, 102 n.38.

CORBRIDGE DEANERY, Northumb.
Diocese of Newcastle
A grant of £1. 10s. towards the est. of a LL was awarded by Bray from funds at his disposal, 1695–9.
References: Kelly, p.259.

CORNHILL, Northumb.
St. Helen Newc.
[nil ?] NRC
One of 92 parishes in the Northumberland Archdeaconry granted a ParLL under a scheme devised by Bishop Shute Barrington, carried out by Archdeacon R. G. Bouyer by 1823 (see p.57), and recorded as still possessing books in visitation returns, 1826–8. In 1858 'a parochial lending library at the rectory' was listed.
References: Day, pp.102 n.38, 103; Post Office Directory, 1858.

CORSTON, Somerset
All Saints. B & W
[nil]
A ParL of 67 vols. was est. in 1710 by the Bray Trustees for the Erection of Parochial Libraries. The books were returned to the Associates of Dr Bray in 1869 at the request of the Secretary, but reluctantly.
Catalogues: no. 28, Bray Associates Records, f.39, pp.29–32; a catalogue of the library founded in 1710, with additonal entries in 1861 (Somerset RO: D/P/cors 23/1).
References: correspondence on the return of the books is entered in the original Library Register (kept at Corston in 1959, but no longer to be found), and in the Bray Associates Records; Kelly, p.263.

COSTOCK, Notts.
St. Giles. S'well
[nil]
In his will proved 20 May 1702, the Revd Thomas Townsend (d.1701) bequeathed 'to my successor the Rector of Cosstock & his successors the rectors of Cosstock for ever. All my books (except manuscripts) together with ye fine deale press or case belonging to them'. The catalogue of books in the same document lists *c.* 309 vols. Henry Twisden, Townsend's successor records the same details in Notitia Parochialis, 1705, adding that 3 catalogues should be made, one for the Archiepiscopal Registry in York, one for the Archidiaconal Registry in Nottingham, and one for the patrons of the church; he also notes that books 'with ye press wch contains yem' were then in his possession. By 1877 the library was no longer to be found.
Catalogues: Archiepiscopal catalogue: 'Catalogue of the books of the Reverend Mr Thomas Townsend late Rector of Codlingstock', Borthwick Institute, Bp. C & P. I/24 (copy in CCC).
References: Notitia Parochialis, no.641; J. T. Godfrey, *Notes on the Churches of Nottinghamshire, Hundred of Rushcliffe*, 1887, p.71; Kelly, p.251; the cat. is analysed in Woolf, pp.192–3.

COVENTRY, Warwicks.
Holy Trinity. Cov.
[3v.] *
DeskL: Bible, 1568; BCP, 1715; BCP, 1727–51. The library, founded 1602 in the Grammar School, was sold in 1908. A grant of £1 towards the est. of a ParLL was awarded by Bray from funds at his disposal 1695–9. No vols. survive from a ParLL est. in 1874 by the Associates of Dr Bray.
References: Shore, p.153; Kelly, pp.106 & n.3, 259.

COXWOLD, Yorks. (N. Yorks.)
St. Michael. York
[1+v.] *
DeskL: Geneva Bible, 1560, and other old Bibles and prayer books.

CRADLEY, Worcs. (W. Mids.)
St. Peter. Worc.
[nil] *
A ParL of 157 vols. was est. by the Associates of Dr Bray in 1823. The patron of the living is the Rector of Halesowen, Worcs.
Catalogues: Cradley ['Cradleigh' in the index], Halesowen. 1823. Bray Associates Records, f.40, pp.83–6.

CRANFIELD, Beds.
St. Peter and St. Paul. St.Alb.
[nil]
A terrier of 1715 records 'a small parochial library'.
References: Terrier, 1715: Beds. CRO.

CRANWICH, Norf.
St. Mary. Nor.
[1v.] Norwich CL
DeskL: Bible, 1659.

CREDITON, Devon
Holy Cross. Ex.
[*c.* 1,000v. & 2,000 pamphlets] Exeter UL
John Grandisson (1292?–1369), Bishop of Exeter, in his will divided his extensive library principally between his Chapter and the collegiate churches of **Ottery**, Crediton and Boseham [Bosham], and Exeter College, Oxford. However most of the extant books were bequeathed to the Governors of the church by Thomas Ley (b. *c.* 1635), vicar 1689–1721, for the use of his successors. There have been few additions since 1721. They were deposited in Exeter UL on permanent loan in 1968. The books are mostly 16th and 17th cent. together with 3 incunables. They include first or early editions of Chaucer, Bacon, More, Milton, Donne and Clarendon, Bibles and early maps. A small quarto contains 16 items printed in London by Richard Pynson between 1520 and 1524 of which 13 are otherwise unknown editions. The pamphlets consist mainly of early 18th cent. works on theology, politics and history . The books were repaired in 1950 by grant aid; there are a number of interesting bindings, and one identified Oxford binding of the period *c.* 1515–1620.
Catalogues: a full catalogue was made by Edmund Tompkins in 1926; card catalogue by Margaret S. G. McLeod (née Hands), 1949; 'An inventory of goods belonging to the parish church at Crediton 1559', *Devon & Cornwall N & Q*, v. 32, no.1 (1971), pp.15–17 (lists 20 liturgical books); Exeter UL OPAC.
References: Foster: Ley; Pilgrim Trust 20th Report, 1950, pp.36–7; Ker, Pastedowns, 183; Kelly, pp.91 n.4, 246; DRB2, p.59.

CREWKERNE, Somerset
St. Bartholomew. B & W
[nil] *
A ParL was est. in 1890, formerly at **Ilminster** (1848), by the Associates of Dr Bray.
References: Bray Associates Annual Report, 1890.

CROFTON, Hants.
Holy Rood. Portsm.
[2v.] Portsmouth City RO
DeskL: BCP, 1794; Bible, 1825.

CROMHALL, Glos.
St. Andrew. Glouc.
[2v.] Glos. RO (temporary deposit, probable transfer to Gloucester CL)
DeskL: Erasmus, *Paraphrases*, n.d. 'presented to the church by order of
Dowager Queen Katherine Parr;' Bible, Novum Testamentum, 1814.
References: CCC Questionnaire, 1950.

CRONDALL, Surrey
All Saints. Guildf.
[1v.]
DeskL: John Jewel, *Apologia*, 17th cent. [could be part of *Works*].
References: NADFAS Report.

CROOK, Westm. (Cumbria)
St. Catherine. Carl.
[nil] *
A ParL of 25 vols. was est. by the Associates of Dr Bray in 1757; it is not
recorded after 1880.
Catalogues: in parish of Kirkby Kendal, Bray Associates Records, f.38, p.45.
References: Bray Associates Annual Reports, 1880; Kelly, p.263.

CROSBY GARRETT, Westm. (Cumbria)
St. Andrew. Carl.
[nil] *
In 1703 Bishop Nicolson reported from his visitation that there were 'some
other books in their chest (as Perkins's *Works* in three voll. &c) which have
been given for ye public use of the parishioners'.
References: Nicolson, 1703, p.41.

CROSBY-ON-EDEN, Cumb. (Cumbria)
St. John the Evangelist. Carl.
[nil]
One of the 10 parishes in the diocese of Carlisle given 16 books in 1687 under
the will of Barnabas Oley (see pp.34–5 and table on pp.444–52).
References: Nicolson, v.8, pp.105–6; Kelly, p.246 & n.1.

CROSBY RAVENSWORTH, Westm. (Cumbria)
St. Lawrence. Carl.
[44v.] Carlisle CL
One of the 10 parishes in the diocese of Carlisle given 16 books in 1687 under

the will of Barnabas Oley (see pp.34–5 and table on pp.444–52). Bishop Nicolson was assured of their safe-keeping in the hand of the vicar at his visitation in 1703. They were reported as missing in 1959, but 11 vols. were discovered in 1993 and deposited in Carlisle CL: nos. 1–2 (Jackson, v.1–2), 1 (Hammond, v.1), 4 (Towerson), 5–7, 9–11 and 13. There are also 19 18th cent. and 14 20th cent. vols. of theology added later.
References: Nicolson, 1703, p.77; Kelly, pp.105, 255 & n.3.

CROSSCRAKE, Westm. (Cumbria)
St. Thomas. Carl.
[nil] *
A ParLL of *c.* 20 vols. was est. in 1761 by the Associates of Dr Bray; in 1849 this library was one of those reported as being 'either wholly lost or reduced to a few tattered volumes'.
Catalogues: 'In the parish of Haversham', Bray Associates Records, f.38, p.86.
References: Select Committee Report, 1849; Kelly, p.263 (as 'Croscake').

CROSTHWAITE, Cumb. (Cumbria)
St. Kentigern (ded. uncertain). Carl.
[nil] *
In Notitia Parochialis, 1705, the incumbent reported 'no library belonging to it, only Josephus works Greek and Latin were bestow'd upon me for my life & afterwards upon my successors at Crosthwaite for ever by one Mr Appleford [Robert Appleford, 1674–1701] late Fellow of St. John's College in Cambridge'. A ParL was est. in 1786 by the Associates of Dr Bray, and augm. in 1872.
References: Notitia Parochialis: no.1182; Kelly, p.261; Venn: Appleford.

CROWMARSH GIFFORD, Bucks.
St. Mary Magdalene. Ox.
[2v.] Berks. RO
DeskL: *Certain Sermons or Homilies*, 1673; *Act for Burying in Woollen*, 1678; and one page from a 1572 Bible.

CRUNDALE, Kent
St. Mary the Blessed Virgin. Cant.
[*c.* 2261 titles in 934v.] Wye College, Ashford (Imperial College, Wye)
The Revd Richard Forster (*c.* 1651–1728/9), rector of Crundale, 1698–1729, in his will dated 15 Nov. 1728 bequeathed his library 'as a parochial library under the protection of the statute of ye seventh year of Queen Ann for the use of all succeeding rectors', that is under the provisions of the 1709 Act. The books were kept at first 'in the study or library of the parsonage house'; they were moved to Godmersham vicarage when the parishes were united, and finally in 1976 were deposited in Wye College, Ashford, Kent. Some books were added by Samuel Pegge (*c.* 1705–96), vicar of Godmersham, 1731–51.

The books reveal Forster's wide interests. In addition to 17th cent. theology and history, especially the Revolution of 1688-9, there are editions of the early Fathers in both Greek and Latin, small collections on mathematics and science, and text-books from his time in Oxford. Most of the books bear his signature, and many have a note of price and sometimes date of purchase. The historical books recorded in Drayton's cat. of 1734 are listed in Woolf, below. A recently discovered Borrowers' Register, covering the years 1729-72, records loans by the incumbent of 81 vols. mainly between 1729 and 1737 to the residents of Crundale and neighbouring villages.

Catalogues: A catalogue of the books present when Silas Drayton [d.1767] was rector of Crundale, 1729 (Canterbury CL Archives, Diocesan records, DCb/J/Y31/; microfilm in Bodl.); 'A copy of a catalogue of books, left by the Reverend Richard Forster, MA, rector of Crundale, to his successors in the said living, for ever; taken and presented to Sr. Edward Filmer of East-Sutton, Bart. Patron of the said living, by me Silas Drayton rector of Crundale AD 1734'. with valuations and a letter (5 Oct. 1734) from Drayton to Filmer: Houghton Lib. MS.f.Eng.789 (MS.Eng.790 is an autograph cat. of the books in Filmer's study taken by him in Nov.1708); Sir Edward Filmer was b. *c.* 1683 and d. in 1705; a catalogue made in 1751 is with the collection (microfilm in Canterbury CL Archives). In the 1729 catalogue there is a pencil total of 940 vols.; in both Canterbury catalogues the absence of Lewis's *History of Faversham Abbey* is noted; a computerised catalogue is in Canterbury CL. The Borrowers' Register is with the collection.

References: Foster: Filmer, Forster; Venn: Drayton, Pegge; Forster's will is in the Canterbury Diocesan Records: PRC17/87, f.14; David Shaw and Mary Lucas, 'The Crundale rectorial library', *Univ. of London Library Resources Co-ordinating Committee Libraries Bulletin*, no.35 (1985), pp.23-4; Yates, 1983, pp.162-3; Sarah Gray and Chris Baggs, 'The English parish library: a celebration', *Libraries & Culture*, v.35 (2000), no.3, pp.423-4; Woolf, pp.184-7 & n.64.

CUBLINGTON, Bucks.
St. Nicholas. Ox.
[6v.] *
DeskL: Bible, 1634 (?); Foxe, *Book of Martyrs*, 1634, 3 vols. (trace of chains); Henry Hammond, *A Paraphrases and Annotations upon all the Books of the New Testament*, 2nd ed, 1659; BCP, Oxford, 1822.

CUDDESDON, Oxon.
All Saints. Ox.
[nil] *
A ParL was est. in 1854 by the Associates of Dr Bray, and augm. in 1872 and 1878.
References: Shore, p.152; Bray Associates Annual Reports, 1880.

CUDWORTH, Somerset
St. Michael. B & W
[nil]
Nothing is known of those books willed by Richard Busby (1606–95) 'to be set apart for the use of the minister of . . . Cudworth . . . and . . . successors . . . to be sent by my executors to the Dean and Chapter of Wells for the use and benefit of the minister . . . giving security . . . for the preservation of them to posterity'. Busby also left books to **Martock** and **Willen**.
References: G. F. R. Barker, *Memoir of Richard Busby*, 1895, p.143; Kelly, p.253.

CUMNOR, Oxon.
St. Michael. Oxf.
[1v.] *
DeskL: Bible, 1611, chained. In Archdeacon Onslow's visitation book, 1786, there is a reference to a Dr Bachelor who 'left five pounds per annum for ever to this parish to purchase books for the use of the poor'.
References: Blades, BIC, p.21; visitation book: Berks. RO: D/EX 1324/1, f.75v.

DACRE, Cumb. (Cumbria)
St. Andrew. Carl.
[1v.] *
DeskL: Bible, 1617, chained

DALSTON, Cumb. (Cumbria)
St. Michael. Carl.
[nil]
One of the 10 parishes in the diocese of Carlisle given 16 books in 1687 under the will of Barnabas Oley (see pp.34–5 and table on pp.444–52). They were all present 'in good order' when Bishop Nicolson visited in 1703; in 1959 there were 9 books remaining in the vicarage: 2 vols. of Hammond and nos. 5–7 and 9–11; also, Richard Fiddes, *Theologica Practica*, 1720; these were still present in the vestry in 1970, but can no longer be found.
References: Nicolson, 1703, p.20; Bill Report, 1970; Barr, p.36.

DALTON, Lancs.
St. Michael and All Angels. Liv.
[nil]
A ParL of 36 vols. was est. in 1757 by the Associates of Dr Bray; a document of 1770 records that Dr Stratford's executors gave books in 1766 which were kept in a bookcase in the chancel.
Catalogues: Bray Associates Records, f.38, p.37.
References: document: Preston RO, DRr/3 (1770); Kelly, p.262.

DARFIELD, Staffs.
All Saints. Sheff.
[2v.] *
DeskL: 2 Books of Homilies, imp. n.d., with chains.

DARLINGTON, Durham
St. Cuthbert. Dur.
[49v.] *
A ParL of 72 vols. was est. in 1711 by the Bray Trustees for erecting Parochial Libraries. The books were reported missing in 1849, but some 49 vols. still remain (nos. 1, 3–10, 12–14, 16–25, 27, 31, 33–34, 42–46, 48, 50, 52–55, 58, 60, 63–65, 68), including the Register, no.9 (see p.48). Now added to this collection are *c.* 12 17th and early 18th cent. books, and a collection of books on local history. They are housed in a bookcase in the N. transept, the door of which forms a memorial panel to the Royal Signals. The books date from 1679 to the early 1700s.
Catalogues: Bray Associates Records, f.39, pp.161–4; Durham Diocesan Records, glebe terriers 1/23, Darlington St. Cuthbert 1806, gives a list of books deposited in 1709 [sic] with a note of their values and details of those remaining and those missing in 1806; a TS catalogue made by Darlington PL is in Lambeth Palace, MS.3094, ff.94–8 (copy in CCC); a new card card catalogue is in preparation.
References: Select Committee Report, 1849; Kelly, p.261 & n.4; Bill Report, 1970.

DARTON, Yorks. (S.Yorks.)
All Saints. Wakef.
[2v.] *
DeskL: Henry More, *Works*, 1708 (presented by Sir Thomas Wentworth); *Book of Homilies*, 1756, with chain.
References: Bill Report, 1970; letter from John Addy, 1969 (in CCC file).

DAVENTRY, Northants.
Holy Cross. Pet.
[*c.* 96 titles in *c.* 118v.]
In 1869 a catalogue was made of 62 titles in 84 vols. at Daventry, mainly ecclesiastical, theological and historical books, dating from *c.* 1590 to *c.* 1689. This catalogue was seen by Neil Ker in 1963 but can no longer be found. The books, save for no.15 in the catalogue, were all present in 1963. From the spine labels there are now 52 titles in 64 vols. surviving from the original collection, including 2 STC, 15 Wing, 6 16th cent. continental, and 27 17th cent. continental books. A number of them have on the title-page, 'Liber Bibliothecæ Daventriensis. Ex dono reverendi admodum et vere docti viri Edvardi Maynard DD Rectoris de Bodington in Com: Northton.', and it seems likely that most of the books were the gift of Edward Maynard (1654–

Daventry: an open eighteenth-century book-cupboard in the north aisle,
normally concealed by a curtain

1740), the antiquary, born at Daventry, and rector of Boddington, where he is buried. He also gave a number of books to **Coleshill**, and some vols. of tracts relating to 17th cent. theological controversies to Magdalen College, Oxford, where he was demy and bursar, 1678–88. The collection is housed in a concealed cupboard at the E. end of the N. aisle behind a red curtain. All the books are in their original bindings, but some have new endpapers, probably made in the 1860s when MS fragments were removed, paper labels with nos. and titles were added to the spines, and the catalogue was completed. Some Oxford bindings, *c.* 1515–1620 have been identified. The additional books now included in the collection are late 18th and early 19th cent. service books and historical works transferred from St. James's, a chapel of ease, to Holy Cross from 1840 (now demolished).

Catalogues: 1869, now lost; a recent TS shelf-list (copies with the collection and in CCC).

References: Kelly, p.251; Bill Report, 1970; DRB2, 1997, p.460 (Magdalen books); Ker, Pastedowns, 640, 661, 664, 688, ccxiii; Pearson 487.1, 675.1, A207.3; Lambeth Palace MSS 3221, ff.252–8, & 3224: notes on provenance and bindings, with rubbings, by N. R. Ker.

DEAL, Kent
St. Leonard. Cant.
[nil]
A ParLL assisted by funds of £2.10s at Bray's disposal, 1695–9, laid the foundation 'of a like library as at Gravesend and left them with the printed form for taking subscriptions towards its enlargement. Together with the rules for the use & preservation of the books'. Bray had begun his journey to Maryland at **Gravesend** and continued to **Plymouth**.

References: George Smith, 'Dr Thomas Bray', *LAR*, 12 (1910), p.250 (quoting from a Bray MS diary letter from Sion College, sold at Sotheby's, 13 June 1977, lot 76); Kelly, pp.106, 258. I am indebted to Dr D. J. McKitterick for the Sotheby reference.

DEARHAM, Cumb. (Cumbria)
St. Mungo. Carl.
[nil]
One of the 10 parishes in the diocese of Carlisle given 16 books in 1687 under the will of Barnabas Oley (see pp.34–5 and table on pp.444–52).

References: Kelly, p.246 & n.1.

DEDHAM, Essex
St. Mary the Virgin. Chelmsf.
[*c.* 150v.]
The library of 2,000v. left by William Burkitt (1650–1703), vicar and lecturer 1692–1703, has not survived, but some of his books in various editions are in the present collection, formed probably by Canon G. H. Rendall (1851–1945),

Dedham: part of a modern bookcase

who lived at Dedham after his retirement as Headmaster of Charterhouse in 1911. His library was moved to the church in *c.* 1938. There are *c.* 9 17th and 12 18th century items, and the remainder are pre-1850; as well as Bibles, commentaries, prayer books and theology, there is a collection of Essex books, pamphlets and periodicals. Rendall's book label occurs in some vols. and also that of Allyn Simmons.

Catalogues: partial TS list of pre-1800 items in CCC.
References: *N & Q*, v.6 ser. 7 (1883), p.117; DRB2, p.80.

DENCHWORTH, Berks.
St. James. ~~Ox.~~
[150v.] Worcester College, Oxford; iv. in situ

The library was begun in 1693 by Ralph Kedden (b. *c.* 1665), vicar 1691–1720, and Gregory Geering (b. *c.* 1664), patron, churchwarden, and owner of the chief manor in the parish, when a room was built over the porch to house the books, all then chained to the shelves. After the restoration of the church in 1852 by G. E. Street the then vicar, E. Horton, removed the books to the vicarage and stripped them of their chains, except for two kept as specimens. Inscriptions and bookplates in the books record that most of them were given by Geering ('to the use of the vicar and his successors . . . for ever'), Edward Brewster, 'Citizen and Stationer of the City of London', and Kedden, 'to his successors . . . for ever'. In July 1828 Archdeacon John Fisher noted 140 vols.; in the 1875 catalogue there were 147 vols. One of the most valuable books, a copy of Caxton's edition of *The Golden Legend*, was sold by an 'erring vicar' in 1843 to Parker, the Oxford bookseller, who in turn sold it to the Bodl. for £20 (it is now at shelfmark Arch.G.b.2). In 1961 the books were deposited on permanent loan at Worcester College, Oxford, with the exception of the Cranmer Bible, [1541?], retained at St. James's Church. Most of the books are in English, and they are all 17th cent. (including *c.* 26 STC items) save for a few 19th and 20th cent. books, and, *Homiliarius Doctorum*, Basel, 1505. The donors, all noted in Tomlinson's catalogue, below, include: Thomas Wilkinson, Richard Hooker (1554?–1600), William Juxon (1582–1663) and Gilbert Burnet (1643–1715). There are some early bindings, including an identified Oxford binding, *c.* 1515–1620, a binding with a fishtail stamp (Oldham 157) and one by Garrett Godfrey.
Catalogues: C. H. Tomlinson, The vicar's library at Denchworth. Supplement to the Denchworth Annual, Wantage, 1875, pp.2–18 (copy in CCC).
References: Foster: Kedden, Geering, Fisher; Notitia Parochialis, 1705: no.1244; visitation book: Berks. RO: D/EX 1324/1, f.55v.; Blades, BIC, p.21; *N & Q* v.6 ser. 4 (1881), p.304; De Ricci, *Census of Caxtons*, p.102; DNB: Hooker, Juxon, Burnet; Lambeth Palace MS.3221: notes on provenance and bindings with rubbings by N. R. Ker; Ker, Pastedowns, 32 & n.1; Plomer, Dictionary: Brewster.

DENT, Yorks. (Cumbria)
St. Andrew. Bradf.
[10v.] Bradford CL
A collection of 25 vols. was given by William Stratford (d.1753), commissary
to the Archdeaconry of Richmond, as listed in terriers of 1788 and 1789. Three
vols. were inscribed as being given in 1754, another, with Stratford's armorial
bookplate, has a MS note 'To the curate of Dent and his successors. Feb.14
1759'. In 1965 Thomas Kelly saw the 9 remaining vols. and these, with one
other vol., were deposited in Bradford CL.
They are mainly 18th cent. theology.
Catalogues: list of 25 vols. in Lambeth Palace MS.3221.
References: Leeds District Archives: Glebe terriers 1778, 1789, 1811; Cæsar
Caine and W. G. Collingwood, 'Dr William Stratford, the benefactor', *Cumb.
and Westm. Antiq. Soc. Trans.* NS 26 (1924), pp.63–76; Kelly, p.256; Barr,
p.37.

DEPTFORD, Kent (G.Lon.)
St. Nicholas. S'wark
[nil ?] NRC
A ParL of 152v. was est. in 1832 by the Associates of Dr Bray.
Catalogues: 1833, Bray Associates Records, f.40, pp.225–7.

DERBY, Derbys.
All Saints (from 1923–4 the Cathedral). Derby
[nil]
There was a small collection of books in All Saints' Church in the 16th cent.
References: Cox, Notes, v.4, p.85; J. C. Cox and W. H. St. J. Hope, *Annals of
the Collegiate Church of All Saints*, 1881, p.175: a list of 10 books chained in
the Lady Chapel *c.* 1527; Read, Supplement, p.160.

DERBY, Derbys.
Holy Trinity. Derby
[nil] *
A lending lib. was in existence at least from 1849 to 1855.
Catalogues: 1849 and 1855. Derby Central PL: BA.027.3 / B732, 13733.

DERBY, Derbys.
St. John the Evangelist. Derby
[nil]
A library existed in the parsonage until 1857, when it was sold at auction.
Catalogues: Catalogue of books at St. John's parsonage to be sold by auction,
1857. Derby Central PL: BA.027.3 / 13750.

DERBY, Derbys.
St. Peter. Derby
[nil] *
A ParLL was est. in 1850 according to a surviving cat.
Catalogues: Catalogue of books, n.d. Derby Central PL: BA.027.3 / 13736.

DETLING, Kent
St. Martin. Cant.
[nil]
A ParL of 72v. was est. in 1710 by the Bray Trustees for Erecting Parochial
Libraries. The books were allegedly sold for £1 in c. 1875.
Catalogues: MS. no.2. 'Debtling', Bray Associates Records, f.39, pp.69–72; 'A
catalogue of the Parochial Library at Debtling', 1730, Canterbury Cathedral
MS.Y.4.30, pp.141–3; a copy of a MS shelflist signed 'John Russell, Vicar of
Debtling, 16 Nov. 1758' is in CCC.
References: Bray Associates Annual Reports, 1877; Kelly, p.262; Yates, 1983,
p.162 & n.8.

DEVIZES, Wilts.
St. Mary. Sarum
[nil] *
There are references in the churchwardens' accounts to the costs of chaining
copies of Foxe and Erasmus. A ParLL of 154v. was est. by the Associates of Dr
Bray in 1841, augm. in 1865 and 1870.
Catalogues: 1841. Bray Associates Records, f.41, pp.59–62.
References: Cox, p.197; Kelly, p.264.

DEWSBURY, Yorks. (W.Yorks.)
All Saints. Wakef.
[nil] *
A ParLL of 172 vols. was est. in 1831 by the Associates of Dr Bray, and augm.
in 1870, 1878 and 1888.
Catalogues: Bray Associates Records, f.40, pp.207–14.
References: Shore, p.152; Bray Associates Annual Reports, 1890; Kelly, p.264.

DIDCOT, Berks. (Oxon.)
All Saints. Ox.
[9v.] Reading UL
DeskL: pre-1900 service books including a 'Vinegar' Bible, Oxford, 1717, and
a fine BCP, William Pickering, 1844, deposited in Reading UL in 1980.
Catalogues: Reading UL OPAC.

DIDSBURY, Lancs. (G.Man.)
St. James. Man.
[nil] *
DeskL: founded in the 17th cent. at the chapel of St. James at Didsbury: there are records for payments for books in 1645 and 1706. In 1842 some large vols., with their chains, were transferred to the vestry, including Jewell's *Apology*, Kettlewell's *Sermons*, Burkitt's *Commentary*, the Homilies, the Great Bible and the sealed BCP. These vols. were present in 1885 but are no longer in situ.
References: Christie, 1885, pp.97–98.

DISS, Norfolk
St. Mary. Norf.
[nil] *
DeskL: Jewell, *Apology*, 1571 and 1611, and 'some old Bibles' were reported in reply to a CCC Questionnaire, 1950, but are no longer present.
References: CCC Questionnaire, 1950.

DOCKING, Norfolk
St. Mary. Nor.
[nil] *
A ParL was est. in 1868 by the Associates of Dr Bray, which incorporated the library from **Sedgfield** in 1872, and was further augm. in 1874. A 'library building' was sold in the 1950s.
References: Shore, p.152.

DODDINGTON, Kent
St. John the Baptist. Cant.
[395v.] Fleur de Lys Heritage Centre, Faversham
A library of 364 books collected by Daniel Somerscales (*c.* 1659–1737), vicar 1694–1737, was given by his executor, Samuel L'Isle (*c.* 1683–1749) in 1743, and housed in travelling cases in the vicarage. Some other books were given in the 19th cent. by John Radcliffe (*c.* 1765–1850), vicar, in *c.* 1820, and others. The books, and four out of probably six of the original cases, were deposited in the attic of the Fleur de Lys Centre in 1983. They are mainly 17th and 18th cent. theology, but there are also a significant no. of linguistic works, editions of the classics, and a few medical, natural history and geographical works. The earliest book is William Lyndewode's *Provinciale*, Paris, Hopyl, 1505 (1506). This book, and others presented by Radcliffe, previously belonged to his kinsman, Francis Barrell, Recorder of Rochester. There are four 16th cent. editions of Calvin; a Geneva Bible of 1588 is stamped with the arms of William Cecil, Lord Burghley (1520–98). A Tacitus of 1588 has the signature of William Camden (1551–1623), and once belonged to Sir Robert Cotton (1571–1631). There are several Oxford centre-piece bindings, an unidentified panel binding (Weale R195, Hobson, Panels, pl.8) and a fine contemporary binding of the André Boule type (on a Cologne 1531 book). Various grants

have been awarded from the CCC for repair and conservation work on the books.

Catalogues: MS catalogue endorsed 'May 2d, 1743. S. Lisle' in Canterbury CL: CCA U3/195/6/1, which lists 71 folios, 30 quartos and 263 octavos, with dates and, usually, places of printing; the books were actually received at Doddington 23 May 1744: MS inventories of 1744 and 1774 are also held in Canterbury CL archives; handlist by John O'Kill, Nov. 1992.

References: Venn: Somerscales; Foster: L'Isle, Radcliffe, Barrell; DNB: Cecil, Camden, Cotton; early 19th cent. notes on the library are in Canterbury CL. Add.MS.21, f.4; Lambeth Palace MS.3221, ff.266–8: additional notes on provenance and rubbings of bindings by N. R. Ker; Yates, pp.163–4; Pearson 1773.3–4, 1907.1–2.

DONCASTER, Yorks. (S.Yorks.)
St. George. Sheff.
[nil, save fragments in Doncaster Borough archives]
Patrick Dujon (1671–1728), vicar of St. George's from 1706, and a frequent correspondent of the SPCK, was the prime mover in the establishment of a 'Society for the improvement of one another in Christian knowledge & for the purchasing such books as may be useful to read', begun in 1714. In 1726, the members, all local clergy, decided to establish a library vested in trustees over the south porch of the church and to make the books available to donors and benefactors as well as members. The rules for members were very similar to those adopted for the SPCK diocesan lending libraries in Wales (see p.411). The Society continued at least until 1793, and the library into the 19th cent., as loans are recorded, but all the books were destroyed when the church was burned down in 1853. The records, kept in the vicarage, survived (as detailed below). The 1726 catalogue of *c.* 400 items is transcribed in Miller, below; an 1821 catalogue (cited in *N & Q* 1882) cannot now be found. A list of books printed before 1550 is in Ballinger, below. The borrowers' register has been analysed in detail by Kaufman and Best (below).

Catalogues: a Minute-Book of the society, 1715–25, and other papers concerning it, 1726–73, are housed in Doncaster Borough archives (P1/5E/1–4), which also holds a vol. (DZ.MD.443, 1–3) containing a copy of the deed of settlement of 1726, a list of benefactors and their gifts, 1717–63, a list of books in the library, *c.* 1726 (pp.177–215), and a register of books issued and returned, Dec. 1726 to Aug. 1773, and a guard book of fragments of books found after the fire of 1853.

References: Edward Miller, *The History and Antiquities of Doncaster*, 1804, pp.98–102; J. Ballinger, 'An old Doncaster library', in W. Smith (ed.), *Old Yorkshire*, iii (1882), pp.149–54; *N & Q*, 6 ser. vi (1882), p.258; Kelly, pp.98, 256; Paul Kaufman, 'New light from parochial libraries: the loan records of St. George's Doncaster', *Libri*, 17.4 (1967), pp.93–101; Best, pp.40–47, 115–63; Manley, pp.238–9.

DONINGTON, Lincs.
St. Mary and the Holy Rood. Linc.
[*c.* 2500v.] Lincoln CL
John Wilson, vicar (d.1869) gave about 2500 vols. which were kept in the vicarage. Many of the books are inscribed by John Wilson or his father. In 1970 the books were reported to be in a damp and very poor condition. In 1993 the collection was transferred into the ownership of Lincoln CL. The main subjects are evangelical / Calvinistic theology, with some books on law, travel and medicine.
Catalogues: a TS list of 17 books of the 17th cent. is held by CCC.
References: Bill Report, 1970.

DORCHESTER, Dorset
All Saints (red.) Sarum
[nil]
DeskL: a 'Breeches' Bible, 1594; John White's *Sermons*, 1647, and his *Troubles of Jerusalems Restauration*, 1645, were reported as present in 1950. A ParL of 67 vols. was est. by the Bray Trustees for Erecting Parochial Libraries in 1710: this library was returned to the Associates in 1871. The church was made redundant in the 1970s and the earlier books cannot now be traced.
Catalogues: no.37, Bray Associates Records, f.39, pp.37–40.
References: Bray Associates Annual Reports, 1871; Kelly, p.261.

DOVER, Kent
St. Mary the Virgin. Cant.
[1v.] Canterbury CL & Archives
DeskL: Homilies, 1652.

DRAYCOTT-LE-MOORS, Staffs.
St. Margaret. Lich.
A Bray Associates Lib. est. here was removed in 1872 to **Cheadle**, Staffs.

DRONFIELD, Derbys.
St. John the Baptist. Derby
[1v.] *
DeskL: Cox in the 1870s noted 5 large folio vols. of Poole's *Synopsis Criticorum*, 1674, and a copy of Jewel's *Apology*, 1569, with a chain attached to the cover in a chest in the upper turret room, which were still present in 1907. The work by Poole can no longer be found; the Jewel is now kept in the vestry.
References: Cox, Notes, 1875–9, v.1, p.207; Cox & Harvey, p.338.

DROXFORD, Hants.

St. Mary and All Saints. Ports.

tsansf

[*c.* 35v.] Southampton UL

A note in a parish register dated 9 Nov. 1745 gives a list of *c.* 150 books with the headnote: 'I Lewis Stephens Rector of Droxford do give the following books and tracts written against popery, to the parish church of Droxford, to remain there forever in a press made at my expence for that purpose, to and for the use of the Curate of Droxford, whenever the Rector of the parish aforesaid does not reside in person'. Stephens (b. *c.* 1689), was rector 1722–47. In the 1972 parish inventory it was stated that the books of interest had been either distributed to members of the congregation, or burned, in 1970. However some 35 vols. are now deposited in Southampton UL, but not kept together as a collection. The surviving books are mainly 17th cent. English theology and sermons.

Catalogues: Foster: Stephens; the 1745 list is in Hants. RO: 66M76/PR3 (TS transcript in CCC); photocopies of Southampton UL catalogue cards and list in Lambeth Palace MS.3221, ff.269–78, and CCC; re-catalogued since 1981 on Southampton UL OPAC.

References: Yates, p.161 and n.5; DRB2, p.90.

DUCKLINGTON, Oxon.

St. Bartholomew. Ox.

[iv.] *

DeskL: at the time of a CCC Questionnaire of 1950 there were: Prayer books of 1710, 1793; Bibles of 1727, 1795, and Greek Testaments of 1706 and 1732. The BCP of 1793 is all that remains.

DUDLESTON, Shrops.

transf

St. Mary the Virgin. Lich.

[102v.] Shrops. RRC

A ParL of 72v. was est. in 1712 by the Bray Trustees for Erecting Parochial Libraries, and augm. by the Associates in 1889. In 1959 62 vols. (nos. 1–6, 8, 11–21, 23, 25–6, 28, 30–48, 50–60, 62–70 and 72) remained in the vicarage. By 1970 the books had been deposited, with later additions, in Shropshire Co.L., together with the original travelling bookcase (the latter is now in the Shrops. Museums Service store at Atcham). They are now stored with other Shrops. PLs in the Shropshire Records and Research Centre, Shrewsbury.

Catalogues: MS. cat. 'Dudliston Chappel' no.33, Bray Associates Records, f.39, pp.213–16 (copies in Lichfield RO: B/A/22/1, and CCC); Shrops. PLC, 1971.

References: Kelly, p.263; Bill Report, 1970.

DUFTON, Westm. (Cumbria)

transf.

St. Cuthbert. Carl.

[28 titles] Cumbria RO, Kendal

It would appear from the vol. nos. given in the list cited below that the 'Dufton

Parish Library', consisting entirely of secular books dating from 1821 to 1880, once contained over 116 vols.
Catalogues: Cumbria RO, Kendal list, WDX/585 (copy in CCC).

DULLINGHAM, Cambs.
St. Mary. Ely
[nil]
A ParL of 72 vols. was est. in 1712 by the Bray Trustees for Erecting Parochial Libraries; it was reported as lost in 1895.
Catalogues: MS cat. no.40, Bray Associates Records, f.39, pp.89–92; three MS catalogues were sold by Quaestor Rare Books in 1991: 1) 'copied from a printed catalogue list in M. Nich. Philips [ ] vicar of that p[ar]ish his hands upon the delivery of the said library to him. this sd library to go [ ] the sd vicrage for ever for the benefit of succeeding vicars, January 21st 1711'; 2) MS catalogue no. 40, Jan. 21, 1713; 3) another MS cat. n.d.
References: Bray Associates Annual Reports, 1895; Kelly, p.261.

DURHAM, Durham
St. Oswald King and Martyr. Dur.
[6+v.] Durham UL (and elsewhere, see below)
John Cock (b. *c.* 1639), vicar of St. Oswald in 1673, lecturer at St. Nicolas, Newcastle 1675–9, and rector of Gateshead 1687–9, was deprived as a non-juror in 1689. In 1701 he bequeathed his books to his successors, the vicars of St. Oswald, with £20 to build a place for their reception. The building in which they were housed is an annex to the vicarage. The catalogue of 1691 records 1,578 vols. Cock's successor, Thomas Rud (*c.* 1667–1732), vicar 1711–25, librarian of the Cathedral, and effectively of Cosin's Library later, added books to the collection and annotated them. The books were sold to Messrs Steadman of Newcastle without faculty in Sept. 1929, soon after the arrival of a new incumbent, Alexander Dunn, vicar 1929–39, and were widely dispersed. Earlier, in a report of 1922, E. V. Stocks, Durham U Librarian, had suggested that the whole collection be transferred to the custody of the Dean and Chapter, or the Trustees of Cosin's Library, but nothing came of his proposal. Stocks had already listed in print 3 foreign incunables, and 144 STC books had been recorded in STC1. A report of 1922 listing 80 other STC books, and books in other categories, e.g. books published by the Plantins and Elseviers, was kept by Stocks in a notebook held by Durham UL, which also possesses *c.* 6 vols. from the library, and maintains a list of books with Cock's bookplate, or Thomas Rud's annotations (see catalogues, below) in catalogues or libraries elsewhere. Books from the collection have been identified in the National Library of Scotland, Cambridge UL, at Urbana, U. of Illinois, and in Sotheby's sale catalogues (e.g. 15 Nov. 1977, lot 281).
Catalogues: Durham UL: 'A catalogue of books belonging to John Cock, 1691', with some additions to 1704/5, in shelf-order (Add.MS.7654); 'Catalogus librorum . . . classicus', in shelf-order by Thomas Rud, including

an incomplete list of the contents of tract vols, a shelf-list of class M, *c.* 1876–81, by A. C. Headlam, and annotations by E. V. Stocks of what he was unable to find in 1916 (Add.MS.766+).
References: Venn: Cock, Rud/Rudd; Robert Surtees, *The History and Antiquities of the County Palatine of Durham*, v.4, pt.2, 1840, p.83; E. V. Stocks, in *Durham University Jnl.*, v.22 (1919), p.57 (nos. 191, 226, 252); Kelly, pp.91 n.4, 247. I am indebted to Dr A. I. Doyle for information in this entry.

DURNFORD, Wilts.
St. Andrew. Sarum
[nil] *
DeskL: a copy of Jewel's *Apology*, [1571?], chained to a Jacobean lectern, was reported in 1950. It was stolen some time before 1977.
References: Blades, BIC, p.25; Cox & Harvey, p.339.

DURSLEY, Glos.
St. James the Great. Glouc.
[iv.] Glos. RO
DeskL: Foxe, *Book of Martyrs*, 8th ed. 1641.
A ParLL was est. in *c.* 1837 with 220 vols. which had increased to 550 by 1857 (but 40 vols. were then described as missing). It was built up with gifts of money or books from 15 local gentry together with a £5 grant from the SPCK. By 1871 the total stock was in the 900s. The fate of the library is unknown.
Catalogues: 1857, 1864 and 1871 (copies in the Bodl.); 1888 (copy in Gloucester PL).
References: Morgan, p.30.

EARDISLEY, Heref.
St. Mary Magdalene. Heref.
[nil]
There is a label reading 'Eardisley Library', a collection almost certainly founded by Canon Charles Samuel Palmer (b. *c.* 1830), vicar 1866–1906, which no longer survives.
References: Foster: Palmer; I am indebted to Brian North Lee for this reference.

EARL STERNDALE, Derbys.
St. Michael and All Angels. Derby
[nil]
James Hill bequeathed books by his will proved at York, 11 June 1712. In 1823 there were 24 books of this gift in a cupboard beside the altar; the names of the books were written on the cupboard doors. The church was destroyed by a landmine in WWII and has been entirely rebuilt.
References: Cox, Notes, vol.2, 1877, p.486 (quoting an account by R. R. Rawlings); CCC file notes.

EASINGTON, Yorks. (N.Yorks.)
All Saints. York
[2v.] York Minster Lib.
DeskL: Bible, A.V. 1683; *A Discourse of Projecting by Sermons*, 1683 (& 5 other tracts, 1683–7). Deposited at York Minster Lib. in 1995.

EAST BEDFONT, Middx.
St. Mary the Virgin. Lon.
[19 titles in 16v.] Hounslow PL
The origin of this library is uncertain: 16 vols. in a parish chest in St. Mary the Virgin church were deposited in Hounslow PL in the 1980s. Each vol. has either the small or the large Bray Library bookplate, but only nos. 7(2), 8, 10, 14 and 63(1) can be identified as from the Oldbury selection, and nos. 10 and 60 from the Whitchurch selection (see pp.53–5). The collection contains books published from 1698 to 1723, including 2 by Bray, 2 by his friend John Kettlewell, and others by local clergy. A number have 'Bedfont Library', and notes of prices paid, in ms. A catalogue (unlocated) of the library provided *c.* 1731 by Lady Anne Hollis and Lady Blount is in Phillipps MS.31985, which later belonged to Wilfred Merton.
Catalogues: MS. cat. above; TS cat. of 16 titles listed at the church by the Middlesex CRO in 1962 (NRA list 8494, copy in CCC).
References: Lambeth Palace MS.3224 (a letter from A. N. L. Munby to N. R. Ker, 16.9.1959, describing the ms. cat. above); Kelly, p.250; Andrea T. Cameron, 'Some parochial libraries of south-west Middlesex', *Ealing Occasional Papers in the History of Libraries*, no.1, 1972, p.8.

EASTBOURNE, Sussex (E.Suss.)
St. Mary. Chich.
[1v.] Bodl.
A 15th cent. Book of Hours, was given in 1929 (?) by Miss Davies-Gilbert.
References: *Sussex Notes and Queries*, v.2 (1929), p.61; Ker, MMBL, II, 1979, p.522.

EAST BUDLEIGH, Devon
All Saints. Ex.
[9v.] *
DeskL: Bible, 1634; Jewel; Foxe, *Book of Martyrs*, 1684, all chained; and Book of sermons / homilies, 1676; Bible, 1739; BCP 1728, 1762, 1768, 1788.
References: Cox & Harvey, p.338.

EAST CARLETON, Norf.
St. Mary. Nor.
[1v.] Norwich CL
DeskL: *Certain Sermons or Homilies*, 1676.

EAST CHALLOW, Berks.
St. Nicolas. Ox.
[3v.] Berks. RO
DeskL: Articles of Religion (1562) and Act of Uniformity (1558), 1630;
Articles, 1688; Archbishop Secker, Letter, 1759.

EAST DEREHAM, Norf.
St. Nicholas. Nor.
[nil] *
A seal bookplate reading 'S. Nicholas Church, East Dereham', is in the Franks
Collection, no.33793.

EAST HADDON, Northants
St. Mary the Virgin. Pet.
[nil] *
A ParL of 67 vols. was est. in 1817 by the Associates of Dr Bray; it is not
recorded after 1880.
Catalogues: sent in Feb. 1817. Bray Associates Records, f.38, pp.267–8.
References: Kelly, p.263; Bray Associates Annual Reports, 1880.

EAST HARLSEY, Yorks. (N. Yorks.)
St. Oswald. York
[c. 600v.] York Minster Lib.
George Lawson (d.1726), who was probably a collateral descendant of the
William Lawson whose books formed the nucleus of **Stainton** parochial
library, and was certainly the benefactor of Leeds Grammar School library,
bequeathed a collection of books 'as a Parochial Library for ye use of ye
Curate of East Harlsey and his succss. &c. dat. March 1st, 1721'. He was also
lord of the manor and patron of the living. In 1734 the library, kept in an attic
room of the vicarage, contained 79 folios, 45 quartos, 339 octavos and over
630 pamphlets. The total has fluctuated over the years: in 1900 there were 540
vols. reported; in 1924, when they were listed by the then vicar, the total was
600; in 1970 the number was again down to 310. When the books were finally
removed in 1976 from the vicarage attic and deposited in York Minster Lib.
there were c. 600 vols. There are a few 16th cent. books, but none before 1550,
and c. 100 pre-1700 items. Many books are signed 'Geo: Lawson' on the title-
page, and 'G.L.' is stamped in gilt on the covers of those he had bound for him.
This library forms part of an important record of the scholarly reading of
Yorkshire laity and clergy in the 17th and early 18th cents.
Catalogues: a MS catalogue drawn up in 1734 was purchased for York
Minster Lib. in 1996: it also contains details of Lawson's will and the codicil
regarding the books; there are notes detailing checks on the books, 1737–83,
and a stamp showing that the Charity Commissioners saw the catalogue in
1919; also in York Minster Lib. are a copy of the list made in 1924 by the
Revd John T. Smith, vicar; a list by David Pearson of all STC / Wing items,
1981; and a copy of Alison Norie's catalogue of part of the collection, 1980;

MS list of 'the principal books', *c.* 1930 (copy in CCC).
References: Venn: Lawson; Bill Report, 1970; Barr, p.36; Pearson 1985.2.

EAST LEAKE, Notts.
St. Mary. S'well
[nil ?] NRC
DeskL: Daniel Featley, *The Dipper Dippe*d, 3rd ed., 1645, chained.
References: Cox & Harvey, p.338; Sidney Potter, *A History of East Leake*,
Nottingham, 1903, pp.60-61. I am indebted to Adrian Henstock for this
reference.

EAST RETFORD, Notts.
St. Swithun. S'well
[nil] *
A ParLL of 150 vols. was est. in 1836 by the Associates of Dr Bray.
Catalogues: 'Clerical Reference Library. 1836'. Bray Associates Records, f.40,
pp.287–91.
References: Kelly, p.263.

EASTWICK, Herts.
St. Botolph. St.Alb.
[iv.]
John Allen (d.1765), rector, 1726–65, gave 1,500 books to Eastwick church,
50 of which were subsequently given to the University of Louvain after 1918
by 'licence'. Cyril Lewis, then rector, noted in the church terrier in 1925 that a
large no. of ancient books had been sold during his incumbency. One book
was returned to the church in 1996: Philippe de Comines, *Memoirs*, 2nd ed,
1723, vol.2, 'given by the Reverend John Allen, Rector of Eastwick, to his
successors in that rectory, 1765'.
References: R. L. Hine, *Charles Lamb and his Hertfordshire*, 1949, p.237;
Lambeth Palace MS.3224: note by N. R. Ker.

EAST WINCH, Norf.
All Saints. Nor.
[nil]
DeskL: Bible, 1611, chain restored in 1884: seen in 1923, but reported missing
from a CCC Questionnaire of 1950.
References: Blades, BIC, p.22; Cox, p.195.

EASTWOOD, Notts.
St. Mary. S'well
[nil]
A ParLL of 66v. was est. in 1819 by the Associates of Dr Bray. The church was
destroyed by fire in 1963.
Catalogues: 1819. Bray Associates Records, f.40, pp.31–3.
References: Kelly, p.263.

ECCLESFIELD, Yorks. (S.Yorks.)
St. Mary the Virgin. Sheff.
[4 titles bound in 2v.]
The earliest remains of a parish library in Yorkshire, comprising 4 items bound in 2 vols. including works by Dionysius and Nicolaus de Lyra, all that has survived from a list in the church accounts of 13 'bookes' given by Charles Parsons (d.1549), vicar 1544–9, rebound by 'Mr. Crofte bookebinder' in 1638. **References**: Venn: Parsons; *N & Q*, 1 ser. v. 8 (1853), p. 273, gives a list; also printed in: Jonathan Eastwood, *History of the Parish of Ecclesfield in the County of York*, 1862, p.517; and in Blades, BIC, p.22, who was informed that the books were very dilapidated and had been removed from the chancel in 1860; Kelly, p.50; Barr, p.33.

ECTON, Northants.
St. Mary Magdalene. Pet.
[nil]
There is a bookplate reading, 'In usum rectorum et incumbentium ecclesiae de Ecton, Johannie Palmer Patronus D.D.D. MDCCLII'. No books survive.
References: I am indebted to Brian North Lee for this reference.

EFFINGHAM, Surrey
St. Lawrence. Guildf.
[2v.] Surrey History Centre, Woking.
By his will John Miller (1666–1724), vicar 1696–1724, gave to his successors in the vicarage 'a useful library which is preserved with great care'. Only two 17th cent. vols. survive, one of which, Ralph Brownrig, *Thirty Five Sermons*, 1664, is inscribed 'The gift of Mr Miller to the vicars of Effingham in Surrey for ever'. The rest of the library was sold by E. F. Bayly, vicar 1882–1929. N. R. Ker noted a copy of Eusebius Pamphilus in Greek, Lyon, 1544, belonging to Effingham in 1746, in the V & A Library.
Catalogues: a brief list of the books left in 1724 is written on the flyleaf of a document containing other notes and writings by Miller, late 17th / early 18th cent.: Surrey History Centre, EFF/23/1.
References: Owen Manning and William Bray, *The History and Antiquities of the County of Surrey*, vol.2, 1809, pp.714–15; transcript by John Harvey of the 'Memorandum Book of the Vicars of Effingham': Surrey History Centre, L4 2440, p.ii; DRB2, p.552; Lambeth Palace MS.3224, f.196: note by N. R. Ker; Kelly, p.254.

EGGINTON, Derbys.
St. Wilfrid. Derby
[3v.] Derbys. RO
DeskL: Bible: New Testament of Erasmus, Basel: Froben, 1548–57 (trace of chain, incomplete); Bible, Oxford, University Printers, 1710; BCP, Oxford, Baskett, 1715.

EGGLESCLIFFE, Durham
St. John the Baptist. Dur.
[3v.] *
DeskL: *Eikon Basilike*, 1662; Jewel's *Apology*, n.d.; BCP, Oxford, 1770.
References: *N & Q*, ser.11, no.6, 17 Aug. 1912.

ELHAM, Kent
St. Mary the Virgin. Cant.
[1338v.] Canterbury CL
A collection of books, constituting a family library, was bequeathed, with
some other endowments, by Lee Warly (1715–1807) 'to the Minister and
Church Warden of the parish of Elham for the time being, for the whole and
sole use of the inhabitants therof . . . with book cases, and writing desk; and
also the sum of fifty-pounds, in aid of fitting up a room, for the reception of the
same' (from a panel in the church). The library was kept in the church, and
after the 'restoration' in 1843 it was arranged in 7 subject sections, each in a
separate case or cases: divinity, elementary works and dictionaries, law,
physics, history, general literature, miscellaneous, and there were then 1443
titles. In 1912, after some items were found to be missing, a cataloguer from
Cambridge UL was asked to produce a catalogue and 200 of the best books
were then deposited in Canterbury CL; the remaining books were deposited in
1956, and in 1970 the deposit became a permanent loan. The library contains
a wide range of material, including late Elizabethan and Jacobean literature
and Civil War tracts collected by Henry Oxinden, of Barham (1609–70);
history, theology, travels, literature and some medical books belonging to his
grandson, John Warly (1674–1732), a Canterbury surgeon; and some law
books from the working library of his son, Lee Warly, an attorney in
Canterbury. The books are heavily annotated both by Henry Oxinden and Lee
Warly, and frequently prices paid are noted.
Catalogues: there are MS lists of the books by Lee Warly dated 1738 and 1760
with the library; two catalogues were published, the first in 1808: *Catalogue of
Books, lately belonging to Lee Warly, . . . bequeathed, for the Benefit of the
Inhabitants of the Parish of Elham*, Canterbury, 1808 (copy in the parish
records: CCA U3/32/28/1/3) and another in 1845: *A catalogue of Mr Lee
Warly's Library bequeathed by him to the Parish of Elham in 1809; restored
by public subscription in 1843*, 1845 (copies with the collection); MS cata-
logue of 1913 with the correspondence on the collection lists 310 titles;
included in Canterbury CL pre-1801 computerised catalogue.
References: Kelly, p.197; Yates, p.165; Sheila Hingley, 'Elham Parish Library', in Peter Isaac and Barry McKay (eds.), *The Reach of Print: Making,
Selling and Using Books*, Winchester and Delaware, 1998, pp.175–90; Sarah
Gray and Chris Baggs, 'The English parish library: a celebration of diversity',
Libraries & Culture, v.35 (2000), no.3, pp.427–30; DNB: Oxinden.

ELLEL, Lancs.
St. John the Evangelist. Blackb.
[nil] *
A ParL of 45 vols. was est. in 1757 by the Associates of Dr Bray.
Catalogues: Ellel in the parish of Cockerham. Bray Associates Records, f.38,
p.40.

ELLESMERE, Shrops.
St. Mary. Lich.
[2v.] *
DeskL: King James Bible, n.d. One vol. survives of the ParL est. in 1871 by the
Associates of Dr Bray, and augm. in 1897.
References: Shore, p.151; Bray Associates Annual Reports, 1900.

ELM GREEN, Worcs.
[place not identified]
A clerical library was est. in c. 1705 by Dr Bray.
References: listed in the Select Committee Report, pp.221–6, but not otherwise
recorded.

ELMLEY CASTLE, Worcs.
St. Mary. Worc.
A ParL of 72 vols. was est. in 1712 at Elmley [Elmley Castle] by the Bray
Trustees for Erecting Parochial Libraries, which by 1877 had been transferred
to **Pershore**, improved and enlarged.
Catalogues: 'Elmly, Worcs. no.12', Bray Associates Records, f.39, pp.169–72.
References: Kelly, p.264.

ELSTON, Notts.
All Saints. S'well
[14 titles in 12v.] Nottingham UL
The remains of the library of the Revd John South (d.1732), rector 1702–32,
were kept in the rectory until a few years before 1959 when they were
deposited in Nottinghamshire Co.L and rebound. In c. 1980 they were
transferred to Nottingham UL. The books are 17th cent. theological works and
mainly in Latin; they are all catalogued on Nottingham UL's OPAC.
Catalogues: TS short-title catalogue, by Peter Hoare, 1996 (with provenances;
copy in CCC).

ELY, Cambs.
St. Mary. Ely
[nil] *
A good library is recorded here in the SPCK MSS, minutes of the Bray
Trustees, 16 July 1711, which state 'all that will may have the free use of it'.
References: Kelly, p.245 & n.3.

EMBSAY, Yorks. (N.Yorks.)
St. Mary the Virgin. York
[nil] *
A ParL was est. in 1853 by the Associates of Dr Bray; it is not recorded after 1900.
References: Shore, p.152; Bray Associates Annual Reports, 1900.

EMLEY, Yorks. (W.Yorks.)
St. Michael the Archangel. Wakef.
[?] W.Yorks. Wakefield RO
Book from the 17th to 19th cent. are stored with the parish records (D8, no list).

ENSTONE, Oxon.
St. Kenelm. Ox.
[7v.] Oxfordshire Archives, Oxford
A collection of books, first recorded in 1756 (see Catalogues, below), all in English, published 1596–1701, consisting of 4 STC books, 3 Wing and 1 18th cent., all with remains of chains, added probably in the latter part of the 17th cent., was deposited in the Bodl. and than transferred to Oxfordshire Archives in 1972.
Catalogues: a list of 8 items on a parchment fragment dated 1756: Bodl. MS.Ch.Oxon.a.11 (154), transcript in CCC; in John Jordan, *A Parochial History of Enstone*, London & Oxford, 1857, pp.372–5; TS list by Paul Morgan, *c.* 1973 (the same items as in the list of 1756 minus 'A Bible & Common Prayer Book') with provenances and details of chaining (copy in CCC).
References: archives list: PR97/17/PR1–7.

EPSOM, Surrey
St. Martin. Guild.
[2v.] *
DeskL: 'Vinegar' Bible, 1717; Biblia Sacra, 1587 (a recent gift).

EVESHAM, Worcs.
All Saints with St. Lawrence. Worc.
[nil] *
A ParL of 67 vols. was est. in 1710 by the Bray Trustees for Erecting Parochial Libraries, and augm. by the Associates in 1870. It was still recorded in 1940 but not in 1946. No books remained in 1959, but the upper half of the original book-cupboard was present, with a catalogue on the inside of the door, marked outside '32'. The cupboard can no longer be found. A copy of the pictorial bookplate dated 1709 is in the Franks Collection: no. 33850.
Catalogues: MS. cat. no.32; received 19 Mar. 1709/10. Bray Associates Records, f.39, pp.13–16.
References: Kelly, p.264.

EVINGTON, Leics.
St. Denys. Leic.
[nil] *
A bookplate for this library, engraved by Orlando Jewitt (1799–1869), is illustrated in Frank Broomhead, *The Book Illustrations of Orlando Jewitt*, 1995, pp.150-1. It is also in the Franks Collection: no.33851.
References: DNB: Jewitt.

EWELL, Surrey
St. Mary the Virgin. Guildf.
[nil] *
A ParLL of 123+ vols. was est. in 1817 by the Associates of Dr Bray.
Catalogues: Bray Associates Records, f.38, pp.269–72.

EWELME, Oxon.
St. Mary the Virgin. Ox.
[iv.]
DeskL: Greek Lexicon, Basel, 1580, given by 'Rev. Steph. Huwman S.J.B. Catt [sic, probably 'Coll.'] Oxon Socij'.
References: NADFAS Report.

EXETER, Devon
St. Edmunds (now a ruin) Ex.
[nil]
A catalogue of books in the parochial lending library in the parish of St. Edmund's Exeter is bound in: *Poems Divine and Moral*, 1823, a vol. in the Westcountry Studies Library, Exeter. The library, est. by the SPCK, has not survived.
References: information from Ian Maxted, Westcountry Studies Librarian, Exeter Central Lib.

FAIRFORD, Glos.
St. Mary the Virgin. Glouc.
[2v.?] NRC
DeskL: copies of an early ed. of Calvin's *Institutes,* and *The Whole Duty of Man*, 1725, were recorded as being chained to a lectern in 1907.
References: Cox & Harvey, p.339.

FAKENHAM, Norf.
St. Peter and St. Paul. Nor.
[nil]
DeskL: once held copies of Jewel, *A Defense of the Apologie*, 1571, and, Erasmus, *Paraphrases*, n.d., in very poor condition: they are now missing.
Catalogues: a list of books, n.d., given to the church by the Rev. Dr Hooper, formerly in Norwich PL, can no longer be found.
References: *Library History,* v.8, no.5, 1990, p.146.

FAVERSHAM, Kent
St. Mary of Charity. Cant.
[nil] *
The Canterbury Cathedral Chapter Act Book, 1711–26, fol. 79v, Midsummer Chapter 1719, has the note: 'Ordered that £5 be given out of the fines of this Chapter towards a parochial library procured by Mr Dean [i.e. George Stanhope] for the use of the incumbent of some benefice in the presentation of this church, & his successors for ever; and that the library be placed at Faversham for the use of the vicar & his successors there'.
References: I am indebted to Dr Nigel Ramsay for this reference.

FECKENHAM, Worcs.
St.John the Baptist. Worc.
[93 titles in 130v.] Worcester CL
A ParL of 72 vols. was est. in 1712 by the Bray Trustees for Erecting Parochial Libraries. This was perhaps the collection referred to by Richard Hurd, Bishop of Worcester, after a visitation as 'a parochial library left by the late Henry Neale, Esq., patron of the vicarage'. In 1888 this collection was reported 'lost', but in 1959 some 69 books still survived; other books, including 12 pre-1800 works, have since been added. In 1997 the collection was deposited in Worcester CL.
Catalogues: no. 39. Bray Associates Records, f.39, pp.35–8; MS list, 19-- in Bodl.MS.Eng.Misc.c.360 (copy in CCC); TS shelf-list, 1998, with collection (copy in CCC).
References: Bray Associates Annual Reports, 1888; Kelly, p.264; Mary Ransome, ed., 'The state of the Bishopric of Worcester, 1782–1808', *Worcs. Hist. Soc.*, N.S. v.6 (1968), p.96.

FELTHAM, Middx.
St. Dunstan. Lon.
[5v.] Hounslow PL; [5 titles in 31v.] Lambeth Palace Lib.
Most of what is known about this library is contained in the 18th cent. MS Register restored to the parish in 1909 and now housed in the Greater London RO. Sir Matthew Decker (1679–1749) est. the library 'for the use of the minister incumbent therein for ever at the expense, books and incident charges of £61–4–0d.' in *c.* 1731. To this gift was added 'an augmentation of books for the immediate use of both catechist and catechumens . . . the condition of the donation to the value of five pounds by the Honourable Lady Blount'. The catalogue, included in the Register after a copy of the printed Parochial Libraries Act of 1709, perhaps in the hand of the vicar of the time, lists 147 titles in *c.* 190 vols. Further notes and additions are recorded by the Revd Colston Carr, vicar in 1792, together with a classification scheme for the library. In 1966, after a long period of neglect at the vicarage, the books were listed by staff from the Greater London Record Office. By this time only 21 titles in *c.* 36 vols. survived from the 18th cent. library (some with the large

Bray Library bookplate, and including nos. 3, 68(2) and 71 from the Oldbury selection, and 15–22 from the Whitchurch selection, see pp.49–53) but with the addition of *c.* 100 vols., mainly published in the 1820s and 1840s, some with SPCK parochial library rules, or a MS note 'Feltham Parochial Library, bought by subscription, 1828'. In 1968 5 titles were deposited in Lambeth Palace Library (2 with the large Bray bookplate, and 2 incomplete sets of SPCK religious tracts, 1827–43, bought by subscription), and shortly after this the remainder of the collection was sold. Recently 5 vols. were retrieved from a Bucks. bookseller and are now deposited in Hounslow PL.

Catalogues: A cat. of the library provided *c.* 1731 by Lady Anne Hollis and Lady Blount is in Phillipps MS.31985, which later belonged to Wilfred Merton (untraced); Register, etc. in Greater London RO: DRO/013/A12/1; TS cat., 1966 (copy in CCC).

References: Lambeth Palace MS.3224 (a letter from A. N. L. Munby to N. R. Ker, 16.9.1959, describing the MS, above); Kelly, p.250; Andrea T. Cameron, 'Some parochial libraries from south-west Middlesex', *Ealing Occasional Papers in the History of Libraries*, no.1, 1972, pp.6–8; Woolf, p.188 & n.70 (which records the preface to a register of Feltham parish library without any listing of books (Folger MS.b.595), founded by 'Sir Nathan Decker', not traced, possibly an error for Sir Matthew Decker).

FENTON, Staffs.
Christ Church. Lich.
[nil ?] NRC
A ParL was est. in 1890 by the Associates of Dr Bray (incorporating that of **Cheadle**).
References: Bray Associates Annual Report, 1890.

FERSFIELD, Norf.
St. Andrew. Nor.
[4v.]
Three vols. only remain from this library: George Stanhope, *Sermons*, v.4, given by Francis Blomefield, Rector; v.1 of Blomefield's *An Essay towards a Topographical History of the County of Norfolk*, Fersfield, 1739; and a BCP, London, Baskett and Hills, 1727. A copy of the bookplate: 'This book belongeth to the Parish Church of St. Andrew in Fersfield, Anno. Dom. 1736. Francis Blomefield, Rector . . . Fersfield: printed, 1736' is in the Franks Collection: no. 33852 (and is reproduced in Lee, below). The church also has the remains of a DeskL: Bible, Cambridge, Hayes, 1674; and BCP, Oxford, 1793, together with other 19th and 20th cent. Bibles and prayer books.
References: Lee, Early, no.368; Lee, British, no.219.

FIELD BROUGHTON, Lancs. (Cumbria)
St. Peter. Carl.
[nil]
A ParL was est. in 1766 by the Associates of Dr Bray. In 1849 this library was reported as being one of those 'either wholly lost or reduced to a few tattered volumes'.
References: Select Committee Report, 1849; Kelly, p.262.

FIELD DALLING, Norf.
St. Andrew. Nor.
[1v.] Norwich CL
DeskL: *Certain Sermons or Homilies*, 1683.

FILBY, Norf.
All Saints. Nor.
[1v.] Norwich CL
DeskL: *Certain Sermons or Homilies*, 1683 (?)

FINEDON, Northants.
St. Mary the Virgin. Pet.
[885v.]
The founder of the library was Sir John Englis Dolben, F.S.A. (1750–1837), and it was dedicated on 21 Sept. 1788 in 'the cell over the south porch . . . for the purpose of a theological and ecclesiastical library for the sole use of the ministers of Finedon for ever, the foundation book being Dr Thomas Bray's Bibliotheca Parochialis'. There are *c.* 1,000 books listed in the 1788 catalogue, but by 1824 59 vols. were missing. There have been later additions to the collection. Some are kept in a glass-fronted case, the remainder on original, but re-arranged, shelving. Most of the books bear the armorial bookplate of Dolben's grandfather 'Sir John Dolben Bart of Finedon in Northamptonshire' (1684–1756), vicar of Finedon, 1719–56. The books include a 12th cent.(?) MS fragment, 4 incunables and *c.* 88 STC items (a possibly unique item is *An Instruction for Children*, London, J. Roux, 1543, STC2 14106.2). The subject content is mainly theology. There is a Garrett Godfrey binding (on a Basel, 1494 book) and some 16th cent. Oxford and Cambridge bindings.
Catalogues: 1788; 1824; 1882 (an unfinished catalogue at the back of a visitors' book); TS list by N. R. Ker of *c.* 31 vols. in Lambeth Palace MS.3221; John L. H. Bailey, 'A catalogue of books in the Monk's Cell Library at St. Mary's Church, Finedon, Northants. Finedon, 1979 (TS, with provenances in the text and a list of the books missing after 1824: copies in Cambridge UL and Northants. RO: ZB 38/2).
References: Architectural notes of the Archdeaconry of Northampton, 1849, p.136; William Roberts, *Book Hunters in London*, 1895, p.56; R. Underwood, *The Pageant of Finedon*, 1942, pp.36–40; Kelly, p.251; John L. H. Bailey, *Finedon, otherwise Thingdon*, 1975; *Finedon Revealed*, 1986; DRB2, p.480.

FLADBURY, Worcs.
St. John the Baptist. Worc.
[1v.] *
DeskL: *Certain Sermons or Homilies*, London, Bill, 1623: formerly kept in the church, now kept in the village museum.

FLAMBOROUGH, Yorks. (E.Riding of Yorks.)
St. Oswald. York
[nil] *
DeskL: the will of Francis Wamsley of Bridlington Key (probate granted 1795) includes 'godly books to be left in a box chained in the Parish Church at Flambrough for the use of the inhabitants of that place', (the books are not specified).
References: Hull UL MS DP/98; *Library History*, v.2:3 (1971), p.120.

FLAXLEY, Glos.
St. Mary the Virgin. Glouc.
[nil] *
A ParL of 72 vols. was est. in 1710 by the Bray Trustees for Erecting Parochial Libraries. The books were 'sold with the effects of the Rectory' in 1948. The original bookcase, present in the rectory in 1959, was disposed of by 1991 when the succeeding rectory was sold.
Catalogues: no.15. Bray Associates Records, f.39, pp.73–6.
References: Kelly, p.262 & n.1; Lambeth Palace MS.3221, ff.288–9: notes by N. R. Ker and 3 photographs of the original bookcase.

FLOOKBURGH, Lancs. (Cumbria)
St. John the Baptist. Carl.
[73v.]
A ParL of 70 vols. was est. in 1725 by the Bray Trustees for Erecting Parochial Libraries. Sir Thomas Lowther was evidently a benefactor to this library (see p.39). The 57 books listed in 1950 match nos. 1–3, 5, 7–11, 15–21, 23–9, 32–7, 39–44, 46–51, 53, 54, 56–61, 63–73, 75, 78, 80, 81 of the Whitchurch 81 vol. catalogue (see pp.53–5), with the addition of: W. Hopkins, *Seventeen Sermons*, 1708, and J. Collier, *Several Discourses upon Practical Subjects*, 1726. Later Bibles and prayer books have been added.
Catalogues: in Lambeth Palace MS.3094, ff.99–100: 'Numb. 63. A catalogue of the Parochial Library at Flookborough . . . Middle Temple April 1725' (photocopy of a MS stamped Leeds Public Library Archives; copy in CCC); MS list, 1950 (copy in CCC). TS cat. by G. E. Marrison, *c.* 1989, with the collection (copy in Cumbria RO, Kendal).
References: Kelly, pp.109 & n.3, 262; Bill Report, 1970; the 1725 cat. is analysed in Woolf, pp.192–3.

FLORDON, Norf.
St. Michael. Nor.
[1v.] Norwich CL
DeskL: John Flavell, *The Whole Works, c.* 1700.

FORD, Northumb.
St. Michael and All Angels Newc.
[nil ?] NRC
One of 92 parishes in the Northumberland Archdeaconry granted a ParLL
under a scheme devised by Bishop Shute Barrington, carried out by Archdeacon R. G. Bouyer by 1823 (see pp.57), and recorded as still possessing books in
visitation returns, 1826–8.
References: Day, p.102 n.38.

FORD, Shrops.
St. Michael. Heref.
[nil]
A ParL of 83 vols. was est. 1760 by the Associates of Dr Bray. In 1849 this
library was one of those reported as being 'either wholly lost or reduced to a
few tattered volumes'.
Catalogues: Bray Associates Records, f.38, pp.11–13.
References: Select Committee Report, 1849; Kelly, p.263.

FRAMPTON COTTEREL, Glos.
St. Peter. Glouc.
[1v.] *
DeskL: Jewel, *Defense of the Apologie*, and other works, London, Norton,
1609 (poor condition), 'under a wooden cover'.
References: Blades, BIC, pp.23–4.

FRANSHAM, Norf.
All Saints. Nor.
[1v.] Norwich CL
DeskL: Bible, 1674.

FRIEZLAND, Yorks. (S.Yorks.)
Christ Church. Man.
[nil] *
A ParL was est. in 1860 by the Associates of Dr Bray; it is not recorded after
1880.
References: Bray Associates Annual Reports, 1880; Shore, p.152; Kelly, p.264
(but no evidence for a library founded in '1800').

FRISBY-ON-THE-WREAKE, Leics.
St. Thomas of Canterbury. Leic.
[nil]
In 1705 it was recorded that 'Mr. Nicholas Sharp about fifty years since . . .
left about 30 books'. Nichols in his *History*, 1800, mentions this gift and notes
some books 'amongst others S. Augustine and Origen and other Fathers in a
wretched condition' in a room at the west end of the church. Listed in Venn are
one Nicholas Sharp of Frisby (d.1614) and another who was B.A. 1641.
References: Notitia Parochialis, 1705: no.761; John Nichols, *History of
Leicestershire*, v.3, 1800, p.262; Kelly, pp.77, 249.

FRODSHAM, Ches.
St. Lawrence. Ches.
[25v.] in the vicarage; [221v.] in Reading UL
The Revd W. C. Cotton (1813–79), vicar from 1857 until his death, bequeathed *c*. 2,614 vols., mainly 19th cent. books, 'as heirlooms to go along
with and be used as far as the rules of law and equity will permit by the person
for the time being entitled as vicar to the Vicarage and Living of Frodsham'. A
catalogue was with the collection at the vicarage, signed by the executors and
dated 1879. It included one incunable: Columella, 1472, *c*. 100 16th cent. and
a larger no. of 17th cent. books. Cotton was founder and first secretary of the
Apiarian Society at Oxford, and in 1932 some 221 books, dating from 1609 to
the 1870s, on all aspects of bees and apiculture in English, French, German,
Italian and Dutch, were deposited on loan at the Ministry of Agriculture,
Fisheries and Food Library, London (kept at the Bee Keeping Unit at
Luddington), and then, in 1987, deposited in Reading UL. The remaining
books were sold in Aug. 1979, save for 25 vols. kept at the vicarage as the
nucleus of a vicarage library.
Catalogues: 1879 catalogue (not located); TS list of books in the Cotton
collection [on bees and apiculture], with additions to 1980 (copies with the
collection and in CCC).
References: Lambeth Palace MS.3224: notes by N. R. Ker; Bill Report, 1970;
'William Charles Cotton, 1813–1879: a centenary exhibition to commemorate
a former vicar of Frodsham in Frodsham Library, 29 October – 17th November 1979' (copy with the collection in Reading UL); DRB2, p.298; Boase:
Cotton.

FROME, Somerset
St. John the Baptist. B & W
[?] *
A ParLL of 169 vols. was est. in 1840 by the Associates of Dr Bray, augm.
in 1871 and amalgamated with **Norton St. Philip**, Somerset. However 'an
extensive collection of early to mid-19th century books' still remains at Frome.
Catalogues: Bray Associates Records, f.40, pp.331–5.
References: Shore, p.151; Kelly, p.263.

GAINSBOROUGH, Lincs.
All Saints (?) Linc.
[nil] *
A ParLL was assisted by Bray from funds at his disposal 1695–9; possibly the same library mentioned in Notitia Parochialis as 'A lending library . . . settled in the town by the voluntary subscriptions of severall persons which was begun A.D. 1696'.
References: Kelly, pp.91, n.2, 259; Notitia Parochialis, 1705: no.879; J. S. English, 'Books and libraries in Gainsborough', *LAR*, v.70.3 (1968), pp.62–3.

GARSDALE, Yorks. (Cumbria)
St. John the Baptist. Bradf.
[2v.] *
A ParL 'for the the parish of Garsdale' was given by Dr Stratford, late commisary of Richmond, in *c.* 1698, and a ParLL is recorded for Garsdale chapel in 1778. A terrier at Chester RO lists *c.* 20 vols. and books are also listed in glebe terriers for 1778, 1789 and 1811. Nothing from these libraries survives save two vols.: Francis Roberts, *Clavis Bibliorum*, 1648, and *Psalms and Hymns for Public Worship*, n.d. (late 18th cent., imp.).
References: Lambeth Palace MS.3224: letters from John Addy; Chester RO: RD/G/Chester/22; W.Yorks Leeds District Archives: CD/RG17; RD/RG11/15–16; Kelly, p.256.

GEDDINGTON, Northants
St. Mary Magdalene. Pet.
[1v.] *
DeskL: Jewel, 1611, chained.
References: Cox, p.195.

GILLINGHAM, Dorset
St. Mary the Virgin. Sarum
[*c.* 265 titles in *c.* 271v.] Salisbury CL
Thomas Freke (d.1718?) bequeathed 619 vols. to the vicar and feoffees of the parish lands of Gillingham; in 1959 *c.* 300 books remained in the vicarage. In 1994 the books were deposited on indefinite loan in Salisbury CL. The books are almost all in English and mainly theological, with a date range of 1594 to 1732 (with 6 later books, 1737–99); there are 29 STC and 175 Wing items. Uncommon books include St. Augustine, *Pretious Booke of Heavely Meditations*, 1640 (STC2 949), and Gilbert Burnet, *A Relation of the Death of the Primitive Persecution*, Amsterdam, 1687 (Wing2 B5863A). A bookplate made for the collection when it was attested by the then vicar, William Newton, 12 April 1735, is reproduced in Lee, below. The bindings are mostly in one style, plain, dark calf, with gilt spines and fore-edge marbling (perhaps made for Thomas Pile, whose name appears in 21 vols. *c.* 1629–1707).
Catalogues: Hutchins, below, mentions an original list of the books appended

to the deed of gift; full catalogue by Paul Morgan, *c.* 1980, includes STC and
Wing nos., original shelf nos. and provenance details (original card cat. and
TS list in CCC).
References: J. M. J. Fletcher, *Proc. of the Dorset Nat. Hist. and Antiq. Field
Club*, v. 35 (1914), p.21; J. Hutchins, *History of Dorset*, v.3, 1868, p.647; Bill
Report, 1970; Lambeth Palace MS.3221, ff.291–302: notes on provenance and
bindings by N. R. Ker; Lee, British, no.365.

GISSING, Norf.
St. Mary the Virgin. Nor.
[2v.] Norwich CL
DeskL: *Certain Sermons or Homilies*, 1676; Jewel, *Works*, 1611.

GOODNESTONE. Kent
ParL: see under **Graveney**

GOODSHAW, Lancs.
St. Mary and All Saints. Man.
[nil] *
A ParL of 129v. was est. in 1840 by the Associates of Dr Bray.
Catalogues: Bray Associates Records, f.41, pp.2–3.
References: Kelly, p.262.

GOOSNARGH, Lancs.
St. Mary the Virgin. Blackb.
[nil] *
A list of 'books lodged in the school closet 1696', 9 titles without authors or
dates, 'all given to the parish by Thomas Waring of London' is recorded in the
Minute Book of the Select Vestry.
References: Minute Book, Lancs. RO: PR/644.

GORTON, Lancs. (G.Man.)
St. James. Man.
[51v.] Chetham's Library; [34v.] in situ
The Gorton Chapel Library was the first of the 5 parochial libraries provided
for under the will of Humphrey Chetham (see under **Manchester**; the others
were at **Bolton [-le-Moors]**, **Turton** and **Walmsley**). 68 vols. (54 titles) were
bought from the £30 bequest and chained in a book-chest or 'presse' in 1658.
The book-chest (one of the two surviving) was originally of the almery type
with a sloping desk in front, similar to the one at Bolton School (p.144). In
c. 1898 the hinged doors were altered to drop-down doors on chains. It bears
the inscription, 'The gift of Humphrey Chetham Esquire 1655'. In 1984 a
faculty was granted for the deposit of the library on indefinite loan in
Chetham's Library, Manchester. The books, reflecting Chetham's puritan
beliefs, date mainly from 1610 to 1656, apart from *The Common Places of*

... *Peter Martyr*, Denham and Middleton, 1583 (STC2 24669). The bindings, original, are well-preserved.

A collection of 34 vols., bequeathed to the rector of Gorton and his successors in the 18th cent., remains in the church.

Catalogues: the 1658 schedule is printed in Christie, pp.64–6, and Evans, appendix 4, pp.43–4; G. J. French, 'Bibliographical notices of the church libraries at Turton and Gorton', *Chetham Soc.*, v. 38 (1855), pp.110–81, prints an annotated catalogue of 36 vols. with reproductions of title-pages; included in Evans, below, in a union catalogue of the extant books in the 5 Chetham libraries, pp.45–53.

References: Blades, BIC, p.24; Streeter, p.303 (and a plate of the bookchest after alteration); Pilgrim Trust 31st Report, 1961, p.40; Evans, pp.22–4 (with illustrations); DRB2, p.437.

GOSFORTH, Northumb.
St. Nicholas. Newc.
[nil] *
Archdeacon Thomas Sharp noted after his 1723 visitation a small library of 'Books left to Gosforth Chappell': 11 vols. of sermons, commentaries, etc. There was no indication of the donor or whether the books were solely for the incumbent. Later this parish was one of 92 in the Northumberland Archdeaconry granted a ParLL under a scheme devised by Bishop Shute Barrington, carried out by Archdeacon R. G. Bouyer by 1823 (see p.57), and recorded as still possessing books in the visitation returns, 1826–8.

References: Northumb. RO: M91, Sharp visitations; Day, p.96, 102 & n.38.

GRANTHAM, Lincs.
St. Wulfram. Linc.
[356 titles in *c.* 318v.]
By an indenture dated 20 Oct. 1598, Francis Trigge (1547?–1606), rector of Welbourn, Lincs., gave books to the value of 'one hundereth poundes or theraboutes' to the Alderman and burgesses of Grantham 'for the better encreasinge of learninge . . . by such of the cleargie & others aswell beinge inhabitantes in or near Grantham & the soake thereof as in other places in the said countie', and that 'the bookes be kept continually bownd with convenient chaines to the staples devised & placed in the library for that purpose' in a 'verie convenient place in a chamber over the sowth porch' of the church. The original benches were removed in 1884, and the books, still with chains, were attached to new shelves with modern split rings. Some books were added by gift in the 17th cent. and later (including 43 books in fine bindings added in 1942). The 1608 catalogue lists 228 titles of which 20 are no longer extant. Blades in 1890 noted 268 vols. of which 74 had chains attached. The books are mainly 16th cent. continental. Among the holdings are one 12th cent. MS law book, 8 incunables (including the only recorded copy of Stephanus de Caieta, *Repetition c. quoniam*, Naples, 1476), 20 STC items (the Year Book 2

Rich. III is not in STC2), and 31 Wing items. Many books were repaired in the
19th cent. and given new endpapers (sometimes the boards were wrongly
replaced; there are notes on the transfer of pastedowns). There are many late
16th cent. bindings, with rolls and stamps, one example of the work of the
'Heavy binder', and 7 identified Oxford bindings, *c.* 1515–1620.

A collection of books bequeathed to the Corporation of Grantham in 1765 by
John Newcome (*c.* 1684–1765), Master of St. John's College, Cambridge,
Dean of Rochester, and born in Grantham, was housed in the vestry of St.
Wulfram's until 1929 when it was transferred to Grantham PL (full description
in DRB2, below). Newcome also gave books to **Offord Cluny.**

Grantham: general view of part of the chained library
established by Francis Trigge in the early seventeenth century

Catalogues: the original indenture of 1598, with the 1609 catalogue attached,
is in the Lincolnshire Archives, Lincoln (Grantham: St. Wulfram's 23/4; TS
transcripts are in CCC); a shelflist compiled by M. E. Phipps in 1939 (copy
with collection); TS corrected by N. R. Ker in Bodl.MS.Eng.Misc.c.360 (copy
in CCC); John Glenn and David Walsh, *Catalogue of the Francis Trigge
Chained library*, Cambridge, 1988 (provenances noted in the text and indexed).

References: Trigge's will is in Lincoln Consistory Court wills 1608, fol.1252; Canon H. Nelson, 'The chained library, Grantham', in *Lincoln Diocesan Magazine*, v.9 (1893); Kelly, pp.81–3, 249; Angela Roberts, 'The chained library, Grantham', *Library History*, v.2:3 (1971), pp.75–90; John Glenn, 'A 16th century chained library', in *Early Tudor England: Proceedings of the 1987 Harlaston Symposium*, ed. D. Williams, Woodbridge, 1989, pp.61–71; D. E. Rhodes, 'More leaves of an incunable by Cornelius Reoelans', *Trans. Camb. Bibliog. Soc.*, v.9 (1987), pp.205–6; *The Chained library of St Wulfram's Church, Grantham*, (pamphlet, Friends of St Wulfram's Church, n.d. [after 1989]; Venn: Newcome; DRB2, 1997, p.117; Lambeth Palace MS.3221: notes by N. R. Ker on provenance and bindings (with rubbings); Pearson 81.1; information from John Glenn, Hon. Librarian. **Photographs**: Blades, BIC, pp.24–5 & pls. 5, 6; Streeter, 1931, p.298; Pearson 81.1.

GRAVELEY, Cambs.
St. Botolph. Ely.
[*c.* 1,092v.] Univ. of London Lib.
According to an inscription in the church, Henry Trotter (d.1766), rector 1723–66, bequeathed his library of 'near 1400 volumes . . . for the use of the neighbouring clergy', together with '£50 to build a room wherein to keep them'. At the time when the rectory was sold, and the books were under threat of destruction, Charles Wilson, Bursar of Jesus College, Cambridge (owners of the advowson) managed to secure their deposit in the College library. In 1960 the college deposited the collection in the Univ. of London Lib. on indefinite loan. The books have a printed bookplate dated 1766 and are numbered 1–1,154, but there are some gaps in the sequence. There are some 23 STC, 242 Wing and 603 18th cent. English books; 11 16th cent. and 99 17th cent. continental books. The subject content is mainly theology (including 19 vols. of separately published sermons) and history, but there is a good deal of science and some English literature. The bindings are mainly plain calf, with a few parchment covers; there is little re-binding.
Catalogues: card catalogue at Jesus College, Cambridge (photocopies with the collection and at CCC); included in Univ. of London Lib. catalogue.
References: DRB2, 1997, pp.34, 407; Lambeth Palace MS.3224: note by A. N. L. Munby; Venn: Trotter.

GRAVENEY, Kent
All Saints. Cant.
[*c.* 41v.]
DeskL / ParL: in an unlocked wooden chest: Foxe's *Book of Martyrs*, 2v, 1550, 1600; Book of Homilies, 1623; BCP, 1700, 1770 (and 19th cent. music and runs of magazines). Many of the smaller books have a label reading: 'Graveney and Goodnestone Parochial Library No . . .' (with MS nos. indicating that there were originally over 100 vols.).
References: Canterbury CL Archives list.

GRAVESEND, Kent
St. George. Roch.
[nil] *
In December 1699 Thomas Bray left London for Maryland and travelled via
Gravesend where, from funds of £2.10s at his disposal, he laid the foundation
for 'a lending library for the use of the Deanery of Rochester, more especially
for the clergy, gentlemen & naval officers that shall abide in the river, for any
time, outward bound'. The parish church of St. George was burned down in
1727: if a library there was not destroyed by fire it had disappeared by 1732
when the new church was ready. Bray continued his journey via **Deal** and
Plymouth.
References: George Smith, 'Dr Thomas Bray', *LAR*, v.12 (1910), p.250
(quoting from a Bray MS diary letter once in Sion College, sold at Sotheby's in
1977: see **Deal**); H. P. Thompson, *Thomas Bray,* 1954, pp.44–5; Kelly,
pp.106, 259.

GRAYRIGG, Westm. (Cumbria)
St. John the Evangelist. Carl.
[nil ?] NRC
A ParL was est. in 1766 by the Associates of Dr Bray, still in place in 1849.
References: Select Committee Report, 1849; Kelly, p.263.

GREAT AYTON, Yorks. (N.Yorks.)
All Saints. York
[8v.] York Minster Lib.
Deposited in 1979. With the bookplate of 'Cholmley Turner of Kirkleatham in
Yorkshire Esq'. Turner (d.1752) acted as patron of Great Ayton in 1727 and
1747, and the books were probably part of his substantial family library at
Kirkleatham Hall.
References: Barr, p.36.

GREAT BRICKHILL, Bucks.
St. Mary. Ox.
[1v.] Bucks. RO, Aylesbury
DeskL: *Book of Homilies,* 1673.

GREAT DODDINGTON, Northants.
St. Nicholas. Pet.
[3v.] *
DeskL: Erasmus, *Paraphrases of Gospels and Acts,* [1548–9?]; Homilies,
1562; Bible, R. Barker, 1613: formerly chained together, now in a display case.

GREAT DRIFFIELD, Yorks. (E.Riding of Yorks.)
All Saints. York.
[nil] *

A ParLL of 169 vols. was est. in 1835 by the Associates of Dr Bray.
Catalogues: 'Great Driffold', Bray Associates Records, f.40, pp.261–5.
References: Kelly, p.264.

GREAT GRANSDEN, Hunts. (Beds.)
St. Bartholomew. Ely
[5v.] Cambs. CRO, Huntingdon
DeskL, and later: George Herbert, *Priest to the Temple*, 1675; Bible (including
an 18th cent. list of parish books, see below), 18th cent.; 3 19th cent. works.
Catalogues: 'Books belonging to the parish of G. Gransden, Hunt.shire. Mar:
18. 1717; Jun. 29, 1742' (19 items lacking Herbert, listed above: Cambs.
CRO, Huntingdon, Acc.3247 (copy in CCC)); 'Catalogue of books belonging
to Mr C: Beauchamp, 1793' (including an armorial bookplate), with accessions up to Oct. 1803, is entirely general history, literature and travels, and
not a parochial library: Cambs. CRO, Huntingdon, 1876/28/1 (copy in CCC).

GREAT MALVERN, Worcs.
St. Mary and St. Michael. Worc.
[27 titles in 31v.] Worcester CL
DeskL: a small theological collection (17th and early 18th cent.) deposited in
Worcester CL in 1982 on permanent loan.
Catalogues: TS list (1981) with the collection (copy in CCC); the chained
books noted by Blades are no longer present.
References: Blades, BIC, p.35.

GREAT MELTON, Norf.
All Saints. Nor.
[1v.] Norwich CL
DeskL: John Jewel, *Defence*, 1567.

GREAT SNORING, Norf.
St. Mary. Nor.
[1v.] Norwich CL
DeskL: Bible, 1611.

GREAT TORRINGTON, Devon
St. Michael. Ex.
[nil] *
On the title-page of John Heydon's *The Discovery of the Wonderful Preservation . . .* 1647 (Wing2 H1678) there is a reference to the library being
preserved when the old church was blown up in 1645. The existing vestry may
have been built to house the library, but there is no record as to the fate of the
books.
References: Pevsner, North Devon, p.92; I am indebted to Peter Hoare for this
reference.

GREAT YARMOUTH, Norf.
St. Nicholas. Nor.
[*c.* 158v.]
Nathaniel Symonds (*c.* 1694–1727), vicar of Ormesby 1718–27, bequeathed
40 shillings a year for 15 years for the purchase of religious books to be chosen
by the minister of Great Yarmouth, half for **Ormesby**, St. Margaret, and half
for Yarmouth or Burgh (with annuities to several other parishes). A list of
books in the library (175 titles) was printed by Swinden (below) in 1772:
all are dated before 1700. 16th cent. books include 9 out of 10 vols. of
St. Augustine's *Works,* Basel, Froben, 1529, with the signature in Latin
of William Redman (d.1602), Bishop of Norwich. Lupson (below) recorded
c. 320 vols. in 1881. St. Nicholas Church was severely damaged in World
War II: the ingenious six-shelf revolving reading-desk was destroyed, and *c.* 50
books badly damaged. During the re-building the remaining books were
deposited in Great Yarmouth PL; in 1961 they were returned to the church and
placed in a newly-constructed bookcase in the vestry lettered at the head,
'Bibliotheca Macronensis'. The collection now includes many later additions
and modern books. There are two versions of a Yarmouth Parochial Library
bookplate (one reading, 'The Parochial Library Great Yarmouth' (late 19th
cent.), and at least one vol. with a Bray Library bookplate and rules (a Bray
Library was est. in 1877).
Catalogues: in Henry Swinden, *The History and Antiquities of Great Yarmouth,* Norwich, 1772, pp.886–92.
References: Venn: Symonds; *N & Q,* 12 (1855), p.55; Edward. J. Lupson, *St.
Nicholas Church, Great Yarmouth,* 1881, pp.138–61 (the 2nd ed., 1897,
contains an illustration of the revolving bookcase); Cox & Harvey, p.336 (a
MS Hebrew roll of Esther is listed); Kelly, pp.75 & n.3, 250; Bill Report,
1970; Lambeth Palace MS.3223, ff.231–2: notes and rubbings of bindings by
N. R. Ker; DNB: Redman. I am indebted to Brian North Lee for the reference
to the late 19th cent. bookplate.

GREENFORD, Middx.
Holy Cross. Lon.
[nil ?] NRC
DeskL: in 1705 the incumbent reported copies of Walton's Polyglot and
Castell's Lexicon, donor unknown (see p.38,n.28).
References: Notitia Parochialis, 1705, no.546.

GRESSINGHAM, Lancs.
St. John the Evangelist. Blackb.
[nil] *
A ParL of 15 vols. was est. in 1762 by the Associates of Dr Bray. In 1849 this
library was reported as being one of those ' either wholly lost or reduced to a
few tattered volumes'. It was refounded in 1858, and augm. in 1870, but is not
recorded after 1900.

Catalogues: Bray Associates Records, f.38, p.88.
References: Select Committee Report, 1849; Shore, p.152; Bray Associates Annual Reports, 1900.

GREYSTOKE, Cumb. (Cumbria)
St. Andrew. Carl.
[nil] *
A catalogue of a library of theology, written in the back of a commonplace book by Dr Alan Smallwood (d.1686), rector 1663–86, is probably of his own collection but was possibly intended for a ParL: there are notes of loans, gifts, stocktaking, etc.
References: Venn: Smallwood; in Cumbria RO, Carlisle (see *Library History*, v.2.3, 1971, p.117).

GRINTON, Yorks. (N.Yorks.)
St. Andrew. Ripon
[iv.] *
DeskL: a copy of Burkitt on the New Testament, 1752, chained in a case and marked 'for the use of the inhabitants of Grinton 1752' and on 'a monastic antiphon stand, *c.* 1420'. First noted in 1950 and still present.
References: CCC Questionnaire, 1950.

GUILDEN MORDEN, Herts.
St. Mary. Ely
[nil] *
A ParL of 70 vols. was est. in 1817 by the Associates of Dr Bray. In 1849 this library was reported as being one of those 'either wholly lost or reduced to a few tattered volumes'.
Catalogues: March 1817. Bray Associates Records, f.38, pp.273–4.
References: Kelly, p.261 (under Cambs.)

GUILDFORD, Surrey
(Ded. unknown). Guildf.
A ParL was est. in 1893 by the Associates of Dr Bray.
References: Bray Associates Annual Report, 1895.

GUIST, Norf.
St. Andrew. Nor.
[5v.] Norwich CL
DeskL: BCP, 1662; *Certain Sermons or Homilies*, 1635; Erasmus, *Paraphrases*, 1548; Bible, 1611; Jewel, *Works*, 1611.

HACKNESS, Yorks. (N.Yorks.)
St. Peter. York
[116v.] York Minster Lib.

transf.

The library was est. in 1700 by Sir Philip Sydenham, bart. (1676?–1739), the owner of Hackness Hall, and was housed in the church vestry. From the catalogues of 1721 and 1862 it would seem that the library reached its maximum size soon after it was created: the 1721 catalogue (with 1726 additions) lists 234 titles of which only 94 remain; in the 1862 catalogue the collection was reduced to 112 vols., each numbered in gold leaf at the foot of the spine. Two more books were lost (nos. 88 and 89) before the collection was finally deposited in York Minster Lib. in 1967. When catalogued again in 1980 the collection contained 138 items in 110 vols., all published between 1515 and 1720. There have been a few recent deposits. The books are mainly in English and mainly theology, often with a puritan bias; but there are also 37 vols. in Latin and Greek and other subjects represented include history, law, language, literature, medicine, philosophy and geography. A Benefactors' Book, begun in 1700 and continued to 1729, makes it clear that the library was for the use of benefactors as well as the incumbent. Some 21 benefactors are listed (who together gave 283 vols.), but many who presented are not listed. There are 17 books signed by Sir Philip Sydenham and 9 by Sir Thomas or Lady Margaret Hoby (including some of the earliest and most valuable books in the collection from the period 1574 to 1631). All the books are in contemporary or early bindings. Two are of note: a Paris, 1515 book, with a cruciform blind-stamp design of London provenance, probably before 1536; and a James I, *Works*, in Latin, 1619, one of a pair bound in London, *c.* 1625 for George Villiers, Duke of Buckingham, in white vellum (the twin is at Jesus College, Oxford). Sydenham also collected MSS (e.g. a 15th cent. Book of Hours with his armorial bookplate was sold at Sotheby's, 24 June 1980).
Catalogues: the 1721 catalogue, by the Revd Richard Richardson, the 1862 catalogue, and the Benefactors' Book, are in the same MS in York Minster Lib.; Susan E. Boorman, 'A catalogue of Hackness parochial library', (M.A. Librarianship, University of Sheffield, 1980) includes provenances in the text (but not indexed), a list of items in the 1721 catalogue which have disappeared, and a transcript of the list of patrons in the Benefactors' Book.
References: VCH, *Yorkshire*, N. Riding, v.2, 1929, pp.529, 531; Barr, p.36; **bindings**: Oldham, Blind-stamped, p.59; Bodleian Library, *Fine Bindings 1500–1700 from Oxford Libraries*, 1968, no.137, pp.78–9 and pl.XXXII.

HADLEIGH, Suffolk
St. Mary. St.E.
[nil]

Dr Thomas Goad (1576–1638), rector of Hadleigh from 1618 until his death, intended to create a public theological library in the S. chapel of St. Mary's church. By 1727 there were still many shelves but no books. The probably incomplete MS catalogue in a late 17th cent. hand in Hadleigh Guildhall lists

144 vols., mostly theology, but with a varied miscellaneous section including books on gardening, accomptmanship, navigation, geometry, geography, history and mineralogy. The Revd Hugh James Rose (1795–1838), rector of Hadleigh 1830–33, attempted to est. a ParLL in 1830 by subscription and by donations of books from the SPCK.

Catalogues: MS, late 17th cent., in Guildhall, Hadleigh, 20/8.

References: DNB: Goad, Rose; Fitch, 1977, p.xiii; Wilkins MS, Hadleigh Deanery; Dorothy M. Barter Snow, 'Hugh James Rose, rector of Hadleigh, Suffolk' (B.Litt. thesis Oxford, 1960).

HALFORD, Warwicks.
Our Blessed Lady. Cov.
[iv.] Warwicks. CRO
DeskL: Homilies, 1673 (bought 1676).

HALIFAX, Yorks. (W.Yorks.)
St. John the Baptist. Wakef.
1. [c. 295 titles in 272v.] York UL
2. [377 titles in c. 400v.] In situ, but probably intended also for York UL. *
From entries in the registers there were MSS and possibly early printed service books, some of which were chained, at least by 1655. There were subsequently two collections:

1. A small library was est. by Robert Clay (c. 1575–1628), vicar 1624–28, which was considerably augmented over the next 200 years. An inventory of 1652 by John Brearcliffe (1609?–82), antiquary, of Halifax, printed by Hanson in 1909 (see below) lists 43 titles, mostly standard works for the use of the clergy. A large collection of books was given by Simon Sterne, of Halifax, in 1710 (commemorated by a plaque in the church), some of which belonged to his father, Richard Sterne (1596?–1683), Archbishop of York, 1664–83. Most of these books bear the signatures of various members of the Sterne family, but the majority prove to be from the library of William Sterne (d.1657), 3rd son of the Archbishop, rector of Glooston, Leics., 1633–57, and they commonly contain his notes. Many of the books are inscribed by their original donors (see Hanson, below). In 1705 the then incumbent did not reply to a questionnaire about the library. In 1710 bookcases were made and the chains struck off. A report was made by Canon F. Harrison, Librarian of York Minster, in 1934, based on the catalogue of 251 vols. made by the Revd P. Gough in c. 1910. The collection (then 263 vols.) was deposited by faculty on permanent loan in York UL in 1966. Not all of the early books survive, but some of the incunables remain, and all the books are pre-1700. They are mainly theological, but the classics are represented, and there are copies of Camden's *Britannia*, 1695, and some rare early scientific and medical works, including the first Latin ed. of Galileo's *Systema Cosmicum*, 1635, and, notably, the first ed. 1624 of *Arithmetica Logarithmica* by Henry Briggs, who presented it to the Halifax library in 1627. A number of books are in

Halifax: open cupboard

contemporary or early tooled or stamped bindings; some still bear evidence of chaining. No.214 was bound by B. Frye, Halifax. There was much rebinding in 1861.

2. In the larger vestry is a library of *c.* 400 vols. bequeathed by William Priestley (d. by 1856), received in 1862, of which *c.* 83 vols. are pre-1800. Priestley also gave £70 to provide the bookcases in which they are still housed.
Catalogues: 1. Brearcliffe 1652 inventory (originals owned by Waterhouse Charity Governors; copy in PRO; printed in Hanson, below); MS catalogue by the Revd Robert Merrick, then curate, and John Lister, *c.* 1883; catalogue of the Revd P. Gough, *c.* 1910 (copies in Bodl.MS.Eng.Misc.c.360, and CCC); card catalogue with the collection. 2. Photostat of ms. catalogue of 'books presented to the vicar of Halifax in aid of the restoration of the ancient library in the crypt of the church of St. John the Baptist, Halifax, by the late William Priestley . . . 1856' in Lambeth Palace MS.3222, ff.3–79 (copy in CCC).
References: Foster: Clay; DNB, Brearcliffe; T. W. Hanson, 'Halifax Parish Church under the Commonwealth', Part III. *Trans. of the Halifax Antiq. Soc.*, (1909), pp.288–98; and 'Halifax Parish church library', *ibid* (1951), pp.37–47; Notitia Parochialis, 1705: no.397; J. Horsfall Turner, *Halifax Books and Authors*, 1906, p.258; A. H. Cash, *Laurence Sterne: the Early and Middle Years*, 1975, p.4; Lambeth Palace MS.3222, ff.3–79: notes on provenance and rubbings of bindings by N. R. Ker, and correspondence by him in CCC file; Pearson A255.4.

HALSTEAD, Essex
St. Andrew. Chelmsf.
[nil] *
A ParL was est. in 1852 by the Associates of Dr Bray.
References: Shore, p.152.

HALTON, Ches.
St. Mary. Ches.
[400+v.]
In 1705 Sir John Chesshyre (1662?–1738) endowed the chapel of ease near Halton Castle; in 1733 he built and furnished with 4 presses of books a separate library-room 'pro communi literatorum usu sub cura Curati Capellæ de Halton', according to a tablet over the door. A unique shelf-list, printed in London in 1733 on vellum in one copy was kept with the collection in 1959 but can no longer be found. According to the 1898 reprint of this list, with additions, there were *c.* 400 vols. in the original bequest but there have been serious losses and neglect over the years. Some 62 19th and 20th cent. vols. have been added to the collection. The original bookcases were destroyed in 1974, as being decayed beyond repair, and the books were transferred to the vicarage. The refurbished library-room was opened in 1976; in *c.* 1983 new bookcases were specially constructed and, after alterations, the books were finally restored to the shelves in 1992 according to the order of the 1733 shelf-

Halton: exterior view of the separate library building
endowed and furnished by Sir John Chesshyre in 1733

Halton: close-up of the memorial inscription concerning the founder,
Sir John Chesshyre

list. The collection consists mainly of divinity, ecclesiastical history and works of the Fathers, with a number of editions of the classics. The earliest book is St. Jerome's *Works*, Basel, Froben, 1516–53. Many books contain Chesshyre's signature, date of purchase, price paid, and names of booksellers (often with warranty). The prices of bindings are given separately. Provenances include the bookplates of William Talbot (1659–1730), Bishop of Oxford, 1702, and Gilbert Burnet (1643–1715), Bishop of Salisbury. After long neglect the bindings are generally in poor condition; 30 vols. were selected for repair / rebinding with grant-aid in 1978.

Catalogues: 1733 catalogue: original now lost; a reprint with additions, including extracts from Chesshyre's will concerning the library, by George Daniel Wray, 1898 (copy in CCC); TS shelf-lists from the Chesshyre Family Papers in Chetham's Lib., Mun.E.1.7 (copy in Lambeth Palace, MS.3222, ff.80–2); TS catalogue by C. D. Wood, 1949, once kept in the vicarage but no longer to be found; computerised catalogue by G. Goodall and P. O'Connor, 1995– .

References: DNB: Chesshyre, Talbot, Burnet; Select Committee Report, 1849; W. E. Axon, 'Sir John Chesshyre's library at Halton, in Cheshire', *Lib. Jnl*, v.4 (1879), pp.35–8; Charles Nickson, *A History of Runcorn*, 1887, pp.114–17.

HALTWHISTLE, Northumb.
Holy Cross. Newc.
[nil] *
One of 92 parishes in the Northumberland Archdeaconry granted a ParLL under a scheme devised by Bishop Shute Barrington, carried out by Archdeacon R. G. Bouyer by 1823 (see p.57), and recorded as still possessing books in the visitation returns, 1826–8. Also noted in 1828 was 'a collection of divinity furnished by Mr. [Nathaniel] Hollingworth', the then incumbent.
References: Day, pp.97, 102 n.38.

HALVERGATE, Norf.
St. Peter and St. Paul. Nor.
[2v.] Norwich CL
DeskL: *Certain Sermons or Homilies*, 1683; Bible, 1685.

HAMBLETON, Rut.
St. Andrew. Pet.
[1v.] *
DeskL: 'Judas' Bible, 1611.

HAMPTON IN ARDEN, Warwicks.
St. Mary and St. Bartholomew. Birm.
[1v.]
DeskL: Collection of articles, canons, injunctions, London, Bill, 1699.
References: NADFAS Report.

HAPTON, Norf.
St. Margaret. Nor.
[3v.] Norwich CL
DeskL: BCP, 1662; *Certain Sermons or Homilies*, 1635 [1633]; Bible, 1611.

HARDRAW, Yorks. (N.Yorks.]
St. Mary and St. John. Ripon
[nil] *
A ParL was est. in 1766 by the Associates of Dr Bray. In 1849 this library was reported as being one of those 'either wholly lost or reduced to a few tattered volumes'.
References: Select Committee Report, 1849; Kelly, p.264.

HARDWICK, Oxon. (otherwise Cokethorpe)
St. Mary the Virgin. Ox.
[nil ?] NRC
DeskL: in 1950 there was a 17th cent. Bible chained on a contemporary shelf in the porch, and 4 18th cent. works.
References: CCC Questionnaire, 1950.

HARTLAND, Devon
St. Nectan. Ex.
[nil] *
DeskL: in reply to a CCC Questionnaire of 1950, Hartland reported a copy of Foxe's *Book of Martyrs*, given in 1686 by Mrs Joanna Tucker of Long Furlong, but this can no longer be found.

HARWICH, Essex
St. Nicholas (ded. uncertain). Chelmsf.
[nil]
The Corporation est. a room in the church for a ParLL or PL, which was in use by 1711. St. Nicholas was the parish church but it is possible that the library was at All Saints as the SPCK correspondent, the Rev. William Curtis, was incumbent of both parishes.
References: Kelly, p.247, citing SPCK MSS, Abstracts of correspondence, vols.1–3, 1709–11.

HASLINGDEN, Lancs.
St. James. Blackb.
[nil] *
A ParL of 65 vols. was est. in 1819 by the Associates of Dr Bray, augm. in 1870.
Catalogues: Bray Associates Records, f.40, pp.27–9.
References: Shore, 1879; Kelly, p.262.

Hatfield Broad Oak: view through the arched door of the room
specially built by Sir Charles Barrington in 1708
to house the collections of George Stirling, vicar *c.* 1684–1728

HASSINGHAM, Norf.
St. Mary. Nor.
[3 items in 2v.] Norwich CL
DeskL: BCP, *c.* 1675; *Book of Psalms*, 1682; *Certain Sermons or Homilies*, 1676.

HATFIELD, Yorks. (S.Yorks.)
St. Lawrence. Sheff.
[nil ?] NRC
DeskL: a copy of Jewel, chained, was present in 1907.
References: Cox & Harvey, p.339.

HATFIELD BROAD OAK, Essex
In situ St. Mary the Virgin. Chelmsf.
[320+v.]
The collection was est. by George Stirling (1648–1728), vicar *c.* 1684–1728, and has been augm. since, mainly by local dignitaries. It was housed in a room specially built to receive it at the E. end of the S. chancel in 1708 by Sir Charles Barrington. The room was enlarged and new shelving provided in 1843, and in 1983 the room was again extensively restored. The collection now contains *c.* 290 pre-1800 works, including 2 incunables, 30 works printed 1501–1600, 135 printed 1601–1700, and 123 printed 1701–1899, and there are 340+ 19th cent. works. The books are mainly theological, with some history, biography, medicine, philosophy, travel, and multilingual diction-aries. Among the earliest books are a copy of Orosius, *Historiae Aversus Paganos*, Venice, 1499, bound with Bartolomeo Platyn, *Historia de Vitis Pontificum*, Venice, 1504; and an Aldine Aristotle, 1498. Most books have an inscription in English or Latin stating that they belong 'to the Church Library at Hatfield Regis alias Broad Oak in ye county of Essex' and a printed no. in white on the spine and inside. Some of the books from the 1840s have SPCK Parochial Lending Library labels with Rules or SPCK blind-stamps on the upper covers, and there is a 19th cent. label, reading 'Hatfield Broad Oak Lending Library', with conditions for lending printed below. There are two 16th cent. stamped bindings, and a number in plain calf stamped with the 17th cent. Barrington arms. The bindings were all in poor condition but many have now been rebound, repaired or boxed with grant- aid.
Catalogues: MS. listing *c.* 320 vols. n.d. (with the collection; copy in Lambeth Palace MS.3222, ff.83–99); computerised catalogue by Brian S. Pugh, 1984 (revised 1994), with the collection (and a copy disk in CCC): includes notes on provenances, bindings, etc.
References: DNB: Stirling; A. D. Jones, 'The church library of Hatfield Regis', *Essex Arch. Soc. Trans*, NS v. 6 (1898), p.339; F. W. Galpin, 'Hatfield Broad Oak', *Essex Rev.* v. 44 (1935), p.83; Kelly, p.247; A. Jones, 'Parochial learning', *Country Life*, 16 Feb. 1978, p.394; Lambeth Palace MS.3222, ff.83–99: notes and rubbings of bindings by N. R. Ker; DRB2, p.80; Pearson

Heathfield (in Chichester Cathedral Library)

A235.2; I am indebted to Brian North Lee for the reference to the 19th cent. bookplate.

HEANTON, Devon
St. Augustine. Ex.
[nil] *
A ParL was projected in 1719.
References: Kelly, p.246, citing SPCK MSS, Abstracts of Correspondence, vol.10, 1719.

HEATHFIELD, Sussex (E.Sussex)
All Saints. Chich.
transf
[221v.] Chichester CL; some in situ *
Richard Wilkin, bookseller of St. Paul's Churchyard (d.1740), son of Richard Wilkin, vicar, 1655–99, bequeathed 'the books in my press and the said press to the use of the residing Vicars of Heathfield and the Curates for ever to be kept in a dry convenient place in the vicaridge house'. The books were kept in the vicarage in the original cupboard which had a MS list inside the doors. A 1745 catalogue states that the books were still 'in the possession of William Preston vicar of that parish'. They were deposited in Chichester CL in 1983. There are *c.* 13 Wing items, the remainder being 18th cent. Apart from religious controversy, there are books of classical scholarship, and works on agriculture, household management, carriers' timetables, heraldry and English literature. Still retained at the vicarage are some brief runs and single vols. from some 6 18th cent. periodicals, probably part of the original collection.
Catalogues: the original book-cupboard has not survived but there is a photograph of the MS list with the collection; the 1745 catalogue in West Sussex RO, Chichester Episcopal Archives EpII/42/3 (copy in CCC) lists 229 vols., by size, with brief authors and titles but no dates.
References: Plomer, *Dictionary*, 1668–1725: Wilkin; Perceval Lucas, *Heathfield Memorials*, 1910, p.26.

HEDGERLEY, Bucks.
St. Mary the Virgin. Ox.
[1v.] Bucks. RO, Aylesbury
DeskL: *A Sermon preached at the Funeral of Mr. Tho. Whitchurch October the 15th 1691 at Chalfont St. Peter, by Henry Parsley, rector of Hedgerley,* 1692.

HEMEL HEMPSTEAD, Herts.
St. Mary. St.Alb.
[2v.] *
DeskL: Foxe, *Book of Martyrs,* 16th / 17th cent. ed.

HENBURY, Glos. (Bristol)
St. Mary the Virgin. Bris.
[nil] *
A printed book label for the Henbury Village & Parish Library, 1808, is in the
Franks Collection: no.33853.

HENLEY-IN-ARDEN, Warwicks (W.Mids.)
St. John the Baptist. Cov.
[nil]
A ParL of 67 vols. was est. in 1710 by the Bray Trustees for Erecting Parochial
Libraries; by 1878 it was untraced. There is a copy of the Bray Library
bookplate in the Franks Collection: no.33854.
Catalogues: Bray Associates Records, f.39, pp.9–11.
References: Bray Associates Annual Reports, 1878.

HENLEY-ON-THAMES, Oxon.
St. Mary. Ox.
[*c.* 400 titles in 475v.] Reading UL, and Christ Church, Oxford.
Charles Aldrich (1681–1737), rector of Henley 1709–37, in his will of 1736
left 'all my study of books to the rectory of Henley, being desirous to lay the
foundation of a parochial library, begging my successor, or the parish, to
provide a room for them, if God should not spare my life to do it'. In 1710
Aldrich had become Librarian at Christ Church, Oxford, where his uncle,
Henry Aldrich (1647–1710) was Dean, an appointment made to facilitate the
carrying out of his wish that his library duplicates should be given to his
nephew. The term 'duplicate' was loosely interpreted, and many early books
and inscribed presentation copies came into Charles Aldrich's library which
should not have left Christ Church. Aldrich's successor, the Revd William
Stockwood, rector 1737–84, apparently took personal possession of the library
for some 40 years until, after a Visitation in 1777, he was persuaded to deliver
up the books to the churchwardens who installed bookshelves in the vestry to
accommodate them. The Visitors devised 'Rules for the government of the
parochial library of Henley', clause 8 of which required 2 catalogues to be
made, one for the church and one for the Diocesan Record Office. The first of
these MS catalogues, *c.* 1780, was discovered at Eton College in 1967 and is
now at Reading UL. It contains a list of 996 titles. A printed catalogue
appeared in 1852, and in 1859 a Henley Library label was put inside all the
books. At the time of an extensive re-ordering of the church in 1853 the books
were removed to St. Mary's Hall (now Kenton Theatre), and a long period of
neglect began. In 1909, after another move to the National School at Gravel
Hill, W. G. Hiscock, later Librarian of Christ Church, 'saved many volumes
from complete disintegration by bringing them back to Oxford', and in 1942
he picked out a further 8 vols. (including 5 presentation copies) for return to
Christ Church. A TS list of 'Books retained at Christ Church' includes *c.* 244
titles (in 283 vols.) of which 171 are definitely from the Henley library (with

bookplates, MS nos., etc) and the remainder probably belonging, with varying degrees of certainty. The residue of the Henley collection, *c.* 475 vols., by then boxed up at Chantry House, was transferred to Reading UL on permanent deposit in 1957. Most of the Henley books were in poor condition; those at Christ Church have in many cases been repaired, and those at Reading UL extensively restored and repaired with the help of an anonymous grant.

Because of its origin, that part of the collection at Reading UL is an unusually catholic one: less than half the books are theological, devotional or biblical, and there are strong groups of books on geography, history and voyages (including De Bry, *India Orientalis*, 1598–1612), science, mathematics (including Archimedes, Basel, 1544; Flamsteed, *Atlas Coelestis*, 1729) and classics, with some books of philosophy, law, literature, art and architecture. There are no incunables but the collection includes 38 STC, 127 Wing and 34 ESTC titles, and 20 continental 16th cent. and 118 18th cent. titles. Some later additions to the collection include books presented by the SPCK, and *c.* 52 vols. of, mainly, Record Commission publications presented in 1834. Bindings in the collection are mainly plain calf, but there is a gold-tooled binding by Henry Seale of Oxford on Epictetus and Theophrastus (1707), edited by Charles Aldrich and dedicated to Henry Aldrich. A copy of Bishop Jewel's *Works*, 1609 (presented 1711) has the remains of a chain and staple. Another clause in the 1777 Rules indicated that books might be borrowed (an unusual provision at the time) and it is evident that some were not returned: at least one vol. with a Henley bookplate is in a private collection. Copies of the pictorial bookplate are in the Franks Collection, nos. 33854–5, dated 1737.

Catalogues: 'A catalogue of the books left to the rectory of Henley by the late Dr Aldrich', *c.* 1780 (RUL MS 411/1/1) also includes dated receipts for books returned from loan, 1802–16, and the TS list of 'Books retained by Christ Church' (copy in CCC marked-up with Christ Church shelf-marks); *A Catalogue of the Old Library at Henley-on-Thames*, 1852 (microfilm copy in RUL: P109); Henley on Thames: the Aldrich Library, TS shelf / subject list, n.d. (Bodl.MS.Eng.Misc.c.360, copy in CCC); catalogue *c.* 1860 of books presented to the library by the SPCK, with some loan records (RUL MS 1172/1/1); Reading UL OPAC (in progress).

References: J. S. Burn, *A History of Henley on Thames*, 1861, pp.103–7; Cox & Harvey, p.334; W. G. Hiscock, *A Christ-Church Miscellany*, 1946, p.64; Kelly, pp.93, 95, 252; Paul Morgan, *Oxford Libraries outside the Bodleian*, 2nd ed., 1980, p.31; J. A. Edwards, 'Manuscript catalogue of Henley Parish Library', *Library History*, v.1.6 (1969), pp.216–17; D. H. Knott, *Rare Book Collections*, Reading UL, 1980 (and later revisions). I am grateful to Matthew Phillips for information on the Henley books at Christ Church.

Hereford: the chained library of All Saints Church bequeathed by
William Brewster in 1715, as housed in Hereford Cathedral (left side)
*(Reproduced by permission of the Dean and Chapter of Hereford
and the Hereford Mappa Mundi Trust)*

Hereford: the chained library of All Saints Church bequeathed by
William Brewster in 1715, as housed in Hereford Cathedral (right side)
*(Reproduced by permission of the Dean and Chapter of Hereford
and the Hereford Mappa Mundi Trust)*

HEREFORD, Heref.
All Saints. Heref.
[*c.* 520 titles in 326v.] Hereford CL

The church inventories from 1619 to 1664 indicate that there were chained books in All Saints during this period, and a desk was made for them: Jewel's *Works*, Erasmus' *Paraphrase*; Greenham's *Works*; and Rufinus' *Catechism*. Neither the books nor the desk have survived. William Brewster, M.D. (1655–1715) bequeathed his substantial and important library to the Bodl. and to St. John's College, Oxford, with some gifts to his friends, and 'to the Rector or vicar of All Saints for the time being and his successors for ever . . . all such my books of divinity, morality and history'. The 'overseers' of the will included other subjects in that part of the bequest to Hereford, which then consisted of 285 vols. In further compliance with the will, two oak presses were made, with a desk across the front within the length of the chains to each book, and two oak benches. The chains of hand-made links, each containing a swivel, are of the same pattern as those in Hereford Cathedral chained library and were perhaps donated by the Cathedral. It was the last substantial library to be chained in its entirety. In 1858, when the parish was in financial difficulties, Mr Head, a churchwarden of All Saints and bookseller in Hereford, sold all the books complete with chains for £100 to a London dealer for shipment to America. The Dean of Windsor (with the canons, patron of the living) intervened and the books were returned to Hereford. Finally in 1995 the books and fittings were sold by faculty to the Mappa Mundi Trust and they are now in a special display in Hereford CL. Apart from books of divinity, morality and history there are works on philosophy, politics and government, science and medicine, and a few works of literature. The oldest book is Alexander Carpenter, *Destructiorium Vitiorum*, Paris, Levet, 1497 (in an early 16th cent. stamped calf binding); other early books include Voragine's *Legende Sanctorum*, Venice, Locatello, 1500 (in original wooden boards), and *Portiforium Secundum vsum Sarum*, London, Whytchurch, 1541 (STC2 15884). There are 336 Wing titles and *c.* 44 STC.

Catalogues: there are catalogues of Brewster's books 1706–16, and papers relating to the disposal of his books and the parochial library in the Brewster Papers, Herf. RO (A.81/IV–); a shelf-list, *c.* 1800; Blades, BIC, pp.26–7, and 53–9, 'Appendix A. A catalogue of the chained library in All Saints' Parish Church, Hereford' has 283 entries (not counting tract vols.); F. C. Morgan, 'Catalogue of the books in All Saints Church, Hereford, bequeathed by Dr William Brewster, 1655–1715', TS, 1963 (photostat in CCC: provenances are noted in the text, and there is a separate index of 25 owners before Brewster).

References: F. H. Mountney, *All Saints' Church Hereford: the Chained Library*, Hereford, 1962; Maura Tallon, *Hereford Cathedral Library, with notes on an Irish Medieval Manuscript there, and on All Saints' Church Chained Library, Hereford*, Athlone printed, 1963 (includes an illustration of 1 case and desk); Pilgrim Trust 33rd Report, 1963, p.16; F. C. Morgan, 'Dr. William Brewster of Hereford (1660–1715): a benefactor to libraries', *Medical*

History, v.8.2 (1964), pp.137–48; 'All Saints Parish Library, Hereford, under threat', *Library History Newsletter* (Summer 1994), pp.1–3. Photographs of the bookcases are in: Blades, BIC, pl.8; Streeter, p.307.

HETHERSETT, Norf.
St. Remigius. Nor.
[4v.] Norwich CL
DeskL: *Certain Sermons or Homilies*, 1635; Erasmus, *Paraphrases*, 1548; Bible, 1613; Jewel, *Works*, 1611.

HEVERSHAM, Westm. (Cumbria)
St. Peter. Carl.
[5 titles in 8v.] Newcastle UL; Cumbria RO, Kendal
The ParLL of *c.* 112 vols. est. in 1766 by the Associates of Dr Bray, and augm. with a further 18 vols. in 1804, was founded in the Free School, later Heversham Grammar School, but intended for the use of local clergy as well as masters and boys of the school. In 1808 there were 163 vols. This collection was deposited in Newcastle UL in 1964. A further 8 vols. are deposited in Cumbria RO, 5 of them 'given to the library of Heversham School by the Reverend Daniel Wilson of Lanca[ster]' in 1772. A later library is said to have been 'founded' at the school by Henry Wilson (b. *c.* 1766), vicar of Heversham, and the Associates of Dr Bray, in 1788.
Catalogues: Bray Associates Records, f.38, p.137; list of 8 vols. Cumbria RO, Kendal: WPR/8 (copy in CCC).
References: Foster: Henry Wilson; Kelly, p.263 & n.3; Edgar Hinchcliffe, 'The Bainbrigg Library of Appleby School' (*History of the Book Trade in the North*, PH73, 1996, p.6); DRB2, 1997, p.54.

HIGH WYCOMBE, Bucks.
All Saints. Ox.
[*c.* 50v.]
A ParLL of *c.* 82 vols. was est. by the Associates of Dr Bray in 1849, and augm. in 1872, 1881, 1884, 1887 and 1896. It is housed in a 16th (?) cent. parish chest, together with deeds and plans. It is mainly a 19th cent. collection but includes Matthew Pole, *Synopsis Criticorum* . . . 5v, 1669–76, Barrow's *Works*, 1716, and Bartholomaeo Gavanto, *Thesaurus Sacrorum Rituum*, Venice, Menasolius, 1682. There are also 20th cent. books, books from other late 19th cent. Bucks. Bray libraries, and 19th cent. music. There is a Borrowers' Register, with some entries from the 1850s to 1870s.
Catalogues: Bray Associates Records, f.41, pp.221–2.
References: Bray Associates Annual Reports, 1900; Kelly, p.261.

HILLINGDON, Middx
St. John the Baptist. Lon.
[2v.?]
Samuel Reynardson (d.1721) in his will dated 1715 gave 'all his printed books
both at Hillingdon and in London, for the use of the Vicar of this parish, and
his successors' and directed 'that all his plants . . . to be sold and money raised
to build a room over the vestry, or over Munsey's porch, and furnishing it with
shelves, a table, a Turkey carpet, or a green cloth, and chairs; and that the
remainder should be appropriated to the purchase of books to add to the
library, which he directed should be kept according to the rules contained in
an Act of Parliament passed in 1708, for the preservation of parochial
libraries'. This room was built over the vestry. Lysons (below) lists 23 selected
titles, 8 16th cent. and the remainder 17th cent., showing that this library
contained valuable early botanical books. A full catalogue was printed in
1851, listing some 522 titles (including those purchased that year). The
collection was 'very good and well-kept' in 1883. According to information
received by the Council in 1950 the books were burnt at the direction of A. M.
Bashford, vicar, 1934–49, except for a copy of *Eikon Basilike*, rescued by the
verger. A Bishops' Bible has also since been discovered.
Catalogues: in Lysons, below; *Catalogue of the Hillingdon Church Library,
preserving the Original Orthography*. Printed for private circulation. The
Lodge, Hillingdon, 1851 (12 copies only; copy in BL: 11913.c.22).
References: Daniel Lysons, *An historical Account of those Parishes in the
County of Middlesex which are nor described in the Environs of London*,
1800, pp.168–9; W. E. Walford, *N & Q*, 6 ser. 8 (1883), p.178; Bill Report,
1970; Andrea T. Cameron, 'Some parochial libraries of south-west Middlesex', *Ealing Occasional Papers in the History of Libraries*, no.1 (1972),
pp.5–6.

HILMARTON, Wilts.
St. Lawrence. Sarum
[3v.?] NRC
DeskL: books present in 1950: Bible, 1611?, chained, rebound 1857; BCPs,
1770 & later; a Bible, tp. missing.
References: CCC Questionnaire, 1950.

HINDRINGHAM, Norf.
St. Martin. Nor.
[1v.] Norwich CL
DeskL: Jewel, *Works*, 1611.

HOCKERING, Norf.
St. Michael. Nor.
[2v.] Norwich CL
DeskL: Bible, 1674; Henry Compton, *Constitutions and Canons*, 1678.

In situ

HODNET, Shrops.
St. Luke. Lich.
[15v.]
DeskL: probably the earliest such collection in Shrops., but its history is unknown. Most of the books were chained and 5 remain chained to the rail of a desk enclosed in a 'Jacobean' style glass case at the E. end of the S. transept; the remaining books are in a parish chest. The 15th cent. Book of Hours was rebound by Roger Powell in 1956; there is one incunable, a Bible, Nuremberg, Koberger, 1479, also repaired by Roger Powell; 3 STC, 1 Wing, 2 18th cent. and 1 19th cent. titles.
Catalogues: a TS list with MS notes and rubbings of 2 bindings by N. R. Ker is in Lambeth Palace MS.3222, ff.119–21; Ker, MMBL, II, 1979, pp.985–6.
References: Kelly, Shrops., p.ix.

Hodnet: part of perhaps the earliest chained library in Shropshire, in a modern Jacobean-style case

HOLDGATE, Shrops.
Holy Trinity. Heref.
[1v.] *
DeskL: a vol. containing 23 printed sermons published 1678–83; 10 of the sermons 1678–9 have the signature of 'Henry Lyttelton' on the title-page.

HOLYWELL, Hunts. (Cambs.)
St. John the Baptist. Ely
[4v.] Cambs. CRO, Huntingdon
DeskL: Jewell, *Works*, 1611; Pulton, *Statutes*, 1632; *Collection of Statutes*, *1640–1667*, 1667; BCP & Psalms, 1669.

HOOLE, Lancs.
St. Michael. Blackb.
[nil]
A ParL of 13 vols. was est. in 1762 by the Associates of Dr Bray. In 1849 this library was reported as being one of those 'either wholly lost or reduced to a few tattered volumes'.
Catalogues: Bray Associates Records, f.38, p.91.
References: Select Committee Report, 1849; Kelly, p.262.

HOOTON ROBERTS, Yorks. (S.Yorks.)
St. John. Sheff.
[1v.] Lambeth Palace Lib.
Known only from a bookplate in: Thomas Roberts, *Short and Plain Instructions for the better Understanding of the Lord's Supper*, 1825, in Lambeth Palace Library.

HORDLE, Hants.
[1v.] Hants. RO
DeskL: John Birket (vicar, 1679–1722), *The God-father's Advice to his Son*, 2nd ed., 1700.

HORNCASTLE, Lincs.
St. Mary the Virgin. Linc.
[4v.] *
DeskL: Foxe, *Book of Martyrs*, 3v. 8th ed. 1684; Nicolas Fontaine [Royaumont, pseud.], trans. Horneck, *History of the Old and New Testament*, 1701, given by a parishioner, Nicholas Shipley, in the late 18th cent. With brass hasps; two vols. have 18–20 inch chains still attached; now housed in a metal chest.

HORNCHURCH, Essex
St. Andrew. Chelmsf.
[nil?]
DeskL: in 1557 a parishioner, after being found guilty of misconduct, was ordered by the church courts to provide a copy of the Bible and 'Mr. Foxe's last book of the monuments', both to be secured by lock and chains to a desk in the church.
References: Woolf, p.190 & n.77, quoting M. M. McIntosh, *A Community Transformed: the Manor and Living of Havering, 150–1620*, Cambridge, 1991, pp.195, 227, 272.

HORSTED KEYNES, Sussex (E.Sussex)
St. Giles. Chich.
[6v.] in situ; [14v.] Chichester CL
The 6v. still at St. Giles consist of Archbishop Leighton's *Sermons,* 1692, his *Select Works,* 1746, and 4 other 18th cent. books. The books now at Chichester CL were originally from Leighton's library (Robert Leighton, 1611–84, Bishop of Dunblane in 1661 and Archbishop of Glasgow in 1669). Shortly after he resigned in 1674 Leighton came to live at Broadhurst in Horsted Keynes, the home of his sister, the widow of Edward Lightmaker, and remained there until his death. The bulk of his library was left to the clergy of the diocese of Dunblane: the Leighton Library at Dunblane is now administered by Stirling UL. The books at Chichester are from the Wing period, and include works by Matthew Hales, Selden and others.
References: DNB: Leighton; DRB2, pp. 559, 624.

HORWICH, Lancs.
Holy Trinity. Man.
[nil] *
Catalogues: A TS catalogue of 'Horwich Parochial Library 1740 Lancs.' is in Lambeth Palace MS.3094 (copy in CCC): it lists 19 titles in 20 vols. (without dates).

HOUNSLOW, Middx
Holy Trinity. Lon.
[nil] *
The minutes of the Bray Trustees for Erecting Parochial Libraries list the conditional allocation of a ParL to Hounslow in the years 1727–9; a catalogue of the library provided *c.* 1731 by Lady Anne Hollis and Lady Blount is in Phillipps MS.31985, which later belonged to Wifred Merton (untraced). The church was destroyed by fire in 1943. A copy of the Bray Library bookplate with 'Hounslow' entered in MS is in the Franks Collection: no. 53856.
References: Kelly, pp.250, 260; Lambeth Palace MS.3224 (a letter from A. N. L. Munby to N. R. Ker, 16.9.1959, describing the MS above).

HOWE, Norf.
St. Mary the Virgin. Nor.
[1v.] *
One vol. has survived from the library of *c.* 76 titles est. by the Bray Trustees for Erecting Parochial Libraries in *c.* 1729 'at the request of Lady Betty Hastings' (see p.39, n.39).
Catalogues: *c.* 1730: Bray Associates Records, loose papers.
References: Kelly, p.263 & n.1.

HUDDERSFIELD, Yorks. (W.Yorks.)
Holy Trinity (ded. uncertain). Wakef.
[nil] *
A ParLL of 216 vols. was est. in 1841 by the Associates of Dr Bray, and augm. in 1872. It is not recorded after 1890.
Catalogues: Bray Associates Records, f.41, pp.53–8.
References: Bray Associates Annual Reports, 1890.

HUGGATE, Yorks. (E. Riding of Yorks.)
St. Mary. York.
[nil]
A Huggate glebe terrier of 1858 lists 'A parochial library in a deal closet in the vestry of nearly 190 volumes', now untraceable.
References: terrier: Humbs. County Archives, Beverley, DDX/200/8.

HUGHENDEN, Bucks.
St. Michael. Ox.
[nil ?] NRC
There are two versions of a seal bookplate in the Franks Collection: nos. 33801–2, which may indicate a 19th cent. ParL.

HULL, Yorks.
Holy Trinity. York
[47 iv.] Hull UL; [iv.] in situ.
Entries in the church accounts noted by Abraham de la Pryme (1672–1704) indicate that Mrs Eleanor Crowle, who gave £5 in 1665 'to be disposed of in books for ye use of the Church', and further sums of £20 and £5 in 1666 and 1667 for the same purpose, was the founder of the library. Pryme made a catalogue of the collection in 1700 which then numbered 331 vols. (see below), and in 1796 John Tickell reported that the library was 'very handsome and neat' and 'continually increasing in number' since the churchwardens had forty shillings a year to buy books at their own discretion. It was early on est. in its own room, a former chapel on the S. side of the choir. A faculty to sell the library was obtained in 1906, but in 1907 it was given by the vicar and churchwardens to the Hull Museums Committee, and then transferred to University College, Hull (now University of Hull) in 1938. There were then 667 vols. The purchases with the annual £2 from 1798 to 1860 are listed in the notebook in Hull UL: they include 17th cent. editions of Basil, Justinus, Strabo, Photius and Salmasius. Most of the books are pre-1700. A MS Bible with historiated initials listed by Pryme, and shown in an exhibition in the town Hall in 1899, was reported missing in 1923 (it bore the signature of Thomas, Lord Fairfax, on the first leaf). A 17th cent. copy of the Visitation of Yorkshire by Robert Glover, Somerset Herald, in 1584–5, with additions, remains at Holy Trinity. Many of the bindings were in a bad state; most of them have EST (Ecclesia Sanctae Trinitatis?) stamped on the front cover.

Catalogues: Abraham de la Pryme's catalogue was included in his 'Short description and account of ye two churches of the Holy Trinity and St. Mary's in Kingston upon Hull', autograph copy in Hull PL (see 'The diary of Abraham de la Pryme', *Surtees Society*, v.54 (1870), p.298); transcripts are in BL.MS Lansdowne 891 (18th cent.) and in Hull PL (19th cent.); another MS catalogue, on vellum, was destroyed in WWII (photostat: Hull UL, DX/51); the notebook in Hull UL is at DX/46; a MS catalogue was made by M. C. Peck in 1870 (Borthwick Institute FAC.1906/25); a TS 'rough list', n.d., is in Bodl.MS.Eng.Misc.c.360 (copy in CCC); the books are being re-catalogued on Hull UL OPAC.

References: DNB: Pryme; John Tickell, *A History of Kingston upon Hull*, 1796, p.793; Blades, BIC, p.28; *Publishers' Circular*, 118, 17 Mar. 1923; Kelly, pp.80, 195, 256; Barr, p.34; Brian Dyson, 'In the line of fire: the library of University College Hull during World War II', *Library History*, v.15:2 (1999), pp.113-23; Lambeth Palace MS.3222, ff.122-3: notes by N. R. Ker.

HULL, Yorks.
St. Mary, Lowgate. York
[164 titles in 145v.] Hull UL
From an inventory of 1684 in the churchwardens' accounts there were copies of Jewel and Harding as well as Bibles and copies of the BCP from an earlier date, and some books still in the collection may have formed a DeskL in the 16th cent. Other inventories record gifts of 16 books given by John Bewley in 1682 and 11 books given by Mr Metcalf in 1684. By 1703 the library had more than doubled in size, which makes the comment in Notitia Parochialis of 1705 of 'weak efforts made towards settling a library in ye parish, but its fallen to nought' somewhat surprising. There were some 18th cent. donors, including William Cogan, alderman, Joshua Claver and James Wilkinson. There were two revivals in the 19th cent., by John Scott, vicar 1816–34, who did much work on rebinding, repairing and collating books, and by his son, John Scott II (d.1865) who succeeded him, and bequeathed *c.* 200 vols., listed in the Record Book in the parish muniments, many belonging to his father or grandfather. There is some evidence for the existence of later library foundations in the form of a few surviving bookplates: 'St. Mary's Library' (which may have had up to *c.* 700 vols.); derived from this, 'St. Mary's Parochial School Library;' and from *c.* 1866, another library, founded with the aid of an SPCK grant. The books were housed finally, in 1877, in cases round the top of the vestry walls. In 1967 they were deposited in Hull UL on permanent loan. The collection contains 19 STC, 12 Wing, 19 18th cent. English titles; 10 16th cent. and 6 17th cent. continental titles.

Catalogues: a detailed description and list is in the Archdeacon's Court books for 1719 and 1720 (Borthwick Institute, R.VI.D.13); a rough list of 1961 came with the collection to Hull UL; P. A. Hoare, 'The Parish Library of Saint Mary Lowgate, Hull: a catalogue . . . with an historical introduction', 1972 (TS, copy in CCC: this is a full catalogue, with descriptions of some of the notable and rarer books, and an index of previous owners, donors and inscriptions); the books are also on Hull UL OPAC.

References: Notitia Parochialis, 1705: no.1044; Kelly, pp.91 n.4, 256; Barr, p.34; B. Dyson, 'Parish library of St. Mary, Lowgate', *Bull. of the Brynmor Jones Lib.*, no.16, (1986), p.2.

HUNGERFORD, Berks.

St. Lawrence. Ox.

[1v.] *

DeskL: 'Breeches' Bible. Nothing survives of the ParLL of 203 vols. est. in 1841 by the Associates of Dr Bray, and augm. in 1870.

Catalogues: Bray Associates Records, f.41, pp.44–9.

References: Kelly, p.261.

HUNMANBY, Yorks. (N.Yorks.)

All Saints. York

[1v.]

DeskL: Bible, 1541, chained. A ParLL of 94 vols. was est. in 1812 for the 'clergy at Hunmanby and its vicinity' by the Associates of Dr Bray. No vols. survive. In *c.* 1807 Archdeacon Francis Wrangham (1769–1842), vicar of Hunmanby from 1795, founded what he himself called 'a small parish library' of *c.* 35 vols. as a lending library, probably mainly recreational, and based on an assumption 'that sermons are less read than tales'. It belonged to a group of libraries categorised by Kelly as 'philanthropic libraries' (another example is **Iron Acton**). No vols. survive.

Catalogues: Bray Associates Records, f.38, pp.244–5.

References: Kelly, pp.199–200, 264; DNB: Wrangham; Francis Wrangham, 'Village libraries', in his *Sermons, Dissertations, and Translations*, v.2, 1816, pp.457–68; Barr, p.38.

HUNTINGDON, Hunts. (Cambs.)

Archdeaconry Library. Ely

[*c.* 500v.] Cambridge UL

A grant of £1 towards the est. of a ParLL was awarded by Bray from funds at his disposal, 1695–9, either at All Saints or at St. Mary's, but no early books survive.

A library was est. by William Wake (1657–1737) by 1716, when he was still Bishop of Lincoln, and housed first in the Bishop's Palace at Buckden for the use of the neighbouring clergy. In 1837 it was placed in the care of the vicar of Buckden. The Archdeaconry of Huntingdon was detached from the diocese of Lincoln in 1837. The collection, incorporating books from the library supported by Bray at St. Mary's **Buckden**, was removed firstly in 1874 from Buckden Palace to Huntingdon Grammar school where it was augm. in 1886, and then in 1890 to a building erected by Archdeacon F. G. Vesey as the Archdeaconry Library. By 1903 there were *c.* 1,000 vols. In the mid-1960s the residue of

books was transferred to Cambridge UL, stored as 'Huntingdon: Rare Books' in the Bible Society Library. In 1999 the Archdeaconry Library was re-est. as a Christian local resource centre under the Huntingdon Team Ministry.
Catalogues: 2 medieval MSS from the Archdeaconry Library are described in Ker, MMBL, II, 1977, pp.988–9.
References: Shore, pp.147, 151; Kelly, pp.248, 258; letter from Barry Jobling, St. Mary, Buckden historian (CCC file); Pearson A236.1.

HUNTSPILL, Somerset
St. Peter and All Hallows. B & W
[2v.] *
DeskL: Bible, London, Robert Barker, 1639–40, in parish chest; pages of Martin Bucer's criticism of Cranmer's Prayer Book, in a glazed frame.

HURLEY, Berks.
St. Mary the Virgin. Ox.
[nil]
In the Notitia Parochialis of 1705 the incumbent records, 'Here are 27 folios (given I believe by ye above named Sir Richard Lovelace) for ye use of ye vicar'. This was presumably Sir Richard Lovelace of Hurley (c. 1586–1634), who was knighted in 1599 and created Baron Lovelace in 1627.
References: Kelly, pp.76, 245; Foster: Lovelace.

IBBERTON, Dorset
St. Eustace. Sarum
[1v.] *
DeskL: Book of Homilies, 1673 (given then); chained, restored in 1917 and now in a display case.

ILLINGWORTH, Yorks. (W.Yorks.)
St. Mary. Wakef.
[nil] *
A ParLL of 165 vols. was est. in 1840 by the Associates of Dr Bray; it is not recorded after 1890.
Catalogues: Bray Associates Records, f.41, pp.27–30.
References: Bray Associates Annual Reports, 1890.

ILMINSTER, Somerset
Blessed Virgin Mary. B & W
[nil] *
A ParLL of 55 vols. was est. in 1848, at Ilminster 'for the use of the clergy of the deanery of Crewkerne', by the Associates of Dr Bray. No vols. remain but some 'Bibles and prayer books 18 & 19 cent.' kept in the church might have formed part of it.
References: Kelly, p.263.

IMPINGTON, Cambs.
St. Andrew. Ely
[3+v.] *
DeskL: several chained vols. including Foxe, *Book of Martyrs* in 3 vols., kept in a chest.
References: Blades, BIC, p.29; Cox, p.196.

INGLETON, Yorks. (N.Yorks.)
St. Mary the Virgin. Bradf.
[nil] *
A ParL of 38 vols. was est. in 1757 at Ingleton 'in the parish of Bentham' by the Associates of Dr Bray, and augm. in 1804 (by 17 vols.).
Catalogues: Bray Associates Records, f.38, p.39, 210.
References: Kelly, p.264.

INGRAM, Northumb.
St. Michael. Newc.
[nil] *
DeskL: a copy of the *Works* of Charles I was reported at Archbishop Thomas Sharp's Visitation, 1723 / 31.
References: Day, p.97.

IPSWICH, Suffolk
St. Mary-le-Tower. St.E.
[*c.* 871 titles in 944v. + 10 MSS] Ipswich School
The founder of the library was William Smarte (d.1599), draper, portman and burgess to Parliament for the borough, who by his will dated 8 January 1598–9 bequeathed 'my latten printed bookes and writen bookes in velum and p'chmente . . . towardes one librarye safelie to be keepte in the vestrye of the parishe church of St. Mary Tower in Ipswich . . . to be used ther by the com'n preacher . . . for the tyme being or any other pre'cher mynded to preache in the saide p'ishe church'. The bequest was quite small, consisting of 8 MSS and 26 printed books, and they were not kept in the vestry but in a chest in the body of the church. All the MSS and 17 of the printed books are still in the collection. From inscriptions it is clear that some books were in use in the church a few years before the bequest. Three, possibly 4 of the MSS were from the Abbey Library of Bury St. Edmunds, and the 100 MSS from the same source, which went to Pembroke College, Cambridge in 1599, may have originally been intended by Smarte for his bequest to Ipswich. In *c.* 1614, after Samuel 'Watch' Ward (1577–1640), the most celebrated of the Town Preachers, had persuaded his colleagues of the need for a working library, the collection was installed in the former dormitory of the Friars Preachers, Christ's Hospital (taken down in the early 1850s) which was fitted out with wall-presses made to order perhaps after the fashion of those in the Arts End at Bodley. The books were removed to a room below in 1748 or shortly after, and there were 5

further moves in the 19th cent. before the entire collection was installed in 1982 in the Holden Library of Ipswich School. The library was chiefly developed and used by Samuel Ward, and later the Ushers and Masters of the Grammar School, and the collections steadily grew until by 1799 there were *c.* 700 titles in 1,000 vols. Gift labels were printed (probably locally) for at least 34 donors. A vellum Benefactors' Book, made and given by William Saire, bookbinder and bookseller of Ipswich, in 1615, records well over 100 donors from 1615 to 1759. The books were mainly theological in the first 50 years. Cave Beck (1623–1706?), Master of the School, 1650–7, added science, philosophy, travel, natural history, local history and topography. John Knight (d.1680), Sergeant- Surgeon to Charles II, left his books in 1680 (including a 2 vol. 17th cent. Sanson and Duval atlas). William Matthews (b.1680), an Ipswich cleric, in a gift of 1725 left 6 vols. containing 158 sermons preached before Parliament, 1641–6, collected and heavily annotated by William Dowsing (1596?–1679), puritan iconoclast. Many books were bequeathed in his will dated 1772 by Thomas Hewett (d.1773) who also founded the library at **Woodbridge**, Suffolk. There are 2 incunables in the collection, 59 STC and 71 Wing titles.

Catalogues: the Benefactors' book (in Ipswich RO) lists many of the earliest gifts with date, author, title, donor and price; MS catalogue of 1705 by Robert Coningsby, Master; John King, *A Numerical Catalogue . . .* Ipswich, 1759 (based on Coningsby; copy in Ipswich RO); a descriptive account of *c.* 50 titles is given in Westhorp, below; MS sheaf catalogue of 1920s in Ipswich PL; catalogue by E. Elizabeth Birkby in Blatchly, 1969, below: gives full descriptions and information on inscriptions, donors, bindings, etc.

References: Sterling Westhorp, 'On the library of the town of Ipswich', *Jnl of the Brit. Arch. Ass.*, v.21 (1865), pp.65–75 (copy in CCC); M. R. James, 'Description of the ancient manuscripts in the Ipswich Public Library', *Proc. Suffolk Inst. of Arch.*, v.22 (1934), pp.86–103; H. R. Hammelmann, 'An ancient public library', *TLS*, v.49 (1950), p.524; Fitch, 1965, pp.52–5; Kelly, pp.71, 73 & n.2, 254; Fitch, 1977, pp.xii–xiii; Ker, MMBL, II, pp.990–3; John Blatchly, 'Ipswich Town Library', *Book Collector*, v.35 (1986), pp.191–8; *idem. The Town Library of Ipswich Provided for the Use of Town Preachers in 1599: a History and Catalogue*, Woodbridge, 1989; Woolf, p.194 & n.84; DRB2, 1997, p.549; DNB: Ward, Beck, Dowsing; Venn: Knight, Matthews.

IRON ACTON, Glos.
St. James the Less. Bris.
[nil]
Known only from the Borrowers' Register which has entries from 1825 to 1840 (now in Bristol RO), studied in detail by Spittal, below. The library contained at least 18 vols. of tracts, in particular runs of *Cheap Repository Tracts*. From the vestry minutes it is possible to identify 87 readers in the Register. In 1826, when more books and tracts were added, a 'parochial library case' was obtained for 21s. and in 1827 100 copies of a library catalogue were printed at

a cost of £1, with a reprint in the following year of 50 more for 9s. 6d. This library clearly belongs to a group categorised by Kelly as 'philanthropic libraries'; for another example see: **Hunmanby.**
References: Kelly, pp.199–200; *Nineteenth Century STC Newsletter*, no.6 (1989), p.28; Jeffrey Spittal, 'A village library in Gloucestershire 1825–40', *The Local Historian*, v.19.4 (1989), pp.147–58.

IRTHLINGBOROUGH, Northants.
St. Peter. Pet.
[nil]
A ParL of 72 vols. was est. in 1710 by the Bray Trustees for Erecting Parochial Libraries. It was reported as lost in 1869.
Catalogues: MS. cat. for 'Attleborough alias Irthlingborough', no.23. Bray Associates Records, f.39, pp.145–8.
References: Bray Associates Annual Reports, 1869; Kelly, p.263.

ISEL, Cumb. (Cumbria)
St. Michael. Carl.
[nil]
One of the 10 parishes in the diocese of Carlisle given 16 books in 1687 under the will of Barnabas Oley (see pp.34–5 and table on pp.444–52). In 1703 the books were 'well kept, in the same chest with the vestments in the choir'. A late 18th cent. vicar recorded that these books were 'kept in a little study along with my own; and are sufficiently distinguished from them by the manner of their binding. For they are all bound after an uniform manner which I take to be calf dressed in imitation of buff. They have been letter'd on the back with these letters B:Oley, but the lettering is so tarnished by length of time that [it] is now scarce legible'. None remain, but there is an original list of the books in the church safe, dated 1687.
Catalogues: transcript of the 1687 list, with other letters, by N. R. Ker, in Bodl.MS.Eng.Misc.c.360 (copy in CCC).
References: Nicolson, 1703, p.80; Kelly, p.246.

ISLIP, Northants.
St. Nicholas. Pet.
[nil ?] NRC
A catalogue of a parochial library dated 1895–6 is held in the Northants. RO.
References: Northants RO, ZA.9132.

IXWORTH, Suffolk
St. Mary. St.E.
[1v.] *
DeskL: BCP, James II.

KENDAL, Westm. (Cumbria)
Holy Trinity. Carl.
[nil ?] NRC
In 1701 the SPCK offered £10 for a ParLL for the Archdeaconry of Richmond, Kendal being considered the best centre. A ParL was est. in 1898 by the Associates of Dr Bray (formerly that of **Old Hutton**).
References: Kelly, p.255 (quoting E. McClure, ed., *A Chapter in English Church History*, 1888, pp.126, 128); Bray Associates Reports, 1890, 1900.

KESWICK, Cumb. (Cumbria)
St. John. Carl.
[nil]
A ParLL was est. in 1786 by the Associates of Dr Bray. What remained of this library, after a long period of neglect, when 'the larger folios . . . were used as platforms for shorter bell-ringers', was dispersed during the 1930s with PCC approval. A surviving copy of the Bray label is dated 1787. In 1849 a 'parochial library of general literature' was founded by the then vicar on a subscription basis 'to encourage the spirit of self-culture, and to promote the continuation of secular and spiritual instruction in this district'. This was active for a long period, eventually being taken over by the Cumberland Co.L in 1958.
References: Kelly, pp.198, 261 (quoting from W. E. Alder-Barrett, 'St. John's Library, Keswick', *LAR*, v.61 (1959), p.35); Scott, p.45, n.13. I am indebted to Brian North Lee for the reference to the Bray label.

KILDWICK, Yorks. (W.Yorks.)
St. Andrew. Bradf.
[*c.* 52 titles in 57v.] Bradford CL
Most of the books were given by members of the Currer family, especially Henry Currer (1651–1722), owner of Kildwick Hall, and Haworth Currer (1690–1744). There were *c.* 70 vols. in 1970. The books were kept in an open-fronted cupboard in the vestry until 1980 when they were deposited in Bradford CL. They consist mainly of 16th and 17th cent. theology.
Catalogues: list with the collection.
References: Kelly, p.256; Bill Report, 1970; Barr, p.37; DRB2, 1997, p.571.

KILLINGTON, Westm. (Cumbria)
All Saints. Bradf.
[1v.] Cumbria RO, Kendal
DeskL: William Allen and Thomas Bray, *Certain Select Discourses*, 1699.

KILMERSDON, Somerset
St. Peter and St. Paul. B & W
[nil]
A ParL of 72 vols. was est. in 1711 by the Bray Trustees for Erecting Parochial

Libraries. A remnant was noted by Blades in 1866. It was reported as lost in 1870.
Catalogues: Bray Associates Records, f.39, pp.45–8.
References: Blades, *Book-Worm*, v.1 (1866), p.158; Bray Associates Annual Reports, 1870; Kelly, p.263.

KIMBOLTON, Hunts. (Cambs.)
St. Andrew. Ely
[nil] *
A ParLL was assisted by Bray from funds at his disposal, 1695–9.
References: Kelly, 1966, p.258.

KINGSBRIDGE, Devon
St. Edmund the King and Martyr. Ex.
[*c.* 650v, + modern pamphlets]
A ParL of 72 vols. was est. in 1711 by the Bray Trustees for Erecting Parochial Libraries. No books have survived from this library, which was reported as 'returned' in 1872 but listed in later Bray Associates Annual Reports until 1938. A Bray bookplate from the Kingsbridge collection is reproduced in *Ex Libris Jnl.*, v.12 (1902), p.79. The present collection, housed in a room above the porch, consists of books from the 4 parishes in the deanery of Woodleigh: Kingsbridge, Thurlestone, Woodleigh and West Alvington, combined into one collection at Kingsbridge for the use of the clergy of the deanery in the period *c.* 1896 to *c.* 1902. The main growth and use of the collection was from 1902 to 1920, after which time it declined in use. The only early books are: St. Augustine, *Works*, in Latin, Paris, 1679 (15 vols.); *Critici Sacra*, Amsterdam, 1698 (9 vols.) and John Walker's *An Attempt towards Recovering an Account of the Numbers and Suffering of the Clergy of the Church of England*, 1714. All other books are late 19th and early 20th cent. publications. Included are survivals from the Clerical Lending Libraries given by the Associates of Dr Bray to **West Alvington** (1871) and Kingsbridge (1902).
Catalogues: MS catalogue 'Kings-bridge', no.24. Bray Associates Records, f.39, pp.165–8 (copies in Devon RO and CCC).
References: Kelly, p.261; a detailed report on this library was made by Dr Margaret Lattimore in 1982 (TS copy in CCC).

KINGS BROMLEY, Staffs.
All Saints. Lich.
[nil] *
A ParL of 115 vols. was est. in 1823 by the Associates of Dr Bray; it is not recorded after 1880.
Catalogues: Bray Associates Records, f.40, pp.69–72.
References: Bray Associates Annual Reports, 1880; Kelly, p.263.

KING'S LYNN, Norf.

St. Nicholas Chapel; St. Margaret. Nor.

[2249 items in 1797v.] King's Lynn PL; iv. in situ

A library was est. in the vestry of St. Nicholas Chapel in *c.* 1617 by the Mayor and Burgesses who ordered £8 derived from a lottery to be used to buy books: Augustine, 6 vols.; Ambrose, 7 vols. and 'The Centuries', 7 vols. Some are described as gifts to St. Nicholas Chapel on the title-page. These books were removed and amalgamated with those of St. Margaret's in 1797.

A library was est. by gifts of money to the Mayor and Burgesses in 1631 and was placed in the chamber over the N. porch of St. Margaret's church. A still extant parchment Register, given in 1641 by John Arrowsmith (1602–59), minister of St. Nicholas Chapel from 1631 and later Master of Trinity College, Cambridge, lists both purchasers and benefactors, 1631–1835. In 1641 319 vols. were listed; in 1714 Thomas Thurlyn (*c.* 1636–1714), rector of Gaywood, bequeathed 441 books valued at £160 (listed in Arrowsmith, below). At about this time the chamber over the N. porch was found to be damp and too small for the collection and a faculty was granted to build a new library in the S. aisle of the chancel, and 7 fine oak bookcases were then made, paid for by public subscription (4 are still in the church and 3 were given to the Grammar School). Two further gifts were made in the 1720s: Robert Barker, M.D. (d.1717) gave 273 vols. in 1720 (listed in Arrowsmith, below), and John Horne (*c.* 1645–1732), Headmaster of the Grammar School 1678–1728, gave 382 vols. and a further 35 vols. at his death (also listed in Arrowsmith, below). From 1661, and for more than a century afterwards, the Usher appointed to the Grammar School was also appointed Librarian. The library was evidently a lending library and not all the books listed in the catalogues still survive. In 1880 the library, then numbering 1777 vols. was moved to the Stanley Library in the 'Athenaeum' Building which eventually became King's Lynn PL in 1905. Some 827 books were stored in St. Nicholas Chapel from 1950, and after several other moves were finally returned to the PL in 1966. The collection was restored and new cases built, 1970–75. The books are chiefly theological; half are in Latin, many printed abroad, especially in Holland and N. Germany. There are 5 incunables, and a large no. of bound vols. of tracts, 1670–90. A printed Sarum Missal of 1529 is still kept at St. Margaret's church. There are roll and panel-stamped bindings, and one identified Oxford 16th cent. binding.

Catalogues: Arrowsmith's Register, 1631–1835, is with the collection; ms. catalogues of 1758, *c.* 1775; 1835 (by the Revd George Munford, copy with the collection); *c.* 1890 (by Father Wrigglesworth, of Lynn, with the collection); card catalogue.

References: King's Lynn Corporation Hall Books (Town Hall); Benjamin Mackerell, *The History and Antiquities of . . . King's Lynn*, 1738, pp.86–8; *Universal Magazine*, v.13 (1753), p.241; Blades, BIC, p.30; Thomas E. Maw, 'The church libraries of King's Lynn', *The Antiquary*, v.40 (1904), pp.235–40; Kelly, pp.75, 95, 250; Raymond Wilson, 'A history of King's Lynn Libraries,

1797–1905' (Library Association, FLA thesis, 1971); 'St. Margaret's Church Library', TS, King's Lynn PL, 1977; and booklet, 1977; Martin, pp.9–27, 55–60; W. M. Jacob, 'Church and borough: King's Lynn 1700–1750', in *Crown and Mitre: Religion and Society in Northern Europe since the Reformation*, ed. W. M. Jacob and Nigel Yates, Woodbridge, 1993, pp.63–80; Ker, *Pastedowns*, cclxxi; Lambeth Palace MS.3222, ff.124–43: notes, rubbings of bindings, rolls and panel stamps, by N. R. Ker; DNB: Arrowsmith; Venn: Horne, Thurlyn, Barker; DRB2, 1997, p.472.

KING'S NORTON, Warwicks. (W.Mids.)
St. Nicholas. Birm.
[*c.* 1140 titles] Birm. PL
The books were given by Thomas Hall (1610–65), appointed curate at St. Nicholas church from 1640 until he was ejected in 1662, 'for a library at Kingsnorton for the use of the minister of Kingsnorton, Mosely and Withal etc. and of the two schoolmasters there' (the heading given in his own catalogue). Another catalogue, not in his own hand but with his own corrections, lists 'Schoole bookes and philosophy given to Kingsnorton library'. The books were kept in cupboards in the old Grammar School building in the churchyard until 1892 when they were deposited on permanent loan in Birmingham PL. The collection consists mainly of 17th cent. theology, but from a surprisingly wide range of persuasions, with some rare foreign treatises. There are a few incunables, including the rare *De Tribus Puellis*, attributed to Ovid, Cologne, *c.* 1500; there are checklists of the STC (215) and Wing (605) items, together with full provenance notes, in the thesis by Vaughan, below; bindings include one with a panel stamp by John Reynes, and an Oxford 16th cent. binding. Another part of Hall's library was given to 'the library at Birmingham', probably **Birmingham, St. Martin.**
Catalogues: Hall's original catalogues in the Hall MS: see Vaughan, below; copies with the collection; ms. catalogue, *c.* 1750; TS catalogue, with report by W. S. Brassington, 1911.
References: W. S. Brassington, 'Thomas Hall and the library founded by him at King's Norton', *Library Chronicle*, v.5 (1888), pp.61-71; Pilgrim Trust 20th Report, 1950, pp.21-2; J.E.Vaughan, 'The Hall manuscript, containing the life, will and catalogues of the Rev. Thomas Hall B.D. (1610–65) transcribed with introduction and notes' (MA, Univ. of Bristol, 1960): the MS at Dr. Williams' Library, London, MS.61.1, Baxter MSS; *idem.* 'The former grammar school of King's Norton', *Trans. of the Worcs. Arch. Soc.*, v.37 (1960), pp.27–36; Kelly, pp.80, 254; Audrey H. Higgs, 'The library of a 17th century puritan priest', *Birmingham Post*, 2 Mar. 1968, p.1; *idem.* 'Two parish libraries and their founders', *Open Access*, N.S.16.3, Spring (1968), pp.2–7; 'The early and fine printing collection', Birmingham Central Library, 1995; Kelly, pp.80, 254; Ker, Pastedowns, 466; Lambeth Palace MS.3222, ff.144–50: notes on provenance and bindings; letter of 1950 with notes on medieval MS and incunable fragments and provenance (with collection).

KINGSTEIGNTON, Devon
St. Michael. Ex.
[2v.] Devon RO
DeskL: Bible, 1660; Foxe, *Book of Martyrs, c.* 1670 (both chained); and 19th cent. liturgical books.
References: Cox & Harvey, p.339.

KINGSTHORPE, Northants.
St. John the Baptist. Pet.
[?] NRC
DeskL: in 1950 there were 5 chained books, all given by Edward Mottershed, d.1643: Erasmus, *Paraphrases,* 1547; Jewel, *Apology,* 1609; Foxe, *Book of Martyrs,* 1641, 3 vol.
References: CCC Questionnaire, 1950.

KINNERSLEY, Heref.
St. James. Heref.
[1v.] * York Minster Lib.
Known only from an inscription in a copy of Thomas Comber, *Short Discourses upon the whole Common-Prayer,* 1684, in York Minster Lib. (XIV. H.3): 'Kynnersley Parish Library, no.17. The gift of the Rev. A. Burn, curate.'
References: Bill Report, 1970.

KINVER, Staffs. (W.Mids.)
St. Peter. Lich.
[nil] *
DeskL: Blades in 1890 reported the presence of a 7 foot oak desk with holes for chains and copies of Foxe, *Book of Martyrs,* 1583 (rebound); Jewel, *Works,* 1609 (a link but no chain); *The Whole duty of Man,* 1703 (with chain, link, clasps and boss); Burkitt, *Expository Notes,* 1716 (with chain, link and clasps). Neither the desk nor books have survived.
References: Blades, BIC, p.30.

KIRKBURTON, Yorks.
All Hallows. Wakef.
[5v.] W. Yorks. Archives Service, Wakefield
DeskL: Jewel, *Apology,* 1587; 'Breeches' Bible, 1594; [Commentary on the BCP, late 17th cent.]; Joseph Briggs, *Catholick Unity,* 1704; Bible, Oxford, Baskett, 1739.
References: list, W.Yorks. Archives Service, Kirkburton, D172 10/1–5 (copy in CCC).

KIRKBY FLEETHAM, Yorks. (N.Yorks.)
St. Mary. Ripon
[81 titles in 98v.] York Minster Lib.

The core of the collection seems to be the theological books given in 1862 by Henry Ingledew, of Angleham in the parish of Kirkby Fleetham, attorney-at-law and alderman of Newcastle 'for the purpose of founding a parochial library, to be preserved for, and appropriated to, the use of the vicar or minister of this parish for the time being, under . . . statute (7th Anne cap.14)'. Earlier owners were local clergy, including Abraham Todd, rector of Welbury 1730–47, and John Todd (c. 1726–86), perpetual curate of Castle Eden, Co. Durham, 1763–86, and a few books were added in 1868 by Thomas Wilson, vicar 1859–75. The books contain a bookplate giving the details of the foundation by Ingledew, above. They were deposited in York Minster Lib. in 1996. One of the earliest books in the collection is Herodian's *History*, 1635.
References: Venn: Todd, John

KIRKBY-IN-CLEVELAND, Yorks. (Cleve.)
St. Augustine. York
[?] NRC
An entry in Baines' Directory, 1823, records 'a parochial library for the free use of the parish, consisting of books selected from the list of the Society for Promoting Christian Knowledge'.
References: Edward Baines, *History, Directory & Gazetteer of the County of York*, v.2, East and North Ridings, Leeds, 1823, p.465.

KIRKBY LONSDALE, Westm. (Lancs.)
St. Mary the Virgin. Carl.
[nil] *
Nicolson & Burn in 1777 recorded that 'Henry Wilson of Blackwell-hall London, a native of Kirkby Lonsdale . . . erected a small library in the church, at the east end of the north ile, over the vestry; and gave several books to it'. None survive.
References: Nicolson & Burn, 1777, vol.1, p.248.

KIRKHAM, Lancs.
St. Michael. Blackb.
[nil]
DeskL: Christie in 1885 recorded 9 titles in the vestry, dating from 1616 to 1776, from a library belonging to the church from the beginning of the 17th cent. They were not present in 1950.
References: Christie, pp.99–100; CCC Questionnaire, 1950.

KIRKLINGTON, Yorks. (N.Yorks.)
St. Michael. Ripon
[iv.]
DeskL: Comber, *Companion to the Altar*, 4th ed., initialled by [the donor?] in 1671.
References: Cox & Harvey, p.339.

KIRKOSWALD, Cumb. (Cumbria)
St. Oswald. Carl.
[9v.] Carlisle CL
A ParLL was assisted by Bray from funds at his disposal 1695–9, and a ParLL of 66 vols. was est. in 1710 by the Bray Trustees for Erecting Parochial Libraries, and augm. by the Associates in 1870 and 1889. By 1900 the library was incorporated into that of **Carlisle** and 9 vols., discovered in the Prescott Library in the Carlisle Diocesan Resources Centre, are now deposited in Carlisle CL on permanent loan.
Catalogues: MS catalogue no.36, received 11 May 1710. Bray Associates Records, f.39, pp.21–4.
References: Shore, 1879; Kelly, pp.258, 261.

KNUTSFORD, Ches.
St. John the Baptist. Ches.
[2v.] *
DeskL: contains a BCP, 1686, previously used in the old chapel, well-bound and preserved; and a BCP, 1687. A ParLL was est. in 1780 by the Associates of Dr Bray; it was withdrawn in 1879.
References: Bray Associates Annual Reports, 1879; Shore, p.151; Richards, p.196; Kelly, p.261.

LAKENHAM, Norf.
St. John the Baptist and All Saints. Nor.
[1v.] Norwich CL
DeskL: Jewel, *Defense of the Apologie,* 1571.

LANCASTER, Lancs.
St. Mary. Blackb.
[nil]
A ParLL of *c.* 161 vols. was est. in 1764 by the Associates of Dr Bray; 43 vols. were added in 1847, and it was further augm. in 1874 and 1896. The books were still present in 1849.
Catalogues: Bray Associates Records, f.38, pp.103–8; f.41, pp.174–5.
References: Select Committee Report, 1849; Bray Associates Annual Reports, 1896; Kelly, p.262.

LANDEWEDNACK, Corn.
St. Wynwallow. Truro
[nil?] NRC
In 1950 there was a pre-1700 Bible in the church.
References: Pearce Survey, 1949–50.

LANE END, Staffs.
Parish unidentified. Lich.
[?]
A ParLL of 50 vols. was 'sent to Lane End, near Newcastle under Lyme, Staffs. Sept. 1814'. 'Lane End' was part of Longton, Stoke-on-Trent, The Potteries.
Catalogues: Bray Associates Records, f.38, pp.255–6.
References: Kelly, p.263; I am grateful to Dr D. J. McKitterick for the identification of this place-name.

LANGLEY MARISH, Bucks. (Berks.)
St. Mary the Virgin. Ox.
[*c.* 191 titles in 269v.]

In situ

Sir John Kedermister (d.1631), of Langley Park, was granted a faculty in 1613/14 to build a room in the church to house a library. In his will, written shortly before his death, he bequeathed a collection 'for the perpetual benefit of the vicar and curate of the parish of Langley, as for all other ministers and preachers of God's word that would resort thither to make use of the books therein'. The 1638 vellum catalogue hanging on the wall is almost certainly that requested by Archbishop Laud's Commissioners on their visitation in 1637. It lists 307 books on 18 shelves; there are now 269 books on 16 shelves. In 1649 Sir John's daughter Elizabeth, and her husband Sir John Parsons, created a Trust to administer the Kedermister charities, which included the contemporary painted cupboards and panels of the library room, described by Rouse (below) as an 'unrivalled example of an early 17th century library interior almost in its original condition'. The room has continued to attract the attention of art-historians (see Jourdain and Croft-Murray, below). The collection contains patristic writings, theology and ecclesiastical history, much in Latin and printed on the continent. Nearly ¾ of the books were printed between 1610 and 1637, and about 80% of these are bound in full contemporary plain calf, with the Kerdermister arms blocked in gold on both covers. There are a number of interesting blind-stamped bindings, including an Origen, Paris, 2 vols., 1522, bound by Garrett Godfrey. There are two medieval MSS: the 13th cent. *Aurora*, of Peter de Riga, and the Kedermister Gospels, an 11th cent. MS on permanent deposit in the British Library since 1932; and Sir John and Dame Mary Kedermister's *Pharmacopolium or a booke of medicine*, a MS of 1630. There are very few signatures or inscriptions in the books; 2 suggesting local provenance are described in Francis, below, p.65. There are 5 visitors' books in the library, covering the period 1878 to date (with a gap from 1968–9). The Charitable Trust est. in 1911 is known as the Sir John Kederminster's Library, and this form of the surname has been used in some of the references below.
Catalogues: 1638 parchment catalogue (transcribed in Francis, below); F. C. Heward, Catalogue of the Kederminster Library, TS (1953); 'Some of the books belonging to the Kederminster Library, Langley Marish, Bucks'. (TS, N. R. Ker, Bodl.MS.Eng.Misc.c.360, copy in CCC); catalogue by Francis, 1966 (below).

Langley Marish: general view of the early seventeenth-century
painted cupboards and panels of the library of
Sir John Kedermister (d. 1631), in near original condition

Langley Marish: another general view

References: 1) **Manuscripts**. Ker, MMBL, III, 1983, pp.14–17; *British Museum Quarterly*, v.6 (1932), p.93, pls.38, 39; Janet Backhouse, and others, eds. *The Golden Age of Anglo-Saxon Art 966–1066*, 1984, no.51, p.69; *Pharmacopolium: Medical History*, v. 2 (1958), p.69. Lambeth Palace MS.3222, ff.151–3: notes on provenance and rubbings of bindings by N. R. Ker. 2) **General**. H. Avray Tipping, 'Langley Church and pew', *Country Life*, 31 July 1909, p.168; E. C. Rouse, 'The Kederminster Library', *Records of Buckinghamshire*, v.14 (1941–6), pp.50–66; E. Croft-Murray, *Decorative Painting in England 1537–1837*, v.1, 1962, p.40; J. Harris, 'A rare and precious room: the Kederminster Library, Langley', *Country Life* (1977), pp.1576–9 and 25 May 1988, p.20; 'Sumptuous Jacobean splendour', *Interiors*, Nov. 1981, pp.133–40; Martin, pp.38–47, 60; Jane Francis, 'The Kedermister Library: an account of its origins and a reconstruction of its contents', *Records of Buckinghamshire*, v.36 (1996), pp.62–85 (includes a transcript of the 1638 catalogue, a reconstruction of the original arrangement of the library based on the 1638 shelf nos., and a short-title catalogue of the present library, including notes on lost books).

transf

LANTEGLOS BY CAMELFORD, Corn.
St. Julitta. Truro
[128 titles in 126v.] Cornwall RO
The library of Daniel Lombard (1679–1747), rector 1713–47, was bequeathed to his successors and kept in the rectory. The 1818 shelf-list of 573 vols. was deposited with the Archdeacon's Registrar at Bodmin in that year. About 120 vols. considered as worthless by the Rt. Revd. J. W. Hunkin, Bishop of Truro, and 'an expert' were burned *c.* 1940. The remaining books were sent to be auctioned at Hodgson's in 1965 (sale cat. 29 April 1965, lots 377–95) but were withdrawn before sale and deposited in April 1966 in Cornwall RO, Truro. There is one 16th cent. book but the remainder are entirely 17th and 18th cent. books of English and continental theology, biblical commentaries and sermons, with some classics and history.
Catalogues: shelf-list by Coryndon Luxmoore, rector, 1818 (with collection: CRO ARD/142); CCC list, *c.* 1956 (Bodl.MS.Eng.Misc.c.360, copy in CCC); Cornwall RO list, 1981 (copy in CCC); TS catalogue by Dr. Margaret Latham, 1982 (with cross-references to nos on earlier lists and a transcript of the 1818 shelf-list: copy in CCC).
References: *N & Q*, 6 ser. 21 Oct. 1882; information from the incumbent in PLCE1; Kelly, p.245 (but ded. incorrect); Lambeth Palace MS 3094, ff.149–56: notes and rubbings of bindings by N. R. Ker; Bill Report, 1970.

LASHAM, Hants.
St. Mary. Win.
[1v.] Hants. RO
DeskL: BCP, 1681, with the bookplate of William Tempest of Inner Temple.

LATHBURY, Bucks.
All Saints. Ox.
[2v.]
DeskL: Bible, Barker, 1617; *Certain Sermons or Homilies*, 1683; and 18th and 19th cent. Bibles and prayer books.
Catalogues: list by Paul Morgan, 1970 (CCC files).

LAWSHALL, Suffolk
All Saints. St.E.
[123 titles in 137v.] Bury St. Edmunds PL
In his will dated 27 Mar. 1704, Stephen Camborne (*c.* 1640–1704), rector of Lawshall from 1681 to his death, bequeathed 'all my library of books to my successor in this liveing of Lawshall to continue here for ever' and directed 'that two catalogues of all the bookes be made by my executors and one part to be delivered to the churchwardens to be kept in the church box and the other to be delivered to the next incumbent to the intent there may be no diminution of the said library but that it may continue for ever'. The MS catalogue of 1709 lists 127 vols. The books remained at the rectory until it was sold in *c.* 1957 when they were removed for safe keeping to the University of London Library, by this time in a very bad physical condition. They were returned briefly to Bury St. Edmunds CL, and were finally deposited in Bury St. Edmunds PL in 1965. Most of the books had by then been repaired with the aid of a grant from the Pilgrim Trust. About half of the collection, which includes a few 19th cent. additions, consists of theology, mostly 17th cent., but some earlier, and mainly in Latin; the rest is miscellaneous, with good holdings of classics. There are 4 STC and 63 Wing items. Most of the vols. are signed by Stephen Camborne; some are from the library of his father, the Revd Thomas Camborne, rector of Campsea Ashe. Lawshall 115 has the bookplate of 'Richard Powlett. May 21. 1653'.
Catalogues: MS cat. of 1709 in Suffolk CRO, Ipswich; TS list of books in the rectory study in 1909 (1910): Bodl.MS.Eng.Misc.c.360 (copy in CCC); TS cat. of books received at the University of London Library, March 1960 (Lambeth Palace MS.3222, ff.189–96); Suffolk PLC; MS cat. by Canon J. A. Fitch, 1986 (copy in CCC).
References: Fitch, 1965, pp.60–2; Kelly, p.254; Lee, Early, no.156.

LEAMINGTON PRIORS, Warwicks.
All Saints. Cov.
[nil?] NRC
A ParL was est. in 1853 by the Associates of Dr Bray; it is not recorded after 1900.
References: Shore, p.153; Bray Associates Annual Reports, 1900.

LECK, Lancs.
St. Peter. Blackb.
[nil]
A ParL of 8 vols. was est. in 1761 by the Associates of Dr Bray; 9 vols. were
'sent before by Dr Stratford & his executors'. In 1849 this library was reported
as being one of those 'either wholly lost or reduced to a few tattered volumes'.
Catalogues: 'sent to Leck chapel in the parish of Tunstall, Lancs.', Bray
Associates Records f.38, p.93.
References: Kelly, p.262.

LEDBURY, Heref.
St. Michael and All Angels. Heref.
[4v.] *
DeskL: Geneva Bibles, 1610 and 1640; Douai New Testament with Fulke
commentary, 1617; Book of Psalms, 1659; & 2 18th cent. prayer books.

LEDSHAM, Yorks.
All Saints. York
[nil]
Bray bequeathed two boxes of books 'to the parish of Ledsham near Ferry
Bridge', probably at the instance of Lady Betty Hastings.
References: Smith, p.58; Kelly, p.256.

LEEDS, Yorks.
St. Peter. Ripon
[nil] *
A ParLL of 163 vols. was est. in 1845 by the Associates of Dr Bray, and augm.
in 1876. A modern library exists in the church but apparently has no
connection with the Bray foundation.
Catalogues: Bray Associates Records, f.41, pp.142–5.
References: Shore, 1879; Kelly, p.256.

LEEK, Staffs.
St. Edward the Confessor. Lich.
[nil]
Margaret Shallcross, widow of Edward, rector of Stockport, gave her husband's books to the vicar of Leek, and 20s. with which to repair them. A 1711
cat. by the then vicar, James Osbourne, lists 44 folio, 67 4to and 17 8vo vols.,
and the succeeding 11 vicars added 34 further vols. The collection was broken
up later in the 18th cent.
Catalogues: the 1711 cat. in the Leek parish records is being transcribed by Mr
M. W. Greenslade of the William Salt Library, Stafford.
References: Woolf, p.196 & n.89.

LEICESTER, Leics.

St. Martin (from 1927 the Cathedral). Leics.

[*c.* 1,000v.] Leics. Guildhall, and Leics. RO

DeskL (in origin): a library was referred to in the churchwardens' accounts from 1586 onwards, apparently housed first in the belfry and then in the chancel of the church. In 1593–4 there were 'receaved 7 bookes that were chaynedd in the Church and geven by Symon Craftes', and another vol. was given by Christopher Bardsey of Leicester in 1598. Henry, Earl of Huntingdon (1535–95), Lord President of York, gave several books 'for the help and benefit of ministers and scholars', and there were numerous other gifts and purchases, including copies of Jewel's *Works,* and Foxe's *Book of Martyrs.* After a motion put forward by John Williams, then Bishop of Lincoln, was approved by John Angell (d.1655), public lecturer and subsequently librarian, the books were put in the care of the Corporation. A room was constructed in the E. range of the Guildhall to house the library, begun in 1632 and completed the following year. A list of benefactors, and brief titles of books given up to *c.* 1743, compiled by Richard Weston, is printed in Nichols, below, who also states that by 1790 there were 948 books and 5 MSS. The collection includes the Leicester Codex of the NT in Greek (given in 1645) and 5 other medieval MSS; the printed books are largely 17th cent. and theological, and include 3 incunables. They are now partly in the Guildhall and partly stored in Leics. RO. A ParL was est. in 1870 in St. Martin's by the Associates of Dr Bray.

Catalogues: General: John Angell, MS cat. of 876 MSS and printed books, *c.* 1632 (once in Leics. PL but now lost: described in Nichols, below); author and subject cats., 1669 (Leics. Museum and Art Gallery, MS.6.D.32/a); Cecil Deedes, J. E. Stokes, J. L. Stocks, *The Old Town Hall Library of Leicester: a Catalogue,* Oxford, 1919 (includes notices of authors, a list of missing books and notes on provenance – not indexed); **Manuscripts:** Historical MSS Commission, 8th Report, 1881, appendix, pp.419–25; Ker, MMBL, III, 1983, pp.75–82.

References: Notitia Parochialis, 1705, no.678; John Nichols, *The History and Antiquities of the County of Leicester,* v.1, 1815, pp.505–10; Thomas North, ed., *The Account of the Churchwardens of St. Martin's, Leicester, 1489–1844,* Leicester, 1884; Frank S. Herne, 'The Town Library, Leicester', *Trans. of the Leics. Lit. & Phil. Soc.,* N.S.3, no.5 (1893), pp.249–50; Shore, p.152; Kelly, p.249; Phillip G. Lindley, *The Town Library of Leicester: a Brief History,* Upton, Wirral, 1975; DNB: Huntingdon, Williams; Foster: Angell.

LEIGH, Lancs.

St. Mary the Virgin. Man.

[2v.] *

DeskL: *A Collection of Cases . . . to recover Dissenters,* 1685, 2 vols. chained; and an 18th cent. music collection. A ParLL of 154 vols. was est. in 1847 by the Associates of Dr Bray; it is not recorded after 1890.

Catalogues: Bray Associates Records, f.41, pp.176–8.

References: Christie, p.101; Bray Associates Annual Reports, 1890; Cox & Harvey, p.339; Kelly, p.262.

LEOMINSTER, Hereford.
St. Peter and St. Paul. Heref.
[nil] *
A ParL of 63 vols. was est. in 1812 by the Associates of Dr Bray. It is not
recorded after 1890. An example of the Bray oval label completed in ms. is
reproduced in *Ex Libris Jnl*, v.12 (1902), p.80.
Catalogues: Bray Associates Records, f.38, p.247.
References: Bray Associates Annual Reports, 1890; Kelly, p.262.

LESSINGHAM, Norf.
All Saints. Nor.
[iv.] *
DeskL: Foxe, *Book of Martyrs, c.* 1603 (imp.), once chained to a lectern.
References: Blades, BIC, p.31; Cox & Harvey, p.339.

LEWES, Sussex (E.Sussex)
St. Anne. Chich.
[nil]
A ParLL was projected here as early as 1708 by the Bray Trustees for Erecting
Parochial Libraries, which, if it was approved and sent, may have been
incorporated into a later bequest, that of Joseph Graves, rector of St. Peter and
St. Mary Westout, who bequeathed his library of 523 vols. in 1717 'in trust for
the benefit of the inhabitants of the town of Lewes'. At the end of the century
the remaining books were being 'left to moulder useless and unknown on a few
shelves in the free school house in St. Anne's; such as were left were finally
sold in 1823 for £53'.
References: *History of Lewes*, 1795, pp.266–7; T. W. Horsfield, *The History
and Antiquities of Lewes and its Vicinity*, 1824, p.315; Charity Commissioners 30th Report, 1837, p.704; Kelly, pp.91, 94, 195, 254.

LEYLAND, Lancs.
St. Andrew. Blackb.
[2v.] *
DeskL: Jewel's *Apology*, Foxe's *Book of Martyrs* and Gibson's *Preservative
against Popery*, 2 vols., 1718, all chained (and 5 other 18th cent. books).
References: Christie, p.101; Blades, BIC, p.31; Cox & Harvey, p.339.

LILLINGTON, Warwicks.
St. Mary Magdalene. Cov.
[iv.] Leamington Spa PL
The only evidence for the existence of this library is a copy of *The Great
Importance of a Religious Life Considered*, 40th ed. 1818, with a label
reading 'A lending library for the use of the parish of Lillington 1822', held by
Leamington Spa PL.
References: I am indebted to the Archivist, Warwicks RO for this reference.

LINCOLN, Lincs.
(Ded. unknown). Linc.
[?]
A ParLL was est. in 1891 by the Associates of Dr Bray.
References: Bray Associates Annual Reports, 1895.

LINDALE, Lancs. (Cumbria)
St. Paul. Carl.
[nil]
A ParL of 11 vols. was est. in 'Lindale Chapel' in 1761 by the Associates of Dr Bray; 3 vols. were 'sent before by Dr Stratford's executors'. In 1849 this library was reported as being one of those 'either wholly lost or reduced to a few tattered volumes'.
Catalogues: Bray Associates Records, f.38, p.89.
References: Select Committee Report, 1849; Kelly, p.262.

LINGFIELD, Surrey
St. Peter and St. Paul. S'wark
[2v.] *
DeskL: Jewel, *Works*, 1570?, chained on a double desk; the companion chained Bible, given by William Saxby in 1688, was stolen in 1996; BCP, 167–?; also, Baskerville Bible, 1763 (presented 1847); Bible, Oxford, Baskett, 1717; BCP, Cambridge, Bentham, 1762; and BCP, Oxford, Jackson & Hamilton, 1788.
References: Cox & Harvey, p.339.

LINTON IN CRAVEN, Yorks. (N.Yorks.)
St. Michael. Bradf.
[2v.] York Minster Lib.
DeskL: Bible, 1613 (Genealogies, 1612–13; Psalms, 1612); BCP, 1618.

LITTLE BOOKHAM, Surrey
(Ded. unknown). Guildf.
[1v.]
DeskL: Vulgate Bible, Lyons, 1675.
References: DRB2, p.552.

LITTLEDALE, Lancs.
St. Anne (red.)
[nil]
A ParL of 9 vols. was est. in 1761 by the Associates of Dr Bray; 5 vols. were 'sent before by Dr Stratford's executors'. In 1849 this library was one of those reported as being 'either wholly lost or reduced to a few tattered volumes'.
Catalogues: sent to Littledale Chapel, in the parish of Lancaster. Bray Associates Records, f.38, p.92.
References: Kelly, p.262.

LITTLE HARROWDEN, Northants.
St. Mary the Virgin. Pet.
[nil]
A ParL of 67 vols. was est. in 1711 by the Bray Trustees for Erecting Parochial Libraries; a further 8 vols. were given by the Hon. Thomas Wentworth (*c.* 1666–1723). It was returned to the Associates in 1871.
Catalogues: no.10, for 'Harrowden-Parva', Bray Associates Records, f.39, pp.141–2; another copy of the Register, including the list of books given by Wentworth in June 1723, is in Northants CRO (YZ 1067).
References: Bray Associates Annual Reports, 1871; Lambeth Palace MS.3224: notes and lists by N. R. Ker; Kelly, p.263; Foster: Wentworth.

LIVERPOOL, Lancs. (M'side)
St. Peter. Liv.
[nil]
John Fells, 'a mariner', gave £30 in 1715 to found a small theological library. The books bought then, and others added by later rectors, numbered 217 vols. in 1818 (107 folio, 50 quarto and 54 octavo). They were originally fastened with rods and chains on open shelves in the vestry but in 1818 they were rebound and placed in glass cases. A ParL was est. in 1890 by the Associates of Dr Bray, and augm. in 1892, 1896 and 1899. Some 305 vols. were listed in Peet's catalogue of 1893. The library was moved to the Diocesan Church House, South John Street, Liverpool, some time before 1903 (it is listed in the catalogue of their library made in that year) and later became part of the Bishop Ryle Library. This library was destroyed by enemy action in World War II. The collection consisted largely of works of the Fathers in 16th and 17th cent. editions from Paris, Geneva and Basel presses. St. Peter's church was also destroyed in World War II.
Catalogues: 2 copies of an 18th cent. MS cat. on vellum once in the church do not survive; Henry Peet, *An Inventory of the Plate . . . in the Two Parish Churches of Liverpool, . . . together with a Catalogue of the Ancient Library in St. Peter's Church*, Liverpool, 1893, pp.vi–vii, 29–52.
References: Bray Associates Annual Reports, 1900; Christie, pp.102–3, gives details of the more interesting books; Kelly, p.249.

LODDON, Norf.
Holy Trinity. Nor.
[2v.] Norwich CL
DeskL: Bible, NT Greek, 1601; *Certain Sermons Appoynted*, 1563, 1600.

LONDON
All Hallows by the Tower. Lon.
[2v.]
DeskL: Lancelot Andrewes, *Sermons*, 3rd ed., 1635; William Laud, *History of the Troubles and Tryal*, 1695, and later Bibles and liturgical works.

A ParL was est. in 1885, and augm. in 1898, by the Associates of Dr Bray (transferred from the Diocesan Missioners' House, Truro).
References: NADFAS Report, 1991–2; Bray Associates Annual Reports, 1885, 1900.

LONDON
All Saints (Chelsea Old Church). Lon.
[5v.] *
DeskL: there are 5 chained books, which were presented some time after he became the Lord of the Manor of Chelsea in 1712, by Sir Hans Sloane (1660–1753), whose monument by Joseph Wilton stands in the churchyard: Bible, 1717; Foxe, *Book of Martyrs*, 9th ed., 1684, vols.1 and 3; BCP, 1723; *Book of Homilies*, 1683, with the signature of Sir Jonathan Trelawney (1650–1721). They are housed in a case which is a copy of the one erected in 1832.
Catalogues: TS list in CCC.
References: Cox & Harvey, p.388.

LONDON
St. Andrew Undershaft. Lon.
[10v.]
DeskL: Erasmus, *Paraphrases*, 1551; Foxe's *Book of Martyrs*, 1596 and 2 copies, n.d., with a chain; William Perkins, *Works*, 1613; Sir Walter Raleigh, *The History of the World*, 1621 (once chained); Henry Mason, *Hearing and Doing*, 1635 and 1653; and *Christian Humiliation*, 2nd ed., 1627; Jewel, *Works*, 1611; and 18th cent. books.
References: Kelly, p.81; NADFAS Report, 1991–2.

LONDON
St. Bartholomew the Great, Smithfield. Lon.
[1v.]
DeskL: John Tillotson, [Works?], 1699.
References: NADFAS Report, 1991–2.

LONDON
St. Botolph without Aldersgate. Lon.
[nil]
Thomas Bray's grant of £1. 5s. towards a parochial library at Aldgate, 1695–9, probably refers to this parish where he was rector from 1708 to 1730. The 330 books from his own library subsequently recorded there in 1808 may have been bequeathed by him to the church in 1730 for the use of probationary missionaries. In 1849 there were 300 books. The Bray Associates came to regard the collection as a Bray library and in 1872 it was transferred to **Stratford**, Essex, and enlarged.
References: Smith, p.79; Select Committee Report, 1849; Kelly, p.250 & n.1.

LONDON
St. Edmund the King. Lon.
[8v.]
DeskL: *'Personal Reign of Christ on Earth'*, 1643; BCP, 1630/50; 1633; Erasmus, *Paraphrases*, 2v. 1548–52 (chained with metal clasps); Bible, 1613; Nathaniel Hardy, *Several Sermons*, 1656; *'Table of Sermons'*, 1652; and 18th cent. vols.
References: NADFAS Reports, 1991–2.

LONDON
St. George the Martyr. Lon.
[nil]
The church was founded in 1706. Robert Nelson (1656–1715), and other prominent members of the SPCK, were among the founders. The library of *c.* 550 vols., mainly of the 17th cent., was sold by Puttick & Simpson, 30 May 1862, lots 577–688, 'by direction of the churchwardens, and with the sanction of the Ecclesiastical Commissioners'.
Catalogues: a copy of the sale cat. was sold by Quaestor Rare Books, cat.22, 1999, no.261.
References: Edwin C. Bedford, *The Story of St. George the Martyr, Queen Square, briefly told . . . compiled chiefly from Notes made by J. L. Miller*, 1910; Kelly, pp.91, n.4, 250; DNB: Nelson.

LONDON
St. Helen, Bishopsgate. Lon.
[3v.]
DeskL: Foxe, *Book of Martyrs*, 3v. 1684 (with chain).
References: NADFAS Reports, 1991–2.

LONDON
St. Leonard, Shoreditch. Lon.
[635v.] Hackney PL, Archives and Local History Dept. (Rose Lipman Library)
Sir Henry Ellis in 1798 noted that: 'in a room on the south side of the communion' of St. Leonard, Shoreditch 'is a library, left by the will of John Dawson, of Hoxton Market-place, bearing date Oct.14, 1763, to the vicar of the parish for the time being, and to his successors for ever. The books, which, together with a catalogue of them, are all bound uniform, amount to 870, and cost him £300. He was 53 years in collecting them, from 1710 to 1763'. John Dawson (1692–1763) was a sailor and excise officer, and his books were bequeathed to John Denne, vicar of Shoreditch 1723–8, under the terms of his will proved 9 Jan. 1765, which laid down strict conditions and compliance with the Parochial Libraries Act of 1709. The conditions were largely ignored: the books were kept in the church, and by 1892, owing to forbidden borrowings, 227 vols. were missing. A ms. cat. by William Burges, parish clerk, 1765, was printed in John Ware's Account of the Charities of Shoreditch in

1836. The books were transferred without faculty to Shoreditch PL on its opening in 1892 by the vicar, Septimus Buss, and kept as a separate collection. After some damage to the library in World War I the books, save for 4 vols, were uniformly re-bound in red morocco (1956–8). They were subsequently brought together with archives from Hackney and Stoke Newington to the Rose Lipman Library. The books are all in English, 1620–1762, and include 4 STC and 49 Wing items. The collection strongly reflects Dawson's methods and habits as a book collector: 493 vols. have his hand-written bookplate with his name, date of accession, book no., case no., shelf and position no.; 231 have his ms. contents list; 42 his ms. text indexes, 24 his ms. illustration indexes, 8 his ms. chronological tables; and 14 his ms. marginal notes. The subjects reveal his professional and wide-ranging interests: mathematics, excise gauging, navigation, travel and voyages, history and English literature, Anglican and general ecclesiastical history, classical and continental literature in translation, moral and political philosophy, law and reference works. A rare, perhaps unique item (though incomplete) is a set of *The Country Journal or the Craftsman*, Nov. 1749 to Dec.1752.

Catalogues: Hackney Archives: ms. cat. by Burgess, 1765 (D/D/DAW/1, including extracts from Dawson's will): printed in John Ware, *An Account of the . . . Charities . . . of St. Leonard's Shoreditch*, 1836, Appendix 17, pp.161–7 (minus details of shelves and cases); 'A catalogue of my books:' ms. of pre-1733 books by Dawson (D/D/DAW/2); card cats. 1894 (dictionary) and 1956 (author); by Brown, 1973, v.2, below.

References: Sir Henry Ellis, *The History and Antiquities of the Parish of Saint Leonard Shoreditch*, 1798, p.12; *Survey of London*, v.8, The Parish of St. Leonard, Shoreditch, 1922, p.102; W. C. Plant, 'John Dawson and his books: or, an exciseman's library of the eighteenth century', *Library Assistant*, v.1.15 (March 1899), pp.165–73; Anthony Brown, 'John Dawson, his life and library' (Library Association FLA thesis, 1973), 3v. (v.2. Catalogue); Kelly, p.250; DNB: Denne; DRB2, pp.230–1 (for further details and references).

LONDON
St. Martin-in-the Fields. Lon.
[500±v.] Lambeth Palace Lib., Westminster City Archives, BL, and elsewhere (see below)
DeskL [?]: a vol. of 12 printed sermons preached by John Williams at St. Martin-in-the-Fields, 1695–6, with some other pre-1700 printed sermons, is deposited with parish records in Westminster City Archives (Acc.1831, 1854). A library was founded in 1684 by Thomas Tenison (1636–1715), vicar 1680–92, later Archbishop of Canterbury. It was housed in a special building designed by Wren and erected in the churchyard. A Benefactors' Book (1685 onwards) while incomplete records early donors and their gifts, including that of John Evelyn, who was also involved in the design of the building. The books were 'to be for public use, but especially for the use of the vicar and lecturer of the said parish, and of the said schoolmaster and usher for the time

being, and the parsons of the parish churches of S. James's and S. Anne's, Westminster, and the King's chaplains in ordinary for the time being'. Later, the parishioners of St. George's Hanover Square were also permitted free use of the library. Some of Tenison's own books, were at one time stored at Lambeth Palace and then retrieved when he became Archbishop in 1695. The endowment for the library and school was only £50 per annum and was soon inadequate. Significant later donations include that of Pierre François Le Courayer (1681-1776) in c. 1772: this collection was strong in works on Church Councils. Other subject strengths of Tenison's library were liturgy, patristics, history (including Americana) and Protestant-Catholic controversy. A loans register was referred to in the early 19th cent. but has not survived. The premises were taken over in 1839 for use as a subscription library which claimed to be linked to Tenison's library and shared the premises for 13 years. The Select Committee in 1849 reported that the 4,000 books were still there but locked up and 'in as bad a state as books can be'. They were sold in two sales in 1861 by Sotheby & Wilkinson: 3 June 1861 (printed books in 1668 lots) and 1 July 1861 (MSS, in 98 lots). In the same year a public subscription, led by A. C. Tait, Bishop of London, enabled Sion College to acquire over 500 of the finest early printed books at the auction. The pre-1850 books in Sion College Library were transferred to Lambeth Palace Library in 1996. Tenison MSS from the 1861 sale are now widely distributed. Locations known are: **London**: British Library (27); Lambeth Palace (1); University College (2); Victoria and Albert Museum (1); **Cambridge** UL (1, a collection of printed fragments); **Dublin**: Trinity College Lib. (1); **Glasgow** UL (1); **Manchester**: John Rylands UL (3); **Norwich** CL (1); **Oxford**: Bodl. (2); **Paris**: Bibliothèque Nationale (1); **USA**: Harvard College L (1); Chicago U Joseph Regenstein L (1); Columbia MO, U of Missouri, Elmer Ellis L (1); Yale UL (1); Pierpont Morgan (1); Folger L (2); 49 MSS have as yet no known location (Dec. 1999). An updated list of the present locations of Tenison MSS is maintained by P. A. Hoare. The library building was finally demolished in 1870.

Catalogues: books, c. 1692–5 (Lambeth Palace MS.1707; c. 1695, ibid., MS.1708); MSS, by Samuel Ayscough, 1786 (BL: copies in 2 states: Add.MS.11,257; Add.5017*, Art.7). There is a detailed analysis of all the cats. in Hoare, below.

References: DNB: Tenison, Wren; Select Committee Report, 1849, pp.64–9; Philip Hale, *A Plea for Archbishop Tenison's Library*, 1851; Armitage Denton, 'Early parochial libraries, with some account of the libraries founded by Dr Bray', *Library Assistant*, 1 (1899), p.204; George Smith, 'Dr. Thomas Bray', *LAR*, 12 (1910), p.244; Kelly, pp.91–2, 194, 250; P. A. Hoare, 'Archbishop Tenison's library at St. Martin-in-the-Fields, with notes on the history of Archbishop Tenison's Grammar School'. (U of London, Diploma in Librarianship, 1963); *idem.* 'St. Martin's Subscription Library, Westminster, 1839-1852: an overlooked library and its links with Edward Edwards', *Library History*, v.12 (1996), pp.62-76; Milton McC. Gatch, 'Fragmenta manuscripta and varia at Missouri and Cambridge', *Trans. Camb. Bib. Soc.*, v.9:5 (1980), pp.434-75; Richard Palmer, 'Sion College Library', *Rare Books Group Newsletter*, 55 (1997), p.43. I am indebted to Peter Hoare for information in this entry.

LONDON
St. Mary Abchurch. Lon.
[3v.]
DeskL: Bible, New Testament, 1617; John Ball, *A Treatise of Faith*, 1631; '*Exposition upon the Difficult and Doubtful Passages of the Seven Epistles called Catholike*', 1627.
References: NADFAS Report, 1991-2.

LONDON
St. Mary Aldermary. Lon.
[nil]
The parish church of St. Thomas the Apostle was destroyed in the Great Fire of 1666 and not rebuilt; the parish was united with that of St. Mary Aldermary in 1670. A ParLL was apparently est. for the united benefice in 1824, but no reference to it can be found in the vestry minutes for that year.
Catalogues: *Catalogue of St. Mary Aldermary and St. Thomas the Apostle Parochial Lending Library, established 1824*, 1851: copy in Guildhall Lib. A4.6 no.53.
References: NADFAS Report, 1991-2; Weinreb & Hibbert, p.767; Vestry minutes: Guildhall Lib. MS.4864/2.

LONDON
St. Mary Woolnoth. Lon.
[1v.]
DeskL: Ralph Robinson, '*Sermons*', 1656.
References: NADFAS Reports, 1991-2.

LONDON
St. Matthew, Bethnal Green. Lon.
[nil] *
A ParLL of 161 vols. was est. in 1844 by the Associates of Dr Bray, and augm. in 1870.
Catalogues: Bray Associates Records, f.41, pp.110-13.
References: Shore, 1879; Kelly, p.263.

LONDON
St. Michael Cornhill. Lon.
[2v.] NRC
DeskL: BCP, 17th cent.? (chained); '*Religious Histories*', 17th cent.? This is possibly the copy of Foxe's *Book of Martyrs* recommended for purchase and chaining in the vestry minutes of 11 Jan. 1571-2 (see p.31, n.11).
References: NADFAS Report, 1991-2.

LONDON
St. Peter's, Cornhill. Lon.
[iv.] Guildhall Lib.
A large library, and one of the few London grammar schools, were attached to
St. Peter's in the Middle Ages. The church was destroyed in the Great Fire,
1666, and rebuilt by Wren, 1677–8. According to Stow, the library was
possibly originally 'formed by Rector Hugh Damlet, who was a learned man
& gave several books to Pembroke College, Cambridge'. Damlet (d.1476) was
rector 1447–76, and Master of Pembroke, 1447–50. A late 13th / early 14th
cent. MS of the Bible, alienated from a chantry chapel, was bought back to the
church in the late 19th cent. and is now on permanent deposit in the Guildhall
Lib.
References: John Stow, *Survey of London . . . 1603*, . . . notes by C. L.
Kingsford, v. 1, 1908, p.194; Ker, MMBL, I, 1969, pp.262–3; Weinreb &
Hibbert, p.764; Venn: Damlet.

LONDON
St. Saviour (in 1905 Cathedral Church of St. Saviour and St. Mary Overie,
Southwark). S'wark
[?]
The priory church of St. Mary Overie, after the ejection of the Augustinian
canons in 1539, became the parish church of St. Saviour, Southwark. The
present library contains books associated with the church from the 16th cent.
onwards.
References: DRB2, 1997, pp.335–6, for a detailed description of the contents.

LONDON
St. Saviour, Pimlico. Lon.
[nil?] NRC
There is a bookplate for 'S. Saviour's Church. Choir', in the Franks Collection:
no.33825.

LONG BENTON, Northumb.
St. Bartholomew. Newc.
[nil] *
One of 92 parishes in the Northumberland Archdeaconry granted a ParLL
under a scheme devised by Bishop Shute Barrington, carried out by Archdeacon R. G. Bouyer by 1823 (see p.57), and recorded as still possessing books in
the visitation returns, 1826–8.
References: Day, p.102 n.38.

LONG HORSLEY, Northumb.
St. Helen. Newc.
[nil] *
One of 92 parishes in the Northumberland Archdeaconry granted a ParLL

under a scheme devised by Bishop Shute Barrington, carried out by Archdeacon R. G. Bouyer by 1823 (see p.57), and recorded as still possessing books in the visitation returns, 1826–8.
References: Day, p.102 n.38.

LONGWORTH, Berks.
St. Mary. Ox.
[1v.] Berks. RO
DeskL: John Fell, *A Sermon preached . . . December 22. 1680*, 1680.

LOSTWITHIEL, Corn.
St. Bartholomew. Truro
[nil?]
A ParL of 72 vols. was est. in 1710 by the Bray Trustees for Erecting Parochial Libraries. In 1889 there were 81 books; by 1950 3 pre-1800 vols. were reported, 2 from the Bray library. The two Bray vols. survived in 1959. According to a report by Dr Margaret Lattimore there is a paper in the parish records stating that this library was presented to the Bishop Phillpotts Library at Truro in 1941 (not confirmed).
Catalogues: 'Lestwithiel' [sic], no.21. Bray Associates Records, f.39, pp.95–8.
References: Pearce Survey, 1949–50; Kelly, p.261; TS Report, 1984 (copy in CCC files).

LOUGHBOROUGH, Leics.
All Saints. Leic.
[*c.* 800v.] Loughborough UL
By his will proved in Jan. 1786, James Bickham (1719–85), rector of Loughborough 1761–85, bequeathed his library to the rectory for ever, for the use of the rectors of Loughborough. He requested that 4 copies of a catalogue should be made and one copy, dated 1786, has survived, now in Leicester UL. The books were originally housed in the medieval rectory, then moved into the church. In 1959 *c.* 200 vols. were kept in a room over the S. porch and 100 vols. on deposit in the College of Further Education. In 1967 the entire collection was deposited in Loughborough Technical College and in 1987 in Loughborough UL. The 1786 catalogue records *c.* 660 titles in *c.* 951 vols.: evidently some books were lost or destroyed during moves in the 19th cent. The library is mainly theological, with some classics, history, and English and foreign literature, mainly of Bickham's period. It is notable for presentation copies of books from his friends Thomas Gray, William Mason, Richard Hurd, and others of their circle. The earliest surviving books are Lyndewode's *Provinciale*, Antwerp, for Francis Birckmann, 1525, and Tyndale's *Works*, Day, 1573. The oldest datable binding is by the binder F.D. on a copy of Plutarch, Basel, Guarinus, 1573 (similar to Oldham, Blind-Stamped, pl.39).
Catalogues: 1786 MS catalogue by 'Mr Adams' (Leics. UL, MS.152, copy in CCC); TS handlist, 1970 (copy in CCC); TS select exhibition catalogue by Ann

Lees and Bob Parsons, 1980 (copy in CCC).
References: G. D. Fletcher, *The Rectors of Loughborough*, 1887, p.34; Kelly, p.249; Geoffrey Wakeman, 'Loughborough Parish Library', *Book Collector*, v.25 (1976), pp.345–53; *idem.* 'Bookbinding styles in the Loughborough and Ashby-de-la-Zouch parish libraries' in G. Wakeman and G. Pollard, *Functional Developments in Bookbinding*, New Castle and Kidlington, 1993.

LOWER PEOVER, Ches.
St. Oswald. Ches.
[iv.] *
DeskL: a copy of John Jewel's *Defence*, 1611 is still chained to the lectern in the Shakerley chapel.
References: Richards, p.202.

LOWICK, Lancs. (Cumbria)
St. Luke. Carl.
[nil]
A ParL of 38 vols. was est. in 1757 by the Associates of Dr Bray. The books were present in 1849 but none had survived by 1950.
Catalogues: in the parish of Ulverstone. Bray Associates Records, f.38, p.38.
References: Select Committee Report, 1849; CCC Questionnaire, 1950; Kelly, p.262.

LUDLOW, Shrops.
St. Laurence. Heref.
[iv.] Bodl.
Two existing books contain an inscription recording that they belonged 'ad librariam ecclesie ludloiensis', by gift of Richard Sparchfoot, Archdeacon of Salop, in 1557. One, Pico della Mirandola, *De Provedentia Dei*, 1508 is now Bodl. D.2.13 Art. Seld.; the other, Appian, *Historia Romana*, Venice, 1477, was in W. & G. Foyle's catalogue, Feb. 1957. A grant of £2.10s towards the est. of a ParLL was awarded by Bray from funds at his disposal, 1695–9, and a ParLL was est. in 1851 by the Associates of Dr Bray (not recorded after 1900).
References: Shore, p.151; Bray Associates Annual Reports, 1900; Kelly, pp.50, 70, 106.n.3, 252.

LUND, Yorks.
All Saints. York
[nil ?] NRC
A MS catalogue dated 1676 of 124 pages, of books in the library of Lund church, apparently in the hand of Sir Thomas Remyngton, was exhibited at the Royal Archaeological Institute, 1878, by A. Hartshorne.
References: *The Archaeological Journal*, v.36 (1879), p.101. I am grateful to Dr Nigel Ramsay for this reference.

LUTTERWORTH, Leics.
St. Mary. Leic.
[1v.] Bodl.
A copy of the Revd W. Jones, *An Essay on the Church*, 1800 with 'Lutterworth Parish Library' stamped in gilt on the cover is now: Bodl. Vet.A5.e.6073. A parochial library est. in 1809 is recorded in White's *Directory of Leicestershire*, 1846.
References: I am grateful to Paul Morgan and Robin Alston for information in this entry.

LYME REGIS, Dorset
St. Michael the Archangel. Sarum
[3v.] *
DeskL: Bible and BCP, 1637 (chained); Bible, 1653; Erasmus, *Paraphrases*, 1559.
References: Cox & Harvey, p.339; Cox, pp.193–8.

LYMINGTON, Hants.
St. Thomas the Apostle. Win.
[3v.]
DeskL: Bible, London, Barker, 1580 (with MS records of the Boyd family in France, America, Ireland and England, 1657–1768); Bible, 1659; BCP Epistles and Gospels, 17th cent.
References: NADFAS Report.

MACCLESFIELD, Ches.
St. Michael and All Angels. Ches.
[nil?] NRC
The churchwardens' accounts suggest that there was a DeskL from at least 1686 containing Bibles, the BCP, Foxe's *Book of Martyrs* and the *Homilies*, with notes on the provision of 'for hingis and 2 book chains' in 1737, a late date for this practice. A ParLL of 150 vols. was est. in 1843 by the Associates of Dr Bray, and augm. in 1869.
Catalogues: Bray Associates Records, f.41, pp.106–9.
References: Shore, 1879; Kelly, 1966, p.261; Richards, p.394.

MAIDSTONE, Kent
All Saints. Cant.
[719v. & 3 MSS] Centre for Kentish Studies, Maidstone
Thomas Ayhurst, a Maidstone merchant, in his will of *c.* 1600, gave money to buy 'Mr Calvin's Institutions in English of the fairest and plainest letter, together with a chain to be fastened to a desk at the lower end of the parish church of Maidstone for the better instruction of the poor and simple there'. In 1658 the Corporation bought a copy of Walton's *Polyglot Bible* in 6 vols. to place in the vestry for the use of ministers. These and other books commonly

found in a DeskL, i.e. Comber on the Common Prayer, a large English Bible, a *Book of Homilies*, and *Constitutions and Canons Ecclesiastical*, were present in the vestry library before 1716, some 32 vols. according to the list in the Burials Register. By 1730 there may have been over 100 vols. in the library. 'A case and shelves with sash'd doors' was set up by a vestry resolution of 1731/2 (the bookcases have not survived). In 1735, largely on the initiative of Samuel Weller (1684–1753), perpetual curate, 1712–53, the library was substantially augmented by the purchase for £50, raised by subscription, of a 'large and choice collection of books' from the library of Thomas Bray, Maidstone having been the town which took advantage of the clause in Bray's will whereby all the historical, chronological, and geographical books in his library, as also the Fathers, the commentaries of Cornelius à Lapide and the works of Luther and Melanchthon, valued at £100, might be sold for £50 'towards the the raising of a lending or publick library in any market town in England'. The original subscribers (listed in Martin, below, pp.61–2) included Lord Fairfax and several local clergymen, including Daniel Somerscales, who founded **Doddington** parochial library. The catalogue of these books lists 559 vols. made up of 238 folios, 129 quartos and 192 octavos. Samuel Weller made a catalogue, printed in 1736, which lists 681 vols., and the Revd Robert Finch's ms catalogue of 1810 lists 724 vols. The library was transferred to the Maidstone Museum in 1867, without a faculty, and finally deposited in Kent Archives Office, later Centre for Kentish Studies, County Hall, Maidstone in 1982. The Maidstone Parochial Library Trust is being formed to manage the library and to raise funds for cataloguing, conservation and purchase. The books range in date from the early 16th to the 18th cent. with particular strengths in history, geography and theology; the works of Luther, Melanchthon and editions of the early Church Fathers are well represented. The 3 medieval MSS consist of a 15th cent. Book of Hours and Psalter, a 13th cent. vol. of sermons, and the 2nd half of the 12th cent. Lambeth Bible (which was certainly in the library by 1716 from an inscription on the pastedown). There are 2 identified Oxford bindings from 1515–1620, and a binding by Garrett Godfrey (A17). Two borrowers' registers survive, covering the years 1717–35 and 1755–1871.
Catalogues: All Saints Burial Registers for 1678–1715 (1716 list); Bodl. MS.Rawl.C.155, ff.286–92 (1735: Bray books, copy in Centre); Robert Finch, cat. 1812; 1882 ms cat. (mainly the same books and shelfmarks as Finch together with a partial list of donors; 22 books listed in both the 1812 and 1882 cats. are now presumed lost); Samuel Weller, *A Catalogue of all the Books in the Parochial Library of the Town and Parish of Maidstone, Kent*, Margate, 1736; Canterbury CL computerised cat.
References: Peter Clark, 'The ownership of books in England, 1560–1640: the example of some Kentish townsfolk'. In: *Schooling and Society: Studies in the History of Education*, ed. Lawrence Stone, 1976, p.96 (also recorded in Canterbury Cathedral Archives: DCb/J/Z.3.15, Precedent Book); Burghmote Records, ff.94v, 96v.; J. M. Russell, *The History of Maidstone*, Maidstone,

1881, pp.121–2; Smith, p.59; Kelly, pp.91 n.4, 97 & n.2, 195, 248; Martin, pp. 48–53, 61–4; Yates, 1983, pp.166–74; *idem*. 'All Saints, Maidstone & the parochial library movement', *Bibliotheca: Historic Libraries Forum Newsletter*, 3, Oct.1996, pp.14–15; Best, pp.61–70, 199–219; Sarah Gray and Chris Baggs, 'The English parish library: a celebration of diversity', *Libraries & Culture*, v.35 (2000), no.3, pp.425–7; Ker, Pastedowns, 1448–9; Ker, MMBL, III, 1983, pp.317–25; Lambeth Palace MS.3222, ff.206–8: notes on provenance and bindings with rubbings by N. R. Ker; Foster: Weller.

MALDON, Essex
St. Peter. Chelmsf.
The collection (included in PLCE1) bequeathed to his native town by Thomas Plume (1630–1704), vicar of Greenwich and later archdeacon of Rochester, and placed by him in a room he had built over the school on the site of St. Peter's church, though probably mainly used by the clergy, was not by definition a parochial library. It was, and remains, under the control of a body of trustees and is housed separately from the church. Thomas Plume was, however, interested in parochial libraries and was one of the early donors of money and books to **Wisbech**.
References: Kelly, pp.91, 94, 96, 195 & n.2, 247 & n.3; RBD2, p.80.

MALLERSTANG, Westm. (Cumbria)
St. Mary. Carl.
[nil]
A ParL of 14 vols. was est. in 1761 by the Associates of Dr Bray. In 1849 this library was reported as being one of those 'either wholly lost or reduced to a few tattered volumes'.
Catalogues: 'Mollerstang', Bray Associates Records, f.38, p.85.
References: Select Committee Report, 1849; Kelly, p.263.

MALMESBURY, Wilts.
St. Peter and St. Paul. Bris.
[3v.]
DeskL: Geneva Bible; medieval MSS: 1. Bible, 4v. 1457?, formerly owned by Mrs Audley Lovell of Cole Park, given in 1914 by the Earl of Suffolk; 2. Biblical History, etc. 14th–15th cent., given by James P. R. Lyell (d.1949).
References: CCC Questionnaire, 1950; Ker, MMBL, III, 1983, pp.331–5.

MANCETTER, Warwicks.
St. Peter. Cov.
[5v.]
DeskL: including Foxe, *Book of Martyrs*, n.d. 2v., Erasmus, *Paraphrases*, n.d. and Jewel, *Apology*, 1560. Blades notes that these are 'probably the books given in 1651 to the church by Humphrey Chetham'. A grant of £2. 10s. was made by Bray to Atherstone towards the cost of a ParLL from funds at his

disposal 1695–9. St. Peter's, Mancetter was the parochial church of Atherstone until 1825.

References: Kelly, p.259 (under Atherstone); Blades, BIC, p.36; Cox & Harvey, p.339; Cox, p.195.

MANCHESTER, Lancs. (G.Man.)
St. Mary (from 1847 the Cathedral). Man.
[nil]
A library was apparently begun in the Jesus Chapel of the Collegiate Church of Manchester in c. 1640 soon after Henry Bury (d.1634) bequeathed £10 'to buy books with them to be payed when they shall have a convenient place of their owne furnished with bookes for the common use of the said parish to the worth of a hundreth pounds'. Bury also gave money and books for the library at **Bury** (St. Mary). Under the terms of his will of 1651, proved in 1653, Humphrey Chetham (1580–1653) made provision for the est. of 5 parochial libraries: 'Also I do hereby give and bequeath the sum of two hundred pounds to be bestowed by my executors in godly English books . . . most proper for the edification of the common people, to be by the discretion of my said executors, chained upon desks or to be fixed to the pillars or in other convenient places in the parish churches of Manchester and Boulton in the Moors, and in the chapels of Turton, Walmesley, and Gorton, in the said county of Lancaster, within one year of my decease'. The Manchester library was the largest of the 5 and contained 131 items in 202 vols. It was not discharged until 26 Jan. 1665 and the books were housed (with the John Prestwich library) in the Jesus Chapel until c. 1830 when the chapel was converted into a registry, and the books were sent to the Chetham's Library. Perhaps because of their scant literary, theological or bibliographical interest, and poor state of repair, the then librarian of Chetham's sold them (minus chains and desks) to booksellers in nearby Shudehill. Some books were purchased by James Crossley (1800–83), President of the Chetham's Society in 1848 and Hon. Librarian from 1877. 6 titles are listed in French (below) and were included in the 1884 sale of Crossley's personal library (but 4 of these were not in the 1665 schedule and presumably were part of the Prestwich library).
A ParL was est. by the Associates of Dr Bray in 1899.

Catalogues: 1665 schedule in Chetham's Hospital and Library Archives (transcribed in Christie, pp.35–48, and Evans, Appendix I, pp.36–8, with prices paid, below); G. J. French, 'Bibliographical notices of the church libraries at Turton and Gorton', Chetham Soc., 1st ser. v.38 (1855), pp.184–95.

References: Christie, pp.5–8, 33–49; Evans, pp.10, 15–16, 36–8; Kelly, pp.83–4, 249; DNB: Crossley; Bray Associates Annual Reports, 1900.

MARGATE, Kent
St. John the Baptist. Cant.
[3v.] *
DeskL: Great Bible; Matthewes Bible, 1537; Geneva Bible, 1616.

MARLBOROUGH, Wilts.
St. Mary the Virgin. Sarum
[c. 760 items in 600+v.] Bodl.
Most of the books were bequeathed by William White (1604–78), master of
Magdalen College School, 1632–48, and rector of Pusey and Appleton, 'to the
Mayre and Corporation of Marlborough in the county of Wilts for the use of
Mr Yate, vicar of S. Maryes, and of his successors for ever'. His will is dated
25 Oct. 1677. They were deposited on permanent loan in Marlborough
College in 1944, and then in the Bodl. in 1985. Of the 237 STC items 8 are the
only known copies and another 45 are rare. The books are mainly theological
and scholarly, with some holdings of classics, literature, political tracts,
history, law and medicine. The school books include 13 examples of the
grammatical treatises of Robert Whittington, and a vol. of 5 tracts by John
Stanbridge, of which 4 are unique. There are many books of interest for their
associations, especially presentation copies, and many are annotated with
date of purchase and price paid. Most of the bindings are by Oxford binders of
the 17th cent. (4 are identified: see Ker, Pastedowns, below) with some earlier
blind-tooled examples (including 7 blind-stamped panels of the 16th cent.).
There is one 16th cent. ms. book of sermons, mostly in English.
Catalogues: Christopher Wordsworth compiled a cat. in 1903.
References: E. G. H. Kempson, 'The Vicar's Library, St. Mary's
Marlborough', *Wilts. Arch. and Nat. Hist. Mag.*, 51 (1947), pp.194–215;
Notes on the Vicar's Library, Marlborough, kept at Marlborough College,
TS, n.d. (list of donors, inscriptions, etc.) (copy in CCC); Kelly, pp.80, 255;
Paul Morgan, in *Bodleian Library Record*, v.12, no.1 (1985), pp.76–7; DRB2,
pp.508–9; Ker, Pastedowns, 1595, 1779, cl, ccxxxix; Pearson 1779.1, A277.3;
Ker, MMBL, III, 1983, pp.471–2; Lambeth Palace MS.3222, ff.219–41:
rubbings of bindings by N. R. Ker.

MARLINGFORD, Norf.
Assumption of the Blessed Virgin Mary. Nor.
[3v.] Norwich CL
DeskL: BCP, 1662; *Certain Sermons or Homilies*, 1635; Bible, 1611.

MARSDEN, Lancs.
St. Paul. Blackb.
[nil] *
A ParLL of 72 vols. was est. in 1820 by the Associates of Dr Bray.
Catalogues: dated 1821. Bray Associates Records, f.40, pp.35–7.
References: Kelly, p.262.

MARSKE, Yorks.
St. Edmund. Ripon
[nil]
A collection of books was given by Matthew Hutton (1639–1711), antiquary, for the use of his nephew, Thomas Hutton (d.1694), rector of Marske, 1659–94, and subsequent rectors. Raine's article, below, includes a list of *c.* 110 titles and 'seventeene little sermon bookes', and he comments that there were 'a few valuable works but, on the whole, the divinity comprised in it was of the most heavy and appalling kind', and that the books 'have long since disappeared'. Although Kelly in 1966 reported that 'a few books remain' none now survive.
Catalogues: in Raine, below (copy in CCC).
References: James Raine, 'Marske', *Arch. Aeliana*, N.S. v.5 (1861), pp.20–22; Kelly, pp.80, 256; DNB: Matthew Hutton; Foster: Thomas Hutton.

MARSKE-BY-THE-SEA, Yorks. (N.Yorks.)
St. Mark. York
[1v.] York Minster Lib.
A ParL of 72 vols. was est. in 1712 by the Bray Trustees for Erecting Parochial Libraries; the library was still extant in 1849; in 1869 it was transferred to **Middlesbrough**. One book, J. F. Ostervald, *The Nature of Uncleanness Consider'd*, 1708, is now in York Minster Lib. (purchased from Murray Hill in 1971): this is Oldbury 22 (see p.449).
Catalogues: no.18, 1712: Borthwick Institute, York: Bp. C and P I/38.
References: Bray Associates Annual Reports, 1869; Bill Report, 1970; Woolf, pp.189, n.72, 192–3.

MARTOCK, Somerset

All Saints. B & W
[13v.] Wells CL
Richard Busby (1606–95) in his will bequeathed books to the parish churches of **Cudworth**, Martock and **Willen**. The 13 vols. for Martock were deposited in Wells CL in the early 1980s. They are all in English and mainly sermons and theological works dating from 1548 to 1689. Each vol. has Busby's arms blocked in gold on the upper cover.
Catalogues: included in Wells CL cat.
References: G. F. Russell Barker, *Memoirs of Richard Busby*, 1895, p.143; Kelly, p.253.

MAUTBY, Norf.
St. Peter and St. Paul. Nor.
[1v.] Norwich CL
DeskL: Edward Boys, *Sixteen Sermons*, 1672.

MELTON MOWBRAY, Leics.
St. Mary. Leic.
[2.v.] *
DeskL: there were once 8 books chained in the N. transept; 2 only remain (now in the vestry): Jewel, *Works*, n.d., and *Defence of the Apology*, n.d. There is no trace of the Melton Clerical Society Library est. in the vestry in *c.* 1839.
References: CCC Questionnaire, 1950; Judith Flint, 'Libraries in Melton Mowbray, 1800–1974' (M.A. in Librarianship thesis, Loughborough U, 1985), p.48.

MENTMORE, Bucks.
St. Mary the Virgin. Ox.
[nil]
William Beasley (1678–1743), rector of Chaddington, Bucks. 1716–42, in his will dated 12 May 1739 left 'to the use of the Vicars of Mentmoore my neighbouring parish my study of books except such English books as my wife shall choose for her use'. In 1744 some 589 vols. were listed in a vellum-bound vol., and in an undated list (after 1880) 219 vols. are recorded. In 1909 the books were deposited on loan in Bucks. Archit. and Arch. Soc. in Aylesbury, catalogued and numbered 1–214, but this cat. has not survived. In 1948, on the instructions of the vicar and churchwardens the books were valued by Blackwells and those of value were then sold, without faculty. Some 131 vols. were seen by Neil Ker in 1956, but only 118 vols. remained from a final sale some time before 1967. Most of the books were printed 1670–1700 and were in bindings of *c.* 1700 or earlier. Many were signed William Beazley 'e Coll. Reg. Cant.', often with a date of purchase (1695 seems to have been the earliest) and were acquired when he was a Scholar at King's College, Cambridge, and during his years as a schoolmaster at Eton, where he had been a pupil.
Catalogues: 1744, in a vellum-bound vol. (Bucks. RO); abbreviated list, *c.* 1800 (Bucks. RO); a list of vols. in the vicarage library and a note on vols. borrowed, 19th cent. (Bucks. RO: PR 146/3/1.2]; by Jane Francis (forthcoming, see below).
References: Lambeth Palace MS.3222: notes by N. R. Ker; Jane Francis, 'Mentmore Library', *Quadrat*, no.8 (1998), pp.21–2.

MERE, Wilts.
St. Michael the Archangel. Sarum
[*c.* 10v.]
A library was probably founded by T. H. Baker, a descendant of Sir Richard Baker, antiquary, who lived at Mere Down, and the Revd J. Lloyd, incumbent 1891–1909. Only *c.* 10 vols. remain, together with miscellaneous later material, in a room over the N. porch accessible by a spiral staircase.
References: CCC files.

MERIDEN, Warwicks.
St. Laurence. Cov.
[1v.] Warwicks. CRO
DeskL: Jewel, *Apology*, 1609.

MERTON, Norf.
St. Peter. Nor.
[1v.] Norwich CL
DeskL: Bible, 1611.

MICKLETON, Glos.
St. Lawrence. Glouc.
[3v.] *
DeskL: Foxe, *Book of Martyrs*, formerly chained, in the parish chest.

MIDDLESBROUGH, Yorks. (N.Yorks.)
St. John the Evangelist (ded. uncertain). York
[nil?] *
A ParL was est., removed and enlarged in 1865 by the Associates of Dr Bray,
and augm. in 1874. It appears in a list of 'lost' libraries in 1869, but some vols.
may have survived in the All Saints Centre for the Deanery of Middlesbrough.
The libraries at **Skelton** and **Stokesley** were consolidated at Middlesborough
in 1869.
References: Lambeth Palace MS.3224: notes by N. R. Ker; Shore, p.150.

MILDEN, Suffolk
St. Peter. St.E.
[1v.] Harvard U, Houghton Lib.
William Burkitt (1650–1703), rector of Milden from 1678, and vicar and
lecturer of **Dedham**, Essex, from 1692, in his will dated 1 Jan. 1700, left to his
nephew 'my library of books to be set up in the studdy at Milding parsonage,
and my will is that they never be sold but . . . for the benefit of succeeding
incumbents'. The library was said to contain *c.* 2,000 vols., easily the largest
of the Suffolk libraries. It was given by A. F. Rivers, rector in 1904, to the
Sudbury Archdeaconry Library (better known as the Abbot Anselm Library).
The old books were then sold, without faculty, and the money raised used to
purchase more modern ones. There is no survivor of the Milden books in the
Abbot Anselm Library today, and no catalogue was ever made. One vol. has
been traced in the Houghton Lib.: a collection of tracts and pamphlets by
Thomas Shepherd (1605–49).
References: N & Q, 6 ser., v. 7 (1883), p.117; Fitch, 1965, pp.58–60.

MILFORD-ON-SEA, Hants.
All Saints. Win.
[1v.]
DeskL: Bible, Geneva, 1606.
References: NADFAS Report.

MILNROW, Lancs.
St. James. Man.
[nil] *
A ParL of 120 vols. was est. in 1833 by the Associates of Dr Bray.
Catalogues: Bray Associates Records, f.40, pp.231–3.
References: Kelly, p.262.

MILTON ABBAS, Dorset
Abbey Church (no longer parochial)
[nil] *
A wall-tablet commemorates the gift of a library by John Tregonwell (d.1680) 'to the use of this abbey church for ever. As a thankfull acknowledgement of God's wonderfull mercy in his preservation, when he fell from the top of this church'. In 1914 there were 66 vols., works of the Fathers and theology, all chained and originally kept in the vestry, but in 1802 they were moved by Gilbert Langdon, the then vicar, to the vicarage house. The books, with 7 exceptions, were handed over for pulping during World War II on a 'peremptory order' from the bishop. 'The order was emphatically resisted by the vicar and churchwardens but insisted upon by the authorities'. The remaining books, together with 2 out of 3 vols. of Foxe's *Book of Martyrs*, with traces of chains (vol.1 with a brass plate inscribed 'The gift of John Chappell citizen and stationer of London') had disappeared by 1970.
Catalogues: TS list of 7 vols. and additions (copy in CCC).
References: John Hutchins, *The History and Antiquities of the County of Dorset*, v.4, 1870, pp.406–7; J. M. J. Fletcher, 'Chained books in Dorset and elsewhere', *Proc. Dorset Nat. Hist. and Antiq. Field Club*, 35 (1914), p.21; Bill Report, 1970.

MILTON KEYNES, Bucks.
All Saints. Ox.
[1v.?] NRC
DeskL: a Bible, 1613, chained, was reported in 1950.
References: CCC Questionnaire, 1950.

MINEHEAD, Somerset
St. Michael. B & W
[14 works in 11v.]
DeskL: originally chained with padlocks to a long desk or book-board near the chancel. The oldest item, a Sarum Missal, 14th / 15th cent., once belonged to

Richard Fitzjames (d.1522), warden of Merton college, Oxford, 1483–1507, vicar of Minehead, 1485–97, and successively Bishop of Rochester, Chichester and London. It was bought for the church at Sotheby's, 29 Nov. 1949. The printed books include 6 STC and 4 Wing items.
Catalogues: TS list, Sept. 1997 (copy in CCC).
References: N & Q, 7. Oct. 1882; Ker, MMBL, III, 1983, pp.472–6.

MISSON, Notts.
St. John the Baptist. S'well
[nil] *
A parish register contains a memorandum about a ParLL est. in 1828, together with a list of subscribers and a catalogue.
References: Notts. Archives: PR 6470.

MITFORD, Northumb.
St. Mary Magdalene. Newc.
[nil] *
One of 92 parishes in the Northumberland Archdeaconry granted a ParLL under a scheme devised by Bishop Shute Barrington, carried out by Archdeacon R. G. Bouyer by 1823 (see p.57), and recorded as still possessing books in the visitation returns, 1826–8.
References: Day, p.102 & n.38.

MITTON, Lancs.
All Hallows. Bradf.
[6v.]
DeskL: 4 vols. each with a 5-link chain and ring attached to the edge of the front board and thought once to have been attached to the screen in the Shireburn Chapel: John Jewel, *The Defence of the Apologie*, n.d.; William Burkitt, *Expository Notes*, 9th ed. (bought in 1726 by William Johnson, vicar of Mitton, 1726–60, for the use of his parishioners); Wheatley's *The Church of England Man's Companion*, [1720?]; Wheatley's *A Book of Commentaries on Prayer*, 1710. Two smaller books, no longer chained: *A Selection of Hymns and Psalms for the Parish Church of Mytton*, n.d., and *The Saints Legacies or a Collection of Certaine Promises out of the Word of God*, 5th ed., 1637.
Catalogues: TS list (copy in CCC).
References: N & Q, 6 ser. v.1, 21 Feb. 1880, p.161.

MONKS KIRBY, Warwicks.
St. Editha. Cov.
[2v.] Warwicks. CRO
DeskL: Foxe, *Book of Martyrs*, 2v. (late 16th cent.)

MORE, Shrops.
St. Peter. Heref.
[*c.* 250 titles in *c.* 270v.] Linley Hall, Shrops.
In an indenture of 1680 Richard More, the younger (d.1698), of Linley Hall, gave *c.* 250 vols. to the church wardens of More 'for their better instruction and the increase of their learning and knowledge and for the encouragement of a good orthodox and preaching ministry of Gods word in the sayd parish', to be placed in 'two wanescote presses standing in the isle', erected by Richard More, the donor's grandfather. An attached document, 'Order and directions for the manageing of the bookes' makes it clear that they were given to the churchwardens 'for the use and benefit of the inhabitants' of the parish. The books were stored in the tower of the church until *c.* 1900, when they were brought down and returned to their original presses (now altered and apparently reduced in size). By 1964 the books had been sent to Shrops. Co.L, catalogued, and again returned to their original presses. In 1995 the books and presses were removed to Linley Hall (the owner is the patron of the living) for security reasons. A contemporary catalogue of the collection, written on parchment perhaps for More himself, was discovered in *c.* 1908 but has since been lost. In comparing it with his catalogue of 1909 Clark-Maxwell noted that 99 vols. had been lost over the years and now that some two thirds of the original collection survived. There are 5 incunables, 151 pre-1600 and 69 1600–1640 books in the collection. From the catalogue of More's personal library in the More family papers it would seem that the parochial library was carefully selected from the poetry, theology, history and geography sections of that library as teaching material, especially in mathematics, Greek and Latin. Most of the pre-1600 books are in Latin. Previous owners, donors and readers are indexed in Codren, below. George Lawson (1598–1678), rector *c.* 1675/6–78, and probably tutor to the More family, owned 8 vols. (some uncertain); Thomas Pierson (d.1633), rector of Bampton Bryan, Herefs., left a library of 450+ books to 14 named local ministers, most of which are dispersed, but 24 vols. are now at More (some of them probably from his marriage to Helen Harvey); and Christopher Harvey (1597–1663) gave 25 vols. (3 uncertain). A deed of 1778 records 'the presentation of a library by Robert More Esq of Linley at More parish church': however there are now only 2 books with the signature of Robert More (1758–1851) in the collection (one uncertain). There is one author's presentation copy: James Ussher, *Gravissimae Quaestiones* (1613). Many of the books have titles lettered on the fore-edge. In 1963 Neil Ker examined the bindings for fragments of medieval MSS: a list of 16 items (not complete) is with the collection. At least 8 early printed books are bound in sheets of illuminated MS and several have leaves as endpapers. Two notable items are a copy of Bertram, *Lucubrationes* (1588) with 2 leaves of an 11th cent. Gospel, and Bèze, *Epistolae* (1575) with a fragment from a 12th cent. Lucan. There are 7 identified Oxford bindings, *c.* 1515–1620, and one by Garrett Godfrey.
Catalogues: by Ridley Relton and W. G. Clark-Maxwell in 1907, below; TS

More: two of the original presses (altered) of the library established by Richard
More the Younger (d. 1698) in St. Peter's Church, now in Linley Hall, Shropshire

cat. 1964 by Shrops. Co.L (Shrops. RRC); Shrops. PLC, 1971 ('most of the surviving books'); Condren, below, pp.150–62.
References: More family papers: Shrops. CRO, 1037/More; W. G. Clark-Maxwell, 'On the library of More Church, Salop', *Trans. of the Shrops. Arch. and Nat. Hist. Soc.*, 3 ser, 7 (1907), pp.115–24; *ibid*. 'The church library of More', 3 ser, v.9, 1909, miscellanea, pp.xxi–xxii; Kelly, pp.96 & n.1, 252; Conal Condren, 'More parish library, Salop', *Library History*, v.7, no.5 (1987), pp.141–62; Jacqueline Eales, 'Thomas Pierson and the transmission of the moderate puritan tradition', *Midland History*, v.20 (1995), pp.73–102; Pierson's will: PRO/PROB.11/164.f.358r–v; Ker, Pastedowns, 287, 1450, 1529, 1596–7, 1861–2; Bill Report, 1971; Foster: Robert More; Lambeth Palace MS.3222, ff.224–54 & 3224: notes and rubbings of bindings by N. R. Ker; I am indebted to Dr Nigel Ramsay for references to Pierson and Robert More.

MORPETH, Northumb.
St. Mary the Virgin. Newc.
[nil] *
A grant of £1. 10s. towards the est. of a ParLL for the Deanery of Morpeth was awarded by Bray from funds at his disposal, 1695–9. This was one of 92 parishes in the Northumberland Archdeaconry granted a ParLL under a scheme devised by Bishop Shute Barrington, carried out by Archdeacon R. G. Bouyer by 1823 (see p.57), and recorded as still possessing books in visitation returns, 1826–8. A cat. was printed in 1825.
Catalogues: 1825: Northumberland RO, Davison collection, ZMD 167, 24/195.
References: Kelly, p.259; Day, pp.102 & n.38, 103.

MUCH MARCLE, Heref.
All Saints. Heref.
[nil?] NRC
A catalogue of books in Yatton (a chapelry in Much Marcle) with a list of borrowers, 1828–30, and a register of 1840 with a list of borrowings, are held in the Heref. & Worcs. RO.
References: Heref. & Worcs. RO: Much Marcle AG56/47 and RC/IV/CC/40 Redcliffe Cooke Colln.

MUCH WENLOCK, Shrops.
Holy Trinity. Heref.
[nil] *
A ParLL of 200 vols. was est. in 1799 by the Associates of Dr Bray. A copy of the Bray Library bookplate is in the Franks Collection: no. 33866; another copy is dated 1798.
Catalogues: 'Wenlock'; received 19 Jan. 1799. Bray Associates Records, f.38, pp.200–2.
References: Kelly, p.263. I am indebted to Brian North Lee for information on the 1798 bookplate.

MUGGINTON, Derbys.
All Saints. Derby
[nil] *
In a bond dated 19 June 1759 'the Reverend Samuel Pole, clerk, late Rector of Mugginton . . . by his last will and testament . . . leave his study of books . . . for the use of the rectors of Mugginton for ever reserving a power to his wife to take such books for her own use as she should think proper'. Pole (d.1758) was rector 1713–58. A catalogue of the books 'valued at ninety pounds or therabouts' was delivered to the Revd. Thomas Blackwall, rector of Mugginton, and a copy to the Lord Bishop: it lists *c.* 532 numbered titles, without dates, mainly theology.
Catalogues: Bond and catalogue: Lichfield RO: B/A/22/2–3 (copy in CCC).
References: Venn: Pole.

MUKER, Yorks. (N.Yorks.)
St. Mary. Ripon
[nil]
A ParLL of 112 vols. was est. in 1821 by the Associates of Dr Bray; it is not recorded after 1880.
Catalogues: Muker, in Par. of Grinton, Yorks. Bray Associates Records, f.40, pp.39–42.
References: Bray Associates Annual Reports, 1880; Kelly, p.264.

MUNGRISDALE, Cumb. (Cumbria)
St. Kentigern. Carl.
[iv.] *
DeskL: Bible, 1617 (with an inscription in the hand of William Forrest, curate and schoolmaster, 'Grisdall Tennants bible booke' purchased 1630 for 44 sh.); and a BCP, 1788.
References: Cox, pp.193–8.

MUNSLOW, Shrops.
St. Michael. Heref.
[iv.] *
DeskL: Jewel, *Apologia*, imperfect, lacking tp but with a ms. note: 'This copy . . . originally placed in this church A.D.1571 according to a pious custom which then prevailed'.

MYDDLE, Shrops.
St. Peter. Lich.
[*c.* 196v.] Shrops. RRC
A small library was est. in 1825 in the rectory of Myddle by Francis Henry Egerton, Earl of Bridgewater (1756–1829), rector, 1781 to 1829 (and of **Whitchurch**, 1797–1829), for the use of the rector for the time being. The bequest was £800, with the income from £150 for its augmentation. After the rectory was sold in 1953, the library (by then at least 2,000 vols.) was

deposited in Shrewsbury PL, but by 1970 was reported as lost. However a
recent search in the Parish Libraries Collection at the Shropshire Records
Centre has shown that *c.* 196 vols. from this collection can still be identified.
There are very few books earlier than 1800.
Catalogues: TS 'Catalogue of the Myddle Parochial Library', n.d.; and
running nos. 5029–5209 in the the Shrops. RRC cat.
References: Select Committee Report, 1849; DNB: Egerton; Thomas Corser,
N & Q, 207, 15.10.1853; John Palmer, annotations to a copy of PLCE1 (held
by BL); Bill Report, 1970; Lambeth Palace MS.3224: note by N. R. Ker.

MYNDTOWN, Shrops.
St. John the Baptist. Heref.
[nil]
A grant of 15*s.* towards the est. of a ParL was awarded by Bray from funds at
his disposal, 1695–9. Any books from this library were probably absorbed into
that founded by Edward Rogers (d.1788), rector of Myndford, which, because
of the amalgamation of livings, was also lodged here and at **Church
Pulverbatch** and **Norbury** before returning to its original home at **Wentnor**.
References: Kelly, pp.252, 253 n.3, 259 & n.3.

NANTWICH, Ches.
St. Mary. Ches.
[135v.]
A grant for a ParLL was included in Bray's Accounts for 1695–9, and the
existence of such a library in 1700 is recorded in a letter to the SPCK. One of
the early members of the SPCK, William Day, may have donated books. In the
Notitia Parochialis of 1705 the incumbent records: 'A library found and
settling by ye clergy of this deanery'. A number of books are inscribed 'E lib e
dono Samuel Edgley de Acton 1699': the Revd Samuel Edgley (d.1721), vicar
of Acton, 1675–1721, was probably the principal early benefactor. 'A catalogue of books in y Library a Nantwich 1712', kept with the collection, lists
181 works of which 85 are now lost. They are still kept in the room above the
S. porch. The earliest book in the library is *Flores Sententiarum Beati Thome
de Acquino*, Lyon, Trechsel, 1496, in a contemporary binding; very rare
books include a Sarum Missal, Wynkyn de Worde, 1502 (STC2 15898) and
Expositio Hymnorum, Wynkyn de Worde, 1502 (STC2 16116a), and there is
a copy of Samuel Purchas, *Purchas his Pilgrimage*, 1613 (STC2 20505) and an
edition of *Eikon Basilike*, 1648. There are in all 13 STC and 36 Wing items,
together with a collection of 18th and 19th cent. books of local interest. A few
books have stamped on the cover: 'Belonging to the library at Namptwich'.
Catalogues: the 1712 cat. is with the collection (TS transcript in CCC), and a
TS edited version by Alan Jeffreys of Keele University is also with the
collection; TS list of 134 items in Bodl.MS.Eng.Misc.c.360 (copy in CCC); TS
cat. of July 1995 with collection (copy in CCC).
References: Notitia Parochialis: 1705, no.1147; James Hall, *A History of the*

Nantwich: general view showing a modern bookcase

Nantwich: the spiral staircase from the library above the south porch

Town and Parish of Nantwich, Nantwich, 1883, pp.301, 331; Venn: Edgley; Kelly, pp.106.n.3, 245, 258; DRB2, p.44; Lambeth Palace MS.3222, ff.255–62: notes by N. R. Ker.

Nayland: a general view of survivals
from the early eighteenth-century library, on modern shelving

NAYLAND, Suffolk
St. James. St.E.
[*c. 47* works in 105v.]
The library was probably est. in the late 18th cent. during the incumbency of the Revd William Jones (1726–1800), vicar, 1777–1800, or his predecessor, the Revd John White (1685?–1755), vicar, 1715–55. A later incumbent, the Revd John Urbin Gray, vicar, 1879–1909, gave 52 vols. The bulk of the collection consists of Anglican divinity from Jewel onwards. There is a copy of the Bible with commentaries by Nicholas de Lyra, Lyon, 1528, 4 out of the 6 vols., with the remains of chains, and all vols. in bindings by John Reynes.
Catalogues: the earliest list is in a terrier of 1834 (Suffolk RO, Bury St. Edmunds: 806/1/112), listing the most valuable works, 17 titles in 27 vols., only 22 of which remain; a list of books in the display case in 1960 by

N. R. Ker (Bodl.MS.Eng.Misc.c.360, copy in CCC); TS cat. with introduction.
by J. A. Fitch, 1968 (copy in CCC).
References: Fitch, 1965, p.77; Lambeth Palace MS.3222, ff.263–72: notes and
rubbings of bindings by N. R. Ker; DNB: Jones; Venn: White.

NECTON, Norf.
All Saints. Nor.
[1v.] Norwich CL
DeskL: Bible, 1549.

NEEDWOOD, Staffs. see Newchurch

NETHER TABLEY, Ches.
Chapel of St. Peter (built 1675–8, re-erected to the W. of Tabley House in
1927–9). Ches.
[2v.] Tabley House
DeskL: Bible, 1619 (bound in green velvet); BCP, 1754.
References: Richards, p.263; Pevsner, Cheshire, 1971, p.349.

NETHERWITTON, Northumb.
St. Giles. Newc.
[nil] *
One of 92 parishes in the Northumberland Archdeaconry granted a ParLL
under a scheme devised by Bishop Shute Barrington, carried out by Archdeacon R. G. Bouyer by 1823 (see p.57), and recorded as still possessing books in
visitation returns, 1826–8.
References: Day, p.102 & n.38.

NEWARK-UPON-TRENT, Notts.
St. Mary Magdalene. S'well
[1256 works in 1300v.]
In his will, proved 19 July 1698, Thomas White (1628–98), vicar 1660–66,
Bishop of Peterborough from 1685, bequeathed 'to the maior, aldermen and
viccar of the towne of Newarke upon Trent for the time being all my printed
bookes to be a library, at least a good beginning of a library for the use of
them and the inhabitants of that towne, and the gentlemen and clergy of the
adjacent countrey'. A room to house the books was built over the S. porch,
then accessible by a gallery. In the 19th cent. Sir George Gilbert Scott built a
stone spiral staircase from the S. porch. In 1742 the Revd George Burghope,
rector of Shelton, Notts., bequeathed his library to Newark (some 55 books
contain his name). The books are mainly theological but a wide range of other
subjects is represented: history, geography, medicine, classics, bee-keeping
and palmistry. Half the books are in Latin, the remainder are mostly in
English, with some Greek, Hebrew, Spanish and Italian. There are 117 works
printed before 1600, some MS material, and 2 identified Oxford bindings of
the period 1515–1620. The Friends of the Bishop White Library was founded

Newark-upon-Trent: a general view of part of the library bequeathed by
Thomas White, vicar 1660–66, and later Bishop of Peterborough

in April 1996 to care for the books and promote the historical significance of the library.

Catalogues: by W. Ridge, printed Newark, 1854; TS 'short list of the more valuable books', n.d., and TS extract from White's will, by N. R. Ker (Bodl.MS.Eng.Misc.c.360, copy in CCC); TS cat. by Oswald Allen, *c.* 1985, deposited in Nottingham UL (copy in Newark Museum).

References: Kelly, pp.91, 94, 251; John Morley, 'Libraries of Newark-upon-Trent, 1698–1960' (FLA thesis, 1969); Bill Report, 1970; Ker, Pastedowns, 1128b, 1529a; Lambeth Palace MS.3022: notes and rubbings of bindings by N. R. Ker; Brenda M. Pask, church guide, 1995; Louise Elizabeth Yirrell, 'An evaluative study for improving access to the Bishop White Library, St. Mary Magdalene Parish Church', (Loughborough U. Dept of Library Studies, dissertation, 1996); Brenda M.Pask, *Newark Parish Church of St.Mary Magdalene*, Newark, 2000; DNB: White; Scott.

NEWBIGGIN-BY-THE-SEA, Northumb.
St. Bartholomew. Newc.
[nil?] NRC
One of 92 parishes in the Northumberland Archdeaconry granted a ParLL under a scheme devised by Bishop Shute Barrington, carried out by Archdeacon R. G. Bouyer by 1823 (see p.57), and recorded as still possessing books in visitation returns, 1826–8.
References: Day, p.102 & n.38.

NEWBURY, Berks.
St. Nicolas. Ox.
[iv.]
A grant of £2. 10s. towards the est. of a ParLL was awarded by Bray from funds at his disposal, 1695–9. A DeskL was in existence at least by 1688: an inventory of that year records '5 bookes in chaines in the south ile'. Archdeacon Onslow's visitation book, 1786, has a record of 'a catalogue to be made of the books belonging to the parochial library'. In 1949 the parish chest with its 'massive padlocks', and a cupboard in the parish room, were found to contain *c.* 40 books of the 17th and early 18th cent., many in Latin. Some were gifts of the local clergy: one was given by Sir Humphrey Forster of Aldermaston. The books were examined by a Keeper from the Bodleian Library who advised that they should be kept together as a collection in a glass-fronted bookcase. In 1973 the clergy of the deanery decided that the books should be sold and that the money raised should be devoted to useful causes. The only vol. recommended for retention is still held: Thomas Bray's *Course of Lectures upon the Church Catechism*, vol.1, 2nd ed., 1697, which is inscribed: 'the gift of the author to ye lending library for ye Deanery of Newbury Berks.', and the lower cover is tooled: 'For the use of the minister and his successors for ever'.
References: Kelly, p.258; Berks. RO, D/P 89 5/1: churchwardens' accounts, 1688; D/EX1324/1: visitation book, 1786; D/P 89 parish magazine, 1949, 1965; MS memorandum, 1973, in the surviving vol.

NEWCASTLE UPON TYNE, Northumb.
St. Nicholas (the Cathedral from 1882). Newc.
[c. 300v.] Newcastle UL

In 1378 Thomas of Farnylaw, chancellor of York, bequeathed a Bible and concordances to be chained in the N. porch 'for the common use'. The church registers suggest that a DeskL containing a few chained vols. was housed in a small room over the vestry at least from 1597. A century later the library was under the control of the Corporation: the Common Council appointed the first salaried library keeper in 1677 (who was normally the curate of St. Nicholas). Under the terms of his will of 17 July 1661 John Cosyn (Cosin), draper of Newcastle, gave to the mayor and burgesses 'an hundred vols. of books . . . all the rest to be bought and provided by my executrix as the ministers shall agree upon, which said books I will shall be added to the library in Saint Nicholas Church'. Later, in the Notitia Parochialis of 1705, it was recorded that 'there is a little library belonging to St. Nic. Church wch was pillag'd by ye Scots in ye late Civil Wars. But since re Restoracion, Mr John Cosin Aldorman gave £80 towards ye furnishing of it with books. Beside 20 volumes out of his own study wch he left by his will to be made choice of by ye vicar'. Under another will in 1721 Nathaniel Ellison, rector of Gateshead, gave books to both the Dean and Chapter of Durham and to the library of St. Nicholas church, Newcastle. In 1735 and 1745 Robert Thomlinson (1668–1747), rector of Wickham, gave c. 4,600 vols. in trust for the library in St. Nicholas, and his friend Walter (later Sir Walter) Blackett of Wallington Hall, Northumberland, and Mayor of Newcastle, 1735–6, erected a handsome building next to the church to house them, and the library became 'a place of great resort for the literary gentlemen of the town' (Mackenzie, below). But the Corporation effectively lost control and after 1750 the library fell into neglect and disuse. However a ParLL of 215 vols. was est. in 1840 by the Associates of Dr Bray, which was augm. in 1870 and 1890. The Thomlinson books were transferred to Newcastle PL in 1885, and the 'Old Library' of St. Nicholas (which included later books in the Chapter Library) was placed on permanent loan in Newcastle UL in 1965. There are 4 medieval MSS with Thomlinson nos. in that collection although there is no evidence that any of them were Thomlinson books, and one (TH1678: a 14th cent. Psalms and canticles in Latin, with Richard Rolle's translation and commentary in English) was given to the church in 1660.

Catalogues: Emerson Charnley, *A Complete Catalogue of the Public Library in St. Nicholas' Church*, Newcastle upon Tyne, 1829; Bray Library 1840 cat.: Bray Associates Records, f.41, pp.31–5; *Newcastle Cathedral Chapter Library: Preliminary Catalogue*, 1888; E. B. Hicks and G. E. Richmond, *A Catalogue of the Newcastle Chapter Library and of the Churchwardens' or Old Parish Library*, Newcastle upon Tyne, 1890 (lists 298 vols. belonging to the old parish library, pp.32–46).

References: Notitia Parochialis: 1705, no.1271; E. Mackenzie, *A Descriptive and Historical Account of Newcastle upon Tyne*, 2v, 1827, v.2, pp.490–6; M.

H. Dodds, 'Wills and inventories', *History Teachers' Miscellany*, v.3 (1925), pp.170–1; Kelly, pp.25, 71, 73–4, 81–2, 96, 195, 251, 263; Joan Knott, 'Newcastle libraries in the early 19th century' (*History of the Book Trade in the North*, PH22, 1974); *idem*. 'A history of the libraries of Newcastle upon Tyne to 1900' (M.Litt., Newcastle U., 1975); Ker, MMBL, III, 1983, pp.490–4; DRB2, p.55, and p.52 (for details of, and references to, the Thomlinson collection).

NEWCHURCH, Staffs.
Christ Church. Lich.
[nil] *
A ParL of 60 vols. was est. in Christ Church on Needwood (now Newchurch) in 1812 by the Associates of Dr Bray, and augm. in 1878; it is not recorded after 1900.
Catalogues: of books sent to Needwood Parsonage, Needwood Forest, Bray Associates Records, f.38, p.246.
References: Bray Associates Annual Reports, 1900; Kelly, p.263.

NEWCHURCH-IN-PENDLE, Lancs.
St. Mary. Blackb.
[nil?] NRC
A ParLL of 142 vols. was est. in 1826 by the Associates of Dr Bray, and augm. in 1870.
Catalogues: Pendle 'New Church', Bray Associates Records, f.40, pp.139–41.
References: Shore, 1879; Kelly, p.262.

NEWENT, Glos.
St. Mary the Virgin. Glouc.
[nil]
John Craister, vicar, by his will dated 1737, 'gave for ever, to the succeeding vicars of Newent, all his study of books'.
References: Charity Commissioners, 18th Report (1828), p.287.

NEW MALTON, Yorks.
St. Leonard (red.) York
[nil]
A ParL of 72 vols. was est. in 1712 by the Bray Trustees for Erecting Parochial Libraries; in 1849 this library was reported as being one of those 'either wholly lost or reduced to a few tattered volumes'.
Catalogues: No.62, with printed rules in: Borthwick Institute, York (Bp C and P II/20, copy in CCC).
References: Select Committee Report, 1849; Bill, 1970; Kelly, p.264; the catalogue is analysed in Woolf, pp.188–9 & n.72, 192–3.

Newport (Essex): part of the library in a fifteenth-century priest's room
over the south porch, and the door to the spiral stone staircase

NEWNHAM, Glos.
St. Peter. Glouc.
[iv.] Glos. RO (temporary deposit)
DeskL: Foxe's, *Book of Martrys*, 1654, and 18th and 19th cent. service books.

NEWPORT, Essex
In situ St. Mary the Virgin. Chelmsf.
[*c.* 800v.]
A DeskL was probably in existence from an early period: a surviving 15th cent. oak lectern still has chains to which Old and New Testaments once were attached. The present library is housed in a 15th cent. priest's room over the S. porch, approached by a spiral stone staircase. A ParL of 72 vols. was est. in 1710 by the Bray Trustees for Erecting Parochial Libraries, and augm. in 1834. This collection was given up in 1870 but re-est. in 1879, and augm. in 1889 and 1896. Of the original collection 49 vols. remained in 1834, and 3 or 4 in 1959. The original Bray cupboard survives with traces on the inside of the hand door of 'A catalogue of the parochial library . . .'. The present library contains *c.* 100 pre-1800 books, the remainder being 19th cent. theology.
Catalogues: MS cat. no.5, Bray Associates Records, f.39, pp.103–6; f.41, pp.239–41 (68 vols.).
References: Bray Associates Annual Reports, 1890; DRB2, p.80.

Newport (Essex): the standard book-cupboard designed for the Bray Trustees library, 1710, with traces of the original catalogue on the inside of the door

NEWPORT, I.O.W.
St. Thomas. Portsm.
[nil] *
A ParLL of 161 vols. was est. in 1834 by the Associates of Dr Bray, and augm.
in 1861, 1869 and 1878.
Catalogues: Bray Associates Records, f.40, pp.254-8.
References:; Bray Associates Annual Reports, 1878; Shore, p.150; Kelly,
p.262.

NEWPORT PAGNELL, Bucks.
St. Peter and St. Paul (red.) Ox.
[nil]
DeskL: chained copies of Jewel and Foxe, and a Bible of 1608, in the church in
1959 are no longer present. In his will (PROB 11 1648) dated 16 Mar. 1730,
Lewis Atterbury (1656–1731) 'left Binnius' Councils to the library at Bedford
and such of my best practical books in divinity as my executors shall thing fitt
to the library of Newport Pagnell aforesaid'. Some 2,000 vols. of pamphlets
were willed to Christ Church, Oxford. The library was apparently placed in
the almshouses known as Queen Anne's Hospital, of which the vicar was the
Master. By 1842 it was in the custody of the Revd George Morley (d.1865),
vicar 1832–65, and Master. A ms. cat. of 1784 lists over 350 vols. (without
dates), including a range of secular works often found in an 18th cent.
gentleman's library.
Catalogues: MS 'catalogue of books in the library at Newport Pagnell made in
1784 by W. Hymers and C. M. Hardy' (Bucks. CRO: PR153/28/1.3).
References: Joseph Staines, *The History of Newport Pagnell and its immediate
Vicinity*, 1842, pp.133–4; Blades, BIC, 1890, p.37; J. S. Antrobus, 'Public
library provision in North Buckinghamshire, 1800–1923', (M.A. Dept. of
Library and Information studies, Loughborough U. of Technology, 1986),
pp.2–3; DNB: Atterbury; Venn: Morley. I am indebted to Jane Francis for the
reference to Atterbury's will.

NEWQUAY, Corn.
St. Michael. Truro
[*c.* 453 titles in 536v.] *
The origins of this library are unclear. John Pearce in a diocesan survey made
in 1949–50 listed 15 titles, 5 pre-1700. Dr Margaret Lattimore visited the
library in Nov. 1982 and reported a total of *c.* 670 books: 3 STC, 2 Wing,
2 17th cent. continental and *c.* 19 18th cent. items; the remainder being 19th
and early 20th cent. theology. The pre-1800 books are still present. There is no
evidence to suggest that the library was in existence much before the first
decade of the 19th cent. Some books have a printed label: 'Ex libris ecclesiae
Sancti Michaelis Archangeli de towan Blystra vel Newquay in Cornubio e
dono A.S. MDCCCX' ('A.S.' has not been identified), and others have labels
or shelf-marks of Bishop Phillpott's Library, **Truro** (probably from a sale of

duplicates), and the Bray lending library at **Truro** (1842). The present church was not completed and consecrated until 1911: the earlier books may have come from the previous parish church, St. Columb Minor, on the outskirts of the town. The library is housed in a small room over the porch. The church was gutted by a fire in 1993, but all the books and records were saved and removed to secure storage. They were returned after re-building in 1998. A new list of the books has been prepared by Mr A. N.Willis, Hon. Librarian.
Catalogues: list of 15 items in the Pearce Survey, 1949–50; list by Willis, 2000 (copy in CCC).
References: Kelly, p.246; TS Lattimore report (copy in CCC file).

NEWTON KYME, Yorks.
St. Andrew. York
[9v. in 4] York Minster Lib.
A set of Jerome, *Opera Omnia*, 9v. in 4, Paris, 1533–4 (Adams J116) was deposited in York Minster Lib. some time before 1996. The vols. have remains of clasps and are in roll-tooled Oxford bindings of *c.* 1537 (Oldham rolls: RC.c(1) 1537 (888); HM.a.(1) [G.F.] 1528–44 (770) & D1.a(5) 1520–45 (595). Vol.4 bears the signature of Elizabeth I on a front flyleaf, and other signatures include Richard Barnes (1532–87), granted licence from Elizabeth to hold 'in commandem' the Chancellorship of York with the Bishopric of Carlisle, and Henry Fairfax (1588–1665), who gave up his fellowship of Trinity College, Cambridge, on accepting the living of Newton Kyme, where he was vicar, 1633–46.
References: Barr, p.40; DNB: Barnes; Venn: Fairfax.

NORBURY, Shrops.
All Saints. Heref.
[iv.] *
A grant of 15s. towards the est. of a ParL was awarded by Bray from funds at his disposal, 1695–9. One vol. survives: Jewel, *Works*, 1609 or 1611 (imp.) The library founded by Edward Rogers at **Wentnor,** because of the amalgamation of livings, was also lodged here and at **Myndtown** and **Church Pulverbatch** before return to Wentnor.
References: Kelly, pp.252, 253 n.3, 259.

NORHAM, Northumb.
St. Cuthbert. Newc.
[nil] *
One of 92 parishes in the Northumberland Archdeaconry granted a ParLL under a scheme devised by Bishop Shute Barrington, carried out by Archdeacon R. G. Bouyer by 1823 (see p.57), and recorded as still possessing books in visitation returns, 1826–8. In 1858 the Northumberland Post Office Directory described the library as 'a parochial lending library for the poorer classes'.
References: Day, p.103.

NORTHAMPTON, Northants.
All Saints. Pet.
[nil]
There was a library in the upper vestry of the N. transept, most of the books in which (from their book labels) were given in 1777 by Edward Crane (1696?–1777), prebendary of Westminster. The earliest donation was a copy of Pliny, 'Liber Bibliothecae Northampton. 1701. Ex dono Edw. Maynard STD'. Maynard (1654–1740) was rector of Passenham and Boddington, Northants. This was perhaps the library assisted by Bray to the sum of £1 from funds at his disposal, 1695–9. A large library in the vestry, including 17th cent. chained books, was recorded in 1907; and an inventory and valuation taken in May 1923 describes a library of c. 1,300 vols., including a Chaucer of 1542 and a Walton Polyglot Bible.
References: R. M. Serjeantson, *A History of the Church of All Saints, North-ampton*, 1901, p.265; *N & Q*, 6 ser. v.6 (1882), p.15; Kelly, pp.91, n.4, 106.n.3, 251, 259; Cox & Harvey, p.335; Lambeth Palace MS.3222, f.275 & MS.3224, citing Northants. RO: an inventory by Woods & Co., Northampton; Venn: Crane.

NORTH CRAVEN, Yorks.
[place not identified]. Ripon
[?]
A ParL of 51 vols. was est. in 1850 by the Associates of Dr Bray.
Catalogues: 'North Craven, Yorks. (Ripon)', Bray Associates Records, f.41, pp.229–30.
References: Kelly, p.264. The deanery of Craven, with others, was formed into an archdeaconry in the diocese of Ripon in 1836.

NORTH GRIMSTON, Yorks. (N.Yorks.)
St. Nicholas. York
[nil]
Timothy Thurscross (d.1671), archdeacon of Cleveland, 1635–8, directed in his will that the greatest part of his 'study of books' should be distributed to 3 Yorkshire churches 'for the vicars therein and their successors for ever'. There is evidence that this happened in only one church, North Grimston, and not until 1685 when Barnabas Oley (1602–86), Thurscross' friend, said in his will: 'The books of Thurscross . . . I have given to Mr Thomas Langley . . . attorney of Furnivall's Inn in London, a near relation of Dr Thurscross, to be preserved for the use of the present vicar of North Grimston'. Langley (1667?–1723) was born in North Grimston. The incumbent in 1705 described them as 'a very useful library'; they were still there in 1731, but missing by 1896.
References: James Raine, *Catalogue of the Printed Books in the Library of the Dean and Chapter of York*, 1896, p.xiii; G. F. Russell Barker, *Memoir of Richard Busby*, 1895, pp.142–3; Notitia Parochialis, 1705: no.1008; Barr, p.35; DNB: Oley; Foster: Thurscross; Venn: Langley.

NORTH MARSTON, Oxon.
Assumption of the Blessed Virgin Mary. Ox.
[1v.]
DeskL: Bible, 1617.

NORTH PIDDLE, Worcs.
St. Michael. Worc.
[nil] *
There is a 19th cent. printed label reading, 'North Piddle Church Library'.
References: I am indebted to Brian North Lee for this reference.

NORTH WALSHAM, Norf.
St. Nicholas. Nor.
[2v.] Mansfield College, Oxford; Los Angeles, U of California, W. A. Clark
Lib.
DeskL: Samuel Otes, *An Explanation of the Generall Epistle of Saint Jude
. . . in One and Forty Sermons,* 1633. Nothing now remains of the ParLL of 67
vols. est. in 1710 by the Bray Trustees for Erecting Parochial Libraries, and
augm. by the Associates in 1788 and in 1870. In 1870 63 of these books
survived in the parish church, together with 85 other books of the 16th, 17th
and 18th cents., and a few of later date. The library was intact until 1938
when, at the instigation of the Secretary of the Bray Associates, 5 of the books
were sold (Blackwells in July), 1 (no.63) was sent to the Principal of Mansfield
College, Oxford, and the remainder were apparently destroyed. The original
'register' and a catalogue of 1870 survived in 1959 but no longer. One
vol. survives in the Clark Lib., Los Angeles, with a Bray bookplate:
Charles Le Cene, *An Essay for a New Translation of the Bible,* 2nd ed, 1727
(*BS530 L45 E1727)
Catalogues: MS. cat. 'North Walsam', no. 4, Bray Associates Records, f.39,
pp.25–8; a TS transcript of the 1870 cat. is in Bodl.MS.Eng.Misc.c.360 (copy
in CCC).
References: Shore, p.152; Kelly, p.263; Lambeth Palace MS.3224: notes by
N. R. Ker.

NORTON, Derbys. (S.Yorks.)
St. James. Sheff.
[508 titles in 446v.] Sheffield UL
In his will dated 1748 Cavendish Nevile (1681–1749), vicar 1710–49, 'did
also give unto the Vicar of Norton . . . for the time being and his successors for
ever the room or building which he . . . had erected there for a library, together
with all the printed books and manuscripts therein or in his house . . . which
were marked with a copper plate of his arms and inscribed to the said library,
and all maps, prints, book cases and shelves . . . which were in the said
library'. Apart from a few post-1750 items all the books in the collection were
from this bequest. They were deposited firstly in Sheffield PL in 1957, and then

in Sheffield UL in 1993. They each have the bookplate (reproduced in Norris, below) added after his death, bearing the arms and crest of Nevile of Chevet, co. York. There is one incunable, *Biblia Latina*, with the postils of Nicholas de Lyra, Nuremberg, Koberger, 1485, once owned by John Argentine (d.1508), Provost of King's College Cambridge, 1501–8. The date range is from 1512 to 1831 with *c.* 91 pre-1640 books (12 STC items); *c.* 234 1641–1700 books (175 Wing items); and 173 18th cent. books. They are arranged, as in both catalogues (below), in chronological order. Most of the books are theological. They include a collection of early Fathers (mainly in Greek), sets of sermons, collections of pamphlets on the 1687 Declaration of Indulgence of James II, the 'Bangorian' controversy, Sherlock, the Sacheverell trial of 1710, and others, with a fair selection of books on history, the classics, poetry, geography, philosophy and languages, and some books on medicine, science and gardening. Provenances (fully recorded in Norris, below, Appendix II) indicate that the library was built up casually rather than systematically. There are many signatures of earlier Neviles, relatives, friends and fellow students, especially from the 30 year period when he was Bursar at University college, Oxford.

Catalogues: TS cat. 1960, 'Norton Parish Library. List of books deposited in Sheffield City Libraries', includes an author index, and provenances in the text but not indexed; Roger C. Norris, 'A catalogue of the parochial library of Norton, Derbyshire', (Postgraduate Diploma in Librarianship, Sheffield U, 1965).

References: 'Extract of the part of Mr Nevile's will relating to the library at Norton'. (Lichfield RO: B/A/22/4–5); Kelly, p.246; DRB1, 1985, p.503 (omitted from 2nd ed.); Lambeth Palace MS.3222, ff.276–333: notes on provenance and rubbings of bindings by N. R. Ker.

NORTON AND LENCHWICK, Worcs.
St. Egwin. Worc.
[3v.] Illinois UL, Urbana
Peter Cassy (d.1784), vicar 1726–84, bequeathed books for the use of his successors in the vicarage, and for consultation by neighbouring clergy. In the *Gentleman's Magazine* in the year of his death he was quoted as saying that 'it cost me, from time to time, much money to purchase books; my successor may peradventure experience the same inconvenience. I will, therefore, as much as in me lies, prevent it, by bequeathing my library, as an heir-loom, to the living'. Each book contained a printed label: 'For the parochial library of Norton & Lenchwick, by P. Cassy, vicar', was numbered outside or inside, and kept in the 'parish room' of the vicarage. A printed list (no longer extant) of 8 leaves, n.d., contained *c.* 362 vols. Most of the books contained the names of previous owners, generally university men. McGovern in 1895 listed 48 missing titles. The collection was sold without faculty in or shortly before 1951. 128 vols. were offered for sale by Countryside Libraries Ltd, Hitchin, Herts. (cat. no.10, 1951, items 313–409). One surviving book in 1959 was

reported missing in 1969. A copy of John Prideaux, *Fasciculus Controversiarum* (Oxford, 1664), with the Norton bookplate, was sold by Arnold Muirhead, cat. winter 1960, The Lime Tree Miscellany, no.25, p.11, item 69; 3 vols. are now in the Illinois UL, Urbana: Baldwin 2266; Baldwin q.480; 81.D92.1718.

Catalogues: inventory by the Revd H. M.Wood (vicar in 1895); TS transcript of Countryside Libraries list, above: Bodl.MS.Eng.Misc.c.360 (copy in CCC). **References:** *Gentleman's Mag.*, v.54, pt.2 (July–Dec. 1784), p.876; W. C. Boulter, 'Peter Cassy's books, at Norton, near Evesham', *N & Q*, 8 ser. v.7 (30 Mar. 1895), pp.241–3; Mary Ransom, ed, 'The state of the Bishopric of Worcester, 1782–1808', *Worcs. Hist. Soc.*, N.S. v.6 (1968), p.78; J. B. McGovern, 'A noteworthy parish and library. The Library', *The Antiquary*, N.S.v.7 (1911), pp.305–10; Kelly, p.255; Bill Report, 1970; Lambeth Palace MSS.3223, ff.1–2, & 3224: notes by N. R. Ker.

NORTON ST. PHILIP, Somerset
St. Philip and St. James. B & W
[nil] *
A ParL of 59 vols. was est. in 1821 by the Associates of Dr Bray, and incorporated that of **Frome**, Somerset in 1871.
Catalogues: Bray Associates Records, f.41, pp.45–7.
References: Bray Associates Annual Reports, 1880; Kelly, p.263.

NORWICH, Norf.
St. Andrew. Nor.
[iv.] Columbia UL
The early history of this library is known largely from a record preserved by the 18th cent. Norfolk antiquary John Kirkpatrick (1680?–1728) who states that in his time (*c.* 1725) there was in the vestry 'a library of some of ye first reformers, commentaries, etc, such as Gualter, Masculus [sic], Calvin, Erasmus, Henry 8th's Bible ye most were given by Tho. Beaumond, alderman in 1586; and, among other books, an ancient MS of Wickliff's translation of ye New Testamt into English (with some things at ye end of it)'. In 1628 the library consisted of 26 works largely of protestant theology, Brentius Calvin, Gualterus, Musculus, Zwingli and a 'New Testament English manuscript'. One of the 26, 'Theophylact in Evan.', was noted as 'belonging to the Citty': the city library had by then been established in an adjoining building. An early 19th cent. cat. (watermarked 1832) lists 13 vols., including a copy of Erasmus, *Paraphrasis in Evangelium S. Matthaei* (Basel, 1522), belonging to Sir John Cheke (1514–71), and with signatures including George Gardiner (1535?–89), Dean of Norwich, and minister of St. Andrew, 1562–71. In 1883 there were only 8 vols. in the vestry library, and today none survive save the New Testament English MS (now in Columbia UL).
Catalogues: early 19th cent. cat. (Cambridge Antiq. Soc. Haddon Library: L. A. S. Cupboard, shelf V).

References: *History of Norfolk*, 1829, v.2, p.1178; John Kirkpatrick, Extracts from MSS relating to Norwich, *c.* 1725 (Norwich PL); F. R. Beecheno, 'Notes on the church of St. Andrew' [quoting from Roger Munde's Charity book, starting in 1574] (Norwich PL: MS.1883); Kelly, pp.71–2, 250; *ibid.* 'Norwich, pioneer of public libraries', *Norfolk Arch.*, v.34, no.2 (1969), p.218; Lambeth Palace MSS.3223, f.3, & 3224: notes by N. R. Ker; DNB: Kirkpatrick, Cheke, Gardiner.

NORWICH, Norf.
St. Augustine. Nor.
[1v.] Norfolk Museums Service
DeskL: Erasmus, *Paraphrases*, 1549.

NORWICH, Norf.
St. Clement with St. Edmund (red.) Nor.
[1v.] Norwich CL
DeskL: *Certain Sermons or Homilies*, 1683.

NORWICH, Norf.
St. George, Colegate (red.) Nor.
[2v.] Norwich CL
DeskL: Jewel, *Works*, 1611; Erasmus, *Paraphrases*, 1548.

NORWICH, Norf.
St. Giles. Nor.
[3v.] Norwich CL
DeskL: BCP, 1662; *Certain Sermons or Homilies*, 1623; Haydn, *Missa in Tempore Belli*, 1st ed., *c.* 1802.

NORWICH, Norf.
St. Gregory (red.) Nor.
[2v.] Norwich CL
DeskL: Bible, 1685; Jewel, *Works*, 1611.

NORWICH, Norf.
St. John de Sepulchre. Nor.
[7v.] Norwich CL
DeskL: Bible. NT Greek, 1633; Bible. NT 1583; BCP, 1636; 1662; *Certain Sermons or Homilies*, 1635; Erasmus, *Paraphrases*, 1548; Jewel, *Works*, 1609.

NORWICH, Norf.
St. John Maddermarket. Nor.
[1v.] Norwich CL
DeskL: Bible, 1611.

NORWICH, Norf.
St. Martin-at-Oak (red.) Nor.
[nil]
Entered in a parish register of the period 1767–81 is: 'A catalogue of books in St. Martin's vestry, given by the Rev. Ephraim Megoe of the parish to his successors in that church for ever'. Megoe (1712?–86) was vicar 1743–86. About 82 titles are listed, nearly all 17th cent., consisting of continental history, theology and classics. By 1829 400 vols. were recorded.
Catalogues: 1767–81, Norfolk RO: PD 15/15 (copy in CCC).
References: *History of Norfolk*, 1829, v.2, p.1237; Venn: Megoe.

NORWICH, Norf.
St. Michael-at-Plea (red.) Nor.
[1v.] Norwich CL
DeskL: *Certain Sermons or Homilies*, 1623.

NORWICH, Norf.
St. Peter Mancroft. Nor.
[17v. including 2 MSS] in situ; Norwich CL; Norwich Co. Hall
DeskL: the remaining MSS and printed books from the library belonging to the church in the 17th cent. and perhaps earlier were re-discovered in chests in the sacristy by members of the Bishop of Norwich's Diocesan Books and Documents Committee in c. 1967. Entries from the churchwardens' accounts mentioning the library in the church in 1629, 1647 and 1652, and a transcript of a late 17th cent. inventory of the books listed under donors with brief titles and a few dates, were printed in 1883 by Rye (below). 12 of the 20 vols. listed still survive. 'A booke to make a cataloge of ye bookes in ye library' was bought in 1682. Of the printed books, 5 (originally 9) vols. were presented by Thomas Tenison (1636–1715), vicar 1674–6, and later vicar and founder of the library at **St. Martin-in-the-Fields, London,** and Archbishop of Canterbury. The medieval MSS are a 13th cent. Bible, and a 12th/13th cent. Pauline Epistles with the glosses of Peter Lombard. Both MSS and books are now in The Mancroft in Heritage Display chapel. A Bible of 1613 and 2 18th cent. books are deposited in Norwich CL, and 25 19th cent. books are deposited in the County Hall basement.
Catalogues: see Rye, below; checklist of 11 titles in 15 vols. in Sayer, below.
References: Walter Rye, St. Peter Mancroft, Norwich: its parish history in the sixteenth and seventeenth centuries', *Norfolk Antiq. Miscellany*, v.2 (1883), pp.345, 359–63; DRB2, p.476; Kelly, pp.75–6, 250; Frank Sayer, 'The Mancroft books', *Mancroft Rev.* [parish magazine], Nov.1967, pp.7, iii; Lambeth Palace MSS.3223, ff.4–15, & 3224: notes on bindings and provenance by N. R. Ker; Ker, MMBL,III, 1983, pp.561–3.

NORWICH, Norf.
St. Stephen. Nor.
[38v.] Norwich CL
The early history of this collection is unknown. In reply to a CCC questionnaire in 1950 it was reported that there was an 'early and interesting
collection' in a chest in the vestry, but it was not until *c.* 1967, after a visit
from a member of the Bishop of Norwich's Diocesan Books & Documents
Committee, that the collection was fully examined. Each of the 38 vols., in the
iron-bound parish chest contained a bookplate dated 1859, 'the gift of Edward
Howman'. The donor was probably Edward John Howman (d.1874), rector of
Boxwell from 1831 until his death, and author of *A Collective Lesson on the
Catechism* [with text], 1843 (his will has not been traced). The books were
removed to Norwich PL by October 1970; they have recently been deposited
in Norwich CL. There is one incunable, Nicholas de Lyra, *Postilla*, Nurem-
berg, Koberger, 1487, and 17 books in English printed before 1663. A copy of
Erasmus, 1522, is in a Spierink binding.
Catalogues: TS list of the books 'temporarily deposited at the Norwich Central
Library' dated 5 Feb. 1970 (copy in CCC).
References: Lambeth Palace MS.3223, ff.16–24: notes and rubbings of bindings by N. R. Ker; Venn: Howman.

NUNEATON, Warwicks.
St. Nicholas (ded. uncertain). Cov.
[1v.] Warwicks. CRO
DeskL: John Innet, *A Sermon preached at the Assizes . . . Warwick August the
1st 1681*, 1681.

OAKHAM, Rut.
All Saints. Pet.
[67 titles in *c.* 150v.] Nottingham UL
A wooden board in the vestry states that 'Lady Harington gave a small library
for the use of the vicar'. James Wright in 1684, below, adds that it was
'founded for the use of the vicar of that church and accommodation of the
neighbouring clergy'. The nucleus of the collection is still that presented in
1616 by Lady Harington (d.1620), widow of John, 1st Baron Harington of
Exton in Rutland (d.1613). She also gave, with Lucy Russell, Countess of
Bedford, a collection of 218 vols. to Sidney Sussex College, Cambridge. It is
possible that both collections may have originally belonged to Anne's son,
John Harington, who died 1613/14, less than a year after his father. From an
inventory of 1806 the collection 'in two large bookcases' probably numbered
118 vols. 'and 4 old bad ones'. When catalogued in 1978 by Anne Herbert (see
below) there were 67 title in *c.* 150 vols. of the original bequest. The collection
was transferred on indefinite loan to Nottingham UL in 1980; the oak
bookcases, early but probably not Jacobean, remain in the church. The books
are nearly all theological, with a few examples of ecclesiastical and canon

law. There are 4 incunables and, of the remainder of the original bequest, all but 2 books were printed before 1600 on the continent, many in Paris and Basel. There are some ms. fore-edge nos. and authors/titles, but no evidence of chaining. In 46 vols. there is a printed book label: 'Ex dono dominae Annae Haringtonae Baronisae', one of the earliest examples of a woman's gift-plate. The incunables and early 16th cent. books are in blind-stamped calf, the remainder in uniform calf; 8 vols. are stamped with a pattern derived from the Harington arms ('Haringtons Knots'). An early 13th cent. Bible, given in 1599, by Thomas Pilkington, is now in Peterborough CL. Further details of provenance are given in Herbert, below.

Catalogues: MS cat. by title, early 20th cent.; TS cat. by Anne L. Herbert (M.A. in Librarianship, U. of Sheffield, 1978); *idem*, 'Books at Oakham belonging to or contemporary with the Harington bequest' (in article below, pp.8–11); author and card cats. with the collection.

References: James Wright, *The History and Antiquities of the County of Rutland*, 1684, p.52; 'Oakham vestry 100 years ago', *Rutland Mag. and County Hist. Record*, v.4 (1909–10), p.188; Anne L. Herbert, 'Oakham parish library', *Library History*, v.6, no.1 (1982), pp.1–11; Kelly, pp.75, 252; Ker, Pastedowns, 133a, appendix, item 56; Ker, MMBL, III, 1983, pp.564–5; Lambeth Palace MS.3223, f.25: notes on ms. fragments by N. R. Ker; DRB2, p.487.

ODIHAM, Hants.
All Saints. Win.
[nil?] NRC
The only record of this library is in a 'Letter from our correspondent', *The Times*, 1 Oct. 1964, reporting on the discovery of a Macaulay letter dated 15 June 1852 in a copy of his Essays 'from the now closed parish library at Odiham, near Basingstoke'. The library at that time was under threat of disposal or sale.
References: I am grateful to John Vaughan for this reference.

OFFORD CLUNY, Hunts. (Cambs.)
All Saints. Ely
[*c*. 11v.] Cambs. CRO, Huntingdon; CCC; Offord Darcy rectory
According to Candlin, below, 'John Newcome, D.D., rector 1730 to 1765 ... left a legacy for the village school and a library of theological works for his successors in Offord Cluny'. Newcome (*c*. 1684–1765) also gave a collection of books to **Grantham** in 1765. There were 'about 60 books' in 1950, kept in a disused loft at Offord Darcy rectory, which, some time before 1959, were transferred to a chest in the church at Offord Cluny. Neil Ker listed the remaining 17 books in 1957, which included 4 Wing items and 13 books published 1704–41, mainly sermons and practical theology. Most of them were signed: 'J' or 'John Newcome'. 5 vols. were deposited in Cambs. RO in 1985; 3 are deposited in the CCC library, and 3 are still in Offord Darcy (new) rectory.

Catalogues: TS list of 17 vols. by N. R. Ker, 1957: Bodl.MS.Eng.Misc.c.360 (copy in CCC); Cambs. RO list of 5 vols. (copy in CCC).
References: Thomas Candlin, *Offord Cluny and Offord Darcy, Huntingdonshire*, 1929, p.24; Venn: Newcome; Kelly, p.248.

OLDBURY, Shrops. (W.Mids.)
Christ Church. Birm.
[iv.] Sandwell District Libraries
DeskL: Bible, BCP, 1578 (poor condition). A ParL of 72 vols. was est. in 1713 by the Bray Trustees for Erecting Parochial Libraries. In 1849 this library was reported as being one of those 'either wholly lost or reduced to a few tattered volumes'.
Catalogues: in Bodl. MS.Rawl.D.834, ff.24–5: TS transcript in Bodl.MS. Eng.Misc.c.360 (copy in CCC, and see pp.49–51 and table on pp.444–52); Bray Associates Records, f.39, pp.217–18.
References: Select Committee Report, 1849; Kelly, p.264 & n.2; Woolf, p.190, n.76.

OLDHAM, Lancs. (G.Man.)
St. Mary with St. Peter. Man.
[nil] *
A ParLL of 145 vols. was est. in 1846 by the Associates of Dr Bray, which was augm. in 1870.
Catalogues: Bray Associates Records, f.41, pp.150–3.
References: Shore, p.152; Kelly, p.262.

OLD HUTTON, Westm. (Cumbria)
St. John the Evangelist. Carl.
[nil?] NRC
A ParLL of *c.* 352 vols. was est. in 1757 (perhaps in the School) by the Associates of Dr Bray. The cat. states that it was 'part of the library of the Revd Dr Evans, Rector of **Uffington** in Lincolnshire'. A copy of the rules and orders and list of trustees is in the Cumbria RO, Westm.
Catalogues: Bray Associates Records, f.38, pp.23–32.
References: rules and orders: Cumbria RO, Westm. Old Hutton WPR/17; Kelly, p.263.

OLD MALTON, Yorks. (N.Yorks.)
St. Mary the Virgin. York
[nil] *
A ParLL of 242 vols. was est. at Old Malton in 1823 'for the deaneries of Buckrose, Bulmer, Pickering and Blyth' by the Associates of Dr Bray.
Catalogues: Bray Associates Records, f.40, pp.89–96; Cambridge UL Dept. of

MSS and Univ. Archives, Add.MS.8887: clerical lending library, annotated catalogue, 1824–47.
References: Kelly, p.264; *Book Trade History Group Newsletter*, 20, (1993), Nov., p.17.

OLNEY, Bucks.
St. Peter and St. Paul. Ox.
[nil] *
A ParL was est. in 1862 by the Associates of Dr Bray, and augm. in 1878.
References: Shore, p.152; Bray Associates Annual Reports, 1878.

ORMESBY, Norf.
St. Margaret. Nor.
[nil?] NRC
Nathaniel Symonds (d.1720) bequeathed 40 sh. p.a. for 15 years for the purchase of religious books chosen by the minister of **Great Yarmouth**, half for Ormesby, St. Margaret and half for Yarmouth or Burgh (with annuities to several other parishes). In 1885 there were 2 vols. in the parish chest, Arthur Lake, *Sermons with some Religious and Divine Meditations*, 1629, and a copy of Jewel's *Works* with an inscription in an early 17th cent. hand: 'Ormisby Snt Margrate owneth this booke'. There were still a few books in 1878 according to Shore.
References: Shore, p.258; Kelly, p.250.

ORTON, Westm. (Cumbria)
All Saints. Carl.
[nil?] NRC
Nicolson in 1703 reported on a 'library, wherein are already deposited Dr Comber's large work on the Common-Prayer, A. B. Tillotson's *Sermons*, and some other good books, lately given (for the use of the parishioners) by Mr Hastwissel, a merchant in London'.
References: Nicolson, p.44.

OSWESTRY, Shrops.
Holy Trinity. Lich.
[nil]
The Bangor Missal in the National Library of Wales (MS.492) has at the end of the Calendar an inscription: 'This booke is geuen to the hye altar of the Paryshe Churche of Oswestry by Sir Morys Griffiths Prist . . . 1554'. A ParLL was est. in 1795 by the Associates of Dr Bray, which was augm. in 1870 and 1878. It is not recorded after 1890. A copy of the bookplate is in the John Johnson Collection in the Bodl.
References: Bray Associates Annual Reports, 1890; Kelly, p.263; Maura Tallon, *Church in Wales Diocesan Libraries*, Athlone, 1962, p.21.

OTLEY, Yorks. (W.Yorks.)
All Saints. Bradf.
[*c.* 90v.] *
A ParL was est. in 1853 by the Associates of Dr Bray, and augm. in 1870, 1877 and 1896. In 1978 the complete library was found in good condition in its original cupboard.
References: Shore, p.152; Barr, p.37.

OTTERY ST MARY, Devon
St. Mary the Virgin. Ex.
[103 titles in 109v.] Exeter UL, and in situ
Books were associated with the church from the 14th cent. John Grandisson (1292?–1369), Bishop of Exeter, in his will divided his extensive library principally between his Chapter and the collegiate churches of Ottery, **Crediton** and Boseham [Bosham], and Exeter College, Oxford. In the next century under the terms of his will, Edmund Lacy (1420–55), Bishop of Exeter, bequeathed all his 36 books, mostly written in his own hand, to be chained in the library at Ottery. A further will of John Hoile, of Ottery St. Mary, 1636, mentions a bequest of 40s. 'towards the furnishing of books in the library . . . in that church'. An account published in 1842 quotes a record of the library in 1672: 'in the gallery in the Lady chapel, called the Library, are a few tattered remains of books . . . such books of value as still exist . . . are forwith to be rebound and catalogued'. Most of the books now deposited at Exeter UL seem to have been acquired in the 19th cent. There are 6 incunables, 17 16th cent. and 50 17th cent. books. Some 19th and 20th cent. books remain in the church.
Catalogues: card cat. with collection.
References: E. A. Savage, *Old English Libraries*, 1911, pp.111–12; The Register of Edmund Lacy, Bishop of Exeter, 1420–1455, Registrum Commune, ed. G. R. Dunstan, v.4, p.52, *Canterbury & York Society*, v.63 (1971); Ker, MLGB2, notes a 'list of 137 books bequeathed in 1445' in the Register, iii, fo.513v; will of John Hoile: Devon RO, 3025 Hole of Bow, P1; 'An account of the church of Ottery St. Mary', *Trans. of the Exeter Diocesan Arch. Soc.*, v.1 (1842), pp.40–1; Kelly, pp.80, 246 (but not 'Holy Cross'); DRB2, p.59; DNB: Grandisson, Lacy.

OUNDLE, Northants.
St. Peter. Pet.
[nil]
A ParL of 72 vols. was est. in 1721 by the Bray Trustees for Erecting Parochial Libraries. It was reported lost in 1896.
Catalogues: Bray Associates Records, MS. cat. no.47, f.39, pp.115–18.
References: Bray Associates Annual Reports, 1896; Kelly, p.263.

OVERSTONE, Northants.
St. Nicholas. Pet.
[4v.] Cambridge UL
DeskL: BCP, 1687; Bible, Oxford, 1770; BCP, 1760, and Bible, Oxford, 1717 (imp.), owned by Sir John Cust (1718–70) and given by his son, Sir Bradley Cust in 1774.
References: DNB: Cust. I am indebted to Paul Morgan for information in this entry.

OVER WHITACRE, Warwicks. (W.Mids.)
St. Leonard. Birm.
[nil]
A ParL of 72 vols, was est. in 1711 by the Bray Trustees for Erecting Parochial Libraries. The church was demolished in 1765 and another built. The library was augm. in 1870, and 125 old vols. and 6 new vols. were noted in 1889, with the rector reporting that he would like to be rid of the old ones. In 1896 the library was reported as lost.
Catalogues: MS. cat. no 42, Bray Associates Records, f.39, pp.121–4 (another copy in Bodl. MS.Rawl. D.834, f.13–14).
References: Bray Associates Annual Reports, 1896; Shore, p.153; Kelly, p.263; Lambeth Palace MS.3224: notes by N. R. Ker.

OVING, Bucks.
All Saints. Ox.
[1v.]
DeskL: BCP, 1662: 'Sealed Book of Charles II'.

OXENHALL, Glos.
St. Anne. Glouc.
[nil]
A ParL of 72 vols. was est. in 1710 by the Bray Trustees for Erecting Parochial Libraries. In 1849 it was reported as being one of those 'either wholly lost or reduced to a few tattered volumes'. The church was almost totally rebuilt after a fire in 1868.
Catalogues: MS. cat. no.16, Bray Association Records, f.39, pp.107–10.
References: Select Committee Report, 1849; Kelly, p.262.

OXFORD, Oxon.
St. Mary the Virgin. Ox.
[nil]
In 1300 there were a few tracts chained or locked in chests in the choir, and later, books also.
References: Blades, BIC, p.68; E. A. Savage, *Old English Libraries*, 1911, p.129.

OXFORD, Oxon.
St. Peter-in-the-East. Ox.
[*c.* 50v.] St. Edmund Hall, Oxford; Bodl.
DeskL: Bible, 1611–12. A library was est. in Aug. 1841 by Walter Kerr Hamilton (1808–69), vicar 1837–41, Bishop of Salisbury 1854–69. The date '1841' and the inscription: 'E. LIBR. BIBL. S.PET. AD. OR. OXON.' are in gilt on the covers of all the books. They were housed in a room over the S. porch. After 12 vols., including a ms. catalogue were deposited in the Bodl. the remainder of the library was sold with faculty in 1959: 38 vols. to the Bodl. and the rest (*c.* 250 vols.) to Messrs Blackwell. Neil Ker listed the books in Blackwell's shop and purchased 6 items (which he subsequently gave to St. Edmund Hall in 1971). The church was closed in 1965. In 1966 the register of borrowers, 1841–76, and the 11 surviving vols. were deposited in Oxfordshire Archives, and in 1982 transferred to St. Edmund Hall . The list shows that most of the books were of Hamilton's gift; 71 were printed before 1800, the earliest being a copy of the *Homilies*, 1623.
Catalogues: Catalogue of the Church Library of St. Peter in the East, 1841; list of 12 surviving vols. above: Oxfordshire Archives: Par/213/17/MS1/1 & Appx. III; TS list by N. R. Ker, 1959, of 197 titles in *c.* 250 vols., with some notes of provenance: Bodl.MS.Eng.Misc.c.360 (copy in CCC); card cat. of books in St. Edmund Hall with the collection.
References: Lambeth Palace MSS.3223, f.26, & 3224; Shore, p.148; *St. Edmund Hall Mag.*, v.9, no.4 (1969); DRB2, p.536; Venn: Hamilton.

OXFORD, Oxon.
St. Peter-le-Bailey. Ox.
[nil]
A ParL was est. in 1721 by the Bray Trustees for Erecting Parochial Libraries. A parchment roll containing a list of 'The books in St. Peter's church' in 1731, held by St. Peter's Hall, includes 31 books, all in English (without dates), together with a note of 'one box with two shelves in it for to put ye books in it with a lock and key to ye sd box'. 10 of the books are the same as those sent out by the Bray Trustees: Burnet, Goodman, Nelson, Ostervald (2), Scott (5): see pp.444–52.
Catalogues: 1731 list in St. Peter's Hall (TS transcript by N. R. Ker in Lambeth Palace MS.3223, f.27); Kelly, p.263.

PAINSWICK, Glos.
St. Mary the Virgin. Glouc.
[*c.* 121 titles in *c.* 45v.] Glos. RO
DeskL (in origin). A collection of 56 books, found in the roof space at The Verlands, Painswick, the vicarage built in 1872, was transferred to the church in 1918 by permission of C. H. Verey, vicar 1917–30. The earlier history of this collection is unknown. On a label attached to an imperfect copy of Jewel's *Works* (item 56) is a note: 'Date 1609. This book is mentioned in the

inventory of goods belong unto our church dated 1685'. There is a note in the churchwardens accounts for 1684: 'Pd for rebinding Bishop Jewell against Harding 0.4.4.' Item 59, a 1660 book, has a cover stamped: 'Painswick Manor, 1660.' A ms. list of 1918 includes records of parish meetings and other archival material as well as printed books. The collection is housed in cupboards in the vestry. It was listed in 1997 by the Gloucester Deputy Diocesan Archivist and includes bound vols. of pamphlets and sermons containing *c.* 15 STC and *c.* 81 Wing items, and a number of, as yet, unidentified items. The greater part of the collection was deposited in Glos. RO in April 2001.

Catalogues: 1918 list with the collection; 1997 list: copy in CCC.

PAKEFIELD, Suffolk
All Saints and St. Margaret. Nor.
[3v.] Norwich CL
DeskL: Bible, 1640, 2v.; *Certain Sermons or Homilies,* 1623.

PASTON, Norf.
St. Margaret. Nor.
[11v.] Norwich CL
DeskL: Archbishop of Canterbury, *Articles to be Enquired,* 1613–14; Erasmus, *Paraphrases,* 1548; *A Forme of Common Prayer,* 1636; Jewel, *Works,* 1611; Archdeacon of Norfolk, *Articles to be Enquired . . . ,* 1635; Bishop of Norwich, *Articles to Enquired . . . ,* 1662; *Certain Prayers Collected out of a Forme of Godly Meditations,* 1603; *A Forme of Common Prayer,* 1625; *A Forme of prayer . . . times of Warre,* 1628; *An Homilie against Disobedience . . . ,* [1571?]; Richard Mocket, *God and the King,* 1615.

PATRIXBOURNE, Kent
St. Mary. Cant.
[nil]
The existence of this library and its contents are known only from an inventory of 1757 found among the parish records. The books belonged to John Bowtell (d.1753), vicar 1698–1752, and were bequeathed by his widow 'to the use of the vicar of Patrixbourne for the time being'. She died in 1757 and an inventory was completed by Herbert Taylor, vicar 1753–63. The books were kept in two studies in the vicarage and numbered 1078 vols. 'besides a large number in prints and simple sermons, pamphlets, &c laid up in a chest under lock & key at the vicarage-house'. There was a copy of Walton's Polyglot Bible, together with popular historical and theological works, a large no. of volumes of sermons and a few topographical works; literature was largely absent.

Catalogues: 1757 inventory: Canterbury CL Diocesan Archives U/3/129/1.
References: Yates, p.164; Venn: Bowtell, Taylor.

PEAKIRK, Northants.
St. Pega. Pet.
[1v.] *
DeskL: Bible, 1613 [?].

PENISTONE, Yorks. (S.Yorks.)
St. John the Baptist. Wakef.
[nil]
A ParL of 43 vols. was est. in 1815 by the Associates of Dr Bray, and augm. in 1872. It is not recorded after 1890, but books were located in the vestry and in the local PL in 1970: they can no longer be found.
Catalogues: sent Feb. 1815, Bray Associates Records, f.38, pp.258–9 (reprinted in Penistone WEA history Group, *A Further History of Penistone*; Penistone, 1965, pp.27–8); lists are also recorded in terriers for 1815 and 1829; TS list of *c.* 32 items: Lambeth Palace MS.3223, ff.28–9.
References: Bray Associates Annual Reports, 1890; Shore, p.152; Kelly, p.264; Bill Report, 1970.

PENSHURST, Kent
St. John the Baptist. Roch.
[4 works in 9v.] Canterbury CL
A catalogue of books belonging to the rectory of Penshurst and kept at the parsonage was made in 1759/60 and given to Archdeacon Potter at his visitation in August 1761. They comprised sets of St. John Chrysostom, Paris, 1621–33, given by Richard Lee, rector 1640–50; Augustine, n.d., given by Francis Sidney (b. *c.* 1567), rector 1617–33, and Matthew Pole, *Synopsis Criticorum*, 1669–76, given by William Egerton (*c.* 1683–1738), rector 1710–38, together with 2 Bibles, a book of Homilies and Joseph Caryl's *An Exposition with Practical Observations upon the Book of Job*, 1676–7: 31 vols. in all. Matthew Nicholas, rector 1786–96, kept a memorandum book listing these works and others. Other books were subsequently added to the collection, but the only vols. to survive, now on deposit in Canterbury CL, are vols.1–6 of Chrysostom's *Works*; vol.2 of his *Homilies*, Heidelberg, 1596 (not on the original list); vol.1 of his *Homilies*, Leiden, 1603 (not on the original list), and the work by Poole: all are marked: 'Penshurst Rectory'.
Catalogues: 1759/60, at the back of the 3rd Penshurst parish register, 1716–1812: Centre for Kentish Studies: P287/1/3 (copy and TS transcript in CCC).
References: Foster: Sidney, Egerton. I am indebted to Sheila Hingley, formerly Librarian, Canterbury Cathedral Library, for information in this entry.

PERSHORE, Worcs.
St. Andrew (red.). Worc.
[nil] *
A ParL of 72 vols. was est. in 1712 at Elmley [**Elmley Castle**] by the Bray Trustees for Erecting Parochial Libraries, which by 1877 had been transferred

to Pershore, improved and enlarged, and again augm. in 1881.
References: Bray Associates Annual Reports, 1885; Shore, p.153; Kelly, p.264 (under Elmsley).

PILLING, Lancs.
St. John the Baptist. Blackb.
[3v.]
DeskL: a chained copy of William Burkitt, *Expository Notes on the New Testament*, given by the Revd George Holden 'to the inhabitants of Pilling for ever', on 29 Sept. 1784, formerly chained to the communion rails of the chapel; Bible, 1717; Geneva Bible, 1560, believed to have survived from Pilling's medieval chapel. A list of 34 books belonging to Pilling Chapel is written at the back of the register for 1760–1798, 'being the gift of the executors of the last will of William Stratford . . . Commissary of the Archdeaconry of Richmond, to the curate and his successors for ever'. A ParL of 15 vols. was est. in 1761 by the Associates of Dr Bray: 4 vols. were noted as 'sent before by Dr Stratford's executors'. None of these books has survived.
Catalogues: list of 34 books: Lancs. RO: PR 2935/1/1, transcribed in David Weston, 'Perpetual curacy 1540–1919, with particular reference to the Chapelry and Parish of Pilling in Lancashire' (PhD thesis, University of Lancaster, 1993), pp.229–32: I am indebted to the author for this reference; 1761 catalogue: Bray Associates Records, f.38, p.87.
References: Kelly, p.262.

PILTON, Somerset
St. John the Baptist. B & W
[nil] *
In 1866 Blades noted 'about 16 old volumes in the parish church'. Neil Ker's notes of 1974 include a TS 'List of books belonging to Pilton church as furnished by Mr P. S. Allen of Merton College, Oct. 1918'. This has 6 titles: 2 incunables and 4 16th cent. continental books. In 1987 the church held copies of the BCP, 1604 and 1662, and a Bible, Oxford, Baskett, 1739, but no longer.
Catalogues: as above, Lambeth Palace MS.3223, ff.30–34, with notes on provenance, including monastic.
References: Blades, *Book-Worm*, Nov. (1866), p.172; Pearson 543.1 (seen by Neil Ker before 1996).

PLEMSTALL, Ches.
St. Peter. Ches.
[4v.] *
DeskL: Bibles, 1549, 1608, 1611; and a Bible, n.d., in 2 vols. both chained, given by Raymond Richards, 1945.
References: Richards, pp.276–7.

PLYMOUTH, Devon

St. Andrew. Ex.

[nil] *

A library was in existence when Bray arrived at Plymouth en route for Maryland which had 'some excellent books in it, as the Polyglot, the Criticks at large, Pools Synopsis, &c., but scarce known to be there, very likely because covered with dust and overwhelmed with rubbish'. Both Bray and the Mayor donated £5 in 1700 towards cleaning and enlarging the library, which was to be a lending library 'for the clergy and other gentlemen in this town and neighbourhood, so for the entertainment of such missionaries as being outward bound and detained here by contrary winds and for the benefit of the naval officers and chaplains of ships which ride in our harbour'. After Bray's departure the project evidently lapsed: such books as were left were probably transferred to the school library est. by Pearde's will in 1669 and did not survive. Nor is there any trace of the ParLL of 132 vols. est. in 1840 by the Associates of Dr Bray (it is not recorded after 1900). Bray had come to Plymouth via **Gravesend** and **Deal**.

Catalogues: 1840 library: Bray Associates Records, f.41, pp.19–21.

References: Bray Associates Annual Reports, 1900; Shore, p.151; Kelly, pp.106 & n.4, 246 & n.4, 258, 261; George Smith, 'Dr Thomas Bray', *LAR*, v.12 (1910), pp.251–2 (quoting from a Bray ms. diary-letter once in Sion College, sold at Sotheby's in 1977: see **Deal**). I am indebted to the staff of the Plymouth Library Local Studies Section for information in this entry, drawn from Dr Margaret Lattimore's 'The history of libraries in Plymouth to 1914', (PhD thesis, University of London, 1982).

PLYMTREE, Devon

St. John the Baptist. Ex.

[nil] *

A terrier / inventory of 1911 in the Devon RO records that 'there is a library of about 700 volumes belonging to the rectory, chiefly the gift of the Revd John Fleming, rector 1778–96', with the additional note, 'this collection of books was disposed of by J. D. Steele, the incumbent prior to his cession of the benefice in July 1963. As far as can be ascertained no faculty or permission was either sought or granted'. The books were kept in the rectory in 1959; by 1970 it was reported that they had been sold to an Exeter bookseller.

References: letter from Dr Margaret Lattimore, 6.12.1963 (in CCC files); Kelly, p.246; Bill Report, 1970.

PORCHESTER, Hants.

St. Mary. Ports.

[1v.] Portsmouth City RO

DeskL: William Perkins, *Works*, v.1, Cambridge, 1612.

PORTSEA, Hants.
St. Mary. Ports.
[1v.] Portsmouth City RO
DeskL: Bible and Bible dictionary, 1578, and 18th and 19th cent. works.

PORTSMOUTH, Hants.
St. Thomas (from 1927 the Cathedral). Ports.
[3v.] Portsmouth City RO
DeskL: Foxe, *Book of Martyrs*, 1583 (v.1 only); BCP, 1662; Andrew Parsons, *Seasonable Councel to an Afflicted People*, 1677.
A ParL of 171 vols. was est. in 1843 by the Associates of Dr Bray. It is not recorded after 1880, but some 18th and 19th cent. vols. on deposit in Portsmouth City RO may be from this collection.
Catalogues: Bray Associates Annual Reports, 1880; 1843: Bray Associates Records, f.41, pp.94–7.

POSLINGFORD, Suffolk
St. Mary. St.E.
[nil]
Terriers in the Suffolk RO, Bury St. Edmunds are our sole knowledge of this library: that for 1716 lists 11 books (in 14 vols.), mostly standard Caroline divinity: Sanderson, Stillingfleet, Hammond, Pearson, Andrewes, Hooker and Laud; the 1827 terrier lists 16 vols. and the 1834 terrier gives 'a catalogue of books in the vestry', listing 12 vols. mainly those in earlier lists, with a few added and a few lost.
Catalogues: terriers, Suffolk RO, Bury St. Edmunds: 806/1/122.
References: Fitch, 1965, p.74; Lambeth Palace MSS.3223, ff.35–6, & 3324: notes by N. R. Ker.

POULTON-LE-FYLDE, Lancs.
St. Chad. Blackb.
[135 titles]. John Rylands UL, Manchester
A ParL of 81 vols. was est. in 1720 by the Bray Trustees for Erecting Parochial Libraries, which was augm. by the Associates in 1757. It was housed in a locked cupboard on the ground floor of the tower. In a review by the Associates in 1885–6 115 vols. were recorded. In 1959 the library included 71 vols. of the Whitchurch selection (see pp.53–5): nos. 1–8, 10, 11, 13, 15–26, 28, 30–62, 64–71, 73, 75–80. It was noted by Christie as a 'complete and excellently preserved Bray library'. The collection was transferred on permanent loan to the John Rylands UL in 1978/79. It now contains Anglican theology and church history, 1690–1720 (two thirds of the books), and 19th cent. theology (the remainder).
Catalogues: the original printed cat. no.56 and a copy of the rules, formerly on a cupboard door, varnished over, are preserved in the Lancs. RO, Preston: PR 3222 acc.6423 (copy in CCC); 1757 cat. of 23 vols. in Bray Associates

Records, f.38, p.49; TS cat. of *c*. 60 titles, n.d.: Lancs. RO, Preston, Blackburn Diocese DR / B; TS cat. of 1967, 44 titles in 63 vols. (copy in CCC).
References: Christie, p.vi; Kelly, p.262; *A Guide to the Special Collections of the John Rylands University Library of Manchester*, Manchester, 1999, p.66; Lambeth Palace MS.3223, ff.37–8: notes by N. R. Ker.

PREES, Shrops.
St. Chad. Lich.
[324v.] Shrops. RRC
At some time before 1817 the Bray Associates sent 30 vols. for a ParLL at 'Press, Herefords.' which may have been intended for Prees, Shrops. The 120 original vols. from this collection, mostly dating from before 1800, with other books, were 'left for the use of the vicars of Prees for ever by John Allen, A. M. Archdeacon of Salop, and sometime vicar of thys said parish. Anno. Dom. MDCCCLXXXIII', as described on the mock antique labels in the books. Allen (*c.* 1811–86) was vicar 1846–83. The books, which include 17th cent. theology, 18th cent. poetry and a run of the *Quarterly Review*, were housed at the vicarage. Sometime before 1957 they were transferred as a gift to the Shropshire CRO and are now in the Records and Research Centre.
Catalogues: Pre-1817 cat. Bray Associates Records, f.38, pp.166–7; a TS list of the books was made by Shrops. CRO in 1957, which includes separate listing of books with and without Allen's bookplate (Bodl.MS.Eng.Misc.c.360, copy in CCC); Shrops. PLC, 1971, nos. 4705–5028.
References: Kelly, Shrops., p.vi; Lambeth Palace MS.3223, ff.39–47: notes by N. R. Ker and rubbings of a binding on a copy of Erasmus, 1549; Venn: Allen.

PRESTBURY, Glos.
St. Mary. Glouc.
[3v.] Gloucester CL
DeskL: Jewel, *A Reply to Mr. Harding's Answer*, 1565, and *A Defence of the Apologie*, 1567; Foxe, *Book of Martyrs*, 1641.

PRESTON, Lancs.
(Ded. unknown). Blackb.
[nil]
A ParLL of 252 vols. was est in 1840 by the Associates of Dr Bray. It was still listed in the Bray Associates Report for 1877, but according to the Archdeacon (in 1996) no parochial libraries survive in the deanery.
Catalogues: Bray Associates Records, f.41, pp.6–11.
References: Shore, p.152; Kelly, p.262.

PRESTON [near Wingham], Kent
St. Mildred. Cant.
[41v.] Canterbury CL
A ParL of 67 vols. was est. in 1710 by the Bray Trustees for Erecting Parochial Libraries. In 1959 41 vols. from the original collection survived, nos. 1–24, 26–35, 38–42, 45–6 (see p.49-52). No.9 was the register: 'The catalogue of the Preston Library April ye 16th 1730. Then exhibited by the vicar at the visitation'. All the books from the top shelf are missing. The travelling bookcase, normally unpainted, was painted white after receipt at the church, with the letters 'Dr Bray's Parochial Library for the use of the vicars of Preston' picked out in black. A copy of the printed 1709 Act originally pasted inside the door has now been removed for conservation. In 1878 the collection was reported as 'withdrawn', but in 1971 it was found to be at the home of the vicar's warden at Preston Court. At some time after 1983 the collection in its bookcase was deposited in Canterbury CL.
Catalogues: MS cat. Bray Associates Records, f.39, pp.65-8; the 1730 register and a ms. cat of 1772: Canterbury CA DCb.JY.4.30; the books are now included in Canterbury CL computerised cat.
References: Bray Associates Annual Reports, 1878; Kelly, p.262; Bill Report, 1970; Yates, p.162; Sarah Gray and Chris Baggs, 'The English parish library: a celebration of diversity', *Libraries & Culture*, v.35 (2000), no.3, pp.420-3, with an illustration of the cupboard (closed). I am indebted to Sheila Hingley and Sarah Gray, Canterbury CL for information in this entry.

PRESTON GUBBALS, Shrops.
St. Martin (CCT). Heref.
[*c*. 86v.] Shrops. RRC
The date of foundation of this library is unknown. It was contained in a wooden chest in the vestry, and numbered 'about 72 books' when recorded in 1903. In 1960 Neil Ker saw a cupboard in the church inscribed 'The gift of Charles Mather Esq.' which contained 61 books, according to the list on the door made in 1896, mainly 18th cent. divinity, with some later additions. The collection was deposited in Shrops. Co.L by 1970, and then in the Shrops. RRC.
Catalogues: Shrops. PLC, 1971.
References: E. C. Peele and R. S. Cleese, eds., *Shropshire Parish Documents*, Shrewsbury, 1903, p.266; Kelly, p.252 (as 'Preston Gobalds', f. by 1798 (?)); Bill Report, 1970; Kelly, Shrops, p.xi; Lambeth Palace MSS.3223, f.48, & 3224: notes by N. R. Ker.

PRINCES RISBOROUGH, Bucks.
St. Mary. Ox.
[nil]
A ParL of 146 vols. was est. in 1816 by the Associates of Dr Bray; by 1879 this library had been amalgamated with that of **Aylesbury**, Bucks.

Catalogues: Bray Associates Records, f.38, pp.262–6.
References: Shore, p.152; Kelly, p.261.

PUDSEY, Yorks. (W.Yorks.)
St. Lawrence and St. Paul. Bradf.
[4 titles in 6v.] Bradford CL
A ParLL of 77 vols. was est. in 1818 by the Associates of Dr Bray. It was not recorded after 1890: the surviving vols. are early 19th cent. theology.
Catalogues: Bray Associates Records. f.40, pp.13–15.
References: Bray Associates Annual Reports, 1890; Kelly, p.264; DRB2, p.571.

PURSE CAUNDLE, Dorset
St. Peter. Sarum
[2v.] *
DeskL: Chained Bible, n.d.; BCP, 1681, 'the property of Lady Victoria Herbert who maintains the charity chapel'.
References: CCC Questionnaire, 1950.

QUAINTON, Bucks.
Holy Cross and St. Mary. Ox.
[57 items] Bucks. RO
DeskL: Printed Forms of Prayer for fast days and special days of prayer: 34 items, 1685–1715; printed Royal Proclamations for fast days, alteration to the Act of Uniformity, request for briefs, etc; also Act for better registering of marriages, births and burials, 1695, Orders in Council relating to the prevention of the spread of distemper in horned cattle: 23 items, 1689–1747.
References: Bucks. RO list (copy in CCC).

QUATFORD, Shrops.
St. Mary Magdalene. Heref.
[1v.]
DeskL: Bible, 1585.
References: CCC file notes.

QUATT, Shrops.
St. Andrew. Heref.
[2v.] Dudmaston Hall *
The 'circular reading desk of very ancient date' (a rotating lectern), noted by Blades in 1890, is still present, but no longer supports 2 vols. of Foxe's *Book of Martyrs* (deposited 'for some years' at Dudmaston Hall).
References: Blades, BIC, 1890, p.37.

RAMPISHAM, Dorset
St. Michael and All Angels. Sarum
[nil] *
A ParLL of 77 vols. was est. in 1818 by the Associates of Dr Bray.
Catalogues: for the united parishes Rampisham, Wroxall, Bray Associates
Records, f.40, pp.9–11.
References: Kelly, p.261.

RAMSEY, Hunts. (Cambs.)
St. Thomas à Becket. Ely
[nil] *
DeskL: a copy of Comber's Paraphrases to the BCP was formerly chained to a
lectern; it was present in 1950, then deposited in a bank, but now cannot be
traced.
References: CCC Questionnaire, 1950.

RANWORTH, Norf.
St. Helen. Nor.
[iv.]
DeskL: a copy of Erasmus, *Paraphrases*, was present in 1950 but can no longer
be found. A 15th cent. antiphonal is probably that bequeathed to the church by
William Cobbe in 1478, and perhaps preserved at the Reformation by the
Holdych family, lords of the manor of Ranworth. It was bought back for the
church at the Huth sale, 16 Nov. 1911, lot 217, via Messrs. Ellis in 1912.
References: CCC Questionnaire, 1950; Ker, MMBL, IV, 1992, pp.194–5.

RATLINGHOPE, Shrops.
St. Margaret. Heref.
[nil]
A grant of 15s. towards the est. of a ParLL was awarded by Bray from funds at
his disposal, 1695–9.
References: Kelly, p.259.

RAUGHTON HEAD, Cumb. (Cumbria)
All Saints. Carl.
[12v.] Carlisle CL
A ParL was est. in 1871 by the Associates of Dr Bray. Lists of library books
dated 1859 and 1867 in the parish records at the Cumbria RO, Carlisle
indicate an earlier collection. By 1900 the collection had been incorporated
into that of **Carlisle**. 12 vols. from the 1871 library have been discovered in the
Prescott Library in the Carlisle Diocesan Resources Centre, and are now
deposited in Carlisle CL on permanent loan.
References: Bray Asscociates Annual Reports, 1900; Shore, p.151.

RAVENSTONEDALE, Westm. (Cumbria)
St. Oswald. Carl.
[nil]
A ParL of 15 vols. was est. in 1762 by the Associates of Dr Bray. In 1849 this
library was reported as one of those 'either wholly lost or reduced to a few
tattered volumes'.
Catalogues: Bray Associates Records, f.78, p.84.
References: Select Committee Report, 1849; Kelly, p.263.

READING, Berks.
St. Giles. Ox.
[9v.] Berks. RO
'A public library at Reading' was recorded in the Bray Trustees minutes of 23
Aug. 1727. Archdeacon Onslow in 1786 noted: 'A parochial library in this
parish. Books given by Mr. Vaughan. Mr. Cadogan has made a catalogue and
they are kept at his house because the vestry is damp'. The remaining books
were deposited with the parish records in Berks. RO by 1970; they range in
date from 1614 to 1815 and include 3 STC items.
No books survive from the ParL est. in 1885 by the Associates of Dr Bray.
Catalogues: list with the parish records: Berks. RO, D/P96 28/50–58 (copies in
Lambeth Palace Lib. and CCC).
References: Bray Associates Annual Reports, 1885; Archdeacon Onslow's
Visitation book, 1786: Berks. RO, D/EX 1324/1, f.27; Kelly, p.245 & n.1; Bill
Report, 1970.

READING, Berks.
St. Laurence. Ox.
[1v.] Berks. RO
DeskL: John Boyes, *Works*, 1629 (1638).

REDMIRE, Yorks. (N.Yorks.)
St. Mary. Ripon
[nil]
A ParLL of *c.* 81 vols. was est. in 1785 by the Associates of Dr Bray. The
bookplate was dated 1786.
Catalogues: Sent Jan. 1786, Bray Associates Records, f.38, pp.178–80.
References: Kelly, p.264. I am indebted to Brian North Lee for the reference to
the bookplate.

REEPHAM, Norf.
St. Mary. Nor.
[nil]
Books marked 'Reepham Church Library' were sold indiscriminately with the
rector's own books at a sale at the rectory *c.* 1843; they included an 8 vol. set
of St. John Chrysostom.
References: *N & Q*, 1 ser., v.7 (1853), p.392.

REEPS WITH BASTWICK, Norf.
St. Peter. Nor.
[1v.] Norwich CL
DeskL: Bible, 1617.

Reigate: shelving above the entrance door with original painted legend

REIGATE, Surrey
St. Mary Magdalene. S'wark
[*c.* 3,000v.]

The library was est. in 1701 by Andrew Cranston (d.1708), vicar 1697–1708, as a library for the clergy of the Archdeaconry of Ewell and the parishioners of Reigate. In a trust deed of 4 Nov. 1708 it was described as 'a publick library for the use and perusall of the freeholders, vicar and inhabitants of the said parish and of the gentlemen and clergymen inhabiting in parts thereunto adjacent'. Cranston provided a comprehensive set of rules for efficient administration, and 44 trustees were appointed to maintain it, with the result that this was the only parochial library exempted from the operation of the Parochial Libraries Act, 1709 'being constituted in another manner than the libraries provided for by this Act' (see: p.442, clause XI). The benefactors' book, started in 1701, shows that *c.* 1,400 books were acquired from 365 donors, whose names were written by Cranston in the books. They include Cranston himself, who gave *c.* 160 books, William Wotton, White Kennet,

Reigate: a general view of part of the library
established in 1701 by Andrew Cranston, vicar 1697–1708,
still housed in a room over the vestry built in 1513

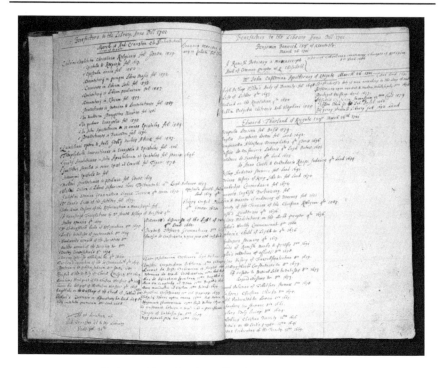

Reigate: Benefactions Register, 1710–1920s

John Evelyn (who gave Walton's Polyglot Bible), and John Flamsteed. Cranston recorded in Notitia Parochialis, 1705 that 'there are at present about 1,600volumes great and small. And the library is daily encreasing'. It was revived and added to by J. N. Harrison (1816–1901), vicar 1847–1901, but at the end of the 19th cent. was in a generally poor state. In 1950 it was est. as a registered charity with a reduced Board of Trustees (Charity no.237990), including a representative from Surrey County Libraries, and received grants from the Pilgrim Trust and the County Council. It is still housed in a room built over the vestry in 1513. There are c. 30 MSS (including 6 medieval MSS), 3 incunables, c. 500 STC, c. 700 Wing and c. 1,000 18th cent. books. The subject field is predominantly theology and 17th–18th cent. controversial works, but there are also books on travel, medicine, history, law, astronomy, mathematics, science, Greek and Latin classics, ecclesiastical history and the Quakers. There are examples of books from most of the important early presses, and presentation copies, including Granville Sharp's anti-slavery works. Identified bindings include several examples with Oldham and Gibson rolls, and works by the Fishtail and Unicorn binders. There is a photograph of the library in Hooper's *Guide* below. With the aid of the Pilgrim Trust and other bodies the library room was restored and some books repaired in 1951, and other books were treated up to c. 1994.

Catalogues: 2 copies of the original ms. cat., one attached to the deed of 1708,

the other with the collection; a cat. drawn up in 1785-8 by Jeoffry Snelson and written out in the register (c. 1,600 entries); printed: *Bibliotheca Reigatiana: Catalogue of the Public Library at Reigate*, 1893 (inaccurate); card index, c. 1969; *The Cranston Library Catalogue*, Trustees of the Cranston Library and Surrey County Council, 1982 (microfilm, including donors' list). An almost complete record of loans, 1707–1920s, survives (there was perhaps a separate book recording those for 1707–11, now lost). From 1711–88 there were 427 loans to 136 borrowers of 233 titles; two fifths of the borrowers were women.
References: Wilfrid Hooper, *Reigate, its Story through the Ages*, Dorking, 1945, pp.62–7; George Smith, 'Dr. Thomas Bray', *LAR*, v.12 (1910), pp.254–5; Notitia Parochialis, 1705: no.535; Wilfrid Hooper, *A Guide to Reigate Church*, 3rd ed, 1951; Martin Roth, 'Rev. Andrew Cranston' in: Audrey Taylor (ed.), *People of Reigate at St.Mary's from 1500-1930*, 1988; Lambeth Palace MS.3223, ff.49–55: notes on provenance and bindings by N. R. Ker; Pearson, 543.2; Kelly, pp.91 n.4, 94, 96, 107, 195, 254 & n.2; Ker, MMBL, IV, 1992, pp. 198-204; Mary C. Spinks, 'The Cranston Library: an eighteenth century parish library at Reigate, Surrey', (U. of Sheffield, Postgraduate Diploma in Librarianship, 1966); Pilgrim Trust, 21st Annual Report, 1951, pp.43–4; Venn: Cranston, Harrison.

REPTON, Derbys.
St.Wystan. Derby
[nil]
A collection of 14 unchained books of a strongly puritan character was 'sent by Mr Willm. Bladone' in 1622 to the vicar and churchwardens for loan to the parishioners, and 'to be emploied for the use of the parrishe, and to be disposed of at the discretion of Mr Thomas Whiteheade' (d.1642), Headmaster of Repton School, 1621–42. Some 15 vols. are listed in the churchwardens' accounts, including a Bible, 'two bookes of Martters' and English theology, e.g. Elton on the Colossians, Perkins on the Creed, Dod and Cleaver on the Commandments, Brinsley's *True Watch* and Dent's *Plain Man's Pathway* and *Sermon of Repentance*. The books could be lent out for up to 3 months provided that they were signed for, the minister and churchwardens keeping a record of borrowings. This was perhaps the earliest recorded free lending library in Great Britain.
Catalogues: books listed (with some errors) in Bigsby and Cox, below.
References: Kelly, pp.82–3, 95, 246, quoting Churchwardens' accounts, Repton, 1622–3, f.365, printed in Robert Bigsby, *Historical and Topographical Description of Repton*, 1854, pp.147–8, and the list of books in J. Charles Cox, *Churchwardens' Accounts*, 1913, pp.121–2.

RIBCHESTER, Lancs.
St.Wilfred. Blackb.
[8v.] Lancaster UL
In 1684 Bradley Hayhurst (d.1685), formerly minister of Macclesfield, 1671–82,

left his library 'to the parish church of Ribchester . . . where I was born'. The churchwardens' accounts, noted by Smith and Shortt, below, suggest that the library was of some size. It was housed above the N. porch when Ralph Thoresby, the antiquary and topographer, visited it in 1702. By 1890 there were apparently only 6 vols. remaining, 'all in a delapidated and disgraceful condition'. But books have since been discovered, and by a minor faculty in 1967, 5 vols. were deposited in Lancaster UL and a further 3 in 1976. From the original collection there are 3 16th cent. continental books, 1 Wing item and 1 17th cent. continental imprint, together with 3 additional items of later date, all liturgical or theological. One vol. (not among those surviving) was marked 'Hayhurst's Library'.

Catalogues: TS list from cat. cards made after deposit (copy in CCC).

References: Tom C. Smith, 'Ribchester parish church library', *The Antiquary*, v.23, no.234 (1891), pp.4, 21–2, 139; Tom C. Smith and Jonathan Shortt, *The History of Ribchester in the County of Lancaster*, 1896, pp.214–19; Ralph Thoresby, *Diary*, v.1, 1902, p.391; Christie, pp.104–5; Kelly, p.249; Lambeth Palace MS.3224: notes by N. R. Ker; Venn: Hayhurst.

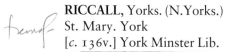

RICCALL, Yorks. (N.Yorks.)
St. Mary. York
[*c.* 136v.] York Minster Lib.
Thomas Cooper, vicar 1721–46, left 'a considerable library' for the use of his successors. None of these books have survived.
In 1886 James Davis of London, perhaps born in the village, presented a library of 334 vols. to the church. A cupboard with a ms. catalogue on the inside of a door was in the vestry, and by 1994, in the entrance to the church. The books were transferred to the vicarage by 1926 and by *c.* 1959 were in the village schoolroom, which was set on fire by vandals, charring the spines of most of them. Between 1965 and 1969 *c.* 15 of the more valuable books (16th to 18th cent.) were sold at Sotheby's. Those remaining, for the most part history, literature and travel, and some religion, were deposited in York Minster Lib. in 1972.

References: VCH, Yorks. East Riding, v.3, p.87; Barr, p.38; York Minster Lib. files.

RICHMOND, Yorks. (N.Yorks.)
Holy Trinity Chapel (red.). Ripon
[nil]
A ParL of 13 vols. was est. in 1761 by the Associates of Dr Bray. In 1849 this library was one of those reported 'either wholly lost or reduced a few tattered volumes'.

Catalogues: sent in 1762, Bray Associates Records, f.38, p.82; the same 13 vol. set was sent to **Arkengarthdale**.

References: Select Committeee Report, 1849; Kelly, p.264.

RICHMOND, Yorks. (N.Yorks.)
St. Mary. Ripon
[6v.] * Ripon CL
DeskL: Foxe, *Book of Martyrs*, 1699; William Allen and Thomas Bray, *Select Discourses*. n.d.; an ed. of Jewel's *Works*; Thomas Comber, *A Companion to the Temple*, v.1–2, 1676; and *Primitive and General Use of the Liturgies in the Christian Church*, 1690. Deposited in Ripon CL in 1976.

RIPON, Yorks. (N.Yorks.)
St. Peter and St. Wilfrid (the Cathedral from 1836). Ripon
[*c.* 758v.]
Most of the 758 vols., bequeathed as a parish library by Anthony Higgin (d.1624) to the Collegiate Church of Ripon, still form part of the collection of the Cathedral (from 1836) where Higgin was Dean, 1608–24.
Catalogues: Jean E. Mortimer, ed. 'The library catalogue of Anthony Higgin, Dean of Ripon (1608–24)', *Proc. Leeds Phil and Lit. Soc.*, v.10 (1962), pp.1–75.
References: Barr, p.34; DRB2, 1997, p.579, for description and references; Venn: Higgin.

RIPPLE, Glos.
St. Mary, Glouc.
[1v.] *
DeskL: 'chained Bible' in a display case.
References: CCC Questionnaire, 1950.

RIVER, Kent
St. Peter and St. Paul. Cant.
[1v.] Canterbury CL & Archives.
DeskL: Edwin Sandys, *Sermons*, 1585.

RIVINGTON, Lancs. (G. Man.)
Dedication not known. Man.
[nil]
A list of 14 vols., chiefly 17th cent. puritan theology, is contained in an 18th cent. minute-book belonging to the church; 4 vols. were present in 1856; none by 1959.
References: Christie, p.106; Kelly, p.249.

ROCHFORD, Essex
St. Andrew. Chelmsf.
[nil] *
John Lister (*c.* 1660–1735), rector 1691–1735, amassed a considerable private library, but none of his books survive at Rochford; nor are there any from the ParLL of 22 vols. est. in 1840 by the Associates of Dr Bray (not recorded after 1880).
Catalogues: Bray Associates Records, f.41, pp.36–40.   *continued*

References: Bray Associates Annual Reports, 1880; Kelly, p.262; Keith Maslen, 'Parson Lister's library', *Trans. Camb. Bib. Soc.*, v.9, no.2 (1987), pp.155–73.

ROOS, Yorks. (Humbs.)
All Saints. York
[nil]
A ParLL was started in May 1833; by 1835 there were 135 vols. and subsequently at least 296 vols. The catalogue is all that survives.
Catalogues: printed, Hull, 1835 (copy in Hull UL).
References: *Library History*, v.2, no.3 (1971), p.120; Barr, p.38.

ROSS-ON-WYE, Herefords.
St. Mary the Virgin. Heref.
[nil]
A ParLL was est. in 1782 by the Associates of Dr Bray, which was augm. in 1873. It is not recorded after 1880.
References: Bray Associates Annual Reports, 1880; Shore, p.151 (wrongly gives date of est. as 1781); Kelly, p.262.

ROTHERHAM, Yorks. (S.Yorks.)
All Saints. Sheff.
[72 titles in 46v.] Rotherham PL
A wooden 'shield' in Rotherham PL has the inscription: 'A lending library founded by Mrs. Frances Mansel, widdw and relict of ye Revd. Edwd. Mansel (late vicar of Ecclesfield) and daughter of George Westby, gentleman of Gilthwaite in ye parish of Rotherham who out of her pious and benevolent intention gave one hundred pound. To be laid out in ye purchase of ye sd library for ye use and advantage of ye clergy and parishioners of Rotherham for ever. Anno domini 1728'. (recorded in brief by Eastwood in 1862, below). Edward Mansel (*c.* 1661–1704) was vicar of Ecclesfield 1693–1704. A ms. vol. in Rotherham PL contains printed catalogues dated 1750, 1758 and 1759, and a fuller listing for 1782 of *c.* 184 titles in *c.* 274 vols. The books remained in the church until 1893 when they were given, with a few associated items such as the 'shield', to Rotherham PL. A special bookcase was to be provided for the books, then numbering 204 vols. In 1925 the building was severely damaged by fire, but one case containing 46 vols. survived. The ms. vol. also contains a borrowers' register recording loans from March 1730 until March 1868, library rules, and names of individual donors. Of the surviving books 13 were published in the 17th cent. and the remainder between 1701 and 1759. Most of the books are religious and in English, with 4 in Latin and 1 in Greek and Latin. There are many sermons, some of local interest, historical works (including Clarendon's *History of the Civil War*), and 5 books by Jeremy Collier.
Catalogues: MS. vol. Rotherham PL (copy in CCC); TS cat. with collection

(copy in CCC); Christopher Casson and Donald Steele, *Catalogue of the Mansel Collection held at Rotherham Library*, 1980 (TS copy in CCC includes an index of publishers, printers and booksellers).

References: Foster: Mansel; Jonathan Eastwood, *History of the Parish of Ecclesfield*, 1862, p.202; John Guest, *Yorkshire. Historic Notices of Rotherham*, Worksop, 1879, pp.202, 209 (names of donors); Kelly, p.256; Best, pp.52–61, 173–98; Freda Crowder, 'The Mansel Library', *Ivanhoe Rev.*, v.8 (1995), pp.44–6.

ROUGHAM, Norf.
St. Mary. Nor.
[nil]
The library of Roger North (1653–1734) was 'so settled as to be a parochial library, to be vested jointly in the occupant of Rougham Hall and the vicar of the parish for the time being'. A new library was built as an adjunct to the N. aisle of the church in 1709. The books of Roger North's niece, Dudleya (1675–1712), were added to the collection in 1714. Anne North bequeathed £20 to the library in 1722. According to Ballard, below, the books were not only for the use of the minister but also 'under certain regulations and restrictions, of the neighbouring clergy also, for ever'. The library building was pulled down and all the books were dispersed before the end of the 18th cent. The parchment cat. of 1714 lists *c.* 1,150 vols. All Dudleya's books, which included works related to the original languages of the OT and oriental learning in general, had an inserted Latin inscription including the name of the late owner and donor, printed by George Ballard.

Catalogues: 1714: Norfolk RO: Norwich Episcopal Records, DN/MSC 2/29; TS summary, 1955 (copy in CCC).

References: Augustus Jessop, ed. *The Lives of the Norths . . .* , v.3, 1890, pp.303, 309; receipt for Ann North: Bodl.MS.North.b.17, f.94; George Ballard, *Memoirs of Several Ladies of Great Britain*, Oxford, 1752, pp.414–15; *N & Q*, 1 ser, v.7, no.188, 190 (1853); DNB: North; Kelly, pp.93–4, 251.

ROYSTON, Herts.
St. John the Baptist. St.Alb.
[~~c. 23v.~~] * ~~Bodl.~~ (and elsewhere, see below)
In 1906 Alfred Kingston (below) described 'a library of some two hundred books presented for the most part by Leonard Chappelow [*c.* 1692–1768], vicar from 1731 to 1739. The books appear to have been little used, many being uncut, though nearly all are decaying and badly worm-eaten. The library includes a Hebrew grammar, published in 1752, by Peter Petit, vicar of the parish'. Chappelow was professor of Arabic at Cambridge from 1720 until his death. 30 vols. from this library were listed in catalogue 13 (1953) of the Cambridge bookseller R. C. Pearson, and 9 others were bought from Pearson by the Bodl. (one bearing Chappelow's name is Vet.a.2.f.135). In addition, a

collection of 'about thirty old books' found during the restoration of the tower roof, was sold 'for £10 to a then parishioner'. 7 vols. dating from 1549 to 1724, have been deposited in Herts. RO, and at least 7 other vols. are now in the library of the U. of Illinois, Urbana . The final residue of this library was bought *c.* 1955 as a 'junked collection' by D. J. de Solla Price, who was able 'to clean and restore about 100 books which were later dispersed, among them a copy of a nice but not uncommon edition of Newton's *Opticks*'. Some waste printed sheets proved to contain some previously unrecorded printed footnotes by Newton on optics, perhaps withdrawn before publication. No faculty was obtained for any of these sales.

References: Alfred A. Kingston, *A History of Royston, Hertfordshire*, 1906, p.96; Foster: Chappelow; Derek J. de Solla Price, 'Newton in a church tower: the discovery of an unknown book by Isaac Newton', *Yale Univ. Lib. Gaz.*, v.34 (1960), pp.124–6; Kelly, p.248.

RYE, Sussex
St. Mary the Virgin. Chich.
[IV.] in situ, and Chichester CL
DeskL: Geneva Bible, 1557–60. Other vols. were restored by Chichester CL on behalf of the church; a Bible, Oxford, Baskett, 1716–17, remains on deposit in Chichester CL.

SACOMBE, Herts.
St. Catherine. St.Alb.
[IV.] Herts. RO.
DeskL: Timothy Puller, *The Moderation of the Church of England*, 1679 (Puller was rector, 1671–93).

ST. ALBANS, Herts.
St. Alban (the Cathedral from 1877). St.Alb.
[nil]
A ParLL of 117 vols. was est. in May 1848 by the Associates of Dr Bray, which was augm. in 1870 and 1878.
Catalogues: Bray Associates Records, f.41, pp.196–8.
References: Bray Associates Annual Reports, 1880; Shore, p.152; Kelly, p.262.

ST. BEES, Cumb. (Cumbria)
St. Mary and St. Bega. Carl.
[nil]
A ParL of 66 vols. was est. in 1712 by the Bray Trustees for Erecting Parochial Libraries, which was augm. in 1818, 1842, 1869 and 1878; it was listed as 'lost' in 1902.
Catalogues: MS. cat. no. 30: Bray Associates Records, f.39, pp.201–4; 'Clerical Institution', 1817 (adding 212 vols.): Bray Associates Records, f.40, pp.1–7; 'L. added 1842' (43 vols.): Bray Associates Records, f.41, p.78.
References: Bray Associates Annual Reports, 1902; Shore, p.151; Kelly, p.261.

ST. COLUMB MAJOR, Corn.
St. Columba. Truro
[nil]
A ParLL of 157 vols. was est. in 1845 by the Associates of Dr Bray, which was augm. in 1871. It is not recorded after 1896, but there were 9 vols. present in 1950. Some books were reported as having been transferred to Truro Theological College (est. in 1878).
Catalogues: Bray Associates Records, f.41, pp.138–41.
References: Bray Associates Annual Reports, 1896; Shore, p.153; Pearce Survey, 1949–50; Kelly, p.261.

ST. DOMINIC, Corn.
St. Dominicia. Truro
[nil ?] NRC
There were 4 pre-1800 Bibles recorded in 1950.
References: Pearce Survey, 1949–50.

ST. IVES, Hunts. (Cambs.)
All Saints. Ely
[nil]
A ParLL was granted £1 from funds at Bray's disposal, 1695–9.
References: Kelly, p.258.

ST. MARTINS, Shrops.
St. Martin. Lich.
[nil]
A ParL of *c.* 95 vols. was est. in 1721 by the Bray Trustees for Erecting Parochial Libraries, which was augm. in 1872. It is not recorded after 1900.
Catalogues: no.61, 'St. Martin's in the Hundred of Oswestry Salop. Dioc. of St. Asaph', printed cat. and rules: NLW, Church in Wales Records SA/MISC/709 (copy in CCC).
References: Bray Associates Annual Reports, 1900; Kelly, p.263.

ST. MARY'S, Scilly Isles
St. Mary. Truro
[nil]
A ParL was est. in 1729 by the Bray Trustees for Erecting Parochial Libraries: in fact, according to the Minutes, two libraries were sent. Later books were 'sent to the Revd Mr Lewis Rtr of St. Mary's in Scilly Island for the use of a school for poor children begun in the year 1777' (10 titles, each in 20-200 copies), and books were also sent in 1780, 1782 and 1878. In 1821 a lending library of 101 vols. was despatched.
Catalogues: 1777: Minutes, pp.167–70; Bray Associates Records. f.38, p.165; 1821: Bray Associates Records, f.40, pp.42–4.
References: Bray Associates Annual Reports, 1880; Kelly, p.261.

St Neots: surviving volumes from the library established by the
Bray Trustees in 1711, and other volumes, housed in a cupboard in the vestry

ST. NEOTS, Hunts. (Cambs.)

St. Mary. Ely

[c. 76v.]

A ParLL was granted £1 by Bray from funds at his disposal, 1695–9; and a
ParL of 72 vols. was est. in 1711 by the Bray Trustees for Erecting Parochial
Libraries, which was augm. in 1869. In 1959 50 vols. survived from this
library, nos. 2–7, 10–20, 26, 28–9, 31–2, 34–48, 50–3, 55–6, 58–60, 63, 65–
7 of the Oldbury selection (see pp.49–51). There were in addition c. 40 other
vols., mainly works of the protestant reformers, given in 1785 by William
Cole (d.1808), rector of Eynesbury, Hunts., 1768–1808. The collection was
originally housed in the 'Dove's Chamber' over the S. porch, but because of
damp was moved in c. 1971 to a cupboard in the vestry.

Catalogues: no.46, Bray Associates Records, f.39, pp.111–4; TS cat. (including some provenances), in Bodl.MS.Eng.Misc.c.360 (copy in CCC).
References: *N & Q*, ser.2, no.112, 20 Feb. 1858; Shore, p.151; Kelly, pp.248 & n.2, 258, 262; Venn: Cole.

ST. PETER PORT, Guernsey (Channel I.)
St. Peter Port. Win.
[nil?] NRC
William Blades in 1866 noted that 'some old and valuable books are in the Parish Church of St Peter Port'.
References: Blades, *Book-Worm*, p.157.

ST. SAVIOUR'S, Guernsey (Channel I.)
St. Saviour. Win.
[nil]
The library bequeathed in the mid 17th cent. by Pierre Carey to the rector and his successors disappeared from the church during the German occupation, 1940–45. A MS list is held in the Priaulx Library, St. Peter Port.
References: DRB2, p.695.

SALFORD, Lancs. (G. Man.)
Sacred Trinity. Man.
[70v.] Salford PL
By his will of 1684 Humphrey Oldfield (d.1690) left his theological books to the church, directing that they should be placed in the chancel, together with £20 to replenish them and £3 for the woodwork and chains that they might not be stolen. They were in fact placed in the tower and then, because of damp, in the vestry. By 1836 many books had disappeared or had been cast out. The collection consisted of 72 vols. when it was presented by the rector and vestry to Salford Central Library in 1876. There are now 70 vols., including books added after Oldfield's death, mainly 17th and 18th cent. but with 2 16th cent. items: Thomas Ryers, *The English Creede*, 1585, and Georgius Agricola, *De Re Metallica Libri XII*, 1556.
Catalogues: TS cat. made after transfer to Salford Central Library, in Bodl.MS.Eng.Misc.c.360 (copy in CCC); card cat. with collection.
References: Christie, pp.107–9; Blades, BIC, 1890, p.38; Cox & Harvey, p.335; DRB2, 1997, p.464.

SALTHOUSE, Norf.
St. Nicholas. Nor.
[2v.] Norwich CL
DeskL: Bible, 1611/13; Jewel, *Works*, 1611.

SANDBACH, Ches.
St. Mary. Ches.
[nil]
A ParLL of 102 vols. was est. in 1810 by the Associates of Dr Bray; it is not recorded after 1900.
Catalogues: Bray Associates Records. f.38, pp.233–5.
References: Bray Associates Annual Reports, 1900; Kelly, p.261.

SCULTHORPE, Norf.
St. Mary and All Saints. Nor.
[1v.] Norwich CL
DeskL: Bible, 1617.

SEATHWAITE, Lancs. (Cumbria)
Holy Trinity. Carl.
[5v.]
A TS cat. dated 1970, 'Catalogue of books, Minister's Library, Seathwaite Church', lists about 41 titles in 70 vols., mainly 18th cent. theology and sermons, but including 6 17th cent. books, e.g. *Synopsis Criticorum Aliorumque*, 4 vols., 1623. This collection was evidently intended to be passed from incumbent to incumbent, and was lent by T. R. Hare, then Honorary Canon, Carlisle Cathedral. None of these books survive but 5 other vols. of sermons and theology dating from 1716 to 1750 are retained.
Catalogues: in Lambeth Palace MS.3094, ff.206–7 (copy in CCC).
References: I am indebted to Dr A. I Doyle for information in this entry.

SEDBERGH, Yorks. (Cumbria)
St. Andrew. Bradf.
[nil] *
A ParL was est. in 1899 by the Associates of Dr Bray.
References: Bray Associates Annual Reports, 1900.

SEDGFORD, Norfolk
St. Mary. Nor.
A ParL est. by the Associates of Dr Bray was removed to **Docking** in 1872.
References: Shore, p.152.

SEFTON, Lancs. (Mers.)
St. Helen. Liv.
[4v.?] NRC
DeskL: in 1950 there were copies of a Bible, 1595, and Foxe, *Book of Martyrs*, 3 vols., 1641 (given by Raymond Richards in 1932).
References: CCC Questionnaire, 1950.

SELBY, Yorks. (N.Yorks.)
Selby Abbey: St. Mary and St. Germain. York
[2v.?] NRC
In 1950 there were copies of Gerard's *Herball*, 1633, and Ambroise Paré, *Works*, 1634, both edited/translated by Thomas Johnson, b. Selby, 1600 (given recently).
References: CCC Questionnaire, 1950.

SELSIDE, Westm. (Cumbria)
St. Thomas. Carl.
[nil] *
A ParL of 30 vols. was est. in 1757 by the Associates of Dr Bray. In 1849 this library was reported as being one of those 'either wholly lost or reduced to a few tattered volumes'.
Catalogues: Selside in parish of Kirkby Kendal, Bray Associates Records, f.38, p.44.
References: Select Committee Report, 1849; Kelly, p.263.

SELWORTHY, Somerset
All Saints. B & W
[1v.] *
DeskL: a copy of Jewel's *Works*, n.d.

SETMURTHY, Cumb. (Cumbria)
St. Barnabas. Carl.
[nil] *
A ParL of 32 vols. was est. in 1757 by the Associates of Dr Bray. In 1849 this library was reported as being one of those 'either wholly lost or reduced to a few tattered volumes'.
Catalogues: 'Secmurthy [sic] in the parish of Brigham', Bray Associates Records, f.86, p.46.
References: Select Committee Report, 1849; Kelly, p.261.

SHAFTESBURY, Dorset
St. Peter. Sarum
[nil] *
A ParLL of 123 vols. was est. in 1846 by the Associates of Dr Bray. No books survive but there is 'a large cupboard which evidently did house a Bray library, there being a notice on the doors to this effect'.
Catalogues: Bray Associates Records, f.41, pp.158–60.
References: Kelly, p.261.

SHAP, Westm. (Cumbria)
St. Michael. Carl.
[nil] *
A grant of £1 towards the est. of a ParLL was awarded by Bray from funds at his disposal, 1695–9.
References: Kelly, p.259.

SHEFFIELD, Yorks. (S.Yorks.)
St. Peter and St. Paul (the Cathedral from 1914). Sheff.
[c. 14 titles in 19v.] Sheffield CL Archives
The incumbent recorded in 1705 that 'a place for a library is fitted up in ye vestry of ye church and a small collection of books made'. Six catalogues of books from the library have survived dating from 1770 to 1786 (see below). The 1786 catalogue lists c. 240 titles. A small collection of 14 works, dating from 1611 to 1765, mainly Bibles, sermons and church history, now in Sheffield Cathedral archives, may be a survival from this library.
Catalogues: 1770 and 1771: Sheffield City Archives, CB/594/1 & 2; 1764, 1777 (parchment), 1781, 1786, attached to Sheffield glebe terriers, Borthwick Institute, York, RIII.F.10.
References: Notitia Parochialis, 1705: no.1014; Barr, p.37; Kelly, p.256.

SHELDON, Warwicks.
St. Giles. Birm.
[371 titles] Birmingham PL
By 1705 a library was est. by 'the present incumbent', i.e. Thomas Bray (1658–1730), rector 1690–1729, and was placed 'in a large room over the Charity School and vestry', built by the patron, William, Lord Digby (1661–1752). This building was replaced by another school building in 1852. Bray gave a grant of £5 to Sheldon from funds at his disposal, 1695–9, and, under the terms of his will, left 'my library at Sheldon . . . to and for the sole use of the incumbent thereof for the time being and his successors for ever'. In another clause he left the residue of his books not otherwise bequeathed 'to be divided, at the discretion of Mr Samuel Smith, to the Parochial Library of Sheldon, and to Professor Hamilton of Edinburgh, for the purposes of distributing them to the Lending Libraries in the Highlands of Scotland'. Books were also given by Bray's predecessor, Digby Bull, and by Thomas Morall, his curate, 1697–1721. The Library after 1852 was housed partly in the vestry and partly in the tower of the church. In 1960 the collection was deposited in Birmingham Reference Library. There is one incunable in the collection, Filelfo's *Epistolæ*, Paris, 1493, in a fine, near-contemporary binding. Many books have the library's panel-stamp and bookplate. The theology books are wide-ranging and include puritan, Catholic and anti-Catholic works, foreign liturgies, and books on the Socinians, Presbyterians and Quakers. Other subjects include dictionaries, mathematics, music, philosophy, history and law. Several of Bray's own works are included.

Catalogues: 'A list of some of the books . . . at St. Giles, Sheldon', n.d. (abbreviated titles and no dates): Bodl.MS.Eng.Misc.c.360 (copy in CCC); Birmingham PL: list by Mary Jones-Bateman (wife of rector in 1867); checklist, 1960; card cat. 1974.

References: Notitia Parochialis, 1705: no.213; Smith, p.59; F. S. Stych, 'The Thomas Bray Library from Sheldon in the Birmingham Reference Library', *Open Access*, v.12, no.2 (1964), pp.1–4; Kelly, pp.104, 107, 255 & n.1, 258–9; DRB2, 1997, p.567; Lambeth Palace MS.3223, ff.58–9, and MS.3224: notes and rubbings by N. R. Ker; DNB: Digby.

SHELFANGER, Norf.
All Saints. Nor.
[1v.] Norwich CL
DeskL: *Certain Sermons or Homilies*, 1623.

SHELLINGFORD, Berks.
St. Faith. Ox.
[1v.] Berks. RO
DeskL: [Articles and Injunctions. 16th cent. fragments].

SHELTON, Norf.
St. Mary. Nor.
[1v] Norwich CL
DeskL: *Certain Sermons or Homilies*, 1635 (1633).

SHELVE, Shrops.
All Saints. Heref.
[nil?] NRC
A grant of 15s. towards the est. of a ParL was awarded by Bray from funds at his disposal, 1695–9.
References: Kelly, p.259.

SHEPSHED, Leics.
St. Botolph. Leic.
[14v.] Leics. RO
A ParL valued at £23. 9s. 3d was est. in 1720 by the Bray Trustees for Erecting Parochial Libraries, which was augm. by the Associates in 1871. It was reported as lost in 1896, but there are some surviving vols. (which suggest that the original collection was the 72 vol. Oldbury selection): they were deposited in Leicester Diocesan Lib. some time before 1959, and then were transferred to Loughborough PL by the Revd John E. Yates when he was Honorary Diocesan Librarian (dates not known), and finally deposited in Leics. RO in 1994. The surviving books are nos. 2, 5, 7, 8, 12 (vol.2) and 52 of the Oldbury selection, and nos. 15–22 (5 out of 8 vols.) of the Whitchurch selection (see pp.49–51 and 53–5. The other 3 vols. are Paoli Sarpi, *The History of the Council of Trent*,

1620, and 2 early 18th cent. works by James Blair.
Catalogues: TS list from Loughborough PL (copy in CCC).
References: Bray Associates Annual Reports, 1896; Shore, p.152; Kelly, p.262.

SHERBORNE, Dorset
Abbey Church of St. Mary. Sarum
[1v.?] *
The churchwardens' accounts for 1670 note the payment of one shilling for
making an old 'table board' fit for the library. A grant of £1. 10s. towards the
est. of a ParL was awarded by Bray from funds at his disposal, 1695–9. A
Bible, with Psalter and Concordances, R. Barker, 1608, and *Sermons or
Homilies*, 1676 (both now lost) were perhaps purchases from this source. 11
other pre-1700 books are 19th or 20th cent. donations.
Catalogues: TS list of pre-1700 books in Sherborne Abbey Library (copy in
CCC).
References: Churchwardens' Accounts: Dorset CRO, PE/SH: CW138; Kelly,
p.258.

SHERBORNE ST JOHN, Hants.
St. Andrew. Win.
[4v.]
DeskL: Foxe, *Book of Martyrs*, 3 vols., 1641, all chained; *Homilies*, 1673.
References: NADFAS Report.

SHERIFF HUTTON, Yorks. (N.Yorks.)
St. Helen and the Holy Cross. York
[1v.] Borthwick Institute, York
DeskL: *Second Tome of Homilies*, 1623.

SHILBOTTLE, Northumb.
St. James. Newc.
[nil] *
One of the 92 parishes in the Northumberland Archdeaconry granted a ParLL
under a scheme devised by Bishop Shute Barrington, carried out by Archdeacon R. G. Bouyer by 1823 (see p.57), and recorded as still possessing books in
visitation returns, 1826–8.
References: Day, p.102 & n.38.

SHIMPLING, Norf.
St. George (CCT). Nor.
[1v.] Norwich CL
DeskL: Bible, 1659.

SHIPDHAM, Norf.

All Saints. Nor.

[*c.* 550v.] Norwich PL; Norwich CL (and elsewhere, see below)

DeskL: Erasmus, *Paraphrases*, 1548; Demosthenes & Aeschines, *Epistolæ*, Paris, Wechel, 1546 (blind-stamped on the cover 'Shipdham Church Porch Library 1720–1950').

By his will of 1764 Thomas Townshend (*c.* 1683–1764), rector 1707–54, bequeathed 'to my son in law Colby Bullock clerk vicar of Shipdham . . . my library of books in the porch chamber of Shipdham . . . and after his decease to his successors in that living for ever'. Colby Bullock (*c.* 1725–1804) was rector 1754–1804. The books, numbering 1,344 vols., were already housed in a small room over the church porch. Many of them contain the name of Peter Needham (1680–1731). All the Shipdham books were at one time, probably in the 19th cent., supplied with nos. written on paper labels and pasted on the upper part of the spine, and most contain the note of the price paid inside. William Blades visited the library in *c.* 1861 in search of Caxtons (which he did not find). The books were first sent to Hodgson's for sale in *c.* 1935 but were not sold because of the Queen Anne Act (see pp.439–42) and were returned. They were again catalogued for sale at Hodgson's 27 April 1950, but the sale was postponed at the last minute. Finally a faculty was obtained and 852 vols. were sold at Hodgson's 29 March 1951 in 220 lots. *The Boke named the Royall*, Wynkyn de Worde for Pynson, 1507, was lot 68 (sold to Quaritch). Some lots were sold to the Huntington Lib., San Marino, California, and others, especially early Americana, to the Folger Lib. The unsold lots, numbering 490 vols., were housed temporarily in Norwich Museum basement before being deposited in Norwich PL. In 1958 34 Shipdham books purchased at the Hodgson's sale were given to Norwich PL by Dr H. C. Frost of Goldhanger, Essex, who later gave a further *c.* 12 vols. The books are mainly 17th cent. and include *c.* 22 STC and 112 Wing items. Two medieval MSS were sold separately to Cambridge UL (now Add.MSS, 7220, 7221). Most of the books are in original bindings: 6 Oxford bindings, *c.* 1515–1620 have been identified.

Catalogues: a cat. made in 1821 was held at the rectory; Hodgson's sale catalogues, no.8, 1949–50; no.6, 1950–51 (31 lots are described in R. C. Pearson's Catalogue 11, nos. 420–47, 467, 757: they range in date from 1556 to 1697); card cat. with the collection at Norwich PL; TS list of STC & Wing nos. in Norwich PL (copy in CCC).

References: Will: Norfolk RO: NRS 24382, 121x6 n.d. 1764; *N & Q*, 2 ser. v.12 (1861), p.469; George Arthur Stephen, *Norfolk Bibliography*, Holt, 1921, pp.42–4; J. E. Hodgson, 'Shipdham Rectorial Library', *Eastern Daily Press*, Nov. (1927); *The Times* (7 Nov. 1927), pp.15, 17; Kelly, p.251; Ker, Pastedowns, 624–5, 1407 (sold), 1462, 1491, 1843; DRB2, p.474; Lambeth Palace MS.3223, ff.60–145: extensive notes on provenance, listings and rubbings by N. R. Ker.

SHIPLAKE, Oxon.
St. Peter and St. Paul. Ox.
[nil] *
DeskL: a ms. note in the Shiplake register, dated 1680 reads: 'Theise books following doe belong to ye parish of Shiplake & should be in ye church, though they are much in ye vicars keeping', and goes on to list Erasmus, *Paraphrases*, 1548; Jewel, *Works*, 1611; the *Book of Homilies* .
References: Shiplake register: Oxfordshire Archives: MS.D.D.Par Shiplake, b.2.f.28 (TS transcript in Bodl.).

SHIPSTON-ON-STOUR, Warwicks.
St. Edmund. Cov.
[2v.] Warwicks. CRO
DeskL: F. Pulton, *A Collection of Sundrie Statutes*, 1632; J. Keble, *The Statutes at Large*, 1676 (given by Henry Parker, 1683). A bookplate exists with this name, perhaps for the personal use of William Parry, rector. It was the gift of the 5th Earl of Northampton.
References: I am indebted to Brian North Lee for the reference to this bookplate.

SHIPTON-UNDER-WYCHWOOD, Oxon.
St. Mary. Ox.
[1v.?] NRC
DeskL: a copy of Foxe, *Book of Martyrs*, n.d. was present in 1989.

SHIRLAND, Derbys.
St. Leonard. Derby
[1v.] *
DeskL: Jewel, *Apology*, 1609, chained to a desk in the chancel.

SHORWELL, I of W
St. Peter. Portsm.
[4v.] *
DeskL: Great Bible, 3rd ed. 1541; Richard Hooker, *Of the Lawes of Ecclesiasticall Politie*, 1622 (?); Bible and BCP, 1706; Bible, Oxford, 1717.

SHUSTOKE, Warwicks.
St. Cuthbert. Birm.
[nil]
A ParL of 81 vols. was est. in 1727 by the Bray Trustees for Erecting Parochial Libraries.
Catalogues: printed cat. with rules, Whitchurch selection: Lichfield RO, B/A/22/6 (copy in CCC).
References: Kelly, p.263.

SIBLE HEDINGHAM, Essex
St. Peter. Chelmsf.
[nil] *
Moses Cook (*c.* 1666–1733), rector 1690–1733, bequeathed a library, kept in the rectory, which was sold with the effects of the rector in 1918 (information from the Dean of Gloucester in 1957).
References: Venn: Cook.

SILVERDALE, Lancs.
St. John. Blackb.
[nil] *
A ParL of 31 vols. was est. in 1757 by the Associates of Dr Bray.
Catalogues: In parish of Warton, Bray Associates Records, f.38, p.47.
References: Kelly, p.262.

SKELTON [near Guisborough], Yorks. (N.Yorks.)
All Saints. York
[nil]
A ParL was est. in 1720 by the Bray Trustees for Erecting Parochial Libraries; the surviving books were transferred to **Middlesbrough** in 1869. One stray vol. is at **Denchworth.**
References: Kelly, p.264; Lambeth Palace MS.3224: notes by N. R. Ker.

SKIPTON, Yorks. (N.Yorks.)
Holy Trinity. Bradf.
[1,700v.] Skipton PL
In 1705 the incumbent recorded that 'a library of indifferent value is setling by Silvester Pettite Esqr of Barnard's Inn'. Silvester Petyt (1640–1719) and his brother William (1636–1707) were natives of Skipton, and by this date William was Keeper of the Records in the Tower of London and Silvester was Principal of Barnard's Inn. They sent a total of 2,204 books in batches over the years, and later Christopher Bateman (fl.1698–1730), a bookseller of Pater-noster Row, also born in Skipton, added *c.* 60 books, and William Busfield, of the Inner Temple, a further 100+ vols. The collection was housed in a small room at the W. end of the church. A sum of £100 was provided for 'the well-being of the library', and trustees were appointed. However the collection was neglected and following two occasions when the trustees tried to sell the books, in 1816 and 1875, the collection was removed, firstly to the newly-opened buildings for the Grammar School, and then in two moves in 1913 and 1938 to the Public Library. The surviving 1,700 books, now carefully restored, are housed in a special room.
Catalogues: a vol. of original catalogues with the collection; *A Catalogue of the Petyt Library at Skipton, Yorkshire*, Gargrave, Coulthurst Trust, 1964.
References: Notitia Parochialis, 1705: no.856; DNB: Petyts; Plomer, Dict.: Bateman; John A.Woods, 'The Petyt Library, Skipton', *Books: National Book*

League Journal, no.289 (Nov.1954); P. S. Baldwin, 'The Petyt Library, Skipton' (Library Association, FLA, 1957), and introduction to the cat. above; Kelly, p.256 & n.4; Barr, p.37; DRB2, p.296: for William Petyt's other donations.

SKIPWITH, Yorks. (N.Yorks.)
St. Helen. York
[1500+v.] York Minster Lib.
In his will Marmaduke Fothergill (d.1731), vicar from 1682 until his enforced retirement as a non-juror in 1689, bequeathed 'all my books whose catalogue is in a paper book distinguished from A to P inclusively, written with my own hand, . . . hereby in trust to the vicars of Howden and Hemingborough for a clerical (not a parochial) liberary [sic] for the Peculiar of that district, to be in the custody of the vicar of Skipwith who shall not lend any books out of that place, but all to be preserved in the common library for the publick good of those who resort thither'. This was on condition that the parishioners find funds to build a library room for them in the churchyard. When after 6 years this condition was not met, Fothergill's widow made over the books to York Minster Lib. by deed of gift in 1737. The collection contains theological and historical books, historical and musical MSS from the widow of the antiquary Matthew Hutton (1639–1711), and a collection of classics assembled by John Price (1600–76?), the classical scholar. It is particularly strong in ms. and printed copies of the English liturgy.
Catalogues: Fothergill's own classed cat., *c.* 1720–30, and ms. cat of *c.* 1774, with collection.
References: Will: copy in Borthwick Institute, Bp.C & P III/12, and printed in Francis Drake, *Eboracum*, 1736, pp.379–80; James Raine, *A Catalogue of the Printed Books in the Library of the Dean and Chapter of York*, York, 1896, pp.xvi–xviii; Barr, p.37; Barr, York Minster, pp.510 & pl.176; Venn: Fothergill; DNB: Hutton, Price.

SLAITHWAITE, Yorks. (N.Yorks.)
St. James. Wakef.
[*c.* 437 titles in 250v.] York UL
In his will Robert Meeke (d.1724), vicar 1685–1724, provided that part of his own library should be kept for the use of his successors. A memorial stone in the churchyard records his bequest which included '133 books for ye use of ye succeeding curates'. Blades recorded *c.* 150 vols. in 1866; in 1959 apparently only 25 vols. remained but the rest of the collection was discovered shortly after and deposited on permanent loan in York UL in 1967. The main collection consists of 17th and 18th cent. theology, but there is also a 17th cent. edition of *Gesta Romanorum*, and some MSS of local interest. Some books have a printed label: 'A bequest from the Rev. R. Meeke, to the Minister of Slaithwaite, for the time being. Walter printer, Ironbridge;' another label records the bequest of Canon C.L. Hulbert in 1888.

Catalogues: Ms list of 25 vols.: in Bodl.MS.Eng.Misc.c.360 (copy in CCC); TS list of *c*. 208 vols. in Lambeth Palace MS.3094, ff.208–11 (copy in CCC)
References: Venn: Meeke; Blades, *Book-Worm*, p.173; Kelly, p.256; Barr, p.37; DRB2, p.583; I am indebted to Dr David J. Shaw for providing me with a picture of the memorial stone.

SLAPTON, Devon
St. James the Great. Ex.
[nil]
A Parl of 72 vols. was est. in 1710 by the Bray Trustees for Erecting Parochial Libraries; it was reported as lost in 1897.
Catalogues: MS. cat. no.22. Bray Associates Records, f.39, pp.99–102, and (with the printed rules): Devon RO: Basket D/17/16 and 43 (copy in CCC); catalogue of the library in 1727 and papers concerning it: Episcopal Registry at Salisbury (see HMC, Various Collections, v.4, 1907, p.22).
References: Bray Associates Annual Reports, 1897; Kelly, p.261.

Sleaford: surviving volumes from a small collection given by Edward Smith, vicar, in 1703, in a modern glazed case designed to show the original chains and rods

In situ

SLEAFORD, Lincs.
St. Denys. Linc.
[19 titles in 20v.]
The Sleaford vestry minute book gives a list of 'the books . . . given by Mr Edw: Smith late Vicar of Sleeford June 1st 1703': some 14 vols., 12 of which are still present. Edward Smith was vicar from 1691 to 1703. Other donors noted there include William Wyche, vicar 1682–9, and Jonah Bowyer, vicar. The incumbent in 1705 reported: 'there is a library fixing in ye parish Mr Edward Smith having given some books towards it, who was ye late vicar'. The books, all in English and mainly late 17th and early 18th cent. theology, were once all chained to a large reading desk but have now been moved to a modern glazed bookcase designed to show the chains and rods: 17 vols. are still chained.
Catalogues: Minute book, 1653–1761: Lincolnshire Archives: Sleaford Par. 10/1; TS list of 15 works, 1969: in Lambeth Palace MS.3094, f.212 (copy in CCC); list of 19 items with collection (copy in CCC).
References: Notitia Parochialis, 1705: no.28; Edward Trollope, *Sleaford*, 1872, pp.165–6; Streeter, p.290 (lists 13 vols. with chains); Kelly, p.249; Pevsner and Harris, *Lincolnshire*, 1964, p.636 (notes 15 chained books); Venn: Smith, Wyche.

SMALLBURGH, Norf.
St. Peter. Nor.
[3v.] Norwich CL
DeskL: Joseph Hall, *The First Centurie of Meditations*, 1617; *Certain Sermons or Homilies*, n.d.; Jewel, *Works*, 1611.

transf

SMARDEN, Kent (formerly Smarden Cranbrook)
St. Dunstan. Cant.
[13+v.] Pusey House, Oxford; Canterbury CL (?)
'Belonging to the rector for the time being . . . a valuable library of 69 volumes in folio' was the gift of William Bedford (1701–83), rector of Smarden 1728–83 (and vicar of Bekesbourne, Kent, 1729–83, where he is buried). The list printed in Haslewood in 1866 (see below) actually contains 68 vols., dating from 1528 to 1744, including 6 16th cent., 20 17th cent. and 4 18th cent. titles, mainly works of the Fathers in continental editions. After the rectory was sold, the books were donated, in May 1940, to St. Augustine's College, Canterbury. The College was closed in 1971–2 and the books were dispersed: at least 13 vols. are known to have been given to the library of Pusey House, Oxford (and identified); some were perhaps deposited in Canterbury CL; and some were sold.
Catalogues: list of authors, nos. of vols. and dates printed in: Francis Haslewood, *The Antiquities of Smarden*, 1866, pp.107–8 (copy in CCC).
References: Blades, *Book-Worm*, p.173; Venn: Bedford. I am indebted to Dr Nigel Ramsay for alerting me to this collection, and to Miss Gladys Clenaghan of Smarden for much of the information in this entry.

SMETHWICK, Warwicks. (W.Mids.)
'Old Church'. Birm.
[1v.] Sandwell District Libraries
DeskL: Richard Allestree, *The Whole Duty of Man*; *The Art of Contentment*,
2nd impression, Oxford, 1675 ('Dorothy Parkes her booke, 1675').

SOLIHULL, Warwicks.
St. Alphege. Birm.
[3v.]
DeskL: NT in Greek and Latin, 2 vols., 1580; BCP, Oxford, 1683; and 18th
cent. books.
References: NADFAS Report.

SOTHERTON, Suffolk
St. Andrew. St.E.
[nil] *
DeskL: in 1965 there was a copy of a book of *Homilies*, which, from an
inscription, cost Robert Freeman, churchwarden, 7s. 6d. in 1635; it no longer
survives.
References: Fitch, 1965, p.47.

SOTTERLEY, Suffolk
St. Margaret. St.E.
[4v.] Suffolk RO, Lowestoft
DeskL: Erasmus, *Paraphrases*, 1548; a fragment of what appears to be the rare
BCP, 1552; Jewel, *Defence of the Apologie of the Churche of Englande*, 1567;
H. Bullinger, *Fifty Godly and Learned Sermons, etc.*, 1587, inscribed on the
flyleaf 'bought for the towne of Sotterley the xvi daye of Maye 1588 in the
thirty year of the reigne of our sovereigne lady Queene Elizabeth. Price viii
shilling. Robt. Edgar gent. and John Warne churchwardens'. Canon Fitch
comments that if these vols. constitute the beginnings of a parochial library
then Sotterley is the earliest in Suffolk, pre-dating Bury St. Edmonds by 7
years.
References: Fitch, 1965, pp.47–8.

SOULDERN, Oxon.
Annunciation of the Blessed Virgin Mary. Ox.
[1v.] Oxfordshire Archives
DeskL: Bible, Cambridge, 1660.

SOUTHAMPTON, Hants.
St. Michael. Win.
[6v.] *
In 1959 there was an empty cupboard in the church with the inscription: 'John,
sonne of John Clungeon of this town, alderman, erected this presse and gave

certain books, who dyed anno 1646'. John Clungeon, the son, was a haber-dasher in London. There are 7 vols. still in the church, not part of this library: Daniel Fealty, *Annotations upon all the Books of the Old and New Testaments*, 2nd ed. 2v. 1651, and Foxe, *Book of Martyrs*, 2v, n.d. (4 vols. once chained, but no longer; 3 chains survive); Bible, 1624, with Concordances, 1613 (given in 1925); Bible, Oxford, 1717 (bookplate: 'Parish of St. Michael, 1812'). A ParLL was est. in 1840 by the Associates of Dr Bray: no books survive. This may have been the Southampton Theological Library (see below). It is not recorded after 1880.

Catalogues: 'List of books presented to the Southampton Theological Library, March 1840'. [128 vols.], Bray Associates Records, f.40, pp.311–3.
References: Bray Associates Annual Reports, 1880; Blades, BIC, p.40; Kelly, pp.75 & n.3, 247, 262.

SOUTH BURLINGHAM, Norf.
St. Edmund. Nor.
[1v.] Norwich CL
DeskL: Jewel, *Works*, 1610. Place-name Burlingham alone in Crockford.

SOUTH COWTON, Yorks. (N.Yorks.)
St. Mary (CCT). York
[nil]
A ParL of 29 vols. was est. in 1761 by the Associates of Dr Bray; in 1849 this library was reported as being one of those 'either wholly lost or reduced to a few tattered volumes'.
Catalogues: sent in 1762, Bray Associates Records, f.38, p.83.
References: Select Committee Report, 1849; Kelly, p.264.

SOUTH ELMHAM, Suffolk
St. Cross. St.E.
[2v.] Bury St. Edmunds CL
DeskL: Wolfgang Musculus, *Commonplaces of the Christian Religion*, 1578; Erasmus, *Paraphrases*, 1548. These 2 vols. were deposited by the rector in *c.* 1955 with the Ipswich PL and then in *c.* 1980 transferred to Bury St. Edmunds CL.
References: note by Canon John Fitch, 1986, in CCC file.

SOUTH WALSHAM, Nor.
St. Mary. Nor.
[3v.] Norwich CL
DeskL: Bible, OT. Greek, 1683; Bible, Pentateuch. Spanish, 1705; Rudolph Walther, *An Hundred, Threescore and Fifteene Homelyes or Sermons*, 1572.

SOUTHWELL, Notts.
Minster Church of St. Mary (from 1884 the Cathedral). S'well
[*c.* 1,200 titles in pre-1800 collection]
In 1705 the incumbent commented on the library in the collegiate (and
parochial) church 'settling by ye prebendaries and neighbouring gentlemen,
but it advances slowly'. The main book purchasing period was *c.* 1670 to
c. 1830. There are now 79 STC, 259 Wing, 118 pre-1600 continental and 142
1600–1700 continental items in the collection, together with 2 medieval MSS,
4 identified Oxford bindings, 1515–1620, and other bindings of interest. A
copy of the collegiate bookplate is in the Franks Collection, no.33831. The
library was housed in various places in the Minster and is shortly to be placed
in the Minster Centre, the former Minster School.
Catalogues: noted in Read, below.
References: Notitia Parochialis, 1705: no.1252; DRB2, p.487; Kelly, pp.63,
252; Ker, MMBL, IV, 1992, pp.349–53; Ker, Pastedowns, 136, 1252, 1408,
xxxiii; Read, p.45; & Read, Supplement, p.153 (for further references);
Lambeth Palace MS.3223, ff.148–59: notes on provenance and bindings by
N. R. Ker (noting Oldham rolls and Hobson panel-stamps).

SPALDING, Lincs.
St. Mary and St. Nicholas. Linc.
[250v.] Spalding Gentleman's Society Library
The library was begun in a room over the church porch in 1637 by Robert
Ram (d.1657), vicar *c.* 1642–56, for the use of the minister and his successors
for ever. In 1661, according to the testimony of William Sneath, aged 68, all
those who had given books to the library 'should with his consent have libertie
to borrow what books they pleased'. A number of these books are signed by
Maurice Johnson (1688–1755), who in 1709 attempted to start a literary
society; this was finally established in 1712 as the Spalding Society of
Gentlemen, with a fund to buy books for its own library and also with the aim
of restoring the parish and Grammar School libraries. The Society added
books to the parish collection and arranged for its transfer to the vestry. The
collection, by then 'upwards of 600 volumes', was moved to the Grammar
school in 1865 when the church was restored internally, and finally in *c.* 1910
was transferred to the Society's Library in the Museum. Some 18 vols. from
the original collection, all 16th and 17th cent. books, were retained in the
church until 1951 when they also were deposited with the Society. The books
from the parochial collection are now housed in a special bookcase. Some of
the 600+ vols. listed earlier may have been absorbed into the main collection,
or the number 600 may have indicated titles rather than vols.: it is unlikely
that any have been lost. The books are mainly theological; there are 2
incunables, *c.* 98 STC and *c.* 150 16th and 17th cent. items. Most of the
original vols. have 'Spalding' on the fore-edge.
Catalogues: 2 ms. cats. by Society members, *c.* 1710–20, with donors'
names, with the collection; TS cat. of 18 vols. transferred in 1951: in

Bodl.MS.Eng.Misc.c.360 (copy in CCC); card cat. *c.* 1994; E.W. Maples and George Goodwin, *Catalogue of the Books, Manuscripts, Pamphlets and Tracts*, Spalding, 1893.
References: *South Holland Mag.*, v.2 (1870), pp.57–9; Edward Mansell Sympson, *Memorials of Old Lincolnshire*, 1911, pp.320, 322, 337; John Nichols, *Literary Anecdotes of the Eighteenth Century*, v.6, pt.1, 1812, p.28; K. A. Manley, 'The S.P.C.K. and English book clubs before 1720', *BLR*, 13 (1989), pp.236–7; Venn: Ram; Kelly, pp.75, 95, 97–8, 122, 195, 249; DRB2, p.118; Lambeth Palace MS.3223, ff.160–5: notes and rubbings by N. R. Ker; Pearson, 545.1, A98(1).1.

SPARSHOLT. Berks. (Oxon)
Holy Cross. Ox.
[2v.] Berks. RO
DeskL: Jewel, *A Defence of the Apologie*, [16th cent.]; [A book of sermons], 1562.

SPETISBURY, Dorset
St. John the Baptist. Sarum
[1v.] *
DeskL: Jewel, *Works*, 1611, chained.

SPIXWORTH, Norf.
St. Peter. Nor.
[3v.] Norwich CL
DeskL: BCP, 1685; Edward Elton, *Exposition of Saint Paul*, 1620; Bible, 1613.

SPONDON, Derbys.
St.Werburgh. Derby
[nil]
A ParL of 120 vols. was est. in 1822 by the Associates of Dr Bray, which was augm. in 1870. It is not recorded after 1890.
Catalogues: 'Spondon cum Membris, Derbys.', Bray Associates Records, f.40, pp.53–6.
References: Bray Associates Annual Reports, 1890; Shore, p.151; Kelly, p.261.

STAINTON, Yorks. (N.Yorks.)
St. Peter and St. Paul. York
[300v.] York Minster Lib.
In his will dated Nov. 1689 Richard Lumley (*c.* 1644–94), vicar 1677–89, bequeathed 'unto the minister or curate for the time being of Stainton the use of my library of bookes'. In 1705 his successor recorded that Lumley had 'bequeathed his library for ever to ye use of the minister or curate for ye time being or whether of them resident there'. The library, kept in the vicarage, was deposited in York Minster Lib. by faculty in 1911. Many of the books have

Lumley's signature; others have the signature of his predecessor John Gillot, vicar 1663–7, and William Lawson, vicar in 1622. There is a very damaged list of books on a parchment sheet attached to the will in the Borthwick Institute in two hands (17th and 18th cent.), and a catalogue of 344 items in a 1764 terrier of Stainton. There are at least 7 incunables and many 16th cent. books. Perhaps the most important item is the Missal of pre-Reformation use of York, printed in Rouen in 1516 by Pierre Olivier, and sold by Jean Gachet, a bookseller from France, who came via Hereford to set up his shop near to York Minster. The collection is very largely in contemporary bindings, with at least 5 notable stamped bindings (3 identified Oxford bindings, 1515–1620).
Catalogues: with the will, 1689: Chancery Court Probate Records, 1689 (copies in Borthwick Institute and CCC); 1764 terrier, with collection.
References: Notitia Parochialis, 1705: no.1058; Elizabeth Brunskill, 'The Stainton Collection', *The Friends of York Minster*, 19th Annual Report (1947), pp.37–9; Kelly, p.256 (but not 'near Guisborough'); place-name in Crockford: 'Stainton-in-Cleveland'; Barr, p.36; Ker, Pastedowns, 628, 1611–2; Venn: Lumley; Foster: Lawson.

STALYBRIDGE, Chcs.
Holy Trinity and Christ Church. Ches.
[1v.] *
DeskL: Great Bible, 6th ed., 1539–41, given by Edward Dain.

STAMFORD, Lincs.
St. Mary. Linc.
[*c.* 118v.]
Richard Banister (d.1612) gave books in his lifetime and prepared a place for them in the chancel. He also bequeathed £10 to the minister and church-wardens to be laid out at 7 per cent and the interest 'bestowed uppon divinity-bookes yearely or once in two yeares: and the same bookes shall bee placed in the library in the said church to remaine for ever'. A catalogue-book given by Banister records purchases from 1633 to 1641, and contains a list of books dated 1720. The library was evidently refounded in *c.* 1720, for the books acquired at this date reveal evidence of being circulated to gentlemen subscribers of a society based at the church. A list of books made in 1928 contains *c.* 119 titles dating from 1506 to 1748. The collection is now housed in a large Victorian glazed bookcase, given in 1946, in a curtained-off area at the base of the tower. There are labels in the books inscribed: 'This book belongs to the library in S. Mary's Church in Stamford, Lincolnshire'. Three vols. were selected for conservation in 1986: Mirabellius, *Polyanthea*, 1522, in a Cambridge binding; Augustine Marlorat, *A Catholike and Ecclestiasticall Exposition of . . . St. Matthewe*, trans. Thomas Tymme, 1570, which bears the inscription: 'This book belongs to the library at S. Maries in Stamford (begun by Richard Banister, anno dni 1625) & was given by William Dugard [*c.* 1607–62], Mr. in Arts & school-master of the Grammar-Schoole in Stamford,

Aprilis 13 anno dni 1636'; and John Whitgift, *The Defense of the Aunswere to the Admonition against the Replie*, 1574, an author's presentation copy dated 1573. **Catalogues**: catalogue-book with the collection; TS list by N. R. Ker in Bodl.MS. Eng.Misc.c.360 (copies in Lambeth Palace MS.3223, ff.166–70, and CCC). **References**: Arnold Sorsby, 'Richard Banister and the beginnings of English ophthalmology', in *Science, Medicine and History: Essays in Honour of Charles Singer*, ed. E. Ashworth Underwood, v.2, 1953, pp.17–18, 50–51; Graham K. Scott, 'English public and semi-public libraries in the provinces, 1750–1850', (Library Association Final Exam, pt.6, 1951), unpublished TS, p.46, n.22; Kelly, pp.75, 250; DNB: Banister; Venn: Dugard.

STANDLAKE, Oxon.
St. Giles. Ox.
[2v.] Oxfordshire Archives
DeskL: *Certain Sermons or Homilies*, 1623 (with 2 17th cent. inscriptions on the tp affirming that the book belonged to the church); Articles, 1628 (inscribed 1635 as being read out by the then incumbent; given by B. H. Blackwell Ltd, 1937); 18th cent. sermons by Matthew Horbery (1706/7–73), incumbent.
References: Foster, ESTC: Horbery.

STANFIELD, Norf.
St. Margaret. Nor.
[5v.] Norwich CL
DeskL: Thomas Bilson, *The Perpetual Gouvernement of Christes Church*, [1610?]; *Certain Sermons or Homilies*, 1683; Henry Compton, *Constitutions and Canons*, 1678; Erasmus, *Paraphrases*, 1548; Jewel, *Works*, 1611.

STANGROUND, Hunts. (Cambs.)
St. John the Baptist. Ely
[nil]
A tablet in the N. aisle records that William Whitehead (1731–54), rector, bequeathed his library 'in usum successorum', appointing the rectors of Woodston and Fletton as trustees 'ut integra semper descendat'. There were 1,000 vols. in the collection. The rector informed the Central Council in 1950 that he had 'sold the library for £90 some years ago; after permission from all concerned'.
References: Walter Debenham Sweeting, *Historical and Architectural Notes on the Parish Churches in and around Peterborough*, 1868, p.196; Kelly, p.248; Venn: Whitehead.

STANSTED MOUNTFICHET, Essex
St. Mary the Virgin. Chelmsf.
[15 titles in 25v.] Colchester PL
A vestry library was in existence from the 1690s. 15 'books belonging to the

vestry' are listed in tithe accounts for 1712–54, and 4 17th cent. books in a late 19th cent. notebook. Two of the books are included in 25 vols. deposited in Colchester PL in 1982. The collection includes 2 STC and 2 Wing items. A copy of Edward Brerewood, *Enquiries Touching the Diversity of Languages*, 1674, was given to the vestry by Sir Stephen Langham in 1693, and William Chillingworth's *The Religion of Protestants*, Oxford, 1638, by Mark Lewis (b. *c*. 1648), vicar 1678–82, in 1696.

Catalogues: TS list *c*. 1980 (copy in CCC); Colchester Library list on receipt, 1982 (copy in CCC).

References: Tithe accounts: Essex RO, Chelmsford, D/P 109/3/2; notebook: T/ P 68/25/3; Kelly, p.247; Venn: Lewis.

STANTON HARCOURT, Oxon.
St. Michael. Ox.
[11 titles in 6v.] Bodl.
DeskL: 5 STC, 4 Wing and 2 pre-1600 continental books: Bibles, prayer books, psalters (including *Psalterium*, Wittenberg, 1564) and Thomas Watson, *A Body of Practical Divinity*, 1692. Deposited in the Bodleian in 1974.
Catalogues: TS list by Paul Morgan, 1974 in Lambeth Palace MS.3094, f.213 (copies in Oxfordshire Archives and CCC); Pearson, 2014b.1.

STARSTON, Norf.
St. Margaret. Nor.
[4 titles in 2v.] Norwich CL
DeskL: BCP, Bible, Psalms, 1580/1; Jewel, *Defense*, 1571.

STAUNTON, Glos.
(Ded. unknown). Glouc.
[1v.] Lambeth Palace Lib.
A bookplate in Henry Isaacson, *Life and Death of Lancelot Andrewes*, 1829, reads, 'Staunton Rectory Library, for the use of future rectors of Staunton by the Rev. Richard Davies [*c*. 1796–1857], M.A. rector from 1823 to 1857'.
References: Foster: Davies.

STAVELEY IN CARTMEL, Lancs. (Cumbria]
St. Mary. Car.
[nil]
A ParL of 28 vols. was est. in 1757 by the Associates of Dr Bray. In 1849 this library was reported as being one of those 'either wholly lost or reduced to a few tattered volumes'.
Catalogues: in Par. of Cartmell, Lancs., Bray Associates Records, f.38, p.35.
References: Select Committee Report, 1849; Kelly, p.262.

Steeple Ashton: general view of a collection mainly given by Samuel Hey, vicar, now housed in a specially-fitted room opened in 1969

STEANE, Northants.
St. Peter. BL *
A Bible of 1660, given to Nathaniel, Lord Crew (1635–1722) by Charles II, and a Psalter of 1643, formerly kept as a rule at Steane Park, were deposited at the British Museum in the late 1970s.
References: CCC Questionnaire, 1950.

STEEPLE ASHTON, Wilts.
St. Mary the Virgin. Sarum
[228 titles in 324v.]   *In situ*
The library was begun by Ellis Wright, vicar 1538–69, who bequeathed a 5 vol. folio edition of St. John Chrysostom, *Opera*, Basel, 1530, 'about the year 1568'. From the churchwardens' account it is probable that other books were given or bequeathed over the succeeding years. The main bequest, however, was by Samuel Hey (*c.* 1745–1828), vicar 1787–1828, who left his personal library of *c.* 175 vols. to the vicarage 'for the use of vicars in succession'. He had earlier in 1816 at his own expense built a room in the vicarage to house his collection, which, from the evidence of an inventory drawn up by his brother Richard, had extensive library furniture and fittings. The library then contained 1,100 vols. and continued to grow with additions from later incumbents until 1932 when the PCC attempted to sell it during an interregnum, a move which was thwarted by the new incumbent. But in 1941, in response to the wartime demand for salvage, the Bishop of Salisbury agreed to the PCC's recommendation for sale but asked Canon Quirk, Salisbury's Canon Librarian, to examine the collection. Most books of value remained at the vicarage, a few vols. were selected for Salisbury CL (but were not in fact deposited), and 8 vols. were sent to Magdalene College, Cambridge, where Hey had been Fellow and later President. The remainder, about 75% of the original collection plus additions, was sold in 1941 for the sum of £3. 7s. In 1968 plans were drawn up for a new vicarage and the remnant of the library was removed to a specially fitted room over the S. porch of the church, opened as 'The Samuel Hey Library' in 1969. In addition to 16th and 17th cent. theology, history and literary works, there are a number of books on America and local topography. The most valuable item is the early 15th cent. MS Book of Hours, with a metrical litany of saints in the vernacular. Many of Hey's books have dates of purchase at Cambridge, 1765–80, and include names of previous owners, especially D. Hughes of Queens' College.
Catalogues: original catalogue prepared by Richard Hey, one of the executors, 1828: Wilts. RO.DI/36/2/2 (copy with the collection); Richard Crawley's cat. of *c.* 1831; Robert Jarrett's cat. of 1832 sent to Magdalene College (and see Smith, below).
References: *Wilts. Notes and Queries*, v.6 (1910), p.371; letters about the bequest of the library of Steeple Ashton from the Rev. Samuel Hey to his successors, 1828–32: Wilts. RO. 1204/2; Christopher Wordsworth, ed., *Horae Eboracensis* (Surtees Soc., v. 132, 1920), Appendix 1, pp.161–4;

E. G. H. Kempson and R. E. Sandell, 'The Vicar's Library', in *Samuel Hey Library at St. Mary's Church, Steeple Ashton*, [*c.* 1970]; William Smith, 'The fifteenth century manuscript Horæ in the parochial library of Steeple Ashton', *Manuscripta*, v.25 (1981), pp.151–63; *idem.* 'The parochial library of Steeple Ashton in Wiltshire', *Library History*, v.6.4 (1983), pp.97–113 (includes appendices: I. Canon Quirk's list (Wilts. RO. 730.80); II. Select items surviving from before 1828 (38 items, with provenances); III. Additions since 1828 still surviving in the Library (15 items with provenances); IV. Books given to Magdalene College, Cambridge (4 items with provenances); Ker, MMBL, IV, 1992, pp.367–8; Lambeth Palace MS.3223, ff.171–3: notes, especially on provenances, by N. R. Ker; Venn: Hey.

STEEPLE ASTON, Oxon.
St. Peter and St. Paul. Ox.
[iv.] Oxfordshire Archives
DeskL: *Two Sermons, the first Preached at Steeple Aston* . . . 1680; and 18th cent. poll books and election pamphlets.

STEEPLE MORDEN, Cambs.
St. Peter and St. Paul. Ely
[nil] *
There was a ParL in Steeple Morden in 1801.
References: A. E. Dobbs, *Education and Social Movements, 1700–1850*, 1919, p.138n.

STETCHWORTH, Suffolk
St. Peter. Ely
[nil]
Cambs. CRO holds a list dated 1845 of *c.* 7 mainly service books (undated) which 'belong to the Church of Stetchworth'.
References: Cambs. CRO: P145/113.

STEVENAGE, Herts.
St. Nicholas. St.Alb.
[nil] *
DeskL: there is a list dated 1575 of 9 titles in 13 vols. in a vestry minute book which includes 'A bible in the greatest volume', the Paraphrases of Erasmus, communion books, psalters and homilies.
References: Herts. RO: Stevenage vestry minutes, D/P105/8/1; Woolf, p.190 & n.75.

STOCKPORT, Ches.
St. Mary (ded. uncertain). Ches.
[nil?] NRC
A ParLL of 159 vols. was est. in 1843 by the Associates of Dr Bray, and augm. in 1872.
Catalogues: Bray Associates Records, f.41, pp.84–8.
References: Shore, p.15; Kelly, p.261.

STOCKTON-ON-TEES, Durham (Cleve.)
St. Thomas. Dur.
[nil]
When a new parish church was built in 1710–12 a room at first floor level on the SW corner off the staircase to the gallery was fitted up as a library with tall bookcases and a bureau. In 1847 there were c. 800 vols., 204 of which, chiefly in Latin, had been left for the church by John Stock, schoolmaster, son of Robert Stock (d.1719), parish clerk. The other vols. belonged to a subscription library started in 1800 by John Brewster (c. 1754–1842), vicar 1799–1805.
References: Thomas Richmond, *The Local Records of Stockton and the Neighbourhood*, 1868, pp.58, 99; William M. Jacob, 'Libraries and philanthropy, 1690—1740', *Bull. of the Ass. of Brit. Theological and Phil. Libraries*, v.4 (1997), p.7; Forster: Brewster.

STOKE-BY-NAYLAND, Suffolk
St. Mary. St.E.
[c. 162 titles in 142v.]
A grant of £2. 10s. towards the est. of a ParLL was awarded by Bray from funds at his disposal, 1695–9, and a library was probably founded by Thomas Reeve (d.1745), vicar 1685–1719, making use of this grant. Charles Martin Torlesse, vicar 1832–81, in his catalogue of 1877 (see below) lists 116 books, most of which still remain; a few others have since been added. From inscriptions in some of the books it is clear that they were intended for loan. They are still housed in a room over the S. porch, since c. 1975 in new bookcases. There are 12 STC and 75 Wing items, 6 Latin works printed in the 16th cent. and a set of Parker Society publications in their original casing. Apart from standard theology, Biblical exegesis and religious controversy there are less commonly found works of literary, historical and scientific interest, e.g. Thomas Digges, *A Geometricall Practicall Treatize named Pantometria*, 1591.
Catalogues: Torlesse's catalogue in his *Some Account of Stoke by Nayland*, 1877, Appendix, pp.97–9; partial lists and notes made by Miss D. M. B. Ellis in 1949, with notes and rubbings of bindings by N. R. Ker: Lambeth Palace MS.3223, ff.174–80; TS cat. of 104 items from Torlesse's list, n.d. (copy in CCC); TS cat. by Canon J. A. Fitch, 1962 (with the collection); Suffolk PLC, 1977.
References: terrier of 1753 (noting existence of library): Suffolk RO, Bury:

Stoke-by-Nayland: a general view of the late seventeenth / early eighteenth century
library, probably founded by Thomas Reeves, vicar 1685–1719,
housed in a room over the south porch

806/1/145; H. Munro Cautley, *Suffolk Churches and their Treasures*, 3rd ed.,
Ipswich, 1954, p.318; Fitch, 1965, pp.75–7; Fitch, 1977, p.xviii; Kelly, pp.254
& n.1, 259; Venn: Reeve, Torlesse.

STOKE DAMEREL, Devon
St. Andrew. Ex.
[nil] *
A ParL was started in 1848 by the Revd W. B. Flower (*c.* 1820–68), late curate
of the parish.
References: *N & Q*, no.226, 25.2.1854; Venn: Flower; CCC Questionnaire
1950.

STOKE HOLY CROSS, Norf.
Holy Cross. Nor.
[4 titles in 3v.] Norwich CL
DeskL: Robert F. Herrey, *Two Right Profitable and Fruitfull Concordances*,
1578; Bible, 1584; *The Whole Book of Psalms, with Hymns Evangelicall*,
1627; with BCP, 1614.

STOKESBY, Norf.
St. Andrew. Nor.
[2v.] Norwich CL
DeskL: Erasmus, *Paraphrases*, 1548; Jewel, *Works*, 1609.

STOKESLEY, Yorks. (N.Yorks.)
St. Peter and St. Paul. York
[?] *
An entry in Baines' *Directory*, 1823, states that: 'in the year 1818, a Society for the promotion of Christian knowledge was established here, under the patronage of the Archdeacon of Cleveland, when a depository of books was formed in the vestry of the parish church, and from which 6,000 volumes have already been dispersed'. This may have been a precursor of the ParLL noted in the Bray reports as est. in 1826 by the Associates of Dr Bray, but the cat. of this lists only 158 vols. This library was reported as being consolidated at **Middlesbrough** in 1869, but part of the collection may have been absorbed into the town's public library in 1845.
Catalogues: Bray Associates Records, f.40, pp.143–6, listed as the Cleveland Deanery Lib. est. at Stokesley.
References: Bray Associates Annual Reports, 1870; Edward Baines, *History, Directory & Gazetteer of the County of York*, v.2, East and North Riding, Leeds, 1823, p.465; Kelly, p.264 & n.4; Paul Hastings, 'Parish libraries in the nineteenth century', *Local Historian*, v.15, no.7 (1983), pp.406–13.

STONE, Staffs.
St. Michael. Lich.
[nil] *
Under her will dated 21 Oct. 1765, Elizabeth Crompton, late of Broseley in the County of Salop., spinster, did 'give and bequeath all and every her books mentioned and set forth in a catalogue or schedule hereunto annexed for the use of the curate of the parish church of Stone and his successors for ever'. The catalogue lists *c.* 454 titles in 518 vols. The entries are undated but early 18th and some 17th cent. books are certainly included in a miscellaneous collection with much theology. It seems likely that the books were removed from the church, and perhaps disposed of, during the incumbency of Eldred Woodland in *c.* 1865.
Catalogues: attached to will, Lichfield RO: B/A/22/7 (copy in CCC).
References: Forster: Woodland.

STONEHOUSE, Glos.
St. Cyr. Glouc.
[nil]
Samson Harris (*c.* 1699–1763), vicar 1727–63, under his will, proved in 1763, left 'unto the churchwardens of the parish of Stonehouse for the time being all my books and furniture in the library in the vicarage house . . . upon trust . . . subject to the provisions . . . governing parochial libraries in a certain Act of Parliament . . . of . . . Queen Anne and upon no other trust'. These books, and others belonging to John Hilton, vicar 1708–23, were removed to the Institute which became the Parish Hall in *c.* 1866, but by 1901 they were stored in an outhouse at the vicarage. The were transferred to the Secondary Modern School in 1958. A valuation for possible sale was made in 1969, but in the same year most of the books were stolen from the school. The residue was 'disposed of or sold' in *c.* 1970. From Hawker's cat. of 1932 there were *c.* 970 titles, of which 746 pre-1763 books were given or bequeathed by Harris. In all there were 15 16th cent., 191 17th cent., 289 18th cent., and 17 19th cent. books, mainly theology and sermons, with a scattering of other subjects.
Catalogues: H. E. Hawker, TS cat. 1932 (Gloucester PL, copy in CCC).
References: Ralph Bigland, *Historical, Monumental and Genealogical Collections relative to the County of Gloucester*, suppl. pt.4., Stonehouse, 1791–2; Kelly, p.247; Lambeth Palace MS.3223, ff.181–4: notes on provenance and bindings with rubbings by N. R. Ker.

STOWEY (near Radstock), Somerset
St. Nicholas and Blessed Virgin Mary. B & W
[nil] *
A ParL was est. in 1720 by the Bray Trustees for Erecting Parochial Libraries, and augm. in 1798. The catalogue of 1800 is signed by Edward Whitley, vicar 1799–1825. It was reported untraced in 1878.
Catalogues: 1720; 1800, with printed rules: Somerset RO: DD/X/ten 1.
References: Bray Associates Annual Reports, 1878; Kelly, p.263; Foster: Whitley.

STRATFIELD SAYE, Hants.
St. Mary. Win.
[iv.] Hants. RO
DeskL: *Sermons and Homilies*, 1640, with a ms. note that it was bought for the church when Andrew Keepe and Richard Keepe were churchwardens in 1662.

STRATFORD, Essex (G.Lon.)
St. John the Evangelist. Chelmsf.
[nil] *
The ParL est. at **London, St. Botolph** by the Associates of Dr Bray was transferred in 1872 to Stratford, and there augm., and again in 1896; it was last listed in 1912.
References: Bray Associates Annual Reports, 1890, 1912; Shore, p.152.

STRATFORD-UPON-AVON, Warwicks.

Holy Trinity. Cov.

[iv.]

DeskL: Bible, 1611, chained, and with an inscription by the churchwardens when it was rebound in 1695.

In the 1870s a Pure Literature Guild had a library of *c.* 388 religious vols., which were subsequently absorbed into a Parish Room Library and increased to 850 vols. The library was active for *c.* 20 years but did not survive beyond the end of the century after the est. of the Public Library.

References: Blades, BIC, p.40; Morgan, p.30.

STREATLEY, Beds.

St. Margaret. St.Alb.

[nil]

A ParL was est. in *c.* 1729 by the Bray Trustees for Erecting Parochial Libraries.

References: see p.39,n.39; Kelly, p.261 & n.1.

STRUMPSHAW, Norf.

St. Peter. Nor.

[iv.] Norwich CL

DeskL: Bible, 1611.

STURRY, Kent.

St. Nicholas. Cant.

[iv.] Canterbury CL & Archives

DeskL: Foxe, *Book of Martyrs*, 1684.

SUDBURY, Suffolk

All Saints. St.E.

[nil]

A ParL of 67 vols. was est. in 1712 by the Bray Associates for Erecting Parochial Libraries. Walter Hackett, vicar, left 5 vols. of Bishop Patrick's *Works* at his death in 1750. From a glebe terrier of 1813 the books were evidently kept in the vicarage house and then numbered 62 vols.; in a terrier of 1834 the number was 61 vols. The library was still extant in 1852, but has long since disappeared. In the Marchmont Bookshop Catalogue 23, June 1966, item 12, John Ellis, *Articulorum XXXIX*, bound with *Articuli Lambethani*, bound with Thomas à Kempis, *De Imitatione Christi*, Paris, 1709, contained the Bray bookplate.

Catalogues: Bray Associates Records, f.39, pp.173–6; 1813 and 1834 terriers: Suffolk RO, Bury: 806/1/148 (copies in Lambeth Palace, MS.3223, ff.185–8).

References: Charles Badham, *The History and Antiquities of All Saints Church, Sudbury*, 1852, pp.105–9; Kelly, p.263; Fitch, 1965, pp.68–9; Fitch, 1977, p.xiii; Fitch, *N & Q* (1976), March, p.115. I am indebted to Michael Tupling for information in this entry.

SUTTON COURTENAY, Berks. (Oxon.)

All Saints. Ox.

transf [15 titles in 19v.] St. George's Chapel Chapter Lib., Windsor

In 1786 Archdeacon Onslow noted 'a parochial library over the church porch'. By 1959 there remained a collection of 24 vols. kept in a long case with glass-fronted doors in the tower vestry. A TS list was made before 1951. The books were mainly given to the church by local gentry and neighbouring clergy from 1686 to 1710, with a few vols. in later years. The bindings of 13 vols. were repaired or renewed by John Gregson, vicar, in 1847. All but 2 have chains or evidence of chaining. They include 4 STC and 10 Wing items. 5 vols. (*c.* 1570–1631) were shown to a local antiquarian society on a visit in 1908, 'the remainder of what was formerly a considerable library'. In 1997 16 vols. from the original collection were deposited in the Chapter Library at Windsor, patron of the living, together with 3 other vols. 8 vols. from the original collection have been lost.

Catalogues: a list of benefactors with a list of books given to the parochial library, *c.* 1720 (mostly still present): Berks. RO. D/P 128 25/1/1–2; TS list of *c.* 1951: in Bodl.MS.Eng.Misc.c.360 (copy in CCC); TS list of books received at Windsor (copies in church and CCC).

References: Archdeacon Onslow's visitation book, 1786: Berks. RO D/EX 1324/1, f.27; *Jnl. of the Berks. Bucks. & Oxon. Archaeol. Soc.*, v.14 (1908–9), p.33; Lambeth Palace MS.3223, ff.189–92: rubbings of bindings and notes by N. R. Ker.

SUTTON ST. MARY, Lincs. (otherwise known as Long Sutton)

In situ St. Mary. Linc.

[62v.] *

A Parl was est. in 1876 by the Associates of Dr Bray, and was still kept in 1907 'in the parvis of the church'. By 1961 there were reckoned to be *c.* 100 vols., about half from the Bray library, with later donations, including 'a very good copy' of William Dugdale's *The History of Imbanking and Drayning of Divers Fenns and Marshes*, 1662, in a glazed bookcase in a room over the porch. 62 vols. remain (but not the vol. by Dugdale).

Catalogues: TS list of authors / brief titles (but no dates) with the collection (copy in CCC).

References: Shore, p.151; letter to N. R. Ker, 9 Oct. 1961 (CCC file); Cox & Harvey, p.335.

SWAFFHAM, Norf.

St. Peter and St. Paul. Nor.

transf [545 titles in 554v.] Norwich CL, and in situ

The library was mainly an amalgamation of a number of collections associated with the Spelman family: there are books from the working collection of Sir Henry Spelman (1560–1641), and the libraries of his sons Sir John (1594–1643) and Sir Clement (1598–1679), together with books and papers of Francis

Willoughby (d.1652), the brother of Clement's wife, Ursula. Sir Clement Spelman, of Narborough, bequeathed the surviving collection, together with a legacy of £100 for the purchase of choice books, to the town of Swaffham in 1679. There is no evidence as to how the £100 bequest was spent: the only recorded purchase is Ortelius, *Theatrum Orbis Mundi*, 1606, for which £1. 10s. 4d was paid in 1709. The library was first housed in the Priest's Chamber over the vestry. The churchwardens paid £2. 14s. 9d 'for fitting up the library' in 1690 and in 1691 2s. for 'carage of books'. In the 18th cent. the books were housed in the vestry, and in 1737 were first catalogued, most of them receiving printed bookplates inscribed 'Swaffham Library. F. Dalton /F. Rayner Church-wardens. 1737' (copy in the Franks Collection: no.33865). They were marked with a letter and no. in white on the spine. The books were re-catalogued in 1879, and the Chamber re-furnished and restored; 47 vols. were then found to be missing. From the latter part of the 19th cent. onwards the library was badly neglected. In the 1970s several grants were made for restoring the Chamber, and for conservation and rebinding of books, but because of further deterioration in the Chamber, and problems concerning local care, considera-tion was given to deposit the library in a number of local repositories. Finally, in 1995, the collection was deposited by faculty in Norwich CL, where 6 new bookcases were specially built to house them, with the aid of a grant from Trinity College, Cambridge. Further grant aid was received from the CCC in 1998 for boxes and slipcases.

The Swaffham books are in subject range much closer to a contemporary Oxford or Cambridge college collection than to a typical parochial or cathedral collection. There are 146 STC books and a substantial no. of 16th and 17th cent. continental imprints, mainly Patristic texts in Latin and Greek and theology in Latin. There is also an important collection of early law books (the cumulative working library of the Spelmans), and a distinctive collection of English late 16th and early to mid 17th cent. recusant imprints from Francis Willoughby's library (44 books are in Allison and Rogers). Individual books of note include a rare Vulgate Bible, Venice, 1483, Holinshed's *Chronicles*, 1577, Bacon's *Essays*, 1629, a Polyglot Bible, 1657, and some rare geograph-ical and mathematical works. Manuscripts include a 14th/15th century Sarum Book of Hours, and the document known as the 'Black Book of Swaffham', compiled by John Botright (d.1474), rector of Swaffham 1435–74. 10 other MSS, mainly legal or recusant, are kept with the books. In the church, mounted on wooden screens, are 10 vellum leaves from 2 15th cent. liturgical MSS.

Catalogues: MS. cat. by Joseph Charles, 1737 (the printed label of Charles, vicar of Swaffham, dated 1729, is reproduced in Lee, below); ms. cat. by Granville Smith, 1879 (with the collection; TS copy with marginal notes on bindings and pastedowns by N. R. Ker: in Lambeth Palace MS.3094, ff.221–34; copies in Norwich PL); 2 undated cats. in Norfolk RO: DN/MSC/ 9/7 and ANL/1/3; Mary Cecelia Lyons, 'Swaffham Parish Library: a catalogue of printed books and manuscripts', Dublin & Norwich, 1987 (unpublished TS, part of M.A. thesis, Loughborough U of Technology, Library and Information Studies, 1986): copies in Norfolk RO & CCC, include notes on authorship (MSS), provenances, fine bindings and binders' waste; shelf-lists and supplements to Lyons are with the collection). The introduction to this cat. was separately published by Norwich CL as *Swaffham Church Library*, 1996.

References: Francis Blomefield, *An Essay towards a Topographical History of the County of Norfolk*, v.6, 1807, p.217; *N & Q*, v.7 (1853), p.438; George Arthur Stephen, *A Norfolk Bibliography*, 1921, p.44; Kelly, pp.76, 251; Martin, pp.68–9; John Pink, *The Parish Church of St. Peter and St. Paul, Swaffham*, rev. ed., Swaffham, 1992, p.9; Ann S. King, 'Swaffham Parish Library: a survey of binder's waste in the collection', Norwich Dean & Chapter, 1997 (unpublished TS); Nicholas Pickwood, 'Swaffham revisited: a review of the earlier conservation work of books in the Swaffham Parish Library'. Preprint from the 9th International Conference of IADA, Copenhagen, 1999; Lambeth Palace MSS.3223, ff.193–201 & 3224: notes on provenance and rubbings by N. R. Ker; Lee, British, no.330; DNB: Spelmans. For much of the early history of the collection I have drawn on the introduction to the catalogue by Lyons, above.

SWINBROOK, Oxon.
St. Mary. Ox.
[iv.]
DeskL: Bible, Cambridge, Hayes, 1674.
References: NADFAS Report.

SWINDERBY, Lincs.
All Saints. Linc.
[nil]
A library, known only from the catalogue at the end of Swinderby Parish Register II, 1681–1802, which lists 108 vols. 'belonging to the parish of Swinderby'. Of these, 73 vols. were bequeathed by the Revd Samuel Disney (d.1721), lecturer at Wakefield, 'as a parochial library for ever'. Some 29 vols. were bequeathed by A. Chambers, vicar, in 1821, and 6 vols. of Walton's Polyglot Bible by John Drake, vicar. All the books on the list are in English; few are dated, those that are dated are theological, 1659 to c. 1738. There is no record of the books at the church after c. 1890.
Catalogues: Swinderby Parish Registers, Lincolnshire Archives (TS transcript in Bodl.MS.Eng.Misc.c.360, copy and another TS transcript in CCC).
References: Kelly, p.250; Venn: Disney.

TADCASTER, Yorks. (N.Yorks.)
St. Mary. York
[nil] *
A ParL of 67 vols. was est. in 1710 by the Bray Associates for Erecting Parochial Libraries; it was withdrawn for return in 1878.

Catalogues: MS. cat. no.26. Bray Associates Records, f.39, pp.61–4.
References: Bray Associates Annual Reports, 1878; Kelly, p.264.

TAMWORTH, Staffs.
St. Editha. Lich.
[nil] *

A grant of £2 towards the est. of a ParLL was awarded by Bray from funds at his disposal, 1695–9. It is possible, but unlikely, that this was the library bequeathed in his will of 1686 by the Revd John Rawlet (c. 1642–86), a native of Tamworth, to Tamworth Grammar School 'to be preserved for the use of succeeding schoole-masters and such students in the towne as shall need them . . . that there may be a public library for the benefit of scholers in the saide town'. A transcript of the cat. of the library lists c. 912 vols. in both shelf-list and author order, but without dates. It contained mainly theology, but also classical and English literature and history, and an imperfect medieval MS Bible, illuminated. It was housed in Guy's Almshouses until 1868 and was then moved to the Grammar School. In 1932 the Trustees of Rawlet's Charity, with the consent of the Charity Commissioners, sold the library at auction and applied the proceeds of the sale to the purposes of the charity.

Catalogues: transcript of the cat. 'sent by Mrs Rawlet to Tamworth' and extracts from Tamworth Charities, Blue Book: Tamworth Lib. (copies in CCC).
References: Kelly, pp.91, 253 & n.5, 259; Venn: Rawlet.

TANKERSLEY, Yorks. (S.Yorks.)
St. Peter. Sheff.
[37 titles in 41v.] Sheffield UL

Robert Booth by his will, proved 10 Jan. 1615, bequeathed books to John Nevinson (d.1634), rector 1601–34, and his successors, for ever. In 1947 the then incumbent, A.W. Douglas, found 32 books in the 'cock-loft', not of his own rectory house but in that of the neighbouring parish of **Worsbrough**, where they had somehow been incorporated into the library of the grammar school. In 1962 the books were deposited in Sheffield PL on unspecified terms, and in 1993 were transferred to Sheffield UL. There are now 41 vols., 34 of which have Robert Booth's standard form of bequest written in: 'Ro. Booth armiger huic libr. reliquit Jo. Nevinsone et suis succesor. rect. Ecclesie de Tankersley in perpetuum'. These are all 16th cent. French, Italian, Swiss and German imprints; there are also 1 Wing item and 5 18th cent. items. The subjects covered are classics, early medicine and theology.

Catalogues: TS cat. after deposit in Sheffield PL, 1963 (also includes a catalogue of the Worsbrough Grammar School Library, with a joint index of authors, editors and commentators: copy in CCC); TS list of 32 items: in Bodl.MS.Eng.Misc.c.360 (copy in CCC).
References: Kelly, pp.76, 256; Barr, pp.33–4; DRB, p.503 (detail omitted in 2nd ed.); Venn: Nevinson.

TARVIN, Ches.
St. Andrew. Ches.
[1v.] * Chester CL
DeskL: a Bible, Cambridge, 1639, and later Bibles and liturgical works, were deposited in Chester CL in 2000. A copy of William Hinde's *A Faithful Remonstrance*, 1641, presented by Raymond Richards, cannot now be found.
References: Richards, p.322.

TATHAM FELLS, Lancs.
Good Shepherd. Blackb.
[nil] *
A terrier of 1778, signed by Geo. Holden curate, records 'the books belonging to the parochial library of Tatham-fell established by Dr Bray's Associates', some 8 titles in 14 vols. This Bray library is otherwise unrecorded. The books include 'Archbishop Sharp's Sermons in seven volumes' (see the Whitchurch selection, 35–8: pp.53–5).
Catalogues: terrier including list in Lancs. RO, Preston: DRB 3/32 Tatham 1778 (copy in CCC).

TAVISTOCK, Devon
St. Eustachius. Ex.
[1v.] *
DeskL: Erasmus, *Paraphrases*, v.1., 1548, chained (from a reference in the churchwardens' accounts this was purchased for 15s. in 1561/2).
References: Blades, BIC, p.41.

TAWSTOCK, Devon
St. Peter. Ex.
[1v.] North Devon RO, Barnstaple
DeskL: Jewel, *Apologie*, n.d.

TEMPLE SOWERBY, Westm. (Cumbria)
St. James. Carl.
[nil] *
A ParLL of 140 vols. was est. in 1811 by the Associates of Dr Bray; it was incorporated into that of **Carlisle** by 1900.
Catalogues: sent Dec.1811 for the clergy of Temple Sowerby 'and its vicinity', Bray Associates Records, f.38, pp.241–3.
References: Bray Associates Annual Reports, 1900; Kelly, p.263.

THORNHAM, Norf.
All Saints. Nor.
[1v.] *
DeskL: Wolfgang Musculus, *Common Places of Christian Religion*, [1578?], disbound, in poor condition. There are no survivals of the 31 vols. given in 1806 to form a parochial library.
Catalogues: in 'Baptisms and burials 1762–1770': Norfolk RO, PO 576/2 (copy in CCC).

THORPE-NEXT-HADDISCOE, Norf.
St. Matthias. Nor.
[1v.] Norwich CL
DeskL: Bible, 1617.

THURGARTON, Norf.
All Saints (CCT). Nor.
[1v.] Norwich CL
DeskL: *Certain Sermons or Homilies*, 1563.

THURLTON, Norf.
All Saints. Nor.
[4v.] Norwich CL
DeskL: BCP, 1683 (2 copies); *Certain Sermons or Homilies*, 1683; Bible, 1613.

THURNHAM, Kent
St. Mary the Virgin. Cant.
[nil]
A collection of books kept formerly in a bookcase in the church is now known only from an inventory of 1751 which lists 126 titles, undated but almost entirely early 18th cent. works in English, including books on charity schools, the sacraments and moral issues, sermons and anti-popish tracts. They may have been the private library of Henry Dering (b. *c.* 1645), vicar 1673–1720.
Catalogues: inventory, 'taken by the minister & churchwardens at Easter 1751': Canterbury Cathedral Archives: DCb. PRC 41 (copy in CCC).
References: Kelly, p.248; Yates, pp.162, 164–5; Foster: Dering.

THURSBY, Cumb. (Cumbria)
St. Andrew. Carl.
[nil]
One of the 10 parishes in the diocese of Carlisle given 16 books in 1687 under the will of Barnabas Oley (see pp.34–5 and table on pp.444–52). They are listed in a terrier of 1830.
References: Kelly, p.246 & n.1; Barr, p.35.

THUXTON, Norf.
St. Paul. Nor.
[1v.] Norwich CL
DeskL: *Certain Sermons or Homilies*, 1676.

THWAITES, Cumb. (Cumbria)
St. Anne. Carl.
[nil]
A ParL of 29 vols. was est. in 1757 by the Associates of Dr Bray. In 1849 this library was reported as being one of those 'either wholly lost or reduced to a few tattered volumes'.
Catalogues: in Parish of Millom, Cumb., Bray Associates Records, f.38, p.36.
References: Select Committee Report, 1849; Kelly, p.261.

TIBENHAM, Norf.
All Saints. Nor.
[1v.] Norwich CL
DeskL: Jewel, *Works*, 1611.

TIDEFORD, Corn.
St. Luke. Truro
[nil] *
Shortly before 1959 some 30–40 calf-bound vols. of 18th cent. theology, an heirloom at the vicarage, disappeared without record. Information from Canon J. H. Adams, then rector of Landulph.
References: Kelly, p.246.

TILSHEAD, Wilts.
St. Thomas à Becket. Sarum
[nil?] NRC
A ParLL of 80 vols. was est. in 1813 by the Associates of Dr Bray.
Catalogues: Bray Associates Records, f.38, pp.251–2.
References: Kelly, p.264.

TILSTOCK, Shrops.
Christ Church. Lich.
[2v.] *
DeskL: Foxe, *Book of Martyrs*, 1684, 2v, once chained.
References: Cox & Harvey, p.340.

TIMSBURY, Hants.
St. Andrew. Win.
[*c.* 7v.] *
DeskL: Bible, 1613, with chain. A collection of *c.* 9 titles was kept in a small cupboard in the vestry with the inscription: 'Bookes given by M. timothy

goodacker Minister of this Parish 1713' on the door. Timothy Goodacker, who was vicar of Willow, Hants. in 1681, died in 1714. 11 books were stolen in 1977. The cupboard (now on the wall) survives with 2 books from the original collection: Symon Patrick, *A Commentary upon the Fourth Book of Moses, called Numbers*, 1699, and, Francis Roberts, *A Treatise on the Four Books of God's Covenants*, 1657.

Catalogues: a printed 'List of books in Timsbury Collection July 1909' signed by 'J. Cooke-Yarborough Vicar of Romsey Priest in charge', in a holder, is screwed to the side of the cupboard.

References: letter from Dereck Smith, 2 Mar. 1977 in Winchester CL: BII.12.Cen.Fol., listing the stolen books; Foster, VCH, Hants., v.4, p.488: Goodaker.

TINSLEY, Yorks. (S.Yorks.)
St. Lawrence. Sheff.
[iv.] BM
A ParL of 72 vols. was est. in 1711 by the Bray Trustees for Erecting Parochial Libraries, and augm. in 1870. In 1877 some 66 vols. still survived; the library is not recorded after 1890. One vol. with the Tinsley bookplate is known, George Herbert's *Country Parson* (see the Whitchurch selection, pp.53–5) in the Franks Collection, no. 33865.

Catalogues: MS. cat. no.7 for 'Tinsy alias Tinshaw', Bray Association Records, f.39, pp.129–32.

References: Bray Associates Annual Reports, 1890; Kelly, p.264; Shore, p.150; Barr, p.37.

TIVERTON, Devon
St. Peter. Ex.
[*c.* 571 titles in 256v.]
A library was collected by Richard Newte (1612–78), rector 1641–54, which was inherited and enlarged by his son, John Newte (1656–1715), rector 1678–1715, who, under the terms of his will of 1716, bequeathed 322 vols. towards 'a parochial library . . . to be forever kept in the chamber over the vestry in the parish church of Tiverton for the use of the several rectors and curates thereof and of the Chilcot's English School for the time being'. About 180 vols. have been added to the collection since the bequest, including *c.* 53 vols. from a Bray library est. in 1853 and augm. in 1872, but not recorded after 1900. In 1814 a survey revealed that 69 vols. from the original bequest were missing. The main strength of the collection is theology, but history is strongly represented, especially in the collection of 331 tracts, mainly of the Commonwealth period, bound up in 16 vols. by John Newte. Nearly all the books are pre-1700. Notable items include a copy of Ptolemy's *Atlas*, Strasburg, 1513, with coloured maps. An illuminated MS Book of Hours (two scribes, early 15th cent. and 1438) was part of the original bequest. John Newte's portrait in the vestry is reproduced in Welsford, below.   *continued*

Tiverton: general view of the library first collected by
Richard Newte, rector 1614–54

Catalogues: an 18th cent. cat. on parchment includes extracts from John
Newte's will, and marks books 'wanting' in the survey of 1814; a cat. of 1817
is chiefly a copy of the 18th cent. cat.; E. S. Chalk, 'A catalogue of the vestry
library', in his *A History of the Church of St. Peter, Tiverton*, Tiverton, 1905,
appendix, pp.xxv–lviii (description of the library, pp.71–3, and of the MS
Book of Hours, pp.73–6); card indexes by Anne Welsford of books and tracts
(copies in Exeter UL and West Country Studies Library, Exeter); A register of
books at the Clerical Lending Library, Tiverton, 1853, with a register of
borrowers 1853–9: Bray Associates Records, f.42.
References: Bray Associates Annual Reports, 1900; Kelly, pp.91 n.4, 96, 246;
Shore, p.151; Anne Welsford, 'Mr. Newte's library in St. Peter's church,
Tiverton', 2pts, *Devonshire Assoc. Report and Trans.*, v.106 (1974), pp.17–
31; v.107 (1975), pp.11–20 (and further refs. therein); Ker, MMBL, IV, 1992,
pp.494–5.

TODDINGTON, Beds.
St. George of England. St.Alb.
[nil] *
Abraham Hartwell (b. *c.* 1541/2), the elder, rector, began a library at
Toddington in 1570. He was the author of *Regina Literata*, 1564, and the
translator of Walter Haddon's *A Sight of the Portugall Pearle*, 1565.
References: Venn: Hartwell (where he is distinguished from Hartwell, the
younger, d.1606; they are confused in DNB); STC2.

TONG, Shrops.
St. Bartholomew. Lich.
[*c.* 454v.] Shrops. RRC

The library was est. by Gervase, Lord Pierrepont (d.1715), of Tong Castle, in 1697 with books which 'Lord Pierrepont should, during his life, appropriate to the use of the minister and his successors'. Lewis Peitier (d.1745), vicar 1695–1745, added 91 vols. 'to make part of it for ever'. It was originally housed at Tong Castle (pulled down in 1954), home of the founder. By 1759 it had been installed in a specially built room in the vicarage, and by 1812 was kept in the church vestry in 4 spacious 17th cent. (?) cupboards, each with 4 shelves and a contents list inside the door. By 1970 the books had been deposited in Shrops. Co.L. and they are now in the Shrops. RRC. There are many leather and parchment-bound folios in the collection, which is largely 17th cent. theology. There are 2 identified Oxford bindings.

Catalogues: a contemporary parchment cat. and a card cat. with the collection; cat. by Beriah Botfield (inaccurate) in *Miscellanies of the Philobiblon Soc.*, v.3 (1856–7), pp.17–42; Shrops. PLC, 1971: NADFAS TS of Tong books extracted from this (copy in CCC).

References: Kelly, p.253 & n.2; Kelly, Shrops, p.x; J. E. Auden, 'The minister's library in Tong church', *Trans. of the Shrops. Archaeol. Soc.*, 4 ser., v.12 (1930), pp.48–60; George A. Griffiths, *A History of Tong*, 2nd ed, Newport, 1894, pp.96, 107; Charity Commissioners, 3rd Report (1820), p.259; Venn: Pierrepont.

TORQUAY, Devon
St. Saviour (red.). Ex.
[nil]

A ParLL of 82 vols. was est. in 1849 by the Associates of Dr Bray, and augm. in 1870; it is not recorded after 1900.

Catalogues: parish of Tor Mohun, Bray Associates Records, f.41, pp.224–5.
References: Bray Associates Annual Reports, 1900; Kelly, p.261; Shore, p.151.

TORTWORTH, Glos.
St. Leonard. Glouc.
[*c.* 207v.] Oriel College Lib., Oxford; Bristol UL

A library was bequeathed by Henry Brooke (1694–1757), rector 1730–57, and also High Master, Manchester Grammar School, which was augm. with that of John Bosworth, rector 1768–86. In 1921 *c.* 200 17th and 18th cent. books, labelled 'Tortworth Rectory' and mostly containing the bookplate of John Bosworth (an Oriel man) were selected for Oriel College, Oxford, including an Aldine *De Rustica*, 1514, and a Coverdale Bible, 1540. In 1949 books from the library may have been included in the sale by Howes, Luce, Williams & Co. of the Tortworth Court, Ducie library, but from the general content of the auction list this would seem to be unlikely. In 1959 there remained *c.* 650 books stored in the rectory, which was subsequently purchased by Lord Ducie.

These books were sold by the Tortworth Estate Company at an auction in Wotton-under-Edge *c.* 1990. Some 61 vols. purchased at the auction by Robert Clark, Fine and Antiquarian Books, Oxford, appeared in his catalogue 26, *c.* 1992, nos. 215–75. There are 7 vols. with dates from 1691 to 1755, in Bristol UL.

Catalogues: copies of the 1949 auction sale cat. and the 1992 Clark cat. in CCC.

References: Kelly, p.247; W. D. Ross, 'The Tortworth Library', *Oriel College Record*, 4, no.4 (1922), pp.105–6; Paul Morgan, *Oxford Libraries Outside the Bodleian*, 2nd ed, Oxford, 1980, p.102; DNB: Brooke.

TOTNES, Devon
St. Mary. Ex.
[302 titles in 293v.] Exeter UL; Totnes Museum
Among the records of the Borough of Totnes there is a vol. covering the period 1631–1705, which describes early bequests and lists some of the books. Gabriel Barber gave £10 in 1619 'towards procuring a library', and there are references to bequests of books and money for books in 1620 and later. The library is referred to as 'publique' in 1635. A vol. still in the collection is inscribed: 'Totnes Library. The gift of Mr. Thomas Southcott, July 10, 1656'. The books were housed in a room over the vestry and suffered badly from damp. A ms. cat. was produced in 1821 and a printed cat. by C. Worthy in 1875 (see below). Neither is complete and Worthy's total of 334 vols. should be 340+ vols. About 17 vols. were deposited in Totnes Museum, and the remainder was deposited on permanent loan in Exeter UL in 1967. The main subject is 17th cent. theology. All but one of the books in Worthy's cat. were printed before 1670. There are now 37 16th cent., 235 17th cent. and 30 18th cent. titles. All the books have a paper label with a no. on the spine. Much rebinding took place in the second quarter of the 17th cent. All the books are now included in the University Library's OPAC, and there is a separate listing of the 16th and 17th bindings of interest.

Catalogues: MS. cat. 1821; cat. by C. Worthy in his *Ashburton and its Neighbourhood*, 1875, pp.xxvii–xxxiii; ms. cat. by W. H. H. Elliott, 1903 (Cambridge UL, MS.Add.6313).

References: Totnes Borough record: Devon RO, DRO 1579A/13/1; Kelly, pp.75, 246; DRB2, p.59; TS report by Dr Margaret Lattimore, Feb. 1983 (copy in CCC file); Lambeth Palace MS.3223, ff.205–9: notes and rubbings of rolls and panel stamps by N. R. Ker; Pearson, 195.1–2, 1408.1, 1843.1.

TOWCESTER, Northants.
St. Lawrence. Pet.
[*c.* 8v.]
DeskL: some vols. on display in a new bookcase (1986) include copies of:
Homilies, 1676; Jewel, *Works*, 1609 (with chain); Great Bible, [1568?] (with chain); Charles Palmer, vicar 1685–1735, *A Perswasive to Parochial Communion*, 2nd ed, 1706; Bible, BCP, 1742; and stored beneath: William Perkins, [a collection of *c.* 21 tracts, mainly 1616–7], copies of a 17th cent. Bible and Foxe, *Book of Martyrs.* Most of the books are imperfect and in poor condition.
References: CCC Questionnaire, 1950.

TREDINGTON, Warwicks.
St. Gregory. Cov.
[1v.] Warwicks. CRO
DeskL: *Certain Sermons or Homilies*, 1640.

TRELYSTAN, Mont. (Powys)
St. Mary the Virgin (ded. uncertain). Heref.
[nil?] NRC
A grant of 15s. towards the est. of a ParLL was awarded by Bray from funds at his disposal, 1695–9.
References: Kelly, p.259 & n.5 (alternative spelling 'Trelytyn').

TROWBRIDGE, Wilts.
St. James (ded. uncertain). Sarum
[nil] *
A ParL was est. in 1890 by the Associates of Dr Bray (formerly at **Bradford-on-Avon**, Wilts.)
References: Bray Associates Annual Report, 1890.

TRURO, Corn.
St. Mary (also the Cathedral from 1877). Truro
[?]
A ParLL of 180 vols. was est. in 1842 by the Associates of Dr Bray, and augm. in 1892. Some vols. from this library were absorbed into the Cathedral Library, and some also into the Bishop Philpotts Library, Truro. Books from these collections are also at **Newquay**, Cornwall. Copies of bookplates for the Bishop Phillpotts Library and the Truro Theological Library are in the Franks Collection, nos. 33833–8.
Catalogues: Bray Associates Records, f.41, pp.70–4.
References: Bray Associates Annual Reports, 1895; Kelly, p.261.

TUNSTALL, Lancs.
St. John the Baptist. Blackb.
[nil?] NRC
A terrier records the gift of 14 titles by 'John Fenwick of Burrow Hall, 1754'.
Catalogues: TS with terrier: Preston RO, Blackburn Diocese, DR/B, no.33.
References: Lambeth Palace MS.3224.

TURTON, Lancs. (G.Man.)
~~St. Anne. Man.~~
[51v.] Turton Tower, Turton
One of the 5 parochial libraries provided for under the will of Humphrey
Chetham (see under: **Manchester**; the others were **Bolton [-le-Moors]**, **Gorton**
and **Walmsley**). A list of 59 titles of books (in 91 vols.) purchased for the
Turton and Walmsley chapel libraries is given in the Chetham Feoffees'
Minute Book, 1659. 15 titles, nos. 45–59 (25 vols.) were originally intended
for Walmsley but were apparently never sent (extant copies are still at
Turton). The collection was kept in the chancel until 1885 when Gilbert
French organised a subscription to enable the books to be restored, the book-
chest cleaned and the books re-chained in it, while he produced an annotated
catalogue. In 1984 the surviving books and 1 surviving 'presse' (out of 2) were
deposited with faculty on permanent loan at Turton Tower (owned by
Chetham, 1628–53) where they are now kept in a box-room, with 3 books
displayed in rotation in a display case next to the book-chest. The books
purchased for Turton and Walmsley show a liberal view of Protestantism,
reflecting various and sometimes opposing opinions.
Catalogues: 1659 list: Chethams' Hospital and Library Archives (printed in
Christie, pp.57–9 and in Evans, Appendix 3, pp.41–2); G. J. French, 'Bibliographical notices of the church libraries at Turton and Gorton', *Chetham Soc*,
v.38 (1855), pp.10–103; Blades, BIC, Appendix B, pp.61–2 (42 entries); ms.
list of 21 items (Bodl.MS.Eng.Misc.c.360, copy in CCC); included in Evans,
below, in a union cat. of the extant books in the five Chetham libraries,
pp.45–53.
References: Christie, pp.57–62; Streeter, pp.304–6 (illustration); Blades, BIC,
pp.41–3, 61–2; Evans, pp.18–22, 41–2, 45–53, and pls. 6, 8–11; Kelly, pp.84,
249 & n.1.

TYNEMOUTH, Northumb. (T & W)
Tynemouth Priory, St. Saviour. Newc.
[nil?] NRC
DeskL: a copy of Foxe's *Book of Martyrs* was noted by Archdeacon Thomas
Sharp in 1723, and this was one of the 92 parishes in the Northumberland
Archdeaconry granted a ParLL under a scheme devised by Bishop Shute
Barrington, carried out by Archdeacon R. G. Bouyer by 1823 (see p.57), and
recorded as still possessing books in visitation returns, 1826–8.
References: Day, pp.99, 102 & n.38.

UBLEY, Somerset
St. Bartholomew. B & W
[IV.] *
DeskL: Erasmus, *Paraphrases*, 1522, chained. A copy of William Thomas, rector of Ubley, *A Preservative of Piety*, 1662, reported in 1950, can no longer be found.
References: CCC Questionnaire, 1950.

UFFINGTON, Lincs.
St. Michael and All Angels. Linc.
[nil] *
A ParLL of *c.* 352 vols. was est. in 1757 at **Old Hutton**, Westm. The cat. states that it was 'part of the library of the Revd Dr. Evans, Rector of Uffington, Lincolnshire'. John Evans, rector, died in 1685.
Catalogues: Bray Associates Records, f.38, pp.23–32.

ULPHA, Cumb. (Cumbria)
St. John. Carl.
[nil]
A ParL of 13 vols. was est. in 1761 by the Associates of Dr Bray, 5 vols. having been 'sent before by Dr. Stratford's executors'. This library was reported in 1849 as being one of those 'either wholly lost or reduced to a few tattered volumes'.
Catalogues: sent 1762 to Ulpha Chapel, Bray Associates Records, f.38, p.95.
References: Select Committee Report, 1849; Kelly, p.261.

ULVERSTON, Lancs. (Cumbria)
St. Mary. Carl.
[nil] *
A ParLL of *c.* 143 vols. was est. in 1753 (but not sent until 1756) and another of 255 vols. was est. in 1824 and augm. in 1869 by the Associates of Dr Bray.
Catalogues: Bray Associates Records: 1756: f.38, pp.5–10; 1825: f.40, pp.121–7.
References: Kelly, p.262.

UPLEADON, Glos.
St. Mary the Virgin. Glouc.
[IV.] *
DeskL: Bible, Robert Barker, 1613.

UPPER HEYFORD, Oxon.
St. Mary. Ox.
[5v.] Oxfordshire Archives, Oxford.
DeskL: Augustine, *Opera*, 10v. in 5, Cologne, 1616 (stamped on upper covers 'S' over 'IC'; deposited 1975).

UPWELL, Norf.
St. Peter. Ely
[nil?] NRC
DeskL: Bishops' Bible, 1568, Jewel, *Apology*, 1578 (both formerly chained); *Homilies*, 1673; Clerke, *Sermons*, 1637. Reported in 1950.
References: CCC Questionnaire, 1950.

WABERTHWAITE, Cumb. (Cumbria)
St. John. Carl.
[nil]
A ParLL of 33 vols. was est. in 1757 by the Associates of Dr Bray. In 1849 this library was one of those reported as being 'either wholly lost or reduced to a few tattered volumes'.
Catalogues: at Waberthwaite & Muncaster, n.d., Bray Associates Records, f.38, p.42.
References: Kelly, p.261.

WAKEFIELD, Yorks. (W.Yorks.)
All Saints (the Cathedral from 1888). Wakef.
[4v.] West Yorkshire Archives, Wakefield
DeskL: Bible, BCP, Robert Barker, 1616 (with notes of Scholey family); *Certain Sermons or Homilies*, 1623; *The Order of Ceremonies . . . at Windsor . . . Order of the Garter*, 1674; *Thirty-Nine Articles*, 2nd ed., 1694 (with inscription of Rob. Wilkes), together with 3 18th cent. books.

WALGRAVE, Northants.
St. Peter. Pet.
[2v.] *
DeskL: Bible, 1611; *Homilies*, 1676, formerly chained.
References: Cox & Harvey, p.340.

WALL, Staffs.
St. John the Baptist. Lich.
[nil] *
A ParL was est. in 1870 by the Associates of Dr Bray.
References: Shore, p.151.

WALMSLEY, Lancs. (G.Man.)
Christ Church. Man.
[11v.] Turton Tower
One of the 5 parochial libraries provided for under the will of Humphrey Chetham (see under: **Manchester**; the others were **Bolton [-le-Moors]**, **Gorton** and **Turton**). A list of 59 titles of books (in 91 vols.) is given in the Chetham Feoffees' Minute Book, 1659. 15 titles, nos.45–59, in 25 vols. were originally intended for Walmsley Chapel but were apparently never sent, and the 11

surviving vols. are now with the **Turton** books at Turton Tower. The inscribed panel for the Walmsley 'presse' was re-worked into an intricately carved oak sideboard in the Chetham's Library (see Evans, below, pl.7).

Catalogues: 1659 list: Chetham's Hospital and Library Archives (printed in Christie, pp.59–60 and in Evans, Appendix 3, pp.41–2); included by Evans, below, in a union cat. of the extant books in the 5 Chetham libraries, pp.45–53.

References: Christie, pp.57–62; Kelly, pp.84 & n.1; 249 & n.1; Evans, pp.18–22 & pl.7.

WALTON, Suffolk
St. Mary. St.E.
[1v.] *
DeskL: Bible, King James.

WANTAGE, Berks.
St. Peter and St. Paul. Ox.
[nil]
DeskL: The churchwardens' accounts in 1629 list all parochial books including a new addition, a copy of Josephus given by Francis Slade, vicar. In 1638 a copy of Foxe's *Book of Martyrs* was added. In 1890 Blades recorded that the then vicar recalled these chained books in his youth, but that they were no longer present.

References: Blades, BIC, p.43; Woolf, p.190 & n.78. quoting from Bodl. MS.Top. Berks.c.44, Wantage churchwardens' accounts, ff.94, 106, 116.

WARMINGHAM, Ches.
St. Leonard. Ches.
[1v.] *
DeskL (?): Sir Thomas Smith, *The Common-welth of England*, 1589.

WARMINSTER, Wilts.
St. Denys (ded. uncertain). Sarum
[nil] *
A ParL of 127 vols. was est. in 1840 by the Associates of Dr Bray, and augm. in 1856, 1870 and 1896.

Catalogues: 'List of books presented to the Warminster Theological Library, March 1840', Bray Associates Records, f.40, pp.317–20.

References: Bray Associates Annual Reports, 1900; Kelly, p.264; Shore, p.152.

WARRINGTON, Lancs. (Ches.)
St. Elphin. Liv.
[*c.* 2v.]
DeskL: Sir Simon Degge, *The Laws of Tythes or Tything*, 1684. A ParLL of 174 vols. was est. in 1844 by the Associates of Dr Bray, and augm. in 1890

and 1896. One book at Warrington has a bookplate indicating that it was from this collection: Arthur Duck, *The Life of Henry Chichele, Archbishop of Canterbury*, 1699, others may be so. A list compiled by Canon J. O. Colling, 1981 shows 34 titles, including 9 18th cent. and 9 19th cent. (pre-1844) books.
Catalogues: Bray Associates Records, f.41, pp.114–7; TS list, 1981 (copy in CCC).
References: Bray Associates Annual Reports, 1900; Kelly, p.262.

WARTON, Lancs.

In situ St. Oswald. Blackb.
[*c.* 48v.] *
A ParLL of 153 vols. was est. in 1846 by the Associates of Dr Bray, and augm. in 1869 and 1896. Some 48 vols. still survive in a cupboard in the vicarage.
Catalogues: Bray Associates Records, f.41, pp.154–7; TS list, 1996 (copy in CCC).
References: Shore, p.152; Bray Associates Annual Reports, 1900; Kelly, p.262.

WARWICK, Warwicks.

Transf St. Mary. Cov.
[1,383v. including bound vols. of pamphlets] Birmingham UL
The antiquary, John Rous (*c.* 1411–91) had a room built over the S. porch in 1464 to house his library (seen by Leland in the 16th cent.), and in the latter part of the 17th cent. books were placed in the vestry behind the Beauchamp Chapel, for which chains were supplied. In 1694 much of the church, including the Rous library, was destroyed but some of the books in the vestry of the Beauchamp Chapel survived. It is possible that the Rous books were dispersed before the fire. A sum of £5 was granted by Bray from funds at his disposal 1695–9, and in 1701 the library was re-founded as a lending library 'for the use of theological readers in Warwick and its neighbourhood', and a Donors' Book to record gifts was begun in the same year. About 500 works were presented by persons with Warwickshire connections, with Thomas Bray's name third in the list. The then vicar, William Edes, reported in the Notitia Parochialis of 1705: 'We are about setling a library, having had encouragement from Dr Bray of Sheldon in this county, Dr. Maynard of Boddington in Northamptonshire, and ye contributions of some of ye neighbouring clergy: the Lord Brook, Ld. Guildford, Ld. Digby, Lady Bowyer and others have been benefactors to it'. A ms. cat. was made by Moses Bray in 1709 and deposited in the Diocesan Register to comply with the Parochial Libraries Act of the same year. The short-lived Warwick Theological Book Society in the 1840s added *c.* 400 vols. to the library. In 1879 an attempt to sell the rare *Myrroure of Oure Ladye*, 1530, was thwarted. The existence of rare books prompted the preparation of another cat. by C. D. Newman and Herbert Hall, published in 1881 'for the use of the subscribers to the library' which was revised by W. J. Carter in 1910 (but repeating many of the errors in the earlier cat.). At some time before 1910 the books were moved from the main vestry to the room

behind the altar in the Beauchamp Chapel (photograph in Carter, below) where their condition deteriorated through lack of ventilation. Some of the badly affected books were treated by the Warwickshire RO, where all the pre-1800 books had been transferred. In 1960 the whole library was placed on loan in Birmingham UL for a term of 20 years, and sold to the University with faculty in 1980/1. In 1956, during re-cataloguing by Paul Morgan, a copy of the *Sarum Legenda* printed by Caxton in 1488, was identified, the most complete copy known (sold to the British Museum in 1958). The collection contains 2 incunables, 96 books printed 1500–99, 615 printed 1600–99; 252 printed 1700–99; 413 printed 1800–99; and 5 printed after 1900. Paul Morgan's article of 1964, below, provides a full list of 'former owners and donors of books, and persons connected with the Library', (pp.44–60), notes on books of unrecorded provenance, and bindings (with references to published descriptions). The books consist mainly of works on theology, patristics, religious polemics and controversy, classics and general literature.

Catalogues: 1709, by Moses Bray, incumbent (copies in Warwicks. RO, DR.97/7 and CCC); Newman & Hill cat. 1881, rev. 1910: Warwicks RO, DR.97/8; TS cat. by Paul Morgan, 1957 (with collection).

References: Notitia Parochialis, 1705: no.627; W. T. Carter, 'The library at St. Mary's Warwick', *Jnl of the Brit. Arch. Ass.*, N.S.16 (1910), pp.53–64; Paul Morgan and G. D. Painter, 'The Caxton Legenda at St. Mary's Warwick', *The Library*, 5 ser., v.12, no.4 (1957), pp.225–39; Paul Morgan, 'St. Mary's Library, Warwick', *Trans. and Proc. of the Birmingham Arch. Soc.*, v.79 (1964), pp.36–60; *idem.* 'A 16th-century Warwickshire library: a problem of provenance', *Book Collector*, v.22, n.3 (1973), pp.337–55; *ibid.* v.23, no.4 (1974), pp.570–2: notes by Morgan and C. B. L. Barr; P. S. Morrish, 'Warwick, Codrington and the future of the past', *Library History*, v.5, no.5 (1981), pp.162–5; DNB: Rous; Kelly, pp.91.n.4, 106.n.3, 255 & n.2, 259; Lambeth Palace MS.3223, ff.210–17: notes on provenance and bindings with rubbings by N. R. Ker.

WASDALE HEAD, Cumb. (Cumbria)
(Ded. unknown). Carl.
[nil]
A ParL was est. in 1766 by the Associates of Dr Bray, and augm. in 1815 with a further 15 vols. A letter from Mr Brockbank the curate, 13 Mar. 1805, stated that only 4 vols. remained of the 1766 library.
Catalogues: 1815. Bray Associates Records, f.38, pp.212–3 (including letter of 1805).
References: Shore, p.151; Kelly, p.261.

WASPERTON, Warwicks.
St. John the Baptist. Cov.
[iv.] Warwicks. CRO
DeskL: *Certain Sermons or Homilies*, 1683.

Wedmore: open bookcase

WEAVERHAM, Ches.
St. Mary the Virgin. Ches.
[1v.] *
DeskL: an early 15th cent. hornbook in a small oak tablet with two sunken panels, for teaching the alphabet and prayers.
References: Richards, p.346.

WEDMORE, Somerset
St. Mary. B & W
[*c.* 66 titles in 125v.]
A collection of 125 vols. was formed by William Andrews (1697–1759), born in Wedmore, a non-juror, during his travels on the continent, 1728–37. After his death in Bath in 1759 the books remained in his house at Wedmore until it was sold in 1792, when they were deposited in the room over the porch at St. Mary's church by his nephew, the Revd Henry Rawlins. Andrews had used the room as his study while working on his translation of Pascal's *Provincial Letters*, published in 1744. While not a parochial library by any definition, the books have been in their cupboard in the custody of the church since that date. They were all published on the continent between 1536 and 1737, and are mostly in French or Latin. The subject range is wide and includes ancient and modern history, the classics, memoirs and some theology, particularly writings on the Jesuits. The bindings are largely original, with gold-tooled spines.
Catalogues: by S. H. A. Hervey in *The Wedmore Chronicle*, v.1 (1887), pp.173–6 (copy in CCC).
References: Cosmo W. H. Rawlins, 'The library and peregrinations of a nonjuror', *Genealogists' Magazine*, v.10 (1947–50), pp.387–97.

WELFORD, Northants.
St. Mary the Virgin. Pet.
[nil?] NRC
John Peck (b. *c.* 1679), vicar from 1702, 'gave to the church vestry of Welford in 1703 Cooper's Dictionary, Theophylact's Works, and some other books'.
References: *Topographer*, v.3 (1790), p.303; Kelly, p.251 & n.2.

WELLS, Somerset
St. Cuthbert. B & W
[1v.] *
DeskL: Bible, 1634.
References: CCC Questionnaire, 1950.

WEM, Shrops.
St. Peter and St. Paul. Lich.
[12 titles in 15v.] Shrops. RRC
DeskL: of 17th and 19th cent. books.
Catalogues: MS cat. with collection (copy in CCC).

WENDLEBURY, Oxon.
St. Giles. Ox.
[nil]
A collection of 65 vols., mainly 17th cent. continental editions of the Greek and Latin Fathers, with 1 STC item, and an 8 vols. set of St. John Chrysostom, Eton, 1613, was bequeathed by Robert Welborne (*c.* 1695–1764), rector, 1730–64, as a parochial library. It was first kept in the N. transept of the church and later removed to the rectory. A notebook, formerly preserved in the church and now deposited in the Bodl. contains Welborne's own list of these books and his directions as to their future custody, with an extract from the Act of 7 Anne, 1709. Three of the directions are that 'the books may be consulted by any of the neighbouring clergy or other litterati, leave being first had of the . . . rector or his curate', that money given for augmenting the library should be spent on completing the collection of the works of the Fathers of the first 6 cents., and that no book in any modern language should be admitted. An added note records that in 1840 the books were repaired, many rebound, and all lettered 'Wendlebury' in gilt on the covers, at the expense of Jacob Ley (*c.* 1804–81), then Censor of Christ Church, Oxford, one of the patrons of the living. Despite this the books 'had become so musty and decayed that they were destroyed some years ago' (information from the rector in 1950).
Catalogues: notebook and list in Bodl. (TS transcript of extracts by N. R. Ker in CCC).
References: *N & Q*, no.180, 9.4.1853; Kelly, pp.93, 252; Palmer, PLCE1.

WENTNOR, Shrops.
St. Michael and All Angels. Heref.
[129v.] Shrops. RRC
Most of the books in the collection were bequeathed by Edward Rogers (1713–88), curate, who was also rector of Myndtown. There were originally *c.* 140 vols. 'over the communion Table in a large cupboard or sort of bookcase . . . chiefly works on divinitie . . . for the use of the clergyman and such of his parishioners who applied for them'. According to Medlicott (below) in 1931 there were 108 vols. including 72 pre-1700 works, the earliest being a Greek-Latin Concordance to the NT dated 1594. Some books were added by 'the Revd Jno. Cooke', rector in 1793. From the evidence of a former rector the collection was at various times, because of the amalgamation of livings, at **Church Pulverbatch, Norbury,** and **Myndtown,** before returning to its original home at Wentnor. The presence of service books and a copy of Jewel's *Works* suggests that a DeskL was absorbed into the collection. It was deposited in Shrops. Co.L by 1964, and then in Shrops. RRC, Shrewsbury.
Catalogues: TS by Shrops. Co.L, 1964; Shrops. PLC, 1971.
References: W. Medlicott, 'The library of Wentnor Church', *Trans. of the Shrops. Arch. and Nat. Hist. Soc.*, 46 (1931–2), miscellanea, pp.i–ii (quoting from BL Add.MS.21018); Kelly, p.253 & n.3; Kelly, Shrops., p.xi; Foster: Rogers.

WENTWORTH, Yorks. (S.Yorks.)
Holy Trinity Old Church (CCT). Sheff.
[nil]
A ParL of 67 vols. was est. in 1711 by the Bray Trustees for Erecting Parochial Libraries; the books were returned to the Associates in 1870.
Catalogues: MS. cat. no.9., Bray Associates Records, f.39, pp.137–40.
References: Bray Associates Annual Reports, 1870; Kelly, p.264.

WEOBLEY, Heref.
St. Peter and St. Paul. Heref.
[nil]
A ParL of 67 vols. was est. in 1710 by the Bray Trustees for Erecting Parochial Libraries; the books were returned to the Associates in 1869.
Catalogues: MS. cat. 'Weobly' no.19., Bray Associates Records, f.39, pp.77–80.
References: Bray Associates Annual Reports, 1869; Kelly, p.262.

WEST ALVINGTON, Devon
All Saints. Ex.
[nil] *
A ParL was est. in 1871 by the Associates of Dr Bray.
References: Shore, p.151.

WESTBURY-ON-SEVERN, Glos.
St. Peter and St. Paul. Glouc.
[1v.] *
DeskL: a copy of Foxe, *Book of Martyrs*, given by Thomas Man, of London, stationer, mutilated, formerly chained.
References: Lambeth Palace MS.3224; McKerrow, Dict. lists Thomas Man, senior, active 1576–1625, and junior, active 1604–10.

WESTERHAM, Kent
St. Mary the Virgin. Roch.
[nil]
Charles West gave several hundred vols. in 1756; by 1856 the books had gone, and the catalogue of them in the parish chest was no longer present when the parish records were deposited in Kent Archives Office in 1982.
References: N & Q, 2 ser., v.2 (1856), p.78; Kelly, p.248; Yates, p.165.

WEST MALVERN, Worcs.
St. James. Worc.
[nil?] NRC
There is a seal armorial bookplate reading, 'St. James's West Malvern. St. James's Library'.
References: I am indebted to Brian North Lee for this reference.

WEST MERSEA, Essex
St. Peter and St. Paul. Chelmsf.
[nil] *
A ParL was est. in 1891 by the Associates of Dr Bray.
References: Bray Associates Annual Report, 1895.

WESTON, Suffolk
St. Peter. St.E.
[1v.] Suffolk RO, Lowestoft
DeskL: BCP, 1662.

WESTON BEGGARD, Heref.
St. John the Baptist. Heref.
[nil?] NRC
DeskL: a list of c. 1650 includes the Great Bible of the largest volume; two copies of the BCP; Jewel's *Works*; 'Mr South his sermons, the second tome of homylies'.
Catalogues: c. 1650 list: Herefords. RO, AA.9/1.

WEST WICKHAM, Cambs.
St. Mary. Ely
[nil]
A note in the Parish Register reads: 'September 26th 1830. Parochial lending library, the gift of Lord Hardwicke, opened' and in another hand below 'But of very little service to this parish. Oct. 1838'.
References: CCC Questionnaire, 1950; Register: Cambs. CRO, P173/114.

WESTWOOD, Warwicks.
St. John the Baptist. Cov.
[nil] *
Surviving catalogues suggest that an SPCK lending library was in existence at least from 1857 to 1871. The 'Westwood Reading Room, established and opened by the Right Hon. Lord Leigh. 1871' had rules and a catalogue by 1878.
Catalogues: 1857, 1867–71; and 1878: Warwicks. CRO, Westwood DR 498/1–2.

WETHERSFIELD, Essex
St. Mary Magdalene. Chelmsf.
[2 titles in 6v.] Durham UL; Reading UL
In 1677 Henry Pelsant (d.1684), vicar 1662–84, after the death of his wife gave to Trinity Hall, Cambridge his house and its contents, including his library of books, on condition that they should be leased to the vicar for the time being at six pounds per annum of which sum £4 was paid to the College chest and the remainder divided among the Master and others. It is probable that the books remained at Wethersfield and were not deposited at Trinity

Hall, although 2 surviving vols. at Reading UL (Milton, *Paradise Lost*, 2 vols., 1751,) have a Trinity Hall bookplate with a 'cancelled' stamp, lifted from a bookplate reading 'Vicars Library, Wethersfield, Essex'. 4 other surviving vols., with the 'Vicars Library' bookplate (Hugo Grotius, *Opera Theologica*, 3v. in 4, Amsterdam, 1679) are in Cosin's Library Durham U. There are no books at St. Mary Magdalene, Wethersfield.

References: Will (microfilm): Essex CRO, Chelmsford: D/AMR7/121; William Warren, *Warren's Book*, ed. A.W.W. Dale, Cambridge, 1911, pp.151, 287–8. I am indebted to Andrew Lacey, Trinity Hall Library, Cambridge, and to Dr A. I. Doyle, Durham UL, for information in this entry.

WHALTON, Northumb.
St. Mary Magdalene. Newc.
[nil] *
DeskL: Archdeacon Sharp noted copies of Jewel's *Works* and Charles I, *Works* on his visitations in 1723–31. This was one of 92 parishes in the Northumberland Archdeaconry granted a ParLL under a scheme devised by Bishop Shute Barrington, carried out by Archdeacon R. G. Bouyer by 1823 (see p.57), and recorded as still possessing books in visitation returns, 1826–8.
References: Day, pp.99, 102 & n.38.

WHICHFORD, Warwicks.
St. Michael. Cov.
[1v.] Warwicks. CRO
DeskL: BCP, 1693.

WHINBURGH, Norf.
St. Mary. Nor.
[3v.] Norwich CL
DeskL: BCP, 1662; *Certain Sermons or Homilies*, 1635 (1633); Bible, 1611.

WHITCHURCH, Hants.
All Hallows. Win.
[2v.] Hants. RO (and elsewhere, see below)
A ParL of 81 vols. was est. in 1720 by the Bray Trustees for Erecting Parochial Libraries. This library was partly withdrawn by the Associates in 1878, and is not recorded after 1880. An inscription on the vestry wall states that 'for any book borrowed out of this place the full value therof shall be laid down untill the same is return'd safe and unblemish'd. 1725'. A monument in the church to Joseph Wood (d.1731), vicar 1691–1731, records that he 'left a handsome library of books for the use of his successors'. There were 587 vols. including a Sarum Breviary, 1525, a Chaucer of *c.* 1545 and a Book of Hours in Slavonic, Moscow, 1639. In 1713 a faculty had been granted for converting part of the N. aisle to house a parish library. It was reported in 1849 that the books had 'fallen into almost total neglect and misuse'. About 660 vols. were

sold with faculty at Sotheby's, 7 Nov. 1927, lots 1–176. The sale cat. describes
329 printed items and 16 MSS. The medieval MS (lot 4) is now in the
Newberry Lib., Chicago, and 2 others are in the Bodl. and the Queen's
College, Oxford. Lots 9, 29 and 64 went to the BM and 166 vols. in 45 lots to
Sir Leicester Harmsworth: 14 of these vols. are now in the Folger Lib.,
Washington (7 Nov. 1927, lots 5, 8, 15, 48, 53, 77, 95, 102, 129, 141, 144,
152, 163, 170, with, respectively, the following red nos. on the spines: 186, 63,
208, 174, 4, 136, 57, 45, 94, 93, 36, 37, 73, 78). Some of the early-printed
books in the library had belonged to Richard Brooke (d.1593), buried in
Whitchurch and with a monument in the church. Two vols. survive in Hants.
RO (PZ1–2): 'A Royal Purveyance, 1575', a ms. given by Joseph Wood, edited
and published by Walter Money, Newbury, 1891 (but omitting the last 2 items
in the MS), and a BCP, printed by Edward Whitchurche, 1552 (imperfect and in
poor condition, with notes related to the Ayliffe family of Whitchurch).

Catalogues: Hants. RO: 1) the Bray library cat. of 1720 (another copy is in
Bodl.Rawlinson D.834, f.31: see pp.53–5); 2) 'A catalogue of the parochial
library (exclusive of those books in the press) at Whitchurch in Hampshire,
August 30th, 1730': listing 587 vols. and omitting the Bray Trustees library; 3)
a 1901 TS copy of Edward Edwards cat. of 1850, listing 1,193 titles, including
all the pamphlets but excluding the MSS. The original vol. containing 1) to 3)
is in the Edward Edwards collection Manchester Central Lib. Edwards' cat.
lists some items which do not appear to have been sold in 1927, e.g. Lyle,
Euphues, 1607; Works of Sir Thomas More, 1557; Augustine, *Meditationes*,
1502. Some of these works were at Whitchurch in 1921 but are no longer
there; 4) Diocesan Records I/I/2/A/282: Catalogue of books in the Whitchurch
Parochial Library, 1844 (c. 618 titles, no dates).

References: Faculty, 1713: Hants. RO, PW9; correspondence and papers
relating to sale at Sotheby's 1927–9, sale cats. marked with prices realized,
faculty, 1927: Hants. RO, PW11; papers of J. F. Williams concerning
Whitchurch ParL (given by N. R. Ker, 1968): Bodl.MS.Top. Hants.c.6.e.11;
Lambeth Palace MSS.3223, ff.218–22 & 3224: notes by N. R. Ker; VCH,
Hants. v.4, p.303; Edward Edwards, Free Town Libraries, 1869, pp.9–11;
Select Committee Report, 1849, p.25; Bray Associates Annual Reports, 1880;
The Times, 13 Oct. 1927, p.12; Kelly, pp.91.n.4, 96, 196, 247, 262 (but not
'All Saints').

WHITCHURCH, Shrops.
St. Alkmund. Lich.
[3,388v.] Shrops. RRC

A library was est. with a collection of 2,250 vols. belonging to Clement
Sankey (or Zanchy) (c. 1632/3–1707), rector from 1684, bought from his
executors by Jane Egerton, Dowager Countess of Bridgewater, in 1707 for
£305 and given by her to the church in 1717, 'for ever for the use of the rectors
for the time being'. It was supplemented by books bequeathed by Francis
Henry, Earl of Bridgewater (1756–1829), rector of Whitchurch from 1797,

and of **Myddle** from 1780, until his death. Bridgewater also left 'the sum of 150l to rectors to be invested in his name, and the dividends thereof to be expended by him, together with the money arising from the sale of his lordship's wines and liquors in his cellars at Whitchurch, in the purchase of printed books for the use of the rectors of that parish for the time being'. In 1849 there were estimated to be 3,077 vols. including 834 folios. The books were kept at the rectory until the 1960s when they were deposited in Shrops. Co.L. and later in the Shrops. RRC, Shrewsbury. They are largely 17th and 18th cent. theology, but history, biography and general literature are also represented. Many of the books were printed on the continent.

Catalogues: a vol. formerly at Whitchurch rectory contained: a) a full list of books without headings and at the end a page in which are listed the books taken out by Jane, Countess of Bridgewater for the use of Mr Henry Egerton; b) a list of the 2,250 books bought by Jane Countess of Bridgewater in 1707 from the executors of Dr Clement Sankey; cat. 1841 (formerly at Whitchurch rectory); Shrops. Co.L card cat. photocopied in 2 vols. 1968 (copies in Bodl. and Reading UL); included in Shrops. PLC, 1971.

References: *N & Q*, v.8 (1853), p.570; Select Committee Report, 1849, p.225; Kelly, pp.95, 253; Kelly, Shrops, pp.viii–ix; Venn: Sankey; DNB: Egertons.

WHITCHURCH, Warwicks.
St. Mary the Virgin. Cov.
[1v.] Warwicks. CRO
DeskL: *Certain Sermons or Homilies*, 1683.

WHITEGATE, Ches.
St. Mary. Ches.
[nil?] NRC
DeskL: in 1973 Richards noted 'a number of early printed prayer books, Bibles and old documents'.
References: Richards, p.354.

WHITTINGHAM, Northumb.
St. Bartholomew. Newc.
[nil] *
One of 92 parishes in the Northumberland Archdeaconry granted a ParLL under a scheme devised by Bishop Shute Barrington, carried out by Archdeacon R. G. Bouyer by 1823 (see p.57), and recorded as still possessing books in visitation returns, 1826–8.
References: Day, p.102 & n.38.

WIGGENHALL, Norf.
St. Mary the Virgin (CCT). Ely
[nil?] NRC
DeskL: William Blades noted books chained to a desk in the chancel in 1866

and 1890, and in Ker's notes, 1950–69, those remaining are described as: Bible, AV, 2nd ed, 1611, and Foxe, *Book of Martyrs*, n.d., 2 of 3 vols. once chained, given in 1633 (one vol. repaired by Gray of Cambridge).

References: Blades, *Book-Worm*, p.173; *idem.* BIC, p.44; Lambeth Palace MS.3224.

WIGTON, Cumb. (Cumbria)
St. Mary. Carl.
[nil]
One of the 10 parishes in the diocese of Carlisle given 16 books in 1687 under the will of Barnabas Oley (see pp.34–5 and table on pp.444–52). Articles of agreement sealed in that year between Thomas Tullie, chancellor of the diocese of Carlisle, Henry Geddes, vicar, and the churchwardens, enforced on Wigton's vicars a covenant whereby they promised not to remove books from the church. This may have been the ParLL granted £1 by Bray from funds at his disposal, 1695–9, later supplemented by a ParL of 67 vols. est. in 1710 by the Bray Trustees for Erecting Parochial Libraries, and a ParLL of 164 vols. est. in 1783 by the Associates of Dr Bray. The Bray library is not recorded after 1890, but in 1956 some books were reported as being stacked in a cupboard in a small study at the back of the vicarage. None now remain.

Catalogues: early 18th cent. cat. and copy of Bray's rules: Cumbria RO, PR/36/42; another copy: MS. cat. no.35, 2 May 1710. Bray Associates Records, f.39, pp.17–20; ParLL of 1783, Bray Associates Records, f.34, pp.168–71.

Reference: articles: Cumbria RO, PR36/40–41; Bray Associates Annual Reports, 1890; Kelly, pp.246, 258, 261; Woolf, pp.188–9 & n.71, 192–3.

WILLEN, Bucks.
St. Mary Magdalene. Ox.
[nil]
Richard Busby (1606–95), headmaster of Westminster School, in his will bequeathed books 'for the use of the ministry to be placed in the library belonging to the church at Willen . . . built . . . by me at my own great charge'. St. Mary Magdalene was constructed 1679–80 by Robert Hooke, who had been a boy in Busby's house. Busby also left books to **Cudworth** and **Martock**. In the 1848 cat. of the library 148 titles are marked 'Willen'. Other books were bequeathed by James Hume (*c.* 1676–1734), rector of Bradwell, Bucks., 1729–34. The library of 619 vols. was moved from the church to the vicarage before 1895 and was destroyed there by fire on 1 May 1946.

Catalogues: *A Catalogue of Books in the Library at Willen*, Newport Pagnell printed, 1848 (preface by George Phillimore, vicar; copies at Westminster School with the Trustees of Dr Busby's Charity, Dean's Yard, Westminster Abbey).

References: G. F. Russell Barker, *Memoir of Richard Busby*, 1895, p.143; Pevsner, *Buckinghamshire*, 1960, p.293; Kelly, p.245; Venn: Hume.

Wimborne Minster: the foot of the spiral staircase in the thirteenth-century vestry leading to the chained library, still housed in the fourteenth-century Treasury above

Wimborne Minster: a general view of the chained library established in 1686 by
William Stone (1615–85)

WIMBORNE MINSTER, Dorset
St. Cuthberga (Cuthburga). Sarum

In situ [380v.]

The churchwardens' accounts, almost complete from 1475, record gifts of
books, and payments for books, desks and chains from 1495 onwards, but the
library was properly est. in 1686 by William Stone (1615–85), one of the three
presbyters conjointly in charge of the Minster church during the Civil War
period and later (1641–5 and 1661–81), with a gift of c. 90 vols. from his
library in Oxford, a collection of the works of the Fathers, mainly in Latin,
with a few books in Greek, Hebrew and English. The books were delivered
before Lady Day 1686 and the churchwardens' accounts for the period record
payments for all the materials for building the library. In a codicil to his will
of 1695, Roger Gillingham (d.1695), of Middle Temple, gave 'unto and for the
use of the new erected library of Wimborne Minster . . . all the books I lately
bought for that purpose that is to say the Poliglott Bible with the lexicon
thereunto belonging . . . [a list of books follows] . . . and so many of my best
folio, 4to, 8vo bookes which are not law bookes as are fittest and most useful
. . . worth £10 . . . not only for the use of the clergy . . . but for the use of the
gent. shopkeepers and better sort of inhabitants in and about the towne . . . my
executors shall not deliver until the bookes already given by . . . William
Stone or any other . . . should be chained to their places as is most usefull in
other public librarys and chain and places be provided for the bookes hereby
given . . . for which purpose . . . I give . . . £10'. The no. of Gillingham's books

is estimated at 88 vols., mostly in English, and on a wide variety of subjects, including history, geography, politics, classics, husbandry, gardening and wine-making. Some of the books have titles and nos. on the fore-edge; they were used as the basis for the first ms. cat. of 1725, which lists works in 279 vols. including the books of 10 later donors, notably Thomas Anstey (c. 1635–68), vicar 1661-8, who gave 25 books, and Samuel Conant (c. 1627–1719), who gave 18 books. The library is still in its original home, the 14th cent. Treasury, access to which is by a spiral staircase from the 13th cent. vestry below. From 1855 to 1857 the library was rebuilt, the roof, shelves, windows and floors were replaced, and the books re-chained. All the library chains from the 17th cent. were removed and have been lost, and those now seen are from the 1850s, and were factory-made. Over 150 vols. are still chained. Under a bequest by William Fitch (d.1740) a reading-desk was provided in the S. choir aisle, with four books chained to it, 'the bible, the Whole duty of Man, Mr. Nelson's Feasts and Fasts, and Doctor Sherlock's concerning death'. At the time of rebuilding, two books survived, *The Whole Duty of Man*, 1702, and a Bible, 1703, which, with their original chains, were placed in the library. During the latter part of the 18th cent. and the first half of the 19th cent. the library was badly neglected, resulting in decay, disbound books, the loss of plates and torn pages. After the rebuilding many books were repaired, and a printed cat. appeared in 1863, showing that 30 books had been lost since 1725, and including provenance information. The oldest work in the library is the MS. Regimen Animarum, dated 1343, and there are other fragments of medieval MSS. The oldest printed book, and the only incunable, is Anselm's *Opuscula*, Basel, 1495 (?), with 8 leaves from another incunable of 1477. There is a fine contemporary binding, with panel-stamps by Reynes, on a copy of Theophylact, *In Quatuor Euangelia*, Coloniae, 1532 (Oldham, Panels, HE21 and REL5; Hobson, Panels, pp.34–5). The library also contains a fine collection of early English church music.

Catalogues: 1725 ms. cat.; W. G.Wilkinson, *Catalogue of the Books in the Minster Library, Wimborne*, Wimborne, 1863 (185 books by title, with notes of donors and former owners; copy in CCC); William Blades, 'Catalogue of the chained library at Wimborne' (Bibliographical Miscellanies, no.2), 1890, pp.14–19 (lists 181 titles); TS cat. by H. B., Salisbury, 1949, by titles and authors (with '24 titles not in the 1863 list and 11 titles of that date now missing', copy in CCC); a complete computerised cat. has been made by Mr W. A. Tandy, to whom I am indebted for much of the information in this entry.

References: Blades, BIC, pp.5–13; *idem*, 'On chained libraries', *The Library*, v.1 (1889), pp.413–5; J.M. J. Fletcher, 'Chained books in Dorset and elsewhere', *Proc. of the Dorset Nat. Hist. Soc. & Antiq. Field Club*, v.35 (1914), pp.8–26; *idem*. in N & Q, 18 Oct. 1913; John Hutchins, *The History and Antiquities of the County of Dorset*, 1796–1815, v.3, p.204; Streeter, pp.295–7; Rigby Graham, 'The manacled books at Wimborne Minster', *The Private Library*, v.7, no.3 (1966), pp.61–4; David M.Williams, 'A chained library', *ABMR*, no.9 (1978), pp.387–8; Helen Hixson, *Chains of Knowledge:*

Wimborne Minster Chained Library, Wimborne, 199–; W. A. Tandy, *The Chained Library in Wimborne Minster*, Wimborne, 2001; Kelly, pp.93, 246; Ker, MMBL, IV, 1992, p.577; Foster: Anstey, Conant; Lambeth Palace MS.3223, f.223: notes on the incunable.

WINDERMERE, Westm. (Cumbria)
St. Martin. Carl.
[3v.] *
DeskL: Erasmus, *Paraphrases*, 1516; Jewel, *Apology*, 1562; Geneva Bible, 1611: all chained.

WINFARTHING, Norf.
St. Mary. Nor.
[3v.] Norwich CL
DeskL: *Certain Sermons or Homilies*, 1683; *A Collection of Articles*, 1675; Jewel, *Defence*, 1567.

WINSHAM, Somerset
St. Stephen. B & W
[1v.] *
DeskL: Foxe, *Book of Martyrs*, 4th ed., 1583.

WINSLOW, Bucks.
St. Laurence. Ox.
[14 items in 21 v.] Bodl.
Under his will dated 30 July 1714, John Croft, vicar 1684–1716, bequeathed 'unto the . . . bishop of London for the tyme being, the . . . Archdeacon of St. Albans for the tyme being and the vicar and churchwardens of the parish of Winslow . . . Nicolaus de Lyra Commentary on the whole Bible the Old Testament and New in six volumes in folio, together with the Repertorium or index which makes a seventh and also Poles Synopsis Criticorum etc in novum Testamentum in two large volumes in folio my poor tribute towards a parochiall library to be contained in the vestry belonging to the parish of Winslow forever for the use of such persons who shall resort thither to consult the meaning of the Holy Scriptures'. Few books were added after this date. They were kept in a locked glass-fronted cupboard inset in the N. aisle wall. 8 vols. were deposited in Bucks. Archit. and Arch. Soc. from 1941–6 and then returned. In 1997 the surviving books were deposited in the Bodl. The Nicolaus de Lyra *Postilla* and *Repertorium*, 6 vols. Basel, J. Petri and J. Froben, 1506–8, have Croft's signature, and that of Henry Jolyffe (d.1573), and are in bindings made at Cambridge by Nicholas Spierinck, who was active there *c.* 1503–31 (see Morgan, below). The Matthew Poole, *Synopsis Criticorum*, v.4, pts. 1–2, 1674–6 is also still present. A first edition of the Bible, AV, 1611 is in a binding by Matthew Dagnall (1658–1736), of Aylesbury, dated 1699.
Catalogues: TS list and rubbings of bindings by N. R. Ker: Lambeth Palace

MS.3223, ff.224–6; TS list by J. S. Antrobus in his 'Public library provision in North Buckinghamshire' (M.A. Dept. of Library and Information Science, Loughborough U of Technology, 1986), p.140; detailed TS list by Paul Morgan, 1986, with notes on provenance and bindings (copy in CCC).
References: Croft's will: Herts. RO, 158 AW8 (I am indebted to Jane Francis for this reference); DNB; Venn: Jolyffe.

WIRKSWORTH, Derbys.
St. Mary. Derby
[nil] *
The catalogue and rules of a parochial library, dated 1853, survive in Derby PL. It may well have been set up in the 1830s by the Revd John Harward (c. 1785–1859) and housed in the old Anthony Gell School in Church Walk on the E. side of the church.
References: Derby PL: HA 027.8/20084; Foster: Harward.

WISBECH, Cambs.
St. Peter and St. Paul. Ely
[c. 1,200v.] * Wisbech and Fenland Museum, Wisbech
It is uncertain when the parochial / town library was est.: a date between 1651 and 1654 is most likely. In 1651 William Coldwell (c. 1624–1702), vicar 1651–1702, gave, with other donations, 'this paper booke', i.e. the ms. record of the town library, which includes catalogues, lists of benefactors and loans. In 1654 William Fisher, High Sheriff of Cambridge and Huntingdon, gave 14 vols. to the library, and John Thurloe (1616–68), Cromwell's Secretary, gave 81 vols. Many books once belonged to Thomas Thurswell (d.1585), of King's College, Cambridge. In the Wisbech Corporation records for 1657 'it was agreed . . . that the Town Bailife should buye two new chaires to sett in the librarye at the church'. Samuel Pepys visited the library on 18 Sept. 1663 and wrote of 'sundry very old abbey manuscripts'. Richard Middleton Massie (1678–1743), appointed first keeper in 1714, in the preface to his printed cat. of 1718 (see below) gives the foundation date as 'about the time of the Restoration' when 'ten Capital Burgesses of the town . . . prepared the chamber over the church-porch with shelves and other necessaries, for the reception of books. And several other gentlemen at the same time liberally contributed both money and books . . . . It was afterwards in a manner quite neglected, till the year 1712. When some of the neighbouring clergy and gentlemen, considering the advantage of parochial libraries, form'd themselves into a club or society; and agreed annually to contribute twenty shillings each to buy books'. There are 23 'gentlemen' listed who gave money and books, including Thomas Plume (1630–1704), the future founder of the library at **Maldon**, Essex, a further 8 benefactors in 1712, and 14 'gentlemen of the club' in 1718. The 1718 cat. lists 697 titles. The town library records include a list of donors drawn up before 1664, catalogues of the 17th, 18th and 19th cents., and entries for loans from 1715 onwards. In 1836 the books were

removed from the room above the porch in the church to the Town Hall, and in 1891 to Wisbech Museum. From 1940–46 the books were kept in what proved to be a damp cellar. In 1952 the MSS and some books were rebound and repaired by J. P. Gray of Cambridge. Of the 9 medieval MSS there is firm evidence that one came from the Abbey of Bury St. Edmunds (see Ker, below); there are 12 English MSS (and 9 others); 12 incunables, and 18 books printed 1500–25. The earliest printed book is: Savonarola, *Practica de Aegritudinibus*, Florence, Bonus Gallus, 1479. There are *c.* 30–40 blind-stamped bindings by named binders, including one by John Reynes of London (after 1597), and 3 identified Oxford bindings, *c.* 1515–1620.

Catalogues: 17th cent, 18th cent. (R. M. Massie) and 19th cent. (by George Thompson, Master of the Grammar School, 1831): in the Wisbech Town Book MS.; *A Catalogue of Books in the Library at Wisbech in the Isle of Ely*, Wisbech [?], 1718, by R.M. Massie (TS transcript in CCC); a cat. drawn up in 1889 by Mr Oliver, curator, can no longer be found; card cat. completed in 1985 (including some provenances but no index).

References: M. R. James, 'On the Abbey of St. Edmund at Bury', *Camb. Antiq. Soc.*, 28 (1895), p.220; F. J. Gardiner, *History of Wisbech*, 1898, pp.214–19; Historical Manuscripts Commission, 9th Report, 1883, pp.293–4 (inaccurate); Ruth Banger, 'Some thoughts on the Town Library', *Wisbech Soc. Mag.* (1983), pp.3–5; Manley, SPCK, pp.237–8; Martin, pp.66–8; Kelly, pp.77 n.3, 96, 98 & n.2, 122, 195, 245; Best, pp.29–39, 82–114; Ker, MMBL, IV, 1992, pp.651–60; Graham K. Scott, 'English public and semi-public libraries in the provinces, 1750–1850', (Library Association Final Exam Essay, 1951), pp.45 n.6, 46 n.23; Ker, Pastedowns, 754, 1845, cclxxvii; Pearson, 870.17; DRB2, p.41 (for the later history of the collections); DNB: Thurloe, Turswell, Plume; Venn: Coldwell, Massie.

WITHAM, Essex
St. Nicholas. Chelmsf.
[nil]
There was a ParLL here from at least as early as 1751 as a surviving register gives details of loans from 1751–75 and 1847–68, together with a list of 282 books added in 1840 or subsequently.
Catalogues: Essex RO, Chelmsford: D/P 81/28/3,4; TS list of 48 books in the library before 1846 from this MS (copy in CCC).
References: noted by E. J. Erith, *Essex Parish Records*, 1950, p.234, and in *Library History*, v.2, no.6 (1972), p.250; Kelly, pp.97, 247; Best, pp.47–51, 164–72.

WITHERSLACK, Westm. (Cumbria)
St. Paul. Carl.
[5v.] Cumbria RO, Kendal
A ParL of 36 vols. was est. in 1757 by the Associates of Dr Bray. 5 vols. from

this library (with dates ranging from 1699 to 1724) are now deposited in the Kendal RO with some later books.
Catalogues: 'in the par. of Beetham', Bray Associates Records, f.38, p.33.
References: Kelly, p.263.

WITHINGTON, Hereford.
St. Peter. Heref.
[nil]
The only evidence for a ParL is a passage in a letter from William Brome of Withington to Thomas Hearne, 13 Feb. 1716–17: 'Pray, do you think Plinie's Natural Hist. Lat. in usum Delp. a proper book for a Parochial Library, to be placed in the church? We are divided about it in our opinions, and I should be glad to know your thoughts of it'.
References: Thomas Hearne, Remains and Collections, *Oxford Hist. Soc.*, v.6 (1902), p.21; Kelly, p.248.

WITNEY, Oxon
St. Mary the Virgin. Ox.
[2v.] Oxfordshire Archives
DeskL: BCP and Psalms, 1687 (2 copies, presented 1753).

WOLLASTON, Northants.
St. Mary. Pet.
[nil]
A ParL of 72 vols. was est. in 1711 by the Bray Trustees for Erecting Parochial Libraries. In 1849 this library was reported as one of those 'either wholly lost or reduced to a few tattered volumes'.
Catalogues: MS. cat. no.48. Bray Associates Records, f.39, pp.125–8; a copy of the original register is now: Bodl. MS.Top.Northants.c.42.
References: Select Committee Report, 1849; Kelly, p.263.

WOLLATON, Notts.
St. Leonard. S'well
[1v.] in situ *; [1v.] Nottingham UL
DeskL: *Certain Sermons or Homilies*, 1683 (on the flyleaf 'Liber Ecclesiae Parochialis Wollton'). The mid 15th cent. Antiphonal, given *c.* 1460, alienated, then restored by the gift of Lord Middleton in 1925, is now deposited in Nottingham UL. There is evidence of a DeskL in the church from the 1460s (Savage, below).
References: Savage, p.129; Ker, MMBL, IV, 1992, pp.667–8.

WOLVERHAMPTON, Staffs. (W.Mids.)
St. Luke. Lich.
DeskL: Geneva Bible, 1597 (given in World War II).
References: *Church Times*, 24.3.2000.

Woodbridge: part of the bookcase high up on the east wall of the vestry housing the library established there by Thomas Hewett, rector of Bucklesham, 1744–73

WOLVERLEY, Worcs.
St. John the Baptist. Worc.
[1v.] * Worcester Diocesan RO
DeskL: Jewel, *Defence of the Apology*, 1611.

WOMERSLEY, Yorks. (S. Yorks.)
St. Martin. Wakef.
[5 titles ~~in 12v.~~] York Minster Lib.
In 1705 the incumbent recorded 'some bookes of ye modern divines as Pareus etc. lately given to ye vicars of Womersley by Samuel Mellish of Doncaster Esqre'. Mellish (d.1707) was a barrister and recorder of Doncaster, where he was buried. The books had long been regarded as lost but were re-discovered in 1978 among the Wakefield Diocesan Records at the West Yorks. Archive Office, and in 1985 they were deposited in York Minster Library. Most of them bear an inscription: 'The gift of Samuel Mellish esq. to the vicar of Womersley and successors, February 16, 1698 [/9], Ebor'. They consist of 8 vols. of a made-up set of Calvin's Latin works, Lyon and Geneva, 1557–1617, with 4 other continental books, 1588–1638.
Catalogues: TS handlist with introduction and notes on bindings by C. B. L. Barr, 1985 (copy in CCC).
References: Notitia Parochialis, 1705: no.575; Kelly, p.256; Barr, pp.36–7.

WOODBRIDGE, Suffolk
St. Mary the Virgin. St.E.
[165 titles in 194v.]
Under a codicil to his will dated 25 Nov. 1772 Thomas Hewett (d.1773), rector of Bucklesham, 1744–73, 'would have the Fathers and that sort of learning sent to Woodbridge with the old cases'. These books, housed in glass-fronted cases, probably the originals, are still high up on the the E. wall of the vestry. In addition to the works of the Fathers, there is a considerable subject range and variety in this library, which includes Caroline divinity, medical treatises, botany, astronomy, and miscellanea. Many of the books have Hewett's neat signature and often the date of purchase and some topical notes. A few books were added to the collection in the 19th cent. There are 11 STC and 50 Wing items. Hewett also bequeathed many books to **Ipswich** library (see Blatchly, below). The deposit of this collection in Suffolk RO was approved in 2001.
Catalogues: A ms. cat. of 1785 is in the parish chest; a detailed ms. cat. and index was compiled by V. B. Redstone in 1736 (copies in the parish chest and on slips in Woodbridge PL; revised version by Canon J. A. Fitch); included in Suffolk PLC, 1971.
References: Fitch, 1964, pp.83–5; John Blatchly, *The Town Library of Ipswich*, 1989, pp.188–9; Kelly, p.254; DRB2, p.551.

WOODCHURCH, Ches.
Holy Cross. Ches.
[*c.* 29v.] Cheshire RO; Liverpool CL
In 1959 there were 45 vols., mainly of the 17th and 18th cents., kept at the rectory, one of which was inscribed: 'July the 9th 1727, the gift of the Revd. Mr. Thos. Green Rectr of Woodchurch for an addition to the library there: and for the perpetual use chiefly of ye ministers yt shall be her'after resident there'. Thomas Green was rector 1705–47. This library was deposited in 1967 in Birkenhead PL and, after reorganisation, the residue was deposited in Chester RO. A ParLL of 146 vols. was est. in 1793 by the Associates of Dr Bray. It would appear that this collection, or part of it, was transferred to the former St. Aidan's College Library at Church House, Liverpool, as 2 items dated 1789 and 1793, one consisting of detached boards only with a Bray Library bookplate for Woodchurch, 1793, are included in the St. Aidan's College Library now deposited in Liverpool CL.
Catalogues: TS list of books at Whitchurch Rectory, n.d. (Bodl.MS. Eng.Misc.c.360, copy in CCC); TS list, Birkenhead Public Libraries, 1967 (copy in CCC); Bray Library: Bray Associates Records, f.38, pp.185–7.
References: Kelly, pp.245, 261; DRB2, p.469. I am indebted to John Vaughan for information in this entry.

WOODPLUMPTON, Lancs.
St. Anne. Blackb.
[nil]
A ParL of 39 vols. was est. in 1757 by the Associates of Dr Bray. In 1849 this library was reported as being one of those 'either wholly lost or reduced to a few tattered volumes'.
Catalogues: Bray Associates Records, f.38, p.34.
References: Select Committee Report, 1849; Kelly, p.262.

WOOLER, Northumb.
St. Mary. Newc.
[nil] *
One of 92 parishes in the Northumberland Archdeaconry granted a ParLL under a scheme devised by Bishop Shute Barrington, carried out by Archdeacon R. G. Bouyer by 1823 (see p.57), and recorded as still possessing books in visitation returns, 1826–8.
References: Day, p.103.

WOOTTON ST LAWRENCE, Hants.
St. Lawrence. Win.
[1v.] Hants. RO
DeskL: Erasmus, *Colloquia*, Amsterdam, 1650.

WOOTTON WAWEN, Warwicks.
St. Peter. Cov.
[12 titles in 9v.]
George Dunscomb (d.1652), vicar 1642–52, 'gave some good books for the use of the parishioners, which were preserved in the vicaredge house, till at the request of the people they were chained to a desk in the south isle of the church, April 11th, 1693'. Thomas Baker, the Cambridge historian, whose quotation this is, was present when this occurred. A description of the desk and chaining system, together with a photograph, is given in Streeter, below. In PLCE1, 1959, this desk was illustrated as plate IV(c); it has since been scandalously altered into a display case. The books include sermons and other theological works published 1578–1673, some signed by Dunscomb.
Catalogues: listed by Blades, BIC, p.46; ms. list n.d. (in Bodl.MS.Eng.Misc.c.360, copy in CCC).
References: Foster: Dunscomb; BL: Thos. Baker Collect. Harl.2045, p.463; Streeter, pp.291–2; *N & Q*, 5 ser., v.8 (1877), p.325; Kelly, pp.77 & n.2, 85 & n. 255; DRB2, p.570.

WORCESTER, Worcs.
All Saints. Worc.
[1v.] *
DeskL: Bible, 1603: rebound but retaining original covers and complete chain.
References: Blades, BIC, p.46.

Wootton Wawen: the display case (after alterations) containing chained books
given by George Dunscomb, vicar 1642–52

WORSBROUGH, Yorks. (S.Yorks.)
St. Mary. York
[516 titles in 556v.] Sheffield UL
Obadiah Walker (1616–99), a native of the village and later Master of
University College, Oxford, in 1673 presented 2 boxes of books 'for the use of
the schole'. Some of the books given later were described as being 'given for
the lecturers and vicars of the church and their successors'. The lecturer or
vicar was often also the schoolmaster, and the clergy and school libraries were
kept together in the vicarage. The collection at some date came to include the
parochial library in the neighbouring parish of **Tankersley**. There were 588
books described in the 1744 cat. In 1959 556 vols. were deposited in Sheffield
PL, and in 1993 the collection was transferred on permanent loan to Sheffield
UL. There are 40 STC books, 90 Wing and 44 books with continental
imprints, 1500–50. The main subjects are classical texts, grammars and
theology, with a few early medical works.
Catalogues: 1675 cat. in Sheffield PL (PR 3/34); 1705 list related to 1675 cat.
in Sheffield PL (modern copy at University College, Oxford); 1774 cat.; TS
cat. after deposit in Sheffield PL, 1963 (includes also a cat. of the Tankersley
ParL, with a joint index of authors, editors and commentators: photocopy in
Lambeth Palace MS.3094, ff.237–323, copy in CCC); Susan M. Cost, 'The
Worsbrough Grammar School Collection: a bibliographical catalogue of the

works in the collection dated 1500–1575' (Sheffield U, MA in Librarianship thesis, 1975).

References: *N & Q*, 1st ser. v.12 (1855), p.298; Joseph Wilkinson, *Worsbrough*, 1879, pp.378–81; P. J.Wallis, in *Yorks. Arch. Jnl*, v.39 (1958), pp.159–60; Kelly, p.256; Bill Report, 1970; Barr, p.32; DRB, p.503 (detail omitted in 2nd ed.); Pearson, A164.3; DNB: Walker.

WORSTEAD, Norfolk.
St. Mary. Nor.
[10 titles in 9v.] Norwich CL
DeskL: BCP, Bible, 1594; Bible, 1611; Jewel, *Works*, 1611; John Trapp, *Commentary*, 1656; Erasmus, *Paraphrases*, 1548; Richard Hooker, *Of the Lawes of Ecclesiastical Politie*, 1617; William Lilly, *Merlini Anglici Ephemeria*, 1650; Psalter, 1638; Henry Wharton, *Fourteen Sermons Preached in Lambeth Palace*, 1697.

WOTTON-UNDER-EDGE, Glos.
St. Mary the Virgin. Glouc.
[*c.* 317v.] Christ Church, Oxford
A library was bequeathed to the parish by John Okes (d.1710), vicar of Whitegate, Cheshire, 1665–90. The books were housed in a room over the S. porch until 1964 when they were deposited on indefinite loan in the library of Christ Church, Oxford, patron of the living, for safe-keeping. According to a report by Bigland (below) in 1889 there were 'sexcentos aut plures libros'. The collection is chiefly 17th cent. theology, with an emphasis on Oriental studies. There are 30+ STC and 135+ Wing items. A number of books are signed by Robert Cholmondeley and other members of his family. He was patron of Oke's living at Whitegate, Cheshire, of which he was deprived as a non-juror in 1689. Some books have prices paid in them and others a pasted slip with a no. The stamps of Edward Gwynn appear on no.212.

Catalogues: TS cat. 1906; modern ms. cat. (with collection); TS list of 'Books not in the typescript catalogue of 1906' (13 items): Bodl.MS.Eng.Mis.C.360 (copy in CCC).

References: Samuel Rudder, *A New History of Gloucestershire*, Cirencester, 1779, p.851; R. Bigland, *Historical, Monumental, Genealogical Collections Relative to the County of Gloucestershire*, suppl. pt.9, 1889, under Wotton-under-Edge; Paul Morgan, *Oxford Libraries outside the Bodleian*, 2nd ed., 1980, p.33; Kelly, p.247; Lambeth Palace MSS.3223, ff.229–30, & 3224: notes on provenance and rubbings of bindings by N. R. Ker; Pearson, 1786.1.

WRINGTON, Somerset
All Saints. B & W
[13v.] * in situ; Somerset RO
DeskL: the churchwardens' accounts, 1650–59, give details of payments 'for tymber & making of the desks & furmes', and 'for chaynes & claspes to

chayne the Bookes of Martires given by Mr fra: Roberts Rector unto the church', and 'for an iron rod to lock the bookes beside the broach, pd for a brass for one of the bookes', and 'for putting a chain & lock to the books of the Covenants of god given . . . by Mr Francis Roberts rector'. Roberts (c. 1609–1675), was rector 1650–75, and the books he gave are still retained. They were originally chained by the spines to a desk in the chancel (a photograph of the desk taken in 1893 is now Bodl. 2589.b.4: it shows 8 chained books). After the restoration of the church in 1859 the books were removed from the desk and a new glazed case made for them, which in 1962 was moved from the vestry to the W. wall of the N. aisle. 7 vols. retain their chains: Bible, Barker, 1617; *Clavis Bibliorum*, 3rd. ed, 1665; *God's Holy Covenant*, 1657; Jewel's *Apology* and *Defence*, 1571, bound together; Foxe's *Book of Martyrs*, 3v, 1570; 5 other pre-1700 books are held by the church, and 2 18th cent. books by Taunton RO.

References: I am grateful to Commander M. C. Lawder, Brook House, Wrington for information in this entry.

WYTHOP, Cumb. (Cumbria)
St. Margaret. Carl.
[nil] *
A ParL of 35 vols. was est. in 1757 by the Associates of Dr Bray; it is not recorded after 1880.
Catalogues: in Par. of Brigham, Cumb., Bray Associates Records, f.38, p.43.
References: Bray Associates Annual Reports, 1880; Kelly, p.261.

YARNTON, Oxon.
St. Bartholomew. Ox.
[6v.] *
In the churchwardens' accounts for 1857/8 there is a record that Vaughan Thomas (c. 1775–1858), vicar from 1803, gave 'to the present and all future vicars and churchwardens of the parish . . . all these pastoral and educational books, bound or unbound which are in the cupboards I lately put up in the Spencer aisle underneath the little desks'. 6 vols. survive, 4 Bibles: 1770, 1842, 1850 and c. 1880, and 2 BCP: 1776, 1815.
Catalogues: detailed TS list by Paul Morgan, 1988 (copy in CCC).
References: Foster: Thomas.

YATTON, Heref.
Chapelry. see: **Much Marcle**

YAXLEY, Suffolk
St. Mary the Virgin. St.E.
[nil]
William Henry Sewell (1836–96), vicar 1861–96, left 1,014 vols. 'in trust to the Archdeacon of Suffolk for the use of his successors in the the benfice of Yaxley subject to the conditions specified in his will'. The books remained at

the vicarage until the benefice was united with Thornham Magna and
Thornham Parva in 1949 when the vicarage was sold and the library,
presumably, with it. From one of the 2 surviving ms cats., the books ranged
over a wide variety of subjects, including bee-keeping, ecclesiology, local
history and novels.
Catalogues: 2 ms. cats. n.d. (one by Thomas Archbold rector of Burgate):
Suffolk RO, Ipswich, FB 128/115/2–3.
References: Fitch, 1965, p.86; Venn: Sewell.

YELDEN, Beds.

St. Mary. St.Alb.
[c. 434v.] Bedford Central Lib.; Stodden Rectory, Huntingdon
A collection of books was bequeathed by Edward Swanton Bunting (1791–
1849), rector 1830–49, and housed in the rectory. The rectory was sold before
1970 and the books deposited in Bedford Central Lib. with the exception of
c. 34 vols, mainly collected plays, retained by the rector. There are c. 20 pre-
1700 books, including editions of Cicero, Amsterdam, Blaeu, 1656 and 1659.
They are mainly theological with a few books on medicine, education and
mechanics.
Catalogues: card cat. with collection; TS 'List of of titles at Stodden Rectory,
April 1995' (copy in CCC).
References: Venn: Bunting; N & Q. 5 ser. v.8 (1877), p.325; Bill Report, 1970;
DRB2, p.11.

YORK, Yorks.
All Saints' Pavement. York
[3v.] *
DeskL: a 16th [?] cent. lectern, removed from St. Crux Church, and copies of
Jewel, *A Reply unto Mr. Harding's Answeare*, 1566 (once chained to it), and
BCP 1678 and 1680.
References: Blades, BIC, 1892, p.81.

YORK, Yorks.
St. Mary Castlegate. York
[6v.] Borthwick Institute, York
Early records state that some service books and others were bequeathed to St.
Mary's Castlegate by the rector, John Pickering in 1394. In 1705 the incumbent recorded: 'Here is a library settling for ye rector and his successors being
in a room in Sr Henry Thomson's hospital late alderman of this city and
parish wch joyns upon ye churchyard, but the room to be in my possession, yet
ye design advances slowly'. 6 vols. were deposited in the Borthwick Institute in
1950, published 1608–1730, including 2 STC items.
References: Barr, p.33 (quoting Savage, p.128 and J. Raine, ed. *Testaments
Eboracensia*, i, pp.194–6); Notitia Parochialis, 1705: no.1128; Kelly, pp.91
n.4, 256.

ISLE OF MAN

ANDREAS, I of M
St. Andrew. S & M
[2 titles in 1v.] Manx National Heritage
A list of books dated 1746 contains 30 titles, including: I of M list, nos. 1–11, 13, 16, 18, 20, 27–33, 34(?), 36–9, and 1 later title (see p.443). 2 books were added on the visitation return for 1754. By 1761 St. Matthew's Gospel in Manx was in the library. The books were kept in the Rectorial Mansion house in the curate's custody. None have survived save 2 titles (bound together) held in the Manx National Heritage: I of M list no.38, and one later deposit.
References: Ferguson, pp.42–3.

ARBORY, I of M
St. Columba. S & M
[nil] *
In the visitation return for 1738 a list of 25 titles is given: I of M list, nos. 1–3, 5–9, 11–18, 20, 23–4, 26, 28–33, 36–8 (see p.443); 9 titles were then missing. In 1759 9 vols. were added. The library was kept in the vicar's house. No books had survived by 1975.
References: Ferguson, pp.54–6.

BALLAUGH, I of M
St. Mary. S & M
[4v.] * Manx National Heritage
The visitation return for 1738 lists 32 titles, including: I of M list, nos. 1–11, 13–24, 27–34, 36–8 (see p.443); 2 titles were then missing. The books were kept at the Mansion house (i.e. the rectory). 7 titles still survived in 1975 at the rectory (but are not there now); I of M list, nos. 2, 29, 31 and 33 have been deposited in Manx National Heritage.
References: Ferguson, pp.38–40, 81.

BRADDON, I of M
St. Brendan. S & M
[nil] *
The visitation return of 1738 lists 25 titles, including: I of M list, nos. 1–9, 12–16, 18, 20–1, 27, 34, 36–8 (see p.443); 9 titles from the list were then missing. In 1757 6 vols. were added, including the Manx Catechism. The books were kept at the minister's house; none had survived by 1975.
References: Ferguson, pp.36–7.

In situ
& trans?

DOUGLAS, I of M
St. Matthew the Apostle. S & M
[18v.] * in situ, and Manx National Heritage
A chapel was built at Douglas to serve the needs of the people and consecrated by Bishop Wilson in 1708. The chaplain from this date was also master of the Grammar school, founded in the early 18th cent. The Douglas Lib. was attached to the School. In 1725 Thomas Bray donated sets of Blair's *Sermons* (I of M list, nos. 29–33), his *Bibliotheca Parochialis*, and *Papal Tyranny* (I of M list, no. 34) and Henry More's English works, to the libraries of Douglas and Castletown. The Convocation return of 1738 lists 51 titles in the Douglas Chapel Lib., and in 1740 Bishop Wilson gave a further 18 titles (2 of which are now in Manx National Heritage: Benjamin Hoadly's *An Answer to Dr. Hare's Sermon*, 1720, and Henry Dodwell's *A Discourse concerning the Rite of Incense in Divine Offices*, 1711). Another list of *c.* 1740 in Bishop Wilson's Notebook is largely a repeat of the 1738 list, but includes the names of donors of some of the books. The library at Douglas was retained in the School house and was a lending library for students. The 16 vols. still at St. Matthew's are from the original foundation. A ParLL was est. in 1859 by the Associates of Dr Bray but has not survived.
References: Bray Associates Annual Reports, 1880; Shore, p.153; Ferguson, ch. 6, pp.72–80.

GERMAN, I of M
St. German. S & M
[nil]
A visitation return of 1738 lists 28 titles, including: I of M list, nos.1–6, 8, 11–23, 27–34, 36–8 (see p.443); 6 vols. from the list were reported as missing. In 1740 Bishop Wilson gave 3 books and a book box with lock 'for the parochial library of this parish'. The visitation list of 1757 noted an additional 4 titles. No books had survived by 1975.
References: Ferguson, pp.60–1.

JURBY, I of M
St. Patrick. S & M
[17v.] Manx National Heritage

Trans?

In the visitation return for 1738 the vicar reported that he had the (then) complete no. of 34 books, including: I of M list, nos. 1–21, 23–34, 36–8 (see p.443); 10 vols. were added in the 1744 list, but 6 vols. were missing. Another 3 vols. appear in the visitation list for 1754. The library was kept in the vicarage 'in a box for the purpose'. 17 vols. have been deposited with parish records in Manx National Heritage: I of M list, nos. 1–3, 5, 6, 14, 17, 18, 27–33, and 2 vols. donated later. The Bray vol., no.18, includes a ms. list of books (copy in CCC) given to the parish; the last dated item is 1740.
References: Ferguson, pp.40–2.

KIRKBRIDE, I of M
St. Bridget. S & M
[2v.] *
In the 1735 visitation list there are 27 titles, including: I of M list, nos. 1–9, 12–18, 20–1, 26–34, 36–8 (see p.443), and a Book of Homilies. 5 vols. were added in 1755, but 5 vols. from the original list were missing. In 1757 the library was kept in the rector's lodgings at Ballakilley. 2 vols. have survived: Pearson on the Creed (I of M list, no. 1), and a copy of Bacon's *Essays*, 1718.
References: Ferguson, pp.43–5.

LEZAYRE, I of M
Holy Trinity. S & M
[3v.] Manx National Heritage
A list of books dated 1729 contains 38 titles, including: I of M list, nos. 1–34, 36–8 (see p.443); 4 vols. were reported missing in 1738; in 1761 I of M list, no. 39 and 7 further titles were added. The collection was kept in the vicarage. 3 vols. are now deposited in Manx National Heritage: I of M list, nos. 1, 3 and 18.
References: Ferguson, pp.45–6.

LONAN, I of M
All Saints. S & M
[nil] *
A list of books dated 1738 contains 29 titles, including: I of M list, nos. 1–10, 12–3, 15–21, 24–34, 36–8 (see p.443). In 1739 a further 8 vols. were sent and in 1757 a further 6 (but 7 were reported as missing). The library was kept at the vicar's house. No books had survived by 1975.
References: Ferguson, pp.48–50.

MALEW, I of M
St. Mark. S & M
[4v?]
In the report for 1738 there is no list but it is stated that 'the Vicar of Malew acknowledges to have all the books of the parochial library'. In 1761, however, this list shows only 25 titles, including: I of M list, nos. 1–4, 6–18, 23, 26, 28–34, 36–8 (see p.443). None of these books had survived in 1975. However, the parish does hold copies of Hooker, 1636; Josephus, 1693; and Erasmus, 1744 (see table on pp.444–52). It is probable that these books came originally from the Castleton Lib., a public lending library and not a ParL, as none of them appear in the ParL lists. They were perhaps borrowed by the Revd John Woods, vicar of Malew in the first half of the 18th cent., and not returned by him or his successors. If this is the case, these books are the only survivors of the Castleton Library, founded in *c.* 1650 and destroyed by fire in 1844.
References: Ferguson, pp.54, 81–2.

MAROWN, I of M
St. Runius. S & M
[nil] *
In the return of 1738 28 titles were listed, including: I of M list, nos. 1–18, 20–23, 27–31, 36–8 (see p.443); 3 vols. were then missing. In 1757 I of M list, no. 39 and 5 other vols. were added. The books were kept in the vicar's house. None had survived by 1975.
References: Ferguson, pp.51–2.

MAUGHOLD, I of M
St. Maughold. S & M
[4 titles in 2v.] * Manx National Heritage
In the 1738 return 31 titles were listed, including: I of M list, nos. 1–23, 26–34, 36–8 (see p.443); 3 titles were then missing. By 1748 they were 'well-secured in a press'. 3 additional titles were listed in 1757. The books were kept in the vicar's study. 2 vols. have been deposited in Manx National Heritage: I of M list, no.10, and 3 titles added later.
References: Ferguson, pp.46–8.

MICHAEL, I of M
St. Michael and All Angels. S & M
[nil] *
The return of 1738 lists 30 titles, including: I of M list, nos. 1–23, 27–34, 36–8, 40 (see p.443); 4 titles from the list are noted as missing. The books were kept at the vicar's mansion house; none had survived by 1975.
References: Ferguson, pp.37–8.

ONCHAN, I of M
St. Peter. S & M
[nil] *
William Gell, vicar, reported that all the books were present in the return of 1738, but no list was provided. A list of 1754, the year before Bishop Wilson's death, contains 37 titles, including: I of M list, nos. 1–23, 27, 29–34, 36–9 (see p.443). St. Matthew's Gospel in Manx was present by 1761. The books were kept in the vicar's house; none had survived by 1975.
References: Ferguson, pp.50–1.

PATRICK, I of M
Holy Trinity. S & M
[nil] *
The return made in 1738 lists 30 titles, including: I of M list, nos. 1, 3–5, 13, 15, 23, 27–33, 36–8 (see p.443). Some 4 titles were missing then, but there were 20 additional titles. Kirk Patrick was not consecrated until 1714 and the library there differed markedly from the others on the Isle of Man since the earlier books for the scheme had been largely distributed. The library was

collected and given by Bishop Wilson himself, together with a large press and lock. No books had survived by 1975.
References: Ferguson, pp.58–60.

RAMSEY, I of M
St. Paul. S & M
[nil] *
In the return of 1754 19 titles are listed, including: I of M list, nos. 4, 17, 26, 28–33, 37 (see p.443), and 13 later titles. A box was provided for the library. The return for 1761 lists 4 additional titles, including St. Matthew's Gospel in Manx. Bishop Wilson gave the library himself, including a press with a lock. No books survived by 1975.
References: Ferguson, pp.61–2.

RUSHEN, I of M
Holy Trinity. S & M
[nil] *
A list submitted in 1738 contains 26 titles, including: I of M list, nos. 1–5, 7, 10–12, 15–20, 23, 35, 37–38 (see p.443); 8 titles were listed as missing. In 1759 14 additional titles were noted. By 1757 the books were kept at the vicar's house. None had survived by 1975.
References: Ferguson, pp.56–8.

SANTAN, I of M
St. Sanctain. S & M
[nil] *
The return of 1738 lists 25 titles, including: I of M list, nos. 4–11, 14–20, 23, 26–34, 36–8 (see p.443) with 5 titles missing, and 6 later books. In 1739 5 further titles were added. No books survived by 1975.
References: Ferguson, pp.52–4.

WALES

ABERGAVENNY, Mon.
St. Mary. Mon.
[?] NLW
A ParLL of 157 vols. was est. in 1784 by the Associates of Dr Bray. A
surviving bookplate is dated 1785. The remains of this library were absorbed
into the Llandaff Diocesan Lib. soon after it was est. in 1883. Some 250 vols.
of the rare and valuable books from the Llandaff collection were deposited in
the NLW in 1943: the Bray library books can no longer be identified.
Catalogues: Bray Associates Records, f.38, pp.176–8.
References: Tallon, p.53; Kelly, p.266 & n.1. I am indebted to Brian North
Lee for the reference to the 1785 bookplate.

ABERNANT, Carm.
St. Lucia. St. D.
[nil] *
A ParL of 35 vols. was est. in 1765 by the Associates of Dr Bray. In 1849 this
library was reported as being 'either wholly lost or reduced to a few tattered
volumes'.
Catalogues: *Catalogues of Libraries in the Diocese of St. David's*, Carmarthen, 1807, no.8, 820–38.
References: the total no. of vols. sent is noted in Bray Associates Records, f.38,
pp.117–20; Select Committee Report, 1849; Kelly, p.265.

ALLTWEN, Glam. (Neath Port Talbot)
St. John the Baptist. Llan.
A ParL was est. in 1896 by the Associates of Dr Bray, and transferred in 1900
to **Pontardawe**, Glam. (in the diocese of St. David's).
References: Bray Associates Annual Report, 1900.

BALA, Mer. (Gwyn.)
Christ Church. St.As.
[nil] *
A ParLL of *c.* 177 vols. was est. in 1763 by the Associates of Dr Bray.
Catalogues: Bray Associates Records, f.38, pp.97–102.
References: Kelly, p.265.

BANGOR, Caer. (Gwyn.)
St. Deiniol (Cathedral). Ban.
[?] Bangor UL
The Bangor Diocesan Lib., created by Deed of Settlement in 1709, was one of
the 4 clerical lending libraries created by the SPCK in each of the Welsh

dioceses, 1708–11 (the others were at **Carmarthen, Cowbridge,** and **St. Asaph**). They were larger than the ordinary Bray parochial libraries, and books could be borrowed by anyone living within 10 miles who was either a clergyman, schoolmaster, trustee, or a contributor to the library of money or books to the value of 10s. The library was first housed in Bangor CL and then, in 1960, deposited in Bangor UL.

References: Tallon, pp.20–21; Kelly, pp.107, 110–11, 260; DRB2, p.678.

BANGOR MONACHORUM, Denbigh. (Wrexham)
St. Dunawd. St.As.
[nil] *
In the Flintshire RO there is 'A catalogue of the books belonging to the Bangor Vestry Library in the year 1833'.
Catalogues: Flints. RO, P/3/1/4 (copy in CCC).

BANGOR TEIFI, Card. (Ceredigion)
St. David. St.D.
[nil] *
A ParL of 36 vols. was est. in 1768 by the Associates of Dr Bray.
References: the total no. of vols. sent is noted in Bray Associates Records, f.38, pp.147–9; Kelly, p.265.

BEAUMARIS, Ang.
St. Mary and St. Nicholas. Ban.
[nil] *
A ParLL of 259 vols. was est. in 1796 by the Associates of Dr Bray, and augm. by 98 vols. in 1840; it is not recorded after 1900.
Catalogues: Bray Associates Records: 1796, f.38, pp.195–7; 1840, f.41, pp.24–6.
References: Shore, p.150; Bray Associates Annual Reports, 1900; Kelly, p.264.

BRECON, Brecon. (Powys)
St. Mary. S & B
[nil?]
A ParLL was est. in 1834 and 're-modelled' in 1845, on a subscription basis. The printed cat. of the later date lists 294 titles; nos. 295–300 are not used, and nos. 301–42 were presented by the Brecknock District Committee of the 'Christian Knowledge Society', 28 Oct. 1845. The books are mainly pastoral and educational.
Catalogues: *Catalogue of the Books belonging to the Brecknock Lending Library in the Vestry Room of St. Mary's,* Brecon, 1845 (copy in NLW, with MS additions; photocopy in CCC).

BRECON, Brecon. (Powys)
St. John the Evangelist (from 1923 the Cathedral). S & B
[?]
The nucleus of the Brecon Diocesan Lib. was the old parochial collection, built up over the years by gifts and bequests, chiefly from the local clergy.
References: Tallon, p.39; DRB2, pp.678–9.

BUTTINGTON, Mont. (Powys)
All Saints. St.A.
[nil] *
A grant of 15s. towards the est. of a ParL was made by Bray from funds at his disposal, 1695–9.
References: Kelly, p.259.

CAERLEON, Mon. (Newport)
St. Cadoc. Mon.
[7v.] NLW; Los Angeles, Clark Lib.
A ParLL of *c.* 113 vols. was est. in 1757 by the Associates of Dr Bray. The remains were absorbed into the Llandaff Diocesan Lib. in the cathedral soon after its est. in 1883. The rare and valuable books from this collection were deposited in the NLW in 1943. 6 vols. from the parochial collection have now been identified: 5 Wing items, 1673–94, and a Greek and Latin Bible, Basel, 1550. The book labels read: 'This book belongs to the parochial library of . . . in the County of. . .' with 'lending' and 'Caerleon' added in ms. (the same label was used at **Llandaff**). A further vol. with this label has been located in the Clark Lib., Los Angeles: Oldbury 66/2 (see p.446).
Catalogues: Bray Associates Records, f.38, pp.18–22.
References: Tallon, p.53; Kelly, p.266 & n.1.

CAERNARFON, Caer. (Gwyn.)
St. Mary. Ban.
[nil] *
A ParLL of *c.* 72 vols. was est. in 1769 by the Associates of Dr Bray, and augm. in 1840; it is not recorded after 1900.
Catalogues: Bray Associates Records, f.38, pp.153–5.
References: Shore, p.150; Bray Associates Annnual Reports, 1900; Kelly, p.264.

CARDIGAN, Card. (Ceredigion)
St. Mary. St.D.
[nil] *
A ParLL of *c.* 151 vols. was est. in 1765 by the Associates of Dr Bray, and augm. by 180 vols. in 1823, and again in 1872, 1883 and 1889.
Catalogues: Bray Associates Records: 1765, f.38, pp.121–7; 1823, f.40, pp.75–80; *Catalogues of Libraries in the Diocese of St. David's*, Carmarthen,

1807, no.6, 656–790; ms. register of books, 1765–1896, with printed rules, 1872, and a borrowers' register, 1872–1915: NLW MS 22706C (copy in CCC).
References: Shore, p.153; Bray Associates Annual Reports, 1890; Kelly, p.265.

CARMARTHEN, Carm.
St. Peter. St.D.
[14v.?] NRC
The Carmarthen Diocesan Lib., est. by deed of settlement in 1708 at Carmarthen (for St. David's), was the first of 4 clerical lending libraries created by the SPCK in each of the Welsh dioceses, 1708–11 (the others were at **Bangor, Cowbridge** and **St. Asaph**). It was set up, largely through the advocacy of John Vaughan (1663–1722), in a room in the charity school given and equipped by the vicar Edmund Meyrick (1636–1713). There were some 4 cases of books to the value of *c*. £60 which could be borrowed by all clergy and schoolmasters living within a radius of *c*. 10 miles. After the collapse of the school building in 1727 the library was removed to the basement of the episcopal palace at Abergwili. By 1807 the books were at the vicarage of St. Peter's, but after 1819 there is no further record of this library. However, in 1895 a ParLL was est. by the Associates of Dr Bray. According to Howells, below, some 14 books still survive in the vestry of St. Peter's. An 18th cent. catalogue lists *c*. 220 vols, including 25 vols. of miscellaneous tracts, 9 16th cent., 97 17th cent., and 72 18th cent. titles.
Catalogues: ms. 'Catalogue of ye books in ye lending library in ye town of Carmarthen', 18th cent.: Flints. RO, D/E/15/8 (copy in CCC; MS. Cat. 1765, NLW MS 15809E; *Catalogues of Libraries in the Diocese of St. David's*, Carmarthen, 1807, no.34, 1624–1843, incorporated into 'A catalogue of the books in the Carmarthen Diocesan Library', vol.2, appendix V of Howells, below.
References: Tallon, pp.9–19 (corrected in Howells); Kelly, pp.107, 110–11, (corrected in Howells); Howells, v.1, ch.4 and v.2, appendix V; DWB: Meyrick, Vaughan.

CELLAN, Card. (Ceredigion)
All Saints. St.D.
[6v.] *
A ParL of 36 vols. was est. in 1765 by the Associates of Dr Bray. 4 books from this library, and 2 other pre-1700 books, have survived.
Catalogues: *Catalogues of Libraries in the Diocese of St. David's*, Carmarthen, 1807, no.15, 960–82.
References: the total no. of vols. sent to 'Kellan' is noted in Bray Associates Records, f.38, pp.117–20; Kelly, p.266.

CHEPSTOW, Mon.
St. Mary. Mon.
[?]
A ParL of 72 vols. was est. in 1712 by the Bray Trustees for Erecting Parochial

Libraries. In 1849 this library was reported as being one of those 'either wholly lost or reduced to a few tattered volumes'.

However, the remains were absorbed into the Llandaff Diocesan Lib. soon after its est. in 1883. The rare and valuable books from Llandaff were deposited in the NLW in 1943, but books from the Chepstow parochial collection cannot now be identified.

Catalogues: MS cat. no.45, Bray Associates Records, f.39, pp.209–12 (another copy in Bodl. MS.Rawl.D.834, ff.20–21).

References: Select Committee Report, 1849; Tallon, p.53; Kelly, p.266 & n.1.

CHIRK, Denbigh (Wrexham)
St. Mary. St.As.
[nil?]
A ParLL was est. by 1853 on a subscription basis. The printed cat. lists *c.* 239 titles in 271 vols. under 12 classes, mainly scriptural, doctrinal and pastoral, but also including books of instructional tales, history, biography, geography and travels, useful arts, natural history and poetry.

Catalogues: *Catalogue of the Parochial Lending Library, Chirk, Denbighshire*, Oswestry, 1853 (copy in NLW; photocopy in CCC).

CHURCH STOKE, Mont. (Powys) see under England

CILIAU AERON, Card. (Ceredigion)
St. Michael. St.D.
[nil?] NRC
A ParL of 35 vols. was est. in 1765 by the Associates of Dr Bray.

Catalogues: *Catalogues of Libraries in the Diocese of St. David's*, Carmarthen, 1807, no.17, 1007–37.

References: the total no. of vols. sent to 'Kilie Ayron' is noted in Bray Association Records, f.38, pp.117–20; Kelly, p.265.

CILMAENLLWYD, Carm.
St. Philip and St. James. St.D.
[?] NLW
A ParLL of *c.* 69 vols. was est. at Cilmaenllwyd in 1764 by the Associates of Dr Bray. The library is listed in the 1807 catalogue of diocesan libraries, where it is stated that the books were then kept at Tenby. The remnants of the library were absorbed into the **Llanboidy** collection, now in the NLW. A no. of vols. have a label similar to those in the **Caerleon** and **Llandaff** collections with 'lending' in ms. preceding 'parochial'.

Catalogues: Kilmaenllwyd [sic]: sent to found a LL May 1764, Bray Associates Records, f.38, pp.111–14; *Catalogues of Libraries in the Diocese of St. David's*, Carmarthen, 1807, no.2, 195–275.

References: Kelly, p.265; Eiluned Rees, *Libri Walliae*, no.4555.

CLYDAU, Pembs.
St. Clydai. St.D.
[nil] *
A ParL of *c*. 35 vols. was est. in 1766 by the Associates of Dr Bray. In 1849 this library was reported as one of those 'either wholly lost or reduced to a few tattered volumes'.
References: the total no. of vols. sent to 'Clydey' is noted in Bray Associates Records, f.38, pp.130–3; Kelly, p.266.

CONWY, Caer. (Gwyn.)
St. Mary. Ban.
[nil?]
A ParLL of 22 titles in 37 vols. was est. in 1880 at Conwy for the rural deanery of Arllechwedd, and transferred in that year to **Llandudno**.
Catalogues: ms. and printed list, printed rules and ms. borrowers' register, 1880–1: NLW, Gwynfryn Richards Collection (copy in CCC).

COWBRIDGE, Glam. (Vale of Glamorgan)
Holy Cross. Llan.
[?] * Ewenny Priory; Representative Body of the Church in Wales, Cardiff
The Cowbridge Diocesan Library, est. by deed of settlement in 1711 for the Llandaff diocese, was one of 4 clerical lending libraries created by the SPCK in each of the Welsh dioceses, 1708–11 (the others were at **Bangor**, **Carmarthen** and **St. Asaph**). In 1736 the local clergy est. the Cowbridge Book Society, with an annual subscription of 5s., to add books to the Diocesan Library (in 1817 this was effectively replaced by the Cowbridge Clerical Book Club). From 1848 onwards, when the room over the vestry in Holy Cross in which they were housed was put to another purpose, the books were apparently lost, but early in the 20th cent. the surving books were discovered in a local cottage from which they were rescued and housed in private hands in Ewenny Priory. In 1827 a ParLL of *c*. 128 vols. was est. in Cowbridge School by William Williams 'for the use of the divinity students of that place' through the Associates of Dr Bray. One bookcase at Holy Cross church with books from one or both of these collections was given to the Representative Body of the Church in Wales, Cardiff.
Catalogues: a printed cat. of 1793, discovered in the parish records, lists over 400 vols., mainly theology (photocopy in Glamorgan RO: D/D Xgc 288; another copy is in the NLW); 1827 cat., Bray Associates Records, f.40, pp.173–6.
References: Tallon, p.50; Ewart Lewis, 'The Cowbridge Diocesan Library, 1711–1848', 2 pts. *Jnl. of the Hist. Soc. of the Church in Wales*, v.4 (1954), pp.36–44; *ibid*. v.7 (1957), pp.81–91; Kelly, pp.107, 110–11, 260 & n.2; Michael Wilcox, 'The Cowbridge Lending Library', Glamorgan Record Office, Annual Report, *c*. 1996, pp.14–17.

CRICCIETH, Caern. (Gwyn.)
St. Catherine. Ban.
A ParL, formerly at Llanystumdwy, was est. in 1880 by the Associates of Dr Bray, and incorporated into **Porthmadog** by 1900.
References: Bray Associates Annual Reports, 1880, 1900.

CYFFIG, Carm. (Dyfed)
St. Cyffig. St.D.
[nil] *
A ParL of 35 vols. was est. in 1766 by the Associates of Dr Bray.
Catalogues: *Catalogues of Libraries in the Diocese of St. David's*, Carmarthen, 1807, no.24, 1210–40.
References: the total no. of vols. sent to 'Kiffig' is noted in Bray Associates Records. f.38, pp.130–3; Kelly, p.265.

DAROWEN, Mont. (Powys)
St. Tudur. Ban.
[58v.] NLW
A ParL of 67 vols. was est. in 1710 by the Bray Trustees for Erecting Parochial Libraries, and augm. in 1872 and 1889. 50 vols. of the original deposit have survived, including: nos. 2–5, 7–8, 10–12, 15–24, 26–7, 33–6, 38–45, 58, 60–65, 67–8, 70 (see pp.49–51). In 1938 the vols. were wrongly reported as having been transferred to Machynlleth. Since 1959 some 12 vols. have been lost, but a further 10 located that were not in the original list. The collection was deposited in the NLW in 1986, and then included an additional 8 vols. from the later Bray deposits.
Catalogues: ms. cat. no.29 for 'Darrowen', Bray Associates Records, f.39, pp.33–6 (copy in NLW, Darrowen Parish Records; photocopy in CCC); ms. cat. 5 Sept. 1749: NLW: SA/MISC 730 (copy in CCC); computer catalogue print-out of Darrowen depost in NLW, 1996 (copy in CCC).
References: Shore, p.151; Bray Associates Annual Reports, 1938; Kelly, p.266.

DENBIGH, Denbigh.
St. Mary. St.As.
[nil] *
A ParLL of 60 vols. was est. in 1814 by the Associates of Dr Bray, and augm. with a further 92 vols. in 1840, and augm. again in 1890.
Catalogues: Bray Associates Records, 1814, f.38, pp.253–4 (visited by the Secretary in 1839 and 34 books marked in the list as still present); 1840, f.41, pp.22–3.
References: Shore, p.152; Bray Associates Annual Reports, 1890; Kelly, p.265.

DEUDDWR, Mont. (Powys). [**Deytheur**]
[place not listed in Crockford]
A ParLL of *c.* 88 vols. was est. in 1767 by the Associates of Dr Bray, and

augm. again in 1870. In 1849 this library was reported as being one of those 'either wholly lost or reduced to a few tattered volumes', but a remnant or later deposit was transferred to **Welshpool** in 1896.

References: the total no. of vols. sent to 'Deuddwyr' is noted in Bray Associates Records, f.38, pp.130–3; Shore, p.153 (as 'Deytheur'); Bray Associates Annual Reports, 1900; Kelly, p.266 (as 'Deythur / Deuddwr').

DOLGELLAU, Mer. (Gwyn.)
St. Mary. Ban.
[c. 208v.]
A ParLL of 271 vols. was est. in 1796 by the Associates of Dr Bray, and augm. in 1840 with 66 vols., and again in 1871, 1889 and 1896. In 1839 David Pugh, curate 1833–41, gave to the Secretary of the Associates a list of books then in the library, marking up only 129 vols. as still present from the original collection. They were housed in 2 old cupboards at the foot of the tower and suffered from damp. The books were cleaned, repaired and listed by Kenneth Kitchin, a local antiquary, some time before 1996, and they are now housed on shelves in the vestry. About 48 vols. from the original Bray library have gold-tooled nos. on the spines. The collection consists of c. 50 vols. of 17th and 18th cent. divinity, including vols. of collected sermons, the remainder being 19th cent. theology.

Catalogues: Bray Associates Records, 1796, f.38, pp.188–94; 1840, f.41, pp.42–3; 4 lists of later Bray books, 1840–96 are with the collection.

References: Bray Associates Annual Reports, 1900; Venn: Pugh; Kelly, p.265.

DOWLAIS, Glam. (Merthyr Tydfil)
St. John the Baptist. Llan.
[nil?] NRC
A ParL was est. in 1883 by the Associates of Dr Bray.

References: Bray Associates Annual Reports, 1885.

EBBW VALE, Mon. (Blaenau Gwent)
Christchurch. Mon.
[nil] *
A ParL was est. in 1896 by the Associates of Dr Bray.

References: Bray Associates Annual Reports, 1900.

EGLWYS GYMYN, Carm.
St. Margaret. St.D.
[nil] *
A ParL of 35 vols. was est. in 1766 by the Associates of Dr Bray. In 1849 this library was reported as being one of those 'either wholly lost or reduced to a few tattered volumes'.

References: the total no. of vols. sent is noted in Bray Associates Records, f.38, pp.130–3; Select Committee Report, 1849; Kelly, p.265 ('Eglwys Cymmin').

EGREMONT, Pembs.
No ded. St.D.
[nil?] NRC
A ParL of 36 vols. was est. in 1768 by the Associates of Dr Bray.
References: the total no. of vols. sent to 'Egremond. Pembs.' is noted in Bray
Associates Records, f.38, pp.147–9; Kelly, p.265.

FISHGUARD, Pembs.
St. Mary. St.D.
[nil] *
A ParL est. by the Associates of Dr Bray was recorded as defunct from 1841;
the date of est. is unknown. In 1849 this library was reported as one of those
'either wholly lost or reduced to a few tattered volumes'.
References: Bray Associates Annual Reports, 1841; Select Committee Report,
1849; Kelly, p.266 & n.2.

FORDEN, Mont. (Powys)
St. Michael. St.A.
[nil] *
A grant of 15s. towards the est. of a ParL was awarded by Bray from funds at
his disposal, 1695–9.
References: Kelly, p.259.

HANMER, Flints. (Wrexham)
St. Chad. St.A.
[nil]
A DeskL of 4 chained books: Foxe, *Book of Martyrs*, 1608, 3v. and Jewel,
Apology, 1570, perished when the church was destroyed by fire in 1889.
References: Blades, BIC, p.26.

HAVERFORDWEST, Pembs.
St. Martin. St.D.
[nil] *
A ParLL of 116 vols. was est. in 1808 'for the benefit of clergy in the deaneries
of Rhos & Dungleddy' by the Associates of Dr Bray, and augm. in 1873. It is
not recorded after 1900.
Catalogues: Bray Associates Records, f.38, pp.220–2.
References: Shore, p.153; Bray Associates Annual Reports, 1900; Kelly, p.266.

HOLYHEAD, Ang.
St. Cybil. Ban.
[nil?]
A ParLL on a subscription basis was est. in 1849. A cat. published in that year
lists 443 titles in *c.* 768 vols., including 26 titles in Welsh 'containing religious
and useful information'.

Catalogues: *A Catalogue of the Books and Rules for the Management of the Holyhead Parochial Lending Library and Reading Room,* Holyhead, 1849 (copy in Cardiff UL: WG40.c; photocopy in CCC).

KERRY, Mont. (Powys)
St. Michael. St.As.
[nil?]
A lending library on a subscription basis, possibly parochial, was est. before 1846. A printed catalogue of 1846 lists 158 titles, mainly pastoral and educational, with prices paid.
Catalogues: *Rules and Catalogue, of the Kerry Lending Library, re-opened November, 1846,* Newtown, 1846 (copy in NLW, with numerous ms. additions; photocopy in CCC).

LAMPETER, Card. (Ceredigion)
St. Peter. St.D.
[nil]
A ParL of 35 vols. was est. in 1765 by the Associates of Dr Bray, and augm. in 1814. No books had survived by 1950.
Catalogues: Bray Associates Records, f.38, pp.117–20; *Catalogues of Libraries in the Diocese of St. David's,* Carmarthen, 1807, no.14, 932–59.
References: Shore, p.153; CCC Questionnaire, 1950; Kelly, p.265.

LAUGHARNE, Carm.
St. Martin. St.D.
[nil] *
A ParL of 35 vols. was est. in 1766 by the Associates of Dr Bray, and augm. in 1872.
Catalogues: *Catalogues of Libraries in the Diocese of St. David's,* Carmarthen, 1807, no.22, 1148–78.
References: the total no. of vols. sent is noted in Bray Associates Records, f.38, pp.130–3; Shore, p.153; Kelly, p.265.

LITTLE NEWCASTLE, Pembs.
St. Peter. St.D.
[nil]
A ParL of 37 vols. was est. in 1766 by the Associates of Dr Bray. In 1849 this library was reported as being one of those 'either wholly lost or reduced to a few tattered volumes'.
References: the total no. of vols. sent is noted in Bray Associates Records, f.38, pp.130–3; Select Committee Report, 1849; Kelly, p.266.

LLANARTH, Card. (Ceredigion)
St. David. St.D.
[nil?] NRC
A ParL of 34 vols. was est. in 1766 by the Associates of Dr Bray, and augm. in
1870.
References: the total no. of vols. sent is noted in Bray Associates Records, f.38,
pp.130–3; Shore, p.153; Kelly, p.265.

LLANBADARN FAWR, Card. (Ceredigion)
St. Padarn. St.D.
[nil]
A ParL of 72 vols. was est. in 1710 by the Bray Trustees for Erecting Parochial
Libraries, and a ParLL of *c.* 105 vols. by the Associates of Dr Bray in 1769.
Many of the books were apparently the gift of a Dr Fowle, with his autograph,
stating that they were given as a 'lending library to the parishioners'. The
library was reported as lost in 1860.
Catalogues: Bray Associates Records: 1710, ms. cat. no.43 for 'Llanbadern-
Vaur', f.39, pp.49–52; 1770, f.38, pp.156–8; *Catalogues of Libraries in the
Diocese of St. David's*, Carmarthen, 1807, no.5, 567–655.
References: Bray Associates Annual Reports, 1860; Blades, BIC, p.31; *N & Q*,
no.216, 17.12.1853; Kelly, pp.257 & n.1, 265.

LLANBADARN TREFEGLWYS, Card. (Ceredigion)
St. Padarn. St.D.
[nil] *
A ParL of 35 vols. was est. in 1765 by the Associates of Dr Bray.
Catalogues: *Catalogues of Libraries in the Diocese of St. David's*,
Carmarthen, 1807, no.18, 1038–65.
References: the total no. of vols. sent is noted in Bray Associates Records, f.38,
pp.117–20; Kelly, p.265.

LLANBOIDY, Carm.
St. Brynach. St.D.
 [61v.] NLW
A ParL was est. in 1833 by the Associates of Dr Bray. This collection,
purchased by the NLW in 1983, includes the remnants of the Bray libraries at
Cilmaenllwyd, in the Llanboidy area, and 'Llandissilis' [sic], probably
Llandysiliogogo, on the Ceredigion coast. The books are all 18th cent.
imprints.
Catalogues: a separate cat. reproduced from cards in the NLW cat.
References: Kelly, p.265 (but not 'Llanboldy'); DRB2, p.671.

LLANDAFF, Glam. (Cardiff)
St. Peter and St. Paul, the Cathedral. Llan.
[20 titles] NLW
The Diocesan Lib. for Llandaff was est. at **Cowbridge** in 1711. A ParLL of
c. 117 vols. was est. in 1760 by the Associates of Dr Bray in the Cathedral (at
that time also the parish church), and augm. in 1872. In 1879 it was reported
that there were 95 books, 1 ms. and 2 printed catalogues in an upper room in
the chapter house. The present Diocesan Lib. est. in 1883 incorporated the
augmented Bray Lib. of 1872 and the remains of the Bray libraries est. at
Abergavenny, Caerleon, Chepstow, Monmouth, Newport, and **Usk**. About
800 items in 200 vols. of the more valuable and rarer printed books from the
Cathedral Lib. were transferred to the NLW in 1943 and purchased in 1984.
Some 20 items from the Llandaff ParLL have now been identified: 3 STC, 4
pre-1600 continental, 11 Wing and 2 17th cent. continental items. They bear
similar labels to books from the **Caerleon** library.
Catalogues: TS, NLW, 1997 (copy in CCC).
References: Shore, p.151; Tallon, pp.53–4; Kelly, pp.260, 265; DRB2, pp.671,
679.

LLANDAWKE, Carm.
St. Odoceus. St.D.
[nil] *
A ParL of 36 vols. was est. in 1766 by the Associates of Dr Bray. In 1849 this
library was reported as being one of those 'wholly lost or reduced to a few
tattered volumes'.
References: the total no. of vols. sent is noted in Bray Associates Records, f.38,
pp.130–3; Select Committee Report, 1849; Kelly, p.265.

LLANDDEUSANT, Carm.
St. Simon and St. Jude. St.D.
[? vacant benefice]
A ParL was est. in 1890 by the Associates of Dr Bray.
References: Bray Associates Annual Reports, 1890.

LLANDDEWI ABERARTH, Card. (Ceredigion)
St. David. St.D.
[nil] *
A ParL of 36 vols. was est. in 1765 by the Associates of Dr Bray. In 1849 this
library was reported as being one of those 'wholly lost or reduced to a few
tattered volumes'.
Catalogues: *Catalogues of Libraries in the Diocese of St. David's,*
Carmarthen, 1807, no.19, 1066–94.
References: Select Committee Report, 1849; Kelly, p.265.

LLANDDOWROR, Carm.
St. Teilo. St.D.
[5v.?] Dyfed Archives, Carm. RO
A ParL of 34 vols. was est. in 1766 by the Associates of Dr Bray. In 1849 this library was reported as being one of those 'wholly lost or reduced to a few tattered volumes'. However 20 18th–19th cent. theology books are included in the parish records preserved at Carm. RO, 5 of which are pre-1766.
Catalogues: *Catalogues of Libraries in the Diocese of St. David's*, Carmarthen, 1807, no.23, 1179–1209; Carm. RO list: Llanddowror CPR/58 (copy in CCC).
References: the total no. of vols. sent is noted in Bray Associates Records. f.38, pp.130–33; Select Committee Report, 1849; Kelly, p.265.

LLANDEILO FAWR, Carm.
St. Teilo. St.D.
[nil] *
A ParL of 34 vols. was est. in 1766 by the Associates of Dr Bray; and a ParLL of 307 vols. was sent in Sept. 1801. The greater part of the latter collection consisted of books bequeathed to the Associates by Thomas Lyttelton (d.1799), a former Secretary; some were given by other benefactors. The donors are noted in the catalogue.
Catalogues: 1801: Bray Associates Records, f.38, pp.205–9; *Catalogues of Libraries in the Diocese of St. David's*, Carmarthen, 1807, no.3, 276–455.
References: the no. of vols. sent in 1766 is noted in Bray Associates Records, f.38, pp.130–3; a note on the library and its stock is in the diocesan visitation return for 1804 (NLW: SD/QA/63); Select Committee Report, 1849; Kelly, p.265.

LLANDEILO TAL-Y-BONT, Glam. (Swansea)
St. Teilo [FFC]. S & B
[nil] *
A ParLL was est. in 1802 by the Associates of Dr Bray.
References: Kelly, p.265 & n.2 ('listed as Llandeilo, Carm. but since Llandilo Fawr is separately entered [. . . Carmarthenshire] the reference is probably to this place, just over the border in Glamorganshire').

LLANDRILLO-YN-RHOS, Denb. (Conwy)
St. Trillo. St.As.
[nil] *
This library is known only from surviving catalogues. A 'catalogue of the books sent by Dr. Tenison to the use of the vicar of Llandrillo in Rhos and his successors' lists 13 works in 18 vols., mainly theology and sermons in English dated 1632–1726; and in the same hand in the same document, 'a catalogue of books the legacy of the Revd Thomas Owen, late vicar of Oswestry, to the vicar of Llandrillo in Rhos and his successors', listing *c.* 80 vols. of 17th and 18th cent. theology. Owen was vicar of Oswestry, 1706–13. A further cat.,

dated 1715, lists by size 100 vols., mainly 17th and 18th cent. theology, with 6 16th cent. items. A copy order dated 7 Mar. 1753 from the Bishop of St. Asaph [Robert Drummond] to David Lloyd, rector of Gwytherin, contains an instruction to lock up the parochial library of Llandrillo until the appointment of a new vicar, in compliance with the Act of Queen Anne.

Catalogues: Tenison / Owen cat.: Denbigh. RO, PD/46/1/1; *c.* 1730 cat.: NLW SA/MISC/1815; copy order: NLW SA/MISC/715 (copies of each in CCC).

References: Foster: Owen.

LLANDUDNO, Caern. (Gwyn.)
St. Tudno. Ban.
[nil] *
A ParL of 37 vols., formerly in **Conwy**, was est. in 1880 by the Associates of Dr Bray, and augm. in 1889.

Catalogues: 2 copies of a ms. list of books, undated: NLW, Gwynfryn Richards Collection (copies in CCC).

References: Bray Associates Annual Reports, 1880, 1890.

LLANDYFAELOG, Carm.
St. Maelog. St.D.
[nil] *
A ParL was est. in 1765 by the Associates of Dr Bray. In 1849 this library was reported as being one of those 'either wholly lost or reduced to a few tattered volumes'.

Catalogues: *Catalogues of Libraries in the Diocese of St. David's,* Carmarthen, 1807, no.12. Llandeveilog, 907–29.

References: Select Committee Report, 1849; Kelly, p.265 ('Llandefeilog').

LLANDYFRIOG, Card. (Ceredigion)
St. Tyfriog. St.D.
[nil?] NRC
A ParL of 36 vols. was est. in 1768 by the Associates of Dr Bray.

Catalogues: *Catalogues of Libraries in the Diocese of St. David's,* Carmarthen, 1807, no.31, 1412–25.

References: the total no. of vols. sent is noted in Bray Associates Records, f.38, pp.147–9; Kelly, p.265.

LLANDYGWYDD, Carm.
St. Tygwydd. St.D.
[nil] *
A ParL of 57 vols. was est. in 1768 by the Associates of Dr Bray.

Catalogues: *Catalogues of Libraries in the Diocese of St. David's,* Carmarthen, 1807, no.26. Llanegwad, 1272–1308.

References: the total no. of vols. sent is noted in Bray Associates Records, f.38, pp.147–9; Kelly, p.265 (alternative spellings of place-name: Llanewydd, Llancwydd).

LLANDYSILIO, Denbigh.

St. Tysilio. St.As.

[nil] *

A ParL of 87 vols. was est. in 1720 by the Bray Trustees for Erecting Parochial Libraries, and augm. by the Associates in 1870. It is not recorded after 1900.

Catalogues: printed cat. with rules, no.57, of the Whitchurch selection (see p.451), endorsed 7 May 1720: NLW, Welsh Church Commission Records 1932 deposit, ff.156–7 (copy in CCC); ms. cat. 1762[?]: NLW, SA/MISC/1816 (copy in CCC).

References: Bray Associates Annual Reports, 1900; Kelly, p.265 (but not 'Llantysilio').

LLANDYSILIO, Pembs.

St. Tysilio. St.D.

[nil]

A ParL of 39 titles was est. in 1766 by the Associates of Dr Bray, and received by John Griffiths (1732–1825), vicar of Llandysilio, on the borders of Carmarthenshire and Pembrokeshire. Griffiths already possessed a private library of 824 titles, recorded in his own catalogue written at the back of a register of births and deaths and dated 18 Feb. 1764. The prices paid are noted against titles 1–588. In the same document is his 'Catalogue of the books I received from Carmarthen, 14th August 1766, which is called a parish library'. In 1770 Griffiths opened his private library to borrowers and began a list of 'books lended' which continued to 1796. Sometimes over 100 books were out on loan, normally to ministers, schoolmasters and the gentry, but sometimes to people in trades and service. The Bray Associates Reports record the grant of a further deposit of books in 1833 to 'Llandissilio, Carmarthenshire', a parish which was on each side of the boundary, the parish church being in Pembrokeshire, now Llandysilio West.

Catalogues: 1764 and 1766: Carm RO, Llandisilio CPR/9/3 (copy in CCC).

References: G. E. Evans, 'John Griffiths, clericus: his curious register and diary', *Trans. Carmarthenshire Antiq. Soc. and Field Club*, v.2 (1906–7), pp.190–5; Kelly, pp.112, 266.

LLANDYSILIOGOGO, Card. (Ceredigion)

St. Tysilio. St.D.

[nil] *

A ParL of 35 vols. was est. in 1766 by the Associates of Dr Bray. In 1849 this library was reported as being one of those 'either wholly lost or reduced to a few tattered volumes'. Several books in the **Llanboidy** collection now in the NLW have a Bray Associates label for a library est. in 1833 with the name 'Llandisillis' added: it is probable that this is Llandysiliogogo.

Catalogues: *Catalogues of Libraries in the Diocese of St. David's*, Carmarthen, 1807, no.21 'Llandisilio-gogof', 1117–47.

References: the total no. of vols. sent is noted in Bray Associates Records, f.38, pp.130–3; Kelly, p.265.

LLANDYSUL, Card. (Ceredigion)
St. Tysul. St.D.
[nil] *
A ParL of 37 vols. was est. in 1765 by the Associates of Dr Bray.
Catalogues: *Catalogues of the Libraries in the Diocese of St. David's,* Carmarthen, 1807, no.11, 898–906.
References: the total no. of vols. sent is noted in Bray Associates Records, f.38, pp.117–20; Kelly, p.265 (but not 'Llandyssul').

LLANDYSUL, Mont. (Powys)
St. Tysul. St.As.
A ParL, probably est. here by the Associates of Dr Bray, was transferred, with that from **Deytheur**, to **Welshpool** in 1896.
References: Bray Associates Annual Reports, 1900.

LLANEGWAD, Carm.
St. Egwad. St.D.
[nil] *
A ParL of 34 vols. was est. in 1766 by the Associates of Dr Bray.
Catalogues: *Catalogues of Libraries in the Diocese of St. David's,* Carmarthen, 1807, no.26, 1272–1308.
References: the total no. of vols. sent is noted in Bray Associates Records, f.38, pp.130–3; Kelly, p.265.

LLANELLI, Carm.
(Ded. unknown). St.D.
[nil] *
A ParL was est. in 1856 by the Associates of Dr Bray, and augm. in 1896; it is not recorded after 1900.
References: Shore, p.153; Bray Associates Annual Reports, 1900.

LLANFAELOG, Ang.
St. Maelog. Ban.
[nil?] NRC
A ParL was est. in 1849 by the Associates of Dr Bray, and augm. in 1879.
References: Bray Associates Annual Reports, 1900; Kelly, p.264 ('Llanfailog').

LLANFAIR CAEREINION, Mont. (Powys)
St. Mary. St.A.
[nil] *
A ParLL of *c.* 124 vols. was est. in 1768 by the Associates of Dr Bray, and augm. in 1870.
Catalogues: 1768. 'Llanfair', Bray Associates Records, f.38, pp.142–6.
References: Shore, p.153; Kelly, p.266.

LLANFIHANGEL-AR-ARTH, Carm.
St. Michael. St.D.
[nil] *
A ParL of 35 vols. was est. in 1765 by the Associates of Dr Bray, and augm. in 1870, 1875, 1889 and 1896.
Catalogues: 'Llanvihangel Yoroth', Bray Associates Records, f.38, pp.117–20; *Catalogues of Libraries in the Diocese of St. David's*, Carmarthen, 1807, no.10, 868–97.
References: Shore, p.153 ('Llanvihangel-ar-arth'); Bray Associates Annual Reports, 1900; Kelly, p.265.

LLANFIHANGEL GENAU'R-GLYN, Card. (Ceredigion)
St. Michael. St.D.
[nil?] NRC
A ParL was est. in 1886 by the Associates of Dr Bray.
References: Bray Associates Annual Reports, 1890.

LLANFWROG, Denb.
St. Mwrog. St.As.
[nil?] NRC
DeskL: an inventory of books and other church possessions, 1683, lists a Great Welsh Bible, a Book of Homilies, Articles of Religion in Welsh, and copies of the BCP, 1668 and 1678.
References: inventory, Denb. RO, Llanfwrog PD/59/1/1/, p.122 (copy in CCC).

LLANFYLLIN, Mont. (Powys)

St. Myllin. St.As.
[369v.] NLW
Llanfyllin was one of a group of libraries granted part of a sum of £34 by Bray from funds at his disposal, 1695–9. Nothing from this period survives, but an SPCK lending library est. in the mid Victorian period was donated to the NLW in 1975/6. It includes 369 vols. of adult and juvenile fiction and non-fiction dating from *c.* 1840 to 1890. About 60 vols. listed in the published cat. of 1858 are still present.
Catalogues: *Catalogue of Books in the Llanfyllin Parochial Lending Library*, Oswestry, 1858; NLW cat. reproduced from cards, 1981.
References: Kelly, p.259 n.4; DRB2, p.671.

LLANGATHEN, Carm.
St. Cathen. St.D.
[nil] *
A ParL of 37 vols. was est. in 1768 by the Associates of Dr Bray. In 1849 this library was reported as being one of those 'either wholly lost or reduced to a few tattered volumes'.

Catalogues: *Catalogues of Libraries in the Diocese of St. David's*, Carmarthen, 1807, no.27, 1309–38.
References: the total no. of vols. sent is noted in Bray Associates Records, f.38, pp.147–9; Select Committee Report, 1849; Kelly, p.265.

LLANGATTOCK, Brecon. (Powys)
St. Catwg. S & M
[nil?] NRC
A ParL was est. in 1899 by the Associates of Dr Bray.
References: Bray Associates Annual Reports, 1900.

LLANGEFNI, Ang.
St. Cyngar. Ban.
[nil?] NRC
A ParLL of 162 vols. was est. in 1823 by the Associates of Dr Bray.
Catalogues: Bray Associates Records, f.40, pp.90–103.
References: Kelly, p.264.

LLANGYNLLO, Radnor. (Powys)
St. Cynllo. S & B
[1v.] *
DeskL: Jeremy Taylor, *A Collection of Polemicall Discourses*, 3rd ed, 1674. A ParLL of 107 vols. was est. in 1811 by the Associates of Dr Bray 'for use of clergy in the rural deanery of Melchoth sub Ithon'. The entire library was returned to the Associates in 1871.
Catalogues: Bray Associates Records, f.38, pp.239–41.
References: Kelly, p.265 (but not 'Card.').

LLANIDLOES, Mont. (Powys)
St. Idloes. Ban.
[nil] *
A copy of *The Whole Duty of Man*, 1687, was once chained to a desk near the altar. This was one of a group of ParLLs granted part of a sum of £34 by Bray from funds at his disposal 1695–9.
References: *The Antiquary*, v.4, 22.11 (1873); Kelly, p.259 & n.4.

LLANLLWCHAEARN, Card. (Ceredigion)
St. Llwchaiarn. St.D.
[nil] *
A ParL of 36 vols. was est. in 1766 by the Associates of Dr Bray. In 1849 this library was reported as being one of those 'either wholly lost or reduced to a few tattered volumes'.
Catalogues: *Catalogues of Libraries in the Diocese of St. David's*, Carmarthen, 1807, no.20, 1095–1116.
References: the total no. of vols. sent is noted in Bray Association Records, f.38, pp.130–3; Select Committee Report, 1849; Kelly, p.265.

LLANOVER, Mon.
St. Bartholomew. Mon.
[nil] *
A ParL of 145 vols. was est. in 1829 by the Associates of Dr Bray.
Catalogues: 'Llandover', Bray Associates Records, f.40, pp.163–5.
References: Kelly, p.266.

LLANRHOS, Caern. (Conwy)
St. Hilary. St.As.
[nil] *
A ParL of 72 vols. was est. in 1712 at Eglwys Rhos by the Bray Trustees for
Erecting Parochial Libraries. In 1849 this library was reported as being one of
those 'either wholly lost or reduced to few tattered volumes', but some books
were returned to the Associates in 1870, and others survived until 1925, when
they were thrown away by a curate (information from the vicar of Doncaster
in 1950). 4 ms. cats. have survived for this collection: the original shelf-list on
receipt, no.11, 26 Dec. 1712 (in 2 copies); another near-identical shelf-list,
signed Evan Ellis, minister (c. 1728–50); another dated 1749 (2 vols. noted as
missing); and another dated 1750, signed Lewis Price, minister (with the same
vols. missing). The original bookcase, with the shelf-list attached to the door,
is still present.
Catalogues: 1712: Bray Associates Records, f.39, pp.185–8; NLW: 1712,
c. 1728–50; 1749; 1750, SA/MISC/720, 732, 729, 731 (copies of each in CCC).
References: Kelly, p.264 & n.; W. K. Lowther Clarke, *The History of the
SPCK*, 1959, p.50: illustrations of the original cupboard and shelf-list.

LLANRWST, Denbigh. (Conwy)
St. Grwst. St.As.
[nil] *
A ParLL of 240 vols. was est. in 1794 by the Associates of Dr Bray, and augm.
by 98 vols. in 1840, and again in 1878. The 1841 cat. lists c. 166 vols.
Catalogues: Bray Associates Records: 1794, f.38, pp.181–4; 1840, f.41,
pp.16–18; *Catalogue of Books belonging to the Clerical Lending Library of
Llanrwst*, Llanrwst, 1841 (copy in NLW: XZ921L79; photocopy in CCC).
References: Shore, p.153; Bray Associates Annual Reports, 1880; Kelly, p.265.

LLANSANTFFRAID GLYNDYFRDWY, Mer. (Denbighshire)
St. Ffraid. St.As.
[nil?] NRC
A ParLL of books and tracts was in existence in 1851. A cat. of Nov. 1851 lists
230 Welsh items (in multiple copies) and 33 English items (also in multiple
copies).
Catalogues: 1851: NLW: SA/MISC/273 (copy in CCC).

LLANTRISANT, Glam. (Rhondda Cynon Taff)
St. Illtyd. Llan.
[nil?] NRC
A ParL was est. in 1896 by the Associates of Dr Bray.
References: Bray Associates Annual Reports, 1900.

LLANWINIO, Carm.
St. Gwynio. St.D.
[nil] *
A ParL of 34 vols. was est. in 1765 by the Associates of Dr Bray. In 1849 this library was reported as being one of those 'either wholly lost or reduced to a few tattered volumes'.
References: the total no. of vols. sent is noted in Bray Associates Records, f.38, pp.117–20; Select Committee Report, 1849; Kelly, p.265.

LLANWNDA, Pembs.
St. Gwyndaf. St.D.
[nil] *
A ParL of 38 vols. was est. in 1768 by the Associates of Dr Bray.
Catalogues: *Catalogues of Libraries in the Diocese of St. David's*, Carmarthen, 1807, no.29, 1368–80.
References: the total no. of vols. sent is noted in Bray Associates Records, f.38, pp.147–9; Kelly, p.266.

LLANWNNEN, Card. (Ceredigion)
St. Lucia. St.D.
[nil] *
A ParL of 36 vols. was est. in 1765 by the Associates of Dr Bray. In 1849 this library was reported as being one of those 'either wholly lost or reduced to a few tattered volumes'.
Catalogues: *Catalogues of Libraries in the Diocese of St. David's*, Carmarthen, 1807, no.13, 930–1.
References: the total no. of vols. sent is noted in Bray Associates Records, f.38, pp.117–20; Select Committee Report, 1849; Kelly, p. 265 (alternative spellings 'Llanwen, Llanwannen').

LLANWNOG, Mont. (Powys)
St. Gwynog. Ban.
[nil?] NRC
A ParL of 28 titles was est. in 1764 by the Associates of Dr Bray, and augm. in 1872 and 1896.
Catalogues: ms. 1765: Bray Associates Records, f.38, p.109, and NLW, Llanwnog Par. Res. 2 (copy in CCC).
References: Shore, p.151; Bray Associates Annual Reports, 1900; Kelly, p.266.

LLANYSTUMDWY, Caer. (Gwynedd)
St. John the Baptist. Ban.
A ParL formerly est. here was transferred to **Criccieth** in 1830.

LLYSFAEN, Denbigh. (Conwy)
St. Cynfran. St.As.
[nil?] NRC
A library was est. by a gift of 12 books 'left by Mr Johnson of Ty Mawr to ye use of the minister of Llysvain & his successours, 1723/4'. A further cat. of 15 titles dated 15 Jan. 1744 was acknowledged to be in the custody of 'Thos. Lloyd Rector'. The books are mainly 17th cent. theology in English, with a book of homilies in Welsh.
Catalogues: 1723/4: Denb. RO, PD/80/1/1; 1744: NLW, SA/MISC/738 (copies of both in CCC).

MENAI BRIDGE, Ang.
St. Mary. Ban.
[nil?] NRC
A ParL was est. in 1900 by the Associates of Dr Bray.
References: Bray Associates Annual Reports, 1900.

MOLD, Flint.
St. Mary. St.As.
[nil] *
A ParLL was est. in 1797 by the Associates of Dr Bray. It is not recorded after 1895. A Bray Associates bookplate for this library, completed in ms. for 'Mold. Flint. St. Asaph, [17]97' is held by Flints. RO: D/DM/736/1.
References: Bray Associates Annual Reports, 1895; Kelly, p.265.

MONMOUTH, Mon.
St. Mary the Virgin. Mon.
[?] NLW
A ParL of 72 vols. was est. in 1710 by the Bray Trustees for Erecting Parochial Libraries, and augm. in 1864, 1880 and 1883. The remains of this library were absorbed into the **Llandaff** Diocesan Lib. soon after its est. in 1883, and the rare and valuable books from the Llandaff collection were deposited in the NLW in 1943. Books from the Monmouth parochial collection can no longer be identified.
Catalogues: Bray Associates Records, f.39, pp.81–4.
References: Shore, p.152; Bray Associates Annual Reports, 1885; Tallon, p.53; Kelly, p.260 & n.1; DRB2, p.671.

MONTGOMERY, Mont. (Powys)
St. Nicholas. St.As.
[nil] *
One of a group of ParLLs granted part of a sum of £34 by Bray from funds at his disposal, 1695–9.
References: Kelly, p.259 & n.4.

NARBERTH, Pembs.
St. Andrew. St.D.
[nil] *
A ParL of 36 vols. was est. in 1768 by the Associates of Dr Bray. In 1849 this library was reported as being one of those 'either wholly lost or reduced to a few tattered volumes'.
References: the total no. of vols. sent is noted in Bray Associates Records, f.38, pp.147–9; Select Committee Report, 1849; Kelly, p.266.

NEWCASTLE EMLYN, Carm.
Holy Trinity. St.D.
[nil?] NRC
A ParL was considered in the Bray Trustees Minutes, 5 Feb. 1718, and was recorded in the Reports, but there is no record of the foundation.
References: Shore, p.153; Kelly, p.265 & n.1.

NEWPORT, Mon. (Newport)
St.Woolos (the Cathedral from 1921). Mon.
[?] NLW
A Parl of 72 vols. was est. in 1711 by the Bray Trustees for Erecting Parochial Libraries, and augm. by the Associates in 1883 and 1889. Nos. 5, 15, 16, 19, 20, 48, 51, 58, 60–2, 64 from the original collection (see pp.49–51), and probably some others, were absorbed into the **Llandaff** Diocesan Lib. soon after it was est. in 1883; c. 250 of the rare and valuable books in the Llandaff collection were deposited in the NLW in 1943. The Newport Bray library books can no longer be identified.
Catalogues: ms. cat. no.50. Bray Associates Records, f.39, pp.153–6; Kelly, p.266 & n.1.
References: Bray Associates Annual Reports, 1890.

NEWTOWN, Mont. (Powys)
St. David. St.As.
[nil] *
One of a group of ParLLs granted part of a sum of £34 by Bray from funds at his disposal, 1695–9.
References: Kelly, p.259 & n.4.

PEN-BRE, Carm.
St. Illtud. St.D.
[nil] *
A ParL was est. before 1807 by the Associates of Dr Bray.
Catalogues: *Catalogues of Libraries in the Diocese of St. David's*, Carmarthen, 1807, no.33, 1473–1623 (as 'Penbrey').

PENBOYR, Carm.
St. Llawddog. St.D.
[nil?] NRC
A ParL of 35 vols. was est. in 1765 by the Associates of Dr Bray.
Catalogues: *Catalogues of Libraries in the Diocese of St. David's*, Carmarthen, 1807, no.9, 839–67.
References: the total no. of vols. sent is noted in Bray Associates Records, f.38, pp.117–20; Kelly, p.265.

PENRHYNDEUDRAETH, Mer. (Gwyn.)
Holy Trinity. Ban.
[nil?] NRC
A ParL was est. in 1879 by the Associates of Dr Bray, and augm. in 1889 and 1896.
References: Bray Associates Reports, 1880, 1890, 1895.

PENTRE, Glam. (Rhondda Cynon Taff)
St. Peter. Llan.
[nil] *
A ParL was est. in 1890 by the Associates of Dr Bray.
References: Bray Associates Annual Reports, 1890.

PONTARDAWE, Glam. (Neath Port Talbot)
(Ded. unknown). S & B
[nil] *
A ParL was est. in 1900 by the Associates of Dr Bray (transferred from **Alltwen** in the diocese of Llandaff).
References: Bray Associates Annual Reports, 1900.

PONTLOTTYN, Glam. (Caerphilly)
St. Tyfaelog. Llan.
[nil?] NRC
A ParL was est. in 1894 by the Associates of Dr Bray, and augm. in 1899.
References: Bray Associates Annual Reports, 1895, 1900.

PORTHMADOG, Caern. (Gwyn.)
(Ded. unknown). Ban.
[nil?] NRC
A ParL was est. in 1892 by the Associates of Dr Bray (incorporating that of **Criccieth** by 1900).
References: Bray Associates Annual Reports, 1895, 1900.

PRENDERGAST, Pembs.
St. David. St.D.
[nil]
A ParL of 72 vols. was est. in 1710 by the Bray Trustees for Erecting Parochial Libraries. It was not recorded after 1878. A copy of the bookplate is in the John Johnson Collection, Bodl.
Catalogues: ms. cat. no.44, Bray Associates Records, f.39, pp.53–6; *Catalogues of Libraries in the Diocese of St. David's*, Carmarthen, 1807, no.32, 1426–72.
References: Bray Associates Annual Reports, 1880; Kelly, p.266.

PRESTEIGNE, Radnor. (Powys)
St. Andrew. S & B
[nil]
A ParLL was est. *c.* 1707 by the Bray Trustees for Erecting Parochial Libraries, perhaps the first Welsh library of any kind est. in Wales.
References: Kelly, pp.110, 257 & n.2, quoting SPCK Minutes of General Meetings, 15 Aug. 1706, and Abstracts of Correspondence. v.1, no.1370, 13 Aug. 1708.

PWLLHELI, Caern. (Gwyn.)
St. Peter, parish of Denio. Ban.
[c. 60v.] *
A ParL of 67 vols. was est. in 1712 by the Bray Trustees for Erecting Parochial Libraries, and this was amalgamated in 1770 with a ParLL of *c.* 233 vols. sent by the Associates of Dr Bray, and augm. in 1861, 1889 and 1896. There are no books surviving from the 1712 or 1770 deposits; those listed on the inventory lists are largely undated, but would seem to be of the 1861 or later deposits, with later gifts and service books.
Catalogues: Bray Associates Records: 1712, ms. cat. no.6, f.39, pp.197–200; 1770, f.30, pp.159–65; parish inventory lists (copy in CCC).
References: Shore, p.151; Bray Associates Annual Reports, 1890, 1900; Kelly, p.265.

RHAYADER, Radnor. (Powys)
St. Clement. S & B
[nil] *
A ParLL of 120 vols. for the 'clergy in Rhayader and its vicinity' was est. in
1810 by the Associates of Dr Bray.
Catalogues: Bray Associates Records, f.38, pp.235–7.
References: Kelly, p.266.

RHOS, Pembs.
St. James. St.D.
[nil?] NRC
A bookplate survives for a ParL est. by the Associates of Dr Bray for 'Rhos &
Dungleddy', Pembs. in 1800 or 1808. It is not otherwise recorded.
References: I am indebted to Brian North Lee for this reference.

ST. ASAPH, Flint. (Denbighshire)
St. Asaph and St. Cyndeyrn (the Cathedral). St.As.
[?] NLW
The St. Asaph Diocesan Lib. est. by deed of settlement in 1711 was one of 4
clerical lending libraries created by the SPCK in each of the Welsh dioceses,
1708–11 (the others were at **Bangor, Carmarthen**, and **Cowbridge**). A schedule
of 22 Oct. 1711 lists 200 vols. (including vols. of bound pamphlets) listed
on 11 shelves in 4 presses, with columns for the booksellers' price and the
lending value. A further *c.* 50 vols. were left to the library in September 1732.
Early donors included William Fleetwood (1656–1723), bishop 1708–14, and
Thomas Tanner (1674–1735), bishop 1732–5. In 1970 the greater part of the
collection (by then *c.* 2,500 vols.) was placed on permanent deposit at the
NLW. Those books from the original clerical lending library are not obviously identifiable. There is a sizeable block in the deposit of books from the ParLL
est. by the Associates of Dr Bray in 1884, and augm. in 1889, bearing the Bray
library labels.
Catalogues: transfer deed and schedule, 1711: NLW SA/MISC/1547 (copy in
CCC); list of books left to St. Asaph L. 1732: NLW SA/MISC/849 (copy in
CCC); list of books given by Fleetwood, Tanner and other donors; list of books
in 1739, and books lent at various times: NLW SA/MB/10.
References: Shore, p.152; Bray Associates Annual Reports, 1890; Tallon,
p.59; Kelly, pp.107, 110–11, 260; DRB2, p.672 (and further refs. cited there);
DNB: Fleetwood, Tanner.

ST. CLEARS, Carm.
St. Mary Magdalen. St.D.
[nil] *
A ParL of 37 vols. was est. in 1768 by the Associates of Dr Bray. In 1888 a
Deanery Clerical Lib. was est. (augm. in 1898) which was added to the
collection and kept in the same cupboard.
Catalogues: *Catalogues of Libraries in the Diocese of St. David's*,
Carmarthen, 1807, no.28, 1339–67.
References: the total no. of vols. sent is noted in Bray Associates Records, f.38,
pp.147–9; Bray Associates Annual Reports, 1900; Kelly, p.265; Lambeth
Palace MS.3224: notes by N. R. Ker.

ST. DAVIDS, Pembs.
St. David and St. Andrew (the Cathedral). St.D.
[?] *
The medieval library at St. Davids was destroyed at the Reformation; another
library was built up over the years but amounted to fewer than 500 vols. by
1795. It was later reorganized and augmented by a ParLL est. in 1807 by the
Associates of Dr Bray. The Bray library books can no longer be identified.
Catalogues: *Catalogues of Libraries in the Diocese of St. David's*,
Carmarthen, 1807, no.1, 1–194.
References: Tallon, p.78; Kelly, pp.62, 266; DRB2, p.687.

SWANSEA, Glam. (Swansea)
St. Mary. S & B
[3v.] West Glamorgan Archives, Swansea
DeskL: according to the churchwardens' accounts Bibles and liturgical works
in both Welsh and English were purchased by the churchwardens over the
period 1559–1626. A ParLL of *c.* 142 vols. was est. in 1793 by the Associates
of Dr Bray, and augm. in 1794 by a ParLL of 210 vols. 'for benefit of clergy of
the Deanery of Gower'. This was further augm. in 1900. St. Mary's church
was burnt down in 1941 and rebuilt in 1954–9. 3 pre–1900 vols. are held in
West Glamorgan Archives.
Catalogues: Bray Associates Records: 1793, f.42, pp.209–11; 1794, f.38,
pp.225–8.
References: Bray Associates Annual Reports, 1900; Kelly, p.265; Margaret
Walker, 'Welsh books in St. Mary's Swansea, 1559–1626', *Bull. of Celtic
Studies*, v.23, pt.4 (1976), pp.397–402.

TREDEGAR, Mon. (Blaenau Gwent)
St. George (ded. uncertain). Mon.
[nil] *
A ParL was est. in 1897 by the Associates of Dr Bray.
References: Bray Associates Annual Reports, 1900.

TREFILAN, Card. (Ceredigion)
St. Hilary. St.D.
[nil?] NRC
A ParL of 34 vols. was est. in 1765 by the Associates of Dr Bray. In 1849 this library was reported as being one of those 'either wholly lost or reduced to a few tattered volumes'.
Catalogues: *Catalogues of Libraries in the Diocese of St. David's,* Carmarthen, 1807, no.16, 983–1006.
References: the total no. of vols. sent is noted in Bray Associates Records, f.38, pp.117–20 ('Trevila'); Kelly, p.265.

TRE-LECH A'R BETWS, Carm.
St. Teilo. St.D.
[nil] *
A ParL of 37 vols. was est. in 1765 by the Associates of Dr Bray.
Catalogues: *Catalogues of Libraries in the Diocese of St. David's,* Carmarthen, 1807, no.7, 791–819 ('Trelech').
References: the total no. of vols. sent is noted in Bray Associates Records, f.38, pp.117–20 ('Treleach'); Kelly, p.265.

TRELYSTAN, Mont. (Powys) see under England

TREVETHIN, Mon. (Torfaen)
St. Cadog. Mon.
[nil] *
A ParL of 72 vols. was est. in 1711 by the Bray Trustees for Erecting Parochial Libraries. Attached to the copy of the original cat. in Gwent RO is a note by John Williams, vicar, 1775, stating that all the books saved 2 marked 'wanting' were still present, together with a further list of the 50 vols. still present in 1827, signed by the curate and churchwarden. A letter from the incumbent in 1959 (CCC file) suggests that the books were disposed of some time after the church was rebuilt in 1846. The library is not recorded after 1870.
Catalogues: Bray Associates Records, f.39, pp.149–52 (another copy in Gwent RO: D/Pa 13.44, with printed Proposal, Rules, and attachments noted above: copy in CCC).
References: Bray Associates Annual Reports, 1870; V.W. T. Rees, *Trevethin: a Short History of the Parish*, Pontypool, 1934, p.62; Kelly, p.266.

USK, Mon.
St. Mary. Mon.
[?] NLW
A ParLL of 126 vols. was est. in 1828, probably in Usk school, by the Associates of Dr Bray, and augm. in 1870 and 1896. The remaining books were absorbed into the **Llandaff** Diocesan Lib. soon after it was est. in 1883;

c. 250 of the rare and valuable books in the Llandaff collection were deposited in the NLW in 1943. The Usk Bray library books can no longer be identified.
Catalogues: Bray Associates Records, f.40, pp.157–60.
References: Shore, p.152; Bray Associates Annual Reports, 1900; Kelly, p.266 & n.1.

WELSHPOOL, Mont. (Powys)
St. Mary. St.As.
[nil] *
A ParL was est. in 1896 by the Associates of Dr Bray (incorporating those of **Deytheur** and **Llandysul (Mont.)**.
References: Bray Associates Annual Reports, 1900.

WHITFORD, Flint.
St. Mary and St. Beuno. St.As.
[nil?]
A ParLL on a subscription basis was est. by 1840. The printed cat. lists *c.* 125 English titles in 153 vols. and 31 Welsh titles in 34 vols., with nos. allocated for additions. The books are mainly pastoral and educational.
Catalogues: *Catalogue of English and Welsh Books, in the Whitford Church Lending Library, 1840,* Holywell, [1840?] (copy in NLW; photocopy in CCC).

WREXHAM, Denbigh. (Wrexham)
St. Giles. St.As.
[nil] *
A ParLL was projected here in 1709, but there is no evidence that it was ever est. A ParLL was est. in 1893 by the Associates of Dr Bray.
References: Bray Associates Annual Reports, 1900; Kelly, p.257 & n.3, quoting SPCK minutes, 15 Aug. 1706, & Abstracts of Correspondence, v.1, 1897, 18 Nov. 1709; a letter from the incumbent quoting the county archivist (CCC file).

YSTRAD MEURIG, Card. (Ceredigion)
St. John the Baptist. St.D.
[nil?] NRC
A ParLL of 92 vols. was est. in 1808 by the Associates of Dr Bray, and augm. in 1809 by 41 vols. , and again in 1872.
Catalogues: Bray Associates Records, f.38, pp.223–5 and 232.
References: Shore, p.153; Kelly, p.265 ('Ystrad Meuric').

THE ACT OF 7 ANNE C.14 [1709]
RELATING TO PAROCHIAL LIBRARIES CAP. XIV

An Act for the better Preservation of Parochial Libraries
in that Part of *Great Britain* called *England*.

'WHEREAS in many Places in the South Parts of *Great
'Britain* called *England* and *Wales*, the Provision for the
'Clergy is so mean, that the necessary Expence of Books
'for the better Prosecution of their Studies cannot be
'defrayed by them; and whereas of late Years, several
'charitable and well-disposed Persons have by charitable
'Contributions erected Libraries within several Parishes
'and Districts in *England*, and *Wales*; but some Provision
'is wanting to preserve the same, and such others as shall
'be provided in the same Manner, from Embezilment;'
Be it therefore enacted by the Queen's most Excellent
Majesty, by and with the Advice and Consent of the
Lords Spiritual and Temporal, and Commons, in this
present Parliament assembled, and by the Authority of
the same, That in every Parish or Place where such a
Library is or shall be erected, the same shall be
preserved for such Use and Uses, as the same is and shall
be given, and the Orders and Rules of the Founder and
Founders of such Libraries shall be observed and kept.

II. And for the Encouragement of such Founders and
Benefactors, and to the Intent they may be satisfied,
that their pious and charitable Intent may not be
frustrated; Be it also enacted by the Authority aforesaid,
That every Incumbent, Rector, Vicar, Minister or Curate
of a Parish, before he shall be permitted to use and enjoy
such Library, shall enter into such Security by Bond or
otherwise, for Preservation of such Library, and due
Observance of the Rules and Orders belonging to the
same, as the proper Ordinaries within their respective
Jurisdictions, in their Discretion shall think fit; and in
case any Book or Books belonging to the said Library
shall be taken away and detained, it shall and may be
lawful for the said Incumbent, Rector, Vicar, Minister or
Curate for the Time being, or any other Person or Persons,
to bring an Action of Trover and Conversion, in the Name

In every Parish where a Library shall be erected, it shall be preserved for the Uses to which it is given, &c.

Incumbents, &c. before they use the Library, shall give Security to preserve it.

If any Book be taken away &c. the Incumbent may bring Trover, and shall recover Treble Damages, to the Use of the Library.

of the proper Ordinaries within their respective Jurisdictions; whereupon Treble Damages shall be given with full Costs of Suit, as if the same were his or their proper Book or Books, which Damages shall be applied to the Use and Benefit of the said Library.

The Ordinary, &c. may inquire into the State of the Library, and amend the Defects; and appoint Persons to inspect the Library.

III. And it is further enacted by the Authority aforesaid, That it shall and may be lawful to and for the proper Ordinary, or his Commissary or Official in his respective Jurisdiction, or the Archdeacon, or by his Direction his Official or Surrogate, if the said Archdeacon be not the Incumbent of the Place where such Library is, in his or their respective Visitation, to enquire into the State and Condition of the said Libraries, and to amend and redress the Grievances and Defects of and concerning the same, as to him or them shall seem meet; and it shall and may be lawful to and for the proper Ordinary, from time to time, as often as shall be thought fit, to appoint such Person or Persons, as he shall think fit, to view the State and Condition of such Libraries, and the said Ordinaries, Archdeacons or Officials respectively, shall have free access to the same at such Times as they shall respectively appoint.

Incumbent, &c. to make a Catalogue of the Books, to be delivered to the Ordinary, and registred without Fee.

IV. And it be also further enacted by the Authority aforesaid, That where any Library is appropriated to the Use of the Minister of any Parish or Place, every Rector, Vicar, Minister or Curate of the same, within six Months after his Institution, Induction or Admission, shall make or cause to be made a new Catalogue of all Books remaining in, or belonging to such Library, and shall sign the said Catalogue thereby acknowledging the Custody and Possession of the said Books; which said Catalogue so signed, shall be delivered to the proper Ordinary within the Time aforesaid, to be kept or registred in his Court, without any Fee or Reward for the same.

Where Libraries are already erected, such Catalogue to be made, &c. before 29 Sept. 1709.

V. And be it further enacted by the Authority aforesaid, That where there are any parochial Libraries already erected, the Incumbent, Rector, Vicar, Minister or Curate of such Parish or Place, shall make or cause to be made a Catalogue of all Books in the same, thereby acknowledging the Custody and Possession thereof; which Catalogue so signed, shall be delivered to the proper Ordinary, on or before the nine and twentieth Day of *September* which shall be in the Year of our Lord one thousand seven hundred and nine; and where any Library shall at any Time hereafter be given and appropriated to the Use

And where any shall be erected, within 6 Months after.

of any Parish or Place, where there shall be an Incumbent, Rector, Vicar, Minister or Curate in Possession, such Incumbent, Rector, Vicar, Minister or Curate, shall make or cause to be made a Catalogue of all the Books, and deliver the same, as aforesaid, within six Months after he shall receive such Library.

Upon the Death or Removal of any Incumbent, the Churchwardens shall lock up the Library.

VI. And to prevent any Imbezilment of Books upon the Death or Removal of any Incumbent, Be it also enacted by the Authority aforesaid, That immediately after the Death or Removal of any Incumbent, Rector, Vicar, Minister, or Curate, the Library belonging to such Parish or Place shall be forthwith shut up, and locked, or otherwise secured by the Churchwarden or Church-wardens for the Time being, or by such Person or Persons as shall be authorized or appointed by the proper Ordinary, or Archdeacon respectively, so that the same shall not be opened again, till a new Incumbent, Rector, Vicar, Minister, or Curate shall be inducted or admitted into the Church of such Parish or Place.

The Vestry, &c. may meet in such Libraries, if they did so formerly.

VII. Provided always, That in case the Place where such Library is or shall be kept, shall be used for any publick Occasion for Meeting of the Vestry, or otherwise, for the Dispatch of any Business of the said Parish, or for any other publick Occasion, for which the said Place hath been ordinarily used, the Place shall nevertheless be made use of as formerly for such Purposes, and after such Business dispatched shall be again forthwith shut and lockt up, or otherwise secured, as is before directed.

The Incumbent shall enter the Benefactions, and Books.

VIII. And be it also further enacted by the Authority aforesaid, That for the better Preservation of the Books belonging to such Libraries, and that the Benefactions given towards the same may appear, a Book shall be kept within the said Library for the entring and registring of all such Benefactions, and such Books as shall be given towards the same, and therein the Minister, Rector, Vicar, or Curate of the said Parish or Place, shall enter or cause to be fairly entered such Benefactions, and an Account of all such Books as shall from time to time be given, and by whom given.

The Ordinary and Donor may make Orders concerning the Library; which shall be entred as aforesaid.

IX. And for the better governing the said Libraries, and preserving of the same, It is hereby further enacted by the Authority aforesaid, That it shall and may be lawful to and for the proper Ordinary, together with the Donor of such Benefaction, (if living) and after the Death of such Donor, for the proper Ordinary alone, to make such other

Rules and Orders concerning the same, over and above, and besides, but not contrary to such as the Donor of such Benefactions shall in his Discretion judge fit and necessary; which said Orders and Rules so to be made, shall, from time to time, be entred in the said Book, or some other Book to be prepared for that Purpose, and kept in the said Library.

Books not to be alienable without Consent of the Ordinary.
If any Book be lost a Justice of Peace may grant a Warrant to search for it; and if found it shall be restored to the Library.

X. And it is further enacted and declared by the Authority aforesaid, That none of the said Books shall in any Case be alienable, nor any Book or Books that shall hereafter be given by any Benefactor or Benefactors shall be alienated, without the Consent of the proper Ordinary, and then only when there is a Duplicate of such Book or Books; and that in case any Book or Books be taken or otherwise lost out of the said Library, it shall and may be lawful to and for any Justice of Peace within the County, Riding, or Division, to grant his Warrant to search for the same, and in case the same be found, such Book or Books so found shall immediately, by Order of such Justice, be restored to the said Library; any Law, Statute, or Usage to the contrary in any wise notwithstanding.

This Act shall not extend to a Library erected in Ryegate in Surrey.

XI. Provided always, That nothing in this Act contained shall extend to a publick Library lately erected in the Parish of *Ryegate* in the County of *Surry*, for the Use of the Freeholders, Vicar, and Inhabitants of the said Parish, and of the Gentlemen and Clergymen inhabiting in Parts thereto adjacent; the said Library being constituted in another Manner than the Libraries provided for by this Act.

APPENDIX B

BISHOP WILSON'S
LIST OF BOOKS, *c.* 1699

A transcript of 'Bishop Wilson's account of books given by himself or friends' from his Notebook (Manx National Heritage, Douglas, Isle of Man: MD 15072)

Parish Library

1. Bishp Pearson on ye Creed. Fol.
2. Bishop Hopkins works. Fol.
3. Mr Craddocks Knowleg. & Pract. Fol.
4. Mr Kettlewels Xn Believer. Fol.
5. ——His Mesures of Xn Obidience. 8vo.
6. Bp Burnets Pastoral care
7. Bp Patrick Xn Sacrifice
8. Lives of Dr. Donne &c.
9. ABp of Canterbury Concerning Swearing
10. Poor Mans Help
11. Christian Monitor
12. Bp of Chichesters Ch. Catechism
13. Mr. Bonnels Life
14. Herbert Country Parson – given by Mr Patten
15. Camfield of Angels
16. Mr. Nelsons Fasts & Feasts
17. Allens Select discourses
18. Brays Lectures on the Ch. Catechism
19. Catechetical Lect.
20. Allen on the 2 Covenants
21. Bp of Man Catechism Manks & Engl.
22. Collection of Psalms out of the new versions
23. Acct. of Societies
24. Help to a National Reformatn.
25. Catalogue of Useful Books
26. Brays Baptismal Covnt.
27. Dr. Rich Sherlocks Pract. Xn. – Bp of Man
28. Lawes Xn. Perfectn.
33. Blairs sermons 5 vol. Oct.
34. Tracts agst. Popery
35. Bp of Man on the Lords Supp.
36. Fox on the New Testament
37. Mr. Auditor Harleys Abstract
38. Mr. Auditor Harley's Harmony
39. Instruction for Indians
40. Dr. Hammond – New Test.

OLEY, BRAY AND WILSON
LIBRARIES

The following table is an attempt to identify and conflate into one sequence the titles listed (with their catalogue nos.) in the following catalogues and lists:

B The Barnabas Oley libraries sent to 10 vicarages in 1687 (pp.34–5)

O The Bray Oldbury 72 vol. library sent to 32 churches 1710–13 (pp.49–51)

N The nearly identical 67 vol. library sent to a further 19 churches over the same period (p.52)

W The Bray Whitchurch 81 vol. library sent to 10 churches, 1720–27 (pp.53–5)

M Bishop Wilson's list of 40 books sent to the 17 libraries he founded in the Isle of Man from 1699 (p.443)

F Isle of Man books added 1699–c. 1740 (Ferguson, pp.36–62).

The first number only is given of of books assigned more than one number. Titles not identified are enclosed in single quotation marks. The dates given are for the first recorded edition (unless another is specified), though in many cases later editions were sent, sometimes in more than one volume, as available at the time of despatch.

Author	Title	B	O	N	W	M	F
Anon.	'An Appendix to a Small Library'						*
Anon.	'A Catalogue of Small Tracts against Vice and Immorality'						*
Anon.	'Catalogue of Useful Books'					25	
Anon.	A Caveat against the Pretender. 1728						*
Anon.	The Christian Belief . . . in answer to . . . Christianity not Mysterious [by John Toland]. 1696						*
Anon.	'A Companion for Candidates for Holy Orders'						*
Anon.	The Country-Parson's Advice to his Parishioners. 1701		69	69			
Anon.	A Discourse against Scoffing at Religion. 1716						*
Anon.	'Heloici ['Hebraica'?] Chronologia'						*
Anon.	Help to a National Reformation. 1700					24	
Anon.	'History of the Life and Death of Our Saviour'						*
Anon.	'Laws of the Church of Rome against Heretics'						*
Anon.	The Notes of the Church, as laid down by Cardinal Bellarmin Examined and Confuted. 1688				25		
Anon.	'Oxford Annotations on St. Paul's Epistles'						*
Anon.	'A Practical Discourse against Lying'						*
Anon.	Reflections on Dr. Fleetwood's Essay upon Miracles. 1706						*

Author	Title	B	O	N	W	M	F
Anon.	'Reflexions on the Holy Scripture'						*
Anon.	The Sacred Succession: or, a Priesthood by Divine Right. 1710						*
Anon.	A Short and Sure Method proposed for the the Extirpation of Popery. 1689						*
Anon.	'Small Tracts for Promoting Christian Knowledge'						*
Addison, Lancelot	The Christian Daily Sacrifice. 1698				77		
Allen, William	A Discourse of Divine Assistance. 1693		70	70	71		
Allen, William	A Discourse of . . . the Two Covenants. 1673		6	6	8	20	
Allen, William & Kettlewell, John	Two Select Discourses on Faith. 2nd ed. 1703		7	7	9	17	
Allestree, Richard	The Works of. 2nd imp. 1687	11					
Allestree, Richard	The Vanity of the Creature. 1684						*
Allestree, Richard	The Whole Duty of Man. 1659						*
Allix, Pierre	The Book of Psalms, with the Argument of of each Psalm. 1701						*
Allix, Pierre	The Judgment of the Ancient Jewish Church against the Unitarians. 1699						*
Amyraut, Moyse	In Symbolum Apostolorum Exercitatio. Salmurii, 1663						*
Andrewes, Lancelot	A Manual of Private Devotions. 1648						*
Andrewes, Lancelot	XCVI Sermons. 4th ed. 1641	5					
Arndt, Johann	De Vero Christianismo. 2v. 1708				39		
Bacon, Francis	The Essays. 1718						*
'Bain'	'Bain. upon Repentance'						*
Bates, William	The Four Last Things. 1691						*
Bennet, Thomas	An Answer to the Dissenters Pleas for Separation. 4th ed. 1707		58	58	45		
Bennet, Thomas	A Confutation of Popery. 3rd ed. 1706		59	59	44		
Bennet, Thomas	A Confutation of Quakerism. 2nd ed. 1709		60	60	43		
Bevan, Thomas	[Hebrew] The Prayer of Prayers. 1673						*
Beveridge, William	The Works . . . containing all his Sermons. 2v. 1720		23				
Beveridge, William	The Church-Catechism Explained [with text]. 1666			27	80		*
Beveridge, William	Private Thoughts upon Religion. 1709		51	51	81		
Beveridge, William	The Great Necessity and Advantage of Publick Prayer. 1708		51	51	81		
Bible. OT	'Collection of Psalms out of the New Version'					22	
Bible. NT	St. Matthew. Manx, trans. William Walker. Lunnyng, 1748						*
Bilson, Thomas	The Survey of Christ's Sufferings. 1604						*
Blackall, Offspring	Practical Discourses upon Our Saviour's Sermon on the Mount. 8v. 1717–18				15		
Blair, Hugh	Our Saviour's Divine Sermon on the on the Mount. 5v. 1722–23					33	
Boyle, Robert	Some Considerations touching the Style of the Holy Scriptures. 1661						*
Bradford, Samuel	The Credibility of the Christian Revelation. 1700				13		

Author	Title	B	O	N	W	M	F
Bragge, Francis	The Passion of Our Saviour. 1694						*
Bragge, Francis	Practical Discourses upon the Parables. 1694						*
Bray, Thomas	Bibliotheca Parochialis. 2nd ed. 1707		14	14			
Bray, Thomas	Catechetical Lectures. 3rd ed. 1703		6	6	8	19	
Bray, Thomas	'A Circular Letter to the Clergy of Man'						*
Bray, Thomas	A Course of Lectures upon the Church Catechism. v.1. Oxford, 1697					18	
Bray, Thomas	Papal Usurpations and Persecution. 2 pts. 1711–12					34	
Bray, Thomas	A Pastoral Discourse to Young Persons. 1704		66	66			
Bray, Thomas	A Short Account of the Several Kinds of Societies. 1700					23	
Bray, Thomas	A Short Discourse upon the Doctrine of our Baptismal Covenant. 1697		66	66		26	
Bray, Thomas	The Whole Course of Catechetical Institution. 1704		66	66	79		
Brett, Thomas	The Independency of the Church upon the State. 1717						*
'Brown, Dr'	'Sermons preached by Dr. Brown'						*
Burkitt, William	The Poor Man's Help. 2nd ed. 1694					10	
Burnet, Gilbert	The Abridgment of the History of the Reformation. 4th ed. 1705		49	49			
Burnet, Gilbert	A Discourse of the Pastoral Care. 1692				63	6	
Burnet, Gilbert	An Exposition of the Thirty-Nine Articles. 1699						*
Calamy, Benjamin	A Collection of Several Sermons. 1659						*
Camfield, Benjamin	A Theological Discourse of Angels. 1678			26		15	
Casas, Bartholomé de las	Popery Truly Display'd. 1689						*
Cave, William	Primitive Christianity. 6th ed. 1702	14	62	62	54		
Chillingworth, William	The Works of. 1704		5	5			
Clagett, William	A Discourse concerning the . . . Holy Spirit . . . additions by Stebbing. 1719						*
Clarke, Samuel	Three Practical Essays viz. on Baptism. 1699		68	68	73		
Comber, Thomas	A Discourse upon . . . Ordaining Bishops. 1699		56	56	23		
Cradock, Samuel	Knowledge & Practice. 4th ed. 1702					3	
Davies, Sir John	Nosce Teipsum. 1599						*
Dodwell, Henry	A Discourse concerning the Use of Incense in Divine Offices. 1711						*
Dorrington, Theophilus	Family Devotions for Sunday Evenings. v.1. 1693						*
Dorrington, Theophilus	Reform'd Devotions in Meditations, Hymns and Petitions. 1686		29				
Dow, Christopher	A Discourse of the Sabbath. 1636						*
Drexel, Jeremias	The Considerations . . . upon Eternitie. Cambridge, 1641				48		
Du Pin, Louis Ellies	A Compendious History of the Church. 4v. 1713				67		
Ellis, Clement	The Self-Deceiver plainly Discover'd to Himself. 1731						*

Author	Title	B	O	N	W	M	F
Ellis, John	Articulorum XXXIX Ecclesiæ Anglicanæ Defensio. Amstelodami, 1700		72	72			
Erasmus	'Of the Dignity of an Ecclesiastic and the Method of forming a Preacher. 1744' MS trans. dedicated by Samuel G. to Bishop Wilson						*
Eusebius	The History of the Church. 2nd ed. 1709		1	1			
Falkner, William	Christian Loyalty. 1679						*
'Farrington' [? Faringdon, Antony]	'Farrington. Faith and Repentance'						*
Fawkner, Antony	Nicodemus for Christ. 1630						*
Featley, Daniel	Annotations upon all the Books of the Old and New Testament [with text]. 1645						*
Fleetwood, William	A Compleat Collection of the Sermons. 1737						*
Fogg, Lawrence	A General View of Christian Religion. Chester, 1714						*
Fogg, Lawrence	Theologiae Speculativae Schema. 1712						*
Fox, Francis	The New Testament with References and Notes. 1722					36	
Gardiner, James	A Practical Exposition of the Beatitudes. 1712						*
Gastrell, Francis	The Christian Institutes. 2nd ed. 1709		50	50	78		*
'Gatsker, Dr'. [? Gataker, Thomas]	'A Discourse against Popery'						*
Godeau, Antoine	Pastoral Instructions and Mediations. 1703		15	15	34		
Goodman, John	The Penitent Pardoned. 1707		27		52		
Goodman, John	A Winter-Evening Conference. 1705		28		63		
Greenhill, William	An Exposition of the First Five Chapters of Ezekeiel. 1645						*
Grotius, Hugo	De Veritate Religionis Christianæ. 1674		30				
'Haddley'	'Haddley's Defence' [?Benjamin Hoadley, A Defence of Episcopal Ordination, 1707]						*
Hamilton, James	The Life and Character of James Bonnel. 3rd ed. 1707		65	65	62	13	
Hammond, Henry	The Works of. 1674–84	1					
Hammond, Henry	A Paraphrase and Annotations upon all the Books of the New Testament [with text]. 1653					40	
Hammond, Henry	A Paraphrase and Annotations . . . Psalms. 1659						*
Harley, Edward	An Abstract of the Historical Part of the Old Testament [with text]. 1730					37	
Harley, Edward	The Harmony between the Psalms and the Other Parts of Scripture [with text]. 1732					38	
Harley, Edward	The Harmony of the Four Gospels [with text]. 1733						*
Harrison, Joseph	An Exposition of the Church Catechism. 1708		70	70			
Herbert, George	A Priest to the Temple. 1671	15	69	69		14	
Hickes, George	An Apologetical Vindication of the Church of England. 2nd ed. 1706		63	63	61		
Hickes, George	Sermons on Various Subjects. 2v. 1713						*
Hoadly, Benjamin	An Answer to . . . Dr. Hare's Sermon. 1720						*

Author	Title	B	O	N	W	M	F
Hooker, Richard	Of the Lawes of Ecclesiasticall Politie. 1593						*
Hopkins, Ezekiel	The Works of. 1701					2	
Hotchkiss, Thomas	A Discourse concerning the Imputation. 1675						*
[Isham, Zacheus]	The Catechism of the Church: with proofs. 1694						*
Isham, Zacheus	Divine Philosophy: containing the Book of of Job . . . [with texts]. 1706				51		
Jackson, Thomas	The Works of. 3v. 1673	1					
Jenkin, Robert	The Reasonableness and Certainty of the Christian Religion. 3rd ed. 1708		52	52	24		
Josephus	The Works of. 1693						*
Jurieu, Pierre	A Critical History . . . of the Church. 2v. 1705						*
Justinus, Martyr	The Apologies of Justin Martyr . . . trans. William Reeves. 2v. 1709		12	12	41		
Ken, Thomas	An Exposition of the Church Catechism. 1685		63	63			
Kettlewell, John	The Measures of Christian Obedience. 5th ed. 1709		48	48	32	5	
Kettlewell, John	Death made Comfortable. 1708		71	71	76		
Kettlewell, John	An Help and Exhortation to Worthy Communication. 1683		47	47	33		
Kettlewell, John	The Practical Believer. 1688		7	7	9	4	
Kidder, Richard	A Demonstration of the Messias. 3 pts. 1684–1700						*
King, William	A Discourse concerning the Inventions of Men in the Worship of God. 1694		32		75		
La Placette, Jean	The Christian Casuist. 1705		15	15	34		
Law, William	A Practical Treatise upon Christian Perfection. 2nd ed. 1728					28	
Law, William	A Serious Call to a Devout and Holy Life. 1729						*
Le Fevre, Isaac	An Historical Account of the Sufferings and Death of. 1704				61		
Leighton, Robert	A Practical Commentary upon the First General Epistle of St. Peter. 1693–4		11	11			
Leslie, Charles	A Short and Easie Method with the Deists. 4th ed. 1709		67	67			
Leslie, Charles	A Short and Easie Method with the Jews. 2nd ed. 1709		67	67			
Lewis, John	The Church Catechism Explained. 2nd ed. 1702						*
Limborg, Philippus van	Theologia Christiana. Amstelaedami, 1686						*
Lips, Joest	A Discourse of Constancy. 1654						*
Lucas, Richard	An Enquiry after Happiness. v.1, pt.1. 1685						*
Lucas, Richard	Practical Christianity. 1677		31	31	72		
Lucas, Richard	Religious Perfection, or a Third Part of the Enquiry after Happiness. 1696						*
Lucas, Richard	Twelve Sermons. 1699					28	
Mapletoft, John	The Principles and Duties of the Christian Religion. 2nd ed. 1710						*
March, John	Sermons. 1693				65		

Author	Title	B	O	N	W	M	F
Mason, Francis	The Authority of the Church in Making Canons . . . a Sermon. 1705				14		
Mede, Joseph	The Works of. 1648	6					
Mocket, Richard	Tractatus de Politia Ecclesiæ Anglicanæ. 1683 [includes 2 works by Zouche, below]				64		
Monro, George	The Just Measures of the Pious Instructions of Youth. Edinburgh, 1700						*
More, Henry	A Collection of Several Philosophical Writings. 2nd ed. 1662				10		
More, Henry	Discourses on Several Texts. 1692						*
More, Henry	Divine Dialogues . . . concerning the Attributes and Providence of God. 1668				58		*
More, Henry	Enchiridion Ethicum. 1668				60		
More, Henry	An Explanation of the Grand Mystery of Godliness. 1660						*
More, Henry	A Modest Enquiry into the Mystery of Iniquity. 1664						*
More, Henry	The Theological Works. 1675		10	10	11		
'Morton'	'Morton. Of Episcopacy'						*
Murrey, Robert	Christ Every Man's Pattern. 1715						*
Nelson, Robert	An Address to Persons of Quality and Estate. 1715				26		
Nelson, Robert	A Companion for the Festivals and Fasts of the Church of England. 1704		54	54	27	16	
Nelson, Robert	The Practice of True Devotion. 1715				66		
Nicholls, William	The Duty of Inferiours. 1701						*
Nourse, Peter	Practical Discourses . . . Select Homilies of the Church of England. 2v. 1708						*
Ostervald, Jean	The Grounds and Principles of the Christian Religion Explain'd. 1704				80		*
Ostervald, Jean	The Nature of Uncleanness Consider'd. 1708		22		47		
Ostervald, Jean	A Treatise concerning the Causes of the Present Corruption among Christians. 1700		21		46		
Parsons, Robert	A Christian Directorie. 1585						*
Patrick, Symon	The Christian Sacrifice. 1671					7	
Patrick, Symon	A Commentary upon the Bookes of Joshua, Judges and Ruth. 1712			21			
Patrick, Symon	A Commentary upon the Fifth Book of Moses called Deuteronomy. 1700			20			
Patrick, Symon	A Commentary upon the First Book of Moses called Genesis. 1695			16			
Patrick, Symon	A Commentary upon the Fourth Book of Moses called Numbers. 1649			19			
Patrick, Symon	A Commentary upon the Second Book of Moses called Exodus. 1697			17			
Patrick, Symon	A Commentary upon the Third Book of Moses called Leviticus. 1698			18			
Patrick, Symon	A Commentary upon the Two Books of Chronicles: Ezra, Nehemiah and Esther. 1706			24			
Patrick, Symon	A Commentary upon the Two Books of Kings. 1705			23			

Author	Title	B	O	N	W	M	F
Patrick, Symon	A Commentary upon the Two Books of Samuel. 1703			22			
Patrick, Symon	The Parables of the Pilgrim. 1665						*
Patrick, Symon	A Treatise of Repentance. 1686						*
Pearson, John	An Exposition of the Creed. 5th ed. 1673	9	8	8	7	1	
Puller, Timothy	The Moderation of the Church of England. 1679						*
Ranew, Nathaniel	Solitude Improved by Divine Meditation. 1670						*
Rawlet, John	The Christian Monitor. 1686				11		
Reynolds, Edward	Three Treatises . . . the Life of Christ. 1631						*
S., J.	Popery Display'd in its Proper Colours. 1681						*
Sale, George, and others	An Universal History. 23v. 1736–65						*
Salmon, William	A Discourse against Transsubtantiation. 1690						*
Sancroft, William	Lex Ignea. 1666						*
Sancroft, William	Occasional Sermons. 1694						*
Sanderson, Robert	Nine Cases of Conscience. 1678	8					
Sanderson, Robert	XXXV Sermons. 7th ed. 1681	7					
Scott, John	The Christian Life. 6th ed. 1704		16	16			
Scott, John	Practical Discourses upon Several Subjects. v.1. 1697						*
Senault, Jean	A Paraphrase upon Job. 1648						*
Sharp, John	Sixteen Sermons. 1691				35		
'Sherlock'	'Sherlock. Immortality of the Soul'						*
Sherlock, Richard	The Practical Christian. 6th ed. 1713					27	
Sherlock, Thomas	Several Discourses preached at the Temple Church. 3rd ed. 1755						*
Sherlock, William	A Defence and Continuation of the Discourse concerning the Knowledge of Jesus Christ. 1675						*
Sherlock, William	A Practical Discourse of Religious Assemblies. 1681						*
Sherlock, William	A Practical Discourse concerning a Future Judgment. 1692						*
Sherlock, William	Sermons Preach'd upon Several Occasions. 1700						*
Smallridge, George	Sixty Sermons. 1724				50		
Sorocold, Thomas	Supplications of Saints. A Booke of Prayers. 3rd ed. 1612						*
Sparrow, Anthony	A Collection of Articles, Injunctions, Canons, Orders [with text]. 4th ed. 1684	13					
Sparrow, Anthony	A Rationale upon the Book of Common Prayer. 1655	12					
Spinckes, Nathaniel	Of Trust in God. 1696		64	64	55		
Stearne, John	Tractatus de Visitatione Infirmiorum. 2nd ed. 1704		67	67			
Stebbing, Henry	Discourses upon Several Subjects: viz. Regeneration. 1722						*
Stillingfleet, Edward	A Discourse concerning the Doctrine of Christ's Satisfaction. 1696–1700		55	55			
Stillingfleet, Edward	A Discourse in Vindication of the Doctrine of the Trinity. 1697		26				

Author	Title	B	O	N	W	M	F
Synge, Edward	A Gentleman's Religion. 1693						*
Talbot, James	The Christian School-Master. 1707						*
Taylor, Jeremy	The Rule and Exercise of Holy Dying. 1651						*
Taylor, Jeremy	The Rule and Exercise of Holy Living. 1650						*
Taylor, Jeremy	Unum Necessarium. 1653						*
Tenison, Thomas	Of Idolatry. 1678						*
Tertullian	Those Two Excellent Monuments . . . Minucius Felix's Octavius and Tertillian's Apology, 1708		13	13	42		*
Thomas à Kempis	'De Imitatione Christi' [? The Christian Pattern. 1642]		72				
Tillotson, John	The Works of. 1696				2		
Tillotson, John	The Works of. 5th ed. 1707		2	2			
Tillotson, John	A Discourse against Transsubstantiation. 1684						*
Tillotson, John	Fifteen Sermons on Several Subjects . . . the Eleventh Volume. 1702		44	44			
Tillotson, John	Fifteen Sermons on Various Subjects . . . the Twelfth Volume. 1703		45	45			
Tillotson, John	Of Sincerity and Constancy in . . . Religion in Fifteen Sermons. 1695		33				
Tillotson, John	'Posthumous Sermons on Several Subjects: 13 scr. 5 vol'.		37	37			
Tillotson, John	The Remaining Discourses upon the Attributes . . . the Seventh Volume. 1700		39	39			
Tillotson, John	Several Discourses . . . the Fourth Volume. 1697		36	36			
Tillotson, John	Several Discourses of Death and Judgement . . . the Ninth Volume. 2nd ed. 1704		41	41			
Tillotson, John	Several Discourses of Repentance . . . the Eighth Volume. 1700		40	40			
Tillotson, John	Several Discourses of the Life . . . of Christ . . . the Tenth Volume. 2nd ed. 1704		42	42			
Tillotson, John	Several Discourses of the Truth of the Christian Religion . . . the Thirteenth Volume.1703		45	45			
Tillotson, John	Several Discourses upon the Attributes of God . . . the Sixth Volume. 1699		38	38			
Tillotson, John	Six sermons. 1694		46	46			
Tillotson, John	Sixteen Sermons . . . on Several Subjects . . . the Second Volume. 1696		34	34			
Tillotson, John	Sixteen Sermons . . . on Several Subjects . . . the Third Volume. 1696		35	35			
Towerson, Gabriel	An Explication of the Catechism of the Church of England [with text]. pt.1. 1678	4					
Twisse, William	The Scripture Sufficiency. 1656						*
Ussher, James	The Principles of Christian Religion; with a Large Bodie of Divinity. 7th ed. 1678	10					*
Wake, William	A Practical Discourse concerning Swearing. 1696					9	
Wake, William	Sermons and Discourses on Several Subjects. 1690					57	
Wall, William	The History of Infant Baptism. 2v. 1705		68	68	74		
'Walls and Evans'	'The Example of St. Paul'						*

Author	Title	B	O	N	W	M	F
Walton, Izaak	The Lives of Dr. John Donne . . . 1670	16				8	
Waple, Edward	Thirty Sermons. 1714						*
Ward, Richard	Life of Dr. H More. 1710				59		
Wensley, Robert	The Form of Sound Words. 1679						*
Wheatly, Charles	The Church of England Man's Companion . . . Book of Common Prayer. 1710		57	57			
Whiston, William	A Short View of the Chronology of the Old Testament. 1710						*
Whitby, Daniel	A Paraphrase and Commentary upon all the Epistles of the New Testament. 2v. 2nd ed. 1706		3	3	5		
Wilkins, John	Of the Principles and Duties of Natural Religion. 5th ed. 1704		61	61	53		
Williams, John	A Brief Exposition of the Church Catechism [with text]. 1689					12	
Wilson, Thomas	An Essay towards an Instruction for the Indians. 1740					39	
Wilson, Thomas	The Principles and Duties of Christianity . . . in English and Manks. 1707 ['The Manks Catechism']					21	
Wilson, Thomas	A Short and Plain Instruction for the Better Understanding of the Lord's Supper. 1734					35	
Wilson, Thomas	The True Christian Method of Educating the Children . . . of the Charity-Schools. 1724						*
Wolseley, Sir Charles	The Reasonableness of Scripture-Belief. 1672						*
Worthington, John	The Great Duty of Self-Resignation. 1675		64	64	56		
Zouche, Richard	'Descriptio Juris et Judicii Ecclesiast. Secund. Can. Anglic'. [This, and the next entry. form part of Mocket, above]				64		
Zouche, Richard	'Descriptio Juris et Judicii Temporalis Secundum Consuetudines Feudales et Normanicas' [see the above entry]				64		

PAROCHIAL COLLECTIONS
AND THEIR CARE

Most of the books in parochial collections belong to the 17th and 18th centuries and, not surprisingly, are mainly theological. The collections nearly always contain volumes of sermons and works of religious controversy, ecclesiastical history and pastoralia. But there are also books on history and geography, Greek and Latin classical authors, and occasionally some small, sometimes surprising collections of books on more specialized subjects. The Index contains references to subject collections when noted in the Directory entries. Books printed from the middle of the 15th century up to and including 1500 are known as incunabula, or incunables. These, and books printed in the first half, at least, of the 16th century are likely to be rare or uncommon and should be treated with special care. There should be separate arrangements for the storage of, and access to, all books printed up to 1800, distinct from those of the 19th and 20th centuries, and the later parish 'working library'. Many churches still possess old Bibles, liturgical works, copies of Erasmus and other books, collectively known as desk-libraries (see index entries), and these too should be carefully preserved, together with single copies of all later prayer books, hymn books, psalters, service sheets, communion booklets, etc., no longer in use, either in situ, or on deposit by arrangement with the diocese.[1]

Some recommendations for looking after a Parochial Library[2]

Arrangement. Original bookcases, book-desks, or other library furniture should continue to be used, provided that the timbers are sound and not rotten or worm-infested, and should not be altered to suit modern needs. If the books and shelves have the same shelf-marks the original order can be preserved. If modern shelving is used an arrangement by size and then subject is probably the least damaging to the books.

Temperature and humidity. Books do not like damp or over-heated conditions: the ideal ambient temperature is in the range 55–61°F (13–16°C), with an ideal relative humidity at a fixed point in the range 45–60%. Air circulation is essential around shelves, between shelves and bookcases and walls, under and within locked bookcases (by bored holes, or grilles instead of glass doors).

Bindings. Books with metal protections or chains should be protected from

1. See also: Peter Wilkinson, 'An unloved heritage: printed books in parish churches', *Churchscape*, no.7, 1988, pp.17–24.
2. I am indebted to Dr D. J. McKitterick for much of the information in this Appendix, drawn from his leaflet, 'How to look after your Parochial Library', prepared for incumbents with collections (available from the CCC).

their fellows by card buffers, and fine blind- or gold-tooled bindings should be kept in special boxes. Leather bindings should be regularly cleaned and treated with leather dressing, but advice on materials and procedures should be sought from skilled local conservators (see Further Reading at the end of this section).

Insect attack. After damp and heat, creatures, such as mice, silver fish and furniture beetles, are the chief enemies of books, especially if undisturbed. The best defence is the regular gentle dusting and opening of individual books, but not 'banging', which can break fragile spines.

Emergency treatment. Books that have suffered from damp should be put on edge in a dry and ventilated (but not heated) area and the pages allowed to separate and dry. Books which have become sodden from a leaking pipe or roof should be placed at once in a freezer bag and then into a deep freezer. The local record office can advise on having the books freeze-dried and treated.

Repairs. Apart from tying on loose boards with acid-free tape, or placing in acid-free boxes, this is a matter that is best left to expert conservators. Books should never be repaired with adhesive tape or modern glues.

Security. Rare and valuable books should not be kept in open access areas, and locks on bookcases and on library doors should be regularly inspected. If possible, alarm systems should be fitted to cases and rooms.

Catalogues. All old library catalogues, lists of donors, and borrowers' registers are valuable documents and should be preserved with care, as they often record books no longer present and preserve the history of the growth of the collections. If there is no basic modern catalogue one should be made: a simple shelf-list with authors' names will suffice for regular checking, but a detailed catalogue, recording details of former owners, bindings, etc., is the preferred long-term aim.

Responsibility. It is important that one person should be responsible for looking after the collection on a day-to-day basis, and for its general security and maintenance.

Further reading and advice.

A. D. Baynes-Cope, *Caring for Books and Documents.* 2nd ed., London, British Library, 1989

Hermione Sandwith and Sheila Stainton, eds., *The National Trust Manual of Housekeeping.* Rev. ed. London, Penguin Books in association with the National Trust, 1993 (ch.2, Books and documents; ch.6, Furniture)

Protecting Archives and Manuscripts against Disasters. (Advisory Memorandum, no.6, March 1998.) Leaflet free of charge from the Royal Commission on Historical Manuscripts, Quality House, Quality Court, Chancery Lane, London WC2A 1HP (020 7242 1198)

Preservation Guidelines. Leaflet free of charge from the National Preservation Office, The British Library, 96 Euston Road, London NW1 2DB (020 7412 7724)

British Standards. BS 5454: 2000. *Recommendations for the Storage and Exhibition of Archival Doocuments.*

Help and advice on all the above matters can also be sought from:

　　1) The Council for the Care of Churches, Church House, Great Smith Street, London SW1P 3NZ (020 7898 1866);

　　2) Record offices; large public or university libraries employing skilled conservators.

PAROCHIAL LIBRARIES
REPORTS AND RECOMMENDATIONS
1709–1991

The Act of 1709. The Act of March 1708–9 (7 Anne c.14) 'for the better preservation of parochial libraries in that part of Great Britain called England' (reproduced on pp.439–42 and discussed on pp.36–7) is still on the statute book, and should afford protection to all parochial libraries established after 1708. It has however frequently not been observed. The only exemption from its provisions are contained in section 4 of the Faculty Jurisdiction Measure, 1938, which states in respect of section X of the Act that (1) 'any book in a parochial library appropriated to the use of the minister of any parish or place within the operation of that Act may be sold under the authority of a faculty issuing out of the consistory court of the diocese in which the parish concerned is situate, and in the case of every sale so authorised the proceedings of sale shall be applied for such of the ecclesiastical purposes of the parish as in such faculty shall be directed', and, (2) 'any question whether a library is within the said Act and is so appropriated shall be finally determined by the Charity Commissioners'. Similarly, the provision under section X of the act stating that books may not be sold except on the authority of the ordinary 'and then only when there is a duplicate of such book or books' was relaxed by the Ecclesiastical Jurisdiction Measure 1963 s6(1)(b)(ii) and the Faculty Jurisdiction Measure 1964 s4 (as amended).

The Report of 1959.[1] In 1949 the Archbishop of Canterbury asked the (then) Central Council for the Care of Churches to make a report on the number and condition of parochial libraries still in existence, and to add recommendations for their future preservation. The Committee was chaired by S. J. A. Evans (d.1984), from 1953 Dean of Gloucester, and the Report was signed by him and by F. C. Morgan (d.1978), Secretary of the Committee. Statistics concerning the libraries mentioned in this Report, and in the alphabetical list appended to it, and in the current Directory, are presented in the table on pp.27–8. The Committee commented, not unexpectedly, on libraries suffering from damp, neglect and vandalism, but also on a sad history of sales without faculty, wanton destruction, disposal and alienation. In addition valuable and sometimes unique furniture had been disposed of or shamefully altered. The Committee urged 'the need to impress upon clergy and laity alike the importance of taking proper care of these libraries', and went on to observe that 'the

---

1. The Report and recommendations were printed in PLCE1, pp.56–62.

witness of the Church of England is perhaps weakest to-day in learned, literary and artistic circles, and the failure to safeguard our bibliographical treasures is hardly likely to strengthen it', an observation as pertinent today as it was in 1959. A summary of the Committee's main recommendations is as follows:

1) That a clause should be added to amend the Faculty Jurisdiction Measure, 1938, section 4: 'any application for the sale of a parochial library or any church books shall be deemed to come within the purview of the Diocesan Advisory Committee who shall be required to advise the petitioners and report to the Chancellor'.

2) Unless circumstances absolutely forbid it a parochial library ought to be retained in its own home.

i. The Diocesan Advisory Committee should supervise parochial libraries and appoint an adviser on the care of church books.

ii. Every library should have an up-to-date catalogue, a copy of which should be appended to the church inventory.

iii. There should be a voluntary local custodian to do regular shelf checks.

3) If a library cannot remain in situ it should be deposited on loan in the local public, county, cathedral or university library, kept as a collection and identified with a bookplate, with formal receipts lodged in the diocesan registry and church safe, and with an entry in the church inventory.

4) The inventory of church goods should include a note of catalogues and books printed before 1501.

5) A desideratum is 'a more detailed combined descriptive catalogue of the libraries and of the books which they contain'.

Bill Report, 1970.[2] In 1970 Dr E. G. W. Bill, Librarian of Lambeth Palace Library, produced a report of a new survey of parochial libraries he had conducted 1969–70 at the request of the Council for the Care of Churches to ascertain how effective the recommendations of the 1959 report had been in the task of preserving parochial libraries. The work of the survey was much aided by the contributions of lay advisers appointed to some (but by no means all) Diocesan Advisory Committees who reported a number of hitherto un-known libraries. The most significant development to emerge from the inquiry was the great increase in the number of libraries deposited in university and other public libraries: 37 in the period 1959–69. While some libraries still in situ were well cared for and were attractive features in their churches, e.g. at Boston, Grantham, Wimborne and Steeple Ashton, others were badly neglect-ed and some had been destroyed. Five more libraries had been sold. It would seem that the Faculty Jurisdiction Measure of 1938 had not been reinforced

2. An unpublished TS Report, revised and endorsed by the Books and Manuscripts Sub-Committee of the Conservation Committee (copies in CCC). Dr Bill's survey is described more fully in his review-article, 'Catalogue of books from the parochial libraries in Shropshire, London, Mansell, 1971', *Library History*, v.2 (1971), no.4, pp.152–7.

and the legal obstacles to sale remained minimal. Reasons for the dispersal and destruction of libraries were not hard to seek. Neglect comes about when, e.g. i. the church in which the library is placed is not the mother church in the benefice; ii. libraries are placed in vicarages and rectories during an interregnum and become especially vulnerable; iii, large, rambling vicarages are replaced by smaller, more convenient ones, and there is no room to store books; iv. the sale of church treasures can seem to solve the short-term financial problem of a hard-pressed church. A summary of Dr Bill's main recommendations is as follows:

1) That under no circumstances should a parochial library be sold.

2) They should be included in the church insurance cover and inventory of church goods.

3) A leaflet of advice on preserving, caring for and maintaining libraries, and on sources of assistance, should be sent to all incumbents with libraries in their care.

4) If a parish can no longer maintain a library, and the local association is strong, efforts should be made to keep it in its place of origin. When the local association is less strong and the books are deteriorating the parish should be actively encouraged by the diocese or diocesan adviser to place the library on deposit in a public or university library in the vicinity.

5) Libraries should be placed on deposit only under the following rigorous conditions:

    i. Books must be kept in at least as good a condition as that in which they were originally received.

    ii. The receiving library must prepare a catalogue within a prescribed period of time, copies of which must be deposited in the parish, diocesan registry and the Bodleian Library.

    iii. Books may be retrieved by the incumbent after due and reasonable notice has been given, with regard however for any expenses incurred by the receiving library on the repair of books.

6) When a library is transferred from one library outside the parish to another library, the consent of the incumbent of the original parish must be obtained.

7) Every library, whether deposited or not, should have a catalogue.

8) That all dioceses should have advisers on books and documents for giving advice, not only on established parochial libraries, but also on smaller collections of books and records not deposited, especially when the church is declared redundant, and also to help enforce recommendations 1) – 7) above.

Treasures on Earth Report, [1973], and later legislation.[3] Appendix V of this report was devoted to Parish Libraries. It contains a brief summary of the main recommendations of the 1959 Report, and a list of the recommend-

---

3. *Treasures on Earth: a Report by a Working Party of the Council for Places of Worship.* General Synod. GS132, [1973].

ations in the Bill Report, 1970, listed above, but not endorsing items 3, 5.iii and 6 from these recommendations. In Item 1 'under no circumstances' is replaced by 'only under exceptional circumstances and after the fullest consultation'. The Care of Churches and Ecclesiastical Jurisdiction Measure 1991 s26(3)(c) made provision for rules covering historic books and records, but so far such rules have not been compiled. [4]

4. For information on post-1959 legislation relating to parochial libraries I am indebted to Jonathan Goodchild, Deputy Secretary (General), CCC.

INDEX

References to matter in the Directory are given by **place-names**, elsewhere by **page-numbers**. Cross-references between place-names are supplied in the Directory. Present locations of deposited parochial collections and desk-libraries are listed under their institutional headings, followed by 'holdings', earlier locations by headings followed by 'former home'. Provenances are cited under individual names with an appropriate epithet (e.g. founder, bequest of, donor, former owner, library of, etc.). Libraries with subject strengths (generally small) are listed under subject headings followed by '[subject]'. Omitted are subjects to be found in most collections, e.g. religion, theology, patristics, ecclesiastical history, sermons, pamphlets on religious controversies, local history and topography. These headings are derived mainly from Directory entries and are certainly not complete. The headings assembled under 'Parochial Libraries: given to, and/or for the use of' are also derived from Directory sources, and may not indicate the exact status of the collection when founded or now.

Francis, Sir Frank (1901–88): work on PLCE1: 23
Franck, Mark (*c.* 1612–64): donor: Barley (?)
Frank, Richard, trustee: Campsall
Frank, Thomas (1663–1730): trustee: Bedford
Freake, Thomas: former owner: Swaffham
Freeman, Robert, churchwarden: donor: Sotherton
Freke, Thomas (d.1718?): bequest of: Gillingham
French, Gilbert J.: subscription: 41, Turton
French, James: donor: Beetham
Frost, Dr H. C., of Goldhanger, Essex: donor: Shipdham
Frye, B., of Halifax: binder: Halifax
Fulham, Edward (*c.* 1608–94): former owner: Compton
Furniture: see Library furniture and fittings

Gainsborough: town library: 38, n.28
Gardemau, Balthazar (*c.* 1656–1739): library of: Coddenham
Gardening [subject]: Hadleigh, Norton, Wimborne Minster
Gardiner, George (1535?–89): former owner: Norwich. St. Andrew
Geale, John (b. *c.* 1685): bequest of: Bishops Lydeard
Geddes, Henry, vicar: Wigton
Geering, Gregory (b. *c.* 1664): founder: Denchworth
Gell, William, vicar: Isle of Man: Onchan
Geography [subject]: Barnstaple, Doddington, Hackness, Hadleigh, Henley-on-
        Thames, Maidstone, More, Newark-upon-Trent, Norton, Swaffham,
        Wimborne Minster; Wales: Chirk
Geology [subject]: Beetham
Geometry [subject]: Hadleigh
Gillingham, Roger (d.1695): bequest of: Wimborne Minster
Gillot, John: former owner: Stainton
Gladman, Ralph (*c.* 1658–1725): bequest of: Aylesbury
Glasgow University Library: holdings: Brent Eleigh, London. St. Martin-in-the-Fields
Gloucester Cathedral Library: holdings: Prestbury
Gloucester County Record Office: holdings: Aschurch, Bledington, Cam, Chalford,
        Coates, Cromhall, Dursley, Newnham, Painswick
Goad, Thomas (1576–1638): intended founder: Hadleigh
Godfrey, Garret: binder: Denchworth, Finedon, Langley Marish, Maidstone, More
Godmersham vicarage: former home: Crundale
Gonville and Caius College, Cambridge: holdings: Bratton Fleming
Goodacker, Timothy (d.1714): donor: Timsbury
Grammatical treatises [subject]: Marlborough
Grandisson, John (1292?–1369), bishop: bequest of: Crediton, Ottery St. Mary
Grantham Public Library: holdings: Grantham
Graves, Joseph: bequest of: Lewes
Gray, John Urbin: donor: Nayland
Gray, Thomas (1716–21): presentation copies of his books: Loughborough
Greater London Record Office: holdings: Feltham
Great Yarmouth Public Library: former home: Great Yarmouth
Green, Thomas, rector: donor: Woodchurch
Gregson, John: binder, or bound for: Sutton Courtenay
Greville, Fulke, 5th Baron: donor: Alcester (?), Warwick
Gribelin, Simon: engraver of the Bray library bookplate: 47–8
Griffiths, John (1732–1825): library of: Wales: Llandysilio (Pembs.)
Griffiths, Sir Morys: donor: Oswestry
Guildhall Library, London: holdings: London. St. Peter's Cornhill

History [subject]: Ash [-by-Wrotham], Barnstaple, Bassingbourn, Beetham, Brent
        Eleigh, Bromham, Castleton, Daventry, Elham, Graveley, Hackness, Hatfield
        Broad Oak, Henley-on-Thames, Hereford, Lanteglos by Camelford, London.
        St. Leonard (Shoreditch), London. St. Martin-in-the-Fields, Loughborough,
        Maidstone, Marlborough, More, Newark-upon-Trent, Norton, Reigate,
        Riccall, Rotherham, Sheldon, Skipwith, Steeple Ashton, Stoke-by-Nayland,
        Tamworth, Whitchurch (Shrops.), Wimborne Minster; Wales: Chirk
    ancient and modern: Wedmore
    Commonwealth tracts: Tiverton
    continental: Norwich. St. Martin-at-Oak
    18th cent.: Crediton
    Revolution, 1688–9: Crundale
Hoare, Henry (1677–1725): donor, Bray Trustees Committee member: 36, 39,
        44, n.50
Hoblyn, Robert (1710–56): former owner: Buckland
Hoby, Lady Margaret: former owner: Hackness
Hoby, Sir Thomas: former owner: Hackness
Hodgson's auctioneers: proposed sale: Lanteglos by Camelford
    sale: Shipdham
Hodson, Robert (d.1680): donor: Broughton (Hunts.)
Hoile, John: bequest of: Ottery St. Mary
Holden, George, curate: donor: Pilling, Tatham Fells
Holdych family, lords of the Manor: Ranworth
Hollingworth, Nathaniel: donor: Haltwhistle
Hollis, Lady Anne: donor: Chertsey, East Bedfont, Feltham, Hounslow
Holmes, Philippe: donor: Broughton (Hunts.)
Hooke, Robert (1635–1703), architect: Willen
Hooker, Richard (1554?–1600): donor: Denchworth
Hooper, Dr: donor: Fakenham
Hopkin-James, Lemuel, rector: Wales: Cowbridge
Horbery, Matthew (1706/7–73): donor: Standlake
Horn-book: example: Weaverham
Horne, John (c. 1645–1732): donor: King's Lynn
Horton, E., vicar: Denchworth
Hounslow Public Library: holdings: East Bedfont, Feltham
Household management [subject]: Heathfield
Howard, Bernard, 12th Duke of Norfolk (1765–1842): donor: Abbeydore
Howard, John (1726?–90): founder: Cardington
Howes, Luce, Williams & Co., auctioneers: Tortworth
Howman, Edward John (d.1874): donor: Norwich. St. Stephen
Hudson, Richard, curate of Flookburgh: addressee: 45–6
Hughes, D., of Queens' College, Cambridge: former owner: Steeple Ashton
Hulbert, Canon C. L.: bequest of: Slaithwaite
Hull. Holy Trinity: 40
Hull Museums Committee: former owner: Hull. Holy Trinity
Hull University Library: holdings: Hull. Holy Trinity, Hull. St. Mary Lowgate
Hume, James (c. 1676–1734): bequest of: Willen
Hunkin, J. W., bishop of Truro: Lanteglos by Camelford
Hunt, William (b.c. 1667): donor: Coleorton
Huntingdon, Henry Hastings, 3rd Earl (1535–95): donor: Leicester
Huntington Library, California: holdings: Bury St. Edmunds, Shipdham
Hurd, Richard (1720–1808), bishop: presentation copies of his books:
        Loughborough
    visitations: Alcester, Feckenham

London: Shoreditch Public Library: former home: London. St. Leonard (Shoreditch)
Los Angeles, University of California: W. A. Clark Library: holdings: North
    Walsham, Wales: Caerleon
Loughborough College of Further Education: former home: Loughborough
Loughborough Public Library: former home: Shepshed
Loughborough University Library: holdings: Ashby-de-la-Zouch, Loughborough
Louvain University Library: holdings: Eastwick
Lovelace, Sir Richard (c. 1568–1634): donor: Hurley
Lovell, Mrs Audley: former owner: Malmesbury
Lowndes, Humphrey, bookseller (active 1587–1629): donor: Astbury
Lowther, Sir Thomas: donor: 39 & n.37, 45–6, Flookburgh
Lumley, Richard (c. 1644–94): bequest of: Stainton
Luther, Martin: works of: Maidstone
Lyell, James P. R. (d.1949): donor: Malmesbury
Lyttelton, Henry: former owner: Holdgate
Lyttelton, Thomas, rector: donor: Bridgnorth
Lyttelton, Thomas (d.1799), Secretary to the Associates: bequest of: Wales:
    Llandeilo Fawr

Mackworth, Sir Humphrey, member of Bray Trustees Committee: 39
Magdalen College, Oxford: books given by Edward Maynard: Daventry
Magdalene College, Cambridge: holdings: Steeple Ashton
Maidstone County Library, Kent: former home: Ash [-by-Wrotham]
Maidstone Museum, Kent: holdings: Maidstone
Mallory, Robert, Jn.: former owner: Abbeydore
Man, Thomas, stationer, senior (active 1576–1625), or junior (active 1604–10):
    donor: Westbury-on-Severn
Mansel, Edward (c. 1661–1704), vicar of Ecclesfield: Rotherham
Mansel, Frances: founder: Rotherham
Mansfield College, Oxford: holdings: North Walsham
Manuscripts: 16th cent.: English: Marlborough
   17th cent.: Langley Marish
   Hebrew: Great Yarmouth
   legal: Swaffham
   local interest: Slaithwaite
   medieval: 30, Appleby Magna, Bath, Beccles, Bedford, Boston, Brent Eleigh,
      Bridgnorth, Bristol. All Saints, Bristol. St. Mary, Bristol. St. Thomas;
      Brockenhurst, Buckingham, Burton Latimer, Bury St. Edmunds,
      Carbrooke, Cartmel, Eastbourne, Finedon, Grantham, Hackness, Hodnet,
      Hull. Holy Trinity, Huntingdon, Ipswich, King's Norton (fragments),
      Langley Marish, Leicester, London: St. Martin-in-the-Fields, London.
      St. Peter's Cornhill, Maidstone, Malmesbury, Minehead, More (fragments),
      Newcastle upon Tyne, Norwich. St. Andrew, Norwich. St. Peter Mancroft,
      Oakham, Oswestry, Ranworth, Reigate, Shipdham, Southwell, Steeple
      Ashton, Swaffham, Tamworth, Tiverton, Whitchurch (Hants.),
      Wimborne Minster, Wisbech, Wollaton
   musical: Bury St. Edmunds
   Phillipps: Chertsey, East Bedfont, Hounslow, London. St. Martin-in-the-Fields
   post-medieval: London. St. Martin-in-the-Fields, Newark-upon-Trent, Reigate,
      Wisbech
   recusant: Swaffham
Manx National Heritage, Douglas, Isle of Man: holdings: I of M: Andreas,Ballaugh,
    Douglas, Jurby, Lezayre, Maughold
Mappa Mundi Trust: Hereford

Nansmoen, Belinus: bequest of: Bristol. St. Mary
National Library of Scotland: holdings: Durham
National Library of Wales: holdings: Oswestry; Wales: Caerleon, Cilmaenllwyd,
        Darowen, Llanboidy, Llandaff, Llanfyllin, St. Asaph, and possibly books
        from Abergavenny, Chepstow, Monmouth, Newport, Usk
Natural history [subject]: Doddington, Ipswich; Wales: Chirk
Navigation [subject]: Hadleigh, London. St. Leonard (Shoreditch)
Neale, Henry, patron: donor: Feckenham
Needham, Peter (1680–1731): former owner: Shipdham
Negus, Gilbert (1698–1763): donor: Bassingbourn
Nelson, Robert (1656–1715), member of Bray Trustees C'ttee and benefactor: 39, 44
    one of church founders: London. St. George the Martyr
Nevile, Cavendish (1681–1749): bequest of: 34, Norton (Derbys.)
Nevinson, John (d.1634), rector: Tankersley
Newberry Library, Chicago: holdings: Whitchurch (Hants.)
Newcastle Cathedral Library: former home: Alnwick
Newcastle Public Library: holdings: Newcastle upon Tyne
Newcastle University Library: holdings: Alnwick, Heversham, Newcastle upon Tyne
Newcome, John (c. 1684–1765): donor: Grantham, Offord Cluny
Newman, Henry, Secretary of the SPCK and of the Bray Trustees Committee: 38, 44–6
Newte, John (1656–1715): bequest of: Tiverton
Newte, Richard (1612–78): library of: Tiverton
Newton, Sir Isaac: unrecorded footnotes: Royston
Newton, William, vicar: Gillingham
Nicholas, Matthew, rector: memorandum book: Penshurst
Nicolson, William (1655–1727), bishop: visitations: 35, Ainstable, Askham,
        Burgh-by-Sands, Crosby Garrett, Crosby Ravensworth, Dalston, Orton
Nightingale, Edward, of Kneesworth Hall, founder: Bassingbourn
Norfolk Museums Service, Norwich: holdings: Norwich. St. Augustine
Norfolk Record Office: holdings: Carbrooke
North, Anne: bequest of: Rougham
North, Dudleya (1675–1712): library of: Rougham
North, Francis, 2nd Baron Guilford: donor: Warwick
North, Roger (1653–1734): library of: Rougham
Northampton, 5th Earl of: donor: Shipston-on Stour
Northamptonshire Record Office: holdings: Burton Latimer
North Devon Athenaeum: former home: Barnstaple
North Devon Record Office, Barnstaple: Tawstock
Northumberland Archdeaconry: parochial lending libraries: 57
Norwich Cathedral Library: holdings: London. St. Martin-in-the-Fields, Norwich.
        St. Peter Mancroft, Norwich. St. Stephen, Shipdham, Swaffham. For the
        survivals from seventy Norfolk and Suffolk desk-libraries now on deposit
        see under the county names in the Table, 83–112
Norwich County Hall: holdings: Norwich. St. Peter Mancroft
Norwich Museum: former home: Shipdham
Norwich Public Library: former home: Norwich. St. Stephen
    holdings: Shipdham
Norwich town library: 32
Notitia Parochialis (1705): 38 & n.28, Beccles, Bicester, Bilston, Bishop's Castle,
        Bury. St. Mary, Chirbury, Costock, Crosthwaite, Denchworth,
        Frisby-on-the-Wreake, Gainsborough, Greenford, Halifax, Hull. St. Mary
        Lowgate, Hurley, Leicester, Myndtown, Nantwich, Newcastle upon Tyne,
        North Grimston, Reigate, Sheffield, Sheldon, Skipton, Sleaford, Southwell,
        Stainton, Warwick, Womersley, York. St. Mary Castlegate

Sunday School libraries: 19th cent: 57
Surrey County Council: donors: Reigate
Surrey History Centre, Woking: holdings: Effingham
Sydenham, Sir Philip, bart. (1676?–1739): founder: Hackness
Symonds, Nathaniel (*c.* 1694–1727): bequest of: Great Yarmouth, Ormesby

Tabley House, Cheshire: holdings: Nether Tabley
Tait, Archibald Campbell (1811–82), archbishop: subscription: London. St. Martin-in-the-Fields
Talbot, William (1659–1730), bishop: donor: Halton
Tanner, Thomas (1674–1735), bishop: donor: Wales: St. Asaph
Taylor, Herbert, vicar: Patrixbourne
Tempest, William, of the Inner Temple: former owner: Lasham
Tenby: former home: Wales: Cilmaenllwyd
Tenison, Edward (1633–1735): donor: Wales: Llandrillo yn Rhos
Tenison, Thomas (1636–1715), archbishop: donor: Norwich. St. Peter Mancroft, founder: London. St. Martin-in-the-Fields
Tennant, Grisdall: former owner: Mungrisdale
Thetford, Thomas: former owner: Swaffham
Thomas, of Farnylaw, Chancellor: donor: Newcastle upon Tyne
Thomas, Vaughan (*c.* 1775–1858): donor: Yarnton
Thomlinson, Robert (1668–1747): donor: Newcastle upon Tyne
Thoresby, Ralph: visitor: Ribchester
Thurloe, John (1616–68): donor: Wisbech
Thurloe, Nicholas, vicar: Brent Eleigh
Thurlyn, Thomas (*c.* 1636–1714): donor: King's Lynn
Thurscross, Timothy (d.1671): bequest of: North Grimston
Thurswell, Thomas (d.1585): former owner: Wisbech
Tinclar, Jonathan, rector of Adlethorpe: founder: Bampton
Todd, Abraham, rector of Welbury: donor: Kirkby Fleetham
Todd, John (*c.* 1726–86): donor: Kirkby Fleetham
Tomkys, John (d.1703): bequest of: Bilston
Tong Castle: former home: Tong
Topography [subject]: Patrixbourne
Toppin, John (d.1756?): donor: Allendale, Alston
Torkington, William (d.1737): founder: Broughton (Hunts.)
Torlesse, Charles Martin (*c.* 1795–1881): vicar: Stoke-by-Nayland
Tortworth Court: Ducie Library: Tortworth
Totnes Museum: holdings: Totnes
Town libraries: 32, Barnstaple, Coleshill, Gainsborough, Grantham, Guildford (32, n.14), Ipswich, Leicester, Lewes, Maldon, Marlborough, Newark-upon-Trent, Newcastle upon Tyne, Norwich. St. Andrew (Norwich), Reigate, Swaffham, Tamworth, Wisbech
   difficulty in distinguishing from school libraries: 32, n.14
Townsend, Thomas (d.1701): bequest of: Costock
Townshend, Thomas (*c.* 1683–1764): bequest of: Shipdham
Travel [subject]: Ash [-by-Wrotham], Bromham, Castleton, Donington, Elham, Hatfield Broad Oak, Ipswich, London. St. Leonard (Shoreditch), Reigate, Riccoll; Wales: Chirk
Treasures on Earth Report (1973): bearing on parochial libraries: 457–8
Tregonwell, John (d.1680): donor: Milton Abbas
Trelawney, Sir Jonathan (1650–1721): former owner: London. All Saints (Chelsea Old Church)
Trevor, John: donor: Bromham